DARK FORCES

New Stories of Suspense and Supernatural Horror

EDITED BY

KIRBY McCAULEY

THE VIKING PRESS NEW YORK

First published by The Viking Press
625 Madison Avenue, New York, N.Y. 10022
Published simultaneously in Canada by
Penguin Books Canada Limited

Printed in the United States of America

Acknowledgments

Portions of lyrics from "Light My Fire," words by The Doors, © 1967, Doors Music Co., are reprinted by permission of the authors and publisher.

Portions of lyrics from "I'm So Afraid," copyright © 1975 Gentoo Music Inc. All rights for the United States and Canada administered by Warner-Tamerlane Publishing Company. All rights reserved. Used by permission.

DARK FORCES

To Lurton Blassingame,
with admiration and affection
and
Deborah Wian, for all kinds
of good reasons

I would like to express my warmest thanks
to Alan Williams, for his enormously helpful
and intelligent editorial input on this book.

CONTENTS

CONTENTS

INTRODUCTION

In more ways than one, the late August Derleth is responsible for the existence of this book.

Back in 1955—when I was in my early teens—my life was permanently and happily altered when I discovered Arkham House, a small publishing firm headed by Derleth based in the village of Sauk City, Wisconsin. Arkham House specialized (and still does) in books of macabre and fantasy fiction, starting up in 1939 with publication of a 1200-copy edition of a large omnibus of H. P. Lovecraft's stories entitled *The Outsider and Others,* which various New York publishers had declined to bring out. Against many negative proclamations, including those of Edmund Wilson, who referred to Lovecraft's stories as "hack work," Derleth campaigned tirelessly for over thirty years to help gain Lovecraft the kind of serious literary recognition he now enjoys.

But Derleth didn't stop with Lovecraft. Before his death, in 1971, he published about a hundred books, including first ones by such notable American fantasists as Ray Bradbury, Robert Bloch, Fritz Leiber, and Carl Jacobi. And from Britain he brought over quality works by such distinguished figures as L. P. Hartley, William Hope Hodgson, Walter de la Mare, A. E. Coppard, H. R. Wakefield, Lord Dunsany, Arthur Machen, and Algernon Blackwood. Derleth bound every book he published in handsome black cloth, stamped them with gold lettering, and usually jacketed them with tasteful and striking dust wrappers. His books were good—and they *looked* it.

Derleth brought out dozens of excellent books—volumes of poetry, anthologies, novels, and story collections—which have never, I believe, been equaled in content or lasting impact by any other single publisher who has tried his hand more than occasionally with the literature of terror and the fantastic. It is true that certain houses brought out the major offerings of a few important writers in the field—Alfred A. Knopf and his list of Machen, de la Mare, and Dahl, come admirably to mind —but only in a context of general publishing, mixing fantasy works with non-fantasy works and lacking Derleth's sensitive focus, which can help an author to endure in a bookselling market increasingly inclined to categorization.

There is a magic about one of Derleth's three thousand-copy edition books of the 1940s and 50s which excites the sophisticated devotee of fantasy fiction far more than almost any best-selling supernatural horror novel of the 1970s. The magic arises out of Derleth's superb taste and aspiration to publish the best he could find, with no particular aim at the commercial jackpot. Derleth set out to prove—and did—that there is an abiding place in publishing for quality supernatural fiction, and he largely proved it with the hard-to-sell and unfashionable form of the short story, collections of which most publishers do with great reservation, if not downright sour looks on their faces. Year in and year out, Derleth brought out remarkably good books of stories which, after they have gone out of print, are eagerly purchased by connoisseurs, for prices ranging up to five hundred dollars. Such enthusiasm by a relatively small, ardent band of collectors does not necessarily signal quality or assure posterity, but I venture to say that at least a few of Derleth's productions, very likely the books of Lovecraft's fiction and Ray Bradbury's remarkable *Dark Carnival,* will stand the test of time.

Derleth did it. He established that there was a permanent place for short fiction of the macabre variety. He was an inspiring force for aficionados of good fantasy fiction and for them the very name Sauk City, in its time, conjured up feelings of reverence. I think, too, he paved the way to some extent for the arrival of quality novels of the supernatural—such as those by Ira Levin, Robert Marasco, John Farris, Stephen King, and Peter Straub—to do well by any standard of book sales. And he certainly made the road to publication for the book you now hold in your hands an easier one to travel.

So, without knowing it, Derleth started me on the course to this book. And it was brought full circle over dinner one night with Anthony Cheetham, the publisher of Futura Publications Limited in England, who suggested I edit an anthology of new stories of horror and the supernatural for him to publish, which we could in turn arrange to have published elsewhere around the world. He liked my only other anthology of original stories, *Frights,* and seemed to feel I was the person to do a more ambitious similar volume for him. At first I was flattered by his offer, but reluctant to accept, because my feeling was, and still is, that people who edit too many anthologies tend to go stale in their selections.

But as the conversation went on, it struck me: why not try to assemble an anthology with the same scope and dynamism of Harlan Ellison's *Dangerous Visions,* but in the supernatural horror field? Ellison's anthology, for those unfamiliar with it, is a two hundred thousand-plus word anthology of new (in 1967) stories of science fiction. Ellison, however, carefully pointed out that his book contained stories of "speculative fiction," tales which weren't shackled by the bonds of strict category, market demands, or editorial taboos. Ellison went after stories that had some roots in science fiction tradition, but which would break new ground, say and do things in new and varied and daring ways. He succeeded brilliantly with both critics and readers. I suggested to Cheetham that we attempt a gambit based in similarly adventurous (though less revolutionary) ambitions, a large book centering on the tale of terror and fantasy. Cheetham liked the notion immediately and promised to back me up in every way feasible—a promise he has splendidly carried through on.

The next step was to find stories. I approached by letter or telephone nearly every writer living who had tried his or her hand at this type of story and whose writing I like personally. Predictably enough, some were able to respond with stories, some were not. I sorely miss here the presence of Jack Finney, Roald Dahl, Elizabeth Jane Howard, Ira Levin, Bernard Malamud, John Farris, Peter Straub, Julio Cortazar, and Nigel Kneale, to name only some. I did what I could to gain contributions from most of the best living practitioners of this kind of story. In addition, I deliberately sought variety, stories ranging wide across the horizon of fantasy fiction. Nothing seems to me more boring than an anthology in one key, having similar backdrops or styles, or which are all variations on a narrow theme. I set out to offer as many of the subjects and moods and general directions the fantastic tale has tended traditionally to take as I could, but hopefully in imaginative, fresh ways.

The pursuit of individual contributions was not without interesting aspects. For example, Stephen King had mentioned to me a year or more before a general idea he had for a story, and I reminded him that it interested me. It sounded just like the kind of story I hankered to have in the book and he phoned one day to say the idea was starting to jell in his mind. A week or so later he called to say the story was under way and looking to run a bit longer than he had originally thought. Would, he asked, twenty thousand words present a space problem? I replied no, my interest heightening. The following week he called to say he had about seventy manuscript pages done—already twenty thousand words or better—but that the end was not in sight. A few days later he called to say that the manuscript was up to eighty-five pages. Soon, another call, and it was over a hundred—and still growing, as was my excitement, of course. And finally the end came: 145 manuscript pages, or about forty thousand words! What King had felt originally to be a novelette of perhaps fifteen thousand words became a novella of forty thousand. I expected an ordinary-length story and ended up with a short novel by the most popular author of supernatural horror stories in the world.

Editing this anthology also provided me with an opportunity to meet Isaac Bashevis Singer. I saw him in his Upper West Side New York apartment on a hot, late spring day in 1978, only a few months before the announcement of his Nobel Prize. He was a gracious and friendly host and it was an hour and a half I shall never forget. Nor will I forget a remark Mr. Singer made in answer to my question as to why he writes so often about demonic and supernatural happenings. He replied, with no hesitation: "It brings me into contact with reality." Mr. Singer's arresting answer speaks of the tip of the iceberg well, I think. And so did Stephen King when he once replied to an interviewer who asked why he writes about fear and terrible manifestations: "What makes you think I have a choice?"

In their own ways, I think Messrs. Singer and King were acknowledging the dominating influence of the subconscious on such stories. Of course all art has its origin in the subconscious, but I believe the uncanny tale retains a stronger foothold there, *in effect as well as origin.* Robert Aickman, who has written thoughtfully and eloquently on the subject of the supernatural story—or "ghost story" as he prefers to call it—has observed:

> The essential quality of the ghost story is that it gives satisfying form to the unanswerable; to thoughts and feelings, even experiences, which are common to all imaginative people, but which cannot be rendered down scientifically into "nothing but" something else. . . . The ghost story, like poetry, deals with the experience behind the experience: behind almost any experience. . . . They should be stories concerned not with appearance and consistency, but with the spirit behind appearance, the void behind the face of order.

I believe Aickman couldn't be more accurate. In reading such stories our goal is more that of mysterious encounter than the prize of resolution or clear moral point. At its best, the tale of the fantastic can convey experiences of a high and exhilarating order because it draws on the power of subconscious truth in both writer and reader, acting as a kind of channel to our submerged self, to that largest part of ourselves we can never fully know, but nevertheless *feel.* Graham Greene once wrote in appreciation of this effect in an essay on the stories of Walter de la Mare: ". . . we are wooed and lulled sometimes to the verge of sleep by the beauty of the prose, until suddenly without warning a sentence breaks in mid-breath and we look up and see the terrified eyes of our fellow-passenger, appealing, hungry, scared, as he watches what we cannot see—'The sediment of an unspeakable possession.'" In contrast to the part of our life devoted to tedious facts and endeavors, it is that contact with the indefinable that can be so satisfying.

A final thought: the tale of horror is almost always about a *breaking down.* In one way or another such stories seem concerned with things coming apart, or slipping out of control, or about sinister encroachments in our lives. Whether the breakdowns are in personal relationships, beliefs, or the social order itself, the assault of dangerous, irrational forces upon normalcy is a preeminent theme of the horror story. Perhaps this kind of story has always been popular because, no less than our forebears, we live in a world where goodwill and reason do not always triumph, as our daily newspapers constantly remind us. There may well be no permanent escape from the inner and outer darkness that troubles us all, but in its way the tale of terror and fantastic encounter mitigates our fears by making them subjects of entertainment. Who is to say that is a bad thing?

—Kirby McCauley
New York City

DARK FORCES

THE LATE SHIFT

By DENNIS ETCHISON

Slowly but surely, over the last dozen years or so, Dennis Etchison has built up an impressive reputation as a distinctive stylist in the fantasy and horror field. He has brought to the form a lyric style and a sharp eye for details, especially those of Southern California, where he has lived most of his life. Etchison has published in magazines ranging from Cavalier *to* Fantasy & Science Fiction *to* Mystery Monthly *and is presently readying his first novel for publication. He is also keenly interested in screen writing and wrote the novelization of John Carpenter's movie,* The Fog. *This story demonstrates his visual sense of the Southern California area and is also a scary projection one step beyond.*

They were driving back from a midnight screening of *The Texas Chainsaw Massacre* ("Who will survive and what will be left of them?") when one of them decided they should make the Stop 'N Start Market on the way home. Macklin couldn't be sure later who said it first, and it didn't really matter; for there was the all-night logo, its bright colors cutting through the fog before they had reached 26th Street, and as soon as he saw it Macklin moved over close to the curb and began coasting toward the only sign of life anywhere in town at a quarter to two in the morning.

They passed through the electric eye at the door, rubbing their faces in the sudden cold light. Macklin peeled off toward the news rack, feeling like a newborn before the LeBoyer Method. He reached into a row of well-thumbed magazines, but they were all chopper, custom car, detective and stroke books, as far as he could see.

"Please, please, sorry, thank you," the night clerk was saying.

"No, no," said a woman's voice, "can't you hear? I want that box, *that* one."

"Please, please," said the night man again.

Macklin glanced up.

A couple of guys were waiting in line behind her, next to the styrofoam ice chests. One of them cleared his throat and moved his feet.

The woman was trying to give back a small, oblong carton, but the clerk didn't seem to understand. He picked up the box, turned to the shelf, back to her again.

Then Macklin saw what it was: a package of one dozen prophylactics from behind the counter, back where they kept the cough syrup and airplane glue and film. That was all she wanted—a pack of Polaroid SX-70 Land Film.

Macklin wandered to the back of the store.

"How's it coming, Whitey?"

"I got the Beer Nuts," said Whitey, "and the Jiffy Pop, but I can't find any Olde English 800." He rummaged through the refrigerated case.

"Then get Schlitz Malt Liquor," said Macklin. "That ought to do the job." He jerked his head at the counter. "Hey, did you catch that action up there?"

"What's that?"

Two more guys hurried in, heading for the wine display. "Never mind. Look, why don't you just take this stuff up there and get a place in line? I'll find us some Schlitz or something. Go on, they won't sell it to us after two o'clock."

He finally found a six-pack hidden behind some bottles, then picked up a quart of milk and a half-dozen eggs. When he got to the counter, the woman had already given up and gone home. The next man in line asked for cigarettes and beef jerky. Somehow the clerk managed to ring it up; the electronic register and UPC code lines helped him a lot.

"Did you get a load of that one?" said Whitey. "Well, I'll be gonged. Old Juano's sure hit the skids, huh? The pits. They should have stood him in an aquarium."

"Who?"

"Juano. It *is* him, right? Take another look." Whitey pretended to study the ceiling.

Macklin stared at the clerk. Slicked-back hair, dyed and greasy and parted in the middle, a phony Hitler mustache, thrift shop clothes that didn't fit. And his skin didn't look right somehow, like he was wearing makeup over a face that hadn't seen the light of day in ages. But Whitey was right. It was Juano. He had waited on Macklin too many times at that little Mexican restaurant over in East L.A., Mama Something's. Yes, that was it, Mama Carnita's on Whittier Boulevard. Macklin and his friends, including Whitey, had eaten there maybe fifty or a hundred times, back when they were taking classes at Cal State. It was Juano for sure.

Whitey set his things on the counter. "How's it going, man?" he said.

"Thank you," said Juano.

Macklin laid out the rest and reached for his money. The milk made a lumpy sound when he let go of it. He gave the carton a shake. "Forget this," he said. "It's gone sour." Then, "Haven't seen you around, old buddy. Juano, wasn't it?"

"Sorry. Sorry," said Juano. He sounded dazed, like a sleepwalker.

Whitey wouldn't give up. "Hey, they still make that good *menudo* over there?" He dug in his jeans for change. "God, I could eat about a gallon of it right now, I bet."

They were both waiting. The seconds ticked by. A radio in the store was playing an old '60s song. *Light My Fire,* Macklin thought. The Doors. "You remember me, don't you? Jim Macklin." He held out his hand. "And my trusted Indian companion, Whitey? He used to come in there with me on Tuesdays and Thursdays."

The clerk dragged his feet to the register, then turned back, turned again. His eyes were half-closed. "Sorry," he said. "Sorry. Please."

Macklin tossed down the bills, and Whitey counted his coins and slapped them on the counter top. "Thanks," said Whitey, his upper lip curling back. He hooked a thumb in the direction of the door. "Come on. This place gives me the creeps."

As he left, Macklin caught a whiff of Juano or whoever he was. The scent was sickeningly sweet, like a gilded lily. His hair? Macklin felt a cold draft blow through his chest, and shuddered; the air conditioning, he thought.

At the door, Whitey spun around and glared.

"So what," said Macklin. "Let's go."

"What time does Tube City here close?"

"Never. Forget it." He touched his friend's arm.

"The hell I will," said Whitey. "I'm coming back when they change fucking shifts. About six o'clock, right? I'm going to be standing right there in the parking lot when he walks out. That son of a bitch still owes me twenty bucks."

"Please," muttered the man behind the counter, his eyes fixed on nothing. "Please. Sorry. Thank you."

The call came around ten. At first he thought it was a gag; he propped his eyelids up and peeked around the apartment half-expecting to find Whitey still there, curled up asleep among the loaded ashtrays and pinched beer cans. But it was no joke.

"Okay, okay, I'll be right there," he grumbled, not yet comprehending, and hung up the phone.

Saint John's Hospital on 14th. In the lobby, families milled about, dressed as if on their way to church, watching the elevators and waiting obediently for the clock to signal the start of visiting hours. Business hours, thought Macklin. He got the room number from the desk and went on up.

A police officer stood stiffly in the hall, taking notes on an accident report form. Macklin got the story from him and from an irritatingly healthy-looking doctor—the official story—and found himself, against his will, believing in it. In some of it.

His friend had been in an accident, sometime after dawn. His friend's car, the old VW, had gone over an embankment, not far from the Arroyo Seco. His friend had been found near the wreckage, covered with blood and reeking of alcohol. His friend had been drunk.

"Let's see here now. Any living relatives?" asked the officer. "All we could get out of him was your name. He was in a pretty bad state of shock, they tell me."

"No relatives," said Macklin. "Maybe back on the reservation. I don't know. I'm not even sure where the—"

A long, angry rumble of thunder sounded outside the windows. A steely light reflected off the clouds and filtered into the corridor. It mixed with the fluorescents in the ceiling, rendering the hospital interior a hard-edged, silvery gray. The faces of the policeman and the passing nurses took on a shaded, unnatural cast.

It made no sense. Whitey couldn't have been that drunk when he left Macklin's apartment. Of course he did not actually remember his friend leaving. But Whitey was going to the Stop 'N Start if he was going anywhere, not halfway across the county to—where? Arroyo Seco? It was crazy.

"Did you say there was liquor in the car?"

"Afraid so. We found an empty fifth of Jack Daniel's wedged between the seats."

But Macklin knew he didn't keep anything hard at his place, and neither did Whitey, he was sure. Where was he supposed to have gotten it, with every liquor counter in the state shut down for the night?

And then it hit him. Whitey never, but never drank sour mash whiskey. In fact, Whitey never drank anything stronger than beer, anytime, anyplace. Because he couldn't. It was supposed to have something to do with his liver, as it did with other Amerinds. He just didn't have the right enzymes.

Macklin waited for the uniforms and coats to move away, then ducked inside.

"Whitey," he said slowly.

For there he was, set up against firm pillows, the upper torso and most of the hand bandaged. The arms were bare, except for an ID bracelet and an odd pattern of zigzag lines from wrist to shoulder. The lines seemed to have been painted by an unsteady hand, using a pale gray dye of some kind.

"Call me by my name," said Whitey groggily. "It's White Feather."

He was probably shot full of painkillers. But at least he was okay. Wasn't he? "So what's with the war paint, old buddy?"

"I saw the Death Angel last night."

Macklin faltered. "I—I hear you're getting out of here real soon," he tried. "You know, you almost had me worried there. But I reckon you're just not ready for the bone orchard yet."

"Did you hear what I said?"

"What? Uh, yeah. Yes." What had they shot him up with? Macklin cleared his throat and met his friend's eyes, which were focused beyond him. "What was it, a dream?"

"A dream," said Whitey. The eyes were glazed, burned out.

What happened? Whitey, he thought. Whitey. "You put that war paint on yourself?" he said gently.

"It's pHisoHex," said Whitey, "mixed with lead pencil. I put it on, the nurse washes it off, I put it on again."

"I see." He didn't, but went on. "So tell me what happened, partner. I couldn't get much out of the doctor."

The mouth smiled humorlessly, the lips cracking back from the teeth. "It was Juano," said Whitey. He started to laugh bitterly. He touched his ribs and stopped himself.

Macklin nodded, trying to get the drift. "Did you tell that to the cop out there?"

"Sure. Cops always believe a drunken Indian. Didn't you know that?"

"Look. I'll take care of Juano. Don't worry."

Whitey laughed suddenly in a high voice that Macklin had never heard before. "*He-he-he!* What are you going to do, kill him?"

"I don't know," he said, trying to think in spite of the clattering in the hall.

"They make a living from death, you know," said Whitey.

Just then a nurse swept into the room, pulling a cart behind her.

"How did you get in here?" she demanded.

"I'm just having a conversation with my friend here."

"Well, you'll have to leave. He's scheduled for surgery this afternoon."

"Do you know about the Trial of the Dead?" asked Whitey.

"Shh, now," said the nurse. "You can talk to your friend as long as you want to, later."

"I want to know," said Whitey, as she prepared a syringe.

"What is it we want to know, now?" she said, preoccupied. "What dead? Where?"

"Where?" repeated Whitey. "Why, here, of course. The dead are here. Aren't they." It was a statement. "Tell me something. What do you do with them?"

"Now what nonsense . . . ?" The nurse swabbed his arm, clucking at the ritual lines on the skin.

"I'm asking you a question," said Whitey.

"Look, I'll be outside," said Macklin, "okay?"

"This is for you, too," said Whitey. "I want you to hear. Now if you'll just tell us, Miss Nurse. What do you do with the people who die in here?"

"Would you please—"

"I can't hear you." Whitey drew his arm away from her.

She sighed. "We take them downstairs. Really, this is most . . ."

But Whitey kept looking at her, nailing her with those expressionless eyes.

"Oh, the remains are tagged and kept in cold storage," she said, humoring him. "Until arrangements can be made with the family for services. There now, can we—?"

"But what happens? Between the time they become 'remains' and the services? How long is that? A couple of days? Three?"

She lost patience and plunged the needle into the arm.

"Listen," said Macklin, "I'll be around if you need me. And hey, buddy," he added, "we're going to have everything all set up for you when this is over. You'll see. A party, I swear. I can go and get them to send up a TV right now, at least."

"Like a bicycle for a fish," said Whitey.

Macklin attempted a laugh. "You take it easy, now."

And then he heard it again, that high, strange voice. *"He-he-he! tamunka sni kun."*

Macklin needed suddenly to be out of there.

"Jim?"

"What?"

"I was wrong about something last night."

"Yeah?"

"Sure was. That place wasn't Tube City. This is. *He-he-he!*"

That's funny, thought Macklin, like an open grave. He walked out. The last thing he saw was the nurse bending over Whitey, drawing her syringe of blood like an old-fashioned phlebotomist.

All he could find out that afternoon was that the operation wasn't critical, and that there would be additional X-rays, tests and a period of "observation," though when pressed for details the hospital remained predictably vague no matter how he put the questions.

Instead of killing time, he made for the Stop 'N Start.

He stood around until the store was more or less empty, then approached the counter. The manager, who Macklin knew slightly, was working the register himself.

Raphael stonewalled Macklin at the first mention of Juano; his beady eyes receded into glacial ignorance. No, the night man was named Dom or Don; he mumbled so that Macklin couldn't be sure. No, Don (or Dom) had been working here for six, seven months; no, no, no.

Until Macklin came up with the magic word: police.

After a few minutes of bobbing and weaving, it started to come out. Raphe sounded almost scared, yet relieved to be able to talk about it to someone, even to Macklin.

"They bring me these guys, my friend," whispered Raphe. "I don't got nothing to do with it, believe me.

"The way it seems to me, it's company policy for all the stores, not just me. Sometimes they call and say to lay off my regular boy, you know, on the graveyard shift. 'Specially when there's been a lot of holdups. Hell, that's right by me. I don't want Dom shot up. He's my best man!

"See, I put the hours down on Dom's pay so it comes out right with the taxes, but he has to kick it back. It don't even go on his check. Then the district office, they got to pay the outfit that supplies these guys, only they don't give 'em the regular wage. I don't know if they're wetbacks or what. I hear they only get maybe a buck twenty-five an hour, or at least the outfit that brings 'em in does, so the office is making money. You know how many stores, how many shifts that adds up to?

"Myself, I'm damn glad they only use 'em after dark, late, when things can get hairy for an all-night man. It's the way they look. But you already seen one, this Juano-Whatever. So you know. Right? You know something else, my friend? They *all* look messed up."

Macklin noticed goose bumps forming on Raphe's arms.

"But I don't personally know nothing about it."

They, thought Macklin, poised outside the Stop 'N Start. Sure enough, like clockwork They had brought Juano to work at midnight. Right on schedule. With raw, burning eyes he had watched Them do something to Juano's shirtfront and then point him at the door and let go. What did They do, wind him up? But They would be back. Macklin was sure of that. They, whoever They were. The Paranoid They.

Well, he was sure as hell going to find out who They were now.

He popped another Dexamyl and swallowed dry until it stayed down.

Threats didn't work any better than questions with Juano himself. Macklin had had to learn that the hard way. The guy was so sublimely creepy it was all he could do to swivel back and forth between register and counter, slithering a hyaline hand over the change machine in the face of the most outraged customers, like Macklin, giving out with only the same pathetic, wheezing *Please, please, sorry, thank you,* like a stretched cassette tape on its last loop.

Which had sent Macklin back to the car with exactly no options, nothing to do that might jar the nightmare loose except to pound the steering wheel and curse and dream redder and redder dreams of revenge. He had burned rubber between the parking lot and Sweeney Todd's Pub, turning over two pints of John Courage and a shot of Irish whiskey before he could think clearly enough to waste another dime calling the hospital, or even to look at his watch.

At six o'clock They would be back for Juano. And then. He would. Find out.

Two or three hours in the all-night movie theater downtown, merging with the shadows on the tattered screen. The popcorn girl wiping stains off her uniform. The ticket girl staring through him, and again when he left. Something about her. He tried to think. Something about the people who work night-owl shifts anywhere. He remembered faces down the years. It didn't matter what they looked like. The nightwalkers, insomniacs, addicts, those without money for a cheap hotel, they would always come back to the only game in town. They had no choice. It didn't matter that the ticket girl was messed up. It didn't matter that Juano was messed up. Why should it?

A blue van glided into the lot.

The Stop 'N Start sign dimmed, paling against the coming morning. The van braked. A man in rumpled clothes climbed out. There was a second figure in the front seat. The driver unlocked the back doors, silencing the birds that were gathering in the trees. Then he entered the store.

Macklin watched. Juano was led out. The a.m. relief man stood by, shaking his head.

Macklin hesitated. He wanted Juano, but what could he do now? What the hell had he been waiting for, exactly? There was still something else, something else. . . . It was like the glimpse of a shape under a sheet in a busy corridor. You didn't know what it was at first, but it was there; you knew what it might be, but you couldn't be sure, not until you got close and stayed next to it long enough to be able to read its true form.

The driver helped Juano into the van. He locked the doors, started the engine and drove away.

Macklin, his lights out, followed.

He stayed with the van as it snaked a path across the city, nearer and nearer the foothills. The sides were unmarked, but he figured it must operate like one of those minibus porta-maid services he had seen leaving Malibu and Bel Air late in the afternoon, or like the loads of kids trucked in to push magazine subscriptions and phony charities in the neighborhoods near where he lived.

The sky was still black, beginning to turn to slate close to the horizon. Once they passed a garbage collector already on his rounds. Macklin kept his distance.

They led him finally to a street that dead-ended at a construction site. Macklin idled by the corner, then saw the van turn back.

He let them pass, cruised to the end and made a slow turn.

Then he saw the van returning.

He pretended to park. He looked up.

They had stopped the van crosswise in front of him, blocking his passage.

The man in rumpled clothes jumped out and opened Macklin's door.

Macklin started to get out but was pushed back.

"You think you're a big enough man to be trailing people around?"

Macklin tried to penetrate the beam of the flashlight. "I saw my old friend Juano get into your truck," he began. "Didn't get a chance to talk to him. Thought I might as well follow him home and see what he's been up to."

The other man got out of the front seat of the van. He was younger, delicate-boned. He stood to one side, listening.

"I saw him get in," said Macklin, "back at the Stop 'N Start on Pico?" He groped under the seat for the tire iron. "I was driving by and—"

"Get out."

"What?"

"We saw you. Out of the car."

He shrugged and swung his legs around, lifting the iron behind him as he stood.

The younger man motioned with his head and the driver yanked Macklin forward by the shirt, kicking the door closed on Macklin's arm at the same time. He let out a yell as the tire iron clanged to the pavement.

"Another accident?" suggested the younger man.

"Too messy, after the one yesterday. Come on, pal, you're going to get to see your friend."

Macklin hunched over in pain. One of them jerked his bad arm up and he screamed. Over it all he felt a needle jab him high, in the armpit, and then he was falling.

The van was bumping along on the freeway when he came out of it. With his good hand he pawed his face, trying to clear his vision. His other arm didn't hurt, but it wouldn't move when he wanted it to.

He was sprawled on his back. He felt a wheel humming under him, below the tirewell. And there were the others. They were sitting up. One was Juano.

He was aware of a stink, sickeningly sweet, with an overlay he remembered from his high-school lab days but couldn't quite place. It sliced into his nostrils.

He didn't recognize the others. Pasty faces. Heads thrown forward, arms distended strangely with the wrists jutting out from the coat sleeves.

"Give me a hand," he said, not really expecting it.

He strained to sit up. He could make out the backs of two heads in the cab, on the other side of the grid.

He dropped his voice to a whisper. "Hey. Can you guys understand me?"

"Let us rest," someone said weakly.

He rose too quickly and his equilibrium failed. He had been shot up with something strong enough to knock him out, but it was probably the Dexamyl that had kept his mind from leaving his body completely. The van yawed, descending an off ramp, as he began to drift. He heard voices. They slipped in and out of his consciousness like fish in darkness, moving between his ears in blurred levels he could not always identify.

"There's still room at the cross." That was the younger, small-boned man, he was almost sure.

"Oh, I've been interested in Jesus for a long time, but I never could get a handle on him. . . ."

"Well, beware the wrath to come. You really should, you know."

He put his head back and became one with a dark dream. There was something he wanted to remember. He did not want to remember it. He turned his mind to doggerel, to the old song. *The time to hesitate is through,* he thought. *No time to wallow in the mire. Try now we can only lose/And our love become a funeral pyre.* The van bumped to a halt. His head bounced off steel.

The door opened. He watched it. It seemed to take forever.

Through slitted eyes: a man in a uniform that barely fit, hobbling his way to the back of the van, supported by the two of them. A line of gasoline pumps and a sign that read WE NEVER CLOSE–NEVER UNDERSOLD. The letters breathed. Before they let go of him, the one with rumpled clothes unbuttoned the attendant's shirt and stabbed a hypodermic into the chest, close to the heart and next to a strap that ran under the arms. The needle darted and flashed dully in the wan morning light.

"This one needs a booster," said the driver, or maybe it was the other one. Their voices ran together. "Just make sure you don't give him the same stuff you gave old Juano's sweetheart there. I want them to walk in on their own hind legs." "You think I want to carry 'em?" "We've done it before, brother. Yesterday, for instance." At that Macklin let his eyelids down the rest of the way, and then he was drifting again.

The wheels drummed under him.

"How much longer?" "Soon now. Soon."

These voices weak, like a folding and unfolding of paper.

Brakes grabbed. The doors opened again. A thin light played over Macklin's lids, forcing them up.

He had another moment of clarity; they were becoming more frequent now. He blinked and felt pain. This time the van was parked between low hills. Two men in Western costumes passed by, one of them leading a horse. The driver stopped a group of figures in togas. He seemed to be asking for directions.

Behind them, a castle lay in ruins. Part of a castle. And over to the side Macklin identified a church steeple, the corner of a turn-of-the-century street, a mock-up of a rocket launching pad and an old brick schoolhouse. Under the flat sky they receded into intersections of angles and vistas which teetered almost imperceptibly, ready to topple.

The driver and the other one set a stretcher on the tailgate. On the litter was a long, crumpled shape, sheeted and encased in a plastic bag. They sloughed it inside and started to secure the doors.

"You got the pacemaker back, I hope." "Stunt director said it's in the body bag." "It better be. Or it's our ass in a sling. *Your* ass. How'd he get so racked up, anyway?" "Ran him over a cliff in a sports car. Or no, maybe this one was the head-on they staged for, you know, that new cop series. That's what they want now, realism. Good thing he's a cremation—ain't no way Kelly or Dee's gonna get this one pretty again by tomorrow." "That's why, man. That's why they picked him. Ashes don't need makeup."

The van started up.

"Going home," someone said weakly.

"Yes . . ."

Macklin was awake now. Crouching by the bag, he scanned the faces, Juano's and the others'. The eyes were staring, fixed on a point as untouchable as the thinnest of plasma membranes, and quite unreadable.

He crawled over next to the one from the self-service gas station. The shirt hung open like folds of skin. He saw the silver box strapped to the flabby chest, directly over the heart. Pacemaker? he thought wildly.

He knelt and put his ear to the box.

He heard a humming, like an electric wristwatch.

What for? To keep the blood pumping just enough so the tissues don't rigor mortis and decay? For God's sake, for how much longer?

He remembered Whitey and the nurse. *"What happens? Between the time they become 'remains' and the services? How long is that? A couple of days? Three?"*

A wave of nausea broke inside him. When he gazed at them again the faces were wavering, because his eyes were filled with tears.

"Where are we?" he asked.

"I wish you could be here," said the gas station attendant.

"And where is that?"

"We have all been here before," said another voice.

"Going home," said another.

Yes, he thought, understanding. Soon you will have your rest; soon you will no longer be objects, commodities. You will be honored and grieved for and your personhood given back, and then you will at last rest in peace. It is not for nothing that you have labored so long and so patiently. You will see, all of you. Soon.

He wanted to tell them, but he couldn't. He hoped they already knew.

The van lurched and slowed. The hand brake ratcheted.

He lay down and closed his eyes.

He heard the door creak back.

"Let's go."

The driver began to herd the bodies out. There was the sound of heavy, dragging feet, and from outside the smell of fresh-cut grass and roses.

"What about this one?" said the driver, kicking Macklin's shoe.

"Oh, he'll do his 48-hours' service, don't worry. It's called utilizing your resources."

"Tell me about it. When do we get the Indian?"

"Soon as Saint John's certificates him. He's overdue. The crash was sloppy."

"This one won't be. But first Dee'll want him to talk, what he knows and who he told. Two doggers in two days is too much. Then we'll probably run him back to his car and do it. And phone it in, so Saint John's gets him. Even if it's DOA. Clean as hammered shit. Grab the other end."

He felt the body bag sliding against his leg. Grunting, they hauled it out and hefted it toward—where?

He opened his eyes. He hesitated only a second, to take a deep breath.

Then he was out of the van and running.

Gravel kicked up under his feet. He heard curses and metal slamming. He just kept his head down and his legs pumping. Once he twisted around and saw a man scurrying after him. The driver paused by the mortuary building and shouted. But Macklin kept moving.

He stayed on the path as long as he dared. It led him past mossy trees and bird-stained statues. Then he jumped and cut across a carpet of matted leaves and into a glade. He passed a gate that spelled DRY LAWN CEMETERY in old iron, kept running until he spotted a break in the fence where it sloped by the edge of the grounds. He tore through huge, dusty ivy and skidded down, down. And then he was on a sidewalk.

Cars revved at a wide intersection, impatient to get to work. He heard coughing and footsteps, but it was only a bus stop at the middle of the block. The air brakes of a commuter special hissed and squealed. A clutch of grim people rose from the bench and filed aboard like sleepwalkers.

He ran for it, but the doors flapped shut and the bus roared on.

More people at the corner, stepping blindly between each other. He hurried and merged with them.

Dry cleaners, laundromat, hamburger stand, parking lot, gas station, all closed. But there was a telephone at the gas station.

He ran against the light. He sealed the booth behind him and nearly collapsed against the glass

He rattled money into the phone, dialed Operator and called for the police.

The air was close in the booth. He smelled hair tonic. Sweat swelled out of his pores and glazed his skin. Somewhere a radio was playing.

A sergeant punched onto the line. Macklin yelled for them to come and get him. Where was he? He looked around frantically, but there were no street signs. Only a newspaper rack chained to a post. NONE OF THE DEAD HAS BEEN IDENTIFIED, read the headline.

His throat tightened, his voice racing. "None of the dead has been identified," he said, practically babbling.

Silence.

So he went ahead, pouring it out about a van and a hospital and a man in rumpled clothes who shot guys up with some kind of super-adrenalin and electric pacemakers and nightclerks and crash tests. He struggled to get it all out before it was too late. A part of him heard what he was saying and wondered if he had lost his mind.

"Who will bury them?" he cried. "What kind of monsters—"

The line clicked off.

He hung on to the phone. His eyes were swimming with sweat. He was aware of his heart and counted the beats, while the moisture from his breath condensed on the glass.

He dropped another coin into the box.

"Good morning, Saint John's. May I help you?"

He couldn't remember the room number. He described the man, the accident, the date. Sixth floor, yes, that was right. He kept talking until she got it.

There was a pause. Hold.

He waited.

"Sir?"

He didn't say anything. It was as if he had no words left.

"I'm terribly sorry . . ."

He felt the blood drain from him. His fingers were cold and numb.

". . . but I'm afraid the surgery wasn't successful. The party did not recover. If you wish I'll connect you with—"

"The party's name was White Feather," he said mechanically. The receiver fell and dangled, swinging like the pendulum of a clock.

He braced his legs against the sides of the booth. After what seemed like a very long time he found himself reaching reflexly for his cigarettes. He took one from the crushed pack, straightened it and hung it on his lips.

On the other side of the frosted glass, featureless shapes lumbered by on the boulevard. He watched them for a while.

He picked a book of matches from the floor, lit two together and held them close to the glass. The flame burned a clear spot through the moisture.

Try to set the night on fire, he thought stupidly, repeating the words until they and any others he could think of lost meaning.

The fire started to burn his fingers. He hardly felt it. He ignited the matchbook cover, too, turning it over and over. He wondered if there was anything else that would burn, anything and everything. He squeezed his eyelids together. When he opened them, he was looking down at his own clothing.

He peered out through the clear spot in the glass.

Outside, the outline fuzzy and distorted but quite unmistakable, was a blue van. It was waiting at the curb.

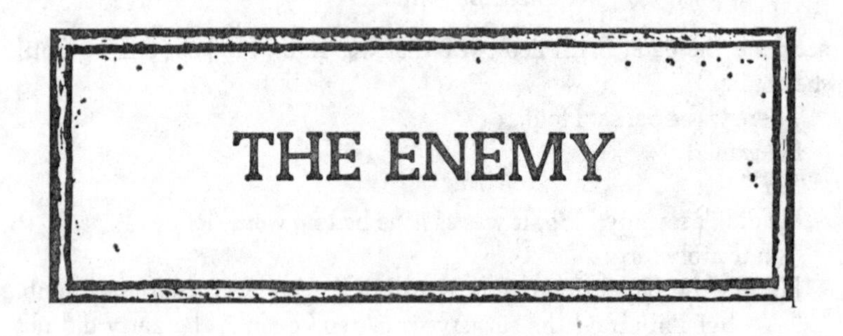

THE ENEMY

By ISAAC BASHEVIS SINGER

The supernatural has long pervaded the work of Isaac Bashevis Singer, the distinguished Yiddish writer and Nobel laureate. Whether set in his native Poland or in the New World, his short stories are frequently populated with demons, departed spirits, and sinister events. The stories are deceptively simple, and though they deal almost exclusively with the ethnic group he knows best, Polish Jewry, they speak to people everywhere: their experiences become the experiences of all men. There is an earthiness in his tales, a frank acceptance of the needs of the flesh, but their chief concern is almost always with the spirit of man. Singer believes most so-called supernatural phenomena to be either lies or people believing what they want to believe, but that there are exceptions to the rule bearing out serious investigation. This Singer tale tells of an apparently innocent refugee from persecution in Europe who finds himself threatened once again.

I

During the Second World War a number of Yiddish writers and journalists managed to reach the United States via Cuba, Morocco, and even Shanghai—all of them refugees from Poland. I did not always follow the news about their arrival in the New York Yiddish press, so I really never knew who among my colleagues had remained alive and who had perished. One evening when I sat in the Public Library on Fifth Avenue and 42nd Street reading *The Phantoms of the Living* by Gurney, Mayers, and Podmor, someone nudged my elbow. A little man with a high forehead and graying black hair looked at me through horn-rimmed glasses, his eyes slanted like those of a Chinese.

He smiled, showing long yellow teeth. He had drawn cheeks, a short nose, a long upper lip. He wore a crumpled shirt and a tie that dangled from his collar like a ribbon. His smile expressed the sly satisfaction of a once close friend who is aware that he has not been recognized—obviously, he enjoyed my confusion. In fact, I remembered the face but could not connect it with any name. Perhaps I had become numb from the hours spent in that chair reading case histories of telepathy, clairvoyance, and the survival of the dead.

"You have forgotten me, eh?" he said. "You should be ashamed of yourself. Chaikin."

The moment he mentioned his name I remembered everything. He was a feuilletonist on a Yiddish newspaper in Warsaw. We had been friends. We had even called each other "thou," though he was twenty years older than I. "So you are alive," I said.

"If this is being alive. Have I really gotten so old?"

"You are the same schlemiel."

"Not exactly the same. You thought I was dead, didn't you? It wouldn't have taken much. Let's go out and have a glass of coffee. What are you reading? You already know English?"

"Enough to read."

"What is this thick book about?"

I told him.

"So you're still interested in this hocus-pocus?"

I got up. We walked out together, passing the Catalogue Room, and took the elevator down to the exit on 42nd Street. There we entered a cafeteria. I wanted to buy Chaikin dinner but he assured me that he had already eaten. All he asked for was a glass of black coffee. "It should be hot," he said. "American coffee is never hot enough. Also, I hate granulated sugar. Do you think you could find me a lump of sugar I can chew on?"

It was not easy for me to make the girl behind the counter pour coffee into a glass and give me a lump of sugar for a greenhorn who missed the old ways. But I did not want Chaikin to attack America. I already had my first papers and I was about to become a citizen. I brought him his glass of black coffee and an egg cookie like the ones they used to bake in Warsaw. With fingers yellowed from tobacco Chaikin broke a piece and tasted it. "Too sweet."

He lit a cigarette and then another, all the time talking, and it was not long before the ashtray on our table was filled with butts and ashes. He was saying: "I guess you know I was living in Rio de Janeiro the last few years. I always used to read your stories in *The Forwerts.* To be frank, until recently I thought of your preoccupation with superstition and miracles as an eccentricity—or perhaps a literary mannerism. But then something happened to me which I haven't been able to cope with."

"Have you seen a ghost?"

"You might say that."

"Well, what are you waiting for? There's nothing I like better than to hear such things, especially from a skeptic like you."

"Really, I'm embarrassed to talk about it. I'm willing to admit that somewhere there may be a God who mismanages this miserable world but I never believed in your kind of hodgepodge. However, sometimes you come up against an event for which there is absolutely no rational explanation. What happened to me was pure madness. Either I was out of my mind during those days or they were one long hallucination. And yet I'm not altogether crazy. You probably know I was in France when the war broke out. When the Vichy government was established I had a chance to escape to Casablanca. From there I went to Brazil. In Rio they have a little Yiddish newspaper and they made me their editor. By the way, I used to reprint all your stuff. Rio is beautiful but what can you do there? I drank their bitter coffee and I scribbled my articles. The women there are another story—it must be the climate. Their demand for love is dangerous for an old bachelor. When I had a chance to leave for New York I grabbed it. I don't have to tell you that getting the visa was not easy. I sailed on an Argentine ship that took twelve days to reach New York.

"Whenever I sail on a ship I go through a crisis. I lose my way on ships and in hotels. I can never find my room. Naturally I traveled tourist class, and I shared a cabin with a Greek fellow and two Italians. That Greek was a wild man, forever mumbling to himself. I don't understand Greek but I am sure he was cursing. Perhaps he had left a young wife and was jealous. At night when the lights were out his eyes shone like a wolf's. The two Italians seemed to be twins—both short, fat, round like barrels. They talked to each other all day long and half through the night. Every few minutes they burst out laughing. Italian is almost as foreign to me as Greek, and I tried to make myself understood in broken French. I could just as well have spoken to the wall. They ignored me completely. The sea always irritates my bladder. Ten times a night I had to urinate, and climbing down the ladder from my berth was an ordeal.

"I was afraid that in the dining room they'd make me sit with other people whose language I didn't understand. But they gave me a small table by myself near the entrance. At first I was happy. I thought I'd be able to eat in peace. But at the very beginning I took one look at my waiter and knew he was my enemy. For hating, no reason is necessary. As a rule Argentines are not especially big, but this guy was very tall, with broad shoulders, a real giant. He had the eyes of a murderer. The first time he came to my table he gave me such a mean look it made me shudder. His face contorted and his eyes bulged. I tried to speak to him in French and then German, but he only shook his head. I made a sign asking for the menu and he let me wait for it half an hour. Whatever I asked for he laughed in my face and brought me something else. He threw down the dishes with a bang. In short, this waiter declared war on me. He was so spiteful it made me sick. Three times a day I was in his power and each time he found new ways to harass me. He tried to serve me pork chops, although I always sent them back. At first I thought the man was a Nazi and wanted to hurt me because I was a Jew. But no. At a neighboring table sat a Jewish family. The woman even wore a Star of David brooch, and still he served them correctly and even chatted with them. I went to the main steward to ask for a different table, but either he did not understand me or pretended he didn't. There were a number of Jews on the ship and I could have easily made acquaintances, but I had fallen into such a mood that I could not speak to anyone. When I finally did make an effort to approach someone he walked away. By that time I really began to suspect that evil powers were at work against me. I could not sleep nights. Each time I dozed off I woke up with a start. My dreams were horrible, as if someone had put a curse on me. The ship had a small library, which included a number of books in French and German. They were locked in a glass case. When I asked the librarian for a book she frowned and turned away.

"I said to myself, 'Millions of Jews are being outraged and tortured in concentration camps. Why should I have it better?' For once I tried to be a Christian and answer hatred with love. It didn't help. I ordered potatoes and the waiter brought me a bowl of cold spaghetti with cheese that smelled to high heaven. I said *'Gracias,'* but that son of a dog did not answer. He looked at me with mockery and scorn. A man's eyes—even his mouth or teeth—sometimes reveal more than any language. I wasn't as much concerned about the wrongs done to me as I was consumed by curiosity. If what was happening to me was not merely a product of my imagination, I'd have to reappraise all values—return to superstitions of the most primitive ages of man. The coffee is ice-cold."

"You let it get cold."
"Well, forget it."

II

Chaikin stamped out the last cigarette of his package. "If you remember, I always smoked a lot. Since that voyage I've been a chain smoker. But let me go on with the story. This trip lasted twelve days and each day was worse than the one before. I almost stopped eating altogether. At first I skipped breakfast. Then I decided that one meal a day was enough, so I only came up for supper. Every day was Yom Kippur. If only I could have found a place to be by myself. But the tourist class was packed. Italian women sat all day long singing songs. In the lounge, men played cards, dominoes, and checkers, and drank huge mugs of beer. When we passed the equator it became like Gehenna. In the middle of the night I would go up to the deck and the heat would hit my face like the draft from a furnace. I had the feeling that a comet was about to collide with the earth and the ocean to boil over. The sunsets on the equator are unbelievably beautiful and frightening, too. Night falls suddenly. One moment it is day, the next is darkness. The moon is as large as the sun and as red as blood. Did you ever travel in those latitudes? I would stretch out on deck and doze just to avoid the two Italians and the Greek. One thing I had learned: to take with me from the table whatever I could: a piece of cheese, a roll, a banana. When my enemy discovered that I took food to the cabin he fell into a rage. Once when I had taken an orange he tore it out of my hand. I was afraid he would beat me up. I really feared that he might poison me and I stopped eating cooked things altogether.

"Two days before the ship was due to land in New York the captain's dinner took place. They decorated the dining room with paper chains, lanterns, and such frippery. When I entered the dining room that evening I barely recognized it. The passengers were dressed in fancy evening dresses, tuxedos, what have you. On the tables there were paper hats and turbans in gold and silver, trumpets, and all this tinsel made for such occasions. The menu cards, with ribbons and tassels, were larger than usual. On my table my enemy had put a foolscap.

"I sat down, and since the table was small and I was in no mood for such nonsense I shoved the hat on the floor. That evening I was kept waiting longer than ever. They served soups, fish, meats, compotes, and cakes and I sat before empty plate. The smells made my mouth water.

After a good hour the waiter, in a great hurry, stuck the menu card into my hand in such a way that it cut the skin between my thumb and index finger. Then he saw the foolscap on the floor. He lifted it up and pushed it over my head so violently it knocked my glasses off. I refused to look ridiculous just to please that scoundrel, and I removed the cap. When he saw that he screamed in Spanish and threatened me with his fist. He did not take my order at all, but just brought me dry bread and a pitcher of sour wine. I was so starved that I ate the bread and drank the wine. South Americans take the captain's dinner very seriously. Every few minutes there would be the pop of a champagne bottle. The band was playing furiously. Fat old couples were dancing. Today the whole thing does not seem so great a tragedy. But then I would have given a year of my life to know why this vicious character was persecuting me. I hoped someone would see how miserably I was being treated, but no one around me seemed to care. It even appeared to me that my immediate neighbors—even the Jews—were laughing at me. You know how the brain works in such situations.

"Since there was nothing more for me to eat I returned to my cabin. Neither the Greek nor the Italians were there. I climbed the ladder to my berth and lay down with my clothes on. Outside, the sea was raging and from the hall above I could hear music, shouts, and laughter. They were having a grand time.

"I was so tired I fell into a heavy sleep. I don't remember ever having slept so deeply. My head sank straight through the pillow. My legs became numb. Perhaps this is the way one dies. Then I awoke with a start. I felt a stabbing pain in my bladder. I had to urinate. My prostate gland is enlarged and who knows what else. My cabin mates had not returned. There was vomit all over the corridors. I attended to my needs and decided to go up on deck for some air. The planks on the deck were clean and wet, as if freshly scrubbed. The sky was overcast, the waves were high, and the ship was pitching violently. I couldn't have stayed there long, it was too cold. Still, I was determined to get a breath of fresh air and I made an effort to walk around.

"And then came the event I still can't believe really happened. I'd reached the railing at the stern of the ship, and turned around. But I was not alone, as I thought. There was my waiter. I trembled. Had he been lurking in the dark waiting for me? Although I knew it was my man, he seemed to be emerging out of the mist. He was coming toward me. I tried to run away but a jerk of the ship threw me right into his hands. I can't describe to you what I felt at that instant. When I was still a yeshiva boy I once heard a cat catch a mouse in the night. It's almost forty years away but the shriek of that mouse still follows me. The despair of everything alive cried out through that mouse. I had fallen into the paws of my enemy and I comprehended his hatred no more than the mouse comprehended that of the cat. I don't need to tell you I'm not much of a hero. Even as a youngster I avoided fights. To raise a hand against anybody was never in my nature. I expected him to lift me up and throw me into the ocean. Nevertheless I found myself fighting back. He pushed me and I pushed him. As we grappled I began to wonder if this could possibly be my arch foe of the dining room. That one could have killed me with a blow. The one I struggled with was not the giant I feared. His arms felt like soft rubber, gelatin, down—I don't know how else to express it. He pushed almost without strength and I was actually able to shove him back. No sound came from him. Why I didn't scream for help, I don't know myself. No one could have heard me anyhow, because the ocean roared and thundered. We struggled silently and stubbornly and the ship kept tossing from one side to the other. I slipped but somehow caught my balance. I don't know how long the duel lasted. Five minutes, ten, or perhaps longer. One thing I remember: I did not despair. I had to fight and I fought without fear. Later it occurred to me that this would be the way two bucks would fight for a doe. Nature dictates to them and they comply. But as the fighting went on I became exhausted. My shirt was drenched. Sparks flew before my eyes. Not sparks—flecks of sun. I was completely absorbed, body and soul, and there was no room for any other sensation. Suddenly I found myself near the railing. I caught the fiend or whatever he was and threw him overboard. He appeared unusually light—sponge or foam. In my panic I did not see what happened to him.

"After that, my legs buckled and I fell onto the deck. I lay there until the gray of dawn. That I did not catch pneumonia is itself a miracle. I was never really asleep, but neither was I awake. At dawn it began to rain and the rain must have revived me. I crawled back to my cabin. The Greek and the Italians were snoring like oxen. I climbed up the ladder and fell on my bed, utterly worn out. When I awoke the cabin was empty. It was one o'clock in the afternoon."

"You struggled with an astral body," I said.

"What? I knew you would say something like that. You have a name for everything. But wait, I haven't finished the story."

"What else?"

"I was still terribly weak when I got up. I went to the dining room anxious to convince myself that the whole thing had been nothing but a nightmare. What else could it have been? I could no more have lifted that bulk of a waiter than you could lift this whole cafeteria. So I dragged myself to my table and sat down. It was lunchtime. In less than a minute a waiter came over to me—not my mortal adversary but another one, short, trim, friendly. He handed me the menu and asked politely what I wanted. In my broken French and then in German I tried to find out where the other waiter was. But he seemed not to understand; anyway, he replied in Spanish. I tried sign language but it was useless. Then I pointed to some items on the menu and he immediately brought me what I asked for. It was my first decent meal on that ship. He was my waiter from then on until we docked in New York. The other one never showed up—as if I really had thrown him into the ocean. That's the whole story."

"A bizarre story."

"What is the sense of all this? Why would he hate me so? And what is an astral body?"

I tried to explain to Chaikin what I had learned about these phenomena in the books of the occult. There is a body within our body: it has the forms and the limbs of our material body but it is of a spiritual substance, a kind of transition between the corporeal and the ghostly—an ethereal being with powers that are above the physical and physiological laws as we know them. Chaikin looked at me through his horn-rimmed glasses sharply, reproachfully, with a hint of a smile.

"There is no such thing as an astral body. I had drunk too much wine on an empty stomach. It was all a play of my fantasy."

"Then why didn't he show up again in the dining room?" I asked.

Chaikin lifted up one of the cigarette stubs and began looking for his matches. "Sometimes waiters change stations. What won't sick nerves conjure up! Besides, I think I saw him a few weeks later in New York. I went into a tavern to make a telephone call and there he was, sitting at the bar—unless this too was a phantom."

We were silent for a long while. Then Chaikin said, "What he had against me, I'll never know."

(Translated from the Yiddish by Friedl Wyler and Herbert Lottman)

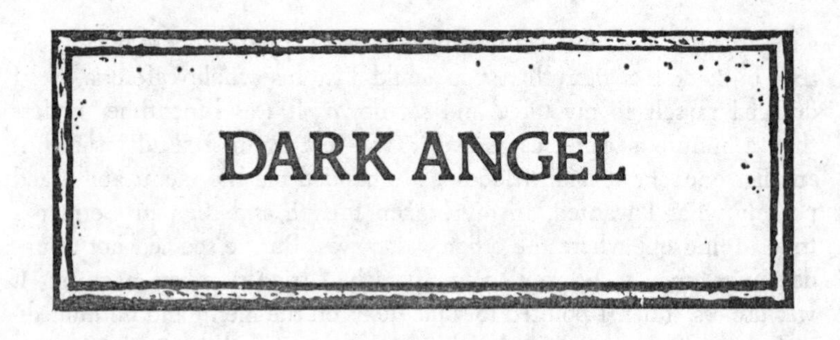

DARK ANGEL

By EDWARD BRYANT

Edward Bryant, now in his mid-thirties, was born in White Plains, New York, but has lived most of his life in the Wyoming-Colorado vicinity. He has worked at a number of jobs, including disc jockey, and has had work published in leading anthologies and magazines, including The National Lampoon. *His books include* Among the Dead *and* Cinnabar, *and he won the Nebula Award in 1979 for his story "Stone." Much of Bryant's work is at once bitterly humorous and visually hard-hitting, and concerns the capacity of people to hurt and be hurt, not unlike his senior co-contributor to this book, Theodore Sturgeon. This story, a fine variation on a classical horror theme, is no exception.*

I can still see the blood. It had been darker than I'd expected; and it ran slowly, like a slow-motion stream in a dream.

Daddy's little girl again . . .

"Was it worth it?" my father had said to me. That was thirty years ago. I was seven.

"So they chased you home from school," he continued. "Danny and his idiot brother. Kids do that. So what? What would they have done if they had caught you?" He'd looked at me speculatively and said, "Never mind." My father claimed to be six feet tall, but he missed that by at least two inches. From my height, he looked as though he were ten feet tall. "Remember what I said yesterday?"

"You said you'd hide in the trees beyond the school. And if they chased me again, you'd help me. You'd throw snowballs."

"You were upset. I meant what I said later," said my father. "After supper."

I said nothing.

My father said, "I asked you if you didn't think it would be unfair for me to help you gang up on them. I waited until you'd calmed down."

"I just wanted you there." My eyes burned, but there were no more tears. "I just wanted you to help me throw snowballs."

He pondered me silently. "Snowballs," he finally said. "Not rocks."

My turn for silence.

"Dan may lose his sight in one eye." My father looked at me, into me, through me. "Was it worth it?"

Thirty years later, I stared past the shoulder of my client, tuning out her prattle. She was self-pitying, a bore. I let my face form a polite mask. I had fulfilled her request, was handling business; I am a professional. But there are some things, some people, with whom I shouldn't be afflicted. I tried to lose myself in the cool, dark recesses of the restaurant.

In the Café Cerberus, beached between a Bloody Mary and the French onion soup, I saw a ghost.

The Café Cerberus can most charitably be described as fashionable. Wood—everything is wood. Oak beams grid the ceiling; the walls are lined with barn-wood bleached by the rural sun. Abstract works of stained and leaded glass fill the frames of the few exterior windows. Occasionally adroit graphics by local artists decorate the walls, a patronage provided by the restaurant management, who changes the displays every two weeks. The pictures are priced and expensive. Greenery—the immaculately groomed plants hang suspended in hand-thrown pots cradled in macrame. When I lunch in the Cerberus I think of the hanging gardens of Nineveh.

Above all, the café is fashionably dark. It was dark even before the energy crises. One peers past the young lawyers in natty suits and the young executives in expensive jogging uniforms to seek out professional athletes, the important local media personalities, entertainment entrepreneurs, the occasional visiting music stars here for club appearances or concerts. It isn't the easiest task to pick out the important people. But then they have an equal handicap trying to figure out if you're a star, too.

It's a grand game, something to do when the conversation palls somewhere between the initial cocktail and the soup and salad. I'm not immune. I sometimes astonish myself with the wit I display on automatic pilot while my mind is taking in the foxy guy at the next table.

Have you ever noticed there sometimes appear to be only about eight distinct physical makeups in the world—and that everybody you know fits one of them? You look at the man across the aisle of the plane, or the woman standing at the corner waiting for the light to change, or the cashier at the bank. And for just a moment you know you know them. The eyes are right, or the mouth. The tilt of the head. The cut of hair. No, you don't know them. But they had you going for a while. The experience disorients you. I suspect for many people it's a pale version of seeing a ghost.

Seeing just any ghost in the Café Cerberus wouldn't have made me spill the remainder of my drink in my lap. But this was a particular specter.

My mind slowed it down, the tomato juice and vodka slopping over the rim of the tilted glass, cascading down, staining me. The Bloody Mary was dark in the dim light of the room, dark against the tan thighs of my slacks. I felt the cold seeping on my skin. Most of the liquid was absorbed. I felt a single large drop run down the back of my calf.

I stared down at myself.

Somewhere in the distance I heard my client start to say, "What's the matter? You look like you saw—"

Everything speeded up to normal. "I'm all right," I said. "It just spilled. I'm clumsy."

My client dipped her napkin in her water glass and handed it over. "I hope that will come out."

"It already is." I rubbed vigorously at the fabric.

"Just like magic." She smiled self-consciously.

"Indeed." I looked back toward the ghost. Alone at a table ten yards away, his attention seemed totally absorbed in the menu. Maybe I was mistaken.

"I'm not sure I can pronounce this," said my client. "You should include a pronunciation guide." She stumbled over the first syllable. I gently took the portfolio from her hands and pulled it to my side of the table. My client was a fiftyish woman, faded blonde with a perpetually timorous expression. I understood her situation. Empathy demanded allowances.

I slowly said, "*Pchagerav monely. Pchagerav tre vodyi.* It's Romany.

It means 'Thrice the candles smoke by me. Thrice thy heart shall broken be.' "

"And they don't have to be special. The candles."

I shook my head. "Buy anything. Cheap is fine. Get them at Woolworth's." I handed her back the portfolio.

She glanced down at the paper. "I doubt I can buy the—" She hesitated. "—the, uh, private parts of a wolf at Woolworth's if this has to be taken a step further."

"It's a big if," I said. "We'll worry about it only if the candle ceremony proves out. I can provide you with the names of several good paraphernalia sellers."

The waitress brought us our lunch. My client had the diet plate with the lean broiled burger. I had the same without the cottage cheese. Things generally have to be paid for, and I had to pay for the carbohydrates in the drink, even if I'd spilled half of it. While we ate, I kept glancing at the ghost—the man I thought I knew. He looked as though he thought he might know me. But he wouldn't sustain eye contact for more than a few seconds at a time.

My client continued talking about her problems and I nodded, frowned, smiled, and said, "Oh"; "Right"; and "Really" at the proper times. We both hesitated a long time when the waitress asked us if we wanted dessert. Finally neither yielded. My client gave the waitress a credit card.

To me she handed an envelope. "Before I run off and forget," she said. Through the tissue I could see that the check was marked "for professional consultation." I put it in my handbag.

"Well . . ." said my client, carefully folding the charge card flimsy. "I've got to pick up my youngest at her violin lesson."

"I'm going to stay here a little while longer," I said. "I need to rest, think a little. Thank you for lunch."

I don't think my client realized how tight she was clutching the portfolio. "Thank you for this."

"Let me know," I said. "All right?"

She nodded and left. I settled back and waited in the cool gloom. The ghost got up from his table and slowly approached me. As he got closer, I was sure. Obviously older, hair thinning, slight paunch, eyes the same. I had loved his eyes. More romantic then, I'd told him his eyes were cold mountain lakes I could dive into. Cold, yes. Yes, I was sure.

"Excuse me," he said. "You look like someone I used to know."

"You do too."

"Angie?" he said. "Angie Black?"

I nodded slightly. "Jerry."

"My God," he said. "It must be fifteen years."

"Twenty."

"Twenty," he repeated. He smiled foolishly. "My God." He was obviously waiting for an invitation.

"Sit down," I said. I could not believe the banality of this all. I could not believe I was talking to the man. I could not believe I was not picking up my salad fork and castrating the son of a bitch.

Jerry pulled out the chair opposite and sat down. "You live here now?"

"Colorado Springs?" I shook my head. "Denver. I'm down here on business."

"Me too," he said. "I mean here on business. I travel. I sell medical instruments. Specialize in gynecological supplies."

I can believe that, I thought. Son of a bitch.

"You said you're here on business?"

"I'm self-employed," I said.

He waited for me to elaborate. I didn't. Twenty years wasn't that long. I could see the wheels turn. His smile widened, became very confident. "Yes, self-employed."

I shrugged. "Girl has to make a living." Maybe I was laying it on a little thick. Jerry's smile never wavered. I doubted two decades had significantly altered his IQ. The son of a bitch.

"This is really incredible," he said. "Running into you like this. I'm here for a regional meeting. Staying at a motel out on East Platte."

I watched him without comment.

"Maybe I'm out of line for suggesting this," he said, "but I'd really like to take you to dinner tonight. I mean, if you're free."

"Well, Jerry," I said. "I really ought to go back to Denver tonight. Business and all. But . . ." He was still not much for eye contact. I saw him staring at my breasts. "I expect I could go back late. After all . . . it's been a long, long time."

"Right," he said. "Where can I pick you up?"

"I'll come to you. You don't mind? Which motel is it?" He told me. We set the time, and then he excused himself to pay his bill and leave because the afternoon session of his conference was about to begin. He paused at the door of the Cerberus and waved back to me. His smile never faltered. I returned him a genteel little wave I hoped was ironic.

He left and I stayed. Story of our lives. I signaled the waitress and asked her to bring me a glass of club soda from the bar. Things were conspiring to make me feel a little rocky. Ovulation definitely is not my favorite time of the month. There are times when I'd like to forget enlightenment and not be so in touch with my body. Feeling something like a mild case of appendicitis twelve times a year is an experience I can do without. Damn mittelschmerz! I felt better than I had earlier, but there was still an abdominal ache.

So I sat and rested and sipped my club soda. And thought about Jerry. And wondered why in hell I was doing what apparently I was doing. Why in hell indeed. That was precisely why. Blood debts die slowly, and hard. And only in blood. Twenty years had changed nothing.

At first the afternoon lull in the Cerberus comforted me. The peace and the darkness soothed. But it gave me time to think and remember. "Is it worth it?" I thought I heard my father say.

I was impressed with the liberal arts division of the Colorado College library. The facsimile translation of Cyranus's *The Magick of Kirani, King of Persia,* London: 1685, hadn't been pulled off the shelf in ages. I literally had to blow the dust off the rough-trimmed pages.

I'd used Cyranus before for a chancier client than myself, so I was fairly confident. I just didn't trust my memory. I took notes: "If therefore you would have conception to be strong and infallible . . . satyrion seed 4 oz.; all the liquor of a roe's gall, honey 3 oz.; mix it up and put it up into a glass vessel. And when there is occasion, give it to a young woman, when it is dry, and let her use coition." The passage added the obvious: to conceive a male, use the gall of a male roe; to conceive a female, use the gall of a female.

I folded my scrap of paper, asked the circulation desk for change, and went to the pay phone. Tracing male exotic deer in Colorado was not so difficult as I'd expected. I could have used the domestic model, but I wanted to be sure. One of my friends and occasional clients spent his summers working for the Cheyenne Mountain Zoo. He owed me a big favor. I hoped he wouldn't ask me questions.

I was slowly realizing soberly, willingly, that I could kill.

As usual, my errands took longer than I'd expected. I called Jerry's motel and left an apologetic message saying I'd be an hour later than planned. I had the feeling Jerry would not cancel our dinner in a fit of pique.

I arrived at the motel shortly after dusk when the neons were still soft against my eyes. Jerry's room was number seven. I wondered if he was superstitious.

Jerry answered the door on the first knock. He'd changed into a tailored blue suit that complemented his eyes. "Want a drink first?" he said. He stepped back and surveyed me. It was the first time in two years I'd worn a dress. I'd bought it this afternoon.

I stood in the doorway. Keane-eyed children stared back at me from the painting above the king-size bed. "Thanks," I said. "Let's wait."

"All right," he said. "Let me get my coat."

He insisted we ride in his Avis Ford. At my suggestion, we drove to the Czech Café in Manitou Springs. "You'll love the roast duckling," I said.

"There's a lot of fat in duck," Jerry answered.

"Makes the flavor."

And that was the general level and tenor of dinner conversation. He seemed to be a little nervous. I realized increasingly that I was. Finally I asked him about his family. I wanted to know about his life. He shifted uncomfortably in his chair.

"Come on," I said.

He looked past my left ear. "It would be—coming up on our fourteenth anniversary," he said. "Linda—my wife—is back in Vegas. She doesn't travel with me."

"Children?"

He shook his head and said nothing.

"Good marriage?"

I hoped he'd tell me it was none of my business. He only hesitated and lit a new cigarette. "Linda doesn't understand me." I must have looked quizzical. He rushed on. "No, really. I know you've probably heard that line a thousand times; but it's true. She doesn't know me. It's just no good."

I leaned back and concentrated on calm. "So why don't you get out of it?"

He looked serious. "There are obligations."

I said, "I'm sure there are."

No one said anything for at least a minute. Then Jerry said, "Does it bother you? I mean, my being married?"

My turn to look away. "No."

More silence.

"What is it that's bothering you?" he said.

"Twenty years."

"What is it?" he said again.

At that moment it took every bit of strength, every resource I possessed, to keep my voice calm, steady, dispassionate. "This is almost a twentieth anniversary," I said. Jerry looked as if he didn't know what expression to adopt. "Not of us first going to bed; not of us breaking up," I said. "Something later on. Twenty years ago I was a seventeen-year-old girl standing in a telephone booth on the main street of her home town. It was past midnight and the city cop car kept circling the block because they couldn't figure out what the hell I was up to. I stood there with twenty dollars in change feeding quarters into the slot. I was calling Stockholm."

Jerry's mouth had dropped open slightly.

"I was calling Sweden because I'd read about the leading columnist for the Stockholm newspaper *Espressen.* He'd traveled around America speaking on legalizing abortion. Drew a lot of fire. I thought maybe he could help me."

Jerry's mouth opened farther.

"He couldn't. I don't know what time it was there, but he was very kind. He apologized and wished me good fortune, but finally said he couldn't help. He could do nothing. I stood in the booth for an hour after that, listening to a dead line. Then I went home and cried.

"Do you know what this state was like then? I was too young and too helpless. I couldn't even get an *illegal* abortion. Even the bad girls in town couldn't help me. Can you believe that?

"I read things, tried to do things to myself. Nothing happened. A little minor mutilation—some blood. Nothing worked.

"Finally I decided to keep the baby. My parents sent me to a home in Wichita. The cover story was that I had a job as a receptionist in an aircraft factory. Do you know what happened then?"

Jerry looked at me transfixed like a rabbit in front of a cobra. He shook his head slowly from side to side. His mouth was still slightly open. He reacted as though he were in an orchestra seat in a live theater.

"The final irony. The baby was born dead. And she almost killed me in dying. As it is, my cervix is damaged. I won't ever be delivering any more children."

"I'm sorry." His voice was little more than a whisper. "I didn't know."

"Of course you didn't know. You were gone. You left after I told you I was pregnant."

His hands made an ineffectual gesture. "It was different then; for both of us. We would have gotten married. I wanted to go to school. I wanted a career. It wouldn't have worked."

I looked at him levelly. "Bullshit. All I wanted was for you to *be* there." I looked for any sign in his face, any evidence at all to deny the truths of twenty years. Nothing. I felt ice all through my belly.

"I just didn't know," he said.

"You already said that."

"I know how you feel," he said.

"*Do* you?"

Jerry looked away silently. He capitulated so easily and I felt cheated. God damn it! He just sat there. Fight me, I thought. Don't let it be one-sided. Prove me wrong if you can. It's on the line. But he only sat staring, saying nothing.

I scooted my chair back. "Come on."

"Where?"

"Back to your motel."

He got up slowly and moved away from the table. The waiter looked agitated.

"Jerry?"

"What."

"Pay the bill."

Jerry seemed to recover his composure in the car; lightly he laid his hand on my left thigh. I had the feeling that while he wasn't sure what was happening, he was now determined to regain control of the situation. Fine. Neither of us spoke all the way down the mountain and back to the motel.

Nor did we speak at first in the room. Jerry silently unlocked the door and switched on a lamp. Equally silently I crossed to the head of the bed and waited for him to close and latch the door. He switched on the Muzak channel on the television. I turned it off.

Standing a foot away from him, I drew the dress over my head. Beneath it, I wore nothing. Then I reached out and undressed him. I knelt to unlace his shoes and felt him shaking slightly. Slowly I stood and moved closer. For a man caught off-balance, he seemed to be recovering nicely.

I kissed him lightly on the lips. Then I moved to the bed, drew down the spread and sheet, lay back against the pillows. He stood over me and I thought I saw the beginning of a smile. His lips and rough hands and body were on me.

He hurried. I was dry, and it hurt. I made him use spittle.

I heard his breath quicken as he massaged my breasts. My nipples were tender, a little sore. "That hurts," I said. He faltered. I waited long enough and said, "I like it. I wouldn't tell that to just any man. Sometimes I enjoy it." His rhythm picked up.

When he climaxed, I watched from a hundred light-years away.

He lay alone in the bed with the sheet drawn up to his waist. He watched me put on the dress and heels. "I wish you'd stay."

"No."

"We have a lot to talk about."

I said patiently, "No, we don't."

"Will I see you again?"

"I doubt it."

He lit a cigarette. "Twenty years ago . . . That was a mistake. A terrible mistake."

"Yes, it was." I wished to God I had a toothbrush. I was not going to ask to borrow his.

"There ought to be some leeway for a mistake."

"Perhaps." In my memory I felt tissue tear.

"I think we could try it."

"Try what?" I said. I smelled the heavy odor of blood from the past.

"To do something about . . . the mistake."

"No," I said. "Too late." I walked toward the door. "It's after midnight, I've got a long drive, and I feel filthy."

His voice was confused and angry. "Was it worth it?"

I didn't return to Denver. Instead I buckled myself into the Audi and drove east out of the Springs on Colorado 24. Beyond the city the street changed to the two-lane blacktop I knew was rarely patrolled. Even if it were, it didn't matter. With the windows down, I floorboarded it across the plains. It was the time of the new moon and overcast hid the stars. I was alone with the raw wind until Kansas loomed ahead and I braked to a stop at the state line.

It probably wasn't worth it. I pulled off on the shoulder and screamed at the stars. I cried myself to sleep still upright in the bucket seat. I awakened shortly before dawn with my mouth tasting like gray cotton. The sun looked swollen, gravid. When I drove back to Denver, I held the car at the speed limit.

I knew the deer-bile potion would insure fertilization.

It was no surprise when I missed my next period, and the one after.

The only suspense was waiting, and allowing my body to work out certain of its own processes without outside influence. While I waited, I worked. Clients came to me with problems and I devised strategies and solutions. My client from the Cerberus confirmed her suspicions about her strayed spouse and returned to me for support and further advice. My friend from the Cheyenne Mountain Zoo came through again marvelously, this time supplying the required private parts of a wolf. As it happened, one of the timber wolves had died of old age, so no one felt ethical qualms. Acquiring desired materials from endangered species is increasingly difficult. Dragons are the worst. Even Cheyenne Mountain can't help.

Between two and three months along, my body decided. I paid with a night of the worst pain I've endured. I paid with fever and blood. In the morning, I scraped a piece of bloody tissue from the soiled towel and sealed it in a bottle. Then I gulped painkillers and slept.

Sleeping and eating and healing took nine days. I was then strong enough for the task. I took a handful of clay from the refrigerator. The best clay for my purposes comes from the red river banks around Ely, Nevada. At room temperature, the consistency feels like flesh.

It took only a short time to mold the doll—legs, arms, head, genitals. For eyes, I pressed two tiny, intense sapphires into the face. I had none of the traditional materials; no hair, no clothing, no nail parings. I possessed something more powerful. For long minutes I held the doll in my hands without moving. Then, with one of my few remaining unbroken fingernails, I slit a neat incision in the belly of the doll.

Next I retrieved the stoppered bottle from the refrigerator. The blood had long since clotted and the tissue was stuck to the bottom. I scraped it loose with a grapefruit spoon. I hated the touch of it, but I took the scrap of flesh between thumb and forefinger and inserted it into the doll's belly. Then I pressed the sides of the incision together and smoothed the scar until the belly was unmarked.

I fasted; I had cleansed myself. In the morning, after my shower, I had sprinkled my body with crushed mandrake root. There was no excuse to delay, no reason to wait longer. A bit unwillingly I realized that events had arranged themselves. The digital watch dial flashed 11:45 p.m. It was Thursday. I drew open the apartment curtains and the full moon shone in.

Naked, I unlocked the wardrobe and drew out the black linen surplice and belt. I daubed saffron perfume on my throat. The carved teak chest provided a jar of ointment with a touch of damiana and some ground clove. I drew the proper pentacle.

The clock in the living room below me began to chime midnight. I set the doll before me and began the words: "*Calicio seou vas dexti fatera crucis patena ante set ad quam! Extersi adsit siti vas seu copula pamini consecrando!*"

I felt something twist within me like a fist made of broken glass.

"I conjure you, Noble One! Come before me at once and perform my bidding without complaint as is the wont of the office you occupy!"

Pain ripped through my abdomen. I wanted to lie down and hug myself with my knees drawn up to my chin.

"I conjure you. Suffer no injury to me, or know the wrath of the Grand Master." The conjuration continued. I thought I saw the doll's tiny limbs writhe.

"*Extersi adsit siti vas seu copula pamini consecrando!*"

I spoke the words of discharge over and over until the passage was complete. Fatigue rushed over me like the surf. I lay on the hardwood floor and wanted to sleep forever. I did sleep, but before I went to my bed, I looked to see if there were blood to clean. I had thought there would be blood.

Weeks passed. The sleek shape of the doll slowly began to distort. So did my dreams. I knew I was having nightmares, but could never remember the precise details in the morning. What I knew full well—and it surprised me—was that I was having doubts. Finally being skeptical of my own feelings and actions.

What was the true cost of retaliation?

Was it worth it?

My friends noticed my disturbance. So did my clients. I hated second-guessing myself. Finally I felt I had no choice. ". . . leeway for a mistake," Jerry had said. People do change over two decades, for better or worse. Perhaps Jerry for the better. Maybe I had made a mistake. I needed to find out.

Playing detective was the easiest part. First I went to the Denver Public Library and looked in the Las Vegas white pages. There was a listing for Jerry Hanford on East Kalahari Court. I called my travel agent and she got me a coach reservation on the next Western flight to Las Vegas. I packed in the next hour, watered the plants, and drove to the airport. In another two hours I was carrying my overnight bag through the terminal at McCarran International Airport. It was noon. I hired a cab to take me to East Kalahari Court. The address turned out to be a sprawling apartment complex on a dusty street running east of the glittering Strip. I got the Hanfords' apartment number from the mailbox rows beside the management building and made my way through a maze of sandy rock gardens and concrete walks.

I found the right number and knocked on the plank door of the pseudo-Spanish villa. Nobody answered. I knocked periodically for five minutes. Finally an elderly woman poked her head out of the door of the adjacent apartment and said, "He ain't here."

"I need to speak with Mr. Hanford," I said. "I have a check to hand-deliver from his insurance company."

"I don't know when he'll be back," she said. "Sometimes he's gone for weeks. Believe this time he's at some convention in Phoenix. Saw him just yesterday."

I don't think she believed my story about the insurance company. I picked up my overnight bag from the sidewalk. "What about Linda—Mrs. Hanford? Is she home?"

"Not hardly," said the woman. "She's dead." My surprise must have been evident. "Didn't know? Yeah, she died quite a ways back. Killed herself with Jerry's pistol. I heard the shot," said the old woman, warming to the subject. "Called the cops."

"I didn't know," I said, hesitating.

"You ain't from no insurance company," said the woman.

I shook my head.

"You got to be one of them women Jerry picks up and drops after a little sweet-talk."

I nodded encouragingly.

"I don't know how that prick does it," said the woman.

I said, "Why did Linda Hanford do it?"

"Well," said the woman, "I don't want to be talking out of school, but—" She didn't hesitate very long. "Jerry treated her like shit, he did. I mean, really bad. Hit her. Hurt her. I could hear it all." She gestured around the apartment mall. "Construction's nothing but crap. Anyhow, Jerry beat her up real bad one night because the doctor said she couldn't have his kid. Next day he was in Oklahoma City sellin' hardware and she blew her brains out. Like I say, he's a prick, and excuse my French."

"What's your name?" I said.

"Finch," she said. "Mrs. Mona T. Finch. Mr. Finch bought a farm in Korea."

"Thank you, Mrs. Finch," I said. "Thanks for talking with me. I've got to go now. I've got a flight to Phoenix to catch."

"Good luck," she said. "You want to use my phone to call a taxi?"

I could get a three-thirty flight for Phoenix. Before I boarded, I called the Phoenix Chamber of Commerce and found out that a major medical-sales-personnel convention was booked into the Hyatt Regency Hotel. I didn't talk to my seatmate on the plane, didn't read the airline magazine, turned down drinks, and rejected the meal. I lay back in my window seat and made my mind as blank a slate as I could. I watched the desert below us.

In Phoenix I took a taxi downtown to the Hyatt Regency, a blocky sand-colored low-rise structure. At the front desk I identified myself as Linda Hanford and asked for my husband, Jerry.

"Uh, right," said the clerk, checking the registration spinner. "Hanford, Jerry. Room 721. You want me to ring him?"

"I want it to be a surprise," I said.

Jerry looked stunned when he answered my knock.

"Have you got a friend in there?"

"I'm alone," he said, and stood back from the door. I walked past him. The room didn't look much different from the room in Colorado Springs.

"Excuse me," said Jerry. "I'll be back in a minute." He went into the bathroom and closed the door; I heard him vomit. I listened to the rasp of brush against teeth and water running in the sink.

When Jerry returned, I said, "You're looking a little peaked."

"I feel terrible," he said. "Been feeling lousy for a while. Goddamned doctors can't tell me why. Absolutely nothing wrong, they say."

A condition of the spell, I thought. No one else can see; nobody else can know. When the time comes, he will be alone. . . . No person can tell him why.

"I can," I said. He looked at me sharply. "And I will. I've already been in Las Vegas today. I heard about Linda."

"Probably had a nice talk with Mona Finch, the big-mouthed bitch. Linda wasn't my fault."

"I wonder," I said. "Let me tell you a few things." I made him sit down, then sat opposite at the writing desk. I started telling him those things.

"You're a *what?*" he said.

"I think 'witch' is an accurate job title."

"You've got to be kidding."

"I'm deadly serious. Now let me tell you more."

He touched his abdomen gingerly and settled back in his chair.

"Why don't you lie on the bed? I think you'll be more comfortable."

He did.

I told him about the doll.

The silence seemed to lengthen beyond endurance for him. "But that's—" He almost choked on the word. "That's voodoo."

"Something like that."

"It's magic. Magic doesn't work unless you believe in it."

"I do."

"I don't," he said.

"The sickness?" I said. "The nausea? The cramps? You didn't know about the doll, remember?"

"Coincidence."

"Today I'm telling you only truths. Later on you'll be more credulous. You'll touch your belly and feel him kick."

Jerry said, "This is sick."

"Kind for kind."

"I think you'd better leave."

"I will," I said. "When I'm sick, I know I'd rather be alone."

"Bitch," he said.

"Yes." I turned back toward him at the door. "One thing I didn't tell you yet."

He stared at me stonily from the bed. "Tell me, Angie, and get out."

"The doll, remember? I modified it radically, but only so far."

"So?"

"I know how proud you are of your penis. I left that. I didn't switch it for a vagina."

He looked at me uncomprehendingly.

"The doll has no birth canal," I said.

Jerry still didn't know what I was saying. He would. I blew him a sad kiss and exited.

In the elevator my legs shook and for a while I had to wedge myself in a corner. Everybody can have one mistake, I told myself. One only. I suddenly wanted to leave the elevator, the hotel, Phoenix. I didn't want to go back to Denver. I wanted to go anywhere else.

I reached the street and wanted to run. The sunset spread clouds the color of blood across the west. I heard screams behind me from the hotel. It was still early in his term. I knew the screams must be echoing only in my head.

THE CREST OF THIRTY-SIX

By DAVIS GRUBB

Davis Grubb, who has been writing short stories and novels for over thirty-five years, had his first success in 1953 with publication of The Night of the Hunter, *that memorable novel of terror and pursuit in the Ohio River valley of West Virginia. Once encountered, Grubb's creation in it of the sinister preacher, who has the words love and hate tattooed on his knuckles, is never forgotten. The author's family has lived in West Virginia for over two hundred years and it provides the setting for most of his work, including such critically praised novels as* The Watchman, Fool's Parade, *and* The Voices of Glory. *His outcry against prejudice and oppression is no less moving for the violence through which he feels compelled to express it. This tale, set on his beloved Ohio River and in his fictional town of Glory, West Virginia, is by turns dark and humorous, gritty and poetical.*

I don't know if she was black or white. Maybe some of both. Or maybe Indian—there was some around Glory, West Virginia, who said she was full Cherokee and descended from the wife of a chief who had broken loose from the March of Tears in the 1840s. Some said not descended at all—that she was that very original woman grown incredibly old. Colonel Bruce theorized that she was the last of the Adena—that vanished civilization who built our great mound here in Glory back a thousand years before Jesus.

What matter whom she was or from whence? Does a seventeen-year-old boy question the race or origin or age of his first true love?

You might well ask, in the first place, what ever possessed the Glory

Town Council to hire on Darly Pogue as wharfmaster? A man whose constant, nagging, gnawing fear—a phobia they call it in the books—whose stuff of nightmare and the theme of at least two attacks of the heebie-jeebies or Whiskey Horrors was the great Ohio River.

Darly feared that great stream like a wild animal fears the forest fire.

There were reasons for that fear. It is said that, as an infant, he had floated adrift in an old cherry-wood pie-safe for six days and six nights of thundering, lightning river storms during the awful flood of 1900.

I read up a lot on reincarnation in those little five-cent Haldemann Julius Blue Books from out Kansas way.

There was one of the little books that says man doesn't reincarnate from his body to another body to another human and so on. It held that our existence as spiritual creatures is divided by God between air and water and land. And we take turns as fish or birds or animals. Or man. A lifetime as a dolphin might be reincarnated as a tiercel to ply the fathomed heavens in splendour and, upon death, to become again a man. Well, somehow, some way, something whispery inside Darly Pogue told him that the good Lord now planned that Darly's next incarnation would, quite specifically, be as an Ohio River catfish.

You can imagine what that did to Darly, what with his phobia of that river.

And where could such mischievous information have originated? Maybe some gypsy fortune-teller—they were always singing and clamoring down the river road in the springtime in their sequined head scarves and candy-colored wagons—maybe one of them told Darly that. In my opinion it was Loll who told him herself: she could be that mean.

And it was, of course, a prediction to rattle a man up pretty sore. I mean, did you ever look eyeball to eyeball with an old flat-headed, rubber-lipped, garbage-eating, mud-covered catfish?

I didn't say *eat* one—God knows that nothing out of God's waters is any tastier rolled in cornmeal and buttermilk batter and fried in country butter.

I said did you ever look a catfish square in the whiskers? Try it next time. It'll shake hell out of you. There's a big, sappy, two-hundred-million-year-old grin on that slippery skewered mug that seems to ask: Homo sapiens, how long you been around? The critter almost winks as much as to remind you that you came from waters as ancient as his—and that you'll probably be going back some day. But, pray the Lord! you'll exclaim, not as one of your ugly horned tribe!

What sense does it make to hire on as wharfmaster a man who fears the very river?

To position such a man twenty-four hours a day, seven days a week in a kind of floating coffin tied with a length of breakable, cuttable rope to the shore?

But, what if that man has ready and unique access to the smallest and greatest of the great river's secrets. Suppose he can locate with unerring accuracy the body of a drowned person. Suppose he can predict with scary certainty the place where a snag is hiding in the channel or the place where a new sandbar is going to form. Suppose he can prognosticate the arrival of steamboats—hours before their putting in. What if he can board one of those boats and at one sweeping glance tell to the ounce—troy or avoirdupois—the weight of its entire cargo?

There wasnt a secret of that old Ohio—that dark, mysterious Belle Rivière—not one that Darly Pogue didn't have instant access to: except one. That One, of course, was the Secret he was married to: Loll, river witch, goddess, woman, whatever—she was the one secret of the great flowing Mistress which Darly did not understand.

But she was, as well, the source of all the rest of the great river's secrets.

Loll.

Dark, strange Loll.

What could possess a man to live with such a woman and on the very breast of that river he feared like a very demon?

The business all began the morning the water first showed sign of rising in the spring of thirty-six. Everybody around Glory came down to the wharfboat full of questions for Darly Pogue and asking him either to confirm or contradict the predictions now crackling in the radio speakers. Wheeling's WWVA.

You see, I have not told you the half of Loll—what kind of creature she really was.

Look at Loll for yourself.

Pretend that it is about ten o'clock in the morning. Wisps of fog still hover like memories above the polished, slow, dark water out in the government channel. Loll creeps mumbling about the little pantry fixing breakfast for me and Darly—cornbread and ramps with home fries and catfish. Mmmmmmm, good. But look at Loll. Her face is like an old dried apple. A little laurel-root pipe is stuck in her withered, toothless gums. Her eyes wind out of deep, leathery wrinkles like mice in an old shoe bag. Look at the hump on her back and her clawlike hands and the long shapeless dotted Swiss of her only dress. This is her —this is Darly Pogue's wife Loll.

So what keeps him with her?

Why does he stay with this old harridan on the river he so disdains? You are on board the wharfboat, in the pantry, looking at this ancient creature. Glance there on the table at the Ingersoll dollar watch with the braided rawhide cord and the watchfob whittled out of a peach pit by a man on Death Row up in Glory prison.

I said about ten o'clock.

Actually, it's five after.

In the morning.

Now turn that nickel-plated watch's hands around to twelve twice—to midnight, that is. Instantly the scene changes, alters magically. The moon appears, imprisoned in the fringes of the violet willow tree up above the brick landing. The stars fox-trot and dip in the glittering river. A sweet, faint wind stirs from the sparkling stream. Breathe in now.

What is that lovely odor?

Laburnum maybe.

Lilac mixed with spicebush and azalea.

With a pinch of cinnamon and musk.

Who is that who stands behind the bedroom door in the small, narrow companionway?

She moves out now into the light—silvered by ardent, panting moonshine—seeming almost like an origin of light rather than someone lit by it. You know you are looking at the same human being you saw at ten —and you know it cannot be but that it is: that, with the coming of nightfall, this is become the most beautiful woman you have ever seen or shall ever look upon again.

Ever.

In your lifetime.

She is naked, save for a little, shimmery see-through skirt and sandals and no brassiere, no chemise, no teddy bear, nor anything else.

And she comes slipping, a little flamewoman, down the companionway, seeming to catch and drag all the moonlight and shadows along with her, and knocks shyly, lovingly, on the stateroom door of Darly Pogue.

Darly has been drinking.

At the first rumor of a flood he panicked.

Loll knocks again.

Y-yes?

It's me, lovey. I have what you've been waiting for. Open up.

Cant you tell me through the door?

But, lovey! I want your arms around me! cried Loll, the starlight seeming to catch and glitter in the lightly tinseled aureole of her nipples. I want to make love! I want to make whoopee!

You know I caint get it up whilst I'm skeert bad, sweetie!

Oh, do let me in!

Aw, shucks, I got a headache, see?

All right, pouted the beautiful girl.

Well? squeaked poor Darly in a teethchattering voice.

Well, what, lovey?

The crest! The crest of thirty-six! cried Darly. What's it going to be? Not as bad as twenty-eight or nineteen and thirteen surely or back in awful eighteen and eighty-four. Is it? O, dont spare me. I can take it. Tell me it haint going to rise that high!

What was the crest of 1913? asked Loll, her pretty face furrowed as she thumbed through her memory. Yes, the crest of 1913 at Glory was sixty-two feet measured on the wall of the Mercantile Bank.

I think so, grunted poor Darly. Yes. That's right.

And the crest of thirty-six—it cant be any higher than that.

The crest of thirty-six, Loll said quietly, lighting a reefer. Will be exactly one hundred and fifteen feet.

Darly was quiet except for an asthmatic squeak.

What? I'm losing my hearing. It sounded exactly like you said, one hundred and fifteen feet!

I did, said Loll, blowing fragrant smoke out of her slender, sensitive nostrils.

Whoooeee! screamed poor Darly, flailing out now through the open stateroom door and galloping toward the gangplank. He was wearing a gaudy pair of underwear which he had sent away for to *Ballyhoo* magazine. He disappeared somewhere under the elms up on Water Street.

That left me alone with her on the wharfboat, peering out through a crack in my own stateroom door at this vision of beauty and light and sweet-smelling womanhood. By damn, it was like standing downwind from an orchard!

She didnt look more than eighteen—about a year older than I, who hadnt ever seen a naked lady except on the backs of well-thumbed and boy-sticky cards that used to get passed around our home room in school.

Nothing at all.

There were lights on the river: boys out gigging for frogs or gathering fish in from trotlines. The gleam of the lanterns flashed on the waters and seemed to stream up through the blowing curtains and glimmer darkling on that girl.

She was so pretty.

She sensed my stare.

She turned and—to my mingled ecstasy and terror—came down the threadbare carpet of the companionway toward my door.

She came in.

A second later we were into the bunk with her wet-lipped and coughing with passion and me not much better.

Afterward she kindly sewed the tear in my shirt and the two ripped-off buttons from our getting me undressed.

Whew!

All the time we were making love I could hear poor Darly Pogue—somewhere up on Water Street reciting the story of the Flood from Genesis, at the top of his voice.

And I haint by God no Noah neither! he'd announce every few minutes, like a candidate declining to run for office. So I haint not your wharfmaster as of this by God hereby date!

Well, I groped and blundered my way into manhood amidst the beautiful limbs of that girl.

The moon fairly blushed to see the things we did.

And with her doing all the teaching.

All through it you could hear the crackle and whisper of static from the old battery Stromberg Carlson—that and the voice of poor Darly Pogue—high atop an old Water Street elm, announcing that the Bible Flood was about to come again.

Who are you? I asked the woman.

I am Loll.

I know that, I said. But I see you in the morning—while you're fixing me and him breakfast and you're *old*—

I am a prisoner of the moon, she said. My beauty waxes and wanes with her phases.

I dont care, I said. I love you. Marry me. I'll borrow for you. I'll even steal for you.

I pondered.

I wont kill for you—but I will *steal*. Will you?

No.

Do you love me at all? I asked then in a ten-year-old's voice.

I am fond of you, she said, giving me a peck of a kiss: her great fog-grey eyes misty from our loving. You are full of lovely aptitudes and you make love marvelously.

She pouted a little and shrugged.

But I do not love you, she said.

I see.

I love *him,* she said. That ridiculous little man who refuses to go with me.

Go? Go where, Loll? You're not leaving Glory are you?

I'm not leaving the river, if that's what you mean. As for Darly Pogue—I adored him in that Other. Before he went away. And now he wont go forward with me again.

Before when, Loll? Forward where?

I got no answer. Her grey eyes were fixed on a circle of streetlamp that illuminated the verdant foliage of the big river elm—and among it the bare legs of poor Darly Pogue.

And now, she said. He must be punished, of course. He has gone too far. He has resisted me long enough. This final insult has done it!

I was getting dressed and in a hurry. I could tell she was talking in other Dimensions about Things and Powers that scared me about as bad as the river did Darly Pogue. Yet I could see what her hold on him was—how she kept him living in that floating casket on top of the moving, living surface of the waters: that great river of pools and shallows, that moving cluster of little lakes, that beloved Ohio. It was her night beauty.

I eased her out of the stateroom as slick and gentle as I could, for I didnt want her passing out one of her punishments onto me.

But I knew I would never be the same.

In fact, I suddenly knew two new things: that I was going to spend my life on the river, and that I would never marry.

Because Loll had spoilt me for even the most loving of mortal caresses.

And, what's more, she sewed my buttons back on that morning. Though the hands that held my repaired garment out to me—they were gnarled and withered like the great roots of old river trees.

Well, you remember the flood of thirty-six. It was a bad one all right.

It was weird—looking down Seventh Street to the streetlight atop the telephone pole by the confectioner's and seeing that streetlight shimmering and shivering just ten inches from the dark, pulsing stream—that streetlamp like a dandelion atop a tall, shimmering stalk of light.

Beautiful.

But kind of deathly, too.

It was a bad, bad flood in the valleys. Crest of fifty-nine feet.

But then Loll had predicted more than one hundred.

Forecast it and scared poor Darly Pogue—who knew she was never wrong—into running for his life and ending up getting himself the corner room on the fifth floor of the Zadok Cramer Hotel. There was only one higher place in Glory and that was the widow's walk atop the old courthouse and this was taller even than the mound. But Darly settled for the fifth floor of the Zadok. It seemed somehow to be the place remotest from the subject of his phobia.

I was living in the hotel by now so I used to take him up his meals—all prepared by the hotel staff: Loll had gone on strike.

Darly didnt eat much.

He just sat on the edge of the painted brass bed toying with the little carved peach pit from Death Row and looking like he was the carver.

She wants me back. And by God I haint going back.

Well, Darly, you could at least go down and see her. I'll lend you my johnboat.

And go back on that wharfboat?

Well, yes, Darly.

Like hell I will, he snaps, pacing the floor in his *Ballyhoo* underwear and walking to the window every few minutes to stare out at block after town block merging liquidly into the great polished expanse of river.

On the wharfboat be damned! he cried. It's farther than that she wants me.

I felt a kind of shiver run over me as Darly seemed to shut his mouth against the Unspeakable. I closed my eyes. All I could see in the dark was the tawny sweet space of skin between Loll's breasts and a tiny mole there, like an island in a golden river.

But I'm safe from her here! he cried out suddenly, sloshing some J. W. Dant into the tumbler from the small washbowl. He drank the half glass of whiskey without winking. Again I shivered.

Aint you even gonna chase it, Darly?

With what?

Well, hell—with water.

Aint got any.

I pointed to the little sink with its twin ornamental brass spigots with the pinheaded cupids for handles.

That's for washing—not drinking. It's—

He shuddered.

—it's *river* water.

He looked miserably at the little spigots and the bowl, golden and browned with use, like an old meerschaum.

I tried to get a room without running water, he said. I do hate this arrangement awfully. Think of it. Those pipes run directly down to . . .

Naturally, he could not finish.

The night of the actual crest of thirty-six I was alone in my own room at the hotel. Since business on the wharfboat had been discontinued during the flood there was no one aboard but Loll. The crest—a mere fifty-nine feet—was registered on the wall of the Purina Feed Warehouse at Seventh and Western. That was the crest of thirty-six. And that was all.

You would think that Darly would have greeted this news with joy.

Or at least relief.

But it sent him into a veritable frenzy against Loll. She had deliberately lied to him. She had frightened him into making himself a laughingstock in Glory. A hundred and fifteen feet, indeed! We shall see about such prevarications!

In his johnboat he rowed his way drunkenly down the cobbled street to where the water lapped against the eaves of the old Traders Hotel and the wharfboat tied in to its staunchstone chimney top.

Loudly Darly began again to read the story of the Flood from Genesis. He got through that and lit into Loll for fair—saying that she had mocked God with predictions of the Flood.

Loll stayed in her stateroom throughout most of these tirades and when she would stand it no more she came out and stood on the narrow little deck looking at him. She was an old crone, now, her rooty knuckles clutched round the moon-silver head of a stick of English furze. Somehow—even in this moon aspect—I felt desire for her again.

You lied, Loll! Darly cried. Damn you, you lied. And you mocked the holy Word!

I did not lie! she cried with a laugh that danced across the renegade water. O, I did not I did not I did not!

You did! screamed Darly and charged down the gangplank from the big johnboat and sprang onto the narrow deck. No one was near enough to intervene as he struck the old woman with the flat of his hand and sent her spinning back into the shadows of the companionway.

The look she cast him in that instant—I saw it.

I tell you I am glad I was never the recipient of such a look.

Darly rowed back to his hotel and went in through a third-story window of the ballroom and up to his room on the fifth.

He was never seen alive on earth again.

He went into that little room on the top of the Zadok Cramer with a hundred and twenty-six pounds of window glazer's putty and began slowly, thoroughly sealing up his room against whatever eventuality.

It was a folly that made the townfolk laugh the harder. Because if the water had risen high as that room—wouldn't it surely sweep the entire structure away?

Yet the flood stage continued to go down. It was plainly a hoax on Loll's part. Yes, the waters kept subsiding. Until by Easter Monday it was down so low that the wharfboat could again tie in onto the big old willow at the foot of Water Street.

Everything was as usual.

Or was it?

There had been a savage electric rainstorm on the last night of the flood of thirty-six. The crest of thirty-six was a grim one and it was near what Loll had warned.

And there was no way to question her about it.

Because during the storm—at some point—she disappeared (as Darly was to do) from off our land of earth.

It all came out the next week.

Toonerville Boso, the desk clerk, hadn't seen nor heard of Darly Pogue in three days and nights. An old lady in four-oh-seven reported a slight leak of brown water in the ceiling of her bedroom. Toonerville approached the sealed room on the morning of the Sunday after Easter and he, too, noted a trickle of yellow, muddy water from under the door of Darly's room. There was also a tiny sunfish flipping helplessly about on the Oriental carpet.

You remember the rest of it—

How a wall of green water and spring mud and live catfish came vomiting out of that door, sweeping poor Boso down the hall and down the winding stairs and out the hotel door and into the sidewalk.

That room had been invaded. Yes, the spigots were wide open.

Everyone in Glory, every one in the riverlands at least, knows that the ceiling of that hotel room was the real crest of thirty-six. Colonel Bruce he worked with transit and scale and plumb bob for a month afterward—measuring it—the real crest of thirty-six. It was exactly one hundred and thirteen feet.

I know, I know—there were catfish in the room and sunfish and gars and a couple of huge goldfish and they all too big to have squeezed up through the hotel plumbing, let alone through those little brass spigots. But they did. The pressure must have been enormous. And it all must have come rushing out and filling up in the space of a few seconds—before Darly Pogue could know what was happening and could scream.

The pressure of Love? I dont know. Some force unknown to us and maybe it's all explained somewhere in one of those little five-cent blue reincarnation books from out Kansas way—I guess it was one I missed. The pressure to get those fish and a few bottles and a lot of mud and water up the pipes and into that room was, as I say, considerable. But nothing compared to the pressure it must have taken to get Darly back out into the river. Out of that room. Into the green, polished, fathomless mother of waters. Love? Maybe it is the strongest force in nature. At least, the love of someone like her.

No trace of her was ever found. No trace of Darly, either—except for his rainbow-hued *Ballyhoo* shorts—they were the one part of him that didnt go through the spigot and which hung there like a beaten flag against the nozzle.

Go there now.

To the river.

When the spring moon is high.

When the lights in the skiffs on the black river look like campfires on stilts of light.

A catfish leaps—porpoising into moonshine and mist and then dipping joyously back into the deeps. Another—smaller—appears by its side. They nuzzle their flat homely faces in the starshine. Their great rubbery lips brush in ecstasy.

And then they are gone in the spring dark—off for a bit of luscious garbage—old lovers at a honeymoon breakfast.

Lucky Darly Pogue! O, lucky Darly!

MARK INGESTRE: THE CUSTOMER'S TALE

By ROBERT AICKMAN

Robert Aickman, the grandson of the Edwardian novelist Richard Marsh, has published a number of collections of macabre stories in both his native England and in America. He explored with Harry Price, the late ghost hunter, Borley Rectory, once reputed to be the most haunted house in England, and served as story adviser on the classic British fantasy film of the 1940s, Dead of Night. *But his ghostly stories are distinctively literary explorations: as he has remarked himself, they are a way of looking at ordinary life. Aickman rarely explains the mysterious happenings in his stories, but rather haunts his reader by a skillful blending of the supernatural with odd aspects of the modern world or allegory. One of his stories, for example, contains an eerie dust storm moving across the grounds of a British manor house about to be given over to the state. Aickman's manifestation of the social storm in a story of the supernatural is typical of his innovational contribution to the form. This story, written more than two years before Sweeney Todd made his musical debut on Broadway, is both a variation on that famous bit of London history and, with its bizarre and erotic aspects, something quite different also.*

I met an old man at the Elephant Theatre, and, though it was not in a pub that we met, we soon found ourselves in one, not in the eponymous establishment, but in a nice, quiet little place down a side turn, which he seemed to know well, but of which, naturally, I knew nothing, since I was only in that district on business, and indeed had been in the great metropolis itself only for a matter of weeks. I may perhaps at the end tell you what the business was. It had some slight bearing upon the old man's tale.

"The Customer's Tale" I call it, because the Geoffrey Chaucer implication may not be far from the truth: a total taradiddle of legend and first-hand experience. As we grow older we frequently become even hazier about the exact chronology of history, and about the boundaries of what is deemed to be historical fact: the king genuinely and sincerely believing that he took part in the Battle of Waterloo; Clement Attlee, after he was made an earl, never doubting that he had the wisdom of Walpole. Was Jowett Ramsey's Lord Chancellor of Clem's? Which one of us can rightly remember that? Well: the old man was a very old man, very old indeed; odd-looking and hairy; conflating one whole century with another whole century, and then sticking his own person in the center of it all, possibly before he was even born.

That first evening, there was, in the nature of things, only a short time before the pubs closed. But we met in the same place again by appointment; and again; and possibly a fourth time, too. That is something I myself cannot exactly recollect; but after that last time, I never saw or heard of him again. I wonder whether anyone did.

I wrote down the old man's tale in my beautiful new shorthand, lately acquired at the college. He was only equal to short installments, but I noticed that, old though he was, he seemed to have no difficulty in picking up each time more or less where he left off. I wrote it all down almost exactly as he spoke it, though of course when I typed it out, I had to punctuate it myself, and no doubt I tidied it up a trifle. For what anyone cares to make of it, here it is.

Fleet Street! If you've only seen it as it is now, you've no idea of what it used to be. I refer to the time when Temple Bar was still there. Fleet Street was never the same after Temple Bar went. Temple Bar was something they simply couldn't replace. Men I knew, and knew well, said that taking it away wrecked not only Fleet Street but the whole City. Perhaps it was the end of England itself. God knows what else was.

It wasn't just the press in those days. All that Canadian newsprint, and those seedy reporters. I don't say you're seedy yet, but you will be. Just give it time. Even a rich journalist has to be seedy. Then there were butchers' shops, and poultry and game shops, and wine merchants passing from father to son, and little places on corners where you could get your watch mended or your old pens sharpened, and proper bookshops too, with everything from *The Complete John Milton* to *The*

Condemned Man's Last Testimony. Of course the "Newgate Calendar" was still going at that time, though one wasn't supposed to care for it. There were a dozen or more pawnbrokers, and all the churches had bread-and-blanket charities. Fancy Fleet Street with only one pawnbroker and all the charity money gone God knows where and better not ask! The only thing left is that little girl dressed as a boy out of Byron's poem. Little Medora. We used to show her to all the new arrivals. People even *lived* in Fleet Street in those days. Thousands of people. Tens of thousands. Some between soft sheets, some on the hard stones. Fancy that! There was room for all, prince and pauper; and women and to spare for almost the lot of them.

Normally, I went round the back, but I remember the first time I walked down Fleet Street itself. It was not a thing you would forget, as I am about to tell you. There were great wagons stuck in the mud, at least I take it to have been mud; and lawyers all over the pavement, some clean, some not. Of course, the lawyers stow themselves away more now. Charles Dickens had something to do with that. And then there were the women I've spoken of: some of them blowsy and brassy, but some soft and appealing, even when they had nothing to deck themselves with but shawls and rags. I took no stock in women at that time. You know why as well as I do. There are a few things that never change. Never. I prided myself upon living clean. Well, I did until that same day. When that day came, I had no choice.

How did I get into the barbershop? I wish I could tell you. I've wondered every time I've thought about the story, and that's been often enough. All I know is that it wasn't to get my hair cut, or to be shaved, and not to be bled either, which was still going on in those days, the accepted thing when you thought that something was the matter with you or were told so, though you didn't set about it in a barbershop if you could afford something better. They took far too much at the barber's. "Bled white" meant something in places of that kind. You can take my word about that.

It's perfectly true that I have always liked my hair cut close, and I was completely clean-shaven as well until I suffered a gash from an assegai when fighting for Queen and Country. You may not believe that, but it's true. I first let this beard grow only to save her Majesty embarrassment, and it's been growing and growing ever since.

As a matter of fact, it was my mother that cut my hair in those days. She knew how *I* liked it and how *she* liked it. She was as thorough as you can imagine, but all the while kissing and joking too. That went on until the episode I am telling you about. Never again afterward.

Often she had been shaving me too; using my dead father's old razors, of which there were dozens and dozens. I never knew my father. I never even saw a likeness of him. I think my mother had destroyed them all, or hidden them away. If ever I asked her about him, she always spoke in the same way. "I prefer you, Paul," she said. "You are the better man. I have nothing to add." Always the same words, or nearly the same. Then she would kiss me very solemnly on the lips, so that there was nothing I could do but change the subject.

How, then, could I possibly have entered that shop? I have an idea that the man was standing outside and simply caught hold of me. That often happened, so that you had to take trouble in looking after yourself. But, as I have told you, I truly do not know. I suspect that things happen from time to time to everyone that they don't understand, and there's simply nothing we can do about them.

I was in the chair immediately, and the man seemed to be clipping at my locks and lathering my face, both at the same time. I daresay he had applied a whiff of chloroform, which, at that period, was something quite new. People always spoke about a whiff of it, as if it had been a Ramón Allones or a Larraniaga.

There were three chairs in the shop, but the man had firmly directed me to a particular one, the one to my left, because that was the one where the light was, or so I supposed was the reason. The man had an assistant, it seemed, in case the shop might suddenly be packed out. The assistant struck me as being pretty well all black, after the style of a Negro, but that might have been only because the whole shop was so dark and smoky. In any case, he could only have been about four feet two inches high, or even less. I wondered how he managed at the chairs. Probably, when at work, he had a box to stand on. All he did now was lean back against the announcements in the far–right-hand corner; waiting until he was needed. The master was as tall as the assistant was short; lean and agile as a daddy longlegs. Also, he was completely clean-shaven and white. One could not help wondering whether anything grew at all, or ever had. Even his hair could well have been some kind of wig. I am sure that it was. It was black and slightly curly and horribly neat. I didn't have my eyes on the pair of them for very long, but I can see them both at this very moment, though, in the case of the assistant, without much definition. Sometimes we can see more without definition than with it. On the marble slab in front of me was a small lighted oil lamp and a single burning candle; smoking heavily, and submerging the other smells. This in the very middle of an ordinary weekday morning. Probably, of course, it was only imitation marble. Probably everything in the shop was an imitation of some kind.

Having your hair cut at that time cost only a few pence, though there was a penny or two more for the tip; and being shaved was often a matter of "Leave it to you, sir." But I knew nothing of that, because, as I have said, I had never had either thing done to me for money in a shop. I began to count up in my head how much I might have in my pocket. I had already begun to support my mother, and, in the nature of things, it can't have been a large sum. Frightening ideas ran about my mind as to how much might be demanded of me. It seemed almost as if I were being treated to everything that the shop had to offer. I tried *not* to think of what might happen were I unable to pay in full.

At one time, the man was holding a bright silvery razor in either hand; which I suppose had its own logic from a commercial point of view. The razors seemed far shinier than those at home. Reflections from the two of them flashed across the ceiling and walls. The razors also seemed far sharper than ours, as was only to be expected. I felt that if an ear were to be streaked off, I should be aware of it because I should see the blood; but that my whole head could go in a second, without my knowing anything at all about it—ever again, of course. I knew how small my head was, and how long and thin my neck. In the mirror I could see something of what was in hand, but not very much, because the mirror was caked and blackened, quite unlike the flickering razors. I doubted whether blood could have been made out in it, even a quite strong flow. I might well see the blood itself, long before the reflection of it.

But the worst thing came suddenly from behind me. Having no knowledge of what went on in these shops, I had never heard about the practice, then taken for granted, of "singeing." The customers regularly used to have the ends of their hair burnt off with a lighted taper. I don't suppose you've even heard of it happening, but it went on until fairly recently, and it only stopped because the shops couldn't get the trained assistant. It was said to "seal" the hairs, as if they had been letters. All that may sound like a good joke, but the thing itself was not at all like a joke.

It was of course the dusky assistant who was doing it—though it suddenly struck me that it might be a disease he had, rather than his natural colouring, perhaps something linked with his being so short. All I know is, and this I can swear to you, that he did not light the taper he held, at either the candle or the lamp. At one moment the bright light behind me was not there, or the assistant there, either. At the next moment the light was so strong and concentrated that, even in the dirty mirror, the reflection was dazzling me.

I think that really it was hypnotizing me. Hypnotism was something else that was fairly new at the time. It wasn't even necessary for the two in the shop to set about it deliberately. The idea of being hypnotized was in the air and fashionable, as different things are at different times. People suddenly went off who would have felt nothing at all a few years earlier.

I felt that my whole body was going round and round like a catherine wheel, feet against head. I felt that my head itself was going round and round in the other dimension, horizontally, so to speak, but faster. At that age, hypnotism had never actually come my way, even though it was being joked about everywhere. As well as all this, there was a sound like a great engine turning over. I think that really I lost myself for a short spell. Fainting was much commoner in those times than it is now, and not only with young girls. What it felt like was a sudden quick fall, with all my blood rushing upward. There were effects on the stage of that kind: clowns with baubles going down through trapdoors and coming up again as demons with pitchforks. They don't show it on the stage anymore, or not so often.

When I came round I was somewhere quite different. Don't ask me exactly how it had come about. Or exactly where I was, for that matter. I can only tell you what happened.

The first thing I knew was a strong smell of cooking.

Baking was what it really smelt like. Everyone at that time knew what baking smelt like, and I more than most, because my mother baked everything—bread, puddings, pies, the lot, even the cat food. I supposed I was down in the cellar of the building. Anyway, I was in *some* cellar. Of course, the kitchen quarters were always in what was called the basement, when the house was good enough to *have* a basement. So the smell was perfectly natural and acceptable.

The only thing was that the place seemed so terribly hot. I thought at first that it might be me, rather than the room, but that became hard to believe.

I was sprawled on a thick mattress. It seemed just as well, and kind of someone, because the floor as a whole was made of stone, not even smooth stone, not smooth at all, but rough. There was enough light for me to see that much. My mattress was considerably fatter than the ones given to the felons in Newgate or to the poorer debtors, and it was most welcome, as I say, but the stuff inside was peeping out everywhere through rents, and the color of the thing was no longer very definite, except that there were marks on it which were almost certainly blood.

I put my hand to my head, but I didn't seem to be actually bleeding through the hair, though it was hard to be sure, as I was sweating so heavily. Then I gave a gulp, like a schoolboy. I suppose I *was* still more or less a schoolboy. Anyway, I nearly fainted all over again.

At the other end of the cellar, if that is what the place was, a huge woman was sitting on a big painted chair, like a throne. The light in the place came from a small lamp on a kind of desk at her side. She had heavy dark hair falling over one shoulder, and a swarthy face, as if she had been a Spanish woman. She wore a dark dress, open all the way down the front to the waist, as if she had just put it on, or could not bear to fasten it owing to the heat, or had been doing some remarkably heavy work. Not that I had ever before seen a woman looking quite like that, not even my mother, when we were alone together. And there was a young girl sitting at her feet, with her head in the woman's lap, so that I could see only that she had dark hair, too, as if she had been the woman's daughter, which of course one would have supposed she was, particularly as the woman was all the time stroking and caressing the girl's hair.

The woman gazed across the cellar at me for some time before she uttered a word. Her eyes were as dark as everything else about her, but they looked very bright and luminous at the same time. Of course, I was little more than a kid, but that was how it all seemed to me. Immediately our eyes met, the woman's and mine, something stirred within me, something quite new and strong. This, although the light was so poor. Or perhaps at first it was *because* of the poor light, like what I said about sometimes seeing more when there is no definition than when there is.

I couldn't utter a word. I wasn't very used to the company of women, in any case. I hadn't much wished for it, as I have said.

So she spoke first. Her voice was as dark as her hair and her eyes. A deep voice. But all she said was: "How old are you?"

"Seventeen and a half, ma'am. A bit more than that, actually."

"So you are still a minor?"

"Yes, ma'am."

"Do you live in the City of London?"

"No, ma'am."

"Where then do you live?"

"In South Clerkenwell, ma'am."

"But you work in the city of London?"

"No, ma'am. I only come to the city on errands."

In those days, we were taught at school how to reply to catechisms of this kind. I had been taught such things very carefully. I must say *that* whatever else I might have to say about education in general. We were told to reply always simply, briefly, and directly. We used to be given exercises and practices.

I must add that the woman was well-spoken, and that she had a highly noticeable mouth. Of course, my faculties were not at their best in all that heat and after the series of odd things that had been happening to me: complete novelties, at that age.

"Whom do you visit on these errands?"

"Mostly people in the backstreets and side streets. We're only in a small way so far." It was customary for everyone who worked for a firm to describe that firm as "we," provided the firm was small enough, and sometimes not only then. With us, even the boozy women who cleaned everything up did it.

"Hardly heard of in the wider world, we might say?"

"I think that could be said, ma'am." I had learned well that boasting was always idle, and led only to still closer interrogation.

"Are your parents living?"

"My father is supposed to be dead, ma'am."

She transfixed me. I was mopping at myself all the time.

"I *think* he's dead, ma'am."

"Was he, or is he, a sailor, or a horsebreaker, or a strolling player, or a hawker?"

"None of those, ma'am."

"A Gay Lothario, perhaps?"

"I don't know, ma'am."

She was gazing at me steadily, but she apparently decided to drop the particular topic. It was a topic I specially disliked, and her dropping it so easily gave me the impression that I had begun to reach her, as well as she me. You know how it can happen. What hypnotism was then, telepathy is now. It's mostly a complete illusion, of course.

"And your mother? Was she pretty?"

"I think she still is pretty, ma'am."

"Describe her as best you can."

"She's very tiny and very frail, ma'am."

"Do you mean she's ill?"

"I don't think she's ill, ma'am."

"Do you dwell with her?"

"I do, ma'am."

"Could she run from end to end of your street, loudly calling out? If the need were to arise. Only then, of course. What do you say?"

At this strange question, the girl on the floor, who had hitherto been still as still, looked up into the woman's face. The woman began to stroke the girl's face and front, though from where I was I could see neither. Besides, it was so hot for caresses.

"I doubt it, ma'am. I hope the need does not arise." We were taught not to make comments, but I could hardly be blamed, I thought, for that one.

"Are you an only child?"

"My sister died, ma'am."

"The family diathesis seems poor, at least on the female side."

I know now that this is what she said, because since then I've worked hard at language and dictionaries and expressing myself, but I did not know then.

"Beg pardon, ma'am?"

But the woman left that topic, too.

"Does your mother know where you are now?"

At school, it might have been taken as rather a joke of a question, but I answered it seriously and accurately.

"She never asks how I spend the day, ma'am."

"You keep yourselves to yourselves?"

"I don't wish my mother to be fussed about me, ma'am."

Here the woman actually looked away for a moment. By now her doing so had a curious effect on me. I should find it difficult to put it into words. I suddenly began to feel queasy. For the first time, I became aware physically of the things that had been happening to me. I longed to escape, but feared for myself if I succeeded.

The woman's eyes came back to me. I could not but go out to meet her.

"Are you or your mother the stronger person?"

"My mother is, ma'am."

"I don't mean physically."

"No, ma'am."

The hot smell, familiar to me as it was, and for that reason all the more incongruous, seemed to have become more overpowering. It was perhaps a part of my newly regained faculties. I had to venture upon a question of my own. At home it was the customary question. It was asked all the time.

"Should not the oven be turned down a little, ma'am?"

The woman never moved a muscle, not even a muscle in her dark eyes. She simply replied "Not yet." But for the first time she smiled at me, and straight at me.

What more could be said on the subject? I knew that overheated ovens burned down houses.

The catechism was resumed.

"How much do you know of women?"

I am sure I blushed, and I am sure that I could make no reply. Our exercises had not included such questions, and I was all but dying of the heat and smell.

"How close have you dared to go?"

I could not withdraw my eyes, though there was nothing that part of me could more deeply wish to do. I hated to be mocked. Mockery was the one thing that could really make me lose control, go completely wild.

"Have you never been close even to your own mother?"

I must all the while have looked more like a turkey than most because my head was so small. You may not allow for that, because it's so much larger now.

You will have gathered that the woman had been drooling slightly, as women do when appealing in a certain way to a man. As I offered no response, she spoke up quite briskly.

"So much the better for all of us," she said, but this time without a trace of the smile that usually goes with remarks of that kind.

Then she added, "So much the better for the customers."

I was certainly not going to inquire what she meant, though I had no idea what I *was* going to do. Events simply had to take their course, as so often in life, though one is always taught otherwise.

Events immediately began to do so. The woman stood up. I could see that the chair, which at first seemed almost like a throne, was in fact hammered together from old sugar boxes and packing cases. The coloring on the outside of it, which had so impressed me, looked much more doubtful now.

"Let's see what you can make of Monica and me," said the woman.

At that the little girl turned to me for the first time. She was a moon-faced child, so pale that it was hard to believe so swarthy a woman could possibly be her mother.

I'm not going to tell you how I replied to what the woman had said. Old though I am, I should still hesitate to do so.

There was a certain amount of dialogue between us.

One factor was that heat. When Monica came to me and started trying to take off my jacket, I could not help feeling a certain relief, even though men, just as much as women, were then used to wearing far heavier clothes, even when it was warm.

Another factor was the woman's bright and steady gaze, though there you will simply think I am making excuses.

Another factor again was that the woman had unlocked something within me that my mother had said should please never be unlocked, never, until she herself had passed away. It was disloyal, but there's usually disloyalty somewhere when one is drawn in that way to a person, and more often than not in several quarters at once.

I did resist. I prevaricated. I did not prevail. I leave it there. I don't know how fond and dutiful you proved at such a time in the case of your own mother.

Monica seemed sweet and gentle, though she never spoke a word. It did, I fear, occur to me that she was accustomed to what she was doing; a quite long and complicated job in those days, which only married ladies and mothers knew about among women. Monica's own dress was made simply of sacking. It was an untrimmed sack. I realized at once that almost certainly she was wearing nothing else. Who could wonder in such heat? Her arms and legs and neck and round face were all skinny to the point of pathos, and white and slimy with the heat. But her hands were gentle, as I say. In the bad light, I could make nothing of her eyes. They seemed soft and blank.

The woman was just standing and gazing and waiting. Her arms rested at her sides, and once more she was quite like a queen, though her dress was still open all down the front to the waist. Of course that made an effect of its own kind too. It was a dark velvet dress, I should say, with torn lace around the neck and around the ends of the sleeves. I could see that she was as bare-footed as little Monica, but that by no means diminished her dignity. She was certainly at her ease, though she was certainly not smiling. She was like a queen directing a battle. Only the once had she smiled; in response to my silly remark about turning down the oven; when I had failed to find the right and unfunny words for what I had meant, and meant so well.

I could now see that the solitary lamp stood on a mere rough ledge rather than on any kind of desk. For that matter, the lamp itself was of a standard and very inexpensive pattern. It was equipped with a movable shade to direct the weak illumination. My mother and I owned a dozen lamps better than that, and used them too, on many, many occasions.

In the end, Monica had me completely naked. She was a most comfortable and competent worker, and, because there was nowhere else to put them, she laid out all my different things neatly on the rough floor, where they looked extremely foolish, as male bits and pieces always do, when not being worn, and often when being worn also.

I stood there gasping and sweating and looking every bit as ridiculous as my things. It is seldom among the most commanding moments in the life of a man. One can see why so many men are drawn to rape and such. Otherwise, if the woman has any force in her at all, the man is at such an utter disadvantage. He is lucky if he doesn't remain so until the end of it. But I don't need to tell you. You'll have formed your own view.

There was no question of that woman lacking a thing. It was doubtless grotesque that I had assented to Monica stripping me, but as soon as Monica had finished, and was moving things about on the floor to make the total effect look even neater, the woman rotated the shade on the lamp, so that the illumination fell on the other end of the cellar, the end that had formerly been in the darkness behind her.

At once she was shedding her velvet dress (yes, it was velvet, I am sure of it) and, even at the time, it struck me as significant that she had put herself in the limelight, so to speak, in order to do so, instead of hiding behind a curtain as most women would have done, more then than now, I believe.

She too proved to be wearing no more than the one garment. Who could wear chemises and drawers and stays in that atmosphere?

The light showed that beneath and around the woman's feet, and I must tell you that they were handsome, well-shaped feet, was a tangle of waste hair, mingled with fur and hide, such as the rag and bone men used to cry, and refuse to pay a farthing for, however earnestly the women selling the stuff might appeal. By no stretch of drink or poetry could one call the heap of it a bed or couch. Our cat would have refused to go near it, let alone lie on it.

None of that made the slightest difference; no more than the heat, the smell, the mystery, or anything else.

The woman, with no clothes on, and with her unleashed hair, was very fine, though no longer a queen. "Let's see," she said, and half-extended her arms toward me.

A real queen might have expressed herself more temptingly, but being a queen is very much a matter of wearing the clothes, as is being a woman. The matter was settled by little Monica giving me a push from behind.

It made me look even more ridiculous, because I fell across the sugar-box throne. In fact, I cut my bare thigh badly. But a flow of blood made no difference in that company, and in a second or two I was wallowing egregiously amid the woman's dark hair and the soft mass of hair and fur from God knows where, and Monica had come in from behind, and begun to help things on.

Almost at once, I became aware of something about Monica, which is scarcely polite to talk about. I only mention it for a reason. The thing was that she herself had no hair, where, even at that time, I knew she should have had hair, she being, I was fairly certain, old enough for it. I refer to that personal matter because it gave me an idea as to who might be Monica's father. On Monica's round head, locks just hung straight around her face, as if they had stopped growing prematurely, and everyone was waiting for them to continue. I began to wonder if there were not some kind of stuck-on wig. I still doubted whether the woman who held me tight was Monica's mother, but for the moment there were other things to think about, especially by such a novice as I was.

There seems to be only one thing worth adding to a scene which you must find obvious enough.

It is that never since have I known a mouth like that woman's mouth. But the entire escapade was of course my first full experience—the first time I was able to go through the whole thing again and again until I was spent and done, sold and paid for.

I suppose I should also say that it was good to have Monica there as well, scrappy though she was, a bit like an undernourished fish. Monica knew many things that she should not have known, and which you can't talk most grown women into bothering about. You'll have come upon what I mean for yourself.

With the two of them, one didn't feel a fool. I even forgot about the heat. I simply can't remember how the woman and Monica managed about that. Perhaps I didn't even notice. I daresay there were creatures making a happy home for themselves in the vast pile of ancient warmth. I should have thought there would have been, but I didn't worry about it at the time. Over the heap, on the dirty wall, was a black-and-white engraving of an old man whose face I knew, because he had been hanged for political reasons. Every now and then, I could see him winking at me through the murk, though I was too pressed to recall his name just then. You remember my telling you that I couldn't keep my hands off the Newgate Calendar and all that went with it. I think his was the only picture in the room.

I keep calling it a room. What else can one call it? A gigantic rat hole, a sewage-overflow chamber, a last resting place for all the world's shorn hair? For me it was an abode of love. My first. Maybe my last.

The woman's hair just smelt of itself. The waste hair was drawn into one's nose and mouth and eyes, even into one's ears, into one's body everywhere. Monica, I believe, had no hair. The tatters of known and unknown fur insinuated themselves between her and me, as if they had been alive. They tickled and chafed but I never so much as tried to hold them back. Joy was all my care, for as long as the appointment lasted.

At the time, it seemed to last more or less for ever. But of course I had no comparisons. The woman and Monica set themselves to one thing after another. Sometimes in turn. Sometimes together. I was half-asphyxiated with heat and hair. I was wet and slimy as a half-skinned eel. I was dead to everything but the precise, immediate half-second. Like the Norseman, I had discovered a new world.

In the end, the woman began tangling her fragrant hair round my crop. I've told you that my neck was like a turkey's in those days. Stringy and very slender.

I am sure that the sweet scent of her hair came from nothing she put on it. In any case, the shop had not struck me as going out for the ladies. For what she was doing, she did not need to have especially long hair either. The ordinary length of hair among women would serve perfectly well. The ordinary length in those days. From what had gone before, I guessed that part of the whole point lay in the tangling process bringing her great mouth harder and tighter than ever against mine. Hair that was too long might have defeated that.

At first the sensation was enough to wake the dead. And by then, as you will gather, that was just about what was needed.

Then it was as if there was a vast shudder in the air. At which the entire spell broke. Nothing had ever taken me more completely by surprise.

It can always be one of the most upsetting experiences in the world, as you may have learned for yourself. I don't know whether it comes worse when one is fully worked up or when the whole miserable point is that one is not.

But that time there was something extra. You won't believe this: I saw a vision of my mother.

She was just standing there, looking tiny and sad, with her arms at her sides, as the woman's had been, and with her own dignity, too. My mother was not wringing her hands or tearing at her wisps of hair or anything fanciful like that. She was just standing very still and looking as if she were a queen, too, a different sort of queen naturally, and this time on the scaffold. That idea of a queen on the scaffold came to me at once.

Until that moment, the huge dark woman had been powerful enough to do exactly what she liked with me. Now, at the first effort I exerted, I broke clean away from her and her hair, and rolled backward on top of Monica. I knew that I had, in fact, dragged a big hank of the woman's hair right away from her head. I could not be mistaken about that because the hank was in my hand. I threw it back among the rest.

I positively leapt to my feet, but even before that the woman was standing, her feet among the garbage, and with a knife in her hand. It was not one of the slim blades that in those days ladies carried in their garters for safety. This lady wore no garters. It was a massive working knife, of the kind employed by butchers who are on the heavier side of the trade. If there had been a little more light, its reflections would have flashed over the walls and ceiling as had happened with the hairdresser's razors.

Monica had climbed up too. She stood between us shuddering and shivering and fishy.

The woman did not come for me. She stepped elegantly across the room, across the place, to the door, and leaned back against it. That was her mistake.

When Monica had undressed me, she could easily have robbed me. I was soon to discover that she had taken nothing. That had been a mistake too.

My few sovereigns and half sovereigns were in a sovereign case, left behind by my father, and among the things given me by my mother when I was confirmed. My other coins were in a purse that had been knitted for me with my name on it. A poor orphan girl named Athene had done that. But there was something else that Monica might have found if she had been tricky enough to look. Wherever I went in those days, I always carried a small pistol. It had been the very first thing I bought with my own money, apart from penny broadsheets and sticks of gob. Even my mother had no idea I possessed it. I did not want her to grieve and fret about what things were like for me in the highways of the world.

She never knew I had it.

Down in that place, the pistol was in my hand more swiftly than thought in my head.

The woman, for her part, gave no time to thinking, or to trying to treat with me. She simply took a leap at me, like a fierce Spanish bull, or a wild Spanish gypsy. There was nothing I could do but allow the pistol to speak for me. I had never discharged it before, except in play on the Heath at night.

I killed the woman. I suppose I am not absolutely certain of that; but I think so. Monica began to whimper and squirm about.

The heat made dressing myself doubly terrible.

I had to decide what to do with Monica. I can truly say that I should have liked very much to rescue her, but I had to drop the idea as impracticable. Apart from everything else, quite a good lot else, I could never have brought her to my home.

I never even kissed her good-bye, or tried in any way to comfort her. I felt extremely bad about that. I still do. It was terrible.

The door opened to me at once, though I had to step over the woman's body to reach it.

Outside, a stone passage ran straight before me to another door, through the glass panels of which I could see daylight. The reek and savor of baking was overwhelming, and the heat, if possible, worse than ever. There were other doors on both sides of the passage. I took it that they led to the different ovens, but I left them unopened.

The door ahead was locked, but the key was on my side of it. Turning it caused me considerable trouble. It called for a knack, and my eyes were full of sweat and my hands beginning to tremble. Nor of course had I any idea what or who might be on the other side of the door. The panels were of obscured glass, but it seemed to me that too little light came through them for the door to open onto the outer world.

Before long, I managed it, perhaps with the new strength I had acquired from somewhere or other. No one had as yet appeared at my rear. I think that, apart from Monica, I was alone down there; and, at that moment, I preferred not to think about Monica.

I flung the door open and found myself in a small, empty, basement shop. It had a single window onto an area; and, beside it, a door. When I say that the shop was empty (and just as well for me that it was), I mean also that it seemed to contain no stock. Nothing at all. There was a small, plain counter, and at the back of it tiers of wooden shelves, all made of dingy polished deal, and all bare as in the nursery rhyme. Brightly colored advertisements were coming in then for the different products, but there was not a bill or a poster in that shop. Nor was there anything like a list of prices, or even a chair for the more decrepit purchasers. I think there was a bit of linoleum on the floor. Nothing more.

I paused long enough to trail my finger down the counter. At least the place seemed to be kept clean, because no mark was left either on the counter or on my finger.

In the shop it was not so hot as in the rest of the establishment, but it was quite hot enough. When later I was allowed to look into a condemned cell, it reminded me of that shop.

But I now had the third door to tackle, the outer door, that might or might not lead to freedom. It looked as if it would, but I had been through too much to be at all sure of anything.

As quietly as I could, I drew the two bolts. They seemed to be in frequent use, because they ran back smoothly. I had expected worse trouble than ever with the lock, but, would you believe it? when the bolts had been drawn, the door simply opened of itself. The protruding part of the lock no longer quite reached into the socket. Perhaps the house was settling slightly. Not that there was any question of seeing much. Outside it was simply the usual, narrow, dirty street with high buildings, and a lot of life going on. A bit of a slum, in fact. Most streets were in those days. That was before the concrete had taken everything over.

I couldn't manage to shut the door. As far as could be seen, one had to be inside to do that. I soon dropped it and started to creep up the area steps. The steps were very worn. Really dangerous for the older people.

For some reason it had never occurred to me that the area gate might be locked, but this time it was. And this time, naturally, there was no key on either side. The area railing was too spiky and too high for me to leap lightly across, even though I was a very long and lanky lad at that time. I was feeling a bit faint as well. For the third time.

A boy came up, dragging a handcart full of stuff from the builders' merchants. He addressed me.

"Come out from under the piecrust, have yer?"

"Which crust?"

The delivery boy pointed over my shoulder. I looked behind me and saw that over the basement door was a sign. It read "Mrs. Lovat's Pie Shop."

At once I thought of the man's name in the picture downstairs. Simon, Lord Lovat. Of course. But Lord Lovat hadn't been hanged, not even with a silken rope. He had been beheaded. Now I should have to think quickly.

"You're wrong," I said to the boy. "I went in to get my hair cut and by mistake came out at the back."

"You was lucky to come out at all," said the boy.

"How's that?" I asked, though I wasn't usually as ready as all this suggests. Not in those days.

"Ask no questions and you'll be told no fibs," said the boy.

"Well," I said, "help me to get out of it."

The boy looked at me. I didn't care for his look.

"I'll watch out for the bobby," said the boy. "He'll help you."

And I had to slip him something before he let me borrow four of his bricks to stand upon on my side of the railing and four to alight upon on the other side. I slipped him a whole five shillings; half as much as his wages for the week in those days. I had taken the place of the barber's assistant who would have had to stand on a box.

After I had helped the boy put the bricks back in his cart, I lost myself in the crowd, as the saying goes. Apart from everything else, I had aroused suspicion by overtipping.

I never heard another thing. Well, not for a very long time, and then not in a personal way.

But I had temporarily lost my appetite for criminal literature. I became out of touch with things for a while. I suffered not only for myself but for my mother. Fortunately, I knew few people who could notice whether I was suffering or not. They might have mocked me if they had, which I could never have endured.

It was a much longer time before I strolled down Fleet Street again. Not until after I was married. And by then Temple Bar had gone, which made a big difference. And manners and customs had changed. Sometimes for the better. Sometimes not. Only on the surface, I daresay, in either case.

I still sometimes break into a sweat when I think of it all. I don't commonly eat meat pies, either. And for a long time I had to cut my own hair, until my wife took over. Since she passed on, I've not bothered with it, as you can see. Why disfigure God's image? as the Russians used to put it. He'll disfigure you fast enough on his own. You can count on that.

The old man was beginning to drool, as, according to him, the woman had done; so that I shut my newly acquired pad and bound it with the still unstretched elastic.

If it had not been in a pub that I had met the old man, where then? I had met him in the auditorium of the Elephant, to which I had been sent as dramatic critic. That too is properly an old man's job, but, in case of need, the smaller papers had, and still have, a habit of sending the youngest person available. I had also to cover boxing matches, swimming matches, dance contests, the running at Herne Hill, and often political and evangelical meetings. Never football matches at one end, or weddings at the other; both of which involved specialists.

The programme for that evening is before me now. I kept it with my notes of the old man's tale, and I have just found the packet, one of hundreds like it.

"Order Tea from the Attendants, who will bring it to you in the Interval. A Cup of Tea and A Plate of Bread and Butter, Price 3d. Also French Pastries, 3d. each."

Wilfrid Lawson, later eminent, played the clean-limbed, overinvolved young hero, Mark Ingestre, in the production we had seen.

There had been a live orchestra, whose opening number had been "Blaze Away."

There were jokes, there were adverts ("Best English Meat Only"), there were even Answers for Correspondents. The price of the programme is printed on the cover: Twopence.

On the other hand, there was a Do You Know? section. "Do You Know," ran the first interrogation, "that *Sweeney Todd* has broken all records for this theatre since it was built?"

"Making him wear a three-cornered hat!" the old man had exclaimed with derision. "And Mrs. Lovat with her hair powdered!"

"David Garrick used to play Macbeth in knee breeches," I replied. Dramatic critics may often, as in my case, know little, but they all know that.

WHERE THE SUMMER ENDS

By KARL EDWARD WAGNER

A psychiatrist by training and a writer by preference, Karl Edward Wagner gave up his practice of medicine to concentrate on his writing, especially his series of stories and novels—about a brooding warrior-adventurer named Kane—which have brought a remarkable new force and depth into the heroic fantasy field established by the late Robert E. Howard. To date, there are a half dozen published books about Kane, but Wagner plans many more. Wagner is also very much interested in the modern tale of terror and his story "Sticks," published first in 1973, is regarded by many as a classic of its kind. In his mid-thirties, he lives presently in North Carolina. Wagner has set this story in his native Knoxville, Tennessee, and focuses chillingly on an increasingly familiar aspect of the Southern landscape.

I

Along Grand Avenue they've torn the houses down, and left emptiness in their place. On one side a tangle of viaducts, railroad yards, and expressways—a scar of concrete and cinder and iron that divides black slum from student ghetto in downtown Knoxville. On the other side, ascending the ridge, shabby relics of Victorian and Edwardian elegance, slowly decaying beneath too many layers of cheap paint and soot and squalor. Most were broken into tawdry apartments—housing for the students at the university that sprawled across the next ridge. Closer to the university, sections had been razed to make room for featureless emplacements of asphalt and imitation used-brick—apartments for the wealthier students. But along Grand Avenue they tore the houses down and left only vacant weed-lots in their place.

Shouldered by the encroaching kudzu, the sidewalks still ran along one side of Grand Avenue, passing beside the tracks and the decrepit shells of disused warehouses. Across the street, against the foot of the ridge, the long blocks of empty lots rotted beneath a jungle of rampant vine—the buried house sites marked by ragged stumps of blackened timbers and low depressions of tumbled-in cellars. Discarded refrigerators and gutted hulks of television sets rusted amidst the weeds and omnipresent litter of beer cans and broken bottles. A green pall over the dismal ruin, the relentless tide of kudzu claimed Grand Avenue.

Once it had been a "grand avenue," Mercer reflected, although those years had passed long before his time. He paused on the cracked pavement to consider the forlorn row of electroliers with their antique lozenge-paned lamps that still lined this block of Grand Avenue. Only the sidewalk and the forgotten electroliers—curiously spared by vandals—remained as evidence that this kudzu-festooned wasteland had ever been an elegant downtown neighborhood.

Mercer wiped his perspiring face and shifted the half-gallon jug of cheap burgundy to his other hand. Cold beer would go better today, but Gradie liked wine. The late-afternoon sun struck a shimmering haze from the expanses of black pavement and riotous weed-lots, reminding Mercer of the whorled distortions viewed through antique windowpanes. The air was heavy with the hot stench of asphalt and decaying refuse and Knoxville's greasy smog. Like the murmur of fretful surf, afternoon traffic grumbled along the nearby expressway.

As he trudged along the skewed paving, he could smell a breath of magnolia through the urban miasma. That would be the sickly tree in the vacant lot across from Gradie's—somehow overlooked when the house there had been pulled down and the shrubbery uprooted—now poisoned by smog and strangled beneath the consuming masses of kudzu. Increasing his pace as he neared Gradie's refuge, Mercer reminded himself that he had less than twenty bucks for the rest of this month, and that there was a matter of groceries.

Traffic on the Western Avenue Viaduct snarled overhead as he passed in the gloom beneath—watchful for the winos who often huddled beneath the concrete arches. He kept his free hand stuffed in his jeans pocket over the double-barreled .357-magnum derringer—carried habitually since a mugging a year ago. The area was deserted at this time of day, and Mercer climbed unchallenged past the railyards and along the unfrequented street to Gradie's house. Here as well, the weeds buried abandoned lots, and the kudzu was denser than he remembered from his previous visit. Trailing vines and smothered trees arcaded the sidewalk, forcing him into the street. Mercer heard a sudden rustle deep beneath the verdant tangle as he crossed to Gradie's gate, and he thought unpleasantly of the gargantuan rats he had glimpsed lying dead in gutters near here.

Gradie's house was one of the last few dwellings left standing in this waste—certainly it was the only one to be regularly inhabited. The other sagging shells of gaping windows and rotting board were almost too dilapidated even to shelter the winos and vagrants who squatted hereabouts.

The gate resisted his hand for an instant—mired over with the fast-growing kudzu that had so overwhelmed the low fence, until Mercer had no impression whether it was of wire or pickets. Chickens flopped and scattered as he shoved past the gate. A brown-and-yellow dog, whose ancestry might once have contained a trace of German shepherd, growled from his post beneath the wooden porch steps. A cluster of silver maples threw a moth-eaten blanket of shade over the yard. Eyes still dazzled from the glare of the pavement, Mercer needed a moment to adjust his vision to the sooty gloom within. By then Gradie was leaning the shotgun back amidst the deeper shadows of the doorway, stepping onto the low porch to greet him.

"Goddamn winos," Gradie muttered, watching Mercer's eyes.

"Much trouble with stealing?" the younger man asked.

"Some," Gradie grunted. "And the goddamn kids. Hush up that growling, Sheriff!"

He glanced protectively across the enclosed yard and its ramshackle dwelling. Beneath the trees, in crates and barrels, crude stands and disordered heaps, lying against the flimsy walls of the house, stuffed into the outbuildings: the plunder of the junk piles of another era.

It was a private junkyard of the sort found throughout any urban slum, smaller than some, perhaps a fraction more tawdry. Certainly it was as out-of-the-way as any. Mercer, who lived in the nearby student quarter, had stumbled upon it quite by accident only a few months before—during an afternoon's hike along the railroad tracks. He had gleaned two rather nice blue-green insulators and a brown-glass Coke bottle by the time he caught sight of Gradie's patch of stunted vegetables between the tracks and the house that Mercer had never noticed from the street. A closer look had disclosed the yard with its moraine of cast-off salvage, and a badly weathered sign that evidently had once read "Red's Second Hand" before a later hand had overpainted "Antiques."

A few purchases—very minor, but then Mercer had never seen another customer here—and several afternoons of digging through Gradie's trove, had spurred that sort of casual friendship that exists between collector and dealer. Mercer's interest in "collectibles" far outstripped his budget; Gradie seemed lonely, liked to talk, very much liked to drink wine. Mercer had hopes of talking the older man down to a reasonable figure on the mahogany mantel he coveted.

"I'll get some glasses." Gradie acknowledged the jug of burgundy. He disappeared into the cluttered interior. From the direction of the kitchen came a clatter and sputter of the tap.

Mercer was examining a stand of old bottles, arrayed on their warped and unpainted shelves like a row of targets balanced on a fence for execution by boys and a new .22. Gradie, two jelly glasses sloshing with burgundy, reappeared at the murkiness of the doorway, squinting blindly against the sun's glare. Mercer thought of a greying groundhog, or a narrow-eyed packrat, crawling out of its burrow—an image tinted grey and green through the shimmering curvatures of the bottles, iridescently filmed with a patina of age and cinder.

He had the thin, worn features that would have been thin and watchful as a child, would only get thinner and more watchful with the years. The limp sandy hair might have been red before the sun bleached it and the years leeched it to a yellow-grey. Gradie was tall, probably had been taller than Mercer before his stance froze into a slouch and then into a stoop, and had a dirty sparseness to his frame that called to mind the scarred mongrel dog that growled from beneath the steps. Mercer guessed he was probably no younger than fifty and probably not much older than eighty.

Reaching between two opalescent-sheened whiskey bottles, Mercer accepted a glass of wine. Distorted through the rows of bottles Gradie's face was watchful. His bright slits of colorless eyes flicked to follow the other's every motion—this through force of habit: Gradie trusted the student well enough.

"Got some more of those over by the fence." Gradie pointed. "In that box there. Got some good ones. This old boy dug them, some place in Vestal, traded the whole lot to me for that R. C. Cola thermometer you was looking at once before." The last with a slight sly smile, flicked lizard-quick across his thin lips: Mercer had argued that the price on the thermometer was too high.

Mercer grunted noncommittally, dutifully followed Gradie's gesture. There might be something in the half-collapsed box. It was a mistake to show interest in any item you really wanted, he had learned—as he had learned that Gradie's eyes were quick to discern the faintest show of interest. The too-quick reach for a certain item, the wrong inflection in a casual "How much?" might make the difference between two bits and two bucks for a dusty book or a rusted skillet. The matter of the mahogany mantelpiece wanted careful handling.

Mercer squatted beside the carton, stirring the bottles gingerly. He was heavyset, too young and too well-muscled to be called beefy. Sporadic employment on construction jobs and a more-or-less-adhered-to program of workouts kept any beer gut from spilling over his wide belt, and his jeans and tank top fitted him as snugly as the older man's faded work clothes hung shapelessly. Mercer had a neatly trimmed beard and subtly receding hairline to his longish black hair that suggested an older grad student as he walked across campus, although he was still working for his bachelor's—in a major that had started out in psychology and eventually meandered into fine arts.

The bottles had been hastily washed. Crusts of cinder and dirt obscured the cracked and chipped exteriors and, within, mats of spiderweb and moldy moss. A cobalt-blue bitters bottle might clean up nicely, catch the sun on the hallway window ledge, if Gradie would take less than a buck.

Mercer nudged a lavender-hued whiskey bottle. "How much for these?"

"I'll sell you those big ones for two, those little ones for one-fifty."

"I could dig them myself for free," Mercer scoffed. "These weed-lots along Grand are full of old junk heaps."

"Take anything in the box for a buck then," Gradie urged him. "Only don't go poking around those goddamn weed-lots. Under that kudzu. I wouldn't crawl into that goddamn vine for any money!"

"Snakes?" Mercer inquired politely.

Gradie shrugged, gulped the rest of his wine. "Snakes or worse. It was in the kudzu they found old Morny."

Mercer tilted his glass. In the afternoon sun the burgundy had a heady reek of hot alcohol, glinted like bright blood. "The cops ever find out who killed him?"

Gradie spat. "Who gives a damn what happens to old winos."

"When they start slicing each other up like that, the cops had damn well better do something."

"Shit!" Gradie contemplated his empty glass, glanced toward the bottle on the porch. "What do they know about knives. You cut a man if you're just fighting; you stab him if you want him dead. You don't slice a man up so there's not a whole strip of skin left on him."

II

"But it had to have been a gang of winos," Linda decided. She selected another yellow flower from the dried bouquet, inserted it into the bitters bottle.

"I think that red one," Mercer suggested.

"Don't you remember that poor old man they found last spring? All beaten to death in an abandoned house. And they caught the creeps who did it to him—they were a couple of his old drinking buddies, and they never did find out why."

"That was over in Lonsdale," Mercer told her. "Around here the pigs decided it was the work of hippy-dope-fiends, hassled a few street people, forgot the whole deal."

Linda trimmed an inch from the dried stalk, jabbed the red strawflower into the narrow neck. Stretching from her bare toes, she reached the bitters bottle to the window shelf. The morning sun, spilling into the foyer of the old house, pierced the cobalt-blue glass in an azure star.

"How much did you say it cost, Jon?" She had spent an hour scrubbing at the bottle with the test tube brushes a former roommate had left behind.

"Fifty cents," Mercer lied. "I think what probably happened was that old Morny got mugged, and the rats got to him before they found his body."

"That's really nice," Linda judged. "I mean, the bottle." Freckled arms akimbo, sleeves rolled up on old blue workshirt, faded blue jeans, morning sun a nimbus through her whiskey-colored close curls, eyes two shades darker than the azure star.

Mercer remembered the half-smoked joint on the hall balustrade, struck a match. "God knows, there are rats big enough to do that to a body down under the kudzu. I'm sure it was rats that killed Midnight last spring."

"Poor old tomcat," Linda mourned. She had moved in with Mercer about a month before it happened, remembered his stony grief when their search had turned up the mutilated cat. "The city ought to clear off these weed-lots."

"All they ever do is knock down the houses," Mercer got out, between puffs. "Condemn them so you can't fix them up again. Tear them down so the winos can't crash inside."

"Wasn't that what Morny was doing? Tearing them down, I mean?"

"Sort of." Mercer coughed. "He and Gradie were partners. Gradie used to run a second-hand store back before the neighborhood had rotted much past the edges. He used to buy and sell salvage from the old houses when they started to go to seed. The last ten years or so, after the neighborhood had completely deteriorated, he started working the condemned houses. Once a house is condemned, you pretty well have to pull it down, and that costs a bundle—either to the owner or, since usually it's abandoned property, to the city. Gradie would work a deal where they'd pay him something to pull a house down—not very much, but he could have whatever he could salvage.

"Gradie would go over the place with Morny, haul off anything Gradie figured was worth saving—and by the time he got the place, there usually wasn't much. Then Gradie would pay Morny maybe five or ten bucks a day to pull the place down—taking it out of whatever *he'd* been paid to do the job. Morny would make a show of it, spend a couple weeks tearing out scrap timber and the like. Then, when they figured they'd done enough, Morny would set fire to the shell. By the time the fire trucks got there, there'd just be a basement full of coals. Firemen would spray some water, blame it on the winos, forget about it. The house would be down, so Gradie was clear of the deal—and the kudzu would spread over the empty lot in another year."

Linda considered the roach, snuffed it out, and swallowed it. Waste not, want not. "Lucky they never burned the whole neighborhood down. Is that how Gradie got that mantel you've been talking about?"

"Probably." Mercer followed her into the front parlor. The mantel had reminded Linda that she wanted to listen to a record.

The parlor—they used it as a living room—was heavy with stale smoke and flat beer and the pungent odor of Brother Jack's barbeque. Mercer scowled at the litter of empty Rolling Rock bottles, crumpled napkins and sauce-stained rinds of bread. He ought to clean up the house today, while Linda was in a domestic mood—but that meant they'd have to tackle the kitchen, and that was an all-day job—and he'd wanted to get her to pose while the sun was right in his upstairs studio.

Linda was having problems deciding on a record. It would be one of hers, Mercer knew, and hoped it wouldn't be Dylan again. She had called his own record library one of the wildest collections of curiosa ever put on vinyl. After half a year of living together, Linda still thought resurrected radio broadcasts of *The Shadow* were a camp joke; Mercer continued to argue that Dylan couldn't sing a note. Withal, she always paid her half of the rent on time. Mercer reflected that he got along with her better than with any previous roommate, and while the house was subdivided into a three-bedroom apartment, they never advertised for a third party.

The speakers, bunched on either side of the hearth, came to life with a scratchy Fleetwood Mac album. It drew Mercer's attention once more to the ravaged fireplace. Some Philistine landlord, in the process of remodeling the dilapidated Edwardian mansion into student apartments, had ripped out the mantel and boarded over the grate with a panel of cheap plywood. In defiance of landlord and fire laws, Mercer had torn away the panel and unblocked the chimney. The fireplace was small, with a grate designed for coal fires, but Mercer found it pleasant on winter nights. The hearth was of chipped ceramic tiles of a blue-and-white pattern—someone had told him they were Dresden. Mercer had scraped away the grime from the tiles, found an ornate brass grille in a flea market near Seymour. It remained to replace the mantel. Behind the plywood panel, where the original mantel had stood, was an ugly smear of bare brick and lathing. And Gradie had such a mantel.

"We ought to straighten up in here," Linda told him. She was doing a sort of half-dance around the room, scooping up debris and singing a line to the record every now and then.

"I was wondering if I could get you to pose for me this morning?"

"Hell, it's too nice a day to stand around your messy old studio."

"Just for a while. While the sun's right. If I don't get my figure studies handed in by the end of the month, I'll lose my incomplete."

"Christ, you've only had all spring to finish them."

"We can run down to Gradie's afterward. You've been wanting to see the place."

"And the famous mantel."

"Perhaps if the two of us work on him?"

The studio—so Mercer dignified it—was an upstairs front room, thrust outward from the face of the house and onto the roof of the veranda, as a sort of cold-weather porch. Three-quarter-length casement windows with diamond panes had at one time swung outward on three sides, giving access onto the tiled porch roof. An enterprising landlord had blocked over the windows on either side, converting it into a small bedroom. The front wall remained a latticed expanse through which the morning sun flooded the room. Mercer had adopted it for his studio, and now Linda's houseplants bunched through his litter of canvases and drawing tables.

"Jesus, it's a nice day!"

Mercer halted his charcoal, scowled at the sheet. "You moved your shoulder again," he accused her.

"Lord, can't you hurry it?"

"Genius can never be hurried."

"Genius, my ass." Linda resumed her pose. She was lean, high-breasted, and thin-hipped, with a suggestion of freckles under her light tan. A bit taller, and she would have had a career as a fashion model. She had taken enough dance to pose quite well—did accept an occasional modeling assignment at the art school when cash was short.

"Going to be a *good* summer." It was that sort of morning.

"Of course." Mercer studied his drawing. Not particularly inspired, but then he never did like to work in charcoal. The sun picked bronze highlights through her helmet of curls, the feathery patches of her mons and axillae. Mercer's charcoal poked dark blotches at his sketch's crotch and armpits. He resisted the impulse to crumple it and start over.

Part of the problem was that she persisted in twitching to the beat of the music that echoed lazily from downstairs. She was playing that Fleetwood Mac album to death—had left the changer arm askew so that the record would repeat until someone changed it. It didn't help him concentrate—although he'd memorized the record to the point he no longer need listen to the words:

I been alone
All the years
So many ways to count the tears
I never change
I never will
I'm so afraid the way I feel
Days when the rain and the sun are gone
Black as night
Agony's torn at my heart too long
So afraid
Slip and I fall and I die

When he glanced at her again, something was wrong. Linda's pose was no longer relaxed. Her body was rigid, her expression tense.

"What is it?"

She twisted her face toward the windows, brought one arm across her breasts. "Someone's watching me."

With an angry grunt, Mercer tossed aside the charcoal, shouldered through the open casement to glare down at the street.

The sidewalks were deserted. Only the usual trickle of Saturday-morning traffic drifted past. Mercer continued to scowl balefully as he studied the parked cars, the vacant weed-lot across the street, the tangle of kudzu in his front yard. Nothing.

"There's nothing out there."

Linda had shrugged into a paint-specked fatigue jacket. Her eyes were worried as she joined him at the window.

"There's something. I felt all crawly all of a sudden."

The roof of the veranda cut off view on the windows from the near sidewalk, and from the far sidewalk it was impossible to see into the studio by day. Across the street, the houses directly opposite had been pulled down. The kudzu-covered lots pitched steeply across more kudzu-covered slope, to the roofs of warehouses along the railyard a block below. If Linda were standing directly at the window, someone on the far sidewalk might look up to see her; otherwise there was no vantage from which a curious eye could peer into the room. It was one of the room's attractions as a studio.

"See. No one's out there."

Linda made a squirming motion with her shoulders. "They walked on then," she insisted.

Mercer snorted, suspecting an excuse to cut short the session. "They'd have had to run. Don't see anyone hiding out there in the weeds, do you?"

She stared out across the tangled heaps of kudzu, waving faintly in the last of the morning's breeze. "Well, there *might* be someone hiding under all that tangle." Mercer's levity annoyed her. "Why can't the city clear off those damn jungles!"

"When enough people raise a stink, they sometimes do—or make the owners clear away the weeds. The trouble is that you can't kill kudzu once the damn vines take over a lot. Gradie and Morny used to try. The stuff grows back as fast as you cut it—impossible to get all the roots and runners. Morny used to try to burn it out—crawl under and set fire to the dead vines and debris underneath the growing surface. But he could never keep a fire going under all that green stuff, and after a few spectacular failures using gasoline on the weed-lots, they made him stick to grubbing it out by hand."

"Awful stuff!" Linda grimaced. "Some of it's started growing up the back of the house."

"I'll have to get to it before it gets started. There's islands in the

TVA lakes where nothing grows but kudzu. Stuff ran wild after the reservoir was filled, smothered out everything else."

"I'm surprised it hasn't covered the whole world."

"Dies down after the frost. Besides, it's not a native vine. It's from Japan. Some genius came up with the idea of using it as an ornamental ground cover on highway cuts and such. You've seen old highway embankments where the stuff has taken over the woods behind. It's spread all over the Southeast."

"Hmmm, yeah? So who's the genius who plants the crap all over the city then?"

"Get dressed, wise-ass."

III

The afternoon was hot and sodden. The sun made the air above the pavement scintillate with heat and the thick odor of tar. In the vacant lots, the kudzu leaves drooped like half-furled umbrellas. The vines stirred somnolently in the musky haze, although the air was stagnant.

Linda had changed into a halter top and a pair of patched cutoffs. "Bet I'll get some tan today."

"And maybe get soaked," Mercer remarked. "Air's got the feel of a thunderstorm."

"Where's the clouds?"

"Just feels heavy."

"That's just the goddamn pollution."

The kudzu vines had overrun the sidewalk, forcing them into street. Tattered strands of vine crept across the gutter into the str their tips crushed by the infrequent traffic. Vines along Gradie's f completely obscured the yard beyond, waved curling tendrils aiml upward. In weather like this, Mercer reflected, you could just abo the stuff grow.

The gate hung again at first push. Mercer shoved harde through the coils of vine that clung there.

"Who's that!" The tone was harsh as a saw blade hitting a nail.

"Jon Mercer, Mr. Gradie. I've brought a friend along."

He led the way into the yard. Linda, who had heard him t the place, followed with eyes bright for adventure. "This Wentworth, Mr. Gradie."

Mercer's voice trailed off as Gradie stumbled out onto the had the rolling slouch of a man who could carry a lot of liq

carrying more liquor than he could. His khakis were the same he'd had on when Mercer last saw him, and had the stains and wrinkles that clothes get when they're slept in by someone who hadn't slept well.

Red-rimmed eyes focused on the half gallon of burgundy Mercer carried. "Guess I was taking a little nap." Gradie's tongue was muddy. "Come on up."

"Where's Sheriff?" Mercer asked. The dog usually warned his master of trespassers.

"Run off," Gradie told him gruffly. "Let me get you a glass." He lurched back into the darkness.

"Owow!" breathed Linda in one syllable. "He looks like something you see sitting hunched over on a bench talking to a bottle in a bag."

"Old Gradie has been hitting the sauce pretty hard last few times I've been by," Mercer allowed.

"I don't think I care for any wine just now," Linda decided, as Gradie reappeared, fingers speared into three damp glasses like a bunch of mismatched bananas. "Too hot."

"Had some beer in the frigidaire, but it's all gone."

"That's all right." She was still fascinated with the enclosed yard. "What a lovely garden!" Linda was into organic foods.

Gradie frowned at the patch of anemic vegetables, beleaguered by encroaching walls of kudzu. "It's not much, but I get a little from it. Damn kudzu is just about to take it all. It's took the whole damn neighborhood—everything but me. Guess they figure to starve me out once the vines crawl over my little garden patch."

"Can't you keep it hoed?"

"Hoe kudzu, miss? No damn way. The vines grow a foot between breakfast and dinner. Can't get to the roots, and it just keeps spreading till the frost; then come spring it starts all over again where the frost left it. I used to keep it back by spraying it regular with 2,4-D. But then the government took 2,4-D off the market, and I can't find nothing else to touch it."

"Herbicides kill other things than weeds," Linda told him righteously.

Gradie's laugh was bitter. "Well, you folks just look all around as you like."

"Do you have any old clothes?" Linda was fond of creating costumes.

"Got some inside there with the books." Gradie indicated a shed that shouldered against his house. "I'll unlock it."

Mercer raised a mental eyebrow as Gradie dragged open the door of the shed, then shuffled back onto the porch. The old man was more in-

terested in punishing the half gallon than in watching his customers. He left Linda to poke through the dusty jumble of warped books and faded clothes, stacked and shelved and hung and heaped within the tin-roofed musty darkness.

Instead he made a desultory tour about the yard—pausing now and again to examine a heap of old hubcaps, a stack of salvaged window frames, or a clutter of plumbing and porcelain fixtures. His deviousness seemed wasted on Gradie today. The old man remained slumped in a broken-down rocker on his porch, staring at nothing. It occurred to Mercer that the loss of Sheriff was bothering Gradie. The old yellow watchdog was about his only companion after Morny's death. Mercer reminded himself to look for the dog around campus.

He ambled back to the porch. A glance into the shed caught Linda trying on an oversized slouch hat. Mercer refilled his glass, noted that Gradie had gone through half the jug in his absence. "All right if I look at some of the stuff inside?"

Gradie nodded, rocked carefully to his feet, followed him in. The doorway opened into the living room of the small frame house. The living room had long since become a warehouse and museum for all of Gradie's choice items. There were a few chairs left to sit on, but the rest of the room had been totally taken over by the treasures of a lifetime of scavenging. Gradie himself had long ago been reduced to the kitchen and back bedroom for his own living quarters.

China closets crouched on lion paws against the wall, showing their treasures behind curved-glass bellies. Paintings and prints in ornate frames crowded the spiderwebs for space along the walls. Mounted deer's heads and stuffed owls gazed fixedly from their moth-eaten poses. Threadbare Oriental carpets lay in a great mound of bright-colored sausages. Mahogany dinner chairs were stacked atop oak and walnut tables. An extravagant brass bed reared from behind a gigantic Victorian buffet. A walnut bookcase displayed choice volumes and bric-a-brac beneath a signed Tiffany lamp. Another bedroom and the dining room were virtually impenetrable with similar storage.

Not everything was for sale. Mercer studied the magnificent walnut china cabinet that Gradie reserved as a showcase for his personal museum. Surrounded by the curving glass sides, the mementos of the junk dealer's lost years of glory reposed in dustless grandeur. Faded photographs of men in uniforms, inscribed snapshots of girls with pompadours and padded-shoulder dresses. Odd items of military uniform, medals and insignia, a brittle silk square emblazoned with the Rising Sun. Gradie was proud of his wartime service in the Pacific.

There were several hara-kiri knives—so Gradie said they were—a Nambu automatic and holster, and a Samurai sword that Gradie swore was five hundred years old. Clippings and souvenirs and odd bits of memorabilia of the Pacific theater, most bearing yellowed labels with painstakingly typed legends. A fist-sized skull—obviously some species of monkey—bore the label: "Jap General's Skull."

"That general would have had a muzzle like a possum." Mercer laughed. "Did you find it in Japan?"

"Bought it during the Occupation," Gradie muttered. "From one little Nip, said it come from a mountain-devil."

Despite the heroic-sounding labels throughout the display—"Flag Taken from Captured Jap Officer"—Mercer guessed that most of the mementos had indeed been purchased while Gradie was stationed in Japan during the Occupation.

Mercer sipped his wine and let his eyes drift about the room. Against one wall leaned the mahogany mantel, and he must have let his interest flicker in his eyes.

"I see you're still interested in the mantel," Gradie slurred, mercantile instincts rising through his alcoholic lethargy.

"Well, I see you haven't sold it yet."

Gradie wiped a trickle of wine from his stubbled chin. "I'll get me a hundred-fifty for that, or I'll keep it until I can get me more. Seen one like it, not half as nice, going for two hundred—place off Chapman Pike."

"They catch the tourists from Gatlinburg," Mercer sneered.

The mantel was of African mahogany, Mercer judged—darker than the reddish Philippine variety. For a miracle only a film of age-blackened lacquer obscured the natural grain—Mercer had spent untold hours stripping layers of cheap paint from the mahogany panel doors of his house.

It was solid mahogany, not a veneer. The broad panels that framed the fireplace were matched from the same log, so that their grains formed a mirror image. The mantelpiece itself was wide and sturdy, bordered by a tiny balustrade. Above that stretched a fine beveled mirror, still perfectly silvered, flanked by lozenge-shaped mirrors on either side. Ornately carved mahogany candlesticks jutted from either side of the mantelpiece, so that a candle flame would reflect against the beveled lozenges. More matched-grain panels continued ceilingward above the mirrors, framed by a second balustraded mantelshelf across the top. Mercer could just about touch it at fullest stretch.

Exquisite, and easily worth Gradie's price. Mercer might raise a hundred of it—if he gave up eating and quit paying rent for a month or three.

"Well, I won't argue it's a beauty," he said. "But a mantel isn't just something you can buy and take home under your arm, brush it off and stick it in your living room. You can always sell a table or a china closet—that's furniture. Thing like this mantel is only useful if you got a fireplace to match it with."

"You think so," Gradie scoffed. "Had a lady in here last spring, fine big house out in west Knoxville. Said she'd like to antique it with one of those paint kits, fasten it against a wall for a stand to display her plants. Wanted to talk me down to one twenty-five though, and I said 'no, ma'am.' "

Linda's scream ripped like tearing glass.

Mercer spun, was out the door and off the porch before he quite knew he was moving. "Linda!"

She was scrambling backward from the shed, silent now but her face ugly with panic. Stumbling, she tore a wrinkled flannel jacket from her shoulders, with revulsion threw it back into the shed.

"Rats!" She shuddered, wiping her hands on her shorts. "In there under the clothes! A great *big* one! Oh, Jesus!"

But Gradie had already burst out of his house, shoved past Mercer—who had pulled short to laugh. The shotgun was a rust-and-blue blur as he lunged past Linda. The shed door slammed to behind him.

"Oh, Jesus!"

The boom of each barrel, megaphoned by the confines of the shed, and in the finger-twitch between each blast, the shrill chitter of pain.

"Jon!"

Then the hysterical cursing from within, and a muffled stomping.

Linda, who had never gotten used to Mercer's guns, was clawing free of his reassuring arm. "Let's go! Let's go!" She was kicking at the gate, as Gradie slid back out of the shed, closing the door on his heel.

"Goddamn big rat, miss." He grinned crookedly. "But I sure done for him."

"Jon, I'm going!"

"Catch you later, Mr. Gradie," Mercer yelled, grimacing in embarrassment. "Linda's just a bit freaked."

If Gradie called after him, Mercer didn't hear. Linda was walking as fast as anyone could without breaking into a run, as close to panic as need be. He loped after her.

"Hey, Linda! Everything's cool! Wait up!"

She didn't seem to hear. Mercer cut across the corner of a weed-lot to intercept her. "Hey! Wait!"

A vine tangled his feet. With a curse, he sprawled headlong. Flinching at the fear of broken glass, he dropped to his hands and knees in the tangle of kudzu. His flailing hands slid on something bulky and foul, and a great swarm of flies choked him.

"Jon!" At his yell, Linda turned about. As he dove into the knee-deep kudzu, she forgot her own near panic and started toward him.

"I'm OK!" he shouted. "Just stay there. Wait for me."

Wiping his hands on the leaves, he heaved himself to his feet, hid the revulsion from his face. He swallowed the rush of bile and grinned. Let her see Sheriff's flayed carcass just now, and she *would* flip out.

IV

Mercer had drawn the curtains across the casement windows, but Linda was still reluctant to pose for him. Mercer decided she had not quite recovered from her trip to Gradie's.

She sneered at the unshaded floor lamp. "You and your morning sunlight."

Mercer batted at a moth. "In the morning we'll be off for the mountains." This, the bribe for her posing. "I want to finish these damn figure studies while I'm in the mood."

She shivered, listened to the nocturnal insects beat against the curtained panes. Mercer thought it was stuffy, but enough of the evening breeze penetrated the cracked casements to draw her nipples taut. From the stairwell arose the scratchy echoes of the Fleetwood Mac album—Mercer wished Linda wouldn't play an album to death when she bought it.

"Why don't we move into the mountains?"

"Be nice." This sketch was worse than the one this morning.

"No." Her tone was sharp. "I'm serious."

The idea was too fanciful, and he was in no mood to argue over another of her whims tonight. "The bears would get us."

"We could fix up an old place maybe. Or put up a log cabin."

"You've been reading *Foxfire Book* too much."

"No, I mean it! Let's get out of here!"

Mercer looked up. Yes, she did seem to mean it. "I'm up for it. But it would be a bit rough for getting to class. And I don't think they just let you homestead anymore."

"Screw classes!" she groaned. "Screw this grungy old dump! Screw this dirty goddamn city!"

"I've got plans to fix this place up into a damn nice townhouse," Mercer reminded her patiently. "Thought this summer I'd open up the side windows in here—tear out this lousy Sheetrock they nailed over the openings. Gradie's got his eye out for some casement windows to match the ones we've got left."

"Oh, Jesus! Why don't you just stay the hell away from Gradie's!"

"Oh, for Christ's sake!" Mercer groaned. "You freak out over a rat, and Gradie blows it away."

"It wasn't just a rat."

"It was the Easter bunny in drag."

"It had paws like a monkey."

Mercer laughed. "I told you this grass was well worth the forty bucks an ounce."

"It wasn't the grass we smoked before going over."

"Wish we didn't have to split the bag with Ron," he mused, wondering if there was any way they might raise the other twenty.

"Oh, screw you!"

Mercer adjusted a fresh sheet onto his easel, started again. This one would be "Pouting Model," or maybe "Uneasy Girl." He sketched in silence for a while. Silence, except for the patter of insects on the windows, and the tireless repetitions of the record downstairs.

"I just want to get away from here," Linda said at last.

In the darkness downstairs, the needle caught on the scratched grooves, and the stereo mindlessly repeated:

"So afraid . . . So afraid . . . So afraid . . . So afraid . . ."

By 1:00 a.m., the heat lightning was close enough to suggest a ghost of thunder, and the night breeze was gusting enough to billow the curtains. His sketches finished—at least, as far as he cared—Mercer rubbed his eyes and debated closing the windows before going to bed. If a storm came up, he'd have to get out of bed in a hurry. If he closed them and it didn't rain, it would be too muggy to sleep. Mechanically he reached for his coffee cup, frowned glumly at the drowned moth that floated there.

The phone was ringing.

Linda was in the shower. Mercer trudged downstairs and scooped up the receiver.

It was Gradie, and from his tone he hadn't been drinking milk.

"Jon, I'm sure as hell sorry about giving your little lady a fright this afternoon."

"No problem, Mr. Gradie. Linda was laughing about it by the time we got home."

"Well, that's good to hear, Jon. I'm sure glad to hear she wasn't scared bad."

"That's quite all right, Mr. Gradie."

"Just a goddamn old rat, wasn't it?"

"Just a rat, Mr. Gradie."

"Well, I'm sure glad to hear that."

"Right you are, Mr. Gradie." He started to hang up.

"Jon, what else I was wanting to talk to you about, though, was to ask you if you really wanted that mantel we was talking about today."

"Well, Mr. Gradie, I'd sure as hell like to buy it, but it's a little too rich for my pocketbook."

"Jon, you're a good old boy. I'll sell it to you for a hundred even."

"Well now, sir—that's a fair enough price, but a hundred dollars is just too much money for a fellow who has maybe ten bucks a week left to buy groceries."

"If you really want that mantel—and I'd sure like for you to have it—I'd take seventy-five for it right now tonight."

"Seventy-five?"

"I got to have it right now, tonight. Cash."

Mercer tried to think. He hadn't paid rent this month. "Mr. Gradie, it's one in the morning. I don't have seventy-five bucks in my pocket."

"How much can you raise, then?"

"I don't know. Maybe fifty."

"You bring me fifty dollars cash tonight, and take that mantel home."

"*Tonight?*"

"You bring it tonight. I got to have it right now."

"All right, Mr. Gradie. See you in an hour."

"You hurry now," Gradie advised him. There was a clattering fumble, and the third try he managed to hang up.

"Who was that?"

Mercer was going through his billfold. "Gradie. Drunk as a skunk. He needs liquor money, I guess. Says he'll sell me the mantel for fifty bucks."

"Is that a bargain?" She toweled her hair petulantly.

"He's been asking one-fifty. I got to give him the money tonight. How much money do you have on you?"

"Jesus, you're not going down to that place tonight?"

"By morning he may have sobered up, forgotten the whole deal."

"Oh, Jesus. You're *not* going to go down there."

Mercer was digging through the litter of his dresser for loose change. "Thirty-eight is all I've got on me. Can you loan me twelve?"

"All I've got is a ten and some change."

"How much change? There's a bunch of bottles in the kitchen—I can return them for the deposit. Who's still open?"

"Hugh's is until two. Jon, we'll be broke for the weekend. How will we get to the mountains?"

"Ron owes us twenty for his half of the ounce. I'll get it from him when I borrow his truck to haul the mantel. Monday I'll dip into the rent money—we can stall."

"You can't get his truck until morning. Ron's working graveyard tonight."

"He's off in six hours. I'll pay Gradie now and get a receipt. I'll pick up the mantel first thing."

Linda rummaged through her shoulder bag. "Just don't forget that we're going to the mountains tomorrow."

"It's probably going to rain anyway."

V

The storm was holding off as Mercer loped toward Gradie's house, but heat lightning fretted behind reefs of cloud. It was a dark night between the filtered flares of lightning, and he was very conscious that this was a bad neighborhood to be out walking with fifty dollars in your pocket. He kept one hand shoved into his jeans pocket, closed over the double-barreled derringer, and walked on the edge of the street, well away from the concealing mounds of kudzu. Once something scrambled noisily through the vines; startled, Mercer almost shot his foot off.

"Who's there!" The voice was cracked with drunken fear.

"Jon Mercer, Mr. Gradie! Jon Mercer!"

"Come on into the light. You bring the money?"

"Right here." Mercer dug a crumpled wad of bills and coins from his pocket. The derringer flashed in his fist.

"Two shots, huh," Gradie observed. "Not enough to do you much good. There's too many of them."

"Just having it to show has pulled me out of a couple bad moments,"

Mercer explained. He dumped the money onto Gradie's shaky palm. "That's fifty. Better count it, and give me a receipt. I'll be back in the morning for the mantel."

"Take it now. I'll be gone in the morning."

Mercer glanced sharply at the other man. Gradie had never been known to leave his yard unattended for longer than a quick trip to the store. "I'll need a truck. I can't borrow the truck until in the morning."

Gradie carelessly shoved the money into a pocket, bent over a lamplit end table to scribble out a receipt. In the dusty glare, his face was haggard with shadowy lines. DT's, Mercer guessed: he needs money bad to buy more booze.

"This is traveling money—I'm leaving tonight," Gradie insisted. His breath was stale with wine. "Talked to an old boy who says he'll give me a good price for my stock. He's coming by in the morning. You're a good old boy, Jon—and I wanted you to have that mantel if you wanted it."

"It's two a.m.," Mercer suggested carefully. "I can be here just after seven."

"I'm leaving tonight."

Mercer swore under his breath. There was no arguing with Gradie in his present state, and by morning the old man might have forgotten the entire transaction. Selling out and leaving? Impossible. This yard was Gradie's world, his life. Once he crawled up out of this binge, he'd get over the willies and not remember a thing from the past week.

"How about if I borrow your truck?"

"I'm taking it."

"I won't be ten minutes with it." Mercer cringed to think of Gradie behind the wheel just now.

Eventually he secured Gradie's key to the aged Studebaker pickup in return for his promise to return immediately upon unloading the mantel. Together they worked the heavy mahogany piece onto the truck bed—Mercer fretting at each threatened scrape against the rusted metal.

"Care to come along to help unload?" Mercer invited. "I got a bottle at the house."

Gradie refused the bait. "I got things to do before I go. You just get back here soon as you're finished."

Grinding dry gears, Mercer edged the pickup out of the kudzu-walled yard, and clattered away into the night.

———

The mantel was really too heavy for the two of them to move—Mercer could handle the weight easily enough, but the bulky piece needed two people. Linda struggled gamely with her end, but the mantel scraped and scuffed as they lowered it from the truck bed and hauled it into the house. By the time they had finished, they both were sticky and exhausted from the effort.

Mercer remembered his watch. "Christ, it's two-thirty. I've got to get this heap back to Gradie."

"Why don't you wait till morning? He's probably passed out cold by now."

"I promised to get right back to him."

Linda hesitated at the doorway. "Wait a second. I'm coming."

"Thought you'd had enough of Gradie's place."

"I don't like waiting here alone this late."

"Since when?" Mercer laughed, climbing into the pickup.

"I don't like the way the kudzu crawls all up the back of the house. Something might be hiding. . . ."

Gradie didn't pop out of his burrow when they rattled into his yard. Linda had been right, Mercer reflected—the old man was sleeping it off. With a pang of guilt, he hoped his fifty bucks wouldn't go toward extending this binge; Gradie had really looked bad tonight. Maybe he should look in on him tomorrow afternoon, get him to eat something.

"I'll just look in to see if he's OK," Mercer told her. "If he's asleep, I'll just leave the keys beside him."

"Leave them in the ignition," Linda argued. "Let's just go."

"Won't take a minute."

Linda swung down from the cab and scrambled after him. Fitful gushes of heat lightning spilled across the crowded yard—picking out the junk-laden stacks and shelves, crouched in fantastic distortions like a Daliesque vision of Hell. The darkness in between bursts was hot and oily, heavy with moisture, and the subdued rumble of thunder seemed like gargantuan breathing.

"Be lucky to make it back before this hits," Mercer grumbled.

The screen door was unlatched. Mercer pushed it open. "Mr. Gradie?" he called softly—not wishing to wake the old man, but remembering the shotgun. "Mr. Gradie? It's Jon."

Within, the table lamps shed a dusty glow across the cluttered room. Without, the sporadic glare of heat lightning popped on and off like a defective neon sign. Mercer squinted into the pools of shadow between cabinets and shelves. Bellies of curved glass, shoulders of polished mahogany smoldered in the flickering light. From the walls, glass eyes glinted watchfully from the mounted deer's heads and stuffed birds.

"Mr. Gradie?"

"Jon. Leave the keys, and let's go."

"I'd better see if he's all right."

Mercer started toward the rear of the house, then paused a moment. One of the glass-fronted cabinets stood open; it had been closed when he was here before. Its door snagged out into the cramped aisle-space; Mercer made to close it as he edged past. It was the walnut cabinet that housed Gradie's wartime memorabilia, and Mercer paused as he closed it because one exhibit was noticeably missing: that of the monkey-like skull that was whimsically labeled "Jap General's Skull."

"Mr. Gradie?"

"Phew!" Linda crinkled her nose. "He's got something scorching on the stove!"

Mercer turned into the kitchen. An overhead bulb glared down upon a squalid confusion of mismatched kitchen furnishings, stacks of chipped, unwashed dishes, empty cans and bottles, scattered remnants of desiccated meals. Mercer winced at the thought of having drunk from these same grimy glasses. The kitchen was deserted. On the stove an overheated saucepan boiled gouts of sour steam, but for the moment Mercer's attention was on the kitchen table.

A space had been cleared by pushing away the debris of dirty dishes and stale food. In that space reposed a possum-jawed monkey's skull, with the yellowed label: "Jap General's Skull."

There was a second skull beside it on the table. Except for a few clinging tatters of dried flesh and greenish fur—the other was bleached white by the sun—this skull was identical to Gradie's Japanese souvenir: a high-domed skull the size of a large, clenched fist, with a jutting, sharp-toothed muzzle. A baboon of sort, Mercer judged, picking it up. A neatly typed label was affixed to the occiput: "Unknown Animal Skull. Found by Fred Morny on Grand Ave. Knoxville, Tenn. 1976."

"Someone lost a pet," Mercer mused, replacing the skull and reaching for the loose paper label that lay beside the two relics.

Linda had gone to the stove to turn off its burner. "Oh, *God!*" she gagged, recoiling from the steaming saucepan.

Mercer stepped across to the stove, followed her sickened gaze. The water had boiled low in the large saucepan, scorching the repellent broth in which the skull simmered. It was a third skull, baboon-like, identical to the others.

"He's *eating* rats!" Linda retched.

"No," Mercer said dully, glancing at the freshly typed label he had scooped from the table. "He's boiling off the flesh so he can exhibit the skull." For the carefully prepared label in his hand read: "Kudzu Devil Skull. Shot by Red Gradie in Yard, Knoxville, Tenn., June 1977."

"Jon, I'm going. This man's stark crazy!"

"Just let me see if he's all right," Mercer insisted. "Or go back by yourself."

"God, no!"

"He's probably in his bedroom then. Fell asleep while he was working on this . . . this . . ." Mercer wasn't sure what to call it. The old man *had* seemed a bit unhinged these last few days.

The bedroom was in the other rear corner of the house, leading off from the small dining room in between. Leaving the glare of the kitchen light, the dining room was lost in shadow. No one had dined here in years obviously, for the area was another of Gradie's store-rooms—stacked and double-stacked with tables, chairs, and bulky items of furniture. Threading his way between the half-seen obstructions, Mercer gingerly approached the bedroom door—a darker blotch against the opposite wall.

"Mr. Gradie? It's Jon Mercer."

He thought he heard a weak groan from the darkness within.

"It's Jon Mercer, Mr. Gradie." He called more loudly, "I've brought your keys back. Are you all right?"

"Jon, let's *go!*"

"Shut up, damn it! I thought I heard him try to answer."

He stepped toward the doorway. An object rolled and crumpled under his foot: It was an empty shotgun shell. There was a strange sweet-sour stench that tugged at Mercer's belly, and he thought he could make out the shape of a body sprawled half out of the bed.

"Mr. Gradie?"

This time a soughing gasp, too liquid for a snore.

Mercer groped for a wall switch, located it, snapped it back and forth. No light came on.

"Mr. Gradie?"

Again a bubbling sigh.

"Get a lamp! Quick!" he told Linda.

"Let him alone, for Christ's sake!"

"Damn it, he's passed out and thrown up! He'll strangle in his own vomit if we don't help him!"

"He had a big flashlight in the kitchen!" Linda whirled to get it, anxious to get away.

Mercer cautiously made his way into the bedroom—treading with care, for broken glass crunched under his foot. The outside shades were drawn, and the room was swallowed in inky blackness, but he was certain he could pick out Gradie's comatose form lying across the bed. Then Linda was back with the flashlight.

Gradie sprawled on his back, skinny legs flung onto the floor, the rest crosswise on the unmade bed. The flashlight beam shimmered on the spreading splotches of blood that soaked the sheets and mattress. Someone had spent a lot of time with him, using a small knife—small-bladed, for if the wounds that all but flayed him had not been shallow, he could not be yet alive.

Mercer flung the flashlight beam about the bedroom. The cluttered furnishings were overturned, smashed. He recognized the charge pattern of a shotgun blast low against one wall, spattered with bits of fur and gore. The shotgun, broken open, lay on the floor; its barrel and stock were matted with bloody fur—Gradie had clubbed it when he had no chance to reload. The flashlight beam probed the blackness at the base of the corner wall, where the termite-riddled floorboards had been torn away. A trail of blood crawled into the darkness beneath.

Then Mercer crouched beside Gradie, shining the light into the tortured face. The eyes opened at the light—one eye was past seeing, the other stared dully. "That you, Jon?"

"It's Jon, Mr. Gradie. You take it easy—we're getting you to the hospital. Did you recognize who did this to you?"

Linda had already caught up the telephone from where it had fallen beneath an overturned nightstand. It seemed impossible that he had survived the blood loss, but Mercer had seen drunks run off after a gutshot that would have killed a sober man from shock.

Gradie laughed horribly. "It was the little green men. Do you think I could have told anybody about the little green men?"

"Take it easy, Mr. Gradie."

"Jon! The phone's dead!"

"Busted in the fall. Help me carry him to the truck." Mercer prodded clumsily with a wad of torn sheets, trying to remember first aid for bleeding. Pressure points? Where? The old man was cut to tatters.

"They're little green devils," Gradie raved weakly. "And they ain't no animals—they're clever as you or me. They *live* under the kudzu. That's what the Nip was trying to tell me when he sold me the skull. Hiding down there beneath the damn vines, living off the roots and whatever they can scavenge. They nurture the goddamn stuff, he said, help it spread around, care for it just like a man looks after his garden.

Winter comes, they burrow down underneath the soil and hibernate."

"Shouldn't we make a litter?"

"How? Just grab his feet."

"Let me lie! Don't you see, Jon? Kudzu was brought over here from Japan, and these damn little devils came with it. I started to put it all together when Morny found the skull—started piecing together all the little hints and suspicions. They like it here, Jon—they're taking over all the waste-lots, got more food than out in the wild, multiplying like rats over here, and nobody knows about them."

Gradie's hysterical voice was growing weaker. Mercer gave up trying to bandage the torn limbs. "Just take it easy, Mr. Gradie. We're getting you to a doctor."

"Too late for a doctor. You scared them off, but they've done for me. Just like they done for old Morny. They're smart, Jon—that's what I didn't understand in time—smart as devils. They knew that I was figuring on them—started spying on me, creeping in to see what I knew—then came to shut me up. They don't want nobody to know about them, Jon! Now they'll come after . . ."

Whatever else Gradie said was swallowed in the crimson froth that bubbled from his lips. The tortured body went rigid for an instant, then Mercer cradled a dead weight in his arms. Clumsily, he felt for a pulse, realized the blood was no longer flowing in weak spurts.

"I think he's gone."

"Oh God, Jon. The police will think we did this!"

"Not if we report it first. Come on! We'll take the truck."

"And just leave him here?"

"He's dead. This is a murder. Best not to disturb things any more than we have."

"Oh, God! Jon, whoever did this may still be around!"

Mercer pulled his derringer from his pocket, flicked back the safety. His chest and arms were covered with Gradie's blood, he noticed. This was not going to be pleasant when they got to the police station. Thank God the cops never patrolled this slum, or else the shotgun blasts would have brought a squad car by now.

Warily he led the way out of the house and into the yard. Wind was whipping the leaves now, and a few spatters of rain were starting to hit the pavement. The erratic light peopled each grotesque shadow with lurking murderers, and against the rush of the wind, Mercer seemed to hear a thousand stealthy assassins.

A flash of electric blue highlighted the yard.

"Jon! Look at the truck!"

All four tires were flat. Slashed.
"Get in! We'll run on the rims!"
Another glare of heat lightning.
All about them, the kudzu erupted from a hundred hidden lairs.
Mercer fired twice.

THE BINGO MASTER

By JOYCE CAROL OATES

Joyce Carol Oates was born and raised in the countryside near Lockport, New York. She received degrees from Syracuse University and the University of Wisconsin. A prolific author—poet, critic, and fiction writer—she has published more than a score of books and has been honored with nearly that many accolades, ranging from the O. Henry Prize to the National Book Award. Her novels include Wonderland *and* Them, *and among her short-story collections are* Marriages and Infidelities *and* Night-Side. *The last, a striking group of stories focusing on the eerie side of relationships and happenings, signaled in 1977 that Joyce Carol Oates has more than a passing interest in the literature of fantasy. She referred to this story as a "mock allegory" and observed: "It would have been impossible for me to translate this parable into conventional naturalistic terms—which is a reason why many of us choose to write, at times, in the surreal mode: the psychological truths to impart are simply too subtle, too complex, for any other technique." This is not a story for those longing for clanking chains and cobwebbed castles or other traditional paraphernalia of the uncanny story. But in a carefully woven and stylish way, Ms. Oates displays here that she is one of our finest living short-story writers, and illuminates along the way some of the higher and most original possibilities of the form. And few who now meet Rose Mallow Odom are likely to soon forget her or her night-side encounter with Joe Pye the Bingo Master.*

Suddenly there appears Joe Pye the Bingo Master, dramatically late by some ten or fifteen minutes, and everyone in the bingo hall except Rose Mallow Odom calls out an ecstatic greeting or at least smiles broadly to show how welcome he is, how forgiven he is for being late—"Just look what he's wearing tonight!" the plump young mother seated across from Rose exclaims, her pretty face dimpling like a child's. "*Isn't* he something," the woman murmurs, catching Rose's reluctant eye.

Joe Pye the Bingo Master. Joe Pye the talk of Tophet—or *some parts* of Tophet—who bought the old Harlequin Amusements Arcade down on Purslane Street by the Gayfeather Hotel (which Rose had been thinking of as boarded up or even razed, but there it is, still in operation) and has made such a success with his bingo hall, even Rose's father's staid old friends at church or at the club are talking about him. The Tophet City Council had tried to shut Joe Pye down last spring, first because too many people crowded into the hall and there was a fire hazard, second because he hadn't paid some fine or other (or was it, Rose Mallow wondered maliciously, a bribe) to the Board of Health and Sanitation, whose inspector had professed to be "astonished and sickened" by the conditions of the rest rooms, and the quality of the foot-longs and cheese-and-sausage pizzas sold at the refreshment stand: and two or three of the churches, jealous of Joe Pye's profits, which might very well eat into *theirs* (for Thursday-evening bingo was a main source of revenue for certain Tophet churches, though not, thank God, Saint Matthias Episcopal Church, where the Odoms worshipped) were agitating that Joe Pye be forced to move outside the city limits, at least, just as those "adult" bookstores and X-rated film outfits had been forced to move. There had been editorials in the paper, and letters pro and con, and though Rose Mallow had only contempt for local politics and hardly knew most of what was going on in her own hometown—her mind, as her father and aunt said, being elsewhere—she had followed the "Joe Pye Controversy" with amusement. It had pleased her when the bingo hall was allowed to remain open, mainly because it upset people in her part of town, by the golf course and the park and along Van Dusen Boulevard; if anyone had suggested that she would be visiting the hall, and even sitting, as she is tonight, at one of the dismayingly long oilcloth-covered tables beneath these ugly bright lights, amid noisily cheerful people who all seem to know one another, and who are happily devouring "refreshments" though it is only seven-thirty and surely they've eaten their dinners beforehand, and *why* are they so goggle-eyed about idiotic Joe Pye!—Rose Mallow would have snorted with laughter, waving her hand in that gesture of dismissal her aunt said was "unbecoming."

Well, Rose Mallow Odom *is* at Joe Pye's Bingo Hall, in fact she has arrived early, and is staring, her arms folded beneath her breasts, at the fabled Bingo Master himself. Of course, there are other workers—attendants—high-school–aged girls with piles of bleached hair and pierced earrings and artfully made-up faces, and even one or two older women, dressed in bright-pink smocks with *Joe Pye* in a spidery green arabesque on their collars, and out front there is a courteous milk-chocolate–skinned young man in a three-piece suit whose function, Rose gathered, was simply to welcome the bingo players and maybe to keep out riffraff, white or black, since the hall *is* in a fairly disreputable part of town. But Joe Pye is the center of attention. Joe Pye is everything. His high rapid chummy chatter at the microphone is as silly, and halfway unintelligible, as any local disc jockey's frantic monologue, picked up by chance as Rose spins the dial looking for something to divert her; yet everyone listens eagerly, and begins giggling even before his jokes are entirely completed.

The Bingo Master is a very handsome man. Rose sees that at once, and concedes the point: no matter that his goatee looks as if it were dyed with ink from the five-and-ten, and his stark-black eyebrows as well, and his skin, smooth as stone, somehow unreal as stone, is as darkly tanned as the skin of one of those men pictured on billboards, squinting into the sun with cigarettes smoking in their fingers; no matter that his lips are too rosy, the upper lip so deeply indented that it looks as if he is pouting, and his getup (what kinder expression?—the poor man is wearing a dazzling white turban, and a tunic threaded with silver and salmon pink, and wide-legged pajama-like trousers made of a material almost as clingy as silk, jet black) makes Rose want to roll her eyes heavenward and walk away. He *is* attractive. Even beautiful, if you are in the habit—Rose isn't—of calling men beautiful. His deep-set eyes shine with an enthusiasm that can't be feigned; or at any rate can't be entirely feigned. His outfit, absurd as it is, hangs well on him, emphasizing his well-proportioned shoulders and his lean waist and hips. His teeth, which he bares often, far too often, in smiles clearly meant to be dazzling, are perfectly white and straight and even: just as Rose Mallow's had been promised to be, though she knew, even as a child of twelve or so, that the ugly painful braces and the uglier "bite" that made her gag wouldn't leave her teeth any more attractive than they already were—which wasn't very attractive at all. Teeth impress her, inspire her to envy, make her resentful. And it's all the more exasperating that Joe Pye smiles so often, rubbing his hands zestfully and gazing out at his adoring giggling audience.

Naturally his voice is mellifluous and intimate, when it isn't busy being "enthusiastic," and Rose thinks that if he were speaking another language—if she didn't have to endure his claptrap about "lovely ladies" and "jackpot prizes" and "mystery cards" and "ten-games-for-the-price-of-seven" (under certain complicated conditions she couldn't follow)—she might find it very attractive indeed. Might find, if she tried, *him* attractive. But his drivel interferes with his seductive power, or powers, and Rose finds herself distracted, handing over money to one of the pink-smocked girls in exchange for a shockingly grimy bingo card, her face flushing with irritation. Of course the evening is an experiment, and not an entirely serious experiment: she has come downtown, by bus, unescorted, wearing stockings and fairly high heels, lipsticked, perfumed, less ostentatiously homely than usual, in order to lose, as the expression goes, her virginity. Or perhaps it would be more accurate, less narcissistic, to say that she has come downtown to acquire a lover? . . .

But no. Rose Mallow Odom doesn't want a lover. She doesn't want a man at all, not in any way, but she supposes one is necessary for the ritual she intends to complete.

"And now, ladies, ladies and gentlemen, if you're all ready, if you're all ready to begin." Joe Pye sings out, as a girl with carrot-colored frizzed hair and an enormous magenta smile turns the handle of the wire basket, in which white balls the size and apparent weight of Ping-Pong balls tumble merrily together, "I am ready to begin, and I wish you each and all the very, very best of luck from the bottom of my heart, and remember there's more than one winner each game, and dozens of winners each night, and in fact Joe Pye's iron-clad law is that *nobody's* going to go away empty-handed—Ah, now, let's see, now: the first number is—"

Despite herself Rose Mallow is crouched over the filthy cardboard square, a kernel of corn between her fingers, her lower lip caught in her teeth. *The first number is—*

It was on the eve of her thirty-ninth birthday, almost two months ago, that Rose Mallow Odom conceived of the notion of going out and "losing" her virginity.

Perhaps the notion wasn't her own, not entirely. It sprang into her head as she was writing one of her dashed-off swashbuckling letters (for which, she knew, her friends cherished her—*isn't Rose hilarious,* they liked to say, *isn't she brave*), this time to Georgene Wescott, who was back in New York City, her second divorce behind her, some sort of complicated, flattering, but not (Rose suspected) very high-paying job at Columbia just begun, and a new book, a collection of essays on contemporary women artists, just contracted for at a prestigious New York publishing house. *Dear Georgene,* Rose wrote, *Life in Tophet is droll as usual what with Papa's & Aunt Olivia's & my own criss-crossing trips to our high-priced $peciali$t pals at that awful clinic I told you about. & it seems there was a scandal of epic proportions at the Tophet Women's Club on acc't of the fact that some sister club which rents the building (I guess they're leftwingdogooder types, you & Ham & Carolyn wld belong if you were misfortunate enough to dwell here-about) includes on its membership rolls some two or three or more Black Persons. Which, tho' it doesn't violate the letter of the Club's charter certainly violates its spirit. & then again,* Rose wrote, very late one night after her Aunt Olivia had retired, and even her father, famously insomniac like Rose herself, had gone to bed, *then again did I tell you about the NSWPP convention here . . . at the Holiday Inn . . . (which wasn't built yet I guess when you & Jack visited) . . . by the interstate expressway? . . . Anyway: (& I fear I did tell you, or was it Carolyn, or maybe both of you) the conference was all set, the rooms & banquet hall booked, & some enterprising muckraking young reporter at the Tophet* Globe-Times *(who has since gone "up north" to Norfolk, to a better-paying job) discovered that the NSWPP stood for National Socialist White People's Party which is (& I do not exaggerate, Georgene, tho' I can see you crinkling up your nose at another of Rose Mallow's silly flights of fancy, "Why doesn't she scramble all that into a story or a* Symboliste *poem as she once did, so she'd have something to show for her exile & her silence & cunning as well," I can hear you mumbling & you are 100% correct) none other than the (are you PREPARED???) American Nazi Party! Yes. Indeed. There is such a party & it overlaps Papa says sourly with the Klan & certain civic-minded organizations hereabouts, tho' he declined to be specific, possibly because his spinster daughter was looking too rapt & incredulous. Anyway, the Nazis were denied the use of the Tophet Holiday Inn & you'd have been impressed by the spirit of the newspaper editorials denouncing them roundly. I hear tell—but maybe it is surreal rumor—that the Nazis not only wear their swastika armbands in secret but have tiny lapel pins on the insides of their lapels, swastikas natcherlly. . . .* And then she'd changed the subject, relaying news of friends, friends' husbands and wives, and former husbands and wives, and acquaintances' latest doings, scandalous and otherwise (for of the lively, gregarious, genius-ridden group that had assembled itself informally in Cambridge, Mass., almost twenty years ago, Rose Mallow Odom was the only really dedicated letter writer—the one who held everyone together through the mails—the one who would continue to write cheerful letter after letter even when she wasn't answered for a year or two), and as a perky little postscript she added that her thirty-ninth birthday was fast approaching and she meant to divest herself of her damned virginity as a kind of present to herself. *As my famous ironing-board figure is flatter than ever, & my breasts the size of Dixie cups after last spring's ritual flu & a rerun of that wretched bronchitis, it will be, as you can imagine, quite a challenge.*

Of course it was nothing more than a joke, one of Rose's whimsical self-mocking jokes, a postscript scribbled when her eyelids had begun to droop with fatigue. And yet . . . And yet when she actually wrote *I intend to divest myself of my damned virginity,* and sealed the letter, she saw that the project was inevitable. She would go through with it. She *would* go through with it, just as in the old days, years ago, when she was the most promising young writer in her circle, and grants and fellowships and prizes had tumbled into her lap, she had forced herself to complete innumerable projects simply because they were challenging, and would give her pain. (Though Rose was scornful of the Odoms' puritanical disdain of pleasure, on intellectual grounds, she nevertheless believed that painful experiences, and even pain itself, had a generally salubrious effect.)

And so she went out, the very next evening, a Thursday, telling her father and her aunt Olivia that she was going to the downtown library. When they asked in alarm, as she knew they would, why on earth she was going at such a time, Rose said with a schoolgirlish scowl that that was her business. But was the library even open at such a strange time, Aunt Olivia wanted to know. Open till nine on Thursdays, Rose said.

That first Thursday Rose had intended to go to a singles bar she had heard about, in the ground floor of a new high-rise office building; but at first she had difficulty finding the place, and circled about the enormous glass-and-concrete tower in her ill-fitting high heels, muttering to herself that no experience would be worth so much effort, even if it was a painful one. (She was of course a chaste young woman, whose general feeling about sex was not much different than it had been in elementary school, when the cruder, more reckless, more knowing children had had the power, by chanting certain words, to make poor Rose

Mallow Odom press her hands over her ears.) Then she discovered the bar—discovered, rather, a long line of young people snaking up some dark concrete steps to the sidewalk, and along the sidewalk for hundreds of feet, evidently waiting to get into the Chanticleer. She was appalled not only by the crowd but by the exuberant youth of the crowd: no one older than twenty-five, no one dressed as she was. (*She* looked dressed for church, which she hated. But however else did people dress?) So she retreated, and went to the downtown library after all, where the librarians all knew her, and asked respectfully after her "work" (though she had made it clear years ago that she was no longer "working"—the demands her mother made upon her during the long years of her illness, and then Rose's father's precarious health, and of course her own history of respiratory illnesses and anemia and easily broken bones had made concentration impossible). Once she shook off the solicitous cackling old ladies she spent what remained of her evening quite profitably—she read *The Oresteia* in a translation new to her, and scribbled notes as she always did, excited by stray thoughts for articles or stories or poems, though in the end she always crumpled the notes up and threw them away. But the evening had not been an entire loss.

The second Thursday, she went to the Park Avenue Hotel, Tophet's only good hotel, fully intending to sit in the dim cocktail lounge until something happened—but she had no more than stepped into the lobby when Barbara Pursley called out to her; and she ended by going to dinner with Barbara and her husband, who were visiting Tophet for a few days, and Barbara's parents, whom she had always liked. Though she hadn't seen Barbara for fifteen years, and in truth hadn't thought of her once during those fifteen years (except to remember that a close friend of Barbara's had been the one, in sixth grade, to think up the cruel but probably fairly accurate nickname The Ostrich for Rose), she did have an enjoyable time. Anyone who had observed their table in the vaulted oak-paneled dining room of the Park Avenue, taking note in particular of the tall, lean, nervously eager woman who laughed frequently, showing her gums, and who seemed unable to keep her hand from patting at her hair (which was baby-fine, a pale brown, in no style at all but not unbecoming), and adjusting her collar or earrings, would have been quite astonished to learn that that woman (of indeterminate age: her "gentle" expressive chocolate-brown eyes might have belonged to a gawky girl of sixteen or to a woman in her fifties) had intended to spend the evening prowling about for a man.

And then the third Thursday (for the Thursdays had become, now, a ritual: her aunt protested only feebly, her father gave her a library book to return) she went to the movies, to the very theater where, at thirteen or fourteen, with her friend Janet Brome, she had met . . . or almost met . . . what were thought to be, then, "older boys" of seventeen or eighteen. (Big boys, farm boys, spending the day in Tophet, prowling about for girls. But even in the darkened Rialto neither Rose nor Janet resembled the kind of girls these boys sought.) And nothing at all happened. Nothing. Rose walked out of the theater when the film—a cloying self-conscious comedy about adultery in Manhattan—was only half over, and took a bus back home, in time to join her father and her aunt for ice cream and Peek Freans biscuits. "You look as if you're coming down with a cold," Rose's father said. "Your eyes are watery." Rose denied it; but came down with a cold the very next day.

She skipped a Thursday, but on the following week ventured out again, eyeing herself cynically and without a trace of affection in her bedroom mirror (which looked wispy and washed-out—but do mirrors actually age, Rose wondered), judging that, yes, she might be called pretty, with her big ostrich eyes and her ostrich height and gawky dignity, by a man who squinted in her direction in just the right degree of dimness. By now she knew the project was doomed but it gave her a kind of angry satisfaction to return to the Park Avenue Hotel, just, as she said in a more recent letter (this to the girl, the woman, with whom she had roomed as a graduate student at Radcliffe, then as virginal as Rose, and possibly even more intimidated by men than Rose—and now Pauline was divorced, with two children, living with an Irish poet in a tower north of Sligo, a tower not unlike Yeats's, with *his* several children) for the brute hell of it.

And the evening had been an initially promising one. Quite by accident Rose wandered into the Second Annual Conference of the Friends of Evolution, and sat at the rear of a crowded ballroom, to hear a paper read by a portly, distinguished gentleman with pince-nez and a red carnation in his buttonhole, and to join in the enthusiastic applause afterward. (The paper had been, Rose imperfectly gathered, about the need for extraterrestrial communication—or was such communication already a fact, and the FBI and "university professors" were united in suppressing it?) A second paper by a woman Rose's age who walked with a cane seemed to be arguing that Christ was in space—"out there in space"—as a close reading of the Book of Saint John the Divine would demonstrate. The applause was even more enthusiastic after this paper, though Rose contributed only politely, for she'd had, over the years, many thoughts about Jesus of Nazareth—and thoughts about those thoughts—and in the end, one fine day, she had taken herself in secret to a psychiatrist at the Mount Yarrow Hospital, confessing in tears, in shame, that she knew very well the whole thing—*the whole thing*—was nonsense, and insipid nonsense at that, but—still—she sometimes caught herself wistfully "believing"; and was she clinically insane? Some inflection in her voice, some droll upward motion of her eyes, must have alerted the man to the fact that Rose Mallow Odom was someone like himself—she'd gone to school in the North, hadn't she?—and so he brushed aside her worries, and told her that of course it was nonsense, but one felt a nagging family loyalty, yes one did quarrel with one's family, and say terrible things, but still the loyalty was there, he would give her a prescription for barbiturates if she was suffering from insomnia, and hadn't she better have a physical examination?—because she was looking (he meant to be kindly, he didn't know how he was breaking her heart) worn out. Rose did not tell him that she had just *had* her six months' checkup and that, for her, she was in excellent health: no chest problems, the anemia under control. By the end of the conversation the psychiatrist remembered who Rose was—"Why, you're famous around here, didn't you publish a novel that shocked everyone?"—and Rose had recovered her composure enough to say stiffly that no one was famous in this part of Alabama; and the original topic had been completely forgotten. And now Jesus of Nazareth was floating about in space . . . or orbiting some moon . . . or was He actually in a spacecraft (the term "spacecraft" was used frequently by the conferees), awaiting His first visitors from planet earth? Rose was befriended by a white-haired gentleman in his seventies who slid across two or three folding chairs to sit beside her, and there was even a somewhat younger man, in his fifties perhaps, with greasy quill-like hair and a mild stammer, whose badge proclaimed him as H. Speedwell of Sion, Florida, who offered to buy her a cup of coffee after the session was over. Rose felt a flicker of—of what?—amusement, interest, despair? She had to put her finger to her lips in a schoolmarmish gesture, since the elderly gentleman on her right and H. Speedwell on her left were both talking rather emphatically, as if trying to impress her, about *their* experiences sighting UFO's, and the third speaker was about to begin.

The topic was "The Next and Final Stage of Evolution," given by the Reverend Jake Gromwell of the New Holland Institute of Religious Studies in Stoneseed, Kentucky. Rose sat very straight, her hands folded on her lap, her knees primly together (for, it must have been by accident, Mr. Speedwell's right knee was pressing against her), and pretended to listen. Her mind was all a flurry, like a chicken coop invaded by a dog, and she couldn't even know what she felt until the fluttering thoughts settled down. Somehow she was in the Regency Ballroom of the Park Avenue Hotel on a Thursday evening in September, listening to a paper given by a porkish-looking man in a tight-fitting gray-and-red plaid suit with a bright-red tie. She had been noticing that many of the conferees were disabled—on canes, on crutches, even in wheelchairs (one of the wheelchairs, operated by a hawk-faced youngish man who might have been Rose's age but looked no more than twelve, was a wonderfully classy affair, with a panel of push-buttons that would evidently do nearly anything for him he wished; Rose had rented a wheelchair some years ago, for herself, when a pinched nerve in her back had crippled her, and *hers* had been a very ordinary model)—and most of them were elderly. There *were* men her own age but they were not promising. And Mr. Speedwell, who smelled of something blandly odd, like tapioca, was not promising. Rose sat for a few more minutes, conscious of being polite, being good, allowing herself to be lulled by the Reverend Gromwell's monotonous voice and by the ballroom's decorations (fluorescent-orange and green and violet snakes undulated in the carpet, voluptuous forty-foot velvet drapes stirred in the tepid air from invisible vents, there was even a garishly inappropriate but mesmerizing mirrored ceiling with "stardust" lighting which gave to the conferees a rakish, faintly lurid air despite their bald heads and trembling necks and crutches) before making her apologetic escape.

Now Rose Mallow Odom sits at one of the long tables in Joe Pye's Bingo Hall, her stomach somewhat uneasy after the Tru-Orange she has just drunk, a promising—a highly promising—card before her. She is wondering if the mounting excitement she feels is legitimate, or whether it has anything to do with the orange soda: or whether it's simple intelligent dread, for of course she doesn't want to win. She can't even imagine herself calling out *Bingo!* in a voice loud enough to be heard. It is after 10:30 p.m. and there have been a number of winners and runners-up, many shrieking, ecstatic *Bingos* and some bellowing *Bingos* and one or two incredulous gasps, and really she should have gone home by now, Joe Pye is the only halfway attractive man in the place (there are no more than a dozen men there) and it isn't likely that Joe Pye in his dashing costume, with his glaring white turban held together by a gold pin, and his graceful shoulders, and his syrupy voice, would pay much attention to *her*. But inertia or curiosity has kept her here. What the hell, Rose thought, pushing kernels of corn about on much-used squares of thick cardboard, becoming acquainted with fellow Tophetians, surely there are worse ways to spend Thursday night? . . . She would dash off letters to Hamilton Frye and Carolyn Sears this weekend, though they owed her letters, describing in detail her newly made friends of the evening (the plump, perspiring, good-natured young woman seated across from her is named Lobelia, and it's ironic that Rose is doing so well this game, because just before it started Lobelia asked to exchange cards, on an impulse—"You give me mine and I'll give you yours, Rose!" she had said, with charming inaccuracy and a big smile, and of course Rose had immediately obliged) and the depressingly bright-lit hall with its disproportionately large American flag up front by Joe Pye's platform, and all the odd, strange, sad, eager, *intent* players, some of them extremely old, their faces wizened, their hands palsied, a few crippled or undersized or in some dim incontestable way not altogether *right*, a number very young (in fact it is something of a scandal, the children up this late, playing bingo beside their mamas, frequently with two or three cards while their mamas greedily work at four cards, which is the limit), and the dreadful taped music that uncoils relentlessly behind Joe Pye's tireless voice, and of course Joe Pye the Bingo Master himself, who has such a warm, toothed smile for everyone in the hall, and who had—unless Rose, her weak eyes unfocused by the lighting, imagined it—actually directed a special smile and a wink in her direction earlier in the evening, apparently sighting her as a new customer. She will make one of her droll charming anecdotes out of the experience. She will be quite characteristically harsh on herself, and will speculate on the phenomenon of suspense, its psychological meaning (isn't there a sense in which all suspense, and not just bingo hall suspense, is asinine?), and life's losers who, even if they win, remain losers (for what possible difference could a home hair dryer, or $100 cash, or an outdoor barbecue grill, or an electric train complete with track, or a huge copy of the Bible, illustrated, bound in simulated white leather, make to any of these people?). She will record the groans of disappointment and dismay when someone screams *Bingo!* and the mutterings when the winner's numbers, read off by one of the bored-looking girl attendants, prove to be legitimate. The winners' frequent tears, the hearty handshaking and cheek-kissing Joe Pye indulges in, as if each winner were specially dear to him, an old friend hurrying forth to be greeted; and the bright-yellow mustard splashed on the foot-longs and their doughy buns; and the several infants whose diapers were changed on a bench unfortunately close by; and Lobelia's superstitious fingering of a tiny gold cross she wears on a chain around her neck; and the worn-out little girl sleeping on the floor, her head on a pink teddy bear someone in her family must have won hours ago; and—

"You won! Here. Hey! She won! Right here! This card, here! Here! Joe Pye, *right here!*"

The grandmotherly woman to Rose's left, with whom she'd exchanged a few pleasant words earlier in the evening (it turns out her name is Cornelia Teasel; she once cleaned house for the Odoms' neighbors the Filarees), is suddenly screaming, and has seized Rose's hand, in her excitement jarring all the kernels off the cards; but no matter, no matter, Rose *does* have a winning card, she has scored bingo, and there will be no avoiding it.

There are the usual groans, half-sobs, mutterings of angry disappointment, but the game comes to an end, and a gum-chewing girl with a brass helmet of hair reads off Rose's numbers to Joe Pye, who punctuates each number not only with a *Yes, right* but *Keep going, honey* and *You're getting there,* and a dazzling wide smile as if he'd never witnessed anything more wonderful in his life. A $100 winner! A first-time customer (unless his eyes deceive him) and a $100 winner!

Rose, her face burning and pulsing with embarrassment, must go to Joe Pye's raised platform to receive her check, and Joe Pye's heartiest warmest congratulations, and a noisy moist kiss that falls uncomfortably near her mouth (she must resist stepping violently back—the man is so physically vivid, so real, so *there*). "*Now* you're smiling, honey, aren't you?" he says happily. Up close he is just as handsome, but the whites of his eyes are perhaps too white. The gold pin in his turban is a crowing cock. His skin is *very* tanned, and the goatee even blacker than Rose had thought. "I been watching you all night, hon, and you'd be a whole lot prettier if you eased up and smiled more," Joe Pye murmurs in her ear. He smells sweetish, like candied fruit or wine.

Rose steps back, offended, but before she can escape Joe Pye reaches out for her hand again, her cold thin hand, which he rubs briskly between his own. "You *are* new here, aren't you? New tonight?" he asks.

"Yes," Rose says, so softly he has to stoop to hear.

"And are you a Tophet girl? Folks live in town?"

"Yes."

"But you never been to Joe Pye's Bingo Hall before tonight?"

"No."

"And here you're walking away a hundred-dollar cash winner! How does that make you feel?"

"Oh, just fine—"

"What?"

"Just fine— I never expected—"

"Are you a bingo player? I mean, y'know, at these churches in town, or anywheres else."

"No."

"Not a player? Just here for the fun of it? A $100 winner, your first night, ain't that excellent luck! —You know, hon, you *are* a real attractive gal, with the color all up in your face, I wonder if you'd like to hang around, oh say another half hour while I wind things up, there's a cozy bar right next door, I noted you are here tonight alone, eh?—might-be we could have a nightcap, just the two of us?"

"Oh I don't think so, Mr. Pye—"

"Joe Pye! Joe Pye's the name," he says, grinning, leaning toward her, "and what might your name be? Something to do with a flower, isn't it?—some kind of a, a flower—"

Rose, very confused, wants only to escape. But he has her hand tightly in his own.

"Too shy to tell Joe Pye your name?" he says.

"It's—it's Olivia," Rose stammers.

"Oh. Olivia. Olivia, is it," Joe Pye says slowly, his smile arrested. "*Olivia,* is it. . . . Well, sometimes I misread, you know; I get a wire crossed or something and I misread; I never claimed to be 100% accurate. Olivia, then. Okay, fine. Olivia. Why are you so skittish, Olivia? The microphone won't pick up a bit of what we say. Are you free for a nightcap around eleven? Yes? Just next door at the Gayfeather where I'm staying, the lounge is a cozy homey place, nice and private, the two of us, no strings attached or nothing. . . ."

"My father is waiting up for me, and—"

"Come *on* now, Olivia, you're a Tophet gal, don't you want to make an out-of-towner feel welcome?"

"It's just that—"

"All right, then? Yes? It's a date? Soon as we close up shop here? Right next door at the Gayfeather?"

Rose stares at the man, at his bright glittering eyes and the glittering heraldic rooster in his turban, and hears herself murmur a weak assent; and only then does Joe Pye release her hand.

And so it has come about, improbably, ludicrously, that Rose Mallow Odom finds herself in the sepulchral Gayfeather Lounge as midnight nears, in the company of Joe Pye the Bingo Master (whose white turban is dazzling even here, in the drifting smoke and the lurid flickering colors from a television set perched high above the bar), and two or three other shadowy figures, derelict and subdued, solitary drinkers who clearly want nothing to do with one another. (One of them, a fairly well-dressed old gentleman with a swollen pug nose, reminds Rose obliquely of her father—except for the alcoholic's nose, of course.) She is sipping nervously at an "orange blossom"—a girlish sweet-acetous concoction she hasn't had since 1962, and has ordered tonight, or has had her escort order for her, only because she could think of nothing else. Joe Pye is telling Rose about his travels to distant lands—Venezuela, Ethiopia, Tibet, Iceland—and Rose makes an effort to appear to believe him, to appear to be naïve enough to believe him, for she has decided to go through with it, to take this outlandish fraud as her lover, for a single night only, or part of a night, however long the transaction will take. "Another drink?" Joe Pye murmurs, laying his hand on her unresisting wrist.

Above the bar the sharply tilted television set crackles with machine-gun fire, and indistinct silhouettes, probably human, race across bright sand, below a bright turquoise sky. Joe Pye, annoyed, turns and signals with a brisk counterclockwise motion of his fingers to the bartender, who lowers the sound almost immediately; the bartender's deference to Joe Pye impresses Rose. But then she is easily impressed. But then she is *not,* ordinarily, easily impressed. But the fizzing stinging orange drink has gone to her head.

"From going north and south on this globe, and east and west, travelling by freighter, by train, sometimes on foot, on foot through the mountains, spending a year here, six months there, two years somewhere else, I made my way finally back home, to the States, and wandered till things, you know, felt right: the way things sometimes feel right about a town or a landscape or another person, and you know it's your destiny," Joe Pye says softly. "If you know what I mean, Olivia."

With two dark fingers he strokes the back of her hand. She shivers, though the sensation is really ticklish.

". . . destiny," Rose says. "Yes. I think I know."

She wants to ask Joe Pye if she won honestly; if, maybe, he hadn't thrown the game her way. Because he'd noticed her earlier. All evening. A stranger, a scowling disbelieving stranger, fixing him with her intelligent skeptical stare, the most conservatively and tastefully dressed player in the hall. But he doesn't seem eager to talk about his business, he wants instead to talk about his life as a "soldier of fortune"—whatever he means by that—and Rose wonders if such a question might be naïve, or insulting, for it would suggest that *he* was dishonest, that the bingo games were rigged. But then perhaps everyone knows they are rigged?—like the horse races?

She wants to ask but cannot. Joe Pye is sitting so close to her in the booth, his skin is so ruddy, his lips so dark, his teeth so white, his goatee Mephistophelian and his manner—now that he is "offstage," now that he can "be himself"—so ingratiatingly intimate that she feels disoriented. She is willing to see her position as comic, even as ludicrous (she, Rose Mallow Odom, disdainful of men and of physical things in general, is going to allow this charlatan to imagine that *he* is seducing *her*—but at the same time she is quite nervous, she isn't even very articulate); she must see it, and interpret it, as *something*. But Joe Pye keeps on talking. As if he were halfway enjoying himself. As if this were a normal conversation. Did she have any hobbies? Pets? Did she grow up in Tophet and go to school here? Were her parents living? What sort of business was her father in?—or was he a professional man? Had *she* travelled much? No? Was she ever married? Did she have a "career"? Had she ever been in love? Did she ever expect to be in love?

Rose blushes, hears herself giggle in embarrassment, her words trip over one another, Joe Pye is leaning close, tickling her forearm, a clown in black silk pajama bottoms and a turban, smelling of something overripe. His dark eyebrows are peaked, the whites of his eyes are luminous, his fleshy lips pout becomingly; he is irresistible. His nostrils even flare with the pretense of passion. . . . Rose begins to giggle and cannot stop.

"You are a highly attractive girl, especially when you let yourself go like right now," Joe Pye says softly. "You know—we could go up to my room where we'd be more private. Would you like that?"

"I am not," Rose says, drawing in a full, shaky breath, to clear her head, "I am not a *girl*. Hardly a girl at the age of thirty-nine."

"We could be more private in my room. No one would interrupt us."

"My father isn't well, he's waiting up for me," Rose says quickly.

"By now he's asleep, most likely!"

"Oh no, no—he suffers from insomnia, like me."

"Like you! Is that so? I suffer from insomnia too," Joe Pye says, squeezing her hand in excitement. "Ever since a bad experience I had in the desert . . . in another part of the world. . . . But I'll tell you about that later, when we're closer acquainted. If we both have insomnia, Olivia, we should keep each other company. The nights in Tophet are so long."

"The nights *are* long," Rose says, blushing.

"But your mother, now: *she* isn't waiting up for you."

"Mother has been dead for years. I won't say what her sickness was but you can guess, it went on forever, and after she died I took all my things—I had this funny career going, I won't bore you with details—all my papers—stories and notes and such—and burnt them in the trash, and I've been at home every day and every night since, and I felt good when I burnt the things and good when I remember it, and—and I feel good right now," Rose says defiantly, finishing her drink. "So I know what I did was a sin."

"Do you believe in sin, a sophisticated girl like yourself?" Joe Pye says, smiling broadly.

The alcohol is a warm golden-glowing breath that fills her lungs and overflows and spreads to every part of her body, to the very tips of her toes, the tips of her ears. Yet her hand is fishlike: let Joe Pye fondle it as he will. So she is being seduced, and it is exactly as silly, as clumsy, as she had imagined it would be, as she imagined such things would be even as a young girl. So. As Descartes saw, I am I, up in my head, and my body is my body, extended in space, *out there,* it will be interesting to observe what happens, Rose thinks calmly. But she is not calm. She has begun to tremble. But she *must* be calm, it is all so absurd.

On their way up to Room 302 (the elevator is out of commission or perhaps there is no elevator, they must take the fire stairs, Rose is fetchingly dizzy and her escort must loop his arm around her) she tells Joe Pye that she didn't deserve to win at bingo and really should give the $100 back or perhaps to Lobelia (but she doesn't know Lobelia's last name!—what a pity) because it was really Lobelia's card that won, not hers. Joe Pye nods though he doesn't appear to understand. As he unlocks his door Rose begins an incoherent story, or is it a confession, about something she did when she was eleven years old and never told anyone about, and Joe Pye leads her into the room, and switches on the lights with a theatrical flourish, and even the television set, though the next moment he switches the set off. Rose is blinking at the complex undulating stripes in the carpet, which are very like snakes, and in a blurry voice she concludes her confession: ". . . she was so popular and so pretty and I hated her, I used to leave for school ahead of her and slow down so she'd catch up, and sometimes that worked, and sometimes it didn't, I just hated her, I bought a valentine, one of those joke valentines, it was about a foot high and glossy and showed some kind of an idiot on the cover, *Mother loved me,* it said, and when you opened it, *but she died,* so I sent it to Sandra, because her mother had died . . . when we were in fifth grade . . . and . . . and . . ."

Joe Pye unclips the golden cock, and undoes his turban, which is impressively long. Rose, her lips grinning, fumbles with the first button of her dress. It is a small button, cloth-covered, and resists her efforts to push it through the hole. But then she gets it through, and stands there panting.

She will think of it, *I must think of it,* as an impersonal event, bodily but not spiritual, *like a gynecological examination.* But then Rose hates those gynecological examinations. Hates and dreads them, and puts them off, canceling appointments at the last minute. *It will serve me right,* she often thinks, *if* . . . But her mother's cancer was elsewhere. Elsewhere in her body, and then everywhere. Perhaps there is no connection.

Joe Pye's skull is covered by mossy, obviously very thick, but close-clipped dark hair; he must have shaved his head a while back and now it is growing unevenly out. The ruddy tan ends at his hairline, where his skin is paste-white as Rose's. He smiles at Rose, fondly and inquisitively and with an abrupt unflinching gesture he rips off the goatee. Rose draws in her breath, shocked.

"But what are *you* doing, Olivia?" he asks.

The floor tilts suddenly so that there is the danger she will fall, stumble into his arms. She takes a step backward. Her weight forces the floor down, keeps it in place. Nervously, angrily, she tears at the prim little ugly buttons on her dress. "I— I'm— I'm hurrying the best I can," she mutters.

Joe Pye rubs at his chin, which is pinkened and somewhat raw-looking, and stares at Rose Mallow Odom. Even without his majestic turban and his goatee he is a striking picture of a man; he holds himself well, his shoulders somewhat raised. He stares at Rose as if he cannot believe what he is seeing.

"Olivia?" he says.

She yanks at the front of her dress and a button pops off, it is hilarious but there's no time to consider it, something is wrong, the dress won't come off, she sees that the belt is still tightly buckled and of course the dress won't come off, if only that idiot wouldn't stare at her, sobbing with frustration she pulls her straps off her skinny shoulders and bares her chest, her tiny breasts, Rose Mallow Odom, who had for years cowered in the girls' locker room at the public school, burning with shame, for the very thought of her body filled her with shame, and now she is contemptuously stripping before a stranger who gapes at her as if he has never seen anything like her before.

"But Olivia what are you *doing?* . . ." he says.

His question is both alarmed and formal. Rose wipes tears out of her eyes and looks at him, baffled.

"But Olivia people don't *do* like this, not this way, not so fast and angry," Joe Pye says. His eyebrows arch, his eyes narrow with disapproval; his stance radiates great dignity. "I think you must have misunderstood the nature of my proposal."

"What do you mean, people don't *do*. . . . What people . . ." Rose whimpers. She must blink rapidly to keep him in focus but the tears keep springing into her eyes and running down her cheeks, they will leave rivulets in her matte makeup which she lavishly if contemptuously applied many hours ago, something has gone wrong, something has gone terribly wrong, why is that idiot staring at her with such pity?

"Decent people," Joe Pye says slowly.

"But I– I–"

"*Decent* people," he says, his voice lowered, one corner of his mouth lifted in a tiny ironic dimple.

Rose has begun to shiver despite the golden-glowing burn in her throat. Her breasts are bluish-white, the pale-brown nipples have gone hard with fear. Fear and cold and clarity. She tries to shield herself from Joe Pye's glittering gaze with her arms, but she cannot: he sees everything. The floor is tilting again, with maddening slowness. She will topple forward if it doesn't stop. She will fall into his arms no matter how she resists, leaning her weight back on her shaky heels.

"But I thought– Don't you– Don't you want–?" she whispers.

Joe Pye draws himself up to his fullest height. He is really a giant of a man: the Bingo Master in his silver tunic and black wide-legged trousers, the rashlike shadow of the goatee framing his small angry smile, his eyes narrowed with disgust. Rose begins to cry as he shakes his head No. And again No. No.

She weeps, she pleads with him, she is stumbling dizzily forward. Something has gone wrong and she cannot comprehend it. In her head things ran their inevitable way, she had already chosen the cold clever words that would most winningly describe them, but Joe Pye knows nothing of her plans, knows nothing of her words, cares nothing for *her*.

"No!" he says sharply, striking out at her.

She must have fallen toward him, her knees must have buckled, for suddenly he has grasped her by her naked shoulders and, his face darkened with blood, he is shaking her violently. Her head whips back and forth. Against the bureau, against the wall, so sudden, so hard, the back of her head striking the wall, her teeth rattling, her eyes wide and blind in their sockets.

"No no no no *no.*"

Suddenly she is on the floor, something has struck the right side of her mouth, she is staring up through layers of agitated air to a bullet-headed man with wet mad eyes whom she has never seen before. The naked lightbulb screwed into the ceiling socket, so far away, burns with the power of a bright blank blinding sun behind his skull.

"But I— I thought—" she whispers.

"Prancing into Joe Pye's Bingo Hall and defiling it, prancing up *here* and defiling my room, what have you got to say for yourself, miss!" Joe Pye says, hauling her to her feet. He tugs her dress up and walks her roughly to the door, grasping her by the shoulders again and squeezing her hard, hard, without the slightest ounce of affection or courtesy, why he doesn't care for her at all!—and then she is out in the corridor, her patent-leather purse tossed after her, and the door to 302 is slammed shut.

It has all happened so quickly, Rose cannot comprehend. She stares at the door as if expecting it to be opened. But it remains closed. Far down the hall someone opens a door and pokes his head out and, seeing her in her disarray, quickly closes *that* door as well. So Rose is left completely alone.

She is too numb to feel much pain: only the pin-prickish sensation in her jaw, and the throbbing in her shoulders where Joe Pye's ghost-fingers still squeeze with such strength. Why, he didn't care for her at all. . . .

Weaving down the corridor like a drunken woman, one hand holding her ripped dress shut, one hand pressing the purse clumsily against her side. Weaving and staggering and muttering to herself like a drunken woman. She *is* a drunken woman. "What do you mean, people— *What* people—"

If only he had cradled her in his arm! If only he had loved her!

On the first landing of the fire stairs she grows very dizzy suddenly, and thinks it wisest to sit down. To sit down at once. Her head is drumming with a pulsebeat she can't control, she believes it is maybe the Bingo Master's pulsebeat, and his angry voice too scrambles about in her head, mixed up with her own thoughts. A puddle grows at the back of her mouth—she spits out blood, gagging—and discovers that one of her front teeth has come loose: one of her front teeth has come loose and the adjacent incisor also rocks back and forth in its socket.

"Oh Joe Pye," she whispers, "oh dear Christ what have you *done*—"

Weeping, sniffing, she fumbles with the fake-gold clasp of her purse and manages to get the purse open and paws inside, whimpering, to see if—but it's gone—she can't find it—ah, but there it *is:* there it is after all, folded small and somewhat crumpled (for she'd felt such embarrassment, she had stuck it quickly into her purse): the check for $100. A plain check that should have Joe Pye's large, bold, black signature on it, if only her eyes could focus long enough for her to see.

"Joe Pye, *what* people," she whimpers, blinking. "I never heard of— *What* people, where—?"

CHILDREN OF THE KINGDOM

By T. E. D. KLEIN

New Yorker T. E. D. Klein is a young fiction writer—his novelette, The Events at Poroth Farm, *was nominated for the World Fantasy Award—who has also written articles for* The New York Times. *While studying at Brown University in Providence, Rhode Island, he became intensely interested in the works of Providence-born fantasy writer H. P. Lovecraft, who combined cosmic horror with a feeling for the atmosphere of New England. The story that follows owes something to Lovecraft, but much more to New York, specifically Manhattan's Upper West Side, where Klein now makes his home. He deals here, in realistic fashion laced with flashes of grim humor, with the tenor of modern-day urban life, its dirt and squalor alongside opulence, its economic and racial tensions, and the sense of life on the edge of danger. He has also richly evoked New York as a city of mystery and fascination, a kind of stage where ancient terrors meet modern ones.*

"Mischief is their occupation, malice their habit, murder their sport, and blasphemy their delight."

—Maturin, *Melmoth the Wanderer*

"They are everywhere, those creatures."

—Derleth, *The House on Curwen Street*

"It taught me the foolishness of *not* being afraid."

—rape victim, New York City

On a certain spring evening several years ago, after an unsuccessful interview in Boston for a job I'd thought was mine, I missed the last train back to New York and was forced to take the eleven-thirty bus. It proved to be a "local," wending its way through the shabby little cities of southern New England and pulling into a succession of dimly lit Greyhound stations far from the highway, usually in the older parts of town—the decaying ethnic neighborhoods, the inner-city slums, the ghettos. I had a bad headache, and soon fell asleep. When I awoke I felt disoriented. All the other passengers were sleeping. I didn't know what time it was, but hesitated to turn on the light and look at my watch lest it disturb the man next to me. Instead, I looked out the window. We were passing through the heart of yet another shabby, nameless city, moving past the same gutted buildings I'd been seeing all night in my dreams, the same lines of cornices and rooftops, empty windows, gaping doorways. In the patches of darkness, familiar shapes seemed strange. Mailboxes and fire hydrants sprouted like tropical plants. Yet somehow it was stranger beneath the streetlights, where garbage cast long shadows on the sidewalk, and vacant lots hid glints of broken glass among the weeds. I remembered what I'd read of those great Mayan cities standing silent and abandoned in the Central American jungle, with no clue to where the inhabitants had gone. Through the window I could now see crumbling rows of tenements, an ugly redbrick housing project, some darkened and filthy-looking shops with alleys blocked by iron gates. Here and there a solitary figure would turn to watch the bus go by. Except for my reflection, I saw not one white face. A pair of little children threw stones at us from behind a fortress made of trash; a grown man stood pissing in the street like an animal, and watched us with amusement as we passed. I wanted to be out of this benighted place, and prayed that the driver would get us through quickly. I longed to be back in New York. Then a street sign caught my eye, and I realized that I'd already arrived. This was my own neighborhood; my home was only three streets down and just across the avenue. As the bus continued south I caught a fleeting glimpse of the apartment building where, less than half a block away, my wife lay awaiting my return.

Less than half a block can make a difference in New York. Different worlds can co-exist side by side, scarcely intersecting. There are places in Manhattan where you can see a modern high-rise, with its terraces and doormen and well-appointed lobby, towering white and immaculate above some soot-stained little remnant of the city's past—a tenement built during the Depression, lines of garbage cans in front, or a nineteenth-century brownstone gone to seed, its brickwork defaced by graffiti, its front door yawning open, its hallway dark, narrow, and forbidding as a tomb. Perhaps the two buildings will be separated by an alley; perhaps not even that. The taller one's shadow may fall across the other, blotting out the sun; the other may disturb the block with loud music, voices raised in argument, the gnawing possibility of crime. Yet to all appearances the people of each group will live their lives without acknowledging the other's existence. The poor will keep their rats, like secrets, to themselves; the cooking smells, the smells of poverty and sickness and backed-up drains, will seldom pass beyond their windows. The sidewalk in front may be lined with the idle and unshaven, men with T-shirts and dark skins and a gaze as sharp as razors, singing, or trading punches, or disputing, perhaps, in Spanish; or they may sit in stony silence on the stoop, passing round a bottle in a paper bag. They are rough-looking and impetuous, these men; but they will seldom leave their kingdom for the alien world next door. And those who inhabit that alien world will move with a certain wariness when they find themselves on the street, and will hurry past the others without meeting their eyes.

My grandfather, Herman Lauterbach, was one of those people who could move in either world. Though his Brooklyn apartment had always seemed a haven of middle-class respectability, at least for as long as I knew him, whatever refinements it displayed were in fact the legacy of his second wife; Herman himself was more at home among the poor. He, too, had been poor for most of his life—a bit of a radical, I suspect—and always thought of my father, his son-in-law, as "nothing but a goddamn stuffshirt" simply because my father had an office job. (As his beloved daughter's only child I was spared such criticisms, although I'm sure he found my lackluster academic career a disappointment and my chosen field, The Puritan Heritage, a bore.) His attitudes never changed, even when, nearing seventy, having outlived two exasperated wives, he himself was forced to don a necktie and go to work for the brother of an old friend in a firm that manufactured watch casings.

He had always been a comical, companionable man, fond of women, jokes, and holidays, but forty-hour weeks went hard with him and soured his temper. So did the death of my mother the following year.

Afterward, things were not the same; he was no longer quite so endearing. One saw a more selfish side, a certain hardness, like that of a child who has grown up in the street. Yet one inevitably forgave him, if only because of his age and lack of consequence, and because there still hung about him a certain air of comedy, as if it was his doom to provide the material for other people's anecdotes. There was, for example, his violent altercation with the driver of a Gravesend Bay bus, which my grandfather had boarded in the belief that it went to Bay Ridge; and then there was the episode in Marinaro's Bar, where jokes about the Mafia were not taken lightly. Several weeks later came a highly injudicious argument with the boss's son, less than half his age, over the recent hike in transit fares for senior citizens, and whether this entitled my grandfather to a corresponding increase in pay. Finally, when the two of them nearly came to blows over an equally minor disagreement—whether or not the city's impending bankruptcy was the fault of Mayor Beame, whom my grandfather somewhat resembled—everyone agreed that it was time for the old man to retire.

For the next three years he managed to get by on his modest savings, augmented by Social Security and regular checks from my father, now remarried and living in New Jersey. Then, suddenly, his age caught up with him: on May 4, 1977, while seated in his kitchen watching the first of the Frost-Nixon interviews (and no doubt shaking his fist at the television set), he suffered a major stroke, toppled backward from his chair, and had to be hospitalized for nearly a month. He was, at this time, eighty-three years old.

Or at least that was what he admitted to. We could never actually be sure, for in the past he'd been known to subtract as much as a decade when applying for a job, and to add it back, with interest, when applying for Golden Age discounts at a local movie house. Whatever the case, during his convalescence it became clear that he was in no shape to return to Brooklyn, where he'd been living on the third floor of a building without elevators. Besides, like his once-robust constitution, the neighborhood had deteriorated over the years; gangs of black and Puerto Rican youths preyed on the elderly of all races, especially those living alone, and an ailing old widower was fair game. On the other hand, he was not yet a candidate for a nursing home, at least not the elaborate kind with oxygen tents and cardiographs attached. What he needed was a rest home. As his doctor explained in private to my wife and me on our second visit, my grandfather was by no means permanently incapacitated; why, just look at Pasteur, who after a series of fifty-eight strokes had gone on to make some of his greatest discoveries.

("And who knows?" the doctor said, "maybe your granddad'll make a few discoveries of his own.") According to the prognosis he was expected to be on his feet within a week or two. Perhaps before that time he would have another stroke; likely, though, it would come later; more than likely it would kill him. Until then, however, he'd be alert and responsive and sufficiently ambulant to care for himself: he would not be walking with his usual speed, perhaps, but he'd be walking.

My grandfather put it more succinctly. "What the hell you think I am," he said, voice gravelly with age, when the question of a rest home was raised, "some vegetable in a wheelchair?" Struggling to sit up in bed, he launched into an extended monologue about how he'd rather die alone and forgotten on Skid Row than in a "home"; but for all its Sturm und Drang the speech sounded curiously insincere, and I had the impression that he'd been rehearsing it for years. No doubt his pride was at stake; when I assured him that what we had in mind was not some thinly disguised terminal ward, nor anything like a day-care center for the senile and decrepit, but rather a sort of boardinghouse where he could live in safety among people his own age, people as active as he was, he calmed down at once. I could see that the idea appealed to him; he had always thrived on conversation, jawboning, even aimless chatter, and the prospect of some company—especially that of fellow retirees with time on their hands—was an inviting one. The truth is, he'd been lonely out in Brooklyn, though of course he would never have admitted it. For my part I was feeling rather guilty; I hadn't come to see him as often as I should have. From now on, I told him, things would be different: I would find him a place in Manhattan, a place where I could visit him once or twice a week. I'd even take him out to dinner, when I got the chance.

He appeared to think it over. Then—for my sake, I think (and somehow I found this horribly depressing)—he screwed his face into a roguish grin, like a small boy boasting to an adult. "Make sure there are plenty of good-looking dames around," he said, "and you got yourself a deal."

The following weekend, with this qualified blessing in mind, Karen and I set about looking for a place. The press had recently brought to light a series of scandals involving various institutions for the aged, and we were particularly anxious to find a reputable one. By Saturday afternoon we'd discovered that many of the private homes were more expensive than we'd counted on—as much as two or three hundred dollars a week—and that in most of them the supervision was too strict; they resembled nothing so much as tiny, smiling prisons. Grandfather would never stand for being cooped up inside all day; he liked to wander. Another, run by nuns, was comfortable, clean, and open to non-Catholics, but its residents were in no condition to feed themselves, much less join in human conversation. These were the unreclaimables, lapsed into senescence; my grandfather, we hoped, would seem positively vigorous beside them.

Finally, early Sunday evening, on the recommendation of a friend, we visited a place on West 81st Street, scarcely a dozen blocks from where we lived. It was called, somewhat optimistically, the Park West Manor for Adults, even though it was rather less than a manor house and nowhere near the park. The owner was a certain Mr. Fetterman, whom we never actually met; it later turned out that he, too, was a bit of a crook, though never in ways that directly affected us. I gather from my wife, who, as accountant for a publishing firm, has always had a better head for business, that the home was part of some statewide franchise operation with vague ties to local government. According to the agreement—common, she informs me—my grandfather's rent was to be paid for out of his now-meager savings; when they were depleted (as, indeed, they would be in a year or so) the cost would be borne by Medicaid for the rest of his life.

The building itself, of dirty red ornamental brick, occupied the south side of the street between Broadway and Amsterdam Avenue, a block and a half from the Museum of Natural History. It consisted of two wings, each nine stories tall, connected by a narrow, recessed entranceway several steps down from the sidewalk. The place seemed respectable enough, though at first sight it was not particularly impressive, especially at the end of the day, with the sun sinking behind the Hudson and long shadows darkening the block. The pavement in front of the building had recently been torn up for some kind of sewer work, and huge brown metal pipes lay stacked on either side like ammunition. My wife and I had to step across a series of planks to reach the front door. Inside it, just before the lobby, was an alcove with a battered wooden desk, behind which, seemingly stupefied with boredom, sat a wrinkled old black man in a guard's uniform—the sort of man one sees at banks these days, ineffectually directing people to the appropriate tellers. He nodded and let us pass through. No doubt he thought he recognized us; it's said that, to whites, all blacks look alike, and years in various city classrooms have convinced me that the reverse is true as well.

The lobby wasn't much of an improvement. Like most lobbies, it was dim, depressing, and cold. The rear wall was lined by a mirror, so that, on entering, my wife and I found ourselves confronted by a rather discouraged-looking little couple approaching from across the room, the woman frowning at the man, no doubt for some trifling thing he had just said, the man glancing with increasing frequency at his watch. To the couple's left ran a long, ornate mantelpiece overhanging a blank expanse of wall where a fireplace should have been. Grouped around this nonexistent fireplace were half a dozen caved-in leather chairs and a pair of dusty rubber plants sagging wearily in their pots, their leaves reflected in the mirror and, on a smaller scale, in the painting hanging just above the mantel: a framed reproduction of Rousseau's *Children of the Kingdom,* the primitive figures peering out at us like a ring of ghosts, their faces pale and impassive against the violets, reds, and greens of the surrounding jungle. The colors were faded, as if from having been stared at by generations of residents.

It was the dinner hour. The lobby was deserted; from somewhere to the right came the sound of voices and the clank of pots and plates, accompanied by a scraping of chairs and the smell of boiled meat. We moved toward it, following the right-hand corridor past a series of turns until we came to a pair of wooden doors with windows in the top. Karen, boldened by fatigue, pushed her way through. Before us stretched the dining room, barely more than half filled, the diners grouped around tables of various shapes and designs. It reminded me of the mess hall at summer camp, as if my fellow campers had aged and withered right there in their seats without ever having gained appreciably in size. Even the waiters looked old: a few, hurrying up the aisles, still sported oily black pompadours, but most looked as if they could easily have traded places with the people they served. White hair was the rule here, with pink skull showing through. This was as true for the women as the men, since by this age the sexes had once more begun to merge; indeed, like babies, the individuals in the room were hard to tell apart. Nor were they any more inclined than children to disguise their curiosity; dozens of old pink heads swiveled in our direction as we stood there in the doorway. We were intruders; I felt as if we'd blundered into a different world. Then I saw the expectation in their faces, and felt doubly bad: each of them had probably been hoping for a visitor, a son or daughter or grandchild, and must have been keenly disappointed by every new arrival that was not the one awaited.

A small, harried-looking man approached us and identified himself as the assistant manager. He looked as if he was about to scold us for having arrived during dinner—he, too, probably assumed we were there to visit someone—but he brightened immediately when we explained why we'd come. "Follow me," he said, moving off at a kind of dogtrot. "I'll show you the place from top to bottom." In the noise and hubbub of the dining room I hadn't caught his name, but as soon as he started toward the nearest exit, my wife and I in tow, a plaintive chorus of "Mr. Calzone" arose behind us. He ignored it and pushed on through the door; I suppose he was glad of the diversion.

We found ourselves in the kitchen, all iron pots and steam, with cooks in white T-shirts and white-jacketed waiters shouting at one another in Spanish. "This used to be kosher," shouted Calzone, "but they cut all that out." I assured him that my grandfather liked his bacon as well as the next man. "Oh, we don't give 'em bacon too often," he said, taking me literally, "but they really go for the pork chops." My wife seemed satisfied, and nodded at the dishwashers and the ranks of aluminum cabinets. As for me, I wasn't sure just what to look for, but am happy to report I saw no worm-eggs and not one dead cat.

Calzone was as good as his word. From the kitchen he conducted us "up top" to the ninth floor via a clanging old elevator of the self-service type, with the numbers beside the buttons printed so large—in raised numerals nearly an inch high—that even a blind man could have run it. (Its speed was such that, had one of the home's frailer residents preferred to take the stairs, she would probably have arrived in time to meet us.) The rooms on the ninth floor, most of them unoccupied, were shabby but clean, with private bathrooms and plenty of closet space. Grandfather would have nothing to complain about. In fact, with its boarders all downstairs at dinner, the place seemed more a college dormitory than an old-folks' home. Aside from the oversized elevator panel and the shiny new aluminum railings we'd noticed everywhere—in easy reach of stairways, tubs, and toilets—about the only concession to age appeared to be a sign-up sheet my wife came across on a bulletin board in the second-floor "game room," for those who wished to make an appointment at some community medical center over on Columbus Avenue.

Our tour ended with the laundry room in the basement. It was hot and uncomfortable and throbbed with the echoes of heavy machinery, like the engine room of a freighter; you could almost feel the weight of the building pressing down on you. The air seemed thick, as if clogged with soapsuds, and moisture dripped from a network of flaking steam pipes suspended from the ceiling. Against one side stood four coin-operated dryers, staring balefully at four squat Maytag washers ranged along the opposite wall. One of the washers, in the farthest corner, appeared to be having a breakdown. It was heaving back and forth on its base like something frantic to escape, a pair of red lights blinking in

alarm above the row of switches. From somewhere in its belly came a frenzied churning sound, as if the thing were delivering itself of a parasite, or perhaps just giving birth. A man in a sweat-stained T-shirt was on his knees before it, scowling at an exposed bit of circuitry where a panel had been removed. Beside him stood an open tool kit, with tools scattered here and there across the concrete floor. He was introduced to us as Reynaldo "Frito" Ley, the building's superintendent, but he barely had time to look up, and when he did the scowl stayed on his face. "She acting up again," he told the assistant manager, in a thick Hispanic accent. "I think somebody messing with the 'lectric wire." Reaching around back to the wall, he yanked out the plug, and the machine ground noisily to a halt.

"Maybe it's rats," I said, feeling somewhat left out. He looked at me indignantly, and I smiled to show that I'd been joking.

But Calzone was taking no chances. "Believe me," he said quickly, "that's one thing they don't complain about." He ran a hand through his thinning hair. "Sure, I know, this building ain't exactly new, and okay, maybe we'll get a little bitty roach now and then, that's only natural. I mean, you're not gonna find a single building in the whole damned city that hasn't got one or two of them babies, am I right? But rats, never. We run a clean place."

"Rats not gonna bother my machines," added the superintendent. "They got no business here. Me, I think it was *los niños*. Kids."

"Kids?" said my wife and I in unison, with Calzone half a beat behind.

"You mean children from the neighborhood?" asked Karen. She had just been reading a series about the revival of youth gangs on the West Side, after more than a decade of peace. "What would they want in a place like this? How could they get in?"

He shrugged. "I don' know, lady. I don' see them. I only know is hard to keep them out. They all the time looking for money. Come down here, try to get the quarters from machines. No good, so they got to go break something—cut up hoses in the back, pull the plug. . . . That kind, they do anything."

Calzone stepped between them. "Don't worry, Mrs. Klein. It's not what you're thinking. What Frito means is, on weekends like this you get people coming in to visit relatives, and sometimes they bring the little kids along. And before you know it the kids are getting bored, and they're running up and down the halls or playing in the elevator. We're trying to put a stop to it, but it's nothing serious. Just pranks, that's all." Moving to the door, he opened it and ushered us outside.

Behind us the superintendent appeared rather annoyed, but when my wife looked back questioningly he turned away. We left him sulking in front of his machine.

"Craziest thing I ever heard of," muttered Calzone, as he led us back to the elevator. "The kids in this neighborhood may cause a bit of trouble now and then, but they sure as hell ain't causing it in here!" The elevator door slid shut with a clang. "Look, I'm not gonna lie to you. We've had our share of problems. I mean, who hasn't, right? But if we've had any break-ins here it's the first time *I've* ever heard of it. Fact is, we've just beefed up our security, and there's no way anyone from outside's getting in. Believe me, your granddad's gonna be as safe here as anywhere else in New York."

Since that very morning's *Times* had carried the story of a wealthy widow and her maid found strangled in their East 62nd Street town house, these words were hardly reassuring.

Nor was my wife's expression when we got out of the elevator. She nudged me with her elbow. "I'd hate to think what the security was like before they beefed it up," she said. Calzone pretended not to hear.

The first battalions of old men and women were marching unsteadily from the dining room as the two of us bid him good-bye. "Come back again and I'll show you our new TV lounge," he called after us, retiring to his little office just beyond the stairs. As soon as he'd closed the door, I approached a pair of well-fed-looking old women who were shuffling arm-in-arm across the lobby. The stouter one had hair as blue as the veins that lined her forehead. Gazing up at me, she broke into a slightly bewildered smile.

I cleared my throat. "Pardon me, but would you two ladies say this is a safe place to live? I mean, from the standpoint of the neighborhood?"

Silence. The smile, the gaze, never wavered.

"Mrs. Hirschfeld doesn't hear so good," explained the other, tightening her grip on the woman's arm. "Even with the new battery you have to shout a little." She spoke with her eyes cast demurely downward, avoiding mine. Her hair was tied in a coquettish little bun. Who knows, I thought, Grandfather might like her. She told me her name was Mrs. Rosenzweig. She and Mrs. Hirschfeld were roommates. "Elsie's very happy here," she said, "and me, I can't complain. Three years already we've been here, and never any trouble." The lashes fluttered. "But of course, we never go outside."

They moved off together toward the elevator, leaning on one another for support. "Well, what do you think?" I asked my wife, as we headed for the exit in front.

She shrugged. "He's your grandfather."

Emerging from the lobby, we found ourselves once more in the presence of the guard, slumped glassy-eyed behind his desk. Here he is in the flesh, I thought, Calzone's beefed-up security. He nodded sleepily to us as we passed.

Outside, dusk had fallen on the block. To the west lay the familiar trees and benches of Broadway, with TV showrooms, banks, and Chinese restaurants. Copperware and cappuccino-makers gleamed in Zabar's window; Sunday browsers chatted by a bookstall on the corner. "Anyway," I said, "it's better than Brooklyn." But when we turned east I wasn't so sure. The building next door was a six-story tenement ribbed with fire escapes and a crumbling succession of ledges. On the front stoop, beneath a rust-stained "No Loitering" sign, sat a conclave of bored-looking young men, one with a gold earring, one fiddling with the dial of a radio as big as an attaché case. I wished we didn't have to walk past them.

"They look like they're posing for a group photo," I said hopefully, taking my wife's hand.

"Yeah—Attica, Class of 1980."

We moved by them silently, drawing hostile glares. Behind us, with a blare of trumpets, the radio exploded into "Soul Soldier." Another group of teenagers was gathered in front of a closed-up shop on the corner of 81st and Amsterdam. "Checks Cashed," a corrugated metal sign proclaimed, and below it, on a faded piece of cardboard taped inside the window, "Food Stamps Sold Here." The place was dark and empty, the window grey with dust.

Snap out of it, I told myself, the neighborhood's not so bad. Just another culture or two, that's all it was, and no worse here than where I lived, half a mile farther uptown. I noted the ancient public library, a shoe-repair shop, a pawnshop with guitars and watches in the window, a place where Haitian magazines were sold, a Puerto Rican social club, a shop whose sign read "Barber" on one side and "Barbería" on the other. Several *botanicas*, shut for the day behind steel gates, displayed windows full of painted plaster figures: Jesus, and Mary, a bearded black man brandishing a snake, an angel with a dagger in his hand. All wore haloes.

Still, the people of the neighborhood did not. The crime rate, in fact, had been climbing that year, and while Park West Manor seemed as good a place as any for my grandfather, I had doubts about the safety of the block. As my wife and I walked home that night, heading up Columbus with the lights of Sunday traffic in our eyes, I thought of the old brick building receding behind us into the shadows of West 81st, and of the doorways, stoops, and street corners surrounding it where unsmiling black youths waited like a threat. I worried about whether they might somehow sneak inside, and about all the damage they might cause—although in view of what actually occurred, these fears now seem, to say the least, rather ironic.

Wednesday, June 8, 1977

If heaven is really populated by the souls of the dead, with their earthly personalities and intellect surviving intact, then the place must be almost as depressing as an old-folks' home. The angels may handle their new wings with a certain finesse, and their haloes may glow bright as gold, but the heads beneath them must be pretty near as empty as the ones I saw the first time I visited my grandfather at Park West Manor. Around me, in the game room, old men and women played leisurely hands of canasta or poker or gin, or sat watching in silence as two of their number shuffled round a pool table, its worn and faded surface just above the spectators' sight. One old man stood talking to himself in the corner; others merely dozed. Contrary to my expectations, there were no twinkle-eyed old Yankee types gathered round a checkerboard puffing corncob pipes, and I looked in vain for bearded Jewish patriarchs immersed in games of chess. No one even had a book. Most of those in the room that day were simply propped up in the lounge chairs like a row of dolls, staring straight ahead as if watching a playback of their lives. My grandfather wasn't among them.

If I sound less than reverent toward my elders, there's a good reason: I am. No doubt I'll be joining their ranks some day myself (unless I'm already food for worms, knocked down by an addict or a bus), and I'll probably spend my time blinking and daydreaming like everyone else. Meanwhile, though, I find it hard to summon up the respect one's supposed to feel for age. Old people have always struck me as rather childish, in fact. Despite their reputation, they've never seemed particularly wise.

Perhaps I just tend to look for wisdom in the wrong places. I remember a faculty party where I introduced myself to a celebrated visiting theologian and asked him a lot of earnest questions, only to discover that he was more interested in making passes at me. I once eavesdropped on the conversation of two well-known writers on the occult who turned out to be engaged in a passionate argument over whether a Thunderbird got better mileage than a Porsche. I bought the book by Dr. Kübler-Ross, the one in which she interviews patients with terminal cancer, and I found, sadly, that the dying have no more insight into life, or death, than the rest of us. But old people have been the biggest disappointment of all; I've yet to hear a one of them say anything profound. They're like that ninety-two-year-old Oxford don who, when asked by some deferential young man what wisdom he had to impart after nearly a century of living, ruminated a moment and then said something like, "Always check your footnotes." I've never found the old to be wiser than anyone else. They've never told me anything I didn't know already.

But Father Pistachio . . . Well, maybe he was different. Maybe he was onto something after all.

At first, though, he seemed no more than an agreeable old humbug. I met him on June 8, when I went to visit Grandfather. It was the spring of '77, with the semester just ending; I had Wednesday afternoons free, and had told Grandfather to expect me. We had installed him in Park West the previous weekend, after collecting some things from his Brooklyn apartment and disposing of the rest. At one-thirty today, unable to find him in his bedroom on the ninth floor, I'd tried the TV lounge and the game room, both in vain, and had finally gone downstairs to ask Miss Pascua, a little Filipino woman who worked as the administrative secretary.

"Mr. Lauterbach likes to spend his time outdoors," she said, a hint of disapproval in her voice. "We let them do what they want here, you know. We don't like to interfere."

"I understand."

"He's doing very well, though," she went on. "He's already made a lot of friends. We're very fond of him."

"Glad to hear it. Any idea where he might be?"

"Well, he seems to have hit it off with some of the local people. They sit out there and talk all day." For a moment I pictured him in dignified conversation with some cronies on a sunny Broadway bench, but then she added: "I'd try looking for him one block down, on the other side of Amsterdam. He's usually on a stoop out there, sitting with a bunch of Puerto Ricans."

I walked out frowning. I should have known he'd do something like that. When you gave him a choice between the jungle to the east—with its fire escapes, its alleyways, its rat-infested basements—and the tamer pastures of Broadway, Broadway didn't have a chance.

The spot he'd picked was a particularly disagreeable one. It was just up the block from an evil-looking bar called Davey's (since closed down by the police), a little bit of Harlem on the West Side: the sort of place where you expect a shoot-out every Saturday night. The buildings beside it were ancient with grime; even the bricks seemed moist, and the concrete foundations were riddled with something curiously like wormholes. I passed a doorway full of teenaged boys who should have been in school. They were hunched furtively against the wall, lighting something out of sight, while others shot craps on the sidewalk, striking poses out of Damon Runyon. In the dim light of an open first-floor window, heavy shapes moved back and forth. A man in dark glasses hurried toward me, angrily dragging a child by the arm. The child said something—he couldn't have been more than five—and as the man passed by he scowled and muttered back, "Don't tell me 'bout your mother, your mother's a goddamn whore!" Already I was beginning to feel depressed. I was glad Karen hadn't come.

My grandfather was three stoops in from the corner, seated beside a large black woman easily twice his weight. On the railing to his right, perched above his shoulder like a raven, sat another old man, with skin like aged parchment and a halo of white hair. He was dressed in black trousers and a black short-sleeved shirt, with the white square of a priest's collar peeking out above it like a window. His mouth was half concealed behind a shaggy white moustache, and the sole incongruous touch was the unnatural redness of his lips, almost as if he were wearing lipstick. On his lap lay a white paper bag.

Grandfather smiled when he saw me, and got to his feet. "Where's that pretty wife of yours?" he asked. I reminded him that Karen was at work. He looked puzzled. "What, *today?*"

"It's Wednesday, remember?"

"My God, you're right!" He broke into astonished laughter. "It felt just like a Sunday!"

I alluded to the trouble I'd had finding him. Here he was, hiding in the shadows, when only one block over—east to the museum, west to Broadway—there were plenty of comfortable benches in the sun.

"Benches are for women," he replied, with a conviction that allowed of no argument—just as, in some long-vanished luncheonette of my childhood, he'd told me, "Straws are for girls." (What does it say about him that he believed this? And what does it say about me that since that time I've never used a straw?)

"Besides," he said, "I wanted you to meet my friends. We get together here because the Father lives upstairs." He nodded toward the old man, but introduced the woman to me first. Her name was Coralette. She was one of those wide, imperturbable creatures who take up two seats or more on the subway. It was impossible to guess her age, but I could hear, each time she spoke, the echoes of a girlhood in the South.

The man was introduced as "Father Pistachio." This was not his name, but it was close enough. My grandfather never got his names or facts exactly right. Perhaps this had something to do with his general rebelliousness. It was certainly not a product of his age, for it had existed as long as I'd known him; half the time, in fact, he confused me with my father. Yet the names he thought up for most people were insidiously appropriate, and often stuck. Father Pistachio was one; I never saw the man without a white paper bag in his hand or, as it was now, crumpled in his lap—a bag that had been filled with those obscene-looking little red nuts, whose dye so stained his lips that he might have passed for some inhabitant of Transylvania.

But he wasn't Transylvanian; nor was he, despite my grandfather's introduction, a Puerto Rican. "No, no," he said quickly, looking somewhat pained, "you no understand, my friend, I say *Costa* Rica my home. Paraíso, Costa Rica. City of Paradise."

My grandfather shrugged. "So if it was paradise, what are you doing up here with an *alter kocker* like me?"

Coralette seemed to find this irresistibly funny, though I suspect the Yiddish escaped her. Pistachio smiled, too.

"My dear Herman," he said, "one is not permitted to stay forever in Eden." He winked at me, and added: "Besides, Paraíso just a name. Paradise *here,* in front of your face."

I nodded dutifully, but could not help noticing the darkened corridor behind him, the graffiti on the crumbling bricks and, just above his head, a filthy window box from which a dead brown ivy plant and two long snakelike tendrils drooped. I wished he'd picked a more convincing spot.

But he was already quoting the authorities for support. "Buddha, he say, 'Every day is a good day.' Jesus Christ say, '*El Reino del Padre*—the Kingdom of the Father—is spread upon the earth, but men are blind and do not see it.' "

"Yeah, where he say that?" asked Coralette. "Ain't in no Bible *I* ever read."

"Is in the one I read," said Pistachio. "The Gospel According to Thomas."

My grandfather chuckled and shook his head. "Thomas," he said, "always this Thomas! That's all you ever talk about."

I knew that Bible talk had always bored my grandfather to tears—he'd said so more than once—but this rudeness seemed uncharacteristic of him, especially to a man he'd known so short a time. Seating myself against the opposite railing, facing the old priest, I searched my mind for more congenial subjects. I forget exactly what we talked of first—the unseasonably warm weather, perhaps—but I do recall that twice again there were references to some private dispute between the two of them.

The first time, I believe, we'd been talking of the news—of the start of Queen Elizabeth's Silver Jubilee, in fact, which my wife and I had watched on TV the night before. Coralette appeared uninterested in the story, but it brought a curious response from Father Pistachio—"I could tell you of another queen"—and an immediate dismissal from my grandfather: "Oh, stop already with your queen!" The second time came much later, and only after the conversation had taken a number of circuitous turns, but once again the starting point was an item from the previous night's news: in this case the repeal of Miami's gay rights ordinance (*"Faygelehs,"* my grandfather snapped, "they oughta send 'em back where they came from!"), which had led to a discussion of Florida in general. Pistachio expressed an interest in settling there eventually—somehow he was under the impression that more than half its citizens spoke Spanish—but my grandfather had had a grudge against the place ever since, during the '20s, he'd made the mistake of investing in some real estate "just off the Everglades" and had lost his shirt. "Hell," he fumed, "they were selling land down there that was still underground!"

I let that one go by me; I could never have touched it. But it did bring a kind of response: Coralette, who read the *Enquirer* each week as religiously as she read the Bible, reported that a colony of derelicts had been discovered living "unnergroun'" in the catacombs below Grand Central Station. (Six months later the story would resurface in the *Times.*) There were as many as forty of these derelicts, pale, frightened, and skinny, subsisting on garbage and handouts from people in the street but spending most of their time down below, amid the steam pipes and the darkness. "Now some folks be wantin' the city to clear 'em outa there," she said, "but it don't make no difference to me. Fact is, I feels kinda sorry for 'em. They just a bunch o' poor, homeless men."

Pistachio sighed, stirred once again by some private memory. "All men are homeless," he said. "We have journeyed for so many year that—"

"Enough with the journey!" said my grandfather. "Can't we ever talk about anything else?"

Hoping to forestall an argument, I tried to change the subject yet again. I had noticed a fat little paperback protruding from Pistachio's back pocket, with *Diccionario* printed at the top. "I see you like to come prepared," I said, pointing to the title.

He gave a shrug both courtly and ambiguous, in true Old World style. "Is for my book," he said. His voice was modest, but there'd been a hint of capitals in it: "My Book."

"You're writing something?" I asked.

He smiled. "Is already written. More than forty years ago I finish it. Then I write it over in Latin, then in *portugués*. Now I am retired, write in English."

So that was why he'd come up north—to work on a translation of his book. It had already been published (at his own expense, he admitted) in Costa Rica and Brazil. The English title, itself the work of almost three days, was to be "A New and Universal Commentary on the Gospel According to Thomas, Revised in Light of Certain Excavations."

"I write it just before I leave the Order," he explained. "It say all I ever want to say. If I live long enough, *si Dios quiere*, I pray that I may see my book in the seven major languages of the world."

This struck me as a shade optimistic, but I didn't want to risk insulting him. He was obviously an extreme case of the proverbial one-book author.

"Who knows," he added, with a nod to my grandfather, "maybe we even do the book in Yiddish."

Grandfather raised his eyebrows and pointedly looked away. I could see that he had heard all this before.

"I gather that it's some sort of religious tract," I said, trying to sound interested. "The Puritans used to go in for that sort of thing. Treatises on doctrine, damnation, the Nativity—"

He shrugged. "Is about a *natividad,* but not the one you think. Is about *natividad* of man."

"Ain't no big mystery in that," said Coralette. "Ain't none of us so different from the monkeys and the lizards and the worms. Lawd done made us outa earth, just like the Bible say. Made each and ever' one of us the same." Reaching back, she took Father Pistachio's dictionary and worked a finger back and forth against the glossy surface of its cover. Soon a little roll of dirt and rubbed-off skin, grey-black in color, had accumulated beneath it; whereupon, taking my own hand between her two much broader ones, she rubbed my fingertip against the same surface. The same material appeared, the same color.

"See?" she said triumphantly. "We's all of us God's clay."

I never got to ask Father Pistachio his own views on the subject because by this time three o'clock had passed and the older children of the neighborhood, released from Brandeis High, were accumulating on the sidewalk before us like Coralette's grey-black matter. My grandfather got unsteadily to his feet just as a trio of teenaged girls swept up the steps, followed by a boy with a pirate's bandana and the straggly beginnings of a moustache. Not one of them was carrying a schoolbook. For a moment Coralette remained where she'd been sitting, blocking half the entranceway, but then she, too, sighed heavily and made as if to stand. I gathered that this was the usual hour for the group to break up.

"I say farewell for now," said Father Pistachio. "Is time for me to go upstairs to sleep. Tonight I work a little on my book." I helped him down from his perch, amazed at how small and fragile he seemed; his feet had barely been able to reach the landing.

"Come on," I said to Grandfather, "I'll walk you back." I told the others that I hoped to see them again. I half believe I meant it.

My grandfather appeared to be in a good mood as we headed up 81st. I, too, was feeling good, if only from relief that he'd adjusted so readily to his new situation. "This life seems to be agreeing with you," I said.

"Yeah, things are always easier when you got a few friends around. That colored girl is good as gold, and so's the Father. He may not speak good English, but I'm telling you, he's one smart cookie. I almost wonder what he sees in me."

I had to admit it seemed an unlikely friendship: a self-professed scholar—a man of the cloth—keeping company with someone, in Whittier's phrase, "innocent of books" and of religion, the one equipped with little English, the other with no Spanish at all. What queer conversations those two old-timers must have had!

"You'll have to come by more often," Grandfather was saying. "I could tell he took to you right away. And he's dying to meet Karen."

"Oh? Why's that?"

"I don't know, he said she sounded interesting."

"That's funny, I wonder why he'd . . ." I paused; I had had a sudden suspicion. "Hey, did you by any chance happen to mention where she works?"

"Sure. She's with that big publishing outfit, isn't she? Something to do with books."

"That's right. *Account* books! She's in the billing department, remember?"

He shrugged. "Books are books."

"I suppose so," I said, and let the matter drop. Inside, though, I was wincing. Poor old Pistachio! No wonder he'd taken such an interest in us: the old geezer probably thought we'd help him sell his book! The truth was, of course, that using Karen as an "in" to the publishing world was like trying to break into Hollywood by dating an usher; but I saw no reason to tell this to Pistachio. He would find out soon enough. Meanwhile, he'd be a good friend for my grandfather.

"'Course, he does go on a bit about that book of his," Grandfather was saying. "He'll talk your ear off if you let him. Some of the theories he's got . . ." He shook his head and laughed. "Know what he told me? That the Indians are a long-lost tribe of Israel!"

I was disappointed; I had heard that one too many times before. It had become something of a joke, in fact, like the Hollow Earth theory and Bigfoot. I didn't mind Pistachio's having a few crackpot notions—at his age he was entitled to believe what he pleased—but couldn't he have been just a bit more original? The long-lost-tribe routine was old hat. Even my grandfather seemed to regard it as a joke.

But typically, he'd gotten it all wrong.

Saturday, June 11

"Is no one safe today," said Father Pistachio. It was a statement, not a question. "Is the same even for an old man like me. Two nights ago I am followed home by six, seven boys. Maybe, in the dark, they do not see I wear the collar of a priest. I think they are getting ready to push me down, but I am lucky. God, He watches. Just as I am asking myself if it is wise to call for help, a car of the police comes slowly up the street, and when I turn around the boys are gone."

"*Po*-lice?" sniffed Coralette. "I don't have no use for them *po*-lice. Kids ain't scared o'them no more, and the law don't mean a thing. Station's sittin' right up there in the middle of 82nd Street, just a block away, and you ever see the house right next door to it? Hmmph! Wouldn't want no daughter o' *mine* livin' there—not these days. Blocks 'round here ain't fit for walkin' down."

"Aw, come on," said my grandfather, "that's no way to talk. Brooklyn's ten times worse than this, believe me. The way I see it, if you're gonna sit inside all day you may as well be dead."

At this moment we, too, were sitting inside, round a greasy little table at Irv's Snack Bar near the corner of 81st and Amsterdam, sipping our afternoon coffee and talking crime, New York's favorite subject. Irv and his wife would let the old folks sit for hours, so Grandfather's friends came here often, especially on weekends, when the stoop of Pistachio's building was occupied by teenagers. Occasionally the blare of their radios penetrated the snack bar's thin walls, along with the pounding rhythms of soul music from the jukebox inside Davey's, just across the street. Saturday nights began early around here, at least when the weather was warm; even at noontime the noise was almost incessant, and continued through the weekend. I don't know how anyone could stand it.

"My cousin's step-sister up on 97th, she say things just as bad up there. Say they's a prowler in the neighborhood." The metal chair sagged noticeably as Coralette shifted her weight. "Some kinda pervert, she say. Lady downstairs from her—Mrs. Jackson, down in 1-B—she hear her little girl just a cryin' out the other night, and see the light go on. Real late it was, and the chile only seven years old. She get up and go into the chile's room to see what happened. Window's wide open to let in the breeze, but she ain't worried, 'cause they's bars across it, like you got to have when you's on the groun' floor. But that chile, she shakin' fit to die. Say she wake up and they's a boy standin' right by her bed, just a lookin' down at her and doin' somethin' evil to hisself. She give a holler and reach for the light, and he take off. Wiggle hisself right out the window, she say. Mrs. Jackson, she look, but she don't see nothin', and she think the chile be havin' bad dreams, 'cause ain't nobody slippery enough to get through them bars. . . . But then she look at the wall above the window, and they's some kinda picture drew up there, higher than the little girl could reach. So Mrs. Jackson know that what the chile say is true. Chile say she seen that boy standin' there, even in the dark. Say it was a *white* boy, that's what she say, and mother-naked, too, 'cept for somethin' he had on over his head, somethin' real ugly like. I tell you, from now on that chile gwin' be sleepin' wid the light on!"

"You mean to say steel bars aren't enough these days?" I laughed, but I'm not sure why; we, too, lived on the ground floor, and not so far from there. "That's all Karen has to hear. She'll be after me again about moving to a more expensive place." I turned to Grandfather. "Do me a favor, don't mention this to her, okay?"

"Of course," he said. "You don't want to go around scaring women."

Father Pistachio cleared his throat. "I would like very much to meet this Karen someday. . . ."

"No question about it," I assured him. "We're going to get the two of you together real soon. Not today, though. Today she's busy painting."

My grandfather squinted at his watch, a souvenir of his years with the watch-casing firm. "Uh oh, speak of the devil, I have to get back. She's probably up there already."

My wife had gotten permission to repaint part of Grandfather's bedroom wall, as well as a few pieces of furniture salvaged from his former apartment. She was convinced she did such things better without my help, and that I would only get in the way—a belief which I'd encouraged, as I was in no hurry to join the two of them. I much preferred to sit here in the snack bar, eating jelly doughnuts and tracing patterns in the sugar on the table. Besides, there were some questions I wanted to ask Father Pistachio. Later, Karen and I were taking Grandfather out to eat, to celebrate his first successful week at the Manor. He'd told us it would be a welcome change.

"I'm looking forward to a decent meal tonight," he was saying, as he got up from his chair. He placed an unsteady hand on my shoulder. "These grandchildren of mine really know how to treat an old man!"

Making his way to the counter, he insisted on paying for my doughnuts and coffee, as well as for the Sanka he'd been restricted to since his stroke. "And give me some quarters, will you, Irv?" he asked, laying another dollar down. "I gotta do some wash, spruce up my wardrobe. My grandchildren are taking me out tonight—someplace swanky." Suddenly a doubt arose; he looked back at me. "Hey, I'm not going to have to wear a tie, am I?"

I shook my head. "It's not going to be *that* swanky!"

"Good," he said. "Just the same, I think I'll wear the socks with the monograms on 'em, the ones your mother gave me. You never can tell who you may be sitting next to." He bid the three of us good-bye, nodded to the counterman—"Take care, Irv, say hello to *Mrs.* Snackbaum for me"—and shuffled out the door.

Irv scratched his head. "I keep tellin' him, my name's Shapiro!"

Across the street the music had grown louder. I could feel the throb of the bass line through the soles of my shoes, and the air rang with grunting and screeching. I was glad I'd stayed inside.

Until now I'd avoided bringing up Pistachio's book. With Grandfather gone it was easier. "I understand," I said, "that you have some rather novel theories about the Indians and the Jews."

His face wrinkled into a grin. "Indian, Jew, Chinese, Turk—is all come from the same place."

"Yes, I remember. You said that's what you deal with in your 'Commentary.'"

"*Exactamente.* Is all there in the Gospel, for those who understand. Thomas, he is very clear, tell you all you want to know. Is through him I discover where man come from."

"Okay, I'll bite. Where *does* he come from?"

"Costa Rica."

The grin remained, but the eyes were absolutely earnest. I waited in vain for a punchline. Beside him Coralette nodded sagely, as if she'd heard all this before and was convinced that it was true.

"That sounds just a little unlikely," I said at last. "Man first walked erect somewhere in East Africa, at least that's what I've always read. They've got it all mapped out. Asia and Europe were next, and then across the Bering Strait and down into America. That was where the Indians came from: they kept on spreading southward till they'd covered the New World."

Pistachio had been listening patiently, mumbling "Yes . . . yes . . ." to himself as he searched his pockets for nuts. Finding one, he split it apart and studied it with the quiet satisfaction of a man contemplating a good cigar. At last he looked up. "Yes," he said, "all this I too have heard, from the time I am *estudiante.* But is all wrong. Is—how you say?—backward. Truth, she is far more strange."

The old man had gotten a faraway look in his eyes. Coralette pushed heavily to her feet and, mumbling excuses, waddled off upon some errand. I could see that it was lecture-time.

For the next half hour or so, as I sipped at still another cup of coffee, while the music from across the street grew steadily more primitive and the afternoon sunlight crept by inches up the wall, Pistachio gave me a short course in human history. It was an idiosyncratic one, to say the least, based as it was on certain Indian myth patterns and a highly selective reading of some fossil remains. According to his theory, the first men had evolved in the warm volcanic uplands of Central America, somewhere in the vicinity of Paraíso, Costa Rica—which was, by sheer coincidence, his own home town. For eons they had dwelled there in a city now gone but for the legends, one great happy tribe beneath a wise and all-powerful queen. Then, hundreds of millennia ago, threatened by invaders from the surrounding jungle—apparently some rival tribe, though I found his account here confusing—they had suddenly abandoned their city and fled northward. What's more, they hadn't paused for rest; as if still in the grip of some feverish need to escape, the tribe had kept on moving, streaming up through the Nicaraguan rain forests, spreading eastward as the land widened before them, but also pressing northward, ever northward, through what was now the United States, Canada, and Alaska, until the more adventurous pushed past the edge of the continent, crossing into Asia and beyond.

I listened to all this in silence, trying to decide just how seriously to take it. The whole thing sounded quite implausible to me, an old man's harmless fantasy, yet like a Velikovsky or a Von Däniken he was able to buttress his argument with a wide array of figures, facts, and names—names such as the Ameghino brothers, a pair of prominent nineteenth-century archaeologists who'd advanced a theory similar to his, but with their own home, Argentina, as the birthplace of mankind. I looked them up the next day in the school library and discovered that they'd actually existed, though their theories had reportedly been "held in disrepute" since the late 1880s.

The name that came up most often, however, was that of Saint Thomas himself. I looked him up as well. His "Gospel" isn't found in standard Bibles, but it's featured in the ancient Gnostic version (an English translation of which, published here in 1959, is on the desk beside me as I write). I should add, by way of a footnote, that Thomas has a special link with America: when the Spaniards first arrived on these shores in the sixteenth century they were shocked to find the Aztecs and other tribes practicing something that looked rather like Christianity, complete with hellfire, resurrections, virgin births, and magic crosses. Rather than admit that their own faith was far from unique, they theorized that Saint Thomas must have journeyed to the New World fifteen hundred years before, and that the Indians were merely practicing a debased form of the religion he had preached.

Somehow Pistachio had managed to scrape together all these queer old theories, folk tales, and fancies into a full-blown explanation of the human race—or at least that's what he claimed. He assured me that none of it conflicted with present-day Catholic doctrine, but then, I doubt he cared a fig for Catholic doctrine; he was obviously no normal priest. It was clear that, like a certain James character, he had "followed strange paths and worshipped strange gods." I wish now that I'd asked him what order he was from. I wonder if he left it voluntarily.

Yet at the time, despite my skepticism, I found the old man's sincerity persuasive. Moved by his description of the vast antediluvian city, with its pyramids, towers, and domes, and carried along by the sound of his voice as he traced man's hasty march across the planet, I could almost picture the course of events as if it were a series of tableaux. It had, I must admit, a certain grandeur: the idyllic tropical beginnings, a civilization sleeping through the centuries of peace, and then, all at once, the panicky flight from an army of invaders and the sudden dramatic surge northward—the first step in a global migration which would see that great primitive tribe break up, branching into other tribes that spread throughout the continent, wave upon wave, to become the Mochicas, the Chibchas, and the Changos, the Paniquitas, Yuncas, and Quechuas, the Aymaras and Atacamenos, the Puquinas and Paezes, the Coconucas, Barbacoas, and Antioquias, the Nicaraguan Zambos and Mosquitos, the Chontals of Honduras, the Maya and the Trahumare of Guatemala and Mexico, the Pueblo and the Navaho, the Paiute and the Crow, the Chinook and the Nootka and the Eskimo. . . .

"Let me get one thing straight," I said. "You're telling me that this accounts for all the races of mankind? Even the Jews?"

He nodded. "They are just another tribe."

So Grandfather had gotten it backward. According to Pistachio, the Israelites were merely a long-lost tribe of Costa Rican Indians!

"But how about family records?" I persisted. "Train tickets, steamship passages, immigration forms? I know for a fact that my family came over here from Eastern Europe."

The old man smiled and patted me on the shoulder. "Then, my son, you have made a circle of the world. Welcome home!"

The elevator shuddered to a halt and I stepped out onto the ninth floor. There was an odor of paint in the hall outside Grandfather's door. I knocked, but no one answered. When there was no response the second time, I pushed my way inside. None of the residents' doors were ever locked, old people being notoriously prone to heart attacks and fainting spells, strokes, broken hips, and other dislocations requiring immediate assistance. Though the supervision here was generally lax, absence from a meal without prior notice brought a visit from the staff. The previous summer, in a locked apartment in the middle of the Bronx, the body of an old man had lain alone and undiscovered for months until, riddled with maggots and swollen to four times its size, it had literally seeped through the floor and into the apartment below. That fate, at least, my grandfather would be spared.

His room, at the moment, was empty, but a radio whispered softly in the corner, tuned to some news station, and I saw my wife's handiwork in the freshly painted nightstand and armoire. I was admiring the job she'd done on the molding round the window when the two of them walked in, looking somewhat out of sorts. I asked them what was the matter.

"It's that laundry room," said Karen. "Only three of the washers are working, and we had a few slowpokes ahead of us. And of course your gallant old grandfather insisted that some women behind us go first, and we ended up waiting till everybody else was done. We just got the clothes in the dryer five minutes ago."

"Now, now," said Grandfather, "it'll just be a few minutes more, and then we can get this show on the road." He turned up the radio, an ancient white plastic Motorola, and for the next half hour we listened to reports of Mrs. Carter's South American tour, South Moluccan terrorists in Holland, and increasingly hot weather in New York. Soon he stretched and began fiddling sleepily with his pipe, which, as long as I'd known him, he'd never been able to keep lit. My wife saw some spots she'd missed beneath the window. I picked up the laundry bag and headed down the hall, attempting to look useful. When the elevator arrived I pressed the lowest button, marked by a "B" as big as my thumb.

Minutes later, when the door slid open once again, I felt momentarily disoriented. Outside the world still lay in daylight; down here, now that the machines were not in use, the corridor was gloomy and silent. It reminded me of a hospital at midnight, tiled walls receding into the distance while, down the middle of the ceiling, a line of dim, caged safety-bulbs made spots of illumination separated by areas of shadow.

The door to the laundry room would normally have stood within the light, but the bulb just above it was missing, leaving that section of the hall somewhat darker than the rest. Opening the door, I reached inside and groped for the light switch while my face was bathed by waves of steamy air. The superintendent's office must have been just beyond the farther wall, because I could hear, very faintly, the drumbeat of some mambo music. Then the fluorescent lights winked on, one after the other, with a loud, insect-like buzzing, but beneath it I could still make out the beat.

I recognized the broken washer at once. It was the unit in the corner at the back, the one that had been out of order weeks ago. Its electrical wire, coiled beside it, had been messily severed near the end, while another length still dangled from the socket in the wall. Evidently Frito had already attempted some repairs, for the unit had been pushed out of line, nearly two feet toward the center of the room. Beneath it, now exposed to view, lay a wide, semicircular drainage hole that extended, from the look of it, hundreds of feet down to some place Coleridge might have dreamed of, where waters flowed in everlasting night. No doubt the machines emptied into an underground spring, or one of those rivers that are said to run beneath Manhattan; only last winter the *Times* had written up a Mercer Street man who fished through a hole in his basement, pulling up eyeless white eels from a subterranean stream.

Leaning over, I caught a whiff of sewage, and could see, very dimly, the swirl of blackish current down below. Within it, outlined against the overhead lights, floated the reflection of my own familiar face, distorted by the movement of the water. It brought back memories of my honeymoon at a Catskill resort where, near the woods, an abandoned well lay covered by a moss-grown granite slab. When workmen lifted it aside my wife and I had peered into the hole, and for an instant had seen, there in the water, a pair of enormous frogs staring back at us, their pale bodies bloated like balloons. Suddenly they'd blinked, turned their bottoms up, and disappeared into the inky depths.

The dryer regarded me silently with its great cyclopean eye. The fluorescent lights buzzed louder. On the wall someone had scratched a crude five-pointed shape halfway between a holly leaf and a hand. I stuffed Grandfather's laundry into the bag and hurried from the room, happy to get out of there. Before closing the door, I switched the lights off. In the darkness, more clearly now, I heard the drumming. Where *was* Frito, anyway? He should have been spending less time on the mambo and more on the machines.

Grandfather appeared to be dozing when I got back to his room, but as soon as I stepped inside he looked up, seized the laundry bag, and dumped it on his bed. "Got to have my lucky socks!" he said, searching through a collection of the rattiest looking underwear I'd ever seen.

"Where's my skirt?" asked Karen, peering over his shoulder.

"You're wearing it," I said.

"No, I mean the one I had on first—that old summer thing I use for painting. It got filthy, so I stuck it in with Grandfather's stuff."

I knew the one she meant—a dowdy old green rag she'd had since college. "I must have left it in the dryer," I said, and walked wearily back down the hall. The elevator hadn't moved since I'd left it.

Yet someone had gotten to the laundry room ahead of me; I saw light streaming under the door, and heard the distant music and a stream of Spanish curses. Inside I found Frito, shoulders heaving as he strained to push the broken washer back against the wall. He looked very angry.

He turned when I came in, and nodded once in greeting. "You give me hand with this, yes? This thing, she weigh six hundred pound."

"How'd you manage to move it out here in the first place?" I asked, eyeing the squat metal body. Six hundred seemed a conservative guess.

"Me?" he said. "I didn't move it." His eye narrowed. "Did *you?*"

"Of course not, I just thought—"

"Why I do this for, huh? Is no reason. Must have been *los niños.* They do anything."

I pointed to the severed wire. "And kids did that? Looks more like rats to me. I mean, look at it! It looks *gnawed.*"

"No," he said, "I tell you once already, rats not gonna bother my machine. They try and eat through this stuff, they break their fuckin' teeth. Same with the cement." He stamped vehemently upon the floor; it sounded sturdy enough. "'Leven year I'm in this place, and never any trouble till a couple weeks ago. I want to buy a lock, but Calzone says—"

But my eye had just been caught by a blob of faded green lying crumpled in the shadow of the dryer by the wall. It was Karen's skirt. Leaving the superintendent to his fulminations, I went to pick it up. I grasped the edge of the cloth—and dropped it with a cry of disgust. The thing was soaking wet, and, as I now saw, it had been lying in a puddle of milky white fluid whose origin seemed all too apparent. About it hung the sour odor I'd smelled before.

"Ugh!" I said. I made a face. I wasn't going to take this back upstairs. Let Karen believe it was lost. Gingerly I prodded it across the floor with my foot and kicked it down the drainage hole. It flashed green for a moment, spreading as it fell, and then was lost from sight in the blackness. I thought I saw the oily waters stir.

Frito shook his head. *"Los niños,"* he said. "They getting in here."

My eye followed the glistening trail that led from the dryer to the hole. "That's not kids," I said. "That's a grown man living in the building. Come on, let's get this covered up before somebody falls through." Bracing myself, I put my shoulder to the machine and pushed. Even when the superintendent joined me it was difficult to budge; it felt like it was bolted to the floor. At last, as metal scraped on concrete with an ugly grating sound, we got the thing back into line.

Just before leaving the room, I looked back to see Frito crouched by the coils of electric cord, glumly poking at the strands of wire that twisted like claws from the end. I sensed that there was something missing, but couldn't decide what it was. With a final wave I stepped into the hall, my mind already on dinner. Behind me, aside from the buzzing of the lights, the place was absolutely silent.

Wednesday, June 15

My grandfather was long overdue for a haircut; he'd last had one in April, well before his stroke, and his hair was beginning to creep over the back of his collar, giving him the appearance of an aged poet or, as he maintained, "an old bum." I'd have thought that he'd be pleased to get it trimmed, and to idle away an afternoon at the barber's, but when I arrived to pick him up in the lobby of the Manor he looked weary and morose.

"Everything's slowing down," he said. "I guess I must be feeling my age. I looked at my face in the mirror when I got up this morning, and it was the face of an old man." He ran his fingers through his hair, which had long ago receded past the top of his head. "Even my hair's slowing down," he said. "Damned stuff doesn't grow half as fast as it used to. I remember how my first wife—your grandmother—used to say I looked distinguished because my hair was prematurely grey." He shook his head. "Well, it's still grey, what's left of it, but it sure as hell ain't premature."

Maybe he was depressed because, after a lifetime of near-perfect health, he'd finally encountered something he couldn't shake off; though the doctor considered him recovered, the stroke had left him weak, uncoordinated, and increasingly impatient with himself. Or maybe it was just the weather. It was one of those heavy, overcast spring days that threaten rain before nightfall and, in the coming weeks, a deadly summer. As we strolled outside the air was humid, the sky as dark as slate. Beneath it earthly objects—the tropical plants for sale outside a florist's shop, an infant in red shorts and halter with her ears already pierced, the gaudy yellow signboard of La Concha Superette—stood out with unnatural clarity, as if imbued with a terrible significance.

"My legs feel like they're ready for the junk heap," said Grandfather. "My mind'll probably go next, and then where will I be?"

He was, in fact, walking even more slowly than usual—he'd stumbled on the planks across the sewage ditch, and I'd had to shorten my steps in order to stay by his side—but I assured him that he had a few good decades left. "If worst comes to worst," I said, "you've still got your looks."

This brought a snort of derision, but I noticed that he stood a little straighter. Screwing up his face, he thrust his hands into his pockets like some actor in a 1930s Warner Brothers' movie. "Nobody wants a man with a mug like mine," he said, "except maybe somebody like Mrs. Rosenzweig."

"Well, there you are." I remembered the little old woman with the deaf roommate. "See? There's someone for everyone." He shook his head and muttered something about its not being right. "Not right?" I said. "What's the matter? Saving yourself for some pretty little blonde?"

He laughed. "There aren't any blondes where I live. They're all old and grey like me."

"So we'll get you someone from the neighborhood."

"Stop already with the dreaming! The closest thing you'll find around here is some colored girl with dyed blond hair."

"Here's one that looks white enough," I said, tapping on the glass. We had reached the Barbería/Barbershop, where an advertising placard in the window, faded by the sun, showed a beefy Mark Spitz look-alike, hair aglisten with Vitalis, attempting to guess the identity of a sinuous young woman who had just crept up behind him. Covering his eyes with two pale, finely manicured hands, she was whispering, "Guess who?" That unwarranted question mark annoyed me.

The shop's front door was open to let in a nonexistent breeze, and the smell of rose water, hair tonic, and sweat hung nostalgically in the doorway. There was only one barber inside, fluttering over a burly *latino* who sat glowering into the mirror, somehow retaining his dignity despite the clumps of shiny black hair that covered his shoulders like fur. Portraits of Kennedy, Pope John, and some unidentified salsa king beamed down at us through a talcum-powder haze. Seating himself by the magazine rack, my grandfather reached instinctively for the *Daily News,* realized he'd already seen it, and passed it on to me. Bored, I scanned the headlines—Spain holding its first free elections in forty-one years, two derelicts found dead and blinded in a men's room at Grand Central Station, James Earl Ray returned to prison following an escape—while Grandfather stared doubtfully at a pile of Spanish-language magazines on the lower shelf. Moments later I saw him frown, lean forward, and extract from beneath the pile a tattered, thumb-stained *Hustler,* which he opened near the middle. His expression changed, more in shock than delight. "Mmmph," he said, "they never had stuff like this back in Brooklyn." Suddenly remembering himself, he shut the magazine. I could see he was embarrassed. "You know," he said, "it's silly for you to sit around here all afternoon. I'll be okay on my own."

"Fine," I said. "We can meet later for coffee." Karen wouldn't be home till after her Wednesday-evening class, and I had plenty of errands to do.

Outside, the sky had grown even darker. As I started up Amsterdam, I could see shopkeepers rolling up their awnings. Davey's Tavern, on the corner ahead, was already noisy with patrons, while soul music, drunks, and broken beer bottles spilled out upon the pavement in front. An overturned garbage can disgorged its contents into the gutter; a few feet past it the opening to a sewer was clogged with bread crusts, wormy lettuce leaves, and pools of curdled cream. "Peewee, huh?" a man on the sidewalk was shouting. He wore greasy overalls and a sleeveless T-shirt dark with perspiration. "Hey, nigger, why they callin' you Peewee for? You needs some o' what I got?" He began digging drunkenly at his fly while the small, goateed man he'd been shouting at hurried toward a nearby car, muttering threats to "get me somethin' an' bust that nigger's ass."

I was just crossing the street to avoid the inevitable fight when I heard my name called. It was Father Pistachio, lounging calmly on his stoop just around the corner from the scene of action and grinning at me beneath his halo of white hair. In truth I'd been hoping to avoid him as well: I just didn't have the time today for another history lesson. Resolving that our meeting would be brief, I waved and circled warily in his direction. He seemed to be alone.

"Where's your friend?" I asked, declining his invitation to sit down.

"Coralette? She call me up this morning, all *dolorosa,* tell me she have trouble in the building where she live. Something about Last Rites. I tell her I am a priest, I can give the Last Rites, but she say is all right, she going to be asking her minister. Then someone else is having to use the telephone—Coralette, you know, she live in a hotel, is not a nice place at all—and so there is no more time for talking. She tell me she will come by later, though. Maybe you will still be here."

"I doubt it," I said. "I really can't stay. I've got to join my grandfather in a little while."

"Ah, yes." The old man smiled. "Herman, he say he gain twenty pound Saturday night at the restaurant. Say he have the best time of his life. And I am thinking to myself, Is good to know that some young people today still have respect for the old."

I nodded uneasily, hoping he wasn't leading up to another request to meet Karen. I hated to keep putting him off.

"Maybe soon you and your wife will be my guests for dinner," he went on. "Real Costa Rican food. How you like that?"

I sighed and said I'd like it very much.

"Good, good." He was visibly pleased. "I am just upstairs. And after I make the dinner, I show you what is to be in my book. Charts, maps, pictures—you understand? *Las ilustraciones.* Some I have already in the first edition, published in Paraíso. I bring it for you next time, yes?"

I said that would be fine.

All this time we had been hearing music from around the corner. Now, suddenly, came the sounds of a scuffle: a taunt, a scream, sporadic bursts of laughter from the crowd.

Pistachio shook his head. "Is a shame. Men, they just want to fight."

"Some men," I said. "But our great-great-granddaddies don't seem to have gone in for it much, at least according to you. They sound pretty cowardly, in fact—pulling up stakes when another tribe showed up, running off like a bunch of kids, leaving the city behind. . . . Sounds to me like they gave up without a fight."

I suppose I was needling him a bit, but it didn't seem to faze him.

"I think you do not understand," he said. "I never say it is another tribe. Is another *raza,* maybe, another people. One cannot be sure. No one knows where they are from. No one knows their name. Maybe they are what God make before He make a man. Legend say that they are soft, like God's first clay, but that they love to fight. Quick like the piranha, and impossible to kill. No use to hit them in the head."

"Oh? Why's that?"

"Is hard to say. Many different stories. In one the Chibcha tell, is because they have something on the face. Flat places, ridges, things like little hooks. Back of head, she is like the front; all look much the same. Me, I think this mean they wear a special thing to cover the head in war." He made a kind of helmet with his hands. "See? This way you cannot hurt them, cannot keep them out. They go where they want, take what they want. Break into the city, steal the food, carry many captives to their king. The lucky ones they kill."

"They don't sound like very nice people."

He gave a short, unmerry laugh. "Some Indians say that they are devils. Chibcha say they are the children of God, but children He make wrong. Is no pity inside them, no love for God or man. When God see that they will not change, He try to get rid of them. They are so strong He have to try one, two, three times! Chibcha call them *Xo Tl'mi-go,* 'The Thrice Accursed.' "

I'm quoting here from memory and my spelling is approximate at best; whatever it was that he actually said, it was unpronounceable. My eyes were held by his plump little red-stained lips, which worked up and down when he talked and which continued to do so even now, as he paused to stuff another nut between them. The fight-sounds down the block had momentarily subsided, but then I heard the jangle of breaking glass—for me, even at a distance, the most unnerving and ugly of sounds—and I realized that the battle was still very much in progress. I'd swear that at one point I could hear the echoes of a faraway war cry; but maybe it was just the effect of the story.

The story—an Indian legend, he claimed—seemed to have been cooked up by a committee of primitive tribesmen sitting round a fire trying to scare themselves. It told of the invaders—clearly a bad bunch, given to all manner of atrocities—and of God's repeated attempts to exterminate them.

"First, they say, God curse the women, make them all *estériles,* barren. But is no good; is not enough. The men, they leave the jungle, raid the city, carry off its women from their bed. As long as they find women, they are still breeding."

"So then God curses the men, right?"

"*Exactamente!*" Raising a finger dramatically, he leaned toward me and lowered his voice, though there was no one else around. "God, He make their *penes* drop off. Their manhood. But again it is no good. Even this is not enough. The fighting, the raiding, she goes on as before. The women, they are taken from the city and—" Here a disapproving little clucking sound, "—just as before."

"But how could they keep on breeding without their, uh . . ."

He gave another one of those all-purpose Latin shrugs, which seemed terribly enigmatic but may just have been embarrassed. "Oh," he said vaguely, "they find a way." He picked a sliver of pistachio from his teeth and stared at it a moment. "But is hard to guess what is truth here, what is *fábula.* Is not history, you know. Is only a story the Indians tell. *Un cuento de hadas.*"

A fairy tale—yes, that's exactly what it was. A prehistoric fairy tale.

"Well," I said, "I guess you can't blame our ancestors for running away. Those outsiders don't sound like the kind of people you want to hang around with. What happened, they take over when the others moved out?"

The old man nodded. "City, she is theirs now. Belong to them. For sport they pull her down—every temple, every tower, every brick. Soon they are making ready to go after the others; is time to breed again, time to bring back food, women, captives for the sacrifice. And now, just before they leave, God make His final curse: He seal their eyes close, every one, forever. No more can they follow the tribe of our fathers. For them, is no more sunlight, no more day. One by one they crawl back to the jungle. One by one they are lost. All of them are dead now, dead and in the earth for two hundred thousand year. Paraíso, she is built upon the place where bodies lie. Farmers turn their bones up with the plow, grind them up for meal. All are *cenizas* now—dust and ashes."

That certainly sounded final enough, I thought. *Exeunt the villains.* At least the fairy tale had a happy ending. . . .

"But hold on," I said, "what if these fellows survived even a third curse? I mean, the first two didn't even slow them down, they adapted right away. And it's not as if losing your sight were a sentence of death. Who's to say the smart ones didn't stick around? Their children could be down there in the jungle right this minute, trying to figure out where all the women went!"

"You think perhaps they are hoping to make a new raid on Paraíso?" The old priest smiled wanly. "No, my friend. The last of them die off down there two hundred thousand year ago. Their story, she is over. *Se termino.*" He clapped his hands. "Now the tribes of man, they are far more interesting. My book tells how they learn to read the stars, build ships, make fire. . . ."

But I wasn't listening. I was thinking once again of those great Mayan cities, Tikal and Copán and the rest, standing silent and deserted in the middle of the jungle—as if, without warning, one afternoon or in the dead of night, all of their inhabitants had simply disappeared, or walked away, or fled.

I wasn't sure just where those cities lay, but I knew they were nowhere near Paraíso.

My grandfather sat waiting for me in the snack bar, lacquered and perfumed and shorn. "You shoulda seen the fight," he said as I settled into my chair. "Those colored boys can really take a beating. Damn thing would still be going on if it wasn't for the weather." He nodded toward the window, against which heavy drops of rain were splattering like gunfire.

For the next few minutes he regaled me with a description of the fight, which he'd viewed from the doorway of the barbershop. The shop itself had disappointed him—"four seventy-five," he said ruefully, "I could've cut my own hair for less than that!"—but its magazines had been a revelation. "It's unbelievable," he said, "they're showing *everything* nowadays. And you could see their faces!"

"What, are you kidding?" Maybe I hadn't heard right. "You mean to say you spent your time looking at the faces, instead of—"

"No, no, I didn't mean that! What the hell you take me for?" He leaned forward and lowered his voice. "What I'm saying is, you could tell who these gals *were*. You'd recognize 'em if you saw 'em on the street. In my day, if some floozie took her clothes off in a magazine, they made damn sure they blocked her eyes out first. Or maybe they'd show you the back of her head. But you hardly ever got to see the face."

I was going to ask him where he'd been living the past twenty years, but he was staring behind me and beginning to get up. I turned to see Coralette squeezing through the door. She saw us and moved ponderously toward our table, shaking rain from her umbrella as she came. "Lawd," she said, "if this ain't just the worst day I ever see!" Heaving herself into a seat, she sighed and shook her head. "Trouble, jus' no end o' trouble."

Coralette, it turned out, was a resident of the Notre Dame Hotel, which stood beside a drug rehabilitation center on West 80th Street. I had passed beneath its awning several times; it was a shabby little place, notable only for the grandiosity of its name and for a Coke machine that all but filled its lobby. Coralette's room was on the second floor, by the rear landing. Across the hall lived a tall, ungainly young black girl, a former addict who'd been enrolled in one of the programs at the building next door. The girl was severely retarded, with impaired speech and a pronounced mongoloid cast to her features, yet according to the scandalized Coralette she spent most of her time with a succession of men—criminals and fellow addicts, to judge by their appearance—from the s.r.o. hotels uptown. Occasionally she would bring one of these men back with her; more often she was out all night, and would return home in the morning barely able to report where she had been.

This spring had seen a change in her. She had stopped going out, and had taken to spending the nights in her room, although it was several weeks before the older woman had realized it. "She been in there all the time," said Coralette, "only I figured she away 'cause I don't never see no light under the door. Then one night I's on the way to the bathroom and hears her voice, but she ain't sayin' nothin'. . . . At first I think maybe she sick, or cryin' out in her sleep. But then I hears this movin' around, and I know she got somebody in there with her. I hears the two of 'em again on my way back. They makin' a lot o' noise, but they ain't talkin', if you knows what I mean."

The noise had been repeated on succeeding nights, and once Coralette had walked by when the visitor apparently was sleeping, "snorin' fit to kill." A few weeks later she had heard somebody coming up the stairs, followed by the closing of the door across the hall. "Now I ain't nosy," she declared, "but I did take me a peek through the keyhole when he pass. Didn't see much, 'cause the light out in the hall and it was dark as sin, but look to me like he didn't have no trousers on."

One night in April she'd encountered the girl outside the bathroom. "She lookin' sorta sick—say she think she got some sorta worm in her—so I asks her to come on in and rest herself. I got me a hot plate, so I cooks up a can o' black bean soup. Poor chile don't even know enough to say thank you, but she drink it all right down. 'Fore she go I asks her how she feelin', and she say she a whole lot better now. Say she think she gwin' be my frien'. Got herself a bran' new boyfrien', too. Sound like she real proud of herself."

For the past two weeks no one had seen her, though from time to time Coralette had heard her moving about in the room. "Sound like she alone now," Coralette recalled. "I figured she was finally settlin' down, takin' that treatment like she s'posed to. But then today the lady from the center come and say that girl ain't showed up for a month."

They had tried her door and found it locked. Knocking had brought no response; neither had an appeal from Coralette. Several other tenants had grown nervous. Finally the manager had been summoned; his passkey had opened the door.

The room, said Coralette, had been a shambles. "They was some kinda mess high up on the walls, and you got to hold your nose when you go in." The girl had been found near the center of the room, hanging naked from the light fixture with a noose around her neck. Oddly, her feet had still been resting on the floor; she must have kept her legs drawn up while dying.

"I guess that boy of hers done left her all alone." Coralette shook her head sorrowfully. "Seems a shame when you think of it, leavin' her like that, 'specially 'cause I recollect how proud she been. Say he was the first white boyfrien' she ever had."

Wednesday, June 29

As one who believes that mornings are for sleeping, I've always tried, both as a student and a teacher, to schedule my classes for later in the day. The earliest I ever ride the subway is ten or ten-thirty a.m., with the executives, the shoppers, and the drones. One morning just before my marriage, however, returning home from Karen's house downtown, I found myself on the subway at halfpast seven. Immediately I knew that I was among a different class of people, virtually a different tribe; I could see it in their work clothes, in the absence of neckties, and in the brown bags and lunch pails that they carried in place of briefcases. But it took me several minutes to discern a more subtle difference: that, instead of the *Times,* the people around me were reading (and now and then moving their lips to) the *Daily News.*

This, as it happens, was my grandfather's favorite—nay, only—reading matter, aside from an occasional racing form. "You see the story on page nine?" he demanded, waving the paper in my face. On an afternoon as hot as this I was grateful for the breeze. We were seated like three wise men, he, Father Pistachio, and I, on the stoop of Pistachio's building. I had joined them only a moment before and was sweating from my walk. Somehow these old men didn't mind the heat as much as I did; I couldn't wait to get back to my air conditioner.

"Recognize this?" said my grandfather, pointing to a photo sandwiched between a paean to the threatened B-1 bomber and a profile of Menachem Begin. "See? Bet you won't find this in your fancy-shmancy *Times!*"

I squinted at the photo. It was dark and rather smudged, but I recognized the awning of the Notre Dame Hotel.

"Wow," I said, "we'll have to send this down to Coralette." Last week, totally without warning, she had packed her bags and gone to stay with a sister in South Carolina, crossing herself and mumbling about "white boys" who were smashing the lights in her hall. I'd had to get the details from Grandfather, as my wife and I had been upstate last week. I hadn't even had a chance to say good-bye.

"I don't know," said Grandfather, "I'm not so sure she'd want to read this."

The article—"Watery Grave for Infant Quints"—was little more than an extended caption. It spoke of the "five tiny bodies . . . shrunken and foul-smelling" that had been discovered in a flooded area of the hotel basement by Con Ed men investigating a broken power line. All five had displayed the same evidence of "albinism and massive birth defects," giving the *News* the opportunity to refer to them as "the doomed quintuplets" and to speculate about the cause of death; "organic causes" seemed likely, but drowning and even strangulation had not been ruled out. "Owing to decomposition," the article noted, "it has not been possible to determine the infants' age at the time of death, nor whether they were male or female. Caseworkers in the Police Department's newly revamped Child Welfare Bureau say that despite recent budget cutbacks they are tracking down several leads."

"Pretty horrible," I said, handing the paper back to my grandfather. "I'm just glad Karen doesn't read things like this."

"But I have brought for you a thing she may like." Father Pistachio was holding up a slim orange book bound in some sort of shiny imitation cloth. It had one of those crude, British-type spines that stick out past the edges of the cover: obviously a foreign job, or else vanity press. This book, as it happened, was both. It was the Costa Rican edition of his "Commentary on Saint Thomas."

"Is a present," he said, placing it reverently in my hand. "For you, also for your wife. I inscribe it to you both."

On the flyleaf, in trembly, old-fashioned script, he had written, *"To my dear American friends: With your help I will spread the truth to all readers of your country,"* and, beneath it, *"'We wander blind as children through a cave; yet though the way be lost, we journey from the darkness to the light.' —Thomas xv:i."*

I read it out loud to Karen after dinner that night while she was in the kitchen washing up. "Gee," she said, "he's really got his heart set on getting that thing published. Sounds to me like a bit of a fanatic."

"He's just old." I flipped through the pages searching for illustrations, since my Spanish was rusty and I didn't feel like struggling through the text. Two Aztecs with a cornstalk flashed past me, then drawings of an arrowhead, a woolly mammoth, and a thing that resembled a swim-fin. *"El guante de un usurpador,"* the latter's caption said. The glove of a usurper. It looked somehow familiar; maybe I'd seen one at the YMCA pool. I turned past it and came to a map. "See this?" I said, holding up the book. "A map of where your ancestors came from. Right on up through Nicaragua."

"Mmm."

"And here's a map of that long-lost city—"

"Looks like something out of *Flash Gordon.*" She went back to the dishes.

"—and a cutaway view of the main temple."

She peered at it skeptically. "Honey, are you sure that old man's not putting you on? I'd swear that's nothing but a blueprint of the Pyramid at Giza. You can find it in any textbook, I've seen it dozens of times. He must have gotten hold of a Xerox machine and— Good God, what's that?"

She was pointing toward a small line drawing on the opposite page. I puzzled out the caption. "That's, um, let me see, '*La cabeza de un usurpador*,' the head of a usurper. . . . Oh, I know, it must be one of the helmets the invaders wore. A sort of battle mask, I guess."

"Really? Looks more like the head of a tapeworm. I'll bet he cribbed it from an old bio book."

"Oh, don't be silly. He wouldn't stoop to that." Frowning, I drifted back to the living room, still staring at the page. From the page the thing stared blankly back. She was right, I had to admit. It certainly didn't look like any helmet I'd ever seen: the alien proportions of the face, with great blank indentations where the eyes should be (unless those two tiny spots were meant for eyes), the round, puckered "mouth" area with rows of hooklike "teeth. . . ."

Shutting the book, I strolled to the window and gazed out through the latticework of bars. Darkness had fallen on the street only half an hour before, yet already the world out there seemed totally transformed.

By day the neighborhood was pleasant enough; we had what was considered a "nice" building, fairly well maintained, and a "nice" block, at least our half of it. The sidewalk lay just outside our windows, level with the floor on which I stood. Living on the bottom meant a savings on the rent, and over the years I'd come to know the area rather well. I knew where the garbage cans were grouped like sentries at the curbside, and how the large brass knocker gleamed on the reconverted brownstone across the street. I knew which of the spindly little sidewalk trees had failed to bud this spring, and where a Mercedes was parked, and what the people looked like in the windows facing mine.

But it suddenly occurred to me, as I stood there watching the night, that a neighborhood can change in half an hour as assuredly as it can change in half a block. After dark it becomes a different place: another neighborhood entirely, coexisting with the first and separated by only a few minutes in time, the first a place where everything is known, the other a place of uncertainty, the first a place of safety, the other one of—

It was time to draw the curtains, but for some reason I hesitated. Instead, I reached over and switched off the noisy little air conditioner, which had been rattling metallically in the next window. As it ground into silence, the noise outside seemed to rise and fill the room. I could hear crickets, and traffic, and the throb of distant drums. Somewhere out there in the darkness they were snapping their fingers, bobbing their heads, maybe even dancing; yet, for all that, the sound struck me as curiously ominous. My eyes kept darting back and forth, from the shadows of the lampposts to the line of strange dark trees—and to that menacing stretch of unfamiliar sidewalk down which, at any moment, anything might walk on any errand.

Stepping back to adjust the curtains, I was startled by the movement of my own pale reflection in the glass, and I had a sudden vision, decidedly unscientific, no doubt inspired by that picture in the book: a vision of a band of huge white tapeworms, with bodies big as men, inching blindly northward toward New York.

Wednesday, July 6

"It was awful. *Awful.*"

"You're telling me! Musta been a real nightmare."

I folded my paper and sat up in the chair, straining to hear above the hum of the fan. The lobby was momentarily deserted, except for an old man dozing in the corner and two old women leafing through a magazine; a third sat numbly by their side, as if waiting for a bus. In the mirror I could see Miss Pascua and Mr. Calzone talking in the office just behind me. They were keeping their voices low.

"You've heard the, uh, details?"

"Nope. Just what I read in yesterday's *News.* Oh, sure, they're all talking about it back in the kitchen. You know how the guys are. Most of 'em got interviewed by the police, and they think they're on *Kojak.* But nobody knows much. I ain't seen Mrs. Hirschfeld all week."

"Her daughter came and took her Monday morning. I doubt if she'll be coming back."

I'd had the same impulse myself last night, when I'd first heard of the incident. I had telephoned my grandfather and asked him if he wanted to move out. He'd sounded angry and upset, but he'd expressed no desire to leave. The Manor, he'd decided, was as safe as anywhere else. A new guard had been hired for the entranceway, and tenants had been told to lock their doors.

"They haven't finished with the room yet," Miss Pascua was saying. "They keep marching through here with their bags and equipment and things. Plus we've got the Con Ed men downstairs. It's a real madhouse."

"And Mrs. Rosenzweig?"

"Ah, the poor thing's still at Saint Luke's. I was the one who telephoned the police. I heard the whole thing."

"Yeah? Bad, huh?" He sounded eager.

"Absolutely awful. She said she was fast asleep, and then something woke her up. I guess it must've been pretty loud, because you know what a racket the air conditioner makes."

"Well, don't forget, *she's* not the one who's got problems there. Her hearing's pretty sharp."

"I guess it must be. She said she could hear somebody snoring. At first, though, she didn't think anything of it. She figured it was just Mrs. Hirschfeld in the next room, so she tries to get back to sleep. But then she hears the snoring getting louder, and it seems to be coming *closer*. She calls out, 'Elsie, is that you?' I mean, she was confused, she didn't know what was going on, she thought maybe Mrs. Hirschfeld was walking in her sleep. But the snoring doesn't stop, it just keeps getting closer to the bed. . . ."

Across the lobby the elevator door slid open with an echoing of metal; several old men and women emerged. I was about to stand, until I saw that Grandfather wasn't among them. He had never been on time in his life.

"That's when she starts getting scared—"

Miss Pascua leaned forward. Above the mantel to my left, the figures in the painting stood frozen gravely at attention, as if listening.

"—because all of a sudden she realizes that the sound's coming from *more than one place*. It's all around her now, like there are dozens of sleepwalkers in the room. She puts out her hand, and she feels a face right next to hers. And the mouth is open—her fingers slide all the way in. She said it was like sticking your hand inside a tin can: all wet and round, with little teeth around the edge."

"Jesus."

"And she couldn't scream, because one of them got his hand over her face and held it there. She said it smelled like something you'd find in the gutter. God knows where he'd been or what he'd been doing. . . ."

My eyebrows rose skyward; I'm sure I must have started from my chair. If what Miss Pascua said was true, I knew *exactly* where the culprit had been and what he'd been doing. I almost turned around and called out to the two of them, but instead I remained silent. There'd be time enough to tell someone later; I would go to the authorities this very afternoon. I sat back, feeling well pleased with myself, and listened to Miss Pascua's voice grow more and more excited.

"I guess she must've thrashed around a lot, because somehow she got free and yelled for Mrs. Hirschfeld to come help her. She's screaming, 'Elsie! Elsie!' "

"A lot of good that'll do her! The old broad's deaf as a post."

"Sure, she'd sleep through anything. Right there in the next room, too. But poor old Mrs. Rosenzweig, she must've got them mad with all her yelling, because they hit her—hard. Oh, you should've seen her face! And they wrapped their arms around her neck and, do you know, they almost strangled her. She was just lying there, trying to breathe, and then she felt some others yank the sheet and blanket down, then they turned her on her stomach and pushed her face into the pillow, and she could feel their hands on her ankles, hauling her legs apart—the nightgown was actually ripped right up the side—and then another one of them pulled it up over her waist. . . ."

Miss Pascua paused for breath. "Jesus," said Calzone, "don't it make you just want to—" He shook his head. "It musta been the blacks. No one else coulda done a thing like that. I mean, to them one woman's the same as any other, they don't care how old she is, or if she's maybe got a handicap or something, just so long as she's white. You know, they caught this guy over on 76th Street, in one of them welfare hotels, he was going around with a stocking over his head—"

The elevator door slid open and my grandfather stepped out. He waved and started across the lobby. Behind me Miss Pascua had interrupted the other's story and was plunging breathlessly on, as if impatient to reach the climax of her own.

"And then, she says, there was this soft, scratching sound, real close to her ear. She says it was like someone rubbing his hands together from the cold. That's when— Well, it sure doesn't sound like any rape I ever heard of. All she'd keep saying was it felt like getting slapped. I mean it, that's just what she said."

My grandfather had reached me in time to overhear this. "God," he whispered, shaking his head, "it's absolutely unbelievable, isn't it? A woman that age—a poor defenseless blind woman. . . ."

"And the most horrible thing of all," Miss Pascua was saying, "she told me that the whole time, with all the things they did to her, they never spoke a single word."

Age-yellowed eyes opened infinitesimally wider. Wrinkled heads turned slowly as I passed. The second floor was crowded that day; I felt as if I were striding through a world of garden gnomes: old folks on the benches by the elevator, old folks standing motionless in the hall, old folks in listless conversation round the doorway to the game room. These were the same ones who congregated in the lobby each morning, waiting for the mailman to arrive, and who began gathering outside the dining room hours before mealtime. Now they had drifted up here, unmindful of the heat, to partake of what little drama yet remained from the events of Sunday night.

I was glad my grandfather wasn't one of them. At least he still got out. I'd said good-bye to him only a minute or two ago when, following the usual coffee and conversation with Pistachio, he'd retired upstairs for his afternoon nap. I hadn't told him about my suspicions, or what I intended to do. He would never have understood.

It wasn't hard to find where Mrs. Rosenzweig had been living; that end of the corridor had been screened off from the rest behind a folding canvas partition, the sort of thing hospitals use to screen the sick from one another and the dead from those alive. A small knot of residents stood chatting in front, as if waiting to see some performance inside. They regarded me with interest as I approached; I suppose that during the past few days they'd been treated to a stream of detectives and police photographers, and took me for another one.

"Have you caught them yet?" one of the ladies demanded.

"Not yet," I said, "but there may be one very good lead."

Indeed, I intended to supply it myself. I must have sounded confident, because they moved respectfully aside for me, and I heard them repeating to each other, "A good lead, he says they have a good lead," as I made my way around the screen.

Mrs. Rosenzweig's door was ajar. Sunlight flooded the room through an open window. Inside, two beefy-looking men sat perspiring over a radio, listening to a Yankees game. Neither of them was in uniform—one wore a plaid short-sleeve shirt, the other just a T-shirt and shorts—but the former, the younger of the two, had a silver badge hanging from his shirt pocket. They had been laughing about some aspect of the game, but when they saw me in the doorway their smiles disappeared.

"You got a reason to be here, buddy?" asked the one with the badge. He got up from the windowsill where he'd been sitting.

"Well, it's nothing very important." I stepped into the room. "There's something I wanted to call to your attention, that's all. Just in case you haven't already considered it. I was downstairs earlier today, and I overheard a woman who works here saying that—"

"Whoa, whoa, hold it," he said. "Now just slow down a second. What's your interest in all this anyway?"

Above the clamor of the radio (which neither of them made a move to turn down) I explained that I'd been visiting my grandfather, who lived here at the Manor. "I come by almost every week," I said. "In fact, I even had a slight acquaintance with Mrs. Rosenzweig and her roommate."

I saw the two cops exchange a quick glance—*Oh my God,* I thought, *what if these bastards think I did it?*—but the attack of paranoia proved short-lived, for I watched their expressions change from wary to indifferent to downright impatient as I told them what Miss Pascua had said.

"She said something about a foul smell, a sort of 'gutter smell.' And so it just occurred to me—I don't know, maybe you've checked this out already—it occurred to me that the logical group of suspects might be right outside." I pointed through the open window, toward the gaping brown sewage ditch that stretched along the sidewalk like a wound. "See? They've been working down there for at least a month or so, and they probably had access to the building."

The man in the T-shirt had already turned back to the game. The other gave me a halfhearted nod. "Believe me, mister," he said, "we're checking out every possibility. We may not look like it to you, but we do a pretty thorough job."

"Fine, that's fine, just so long as you intend to talk to them—"

The man in the T-shirt looked up. "We *do,*" he said. "It's being done. Thank you very much for coming forward. Now why don't you just give my partner here your name, address, and phone number in case we have to contact you." He reached out and turned up the volume on the radio.

Laboriously the other one took down the information; he seemed far more concerned with getting the spelling of my name right than with anything else I'd had to say. While he wrote I looked around the room—at the discolorations in the plaster, the faded yellow drapes, a lilac sachet on the bureau, a collection of music boxes on a shelf. It didn't look much like the scene of a crime, except for strips of black masking tape directing one's attention to certain parts of the walls and floor. Four strips framed the light switch, another four an overturned table lamp, presumably for guests. Beside it stood a clock with its dial exposed so that a blind person could read it. The bed, too, was bordered by tape, the sheet and blanket still in violent disarray. With sunlight streaming in it was hard to imagine what had happened here: the old woman, the darkness, the sounds. . . .

Snapping shut his notebook, the younger cop thanked me and walked with me to the door. Beyond it stood the canvas screen, blocking out the view, though in the space between the canvas and the floor I could see a line of stubby little shoes and hear the shrill chatter of old ladies. Well, I told myself, maybe I didn't get to play Sherlock Holmes, but at least I've done my duty.

"We'll call you if there's anything we need," said the cop, practically shutting the door in my face. As it swung closed I saw, for the first time, that there were four strips of masking tape near the top, around a foot square, enclosing a familiar-looking shape.

"Wait a second," I said. "What's that?"

The door swung back. He saw where I was pointing. "Don't touch it," he said. "We found it there on the door. That tape's for the photographer and the fingerprint guys."

Standing on tiptoe, I took a closer look. Yes, I had seen it before—the outline of a crude, five-pointed holly leaf scratched lightly into the wood. The scratch marks extended outward from the shape in messy profusion, but none penetrated inside.

"You know," I said, "I saw the same thing a few weeks ago on the wall of the laundry room."

"Yeah, the super already told us. Anything else?"

I shook my head. It wasn't till hours later, back in the solitude of my apartment, that I realized I had seen the shape in still another place.

They say the night remembers what the day forgets. Pulling out the crudely bound orange book, I opened it to one of the drawings. There it was, that shape again, in the outline of the flipper-like gauntlets which Pistachio claimed his *usurpadores* had worn.

I got up and made myself some tea, then returned to the living room. Karen was still at her Wednesday-evening class, and would not be back till nearly ten. For a long time I sat very still, with the book open on my lap, listening to the comforting rattle of the air conditioner as it blotted out the night. One memory kept intruding: how, as a child, I liked to take a pencil and trace around the edges of my hand. This shape, I knew, is one that every child learns to draw.

I wondered what it would look like if the child's hands were webbed.

Wednesday, July 13

Certain things are not supposed to happen before midnight. There's a certain category of events—certain freak encounters and discoveries, certain crimes—for which mere nighttime doesn't seem quite dark enough. Only after midnight, after most of the world is asleep and the laws of the commonplace suspended, only then are we prepared for a touch, however brief, of the impossible.

But that night the impossible didn't wait.

The sun had been down for exactly an hour. It was twenty minutes after nine o'clock. My grandfather and I were sitting edgily in his room, listening to news on the radio and waiting for the weather to come on. The past three days had been exceptionally hot, but tonight there was a certain tension, that feeling of impending rain. In the window beside us churned an antiquated little air conditioner, competing with the blare of soul and salsa from the street below. Occasionally we could see flashes of heat lightning far away to the north, lighting up the sky like distant bombs.

We were waiting for Father Pistachio, who was already several minutes late. I had promised to take both of them to an evening flute recital at Temple Ohav Sholom on 84th Street, on the other side of Broadway. There'd be a lot of old people in attendance, or so Grandfather believed. According to his calculations, the "boring part"—that is, the actual flute playing—would be over soon, and with a little luck the three of us would arrive just in time for the refreshments. I wondered if Pistachio was going to show up in his priest's collar, and what they'd make of it at the temple.

The radio announced the time. It was nine twenty-two.

"What the hell's keeping him?" said my grandfather. "We really ought to be getting over there. The ladies always leave early." He got up from the bed. "What do you think? This shirt look okay?"

"You're not wearing any socks."

"What?" He glared down at his feet. "*Oy gevalt*, it's a wonder I remember my own name!" Looking extremely dejected, he sat back on the bed but immediately jumped up again. "I know where the damn things are. I stuck them in with Esther Feinbaum's wash." He began moving toward the door.

"Wait a second," I said. "Where are you going?"

"Downstairs. I'll be right back."

"But that's ridiculous! Why make a special trip?" I fought down my exasperation. "Look, you've got plenty of socks right there in your drawer. Karen just bought you some, remember? The others'll wait till tomorrow."

"They may not be there tomorrow. Old Esther leaves 'em hanging down by the dryers. She doesn't like to have men in her room!" He grinned. "Anyway, you don't understand. They're my lucky socks, the ones your mother made. I had 'em washed special for tonight, and I'm not going without 'em."

I watched him shuffle out the door. He seemed to be aging faster, and moving slower, with each passing week.

"The time," said the radio, "is nine twenty-five."

I went to the window and looked down. Plenty of people were out on the sidewalk, drinking or dancing or sitting on the stoop, but there was no sign of Pistachio. He had said something about bringing me some "new proof" of his theory, and I tried to imagine what it could be. A rabbi with a Costa Rican accent, perhaps, or a *Xo Tl'mi-go* skull. Or maybe just a photo of the back of his own head. I stood there while the wind from the air conditioner blew cold against my skin, watching heat lightning flash in the distance. Then I sat down and returned to the news. Karen would be on her way home, just about now, from her class up at Lehman in the Bronx. I wondered if it was raining up there. The radio didn't say.

Nine minutes later it happened. Suddenly the lights in Grandfather's room dimmed, flickered, and died. The radio fell silent. The air conditioner clattered to a halt.

I sat there in the darkness feeling faintly annoyed. The first thing that crossed my mind, I remember, was that somehow, perhaps in opening one of the dryers, Grandfather had inadvertently triggered a short circuit. Yes, I thought, that would be just like him!

In the unaccustomed silence I heard a frightened yell, then another, coming from the hall. They were joined, in a moment, by shouts from down in the street. Only then did I realize that more than just the building was affected. It was the whole city. We were having a blackout.

Still, even then, it seemed a minor annoyance. We'd had many such episodes before, in summers past, and I thought I knew what to expect. The city's overloaded current would dip momentarily; lights would flicker, clocks lose time, record players slow so that the voices turned to growls—and then, a few seconds later, the current would come back. Afterward we'd get the usual warnings about going easy on appliances, and everyone would turn his air conditioner down a degree or two. Perhaps this time the problem might be a little more severe, but it was still nothing to get excited about. Con Ed would fix things in a moment. They always had. . . .

Already it had grown hot inside the room. I switched the lamp on and off, on and off, with that sense of incomprehension and resentment one feels when a familiar object, something that's supposed to work, suddenly and mysteriously does not. Well, well, I thought, The Machine Stops. I went to the window, opened it, and peered into the darkness. There were no streetlights to be seen, and the sidewalk below me was almost invisible; it was as if I were looking down upon a courtyard or a river, though I could hear a babble of excited voices down there, voices and pounding feet and slamming doors. Buildings I could see a little better, and all of them looked dead, massive black monoliths against a black sky, with the moon just a sliver on the horizon. Across the water New Jersey was still lit, its brightness reflected in the Hudson, but here the only light came from the files of cars moving tentatively up Amsterdam and Broadway. In the glow of their headlights I could see faces at the windows of some of the other buildings, gazing out as I was, with varying degrees of wonder or curiosity or fear. From the street below came the sound of breaking glass.

It roused my sense of urgency, that sound. I wasn't worried about Karen—she'd get home okay—and no doubt old Pistachio, if he hadn't left yet, would have the sense to sit tight till the lights came on again.

But Grandfather was another story. For all I knew the old fool was trapped down there in a pitch-black laundry room without a single sound or ray of light to guide him. Perhaps he was unable to locate the door; perhaps he was terrified. I had to get down there to him. Feeling my way to the night table, I pocketed a book of matches from beside his pipe rack and moved slowly toward the hall.

Outside I could hear the residents shouting to one another from their doorways, their voices querulous and frightened. "Frito!" they were shouting. "Where's Frito?" Blindly I continued toward the stairs, inching my way across the polished floor. "Frito? Is that Frito?" an old lady called out as I passed. She sounded on the edge of panic. Immediately others up and down the hall took up the cry. "Frito, is it a blackout?" "Frito, do you have a flashlight?" "Frito, I want to call my son!"

"For God's sake, stop it!" I shouted. "I'm not Frito—see?" I lit a match in front of my face. It probably made me look like a cadaver. "Now just stay in your rooms and keep calm," I said. "We'll get the lights on for you as soon as we can."

I felt my way past the elevator, now useless, and went on until I'd reached the top of the stairs, where I lit another match. The first step lay just beneath my foot. Holding onto the metal railing, I started down.

As a boy I'd been afraid of the dark—or, more specifically, of monsters. I knew they only inhabited the world of movies, but sometimes in the dark it would occur to me that I, too, might be performing, all unwittingly, in a movie, perhaps even in the dread role of victim. There were two things movie victims never did, at least (alas) in my day: they never swore, and they never uttered brand names. Knowing this, I'd hit upon an ingenious way to keep my courage up. Whenever I was forced to brave the darkness, whether in the cellar or the attic or even my own room, I'd chant the magic words *"Fuck"* and *"Pepsi-Cola"* and I knew that I'd be safe.

Somehow, though, I doubted that these words—or any words, in any tongue—would still be so effective. Magic wasn't what it used to be; I would simply have to put one foot in front of the other and take my chances.

Echoes of voices floated up the stairwell—cries for assistance, for candles, for news. Others were calling out to friends. At each floor the cries would get louder, diminishing again as I passed on toward the next. While I descended I kept a tight grip on the railing, nervously feeling my way around the landings where the railing came to an end. The eighth floor disappeared behind me, and the seventh; I counted them off in my head. The sixth . . . The fifth . . . Passing the fourth floor, I saw a moving light on the stairway beneath and heard footsteps advancing upward. Then the light veered through a doorway and was lost from sight. One floor down I heard Calzone's voice and saw a flashlight beam receding down the hall. "No, you can't go *nowhere,*" he was shouting, "it's blacked out all the way to Westchester. Con Ed says they're working on it now. They'll get it all fixed up before too long." I hoped he was right.

As I passed the second floor I began to hear a noise which, at the time, I couldn't identify: a hollow, rhythmic, banging noise from down below, like someone hammering on a coffin. I couldn't even tell where it was coming from, unless from the wall itself, for the hammering became louder as I continued my descent, reaching its loudest point almost midway between the two floors—after which, unlike the voices, it began growing fainter again. By the time I reached the first floor it was lost amid the noises from the street.

They were having a festival out there, or a riot. I could hear shouts, laughter, and Latin music from some battery-driven tape deck. I also heard the shattering of glass, and what I first mistook for gunshots, but which I later realized were only firecrackers left over from the Fourth. Despite the clamor outside, the lobby wore an air of desolation, like an abandoned palace in time of war. As I rounded the stairs I caught a glimpse of its high, mirrored wall and, in it, dim reflections of the rubber plants, the mantelpiece, the sagging, empty chairs. The room was illuminated by a lantern that flickered in the alcove in front. Nearby stood the new security guard, talking to a group of shadowy figures in the doorway. I remember wondering whether he'd be called upon to keep the neighborhood at bay tonight, and whether he'd be able to do so.

But at the moment that didn't seem important. Finding the railing again, I continued downward. The lantern light vanished with a turn in the stairs, and I found myself once more in total darkness. Already the first floor's noise seemed far behind; my footsteps, deliberate as they were, echoed softly from the walls. Seconds later I felt the railing end, and knew I'd reached the landing. Here I paused for breath, fingers pressed against the rough concrete. The air was suffocating; I felt as if I were chin-deep in warm water, and that if I stepped forward I would drown. Digging into my pocket, I found a match and, like a blind man, lit it. Walls leapt into view around me. I felt better now—though for a moment an old warning flashed through my mind about people smothering in locked vaults because they'd lit matches and burned up their oxygen. Silly, I thought, it's nothing but a basement—and proceeded down the final flight of steps.

At last my feet touched bottom. I lit another match and saw, ahead of me, the narrow corridor stretching into darkness. As I followed it, I listened. There was no sound. The match burned my fingers and I dropped it. "Grandfather?" I called, in the half-embarrassed voice of one not sure of a response. "Grandfather?" I thought I heard a stirring from farther down the hall, like something being scraped across a cement floor. "It's okay, I'm coming!" Lighting still another match, I made my way toward the door to the laundry room. Even at this distance I could smell the moist, sweet laundry smell and, beneath it, something sour, like a backed-up drain. *Sewer men,* I thought, and shook my head.

When I was still a step or two away, the match went. Blindly I groped for the door. I could hear someone on the other side, scrabbling to get out. At last my fingers found the knob. "It's okay," I said, turning it, "I'm here—"

The door exploded in my face. I went down beneath a mob of twisting bodies pouring through the doorway, tumbling out upon me like a wave. I was kicked, tripped over, stepped on; I struggled to rise, and felt, in the darkness, the touch of naked limbs, smooth, rubbery flesh, hands that scuttled over me like starfish. In seconds the mob had swept past me and was gone; I heard them padding lightly up the hall, heading toward the stairs.

Then silence.

I lay back on the floor, exhausted, unable to believe it was over. I knew that, in a little while, I would not be able to believe it had happened at all. Though they'd left the stench of sewage in my nostrils, the gang—whatever they were, wherever they had gone—already seemed a crazy dream born of the darkness and the heat.

But Grandfather was real. What had they done to him? Trembling, head spinning, I staggered to my feet and found the doorway to the laundry room. Inside I lit one last match. The floor shone wet and slippery; the four washers lay scattered across it like children's discarded toys. There was no sign of my grandfather.

Hours later, when they pulled him from the elevator stalled midway between the first and second floors—Frito with his crowbar, Calzone holding the light—all my grandfather would say (feebly waving the two little pieces of dark cloth as if they were trophies) was, "I found my socks."

Karen, all this time, was fifty blocks uptown.

At nine-thirty she and her friend Marcia had been driving home in Marcia's little white Toyota, returning from their evening class at Lehman. There'd been an obstruction at 145th Street, and Marcia had turned south onto Lenox Avenue, past the Lenox Terrace project and the blocks of ancient brownstones. Though the traffic was heavy tonight, they were making good time; a mile ahead, at Central Park, they would be turning west. The air inside the car was hot and stuffy, but they kept the doors locked and the windows rolled up tight. This was, after all, the middle of Harlem.

Suddenly, as if some child had yanked the plug, the lights went out.

Marcia's foot went instinctively to the brakes; the car slowed to a crawl. So did the cars in front and behind. A few, elsewhere, did not. From somewhere up ahead came a grinding crash and the sound of tearing metal. Horns blared, bumpers smashed against bumpers, and the traffic rolled to a standstill. Beyond the unmoving line of headlights there was nothing but darkness.

But all at once the darkness was filled with moving shapes.

"Oh my God," said Marcia. "Look!"

Up and down the blackened street, hordes of figures were rushing from the houses, cheering, clapping, arms waving, as if they'd been waiting all their lives for this moment. It reminded the women of a prison break, an end of school, a day of liberation. They saw one tall, gangling figure burst through a doorway and dash into the street directly in front of them. Suddenly, in sheer exuberance, he bounded high into the air, feet kicking like a ballet dancer's, and sailed clear across the hood of the car, landing moments later on the other side and disappearing into the night. Karen never got to see his face, but there was one image she'd remember long afterward, whenever the blackout was discussed: the image of those two white sneakers dancing high above the beam of the headlights, six feet in the air, as if somehow released, not just from man's law, but from the law of gravity as well.

It was nearly one o'clock, and I still couldn't reach her.

I was sitting in Grandfather's room with the phone cradled in my lap. Beside me the old man lay snoring. I had put him to bed only a few minutes before but he'd already fallen asleep, exhausted from his ordeal in the elevator. There would be no sleep for me, though: I was too worried about Karen, and events outside the window only made me worry more. I heard hoarse shouts, the shattering of glass, and gangs of youths passing unseen in the streets below, bragging to each other about the jewelry, clothes, and radios they'd robbed. On Amsterdam Avenue a crowd had formed in front of the pawnshop, and three dark burly men, naked to the waist, were struggling to tear down the metal security gate that stretched across the window and the door. Others, holding flashlights, were egging them on. There were distant fires to the north, and sirens, and the echoes of explosions. I was almost beginning to think of myself as a widower.

Suddenly, on my lap, the phone began to ring. (Telephones were not affected by the power failure, being part of a separate electrical system.) I snatched it to my ear before Grandfather awoke.

"Goddammit, Karen, where the hell *were* you all this time? I've been trying you for hours. Couldn't you at least have picked up a phone—"

"I couldn't," she said. "Honestly. I haven't been near a phone all night."

Her voice sounded far away. "Where are you now," I said, "at Marcia's? I tried there, too."

"Believe it or not, I'm up here at the Cloisters."

"What?"

"It's true—the castle's right behind me, completely dark. I'm in a phone booth near the parking lot. There's a whole bunch of people up here, it's really beautiful. I can see stars I've never seen before."

For all her seeming rapture, I thought I detected a thin edge of hysteria in her voice—and when she told me what had happened, I understood why.

She and Marcia had spent the first part of the blackout sitting terrified in their car, watching things go to pieces around them. Store windows were being smashed, doors broken down; people were running past them waving torches. Others hurried back and forth along the avenue in a travesty of Christmas shopping, their arms weighed down with merchandise. Amid such activity those trapped within the cars had been ignored, but there'd been a few bad moments, and help had been slow to arrive. With stoplights out all over the city and traffic tied up everywhere at once, the accident had cost them nearly an hour.

Even when the line of cars began rolling again, they made little speed, creeping through the dark streets like a funeral cortege, their headlights providing the sole illumination—though here and there the eastern sky across the Harlem River seemed to glow with unseen fires. As they drew farther south the crowds grew thicker, crowds who made no effort to move aside for them. More than once their way was blocked by piles of burning refuse; more than once a fist would pound against the car door and a black face would glare fiercely through the window. Continuing in their present course seemed madness, and when some obstruction several blocks ahead seemed likely to halt them a second time, Marcia turned up the first wide thoroughfare they came to, 125th Street, and drove west in the direction of the Hudson, narrowly avoiding the bands of looters stockpiling food crates in the center of the street. At Riverside Drive, instead of resuming their way south, on impulse they had headed in the opposite direction, eager to get as far from the city as they could. They had driven all the way to Fort Tryon Park, at the northern tip of the island.

"We've both had a chance to calm down now," she added. "We're ready to start back. Marcia's getting tired, and both of us want to get home. We're going to take the West Side Highway all the way to 96th, so we shouldn't have any problems. But I swear to God, if we see another black I hope we hit him!"

I said I hoped that wouldn't be necessary, and made her promise to call me as soon as she got home. I was going to spend the night here in Grandfather's room.

After hanging up, I turned back to the action in the street below. Over on Amsterdam the crowd had succeeded in pulling down the pawnshop's metal gate. The large display window had already been stripped bare; glass littered the sidewalk. Now they were lined up in front of the shop like patrons at a movie theater, patiently awaiting their turn to file inside and take something. It was clear that the ones at the end of the line were not going to find much left. They passed the time by breaking the shards of glass into smaller pieces. The sound reminded me, somehow, of films I'd seen of Nazi Germany. It set my teeth on edge.

Suddenly there was a cry of "*Cuidado!*" and the crowd melted away. A minute passed, and then, like twin spaceships from another world, a pair of blue-and-white police cars rolled silently up the avenue, red lights whirling on their roofs. They paused, and from each car a searchlight beam swept dispassionately over the ruins of the shop. Then the searchlights were switched off, and the cars moved on, unhurried and silent. The crowd returned moments later. The sound of breaking glass continued through the night.

There were thousands of similar stories that night. There was the story of the man who pulled up before an appliance store in a rented truck and carted off a whole block of refrigerators; and the story of the twelve-year-old black boy who walked up to a white woman on the street and nearly strangled her when he tried to wrench a string of pearls from her neck; and the story, repeated many times, of mobs racing through the aisles of five-and-tens, stealing ribbons, erasers, spools of thread, shoes that didn't fit—anything they could lay their hands on, anything they saw. For months afterward the people of the poorer black sections of Brooklyn were forced to do their shopping miles from home because the stores in their own neighborhoods had been destroyed. By the time the blackout was over, nine million people had gone a day without electricity, three thousand had been arrested for looting with thousands more unpunished, and a billion dollars in damages had been lost.

But amid the statistics and postmortems, the newspaper stories and police reports, there were other reports—"unsubstantiated rumors," the *Times* called them—of roaming whites glimpsed here and there in the darker corners of the city, whites dressed "oddly," or undressed, or "emaciated" looking, or "masked," terrorizing the women of the neighborhood and hiding from the light. A woman in Crown Heights said she'd come upon a "white boy" thrusting his hand between her infant daughter's legs, but that he'd run away before she got a look at him. A Hunts Point girl swore that, minutes after the blackout began, a pack of "skinny old men" had come swarming up from the basement of an abandoned building and had chased her up the block. At the Astoria Boulevard subway stop near Hell Gate, an electrical worker had heard someone—a woman or a child—sobbing on the tracks where, hours before, a stalled train had been evacuated, and had seen, in his flashlight's beam, a group of distant figures fleeing through the tunnel. Hours later a man with a Spanish accent had telephoned the police to complain, in broken English, that his wife had been molested by "kids" living in the subway. He had rung off without giving his name. A certain shopping-bag lady, subject of a humorous feature in the *Enquirer,* even claimed to have had sexual relations with a "Martian" who, after rubbing his naked groin, had groped blindly beneath her dress; she had a long history of alcoholism, though, and her account was treated as a joke. The following September the *News* and the *Post* ran indignant reports on the sudden hike in abortions among the city's poor—but then, such stories, like those of climbing birth rates nine months later, are part and parcel of every blackout.

If I seem to credit these stories unduly—to dwell on them, even—it's because of what had happened to me in the basement, at the start of the blackout, and because of another incident, far more terrible, which occurred later that night. Since then some years have elapsed; and now, with Karen's permission, I can speak of it.

The two of them had driven back without mishap. Marcia had left Karen off in front of our apartment and had waited till she got inside. After all that they had been through that night, the neighborhood seemed an oasis of safety. There'd been stores broken into on Columbus, but our block, by this time, was relatively quiet. It was 2:15 a.m.

Unlocking the door, Karen felt her way into the kitchen and, with some difficulty, located a dusty box of Sabbath candles, one of which she lit on the top burner of the stove. A thin white stream of candle wax ran, wormlike, down her hand; she stood the candle upon a saucer to protect the rug. Moving slowly so that the flame would not go out, she walked into the bedroom, pausing to open the window and let some air into the room. She noticed, with some irritation, that it was already halfway open; someone had been careless, and it wasn't her. She would have to remember to mention it to me when she called. The phone was there before her on the night table. Carefully, in the flickering light, she dialed Grandfather's number.

I had been nodding off, lulled by the rhythm of Grandfather's snoring, when the telephone jerked me awake. For a moment I forgot where I was, but then I heard Karen's voice.

"Well," she said, "here I am, safe and sound, and absolutely exhausted. One thing's good, at least I won't have to go to work tomorrow. I feel like I could use a good twelve hours' sleep, though it'll probably be pretty unbearable in here tonight without the air conditioner. There's a funny smell, too. I just took a peek in the refrigerator, and all that meat you bought's going to spoil unless—*Oh God, what's that?*"

I heard her scream. She screamed several times. Then there was a thud, and then a jarring succession of bangs as the phone was dropped and left dangling from the edge of the table.

And then, in the background, I heard it: a sound so similar to the one coming from the bed behind me that for one horrifying second I'd confused the two.

It was the sound of snoring.

Nine flights of stairs and a dozen blocks later I stumbled from the darkness into the darkness of our apartment. The police had not arrived yet, but Karen had already regained consciousness, and a candle burned once more upon the table. A two-inch purple welt just below her hairline showed where, in falling, she had hit the table's edge.

I was impressed by how well she was bearing up. Even though she'd awakened alone in the dark, she had managed to keep herself busy: after relighting the candle and replacing the telephone, she had methodically gone about locking all the windows and had carefully washed the stickiness from her legs. In fact, by the time I got there she seemed remarkably composed, at least for the moment—composed enough to tell me, in a fairly level voice, about the thing she'd seen drop soundlessly into the room, through the open window, just as another one leaped toward her from the hall and a third, crouched gaunt and pale behind the bed, rose up and, reaching forward, pinched the candle out.

Her composure slipped a bit—and so did mine—when, six hours later, the morning sunlight revealed a certain shape scratched like a marker in the brick outside our bedroom window.

Six weeks later, while we were still living at her mother's house in Westchester, the morning bouts of queasiness began. The tests came back negative, negative again, then positive. Whatever was inside her might well have been mine—we had, ironically, decided some time before to let nature take its course—but we took no chances. The abortion cost only $150, and we got a free lecture from a Right to Life group picketing in front. We never asked the doctor what the wretched little thing inside her looked like, and he never showed the least inclination to tell us.

Wednesday, February 14, 1979

"'Young men think that old men are fools,'" said Mrs. Rosenzweig, quoting with approval one of my grandfather's favorite sayings, "'but old men *know* that young men are fools.'" She pursed her lips doubtfully. "Of course," she added, "that wouldn't apply to you."

I laughed. "Of course not! Besides, I'm not so young anymore."

It had been exactly a year since I'd last seen her; having arrived today with a big red box of Valentine's Day chocolates for her, I was glad to find her still alive—and still living at the Manor. Despite the night of terror she'd suffered back in '77, she had returned here as soon as she'd been discharged from the hospital, believing herself too old for a change of scene, too old to make new friends. The Manor was her home, and she was determined to stay.

Here, inside her own room, it was virtually impossible to tell that she was blind (just as I had been fooled the first time I'd met her); habit had taught her the location of every article, every piece of furniture. But elsewhere in the building, with her former roommate, Mrs. Hirschfeld, no longer there to lean on, she'd felt helpless and alone—until my grandfather'd acted the gentleman. He had befriended her, made her feel secure; they had walked along Broadway together, traded stories of the past, and kept each other company through the long summer afternoons. For a while, he had replaced Mrs. Hirschfeld in her life; she had replaced poor old Father Pistachio in his. . . .

"Did I ever show you what Herman gave me?" Unerringly she picked a small round object from the shelf beside her and began winding a key in its base. It appeared to be a miniature globe of the world, with a decal on the base proclaiming *"Souvenir of Hayden Planetarium."* When she set it back on the shelf, it played the opening bars of "Home Sweet Home."

"That's very nice."

The music ran on a few seconds more, then died in the air. The old woman sighed.

"It was nice of you to bring that chocolate. That's just the kind of thing your grandfather would have done. He was always very generous."

"Yes," I said, "he was. He never had much, but he was devoted to his friends."

The chocolate—in fact, the visit itself—had been my way of commemorating this day. It was the first anniversary of his death.

He had died following another stroke, just as the doctors had predicted—one of the few times in his life that he'd acted according to prediction. It had happened after dinner, while he'd been sitting in the game room with several of his cronies, laughing heartily at one of his own jokes. Laughter, Svevo tells us, is the only form of violent exercise old men are still permitted, but perhaps in this case the violence had been too much. Rushed to the hospital, he had lingered less than a week. I don't believe his end was a hard one. His last words are unrecorded, which is probably just as well—what are anyone's last words, after all, except a curse, a cry for help, or a string of nonsense?—but the last words I ever heard him say, and which have now become a family legend, were addressed to a young intern, fresh out of med school, who had come to take his blood pressure. During this process the old man had remained silent—speaking had become extremely difficult—and his eyes were closed; I assumed he was unconscious. But when the intern, putting away his instruments, happened to mention that he had a date waiting for him that night as soon as he got off work, my grandfather opened his eyes and said, in what was little more than a whisper, "Ask her if she's got a friend for me."

And Father Pistachio—he, too, is gone now, gone even before my grandfather. Although he has never been listed as such, he remains, as far as I'm concerned, the only likely fatality of the 1977 Blackout. It appears that, at the moment the power failed, he'd been on his way to visit Grandfather and me in the Manor, a short walk up the street. Beyond that it's impossible to say, for no one saw what happened to him. Maybe, in the darkness, he got frightened and ran off, maybe he had a run-in with the same gang that attacked me, maybe he simply fell down a rabbit hole and disappeared. I have one or two suspicions of my own—suspicions about the Blackout itself, in fact, and whether it was really Con Ed's fault—but such speculations only get my wife upset. All we really know is that the old man vanished without a trace, though Grandfather later claimed to have seen a white paper bag lying crumpled and torn near the stoop of Pistachio's house.

As for his effects, the contents of his room, I am not the one to ask—and the one to ask is dead. Grandfather was supposed to have gone over and inquired about them, but he told me he'd been "given the runaround" by the superintendent of the building, a gruff Puerto Rican man who understood almost no English. The super had maintained that he'd given all Pistachio's belongings to the "*policía,*" but I wouldn't be surprised if, in fact, he'd kept for himself the things he thought of value and had thrown away the rest. Still, I like to pretend that somewhere, in a storeroom down the dusty corridors of some obscure city department, hidden away in some footlocker or cubbyhole or file shelf, there lies the old priest's great work—the notes and maps and photos, the pages of English translation—complete with all the "new material" he'd hinted of.

One thing, at least, has survived. The super, a religious man (or perhaps just superstitious), had held back one of Pistachio's books, believing it to be a Bible, and this he allowed my grandfather to take. In a sense he was right, it was a Bible—the 1959 Harper & Row edition of *The Gospel According to Thomas,* which now stands on my desk looking very scholarly next to the cheap Spanish version of his "Commentary." The book holds little interest for me, nor is it particularly rare, but I find it makes an excellent memento of its former owner, thanks to the hundreds of annotations in Pistachio's crabbed hand: tiny comments scribbled in the margins, *"sí!"* and *"indudable!"* and even one *"caramba!"* along with some more cryptic—*"Ync."* and *"Qch."* and *"X.T."*—and pages and pages of underlinings. One passage, attributed to Christ himself, was actually circled in red ink:

> Whoever feels the touch of my hand shall become as I am, and the hidden things shall be revealed to him. . . . I am the All, and the All came forth from me. Cleave a piece of wood and you will find me; lift up a stone and I am there.

Beneath it he had written, *"Está hecho."* It is done.

I was feeling depressed as I said good-bye to Mrs. Rosenzweig. Though I agreed to visit her again soon, privately I doubted I'd be back before next year. Coming here aroused too many painful memories.

Outside, the world looked even bleaker. It was not yet 5:00 p.m., and already getting dark. We'd had below-freezing temperatures throughout the week and the pavement was covered with patches of snow. Turning up my collar against the icy wind, I headed up the block.

Now, one of the hoariest clichés of a certain type of cheap fiction—along with the mind that "suddenly goes blank," and the fearful town where everyone "clams up" when a stranger arrives, and the victimized industrialist who won't go to the police because "I don't want the publicity," and the underworld informer who says "I know who did it but I can't tell you over the phone"—along with these is the feeling of "being watched." One's flesh is supposed to crawl, one's hair to stand on end; one is supposed to have an "indefinable sense" that one is under scrutiny. The truth is not so mystical. In the course of my life I have stared, and stared hard, at thousands of people who, were they the least bit sensitive, would have shivered or turned or perhaps even jumped in the air. None has ever done so. For that matter, I've undoubtedly been glared at by hundreds of people in my time without ever realizing it.

This time was the same. I was standing on the corner of 81st and Amsterdam, hunching my shoulders against the cold and waiting impatiently for the light to change. My mind was on the clean new restaurant across the street that advertised "Dominican and American Cuisine," right where Davey's Tavern used to stand. *How nice,* I said to myself. *Things are looking up.*

The light changed. I took one step off the curb, and heard something crackle underfoot. That was why I happened to look down. I saw that I had stepped upon a little mound of pistachio shells, red against the snow, piled by the opening to a sewer.

And I froze—for there was something in the opening, just beside my shoe: something watching intently, its face pressed up against the metal grating, its pale hands clinging tightly to the bars. I saw, dimly in the streetlight, the empty craters where its eyes had been—empty but for two red dots, like tiny beads—and the gaping red ring of its mouth, like the sucker of some undersea creature. The face was alien and cold, without human expression, yet I swear that those eyes regarded me with utter malevolence—and that they recognized me.

It must have realized that I'd seen it—surely it heard me cry out—for at that moment, like two exploding white stars, the hands flashed open and the figure dropped back into the earth, back to that kingdom, older than ours, that calls the dark its home.

THE DETECTIVE OF DREAMS

By GENE WOLFE

Born in Brooklyn, a veteran of the Korean War, and now living in Barrington, Illinois, Gene Wolfe has been publishing fantasy and science-fiction stories and novels for about a dozen years. He has been frequently nominated for Hugo and Nebula awards in science fiction, and his 1973 novella, The Death of Dr. Island, *won the latter prize, which is voted upon by the membership of the Science Fiction Writers of America. Wolfe's work is elegant in its style and always carefully thought out and constructed. This story is that way, but it is also like nothing else he has published. To the casual reader, it might seem a parody on a certain kind of nineteenth-century style and genre, but a closer look reveals a statement of deep personal belief and commitment, wrapped in the manners and atmosphere of another century, one he perhaps sees as especially significant to the close of this one.*

I was writing in my office in the rue Madeleine when Andrée, my secretary, announced the arrival of Herr D_____. I rose, put away my correspondence, and offered him my hand. He was, I should say, just short of fifty, had the high, clear complexion characteristic of those who in youth (now unhappily past for both of us) have found more pleasure in the company of horses and dogs and the excitement of the chase than in the bottles and bordels of city life, and wore a beard and mustache of the style popularized by the late emperor. Accepting my invitation to a chair, he showed me his papers.

"You see," he said, "I am accustomed to acting as the representative of my government. In this matter I hold no such position, and it is possible that I feel a trifle lost."

"Many people who come here feel lost," I said. "But it is my boast that I find most of them again. Your problem, I take it, is purely a private matter?"

"Not at all. It is a public matter in the truest sense of the words."

"Yet none of the documents before me—admirably stamped, sealed, and beribboned though they are—indicates that you are other than a private gentleman traveling abroad. And you say you do not represent your government. What am I to think? What is this matter?"

"I act in the public interest," Herr D_____ told me. "My fortune is not great, but I can assure you that in the event of your success you will be well recompensed; although you are to take it that I alone am your principal, yet there are substantial resources available to me."

"Perhaps it would be best if you described the problem to me?"

"You are not averse to travel?"

"No."

"Very well then," he said, and so saying launched into one of the most astonishing relations—no, *the* most astonishing relation—I have ever been privileged to hear. Even I, who had at first hand the account of the man who found Paulette Renan with the quince seed still lodged in her throat; who had received Captain Brotte's testimony concerning his finds amid the antarctic ice; who had heard the history of the woman called Joan O'Neil, who lived for two years behind a painting of herself in the Louvre, from her own lips—even I sat like a child while this man spoke.

When he fell silent, I said, "Herr D_____, after all you have told me, I would accept this mission though there were not a *sou* to be made from it. Perhaps once in a lifetime one comes across a case that must be pursued for its own sake; I think I have found mine."

He leaned forward and grasped my hand with a warmth of feeling that was, I believe, very foreign to his usual nature. "Find and destroy the Dream-Master," he said, "and you shall sit upon a chair of gold, if that is your wish, and eat from a table of gold as well. When will you come to our country?"

"Tomorrow morning," I said. "There are one or two arrangements I must make here before I go."

"I am returning tonight. You may call upon me at any time, and I will apprise you of new developments." He handed me a card. "I am always to be found at this address—if not I, then one who is to be trusted, acting in my behalf."

"I understand."

"This should be sufficient for your initial expenses. You may call on me should you require more." The cheque he gave me as he turned to leave represented a comfortable fortune.

I waited until he was nearly out the door before saying, "I thank you, Herr Baron." To his credit, he did not turn; but I had the satisfaction of seeing a flush red rising above the precise white line of his collar before the door closed.

Andrée entered as soon as he had left. "Who was that man? When you spoke to him—just as he was stepping out of your office—he looked as if you had struck him with a whip."

"He will recover," I told her. "He is the Baron H_____, of the secret police of K_____. D_____ was his mother's name. He assumed that because his own desk is a few hundred kilometers from mine, and because he does not permit his likeness to appear in the daily papers, I would not know him; but it was necessary, both for the sake of his opinion of me and my own of myself, that he should discover that I am not so easily deceived. When he recovers from his initial irritation, he will retire tonight with greater confidence in the abilities I will devote to the mission he has entrusted to me."

"It is typical of you, monsieur," Andrée said kindly, "that you are concerned that your clients sleep well."

Her pretty cheek tempted me, and I pinched it. "I am concerned," I replied; "but the Baron will not sleep well."

My train roared out of Paris through meadows sweet with wild flowers, to penetrate mountain passes in which the danger of avalanches was only just past. The glitter of rushing water, sprung from on high, was everywhere; and when the express slowed to climb a grade, the song of water was everywhere, too, water running and shouting down the gray rocks of the Alps. I fell asleep that night with the descant of that icy purity sounding through the plainsong of the rails, and I woke in the station of I_____, the old capital of J_____, now a province of K_____.

I engaged a porter to convey my trunk to the hotel where I had made reservations by telegraph the day before, and amused myself for a few hours by strolling about the city. Here I found the Middle Ages might almost be said to have remained rather than lingered. The city wall was complete on three sides, with its merloned towers in repair; and the cobbled streets surely dated from a period when wheeled traffic of any kind was scarce. As for the buildings—Puss in Boots and his friends must have loved them dearly: there were bulging walls and little panes of bull's-eye glass, and overhanging upper floors one above another until the structures seemed unbalanced as tops. Upon one grey old pile with narrow windows and massive doors, I found a plaque informing me that though it had been first built as a church, it had been successively a prison, a customhouse, a private home, and a school. I investigated further, and discovered it was now an arcade, having been divided, I should think at about the time of the first Louis, into a multitude of dank little stalls. Since it was, as it happened, one of the addresses mentioned by Baron H_____, I went in.

Gas flared everywhere, yet the interior could not have been said to be well lit—each jet was sullen and secretive, as if the proprietor in whose cubicle it was located wished it to light none but his own wares. These cubicles were in no order; nor could I find any directory or guide to lead me to the one I sought. A few customers, who seemed to have visited the place for years, so that they understood where everything was, drifted from one display to the next. When they arrived at each, the proprietor came out, silent (so it seemed to me) as a specter, ready to answer questions or accept a payment; but I never heard a question asked, or saw any money tendered—the customer would finger the edge of a kitchen knife, or hold a garment up to her own shoulders, or turn the pages of some moldering book; and then put the thing down again, and go away.

At last, when I had tired of peeping into alcoves lined with booths still gloomier than the ones on the main concourse outside, I stopped at a leather merchant's and asked the man to direct me to Fräulein A_____.

"I do not know her," he said.

"I am told on good authority that her business is conducted in this building, and that she buys and sells antiques."

"We have several antique dealers here. Herr M_____—"

"I am searching for a young woman. Has your Herr M_____ a niece or a cousin?"

"—handles chairs and chests, largely. Herr O_____, near the guildhall—"

"It is within this building."

"—stocks pictures, mostly. A few mirrors. What is it you wish to buy?"

At this point we were interrupted, mercifully, by a woman from the next booth. "He wants Fräulein A_____. Out of here, and to your left;

past the wigmaker's, then right to the stationer's, then left again. She sells old lace."

I found the place at last, and sitting at the very back of her booth Fräulein A_____ herself, a pretty, slender, timid-looking young woman. Her merchandise was spread on two tables; I pretended to examine it and found that it was not old lace she sold but old clothing, much of it trimmed with lace. After a few moments she rose and came out to talk to me, saying, "If you could tell me what you require? . . ." She was taller than I had anticipated, and her flaxen hair would have been very attractive if it were ever released from the tight braids coiled round her head.

"I am only looking. Many of these are beautiful—are they expensive?"

"Not for what you get. The one you are holding is only fifty marks."

"That seems like a great deal."

"They are the fine dresses of long ago—for visiting, or going to the ball. The dresses of wealthy women of aristocratic taste. All are like new; I will not handle anything else. Look at the seams in that one you hold, the tiny stitches all done by hand. Those were the work of dressmakers who created only four or five in a year, and worked twelve and fourteen hours a day, sewing at the first light, and continuing under the lamp, past midnight."

I said, "I see that you have been crying, Fräulein. Their lives were indeed miserable, though no doubt there are people today who suffer equally."

"No doubt there are," the young woman said. "I, however, am not one of them." And she turned away so that I should not see her tears.

"I was informed otherwise."

She whirled about to face me. "You know him? Oh, tell him I am not a wealthy woman, but I will pay whatever I can. Do you really know him?"

"No." I shook my head. "I was informed by your own police."

She stared at me. "But you are an outlander. So is he, I think."

"Ah, we progress. Is there another chair in the rear of your booth? Your police are not above going outside your own country for help, you see, and we should have a little talk."

"They are not our police," the young woman said bitterly, "but I will talk to you. The truth is that I would sooner talk to you, though you are French. You will not tell them that?"

I assured her that I would not; we borrowed a chair from the flower stall across the corridor, and she poured forth her story.

"My father died when I was very small. My mother opened this booth to earn our living—old dresses that had belonged to her own mother were the core of her original stock. She died two years ago, and since that time I have taken charge of our business and used it to support myself. Most of my sales are to collectors and theatrical companies. I do not make a great deal of money, but I do not require a great deal, and I have managed to save some. I live alone at Number 877 ——strasse; it is an old house divided into six apartments, and mine is the gable apartment."

"You are young and charming," I said, "and you tell me you have a little money saved. I am surprised you are not married."

"Many others have said the same thing."

"And what did you tell them, Fräulein?"

"To take care of their own affairs. They have called me a manhater—Frau G——, who has the confections in the next corridor but two, called me that because I would not receive her son. The truth is that I do not care for people of either sex, young or old. If I want to live by myself and keep my own things to myself, is not it my right to do so?"

"I am sure it is; but undoubtedly it has occurred to you that this person you fear so much may be a rejected suitor who is taking his revenge on you."

"But how could he enter and control my dreams?"

"I do not know, Fräulein. It is you who say that he does these things."

"I should remember him, I think, if he had ever called on me. As it is, I am quite certain I have seen him somewhere, but I cannot recall where. Still . . ."

"Perhaps you had better describe your dream to me. You have the same one again and again, as I understand it?"

"Yes. It is like this. I am walking down a dark road. I am both frightened and pleasurably excited, if you know what I mean. Sometimes I walk for a long time, sometimes for what seems to be only a few moments. I think there is moonlight, and once or twice I have noticed stars. Anyway, there is a high, dark hedge, or perhaps a wall, on my right. There are fields to the left, I believe. Eventually I reach a gate of iron bars, standing open—it's not a large gate for wagons or carriages, but a small one, so narrow I can hardly get through. Have you read the writings of Dr. Freud of Vienna? One of the women here mentioned once that he had written concerning dreams, and so I got them from the library, and if I were a man I am sure he would say that entering that gate meant sexual commerce. Do you think I might have unnatural leanings?" Her voice had dropped to a whisper.

"Have you ever felt such desires?"

"Oh, no. Quite the reverse."

"Then I doubt it very much," I said. "Go on with your dream. How do you feel as you pass through the gate?"

"As I did when walking down the road, but more so—more frightened, and yet happy and excited. Triumphant, in a way."

"Go on."

"I am in the garden now. There are fountains playing, and nightingales singing in the willows. The air smells of lilies, and a cherry tree in blossom looks like a giantess in her bridal gown. I walk on a straight, smooth path; I think it must be paved with marble chips, because it is white in the moonlight. Ahead of me is the *Schloss*—a great building. There is music coming from inside."

"What sort of music?"

"Magnificent—joyous, if you know what I am trying to say, but not the tinklings of a theater orchestra. A great symphony. I have never been to the opera at Bayreuth; but I think it must be like that—yet a happy, quick tune."

She paused, and for an instant her smile recovered the remembered music. "There are pillars, and a grand entrance, with broad steps. I run up—I am so happy to be there—and throw open the door. It is brightly lit inside; a wave of golden light, almost like a wave from the ocean, strikes me. The room is a great hall, with a high ceiling. A long table is set in the middle and there are hundreds of people seated at it, but one place, the one nearest me, is empty. I cross to it and sit down; there are beautiful golden loaves on the table, and bowls of honey with roses floating at their centers, and crystal carafes of wine, and many other good things I cannot remember when I awake. Everyone is eating and drinking and talking, and I begin to eat too."

I said, "It is only a dream, Fräulein. There is no reason to weep."

"I dream this each night—I have dreamed so every night for months."

"Go on."

"Then he comes. I am sure he is the one who is causing me to dream like this because I can see his face clearly, and remember it when the dream is over. Sometimes it is very vivid for an hour or more after I wake—so vivid that I have only to close my eyes to see it before me."

"I will ask you to describe him in detail later. For the present, continue with your dream."

"He is tall, and robed like a king, and there is a strange crown on his head. He stands beside me, and though he says nothing, I know that the etiquette of the place demands that I rise and face him. I do this. Sometimes I am sucking my fingers as I get up from his table."

"He owns the dream palace, then."

"Yes, I am sure of that. It is his castle, his home; he is my host. I stand and face him, and I am conscious of wanting very much to please him, but not knowing what it is I should do."

"That must be painful."

"It is. But as I stand there, I become aware of how I am clothed, and—"

"How are you clothed?"

"As you see me now. In a plain, dark dress—the dress I wear here at the arcade. But the others—all up and down the hall, all up and down the table—are wearing the dresses I sell here. These dresses." She held one up for me to see, a beautiful creation of many layers of lace, with buttons of polished jet. "I know then that I cannot remain; but the king signals to the others, and they seize me and push me toward the door."

"You are humiliated then?"

"Yes, but the worst thing is that I am aware that he knows that I could never drive myself to leave, and he wishes to spare me the struggle. But outside—some terrible beast has entered the garden. I smell it—like the hyena cage at the *Tiergarten*—as the door opens. And then I wake up."

"It is a harrowing dream."

"You have seen the dresses I sell. Would you credit it that for weeks I slept in one, and then another, and then another of them?"

"You reaped no benefit from that?"

"No. In the dream I was clad as now. For a time I wore the dresses always—even here to the stall, and when I bought food at the market. But it did no good."

"Have you tried sleeping somewhere else?"

"With my cousin who lives on the other side of the city. That made no difference. I am certain that this man I see is a real man. He is in my dream, and the cause of it; but he is not sleeping."

"Yet you have never seen him when you are awake?"

She paused, and I saw her bite at her full lower lip. "I am certain I have."

"Ah!"

"But I cannot remember when. Yet I am sure I have seen him—that I have passed him in the street."

"Think! Does his face associate itself in your mind with some particular section of the city?"

She shook her head.

When I left her at last, it was with a description of the Dream-Master less precise than I had hoped, though still detailed. It tallied in almost all respects with the one given me by Baron H——; but that proved nothing, since the baron's description might have been based largely on Fräulein A——'s.

The bank of Herr R—— was a private one, as all the greatest banks in Europe are. It was located in what had once been the town house of some noble family (their arms, overgrown now with ivy, were still visible above the door) and bore no identification other than a small brass plate engraved with the names of Herr R—— and his partners. Within, the atmosphere was more dignified—even if, perhaps, less tasteful—than it could possibly have been in the noble family's time. Dark pictures in gilded frames lined the walls, and the clerks sat at inlaid tables upon chairs upholstered in tapestry. When I asked for Herr R——, I was told that it would be impossible to see him that afternoon; I sent in a note with a sidelong allusion to "unquiet dreams," and within five minutes I was ushered into a luxurious office that must once have been the bedroom of the head of the household.

Herr R—— was a large man—tall, and heavier (I thought) than his physician was likely to have approved. He appeared to be about fifty; there was strength in his wide, fleshy face; his high forehead and capacious cranium suggested intellect; and his small, dark eyes, forever flickering as they took in the appearance of my person, the expression of my face, and the position of my hands and feet, ingenuity.

No pretense was apt to be of service with such a man, and I told him flatly that I had come as the emissary of Baron H——, that I knew what troubled him, and that if he would cooperate with me I would help him if I could.

"I know you, monsieur," he said, "by reputation. A business with which I am associated employed you three years ago in the matter of a certain mummy." He named the firm. "I should have thought of you myself."

"I did not know that you were connected with them."

"I am not, when you leave this room. I do not know what reward Baron H—— has offered you should you apprehend the man who is oppressing me, but I will give you, in addition to that, a sum equal to that you were paid for the mummy. You should be able to retire to the south then, should you choose, with the rent of a dozen villas."

"I do not choose," I told him, "and I could have retired long before. But what you just said interests me. You are certain that your persecutor is a living man?"

"I know men." Herr R_____ leaned back in his chair and stared at the painted ceiling. "As a boy I sold stuffed cabbage-leaf rolls in the street—did you know that? My mother cooked them over wood she collected herself where buildings were being demolished, and I sold them from a little cart for her. I lived to see her with half a score of footmen and the finest house in Lindau. I never went to school; I learned to add and subtract in the streets—when I must multiply and divide I have my clerk do it. But I learned men. Do you think that now, after forty years of practice, I could be deceived by a phantom? No, he is a man—let me confess it, a stronger man than I—a man of flesh and blood and brain, a man I have seen somewhere, sometime, here in this city—and more than once."

"Describe him."

"As tall as I. Younger—perhaps thirty or thirty-five. A brown, forked beard, so long." (He held his hand about fifteen centimeters beneath his chin.) "Brown hair. His hair is not yet grey, but I think it may be thinning a little at the temples."

"Don't you remember?"

"In my dream he wears a garland of roses—I cannot be sure."

"Is there anything else? Any scars or identifying marks?"

Herr R_____ nodded. "He has hurt his hand. In my dream, when he holds out his hand for the money, I see blood in it—it is his own, you understand, as though a recent injury had reopened and was beginning to bleed again. His hands are long and slender—like a pianist's."

"Perhaps you had better tell me your dream."

"Of course." He paused, and his face clouded, as though to recount the dream were to return to it. "I am in a great house. I am a person of importance there, almost as though I were the owner; yet I am not the owner—"

"Wait," I interrupted. "Does this house have a banquet hall? Has it a pillared portico, and is it set in a garden?"

For a moment Herr R_____'s eyes widened. "Have you also had such dreams?"

"No," I said. "It is only that I think I have heard of this house before. Please continue."

"There are many servants—some work in the fields beyond the garden. I give instructions to them—the details differ each night, you understand. Sometimes I am concerned with the kitchen, sometimes with the livestock, sometimes with the draining of a field. We grow wheat, principally, it seems; but there is a vineyard too, and a kitchen garden. And of course the house itself must be cleaned and swept and kept in repair. There is no wife; the owner's mother lives with us, I think, but she does not much concern herself with the housekeeping—that is up to me. To tell the truth, I have never actually seen her, though I have the feeling that she is there."

"Does this house resemble the one you bought for your own mother in Lindau?"

"Only as one large house must resemble another."

"I see. Proceed."

"For a long time each night I continue like that, giving orders, and sometimes going over the accounts. Then a servant, usually it is a maid, arrives to tell me that the owner wishes to speak to me. I stand before a mirror—I can see myself there as plainly as I see you now—and arrange my clothing. The maid brings rose-scented water and a cloth, and I wipe my face; then I go in to him.

"He is always in one of the upper rooms, seated at a table with his own account book spread before him. There is an open window behind him, and through it I can see the top of a cherry tree in bloom. For a long time—oh, I suppose ten minutes—I stand before him while he turns over the pages of his ledger."

"You appear somewhat at a loss, Herr R——not a common condition for you, I believe. What happens then?"

"He says, 'You owe . . .'" Herr R—— paused. "That is the problem, monsieur, I can never recall the amount. But it is a large sum. He says, 'And I must require that you make payment at once.'

"I do not have the amount, and I tell him so. He says, 'Then you must leave my employment.' I fall to my knees at this and beg that he will retain me, pointing out that if he dismisses me I will have lost my source of income, and will never be able to make payment. I do not enjoy telling you this, but I weep. Sometimes I beat the floor with my fists."

"Continue. Is the Dream-Master moved by your pleading?"

"No. He again demands that I pay the entire sum. Several times I have told him that I am a wealthy man in this world, and that if only he would permit me to make payment in its currency, I would do so immediately."

"That is interesting—most of us lack your presence of mind in our nightmares. What does he say then?"

"Usually he tells me not to be a fool. But once he said, 'That is a dream—you must know it by now. You cannot expect to pay a real debt with the currency of sleep.' He holds out his hand for the money as he speaks to me. It is then that I see the blood in his palm."

"You are afraid of him?"

"Oh, very much so. I understand that he has the most complete power over me. I weep, and at last I throw myself at his feet—with my head under the table, if you can credit it, crying like an infant.

"Then he stands and pulls me erect, and says, 'You would never be able to pay all you owe, and you are a false and dishonest servant. But your debt is forgiven, forever.' And as I watch, he tears a leaf from his account book and hands it to me."

"Your dream has a happy conclusion, then."

"No. It is not yet over. I thrust the paper into the front of my shirt and go out, wiping my face on my sleeve. I am conscious that if any of the other servants should see me, they will know at once what has happened. I hurry to reach my own counting room; there is a brazier there, and I wish to burn the page from the owner's book."

"I see."

"But just outside the door of my own room, I meet another servant—an upper-servant like myself, I think, since he is well dressed. As it happens, this man owes me a considerable sum of money, and to conceal from him what I have just endured, I demand that he pay at once." Herr R—— rose from his chair and began to pace the room, looking sometimes at the painted scenes on the walls, sometimes at the Turkish carpet at his feet. "I have had reason to demand money like that often, you understand. Here in this room.

"The man falls to his knees, weeping and begging for additional time; but I reach down, like this, and seize him by the throat."

"And then?"

"And then the door of my counting room opens. But it is not my counting room with my desk and the charcoal brazier, but the owner's own room. He is standing in the doorway, and behind him I can see the open window, and the blossoms of the cherry tree."

"What does he say to you?"

"Nothing. He says nothing to me. I release the other man's throat, and he slinks away."

"You awaken then?"

"How can I explain it? Yes, I wake up. But first we stand there; and while we do I am conscious of . . . certain sounds."

"If it is too painful for you, you need not say more."

Herr R—— drew a silk handkerchief from his pocket and wiped his face. "How can I explain?" he said again. "When I hear those sounds, I am aware that the owner possesses certain other servants, who have never been under my direction. It is as though I have always known this, but had no reason to think of it before."

"I understand."

"They are quartered in another part of the house—in the vaults beneath the wine cellar, I think sometimes. I have never seen them, but I know—then—that they are hideous, vile and cruel; I know too that he thinks me but little better than they, and that as he permits me to serve him, so he allows them to serve him also. I stand—we stand—and listen to them coming through the house. At last a door at the end of the hall begins to swing open. There is a hand like the paw of some filthy reptile on the latch."

"Is that the end of the dream?"

"Yes." Herr R—— threw himself into his chair again, mopping his face.

"You have this experience each night?"

"It differs," he said slowly, "in some details."

"You have told me that the orders you give the under-servants vary."

"There is another difference. When the dreams began, I woke when the hinges of the door at the passage-end creaked. Each night now the dream endures a moment longer. Perhaps a tenth of a second. Now I see the arm of the creature who opens that door, nearly to the elbow."

I took the address of his home, which he was glad enough to give me, and leaving the bank made my way to my hotel.

When I had eaten my roll and drunk my coffee the next morning, I went to the place indicated by the card given me by Baron H——, and in a few minutes was sitting with him in a room as bare as those tents from which armies in the field are cast into battle. "You are ready to begin the case this morning?" he asked.

"On the contrary. I have already begun; indeed, I am about to enter a new phase of my investigation. You would not have come to me if your Dream-Master were not torturing someone other than the people whose names you gave me. I wish to know the identity of that person, and to interrogate him."

"I told you that there were many other reports. I—"

"Provided me with a list. They are all of the petite bourgeoisie, when they are not persons still less important. I believed at first that it might be because of the urgings of Herr R_____ that you engaged me; but when I had time to reflect on what I know of your methods, I realized that you would have demanded that he provide my fee had that been the case. So you are sheltering someone of greater importance, and I wish to speak to him."

"The Countess—" Baron H_____ began.

"Ah!"

"The Countess herself has expressed some desire that you should be presented to her. The Count opposes it."

"We are speaking, I take it, of the governor of this province?"

The Baron nodded. "Of Count von V_____. He is responsible, you understand, only to the Queen Regent herself."

"Very well. I wish to hear the Countess, and she wishes to talk with me. I assure you, Baron, that we will meet; the only question is whether it will be under your auspices."

The Countess, to whom I was introduced that afternoon, was a woman in her early twenties, deep-breasted and somber-haired, with skin like milk, and great dark eyes welling with fear and (I thought) pity, set in a perfect oval face.

"I am glad you have come, monsieur. For seven weeks now our good Baron H_____ has sought this man for me, but he has not found him."

"If I had known my presence here would please you, Countess, I would have come long ago, whatever the obstacles. You then, like the others, are certain it is a real man we seek?"

"I seldom go out, monsieur. My husband feels we are in constant danger of assassination."

"I believe he is correct."

"But on state occasions we sometimes ride in a glass coach to the *Rathaus*. There are uhlans all around us to protect us then. I am certain that—before the dreams began—I saw the face of this man in the crowd."

"Very well. Now tell me your dream."

"I am here, at home—"

"In this palace, where we sit now?"

She nodded.

"That is a new feature, then. Continue, please."

"There is to be an execution. In the garden." A fleeting smile crossed the Countess's lovely face. "I need not tell you that that is not where the executions are held; but it does not seem strange to me when I dream.

"I have been away, I think, and have only just heard of what is to take place. I rush into the garden. The man Baron H_____ calls the Dream-Master is there, tied to the trunk of the big cherry tree; a squad of soldiers faces him, holding their rifles; their officer stands beside them with his saber drawn, and my husband is watching from a pace or two away. I call out for them to stop, and my husband turns to look at me. I say: 'You must not do it, Karl. You must not kill this man.' But I see by his expression that he believes that I am only a foolish, tender-hearted child. Karl is . . . several years older than I."

"I am aware of it."

"The Dream-Master turns his head to look at me. People tell me that my eyes are large—do you think them large, monsieur?"

"Very large, and very beautiful."

"In my dream, quite suddenly, his eyes seem far, far larger than mine, and far more beautiful; and in them I see reflected the figure of my husband. Please listen carefully now, because what I am going to say is very important, though it makes very little sense, I am afraid."

"Anything may happen in a dream, Countess."

"When I see my husband reflected in this man's eyes, I know—I cannot say how—that it is this reflection, and not the man who stands near me, who is the real Karl. The man I have thought real is only a reflection of that reflection. Do you follow what I say?"

I nodded. "I believe so."

"I plead again: 'Do not kill him. Nothing good can come of it. . . .' My husband nods to the officer, the soldiers raise their rifles, and . . . and . . ."

"You wake. Would you like my handkerchief, Countess? It is of coarse weave; but it is clean, and much larger than your own."

"Karl is right—I am only a foolish little girl. No, monsieur, I do not wake—not yet. The soldiers fire. The Dream-Master falls forward, though his bonds hold him to the tree. And Karl flies to bloody rags beside me."

On my way back to my hotel, I purchased a map of the city; and when I reached my room I laid it flat on the table there. There could be no question of the route of the Countess's glass coach—straight down the Hauptstrasse, the only street in the city wide enough to take a carriage surrounded by cavalrymen. The most probable route by which Herr R_____ might go from his house to his bank coincided with the Hauptstrasse for several blocks. The path Fräulein A_____ would travel from her flat to the arcade crossed the Hauptstrasse at a point contained by that interval. I needed to know no more.

Very early the next morning I took up my post at the intersection. If my man were still alive after the fusillade Count von V_____ fired at him each night, it seemed certain that he would appear at this spot within a few days, and I am hardened to waiting. I smoked cigarettes while I watched the citizens of I_____ walk up and down before me. When an hour had passed, I bought a newspaper from a vendor, and stole a few glances at its pages when foot traffic was light.

Gradually I became aware that I was watched—we boast of reason, but there are senses over which reason holds no authority. I did not know where my watcher was, yet I felt his gaze on me, whichever way I turned. So, I thought, you know me, my friend. Will I too dream now? What has attracted your attention to a mere foreigner, a stranger, waiting for who-knows-what at this corner? Have you been talking to Fräulein A_____? Or to someone who has spoken with her?

Without appearing to do so, I looked up and down both streets in search of another lounger like myself. There was no one—not a drowsing grandfather, not a woman or a child, not even a dog. Certainly no tall man with a forked beard and piercing eyes. The windows then—I studied them all, looking for some movement in a dark room behind a seemingly innocent opening. Nothing.

Only the buildings behind me remained. I crossed to the opposite side of the Hauptstrasse and looked once more. Then I laughed.

They must have thought me mad, all those dour burghers, for I fairly doubled over, spitting my cigarette to the sidewalk and clasping my hands to my waist for fear my belt would burst. The presumption, the impudence, the brazen insolence of the fellow! The stupidity, the wonderful stupidity of myself, who had not recognized his old stories! For the remainder of my life now, I could accept any case with pleasure, pursue the most inept criminal with zest, knowing that there was always a chance he might outwit such an idiot as I.

For the Dream-Master had set up His own picture, and full-length and in the most gorgeous colors, in His window. Choking and spluttering I saluted it, and then, still filled with laughter, I crossed the street once more and went inside, where I knew I would find Him. A man awaited me there—not the one I sought, but one who understood Whom it was I had come for, and knew as well as I that His capture was beyond any thief-taker's power. I knelt, and there, though not to the satisfaction I suppose of Baron H_____, Fräulein A_____, Herr R_____, and the Count and Countess von V_____, I destroyed the Dream-Master as He has been sacrificed so often, devouring His white, wheaten flesh that we might all possess life without end.

Dear people, dream on.

VENGEANCE IS.

By THEODORE STURGEON

Theodore Sturgeon, born on Staten Island, New York, of old American stock dating back to 1640, is one of the acknowledged masters of modern fantasy and science fiction, both in his short work and in such fine novels as More Than Human *and* The Dreaming Jewels. *His styles are many: witty, spare, hardboiled, and lyrically expressive. He's a remarkably inventive and powerful writer and there is reason to suspect his best stories will be remembered long after those of nearly all now posing for posterity in academic circles and in the literary quarterlies. Harlan Ellison once observed that Theodore Sturgeon knows more about love than anyone he'd ever met. And, in fact, the Sturgeon you might meet is earnest, warm, and sympathetic, a man whom you immediately feel cares and understands. But, as this story testifies, he also understands the hurtful, twisted side of human nature.*

"You have a dark beer?"

"In a place like this you want dark beer?"

"Whatever, then."

The bartender drew a thick-walled stein and slid it across. "I worked in the city. I know about dark beer and Guinness and like that. These yokels around here," he added, his tone of voice finishing the sentence.

The customer was a small man with glasses and not much of a beard. He had a gentle voice. "A man called Grinny . . ."

"Grimme," the barman corrected. "So you heard. Him and his brother."

The customer didn't say anything. The bartender wiped. The customer told him to pour one for himself.

"I don't usual." But the barman poured. "Grimme and that brother Dave, the worst." He drank. "I hate it a lot out here, yokels like that is why."

"There's still the city."

"Not for me. The wife."

"Oh." And he waited.

"They lied a lot. Come in here, get drunk, tell about what they done, mostly women. Bad, what they said they done. Worse when it wasn't lies. You want another?"

"Not yet."

"No lie about the Fannen kid, Marcy. Fourteen, fifteen maybe. Tooken her out behind the Johnson's silo, what they done to her. And then they said they'd kill her, she said anything. She didn't. Not about that, not about anything, ever again, two years. Until the fever last November, she told her mom. She died. Mom came told me 'fore she moved out."

The customer waited.

"Hear them tell it, they were into every woman, wife, daughter in the valley, anytime they wanted."

The customer blew through his nostrils, once, gently. A man came in for two six-packs and a hip-sized Southern Comfort and went away in a pickup truck. "'Monday-busy' I call this," said the barman, looking around the empty room. "And here it's Wednesday." Without being asked, he drew another beer for the customer. "To have somebody to talk to," he said in explanation. Then he said nothing at all for a long time.

The customer took some beer. "They just went after local folks, then."

"Grimme and David? Well yes, they had the run of it, the most of the men off with the lumbering, nothing grows in these rocks around here. Except maybe chickens, and who cares for chickens? Old folks, and the women. Anyway, that Grimme, shoulders *this* wide. Eyes *that* close together, and hairy. The brother, maybe you'd say a good-lookin' guy for a yokel, but, well, scary." He nodded at his choice of words and said it again. "Scary."

"Crazy eyes," said the customer.

"You got it. So the times they wasn't just lyin', the women didn't want to tell and I got to say it, the men just as soon not know."

"But they never bothered anyone except their own valley people."

"Who else is ever around here to bother? Oh, they bragged about this one and that one they got to on the road, you know, blonde in the big convertible, give them the eye, give them whiskey, give them a good time up on the back roads. All lies and you know it. They got this big old van. Gal hitchhiker, they say the first woman ever used 'em both up. Braggin', lyin'. Shagged a couple city people in a little hatchback, leaned on them 'til the husband begged 'em to ball the wife. I don't believe that at all."

"You don't."

"What man would say that to a couple hairy yokels, no matter what? Man got to be yellow or downright kinky."

"What happened?"

"Nothing happened, I told you I don't believe it! It's lies, brags and lies. Said they found 'em driving the quarry road, 'way yonder. Passed 'em and parked the van to let 'em by, look 'em over. Passed 'em and got ahead, when they caught up David was lying on the road and Grimme made like artificial you know, lifeguards do it."

"Respiration."

"Yeah, that. They seen that and they stopped, the couple in the hatchback, got out, Grimme and David jumped 'em. Said the man's a shrimpy little guy looked like a perfessor, woman's a dish, too good for him. But that's what they said. I don't believe any of it."

"You mean they'd never do a thing like that."

"Oh they would all right. Cutting off the woman's clo'es to see what she got with a big old skinning knife. Took awhile, they said it was a lot of laughs. David holdin' both her arms behind her back one-handed, cuttin' away her clo'es and makin' jokes, Grimme holdin' the little perfessor man around the neck with the one elbow, laughin', 'til the man snatched his head clear and that's when he said it. 'Give it to him,' he told the woman, 'Go on, give it to him,' and she says 'For the love of God don't ask me to do that.' I don't believe any man ever would say a thing like that."

"You really don't."

"No way. Because listen, when the man jerked out his head and said that, and the woman said don't ask her to do that, *then* the perfessor guy tried to fight Grimme. You see what I'm saying? If Grimme breaks him up and stomps on the pieces, then you could maybe understand him beggin' the woman to quit and give in. The way Grimme told it right here standing where you are, the man said it when Grimme hadn't done nothing yet but hold his neck. That's the part Grimme told over and over, laughin'. 'Give it to him,' the man kept telling her. And Grimme never even hit him yet. 'Course when the little man tried to fight him Grimme just laughed and clobbered him once side of the neck, laid him out cold. That was when the woman turned into a wildcat, to hear them tell it. It was all David could do to hold her, let alone mess around. Grimme left him to it and went around back to see what they got in their car. Mind you, I don't know if he really done all this; I'm just telling you what he said. I heard it three, four times just that first week.

"So he opened up the back and there was a stack of pictures, you know, painting like on canvas. He hauled 'em all out and put 'em all down flat on the ground and walked up and back looking at them. He says 'David, you like these?' and David he said 'Hell no' and Grimme walked the whole line, one big boot in the middle of each and every picture. And he says at the first step that woman screamed like it was her face he was stepping on and she hollered 'Don't, don't, they mean everything in the world to him!' she meant the perfessor, but Grimme went ahead anyway. And then she just quit, she said go ahead, and Dave tooken her into the van and Grimme sat on the perfessor till he was done, then Grimme went in and got his while Dave sat on the man, and after that they got in their van and come here to get drunk and tell about it. And if you really want to know why I don't believe any of it, those people never tried to call the law." And the barman gave a vehement nod and drank deep.

"So what happened to them?"

"Who—the city people? I told you—I don't even believe there was any."

"Grimme."

"Oh. Them." The barman gave a strange chuckle and said with sudden piety, "The Lord has strange ways of fighting evil."

The customer waited. The barman drew him another beer and poured a jigger for himself.

"Next time I see Grimme it's a week, ten days after. It's like tonight, nobody here. He comes in for a fifth of sourmash. He's walking funny, kind of bowlegged. I thought at first trying to clown, he'd do that. But every step he kind of grunted, like you would if I stuck a knife in you, but every step. And the look on his face I never saw the like before. I tell you, it scared me. I went for the whiskey and outside there was screaming."

As he talked his gaze went to the far wall and somehow through it, his eyes very round and bulging. "I said 'What in God's name is that?' and Grimme said, 'It's David, he's out in the van, he's hurting.' And I said, 'Better get him to the doctor,' and he said they just came from there, full of painkiller but it wasn't enough, and he tooken his whiskey and left, walking that way and grunting every step, and drove off. Last time I saw him."

His eyes withdrew from elsewhere, back into the room, and became more normal. "He never paid for the whiskey. I don't think he meant to stiff me, the one thing he never did. He just didn't think of it at the time. Couldn't," he added.

"What was wrong with him?"

"I don't know. The doc didn't know."

"That would be Dr. McCabe?"

"McCabe? I don't know any Dr. McCabe around here. It was Dr. Thetford over the Allersville Corners."

"Ah. And how are they now, Grimme and David?"

"Dead is how they are."

"Dead? . . . You didn't say that."

"I didn't?"

"Not until now." The customer got off his stool and put money on the bar and picked up his car keys. He said, his voice quite as gentle as it had been all along, "The man wasn't yellow and he wasn't kinky. It was something far worse." Not caring at all what this might mean to the bartender, he walked out and got into his car.

He drove until he found a telephone booth—the vanishing kind with a door that would shut. First he called Information and got a number; then he dialed it.

"Dr. Thetford? Hello . . . I want to ease your mind about something. You recently had two fatalities, brothers. . . . No, I will not tell you my name. Bear with me, please. You attended these two and you probably performed the autopsies, right? Good. I hoped you had. And you couldn't diagnose, correct? You probably certified peritonitis, with good reason. . . . No, I will *not* tell you my name! And I am not calling to question your competence. Far from it. My purpose is only to ease your mind, which presupposes that you are good at your job and you really care about a medical anomaly. Do we understand each other? Not yet? Then hear me out. . . . Good."

Rather less urgently, he went on: "An analogy is a disease called granuloma inguinale, which, I don't have to tell you, can destroy the whole sexual apparatus with ulcerations and necrosis, and penetrate the body to and all through the peritoneum. . . . Yes, I know you considered that and I know you rejected it, and I know why. . . . Right. Just too damn fast. I'm sure you looked for characteristic bacterial and viral evidence as well, and didn't find any.

". . . Yes, of course, Doctor—you're right and I'm sorry, going on about all the things it isn't without saying what it is.

"Actually, it's a hormone poison, resulting from a biochemical mutation in—in the carrier. It's synergistic, wildly accelerating—as you saw. One effect is something you couldn't possibly know—it affects the tactile neurones in such a way that morphine and its derivatives have an inverted effect—in much the same way that amphetamines have a calmative effect on children. In other words, the morphine aggravated and intensified their pain. . . . I know, I know; I'm sorry. I made a real effort to get to you and tell you this in time to spare them some of that agony, but—as you say, it's just too damn fast.

". . . Vectors? Ah. That's something you do not have to worry about. I mean it, Doctor—it is totally unlikely that you will ever see another case.

". . . Where did it come from? I can tell you that. The two brothers assaulted and raped a woman—very probably the only woman on earth to have this mutated hormone poison. . . . Yes, I *can* be sure. I have spent most of the last six years in researching this thing. There have been only two other cases of it—yes, just as fast, just as lethal. Both occurred before she was aware of it. She—she is a woman of great sensitivity and a profound sense of responsibility. One was a man she cared very little about, hardly knew. The other was someone she cared very much indeed about. The cost to her when she discovered what had happened was—well, you can imagine.

"She is a gentle and compassionate person with a profound sense of ethical responsibility. Please believe me when I tell you that at the time of the assault she would have done anything in her power to protect those—those men from the effects of that . . . contact. When her husband—yes, she has a husband, I'll come to that—when he became infuriated at the indignities they were putting on her, and begged her to give in and let them get what they deserved, she was horrified—actually hated him for a while for having given in to such a murderous suggestion. It was only when they vandalized some things that were especially precious to her husband—priceless—that she too experienced the same deadly fury and let them go ahead. The reaction has been terrible for her—first to see her husband seeking vengeance, when she was convinced he could rise above that—and in a moment find that she herself could be swept away by the same thing. . . . But I'm sorry, Dr. Thetford—I've come far afield from medical concerns. I meant only to reassure you that you are not looking at some mysterious new plague. You can be sure that every possible precaution is being taken against its recurrence. . . . I admit that total precautions against the likes of those two may not be possible, but there's little chance of its happening again. And that, sir, is all I am going to say, so good—

"What? Unfair? . . . I suppose you're right at that—to tell you so much and so little all at once. And I do owe it to you to explain what my concern is in all this. Please—give me a moment to get my thoughts together.

". . . Very well. I was commissioned by that lady to make some discreet inquiries about what happened to those two, and if possible to get to their doctor in time to inform him—you—about the inverted effect of morphine. There would be no way to save their lives, but they might have been spared the agony. Further, she found that not knowing for sure if they were indeed victims was unbearable. This news is going to be hard for her to take, but she will survive it somehow; she's done it before. Hardest of all for her—and her husband—will be to come to terms with the fact that, under pressure, they both found themselves capable of murderous vengefulness. She has always believed, and by her example he came to believe, that vengeance is unthinkable. And he failed her. And she failed herself." Without a trace of humor, he laughed. " 'Vengeance is mine, saith the Lord.' I can't interpret that, Doctor, or vouch for it. All I can derive from this—episode—is that vengeance *is*. And that's all I intend to say to you—what?

". . . One more question? . . . Ah—the husband. Yes, you have the right to ask that. I'll say it this way: there was a wedding seven years ago. It was three years before there was a marriage, you follow? Three years of the most intensive research and the most meticulous experimentation. And you can accept as fact that she is the only woman in the world who can cause this affliction—and he is the only man who is immune.

"Doctor Thetford: good night."

He hung up and stood for a long while with his forehead against the cool glass of the booth. At length he shuddered, pulled himself together, went out and drove away in his little hatchback.

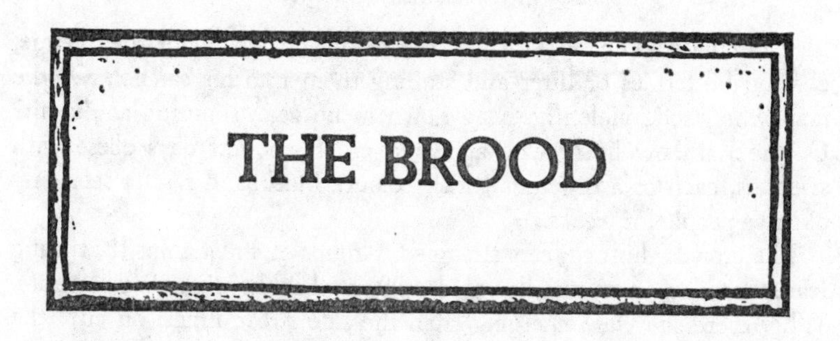

THE BROOD

By RAMSEY CAMPBELL

A lifelong resident of Liverpool, Ramsey Campbell began his writing career as a transatlantic protégé-by-mail of August Derleth. Derleth brought out Campbell's first collection of stories in 1964, when he was only eighteen. Since then Campbell has published several further books, including a much praised collection, Demons by Daylight, *and a fine, long horror novel,* The Parasite. *Campbell's approach to the contemporary horror tale is oblique and subtle and colored by a gray view of the world that often has the cumulative effect of a nightmare from which one cannot awaken. The story at hand, set in his native Liverpool, conjures up fearful things in a distinctly urban setting, not unlike the manner in which his friend and fellow fantasist T. E. D. Klein does in New York.*

He'd had an almost unbearable day. As he walked home his self-control still oppressed him, like rusty armour. Climbing the stairs, he tore open his mail: a glossy pamphlet from a binoculars firm, a humbler folder from the Wild Life Preservation Society. Irritably he threw them on the bed and sat by the window, to relax.

It was autumn. Night had begun to cramp the days. Beneath golden trees, a procession of cars advanced along Princes Avenue, as though to a funeral; crowds hurried home. The incessant anonymous parade, dwarfed by three stories, depressed him. Faces like these vague twilit miniatures—selfishly ingrown, convinced that nothing was their fault—brought their pets to his office.

But where were all the local characters? He enjoyed watching them, they fascinated him. Where was the man who ran about the avenue, chasing butterflies of litter and stuffing them into his satchel? Or the man who strode violently, head down in no gale, shouting at the air? Or the Rainbow Man, who appeared on the hottest days obese with sweaters, each of a different garish colour? Blackband hadn't seen any of these people for weeks.

The crowds thinned; cars straggled. Groups of streetlamps lit, tinting leaves sodium, unnaturally gold. Often that lighting had meant—Why, there she was, emerging from the side street almost on cue: the Lady of the Lamp.

Her gait was elderly. Her face was withered as an old blanched apple; the rest of her head was wrapped in a tattered grey scarf. Her voluminous ankle-length coat, patched with remnants of colour, swayed as she walked. She reached the central reservation of the avenue, and stood beneath a lamp.

Though there was a pedestrian crossing beside her, people deliberately crossed elsewhere. They would, Blackband thought sourly: just as they ignored the packs of stray dogs that were always someone else's responsibility—ignored them, or hoped someone would put them to sleep. Perhaps they felt the human strays should be put to sleep, perhaps that was where the Rainbow Man and the rest had gone!

The woman was pacing restlessly. She circled the lamp, as though the blurred disc of light at its foot were a stage. Her shadow resembled the elaborate hand of a clock.

Surely she was too old to be a prostitute. Might she have been one, who was now compelled to enact her memories? His binoculars drew her face closer: intent as a sleepwalker's, introverted as a foetus. Her head bobbed against gravel, foreshortened by the false perspective of the lenses. She moved offscreen.

Three months ago, when he'd moved to this flat, there had been two old women. One night he had seen them, circling adjacent lamps. The other woman had been slower, more sleepy. At last the Lady of the Lamp had led her home; they'd moved slowly as exhausted sleepers. For days he'd thought of the two women in their long faded coats, trudging around the lamps in the deserted avenue, as though afraid to go home in the growing dark.

The sight of the lone woman still unnerved him, a little. Darkness was crowding his flat. He drew the curtains, which the lamps stained orange. Watching had relaxed him somewhat. Time to make a salad.

The kitchen overlooked the old women's house. See The World from the Attics of Princes Avenue. All Human Life Is Here. Backyards penned in rubble and crumbling toilet sheds; on the far side of the back street, houses were lidless boxes of smoke. The house directly beneath his window was dark, as always. How could the two women—if both were still alive—survive in there? But at least they could look after themselves, or call for aid; they were human, after all. It was their pets that bothered him.

He had never seen the torpid woman again. Since she had vanished, her companion had begun to take animals home; he'd seen her coaxing them toward the house. No doubt they were company for her friend; but what life could animals enjoy in the lightless, probably condemnable house? And why so many? Did they escape to their homes, or stray again? He shook his head: the women's loneliness was no excuse. They cared as little for their pets as did those owners who came, whining like their dogs, to his office.

Perhaps the woman was waiting beneath the lamps for cats to drop from the trees, like fruit. He meant the thought as a joke. But when he'd finished preparing dinner, the idea troubled him sufficiently that he switched off the light in the main room and peered through the curtains.

The bright gravel was bare. Parting the curtains, he saw the woman hurrying unsteadily toward her street. She was carrying a kitten: her head bowed over the fur cradled in her arms; her whole body seemed to enfold it. As he emerged from the kitchen again, carrying plates, he heard her door creak open and shut. Another one, he thought uneasily.

By the end of the week she'd taken in a stray dog, and Blackband was wondering what should be done.

The women would have to move eventually. The houses adjoining theirs were empty, the windows shattered targets. But how could they take their menagerie with them? They'd set them loose to roam or, weeping, take them to be put to sleep.

Something ought to be done, but not by him. He came home to rest. He was used to removing chicken bones from throats; it was suffering the excuses that exhausted him—Fido always had his bit of chicken, it had never happened before, they couldn't understand. He would nod curtly, with a slight pained smile. "Oh yes?" he would repeat tonelessly. "Oh yes?"

Not that that would work with the Lady of the Lamp. But then, he didn't intend to confront her: what on earth could he have said? That he'd take all the animals off her hands? Hardly. Besides, the thought of confronting her made him uncomfortable.

She was growing more eccentric. Each day she appeared a little earlier. Often she would move away into the dark, then hurry back into the flat bright pool. It was as though light were her drug.

People stared at her, and fled. They disliked her because she was odd. All she had to do to please them, Blackband thought, was be normal: overfeed her pets until their stomachs scraped the ground, lock them in cars to suffocate in the heat, leave them alone in the house all day then beat them for chewing. Compared to most of the owners he met, she was Saint Francis.

He watched television. Insects were courting and mating. Their ritual dances engrossed and moved him: the play of colours, the elaborate racial patterns of the life-force which they instinctively decoded and enacted. Microphotography presented them to him. If only people were as beautiful and fascinating!

Even his fascination with the Lady of the Lamp was no longer unalloyed; he resented that. Was she falling ill? She walked painfully slowly, stooped over, and looked shrunken. Nevertheless, each night she kept her vigil, wandering sluggishly in the pools of light like a sleepwalker.

How could she cope with her animals now? How might she be treating them? Surely there were social workers in some of the cars nosing home, someone must notice how much she needed help. Once he made for the door to the stairs, but already his throat was parched of words. The thought of speaking to her wound him tight inside. It wasn't his job, he had enough to confront. The spring in his guts coiled tighter, until he moved away from the door.

One night an early policeman appeared. Usually the police emerged near midnight, disarming people of knives and broken glass, forcing them into the vans. Blackband watched eagerly. Surely the man must escort her home, see what the house hid. Blackband glanced back to the splash of light beneath the lamp. It was deserted.

How could she had moved so fast? He stared, baffled. A dim shape lurked at the corner of his eyes. Glancing nervously, he saw the woman standing on a bright disc several lamps away, considerably farther from the policeman than he'd thought. Why should he have been so mistaken?

Before he could ponder, a sound distracted him: a loud fluttering, as though a bird were trapped and frantic in the kitchen. But the room was empty. Any bird must have escaped through the open window. Was that a flicker of movement below, in the dark house? Perhaps the bird had flown in there.

The policeman had moved on. The woman was trudging her island of light; her coat's hem dragged over the gravel. For a while Blackband watched, musing uneasily, trying to think what the fluttering had resembled more than the sound of a bird's wings.

Perhaps that was why, in the early hours, he saw a man stumbling through the derelict back streets. Jagged hurdles of rubble blocked the way; the man clambered, panting dryly, gulping dust as well as breath. He seemed only exhausted and uneasy, but Blackband could see what was pursuing him: a great wide shadow-colored stain, creeping vaguely over the rooftops. The stain was alive, for its face mouthed—though at first, from its color and texture, he thought the head was the moon. Its eyes gleamed hungrily. As the fluttering made the man turn and scream, the face sailed down on its stain toward him.

Next day was unusually trying: a dog with a broken leg and a suffering owner, you'll hurt his leg, can't you be more gentle, oh come here, baby, what did the nasty man do to you; a senile cat and its protector, isn't the usual vet here today, he never used to do that, are you sure you know what you're doing. But later, as he watched the woman's obsessive trudging, the dream of the stain returned to him. Suddenly he realized he had never seen her during daylight.

So that was it! he thought, sniggering. She'd been a vampire all the time! A difficult job to keep when you hadn't a tooth in your head. He reeled in her face with the focusing-screw. Yes, she was toothless. Perhaps she used false fangs, or sucked through her gums. But he couldn't sustain his joke for long. Her face peered out of the frame of her grey scarf, as though from a web. As she circled she was muttering incessantly. Her tongue worked as though her mouth were too small for it. Her eyes were fixed as the heads of grey nails impaling her skull.

He laid the binoculars aside, and was glad that she'd become more distant. But even the sight of her trudging in miniature troubled him. In her eyes he had seen that she didn't want to do what she was doing.

She was crossing the roadway, advancing toward his gate. For a moment, unreasonably and with a sour uprush of dread, he was sure she intended to come in. But she was staring at the hedge. Her hands fluttered, warding off a fear; her eyes and her mouth were stretched wide. She stood quivering, then she stumbled toward her street, almost running.

He made himself go down. Each leaf of the hedge held an orange-sodium glow, like wet paint. But there was nothing among the leaves, and nothing could have struggled out, for the twigs were intricately bound by spiderwebs, gleaming like gold wire.

The next day was Sunday. He rode a train beneath the Mersey and went tramping the Wirral Way nature trail. Red-faced men, and women who had paralyzed their hair with spray, stared as though he'd invaded their garden. A few butterflies perched on flowers; their wings settled together delicately, then they flickered away above the banks of the abandoned railway cutting. They were too quick for him to enjoy, even with his binoculars; he kept remembering how near death their species were. His moping had slowed him, he felt barred from his surroundings by his inability to confront the old woman. He couldn't speak to her, there were no words he could use, but meanwhile her animals might be suffering. He dreaded going home to another night of helpless watching.

Could he look into the house while she was wandering? She might leave the door unlocked. At some time he had become intuitively sure that her companion was dead. Twilight gained on him, urging him back to Liverpool.

He gazed nervously down at the lamps. Anything was preferable to his impotence. But his feelings had trapped him into committing himself before he was ready. Could he really go down when she emerged? Suppose the other woman was still alive, and screamed? Good God, he needn't go in if he didn't want to. On the gravel, light lay bare as a row of plates on a shelf. He found himself thinking, with a secret eagerness, that she might already have had her wander.

As he made dinner, he kept hurrying irritably to the front window. Television failed to engross him; he watched the avenue instead. Discs of light dwindled away, impaled by their lamps. Below the kitchen window stood a block of night and silence. Eventually he went to bed, but heard fluttering—flights of litter in the derelict streets, no doubt. His dreams gave the litter a human face.

Throughout Monday he was on edge, anxious to hurry home and be done; he was distracted. Oh poor Chubbles, is the man hurting you! He managed to leave early. Day was trailing down the sky as he reached the avenue. Swiftly he brewed coffee and sat sipping, watching.

The caravan of cars faltered, interrupted by gaps. The last homecomers hurried away, clearing the stage. But the woman failed to take her cue. His cooking of dinner was fragmented; he hurried repeatedly back to the window. Where was the bloody woman, was she on strike? Not until the following night, when she had still not appeared, did he begin to suspect he'd seen the last of her.

His intense relief was short-lived. If she had died of whatever had been shrinking her, what would happen to her animals? Should he find out what was wrong? But there was no reason to think she'd died. Probably she, and her friend before her, had gone to stay with relatives. No doubt the animals had escaped long before—he'd never seen or heard any of them since she had taken them in. Darkness stood hushed and bulky beneath his kitchen window.

For several days the back streets were quiet, except for the flapping of litter or birds. It became easier to glance at the dark house. Soon they'd demolish it; already children had shattered all the windows. Now, when he lay awaiting sleep, the thought of the vague house soothed him, weighed his mind down gently.

That night he awoke twice. He'd left the kitchen window ajar, hoping to lose some of the unseasonable heat. Drifting through the window came a man's low moaning. Was he trying to form words? His voice was muffled, blurred as a dying radio. He must be drunk; perhaps he had fallen, for there was a faint scrape of rubble. Blackband hid within his eyelids, courting sleep. At last the shapeless moaning faded. There was silence, except for the feeble, stony scraping. Blackband lay and grumbled, until sleep led him to a face that crept over heaps of rubble.

Some hours later he woke again. The lifelessness of four o'clock surrounded him, the dim air seemed sluggish and ponderous. Had he dreamed the new sound? It returned, and made him flinch: a chorus of thin, piteous wailing, reaching weakly upward toward the kitchen. For a moment, on the edge of dream, it sounded like babies. How could babies be crying in an abandoned house? The voices were too thin. They were kittens.

He lay in the heavy dark, hemmed in by shapes that the night deformed. He willed the sounds to cease, and eventually they did. When he awoke again, belatedly, he had time only to hurry to work.

In the evening the house was silent as a draped cage. Someone must have rescued the kittens. But in the early hours the crying woke him: fretful, bewildered, famished. He couldn't go down now, he had no light. The crying was muffled, as though beneath stone. Again it kept him awake, again he was late for work.

His loss of sleep nagged him. His smile sagged impatiently, his nods were contemptuous twitches. "Yes," he agreed with a woman who said she'd been careless to slam her dog's paw in a door, and when she raised her eyebrows haughtily: "Yes, I can see that." He could see her deciding to find another vet. Let her, let someone else suffer her. He had problems of his own.

He borrowed the office flashlight, to placate his anxiety. Surely he wouldn't need to enter the house, surely someone else—He walked home, toward the darker sky. Night thickened like soot on the buildings.

He prepared dinner quickly. No need to dawdle in the kitchen, no point in staring down. He was hurrying; he dropped a spoon, which reverberated shrilly in his mind, nerve-racking. Slow down, slow down. A breeze piped incessantly outside, in the rubble. No, not a breeze. When he made himself raise the sash he heard the crying, thin as wind in crevices.

It seemed weaker now, dismal and desperate: intolerable. Could nobody else hear it, did nobody care? He gripped the windowsill; a breeze tried feebly to tug at his fingers. Suddenly, compelled by vague anger, he grabbed the flashlight and trudged reluctantly downstairs.

A pigeon hobbled on the avenue, dangling the stump of one leg, twitching clogged wings; cars brisked by. The back street was scattered with debris, as though a herd had moved on, leaving its refuse to manure the paving stones. His flashlight groped over the heaped pavement, trying to determine which house had been troubling him.

Only by standing back to align his own window with the house could he decide, and even then he was unsure. How could the old woman have clambered over the jagged pile that blocked the doorway? The front door sprawled splintered in the hall, on a heap of the fallen ceiling, amid peelings of wallpaper. He must be mistaken. But as his flashlight dodged about the hall, picking up debris then letting it drop back into the dark, he heard the crying, faint and muffled. It was somewhere within.

He ventured forward, treading carefully. He had to drag the door into the street before he could proceed. Beyond the door the floorboards were cobbled with rubble. Plaster swayed about him, glistening. His light wobbled ahead of him, then led him toward a gaping doorway on the right. The light spread into the room, dimming.

A door lay on its back. Boards poked like exposed ribs through the plaster of the ceiling; torn paper dangled. There was no carton full of starving kittens; in fact, the room was bare. Moist stains engulfed the walls.

He groped along the hall, to the kitchen. The stove was fat with grime. The wallpaper had collapsed entirely, draping indistinguishable shapes that stirred as the flashlight glanced at them. Through the furred window, he made out the light in his own kitchen, orange-shaded, blurred. How could two women have survived here?

At once he regretted that thought. The old woman's face loomed behind him: eyes still as metal, skin the colour of pale bone. He turned nervously; the light capered. Of course there was only the quivering mouth of the hall. But the face was present now, peering from behind the draped shapes around him.

He was about to give up—he was already full of the gasp of relief he would give when he reached the avenue—when he heard the crying. It was almost breathless, as though close to death: a shrill feeble wheezing. He couldn't bear it. He hurried into the hall.

Might the creatures be upstairs? His light showed splintered holes in most of the stairs; through them he glimpsed a huge symmetrical stain on the wall. Surely the woman could never have climbed up there—but that left only the cellar.

The door was beside him. The flashlight, followed by his hand, groped for the knob. The face was near him in the shadows; its fixed eyes gleamed. He dreaded finding her fallen on the cellar steps. But the crying pleaded. He dragged the door open; it scraped over rubble. He thrust the flashlight into the dank opening. He stood gaping, bewildered.

Beneath him lay a low stone room. Its walls glistened darkly. The place was full of debris: bricks, planks, broken lengths of wood. Draping the debris, or tangled beneath it, were numerous old clothes. Threads of a white substance were tethered to everything, and drifted feebly now the door was opened.

In one corner loomed a large pale bulk. His light twitched toward it. It was a white bag of some material, not cloth. It had been torn open; except for a sifting of rubble, and a tangle of what might have been fragments of dully painted cardboard, it was empty.

The crying wailed, somewhere beneath the planks. Several sweeps of the light showed that the cellar was otherwise deserted. Though the face mouthed behind him, he ventured down. For God's sake, get it over with; he knew he would never dare return. A swath had been cleared through the dust on the steps, as though something had dragged itself out of the cellar, or had been dragged in.

His movements disturbed the tethered threads; they rose like feelers, fluttering delicately. The white bag stirred, its torn mouth worked. Without knowing why, he stayed as far from that corner as he could.

The crying had come from the far end of the cellar. As he picked his way hurriedly over the rubble he caught sight of a group of clothes. They were violently coloured sweaters, which the Rainbow Man had worn. They slumped over planks; they nestled inside one another, as though the man had withered or had been sucked out.

Staring uneasily about, Blackband saw that all the clothes were stained. There was blood on all of them, though not a great deal on any. The ceiling hung close to him, oppressive and vague. Darkness had blotted out the steps and the door. He caught at them with the light, and stumbled toward them.

The crying made him falter. Surely there were fewer voices, and they seemed to sob. He was nearer the voices than the steps. If he could find the creatures at once, snatch them up and flee—He clambered over the treacherous debris, toward a gap in the rubble. The bag mouthed emptily; threads plucked at him, almost impalpably. As he thrust the flashlight's beam into the gap, darkness rushed to surround him.

Beneath the debris a pit had been dug. Parts of its earth walls had collapsed, but protruding from the fallen soil he could see bones. They looked too large for an animal's. In the centre of the pit, sprinkled with earth, lay a cat. Little of it remained, except for its skin and bones; its skin was covered with deep pockmarks. But its eyes seemed to move feebly.

Appalled, he stooped. He had no idea what to do. He never knew, for the walls of the pit were shifting. Soil trickled scattering as a face the size of his fist emerged. There were several; their limbless bodies squirmed from the earth, all around the pit. From toothless mouths, their sharp tongues flickered out toward the cat. As he fled they began wailing dreadfully.

He chased the light toward the steps. He fell, cutting his knees. He thought the face with its gleaming eyes would meet him in the hall. He ran from the cellar, flailing his flashlight at the air. As he stumbled down the street he could still see the faces that had crawled from the soil: rudimentary beneath translucent skin, but beginning to be human.

He leaned against his gatepost in the lamplight, retching. Images and memories tumbled disordered through his mind. The face crawling over the roofs. Only seen at night. Vampire. The fluttering at the window. Her terror at the hedge full of spiders. *Calyptra,* what was it, *Calyptra eustrigata.* Vampire moth.

Vague though they were, the implications terrified him. He fled into his building, but halted fearfully on the stairs. The things must be destroyed: to delay would be insane. Suppose their hunger brought them crawling out of the cellar tonight, toward his flat—Absurd though it must be, he couldn't forget that they might have seen his face.

He stood giggling, dismayed. Whom did you call in these circumstances? The police, an exterminator? Nothing would relieve his horror until he saw the brood destroyed, and the only way to see that was to do the job himself. Burn. Petrol. He dawdled on the stairs, delaying, thinking he knew none of the other tenants from whom to borrow the fuel.

He ran to the nearby garage. "Have you got any petrol?"

The man glared at him, suspecting a joke. "You'd be surprised. How much do you want?"

How much indeed! He restrained his giggling. Perhaps he should ask the man's advice! Excuse me, how much petrol do you need for—"A gallon," he stammered.

As soon as he reached the back street he switched on his flashlight. Crowds of rubble lined the pavements. Far above the dark house he saw his orange light. He stepped over the debris into the hall. The swaying light brought the face forward to meet him. Of course the hall was empty.

He forced himself forward. Plucked by the flashlight, the cellar door flapped soundlessly. Couldn't he just set fire to the house? But that might leave the brood untouched. Don't think, go down quickly. Above the stairs the stain loomed.

In the cellar nothing had changed. The bag gaped, the clothes lay emptied. Struggling to unscrew the cap of the petrol can, he almost dropped the flashlight. He kicked wood into the pit and began to pour the petrol. At once he heard the wailing beneath him. "Shut up!" he screamed, to drown out the sound. "Shut up! Shut up!"

The can took its time in gulping itself empty; the petrol seemed thick as oil. He hurled the can clattering away, and ran to the steps. He fumbled with matches, gripping the flashlight between his knees. As he threw them, the lit matches went out. Not until he ventured back to the pit, clutching a ball of paper from his pocket, did he succeed in making a flame that reached his goal. There was a whoof of fire, and a chorus of interminable feeble shrieking.

As he clambered sickened toward the hall, he heard a fluttering above him. Wallpaper, stirring in a wind: it sounded moist. But there was no wind, for the air clung clammily to him. He slithered over the rubble into the hall, darting his light about. Something white bulked at the top of the stairs.

It was another torn bag. He hadn't been able to see it before. It slumped emptily. Beside it the stain spread over the wall. That stain was too symmetrical; it resembled an inverted coat. Momentarily he thought the paper was drooping, tugged perhaps by his unsteady light, for the stain had begun to creep down toward him. Eyes glared at him from its dangling face. Though the face was upside down he knew it at once. From its gargoyle mouth a tongue reached for him.

He whirled to flee. But the darkness that filled the front door was more than night, for it was advancing audibly. He stumbled, panicking, and rubble slipped from beneath his feet. He fell from the cellar steps, onto piled stone. Though he felt almost no pain, he heard his spine break.

His mind writhed helplessly. His body refused to heed it in any way, and lay on the rubble, trapping him. He could hear cars on the avenue, radio sets and the sounds of cutlery in flats, distant and indifferent. The cries were petering out now. He tried to scream, but only his eyes could move. As they struggled, he glimpsed through a slit in the cellar wall the orange light in his kitchen.

His flashlight lay on the steps, dimmed by its fall. Before long a rustling darkness came slowly down the steps, blotting out the light. He heard sounds in the dark, and something that was not flesh nestled against him. His throat managed a choked shriek that was almost inaudible, even to him. Eventually the face crawled away toward the hall, and the light returned. From the corner of his eye he could see what surrounded him. They were round, still, practically featureless: as yet, hardly even alive.

THE WHISTLING WELL

By CLIFFORD D. SIMAK

Clifford D. Simak's fiction is noted for its warm attention to human values and love for the American rural countryside. Simak is, in fact, a kind of folk writer, juxtaposing details of middle American life against the vastness of cosmic space. This vision sustains such science fiction classics as City *and* Way Station *and has made Simak one of the field's foremost writers. Now retired, he spent most of his career as a Minneapolis newspaperman, covering everything from medical science to the Wisconsin murder case which inspired the famous novel and film* Psycho. *Now a resident of Minnetonka, Minnesota, he was raised on a farm in southwestern Wisconsin, the area that forms the setting for the story that follows, with its unique Simakian statement.*

He walked the ridge, so high against the sky, so windswept, so clean, so open, so far-seeing. As if the very land itself, the soil, the stone, were reaching up, standing on tiptoe, to lift itself, stretching toward the sky. So high that one, looking down, could see the backs of hawks that swung in steady hunting circles above the river valley.

The highness was not all. There was, as well, the sense of ancientness and the smell of time. And the intimacy, as if this great high ridge might be transferring to him its personality. A personality, he admitted to himself, for which he had a liking, a thing that he could wrap, as a cloak, around himself.

And through it all, he heard the creaking of the rocker as it went back and forth, with the hunched and shriveled, but still energetic, old lady crouched upon it, rocking back and forth, so small, so dried up, so emaciated that she seemed to have shrunken into the very structure of the chair, her feet dangling, not reaching the floor. Like a child in a great-grandfather chair. Her feet not touching, not even reaching out a toe to make the rocker go. And, yet, the rocker kept on rocking, never stopping. How the hell, Thomas Parker asked himself, had she made the rocker go?

He had reached the ultimate point of the ridge where steep, high limestone cliffs plunged down toward the river. Cliffs that swung east and from this point continued along the river valley, a stony rampart that fenced in the ridge against the deepness of the valley.

He turned and looked back along the ridge and there, a mile or so away, stood the spidery structure of the windmill, the great wheel facing west, toward him, its blades a whir of silver movement in the light of the setting sun.

The windmill, he knew, was clattering and clanking, but from this distance, he could hear no sound of it, for the strong wind blowing from the west so filled his ears that he could pick up no sound but the blowing of the wind. The wind whipped at his loose jacket and made his pants legs ripple and he could feel its steady pressure at his back.

And, yet, within his mind, if not within his ears, he still could hear the creaking of the rocker, moving back and forth within that room where a bygone gentility warred against the brusqueness of present time. The fireplace was built of rosy brick, with white paneling placed around the brick, the mantel loaded with old figurines, with framed photographs from another time, with an ornate, squatty clock that chimed each quarter hour. There had been furniture of solid oak, a threadbare carpet on the floor. The drapes at the large bow windows, with deep window seats, were of some heavy material, faded over the years to a nondeterminate coloring. Paintings with heavy gilt frames hung on the walls, but the gloom within the room was so deep that there was no way of seeing what they were.

The woman-of-all-work, the companion, the housekeeper, the practical nurse, the cook, brought in the tea, with bread-and-butter sandwiches piled on one plate and delicate cakes ranged on another. She had set the tray on the table in front of the rocking old lady and then had gone away, back into the dark and mysterious depths of the ancient house.

The old lady spoke in her brittle voice, "Thomas," she said, "if you will pour. Two lumps for me, no cream."

Awkwardly, he had risen from the horsehair chair. Awkwardly he had poured. He had never poured before. There was a feeling that he should do it charmingly and delicately and with a certain genteel flair, but he did not have the flair. He had nothing that this house or this old lady had. His was another world.

He had been summoned here, imperatively summoned, in a crisp little note on paper that had a faint scent of lavender, the script of the writing more bold than he would have expected, the letters a flowing dignity in old copperplate.

I shall expect you, she had written, *on the afternoon of the 17th. We have matters to discuss.*

A summons from the past and from seven hundred miles away and he had responded, driving his beaten-up, weather-stained, lumbering camper through the flaming hills of a New England autumn.

The wind still tugged and pushed at him, the windmill blades still a swirl of movement and below him, above the river, the small, dark shape of the circling hawk. Autumn then, he told himself, and here another autumn, with the trees of the river valley, the trees of other far-off vistas, taking on the color of the season.

The ridge itself was bare of trees, except for a few that still clustered around the sites of homesteads, the homesteads now gone, burned down or weathered away or fallen with the passage of the years. In time long past, there might have been trees, but more than a hundred years ago, if there had been any, they had fallen to the ax to clear the land for fields. The fields were still here, but no longer fields; they had known no plow for decades.

He stood at the end of the ridge and looked back across it, seeing all the miles he had tramped that day, exploring it, getting to know it, although why he felt he should get to know it, he did not understand. But there was some sort of strange compulsion within him that, until this moment, he had not even questioned.

Ancestors of his had trod this land, had lived on it and slept on it, had procreated on it, had known it as he, in a few short days, would never know it. Had known it and had left. Fleeing from some undefinable thing. And that was wrong, he told himself, that was very wrong. The information he'd been given had been somehow garbled. There was nothing here to flee from. Rather, there was something here to live for, to stay for—the closeness to the sky, the cleansing action of the wind, the feeling of intimacy with the soil, the stone, the air, the storm, the very sky itself.

Here his ancestors had walked the land, the last of many who had walked it. For millions of years unknown, perhaps unsuspected, creatures had walked along this ridge. The land was unchanging, geologically ancient, a sentinel of land standing as a milepost amidst other lands that had been forever changing. No great mountain-building surges had distorted it, no glacial action had ground it down, no intercontinental seas had crept over it. For hundreds of millions of years, it had been a freestanding land. It had stayed as it was through all that time, with only the slow and subtle changes brought about by weathering.

He had sat in that room from out of the past and across the table from him had been the rocking woman, rocking even as she drank the tea and nibbled at the bread-and-butter sandwich.

"Thomas," she had said, speaking in her old brittle voice, "I have a job for you to do. It's a job that you must do, that only you can do. It's something that's important to me."

Important to her. Not to someone else, to no one else but her. It made no difference to whom else it might be important or unimportant. To her, it was important and that was all that counted.

He said, amused at her, at her rocking and her intensity, the amusement struggling up through the out-of-placeness of the room, the woman and the house, "Yes, Auntie, what kind of job? If it's one that I can do . . ."

"You can do it," she said, tartly. "Thomas, don't get cute with me. It's something you can do. I want you to write a history of our family, of our branch of the Parkers. I am aware there are many Parkers in the world, but it's our direct line in which my interest lies. You can ignore all collateral branches."

He had stuttered at the thought. "But, Auntie, that would take a long time. It might take years."

"I'll pay you for your time," she'd said. "You write books about other things. Why not about the family? You've just finished a book about paleontology. You spent three years or more on that. You've written books on archaeology, on the old Egyptians, on the ancient trade routes of the world. Even a book on old folklore and superstitions and, if you don't mind my saying so, that was the silliest book I ever read. Popular science, you call it, but it takes a lot of work. You talk to many different people, you dig into dusty records. You could do as much for me."

"But there'd be no market for such a book. No one would be interested."

"I would be interested," she said sharply, the brittle voice cracking. "And who said anything about publication? I simply want to know. I want to know, Thomas, where we came from and who we are and what kind of folks we are. I'll pay you for the job. I'll insist on paying you. I'll pay you . . ."

And she named a sum that quite took his breath away. He had never dreamed she had that kind of money.

"And expenses," she said. "You must keep a very close accounting of everything you spend."

He tried to be gentle with her, for quite obviously she was mad. "But, Auntie, you can get it at a much cheaper figure. There are genealogy people who make a business of tracing back old family histories."

She sniffed at him. "I've had them do the tracing. I'll give you what I have. That should make it easier for you."

"But if you have that—"

"I suspect what they have told me. The record is unclear. To my mind, it is. They try too hard to give you something for your money. They set out to please you. They gild the lily, Thomas. They tell about the manor house in Shropshire, but I'm not sure there ever was a manor house. It sounds just a bit too pat. I want to know if there ever was or not. There was a merchant in London. He dealt in cutlery, they say. That's not enough for me; I must know more of him. Even in our New England, the record is a fuzzy one. Another thing, Thomas. There are no horse thieves mentioned. There are no gallows birds. If there are horse thieves and gallows birds, I want to know of them."

"But, why, Auntie? Why go to all the bother? If it is written, it will never be published. No one but you and I will know. I hand you the manuscript and that is all that happens."

"Thomas," she had said, "I am a mad old woman, a senile old woman, with only a few years left of madness and senility. I should hate to have to beg you."

"You will not have to beg me," he had said. "My feet, my brain, my typewriter are for hire. But I don't understand."

"Don't try to understand," she'd told him. "I've had my way my entire life. Let me continue to."

And, now, it had finally come to this. The long trail of the Parkers had finally come down to this high and windswept ridge with its clattering windmill and the little clumps of trees that had stood around the farmsteads that were no longer there, to the fields that had long been fallow fields, to the little spring beside which he had parked the camper.

He stood there above the cliffs and looked down the slope to where a tangled mass of boulders, some of them barn-size or better, clustered on the hillside, with a few clumps of paper birch growing among them.

Strange, he thought. These were the only trees, other than the homestead trees, that grew upon the ridge, and the only boulder clump. Not, certainly, the residue of glaciation, for the many Ice Age glaciers that had come down across the Middle West had stopped north of here. This country, for many miles around, was known as the driftless area, a magic little pocket that, for some reason not yet known, had been bypassed by the glaciers while they crunched far south on each side of it.

Perhaps, at one time, he told himself, there had been an extrusive rock formation jutting from the ridge, now reduced by weathering to the boulder cluster.

Idly, with no reason to do so, without really intending to, he went down the slope to the cluster with its growth of paper birch.

Close up, the boulders were fully as large as they had appeared from the top of the ridge. Lying among the half dozen or so larger ones were many others, broken fragments that had been chipped off by frost or running water, perhaps aided by the spalling effect of sunlight.

Thomas grinned to himself as he climbed among them, working his way through the cracks and intervals that separated them. A great place for kids to play, he thought. A castle, a fort, a mountain to childish imagination. Blowing dust and fallen leaves through the centuries had found refuge among them and had formed a soil in which were rooted many plants, including an array of wild asters and goldenrod, now coming into bloom.

He found, toward the center of the cluster, a cave or what amounted to a cave. Two of the larger boulders, tipped together, formed a roofed tunnel that ran for a dozen feet or more, six feet wide, the sides of the boulders sloping inward to meet some eight feet above the tunnel's floor. In the center of the tunnel lay a heaped pile of stones. Some kid, perhaps, Thomas told himself, had gathered them many years ago and had hidden them here as an imagined treasure trove.

Walking forward, he stooped, and picked up a fistful of the stones. As his fingers touched them, he knew there was something wrong. These were not ordinary stones. They felt polished and sleek beneath his fingertips, with an oily texture to them.

A year or more ago, in a museum somewhere in the west—perhaps Colorado, although he could not be sure—he had first seen and handled other stones like these.

"Gastroliths," the grey-bearded curator had told him. "Gizzard stones.

We think they came from the stomachs of herbivorous dinosaurs—perhaps all dinosaurs. We can't be certain."

"Like the grit you find in a chicken's craw?" Thomas had asked.

"Exactly," the curator said. "Chickens pick up and swallow tiny stones, grains of sand, bits of shell to help in the digestion of their food. They simply swallow their food. They have no way to chew it. The grit in the gizzard does the chewing for them. There's a good possibility, one might even say, a high possibility, the dinosaurs did the same, ingesting pebbles to do the chewing for them. During their lifetime, they carried these stones, which became highly polished, and then when they died—"

"But the greasiness? The oily feeling?"

The curator shook his head. "We don't know. Dinosaur oil? Oil picked up from being so long in the body?"

"Hasn't anyone tried to extract it? To find out if there is really oil?"

"I don't believe anyone has," the curator said.

And here, in this tunnel, in this cave, whatever one might call it, a pile of gizzard stones.

Squatting, Thomas picked them over, gathering a half dozen of the larger ones, the size of small hen's eggs, or less, feeling the short hairs on his neck tingling with an ancient, atavistic fear that should have been too far in the distant past to have been felt at all.

Here, millions of years ago, perhaps a hundred million years ago, a sick, or injured, dinosaur had crept in to die. Since that time, the flesh was gone, the bones turned into dust, but remaining was the pile of pebbles the long-gone dinosaur had carried in its gizzard.

Clutching the stones in his hand, Thomas settled back on his heels and tried to re-create, within his mind, what had happened here. Here the creature had lain, crouched and quivering, forcing itself, for protection, as deeply into this rock-girt hole as had been possible. It had snorted in its sickness, whimpered with its pain. And it had died here, in this same spot he now occupied. Later had come the little scavenging mammals, tearing at its flesh. . . .

This was not dinosaur land, he thought, not the kind of place the fossil hunters came to hunt the significant debris of the past. There had been dinosaurs here, of course, but there had not been the violent geological processes which would have resulted in the burying and preservation of their bones. Although, if there had been, they'd still be here, for this was ancient land, untouched by the grinding glaciers that must have destroyed, or deeply buried, so many fossil caches.

But here, in this cluster of shattered boulders, he had stumbled on the dying place of a thing that no longer walked on earth. He tried to imagine what form that now extinct creature might have taken, what it would have looked like when it still had life within it. But there was no way that he could know. There had been so many different shapes of them, some of them known by their fossils, perhaps many still unknown.

He fed the selected gizzard stones into the pocket of his jacket and when he crawled from the tunnel and walked out of the pile of boulders, the sun was bisected by the jagged hills far to the west. The wind had fallen with the coming of the evening hours and he walked in a hushed peace along the ridge. Ahead of him, the windmill clattered with subdued tone, clanking as the wheel went slowly round and round.

Short of the windmill, he went down the slope to the head of a deep ravine that plunged down toward the river. Here, beside the spring, parked beneath a massive cottonwood, his camper shone whitely in the creeping dusk. Well before he reached it, he could hear the sound of water gushing from the hillside. In the woods farther down the slope, he could hear the sound of birds settling for the coming night.

He rekindled the campfire and cooked his supper and later sat beside the fire, knowing that now it was time to leave. His job was finished. He had traced out the long line of Parkers to this final place, where shortly after the Civil War, Ned Parker had come to carve out a farm.

In Shropshire there had been, indeed, a manor house, but, if one were to be truthful, not much of a manor house. And he had found, as well, that the London merchant had not dealt in cutlery, but in wool. There had been no horse thieves, no gallows birds, no traitors, no real scamps of any kind. The Parkers had been, in fact, a plodding sort of people, not given to greatness, nor to evil. They had existed nonspectacularly, as honest yeomen, honest merchants, farming their small acres, managing their small businesses. And finally crossing the water to New England, not as pioneers, but as settlers. A few of them had fought in the Revolutionary War, but were not distinguished warriors. Others had fought in the Civil War, but had been undistinguished there, as well.

There had, of course, been a few notable, but not spectacular exceptions. There had been Molly Parker, who had been sentenced to the ducking stool because she talked too freely about certain neighbors. There had been Jonathon, who had been sentenced to the colonies because he had the bad judgment of having fallen into debt. There had been a certain Teddy Parker, a churchman of some sort (the evidence was not entirely clear), who had fought a prolonged and bitter battle in the court with a parishioner over pasture rights held by the church which had been brought into question.

But these were minor matters. They scarcely caused a ripple on the placidity of the Parker tribe.

It was time to leave, he told himself. He had tracked the family, or this one branch of the family, down to this high ridge. He had found the old homestead, the house burned many years ago, now marked only by the cellar excavation, half filled with the litter of many years. He had seen the windmill and had stood beside the whistling well, which had not whistled for him.

Time to leave, but he did not want to leave. He felt a strange reluctance at stirring from this place. As if there were more to come, more that might be learned—although he knew there wasn't.

Was this reluctance because he had fallen in love with this high and windy hill, finding in it some of the undefinable charm that must have been felt by his great-great-grandfather? He had the feeling of being trapped and chained, of having found the one place he was meant to be. He had, he admitted to himself, the sense of belonging, drawn and bound by ancestral roots.

That was ridiculous, he told himself. By no matter what weird biochemistry within his body he had come to think so, he could have no real attachment to this place. He'd give himself another day or two and then he'd leave. He'd make that much concession to this feeling of attachment. Perhaps, by the end of another day or two, he'd have enough of it, the enchantment fallen from him.

He pushed the fire more closely together, heaped more wood upon it. The flames caught and flared up. He leaned back in his camp chair and stared out into the darkness, beyond the firelit circle. Out in the dark were darker humps, waiting, watching shapes, but they were, he knew, no more than clumps of bushes—a small plum tree or a patch of hazel. A glow in the eastern sky forecast a rising moon. A quickening breeze, risen after the sunset calm, rattled the leaves of the big cottonwood that stood above the camp.

He scrooched around to sit sidewise in the chair and when he did, the gizzard stones in his jacket pocket caught against the chair arm and pressed hard against his hip.

Reaching a hand into his pocket, he took them out. Flat upon his palm, he held them out so the firelight fell upon them. He rubbed a thumb against them. They had the feel and look of velvet. They glistened in the dancing firelight. The gloss on them was higher than was ever found in the polished pebbles that turned up in river gravel. Turning them, he saw that all the depressions, all the concave surfaces, were as highly polished as the rest of the stone.

The stones found in river gravel had obtained their polish by sand action, swirling or washed along the riverbed. The gizzard stones had been polished by being rubbed together by the tough contracting muscles of a gizzard. Perhaps some sand in the gizzard, as well, he thought, for in jerking up a plant from sandy soil, the dinosaur would not be too finicky. It would ingest the sand, the clinging bits of soil, along with the plant. For years, these stones had been subjected to continuous polishing action.

Slowly, he kept turning the stones with a thumb and finger of the other hand, fascinated by them. Suddenly, one of them flashed in the firelight. He turned it back and it flashed again. There was, he saw, some sort of an irregularity on its surface.

He dropped the other two into his pocket and leaned forward toward the fire with the one that had flashed lying in his palm. Turning it so that the firelight fell full upon it, he bent his head close above it, trying to puzzle out what might be there. It looked like a line of writing, but in characters he had never seen before. And that had to be wrong, of course, for at the time the dinosaur swallowed the stone, there had been no such thing as writing. Unless someone, later on, within the last century or so— He shook his head in puzzlement. That made no sense, either.

With the stone clutched in his hand, he went into the camper, rummaged in a desk drawer until he found a small magnifying glass. He lit a gas lantern and turned it up, placed it on the desk top. Pulling over a chair, he sat down, held the stone in the lantern light, and peered at it through the glass.

If not writing, there was something there, engraved into the stone—the engraving worn as smooth and sleek as all the rest of it. It was no recent work. There was no possibility, he told himself, that the line that resembled engraving could be due to natural causes. He tried to make out exactly what it was, but in the flicker of the lantern, it was difficult to do so. There seemed to be two triangles, apex pointing down in one, up in the other and the two of them connected midpoint by a squiggly line.

But that was as much as he could make of it. The engraving, if that was what it was, was so fine, so delicate, that it was hard to see the details, even with the glass. Perhaps a higher-power glass might show more, but this was the only magnifier he had.

He laid the stone and glass on the desk top and went outside. As he came down the steps, he felt the differentness. There had been blacker shapes out in the darkness and he had recognized them as clumps of hazel or small trees. But now the shapes were bigger and were moving.

He stopped at the foot of the steps and tried to make them out, to pinpoint the moving shapes, but his eyes failed to delineate the shapes, although at times they seemed to catch the movement.

You're insane, he told himself. There is nothing out there. A cow or steer, perhaps. He had been told, he remembered, that the present owners of the land, at times, ran cattle on it, pasturing them through the summer, penning them for finishing in the fall. But in his walks about the ridge, he'd not seen any cattle and if there were cattle out there, he thought that he would know it. If cattle moved about, there should be a crackling of their hocks, snuffling as they nosed at grass or leaves.

He went to the chair and sat down solidly in it. He reached for a stick and pushed the fire together, then settled back. He was too old a hand at camping, he assured himself, to allow himself to imagine things out in the dark. Yet, somehow, he had got the wind up.

Nothing moved beyond the reaches of the firelight and still, despite all his arguments with himself, he could feel them out there, sense them with a sense he had not known before, had never used before. What unsuspected abilities and capacities, he wondered, might lie within the human mind?

Great dark shapes that moved sluggishly, that hitched along by inches, always out of actual sight, but still circling in close to the edge of light, just beyond its reach.

He sat rigid in the chair, feeling his body tightening up, his nerves stretching to the tension of a violin string. Sitting there and listening for the sound that never came, for the movement that could only be sensed, not seen.

They were out there, said this strange sense he had never known before, while his mind, his logical human mind, cried out against it. There is no evidence, said his human mind. There need be no evidence, said this other part of him; we know.

They kept moving in. They were piling up, for there were a lot of them. They were deadly silent and deliberate in the way they moved. If he threw a chunk of wood out into the darkness, the chunk of wood would hit them.

He did not throw the wood.

He sat, unmoving, in the chair. I'll wear them out, he told himself.

If they are really out there, I will wear them out. This is my fire, this is my ground. I have a right to be here.

He tried to analyze himself. Was he frightened? He wasn't sure. Perhaps not gibbering frightened, but probably frightened otherwise. And, despite what he said, did he have the right to be here? He had a right to build the fire, for it had been mankind, only mankind, who had made use of fire. None of the others did. But the land might be another thing; the land might not be his. There might be a long-term mortgage on it from another time.

The fire died down and the moon came up over the ridgetop. It was almost full, but its light was feeble-ghostly. The light showed nothing out beyond the campfire, although, watching closely, it seemed to Thomas that he could see massive movement farther down the slope, among the trees.

The wind had risen and from far off, he heard the faint clatter of the windmill. He craned his head to try to see the windmill, but the moonlight was too pale to see it.

By degrees, he relaxed. He asked himself, in something approaching fuzzy wonder, what the hell had happened? He was not a man given to great imagination. He did not conjure ghosts. That something incomprehensible had taken place, there could be little doubt—but his interpretation of it? That was the catch; he had made no interpretation. He had held fast to his life-long position as observer.

He went into the camper and found the bottle of whiskey and brought it out to the fire, not bothering with a glass. He sat sprawled in the chair, holding the bottle with one hand, resting the bottom of it on his gut. The bottom of the bottle was a small circle of coldness against his gut.

Sitting there, he remembered the old black man he had talked with one afternoon, deep in Alabama, sitting on the ramshackle porch of the neat, ramshackle house, with the shade of a chinaberry tree shielding them from the heat of the late-afternoon sun. The old man sat easily in his chair, every now and then twirling the cane he held, its point against the porch floor, holding it easily by the shaft, twirling it every now and then, so that the crook of it went round and round.

"If you're going to write your book the way it should be written," the old black man had said, "you got to look deeper than the Devil. I don't suppose I should be saying this, but since you promise you will not use my name . . ."

"I won't use your name," Thomas had told him.

"I was a preacher for years," the old man said. "And in those years, I leaned plenty on the Devil. I held him up in scorn; I threatened people with him. I said, 'If you don't behave yourselves, Old Devil, he will drag you down them long, long stairs, hauling you by your heels, with your head bumping on the steps, while you scream and plead and cry. But Old Devil, he won't pay no attention to your screaming and your pleading. He won't even hear you. He'll just haul you down those stairs and cast you in the pit.' The Devil, he was something those people could understand. They'd heard of him for years. They knew what he looked like and the kind of manners that he had. . . ."

"Did it ever help?" Thomas had asked. "Threatening them with the Devil, I mean."

"I can't be sure. I think sometimes it did. Not always, but sometimes. It was worth the try."

"But you tell me I must go beyond the Devil."

"You white folks don't know. You don't feel it in your bones. You're too far from the jungle. My people, we know. Or some of us do. We're only a few lifetimes out of Africa."

"You mean—"

"I mean you must go way back. Back beyond the time when there were any men at all. Back to the older eons. The Devil is a Christian evil—a gentle evil, if you will, a watered-down version of real evil, a shadow of what there was and maybe is. He came to us by way of Babylon and Egypt and even the Babylonians and Egyptians had forgotten, or had never known, what evil really was. I tell you the Devil isn't a patch on the idea he is based on. Only a faint glimmer of the evil that was sensed by early men—not seen, but sensed, in those days when men chipped the first flint tools, while he fumbled with the idea of the use of fire."

"You're saying that there was evil before man? That figures of evil are not man's imagining?"

The old man grinned, a bit lopsidedly, at him, but still a serious grin. "Why should man," he asked, "take to himself the sole responsibility for the concept of evil?"

He'd spent, Thomas remembered, a pleasant afternoon on the porch, in the shade of the chinaberry tree, talking with the old man and drinking elderberry wine. And, at other times and in other places, he had talked with other men and from what they'd told him had been able to write a short and not too convincing chapter on the proposition that a primal evil may have been the basis for all the evil figures mankind had conjured up. The book had sold well, still was selling. It had been worth all the work he had put into it. And the best part of it was that he had escaped scot-free. He did not believe in the Devil or any of the rest of it. Although, reading his book, a lot of other people did.

The fire burned down, the bottle was appreciably less full than when he'd started on it. The landscape lay mellow in the faint moonlight. Tomorrow, he told himself, I'll spend tomorrow here, then I'll be off again. Aunt Elsie's job is finished.

He got up from the chair and went in to bed. Just before he went to bed, it seemed to him that he could hear, again, the creaking and the scuffing of Auntie's rocking chair.

After breakfast, he climbed the ridge again to the site of the Parker homestead. He'd walked past it on his first quick tour of the ridge, only pausing long enough to identify it.

A massive maple tree stood at one corner of the cellar hole. Inside the hole, raspberry bushes had taken root. Squatting on the edge of the hole, he used a stick he had picked up to pry into the loam. Just beneath the surface lay flakes of charcoal, adding a blackness to the soil.

He found a bed of rosemary. Picking a few of the leaves, he crushed them in his fingers, releasing the sharp smell of mint. To the east of the cellar hole, a half dozen apple trees still survived, scraggly, branches broken by the winds, but still bearing small fruit. He picked one of the apples and when he bit into it, he sensed a taste out of another time, a flavor not to be found in an apple presently marketed. He found a still flourishing patch of rhubarb, a few scrawny rosebushes with red hips waiting for the winter birds, a patch of iris so crowded that corms had been pushed above the surface of the ground.

Standing beside the patch of iris, he looked around. Here, at one time, more than a century ago, his ancestor had built a homestead—a house, a barn, a chicken house, a stable, a granary, a corncrib, and perhaps other buildings, had settled down as a farmer, a soldier returned from the wars, had lived here for a term of years and then had left. Not only he but all the others who had lived on this ridge as well.

On this, his last trip to complete the charge that had been put upon him by that strange old lady hunched in her rocking chair, he had stopped at the little town of Patch Grove to ask his way. A couple of farmers sitting on a bench outside a barbershop had looked at him—reticent, disbelieving, perhaps somewhat uneasy.

"Parker's Ridge?" they'd asked. "You want to know the way to Parker's Ridge?"

"I have business there," he'd told them.

"There ain't no one to do business with on Parker's Ridge," they'd told him. "No one ever goes there."

But when he'd insisted, they'd finally told him. "There's only one ridge, really," they'd said, "but it's divided into two parts. You go north of town until you reach a cemetery. Just short of the cemetery, you take a left. That puts you on Military Ridge. You keep to the high ground. There are some roads turning off, but you stay on top the ridge."

"But that you say is Military Ridge. What I want is Parker's Ridge."

"One and the same," said one of the men. "When you reach the end of it, that's Parker's Ridge. It stands high above the river. Ask along the way."

So he'd gone north of town and taken a left before he reached the cemetery. The ridge road was a secondary route, a farm road, either unpaved or paved so long ago and so long neglected that it bore little trace of paving. Small farms were strung along it, little ridgetop farms, groups of falling-down buildings surrounded by scant and runty fields. Farm dogs raced out to bark at him as he passed the farms.

Five miles down the road a man was taking mail out of a mailbox. Thomas pulled up. "I'm looking for Parker's Ridge," he said. "Am I getting close?"

The man stuffed the three or four letters he'd taken from the box into the rear pocket of his overalls. He stepped down to the road and stood beside the car. He was a large man, rawboned. His face was creased and wrinkled and wore a week of beard.

"You're almost there," he said. "Another three miles or so. But would you tell me, stranger, why you want to go there?"

"Just to look around," said Thomas.

The man shook his head. "Nothing there to look at. No one there. Used to be people there. Half a dozen farms. People living on them, working the farms. But that was long ago. Sixty years ago—no, maybe more than that. Now they all are gone. Someone owns the land, but I don't know who. Someone runs cattle there. Goes out West in the spring to buy them, runs them on pasture until fall, then rounds them up and feeds them grain, finishing them for the market."

"You're sure there's no one there?"

"No one there now. Used to be. Buildings, too. Houses and old farm buildings. Not any longer. Some of them burned. Kids, most likely, setting a match to them. Kids probably thought they were doing right. The ridge has a bad reputation."

"What do you mean, a bad reputation? How come a bad—"

"There's a whistling well, for one thing. Although I don't know what the well has to do with it."

"I don't understand. I've never heard of a whistling well."

The man laughed. "That was old Ned Parker's well. He was one of the first settlers out there on the ridge. Come home from the Civil War and bought land out there. Got it cheap. Civil War veterans could buy government land at a dollar an acre and, at that time, this was all government land. Ned could have bought rich, level land out on Blake's Prairie, some twenty miles or so from here, for the same dollar an acre. But not him. He knew what he wanted. He wanted a place where timber would be handy, where there'd be a running spring for water, where he'd be close to hunting and fishing."

"I take it the place didn't work out too well."

"Worked out all right except for the water. There was one big spring he counted on, but a few dry years came along and the spring began running dry. It never did run dry, but Ned was afraid it would. It is still running. But Ned, he wasn't going to be caught without water, so, by God, he drilled a well. Right on top that ridge. Got in a well driller and put him to work. Hit a little water, but not much. Went deeper and deeper and still not enough. Until the well driller said, 'Ned, the only way to get water is to go down to the river level. But the rest of the way it is going to cost you a dollar and a quarter a foot.' Now, in those days, a dollar and a quarter was a lot of money, but Ned had so much money sunk in the well already that he said to go ahead. So the well driller went ahead. Deepest well anyone had ever heard of. People used to come and just stand there, watching the well being drilled. My grandfather told me this, having heard it from his father. When the hole reached river level, they did find water, a lot of water. A well that would never run dry. But pumping was a problem. That water had to be pumped straight up a long way. So Ned bought the biggest, heaviest, strongest windmill that was made and that windmill set him back a lot of cash. But Ned never complained. He wanted water and now he had it. The windmill never gave no trouble, like a lot of windmills did. It was built to last. It's still there and still running, although it's not pumping water anymore. The pump shaft broke years ago. So did the vane control, the lever to shut off the wheel. Now that mill runs all the time. There's no way to shut it off. Running without grease, it's gotten noiser and noisier. Some day, of course, it will stop, just break down."

"You told me a whistling well. You told me everything else, but nothing about a whistling well."

"Now that's a funny thing," the farmer said. "At times, the well whistled. Standing on the platform, over the bore, you can feel a rush of wind. When the rush gets strong enough, it is said to make a whistling sound. People say it still does, although I couldn't say. Some people used to say it only whistled when the wind was from the north, but I can't swear to that, either. You know how people are. They always have answers for everything whether they know anything about it or not. I understand that those who said it only whistled when the wind was from the north explained it by saying that a strong north wind would blow directly against the cliffs facing the river. There are caves and crevices in those cliffs and they said some of the crevices ran back into the ridge and that the well cut through some of them. So a north wind would blow straight back along the crevices until it hit the well and then come rushing up the bore."

"It sounds a bit far-fetched to me," said Thomas.

The farmer scratched his head. "Well, I don't know. I can't tell you. It's only what the old-time people said. And they're all gone now. Left their places many years ago. Just pulled up and left."

"All at once?"

"Can't tell you that, either. I don't think so. Not all in a bunch. First one family and then another, until they all were gone. That happened long ago. No one would remember now. No one knows why they left. There are strange stories—not stories, really, just things you hear. I don't know what went on. No one killed, so far as I know. No one hurt. Just strange things. I tell you, young man, unless I had urgent business there, I wouldn't venture out on Parker's Ridge. Neither would any of my neighbors. None of us could give you reasons, but we wouldn't go."

"I'll be careful," Thomas promised.

Although, as it turned out, there'd been no reason to be careful. Rather, once he'd reached the ridge, he'd felt that inexplicable sense of belonging, of being in a place where he was supposed to be. Walking the ridge, he'd felt that this barren backbone of land had transferred, or was in the process of transferring, its personality to him and he'd taken it and made it fit him like a cloak, wrapping himself in it, asking himself: Can a land have a personality?

The road, once Military Ridge had ended beyond the last farmhouse and Parker's Ridge began, had dwindled to a track, only a grassy hint that a road once had existed there. Far down the ridge he had sighted the windmill, a spidery construction reared against the sky, its wheel clanking in the breeze. He had driven on past it and then had stopped the camper, walking down the slope until he had located the still-flowing spring at the head of the ravine. Going back to the camper, he had driven it off the track and down the sloping hillside, to park it beneath the cottonwood that stood above the spring. That had been the day before yesterday and he had one more day left before he had to leave.

Standing now, beside the iris bed, he looked around him and tried to imagine the kind of place this may have been—to see it with the eyes of his old ancestor, home from the wars and settled on acres of his own. There would still have been deer, for this old man had wanted hunting, and it had not been until the great blizzard of the early 1880s that the wild game of this country had been decimated. There would have been wolves to play havoc with the sheep, for in those days, everyone kept sheep. There would have been guinea fowls whistling in the hedgerows, for, in those days, as well, everyone kept guineas. And the chances were that there would have been peacocks, geese, ducks, chickens wandering the yards. Good horses in the stable, for everyone in those days placed great emphasis on good horses. And, above all, the great pride in one's own acreage, in the well-kept barns, the herds of cattle, the wheat, the corn, the newly planted orchard. And the old man, himself, he wondered—what kind of man was old Ned Parker, walking the path from the house up to the windmill. A stout and stocky man, perhaps, for the Parkers ran to stocky. An erect old man, for he'd been four years a soldier in the Union Army. Walking, perhaps, with his hands clasped behind his back, and head thrown back to stare up at the windmill, his present pride and glory.

Grandfather, Thomas asked himself, what happened? What is this all about? Did you feel belonging as I feel belonging? Did you feel the openness of this high ridge, the windswept sense of intimacy, the personality of the land as I feel it now? Was it here then, as well as now? And if that should have been the case, as it certainly must have been, why did you leave?

There was no answer, of course. He knew there would not be. There was no one now to answer. But even as he asked the question, he knew that this was a land loaded with information, with answers if one could only dig them out. There is something worth knowing here, he told himself, if one could only find it. The land was ancient. It had stood and watched and waited as ages swept over it, like cloud shadows passing across the land. Since time immemorial, it had stood sentinel above the river and had noted all that had come to pass.

There had been amphibians floundering and bellowing in the river swamps, there had been herds of dinosaurs and those lonely ones that had preyed upon the herds, there had been rampaging titanotheres and the lordly mammoth and the mastodon. There had been much to see and note.

The old black man had said look back, look back beyond the time of man, to the forgotten primal days. To the day, Thomas wondered, when each worshipping dinosaur had swallowed one stone encised with a magic line of cryptic symbols as an earnest that it held faith in a primal god?

Thomas shook himself. You're mad, he told himself. Dinosaurs had no gods. Only men had the intelligence that enabled them to create their gods.

He left the iris patch and paced slowly up the hill, heading for the windmill, following the now nonexistent path that old Ned Parker must have followed more than a hundred years before.

He tilted back his head to look up at the spinning wheel, moving slowly in the gentle morning breeze. So high against the sky, he thought, so high above the world.

The platform of the well was built of hewn oak timbers, weathered by the years, but still as sound as the day they had been laid. The outer edge of them was powdery and crumbling, but the powdering and the crumbling did not go deep. Thomas stooped and flicked at the wood with a fingernail and a small fragment of the oak came free, but beneath it the wood was solid. The timbers would last, he knew, for another hundred years, perhaps several hundred years.

As he stood beside the platform, he became aware of the sound that came from the well. Nothing like a whistle, but a slight moaning, as if an animal somewhere near its bottom were moaning in its sleep. Something alive, he told himself, something moaning gently far beneath the surface, a great heart and a great brain beating somewhere far below in the solid rock.

The brains and hearts of olden dinosaurs, he thought, or the gods of dinosaurs. And brought himself up short. You're at it again, he told himself, unable to shake this nightmare fantasy of the dinosaur. The finding of the heap of gizzard stones must have left a greater mark upon him than he had thought at first.

It was ridiculous on the face of it. The dinosaurs had had dim intellects that had done no more than drive them to the preservation of their own lives and the procreation of their kind. But logic did not help; illogic surged within him. No brain capacity, of course, but some other organ—perhaps supplementary to the brain—that was concerned with faith?

He grew rigid with anger at himself, with disgust at such flabby thinking, at a thought that could be little better than the thinking of the rankest cult enthusiast, laced with juvenility.

He left the well and walked up to the track he had followed coming in. He walked along it rapidly, bemused at the paths his mind had taken. The place, he thought, for all its openness, all its reaching toward the sky, all its geographic personality, worked a strange effect upon one. As if it were not of a piece with the rest of the earth, as if it stood apart, wondering, as he thought this, if that could have been the reason all the families left.

He spent the day upon the ridge, covering the miles of it, poking in its corners, forgetting the bemusement and the anger, forgetting even the very strangeness of it, glorying, rather, in the strangeness and that fascinating sense of freedom and of oneness with the sky. The rising wind from the west tugged and pulled at him. The land was clean, not with a washed cleanness but with the clean of a thing that had never been dirty, that had stayed fresh and bright from the day of its creation, untouched by the greasy fingers of the world.

He found the gaping cellar-holes of other farmhouses and squatted near them almost worshipfully, seeking out the lilac clumps, the crumbling remains of vanished fences, the still remaining stretches of earlier paths, now not going anywhere, the flat limestone slabs that had formed doorsteps or patios. And, from these, he formed within his mind the profiles of the families that had lived here for a time, perhaps attracted to it even as he found himself attracted to it, and who, in the end, had fled. He tested the wind and the highness, the antiseptic ancientness and tried to find within them the element of horror that might have brought about their fleeing. But he found no horror; all he found was a rough sort of serenity.

He thought again of the old lady in the rocking chair that day he had sat with her at tea in an old New England house, eating thin-sliced bread and butter. She was touched, of course. She had to be. There was no earthly reason she should want to know so desperately the details of the family line.

He had told her nothing of his investigations. He had reported every now and then by very formal letters to let her know he was still working on the project. But she would not know the story of the Parkers until he had put the manuscript into her clawlike hands. She would find some surprises, he was sure. No horse thieves, no gallows birds, but there had been others she could not have guessed and in whom she could take no pride. If it was pride that she was seeking. He was not sure it was. There had been the medicine-show Parker of the early nineteenth century who had been run out of many towns because of his arrogance and the inferiority of his product. There had been a renegade slave trader in the middle of the century, the barber in an Ohio town who had run off with the wife of the Baptist minister, the desperado who had died in a hail of withering gunfire in a Western cattle town. Perhaps, he thought, Aunt Elsie might like the desperado. A strange tribe, this branch of the Parkers, ending with the man who had drilled a well that could have loosed upon the countryside the spawn of ancient evil. And stopped himself at that. You do not know it for a fact, he sternly told himself. You don't even have the smallest ground for slightest speculation. You're letting this place get to you.

The sun was setting when he came back down the track, turning off to go down to the camper parked beside the spring. He had spent the day upon the ridge and he would not spend another. Tomorrow he would leave. There was no reason for staying longer. There might be something here that needed finding, but nothing he could find.

He was hungry, for he had not eaten since breakfast. The fire was dead and he rekindled it, cooked a meal and ate it as the early-autumn dusk crept in. Tired from his day of tramping, he still felt no need of sleep. He sat in the camp chair and listened to the night close down. The eastern sky flushed with the rising moon and down in the hills that rose above the river valley a couple of owls chortled back and forth.

Finally, he rose from the chair and went into the camper to get the bottle. There was some whiskey left and he might as well finish it off. Tomorrow, if he wished, he could buy another. In the camper, he lit the lantern and placed it on the desk. In the light of the lantern, he saw the gizzard stone, where he had left it on the desk top the night before. He picked it up and turned it until he could see the faint inscription on it. He bent forward to try to study the faint line, wondering if he might have mistaken some small imperfection in the stone as writing, feeling a nagging doubt as to the validity of his examination of it the night before. But the cryptic symbols still were there. They were not the sort of tracery that could occur naturally. Was there anyone on earth, he wondered, who could decipher the message on the stone? And even asking it, he doubted it. Whatever the characters might be, they had been graven millions of years before the first thing even faintly resembling man had walked upon the earth. He dropped the stone in his jacket pocket, found the bottle, and went out to the fire.

There was an uneasiness in him, an uneasiness that seemed to hang in the very air. Which was strange, because he had not noted the uneasiness when he had left the fire to go into the camper. It was something that had come in that small space of time he'd spent inside the camper.

He studied the darkening terrain carefully and there was movement out beyond the campfire circle, but it was, he decided, only the movement of trees shaken by the wind. For in the short time since early evening, the wind had shifted to the north and was blowing up a gale. The leaves of the huge cottonwood under which the camper sat were singing, that eerie kind of song that leaves sing in a heavy wind. From the ridge above came the banging clatter of the windmill—and something else as well. A whistle. The well was whistling. He heard the whistle only at intervals, but as he listened more attentively to catch the sound of it, it became louder and consistent, a high, unbroken whistling that had no break or rhythm, going on and on.

Now there was movement, he was certain, beyond the campfire light that could not be accounted for by the thrashing of the trees. There were heavy thumpings and bumpings, as if great ungainly bodies were moving in the dark. He leaped from the chair and stood rigid in the flickering firelight. The bottle slipped from his fingers and he did not stoop to pick it up. He felt the panic rising in him and even as he tried to brush it off, his nerves and muscles tightened involuntarily in an atavistic fear—fear of the unknown, of the bumping in the dark, of the uncanny whistling of the well. He yelled, not at what might be out beyond the campfire, but at himself, what remained of logic, what remained of mind raging at the terrible fear that had gripped his body. Then the logic and the mind succumbed to the fear and, in blind panic, he ran for the camper.

He leaped into the cab, slammed himself into the seat, reached out for the starting key. At the first turn of the key, the motor exploded into life. When he turned on the headlights, he seemed to see the bumping, humping shapes, although even in the light he could not be sure. They were, if they were there at all, no more than heavier shadows among all the other shadows.

Sobbing in haste, he put the engine into gear, backed the camper up the slope and in a semicircle. Then, with it headed up the slope, he pushed the gear to forward. The four-wheel drive responded and, slowly gathering speed, the camper went charging up the hill toward the track down which he had come, past the thumping windmill, only hours before.

The spidery structure of the windmill stood stark against the moonwashed sky. The blades of the rotating wheel were splashes of light, catching and shattering the feeble light of the newly risen moon. Over it all rose the shrieking whistle of the well. The farmer, Thomas remembered, had said that the well whistled only when the wind blew from the north.

The camper reached the track, barely visible in the flare of headlights, and Thomas jerked the wheel to follow it. The windmill now was a quarter of a mile away, perhaps less than a quarter mile. In less than a minute, he would be past it, running down the ridge, heading for the safety of another world. For this ridge, he told himself, was not of this world. It was a place set apart, a small wedge of geography that did not quite belong. Perhaps, he thought, that had been a part of its special charm, that when one entered here, he shed the sorrows and the worries of the real world. But, to counter-balance that, he also found something more frightening than the real world could conjure up.

Peering through the windshield, it seemed to Thomas that the windmill had somehow altered, had lost some of its starkness, that it had blurred and changed—that, in fact, it had come alive and was engaging in a clumsy sort of dance, although there was a certain flowing smoothness to the clumsiness.

He had lost some of his fear, was marginally less paralyzed with fear than he had been before. For now he was in control, to a certain extent at least, and not hemmed in by horrors from which he could not escape. In a few more seconds, he would be past the windmill, fleeing downwind from the whistle, putting the nightmare all behind him. Putting, more than likely, his imagination all behind him, for the windmill could not be alive, there were no humping shapes . . .

Then he realized that he was wrong. It was not imagination. The windmill was alive. He could see its aliveness more clearly than imagination could have shown it. The structure was festooned and enwrapped by wriggling, climbing shapes, none of which he could see in their entirety, for they were so entangled in their climbing that no one of them could be seen in their entirety. There was about them a drippiness, a loathesomeness, a scaliness that left him gulping in abject terror. And there were, as well, he saw, others of them on the ground surrounding the well, great dark, humped figures that lurched along until they crossed the track.

Instinctively, without any thought at all, he pushed the accelerator to the floorboards and the camper leaped beneath him, heading for the massed bodies. He would crash into them, he thought, and it had been a silly thing to do. He should have tried to go around them. But now it was too late; panic had taken over and there was nothing he could do.

The engine spit and coughed, then slobbered to a halt. The camper rolled forward, came to a staggering stop. Thomas twisted the starter key. The motor turned and coughed. But it would not start. All the dark humps bumped themselves around to look at him. He could see no eyes, but he could feel them looking. Frantically, he cranked the engine. Now it didn't even cough. The damn thing's flooded, said one corner of his mind, the one corner of his mind not flooded by his fear.

He took his hand off the key and sat back. A terrible coldness came upon him—a coldness and a hardness. The fear was gone, the panic gone; all that remained was the coldness and the hardness. He unlatched the door and pushed it open. Deliberately, he stepped down to the ground and moved away from the camper. The windmill, freighted with its monsters, loomed directly overhead. The massed humped shapes blocked the track. Heads, if they were heads, moved back and forth. There was the sense of twitching tails, although he could see no tails. The whistling filled the universe, shrill, insistent, unending. The windmill blades, unhampered by the climbing shapes, clattered in the wind.

Thomas moved forward. "I'm coming through," he said, aloud. "Make way for me. I am coming through." And it seemed to him that as he walked slowly forward, he was walking to a certain beat, to a drum that only he could hear. Startled, he realized that the beat he was walking to was the creaking of that rocking chair in the old New England house.

Illogic said to him, *It's all that you can do. It's the only thing to do. You cannot run, to be pulled down squealing. It's the one thing a man can do.*

He walked slowly, but deliberately, marching to the slow, deliberate creaking of the rocking chair. "Make way," he said. "I am the thing that came after you."

And they seemed to say to him, through the shrill whistling of the well, the clatter of the windmill blades, the creaking of the chair, *Pass, strange one. For you carry with you the talisman we gave our people. You have with you the token of your faith.*

Not my faith, he thought. Not my talisman. That's not the reason you do not dare to touch me. I swallowed no gizzard stone.

But you are brother, they told him, *to the one who did.*

They parted, pulled aside to clear the track for him, to make way for him. He glanced to neither left nor right, pretending they were not there at all, although he knew they were. He could smell the rancid, swamp-smell of them. He could feel the presence of them. He could feel the reaching out, as if they meant to stroke him, to pet him as one might a dog or cat, but staying the touch before it came upon him.

He walked the track and left them behind, grouped in their humpiness all about the well. He left them deep in time. He left them in another world and headed for his own, striding, still slowly, slow enough so they would not think that he was running from them, but a bit faster than he had before, down the track that bisected Parker's Ridge.

He put his hand into the pocket of the jacket, his fingers gripping the greasy smoothness of the gizzard stone. The creaking of the chair still was in his mind and he still marched to it, although it was growing fainter now.

Brother, he thought, they said brother to me. And indeed I am. All life on earth is brother and each of us can carry, if we wish, the token of our faith.

He said aloud, to that ancient dinosaur that had died so long ago among the tumbled boulders, "Brother, I am glad to know you. I am glad I found you. Glad to carry the token of your faith."

THE PECULIAR DEMESNE

By RUSSELL KIRK

Russell Kirk is a political theorist, essayist, lecturer, scholar, novelist, and short-story writer, and author of the watershed book The Conservative Mind. *From his home in the small town of Mecosta, Michigan, Kirk contributes regularly to William F. Buckley, Jr.'s,* The National Review, *and his polemic writings are valued and respected by those on both sides of the political aisle. Dr. Kirk has written a number of remarkable uncanny tales, which at once are firmly traditional, often noticeably allegorical, and tinged with Old Testament morality. This one, an episode in the career of his shadowy hero Manfred Arcane—who figures in two of Kirk's novels,* A Creature of the Twilight *and* Lord of the Hollow Dark*—is a baroque entertainment of uncommon quality, set in an Africa on no known map.*

"The imagination of man's heart is evil from his youth."
—Gen. VIII: 21

Two black torch-bearers preceding us and two following, Mr. Thomas Whiston and I walked through twilight alleys of Haggat toward Manfred Arcane's huge house, on Christmas Eve. Big flashlights would have done as well as torches, and there were some few streetlamps even in the lanes of the ancient dyers' quarter, where Arcane, disdaining modernity, chose to live; but Arcane, with his baroque conceits and crotchets, had insisted upon sending his linkmen for us.

The gesture pleased burly Tom Whiston, executive vice-president for African imports of Cosmopolitan-Anarch Oil Corporation. Whiston had not been in Haggat before, or anywhere in Hamnegri. Considerably to his vexation, he had not been granted an audience with Achmet ben Ali, Hereditary President of Hamnegri and Sultan in Kalidu. With a sellers' market in petroleum, sultans may be so haughty as they please, and Achmet the Pious disliked men of commerce.

Yet His Excellency Manfred Arcane, Minister without Portfolio in the Sultan's cabinet, had sent to Whiston and to me holograph invitations to his Christmas Eve party—an event of a sort infrequent in the Moslem city of Haggat, ever since most of the French had departed during the civil wars. I had assured Whiston that Arcane was urbane and amusing, and that under the Sultan Achmet, no one was more powerful than Manfred Arcane. So this invitation consoled Tom Whiston considerably.

"If this Arcane is more or less European," Whiston asked me, "how can he be a kind of grand vizier in a country like this? Is the contract really up to him, Mr. Yawby?"

"Why," I said, "Arcane can be what he likes: when he wants to be taken for a native of Haggat, he can look it. The Hereditary President and Sultan couldn't manage without him. Arcane commands the mercenaries, and for all practical purposes he directs foreign relations—including the oil contracts. In Hamnegri, he's what Glubb Pasha was in Jordan once, and more. I was consul here at Haggat for six years, and was made consul general three years ago, so I know Arcane as well as any foreigner knows him. Age does not stale, nor custom wither, this Manfred Arcane."

Now we stood at the massive carved wooden doors of Arcane's house, which had been built in the seventeenth century by some purse-proud Kalidu slave trader. Two black porters with curved swords at their belts bowed to us and swung the doors wide. Whiston hesitated just a moment before entering, not to my surprise; there was a kind of magnificent grimness about the place which might give one a grue.

From somewhere inside that vast hulking old house, a soprano voice, sweet and strong, drifted to us. "There'll be women at this party?" Whiston wanted to know.

"That must be Melchiora singing—Madame Arcane. She's Sicilian, and looks like a *femme fatale.*" I lowered my voice. "For that matter, she *is* a *femme fatale*. During the insurrection four years ago, she shot a half dozen rebels with her own rifle. Yes, there will be a few ladies: not a harem. Arcane's a Christian of sorts. I expect our party will be pretty much *en famille*—which is to say, more or less British, Arcane having been educated in England long ago. This house is managed by a kind of chatelaine, a very old Englishwoman, Lady Grizel Fergusson. You'll meet some officers of the IPV—the Interracial Peace Volunteers, the mercenaries who keep your oil flowing—and three or four French couples, and perhaps Mohammed ben Ibrahim, who's the Internal-Security Minister nowadays, and quite civilized. I believe there's an Ethiopian noble, an exile, staying with Arcane. And of course there's Arcane's usual ménage, a lively household. There should be English-style games and stories. The Minister without Portfolio is a raconteur."

"From what I hear about him," Tom Whiston remarked *sotto voce*, "he should have plenty of stories to tell. They say he knows where the bodies are buried, and gets a two percent royalty on every barrel of oil."

I put my finger on my lips. "Phrases more or less figurative in America," I suggested, "are taken literally in Hamnegri, Mr. Whiston—because things are done literally here. You'll find that Mr. Arcane's manners are perfect: somewhat English, somewhat Austrian, somewhat African grandee, but perfect. His Excellency has been a soldier and a diplomat, and he is subtle. The common people in this town call him 'the Father of Shadows.' So to speak of bodies . . ."

We had been led by a manservant in a scarlet robe up broad stairs and along a corridor hung with carpets—some of them splendid old Persians, others from the cruder looms of the Sultanate of Kalidu. Now a rotund black man with a golden chain about his neck, a kind of majordomo, bowed us into an immense room with a fountain playing in the middle of it. In tolerable English, the majordomo called out, after I had whispered to him, "Mr. Thomas Whiston, from Texas, America; and Mr. Harry Yawby, Consul General of the United States!"

There swept toward us Melchiora, Arcane's young wife, or rather consort: the splendid Melchiora, sibylline and haughty, her mass of black hair piled high upon her head, her black eyes gleaming in the lamplight. She extended her slim hand for Tom Whiston to kiss; he was uncertain how to do that.

"Do come over to the divan by the fountain," she said in flawless English, "and I'll bring my husband to you." A fair number of people were talking and sipping punch in that high-ceilinged vaulted hall—once the harem of the palace—but they seemed few and lonely in its shadowy vastness. A string quartet, apparently French, were playing; black servingmen in ankle-length green gowns were carrying about brass trays of refreshments. Madame Arcane presented Whiston to some of the guests I knew already: "Colonel Fuentes . . . Major MacIlwraith, the Volunteers' executive officer . . . Monsieur and Madame Courtemanche . . ." We progressed slowly toward the divan. "His Excellency Mohammed ben Ibrahim, Minister for Internal Security . . . And a new friend, the Fitaurari Wolde Mariam, from Gondar."

The Fitaurari was a grizzle-headed veteran with aquiline features who had been great in the Abyssinian struggle against Italy, but now was lucky to have fled out of his country, through Gallabat, before the military junta could snare him. He seemed uncomfortable in so eccentrically cosmopolitan a gathering; his wide oval eyes, like those in an Ethiopian fresco, looked anxiously about for someone to rescue him from the voluble attentions of a middle-aged French lady; so Melchiora swept him along with us toward the divan.

Ancient, ancient Lady Grizel Fergusson, who had spent most of her many decades in India and Africa, and whose husband had been tortured to death in Kenya, was serving punch from a barbaric, capacious silver bowl beside the divan. "Ah, Mr. Whiston? You've come for our petrol, I understand. Isn't it shockingly dear? But I'm obstructing your way. Now where has His Excellency got to? Oh, the Spanish consul has his ear; we'll extricate him in a moment. Did you hear Madame Arcane singing as you came in? Don't you love her voice?"

"Yes, but I didn't understand the words," Tom Whiston said. "Does she know 'Rudolph the Red-Nosed Reindeer'?"

"Actually, I rather doubt— Ah, there she has dragged His Excellency away from the Spaniard, clever girl. Your Excellency, may I present Mr. Whiston—from Texas, I believe?"

Manfred Arcane, who among other accomplishments had won the civil war for the Sultan through his astounding victory at the Fords of Krokul, came cordially toward us, his erect figure brisk and elegant. Two little wolfish black men, more barbaric foster sons than servants, made way for him among the guests, bowing, smiling with their long teeth, begging pardon in their incomprehensible dialect. These two had saved Arcane's life at the Fords, where he had taken a traitor's bullet in the back; but Arcane seemed wholly recovered from that injury now.

Manfred Arcane nodded familiarly to me and took Whiston's hand. "It's kind of you to join our pathetic little assembly here; and good of you to bring him, Yawby. I see you've been given some punch; it's my own formula. I'm told that you and I, Mr. Whiston, are to have, tête-à-tête and candidly, a base commercial conversation on Tuesday. To-night we play, Mr. Whiston. Do you fancy snapdragon, that fiery old Christmas sport? Don't know it? It's virtually forgotten in England now, I understand, but once upon a time before the deluge, when I was at Wellington School, I became the nimblest boy for it. They insist that I preside over the revels tonight. Do you mind having your fingers well burnt?"

His was public-school English, and Arcane was fluent in a dozen other languages. Tom Whiston, accustomed enough to Arab sheikhs and African pomposities, looked startled at this bouncing handsome white-haired old man. Energy seemed to start from Arcane's fingertips; his swarthy face—inherited, report said, from a Montenegrin gypsy mother—was mobile, nearly unlined, at once jolly and faintly sinister. Arcane's underlying antique grandeur was veiled by ease and openness of manners. I knew how deceptive those manners could be. But for him, the "emergent" Commonwealth of Hamnegri would have fallen to bits.

Motioning Whiston and me to French chairs, Arcane clapped his hands. Two of the servingmen hurried up with a vast brass tray, elaborately worked, and set it upon a low stand; one of them scattered handfuls of raisins upon the tray, and over these the other poured a flagon of warmed brandy.

The guests, with their spectrum of complexions, gathered in a circle round the tray. An olive-skinned European boy—"the son," I murmured to Whiston—solemnly came forward with a long lighted match, which he presented to Arcane. Servants turned out the lamps, so that the old harem was pitch-black except for Arcane's tiny flame.

"Now we join reverently in the ancient and honorable pastime of snapdragon," Arcane's voice came, with mock portentousness. In the match-flame, one could make out only his short white beard. "Whosoever snatches and devours the most flaming raisins shall be awarded the handsome tray on which they are scattered, the creation of the finest worker in brass in Haggat. Friends, I offer you a foretaste of Hell! Hey presto!"

He set his long match to the brandy, at three points, and blue flames sprang up. In a moment they were ranging over the whole surface of the tray. "At them, brave companions!" Few present knowing the game, most held back. Arcane himself thrust a hand into the flames, plucked out a handful of raisins, and flung them burning into his mouth, shrieking in simulated agony. "Ah! Ahhh! I burn, I burn! What torment!"

Lady Fergusson tottered forward to emulate His Excellency; and I snatched my raisins, too, knowing that it is well to share in the play of those who sit in the seats of the mighty. Melchiora joined us, and the boy, and the Spanish consul, and the voluble French lady, and others.

When the flames lagged, Arcane shifted the big tray slightly, to keep up the blaze.

"Mr. Whiston, are you craven?" he called. "Some of you ladies, drag our American guest to the torment!" Poor Whiston was thrust forward, grabbed awkwardly at the raisins—and upset the tray. It rang upon the tiled floor, the flames went out, and the women's screams echoed in total darkness.

"So!" Arcane declared, laughing. The servants lit the lamps. "Rodríguez," he told the Spanish consul, "you've proved the greatest glutton tonight, and the tray is yours, after it has been washed. Why, Mr. Texas Whiston, I took you for a Machiavelli of oil contracts, but the booby prize is yours. Here, I bestow it upon you." There appeared magically in his hand a tiny gold candlesnuffer, and he presented it to Whiston.

Seeing Whiston red-faced and rather angry, Arcane smoothed his plumage, an art at which he was accomplished. With a few minutes' flattering talk, he had his Texas guest jovial. The quartet had struck up a waltz; many of the guests were dancing on the tiles; it was a successful party.

"Your Excellency," Grizel Fergusson was saying in her shrill old voice, "are we to have our Christmas ghost story?" Melchiora and the boy, Guido, joined in her entreaty.

"That depends on whether our American guest has a relish for such yarn-spinning," Arcane told them. "What's dreamt of in your philosophy, Mr. Whiston?"

In the shadows about the fountain, I nudged Whiston discreetly: Arcane liked an appreciative audience, and he was a tale-teller worth hearing.

"Well, I never saw any ghosts myself," Whiston ventured, reluctantly, "but maybe it's different in Africa. I've heard about conjure men and voodoo and witch doctors. . . ."

Arcane gave him a curious smile. "Wolde Mariam here—he and I were much together in the years when I served the Negus Negusti, rest his soul—could tell you more than a little of that. Those Gondar people are eldritch folk, and I suspect that Wolde Mariam himself could sow dragon's teeth."

The Abyssinian probably could not catch the classical allusion, but he smiled ominously in his lean way with his sharp teeth. "Let us hear him, then," Melchiora demanded. "It needn't be precisely a ghost story."

"And Manfred—Your Excellency—do tell us again about Archvicar

Gerontion," Lady Fergusson put in. "Really, you tell that adventure best of all."

Arcane's subtle smile vanished for a moment, and Melchiora raised a hand as if to dissuade him; but he sighed slightly, smiled again, and motioned toward a doorway in line with the fountain. "I'd prefer being toasted as a snapdragon raisin to enduring that experience afresh," he said, "but so long as Wolde Mariam doesn't resurrect the Archvicar, I'll try to please you. Our dancing friends seem happy; why affright them? Here, come into Whitebeard's Closet, and Wolde Mariam and I will chill you." He led the way toward that door in the thick wall, and down a little corridor into a small whitewashed room deep within the old house.

There were seven of us: Melchiora, Guido, Lady Fergusson, Whiston, Wolde Mariam, Arcane, and myself. The room's only ornament was one of those terrible agonized Spanish Christ-figures, hung high upon a wall. There were no European chairs, but a divan and several leather stools or cushions. An oil lamp suspended from the ceiling supplied the only light. We squatted or crouched or lounged about the Minister without Portfolio and Wolde Mariam. Tom Whiston looked embarrassed. Melchiora rang a little bell, and a servant brought tea and sweet cakes.

"Old friend," Arcane told Wolde Mariam, "it is an English custom, Lord knows why, to tell uncanny tales at Christmas, and Grizel Fergusson must be pleased, and Mr. Whiston impressed. Tell us something of your Gondar conjurers and shape-shifters."

I suspect that Whiston did not like this soiree in the least, but he knew better than to offend Arcane, upon whose good humor so many barrels of oil depended. "Sure, we'd like to hear about them," he offered, if feebly.

By some unnoticed trick or other, Arcane caused the flame in the lamp overhead to sink down almost to vanishing point. We could see dimly the face of the tormented Christ upon the wall, but little else. As the light had diminished, Melchiora had taken Arcane's hand in hers. We seven at once in the heart of Africa, and yet out of it—out of time, out of space. "Instruct us, old friend," said Arcane to Wolde Mariam. "We'll not laugh at you, and when you've done, I'll reinforce you."

Although the Ethiopian soldier's eyes and teeth were dramatic in the dim lamplight, he was no skilled narrator in English. Now and then he groped for an English word, could not find it, and used Amharic or Italian. He told of deacons who worked magic, and could set papers afire though they sat many feet away from them; of spells that made men's eyes bleed continuously, until they submitted to what the conjurers demanded of them; of Falasha who could transform themselves into hyenas, and Galla women who commanded spirits. Because I collect folktales of East Africa, all this was very interesting to me. But Tom Whiston did not understand half of what Wolde Mariam said, and grew bored, not believing the other half; I had to nudge him twice to keep him from snoring. Wolde Mariam himself was diffident, no doubt fearing that he, who had been a power in Gondar, would be taken for a superstitious fool. He finished lamely: "So some people believe."

But Melchiora, who came from sinister Agrigento in Sicily, had listened closely, and so had the boy. Now Manfred Arcane, sitting directly under the lamp, softly ended the awkward pause.

"Some of you have heard all this before," Arcane commenced, "but you protest that it does not bore you. It alarms me still: so many frightening questions are raised by what occurred two years ago. The Archvicar Gerontion—how harmoniously perfect in his evil, his 'unblemished turpitude'—was as smoothly foul a being as one might hope to meet. Yet who am I to sit in judgment? Where Gerontion slew his few victims, I slew my myriads."

"Oh, come, Your Excellency," Grizel Fergusson broke in, "your killing was done in fair fight, and honorable."

The old adventurer bowed his handsome head to her. "Honorable—with a few exceptions—in a rude *condottiere*, perhaps. However that may be, our damned Archvicar may have been sent to give this old evildoer a foretaste of the Inferno—through a devilish game of snapdragon, with raisins, brandy, and all. What a dragon Gerontion was, and what a peculiar dragon-land he fetched me into!" He sipped his tea before resuming.

"Mr. Whiston, I doubt whether you gave full credence to the Fitaurari's narration. Let me tell you that in my own Abyssinian years I saw with these eyes some of the phenomena he described; that these eyes of mine, indeed, have bled as he told, from a sorcerer's curse in Kaffa. O ye of little faith! But though hideous wonders are worked in Gondar and Kaffa and other Ethiopian lands, the Indian enchanters are greater than the African. This Archvicar Gerontion—he was a curiously well-read scoundrel, and took his alias from Eliot's poem, I do believe—combined the craft of India with the craft of Africa."

This story was new to me, but I had heard that name "Gerontion" somewhere, two or three years earlier. "Your Excellency, wasn't somebody of that name a pharmacist here in Haggat?" I ventured.

Arcane nodded. "And a marvelous chemist he was, too. He used his chemistry on me, and something more. Now look here, Yawby: if my memory serves me, Aquinas holds that a soul must have a body to inhabit, and that has been my doctrine. Yet it is an arcane doctrine"—here he smiled, knowing that we thought of his own name or alias—"and requires much interpretation. Now was I out of my body, or in it, there within the Archvicar's peculiar demesne? I'll be damned if I know—and if I don't, probably. But how I run on, senile creature that I am! Let me try to put some order into this garrulity."

Whiston had sat up straight and was paying sharp attention. There was electricity in Arcane's voice, as in his body.

"You may be unaware, Mr. Whiston," Manfred Arcane told him, "that throughout Hamnegri, in addition to my military and diplomatic responsibilities, I exercise certain judicial functions. To put it simply, I constitute in my person a court of appeal for Europeans who have been accused under Hamnegrian law. Such special tribunals once were common enough in Africa; one survives here, chiefly for diplomatic reasons. The laws of Hamnegri are somewhat harsh, perhaps, and so I am authorized by the Hereditary President and Sultan to administer a kind of *jus gentium* when European foreigners—and Americans, too—are brought to book. Otherwise European technicians and merchants might leave Hamnegri, and we might become involved in diplomatic controversies with certain humanitarian European and American governments.

"So! Two years ago there was appealed to me, in this capacity of mine, the case of a certain T. M. A. Gerontion, who styled himself Archvicar in the Church of the Divine Mystery—a quasi-Christian sect with a small following in Madras and South Africa, I believe. This Archvicar Gerontion, who previously had passed under the name of Omanwallah and other aliases, was a chemist with a shop in one of the more obscure lanes of Haggat. He had been found guilty of unlicensed trafficking in narcotics and of homicides resulting from such traffic. He had been tried by the Administrative Tribunal of Post and Customs. You may perceive, Mr. Whiston, that in Hamnegri we have a juridical structure unfamiliar to you; there are reasons for that—among them the political influence of the Postmaster-General, Gabriel M'Rundu. At any rate, jurisdiction over the narcotics traffic is enjoyed by that tribunal, which may impose capital punishment—and did impose a death sentence upon Gerontion.

"The Archvicar, a very clever man, contrived to smuggle an appeal to me, on the ground that he was a British subject, or rather a citizen of the British Commonwealth. 'To Caesar thou must go.' He presented a *prima facie* case for this claim of citizenship; whether or not it was a true claim, I never succeeded in ascertaining to my satisfaction; the man's whole life had been a labyrinth of deceptions. I believe that Gerontion was the son of a Parsee father, and born in Bombay. But with his very personal identity in question—he was so old, and had lived in so many lands, under so many aliases and false papers, and with so many inconsistencies in police records—why, how might one accurately ascertain his mere nationality? Repeatedly he had changed his name, his residence, his occupation, seemingly his very shape."

"He was fat and squat as a toad," Melchiora said, squeezing the minister's hand.

"Yes, indeed," Arcane assented, "an ugly-looking customer—though about my own height, really, Best Beloved—and a worse-behaved customer. Nevertheless, I accepted his appeal, and took him out of the custody of the Postmaster-General before sentence could be put into execution. M'Rundu, who fears me more than he loves me, was extremely vexed at this; he had expected to extract some curious information, and a large sum of money, from the Archvicar—though he would have put him to death in the end. But I grow indiscreet; all this is *entre nous*, friends.

"I accepted the Archvicar's appeal because the complexities of his case interested me. As some of you know, often I am bored, and this appeal came to me in one of my idle periods. Clearly the condemned man was a remarkable person, accomplished in all manner of mischief: a paragon of vice. For decades he had slipped almost scatheless through the hands of the police of a score of countries, though repeatedly indicted—and acquitted. He seemed to play a deadly criminal game for the game's sake, and to profit substantially by it, even if he threw away most of his gains at the gaming tables. I obtained from Interpol and other sources a mass of information about this appellant.

"Gerontion, or Omanwallah, or the person masquerading under yet other names, seemed to have come off free, though accused of capital crimes, chiefly because of the prosecutors' difficulty in establishing that the prisoner in the dock actually was the person whose name had appeared on the warrants of arrest. I myself have been artful in disguises and pseudonyms. Yet this Gerontion, or whoever he was, far excelled me. At different periods of his career, police descriptions of the offender deviated radically from earlier descriptions; it seemed as if he must be three men in one; most surprising, certain sets of fingerprints I obtained from five or six countries in Asia and Africa, purporting to be those of the condemned chemist of Haggat, did not match one another. What an eel! I suspected him of astute bribery of record-custodians, policemen, and even judges; he could afford it.

"He had been tried for necromancy in the Shan States, charged with having raised a little child from the grave and making the thing do his bidding; tried also for poisoning two widows in Madras; for a colossal criminal fraud in Johannesburg; for kidnapping a young woman—never found—in Ceylon; repeatedly, for manufacturing and selling dangerous narcotic preparations. The catalogue of accusations ran on and on. And yet, except for brief periods, this Archvicar Gerontion had remained at a licentious liberty all those decades."

Guido, an informed ten years of age, apparently had not been permitted to hear this strange narration before; he had crept close to Arcane's knees. "Father, what had he done here in Haggat?"

"Much, Guido. Will you find me a cigar?" This being produced from a sandalwood box, Arcane lit his Burma cheroot and puffed as he went on.

"I've already stated the indictment and conviction by the Tribunal of Post and Customs. It is possible for vendors to sell hashish and certain other narcotics, lawfully, here in Hamnegri—supposing that the dealer has paid a tidy license fee and obtained a license which subjects him to regulation and inspection. Although Gerontion had ample capital, he had not secured such documents. Why not? In part, I suppose, because of his intense pleasure in running risks; for one type of criminal, evasion of the law is a joyous pursuit in its own right. But chiefly his motive must have been that he dared not invite official scrutiny of his operations. The local sale of narcotics was a small item for him; he was an exporter on a large scale, and Hamnegri has subscribed to treaties against that. More, he was not simply marketing drugs but manufacturing them from secret formulas—and experimenting with his products upon the bodies of such as he might entice to take his privy doses.

"Three beggars, of the sort that would do anything for the sake of a few coppers, were Gerontion's undoing. One was found dead in an alley, the other two lying in their hovels outside the Gate of the Heads. The reported hallucinations of the dying pair were of a complex and fantastic character—something I was to understand better at a later time. One beggar recovered enough reason before expiring to drop the Archvicar's name; and so M'Rundu's people caught Gerontion. Apparently Gerontion had kept the three beggars confined in his house, but there must have been a blunder, and somehow in their delirium the three had contrived to get into the streets. Two other wretched mendicants were found by the Post Office Police locked, comatose, into the Archvicar's cellar. They also died later.

"M'Rundu, while he had the chemist in charge, kept the whole business quiet; and so did I, when I had Gerontion in this house later. I take it that some rumor of the affair came to your keen ears, Yawby. Our reason for secrecy was that Gerontion appeared to have connections with some sort of international ring or clique or sect, and we hoped to snare confederates. Eventually I found that the scent led to Scotland; but that's another story."

Wolde Mariam raised a hand, almost like a child at school. "Ras Arcane, you say that this poisoner was a Christian? Or was he a Parsee?"

The Minister without Portfolio seemed gratified by his newly conferred Abyssinian title. "Would that the Negus had thought so well of me as you do, old comrade! Why, I suppose I have become a kind of *ras* here in Hamnegri, but I like your mountains better than this barren shore. As for Gerontion's profession of faith, his Church of the Divine Mystery was an instrument for deception and extortion, working principally upon silly old women; yet unquestionably he did believe fervently in a supernatural realm. His creed seemed to have been a debauched Manichaeism—that perennial heresy. I don't suppose you follow me, Wolde Mariam; you may not even know that you're a heretic yourself, you Abyssinian Monophysite: no offense intended, old friend. Well, then, the many Manichees believe that the world is divided between the forces of light and of darkness; and Gerontion had chosen to side with the darkness. Don't stir so impatiently, little Guido, for I don't mean to give you a lecture on theology."

I feared, nevertheless, that Arcane might launch into precisely that, he being given to long and rather learned, if interesting, digressions; and like the others, I was eager for the puzzling Gerontion to stride upon the stage in all his outer and inner hideousness. So I said, "Did Your Excellency actually keep this desperate Archvicar here in this house?"

"There was small risk in that, or so I fancied," Arcane answered. "When he was fetched from M'Rundu's prison, I found him in shabby condition. I never allow to police or troops under my command such methods of interrogation as M'Rundu's people employ. One of the Archvicar's legs had been broken; he was startlingly sunken, like a pricked balloon; he had been denied medicines—but it would be distressing to go on. For all that, M'Rundu had got precious little information out of him; I obtained more, far more, through my beguiling kindliness. He could not have crawled out of this house, and of course I have guards at the doors and elsewhere.

"And do you know, I found that he and I were like peas in a pod—"

"No!" Melchiora interrupted passionately. "He didn't look in the least like you, and he was a murdering devil!"

"To every coin there are two sides, Best Beloved," Arcane instructed her. " 'The brave man does it with a sword, the coward with a kiss.' Not that Gerontion was a thorough coward; in some respects he was a hero of villainy, taking ghastly risks for the satisfaction of triumphing over law and morals. I mean this: he and I both had done much evil. Yet the evil that I had committed, I had worked for some seeming good —the more fool I—or in the fell clutch of circumstance; and I repented it all. 'I do the evil I'd eschew'—often the necessary evil committed by those who are made magistrates and commanders in the field.

"For his part, however, Gerontion had said in his heart, from the beginning, 'Evil, be thou my good.' I've always thought that Socrates spoke rubbish when he argued that all men seek the good, falling into vice only through ignorance. Socrates had his own *daimon,* but he did not know the Demon. Evil is pursued for its own sake by some men—though not, praise be, by most. There exist fallen natures which rejoice in pain, death, corruption, every manner of violence and fraud and treachery. Behind all these sins and crimes lies the monstrous ego."

The boy was listening to Arcane intently, and got his head patted, as reward, by the Minister without Portfolio. "These evil-adoring natures fascinate me morbidly," Arcane ran on, "for deep cries unto deep, and the evil in me peers lewdly at the evil in them. Well, Archvicar Gerontion's was a diabolic nature, in rebellion against all order here below. His nature charmed me as a dragon is said to charm. In time, or perhaps out of it, that dragon snapped, as you shall learn.

"Yes, pure evil, defecated evil, can be charming—supposing that it doesn't take one by the throat. Gerontion had manners—though something of a chichi accent—wit, cunning, breadth of bookish knowledge, a fund of ready allusion and quotation, penetration into human motives and types of character, immense sardonic experience of the world, even an impish malicious gaiety. Do you know anyone like that, Melchiora—your husband, perhaps?" The beauty compressed her lips.

"So am I quite wrong to say that he and I were like peas in a pod?" Arcane spread out his hands gracefully toward Melchiora. "There existed but one barrier between the Archvicar and myself, made up of my feeble good intentions on one side and of his strong malice on the other side; or, to put this in a different fashion, I was an unworthy servant of the light, and he was a worthy servant of the darkness." Arcane elegantly knocked the ash off his cigar.

"How long did this crazy fellow stay here with you?" Tom Whiston asked. He was genuinely interested in the yarn.

"Very nearly a fortnight, my Texan friend. Melchiora was away visiting people in Rome at the time; this city and this whole land were relatively free of contention and violence that month—a consummation much to be desired but rare in Hamnegri. Idle, I spent many hours in the Archvicar's reverend company. So far as he could navigate in a wheelchair, Gerontion had almost the run of the house. He was well fed, well lodged, well attended by a physician, civilly waited upon by the servants, almost cosseted. What did I have to fear from this infirm old scoundrel? His life depended upon mine; had he injured me, back he would have gone to the torments of M'Rundu's prison.

"So we grew almost intimates. The longer I kept him with me, the more I might learn of the Archvicar's international machinations and confederates. Of evenings, often we would sit together—no, not in this little cell, but in the great hall, where the Christmas party is in progress now. Perhaps from deep instinct, I did not like to be confined with him in a small space. We exchanged innumerable anecdotes of eventful lives.

"What he expected to gain from learning more about me, his dim future considered, I couldn't imagine. But he questioned me with a flattering assiduity about many episodes of my variegated career, my friends, my political responsibilities, my petty tastes and preferences. We found that we had all sorts of traits in common—an inordinate relish for figs and raisins, for instance. I told him much more about myself than I would have told any man with a chance of living long. Why not indulge the curiosity, idle though it might be, of a man under sentence of death?

"And for my part, I ferreted out of him, slyly, bits and pieces that eventually I fitted together after a fashion. I learnt enough, for one thing, to lead me later to his unpleasant confederates in Britain, and to break them. Couldn't he see that I was worming out of him information which might be used against others? Perhaps, or even probably, he did perceive that. Was he actually betraying his collaborators to me, deliberately enough, while pretending to be unaware of how much he gave away? Was this tacit implication of others meant to please me, and so curry favor with the magistrate who held his life in his hands—yet without anyone being able to say that he, Gerontion, had let the cat out of the bag? This subtle treachery would have accorded well with his whole life.

"What hadn't this charlatan done, at one time or another? He had been deep in tantric magic, for one thing, and other occult studies; he knew all the conjurers' craft of India and Africa, and had practiced it. He had high pharmaceutical learning, from which I was not prepared to profit much, though I listened to him attentively; he had invented or compounded recently a narcotic, previously unknown, to which he gave the name *kalanzi;* from his testing of that, the five beggars had perished —'a mere act of God, Your Excellency,' he said. He had hoodwinked great and obscure. And how entertainingly he could talk of it all, with seeming candor!

"On one subject alone was he reticent: his several identities, or masks and assumed names. He did not deny having played many parts; indeed, he smilingly gave me a cryptic quotation from Eliot: 'Let me also wear/Such deliberate disguises/Rat's coat, crowskin, crossed staves. . . .' When I put it to him that police descriptions of him varied absurdly, even as to fingerprints, he merely nodded complacently. I marveled at how old he must be—even older than the broken creature looked—for his anecdotes went back a generation before my time, and I am no young man. He spoke as if his life had known no beginning and would know no end—this man, under sentence of death! He seemed to entertain some quasi-Platonic doctrine of transmigration of souls; but, intent on the track of his confederates, I did not probe deeply into his peculiar theology.

"Yes, a fascinating man, wickedly wise! Yet this rather ghoulish entertainer of my idle hours, like all remarkable things, had to end. One evening, in a genteel way, he endeavored to bribe me. I was not insulted, for I awaited precisely that from such a one—what else? In exchange for his freedom—'After all, what were those five dead beggars to you or to me?'—he would give me a very large sum of money; he would have it brought to me before I should let him depart. This was almost touching: it showed that he trusted to my honor, he who had no stitch of honor himself. Of course he would not have made such an offer to M'Rundu, being aware that the Postmaster-General would have kept both bribe and briber.

"I told him, civilly, that I was rich already, and always had preferred glory to wealth. He accepted that without argument, having come to understand me reasonably well. But I was surprised at how calmly he seemed to take the vanishing of his last forlorn hope of escape from execution.

"For he knew well enough by now that I must confirm the death sentence of the Administrative Tribunal of Post and Customs, denying his appeal. He was guilty, damnably guilty, as charged; he had no powerful friends anywhere in the world to win him a pardon through diplomatic channels; and even had there been any doubt of his wickedness in Haggat, I was aware of his unpunished crimes in other lands. Having caught such a creature, poisonous and malign, in conscience I could not set it free to ravage the world again.

"The next evening, then, I said—with a sentimental qualm, we two having had such lively talk together, over brandy and raisins, those past several days—that I could not overturn his condemnation. Yet I would not return him to M'Rundu's dungeon. As the best I might do for him, I would arrange a private execution, so painless as possible; in token of our mutual esteem and comparable characteristics, I would administer *le coup de grâce* with my own hand. This had best occur the next day; I would sit in formal judgment during the morning, and he would be dispatched in the afternoon. I expressed my regrets—which, in some degree, were sincere, for Gerontion had been one of the more amusing specimens in my collection of lost souls.

"I could not let him tarry with me longer. For even an experienced snake handler ought not to toy overlong with his pet cobra, there still being venom in the fangs. This reflection I kept politely to myself. 'Then linger not in Attalus his garden. . . .'

" 'If you desire to draw up a will or to talk with a clergyman, I am prepared to arrange such matters for you in the morning, after endorsement of sentence, Archvicar,' I told him.

"At this, to my astonishment, old Gerontion seemed to choke with emotion; why, a tear or two strayed from his eyes. He had difficulty getting his words out, but he managed a quotation and even a pitiful smile of sorts: 'After such pleasures, that would be a dreadful thing to do.' I was the Walrus or the Carpenter, and he a hapless innocent oyster!

"What could he have hoped to get from me, at that hour? He scarcely could have expected, knowing how many lies I had on my vestigial conscience already, that I would have spared him for the sake of a tear, as if he had been a young girl arrested for her first traffic violation. I raised my eyebrows and asked him what possible alternative existed.

" 'Commutation to life imprisonment, Your Excellency,' he answered, pathetically.

"True, I had that power. But Gerontion must have known what Hamnegri's desert camps for perpetual imprisonment were like: in those hard places, the word 'perpetual' was a mockery. An old man in his condition could not have lasted out a month in such a camp, and a bullet would have been more merciful far.

"I told him as much. Still he implored me for commutation of his sentence: 'We both are old men, Your Excellency: live and let live!' He actually sniveled like a fag at school, this old terror! True, if he had in mind that question so often put by evangelicals—'Where will you spend eternity?'—why, his anxiety was readily understood.

"I remarked merely, 'You hope to escape, if sent to a prison camp. But that is foolish, your age and your body considered, unless you mean to do it by bribery. Against that, I would give orders that any guard who might let you flee would be shot summarily. And, as the Irish say, "What's all the world to a man when his wife's a widdy?" No, Archvicar, we must end it tomorrow.'

"He scowled intently at me; his whining and his tears ceased. 'Then let me thank Your Excellency for your kindnesses to me in my closing days,' he said, in a controlled voice. 'I thank you for the good talk, the good food, the good cognac. You have entertained me well in this demesne of yours, and when opportunity offers I hope to be privileged to entertain Your Excellency in my demesne.'

"*His* demesne! I suppose we all tend to think our own selves immortal. But this fatuous expectation of living, and even prospering, after the stern announcement I had made to him only moments before—why, could it be, after all, that this Archvicar was a lunatic merely? He had seemed so self-seekingly rational, at least within his own inverted deadly logic. No, this invitation must be irony, and so I replied in kind: 'I thank you, most reverend Archvicar, for your thoughtful invitation, and will accept it whenever room may be found for me.'

"He stared at me for a long moment, as a dragon in the legends paralyzes by its baleful eye. It was discomfiting, I assure you, the Archvicar's prolonged gaze, and I chafed under it; he seemed to be drawing the essence out of me. Then he asked, 'May I trouble Your Excellency with one more importunity? These past few days, we have become friends almost; and then, if I may say so, there are ties and correspondences between us, are there not? I never met a gentleman more like myself, or whom I liked better—take that as a compliment, sir. We have learnt so much about each other; something of our acquaintance will endure long. Well'—the intensity of his stare diminished slightly—'I mentioned cognac the other moment, your good brandy. Might we have a cheering last drink together, this evening? Perhaps that really admirable Napoleon cognac we had on this table day before yesterday?'

" 'Of course.' I went over to the bellpull and summoned a servant, who brought the decanter of cognac and two glasses—and went away, after I had instructed him that we were not to be disturbed for two or three hours. I meant this to be the final opportunity to see whether a tipsy Archvicar might be induced to tell me still more about his confederates overseas.

"I poured the brandy. A bowl of raisins rested on the table between us, and the Archvicar took a handful, munching them between sips of cognac; so did I.

"The strong spirit enlivened him; his deep-set eyes glowed piercingly; he spoke confidently again, almost as if he were master in the house.

"'What is this phenomenon we call dying?' he inquired. 'You and I, when all's said, are only collections of electrical particles, positive and negative. These particles, which cannot be destroyed but may be induced to rearrange themselves, are linked temporarily by some force or power we do not understand—though some of us may be more ignorant of that power than others are. Illusion, illusion! Our bodies are feeble things, inhabited by ghosts—ghosts in a machine that functions imperfectly. When the machine collapses, or falls under the influence of chemicals, our ghosts seek other lodging. *Maya!* I sought the secret of all this. What were those five dead beggars for whose sake you would have me shot? Why, things of no consequence, those rascals. I do not dread their ghosts: they are gone to my demesne. Having done with a thing, I dispose of it—even Your Excellency.'

"Were his wits wandering? Abruptly the Archvicar sagged in his wheelchair; his eyelids began to close; but for a moment he recovered, and said with strong emphasis, 'Welcome to my demesne.' He gasped for breath, but contrived to whisper, 'I shall take your body.'

"I thought he was about to slide out of the wheelchair altogether; his face had gone death-pale, and his teeth were clenched. 'What is it, man?' I demanded. I started up to catch him.

"Or rather, I intended to rise. I found that I was too weak. My face also must be turning livid, and my brain was sunk in torpor suddenly; my eyelids were closing against my will. 'The ancient limb of Satan!' I thought in that last instant. 'He's poisoned the raisins with that infernal *kalanzi* powder of his, a final act of malice, and we're to die together!' After that maddening reflection I ceased to be conscious."

Mr. Tom Whiston drew a sighing breath: "But you're still with us." Melchiora had taken both of Arcane's hands now. Wolde Mariam was crossing himself.

"By the grace of God," said Manfred Arcane. The words were uttered slowly, and Arcane glanced at the Spanish crucifix on the wall as he spoke them. "But I've not finished, Mr. Whiston: the worst is to come. Melchiora, do let us have cognac."

She took a bottle from a little carved cupboard. Except Guido, everybody else in the room accepted brandy too.

"When consciousness returned," Arcane went on, "I was in a different place. I still do not know where or what that place was. My first speculation was that I had been kidnapped. For the moment, I was alone, cold, unarmed, in the dark.

"I found myself crouching on a rough stone pavement in a town—not an African town, I think. It was an ancient place, and desolate, and silent. It was a town that had been sacked—I have seen such towns—but sacked long ago.

"Do any of you know Stari Bar, near the Dalmatian coast, a few miles north of the Albanian frontier? No? I have visited that ruined city several times; my mother was born not far from there. Well, this cold and dark town, so thoroughly sacked, in which I found myself was somewhat like Stari Bar. It seemed a Mediterranean place, with mingled Gothic and Turkish—not Arabic—buildings, most of them unroofed. But you may be sure that I did not take time to study the architecture.

"I rose to my feet. It was a black night, with no moon or stars, but I could make out things tolerably well, somehow. There was no one about, no one at all. The doors were gone from most of the houses, and as for those which still had doors—why, I did not feel inclined to knock.

"Often I have been in tight corners. Without such previous trying experiences, I should have despaired in this strange clammy place. I did not know how I had come there, nor where to go. But I suppose the adrenalin began to rise in me—what are men and rats, those natural destroyers, without ready adrenalin?—and I took stock of my predicament.

"My immediate necessity was to explore the place. I felt giddy, and somewhat uneasy at the pit of my stomach, but I compelled myself to walk up that steep street, meaning to reach the highest point in this broken city and take a general view. I found no living soul.

"The place was walled all about. I made my way through what must have been the gateway of the citadel, high up, and ascended with some difficulty, by a crumbling stair, a precarious tower on the battlements. I seemed to be far above a plain, but it was too dark to make out much. There was no tolerable descent out of the town from this precipice;

presumably I must return all the way back through those desolate streets and find the town gates.

"But just as I was about to descend, I perceived with a start a distant glimmer of light, away down there where the town must meet the plain. It may not have been a strong light, yet it had no competitor. It seemed to be moving erratically—and moving toward me, perhaps, though we were far, far apart. I would hurry down to meet it; anything would be better than this accursed solitude.

"Having scrambled back out of the citadel, I became confused in the complex of streets and alleys, which here and there were nearly choked with fallen stones. Once this town must have pullulated people, for it was close-built with high old houses of masonry; but it seemed perfectly empty now. Would I miss that flickering faint light, somewhere in this fell maze of ashlar and rubble? I dashed on, downward, barking my shins more than once. Yes, I felt strong physical sensations in that ravaged town, where everyone must have been slaughtered by remorseless enemies. 'The owl and bat their revel keep. . . .' It was only later that I became aware of the absence of either owl or bat. Just one animate thing showed itself: beside a building that seemed to have been a domed Turkish bathhouse, a thick nasty snake writhed away, as I ran past; but that may have been an illusion.

"Down I scuttled like a frightened hare, often leaping or dodging those tumbled building-stones, often slipping and stumbling, unable to fathom how I had got to this grisly place, but wildly eager to seek out some other human being.

"I trotted presently into a large piazza, one side of it occupied by a derelict vast church, perhaps Venetian Gothic, or some jumble or antique styles. It seemed to be still roofed, but I did not venture in then. Instead I scurried down a lane, steep-pitched, which ran beside the church; for that lane would lead me, I fancied, in the direction of the glimmering light.

"Behind the church, just off the lane, was a large open space, surrounded by a low wall that was broken at various points. Had I gone astray? Then, far down at the bottom of the steep lane which stretched before me, I saw the light again. It seemed to be moving up toward me. It was not a lantern of any sort, but rather a mass of glowing stuff, more phosphorescent than incandescent, and it seemed to be about the height of a man.

"We all are cowards—yes, Melchiora, your husband too. That strange light, if light it could be called, sent me quivering all over. I must not confront it directly until I should have some notion of what it was. So I dodged out of the lane, to my left, through one of the gaps in the low wall which paralleled the alley.

"Now I was among tombs. This open space was the graveyard behind that enormous church. Even the cemetery of this horrid town had been sacked. Monuments had been toppled, graves dug open and pillaged. I stumbled over a crumbling skull, and fell to earth in this open charnel house.

"That fall, it turned out, was all to the good. For while I lay prone, that light came opposite a gap in the enclosing wall, and hesitated there. I had a fair view of it from where I lay.

"Yes, it was a man's height, but an amorphous thing, an immense corpse-candle, or will-o'-the-wisp, so far as it may be described at all. It wavered and shrank and expanded again, lingering there, lambent.

"And out of this abominable corpse-candle, if I may call it that, came a voice. I suppose it may have been no more than a low murmur, but in that utter silence of the empty town it was tremendous. At first it gabbled and moaned, but then I made out words, and those words paralyzed me. They were these: 'I must have your body.'

"Had the thing set upon me at that moment, I should have been lost: I could stir no muscle. But after wobbling near the wall-gap, the corpse-candle shifted away and went uncertainly up the lane toward the church and the square. I could see the top of it glowing above the wall until it passed out of the lane at the top.

"I lay unmoving, though conscious. Where might I have run to? The thing was not just here now; it might be anywhere else, lurking. And it sent into me a dread more unnerving than ever I have felt from the menace of living men.

"Memory flooded upon me in that instant. In my mind's eye, I saw the great hall here in this house at Haggat, and the Archvicar and myself sitting at brandy and raisins, and his last words rang in my ears. Indeed I had been transported, or rather translated, to the Archvicar's peculiar demesne, to which he consigned those wretches with whom he had finished.

"Was this ruined town a 'real' place? I cannot tell you. I am certain that I was not then experiencing a dream or vision, as we ordinarily employ those words. My circumstances were actual; my peril was genuine and acute. Whether such an object as that sacked city exists in stone somewhere in this world—I do not mean to seek it out—or whether it was an illusion conjured out of the Archvicar's imagination, or out of mine, I do not know. *Maya!* But I sensed powerfully that whatever the nature of this accursed place, this City of Dis, I might never get out of it—certainly not if the corpse-candle came upon me.

"For that corpse-candle must be in some way the Archvicar Gerontion, seeking whom he might devour. He had, after all, a way out of the body of this death: and that was to take my body. Had he done the thing before, twice or thrice before, in his long course of evil? Had he meant to do it with one of those beggars upon whom he had experimented, and been interrupted before his venture could be completed?

"It must be a most perilous chance, a desperate last recourse, for Gerontion was enfeebled and past the height of his powers. But his only alternative was the executioner's bullet. He meant to enter into me, to penetrate me utterly, to perpetuate his essence in my flesh; and I would be left here—or the essence, the ghost of me, rather—in this place of desolation beyond time and space. The Archvicar, master of some Tantra, had fastened upon me for his prey because only I had lain within his reach on the eve of his execution. And also there were those correspondences between us, which would diminish the obstacles to the transmigration of Gerontion's malign essence from one mortal vessel to another: the obverse of the coin would make itself the reverse. Deep cried unto deep, evil unto evil.

"Lying there among dry bones in the plundered graveyard, I had no notion of how to save myself. This town, its secrets, its laws, were Gerontion's. Still—that corpse-candle form, gabbling and moaning as if in extremity, must be limited in its perceptions, or else it would have come through the wall-gap to take me a few minutes earlier. Was it like a hound on the scent, and did it have forever to track me down?

"'Arcane! Arcane!' My name was mouthed hideously; the vocal *ignis fatuus* was crying from somewhere. I turned my head, quick as an owl. The loathsome glow now appeared behind the church, up the slope of the great graveyard; it was groping its way toward me.

"I leaped up. As if it sensed my movement, the sightless thing swayed and floated in my direction. I dodged among tall grotesque tombstones; the corpse-candle drifted more directly toward me. This was to be hide-and-seek, blindman's buff, with the end foreordained. 'Here we go round the prickly pear at five o'clock in the morning!'

"On the vague shape of phosphorescence came, with a hideous fluttering urgency; but by the time it got to the tall tombstones, I was a hundred yards distant, behind the wreck of a small mausoleum.

"I never have been hunted by tiger or polar bear, but I am sure that what I experienced in that boneyard was worse than the helpless terror of Indian villager or wounded Eskimo. To even the worst ruffian storming an outpost at the back of beyond, the loser may appeal for mercy with some faint hope of being spared. I knew that I could not surrender at discretion to this *ignis fatuus,* any more than to tiger or bear. It meant to devour me.

"Along the thing came, already halfway to the mausoleum. There loomed up a sort of pyramid-monument some distance to my right; I ran hard for it. At the lower end of the cemetery, which I now approached, the enclosing wall looked too high to scale. I gained the little stone pyramid, but the corpse-candle already had skirted the mausoleum and was making for me.

"What way to turn? Hardly knowing why, I ran upward, back toward the dark hulk of the church. I dared not glance over my shoulder —no tenth of a second to spare.

"This was no time to behave like Lot's wife. Frantically scrambling, I reached a side doorway of the church, and only there paused for a fraction of a second to see what was on my heels. The corpse-candle was some distance to the rear of me, drifting slowly, and I fancied that its glow had diminished. Yet I think I heard something moan the word 'body.' I dashed into the immensity of that church.

"Where might I possibly conceal myself from the faceless hunter? I blundered into a side-chapel, its floor strewn with fallen plaster. Over its battered altar, an icon of Christ the King still was fixed, though lance-thrusts had mutilated the face. I clambered upon the altar and clasped the picture.

"From where I clung, I could see the doorway by which I had entered the church. The tall glow of corruption had got so far as that doorway, and now lingered upon the threshold. For a moment, as if by a final frantic effort, it shone brightly. Then the corpse-candle went out as if an extinguisher had been clapped over it. The damaged icon broke loose from the wall, and with it in my arms I fell from the altar."

I felt acute pain in my right arm: Whiston had been clutching it fiercely for some minutes, I suppose, but I had not noticed until now. Guido was crying hard from fright, his head in Melchiora's lap. No one said anything, until Arcane asked Grizel Fergusson, "Will you turn up the lamp a trifle? The play is played out; be comforted, little Guido."

"You returned, Ras Arcane," Wolde Mariam's deep voice said, quavering just noticeably. "What did you do with the bad priest?"

"It was unnecessary for me to do anything—not that I could have done it, being out of my head for the next week. They say I screamed a good deal during the nights. It was a month before I was well enough to walk. And even then, for another two or three months, I avoided dark corners."

"What about the Archvicar's health?" I ventured.

"About ten o'clock, Yawby, the servants had entered the old harem to tidy it, assuming that the Archvicar and I had retired. They had found that the Archvicar had fallen out of his wheelchair, and was stretched very dead on the floor. After a short search, they discovered me in this little room where we sit now. I was not conscious, and had suffered some cuts and bruises. Apparently I had crawled here in a daze, grasped the feet of Our Lord there"—nodding toward the Spanish Christ upon the wall—"and the crucifix had fallen upon me, as the icon had fallen in that desecrated church. These correspondences!"

Tom Whiston asked hoarsely, "How long had it been since you were left alone with the Archvicar?"

"Perhaps two hours and a half—nearly the length of time I seemed to spend in his damned ruined demesne."

"Only you, Manfred, could have had will strong enough to come back from that place," Melchiora told her husband. She murmured softly what I took for Sicilian endearments. Her fine eyes were wet, though she must have heard the fearful story many times before, and her hands trembled badly.

"Only a man sufficiently evil in his heart could have been snared there at all, my delight," Arcane responded. He glanced around our unnerved little circle. "Do you suppose, friends, that the Archvicar wanders there still, among the open graves, forlorn old ghoul, burning, burning, burning, a corpse-candle forever and a day?"

Even the Fitaurari was affected by this image. I wanted to know what had undone Gerontion.

"Why," Arcane suggested, "I suppose that what for me was an underdose of his *kalanzi* must have been an overdose for the poisoner himself: he had been given only a few seconds, while my back was turned, to fiddle with those raisins. What with his physical feebleness, the strain upon his nerves, and the haste with which he had to act, the odds must have run against the Archvicar. But I did not think so while I was in his demesne." Arcane was stroking the boy's averted head.

"I was in no condition to give his mortal envelope a funeral. But our trustworthy Mohammed ben Ibrahim, that unsmiling young statesman, knew something of the case; and in my absence, he took no chances. He had Gerontion's flaccid husk burnt that midnight, and stood by while the smoke and the stench went up. Tantric magic, or whatever occult skill Gerontion exercised upon me, lost a grand artist.

"Had the creature succeeded in such an undertaking before—twice perhaps, or even three times? I fancy so; but we have no witnesses surviving."

"Now I don't want to sound like an idiot, and I don't get half of this," Whiston stammered, "but suppose that the Archvicar could have brought the thing off. . . . He couldn't, of course, but suppose he could have—what would he have done then?"

"Why, Mr. Whiston, if he had possessed himself of my rather battered body, and there had been signs of life remaining in that discarded body of his—though I doubt whether he had power or desire to shift the ghost called Manfred Arcane into his own old carcass—presumably he would have had the other thing shot the next day; after all, that body of his lay under sentence of death." Arcane finished his glass of cognac, and chuckled deeply.

"How our malicious Archvicar Gerontion would have exulted in the downfall of his host! How he would have enjoyed that magnificent irony! I almost regret having disobliged him. Then he would have assumed a new identity: that of Manfred Arcane, Minister without Portfolio. He had studied me most intensely, and his acting would have adorned any stage. So certainly he could have carried on the performance long enough to have flown abroad and hidden himself. Or conceivably he might have been so pleased with his new identity, and so letter-perfect at realizing it, that he merely could have stepped into my shoes and fulfilled my several duties. That role would have given him more power for mischief than ever he had known before. A piquant situation, friends?"

Out of the corner of my eye, I saw the splendid Melchiora shudder from top to toe.

"Then how do we know that he failed?" my charge Tom Whiston inquired facetiously, with an awkward laugh.

"Mr. Whiston!" Melchiora and Grizel Fergusson cried with simultaneous indignation.

Manfred Arcane, tough old charmer, smiled amicably. "On Tuesday morning, when we negotiate our new oil contract over brandy and raisins, my Doubting Thomas of Texas, you shall discover that, after all, Archvicar Gerontion succeeded. For you shall behold in me a snapdragon, Evil Incarnate." Yet before leading us out of that little room and back to the Christmas waltzers, Arcane genuflected before the crucified figure on the wall.

WHERE THE STONES GROW

By LISA TUTTLE

Lisa Tuttle, still in her late twenties, is a Texan. Born in Houston, she attended college at Syracuse University, and once wrote a daily column about television for the Austin American-Statesman. *Ms. Tuttle has published about two dozen stories to date, mainly in the genres of fantasy, horror, and science fiction. She collaborated with George R. R. Martin on* The Storms of Windhaven, *which was nominated for a Nebula Award as the best science-fiction novella of 1975. She and Martin later added to that novella and published a novel simply entitled* Windhaven. *Her interests include occult investigation and membership in the National Organization for Women (NOW).*

He saw the stone move. Smoothly as a door falling shut, it swung slightly around and settled back into the place where it had stood for centuries.

They'll kill anyone who sees them.

Terrified, Paul backed away, ready to run, when he saw something that didn't belong in that high, empty field which smelled of the sea. Lying half-in, half-out of the triangle formed by the three tall stones called the Sisters was Paul's father, his face bloody and his body permanently stilled.

When he was twenty-six, his company offered to send Paul Staunton to England for a special training course, the offer a token of better things to come. In a panic, Paul refused, much too vehemently. His only reason—that his father had died violently in England eighteen years before—was not considered a reason at all. Before the end of the year, Paul had been transferred away from the main office in Houston to the branch in San Antonio.

He knew he should be unhappy, but, oddly enough, the move suited him. He was still being paid well for work he enjoyed, and he found the climate and pace of life in San Antonio more congenial than that of Houston. He decided to buy a house and settle down.

The house he chose was about forty years old, built of native white limestone and set in a bucolic neighborhood on the west side of the city. It was a simple rectangle, long and low to the ground, like a railway car. The roof was flat and the gutters and window frames peeled green paint. The four rooms offered him no more space than the average mobile home, but it was enough for him.

A yard of impressive size surrounded the house with thick green grass shaded by mimosas, pecans, a magnolia, and two massive, spreading fig trees. A chain-link fence defined the boundaries of the property, although one section at the back was torn and sagging and would have to be repaired. There were neighboring houses on either side, also set in large yards, but beyond the fence at the back of the house was a wild mass of bushes and high weeds, ten or more undeveloped acres separating his house from a state highway.

Paul Staunton moved into his house on a day in June, a few days shy of the nineteenth anniversary of his father's death. The problems and sheer physical labor involved in moving had kept him from brooding about the past until something unexpected happened. As he was unrolling a new rug to cover the ugly checkerboard linoleum in the living room, something spilled softly out: less than a handful of grey grit, the pieces too small even to be called pebbles. Just rock-shards.

Paul broke into a sweat and let go of the rug as if it were contaminated. He was breathing quickly and shallowly as he stared at the debris.

His reaction was absurd, all out of proportion. He forced himself to take hold of the rug again and finish unrolling it. Then—he could not make himself pick them up—he took the carpet sweeper and rolled it over the rug, back and forth, until all the hard grey crumbs were gone.

It was time for a break. Paul got himself a beer from the refrigerator and a folding chair from the kitchen and went out to sit in the backyard. He stationed himself beneath one of the mimosa trees and stared out at the lush green profusion. He wouldn't even mind mowing it, he thought as he drank the beer. It was his property, the first he'd ever owned. Soon the figs would be ripe. He'd never had a fig before, except inside a cookie.

When the beer was all gone, and he was calmer, he let himself think about his father.

Paul's father, Edward Staunton, had always been lured by the thought of England. It was a place of magic and history, the land his ancestors had come from. From childhood he had dreamed of going there, but it was not until he was twenty-seven, with a wife and an eight-year-old son, that a trip to England had been possible.

Paul had a few dim memories of London, of the smell of the streets, and riding on top of a bus, and drinking sweet, milky tea—but most of these earlier memories had been obliterated by the horror that followed.

It began in a seaside village in Devon. It was a picturesque little place, but famous for nothing. Paul never knew why they had gone there.

They arrived in the late afternoon and walked through cobbled streets, dappled with slanting sun-rays. The smell of the sea was strong on the wind, and the cry of gulls carried even into the center of town. One street had looked like a mountain to Paul, a straight drop down to the grey, shining ocean, with neatly kept stone cottages staggered on both sides. At the sight of it, Paul's mother had laughed and gasped and exclaimed that she didn't dare, not in *her* shoes, but the three of them had held hands and, calling out warnings to each other like intrepid mountaineers, the Stauntons had, at last, descended.

At the bottom was a narrow pebble beach, and steep, pale cliffs rose up on either side of the town, curving around like protecting wings.

"It's magnificent," said Charlotte Staunton, looking from the cliffs to the grey-and-white movement of the water, and then back up at the town.

Paul bent down to pick up a pebble. It was smooth and dark brown, more like a piece of wood or a nut than a stone. Then another: smaller, nearly round, milky. And then a flat black one that looked like a drop of ink. He put them in his pocket and continued to search hunched over, his eyes on the ground.

He heard his father say, "I wonder if there's another way up?" And then another voice, a stranger's, responded, "Oh, aye, there is. There is the Sisters' Way."

Paul looked up in surprise and saw an elderly man with a stick and a pipe and a little black dog who stood on the beach with them as if he'd grown there, and regarded the three Americans with a mild, benevolent interest.

"The Sisters' Way?" said Paul's father.

The old man gestured with his knobby walking stick toward the cliffs to their right. "I was headed that way myself," he said. "Would you care to walk along with me? It's an easier path than the High Street."

"I think we'd like that," said Staunton. "Thank you. But who are the Sisters?"

"You'll see them soon enough," said the man as they all began to walk together. "They're at the top."

At first sight, the cliffs had looked dauntingly steep. But as they drew closer they appeared accessible. Paul thought it would be fun to climb straight up, taking advantage of footholds and ledges he could now see, but that was not necessary. The old man led them to a narrow pathway which led gently up the cliffs in a circuitous way, turning and winding, so that it was not a difficult ascent at all. The way was not quite wide enough to walk two abreast, so the Stauntons fell into a single file after the old man, with the dog bringing up the rear.

"Now," said their guide when they reached the top. "Here we are! And there stand the Sisters."

They stood in a weedy, empty meadow just outside town—rooftops could be seen just beyond a stand of trees about a half a mile away. And the Sisters, to judge from the old man's gesture, could be nothing more than some rough grey boulders.

"Standing stones," said Edward Staunton in a tone of great interest. He walked toward the boulders and his wife and son followed.

They were massive pieces of grey granite, each one perhaps eight feet tall, rearing out of the porous soil in a roughly triangular formation. The elder Staunton walked among them, touching them, a reverent look on his face. "These must be incredibly old," he said. He looked back at their guide and raised his voice slightly. "Why are they called the 'Sisters'?"

The old man shrugged. "That's what they be."

"But what's the story?" Staunton asked. "There must be some legend—a tradition—maybe a ritual the local people perform."

"We're good Christians here," the old man said, sounding indignant. "No rituals here. We leave them stones alone!" As he spoke, the little dog trotted forward, seemingly headed for the stones, but a hand gesture from the man froze it, and it sat obediently at his side.

"But surely there's a story about how they came to be here? Why is that path we came up named after them?"

"Ah, that," said the man. "That is called the Sisters' Way because on certain nights of the year the Sisters go down that path to bathe in the sea."

Paul felt his stomach jump uneasily at those words, and he stepped back a little, not wanting to be too close to the stones. He had never heard of stones that could move by themselves, and he was fairly certain such a thing was not possible, but the idea still frightened him.

"They move!" exclaimed Staunton. He sounded pleased. "Have you ever seen them do it?"

"Oh, no. Not I, or any man alive. The Sisters don't like to be spied on. They'll kill anyone who sees them."

"Mama," said Paul, urgently. "Let's go back. I'm hungry."

She patted his shoulder absently. "Soon, dear."

"I wonder if anyone has tried," said Staunton. "I wonder where such a story comes from. When exactly are they supposed to travel?"

"Certain nights," said the old man. He sounded uneasy.

"Sacred times? Like Allhallows maybe?"

The old man looked away toward the trees and the village and he said: "My wife will have my tea waiting for me. She worries if I'm late. I'll just say good day to you then." He slapped his hip, the dog sprang up, and they walked away together, moving quickly.

"He believes it," Staunton said. "It's not just a story to him. I wonder what made him so nervous? Did he think the stones would take offense at his talking about them?"

"Maybe tonight is one of those nights," his wife said thoughtfully. "Isn't Midsummer Night supposed to be magical?"

"Let's go," said Paul again. He was afraid even to look at the stones. From the corner of his eye he could catch a glimpse of them, and it seemed to him that they were leaning toward his parents threateningly, listening.

"Paul's got a good idea," his mother said cheerfully. "I could do with something to eat myself. Shall we go?"

The Stauntons found lodging for the night in a green-shuttered cottage with a Bed and Breakfast sign hanging over the gate. It was the home of Mr. and Mrs. Winkle, a weathered-looking couple, who raised cats and rose bushes and treated their visitors like old friends. After the light had faded from the sky, the Stauntons sat with the Winkles in their cozy parlor and talked. Paul was given a jigsaw puzzle to work, and he sat with it in a corner, listening to the adults and hoping he would not be noticed and sent to bed.

"One thing I like about this country is the way the old legends live on," Staunton said. "We met an old man this afternoon on the beach, and he led us up a path called the Sisters' Way, and showed us the stones at the top. But I couldn't get much out of him about why the stones should be called the Sisters—I got the idea that he was afraid of them."

"Many are," said Mr. Winkle equably. "Better safe than sorry."

"What's the story about those stones? Do you know it?"

"When I was a girl," Mrs. Winkle offered, "people said that they were three sisters who long ago had been turned to stone for sea-bathing on the Sabbath. And so wicked were they that, instead of repenting their sin, they continue to climb down the cliff to bathe whenever they get the chance."

Mr. Winkle shook his head. "That's just the sort of tale you might expect from a minister's daughter," he said. "Bathing on the Sabbath indeed! That's not the story at all. I don't know all the details of it—different folks say it different ways—but there were once three girls who made the mistake of staying overnight in that field, long before there was a town here. And when morning came, the girls had turned to stone.

"But even as stones they had the power to move at certain times of the year, and so they did. They wore away a path down the cliff by going to the sea and trying to wash away the stone that covered them. But even though the beach now is littered with little bits of the stone that the sea has worn away, it will take them till doomsday to be rid of it all." Mr. Winkle picked up his pipe and began to clean it.

Staunton leaned forward in his chair. "But why should spending the night in that field cause them to turn to stone?"

"Didn't I say? Oh, well, the name of that place is the place where the stones grow. And that's what it is. Those girls just picked the wrong time and the wrong place to rest, and when the stones came up from the ground the girls were covered by them."

"But that doesn't make sense," Staunton said. "There are standing stones all over England—I've read a lot about them. And I've never heard a story like that. People don't just turn to stone for no reason."

"Of course not, Mr. Staunton. I didn't say it was for no reason. It was the place they were in, and the time. I don't say that sort of thing—people turning into stones—happens in this day, but I don't say it doesn't. People avoid that place where the stones grow, even though it lies so close upon the town. The cows don't graze there, and no one would build there."

"You mean there's some sort of a curse on it?"

"No, Mr. Staunton. No more than an apple orchard or an oyster bed is cursed. It's just a place where stones grow."

"But stones don't grow."

"Edward," murmured his wife warningly.

But Mr. Winkle did not seem to be offended by Staunton's bluntness. He smiled. "You're a city man, aren't you, Mr. Staunton? You know, I heard a tale once about a little boy in London who believed the greengrocer made vegetables out of a greenish paste and baked them, just the way his mother made biscuits. He'd never seen them growing—he'd never seen *anything* growing, except flowers in window boxes, and grass in the parks—and grass and flowers aren't good to eat, so how should he know?

"But the countryman knows that everything that lives grows, following its own rhythm, whether it is a tree, a stone, a beast, or a man."

"But a stone's not alive. It's not like a plant or an animal." Staunton cast about for an effective argument. "You could prove it for yourself. Take a rock, from that field or anywhere else, and put it on your windowsill and watch it for ten years, and it wouldn't grow a bit!"

"You could try that same experiment with a potato, Mr. Staunton," Mr. Winkle responded. "And would you then tell me that a potato, because it didn't grow in ten years on my windowsill, never grew and never grows? There's a place and a time for everything. To everything there is a season," he said, reaching over to pat his wife's hand. "As my wife's late father was fond of reminding us."

As a child, Paul Staunton had been convinced that the stones had killed his father. He had been afraid when his mother had sent him out into the chilly, dark morning to find his father and bring him back to have breakfast, and when he had seen the stone, still moving, he had known. Had known, and been afraid that the stones would pursue him, to punish him for his knowledge, the old man's warning echoing in his mind. *They'll kill anyone who sees them.*

But as he had grown older, Paul had sought other, more rational, explanations for his father's death. An accident. A mugging. An escaped lunatic. A coven of witches, surprised at their rites. An unknown enemy who had trailed his father for years. But nothing, to Paul, carried the conviction of his first answer. That the stones themselves had killed his father, horribly and unnaturally moving, crushing his father when he stood in their way.

It had grown nearly dark as he brooded, and the mosquitoes were beginning to bite. He still had work to do inside. He stood up and folded the chair, carrying it in one hand, and walked toward the door. As he reached it, his glance fell on the window ledge beside him. On it were three light-colored pebbles.

He stopped breathing for a moment. He remembered the pebbles he had picked up on that beach in England, and how they had come back to haunt him more than a week later, back at home in the United States, when they fell out of the pocket where he had put them so carelessly. Nasty reminders of his father's death, then, and he had stared at them, trembling violently, afraid to pick them up. Finally he had called his mother, and she had gotten rid of them for him somehow. Or perhaps she had kept them—Paul had never asked.

But that had nothing to do with these stones. He scooped them off the ledge with one hand, half-turned, and flung them away as far as he could. He thought they went over the sagging back fence, but he could not see where, amid the shadows and the weeds, they fell.

He had done a lot in two days, and Paul Staunton was pleased with himself. All his possessions were inside and in their place, the house was clean, the telephone had been installed, and he had fixed the broken latch on the bathroom window. Some things remained to be done—he needed a dining-room table, he didn't like the wallpaper in the bathroom, and the backyard would have to be mowed very soon—but all in all he thought he had a right to be proud of what he had done. There was still some light left in the day, which made it worthwhile to relax outside and enjoy the cooler evening air.

He took a chair out, thinking about the need for some lawn furniture, and put it in the same spot where he had sat before, beneath the gentle mimosa. But this time, before sitting down, he began to walk around the yard, pacing off his property and luxuriating in the feeling of being a landowner.

Something pale, glimmering in the twilight, caught his eye, and Paul stood still, frowning. It was entirely the wrong color for anything that should be on the other side of the fence, amid that tumbled blur of greens and browns. He began to walk toward the back fence, trying to make out what it was, but was able only to catch maddeningly incomplete glimpses. Probably just trash, paper blown in from the road, he thought, but still . . . He didn't trust his weight to the sagging portion of the fence, but climbed another section. He paused at the top, not entirely willing to climb over, and strained his eyes for whatever it was and, seeing it at last, nearly fell off the fence.

He caught himself in time to make it a jump, rather than an undignified tumble, but at the end of it he was on the other side of the fence and his heart was pounding wildly.

Standing stones. Three rocks in a roughly triangular formation.

He wished he had not seen them. He wanted to be back in his own yard. But it was too late for that. And now he wanted to be sure of what he had seen. He pressed on through the high weeds and thick plants, burrs catching on his jeans, his socks, and his T-shirt.

There they were.

His throat was tight and his muscles unwilling, but Paul made himself approach and walk around them. Yes, there were three standing stones, but beyond the formation, and the idea of them, there was no real resemblance to the rocks in England. These stones were no more than four feet high, and less than two across. Unlike the standing stones of the Old World, these had not been shaped and set in their places—they were just masses of native white limestone jutting out of the thin soil. San Antonio lies on the Edwards Plateau, a big slab of limestone laid down as ocean sediment during the Cretaceous, covered now with seldom more than a few inches of soil. There was nothing unusual about these stones, and they had nothing to do with the legends of growing, walking stones in another country.

Paul knew that. But, as he turned away from the stones and made his way back through the underbrush to his own yard, one question nagged him, a problem he could not answer to his own satisfaction, and that was: Why didn't I see them before?

Although he had not been over the fence before, he had often enough walked around the yard—even before buying the house—and once had climbed the fence and gazed out at the land on the other side.

Why hadn't he seen the stones then? They were visible from the fence, so why hadn't he seen them more than a week earlier? He should have seen them. If they were there.

But they must have been there. They couldn't have popped up out of the ground overnight; and why should anyone transport stones to such an unlikely place? They must have been there. So why hadn't he seen them before?

The place where the stones grow, he thought.

Going into the house, he locked the back door behind him.

The next night was Midsummer Eve, the anniversary of his father's death, and Paul did not want to spend it alone.

He had drinks with a pretty young woman named Alice Croy after work—she had been working as a temporary secretary in his office—and then took her out to dinner, and then for more drinks, and then, after a minor altercation about efficiency, saving gas, and who was not too drunk to drive, she followed him in her own car to his house where they had a mutually satisfying if not terribly meaningful encounter.

Paul was drifting off to sleep when he realized that Alice had gotten up and was moving about the room.

He looked at the clock: it was almost two.

"What're you doing?" he asked drowsily.

"You don't have to get up." She patted his shoulder kindly, as if he were a dog or a very old man.

He sat up and saw that she was dressed except for her shoes. "What are you doing?" he repeated.

She sighed. "Look, don't take this wrong, okay? I like you. I think what we had was really great, and I hope we can get together again. But I just don't feel comfortable in a strange bed. I don't know you well enough to—it would be awkward in the morning for both of us. So I'm just going on home."

"So that's why you brought your own car."

"Go back to sleep. I didn't mean to disturb you."

"Your leaving disturbs me."

She made a face.

Paul sighed and rubbed his eyes. It would be pointless to argue with her. And, he realized, he didn't like her very much—on any other night he might have been relieved to see her go.

"All right," he said. "If you change your mind, you know where I live."

She kissed him lightly. "I'll find my way out. You go back to sleep, now."

But he was wide awake, and he didn't think he would sleep again that night. He was safe in his own bed, in his own house, surely. If his father had been content to stay inside, instead of going out alone, in the grey, predawn light, to look at three stones in a field, he might be alive now.

It's over, thought Paul. Whatever happened, happened long ago, and to my father, not me. (But he had seen the stone move.)

He sat up and turned on the light before that old childhood nightmare could appear before him: the towering rocks lumbering across the grassy field to crush his father. He wished he knew someone in San

Antonio well enough to call at this hour. Someone to visit. Another presence to keep away the nightmares. Since there was no one, Paul knew that he would settle for lots of Jack Daniel's over ice, with Bach on the stereo—supreme products of civilization to keep the ghosts away.

But he didn't expect it to work.

In the living room, sipping his drink, the uncurtained glass of the windows disturbed him. He couldn't see out, but the light in the room cast his reflection onto the glass, so that he was continually being startled by his own movements. He settled that by turning out the lights. There was a full moon, and he could see well enough by the light that it cast, and the faint glow from the stereo console. The windows were tightly shut and the air-conditioning unit was laboring steadily: the cool, laundered air and the steady hum shut out the night even more effectively than the Brandenburg Concerti.

Not for the first time, he thought of seeing a psychiatrist. In the morning he would get the name of a good one. Tough on a young boy to lose his father, he thought, killing his third drink. So much worse for the boy who finds his father's dead body in mysterious circumstances. But one had to move beyond that. There was so much more to life than the details of an early trauma.

As he rose and crossed the room for another drink (silly to have left the bottle all the way over there, he thought), a motion from the yard outside caught his eye, and he slowly turned his head to look.

It wasn't just his reflection that time. There had been something moving in the far corner of the yard, near the broken-down fence. But now that he looked for it, he could see nothing. Unless, perhaps, was that something there in the shadows near one of the fig trees? Something about four feet high, pale-colored, and now very still?

Paul had a sudden urge, which he killed almost at once, to take a flashlight and go outside, to climb the fence and make sure those three rocks were still there. *They want me to come out,* he thought—and stifled that thought, too.

He realized he was sweating. The air conditioner didn't seem to be doing much good. He poured himself another drink and pulled his chair around to face the window. Then he sat there in the dark, sipping his whiskey and staring out into the night. He didn't bother to replace the record when the stereo clicked itself off, and he didn't get up for another drink when his glass was empty. He waited and watched for nearly an hour, and he saw nothing in the dark yard move. Still he waited, thinking, *They have their own time, and it isn't ours. They grow at their own pace, in their own place, like everything else alive.*

Something was happening, he knew. He would soon see the stones move, just as his father had. But he wouldn't make his father's mistake and get in their way. He wouldn't let himself be killed.

Then, at last—he had no idea of the time now—the white mass in the shadows rippled, and the stone moved, emerging onto the moonlit grass. Another stone was behind it, and another. Three white rocks moving across the grass.

They were flowing. The solid white rock rippled and lost its solid contours and re-formed again in another place, slightly closer to the house. Flowing—not like water, like rock.

Paul thought of molten rock and of lava flows. But molten rock did not start and stop like that, and it did not keep its original form intact, forming and re-forming like that. He tried to comprehend what he was seeing. He knew he was no longer drunk. How could a rock move? Under great heat or intense pressure, perhaps. What were rocks? Inorganic material, but made of atoms like everything else. And atoms could change, could be changed—forms could change—

But the simple fact was that rocks did not move. Not by themselves. They did not wear paths down cliffs to the sea. They did not give birth. They did not grow. They did not commit murder. They did not seek revenge.

Everyone knew this, he thought, as he watched the rocks move in his backyard. No one had ever seen a rock move.

Because they kill anyone who sees them.

They had killed his father, and now they had come to kill him.

Paul sprang up from his chair, overturning it, thinking of escape. Then he remembered. He *was* safe. Safe inside his own home. His hand came down on the windowsill and he stroked it. Solid walls between him and those things out there: walls built of sturdy, comforting stone.

Staring down at his hand on the white rock ledge, a half-smile of relief still on his lips, he saw it change. The stone beneath his hand rippled and crawled. It felt to his fingertips like warm putty. It was living. It flowed up to embrace his hand, to engulf it, and then solidified. He screamed and tried to pull his hand free. He felt no physical pain, but his hand was buried firmly in the solid rock, and he could not move it.

He looked around in terror and saw that the walls were now molten and throbbing. They began to flow together. A stream of living rock surged across the window-glass. Dimly, he heard the glass shatter. The walls were merging, streaming across floor and ceiling, greedily filling all the empty space. The living, liquid rock lapped about his ankles, closing about him, absorbing him, turning him to stone.

THE NIGHT BEFORE CHRISTMAS

By ROBERT BLOCH

Robert Bloch has been contributing to the field of suspense and supernatural horror for more than forty years. Born in Chicago, he has been living in southern California for the last two decades, devoting much of his time to movie and television work. His most famous book is Psycho, *but he has written several other fine novels of suspense, including* The Scarf *and* Firebug. *And he has published hundreds of short stories, the best of them being among the finest supernatural horror stories of our time, such as, "That Hell-Bound Train," "The Animal Fair," and "Yours Truly, Jack The Ripper." Very few writers can match his skill at portraying the ticking mechanism of the psychopath, as this story powerfully demonstrates.*

I don't know how it ends.

Maybe it ended when I heard the shot from behind the closed door to the living room—or when I ran out and found him lying there.

Perhaps the ending came after the police arrived; after the interrogation and explanation and all that lurid publicity in the media.

Possibly the real end was my own breakdown and eventual recovery—if indeed I ever fully recovered.

It could be, of course, that something like this never truly ends as long as memory remains. And I remember it all, from the very beginning.

Everything started on an autumn afternoon with Dirk Otjens, at his gallery on La Cienega. We met at the door just as he returned from lunch. Otjens was late; very probably he'd been with one of his wealthy customers and such people seem to favor late luncheons.

"Brandon!" he said. "Where've you been? I tried to get hold of you all morning."

"Sorry—an appointment—"

Dirk shook his head impatiently. "You ought to get yourself an answering service."

No sense telling him I couldn't afford one, or that my appointment had been with the unemployment office. Dirk may have known poverty himself at one time, but that was many expensive luncheons ago, and now he moved in a different milieu. The notion of a starving artist turned him off, and letting him picture me in that role was—like hiring an answering service—something I could not now afford. It had been a break for me to be taken on as one of his clients, even though nothing had happened so far.

Or had it?

"You've made a sale?" I tried to sound casual, but my heart was pounding.

"No. But I think I've got you a commission. Ever hear of Carlos Santiago?"

"Can't say that I have."

"Customer of mine. In here all the time. He saw that oil you did—you know, the one hanging in the upstairs gallery—and he wants a portrait."

"What's he like?"

Dirk shrugged. "Foreigner. Heavy accent." He spoke with all of the disdain of a naturalized American citizen. "Some kind of shipping magnate, I gather. But the money's there."

"How much?"

"I quoted him twenty-five hundred. Not top dollar, but it's a start."

Indeed it was. Even allowing for his cut, I'd still clear enough to keep me going. The roadblock had been broken, and somewhere up ahead was the enchanted realm where everybody has an answering service to take messages while they're out enjoying expensive lunches of their own. Still—

"I don't know," I said. "Maybe he's not a good subject for me. A Spanish shipping tycoon doesn't sound like my line of work. You know I'm not one of those artsy-craftsy temperamental types, but there has to be a certain chemistry between artist and sitter or it just doesn't come off."

From Dirk's scowl I could see that what I was saying didn't come off, either, but it had to be stated. I am, after all, an artist. I spent nine years learning my craft here and abroad—nine long hard years of self-sacrifice and self-discovery that I didn't intend to toss away the first time somebody waved a dollar bill in my direction. If that's all I cared about, I might as well go into mass-production, turning out thirty-five dollar clowns by the gross to sell in open-air shows on supermarket lots. On the other hand—

"I'd have to see him first," I said.

"And so you shall." Dirk nodded. "You've got a three-o'clock appointment at his place."

"Office?"

"No, the house. Up in Trousdale. Here, I wrote down the address for you. Now get going, and good luck."

I remember driving along Coldwater, then making a right turn onto one of those streets leading into the Trousdale Estates. I remember it very well, because the road ahead climbed steeply along the hillside and I kept wondering if the car would make the grade. The old heap had an inferiority complex and I could imagine how it felt, wheezing its way past the semicircular driveways clogged with shiny new Cadillacs, Lancias, Alfa-Romeos, and the inevitable Rolls. This was a neighborhood in which the Mercedes was the household's second car. I didn't much care for it myself, but Dirk was right; the money was here.

And so was Carlos Santiago.

The car in his driveway was a Ferrari. I parked behind it, hoping no one was watching from the picture window of the sprawling two-story pseudo-*palazzo* towering above the cypress-lined drive. The house was new and the trees were still small, but who was I to pass judgment? The money was here.

I rang the bell. Chimes susurrated softly from behind the heavy door; it opened, and a dark-haired, uniformed maid confronted me. "Yes, please?"

"Arnold Brandon. I have an appointment with Mr. Santiago."

She nodded. "This way. The Señor waits for you."

I moved from warm afternoon sunlight into the air-conditioned chill of the shadowy hall, following the maid to the arched doorway of the living room at our left.

The room, with its high ceiling and recessed fireplace, was larger than I'd expected. And so was my host.

Carlos Santiago called himself a Spaniard; I later learned he'd been born in Argentina and undoubtedly there was Indio blood in his veins. But he reminded me of a native of Crete.

The Minotaur.

Not literally, of course. Here was no hybrid, no man's body topped by the head of a bull. The greying curly hair fell over a forehead unadorned by horns, but the heavily lidded eyes, flaring nostrils, and neckless merging of huge head and barrel chest somehow suggested a mingling of the taurine and the human. As an artist, I saw in Santiago the image of the man-bull, the bull-man, the incarnation of *macho*.

And I hated him at first sight.

The truth is, I've always feared such men; the big, burly, arrogant men who swagger and bluster and brawl their way through life. I do not trust their kind, for they have always been the enemies of art, the book-burners, smashers of statues, contemptuous of all creation which does not spurt from their own loins. I fear them even more when they don the mask of cordiality for their own purposes.

And Carlos Santiago was cordial.

He seated me in a huge leather chair, poured drinks, inquired after my welfare, complimented the sample of my work he'd seen at the gallery. But the fear remained, and so did the image of the Minotaur. *Welcome to my labyrinth.*

I must admit the labyrinth was elaborately and expensively designed and tastefully furnished. All of which only emphasized the discordant note in the decor—the display above the fireplace mantel. The rusty, broad-bladed weapon affixed to the wall and flanked by grainy, poorly framed photographs seemed as out of place in this room as the hulking presence of my host.

He noted my stare, and his chuckle was a bovine rumble.

"I know what you are thinking, *amigo*. The oh-so-proper interior decorator was shocked when I insisted on placing those objects in such a setting. But I am a man of sentiment, and I am not ashamed.

"The machete—once it was all I possessed, except for the rags on my back. With it I sweated in the fields for three long years as a common laborer. At the end I still wore the same rags and it was still my only possession. But with the money I had saved I made my first investment —a few tiny shares in a condemned oil tanker, making its last voyage. The success of its final venture proved the beginning of my own. I spare you details; the story is in those photographs. These are the ships I came to acquire over the years, the Santiago fleet. Many of them are old and rusty now, like the machete—like myself, for that matter. But we belong together."

Santiago poured another drink. "But I bore you, Mr. Brandon. Let us speak now of the portrait."

I knew what was coming. He would tell me what and how to paint, and insist that I include his ships in the background; perhaps he intended to be shown holding the machete in his hand.

He was entitled to his pride, but I had mine. God knows I needed the money, but I wasn't going to paint the Minotaur in any setting. No sense avoiding the issue; I'd have to take the bull by the horns—

"Louise!"

Santiago turned and rose, smiling as she entered. I stared at the girl—tall, slim, tawny-haired, with flawless features dominated by hazel eyes. The room was radiant with her presence.

"Allow me to present my wife."

Both of us must have spoken, acknowledging the introduction, but I can't recall what we said. All I remember is that my mouth was dry, my words meaningless. It was Santiago's words that were important.

"You will paint her portrait," he said.

That was the beginning.

Sittings were arranged for in the den just beyond the living room; north light made afternoon sessions ideal. Three times a week I came—first to sketch, then to fill in the background. Reversing the usual procedure, I reserved work on the actual portraiture until all of the other elements were resolved and completed. I wanted her flesh tones to subtly reflect the coloration of setting and costume. Only then would I concentrate on pose and expression, capturing the essence. But how to capture the sound of the soft voice, the elusive scent of perfume, the unconscious grace of movement, the totality of her sensual impact?

I must concede that Santiago, to his credit, proved cooperative. He never intruded upon the sittings, nor inquired as to their progress. I'd stipulated that neither he nor my subject inspect the work before completion; the canvas was covered during my absence. He did not disturb me with questions, and after the second week he flew off to the Middle East on business, loading tankers for a voyage.

While he poured oil across troubled waters, Louise and I were alone.

We were, of course, on a first-name basis now. And during our sessions we talked. *She* talked, rather; I concentrated on my work. But in order to raise portraiture beyond mere representationalism the artist must come to know his subject, and so I encouraged such conversation in order to listen and learn.

Inevitably, under such circumstances, a certain confidential relationship evolves. The exchange, if tape-recorded, might very well be mistaken for words spoken in psychiatric therapy or uttered within the confines of the confessional booth.

But what Louise said was not recorded. And while I was an artist, exulting in the realization that I was working to the fullest extent of my powers, I was neither psychiatrist nor priest. I listened, but did not judge.

What I heard was ordinary enough. She was not María Cayetano, Duchess of Alba, any more than I was Francisco José de Goya y Lucientes.

I'd already guessed something of her background, and my surmise proved correct. Hers was the usual story of the unusually attractive girl from a poor family. Cinderella at the high-school prom, graduating at the stroke of midnight to find herself right back in the kitchen. Then the frantic effort to escape—runner-up in a beauty contest, failed fashion model, actress ambitions discouraged by the cattle-calls where she found herself to be merely one of a dozen duplicates. Of course there were many who volunteered their help as agents, business managers, or outright pimps; all of them expected servicing for their services. To her credit, Louise was too street-smart to comply. She still had hopes of finding her Prince. Instead, she met the Minotaur.

One night she was escorted to an affair where she could meet "important people." One of them proved to be Carlos Santiago, and before the evening ended he'd made his intentions clear.

Louise had the sense to reject the obvious, and when he attempted to force the issue she raked his face with her nails. Apparently the impression she made was more than merely physical, and next day the flowers began to arrive. Once he progressed to earrings and bracelets, the ring was not far behind.

So Cinderella married the Minotaur, only to find life in the labyrinth not to her liking. The bull, it seemed, did a great deal of bellowing, but in truth he was merely a steer.

All this, and a great deal more, gradually came out during our sessions together. And led, of course, to the expected conclusion.

I put horns on the bull.

Justification? These things aren't a question of morality. In any case, Louise had no scruples. She'd sold herself to the highest bidder and it proved a bad bargain; I neither condemned nor condoned her. Cinderella had wanted out of the kitchen and took the obvious steps to escape. She lacked the intellectual equipment to find another route, and in our society—despite the earnest disclaimers of Women's Lib—Beauty usually ends up with the Beast. Sometimes it's a young Beast with nothing to offer but a state of perpetual rut; more often it's an aging Beast who provides status and security in return for occasional coupling. But even that had been denied Louise; her Beast was an old bull whose pawings and snortings she could no longer endure. Meeting me had intensified natural need; it was lust at first sight.

As for me, I soon realized that behind the flawless façade of face and form there was only a vain and greedy child. She'd created Cinderella out of costume and coiffure and cosmetics; I'd perpetuated the pretense in pigment. It was not Cinderella who writhed and panted in my arms. But knowing this, knowing the truth, didn't help me. I loved the scullery-maid.

Time was short, and we didn't waste it in idle declarations or decisions about the future. Afternoons prolonged into evenings and we welcomed each night, celebrating its concealing presence.

Harsh daylight followed quickly enough. It was on December eighteenth, just a week before Christmas, that Carlos Santiago returned. And on the following afternoon Louise and I met for a final sitting in the sunlit den.

She watched very quietly as I applied last-minute touches to the portrait—a few highlights in the burnished halo of hair, a softening of feral fire in the emerald-flecked hazel eyes.

"Almost done?" she murmured.

"Almost."

"Then it's over." Her pose remained rigid but her voice trembled.

I glanced quickly toward the doorway, my voice softening to a guarded whisper.

"Does he know?"

"Of course not."

"The maid—"

"You always left after a sitting. She never suspected that you came back after she was gone for the night."

"Then we're safe."

"Is that all you have to say?" Her voice began to rise and I gestured quickly.

"Please—lower your head just a trifle—there, that's it—"

I put down my brush and stepped back. Louise glanced up at me.

"Can I look now?"

"Yes."

She rose, moved to stand beside me. For a long moment she stared without speaking, her eyes troubled.

"What's the matter?" I said. "Don't you like it?"

"Oh yes—it's wonderful—"

"Then why so sad?"

"Because it's finished."

"All things come to an end," I said.

"Must they?" she murmured. "Must they?"

"Mr. Brandon is right."

Carlos Santiago stood in the doorway, nodding. "It has been finished for some time now," he said.

I blinked. "How do you know?"

"It is the business of every man to know what goes on in his own house."

"You mean you looked at the portrait?" Louise frowned. "But you gave Mr. Brandon your word—"

"My apologies." Santiago smiled at me. "I could not rest until I satisfied myself as to just what you were doing."

I forced myself to return his smile. "You are satisfied now?"

"Quite." He glanced at the portrait. "A magnificent achievement. You seem to have captured my wife in her happiest mood. I wish it were within my power to bring such a smile to her face."

Was there mockery in his voice, or just the echo of my own guilt?

"The portrait can't be touched for several weeks now," I said. "The paint must dry. Then I'll varnish it and we can select the proper frame."

"Of course," said Santiago. "But first things first." He produced a check from his pocket and handed it to me. "Here you are. Paid in full."

"That's very thoughtful of you—"

"You will find me a thoughtful man." He turned as the maid entered, carrying a tray which held a brandy decanter and globular glasses.

She set it down and withdrew. Santiago poured three drinks. "As you see, I anticipated this moment." He extended glasses to Louise and myself, then raised his own. "A toast to you, Mr. Brandon. I appreciate your great talent, and your even greater wisdom."

"Wisdom?" Louise gave him a puzzled glance.

"Exactly." He nodded. "I have no schooling in art, but I do know that a project such as this can be dangerous."

"I don't understand."

"There is always the temptation to go on, to overdo. But Mr. Brandon knows when to stop. He has demonstrated, shall we say, the artistic conscience. Let us drink to his decision."

Santiago sipped his brandy. Louise took a token swallow and I followed suit. Again I wondered how much he knew.

"You do not know just what this moment means to me," he said. "To stand here in this house, with this portrait of the one I love—it is the dream of a poor boy come true."

"But you weren't always poor," Louise said. "You told me yourself that your father was a wealthy man."

"So he was." Santiago paused to drink again. "I passed my childhood in luxury; I lacked for nothing until my father died. But then my older brother inherited the *estancia* and I left home to make my own way in the world. Perhaps it is just as well, for there is much in the past which does not bear looking into. But I have heard stories." He smiled at me. "There is one in particular which may interest you," he said.

"Several years after I left, my brother's wife died in childbirth. Naturally he married again, but no one anticipated his choice. A nobody, a girl without breeding or background, but one imagines her youth and beauty enticed him."

Did his sidelong glance at Louise hold a meaning or was that just my imagination? Now his eyes were fixed on me again.

"Unlike his first wife, his new bride did not conceive, and it troubled him. To make certain he was not at fault, during this period he fathered several children by various serving-maids at the *estancia*. But my brother did not reproach his wife for her defects; instead he summoned a physician. His examination was inconclusive, but during its course he made another discovery—my brother's wife had the symptoms of an obscure eye condition, a malady which might some day bring blindness.

"The physician advised immediate surgery, but she was afraid the operation itself could blind her. So great was this fear that she made my brother swear a solemn oath upon the Blessed Virgin that, no matter what happened, no one would be allowed to touch her eyes."

"Poor woman!" Louise repressed a shudder. "What happened?"

"Naturally, after learning of her condition, my brother abstained from the further exercise of his conjugal rights. According to the physician it was still possible she might conceive, and if so perhaps her malady might be transmitted to the child. Since my brother had no wish to bring suffering into the world he turned elsewhere for his pleasures. Never once did he complain of the inconvenience she caused him in this regard. His was the patience of a saint. One would expect her to be grateful for his thoughtfulness, but it is the nature of women to lack true understanding."

Santiago took another swallow of his drink. "To his horror, my brother discovered that his wife had taken a lover. A young boy who worked as a gardener at the *estancia.* The betrayal took place while he was away; he now spent much time in Buenos Aires, where he had business affairs and the consolation of a sympathetic and understanding mistress.

"When the scandal was reported to him he at first refused to believe, but within weeks the evidence was unmistakable. His wife was pregnant."

"He divorced her?" Louise murmured.

Santiago shrugged. "Impossible. My brother was a religious man. But there was a need to deal with the gossip, the sly winks, the laughter behind his back. His reputation, his very honor, was at stake."

I took advantage of his pause to jump in. "Let me finish the story for you," I said. "Knowing his wife's fear of blindness, he insisted on the operation and bribed the surgeon to destroy her eyesight."

Santiago shook his head. "You forgot—he had sworn to the *pobrecita* that her eyes would not be touched."

"What did he do?" Louise said.

"He sewed up her eyelids." Santiago nodded. "Never once did he touch the eyes themselves. He sewed her eyelids shut with catgut and banished her to a guesthouse with a servingwoman to attend her every need."

"Horrible!" Louise whispered.

"I am sure she suffered," Santiago said. "But mercifully, not for long. One night a fire broke out in the bedroom of the guesthouse while the servingwoman was away. No one knows how it started—perhaps my brother's wife knocked over a candle. Unfortunately the door was locked and the servingwoman had the only key. A great tragedy."

I couldn't look at Louise, but I had to face him. "And her lover?" I asked.

"He ran for his life, into the pampas. It was there that my brother tracked him down with the dogs and administered a suitable punishment."

"What sort of punishment would that be?"

Santiago raised his glass. "The young man was stripped and tied to a tree. His genitals were smeared with wild honey. You have heard of the fire ants, *amigo?* They swarmed in this area—and they will devour anything which bears even the scent of honey."

Louise made a strangled sound in her throat, then turned and ran from the room.

Santiago gulped the rest of his drink. "It would seem I have upset her," he said. "This was not my intention—"

"Just what was your intention?" I met the bull-man's gaze. "Your story doesn't upset me. This is not the jungle. And you are not your brother."

Santiago smiled. "I have no brother," he said.

I drove through dusk. Lights winked on along Hollywood Boulevard from the Christmas decorations festooning lampposts and arching overhead. Glare and glow could not completely conceal the shabbiness of sleazy storefronts or blot out the shadows moving past them. Twilight beckoned those shadows from their hiding places; no holiday halted the perpetual parade of pimps and pushers, chickenhawks and hookers, winos and heads. Christmas was coming, but the blaring of tape-deck carols held little promise for such as these, and none for me.

Stonewalling it with Santiago had settled nothing. The truth was that I'd made a little token gesture of defiance, then ran off to let Louise face the music.

It hadn't been a pretty tune he'd played for the two of us, and now that she was alone with him he'd be free to orchestrate his fury. Was he really suspicious? How much did he actually know? And what would he do?

For a moment I was prompted to turn and go back. But what then? Would I hold Santiago at bay with a tire iron while Louise packed her things? Suppose she didn't want to leave with me? Did I really love her enough to force the issue?

I kept to my course but the questions pursued me as I headed home.

The phone was ringing as I entered the apartment. My hand wasn't steady as I lifted the receiver and my voice wasn't steady either.

"Yes?"

"Darling, I've been trying to reach you—"

"What's the matter?"

"Nothing's the matter. He's gone."

"Gone?"

"Please—I'll tell you all about it when I see you. But hurry—"

I hurried.

And after I parked my car in the empty driveway, after we'd clung to one another in the darkened hall, after we settled on the sofa before the fireplace, Louise dropped her bombshell.

"I'm getting a divorce," she said.

"Divorce? . . ."

"When you left he came to my room. He said he wanted to apologize for upsetting me, but that wasn't the real reason. What he really wanted to do was tell me how he'd scared you off with that story he'd made up."

"And you believed him?"

"Of course not, darling! I told him he was a liar. I told him you had nothing to be afraid of, and he had no right to humiliate me. I said I was fed up listening to his sick raving, and I was moving out. That wiped the grin off his face in a hurry. You should have seen him—he looked like he'd been hit with a club!"

I didn't say anything, because I hadn't seen him. But I was seeing Louise now. Not the ethereal Cinderella of the portrait, and not the scullery-maid—this was another woman entirely; hot-eyed, harsh-voiced, implacable in her fury.

Santiago must have seen as much, and more. He blustered, he protested, but in the end he pleaded. And when he tried to embrace her, things came full circle again. Once more she raked his face with her nails, but this time in final farewell. And it was he who left, stunned and shaken, without even stopping to pack a bag.

"He actually agreed to a divorce?" I said.

Louise shrugged. "Oh, he told me he was going to fight it, but that's just talk. I warned him that if he tried to stop me in court I'd let it all hang out—the jealousy, the drinking, everything. I'd even testify about how he couldn't get it up." She laughed. "Don't worry, I know Carlos. That's one kind of publicity he'd do anything to avoid."

"Where is he now?"

"I don't know and I don't care." The hot eyes blazed, the harsh voice sounded huskily in my ear. "You're here," she whispered.

And as her mouth met mine, I felt the fury.

I left before the maid arrived in the morning, just as I'd always done, even though Louise wanted me to stay.

"Don't you understand?" I said. "If you want an uncontested divorce, you can't afford to have me here."

Dirk Otjens recommended an attorney named Bernie Prager; she went to him and he agreed. He warned Louise not to be seen privately or in public with another man unless there was a third party present.

Louise reported to me by phone. "I don't think I can stand it, darling —not seeing you—"

"Do you still have the maid?"

"Josefina? She comes in every day, as usual."

"Then so can I. As long as she's there we have no problem. I'll just show up to put a few more finishing touches on the portrait in the afternoons."

"And in the evenings—"

"That's when we can blow the whole deal," I said. "Santiago has probably hired somebody to check on you."

"No way."

"How can you be sure?"

"Prager's nobody's fool. He's used to handling messy divorce cases and he knows it's money in his pocket if he gets a good settlement." Louise laughed. "Turns out he's got private investigators on his own payroll. So Carlos is the one being tailed."

"Where is your husband?"

"He moved into the Sepulveda Athletic Club last night, went to his office today—business as usual."

"Suppose he hired a private eye by phone?"

"The office lines and the one in his room are already bugged. I told you, Prager's nobody's fool."

"Sounds like an expensive operation."

"Who cares? Darling, don't you understand? Carlos has money coming out of his ears. And we're going to squeeze out more. When this is over, I'll be set for life. We'll both be set for life." She laughed again.

I didn't share her amusement. Granted, Carlos Santiago wasn't exactly Mr. Nice. Maybe he deserved to be cuckolded, deserved to lose Louise. But was she really justified in taking him for a bundle under false pretenses?

And was I any better if I stood still for it? I thought about what would happen after the divorce settlement was made. No more painting, no more hustling for commissions. I could see myself with Louise, sharing the sweet life, the big house, big cars, travel, leisure, luxuries. And yet, as I sketched a mental portrait of my future, my artist's eye noted a shadow. The shadow of one of those pimps prowling Hollywood Boulevard.

It wasn't a pretty picture.

But when I arrived in the afternoon sunshine of Louise's living room, the shadow vanished in the glow of her gaiety.

"Wonderful news, darling!" she greeted me. "Carlos is gone."

"You already told me—"

She shook her head. "I mean really gone," she said. "Prager's people just came through with a report. He phoned in for reservations on the noon flight to New Orleans. One of his tankers is arriving there and he's going to supervise unloading operations. He won't be back until after the holidays."

"Are you absolutely sure?"

"Prager sent a man to LAX. He saw Carlos take off. And all his calls are being referred to the company office in New Orleans."

She hugged me. "Isn't that marvelous? Now we can spend Christmas together." Her eyes and voice softened. "That's what I've missed the most. A real old-fashioned Christmas, with a tree and everything."

"But didn't you and Carlos—"

Louise shook her head. "Something always came up at the last minute—like this New Orleans trip. If we hadn't split, I'd be on that plane with him right now.

"Did you ever celebrate Christmas in Kuwait? That's where we were last year, eating lamb curry with some greasy port official. Carlos promised, no more holiday business trips, this year we'd stay home and have a regular Christmas together. You see how he kept his word."

"Be reasonable," I said. "Under the circumstances what do you expect?"

"Even if this hadn't happened, it wouldn't change anything." Once again her eyes smoldered and her voice harshened. "He'd still go and drag me with him, just to show off in front of his business friends. 'Look what I've got—hot stuff, isn't she? See how I dress her, cover her with fancy jewelry?' Oh yes, nothing's too good for Carlos Santiago—he always buys the best!"

Suddenly the hot eyes brimmed and the strident voice dissolved into a soft sobbing.

I held her very close. "Come on," I said. "Fix your face and get your things."

"Where are we going?"

"Shopping. For ornaments—and the biggest damned Christmas tree in town."

If you've ever gone Christmas shopping with a child, perhaps you can understand what the next few days were like. We picked up our ornaments in the big stores along Wilshire; like Hollywood Boulevard, this street too was alive with holiday decorations and the sound of Yuletide carols. But there was nothing tawdry behind the tinsel, nothing mechanical about the music, no shadows to blur the sparkle in Louise's eyes. To her this make-believe was reality; each day she became a kid again, eager and expectant.

ou get here?" I said.
aid had left. Our privacy was not interrupted."
ouise tell you?"
amigo. I had suspected, of course, but I could not be
admitted it. No matter, for our differences are resolved."
ouise? Tell me—"
I will be frank with you, as she was with me. She told
—how much she loved you, what you planned to do to-
er foolish wish to decorate the tree in the den. Her plead-
e melted a heart of stone, *amigo*. I found it impossible to

armed her—"
her wish. She is in the den now." Santiago chuckled
e trailing off into a spasm of coughing.
already groping my way to the door of the den, flinging it

from the tree-bulbs was dim, barely enough for me to
ing over the machete on the floor. Quickly I looked up at
the corner, half-expecting to see the painting slashed. But
ait was untouched.
myself to gaze down at the floor again, dreading what I
hen breathed a sigh of relief. There was nothing on the
machete.
I picked it up, and now I noticed the stains on the rusty
ed stains slowly oozing in tiny droplets to the floor.
ment I fancied I could actually hear them fall, then realized
oo minute and too few to account for the steady dripping
ame from—
en that Santiago must have shot himself in the other room,
ot the sudden sound which prompted my scream.
t the Christmas tree, at the twinkling lights twining gaily
uge boughs, and at the oddly shaped ornaments draped and
spiky branches. Stared, and screamed, because the madman
e truth.
as decorating the Christmas tree.

Nights found her eager and expectant too, but no longer a child. The contrast was exciting, and each mood held its special treasures.

All but one.

It came upon her late in the afternoon of the twenty-third, when the tree arrived. The deliveryman set it up on a stand in the den and after he left we gazed at it together in the gathering twilight.

All at once she was shivering in my arms.

"What's the matter?" I murmured.

"I don't know. Something's wrong—it feels like there's someone watching us."

"Of course." I gestured toward the easel in the corner. "It's your portrait."

"No, not that." She glanced up at me. "Darling, I'm scared. Suppose Carlos comes back?"

"I phoned Prager an hour ago. He has transcripts of all your husband's calls up until noon today. Carlos phoned his secretary from New Orleans and said he'll be there through the twenty-seventh."

"Suppose he comes back without notifying the office?"

"If he does he'll be spotted—Prager's keeping the airport staked out, just in case." I kissed her. "Now stop worrying. There's no sense being paranoid—"

"Paranoid." I could feel her shivering again. "Carlos is the one who's paranoid. Remember that horrible story he told us—"

"But it was only a story. He has no brother."

"I think it's true. *He* did those things."

"That's what he wanted us to think. It was a bluff, and it didn't work. And we're not going to let him spoil our holiday."

"All right." Louise nodded, brightening. "When do we decorate the tree?"

"Christmas Eve," I said. "Tomorrow night."

It was late the following morning when I left—almost noon—and already Josefina was getting ready to depart. She had some last-minute shopping to do, she said, for her family.

And so did I.

"When will you be back?" Louise asked.

"A few hours."

"Take me with you."

"I can't—it's a surprise."

"Promise you'll hurry then, darling." Her eyes were radiant. "I can't wait to trim the tree."

"I'll make it as soon as possible."

But "soon" is a relative term and—when applied to parking and shopping on the day before Christmas—an unrealistic one.

I knew exactly what I was looking for, but it was close to closing-time in the little custom-jewelry place where I finally found it.

I'd never bought an engagement ring before and didn't know if Louise would approve of my choice. The stone was marquise-cut but it looked tiny and insignificant in comparison with the diamonds Santiago had given her. Still, people are always saying it's the sentiment that counts. I hoped she'd feel that way.

When I stepped out onto the street again it was already ablaze with lights and the sky above had dimmed from dusk to darkness. On the way to my car I found a phone booth and put in a call to Prager's office.

There was no answer.

I might have anticipated his office would be closed—if there'd been a party, it was over now. Perhaps I could reach him at home after I got back to the house. On the other hand, why bother? If there'd been anything to report he'd have phoned Louise immediately.

The real problem right now was fighting my way back to the parking lot, jockeying the car out into the street, and then enduring the start-stop torture of the traffic.

Celestial choirs sounded from the speaker system overhead.

"Silent night, holy night,
All is calm, all is bright—"

The honking of horns shattered silence with an unholy din; none of my fellow drivers were calm and I doubted if they were bright.

But eventually I battled my way onto Beverly Drive, crawling toward Coldwater Canyon. Here traffic was once again bumper-to-bumper; the hands of my watch inched to seven-thirty. I should have called Louise from that phone booth while I was at it and told her not to worry. Too late now; no public phones in this residential area. Besides, I'd be home soon.

Home.

As I edged into the turnoff which led up through the hillside, the word echoed strangely. This was my home now, or soon would be. *Our* home, that is. Our home, our cars, our money, Louise's and mine—

Nothing is yours. It's his home, his money, his wife. You're a thief. Stealing his honor, his very life—

I shook my head. *Crazy.*
the crazy one.

I thought about the expre
the story of his brother's b
about himself? If so, he had t

And even if it was just a
madman's cunning. Swearin
eyes, and then sewing her e
tion was capable of anything.

Suddenly my foot was floo
careening around the rising
hands streaked by sweat, hu
with their outdoor decoratio
windows.

There were no lights at all
when I saw the Ferrari parked i

I jammed to a stop behind
given me a duplicate house key
ing hand.

The door swung open on d
the archway at my left.

"Louise!" I called. "Louise—w
Silence.

Or almost silence.

As I entered the living room
coming from the direction of the
My hand moved to the light sw

"Don't turn it on."

The voice was slurred, but I rec

"Santiago—what are you doing h

"Waiting for you, *amigo.*"

"But I thought—"

"That I was gone? So did Lou
darkness.

I took a step forward, and now I
slurred whisper sounded again.

"You see, I know about the bug
lance. So when I returned this mor
connecting flight from Denver. No
ing arrivals from that city. I meant
who surprised me."

"When did
"After the m
"What did I
"The truth,
sure until she
"Where is L
"Of course.
me everythin
gether, even
ing would ha
resist."
"If you've
"I granted
again, his voi
But I was
open.
The light
avoid stumb
the easel in
Louise's port
I forced
might see,
floor but the
Stooping,
blade—the
For a mo
they were
sound that
It was th
but it was n
I stared
across its h
affixed to i
had told th
Louise w

Edward Gorey, a Midwesterner by birth, has been a unique fixture of the New York literary and artistic scene for over a quarter of a century, delighting a band of enthusiasts with wonderfully droll and macabre illustrated books brought out in limited editions. It has only been in recent years—with the publication of the two volumes of his collected works, Amphigorey *and* Amphigorey Too*—that he's gained a large popular following. Gorey's work is witty, sad, ironic, elegant. It hearkens back to Victorian and Edwardian times, and is filled with references to opera, theater, and the ballet. Yet beneath the sophistication and stylization there is a vulnerable innocence—a kind of baffled and helpless awareness of the unhappy things fate holds in store for so many. The cumulative effect of his illustrated stories, beautifully drawn and written, is both touching and haunting.*

One winter morning Friedrich woke
With an idea for a joke.

"I won't get up to-day"; he said,
"I'll spend it lying here in bed."

They came and called him through the door;
He only went to sleep once more.

They wondered if he'd fallen ill,
And asked if he would like a pill.

They offered, as a special treat,
To give him anything to eat.

That afternoon they brought new toys,
And other things for making noise.

They said he could do what he chose;
He only hid beneath the clothes.

As they gave up and left to stay,
The light was fading from the day.

"I'll get up now," he thought, "and go
And play till supper in the snow."

But when he tried to rise at last
The sheets and blankets held him fast.

A dreadful twang came from the springs;
The bed unfolded great black wings.

While Friedrich shrieked, the bed took flight,
And flapped away into the night.

They could not see it very soon
Because there wasn't any moon.

The bed came down again at dawn,
Both Friedrich and the bed-clothes gone.

A TOUCH OF PETULANCE

By RAY BRADBURY

A book such as this would be incomplete without a story from Ray Bradbury. He is a multitalented author: poet, playwright, essayist, screenwriter, short-story writer, and novelist. But Bradbury's first important work was in the genre of modern fantasy and horror stories, beginning in the early 1940s in the pulp magazine, Weird Tales. *His early stories of fantasy, set mainly in the Midwest of his dreams and evoking the poetic memory of childhood and small-town life, opened up the form in an important way. In contrast to Lovecraft and most of the Victorian and Edwardian writers of fantasy, with their relatively impersonal protagonists or narrators, Bradbury depicted the supernatural in believable modern settings, and populated his stories with identifiable, ordinary people. After publication of* Dark Carnival *in 1947, with notable exceptions such as his masterful novel,* Something Wicked This Way Comes, *Bradbury has tended to focus on science fiction, creating such famous works as* The Martian Chronicles *and* Fahrenheit 451. *His contributions to both fields are enormous in both influence and artistry and it's a privilege to offer here a new story of fantasy by Ray Bradbury.*

On an otherwise ordinary evening in May, a week before his twenty-ninth birthday, Johnathen Hughes met his fate, commuting from another time, another year, another life.

His fate was unrecognizable at first, of course, and boarded the train at the same hour, in Pennsylvania Station, and sat with Hughes for the dinnertime journey across Long Island. It was the newspaper held by this fate disguised as an older man that caused Johnathen Hughes to stare and finally say:

"Sir, pardon me, your *New York Times* seems different from mine. The typeface on your front page seems more modern. Is that a later edition?"

"No!" The older man stopped, swallowed hard, and at last managed to say, "Yes. A very late edition."

Hughes glanced around. "Excuse me, but—all the other editions look the same. Is yours a trial copy for a future change?"

"Future?" The older man's mouth barely moved. His entire body seemed to wither in his clothes, as if he had lost weight with a single exhalation. "Indeed," he whispered. "Future change. God, what a joke."

Johnathen Hughes blinked at the newspaper's dateline:

May 2nd, 1999

"Now, see here—" he protested, and then his eyes moved down to find a small story, minus picture, in the upper-left-hand corner of the front page:

> WOMAN MURDERED.
> POLICE SEEK HUSBAND.
> "Body of Mrs. Alice Hughes
> found shot to death—"

The train thundered over a bridge. Outside the window, a billion trees rose up, flourished their green branches in convulsions of wind, then fell as if chopped to earth.

The train rolled into a station as if nothing at all in the world had happened.

In the silence, the young man's eyes returned to the text:

> Johnathen Hughes, certified
> public accountant, of 112
> Plandome Avenue, Plandome—"

"My God!" he cried. "Get away!"

But he himself rose and ran a few steps back before the older man could move. The train jolted and threw him into an empty seat where he stared wildly out at a river of green light that rushed past the windows.

Christ, he thought, who would *do* such a thing? Who'd try to hurt us—*us*? What kind of joke? To mock a new marriage with a fine wife? Damn! And again, trembling, Damn, oh, damn!

The train rounded a curve and all but threw him to his feet. Like a man drunk with traveling, gravity, and simple rage, he swung about and lurched back to confront the old man, bent now into his newspaper, gone to earth, hiding in print. Hughes brushed the paper out of the way, and clutched the old man's shoulder. The old man, startled, glanced up, tears running from his eyes. They were both held in a long moment of thunderous traveling. Hughes felt his soul rise to leave his body.

"Who *are* you!?"

Someone must have shouted that.

The train rocked as if it might derail.

The old man stood up as if shot in the heart, blindly crammed something in Johnathen Hughes's hand, and blundered away down the aisle and into the next car.

The younger man opened his fist and turned a card over and read a few words that moved him heavily down to sit and read the words again:

JOHNATHEN HUGHES, CPA
679-4990. Plandome.

"No!" someone shouted.

Me, thought the young man. Why, that old man is . . . *me.*

There was a conspiracy, no, several conspiracies. Someone had contrived a joke about murder and played it on him. The train roared on with five hundred commuters who all rode, swaying like a team of drunken intellectuals behind their masking books and papers, while the old man, as if pursued by demons, fled off away from car to car. By the time Johnathen Hughes had rampaged his blood and completely thrown his sanity off balance, the old man had plunged, as if falling, to the farthest end of the commuter's special.

The two men met again in the last car, which was almost empty. Johnathen Hughes came and stood over the old man, who refused to look up. He was crying so hard now that conversation would have been impossible.

Who, thought the young man, who is he crying for? Stop, please, stop.

The old man, as if commanded, sat up, wiped his eyes, blew his nose, and began to speak in a frail voice that drew Johnathen Hughes near and finally caused him to sit and listen to the whispers:

"We were born—"

"We?" cried the young man.

"We," whispered the old man, looking out at the gathering dusk that traveled like smokes and burnings past the window, "we, yes, we, the two of us, we were born in Quincy in 1950, August twenty-second—"

Yes, thought Hughes.

"—and lived at Forty-nine Washington Street and went to Central School and walked to that school all through first grade with Isabel Perry—"

Isabel, thought the young man.

"we . . ." murmured the old man. "our" whispered the old man. "us" And went on and on with it:

"Our woodshop teacher, Mr. Bisbee. History teacher, Miss Monks. We broke our right ankle, age ten, ice-skating. Almost drowned, age eleven; Father saved us. Fell in love, age twelve, Impi Johnson—"

Seventh grade, lovely lady, long since dead, Jesus God, thought the young man, growing old.

And that's what happened. In the next minute, two minutes, three, the old man talked and talked and gradually became younger with talking, so his cheeks glowed and his eyes brightened, while the young man, weighted with old knowledge given, sank lower in his seat and grew pale so that both almost met in mid-talking, mid-listening, and became twins in passing. There was a moment when Johnathen Hughes knew for an absolute insane certainty, that if he dared glance up he would see identical twins in the mirrored window of a night-rushing world.

He did not look up.

The old man finished, his frame erect now, his head somehow driven high by the talking out, the long-lost revelations.

"That's the past," he said.

I should hit him, thought Hughes. Accuse him. Shout at him. Why aren't I hitting, accusing, shouting.

Because . . .

The old man sensed the question and said, "You know I'm who I say I am. I know everything there is to know about us. Now—the future?"

"Mine?"

"Ours," said the old man.

Johnathen Hughes nodded, staring at the newspaper clutched in the old man's right hand. The old man folded it and put it away.

"Your business will slowly become less than good. For what reasons, who can say? A child will be born and die. A mistress will be taken and lost. A wife will become less than good. And at last, oh believe it, yes, do, very slowly, you will come to—how shall I say it—hate her living presence. There, I see I've upset you. I'll shut up."

They rode in silence for a long while, and the old man grew old again, and the young man along with him. When he had aged just the proper amount, the young man nodded the talk to continue, not looking at the other who now said:

"Impossible, yes, you've been married only a year, a great year, the best. Hard to think that a single drop of ink could color a whole pitcher of clear fresh water. But color it could and color it did. And at last the entire world changed, not just our wife, not just the beautiful woman, the fine dream."

"You—" Johnathen Hughes started and stopped. "You—killed her?"

"We did. Both of us. But if I have my way, if I can convince you, neither of us will, she will live, and you will grow old to become a happier, finer me. I pray for that. I weep for that. There's still time. Across the years, I intend to shake you up, change your blood, shape your mind. God, if people knew what murder is. So silly, so stupid, so—ugly. But there is hope, for I have somehow got here, touched you, begun the change that will save our souls. Now, listen. You do admit, do you not, that we are one and the same, that the twins of time ride this train this hour this night?"

The train whistled ahead of them, clearing the track of an encumbrance of years.

The young man nodded the most infinitely microscopic of nods. The old man needed no more.

"I ran away. I ran to you. That's all I can say. She's been dead only a day, and I ran. Where to go? Nowhere to hide, save Time. No one to plead with, no judge, no jury, no proper witnesses save—you. Only you can wash the blood away, do you see? You *drew* me, then. Your youngness, your innocence, your good hours, your fine life still untouched, was the machine that seized me down the track. All of my sanity lies in you. If you turn away, great God, I'm lost, no, *we* are lost. We'll share a grave and never rise and be buried forever in misery. Shall I tell you what you must do?"

The young man rose.

"Plandome," a voice cried. "Plandome."

And they were out on the platform with the old man running after,

the young man blundering into walls, into people, feeling as if his limbs might fly apart.

"Wait!" cried the old man. "Oh, please."

The young man kept moving.

"Don't you see, we're in this together, we must think of it together, solve it together, so you won't become me and I won't have to come impossibly in search of you, oh, it's all mad, insane, I know, I know, but listen!"

The young man stopped at the edge of the platform where cars were pulling in, with joyful cries or muted greetings, brief honkings, gunnings of motors, lights vanishing away. The old man grasped the young man's elbow.

"Good God, your wife, mine, will be here in a moment, there's so much to tell, you *can't* know what I know, there's twenty years of unfound information lost between which we must trade and understand! Are you listening? God, you *don't* believe!"

Johnathen Hughes was watching the street. A long way off a final car was approaching. He said: "What happened in the attic at my grandmother's house in the summer of 1958? No one knows that but me. Well?"

The old man's shoulders slumped. He breathed more easily, and as if reciting from a promptboard said: "We hid ourselves there for two days, alone. No one ever knew where we hid. Everyone thought we had run away to drown in the lake or fall in the river. But all the time, crying, not feeling wanted, we hid up above and . . . listened to the wind and wanted to die."

The young man turned at last to stare fixedly at his older self, tears in his eyes. "*You* love me, then?"

"I had better," said the old man. "I'm all you have."

The car was pulling up at the station. A young woman smiled and waved behind the glass.

"Quick," said the old man, quietly. "Let me come home, watch, show you, teach you, find where things went wrong, correct them now, maybe hand you a fine life forever, let me—"

The car horn sounded, the car stopped, the young woman leaned out.

"Hello, lovely man!" she cried.

Johnathen Hughes exploded a laugh and burst into a manic run. "Lovely lady, hi—"

"Wait."

He stopped and turned to look at the old man with the newspaper, trembling there on the station platform. The old man raised one hand, questioningly.

"Haven't you forgotten something?"

Silence. At last: "You," said Johnathen Hughes. "You."

The car rounded a turn in the night. The woman, the old man, the young, swayed with the motion.

"What did you say your name was?" the young woman said, above the rush and run of country and road.

"He didn't say," said Johnathen Hughes quickly.

"Weldon," said the old man, blinking.

"Why," said Alice Hughes. "That's *my* maiden name."

The old man gasped inaudibly, but recovered. "Well, *is* it? How curious!"

"I wonder if we're related? You—"

"He was my teacher at Central High," said Johnathen Hughes, quickly.

"And still am," said the old man. "And still am."

And they were home.

He could not stop staring. All through dinner, the old man simply sat with his hands empty half the time and stared at the lovely woman across the table from him. Johnathen Hughes fidgeted, talked much too loudly to cover the silences, and ate sparsely. The old man continued to stare as if a miracle was happening every ten seconds. He watched Alice's mouth as if it were giving forth fountains of diamonds. He watched her eyes as if all the hidden wisdoms of the world were there, and now found for the first time. By the look of his face, the old man, stunned, had forgotten why he was there.

"Have I a crumb on my chin?" cried Alice Hughes, suddenly. "Why is everyone *watching* me?"

Whereupon the old man burst into tears that shocked everyone. He could not seem to stop, until at last Alice came around the table to touch his shoulder.

"Forgive me," he said. "It's just that you're so lovely. Please sit down. Forgive."

They finished off the dessert and with a great display of tossing down his fork and wiping his mouth with his napkin, Johnathen Hughes cried, "That was fabulous. Dear wife, I love you!" He kissed her on the cheek, thought better of it, and rekissed her, on the mouth. "You see?" He glanced at the old man. "I very *much* love my wife."

The old man nodded quietly and said, "Yes, yes, I remember."

"You *remember?*" said Alice, staring.

"A toast!" said Johnathen Hughes, quickly. "To a fine wife, a grand future!"

His wife laughed. She raised her glass.

"Mr. Weldon," she said, after a moment. "You're not drinking? . . ."

It was strange seeing the old man at the door to the living room.

"Watch this," he said, and closed his eyes. He began to move certainly and surely about the room, eyes shut. "Over here is the pipestand, over here the books. On the fourth shelf down a copy of Eiseley's *The Star Thrower*. One shelf up H. G. Wells's *Time Machine,* most appropriate, and over here the special chair, and me in it."

He sat. He opened his eyes.

Watching from the door, Johnathen Hughes said, "You're not going to cry again, are you?"

"No. No more crying."

There were sounds of washing up from the kitchen. The lovely woman out there hummed under her breath. Both men turned to look out of the room toward that humming.

"Some day," said Johnathen Hughes, "I will hate her? Some day, I will kill her?"

"It doesn't seem possible, does it? I've watched her for an hour and found nothing, no hint, no clue, not the merest period, semicolon or exclamation point of blemish, bump, or hair out of place with her. I've watched you, too, to see if *you* were at fault, *we* were at fault, in all this."

"And?" The young man poured sherry for both of them, and handed over a glass.

"You drink too much is about the sum. Watch it."

Hughes put his drink down without sipping it. "What else?"

"I suppose I should give you a list, make you keep it, look at it every day. Advice from the old crazy to the young fool."

"Whatever you say, I'll remember."

"Will you? For how long? A month, a year, then, like everything else, it'll go. You'll be busy living. You'll be slowly turning into . . . me. She will slowly be turning into someone worth putting out of the world. Tell her you love her."

"Every day."

"Promise! It's *that* important! Maybe that's where I failed myself, failed us. Every day, without fail!" The old man leaned forward, his face taking fire with his words. "Every day. Every day!"

Alice stood in the doorway, faintly alarmed.

"Anything wrong?"

"No, no." Johnathen Hughes smiled. "We were trying to decide which of us likes you best."

She laughed, shrugged, and went away.

"I think," said Johnathen Hughes, and stopped and closed his eyes, forcing himself to say it, "it's time for you to go."

"Yes, time." But the old man did not move. His voice was very tired, exhausted, sad. "I've been sitting here feeling defeated. I can't find anything wrong. I can't find the flaw. I can't advise you, my God, it's so stupid, I shouldn't have come to upset you, worry you, disturb your life, when I have nothing to offer but vague suggestions, inane cryings of doom. I sat here a moment ago and thought: I'll kill her now, get rid of her now, take the blame now, as an old man, so the young man there, you, can go on into the future and be free of her. Isn't that silly? I wonder if it would work? It's that old time-travel paradox, isn't it? Would I foul up the time flow, the world, the universe, what? Don't worry, no, no, don't look that way. No murder now. It's all been done up ahead, twenty years in your future. The old man having done nothing whatever, having been no help, will now open the door and run away to his madness."

He arose and shut his eyes again.

"Let me see if I can find my way out of my own house, in the dark."

He moved, the young man moved with him to find the closet by the front door and open it and take out the old man's overcoat and slowly shrug him into it.

"You *have* helped," said Johnathen Hughes. "You have told me to tell her I love her."

"Yes, I *did* do that, didn't I?"

They turned to the door.

"Is there hope for us?" the old man asked, suddenly, fiercely.

"Yes. I'll make sure of it," said Johnathen Hughes.

"Good, oh, good. I almost believe!"

The old man put one hand out and blindly opened the front door.

"I won't say good-bye to her. I couldn't stand looking at that lovely face. Tell her the old fool's gone. Where? Up the road to wait for you. You'll arrive someday."

"To become you? Not a chance," said the young man.

"Keep saying that. And—my God—here—" The old man fumbled in

his pocket and drew forth a small object wrapped in crumpled newspaper. "You'd better keep this. I can't be trusted, even now. I might do something wild. Here. Here."

He thrust the object into the young man's hands. "Good-bye. Doesn't that mean: God be with you? Yes. Good-bye."

The old man hurried down the walk into the night. A wind shook the trees. A long way off, a train moved in darkness, arriving or departing, no one could tell.

Johnathen Hughes stood in the doorway for a long while, trying to see if there really was someone out there vanishing in the dark.

"Darling," his wife called.

He began to unwrap the small object.

She was in the parlor door behind him now, but her voice sounded as remote as the fading footsteps along the dark street.

"Don't stand there letting the draft in," she said.

He stiffened as he finished unwrapping the object. It lay in his hand, a small revolver.

Far away the train sounded a final cry which failed in the wind.

"Shut the door," said his wife.

His face was cold. He closed his eyes.

Her voice. Wasn't there just the *tiniest* touch of petulance there?

He turned slowly, off-balance. His shoulder brushed the door. It drifted. Then:

The wind, all by itself, slammed the door with a bang.

LINDSAY AND THE RED CITY BLUES

By JOE HALDEMAN

Born in Oklahoma City, raised in the Washington, D.C., area and now living in Florida, Joe Haldeman is widely regarded as one of the finest younger science fiction writers in America. His novel The Forever War, *which won both of the major science fiction awards of its year, the Nebula and the Hugo, drew powerfully on his experiences in Vietnam as a combat demolition specialist. Haldeman holds a masters degree in English and taught a course on creative writing at the University of Iowa before devoting himself to full-time writing in 1975. His fiction is noted for its lean, realistic style and wry point of view. This story, which interestingly parallels Edward Bryant's, "Dark Angel," grew out of a visit Haldeman made to North Africa and expresses effectively some of the fears involved in contact with exotic foreign cultures.*

"The ancient red city of Marrakesh," his guidebook said, "is the last large oasis for travelers moving south into the Sahara. It is the most exotic of Moroccan cities, where Arab Africa and Black Africa meet in a setting that has changed but little in the past thousand years."

In midafternoon, the book did not mention, it becomes so hot that even the flies stop moving.

The air conditioner in his window hummed impressively but neither moved nor cooled the air. He had complained three times and the desk clerk responded with two shrugs and a blank stare. By two o'clock his little warren was unbearable. He fled to the street, where it was hotter.

Scott Lindsay was a salesman who demonstrated chemical glassware for a large scientific-supply house in the suburbs of Washington, D.C. Like all Washingtonians, Lindsay thought that a person who could survive summer on the banks of the Potomac could survive it anywhere. He saved up six weeks of vacation time and flew to Europe in late July. Paris was pleasant enough, and the Pyrenees were even cool, but nobody had told him that on August first all of Europe goes on vacation; every good hotel room has been sewed up for six months, restaurants are jammed or closed, and you spend all your time making bad travel connections to cities where only the most expensive hotels have accommodations.

In Nice a Canadian said he had just come from Morocco, where it was hotter than hell but there were practically no tourists, this time of year. Scott looked wistfully over the poisoned but still blue Mediterranean, felt the pressure of twenty million fellow travelers at his back, remembered Bogie, and booked the next flight to Casablanca.

Casablanca combined the charm of Pittsburgh with the climate of Dallas. The still air was thick with dust from high-rise construction. He picked up a guidebook and riffled through it and, on the basis of a few paragraphs, took the predawn train to Marrakesh.

"The Red City," it went on, "takes its name from the color of the local sandstone from which the city and its ramparts were built." It would be more accurate, Scott reflected, though less alluring, to call it the Pink City. The Dirty Pink City. He stumbled along the sidewalk on the shady side of the street. The twelve-inch strip of shade at the edge of the sidewalk was crowded with sleeping beggars. The heat was so dry he couldn't even sweat.

He passed two bars that were closed and stepped gratefully into a third. It was a Moslem bar, a milk bar, no booze, but at least it was shade. Two young men slumped at the bar, arguing in guttural whispers, and a pair of ancients in burnooses sat at a table playing a static game of checkers. An oscillating fan pushed the hot air and dust around. He raised a finger at the bartender, who regarded him with stolid hostility, and ordered in schoolboy French a small bottle of Vichy water, carbonated, without ice, and, out of deference to the guidebook, a glass of hot mint tea. The bartender brought the mint tea and a liter bottle of Sidi Harazim water, not carbonated, with a glass of ice. Scott tried to argue with the man but he only stared and kept repeating the price. He finally paid and dumped the ice (which the guidebook had warned him about) into the ashtray. The young men at the bar watched the transaction with sleepy indifference.

The mint tea was an aromatic infusion of mint leaves in hot sugar water. He sipped and was surprised, and perversely annoyed, to find it quite pleasant. He took a paperback novel out of his pocket and read the same two paragraphs over and over, feeling his eyes track, unable to concentrate in the heat.

He put the book down and looked around with slow deliberation, trying to be impressed by the alienness of the place. Through the open front of the bar he could see across the street, where a small park shaded the outskirts of the Djemaa El Fna, the largest open-air market in Morocco and, according to the guidebook, the most exciting and colorful; which itself was the gateway to the mysterious labyrinthine medina, where even this moment someone was being murdered for his pocket change, goats were being used in ways of which Allah did not approve, men were smoking a mixture of camel dung and opium, children were merchandised like groceries; where dark men and women would do anything for a price, and the price would not be high. Scott touched his pocket unconsciously and the hard bulge of the condom was still there.

The best condoms in the world are packaged in a blue plastic cylinder, squared off along the prolate axis, about the size of a small matchbox. The package is a marvel of technology, held fast by a combination of geometry and sticky tape, and a cool-headed man, under good lighting conditions, can open it in less than a minute. Scott had bought six of them in the drugstore in Dulles International, and had only opened one. He hadn't opened it for the Parisian woman who had looked like a prostitute but had returned his polite proposition with a storm of outrage. He opened it for the fat customs inspector at the Casablanca airport, who had to have its function explained to him, who held it between two dainty fingers like a dead sea thing, and called his compatriots over for a look.

The Djemaa El Fna was closed against the heat, pale-orange dusty tents slack and pallid in the stillness. And the trees through which he stared at the open-air market, the souk, they were also covered with pale dust; the sky was so pale as to be almost white, and the street and sidewalk were the color of dirty chalk. It was like a faded watercolor displayed under too strong a light.

"Hey, mister." A slim Arab boy, evidently in his early teens, had slipped into the place and was standing beside Lindsay. He was well scrubbed and wore Western-style clothing, discreetly patched.

"Hey, mister," he repeated. "You American?"

"Nu. Eeg bin Jugoslav."

The boy nodded. "You from New York? I got four friends New York."

"Jugoslav."

"You from Chicago? I got four friends Chicago. No, five. Five friends Chicago."

"Jugoslav," he said.

"Where in U.S. you from?" He took a melting ice cube from the ashtray, buffed it on his sleeve, popped it into his mouth, crunched.

"New Caledonia," Scott said.

"Don't like ice? Ice is good this time day." He repeated the process with another cube. "New what?" he mumbled.

"New Caledonia. Little place in the Rockies, between Georgia and Wisconsin. I don't like polluted ice."

"No, mister, this ice okay. Bottle-water ice." He rattled off a stream of Arabic at the bartender, who answered with a single harsh syllable. "Come on, I guide you through medina."

"No."

"I guide you free. Student, English student. I take you free, take you my father's factory."

"You'll take me, all right."

"Okay, we go now. No touris' shit, make good deal."

Well, Lindsay, you wanted experiences. How about being knocked over the head and raped by a goat? "All right, I'll go. But no pay."

"Sure, no pay." He took Scott by the hand and dragged him out of the bar, into the park.

"Is there any place in the medina where you can buy cold beer?"

"Sure, lots of place. Ice beer. You got cigarette?"

"Don't smoke."

"That's okay, you buy pack up here." He pointed at a gazebo-shaped concession on the edge of the park.

"Hell, no. You find me a beer and I might buy you some cigarettes." They came out of the shady park and crossed the packed-earth plaza of the Djemaa El Fna. Dust stung his throat and nostrils, but it wasn't quite as hot as it had been earlier; a slight breeze had come up. One industrious merchant was rolling up the front flap of his tent, exposing racks of leather goods. He called out "Hey, you buy!" but Scott ignored him, and the boy made a fist gesture, thumb erect between the two first fingers.

Scott had missed one section of the guidebook: "Never visit the medina without a guide; the streets are laid out in crazy, unpredictable angles and someone who doesn't live there will be hopelessly lost in minutes. The best guides are older men or young Americans who live there for the cheap narcotics; with them you can arrange the price ahead of time, usually about 5 dirham ($1.10). *Under no circumstances* hire one of the street urchins who pose as students and offer to guide you for free; you will be cheated or even beaten up and robbed."

They passed behind the long double row of tents and entered the medina through the Bab Agnou gateway. The main street of the place was a dirt alley some eight feet wide, flanked on both sides by small shops and stalls, most of which were closed, either with curtains or steel shutters or with the proprietor dozing on the stoop. None of the shops had a wall on the side fronting the alley, but the ones that served food usually had chest-high counters. If they passed an open shop the merchant would block their way and importune them in urgent simple French or English, plucking at Scott's sleeve as they passed.

It was surprisingly cool in the medina, the sun's rays partially blocked by wooden lattices suspended over the alleyway. There was a roast-chestnut smell of semolina being parched, with accents of garlic and strange herbs smoldering. Slight tang of exhaust fumes and sickly-sweet hint of garbage and sewage hidden from the sun. The boy led him down a side street, and then another. Scott couldn't tell the position of the sun and was quickly disoriented.

"Where the hell are we going?"

"Cold beer. You see." He plunged down an even smaller alley, dark and sinister, and Lindsay followed, feeling unarmed.

They huddled against a damp wall while a white-haired man on an antique one-cylinder motor scooter hammered by. "How much farther is this place? I'm not going to—"

"Here, one corner." The boy dragged him around the corner and into a musty-smelling, dark shop. The shopkeeper, small and round, smiled gold teeth and greeted the boy by name, Abdul. "The word for beer is 'bera,' " he said. Scott repeated the word to the fat little man and Abdul added something. The man opened two beers and set them down on the counter, along with a pack of cigarettes.

It's a new little Arab, Lindsay, but I think you'll be amused by its presumption. He paid and gave Abdul his cigarettes and beer. "Aren't you Moslem? I thought Moslems didn't drink."

"Hell yes, man." He stuck his finger down the neck of the bottle and flicked away a drop of beer, then tilted the bottle up and drained half of it in one gulp. Lindsay sipped at his. It was warm and sour.

"What you do in the States, man?" He lit a cigarette and held it awkwardly.

Chemical glassware salesman? "I drive a truck." The acrid Turkish tobacco smoke stung his eyes.

"Make lots of money."

"No, I don't." He felt foolish saying it. World traveler, Lindsay, you spent more on your ticket than this boy will see in his life.

"Let's go my father's factory."

"What does your father make?"

"All kinds things. Rugs."

"I wouldn't know what to do with a rug."

"We wrap it, mail to New Caledonia."

"No. Let's go back to—"

"I take you my uncle's factory. Brass, very pretty."

"No. Back to the plaza, you got your cig—"

"Sure, let's go." He gulped down the rest of his beer and stepped back into the alley, Scott following. After a couple of twists and turns they passed an antique-weapons shop that Scott knew he would have noticed, if they'd come by it before. He stopped.

"Where are you taking me now?"

He looked hurt. "Back to Djemaa El Fna. Like you say."

"The hell you are. Get lost, Abdul. I'll find my own way back." He turned and started retracing their path. The boy followed about ten paces behind him, smoking.

He walked for twenty minutes or so, trying to find the relatively broad alleyway that would lead back to the gate. The character of the medina changed: there were fewer and fewer places selling souvenirs, and then none; only residences and little general-merchandise stores, and some small-craft factories, where one or two men, working at a feverish pace, cranked out the items that were sold in the shops. No one tried to sell him anything, and when a little girl held out her hand to beg, an old woman shuffled over and slapped her. Everybody stared when he passed.

Finally he stopped and let Abdul catch up with him. "All right, you win. How much to lead me out?"

"Ten dirham."

"Stuff it. I'll give you two."

Abdul looked at him for a long time, hands in pockets. "Nine dirham." They haggled for a while and finally settled on seven dirham, about $1.50, half now and half at the gate.

They walked through yet another part of the medina, single file through narrow streets, Abdul smoking silently in the lead. Suddenly he stopped.

Scott almost ran into him. "Say, you want girl?"

"Uh . . . I'm not sure," Scott said, startled into honesty.

He laughed, surprisingly deep and lewd. "A boy, then?"

"No, no." Composure, Lindsay. "Your sister, no doubt."

"*What?*" Wrong thing to say.

"American joke. She a friend of yours?"

"Good friend, good fuck. Fifty dirham."

Scott sighed. "Ten." Eventually they settled on thirty-two, Abdul to wait outside until Scott needed his services as a guide again.

Abdul took him to a caftan shop, where he spoke in whispers with the fat owner, and gave him part of the money. They led Lindsay to the rear of the place, behind a curtain. A woman sat on her heels beside the bed, patiently crocheting. She stood up gracelessly. She was short and slight, the top of her head barely reaching Scott's shoulders, and was dressed in traditional costume: lower part of the face veiled, dark blue caftan reaching her ankles. At a command from the owner, she hiked the caftan up around her hips and sat down on the bed with her legs spread apart.

"You see, very clean," Abdul said. She was the skinniest woman Scott had ever seen naked, partially naked, her pelvic girdle prominent under smooth brown skin. She had very little pubic hair and the lips of her vulva were dry and grey. But she was only in her early teens, Scott estimated; that, and the bizarre prospect of screwing a fully clothed masked stranger stimulated him instantly, urgently.

"All right," he said, hoarse. "I'll meet you outside."

She watched with alert curiosity as he fumbled with the condom package, and the only sound she made throughout their encounter was to giggle when he fitted the device over his penis. It was manufactured to accommodate the complete range of possible sizes, and on Scott it had a couple of inches to spare.

This wonder condom, first-class special-delivery French letter is coated with a fluid so similar to natural female secretions, so perfectly intermiscible and isotonic, that it could fool the inside of a vagina. But Scott's ran out of juice in seconds, and the aloof lady's physiology didn't supply any replacement, so he had to fall back on saliva and an old familiar fantasy. It was a long dry haul, the bedding straw crunching monotonously under them, she constantly shifting to more comfortable positions as he angrily pressed his weight into her, finally a draining that was more hydrostatics than passion, which left him jumpy rather than satisfied. When he rolled off her the condom stayed put, there being more lubrication inside it than out. The woman extracted it and, out of some obscure motive, twisted a knot in the end and dropped it behind the bed.

When he'd finished dressing, she held out her hand for a tip. He laughed and told her in English that he was the one who ought to be paid, he'd done all the work, but gave her five dirham anyhow, for the first rush of excitement and her vulnerable eyes.

Abdul was not waiting for him. He tried to interrogate the caftan dealer in French, but got only an interesting spectrum of shrugs. He stepped out onto the street, saw no trace of the little scoundrel, went back inside and gave the dealer a five while asking the way to Djemaa El Fna. He nodded once and wrote them down on a slip of paper in clear, copybook English.

"You speak English?"

"No," he said with an Oxford vowel.

Scott threaded his way through the maze of narrow streets, carefully memorizing the appearance of each corner in case he had to backtrack. None of the streets was identified by name. The sun was down far enough for the medina to be completely in shadow, and it was getting cooler. He stopped at a counter to drink a bottle of beer, and a pleasant lassitude fell over him, the first time he had not felt keyed-up since the Casablanca airport. He strolled on, taking a left at the corner of dye shop and motor scooter.

Halfway down the street, Abdul stood with seven or eight other boys, chattering away, laughing.

Scott half-ran toward the group and Abdul looked up, startled, when he roared "You little bastard!"—but Abdul only smiled and muttered something to his companions, and all of them rushed him.

Not a violent man by any means, Scott had nevertheless suffered enough at the hands of this boy, and he planted his feet, balled his fists, bared his teeth and listened with his whole body to the sweet singing adrenalin. He'd had twelve hours of hand-to-hand combat instruction in basic training, the first rule of which (*If you're outnumbered, run*) he ignored; the second rule of which (*Kick, don't punch*) he forgot, and swung a satisfying roundhouse into the first face that came within reach, breaking lips and teeth and one knuckle (he would realize later); then assayed a side-kick to the groin, which only hit a hip but did put the victim out of the fray; touched the ground for balance and bounced up, shaking a child off his right arm while swinging his left at Abdul's neck, and missing; another side-kick, this time straight to a kidney, producing a good loud shriek; Abdul hanging out of reach, boys all over him, kicking, punching, finally dragging him to his knees;

Abdul stepping forward and kicking him in the chest, then the solar plexus; the taste of dust as someone keeps kicking his head; losing it, losing it, fading out as someone takes his wallet, then from the other pocket, his traveler's checks, Lindsay, tell them to leave the checks, they can't, nobody will, just doing it to annoy me, fuck them.

It was raining and singing. He opened one eye and saw dark brown. His tongue was flat on the dirt, interesting crunchy dirt-taste in his mouth, Lindsay, reel in your tongue, this is stupid, people piss in this street. Raining and singing, I have died and gone to Marrakesh. He slid forearm and elbow under his chest and pushed up a few inches. An irregular stain of blood caked the dust in front of him, and blood was why he couldn't open the other eye. He wiped the mud off his tongue with his sleeve, then used the other sleeve to unstick his eyelid.

The rain was a wrinkled old woman without a veil, patiently sprinkling water on his head, from a pitcher, looking very old and sad. When he sat up, she offered him two white tablets with the letter "A" impressed on them, and a glass of the same water. He took them gratefully, gagged on them, used another glass of water to wash them farther down. Thanked the impassive woman in three languages, hoped it was bottled water, stood up shakily, sledgehammer headache. The slip of paper with directions lay crumpled in the dust, scuffed but still legible. He continued on his way.

The singing was a muezzin, calling the faithful to prayer. He could hear others singing, in more distant parts of the city. Should he take off his hat? No hat. Some natives were simply walking around, going about their business. An old man was prostrate on a prayer rug in the middle of the street; Scott tiptoed around him.

He came out of the medina through a different gate, and the Djemaa El Fna was spread out in front of him in all its early-evening frenzy. A troupe of black dancers did amazing things to machine-gun drum rhythms; acrobats formed high shaky pyramids, dropped, re-formed; people sang, shouted, laughed.

He watched a snake handler for a long time, going through a creepy repertoire of cobras, vipers, scorpions, tarantulas. He dropped a half-dirham in the man's cup and went on. A large loud group was crowded around a bedsheet-size game board where roosters strutted from one chalked area to another, pecking at a vase of plastic flowers here, a broken doll there, a painted tin can or torn deck of playing cards elsewhere; men laying down incomprehensible bets, collecting money, shouting at the roosters, baby needs a new pair of sandals.

Then a quiet, patient line, men and women squatting, waiting for the services of a healer. The woman being treated had her dress tucked modestly between her thighs, back bared from shoulders to buttocks, while the healer burned angry welts in a symmetrical pattern with the smoldering end of a length of clothesline, and Scott walked on, charmed in the old sense of the word, hypnotized.

People shrank from his bloody face and he laughed at them, feeling like part of the show, then feeling like something apart, a visitation. Drifting down the rows of merchants: leather, brass, ceramics, carvings, textiles, books, junk, blankets, weapons, hardware, jewelry, food. Stopping to buy a bag of green pistachio nuts, the vendor gives him the bag and then waves him away, flapping; no pay, just leave.

Gathering darkness and most of the merchants closed their tents but the thousands of people didn't leave the square. They moved in around men, perhaps a dozen of them, who sat on blankets scattered around the square, in the flickering light of kerosene lanterns, droning the same singsong words over and over. Scott moved to the closest and shouldered his way to the edge of the blanket and squatted there, an American gargoyle, staring. Most of the people gave him room but light fingers tested his hip pocket; he swatted the hand away without looking back. The man in the center of the blanket fixed on his bloody stare and smiled back a tight smile, eyes bright with excitement. He raised both arms and the crowd fell silent, switched off.

A hundred people breathed in at once when he whispered the first words, barely audible words that must have been the Arabic equivalent of "Once upon a time." And then the storyteller shouted and began to pace back and forth, playing out his tale in a dramatic staccato voice, waving his arms, hugging himself, whispering, moaning—and Lindsay followed it perfectly, laughing on cue, crying when the storyteller cried, understanding nothing and everything. When it was over, the man held out his cap first to the big American with the bloody face, and Scott emptied his left pocket into the cap: dirham and half-dirham pieces and leftover francs and one rogue dime.

And he stood up and turned around and watched his long broad shadow dance over the crowd as the storyteller with his lantern moved on around the blanket, and he spotted his hotel and pushed toward it through the mob.

It was worth it. The magic was worth the pain and humiliation.

He forced himself to think of practical things, as he approached the hotel. He had no money, no credit cards, no traveler's checks, no identification. Should he go to the police? Probably it would be best to go to American Express first. Collect phone call to the office. Have some money wired. Identity established, so he could have the checks replaced. Police here unlikely to help unless "tipped."

Ah, simplicity. He did have identification; his passport, that he'd left at the hotel desk. That had been annoying, now a lifesaver. Numbers of traveler's checks in his suitcase.

There was a woman in the dusty dim lobby of the hotel. He walked right by her and she whispered "Lin—say."

He remembered the eyes and stopped. "What do you want?"

"I have something of yours." Absurdly, he thought of the knotted condom. But what she held up was a fifty-dollar traveler's check. He snatched it from her; she didn't attempt to stop him.

"You sign that to me," she said. "I bring you everything else the boys took."

"Even the money?" He had over five hundred dirhams' cash.

"What they gave me, I bring you."

"Well, you bring it here, and we'll see."

She shook her head angrily. "No, I bring *you*. I bring you . . . *to* it. Right now. You sign that to me."

He was tempted. "At the caftan shop?"

"That's right. Wallet and 'merican 'spress check. You come."

The medina at night. A little sense emerged. "Not now. I'll come with you in the morning."

"Come now."

"I'll see you here in the morning." He turned and walked up the stairs.

Well, he had fifty out of the twelve hundred dollars. He checked the suitcase and the list of numbers was where he'd remembered. If she wasn't there in the morning, he would be able to survive the loss. He caressed the dry leather sheath of the antique dagger he'd bought in the Paris flea market. If she was waiting, he would go into the medina armed. It would simplify things to have the credit cards. He fell asleep and had violent dreams.

He woke at dawn. Washed up and shaved. The apparition that peered back from the mirror looked worse than he felt; he was still more exhilarated than otherwise. He took a healing drink of brandy and stuck the dagger in his belt, in the back so he wouldn't have to button his sport coat. The muezzin's morning wail stopped.

She was sitting in the lobby's only chair, and stood when he came down the stairs.

"No tricks," he said. "If you have what you say, you get the fifty dollars."

They went out of the hotel and the air was almost cool, damp smell of garbage. "Why did the boys give this to you?"

"Not *give*. Business deal, I get half."

There was no magic in the Djemaa El Fna in the morning, just dozens of people walking through the dust. They entered the medina and it was likewise bereft of mystery and danger. Sleepy collection of closed-off shopfronts, everything beaded with dew, quiet and stinking. She led him back the way he had come yesterday afternoon. Passing the alley where he had encountered the boys, he noticed there was no sign of blood. Had the old woman neatly cleaned up, or was it simply scuffed away on the sandals of negligent passersby? Thinking about the fight, he touched the dagger, loosening it in its sheath. Not for the first time, he wondered whether he was walking into a trap. He almost hoped so. But all he had left of value was his signature.

Lindsay had gotten combat pay in Vietnam, but the closest he'd come to fighting was to sit in a bunker while mortars and rockets slammed around in the night. He'd never fired a shot in anger, never seen a dead man, never this never that, and he vaguely felt unproven. The press of the knife both comforted and frightened him.

They entered the caftan shop, Lindsay careful to leave the door open behind them. The fat caftan dealer was seated behind a table. On the table were Lindsay's wallet and a china plate with a small pile of dried mud.

The dealer watched impassively while Lindsay snatched up his wallet. "The checks."

The dealer nodded. "I have a proposition for you."

"You've learned English."

"I believe I have something you would like to buy with those checks."

Lindsay jerked out the dagger and pointed it at the man's neck. His hand and voice shook with rage. "I'll cut your throat first. Honest to God, I will."

There was a childish giggle and the curtain to the "bedroom" parted, revealing Abdul with a pistol. The pistol was so large he had to hold it with both hands, but he held it steadily, aimed at Lindsay's chest.

"Drop the knife," the dealer said.

Lindsay didn't. "This won't work. Not even here."

"A merchant has a right to protect himself."

"That's not what I mean. You can kill me, I know, but you can't force me to sign those checks at gunpoint. *I will not do it!*"

He chuckled. "That is not what I had in mind, not at all. I truly do have something to sell you, something beyond worth. The gun is only for my protection; I assumed you were wise enough to come armed. Relinquish the knife and Abdul will leave."

Lindsay hesitated, weighing obscure odds, balancing the will to live against his newly born passion. He dropped the dagger.

The merchant said something in Arabic while the prostitute picked up the knife and set it on the table. Abdul emerged from the room with no gun and two straight wooden chairs. He set one next to the table and one behind Lindsay, and left, slamming the door.

"Please sign the check you have and give it to the woman. You promised."

He signed it and asked in a shaking voice, "What do you have that you think I'll pay twelve hundred dollars for?"

The woman reached into her skirts and pulled out the tied-up condom. She dropped it on the plate.

"This," he said, "your blood and seed." With the point of the dagger he opened the condom and its contents spilled into the dirt. He stirred them into mud.

"You are a modern man—"

"What kind of mumbo-jumbo—"

"—a modern man who certainly doesn't believe in magic. Are you Christian?"

"Yes. No." He was born Baptist but hadn't gone inside a church since he was eighteen.

He nodded. "I was confident the boys could bring back some of your blood last night. More than I needed, really." He dipped his thumb in the vile mud and smeared a rough cross on the woman's forehead.

"I can't believe this."

"But you can." He held out a small piece of string. "This is a symbolic restraint." He laid it over the glob of mud and pressed down on it.

Lindsay felt himself being pushed back into the chair. Cold sweat peppered his back and palms.

"Try to get up."

"Why should I?" Lindsay said, trying to control his voice. "I find this fascinating." Insane, Lindsay, voodoo only works on people who believe in it. Psychosomatic.

"It gets even better." He reached into a drawer and pulled out Lindsay's checkbook; opened it and set it in front of Lindsay with a pen. "Sign."

Get up get up. "No."

He took four long sharp needles out of the drawer, and began talking in a low monotone, mostly Arabic but some nonsense English. The woman's eyes drooped half-shut and she slumped in the chair.

"Now," he said in a normal voice, "I can do anything to this woman, and she won't feel it. You will." He pulled up her left sleeve and pinched her arm. "Do you feel like writing your name?"

Lindsay tried to ignore the feeling. You can't hypnotize an unwilling subject. Get up get up get up.

The man ran a needle into the woman's left triceps. Lindsay flinched and cried out. Deny him, get up.

He murmured something and the woman lifted her veil and stuck out her tongue, which was long and stained blue. He drove a needle through it and Lindsay's chin jerked back onto his chest, tongue on fire, bile foaming up in his throat. His right hand scrabbled for the pen and the man withdrew the needles.

He scrawled his name on the fifties and hundreds. The merchant took them wordlessly and went to the door. He came back with Abdul, armed again.

"I am going to the bank. When I return, you will be free to go." He lifted the piece of string out of the mud. "In the meantime, you may do as you wish with this woman; she is being paid well. I advise you not to hurt her, of course."

Lindsay pushed her into the back room. It wasn't proper rape, since she didn't resist, but whatever it was he did it twice, and was sore for a week. He left her there and sat at the merchant's table, glaring at Abdul. When he came back, the merchant told Lindsay to gather up the mud and hold it in his hand for at least a half hour. And get out of Marrakesh.

Out in the bright sun he felt silly with the handful of crud, and ineffably angry with himself, and he flung it away and rubbed the offended hand in the dirt. He got a couple of hundred dollars on his credit cards, at an outrageous rate of exchange, and got the first train back to Casablanca and the first plane back to the United States.

Where he found himself to be infected with gonorrhea.

And over the next few months paid a psychotherapist and a hypnotist over two thousand dollars, and nevertheless felt rotten for no organic reason.

And nine months later lay on an examining table in the emergency room of Suburban Hospital, with terrible abdominal pains of apparently psychogenic origin, not responding to muscle relaxants or tranquilizers, while a doctor and two aides watched in helpless horror as his own muscles cracked his pelvic girdle into sharp knives of bone, and his child was born without pain four thousand miles away.

A GARDEN OF BLACKRED ROSES

By CHARLES L. GRANT

Charles L. Grant is a versatile and talented New Jersey writer in his late thirties, who has made his mark in a number of fields, from science fiction to historical novels, but his first allegiance has always been to the tale of supernatural fantasy. In that field he has written a series of novels set in the fictional Connecticut town of Oxrun Station, beginning with The Hour of the Oxrun Dead *in 1977. His work in fantasy is distinguished by its poetic imagery and subtle, delicate handling of fear—fear of loneliness, of loss, of the unknown. Those qualities, together with his feeling for the realities and mysteries of small-town America—a different approach to some of the same themes as the early Bradbury—makes for a compelling combination of the strange and familiar.*

1. Bouquet

A comfortable February warmth expanded throughout the house as the furnace droned on, and the cold outside was reduced to a lurking wind skittering through leafless brown trees, the ragged tail of a stray dog tucked between scrawny haunches, and glimpses of bright white snow through lightly fogged windows. Steven paused at the front door, his left hand on the knob, his gloves stuffed into his overcoat pockets. The girls were in their rooms, either napping fitfully or lying on the floor staring at the carpet, hoping for something to do. Rachel was in the kitchen, arranging in a Wedgwood vase the flowers he had slipped out of old man Dimmesdale's garden. He glanced into the living room, at the fireplace and the logs stacked neatly to be charred into ash; up the stairs at ancient Tambor's tail poking around the corner while the rest of his dark brown-and-tan bulk slept in front of the furnace's baseboard outlet; then down to his hand on the knob. Barely trembling, as he waited.

"Steven, have you gone yet?"

The voice was muffled but the apology was evident. In the beauty of the roses, she had forgiven him the act of stealing. He grinned, rubbed once at a freshly shaven jaw, and slipped on his gloves. There would be no need now for penance.

"No, not yet," he called. "Just going."

"Well, look, on your way back would you stop in Eben's for some milk? I want to make some pudding."

"Chocolate?"

"Butterscotch."

His grin broadened; the peace was complete. "Shouldn't be more than an hour," he said.

"Love you."

"Me, too."

The door opened and he was on the stoop, his face tightening against the cold, his breath taken in small, metal-cold stabs. Using his boots to clear the way, he kicked a narrow path down the concrete walk and past the barberry hedge. There were no cars yet on Hawthorne Street, it was too soon for the returning commuters, but the snow at the gutters was already turning a desecrating brown, though the fall had stopped only an hour before. He wondered what it was about the physics of weather that caused flakes to drift here an unbearable white, and there become slush that could only be described, and charitably so, as unspeakably evil. It seemed to be automatic, needing neither cars nor trucks nor plows to make the transformation. It was, he decided finally, not physics but magic, the word he used when nothing else made sense.

Several women and not a few young children were already out, shovels scraping against stone as they pushed aside the several inches accumulation amid temptations of snowballs and snowmen, and the lingering grey threat of another fall. He waved to several, stopped and spoke with two or three, laughed when a missile struck his back and he was delayed for a block fighting a roaring action against an army of seven. But finally he broke and ran, waving, and warning that he would be back. The children, pompously waddling in overstuffed coats, shrieked and scattered, and the street was suddenly quiet.

No place like it, Steven thought with a smile that would not vanish. Then he looked to his left across the street, and the smile became a remembering grin. Where else, he wondered, except on our Hawthorne Street would there also be a house that belonged to a man named

Dimmesdale, the damned and adulterous minister who rightfully belonged in *The Scarlet Letter*? He paused, then, a momentary guilt darkening his mood as he stared covetously at the garden the old man had planted at the side of the blue Cape Cod. While the rest of the street's gardens were brittle and waiting for spring, Dimmesdale had discovered a way to bring color to snow.

Magic, Steven thought: no two ways about it.

The flowers were mostly roses, and at the back of the house-long garden a thicket of rosebushes with blossoms so deeply red they seemed at a glance to be midnight black.

The night before, as he and Rachel were returning from bridge at Barney and Edna Hawkins' apartment over the luncheonette, Steven had bet his wife he could steal a few of the flowers without being caught. She had grown angry at his sudden childish turn, but he had sent her on in stubborn defiance and had crept, nearly giggling, along the side of the house until he had reached the rear of the garden's bed. There, with a prickling at the back of his neck (though he refused to turn around), he had risked the stab of thorns to break off and race away with a double handful.

Rachel had not spoken to him when he finally returned, out of breath and grinning stupidly, and he had placed the roses in the refrigerator. And the next morning he found her standing over them, each lying neatly and apart from the others on the kitchen table. Her brushed black hair was pulled over one shoulder and she tugged at it, and worried. When he had brought out the vase, she'd glared at him but did not throw the flowers away.

"Amazing," he whispered to the silent house; and when he returned from the office with the papers he'd wanted and had run the gauntlet of children again, Rachel was waiting for him in the living room, smiling proudly at the roses displayed in the bay window.

"You're incorrigible," she said, dark lips brushing his cheek.

"You love it," he answered, shrugging out of his coat and tossing it onto a nearby chair. "Where are the kids?"

"Out. I chased them and the cat into the yard when Sue decided to fingerpaint her room."

"Ah . . . damn," Steven muttered.

Rachel laughed and sat on the broad window ledge, her blue tartan skirt riding to her thighs, her black sweater pulled snug. "Watercolors, dope. It came right off."

"You know," he said, sitting by her feet and lighting a cigarette, "I don't know where they get it. Honestly, I don't. Certainly not from their father."

"Oh, certainly not," she said. "And I'm too demure and staid. It must be in the genes."

"Gene who?"

"The milkman, fool."

"As I thought," he said, holding his cigarette up as though it were a glass of wine, turning it slowly, swinging it gently back and forth. "It's always the husband who's the—"

The scream was faint, but enough to scramble Steven to his feet and race out onto the back porch. His daughters were running toward him, arms waving, hair streaming; four girls, and all of them crying. Rachel came up behind him as he jumped the steps to the ground and knelt, sweeping his girls into his arms, listening through their babbled hysteria until, finally, he understood. And rose.

"Keep them here," he said quietly.

Rachel, who had heard, was fighting not to cry.

He walked across the yard, his legs leaden, his head suddenly too heavy to keep upright. Oblivious to the cold wind blowing down from the grey, heedless of the snow tipping into his shoes.

Tambor. A Siamese that had been with him since before he had met and married Rachel. Seventeen years, fat, content, extraordinarily patient with the babies who yanked at his crooked tail, pounded his back, poked at his slightly crossed eyes and pulled his whiskers.

Tambor. Who loved laps and the bay window and the hearth and thick quilts. Who dug into paper bags and under rugs and as far as he could get into anyone's shoes.

He was lying beneath the crab apple tree at the back of the yard. The children had cleared the snow away from the knees of protruding roots, and the grass was still green, and the earth was still warm. Steven knelt, and was not ashamed when the tears came in mourning for nearly two decades of his life. He buried Tambor where he lay and, as an afterthought, took one of the roses and placed it on the freshly turned, clayed dirt.

"He was old," he said late that night as Rachel hugged him tightly in their bed, her head on his chest. "He was . . . tired."

"I expect him to be there in the morning, big as life, with the rose in his mouth."

Steven smiled. Tambor ate flowers as much as his own food.

"I don't want him to die," she whimpered, much like his daughters. "He introduced us."

"I'll get Dimmesdale to bring him back. He's sure spooky enough."

"Not funny, Steve," she said; and, after a minute: "What are we going to do? I want him back."

"So do I, love."

"Steve, what are we going to do?"

There was nothing he could say. Rachel had hated cats when they'd met, but Tambor had sat in front of her in the apartment, his crossed blue eyes regarding her steadily. Then, as she'd reached out politely to stroke his cocked head, Tambor had gently taken her finger into his mouth, released it and licked it, and Rachel had been besieged and captured in less than a minute.

To replace him was unthinkable.

Yet, the following morning as he trudged glumly down the street to fetch the morning papers, Steven could not get the idea out of his head.

The children were inconsolable. They'd moped over breakfast and refused to listen to his multivoiced rendering of the Sunday comics. When he suggested they go outside and play, they pointedly used the front door and lined up on the sidewalk, watching the rest of the neighborhood, but not joining in.

Lunch was bad, supper was worse, and his temper grew shorter when Rachel took the remaining roses and threw them into the backyard.

"They're too dark," she said to his puzzled glare. "We have enough dark things around here, don't you think?"

And as he lay still in bed again, Rachel sighing in her sleep, he listened to the wind scrape at the house with claws of frozen snow. Listened to the shudder of the eaves, the groan of the doors, and tried to remember how it had been when he had brought Tambor home for the first time. How small, how helpless, stumbling across the bare apartment floor with Steven trailing anxiously behind him, waiting for the opportunity to teach him of litter boxes and sanitation.

The cry made him blink.

Sue, Bess, Annie, Holly. Damn, he thought, someone was having a nightmare again.

Sighing, he waited for Rachel to hear and to move, and when she didn't, he threw back the quilt and stuffed his feet into his slippers. A robe on the bureau found its woolen way around his shoulders and he slipped into the corridor without a light.

A baby crying, wailing plaintively.

He looked into Bess's room, into Holly's, but each was silent.

A baby. Begging.

The other two rooms were equally still.

He pulled the robe tightly across his throat and, after a check to see if Rachel had awakened, he moved downstairs, head cocked, listening, drawn finally into the kitchen. He stood at the back door after flicking on the porch light and peered through the small panes into the yard beyond.

The crying was there.

We were partners, Tambor and I, he thought; friends, buddies, my . . . my conscience.

Remembering, then, the look on the cat's face when he'd crept into the house with the roses in his hands.

Tambor?

You're dreaming, son, he told himself, but could not stop his legs from taking him to the hall closet, his hands grabbing boots and coat and fur-lined gloves. Then he rushed back into the kitchen and yanked open the door.

The crying was there.

And the snow.

Silently now, sifting through the black curtain beyond the reach of the light.

"Tambor!" he whispered harshly.

A shadow moved just to one side of him. He whirled, and it was gone. A faint flicker of red.

He stumbled across the yard to the crab apple tree, pulling from his pocket the flashlight grabbed from the kitchen and aiming it at the grave. It was, in spite of the snow, still cleared; and the rose still lay there, its petals toward the bole.

"Tam, where are you?"

The crying.

He spun around, flashlight following, and in the sweep the darts of red . . . eyes reflecting. He slowed, and there was only the falling, sifting, gently blowing white.

Something else . . . something crouched beyond the cleared space of the grave. He knelt, poked at it with a stiffly trembling finger and saw another rose, one of those Rachel had thrown away. And, still kneeling, he suddenly looked back over his shoulder and saw the shadow, and the steadily gleaming twin points of red.

Big as life, Rachel had said.

One rose . . . big as life.

Two . . .

Suddenly, choking, he threw the flashlight at the now glaring red, at the eyes that told him they did not like being alone. Then he fell to his hands and knees, digging at the snow, thrashing, casting it aside in waves, in splashes. Another rose, and another, as he made his cold and slow way back toward the light, the porch, the safety of the house.

The crying was louder, no longer begging.

The snow was heavier, no longer drifting.

And just before the porch light winked out and the shadow grew, he wondered just how many roses he had stolen from the garden.

2. *Corsage*

A sea of clouds in shades of grey. Breakers of wind that scattered spray. And Barney Hawkins—short, large, nearly sixty—stood by the fence and chewed on his lip. As he had been for an hour, and as he would be doing for an hour more, for the rest of the day, if he didn't make up his mind one way or the other.

He was the owner of the only luncheonette on Hawthorne Street, and he was proud of it, and of the fact that what he called the "nice kids" had chosen his corner establishment for their base, their rendezvous, their home away from school. With long hair and short, short skirts and jeans, they had somehow decided that the red false-leather booths and the green stools lining the white counter were peaceable places undisturbed by disdaining adults and scornful police. He never bothered them, never tried to be more than a friendly ear, except when he tried to show them by his example that romance both capitalized and small was something that did not belong in the modern world. They might argue, then, through a barrier of what he called reality; but as he tolerated their flowers and their causes, so they tolerated his cynicism and his acid.

And he wished that tolerance extended to his wife.

Just that morning a quartet of boys had been huddled over a small tape recorder in the back booth, poking at it apprehensively, looking at one another and at Barney, but not touching it.

Brian was a junior, and the bravest of the lot, and as Barney stared over their heads through the plate-glass window into the drizzle beyond, he listened with half an ear while the boy made his case.

"Look, I was there! And there ain't nothing there at all. You guys don't understand these things, do you? I mean, if there's nothing there, then there's nothing there. That's all there is to it."

"Brian, you're a . . ." The speaker looked toward Barney and grinned. "You're a jerk." It was Syd, bespectacled and tall, somewhat respected and definitely feared for the brains he had, and used, but seldom flaunted. He pushed back his wire-rim glasses and poked at Brian's arm, then at the recorder. "I was there, understand? And I got it all down on tape. Tapes don't lie. I wouldn't fool you."

The other two only nodded; for whom, Barney could not tell.

"All right," Syd said finally. "You want to hear it or not? I haven't got all day. My dad's coming home this afternoon and I got to be there."

Barney pushed reluctantly away from the counter when Edna called him from the back. Shaking his head, he took a swipe at the grill with a damp cloth and pushed aside the bright-blue curtains that kept the wrong eyes from peering into the sanctuary he used when things out front got a little too sticky, lovey, and loud. Edna, her dimming red hair bunned tightly at her nape, was seated at a battered Formica table, a cup of cold tea cradled in her wash-red hands.

"What's up?" he said, taking the chair opposite, hoping she wouldn't want, for the thirty-fifth time, to do something silly and candle-lighted for their anniversary.

She pointed to the pay phone on the wall by the curtain. "Amos called again."

"For God's sake, now what? Didn't I pay for that damned parking ticket last Saturday, for crying out loud?"

Edna's smile was weakly tolerant, and he scratched a large hand through his still blond hair. Amos Russo might be the best cop in town, he thought, but there were times when he could be too damned efficient. And Barney could not convince him that he was not the father of every stray kid who wandered into the shop.

"Well, is it the ticket?" he asked again; and when she shook her head, he groaned. "Then who's in trouble, and why the hell doesn't he call their parents?"

"It's Syd," she said, lowering her voice and glancing toward the front. "That's why I called you in here instead of coming out." Her voice had scaled into a whine, and only by staring at the grease-pocked ceiling could he stop himself from wincing. "It's Syd. The nice one."

"Syd? My God, that kid's got more brains than any twelve of those kids put together. What could he possibly do to rile Amos?"

"He's been prowling around the Yardley place."

"So who hasn't?"

"And he insists that someone is living in there. Amos wants you to tell him to stop bothering the police."

"No," Barney said, straightening and glaring. "No one lives there."

"Now, Barney . . ."

He tightened his lips and stared over her head. The last people, he remembered, to ever live in that run-down firetrap was a young couple who moved in about ten years ago. One weekend they and their van showed up, and two months later the windows were blank and no one knew what had happened. It wasn't the only house in the world like it, he thought, and wouldn't be the last: a relic from an age when high ceilings and wall-sized fireplaces were considered quite romantic and necessary—but to heat such a place now, to replace the outmoded wiring, the plumbing, put on a new roof and drains . . . he himself had once considered buying the house when he was younger, but the money had not been there and the dream soon faded.

Like all the dreams he had had when he was young, of wealth and power and a vast legacy for his children.

Now, there was only the luncheonette and the apartment above it. And children . . . none.

"I'd like to burn the place down," he said.

"Barney!"

He almost laughed at the shock in her face, and the quick resignation that he would never understand. Then, before the fight could begin—as it always did when he tried to explain what reality was—she reached down into her lap, lifted her hands and placed on the table three deep red blossoms wired together. He stared at them, at Edna, and she smiled as she held the flowers to her left shoulder.

"Pretty?"

"Where'd you get them?"

"Dimmesdale's."

"You're not telling me he gave them to you!"

Her smile drifted, returned, and faded. "No. I . . . I took them."

"For God's sake, why?"

"Because they're better than plastic, damnit!" she snapped.

Again he stared, then pushed himself to his feet. "I'll talk to Syd. He's as crazy as you are."

She doesn't know what love is, he thought sadly; she reads too many books and sees too many movies.

He stepped back through the curtain, stopped, and heard the voices.

Edward, it's cold!

It's only the fog, dear. Nothing to fear, nothing at all. Up from the river. Something to do with temperature change and moisture in the air, things like that.

I don't like it. And I'm tired of waiting.

We won't have to wait long, I promise you. Besides, it's peaceful, you have to admit that.

It is. Yes. It is. Quiet, like just before the sun goes down. Would you light a fire? We can sit while we're waiting, and look at the flames.

A click, and the voices changed.

Andrew, it's cold.

Shall I light a fire?

Yes, and draw the curtains, too. I don't like the fog.

Oh, I don't know. I rather enjoy it. It cuts us off, and it's as though we had no problems, no one in the world but you and me. I kind of like it.

It reminds me of graveyards.

You have no romance in your soul, Eloise.

Enough to marry you, didn't I? Kiss me once and light the fire.

All right. But I still like the fog.

And yet again.

I love you, Simon.

It's a beautiful house.

Are you sure you had no one else in mind?

No one, no one at all. It was built just for you.

Do we have to wait long?

Charity, I love you, but you have no patience.

Let's stand on the porch, then, and look at the fog.

I'd rather stay inside and look at the fire.

The four boys had been joined by two girls in cheerleader jackets and short skirts, high white socks and buffed white shoes. They were giggling, and the boys were laughing silently. Barney glared, then rushed around the counter and slammed his hand down on the table, hard enough to jolt the recorder, pop the lid and send the cassette skittering. He snatched it up and jammed it into his pocket, at the same time backing away and ordering the kids out.

There were protests, though muted, and one of the girls stopped at the door and looked back at him.

"Mr. Hawkins, you ain't got no soul," she said.

He grinned tightly. "I do. I just know what to do with it."

"Well," she said as Syd returned to tug at her arm, "you won't have it for long if you don't loosen up."

They vanished, then, into a rusted Pontiac that howled angrily away from the curb toward the football field. He watched a plume of exhaust twist into the rain, blinked, and wondered what in hell had made him react that way.

"Barney?"

He felt the bulge of the cassette in his pocket. Edna moved to stand beside him, one hand on his arm, lightly.

"Syd," he said, "has a perverted sense of humor. He's been sneaking around the neighborhood at night, taping people in their houses. People doing . . . getting ready to do . . . things. He's been using the fog for cover."

"What fog?"

He blinked and looked down at her, stepped back suddenly when she shimmered slightly and her hair brightened, her face softened, and her figure lost the pounds it had gained. Quickly, then, he began untying his apron.

"Why," he said, "the fog. You know what a fog is, don't you? Last night, the night before, I don't know when. Syd's been—"

"Barney, there hasn't been a decent fog around here for . . . for weeks." She stepped toward him, her hand outstretched. "Come on, love, we have sandwiches to get ready before the game is over."

"I don't want them back in here."

"Barney, you're being ridiculous."

He snatched his arm away and tossed the apron into a booth, snatched down his overcoat from the rack by the register and grabbed the cassette. "I'm going out for a minute," he said as he left. "I'll be back in time, don't worry."

"Barney! Please . . . don't—"

He stood outside and saw her through the window, her hands clasped in front of her stomach, and was more than somewhat startled to see the hatred in her face.

Now, an hour later, he could still imagine the uncharacteristic hardening around her eyes, the tight set of her mouth, and the way she stared when he had walked away.

He shuddered and pulled at his collar. Only a few degrees cooler and the rain would be snow. The road was slick and black, and there were puddles skimmed with thin ice. He hunched his shoulders and wished he had brought his hat, wiped a hand over his face and looked out over the lawn beyond the fence. To the Yardley house.

He had only been inside that Victorian mockery of a rich man's mansion once. And once had been enough, more than enough. It had been with Edna, before they were married and while they still watched sunsets and sunrises and delighted at the way young birds learned to fly.

They had crept in through the back door, each carrying a blanket, had made their way to the front of the house and set the blankets atop each other on the floor before the hearth. Edna brought a single candle from which she dripped wax to set it on the mantel. It cast shadows, and as he undressed her, she made stories of them, turning men into knights and women into Guineveres; and when they had done and lay sweated and sated, he tried, tenderly, to tell her what she had done wrong, and they had fought. In the shadows. While the candle burned to the end of its wick.

In the three and a half decades since that night, neither had mentioned it, and Barney only tried to keep boys like Syd from thinking there was something . . . special . . . about a house that overlooked the river.

Finally, he pushed at the gate in the middle of the fence and walked slowly to the porch. As he expected, the front door was locked, and all the windows were grey with dust. He moved down the side steps and made his way through the sodden weeds to the back. Looking through the rain to the blur of the river and the hillside beyond.

There was no fog. There was obviously no one in or near the house. He began to feel foolish, and wondered who Syd had enlisted to make the tape. But since, he thought, he had come this far he might as well lay all the ghosts to rest so the kids could come back, so they could come back to the store and learn what he knew, and what he had lived.

He tried the back door and, when it opened, hesitated only long enough to pass his fingers over his face before stepping over the threshold and closing the door behind him. The light was dim, and he hurried through the kitchen and down the long narrow corridor to the living room. And it was as he remembered: empty and dusty and more damp than his bones could take. There was a fireplace on the back wall, and he knelt on the hearth and passed his hand over the blackened stone. Cold. And iced.

He jammed his hands into his coat pockets. The left curled around Syd's cassette, and there was reluctant admiration for the thought behind the prank. He knew, then, that it had all been planned; that the kids would know he would listen and become angry at the soap-opera dialogue and the shy giggles of the girls. He licked his lips and laughed.

Stopped.

His right hand felt velvet.

He pulled out the roses Edna had taken from the garden, stared, glared, and tossed them angrily into the fireplace, the curse on his lips dying unborn when he looked at the windows.

And saw the fog.

Tried the doors, and all of them locked.

Raced through the house, tripping over dust, throwing his weight against glass and none of it breaking.

It was cold, and he was sweating.

He stood in the middle of the living room, shaking his fist at the windows, the fog, the roses in the fireplace, and the single lighted candle that glowed on the mantel.

Dropped to his knees and opened his hand.

And the shadows of mournful vengeance pulsed in the corners and *sighed.*

3. *Blossom*

When Syd gave the rose to Ginny, she was obviously unimpressed and perhaps even a little scornful. It would not matter then, explaining to her (and somewhat embellishing) the risks he had taken in sneaking it out of Dimmesdale's garden. Had he been caught, the police in general and Russo in particular, would have followed tradition and forced him into a public restitution for his stealing; and how, he wondered, do you replace a rose?

He glanced across the classroom aisle and watched with weary bitterness as Ginny toyed with the petals, poking at them with her pen and jabbing at them once. So far as he could tell, she had not lifted it to enjoy the scent, nor glided a finger over the velvet to close her eyes at the touch. He saw her shrug. And when the last bell rang he sat there until the room had emptied. He, and the rose . . . lonely on the floor where a half-dozen feet had trampled it to a pulp.

His first reaction was self-pity: while not exactly homely, neither was he quarterback-handsome. And to get Ginny, in any sense of the word, was apparently and finally impossible. He loved her. And he could not have her.

Then, as quickly, he became vindictive: he'd pour the blackest ink he could find over her collection of snug cashmere sweaters, tangle forever that cloudsoft sable hair, use a razor and define in blood the gentle lines of her face.

He snorted, knelt on the floor and used his handkerchief to cover the rose and lift it into his hip pocket.

Another time, another ploy, he thought as he walked home; but Ginny seemed so cold not even the equator could warm her.

After turning onto Hawthorne Street, he quickened his pace. His mother would be more than annoyed if he were late one more time. It was bad enough that his father had taken a job that required him to travel over two dozen days a month; should he himself now be absent, he knew his mother would cry. Not loudly. Standing in front of the living-room window perhaps, or by the stove, or just in the middle of the upstairs hall . . . tears, not sobs, and as quickly wiped away as they appeared. And were denied when he asked. When he left for college in the fall, he wondered how she would be able to stand the empty bed in his room.

Someone called him, then, but he was in too much of a hurry to do more than lift a hand in blind greeting. The only time he stopped was at Dimmesdale's house, where he stared boldly at the flourishing garden, the Cape Cod, delighting as he did so in the brightness of the afternoon, the shimmering new green of leaves and grass, the fresh cool bite of the early spring breeze. And then he blinked, thinking he saw a figure behind one of the first-floor windows. Certainly a curtain moved, but there was a window opened and he decided it was wishful thinking. Wishful . . . he gnawed on his lower lip, one hand guiltily at his hip pocket, and he whispered: "Ginny. I want to be like one of her candies."

How many boxes had he sent her over the past four months. Anonymously. Painfully. Watching her share the chocolates and the creams with everyone. Or nearly so.

"A wishbone would be better," a voice said behind him, and he spun around, angered and embarrassed. Flo Joiner stood looking at him through green-tinted glasses and ruffled black bangs, her lips in a slight smile, her arms folded around books held protectively in front of her breasts.

"I don't like people who do that," he said, walking again, and cursing silently when she kept his pace.

"Sorry," she said, "but when you waved at me, I thought you wanted to walk me home. I didn't know you were going to have a séance."

"A what?" The sun was in his eyes and he squinted as he stared down at her.

"A séance. You know. Disembodied heads and tambourines and stuff like that. I thought you were holding a private séance at the creep's house."

"How do you know he's a creep?"

She laughed and blew at her bangs to drive them up and away from her glasses. The habit annoyed him; Flo thought it made her look cute. "Anyone who lives the way that old man does has got to be a creep. But . . . sometimes wishing works, I guess. Right?"

"No," he said, stopping as she did in front of a low white ranch house. She took a step up the walk, turned, and asked if he would like something to eat, cake or whatever. "Never say whatever," he said with a grin that apologized for his brusqueness. "It puts evil thoughts in a senior's head."

"Oh, really?" she said with a smile he couldn't quite read. "And yes, wishing does too sometimes work. My dad said he wished for a new car and got it. My brother wanted a new glove and he got it, too. I'm not telling you what I'm going to wish for."

"You guys are just lucky, that's all. I never saw so much luck in one place in my life."

Flo shrugged as though she weren't interested. "Probably. Besides, my stupid brother says you got to have a flower first. Something from the creep's garden." She lowered voice and head, then, and stared at him over her glasses. "But not the roses, Sydney, definitely not the roses."

"Are you trying to imitate someone?"

"You'll never know, Sydney, you'll never know."

"Oh, for God's sake, Flo!"

Once again, irritatingly, she laughed, and Syd waved her a curt good-bye.

Once in the house, he yelled for his mother, raced up the stairs, and dumped his books on the bed before changing his clothes. The handkerchief he set very carefully on the windowsill and gazed at it a moment, scratching thoughtfully at his waist, his jaw, the back of his neck. Then he was downstairs again and in the kitchen, kissing his mother quickly on the cheek while he looked over her shoulder at the pot of split-pea soup simmering under steam on the stove.

"Ugh," he said.

"You know you love it," she laughed and aimed a slap at his rump.

He sprawled on one of the kitchen chairs and nodded when she lifted a bottle of ginger ale, watched as the carbonation gathered and leaped, foamed and dripped over the side of the glass. His mother moved back to her cooking, and for a long and peaceful while they listened to the sounds of the neighborhood winding down toward supper.

"Do you have any homework?"

He grunted.

There was a card from his father propped against a saltshaker in the middle of the table. He turned it around and stared at the picture: a Hopi Indian summoning spirits for the tourists. He thought it disgusting and turned it back, not bothering to read the message done in red ink.

"He'll be home on Saturday."

Syd grunted.

In spite of the bubbles, his soda tasted flat.

"Mom, I'm wondering . . . I've been thinking for a long time that maybe . . . well, maybe I shouldn't go to college this fall. I mean, what with Dad—"

"Don't," she said, turning from the stove, her face pale with anger. "Don't ever say that! Never say that in this house again."

"But, Mom—"

"It's that Ginny girl, isn't it? You want to run away and marry her or something. Always going out with her four or five times a week, coming home late at night even though you know you have school the next day, sneaking in and thinking I'm asleep so I don't know how late. How stupid do you think I am, Sydney?"

He saw the tears brimming in rage and shook his head, in slow defeat. "All right," he said sullenly. "I'm sorry. I just wanted to save you and Dad some money, that's all."

"No," she said, anger fled and her voice suddenly soft. "You just don't want to leave me alone."

He allowed her to hug him tightly as he sat there, his head pushed into her small breasts; and he was ashamed and annoyed that an image of Ginny sprang instantly into his mind, chewing thoughtfully on her precious chocolates and smiling at . . . someone else. His mother began rocking him, crooning wordlessly, and he wondered if she suspected how much he loved her, and how much he needed someone else to love, suspected that his dates with Ginny were solitary walks in the park, along the back streets, along the river. He wondered, and suddenly cared that she did not know.

Later that night, when supper was done and the dishes washed and his mother was working her needlepoint in front of the television, he walked down to the luncheonette to see what was happening, and on the way home a few minutes later plucked four huge golden mums from Dimmesdale's garden, saluted Flo's house as he passed it on the run, and gave the flowers to his mother. As she cried. And he stood

awkwardly in the middle of the room, waiting, then mumbling something about his homework and retreating to his room.

The following afternoon he saw his father's car in the driveway. Their reunion was, as always, noisy and emotional, and he whooped through an improvised dance when he learned that his dad had been transferred to the home office and would no longer travel. His mother grinned, he grinned, and for the first time that year they went out to dinner.

And in the restaurant he saw Ginny sitting with her parents. When she spotted his staring, she smiled and held it. He choked and dared a smile back.

In school the next day she passed him a note. He did not read it, did not want to—the last time she had done it was to beg him for an introduction to his ex-best friend. He stood in the hall after class and held the folded paper dumbly in his hand, and didn't even notice when Flo asked him a question, saw the note and took it, opened it and read it with one eye closed. When she had done, her lips were tight and, he thought, she looked rather saddened. She handed it back to him and left without speaking. He knew why when he followed, unbelieving, the words that directed him to meet her after supper, in the park, and alone.

No, he thought; not me, it's a mistake.

But he showered twice when he finally made it home, tried on four pairs of jeans and three shirts before he achieved the effect he thought she would like.

When he left, his mother and father were sitting in the living room, holding hands on the sofa and watching a blank-screened television.

Hot damn, he thought, and smiled.

The park was small, scarcely two blocks long and three blocks deep, but once inside he walked hurriedly through the trees and across a small baseball field, around an even smaller pond and back into the trees again. The wind had picked up somewhat, and the leaves and brush whispered at him as he passed, stroked at his arms and face, scuttled underfoot like small furless animals. Here the sounds of the street were smothered in shadows, and the shadows themselves were tantalizing and deep. Yet he refused to allow himself to fantasize. Whatever Ginny wanted to do was all right with him. Just talking with her would be the improvement he had searched for, prayed for, wished . . . his hand slapped at his hip pocket. The handkerchief with the rose was still at the window, but he grinned when he realized he would need no talisman this time. Be yourself, his mother had told him often enough; and so he would be, if that's what Ginny wanted.

She was standing when he found her, almost despairing that he wouldn't, leaning against the curved trunk of a birch, dressed in powder-blue cardigan and tartan skirt, her hair feathered down over her shoulders. He stopped until she noticed him and nodded, and held out her hand. He took it, felt its cool, its soft, felt her press against him and lift her head, her face, her lips to his.

Lord, he thought; and thought no more until they were sitting side by side against the tree, staring through the foliage at the first glare of stars.

"I've wanted you for a long time," she said finally, quietly, almost shyly.

"Me, too," he said, grimacing at the brilliance of his response.

"I thought you were the one who was sending me all those chocolates."

"I was," he admitted, looking away and smiling. "I knew you liked them."

"You'll get me fat."

"Never," he said seriously. "Ginny, you'll never get fat."

In silence they listened to a mockingbird's sigh.

"Ginny . . . why did you send me that note?"

"I don't know. Suddenly, I just felt like it."

She took his hand and nuzzled it. Her lips were soft, moist, and he thought of the rose.

"I'm glad you liked the candy."

She laughed and lay her head on his arm. "I couldn't live without them."

He grinned as she kissed his palm, and wondered how long she would keep him there, in the park, beneath the trees, on the grass.

"Ginny, do you . . . this is dumb, but do you believe in wishes?"

"You're right, that's dumb. You're the smartest kid in the class. You should know better."

"No, I mean it." He felt his face grow warm as she stared at him, her eyes moist, her lips gleaming darkly. "You know, the other day I was so mad when you . . . well, I wanted you so much I even wished I could have been one of the chocolates or something."

"Now that," she said, "is not so dumb. It's not. It's beautiful."

Her tongue flicked over his thumb. Kissed it. Moved to his lips and he drew her down on top of him.

A rustling in the branches above them. The feel of grass on the back of his neck. And suddenly, as she wriggled over his chest, he thought of poor Flo and the sad look on her face.

Something drifted down to his cheek, and he thought of the mums he had given his mother . . . and his father's car parked in the drive.

The Joiners' luck.

The blackred rose. In his handkerchief on the windowsill. Crushed. Dead.

"You're sweet," she whispered as she took the first bite.

4. Thorn

The window. Framed on the inside by pale white curtains. Framed on the outside by two spikes of juniper.

The cobbler's bench. Roughly hewn and edged with splinters.

The man on the bench seated before the window. Dressed in a preacher's black jacket, black trousers, black shoes. His hair a trapped cloud of angry grey. His eyes only shadows. His mouth just air.

Watching: the eldest and the youngest pass to the opposite side of the street, while those in between quickened their pace but kept to the sidewalk; the traffic pass in pendulum waves; the wind, the rain, the sun light to dark.

Listening: the laughter stifled, giggling bitten back, footfalls and running and not a few dares; the snarl of dogs, the spitting of cats, the wingbeats of birds that deserted his trees; and the wind, and the rain, and the sun light to dark.

And when the moon had gone and the street was a grave, he stood and stretched and moved out to his garden where he grabbed with powerful hands what remained of the flowers stolen during the day. He carried the debris into the kitchen, down the cellar stairs, and dumped it all on a pile in the corner.

Then he turned to the center of the floor where strings of artificial suns glared brightly over beds of new-growing flowers. Violets, pansies, mums, and lilies. He considered them carefully, and the promises they would bring.

But sooner or later someone would come inside. A young boy on a lark, a man simply curious. Perhaps even a girl who was braver than most.

No, he thought; there was still too much laughter.

Around the furnace, then, and into the corner where the lights did not reach and the warmth would not spread. He blinked slowly, forcing his eyes to adjust until they could barely discern a row of low bushes like miniature Gorgons, with twigs instead of snakes and buds instead of fangs. He took a deep breath of the swirling dark air, released it slowly and dropped to his knees.

His fingers moved with ritual slowness over the buttons of his shirt and parted the edges to expose his chest. He leaned over, and touched a forefinger to his skin, probing, tracing, then taking his nail and digging into the flesh that would never form scars. There was no pain. Only the practiced identification of smooth sticky wetness. With the fingertip, then, he touched at his chest, at the letter drawn there, and on each waiting bud (with the sigh of a name) he placed one shimmering drop (with the remembrance of a name), and sat back and watched as the buds drank in the blood . . . and the dark . . . and the air never warm.

Were roses.

Blackred.

Blackred . . . and waiting.

OWLS HOOT IN THE DAYTIME

By MANLY WADE WELLMAN

In his long and varied career, spanning more than half a century, Manly Wade Wellman has published dozens of books and hundreds of stories. One of his Southern regional histories, Rebel Boast, *garnered him a nomination for a Pulitzer Prize. He is perhaps most appreciated, however, for his tales of horror and the supernatural, many of them set in the rural South and revolving around a character named, simply, John, a wandering ballad singer who, silver-stringed guitar in hand, travels through the Southern mountains seeing all manner of strange things. Wellman's stories are a bit in the tradition of Mark Twain and Irvin S. Cobb. They have a wonderful simplicity about them and abound in local color and the true Southern rural spirit.*

That time back yonder, I found the place myself, the way folks in those mountains allowed I had to.

I was rough hours on the way, high up and then down, over ridges and across bottoms, where once there'd been a road. I found a bridge across a creek, but it was busted down in the middle, like a warning not to use it. I splashed across there. It got late when I reached a cove pushed in amongst close-grown trees on a climbing slope.

An owl hooted toward where the sun sank, so maybe I was on the right track, a path faint through the woods. I found where a gate had been, a rotted post with rusty hinges on it. The trees beyond looked dark as the way to hell, but I headed along that snaky-winding path till I saw the housefront. The owl hooted again, off where the gloom grayed off for the last of daylight.

That house was half logs, half ancient whipsawed planks, weathered to dust color. Trees crowded the sides, branches crossed above the shake roof. The front-sill timber squatted on pale rocks. The door had come down off its old leather hinges. Darkness inside. Two windows stared, with flowered bushes beneath them. The grassy yard space wasn't a great much bigger than a parlor floor.

"What ye wish, young sir?" a scrapy voice inquired me, and I saw somebody a-sitting on a slaty rock at the house's left corner.

"I didn't know anybody was here," I said, and looked at him and he looked at me.

I saw a gnarly old man, his ruined face half-hid in a blizzardy white beard, his body wrapped in a brown robe. Beside him hunkered down what looked like a dark-haired dog. Both of them looked with bright, squinty eyes, a-making me recollect that my shirt was rumpled, that I sweated under my pack straps, that I had mud on my boots and my dungaree pant cuffs.

"If ye nair knowed nobody was here, why'd ye come?" scraped his voice.

"It might could be hard to explain."

"I got a lavish of time to hark at yore explanation."

I grinned at him. "I go up and down, a-viewing the country over. I've heard time and again about a place so far off of the beaten way that owls hoot in the daytime and they have possums for yard dogs."

An owl hooted somewhere.

"That's a saying amongst folks here and yonder," said the old man, his broad brown hand a-stroking his beard.

"Yes, sir," I agreed him, "but I heard tell it was in this part of the country, so I thought I'd find out."

The beard stirred as he clamped his mouth. "Is that all ye got to do with yore young life?"

"Mostly so," I told him the truth. "I find out things."

The animal alongside him hiked up its long snout.

It was the almightiest big possum I'd ever seen, big as a middling-sized dog. Likely it weighed more than fifty pounds. Its eyes dug at me.

"Folks at the county seat just gave me general directions," I went on. "I found an old road in the woods. Then I heard the owl hoot and it was still daytime, so I followed the sound here."

I felt funny, a-standing with my pack straps galled into me, to say all that.

"I've heard tell an owl hoot by daytime is bad luck," scraped the voice in the beard. "Heap of that a-going, if it's so."

"Over in Wales, they say an owl hooting means that a girl's a-losing her virginity," I tried to make a joke.

"Hum." Not exactly a laugh. "Owls must be kept busy a-hooting for that, too." He and the possum looked me up and down. "Well, since ye come from so far off, why don't me bid ye set and rest?"

"Thank you, sir." I unslung my pack and put it down and laid my guitar on it. Then I stepped toward the dark door hole.

"Stay out of yonder," came quick warning words. "What's inside is one reason why nobody comes here but me. Set down on that stump acrost from me. What might I call ye?"

I dropped down on the stump. "My name's John. And I wish you'd tell me more about how is it folks don't come here."

"I'm Maltby Sanger, and this here good friend I got with me is named Ung. The rest of the saying's fact, too. I keep him for a yard dog."

Ung kept his black eyes on me. His coarse fur was grizzled gray. His forepaws clasped like hands under his shallow chin.

"Maybe I'd ought to fix us some supper while we talk," said Maltby Sanger.

"Don't bother," I said. "I'll be a-heading back directly."

"Hark at me," he said, scrapier than ever. "There ain't no luck a-walking these here woods by night."

"There'll be a good moon."

"That there's the worst part. The moon shows ye to what's afoot in the woods. Eat here tonight and then sleep here."

"Well, all right." I leaned down and unbuckled my pack. "But let me fix the supper, since I came without bidding." I fetched out a little poke of meal, a big old can of sardines in tomatoes. "If I could have some water, Mr. Sanger."

" 'Round here, there's water where I stay at."

He got off his rock, and I saw that he was dwarfed. His legs under that robe couldn't be much more than knees and feet. He wouldn't stand higher than my elbow.

"Come on, John," he said, and I picked up a tin pan and followed him round the house corner.

Betwixt two trees was built a little shackly hut, poles up and down and clay-daubed for walls, other poles laid up top and covered with twigs and grass for a roof. In front of it, in what light was left, flowed a spring. I filled my pan and started back.

"Is that all the water ye want?" he asked after me.

"Just to make us some pone. I've got two bottles of beer to drink."

"Beer," he said, like as if he loved the word.

He waddled back, a-picking up wood as he came. We piled twigs for me to light with a match, then put bigger pieces on top. I poured meal into the water in the pan and worked up a batter. Then I found a flat rock and rubbed it with ham rind and propped it close to the fire to pour the batter on. Afterward I opened the sardines and got my fork for Maltby Sanger and took my spoon for myself. When the top of the pone looked brown enough, I turned it over with my spoon and knife, and I dug out those bottles of beer and twisted off the caps.

We ate, squatted on two sides of the fire. Maltby Sanger appeared to enjoy the sardines and pone, and he gave some to Ung, who held chunks in his paws to eat. When we'd done, not a crumb was left. "I relished that," allowed Maltby Sanger.

It had turned full dark, and I was glad for the fire.

"Ye pick that guitar, John?" he inquired. "Why not pick it some right now?"

I tuned my silver strings and struck chords for an old song I recollected. One verse went like this:

> *"We sang good songs that came out new,*
> *But now they're old amongst the young,*
> *And when we're gone, it's just a few*
> *Will know the songs that we have sung."*

"I God and that's a true word," said Maltby Sanger when I finished. "Them old songs is a-dying like flies."

I hushed the silver strings with my palm. "I don't hear that owl hoot," I said.

"It ain't daytime no more," said Maltby Sanger.

"Hark at me, sir," I spoke up. "Why don't you tell me just what's a-happening here, or anyway a-trying to happen?"

He gave me one of his beady looks and sighed a tired-out sigh. "How'll I start in to tell ye?"

"Start in at the beginning."

"Ain't no beginning I know of. The business is as old as this here mountain itself."

"Then it's right old, Mr. Sanger," I said. "I've heard say these are the oldest mountains on all this earth. They go back before Adam and Eve, before the first of living things. But here we've got a house, made with hands." I looked at the logs, the planks. "Some man's hands."

"John," he said, "that there's just a housefront, built up against the rock, and maybe not by no man's hands, no such thing. I reckon it was put there to tole folks in. But I been here all these years to warn folks off, the way I tried to warn ye." He looked at me, and so did Ung, next to him. "Till I seen ye was set in yore mind to stay, so I let ye."

I studied the open door hole, so dark inside. "Why should folks be toled in, Mr. Sanger?"

"I've thought on that, and come to reckon the mountain wants folks right into its heart or its belly." He sort of stared his words into me. "Science allows this here whole earth started out just a ball of fire. The outside cooled down. Water come in for the sea, and trees and living things got born onto the land. But they say the fire's still inside. And fire's got to have something to feed on."

I looked at our own fire. It was burning small and hot, but if it got loose it could eat up that whole woods. "You remind me of old history things," I said, "when gods had furnaces inside them and sacrifices were flung into them."

"Right, John," he nodded me. "Moloch's the name in the Bible, fifth chapter of Amos, and I likewise think somewheres in Acts."

"The name's Molech another place," I said. "Second Kings; Preacher Ricks had it for a text one time. How King Joash ruled that no man would make his son or daughter pass through the fire to Molech. You reckon this place is some way like that?"

"Might could be this here place, and places like it in other lands, gave men the idee of fiery gods to burn up their children."

I hugged my guitar to me, for what comfort it could give. "You wouldn't tell me all this," I said, "if you wanted to fool me into the belly of the mountain."

"I don't worship no such," he snapped. "I told ye, I'm here to keep folks from a-meddling into there and not come out no more. It was long years back when I come here to get away from outside things. I wasn't much good at a man's work, and folks laughed at how dwarfished-down I was."

"I don't laugh," I said.

"No, I see ye don't. But don't either pity me. I wouldn't like that no more than I'd like laughter."

"I don't either pity you, Mr. Sanger. I judge you play the man the best you can, and nobody can do more than that."

He patted Ung's grizzled back. "I come here," he said again, "and I heard tell about this place from the old man who was here then. I allowed I'd take over from him if he wanted to leave, so he left. It wonders me if this sounds like a made-up tale to ye."

"No, sir, I hark at air word you speak."

"If ye reckon this here is just some common spot, look on them flowers at the window by ye."

It was a shaggy bush in the firelight. There were blue flowers. But likewise pinky ones, the color of blood-drawn meat. And dead white ones, with dark spots in them, like eyes.

"Three different flowers on one bush," he said. "I don't reckon there's the like of that, nowheres else on this earth."

"Sassafras has three different leaves on one branch," I said. "There'll be a mitten leaf, and a toad-foot leaf next to it, and then just a plain smooth-edged leaf." I studied the bush. "But those flowers would be special, even if there was just one of a kind on a twig."

"Ye done harked at what I told, John," said Maltby Sanger, and put his bottle up to his beard to drink the last drop. "Suit yourself if it makes sense."

"Sense is what it makes," I said. "All right, you've been here for years. I reckon you live in that little cabin 'round the corner. Does that suit you?"

"It's got to suit somebody. Somebody's needed. To guard folks off from a-going in yonder and then not come out."

I strummed my guitar, tried to think of what to sing. Finally:

> *"Yonder comes the Devil*
> *From hell's last bottom floor,*
> *A-shouting and a-singing,*
> *'There's room for many a more.' "*

"I enjoy to hear ye make music, John," said Maltby Sanger. "It was all right for ye to come here tonight. No foolishness. I won't say no danger, but ye'll escape danger, I reckon."

I looked toward the open door. It was all black inside—no, not all black. I saw a couple of red points in there. I told myself they were reflected from our fire.

"I've been a-putting my mind on what's likely to be down yonder," I said. "Recollected all I was told when I was little, about how hell was an everlasting fire down under our feet, like the way heaven was up in the sky over us."

"Have ye thought lately, the sky ain't truly up over us no more?" he inquired me. "It's more like off from us now, since men have gone a-flying off to the moon and are a-fixing to fly farther than that, to the stars. Stars is what's in the sky, and heaven's got to be somewheres else.

But I ain't made up my mind on hell, not yet. Maybe it's truly a-burning away, down below our feet, right this minute."

"Or either, the fire down in there is what made folks decide what hell was."

"Maybe that," he halfway agreed me. "John, it's nigh onto when I go to sleep. I wish there was two beds in my cabin, but—"

"Just let me sleep out here and keep our fire a-going," I said. "Keep it a-going, and not let it get away and seek what it might devour."

"Sure thing, if ye want to." He got up on his stumpy legs and dragged something out from under that robe he wore. "Ye might could like to have this with ye."

I took it. It was a great big Bible, so old its leather covers were worn and scrapped near about away.

"I thank you, sir," I said. "I'll lay a little lightwood on the fire and read in this."

"Then I'll see ye when the sun comes up."

He shuffled off to his shack. Ung stayed there and looked at me. I didn't mind that, I was a-getting used to him.

Well, gentlemen, I stirred up the fire and put on some chunks of pine so it would burn up strong and bright. I opened the Bible and looked through to the Book of Isaiah, thirty-fourth chapter. I found what I'd recollected to be there:

> *It shall not be quenched night nor day: the smoke thereof shall go up for ever; from generation to generation it shall lie waste . . .*

On past that verse, there's talk about dragons and satyrs and such like things they don't want you to believe in these days. In the midst of my reading, I heard something from that open door, a long, grumbling sigh of sound, and I looked over to see what.

The two red lights moved closer together, and this time they seemed to be set in a lump of something, like eyes in a head.

I got up quick, the Bible in my hand. Those eyes looked out at me, and the red of them burned up bright, then went dim, then bright again. Ung, at my foot, made a burbling noise, like as if it pestered him.

I put down the Bible and picked up a burning chunk from the fire. I made myself walk to the door. My chunk gave me some light to see inside. Sure enough it was a cave in there; what looked like a house outside was just a front, built on by whatever had built it for whatever reason. The cave was hollowed back into the mountain and it had a smooth-looking floor, almost polished, of black rock. Inside, the space slanted inward both ways, to narrowness farther in. It was more like a throat than anything I could say for it. A great big throat, big enough to swallow a man, or more than one man.

Far back hung whatever it was had those eyes. I saw the eyes shine, not just from my flashlight. They had light of their own.

"All right," I said out loud to the eyes. "Here I am. I look for the truth. What's the truth about you?"

No answer but a grumble. The thing moved, deep in there. I saw it had, not just that black head with red eyes, it had shoulders and things like arms. It didn't come close, but it didn't pull back. It waited for me.

"What's the truth about you?" I inquired it again. "Might could your name be Molech?"

It made nair sound, but it lifted those long arms. I saw hands like pitchforks. It was bigger than I was, maybe half again bigger. Was it stronger?

A man's got to be a man sometime, I told myself inside me. I'd come there to find out what was what. There was some strange old truth in there, not a pretty truth maybe, but I'd come to see what it was.

I walked to where the door was fallen off the leather hinges. The red eyes came up bright and died down dull and watched me a-coming. They waited for me, they hoped I'd get close.

I put my foot on where the door log had been once. It was long ago rotted to punk, it crumbled under my boot. I took hold of the jamb and leaned in.

"You been having a time for yourself?" I asked the eyes.

There was light from the chunk I carried, but other light, a ghost of a show of it, was inside. It came from on back in there. It was a kind of smoky reddish light, I thought, you might have called it rosy. It made a glitter on something two–three steps inside.

I spared a look down there to the floor. Gentlemen, it was a jewel, a bunch of jewels, a-shining white and red and green. And big. They were like a bunch of glass bottles for size. Only they weren't bottles. They shone too bright, too clear, strewed out there by my foot.

There for the picking up—but if I bent over, there was that one with the red eyes and the black shape, and he could pick me up.

"No," I said to him, "you don't get hold of me thattaway," and I whirled my chunk of fire, to get more light.

There he was, dark and a-standing two-legged like a man, but he was taller than I was, by the height of that round head with the red eyes. And no hair to his black hide, it was as slick as a snake. Long arms and pitchfork hands sort of pawed out toward me, the way a praying mantis does. The head cocked itself. I saw it had something in it besides eyes, it had a mouth, open and as wide as a gravy boat, wet and black, like a mess of hot tar.

"You must have tricked a many a man in here with those jewels," I said.

He heard me, he knew what I said, knew that I wouldn't stoop down. He moved in on me.

Those legs straddled. Their knees bent backward, like a frog's, the feet slapped flat and wide on the floor of the cave, amongst more jewels everywhere. Enough in there to pay a country's national debt. He reached for me again. His fingers were lumpy-jointed and they had sharp claws, like on the feet of a great big hawk. I moved backward, I reckoned I'd better. And he followed right along. He wanted to get those claws into me.

I backed to the old door-log and near about tripped on it. I dropped the burning chunk and grabbed hold of the fallen-down door with both hands, to stay on my feet. I got hold of its two edges and hiked it between me and that snake-skinned thing that lived inside. I looked past one edge of the door, and all of a sudden I saw him stop.

There was the rosy light in yonder, and outside my chunk blazed where it had fallen. I could see that door rightly for the first time.

It was one of those you used to see in lots of places, made with a thick center piece running from top to bottom betwixt the panels, and two more thick pieces set midpoint of the long one to go right and left to make a cross. In amongst these were set the four old, half-rotted panels. But the cross stood there. And often, I'd heard tell, such doors were made thattaway to keep evil from a-coming through.

So, in the second I did my figuring, I saw why the front had been built on the cave, why that door had been hung there. It was to hold in whatever was inside. And it had worked right well till the door dropped down.

It was a heavy old door, but I muscled it up. I shoved on back into the cave, with the door in front of me like a shield.

Nothing shoved back. I took one step after another amongst those shining jewels, careful to keep from a-tripping on them. I cocked my head leftways to look past the door. That big black somebody moved away from me. I saw the flicker of the rose light from where it came into the cave.

The cross, was it a help? I'd been told that there were crosses long before the one on Calvary, made for power's sake in old, old lands beyond the sea. Yes, and in this land too, by Indian tribes one place and another. My foot near about skidded on a rolling jewel, but I stayed up.

"In this sign we conquer," I said, after some king in the olden days, and I believed it. And I went on forward with the door for my sign.

For as long as a breath I shoved up against him. I felt him lean against the other side, like high wind a-blowing. I fought to keep the door on him to push him back, and took a long step and dug in with my foot.

And almighty near fell down a hole all full of the rosy light.

He'd tricked me there where his light came up from. I hung on its edge, a-looking down a hole three–four feet across, deeper than I could ask myself to judge, and away down there was fire, a-dancing and a-streaming—a world, it looked to me, of fire.

On the other side of the door he made a noise. It was a whiny buzz, what you'd expect from a bee as big as a dog. His long old arm snaked round the edge of the door, a-raking with its claws. They snagged into my shirt—I heard it rip. I managed to sidestep clear of that hole, and he buzzed and came again. I shoved hard with the door, put all I could put into it. Heat come in all round me, it was like when you sit in a close room with a hot stove. I smelt something worse than a skunk.

The pressure was there, and then the pressure was all of a sudden gone. I went down, the door in front of me, to slam on the floor with a rattly bang.

I got up quick, without the door. I wondered how to face him. But he wasn't there. Nowhere.

I stood and trembled and gulped for air. Sweat streamed all over me. I looked up, all 'round me. Sure enough, he was gone. I was all alone in that dark cave, me and the door. And the rosy light was gone.

For the door had fallen whack down on top of it.

I put a knee down on the panel. I could feel a tremble and stir underneath.

"By God Almighty, I've got you penned in!" I yelled down to what made the stir in that fiery hole.

It was a-humping to me there. I reached out and grabbed a shiny green jewel. It must have weighed eight pounds or so. I put it on a plank of the cross. I got up on my feet, found more jewels. I laid them on, one next to another, along both arms, to make the cross twice as strong.

"You're shut up in there now," I said down to the hole it covered.

The door lay still and solid. No more hum below.

I headed out toward the gleam of the cooking fire. My feet felt weak under me. Ung sat out there and looked at me. I wondered if I should ought to get a blanket. Then I didn't bother. I must have slept.

It was morning's first gray again, with the stars a-paling out of the sky, when I sat up awake. Maltby Sanger was there, a-building up the fire. "Ye look to have had ye a quiet night," he said.

"Me?" I said, and he laughed. Next to the fire he set a saucepan with eggs in it.

"Duck eggs," he told me. "Ung found them for our breakfast. And I got parched corn, and tomatoes from my garden."

"And I've got a few pinches of coffee, we can boil it in my canteen cup," I said. "Looky over yonder at the cave."

He looked. He pulled his whiskers. "Bless my soul," he said, "the door's plumb gone off it."

"The door's inside, to bottle up what was the trouble in there," I said.

While he was a-cooking, I told him what I'd met in the cave. He got up with a can of hot coffee in his hand and stumped inside. Out again, he filled one of his old buckets with dirt and stones and fetched it into the cave. Then back for another bucketful of the same stuff, and then another. Finally he came out and washed his hands and served up the eggs. We ate them before the either of us said a word.

"Moloch," Maltby Sanger said then. "Ye reckon that's who he is?"

"He didn't speak his name," I replied him. "All I guess is, he'll likely stay under that door with the cross and the weight on it, so long as it's left to pen him in."

"So long as it's left," he agreed me. "Only ye used them jewels for weight. If somebody comes a-using 'round here and sees them, he might could wag them off. So I put a heap of dirt over them to hide them best I could. Nobody's a-going to scrabble there so long's I'm here to keep them from it."

He stroked his beard and grinned his teeth at me.

"My time's been long hereabouts, and it'll be longer. Only after I'm gone can somebody stir him up in yonder. Then the world can suit itself about what to do about him."

He squinted his eyes to study me. "Now," he said, "ye'll likely be a-going yore way."

"Yes, sir, and I'm honest to thank you for a-letting me found out what I wanted to know."

I stowed my pack and strapped on the blanket roll.

"Last night," he said from across the fire, "I'd meant to ask ye to stay on watch here and let me go."

"Ask me to stay?"

"That's what. And ye'd have stayed, John, if I'd asked ye the right way. Stayed and kept the watch here."

I couldn't tell myself for certain if that was so.

"I aimed for to ask ye," he said again, "but if I was to go, where'd I go? Hellfire, John, I been here so long it's home."

Ung twinkled an eye, like as if he heard and understood.

"I'll just stay a-setting here and warn other folks off from a-messing round where that door is," said Maltby Sanger.

I slung my pack on my shoulders and picked up my guitar. "Sunrise now," I said.

"Sure enough, sunrise. Good-bye, John. I was proud to have ye here overnight."

We shook hands. He didn't seem so dwarfish right then. I found the path I'd come in by, that would take me back to people.

The sun was up. Daytime was come. Back on the way I went, I heard the long, soft hoot of an owl.

WHERE THERE'S A WILL

By RICHARD MATHESON and
RICHARD CHRISTIAN MATHESON

It is not unusual for a son to follow in the writing footsteps of his father, but it's uncommon for the two to collaborate. Here is a rare and fortunate exception. Richard Matheson is a successful Hollywood screenwriter, author of many classic throat-gripping short stories and novels of terror—"Duel," "Prey," A Stir of Echoes, The Shrinking Man, I Am Legend—*as well as one of the key writers to work with the late Rod Serling on the famous* Twilight Zone *television series. His son, Richard Christian Matheson, still in his mid-twenties, has already sold a number of short stories to magazines and anthologies and has begun a career in television scripting. He shows promise of making a strong mark of his own. Their combined talents concentrate here on the claustrophobic aspects of terror.*

He awoke.

It was dark and cold. Silent.

I'm thirsty, he thought. He yawned and sat up; fell back with a cry of pain. He'd hit his head on something. He rubbed at the pulsing tissue of his brow, feeling the ache spread back to his hairline.

Slowly, he began to sit up again but hit his head once more. He was jammed between the mattress and something overhead. He raised his hands to feel it. It was soft and pliable, its texture yielding beneath the push of his fingers. He felt along its surface. It extended as far as he could reach. He swallowed anxiously and shivered.

What in God's name was it?

He began to roll to his left and stopped with a gasp. The surface was blocking him there, as well. He reached to his right and his heart beat faster. It was on the other side, as well. He was surrounded on four sides. His heart compressed like a smashed soft-drink can, the blood spurting a hundred times faster.

Within seconds, he sensed that he was dressed. He felt trousers, a coat, a shirt and tie, a belt. There were shoes on his feet.

He slid his right hand to his trouser pocket and reached in. He palmed a cold, metal square and pulled his hand from the pocket, bringing it to his face. Fingers trembling, he hinged the top open and spun the wheel with his thumb. A few sparks glinted but no flame. Another turn and it lit.

He looked down at the orange cast of his body and shivered again. In the light of the flame, he could see all around himself.

He wanted to scream at what he saw.

He was in a casket.

He dropped the lighter and the flame striped the air with a yellow tracer before going out. He was in total darkness, once more. He could see nothing. All he heard was his terrified breathing as it lurched forward, jumping from his throat.

How long had he been here? Minutes? Hours?

Days?

His hopes lunged at the possibility of a nightmare; that he was only dreaming, his sleeping mind caught in some kind of twisted vision. But he knew it wasn't so. He knew, horribly enough, exactly what had happened.

They had put him in the one place he was terrified of. The one place he had made the fatal mistake of speaking about to them. They couldn't have selected a better torture. Not if they'd thought about it for a hundred years.

God, did they loathe him that much? To do *this* to him?

He started shaking helplessly, then caught himself. He wouldn't let them do it. Take his life and his business all at once? No, goddamn them, *no!*

He searched hurriedly for the lighter. That was their mistake, he thought. Stupid bastards. They'd probably thought it was a final, fitting irony: A gold-engraved thank you for making the corporation what it was. On the lighter were the words: *To Charlie/Where there's a Will . . .*

"Right," he muttered. He'd beat the lousy sons of bitches. They weren't going to murder him and steal the business he owned and built. There *was* a will.

His.

He closed his fingers around the lighter and, holding it with a white-knuckled fist, lifted it above the heaving of his chest. The wheel ground against the flint as he spun it back with his thumb. The flame caught and he quieted his breathing as he surveyed what space he had in the coffin.

Only inches on all four sides.

How much air could there be in so small a space, he wondered? He clicked off the lighter. Don't burn it up, he told himself. Work in the dark.

Immediately, his hands shot up and he tried to push the lid up. He pressed as hard as he could, his forearms straining. The lid remained fixed. He closed both hands into tightly balled fists and pounded them against the lid until he was coated with perspiration, his hair moist.

He reached down to his left-trouser pocket and pulled out a chain with two keys attached. They had placed those with him, too. *Stupid bastards.* Did they really think he'd be so terrified he couldn't *think?* Another amusing joke on their part. A way to lock up his life completely. He wouldn't need the keys to his car and to the office again so why not put them in the casket with him?

Wrong, he thought. He *would* use them again.

Bringing the keys above his face, he began to pick at the lining with the sharp edge of one key. He tore through the threads and began to rip apart the lining. He pulled at it with his fingers until it popped free from its fastenings. Working quickly, he pulled at the downy stuffing, tugging it free and placing it at his sides. He tried not to breathe too hard. The air had to be preserved.

He flicked on the lighter and looking at the cleared area, above, knocked against it with the knuckles of his free hand. He sighed with relief. It was oak not metal. Another mistake on their part. He smiled with contempt. It was easy to see why he had always been so far ahead of them.

"Stupid bastards," he muttered, as he stared at the thick wood. Gripping the keys together firmly, he began to dig their serrated edges against the oak. The flame of the lighter shook as he watched small pieces of the lid being chewed off by the gouging of the keys. Fragment after fragment fell. The lighter kept going out and he had to spin the flint over and over, repeating each move, until his hands felt numb. Fearing that he would use up the air, he turned the lighter off again, and continued to chisel at the wood, splinters of it falling on his neck and chin.

His arm began to ache.

He was losing strength. Wood no longer coming off as steadily. He laid the keys on his chest and flicked on the lighter again. He could see only a tattered path of wood where he had dug but it was only inches long. It's not enough, he thought. It's not enough.

He slumped and took a deep breath, stopping halfway through. The air was thinning. He reached up and pounded against the lid.

"Open this thing, goddammit," he shouted, the veins in his neck rising beneath the skin. *"Open this thing and let me out!"*

I'll die if I don't do something more, he thought.

They'll win.

His face began to tighten. He had never given up before. Never. And they weren't going to win. There was no way to stop him once he made up his mind.

He'd show those bastards what willpower was.

Quickly, he took the lighter in his right hand and turned the wheel several times. The flame rose like a streamer, fluttering back and forth before his eyes. Steadying his left arm with his right, he held the flame to the casket wood and began to scorch the ripped grain.

He breathed in short, shallow breaths, smelling the butane and wood odor as it filled the casket. The lid started to speckle with tiny sparks as he ran the flame along the gouge. He held it to one spot for several moments then slid it to another spot. The wood made faint crackling sounds.

Suddenly, a flame formed on the surface of the wood. He coughed as the burning oak began to produce grey pulpy smoke. The air in the casket continued to thin and he felt his lungs working harder. What air was available tasted like gummy smoke, as if he were lying in a horizontal smokestack. He felt as though he might faint and his body began to lose feeling.

Desperately, he struggled to remove his shirt, ripping several of the buttons off. He tore away part of the shirt and wrapped it around his right hand and wrist. A section of the lid was beginning to char and had become brittle. He slammed his swathed fist and forearm against the smoking wood and it crumbled down on him, glowing embers falling on his face and neck. His arms scrambled frantically to slap them out. Several burned his chest and palms and he cried out in pain.

Now a portion of the lid had become a glowing skeleton of wood, the heat radiating downward at his face. He squirmed away from it, turning his head to avoid the falling pieces of wood. The casket was filled with smoke and he could breathe only the choking, burning smell of it. He coughed his throat hot and raw. Fine-powder ash filled his mouth and nose as he pounded at the lid with his wrapped fist. Come on, he thought. Come on.

"Come on!" he screamed.

The section of lid gave suddenly and fell around him. He slapped at his face, neck and chest but the hot particles sizzled on his skin and he had to bear the pain as he tried to smother them.

The embers began to darken, one by one and now he smelled something new and strange. He searched for the lighter at his side, found it, and flicked it on.

He shuddered at what he saw.

Moist, root laden soil packed firmly overhead.

Reaching up, he ran his fingers across it. In the flickering light, he saw burrowing insects and the whiteness of earthworms, dangling inches from his face. He drew down as far as he could, pulling his face from their wriggling movements.

Unexpectedly, one of the larva pulled free and dropped. It fell to his face and its jelly-like casing stuck to his upper lip. His mind erupted with revulsion and he thrust both hands upward, digging at the soil. He shook his head wildly as the larva were thrown off. He continued to dig, the dirt falling in on him. It poured into his nose and he could barely breathe. It stuck to his lips and slipped into his mouth. He closed his eyes tightly but could feel it clumping on the lids. He held his breath as he pistoned his hands upward and forward like a maniacal digging machine. He eased his body up, a little at a time, letting the dirt collect under him. His lungs were laboring, hungry for air. He didn't dare open his eyes. His fingers became raw from digging, nails bent backward on several fingers, breaking off. He couldn't even feel the pain or the running blood but knew the dirt was being stained by its flow. The pain in his arms and lungs grew worse with each passing second until shearing agony filled his body. He continued to press himself upward, pulling his feet and knees closer to his chest. He began to wrestle himself into a kind of spasmed crouch, hands above his head, upper arms gathered around his face. He clawed fiercely at the dirt which gave way with each shoveling gouge of his fingers. Keep going, he told himself. *Keep going.* He refused to lose control. Refused to stop and die in the earth. He bit down hard, his teeth nearly breaking from the tension of his jaws. *Keep going,* he thought. *Keep going!* He pushed up harder and harder, dirt cascading over his body, gathering in his hair and on his shoulders. Filth surrounded him. His lungs felt ready to burst. It seemed like minutes since he'd taken a breath. He wanted to scream from his need for air but couldn't. His fingernails began to sting and throb, exposed cuticles and nerves rubbing against the granules of dirt. His mouth opened in pain and was filled with dirt, covering his tongue and gathering in his throat. His gag reflex jumped and he began retching, vomit and dirt mixing as it exploded from his mouth. His head began to empty of life as he felt himself breathing in more dirt, dying of asphyxiation. The clogging dirt began to fill his air passages, the beat of his heart doubled. *I'm losing!* he thought in anguish.

Suddenly, one finger thrust up through the crust of earth. Unthinkingly, he moved his hand like a trowel and drove it through to the surface. Now, his arms went crazy, pulling and punching at the dirt until an opening expanded. He kept thrashing at the opening, his entire system glutted with dirt. His chest felt as if it would tear down the middle.

Then his arms were poking themselves out of the grave and within several seconds he had managed to pull his upper body from the ground. He kept pulling, hooking his shredded fingers into the earth and sliding his legs from the hole. They yanked out and he lay on the ground completely, trying to fill his lungs with gulps of air. But no air could get through the dirt which had collected in his windpipe and mouth. He writhed on the ground, turning on his back and side until he'd finally raised himself to a forward kneel and began hacking phlegm-covered mud from his air passages. Black saliva ran down his chin as he continued to throw up violently, dirt falling from his mouth to the ground. When most of it was out he began to gasp, as oxygen rushed into his body, cool air filling his body with life.

I've *won,* he thought. I've beaten the bastards, *beaten* them! He began to laugh in victorious rage until his eyes pried open and he looked around, rubbing at his blood-covered lids. He heard the sound of traffic and blinding lights glared at him. They crisscrossed on his face, rushing at him from left and right. He winced, struck dumb by their glare, then realized where he was.

The cemetery by the highway.

Cars and trucks roared back and forth, tires humming. He breathed a sigh at being near life again; near movement and people. A grunting smile raised his lips.

Looking to his right, he saw a gas-station sign high on a metal pole several hundred yards up the highway.

Struggling to his feet, he ran.

As he did, he made a plan. He would go to the station, wash up in the rest room, then borrow a dime and call for a limo from the company to come and get him. No. Better a cab. That way he could fool those sons of bitches. Catch them by surprise. They undoubtedly assumed he was long gone by now. Well, he had beat them. He knew it as he picked up the pace of his run. Nobody could stop you when you really wanted something, he told himself, glancing back in the direction of the grave he had just escaped.

He ran into the station from the back and made his way to the bathroom. He didn't want anyone to see his dirtied, bloodied state.

There was a pay phone in the bathroom and he locked the door before plowing into his pocket for change. He found two pennies and a quarter and deposited the silver coin, they'd even provided him with money, he thought; the stupid bastards.

He dialed his wife.

She answered and screamed when he told her what had happened. She screamed and screamed. What a hideous joke she said. Whoever was doing this was making a hideous joke. She hung up before he could stop her. He dropped the phone and turned to face the bathroom mirror.

He couldn't even scream. He could only stare in silence.

Staring back at him was a face that was missing sections of flesh. Its skin was grey, and withered yellow bone showed through.

Then he remembered what else his wife had said and began to weep. His shock began to turn to hopeless fatalism.

It had been over seven months, she'd said.

Seven months.

He looked at himself in the mirror again, and realized there was nowhere he could go.

And, somehow all he could think about was the engraving on his lighter.

TRAPS

By GAHAN WILSON

A native of Evanston, Illinois, Gahan Wilson once remarked humorously that he is the only "admitted cartoonist" to have graduated from the Chicago School of Art. His cartoons—a sort of combination of Charles Addams and James Thurber—have appeared in The New Yorker, Playboy, The Magazine of Fantasy and Science Fiction, *and* The National Lampoon, *where, even at their most ghoulish, they are considerably more wistful and gentle than most of the other things in that magazine. Wilson's interest in the macabre goes far beyond the comic concerns of his cartoons, however. He has a considerable knowledge of, and respect for, the supernatural tradition in literature, and has, when prevailed upon, produced superb short stories. Because of the steady demand for his cartoons, Wilson has regrettably had time to write only a half dozen or so stories to date, this deliciously macabre and funny example being the latest.*

Lester adjusted his brand new cap with ROSE BROTHERS EXTERMINATORS stitched in bright scarlet on its front and stared gloomily down at the last of the traps and poisons he had set the week before.

"It's just like I told you it would be, Lester Bailey," hissed Miss Dinwittie. "They're too smart for you is what it is!"

Lester winced away from Miss Dinwittie's fierce, wrinkled frown and considered the trap the Rose Brothers Exterminators people had given him to lay on the floor of her basement.

It was a very impressive machine. When you touched the bait it slapped shut sharp serrated jaws, which not only prevented your going elsewhere but insured your bleeding to death as you lingered. If you were a rat, that is. A man would probably only lose a finger.

This time, in spite of the bait being removed, the trap remained unsprung. Impossibly, its shiny teeth continued to gape wide around the tiny platform which they were supposed to have infallibly guarded. Lester shook his large, rather square head, in mortification.

It was not bad enough that the trap had been gulled. The bait, which had been carefully poisoned, was uneaten. It lay demurely five inches from the trap. Outside of one light toothmark, evidence of the gentlest and most tentative of tastes, it was spurned and virginal.

"I ain't never seen nothing like it, Miss Dinwittie," admitted Lester with a sign.

"That's quite obvious from the expression on your face," she piped. "All this folderol you've put around hasn't done a thing except stir them up!"

She snorted and kicked at the trap with one high-button shoe. The mechanism described a small parabola, snapped ineffectually at the apogee, and fell with a tinny clatter.

Lester was not surprised by this contemptuous action of Miss Dinwittie. Miss Dinwittie was customarily contemptuous for the simple reason that she felt she had every right to be. Her father had been a remarkably greedy man, and by the time he'd died had managed to pretty well own the small town he'd settled in, and Miss Dinwittie had not let go a foot of it. The children believed she was a witch.

"They get brighter every day," she snapped. "And now you've gone and got them really mad!"

She looked around the gloom of the basement, moving her small, grey head in quick, darting movements.

"Listen!"

Lester stood beside her in the musty air and did as he was told. After a time he could make out nasty little noises all around. Shufflings and scratchings and tiny draggings. He peered at the ancient tubes and pipes running along the walls and snaking under the beams and flooring.

"They're just snickering at you, Lester Bailey," said Miss Dinwittie.

She sniffed and marched up the basement steps with Lester dutifully following, looking up at her thin, sexless behind. When they reached the kitchen she made him sit on one of the rickety chairs, which were arranged around the oilcloth-covered table, and poured him some bitter coffee. He drank it without complaint. He had no wish to further offend Miss Dinwittie.

She prowled briefly around the room and then surprised him by suddenly sitting by his side and leaning closely toward him in a conspiratorial manner. She smelled dry and sour.

"They've got together!" she whispered.

She clutched her bony hands on the shiny white oilcloth. Lester could hear the air rustling in the passages of her nose. She frowned and her eyes shown with a dark revelation.

"They've got together," she said again. "It used to be you could pick them off, one by one. It was each rat for himself. But now it's not the same."

She leaned even closer to him. She actually poked a thin finger into his chest.

"Now they've *organized!*"

Lester studied her carefully. The people at Rose Brothers Exterminators had in no way prepared him for this sort of thing. Miss Dinwittie sat back and crossed her arms in a satisfied way. She smiled grimly, and nodded to herself.

"Organized," she said again, quietly.

Lester fumbled uncertainly over the limited information he had at his disposal concerning the handling of the violently insane. There was not much, but he did recall it was very important to humor them. You've got to humor them or they'll go for the ax or the bread knife.

"They're like an army," said Miss Dinwittie, leaning forward again, too self-absorbed to notice Lester's reflex leaning away. "I believe they have officers and everything. I *know* they've got scouts!"

She looked at him expectantly. Lester's reaction, a blank, wide-eyed look, irritated her.

"Well?" she snapped. "Aren't you going to ask me *how* I know?"

"About what, Miss Dinwittie?"

"Ask me *how I know* they've got scouts, you silly boob!"

"How do you come to know that, Miss Dinwittie?"

She stood and, beckoning Lester to follow, crossed the cold linoleum floor. When he reached her side at a particularly dark corner of the kitchen, she pointed to the base of the wall. Lester squinted. He believed he could make out something on the molding. He squatted down to have a better look at it. Scrawled clumsily on the cracked paint with what seemed to be a grease pencil was a tiny arrow and a cross and a squiggle that looked like it came from a miniature alphabet.

"It's some kind of *instruction,* isn't it?" hissed Miss Dinwittie. "It's put there to *guide the others!*"

Lester stood, unobtrusively. It had suddenly occurred to him that the old woman could have crowned him easily with a pan as he'd hunkered down at her feet. She glared at the weird little marks and snarled faintly.

"They're all over the house," she said. "In the closets, on the stairs, inside cabinets—everywhere!"

Suddenly her mood changed and, giving a small, vindictive laugh, she once again poked Lester in the chest.

"Gives them clean away, doesn't it?" she asked. "And there's *something else!* I'll go up and bring it down and you take it over to those silly fools who hired you, so they'll see what they're dealing with and give me some *service* for my money!"

Putting a thin finger to her lips, she backed out of the room. Smiling, she closed the door.

Lester stared after her and then a sudden hissing behind him made him wheel to see coffee boiling from its pot onto the stove. He turned off the burner, frightened at the way his heart was thumping in his chest. He wished to God he could have a cigarette, but he knew Miss Dinwittie didn't hold with smoking or anything else along those lines.

He could hear the rats. He decided he had never seen such a house for rats in all his life. One of them was making scuttling noises in the wall before him so he thumped the wall, but the rat just scuttled right along, behind the dead flowers printed on the paper, paying him no mind. Lester sighed and sat down in one of the inhospitable chairs.

Another rat started scratching over at the wall where those funny marks were, and then another in some other part, and then a third and then a fourth. Lester began to estimate how many rats there might be in the old house and then decided maybe that wasn't such a good idea, his being alone in this gloomy kitchen and all.

He wiped the back of his hand against his lips and wished again for a cigarette. He stood and went to the hall door and opened it, looking up at the narrow staircase leading to the second floor. The carpeting on the stairs and floor was a smudgy brown.

He went back into the kitchen and took out his cigarettes and lit one. To hell with Miss Dinwittie, anyways. Besides, he'd hear her coming and snuff it out. He bet those steps creaked something awful.

If you could hear them over the sound of the rats, that is. They'd gotten louder, he could swear to it. He let the smoke drift out of his mouth and listened carefully. They said you could hear better if your mouth was open. He pressed his ear to the ugly floral paper and then drew back in fright when the sound of them instantly spread away from where he'd touched the wall. He ground the cigarette out on the sole of his shoe and dropped it in a box of garbage by the sink. He went to the hall again and called out, "Miss Dinwittie?"

He gaped up into the darkness of the second floor. Had something moved up there?

"Miss Dinwittie? You all right?"

He shuffled his feet on the dusty carpet. It looked a little like rat skin itself, come to think of it. Was something rustling up there?

"Miss Dinwittie? I'm coming up!"

That would get a rise out of the old bitch if anything would. She wouldn't tolerate folks like him coming where they hadn't been asked.

But there was no objection of any kind, so he rubbed his nose and began, slowly, to climb the stairs. The banister was repulsively smooth and slick. Like a rat's tail, he thought.

"Miss Dinwittie?"

It was dark as hell up here. He took the flashlight from his belt and turned it this way and that, continuing to call as he peered through old doorways. When he came to her bedroom he was careful to call her name three times before he went in.

On the dresser, between a silver comb and brush, lying right in the center of a dainty antimacassar doily, was the desiccated body of a rat in the convulsions of a violent rigor mortis. Its dried fingers clawed the air and its withered lips pulled back from dully gleaming teeth. It looked furious.

"Shit!" said Lester.

The top of its head had been flattened, perhaps by the heel of one of Miss Dinwittie's shoes. Around its waist was tied a bit of grey string, and fixed to one side of this crude belt, by means of a tiny loop, was a small sliver of glass tapered on one end to a vicious point and wrapped about the other with a fragment of electrician's tape so as to form a kind of handle. It was an efficient-looking miniature sword.

Why that goddamn old bitch's gone right out of her goddamn head, thought Lester; she's dressed that goddamn dead rat up just like a little girl dresses up a doll!

He heard a faint noise in the hall and turned, sweating in the clammy chill of the room. Was she out there waiting for him with a sword of her own? You read all the time in the papers about the awful things crazy people do!

He tiptoed out of the room and peered down the hall and his breath stopped. The beam of his flashlight pointed at the bottom of the door leading to the attic and revealed Miss Dinwittie's high-button shoes with their toes up in the air. Even as he gaped at them they edged out of sight in uneven little starts to the sounds of a faint bumping and an even fainter scrabbling.

Oh my God, thought Lester, oh my Jesus God, oh please don't let none of this happen to me, please, God!

Still on tiptoe, even more on tiptoe, he worked his way to the stairs. He wanted to sob but he told himself he musn't do it because he'd never be able to hear the rats if he was sobbing. He started down the stairs and was halfway when a dim instinct made him look back up to the top.

There, peering down at him, was a lone rat holding a discarded plastic knitting needle proudly upright. Fixed to the needle's top was a tiny rectangle of foul, tattered cloth. It took Lester several horrible seconds to realize he was looking at the flag of the rats.

"I didn't mean nothing!" he whispered, groping his way backwards down the stairs. He plucked the cap with ROSE BROTHERS EXTERMINATORS from his head and flung it from him, crying: *"It was just a goddam way to make a living!"*

But the time for all that was long since past, and the rat army, in perfect ranks and files on the floor below, watched its enemy approaching, step by step, and eagerly awaited its general's command.

THE MIST

By STEPHEN KING

Stephen King is a literary phenomenon. While in his twenties, he burst on to the book scene with a best-selling novel of horror called Carrie, *about a lonely high-school girl with awesome psychic powers. He has followed that with other astonishing successes, one after the other, making him one of the most popular writers in the world. King has a remarkable eye and feeling for the lives of ordinary Americans and the places they live. They're the people you might see buying a McDonald's hamburger, or at a local baseball game, or your neighborhood hardware store. And, indeed, that's a key to understanding King's way. He has carried on what Ray Bradbury pioneered: his stories are always about identifiable people whose lives are altered by paranormal events and forces. His characters and their worlds ring uncannily right, and he* involves one intensely *in their predicaments. That, as much as his superb touch with terror, is what readers respond to. All those King qualities are evident in the terrifying short novel that follows, as well as his gift for visually rich, well-paced, gripping storytelling. In true King fashion, ordinary people come face-to-face with the stuff their nightmares are made of, in a familiar place not far from home.*

I. The Coming of the Storm.

This is what happened. On the night that the worst heat wave in northern New England history finally broke—the night of July 19—the entire western Maine region was lashed with the most vicious thunderstorms I have ever seen.

We lived on Long Lake, and we saw the first of the storms beating its way across the water toward us just before dark. For an hour before the air had been utterly still. The American flag that my father put up on our boathouse in 1936 lay limp against its pole. Not even its hem fluttered. The heat was like a solid thing, and it seemed as deep as sullen quarry-water. That afternoon the three of us had gone swimming, but the water was no relief unless you went out deep. Neither Steffy or I wanted to go deep because Billy couldn't. Billy is five.

We ate a cold supper at five-thirty, picking listlessly at ham sandwiches and potato salad out on the deck that faces the lake. Nobody seemed to want anything but the Pepsi, which was in a steel bucket of ice cubes.

After supper Billy went out back to play on his monkey bars for a while. Steff and I sat without talking much, smoking and looking across the sullen flat mirror of the lake to Harrison on the far side. A few power boats droned back and forth. The evergreens over there looked dusty and beaten. In the west, great purple thunderheads were slowly building up, massing like an army. Lightning flashed inside them. Next door, Brent Norton's radio, tuned to that classical-music station that broadcasts from the top of Mount Washington, sent out a loud bray of static each time the lightning flashed. Norton was a lawyer from New Jersey and his place on Long Lake was only a summer cottage with no furnace or insulation. Two years before we had a boundary dispute that finally wound up in county court. I won. Norton claimed I won because he was an out-of-towner. There was no love lost between us.

Steff sighed and fanned the tops of her breasts with the edge of her halter. I doubted if it cooled her off much but it improved the view a lot.

"I don't want to scare you," I said, "but there's a bad storm on the way, I think."

She looked at me doubtfully. "There were thunderheads last night and the night before, David. They just broke up."

"They won't do that tonight."

"No?"

"If it gets bad enough, we're going to go downstairs."

"How bad do you think it can get?"

My dad was the first to build a year-round home on this side of the lake. When he was hardly more than a kid he and his brothers put up a summer place where the house now stood, and in 1938 a summer storm knocked it flat, stone walls and all. Only the boathouse escaped. A year later he started the big house. It's the trees that do the damage in a bad blow. They get old, and the wind knocks them over. It's mother nature's way of cleaning house periodically.

"I don't really know," I said, truthfully enough. I had only heard stories about the great storm of thirty-eight. "But the wind can come off the lake like an express train."

Billy came back a while later, complaining that the monkey bars were no fun because he was "all sweated up." I ruffled his hair and gave him another Pepsi. More work for the dentist.

The thunderheads were getting closer, pushing away the blue. There was no doubt now that a storm was coming. Norton had turned off his radio. Billy sat between his mother and me, watching the sky, fascinated. Thunder boomed, rolling slowly across the lake and then echoing back again. The clouds twisted and roiled, now black, now purple, now veined, now black again. They gradually overspread the lake, and I could see a delicate caul of rain extending down from them. It was still a distance away. As we watched, it was probably raining on Bolster's Mills, or maybe Norway.

The air began to move, jerkily at first, lifting the flag and then dropping it again. It began to freshen and grew steady, first cooling the perspiration on our bodies and then seeming to freeze it.

That was when I saw the silver veil rolling across the lake. It blotted out Harrison in seconds and then came straight at us. The power boats had vacated the scene.

Billy stood up from his chair, which was a miniature replica of our director's chairs, complete with his name printed on the back. "Daddy! Look!"

"Let's go in," I said. I stood up and put my arm around his shoulders.

"But do you see it? Dad, what is it?"

"A water-cyclone. Let's go in."

Steff threw a quick, startled glance at my face and then said, "Come on, Billy. Do what your father says."

We went in through the sliding glass doors that give on the living room. I slid the door shut on its track and paused for another look out. The silver veil was three-quarters of the way across the lake. It had resolved itself into a crazily-spinning teacup between the lowering black sky and the surface of the water, which had gone the color of lead streaked with white chrome. The lake had begun to look eerily like the ocean, with high waves rolling in and sending spume up from the docks and breakwaters. Out in the middle, big whitecaps were tossing their heads back and forth.

Watching the water-cyclone was hypnotic. It was nearly on top of us when lightning flashed so brightly that it printed everything on my eyes in negative for thirty seconds afterward. The telephone gave out a startled *ting!* and I turned to see my wife and son standing directly in front of the big picture window that gives us a panoramic view of the lake to the northwest.

One of those terrible visions came to me—I think they are reserved exclusively for husbands and fathers—of the picture window blowing in with a low hard coughing sound and sending jagged arrows of glass into my wife's bare stomach, into my boy's face and neck. The horrors of the Inquisition are nothing compared to the fates your mind can imagine for your loved ones.

I grabbed them both hard and jerked them away. "What the hell are you doing? Get away from there!"

Steff gave me a startled glance. Billy only looked at me as if he had been partially awakened from a deep dream. I led them into the kitchen and hit the light switch. The phone ting-a-linged again.

Then the wind came. It was as if the house had taken off like a 747. It was a high, breathless whistling, sometimes deepening to a bass roar before glissading up to a whooping scream.

"Go downstairs," I told Steff, and now I had to shout to make myself heard. Directly over the house thunder whacked mammoth planks together and Billy shrank against my leg.

"You come too!" Steff yelled back.

I nodded and made shooing gestures. I had to pry Billy off my leg. "Go with your mother. I want to get some candles in case the lights go off."

He went with her, and I started opening cabinets. Candles are funny things, you know. You lay them by every spring, knowing that a summer storm may knock out the power. And when the time comes, they hide.

I was pawing through the fourth cabinet, past the half-ounce of grass that Steff and I bought four years ago and had still not smoked much of, past Billy's wind-up set of chattering teeth from the Auburn Novelty Shop, past the drifts of photos Steffy kept forgetting to glue in our album. I looked under a Sears catalogue and behind a Kewpie doll from Taiwan that I had won at the Fryeburg fair knocking over wooden milk bottles with tennis balls.

I found the candles behind the Kewpie doll with its glazed dead man's eyes. They were still wrapped in their cellophane. As my hand closed around them the lights went out and the only electricity was the stuff in the sky. The dining room was lit in a series of shutter-flashes that were white and purple. Downstairs I heard Billy start to cry and the low murmur of Steff soothing him.

I had to have one more look at the storm.

The water-cyclone had either passed us or broken up when it reached the shoreline, but I still couldn't see twenty yards out onto the lake. The water was in complete turmoil. I saw someone's dock—the Jassers', maybe—hurry by with its main supports alternately turned up to the sky and buried in the churning water.

I went downstairs. Billy ran to me and clung to my legs. I lifted him up and gave him a hug. Then I lit the candles. We sat in the guest room down the hall from my little studio and looked at each other's faces in the flickering yellow glow and listened to the storm roar and bash at our house. About twenty minutes later we heard a ripping, rending crash as one of the big pines went down nearby. Then there was a lull.

"Is it over?" Steff asked.

"Maybe," I said. "Maybe only for a while."

We went upstairs, each of us carrying a candle, like monks going to vespers. Billy carried his proudly and carefully. Carrying a candle, carrying the *fire,* was a very big deal for him. It helped him forget about being afraid.

It was too dark to see what damage had been done around the house. It was past Billy's bedtime, but neither of us suggested putting him in. We sat in the living room, listened to the wind, and looked at the lightning.

About an hour later it began to crank up again. For three weeks the temperature had been over ninety, and on six of those twenty-one days the National Weather Service station at the Portland Jetport had reported temperatures of over one hundred degrees. Queer weather. Coupled with the grueling winter we had come through and the late spring, some people had dragged out that old chestnut about the long-range results of the fifties A-bomb tests again. That, and of course, the end of the world. The oldest chestnut of them all.

The second squall wasn't so hard, but we heard the crash of several trees weakened by the first onslaught. As the wind began to die down again, one thudded heavily on the roof, like a fist dropped on a coffin lid. Billy jumped and looked apprehensively upward.

"It'll hold, champ," I said.

Billy smiled nervously.

Around ten o'clock the last squall came. It was bad. The wind howled almost as loudly as it had the first time, and lightning seemed to be flashing all around us. More trees fell, and there was a splintering crash down by the water that made Steff utter a low cry. Billy had gone to sleep on her lap.

"David, what was that?"

"I think it was the boathouse."

"Oh. Oh, Jesus."

"Steffy, I want us to go downstairs again." I took Billy in my arms and stood up with him. Steff's eyes were big and frightened.

"David, are we going to be all right?"

"Yes."

"Really?"

"Yes."

We went downstairs. Ten minutes later, as the final squall peaked, there was a splintering crash from upstairs—the picture window. So maybe my vision earlier hadn't been so crazy after all. Steff, who had been dozing, woke up with a little shriek, and Billy stirred uneasily in the guest bed.

"The rain will come in," she said. "It'll ruin the furniture."

"If it does, it does. It's insured."

"That doesn't make it any better," she said in an upset, scolding voice. "Your mother's dresser . . . our new sofa . . . the color TV . . ."

"Shhh," I said. "Go to sleep."

"I can't," she said, and five minutes later she had.

I stayed awake for another half hour with one lit candle for company, listening to the thunder walk and talk outside. I had a feeling that there were going to be a lot of people from the lakefront communities calling their insurance agents in the morning. A lot of chainsaws burring as cottage owners cut up the trees that had fallen on their roofs and battered through their windows, and a lot of orange CMP trucks on the road.

The storm was fading now, with no sign of a new squall coming in. I went back upstairs, leaving Steff and Billy on the bed, and looked into the living room. The sliding-glass door had held. But where the picture window had been there was now a jagged hole stuffed with birch leaves. It was the top of the old tree that had stood by our outside basement access for as long as I could remember. Looking at its top, now visiting in our living room, I could understand what Steffy had meant by saying insurance didn't make it any better. I had loved that tree. It had been a hard campaigner of many winters, the one tree on the lakeside of the house that was exempt from my own chainsaw. Big chunks of glass on the rug reflected my candle-flame over and over. I reminded myself to warn Steff and Billy. They would want to wear their slippers in here. Both of them liked to slop around barefoot in the morning.

I went downstairs again. All three of us slept together in the guest bed, Billy between Steff and me. I had a dream that I saw God walking across Harrison on the far side of the lake, a God so gigantic that above the waist He was lost in a clear blue sky. In the dream I could hear the rending crack and splinter of breaking trees as God stamped the woods into the shape of His footsteps. He was circling the lake, coming toward the Bridgton side, toward us, and behind Him everything that had been green turned a bad gray and all the houses and cottages and summer places were bursting into purple-white flame like lightning, and soon the smoke covered everything. The smoke covered everything like a mist.

II. After the Storm. Norton.
A Trip to Town.

"*Jeee*-pers," Billy said.

He was standing by the fence that separates our property from Norton's and looking down our driveway. The driveway runs a quarter of a mile to a camp road which, in its turn, runs about three-quarters of a mile to a stretch of two-lane blacktop called Kansas Road. From Kansas Road you can go anywhere you want, as long as it's Bridgton.

I saw what Billy was looking at and my heart went cold.

"Don't go any closer, champ. Right there is close enough."

Billy didn't argue.

The morning was bright and as clear as a bell. The sky, which had been a mushy, hazy color during the heat wave, had regained a deep, crisp blue that was nearly autumnal. There was a light breeze, making cheerful sun-dapples move back and forth in the driveway. Not far from where Billy was standing there was a steady hissing noise, and in the grass there was what you might at first have taken for a writhing bundle of snakes. The bundle wasn't snakes. The power lines leading to our house had fallen in an untidy tangle about twenty feet away and lay in a burned patch of grass. They were twisting lazily and spitting. If the trees and grass hadn't been so completely damped down by the torrential rains, the house might have gone up. As it was, there was only that black patch where the wires had touched directly.

"Could that lectercute a person, Daddy?"

"Yeah. It could."

mid-May storm dropped nearly a foot of wet, heavy snow on the region, covering the new grass and flowers. Giosti had been in his cups for fair, and happy to pass along the Black Spring story, along with his own original twist. But we get snow in May sometimes; it comes and it's gone two days later. It's no big deal.

Steff was glancing doubtfully at the downed wires again. "When will the power company come?"

"Just as soon as they can. It won't be long. I just don't want you to worry about Billy. His head's on pretty straight. He forgets to pick up his clothes, but he isn't going to go and step on a bunch of live lines. He's got a good, healthy dose of self-interest." I touched a corner of her mouth and it obliged by turning up in the beginning of a smile. "Better?"

"You always make it seem better," she said, and that made me feel good.

From the lakeside of the house Billy was yelling for us to come and see.

"Come on," I said. "Let's go look at the damage."

She snorted ruefully. "If I want to look at damage, I can go sit in my living room."

"Make a little kid happy, then."

We walked down the stone steps hand in hand. We had just reached the first turn in them when Billy came from the other direction at speed, almost knocking us over.

"Take it easy," Steff said, frowning a little. Maybe, in her mind, she was seeing him skidding into that deadly nest of live wires instead of the two of us.

"You gotta come see!" Billy panted. "The boathouse is all bashed! There's a dock on the rocks . . . and trees in the boat cove. . . . Jesus *Christ!*"

"Billy Drayton!" Steff thundered.

"Sorry, Ma—but you gotta—wow!" He was gone again.

"Having spoken, the doomsayer departs," I said, and that made Steff giggle again. "Listen, after I cut up those trees across the driveway, I'll go by the Central Maine Power office on Portland Road. Tell them what we got. Okay?"

"Okay," she said gratefully. "When do you think you can go?"

Except for the big tree—the one with the moldy corset of moss—it would have been an hour's work. With the big one added in, I didn't think the job would be done until eleven or so.

"I'll give you lunch here, then. But you'll have to get some things at

"What are we going to do about it?"

"Nothing. Wait for the CMP."

"When will they come?"

"I don't know." Five-year-olds have as many questions as Hallmark has cards. "I imagine they're pretty busy this morning. Want to take a walk up to the end of the driveway with me?"

He started to come and then stopped, eyeing the wire nervously. One of them humped up and turned over lazily, as if beckoning.

"Daddy, can lectricity shoot through the ground?"

A fair enough question. "Yes, but don't worry. Electricity wants the ground, not you, Billy. You'll be all right if you stay away from the wires."

"Wants the ground," he muttered, and then came to me. We walked up the driveway holding hands.

It was worse than I had imagined. Trees had fallen across the drive in four different places, one of them small, two of them middling, and one old baby that must have been five feet through the middle. Moss was crusted onto it like a moldy corset.

Branches, some half-stripped of their leaves, lay everywhere in jack-straw profusion. Billy and I walked up to the camp road, tossing the smaller branches off into the woods on either side. It reminded me of a summer's day that had been maybe twenty-five years before; I couldn't have been much older than Billy was now. All my uncles had been here, and they had spent the day in the woods with axes and hatchets and Darcy-poles, cutting brush. Later that afternoon they had all sat down to the trestle picnic table my dad and mom used to have and there had been a monster meal of hot dogs and hamburgers and potato salad. The Gansett beer had flowed like water and my uncle Reuben took a dive into the lake with all his clothes on, even his deck-shoes. In those days there were still deer in these woods.

"Daddy, can I go down to the lake?"

He was tired of throwing branches, and the thing to do with a little boy when he's tired is to let him go do something else. "Sure."

We walked back to the house together and then Billy cut right, going around the house and giving the downed wires a large berth. I went left, into the garage, to get my McCullough. As I had suspected, I could already hear the unpleasant song of the chainsaw up and down the lake.

I topped up the tank, took off my shirt, and was starting back up the driveway when Steff came out. She eyed the downed trees lying across the driveway nervously.

"How bad is it?"

"I can cut it up. How bad is it in there?"

"Well, I got the glass up, but you're going to have to do something about that tree, David. We can't have a tree in the living room."

"No," I said. "I guess we can't."

We looked at each other in the morning sunlight and got giggling. I set the McCullough down on the cement areaway and kissed her, holding her buttocks firmly.

"Don't," she murmured. "Billy's—"

He came tearing around the corner of the house just then. "Dad! Daddy! Y'oughta see the—"

Steffy saw the live wires and screamed for him to watch out. Billy, who was a good distance away from them, pulled up short and stared at his mother as if she had gone mad.

"I'm okay, Mom," he said in the careful tone of voice you use to placate the very old and senile. He walked toward us, showing us how all right he was, and Steff began to tremble in my arms.

"It's all right," I said in her ear. "He knows about them."

"Yes, but people get killed," she said. "They have ads all the time on television about live wires, people get— Billy, I want you to come in the house right now!"

"Aw, come on, Mom! I wanna show Dad the boathouse!" He was almost bug-eyed with excitement and disappointment. He had gotten a taste of poststorm apocalypse and wanted to share it.

"You go in right now! Those wires are dangerous and—"

"Dad said they want the ground, not me—"

"Billy, don't you argue with me!"

"I'll come down and look, champ. Go on down yourself." I could feel Steff tensing against me. "Go around the other side, kiddo."

"Yeah! Okay!"

He tore past us, taking the stone steps that led around the west end of the house two by two. He disappeared with his shirttail flying, trailing back one word—"Wow!"—as he spotted some other novel piece of destruction.

"He knows about the wires, Steffy." I took her gently by the shoulders. "He's scared of them. That's good. It makes him safe."

One tear tracked down her cheek. "David, I'm scared."

"Come on! It's over."

"Is it? Last winter . . . and the late spring . . . they called it a black spring in town . . . they said there hadn't been one in these parts since 1888—"

"They" undoubtedly meant Mrs. Carmody, who kept the Antiquary, a junk shop that Steff liked to rummage around times. Billy loved to go with her. In one of the shadowy, du rooms, stuffed owls with gold-ringed eyes spread their wings fo their feet endlessly grasped varnished logs; stuffed raccoons sto trio around a "stream" that was a long fragment of dusty mirr one moth-eaten wolf, which was foaming sawdust instead of around his muzzle, snarled a creepy eternal snarl. Mrs. Ca claimed the wolf was shot by her father as it came to drink Stevens Brook one September afternoon in 1901.

The expeditions to Mrs. Carmody's Antiquary shop worked we my wife and son. She was into carnival glass and he was into dea the name of taxidermy. But I thought that the old woman exercis rather unpleasant hold over Steff's mind, which was in all other v practical and hardheaded. She had found Steff's vulnerable spo mental Achilles' heel. Nor was she the only one in town who was cinated by Mrs. Carmody's gothic pronouncements and folk remec (which were always prescribed in God's name).

Stump-water would take off bruises if your husband was the sc who got a bit too free with his fists after three drinks. You could te what kind of a winter was coming by counting the rings on the cate pillars in June or by measuring the thickness of August honeycomb And now, good God protect and preserve us, THE BLACK SPRING OI 1888 (add your own exclamation points, as many as you think it deserves). I had also heard the story. It's one they like to pass around up here—if the spring is cold enough, the ice on the lakes will eventually turn as black as a rotted tooth. It's rare, but hardly a once-in-a-century occurrence. They like to pass it around, but I doubt that many could pass it around with as much conviction as Mrs. Carmody.

"We had a hard winter and a late spring," I said. "Now we're having a hot summer. And we had a storm but it's over. You're not acting like yourself, Stephanie."

"That wasn't an ordinary storm," she said in that same husky voice.

"No," I said. "I'll go along with you there."

I had heard the Black Spring story from Bill Giosti, who owned and operated—after a fashion—Giosti's Mobil in Casco Village. Bill ran the place with his three tosspot sons (with occasional help from his four tosspot grandsons . . . when they could take time off from tinkering with their snowmobiles and dirtbikes). Bill was seventy, looked eighty, and could still drink like twenty-three when the mood was on him. Billy and I had taken the Scout in for a fill-up the day after a surprise

the market for me . . . we're almost out of milk and butter. Also . . . well, I'll have to make you a list."

Give a woman a disaster and she turns squirrel. I gave her a hug and nodded. We went on around the house. It didn't take more than a glance to understand why Billy had been a little overwhelmed.

"Lordy," Steff said in a faint voice.

From where we stood we had enough elevation to be able to see almost a quarter of a mile of shoreline—the Bibber property to our left, our own, and Brent Norton's to our right.

The huge old pine that had guarded our boat cove had been sheared off halfway up. What was left looked like a brutally sharpened pencil, and the inside of the tree seemed a glistening and defenseless white against the age- and weather-darkened outer bark. A hundred feet of tree, the old pine's top half, lay partly submerged in our shallow cove. It occurred to me that we were very lucky our little Star-Cruiser wasn't sunk underneath it. The week before it had developed engine trouble and it was still at the Naples marina, patiently waiting its turn.

On the other side of our little piece of shorefront, the boathouse my father had built—the boathouse that had once housed a sixty-foot Chris-Craft when the Drayton family fortunes had been at a higher mark than they were today—lay under another big tree. It was the one that had stood on Norton's side of the property line, I saw. That raised the first flush of anger. The tree had been dead for five years and he should have long since had it taken down. Now it was three-quarters of the way down; our boathouse was propping it up. The roof had taken on a drunken, swaybacked look. The wind had swirled shingles from the hole the tree had made all over the point of land the boathouse stood on. Billy's description, "bashed," was as good as any.

"That's Norton's tree!" Steff said, and she said it with such hurt indignation that I had to smile in spite of the pain I felt. The flagpole was lying in the water and Old Glory floated soggily beside it in a tangle of lanyard. And I could imagine Norton's response: Sue me.

Billy was on the rock breakwater, examining the dock that had washed up on the stones. It was painted in jaunty blue-and-yellow stripes. He looked back over his shoulder at us and yelled gleefully, "It's the Martinses', isn't it?"

"Yeah, it is," I said. "Wade in and fish the flag out, would you, Big Bill?"

"Sure!"

To the right of the breakwater was a small sandy beach. In 1941, before Pearl Harbor paid off the Great Depression in blood, my dad hired a man to truck in that fine beach sand—six dumptrucks full—and to spread it out to a depth that is about nipple-high on me, say five feet. The workman charged eighty bucks for the job and the sand has never moved. Just as well, you know; you can't put a sandy beach in on your land now. Now that the sewerage runoff from the booming cottage-building industry has killed most of the fish and made the rest of them unsafe to eat, the EPA has forbidden installing sand beaches. They might upset the ecology of the lake, you see, and it is presently against the law for anyone except land developers to do that.

Billy went for the flag—then stopped. At the same moment I felt Steff go rigid against me, and I saw it myself. The Harrison side of the lake was gone. It had been buried under a line of bright-white mist, like a fair-weather cloud fallen to earth.

My dream of the night before recurred, and when Steff asked me what it was, the word that nearly jumped first from my mouth was *God.*

"David?"

You couldn't see even a hint of the shoreline over there, but years of looking at Long Lake made me believe that the shoreline wasn't hidden by much; only yards, maybe. The edge of the mist was nearly ruler-straight.

"What is it, Dad?" Billy yelled. He was in the water up to his knees, groping for the soggy flag.

"Fogbank," I said.

"On the *lake?*" Steff asked doubtfully, and I could see Mrs. Carmody's influence in her eyes. Damn the woman. My own moment of unease was passing. Dreams, after all, are insubstantial things, like mist itself.

"Sure. You've seen fog on the lake before."

"Never like that. That looks more like a cloud."

"It's the brightness of the sun," I said. "It's the same way clouds look from an airplane when you fly over them."

"What would do it? We only get fog in damp weather."

"No, we've got it right now," I said. "Harrison does, anyway. It's a little leftover from the storm, that's all. Two fronts meeting. Something along that line."

"David, are you sure?"

I laughed and hauled my arm around her neck. "No. Actually, I'm bullshitting like crazy. If I was sure, I'd be doing the weather on the six-o'clock news. Go on and make your shopping list."

She gave me one more doubtful glance, looked at the fogbank for a moment or two with the flat of her hand held up to shade her eyes, and then shook her head. "Weird," she said, and walked away.

For Billy, the mist had lost its novelty. He had fished the flag and a tangle of lanyard out of the water. We spread it on the lawn to dry.

"I heard it was wrong to ever let the flag touch the ground, Daddy," he said in a businesslike, let's-get-this-out-of-the-way tone.

"Yeah?"

"Yeah. Victor McAllister says they lectercute people for it."

"Well, you tell Vic he's full of what makes the grass grow green."

"Horseshit, right?" Billy is a bright boy, but oddly humorless. To the champ, everything is serious business. I'm hoping that he'll live long enough to learn that in this world that is a very dangerous attitude.

"Yeah, right, but don't tell your mother I said so. When the flag's dry, we'll put it away. We'll even fold it into a cocked hat, so we'll be on safe ground there."

"Daddy, will we fix the boathouse roof and get a new flagpole?" For the first time he looked anxious. He'd maybe had enough destruction for a while.

I clapped him on the shoulder. "You're damn tooting."

"Can I go over to the Bibbers' and see what happened there?"

"Just for a couple of minutes. They'll be cleaning up, too, and sometimes that makes people feel a little ugly." The way I presently felt about Norton.

"Okay. 'Bye!" He was off.

"Stay out of their way, champ. And Billy?"

He glanced back.

"Remember about the live wires. If you see more, steer clear of them."

"Sure, Dad."

I stood there for a moment, first surveying the damage, then glancing out at the mist again. It seemed closer, but it was very hard to tell for sure. If it was closer, it was defying all the laws of nature, because the wind—a very gentle breeze—was against it. That, of course, was patently impossible. It was very, very white. The only thing I can compare it to would be fresh-fallen snow lying in dazzling contrast to the deep-blue brilliance of the winter sky. But snow reflects hundreds and hundreds of diamond points in the sun, and this peculiar fogbank, although bright and clean-looking, did not sparkle. In spite of what Steff had said, mist isn't uncommon on clear days, but when there's a lot of it, the suspended moisture almost always causes a rainbow. But there was no rainbow here.

The unease was back, tugging at me, but before it could deepen I heard a low mechanical sound—*whut-whut-whut!*—followed by a barely-audible "Shit!" The mechanical sound was repeated, but this time there was no oath. The third time the chuffing sound was followed by "Mother-*fuck!*" in that same low I'm-all-by-myself-but-boy-am-I-pissed tone.

Whut-whut-whut-whut—

—silence—

—then: "You cunt."

I began to grin. Sound carries well out here, and all the buzzing chainsaws were fairly distant. Distant enough for me to recognize the not-so-dulcet tones of my next-door neighbor, the renowned lawyer and lakefront-property–owner, Brenton Norton.

I moved down a little closer to the water, pretending to stroll toward the dock beached on our breakwater. Now I could see Norton. He was in the clearing beside his screened-in porch, standing on a carpet of old pine needles and dressed in paint-spotted jeans and a white strappy T-shirt. His forty-dollar haircut was in disarray and sweat poured down his face. He was down on one knee, laboring over his own chainsaw. It was much bigger and fancier than my little $79.95 Value House job. It seemed to have everything, in fact, but a starter button. He was yanking a cord, producing the listless *whut-whut-whut* sounds and nothing more. I was gladdened in my heart to see that a yellow birch had fallen across his picnic table and smashed it in two.

Norton gave a tremendous yank on the starter cord.

Whut-whut-whutwhutwhut-WHAT!WHAT!WHAT! . . . WHAT! . . . Whut.

Almost had it there for a minute, fella.

Another Herculean tug.

Whut-whut-whut.

"Cocksucker," Norton whispered fiercely, and bared his teeth at his fancy chainsaw.

I went back around the house, feeling really good for the first time since I got up. My own saw started on the first tug, and I went to work.

Around ten o'clock there was a tap on my shoulder. It was Billy with a can of beer in one hand and Steff's list in the other. I stuffed the list in the back pocket of my jeans and took the beer, which was not exactly frosty-cold but at least cool. I chugged almost half of it at once—rarely does a beer taste that good—and tipped the can in salute at Billy. "Thanks, champ."

"Can I have some?"

I let him have a swallow. He grimaced and handed the can back. I offed the rest and just caught myself as I started to scrunch it up in the middle. The deposit law on bottles and cans has been in effect for over three years, but old ways die hard.

"She wrote something across the bottom of the list, but I can't read her writing," Billy said.

I took out the list again. "I can't get WOXO on the radio," Steff's note read. "Do you think the storm knocked them off the air?"

WOXO is the local automated FM rock outlet. It broadcast from Norway, about twenty miles north, and was all that our old and feeble FM receiver would haul in.

"Tell her probably," I said, after reading the question over to him. "Ask her if she can get Portland on the AM band."

"Okay. Daddy, can I come when you go to town?"

"Sure. You and Mommy both, if you want."

"Okay." He ran back to the house with the empty can.

I had worked my way up to the big tree. I made my first cut, sawed through, then turned the saw off for a few moments to let it cool down —the tree was really too big for it, but I thought it would be all right if I didn't rush it. I wondered if the dirt road leading up to Kansas Road was clear of falls, and just as I was wondering, an orange CMP truck lumbered past, probably on its way to the far end of our little road. So that was all right. The road was clear and the power guys would be here by noon to take care of the live lines.

I cut a big chunk off the tree, dragged it to the side of the driveway, and tumbled it over the edge. It rolled down the slope and into the underbrush that had crept back since that long-ago day when my dad and his brothers—all of them artists, we have always been an artistic family, the Draytons—had cleared it away.

I wiped sweat off my face with my arm and wished for another beer; one really only sets your mouth. I picked up the chainsaw and thought about WOXO being off the air. That was the direction that funny fogbank had come from. And it was the direction Shaymore (pronounced *Shammore* by the locals) lay in. Shaymore was where the Arrowhead Project was.

That was old Bill Giosti's theory about the so-called black spring; the Arrowhead Project. In the western part of Shaymore, not far from where the town borders on Stoneham, there was a small government preserve surrounded with wire. There were sentries and closed-circuit television cameras and God knew what else. Or so I had heard; I'd never actually seen it, although the Old Shaymore Road runs along the eastern side of the government land for a mile or so.

No one knew for sure where the name Arrowhead Project came from, and no one could tell you for one hundred percent sure that that really was the name of the project—if there was a project. Bill Giosti said there was, but when you asked him how and where he came by his information, he got vague. His niece, he said, worked for the Continental Phone Company, and she had heard things. It got like that.

"Atomic things," Bill said that day, leaning in the Scout's window and blowing a healthy draught of Pabst into my face. "That's what they're fooling around with up there. Shooting atoms into the air and all that."

"Mr. Giosti, the air's full of atoms," Billy had said. "That's what Mrs. Neary says. Mrs. Neary says everything's full of atoms."

Bill Giosti gave my son Bill a long, bloodshot glance that finally deflated him. "These are *different* atoms, son."

"Oh, yeah," Billy muttered, giving in.

Dick Muehler, our insurance agent, said the Arrowhead Project was an agricultural station the government was running, no more or less. "Bigger tomatoes with a longer growing season," Dick said sagely, and then went back to showing me how I could help my family most efficiently by dying young. Janine Lawless, our postlady, said it was a geological survey having something to do with shale oil. She knew for a fact, because her husband's brother worked for a man who had—

Mrs. Carmody, now . . . she probably leaned more to Bill Giosti's view of the matter. Not just atoms, but *different* atoms.

I cut two more chunks off the big tree and dropped them over the side before Billy came back with a fresh beer in one hand and a note from Steff in the other. If there's anything Big Bill likes to do more than run messages, I don't know what it could be.

"Thanks," I said, taking them both.

"Can I have a swallow?"

"Just one. You took two last time. Can't have you running around drunk at ten in the morning."

"Quarter past," he said, and smiled shyly over the top of the can. I smiled back—not that it was such a great joke, you know, but Billy makes them so rarely—and then read the note.

"Got JBQ on the radio," Steffy had written. "Don't get drunk before you go to town. You can have one more, but that's it before lunch. Do you think you can get up our road okay?"

I handed him the note back and took my beer. "Tell her the road's okay because a power truck just went by. They'll be working their way up here."

"Okay."

"Champ?"

"What, Dad?"

"Tell her everything's okay."

He smiled again, maybe telling himself first. "Okay."

He ran back and I watched him go, legs pumping, soles of his zori showing. I love him. It's his face and sometimes the way his eyes turn up to mine that make me feel as if things are really okay. It's a lie, of course—things are not okay and never have been—but my kid makes me believe the lie.

I drank some beer, set the can down carefully on a rock, and got the chainsaw going again. About twenty minutes later I felt a light tap on my shoulder and turned, expecting to see Billy again. Instead it was Brent Norton. I turned off the chainsaw.

He didn't look the way Norton usually looks. He looked hot and tired and unhappy and a little bewildered.

"Hi, Brent," I said. Our last words had been hard ones, and I was a little unsure how to proceed. I had a funny feeling that he had been standing behind me for the last five minutes or so, clearing his throat decorously under the chainsaw's aggressive roar. I hadn't gotten a really good look at him this summer. He had lost weight, but it didn't look good. It should have, because he had been carrying around an extra twenty pounds, but it didn't. His wife had died the previous November. Cancer. Aggie Bibber told Steffy that. Aggie was our resident necrologist. Every neighborhood has one. From the casual way Norton had of ragging his wife and belittling her (doing it with the contemptuous ease of a veteran matador inserting *bandilleras* in an old bull's lumbering body), I would have guessed he'd be glad to have her gone. If asked, I might even have speculated that he'd show up this summer with a girl twenty years younger than he was on his arm and a silly my-cock-has-died-and-gone-to-heaven grin on his face. But instead of the silly grin there was only a new batch of age-lines, and the weight had come off in all the wrong places, leaving sags and folds and dewlaps that told their own story. For one passing moment I wanted only to lead Norton to a patch of sun and sit him beside one of the fallen trees with my can of beer in his hand, and do a charcoal sketch of him.

"Hi, Dave," he said, after a long moment of awkward silence—a silence that was made even louder by the absence of the chainsaw's racket and roar. He stopped, then blurted: "That tree. That damn tree. I'm sorry. You were right."

I shrugged.

He said, "Another tree fell on my car."

"I'm sorry to h—" I began, and then a horrid suspicion dawned. "It wasn't the T-Bird, was it?"

"Yeah. It was."

Norton had a 1960 Thunderbird in mint condition, only thirty thousand miles. It was a deep midnight blue inside and out. He drove it only summers, and then only rarely. He loved that Bird the way some men love electric trains or model ships or target-shooting pistols.

"That's a bitch," I said, and meant it.

He shook his head slowly. "I almost didn't bring it up. Almost brought the station wagon, you know. Then I said what the hell. I drove it up and a big old rotten pine fell on it. The roof of it's all bashed in. And I thought I'd cut it up . . . the tree, I mean . . . but I can't get my chainsaw to fire up. . . . I paid two hundred dollars for that sucker . . . and . . . and . . ."

His throat began to emit little clicking sounds. His mouth worked as if he were toothless and chewing dates. For one helpless second I thought he was going to just stand there and bawl like a kid on a sandlot. Then he got himself under some halfway kind of control, shrugged, and turned away as if to look at the chunks of wood I had cut up.

"Well, we can look at your saw," I said. "Your T-Bird insured?"

"Yeah," he said, "like your boathouse."

I saw what he meant, and remembered again what Steff had said about insurance.

"Listen, Dave, I wondered if I could borrow your Saab and take a run up to town. I thought I'd get some bread and coldcuts and beer. A lot of beer."

"Billy and I are going up in the Scout," I said. "Come with us if you want. That is, if you'll give me a hand dragging the rest of this tree off to one side."

"Happy to."

He grabbed one end but couldn't quite lift it up. I had to do most of the work. Between the two of us we were able to tumble it into the underbrush. Norton was puffing and panting, his cheeks nearly purple. After all the yanking he had done on that chainsaw starter pull, I was a little worried about his ticker.

"Okay?" I asked, and he nodded, still breathing fast. "Come on back to the house, then. I can fix you up with a beer."

"Thank you," he said. "How is Stephanie?" He was regaining some of the old smooth pomposity that I disliked.

"Very well, thanks."

"And your son?"

"He's fine, too."

"Glad to hear it."

Steff came out, and a moment's surprise passed over her face when she saw who was with me. Norton smiled and his eyes crawled over her tight T-shirt. He hadn't changed that much after all.

"Hello, Brent," she said cautiously. Billy poked his head out from under her arm.

"Hello, Stephanie. Hi, Billy."

"Brent's T-Bird took a pretty good rap in the storm," I told her. "Stove in the roof, he says."

"Oh, no!"

Norton told it again while he drank one of our beers. I was sipping a third, but I had no kind of buzz on; apparently I had sweat the beer out as rapidly as I drank it.

"He's going to come to town with Billy and me."

"Well, I won't expect you for a while. You may have to go to the Shop-and-Save in Norway."

"Oh? Why?"

"Well, if the power's off in Bridgton—"

"Mom says all the cash registers and things run on electricity," Billy supplied.

It was a good point.

"Have you still got the list?"

I patted my hip pocket.

Her eyes shifted to Norton. "I'm very sorry about Carla, Brent. We all were."

"Thank you," he said. "Thank you very much."

There was another moment of awkward silence which Billy broke. "Can we go now, Daddy?" He had changed to jeans and sneakers.

"Yeah, I guess so. You ready, Brent?"

"Give me another beer for the road and I will be."

Steffy's brow creased. She has never approved of the one-for-the-road philosophy, or of men who drive with a can of Bud leaning against their crotches. I gave her a bare nod and she shrugged. I didn't want to reopen things with Norton now. She got him a beer.

"Thanks," he said to Steffy, not really thanking her but only mouthing a word. It was the way you thank a waitress in a restaurant. He turned back to me. "Lead on, Macduff."

"Be right with you," I said, and went into the living room.

Norton followed, and exclaimed over the birch, but I wasn't interested in that or in the cost of replacing the window just then. I was looking at the lake through the sliding-glass panel that gave on our deck. The breeze had freshened a little and the day had warmed up five degrees or so while I was cutting wood. I thought the odd mist we'd noticed earlier would surely have broken up, but it hadn't. It was closer, too. Halfway across the lake, now.

"I noticed that earlier," Norton said, pontificating. "Some kind of temperature inversion, that's my guess."

I didn't like it. I felt very strongly that I had never seen a mist exactly like this one. Part of it was the unnerving straight edge of its leading front. Nothing in nature is that even; man is the inventor of straight edges. Part of it was that pure, dazzling whiteness, with no variation but also without the sparkle of moisture. It was only half a mile or so off now, and the contrast between it and the blues of the lake and sky were more striking than ever.

"Come on, Dad!" Billy was tugging at my pants.

We all went back to the kitchen. Brent Norton spared one final glance at the tree that had crashed into our living room.

"Too bad it wasn't an apple tree, huh?" Billy remarked brightly. "That's what my mom said. Pretty funny, don't you think?"

"Your mother's a real card, Billy," Norton said. He ruffled Billy's hair in a perfunctory way and his eyes went to the front of Steff's T-shirt again. No, he was not a man I was ever going to be able to really like.

"Listen, why don't you come with us, Steff?" I asked. For no concrete reason I suddenly wanted her to come along.

"No, I think I'll stay here and pull some weeds in the garden," she said. Her eyes shifted slightly toward Norton and then back to me. "This morning it seems like I'm the only thing around here that doesn't run on electricity."

Norton laughed too heartily.

I was getting her message, but tried one more time. "You sure?"

"Sure," she said firmly. "The old bend-and-stretch will do me good."

"Well, don't get too much sun."

"I'll put on my straw hat. We'll have sandwiches when you get back."

"Good."

She turned her face up to be kissed. "Be careful. There might be blowdowns on Kansas Road too, you know."

"I'll be careful."

"You be careful, too," she told Billy, and kissed his cheek.

"Right, Mom." He banged out of the door and the screen cracked shut behind him.

Norton and I walked out after him. "Why don't we go over to your place and cut the tree off your Bird?" I asked him. All of a sudden I could think of lots of reasons to delay leaving for town.

"I don't even want to look at it until after lunch and a few more of these," Norton said, holding up his beer can. "The damage has been done, Dave old buddy."

I didn't like him calling me buddy, either.

We all got into the front seat of the Scout (in the far corner of the garage my scarred Fisher plow blade sat glimmering yellow, like the ghost of Christmas yet-to-come) and I backed out, crunching over a litter of storm-blown twigs. Steff was standing on the cement path which leads to the vegetable patch at the extreme west end of our property. She had a pair of clippers in one gloved hand and the weeding claw in the other. She had put on her old floppy sunhat, and it cast a band of shadow over her face. I tapped the horn twice, lightly, and she raised the hand holding the clippers in answer. We pulled out. I haven't seen my wife since then.

We had to stop once on our way up to Kansas Road. Since the power truck had driven through, a pretty fair-sized pine had dropped across the road. Norton and I got out and moved it enough so I could inch the Scout by, getting our hands all pitchy in the process. Billy wanted to help but I waved him back. I was afraid he might get poked in the eye. Old trees have always reminded me of the Ents in Tolkien's wonderful Rings saga, only Ents that have gone bad. Old trees want to hurt you. It doesn't matter if you're snowshoeing, cross-country skiing, or just taking a walk in the woods. Old trees want to hurt you, and I think they'd kill you if they could.

Kansas Road itself was clear, but in several places we saw more lines down. About a quarter-mile past the Vicki-Linn Campground there was a power pole lying full-length in the ditch, heavy wires snarled around its top like wild hair.

"That was some storm," Norton said in his mellifluous, courtroom-trained voice; but he didn't seem to be pontificating now, only solemn.

"Yeah, it was."

"Look, Dad!"

He was pointing at the remains of the Ellitches' barn. For twelve years it had been sagging tiredly in Tommy Ellitch's back field, up to its hips in sunflowers, goldenrod, and Lolly-come-see-me. Every fall I would think it could not last through another winter. And every spring it would still be there. But it wasn't anymore. All that remained was splintered wreckage and a roof that had been mostly stripped of shingles. Its number had come up. And for some reason that echoed solemnly, even ominously, inside me. The storm had come and smashed it flat.

Norton drained his beer, crushed the can in one hand, and dropped it indifferently to the floor of the Scout. Billy opened his mouth to say something and then closed it again—good boy. Norton came from New Jersey, where there was no bottle-and-can law; I guess he could be forgiven for squashing my nickel when I could barely remember not to do it myself.

Billy started fooling with the radio, and I asked him to see if WOXO was back on the air. He dialed up to FM 92 and got nothing but a blank hum. He looked at me and shrugged. I thought for a moment. What other stations were on the far side of that peculiar fog front?

"Try WBLM," I said.

He dialed down to the other end, passing WJBQ-FM and WIGY-FM on the way. They were there, doing business as usual . . . but WBLM, Maine's premier progressive-rock station, was off the air.

"Funny," I said.

"What's that?" Norton asked.

"Nothing. Just thinking out loud."

Billy had tuned back to the musical cereal on WJBQ. Pretty soon we got to town.

The Norge Washateria in the shopping center was closed, it being impossible to run a coin-op laundry without electricity, but both the Bridgton Pharmacy and the Federal Foods Supermarket were open. The parking lot was pretty full, and, as always in the middle of the summer, a lot of the cars had out-of-state plates. Little knots of people stood here and there in the sun, noodling about the storm, women with women, men with men.

I saw Mrs. Carmody, she of the stuffed animals and the stump-water lore. She sailed into the supermarket decked out in an amazing canary-yellow pantsuit. A purse that looked the size of a small Samsonite suitcase was slung over one forearm. Then an idiot on a Yamaha roared past me, missing my front bumper by a few scant inches. He wore a denim jacket, mirror sunglasses, and no helmet.

"Look at that stupid shit," Norton growled.

I circled the parking lot once, looking for a good space. There were none. I was just resigning myself to a long walk from the far end of the lot when I got lucky. A lime-green Cadillac the size of a small cabin cruiser was easing out of a slot in the rank closest to the market's doors. The moment it was gone, I slid into the space.

I gave Billy Steff's shopping list. "Get a cart and get started. I want to give your mother a jingle. Mr. Norton will help you. And I'll be right along."

We got out and Billy immediately grabbed Mr. Norton's hand. He'd been taught not to cross the parking lot without holding an adult's hand when he was younger and hadn't yet lost the habit. Norton looked surprised for a moment, and then smiled a little. I could almost forgive him for feeling Steff up with his eyes. The two of them went into the market.

I strolled over to the pay phone, which was on the wall between the drugstore and the Norge. A sweltering woman in a purple sunsuit was jogging the cut-off switch up and down. I stood behind her with my hands in my pockets, wondering why I felt so uneasy about Steff, and why the unease should be all wrapped up with that line of white but unsparkling fog, the radio stations that were off the air . . . and the Arrowhead Project.

The woman in the purple sunsuit had a sunburn and freckles on her fat shoulders. She looked like a sweaty overage baby. She slammed the phone back down in its cradle, turned toward the drugstore, and saw me there.

"Save your dime," she said. "Just dah-dah-dah." She walked grumpily away.

I almost slapped my forehead. The phone lines were down someplace, of course. Some of them were underground, but nowhere near all of them. I tried the phone anyway. The pay phones in the area are what Steff calls Paranoid Pay Phones. Instead of putting your dime right in, you get a dial tone and make your call. When someone answers, there's an automatic cutoff and you have to shove your dime in before your party hangs up. They're irritating, but that day it did save me my dime. There was no dial tone. As the lady had said, it was just dah-dah-dah.

I hung up and walked slowly toward the market, just in time to see an amusing little incident. An elderly couple walked toward the IN door, chatting together. And still chatting, they walked right into it. They stopped talking in a jangle and the woman squawked her surprise. They stared at each other comically. Then they laughed, and the old guy pushed the door open for his wife with some effort—those electric-eye doors are heavy—and they went in. When the electricity goes off, it catches you in a hundred different ways.

I pushed the door open myself and noticed the lack of air conditioning first thing. Usually in the summer they have it cranked up high enough to give you frostbite if you stay in the market more than an hour at a stretch.

Like most modern markets, the Federal was constructed like a Skinner box—modern marketing techniques turn all customers into white rats. The stuff you really needed, staples like bread, milk, meat, beer, and frozen dinners, was all on the far side of the store. To get there you had to walk past all the impulse items known to modern man—everything from Cricket lighters to rubber dog bones.

Beyond the IN door is the fruit and vegetable aisle. I looked up it, but there was no sign of Norton or my son. The old lady who had run into the door was examining the grapefruits. Her husband had produced a net sack to store purchases in.

I walked up the aisle and went left. I found them in the third aisle, Billy mulling over the ranks of Jell-O packages and instant puddings. Norton was standing directly behind him, peering at Steff's list. I had to grin a little at his nonplussed expression.

I threaded my way down to them, past half-loaded carriages (Steff hadn't been the only one struck by the squirreling impulse, apparently) and browsing shoppers. Norton took two cans of pie filling down from the top shelf and put them in the cart.

"How you doing?" I asked, and Norton looked around with unmistakable relief.

"All right, aren't we, Billy?"

"Sure," Billy said, and couldn't resist adding in a rather smug tone: "But there's lots of stuff Mr. Norton can't read either, Dad."

"Let me see." I took the list.

Norton had made a neat, lawyerly check beside each of the items he and Billy had picked up—half a dozen or so, including the milk and a six-pack of Coke. There were maybe ten other things that she wanted.

"We ought to go back to the fruits and vegetables," I said. "She wants some tomatoes and cucumbers."

Billy started to turn the cart around and Norton said, "You ought to go have a look at the checkout, Dave."

I went and had a look. It was the sort of thing you sometimes see photos of in the paper on a slow newsday, with a humorous caption beneath. Only two lanes were open, and the double line of people waiting to check their purchases out stretched past the mostly denuded bread racks, then made a jig to the right and went out of sight along the frozen-food coolers. All of the new computerized NCR registers were hooded. At each of the two open positions, a harried-looking girl was totting up purchases on a battery-powered pocket calculator. Standing with each girl was one of the Federal's two managers, Bud Brown and Ollie Weeks. I liked Ollie but didn't care much for Bud Brown, who seemed to fancy himself the Charles de Gaulle of the supermarket world.

As each girl finished checking her order, Bud or Ollie would paperclip a chit to the customer's cash or check and toss it into the box he was using as a cash repository. They all looked hot and tired.

"Hope you brought a good book," Norton said, joining me. "We're going to be in line for a while."

I thought of Steff again, at home alone, and had another flash of unease. "You go on and get your stuff," I said. "Billy and I can handle the rest of this."

"Want me to grab a few more beers for you too?"

I thought about it, but in spite of the rapprochement, I didn't want to spend the afternoon with Brent Norton getting drunk. Not with the mess things were in around the house.

"Sorry," I said. "I've got to take a raincheck, Brent."

I thought his face stiffened a little. "Okay," he said shortly, and walked off. I watched him go, and then Billy was tugging at my shirt.

"Did you talk to Mommy?"

"Nope. The phone wasn't working. Those lines are down too, I guess."

"Are you worried about her?"

"No," I said, lying. I was worried, all right, but had no idea why I should be. "No, of course I'm not. Are you?"

"No-ooo . . ." But he was. His face had a pinched look. We should have gone back then. But even then it might have been too late.

III. The Coming of the Mist.

We worked our way back to the fruits and vegetables like salmon fighting their way upstream. I saw some familiar faces—Mike Hatlen, one of our selectmen, Mrs. Reppler from the grammar school (she, who had terrified generations of third graders, was currently sneering at the cantaloupes), Mrs. Turman, who sometimes sat Billy when Steff and I went out—but mostly they were summer people stocking up on no-cook items and joshing each other about "roughing it." The cold cuts had been picked over as thoroughly as the dime-book tray at a rummage sale; there was nothing left but a few packages of bologna, some macaroni loaf, and one lonely, phallic kielbasa sausage.

I got tomatoes, cukes, and a jar of mayonnaise. She wanted bacon, but all the bacon was gone. I picked up some of the bologna as a substitute, although I've never been able to eat the stuff with any real enthusiasm since the FDA reported that each package contained a small amount of insect filth—a little something extra for your money.

"Look," Billy said as we rounded the corner into the fourth aisle. "There's some army guys."

There were two of them, their dun uniforms standing out against the much brighter background of summer clothes and sportswear. We had gotten used to seeing a scattering of army personnel with the Arrowhead Project only thirty miles or so away. These two looked hardly old enough to shave yet.

I glanced back down at Steff's list and saw that we had everything . . . no, almost but not quite. At the bottom, as an afterthought, she had scribbled: *Bottle of Lancer's?* That sounded good to me. A couple of glasses of wine tonight after Billy had sacked out, then maybe a long slow bout of lovemaking before sleep.

I left the cart and worked my way down to the wine and got a bottle. As I walked back I passed the big double doors leading to the storage area and heard the steady roar of a good-sized generator. I decided it was probably just big enough to keep the cold cases cold, but not large enough to power the doors and cash registers and all the other electrical equipment. It sounded like a motorcycle back there.

Norton appeared just as we got into line, balancing two six-packs of Schlitz Light, a loaf of bread, and the kielbasa I had spotted a few minutes earlier. He got in line with Billy and me. It seemed very warm in the market with the air conditioning off, and I wondered why none of the stockboys hadn't at least chocked the doors open. I had seen Buddy Eagleton in his red apron two aisles back, doing nothing and piling it up. The generator roared monotonously. I had the beginnings of a headache.

"Put your stuff in here before you drop something," I said.

"Thanks."

The lines were up past the frozen food now; people had to cut through to get what they wanted and there was much excuse me-ing and pardon me-ing. "This is going to be a cunt," Norton said morosely, and I frowned a little. That sort of language is rougher than I'd like Billy to hear.

The generator's roar muted a little as the line shuffled forward. Norton and I made desultory conversation, skirting around the ugly property dispute that had landed us in district court and sticking with things like the Red Sox's chances and the weather. At last we exhausted our little store of small talk and fell silent. Billy fidgeted beside me. The line crawled along. Now we had frozen dinners on our right and the more expensive wines and champagnes on our left. As the line progressed down to the cheaper wines, I toyed briefly with the idea of picking up a bottle of Ripple, the wine of my flaming youth. I didn't do it. My youth never flamed that much anyway.

"Jeez, why can't they hurry up, Dad?" Billy asked. That pinched look was still on his face, and suddenly, briefly, the mist of disquiet that had settled over me rifted, and something terrible peered through from the other side—the bright and metallic face of pure terror. Then it passed.

"Keep cool, champ," I said.

We had made it up to the bread racks—to the point where the double line bent to the left. We could see the check-out lanes now, the two that were open and the other four, deserted, each with a little sign on the stationary conveyor belt, signs that read PLEASE CHOOSE ANOTHER LANE and WINSTON. Beyond the lanes was the big sectioned plate-glass window which gave a view of the parking lot and the intersection of Routes 117 and 302 beyond. The view was partially obscured by the white-paper backs of signs advertising current specials and the latest giveaway, which happened to be a set of books called *The Mother Nature Encyclopedia.* We were in the line that would eventually lead us to the checkout where Bud Brown was standing. There were still maybe thirty people in front of us. The easiest one to pick out was Mrs. Carmody in her blazing-yellow pantsuit. She looked like an advertisement for yellow fever.

Suddenly a shrieking noise began in the distance. It quickly built up in volume and resolved itself into the crazy warble of a police siren. A horn blared at the intersection and there was a shriek of brakes and burning rubber. I couldn't see—the angle was all wrong—but the siren reached its loudest as it approached the market and then began to fade as the police car went past. A few people broke out of line to look, but not many. They had waited too long to chance losing their places for good.

Norton went; his stuff was tucked into my cart. After a few moments he came back and got into line again. "Local fuzz," he said.

Then the town fire whistle began to wail, slowly cranking up to a shriek of its own, falling off, then rising again. Billy grabbed my hand —clutched it. "What is it, Daddy?" he asked, and then, immediately: "Is Mommy all right?"

"Must be a fire on the Kansas Road," Norton said. "Those damn live lines from the storm. The fire trucks will go through in a minute."

That gave my disquiet something to crystallize on. There were live lines down in *our* yard.

Bud Brown said something to the checker he was supervising; she had been craning around to see what was happening. She flushed and began to run her calculator again.

I didn't want to be in this line. All of a sudden I very badly didn't want to be in it. But it was moving again, and it seemed foolish to leave now. We had gotten down by the cartons of cigarettes.

Someone pushed through the IN door, some teenager. I think it was the kid we almost hit coming in, the one on the Yamaha with no helmet. "The fog!" he yelled. "Y'oughta see the fog! It's rolling right up Kansas Road!" People looked around at him. He was panting, as if he had run a long distance. Nobody said anything. "Well, y'oughta see it," he repeated, sounding defensive this time. People eyed him and some of them shuffled, but no one wanted to lose his or her place in line. A few people who hadn't reached the lines yet left their carts and strolled through the empty check-out lanes to see if they could see what he was talking about. A big guy in a summer hat with a paisley band—the kind of hat you almost never see except in beer commercials with backyard barbecues as their settings—yanked open the OUT door and several people—ten, maybe a dozen—went out with him. The kid went along.

"Don't let out all the air conditioning," one of the army kids cracked, and there were a few chuckles. I wasn't chuckling. I had seen the mist coming across the lake.

"Billy, why don't you go have a look?" Norton said.

"No," I said at once, for no concrete reason.

The line moved forward again. People craned their necks, looking for the fog the kid had mentioned, but there was nothing on view except bright-blue sky. I heard someone say that the kid must have been joking. Someone else responded that he had seen a funny line of mist on Long Lake not an hour ago. The fire whistle whooped and screamed. I didn't like it. It sounded like big-league doom blowing that way.

More people went out. A few even left their places in line, which speeded up the proceedings a bit. Then grizzled old John Lee Frovin, who works as a mechanic at the Texaco station, came ducking in and yelled: "Hey! Anybody got a camera?" He looked around then ducked back out again.

That caused something of a rush. If it was worth taking a picture of, it was worth seeing.

Suddenly Mrs. Carmody cried in her rusty but powerful old voice, "Don't go out there!"

People turned around to look at her. The orderly shape of the lines had grown fuzzy as people left to get a look at the mist, or as they drew away from Mrs. Carmody, or as they milled around, seeking out their friends. A pretty young woman in a cranberry-colored sweatshirt and dark-green slacks was looking at Mrs. Carmody in a thoughtful, evaluating way. A few opportunists were taking advantage of whatever the situation was to move up a couple of places. The checker beside Bud Brown looked over her shoulder again, and Brown tapped her shoulder with a long brown finger. "Keep your mind on what you're doing, Sally."

"Don't go out there!" Mrs. Carmody yelled. "It's death! I feel that it's death out there!"

Bud and Ollie Weeks, who both knew her, just looked impatient and irritated, but any summer people around her stepped smartly away, never minding their places in line. The bag-ladies in big cities seem to have the same effect on people, as if they were carriers of some contagious disease. Who knows? Maybe they are.

Things began to happen at an accelerating, confusing pace then. A man staggered into the market, shoving the IN door open. His nose was bleeding. "Something in the fog!" he screamed, and Billy shrank against me—whether because of the man's bloody nose or what he was saying, I don't know. "Something in the fog! Something in the fog took John Lee! Something—" He staggered back against a display of lawn food stacked by the window and sat down there. *"Something in the fog took John Lee and I heard him screaming!"*

The situation changed. Made nervous by the storm, by the police siren and the fire whistle, by the subtle dislocation any power outage causes in the American psyche, and by the steadily mounting atmosphere of unease as things somehow . . . somehow *changed* (I don't know how to put it any better than that), people began to move in a body.

They didn't bolt. If I told you that, I would be giving you entirely the wrong impression. It wasn't exactly a panic. They didn't run—or at least, most of them didn't. But they went. Some of them just went to the big show-window on the far side of the check-out lanes to look out. Others went out the IN door, some still carrying their intended purchases. Bud Brown, harried and officious, began yelling: "Hey! You haven't paid for that! Hey, you! Come back with those hotdog rolls!"

Someone laughed at him, a crazy, yodeling sound that made other people smile. Even as they smiled they looked bewildered, confused, and nervous. Then someone else laughed and Brown flushed. He grabbed a box of mushrooms away from a lady who was crowding past him to look out the window—the segments of glass were lined with people now, they were like the folks you see looking through loopholes into a building site—and the lady screamed, "Give me back my mushies!" This bizarre term of affection caused two men standing nearby to break into crazy laughter—and there was something of the old English Bedlam about all of it, now. Mrs. Carmody trumpeted again not to go out there. The fire whistle whooped breathlessly, a strong old woman who had scared up a prowler in the house. And Billy burst into tears.

"Daddy, what's that bloody man? Why is that bloody man?"

"It's okay, Big Bill, it's his nose, just his nose, he's okay."

"What did he mean, something in the fog?" Norton asked. He was frowning ponderously, which was probably Norton's way of looking confused.

"Daddy, I'm scared," Billy said through his tears. "Can we please go home?"

Someone bumped past me roughly, jolting me on my feet, and I picked Billy up. I was getting scared, too. The confusion was mounting. Sally, the checker by Bud Brown, started away and he grabbed her back by the collar of her red smock. It ripped. She slap-clawed out at him, her face twisting. *"Get your fucking hands off me!"* she screamed.

"Oh, shut up, you little bitch," Brown said, but he sounded totally astounded.

He reached for her again and Ollie Weeks said sharply: "Bud! Cool it!"

Someone else screamed. It hadn't been a panic before—not quite—but it was getting to be one. People streamed out of both doors. There was a crash of breaking glass and Coke fizzed suddenly across the floor.

"What the Christ *is* this?" Norton exclaimed.

That was when it started getting dark . . . but no, that's not exactly right. My thought at the time was not that it was getting dark but that all the lights in the market had gone out. I looked up at the fluorescents in a quick reflex action, and I wasn't alone. And at first, until I remembered the power failure, it seemed that was it, that was what had changed the quality of the light. Then I remembered they had been out all the time we had been in the market and things hadn't seemed dark before. Then I knew, even before the people at the window started to yell and point.

The mist was coming.

It came from the Kansas Road entrance to the parking lot, and even this close it looked no different than it had when we first noticed it on the far side of the lake. It was white and bright but non-reflecting. It was moving fast and it had blotted out most of the sun. Where the sun had been there was now a silver coin in the sky, like a full moon in winter seen through a thin scud of cloud.

It came with lazy speed. Watching it reminded me somehow of last evening's waterspout. There are big forces in nature that you hardly ever see—earthquakes, hurricanes, tornadoes—and I haven't seen them all but I've seen enough to guess that they all move with that lazy, hypnotizing speed. They hold you spellbound, the way Billy and Steffy had been in front of the picture window last night.

It rolled impartially across the two-lane blacktop and erased it from view. The McKeons' nice restored Dutch Colonial was swallowed whole. For a moment the second floor of the ramshackle apartment building next door jutted out of the whiteness, and then it went, too. The KEEP RIGHT sign at the entrance and exit points to the Federal's parking lot disappeared, the black letters on the sign seeming to float for a moment in limbo after the sign's dirty-white background was gone. The cars in the parking lot began to disappear next.

"What the Christ *is* this?" Norton asked again, and there was a breathy, frightened catch in his voice.

It came on, eating up the blue sky and the fresh black hottop with equal ease. Even twenty feet away the line of demarcation was perfectly clear. I had the nutty feeling that I was watching some extra-good piece of visual effects, something dreamed up by Willys O'Brian or Douglas Trumbull. It happened so quickly. The blue sky disappeared to a wide swipe, then to a stripe, then to a pencil line. Then it was gone. Blank white pressed against the glass of the wide show window. I could see as far as the litter barrel that stood maybe four feet away, but not much farther. I could see the front bumper of my Scout, but that was all.

A woman screamed, very loud and long. Billy pressed himself more tightly against me. His body was trembling like a loose bundle of wires with high voltage running through them.

A man yelled and bolted through one of the deserted lanes toward the door. I think that was what finally started the stampede. People rushed pell-mell into the fog.

"Hey!" Brown roared. I don't know if he was angry, scared, or both. His face was nearly purple. Veins stood out on his neck, looking almost as thick as battery cables. *"Hey you people, you can't take that stuff! Get back here with that stuff, you're shoplifting!"*

They kept going, but some of them tossed their stuff aside. Some were laughing and excited, but they were a minority. They poured out into the fog, and none of us who stayed ever saw them again. There was a faint, acrid smell drifting in through the open door. People began to jam up there. Some pushing and shoving started. I was getting an ache in my shoulders from holding Billy. He was good-sized; Steff sometimes called him her young heifer.

Norton started to wander off, his face preoccupied and rather bemused. He was heading for the door.

I switched Billy to the other arm so I could grab Norton's arm before he drifted out of reach. "No, man, I wouldn't," I said.

He turned back. "What?"

"Better wait and see."

"See what?"

"I don't know," I said.

"You don't think—" He began, and a shriek came out of the fog.

Norton shut up. The tight jam at the OUT door loosened and then reversed itself. The babble of excited conversation, shouts and calls, subsided. The faces of the people by the door suddenly looked flat and pale and two dimensional.

The shriek went on and on, competing with the fire whistle. It seemed impossible that any human pair of lungs could have enough air in them to sustain such a shriek. Norton muttered, "Oh my God," and ran his hands through his hair.

The shriek ended abruptly. It did not dwindle; it was cut off. One more man went outside, a beefy guy in chino workpants. I think he was set on rescuing the shrieker. For a moment he was out there, visible through the glass and the mist, like a figure seen through a milk-scum on a tumbler. Then (and as far as I know, I was the only one to see this) something beyond him appeared to move, a gray shadow in all that white. And it seemed to me that instead of running into the fog, the bald man in the chino pants was *jerked* into it, his hands flailing upward as if in surprise.

For a moment there was total silence in the market.

A constellation of moons suddenly glowed into being outside. The parking-lot sodium lights, undoubtedly supplied by underground electrical cables, had just gone on.

"Don't go out there," Mrs. Carmody said in her best gore-crow voice. "It's death to go out there."

All at once no one seemed disposed to argue or laugh.

Another scream came from outside, this one muffled and rather distant-sounding. Billy tensed against me again.

"David, what's going on?" Ollie Weeks asked. He had left his position. There were big beads of sweat on his round, smooth face. "What is this?"

"I'll be goddamned if I have any idea," I said. Ollie looked badly scared. He was a bachelor who lived in a nice little house up by Highland Lake and who liked to drink in the bar at Pleasant Mountain. On the pudgy little finger of his left hand was a star-sapphire ring. The February before he won some money in the state lottery. He bought the ring out of his winnings. I always had the idea that Ollie was a little afraid of girls.

"I don't dig this," he said.

"No. Billy, I have to put you down. I'll hold your hand, but you're breaking my arms, okay?"

"Mommy," he whispered.

"She's okay," I told him. It was something to say.

The old geezer who runs the second-hand shop near Jon's Restaurant walked past us, bundled into the old collegiate letter-sweater he wears year-round. He said loudly: "It's one of those pollution clouds. The mills at Rumford and South Paris. Chemicals." With that, he made off up the Aisle 4, past the patent medicines and toilet paper.

"Let's get out of here, David," Norton said with no conviction at all. "What do you say we—"

There was a thud. An odd, twisting thud that I felt mostly in my feet, as if the entire building had suddenly dropped three feet. Several people cried out in fear and surprise. There was a musical jingle of bottles leaning off their shelves and destroying themselves upon the tile floor. A chunk of glass shaped like a pie wedge fell out of one of the segments of the wide front window, and I saw that the wooden frames banding the heavy sections of glass had buckled and splintered in some places.

The fire whistle stopped in mid-whoop.

The quiet that followed was the baited silence of people waiting for something else, something more. I was shocked and numb, and my mind made a strange cross-patch connection with the past. Back when Bridgton was little more than a crossroads, my dad would take me in with him and stand talking at the counter while I looked through the glass at the penny candy and two-cent chews. It was January thaw. No sound but the drip of meltwater falling from the galvanized tin gutters to the rain barrels on either side of the store. Me looking at the jaw-breakers and buttons and pinwheels. The mystic yellow globes of light overhead showing up the monstrous, projected shadows of last summer's battalion of dead flies. A little boy named David Drayton with his father, the famous artist Andrew Drayton, whose painting *Christine Standing Alone* hung in the White House. A little boy named David Drayton looking at the candy and the Davy Crockett bub-ble-gum cards and vaguely needing to go pee. And outside the pressing, billowing yellow fog of January thaw.

The memory passed, but very slowly.

"You people!" Norton bellowed. "All you people, listen to me!"

They looked around. Norton was holding up both hands, the fingers splayed like a political candidate accepting accolades.

"It may be dangerous to go outside!" Norton yelled.

"Why?" a woman screamed back. "My kids're at home! I got to get back to my kids!"

"It's death to go out there!" Mrs. Carmody came back smartly. She was standing by the twenty-five pound sacks of fertilizer stacked below the window, and her face seemed to *bulge* somehow, as if she were swelling.

A teenager gave her a sudden hard push and she sat down on the bags with a surprised grunt. "Stop saying that, you old bag! Stop rap-pin that crazy bullshit!"

"Please!" Norton yelled. "If we just wait a few moments until it blows over and we can see—"

A babble of conflicting shouts greeted this.

"He's right," I said, shouting to be heard over the noise. "Let's just try to keep cool."

"I think that was an earthquake," a bespectacled man said. His voice was soft, with awe, fear, or both. In one hand he held a package of hamburger and a bag of buns. The other hand was holding the hand of a little girl, maybe a year younger than Billy. "I really think that was an earthquake."

"They had one over in Naples four years ago," a fat local man said.

"That was in Casco," his wife contradicted immediately. She spoke in the unmistakable tones of a veteran contradictor.

"Naples," the fat local man said, but with less assurance.

"Casco," his wife said firmly, and he gave up.

Somewhere a can that had been jostled to the very edge of its shelf by the thump, earthquake, whatever it had been, fell off with a delayed clatter. Billy burst into tears. "I want to go *home! I want my MOTHER!*"

"Can't you shut that kid up?" Bud Brown asked. His eyes were darting rapidly but aimlessly from place to place.

"Would you like a shot in the teeth, motormouth?" I asked him.

"Come on, Dave, that's not helping," Norton said distractedly.

"I'm sorry," the woman who had screamed earlier said. "I'm sorry, but I can't stay here. I've got to get home and see to my kids."

She looked around at us, a blond woman with a tired, pretty face.

"Wanda's looking after little Victor, you see. Wanda's only eight and sometimes she forgets . . . forgets she's supposed to be . . . well, watching him, you know. And little Victor . . . he likes to turn on the stove burners to see the little red light come on . . . he likes that light . . . and sometimes he pulls out the plugs . . . little Victor does . . . and Wanda gets . . . bored watching him after a while . . . she's just eight . . ." She stopped talking and just looked at us. I imagine that we must have looked like nothing but a bank of merciless eyes to her right then, not human beings at all, just eyes. *"Isn't anyone going to help me?"* she screamed. Her lips began to tremble. "Won't . . . won't anybody here see a lady home?"

No one replied. People shuffled their feet. She looked from face to face with her own broken face. The fat local man took a hesitant half-step forward and his wife jerked him back with one quick tug, her hand clapped over his wrist like a manacle.

"You?" the blond woman asked Ollie. He shook his head. "You?" she said to Bud. He put his hand over the Texas Instruments calculator on the counter and made no reply. "You?" she said to Norton, and Norton began to say something in his big lawyer's voice, something about how no one should go off half-cocked, and . . . and she dismissed him and Norton just trailed off.

"You?" she said to me, and I picked Billy up again and held him in my arms like a shield to ward off her terrible broken face.

"I hope you all rot in hell," she said. She didn't scream it. Her voice was dead tired. She went to the OUT door and pulled it open, using both hands. I wanted to say something to her, call her back, but my mouth was too dry.

"Aw, lady, listen—" the teenage kid who had shouted at Mrs. Carmody began. He held her arm. She looked down at his hand and he let her go, shamefaced. She slipped out into the fog. We watched her go and no one said anything. We watched the fog overlay her and make her insubstantial, not a human being anymore but a pen-and-ink sketch of a human being done on the world's whitest paper, and no one said anything. For a moment it was like the letters of the KEEP RIGHT sign that had seemed to float on nothingness; her arms and legs and pallid blond hair were all gone and only the misty remnants of her red summer dress remained, seeming to dance in white limbo. Then her dress was gone, too, and no one said anything.

IV. The Storage Area. Problems with the Generator. What Happened to the Bag-Boy.

Billy began to act hysterical and tantrumy, screaming for his mother in a hoarse, demanding way through his tears, instantly regressing to the age of two. Snot was lathered on his upper lip. I led him away, walking down one of the middle aisles with my arm around his shoulders, trying to soothe him. I took him back by the long, white meat cabinet that ran the length of the store at the back. Mr. McVey, the butcher, was still there. We nodded at each other, the best we could do under the circumstances.

I sat down on the floor and took Billy on my lap and held his face against my chest and rocked him and talked to him. I told him all the lies parents keep in reserve for bad situations, the ones that sound so damn plausible to a child, and I told them in a tone of perfect conviction.

"That's not regular fog," Billy said. He looked up at me, his eyes dark-circled and tear-streaked. "It isn't, is it, Daddy?"

"No, I don't think so." I didn't want to lie about that.

Kids don't fight shock the way adults do; they go with it, maybe because kids are in a semipermanent state of shock until they're thirteen or so. Billy started to doze off. I held him, thinking he might snap awake again, but his doze deepened into a real sleep. Maybe he had been awake part of the night before, when we had slept three-in-a-bed for the first time since Billy was an infant. And maybe—I felt a cold eddy slip through me at the thought—maybe he had sensed something coming.

When I was sure he was solidly out, I laid him on the floor and went looking for something to cover him up with. Most of the people were still up front, looking out into the thick blanket of mist. Norton had gathered a little crowd of listeners and was busy spell-binding—or trying to. Bud Brown stood rigidly at his post, but Ollie Weeks had left his.

There were a few people in the aisles, wandering like ghosts, their faces greasy with shock. I went into the storage area through the big double doors between the meat cabinet and the beer cooler.

The generator roared steadily behind its plywood partition, but something had gone wrong. I could smell diesel fumes, and they were much too strong. I walked toward the partition, taking shallow breaths. At last I unbuttoned my shirt and put part of it over my mouth and nose.

The storage area was long and narrow, feebly lit by two sets of emergency lights. Cartons were stacked everywhere—bleach on one side, cases of soft drinks on the far side of the partition, stacked cases of Beefaroni and catsup. One of those had fallen over and the cardboard carton appeared to be bleeding.

I unlatched the door in the generator partition and stepped through. The machine was obscured in drifting, oily clouds of blue smoke. The exhaust pipe ran out through a hole in the wall. Something must have blocked off the outside end of the pipe. There was a simple on/off switch and I flipped it. The generator hitched, belched, coughed, and died. Then it ran down in a diminishing series of popping sounds that reminded me of Norton's stubborn chainsaw.

The emergency lights faded out and I was left in darkness. I got scared very quickly, and I got disoriented. My breathing sounded like a low wind rattling in straw. I bumped my nose on the flimsy plywood door going out and my heart lurched. There were windows in the double doors, but for some reason they had been painted black, and the darkness was nearly total. I got off course and ran into a stack of the Snowy Bleach cartons. They tumbled and fell. One came close enough to my head to make me step backward, and I tripped over another carton that had landed behind me and fell down, thumping my head hard enough to see bright stars in the darkness. Good show.

I lay there cursing myself and rubbing my head, telling myself to just take it easy, just get up and get out of here, get back to Billy, telling myself nothing soft and slimy was going to close over my ankle or slip into one groping hand. I told myself not to lose control, or I would end up blundering around back here in a panic, knocking things over and creating a mad obstacle course for myself.

I stood up carefully, looking for a pencil line of light between the double doors. I found it, a faint but unmistakable scratch of light on the darkness. I started toward it, and then stopped.

There was a sound. A soft sliding sound. It stopped, then started again with a stealthy little bump. Everything inside me went loose. I regressed magically to four years of age. That sound wasn't coming from the market. It was coming from behind me. From outside. Where the mist was. Something that was slipping and sliding and scraping over the cinderblocks. And, maybe, looking for a way in.

Or maybe it was already in, and it was looking for me. Maybe in a moment I would feel whatever was making that sound on my shoe. Or on my neck.

It came again. I was positive it was outside. But the terror didn't loosen. I told my legs to go and they refused the order. Then the quality of the noise changed. Something *rasped* across the darkness and my heart leaped in my chest and I lunged at that thin vertical line of light. I hit the doors straight-arm and burst through into the market.

Three or four people were right outside the double doors—Ollie Weeks was one of them—and they all jumped back in surprise. Ollie grabbed at his chest. "David!" he said in a pinched voice. "Jesus Christ, you want to take ten years off my—" He saw my face. "What's the matter with you?"

"Did you hear it?" I asked. My voice sounded strange in my own ears, high and squeaking. "Did any of you hear it?"

They hadn't heard anything, of course. They had come up to see why the generator had gone off. As Ollie told me that, one of the bagboys bustled up with an armload of flashlights. He looked from Ollie to me curiously.

"I turned the generator off," I said, and explained why.

"What did you hear?" one of the other men asked. He worked for the town road department; his name was Jim something.

"I don't know. A scraping noise. Slithery. I don't want to hear it again."

"Nerves," the other fellow with Ollie said.

"No. It was not nerves."

"Did you hear it before the lights went out?"

"No, only after. But . . ." But nothing. I could see the way they were looking at me. They didn't want any more bad news, anything else frightening or off-kilter. There was enough of that already. Only Ollie looked as if he believed me.

"Let's go in and start her up again," the bag-boy said, handing out the flashlights. Ollie took his doubtfully. The bag-boy offered me one, a slightly contemptuous shine in his eyes. He was maybe eighteen. After a moment's thought, I took the light. I still needed something to cover Billy with.

Ollie opened the doors and chocked them, letting in some light. The Snowy Bleach cartons lay scattered around the half-open door in the plywood partition.

The fellow named Jim sniffed and said, "Smells pretty rank, all right. Guess you was right to shut her down."

The flashlight beams bobbed and danced across cartons of canned goods, toilet paper, dog food. The beams were smoky in the drifting fumes the blocked exhaust had turned back into the storage area. The bag-boy trained his light briefly on the wide loading door at the extreme right.

The two men and Ollie went inside the generator compartment. Their lights flashed uneasily back and forth, reminding me of something out of a boy's adventure story—and I illustrated a series of them while I was still in college. Pirates burying their bloody gold at midnight, or maybe the mad doctor and his assistant snatching a body. Shadows, made twisted and monstrous by the shifting, conflicting flashlight beams, bobbed on the walls. The generator ticked irregularly as it cooled.

The bag-boy was walking toward the loading door, flashing his light ahead of him. "I wouldn't go over there," I said.

"No, I know *you* wouldn't."

"Try it now, Ollie," one of the men said. The generator wheezed, then roared.

"Jesus! Shut her down! Holy crow, don't that *stink!*"

The generator died again.

The bag-boy walked back from the loading door just as they came out. "Something's plugged that exhaust, all right," one of the men said.

"I'll tell you what," the bag-boy said. His eyes were shining in the glow of the flashlights, and there was a devil-may-care expression on his face that I had sketched too many times as part of the frontispieces for my boys' adventure series. "Get it running long enough for me to raise the loading door back there. I'll go around and clear away whatever it is."

"Norm, I don't think that's a very good idea," Ollie said doubtfully.

"Is it an electric door?" the one called Jim asked.

"Sure," Ollie said. "But I just don't think it would be wise for—"

"That's okay," the other guy said. He tipped his baseball cap back on his head. "I'll do it."

"No, you don't understand," Ollie began again. "I really don't think anyone should—"

"Don't worry," he said indulgently to Ollie, dismissing him.

Norm, the bag-boy, was indignant. "Listen, it was my idea," he said. All at once, by some magic, they had gotten around to arguing about who was going to do it instead of whether or not it should be done at all. But of course, none of them had heard that nasty slithering sound.

"Stop it!" I said loudly.

They looked around at me.

"You don't seem to understand, or you're trying as hard as you can *not* to understand. This is no ordinary fog. Nobody has come into the market since it hit. If you open that loading door and something comes in—"

"Something like what?" Norm said with perfect eighteen-year-old macho contempt.

"Whatever made the noise I heard."

"Mr. Drayton," Jim said. "Pardon me, but I'm not convinced you heard anything. I know you're a big-shot artist with connections in New York and Hollywood and all, but that doesn't make you any different from anyone else, in my book. Way I figure, you got in here in the dark and maybe you just . . . got a little confused."

"Maybe I did," I said. "And maybe if you want to start screwing around outside, you ought to start by making sure that lady got home safe to her kids." His attitude—and that of his buddy and of Norm the bag-boy—was making me mad and scaring me more at the same time. They had the sort of light in their eyes that some men get when they go shooting rats at the town dump.

"Hey," Jim's buddy said. "When any of us here want your advice, we'll ask for it."

Hesitantly, Ollie said: "The generator really isn't that important, you know. The food in the cold-cases will keep for twelve hours or more with absolutely no—"

"Okay, kid, you're it," Jim said brusquely. "I'll start the motor, you raise the door just high enough to duck underneath, then I'll shut her down so that the place doesn't stink up too bad. Me and Myron will be standing by the exhaust outflow. Give us a yell when it's clear."

"Sure," Norm said, and bustled excitedly away.

"This is crazy," I said. "You let that lady go by herself—"

"I didn't notice you breaking your ass to escort her," Jim's buddy Myron said. A dull, brick-colored flush was creeping out of his collar.

"—but you're going to let this kid risk his life over a generator that doesn't even matter?"

"Why don't you just shut the fuck up!" Norm yelled.

"Listen, Mr. Drayton," Jim said, and smiled at me coldly. "I'll tell you what. If you've got anything else to say, I think you better count your teeth first, because I'm tired of listening to your bullshit."

Ollie looked at me, plainly frightened. I shrugged. They were crazy, that was all. Their sense of proportion was temporarily gone. Out there they had been confused and scared. In here was a straightforward mechanical problem: a balky generator. It was possible to solve this problem. Solving the problem would help make them feel less confused and helpless. Therefore they would solve it.

Jim and his friend Myron decided I knew when I was licked and went back into the generator compartment. "Ready, Norm?" Jim asked.

Norm nodded, then realized they couldn't hear a nod. "Yeah," he said.

"Norm," I said. "Don't be a fool."

"It's a mistake," Ollie added.

He looked at us, and suddenly his face was much younger than eighteen. It was the face of a boy. His Adam's apple bobbed convulsively, and I saw that he was scared green. He opened his mouth to say something—I think he was going to call it off—and then the generator roared into life again, and when it was running smoothly, Norm lunged at the button to the right of the door and it began to rattle upward on its dual steel tracks. The emergency lights had come back on when the generator started. Now they dimmed down as the motor which lifted the door sucked away the juice.

The shadows ran backward and melted. The storage area began to fill with the mellow white light of an overcast late-winter day. I noticed that odd, acrid smell again.

The loading door went up two feet, then four. Beyond I could see a square cement platform outlined around the edges with a yellow stripe. The yellow faded and washed out in just three feet. The fog was incredibly thick.

"Ho up!" Norm yelled.

Tendrils of mist, as white and fine as floating lace, eddied inside. The air was cold. It had been noticeably cool all morning long, especially after the sticky heat of the last three weeks, but it had been a summery coolness. This was *cold.* It was like March. I shivered. And I thought of Steff.

The generator died. Jim came out just as Norm ducked under the door. He saw it. So did I. So did Ollie.

A tentacle came over the far lip of the concrete loading platform and grabbed Norm around the calf. My mouth dropped wide open. Ollie made a very short glottal sound of surprise—*uk!* The tentacle tapered from a thickness of a foot—the size of a grass snake—at the point where it had wrapped itself around Norm's lower leg to a thickness of maybe four or five feet where it disappeared into the mist. It was slate gray on top, shading to a fleshy pink underneath. And there were rows of suckers on the underside. They were moving and writhing like hundreds of small, puckering mouths.

Norm looked down. He saw what had him. His eyes bulged. *"Get it off me! Hey, get it off me! Christ Jesus, get this frigging thing off me!"*

"Oh my God," Jim whimpered.

Norm grabbed the bottom edge of the loading door and yanked himself back in. The tentacle seemed to bulge, the way your arm will when you flex it. Norm was yanked back against the corrugated steel door—his head clanged against it. The tentacle bulged more, and Norm's legs and torso began to slip back out. The bottom edge of the loading door scraped the shirttail out of his pants. He yanked savagely and pulled himself back in like a man doing a chin-up.

"Help me," he was sobbing. "Help me, you guys, please, please."

"Jesus, Mary, and Joseph," Myron said. He had come out of the generator compartment to see what was going on.

I was the closest, and I grabbed him around the waist and yanked as hard as I could, rocking way back on my heels. For a moment we moved backward, but only for a moment. It was like stretching a rubber band or pulling taffy. The tentacle yielded but gave up its basic grip not at all. Then three more tentacles floated out of the mist toward us. One curled around Norm's flapping red Federal apron and tore it away. It disappeared back into the mist with the red cloth curled in its grip and I thought of something my mother used to say when my brother and I would beg for something she didn't want us to have—candy, a comic book, some toy. "You need that like a hen needs a flag," she'd say. I thought of that, and I thought of that tentacle waving Norm's red apron around, and I got laughing. I got laughing except my laughter and Norm's screams sounded about the same. Maybe no one even knew I was laughing except me.

The other two tentacles slithered aimlessly back and forth on the loading platform for a moment, making those low scraping sounds I had heard earlier. Then one of them slapped against Norm's left hip and slipped around it. I felt it touch my arm. It was warm and pulsing and smooth. I think now that if it had gripped me with those suckers, I would have gone out into the mist too. But it didn't. It grabbed Norm. And the third tentacle ringleted his other ankle.

Now he was being pulled away from me. "Help me!" I shouted. "Ollie! Someone! Give me a hand here!"

But they didn't come. I don't know what they were doing, but they didn't come.

I looked down and saw the tentacle around Norm's waist working into his skin. The suckers were *eating* him where his shirt had pulled out of his pants. Blood, as red as his missing apron, began to seep out from around the trench the pulsing tentacle had made for itself.

I banged my head on the lower edge of the partly raised door.

Norm's legs were outside again. One of his loafers had fallen off. A new tentacle came out of the mist, wrapped its tip firmly around the shoe, and made off with it. Norm's fingers clutched at the door's lower edge. He had it in a death-grip. His fingers were livid. He was not screaming anymore; he was beyond that. His head whipped back and forth in an endless gesture of negation, and his long black hair flew wildly.

I looked over his shoulder and saw more tentacles coming, dozens of them, a forest of them. Some were small, but a few were gigantic, as thick as the moss-corseted tree that had been lying across our driveway that morning. The big ones had candy-pink suckers that seemed the size of manhole covers. One of these big ones struck the concrete loading platform with a loud and rolling *thrrrrap!* sound and moved sluggishly toward us like a great blind earthworm. I gave one final gigantic tug, and the tentacle holding Norm's right calf slipped a little. That was all. But before it reestablished its grip, I saw that the thing was eating him away.

One of the tentacles brushed delicately past my cheek and then wavered in the air, as if debating. I thought of Billy then. Billy was lying asleep in the market by Mr. McVey's long, white meat cooler. I had come in here to find something to cover him up with. If one of those things got hold of me, there would be no one to watch out for him—except maybe Norton.

So I let go of Norm and dropped to my hands and knees.

I was half in and half out, directly under the raised door. A tentacle passed by on my left, seeming to walk on its suckers. It attached itself to one of Norm's bulging upper arms, paused for a second, and then slid around it in coils.

Now Norm looked like something out of a madman's dream of snake charming. Tentacles twisted over him uneasily almost everywhere . . . and they were all around me, as well. I made a clumsy leapfrog jump back inside, landed on my shoulder and rolled. Jim, Ollie, and Myron were still there. They stood like a tableau of waxworks in Madame Tussaud's, their faces pale, their eyes too bright. Jim and Myron flanked the door to the generator compartment.

"Start the generator!" I yelled at them.

Neither moved. They were staring with a drugged, thanatotic avidity at the loading bay.

I groped on the floor, picked up the first thing that came to hand—a box of Snowy Bleach—and chucked it at Jim. It hit him in the gut, just above the belt buckle. He grunted and grabbed at himself. His eyes flickered back into some semblance of normality.

"Go start that fucking generator!" I screamed so loudly it hurt my throat.

He didn't move; instead he began to defend himself, apparently having decided that, with Norm being eaten alive by some insane horror from the mist, the time had come for rebuttals.

"I'm sorry," he whined. "I didn't know, how the hell was I supposed to know? You said you heard something but I didn't know what you meant, you should have said what you meant better, I thought, I dunno, maybe a bird, or something—"

So then Ollie moved, bunting him aside with one thick shoulder and blundering into the generator room. Jim stumbled over one of the bleach cartons and fell down, just as I had done in the dark. "I'm sorry," he said again. His red hair had tumbled over his brow. His cheeks were cheese-white. His eyes were those of a horrified little boy. Seconds later the generator coughed and rumbled into life.

I turned back to the loading door. Norm was almost gone, yet he clung grimly with one hand. The other had been ripped away. His body boiled with tentacles, and blood pattered serenely down on the concrete in dime-size droplets. His head whipped back and forth and his eyes bulged with terror as they stared off into the mist.

Other tentacles now crept and crawled over the floor inside. There were too many near the button that controlled the loading door to even think of approaching it. One of them closed around a half-liter bottle of Pepsi and carried it off. Another slipped around a cardboard carton and squeezed. The carton ruptured and rolls of toilet paper, two-packs of Delsey wrapped in cellophane, geysered upward, came down, and rolled everywhere. Tentacles seized them eagerly.

One of the big ones slipped in. Its tip rose from the floor and it seemed to sniff the air. It began to advance toward Myron and he stepped mincingly away from it, his eyes rolling madly in their sockets. A high-pitched little moan escaped his slack lips.

I looked around for something, anything at all long enough to reach over the questing tentacles and punch the SHUT button on the wall. I saw a janitor's push broom leaning against a stack-up of beer cases and grabbed it.

Norm's good hand was ripped loose. He thudded down onto the concrete loading platform and scrabbled madly for a grip with his one free hand. His eyes met mine for a moment. They were hellishly bright and aware. He knew what was happening to him. Then he was pulled, bumping and rolling, into the mist. There was another scream, choked off. Norm was gone.

I pushed the tip of the broom handle onto the button and the motor whined. The door began to slide back down. It touched the thickest of the tentacles first, the one that had been investigating in Myron's direction. It indented its hide–skin, whatever–and then pierced it. A black goo began to spurt from it. It writhed madly, whipping across the concrete storage-area floor like an obscene bullwhip, and then it seemed to flatten out. A moment later it was gone. The others began to withdraw.

One of them had a five-pound bag of Gaines dog food, and it wouldn't let go. The descending door cut it in two before thumping home in its grooved slot. The severed chunk of tentacle squeezed convulsively tighter, splitting the bag open and sending brown nuggets of dog food everywhere. Then it began to flop on the floor like a fish out of water, curling and uncurling, but ever more slowly, until it lay still. I prodded it with the tip of the broom. The piece of tentacle, maybe three feet long, closed on it savagely for a moment, then loosened and lay limp again in the confused litter of toilet paper, dog food, and bleach cartons.

There was no sound except the roar of the generator and Ollie, crying inside the plywood compartment. I could see him sitting on a stool in there with his face clutched in his hands.

Then I became aware of another sound. The soft, slithery sound I had heard in the dark. Only now the sound was multiplied tenfold. It was the sound of tentacles squirming over the outside of the loading door, trying to find a way in.

Myron took a couple of steps toward me. "Look," he said. "You got to understand—"

I looped a fist at his face. He was too surprised to even try to block it. It landed just below his nose and mashed his upper lip into his teeth. Blood flowed into his mouth.

"You got him killed!" I shouted. "Did you get a good look at it? Did you get a good look at what you did?"

I started to pummel him, throwing wild rights and lefts, not punching the way I had been taught in my college boxing classes but only hitting out. He stepped back, shaking some of them off, taking others with a numbness that seemed like a kind of resignation or penance. That made me angrier. I bloodied his nose. I raised a mouse under one of his eyes that was going to black just beautifully. I clipped him a hard one on the chin. After that one, his eyes went cloudy and semi-vacant.

"Look," he kept saying, "look, look," and then I punched him low in the stomach and the air went out of him and he didn't say "Look, look" anymore. I don't know how long I would have gone on punching him, but someone grabbed my arms. I jerked free and turned around. I was hoping it was Jim. I wanted to punch Jim out, too.

But it wasn't Jim. It was Ollie, his round face dead-pale, except for the dark circles around his eyes—eyes that were still shiny from his tears. "Don't, David," he said. "Don't hit him anymore. It doesn't solve anything."

Jim was standing off to one side, his face a bewildered blank. I kicked a carton of something at him. It struck one of his Dingo boots and bounced away.

"You and your buddy are a couple of stupid assholes," I said.

"Come on, David," Ollie said unhappily. "Quit it."

"You two assholes got that kid killed."

Jim looked down at his Dingo boots. Myron sat on the floor and held his beer belly. I was breathing hard. The blood was roaring in my ears and I was trembling all over. I sat down on a couple of cartons and put my head down between my knees and gripped my legs hard just above the ankles. I sat that way for a while with my hair in my face, waiting to see if I was going to black out or puke or what.

After a bit the feeling began to pass and I looked up at Ollie. His pink ring flashed subdued fire in the glow of the emergency lights.

"Okay," I said dully. "I'm done."

"Good," Ollie said. "We've got to think what to do next."

The storage area was beginning to stink of exhaust again. "Shut the generator down. That's the first thing."

"Yeah, let's get out of here," Myron said. His eyes appealed to me. "I'm sorry about the kid. But you got to understand–"

"I don't got to understand anything. You and your buddy go back into the market, but you wait right there by the beer cooler. And don't say a word to anybody. Not yet."

They went willingly enough, huddling together as they passed through the swinging doors. Ollie killed the generator, and just as the lights started to fail, I saw a quilted rug–the sort of thing movers use to pad breakable things–flopped over a stack of returnable soda bottles. I reached up and grabbed it for Billy.

There was the shuffling, blundering sound of Ollie coming out of the generator compartment. Like a great many overweight men, his breathing had a slightly heavy, wheezing sound.

"David?" His voice wavered a little. "You still here?"

"Right here, Ollie. You want to watch out for all those bleach cartons."

"Yeah."

I guided him with my voice and in thirty seconds or so he reached out of the dark and gripped my shoulder. He gave a long, trembling sigh.

"Christ, let's get out of here." I could smell the Rolaids he always chewed on his breath. "This dark is . . . is bad."

"It is," I said. "But hang tight a minute, Ollie. I wanted to talk to you and I didn't want those other two fuckheads listening."

"Dave . . . they didn't twist Norm's arm. You ought to remember that."

"Norm was a kid, and they weren't. But never mind, that's over. We've got to tell them, Ollie. The people in the market."

"If they panic–" Ollie's voice was doubtful.

"Maybe they will and maybe they won't. But it will make them think twice about going out, which is what most of them want to do. Why shouldn't they? Most of them will have people they left at home. I do myself. We have to make them understand what they're risking if they go out there."

His hand was gripping my arm hard. "All right," he said. "Yes. I just keep asking myself . . . all those tentacles . . . like a squid or something. . . . David, what were they hooked to? *What were those tentacles hooked to?"*

"I don't know. But I don't want those two telling people on their own. That *would* start a panic. Let's go."

I looked around, and after a moment or two located the thin line of vertical light between the swing doors. We started to shuffle toward it, wary of scattered cartons, one of Ollie's pudgy hands clamped over my forearm. It occurred to me that all of us had lost our flashlights.

As we reached the doors, Ollie said flatly: "What we saw . . . it's impossible, David. You know that, don't you? Even if a van from the Boston Seaquarium drove out back and dumped out one of those gigantic squids like in *Twenty Thousand Leagues under the Sea,* it would die. *It would just die.*"

"Yes," I said. "That's right."

"So what happened? Huh? What happened? What is that damned mist?"

"Ollie, I don't know."

We went out.

V. An Argument with Norton. A Discussion Near the Beer Cooler. Verification.

Jim and his good buddy Myron were just outside the doors, each with a Budweiser in his fist. I looked at Billy, saw he was still asleep, and covered him with the ruglike mover's pad. He moved a little, muttered something, and then lay still again. I looked at my watch. It was 12:15 p.m. That seemed utterly impossible; it felt as if at least five hours had passed since I had first gone in there to look for something to cover him with. But the whole thing, from first to last, had taken only about thirty-five minutes.

I went back to where Ollie stood with Jim and Myron. Ollie had taken a beer and he offered me one. I took it and gulped down half the can at once, as I had that morning cutting wood. It bucked me up a little.

Jim was Jim Grondin. Myron's last name was LaFleur—that had its comic side, all right. Myron the flower had drying blood on his lips, chin, and cheek. The eye with the mouse under it was already swelling up. The girl in the cranberry-colored sweatshirt walked by aimlessly and gave Myron a cautious look. I could have told her that Myron was only dangerous to teenaged boys intent on proving their manhood, but saved my breath. After all, Ollie was right—they *had* only been doing what they thought was best, although in a blind, fearful way rather than in any real common interest. And now I needed them to do what *I* thought was best. I didn't think that would be a problem. They had both had the stuffing knocked out of them. Neither—especially Myron the flower—were going to be good for anything for some time to come. Something that had been in their eyes when they were fixing to send Norm out to unplug the exhaust vent had gone now. Their peckers were no longer up.

"We're going to have to tell these people something," I said.

Jim opened his mouth to protest.

"Ollie and I will leave out any part you and Myron had in sending Norm out there if you'll back up what he and I say about . . . well, about what got him."

"Sure," Jim said, pitifully eager. "Sure, if we don't tell, people might go out there . . . like that woman . . . that woman who . . ." He wiped his hand across his mouth and then drank more beer quickly. "Christ, what a mess."

"David," Ollie said. "What—" He stopped, then made himself go on. "What if they get in? The tentacles?"

"How could they?" Jim asked. "You guys shut the door."

"Sure," Ollie said. "But the whole front wall of this place is plate glass."

An elevator shot my stomach down about twenty floors. I had known that, but had somehow been successfully ignoring it. I looked over at where Billy lay asleep. I thought of those tentacles swarming over Norm. I thought about that happening to Billy.

"Plate glass," Myron LaFleur whispered. "Jesus Christ in a chariot-driven sidecar."

I left the three of them standing by the cooler, each working a second can of beer, and went looking for Brent Norton. I found him in sober-sided conversation with Bud Brown at Register 2. The pair of them—Norton with his styled gray hair and his elderly-stud good looks, Brown with his dour New England phiz—looked like something out of a *New Yorker* cartoon.

As many as two dozen people milled restlessly in the space between the end of the check-out lanes and the long show window. A lot of them were lined up at the glass, looking out into the mist. I was again reminded of the people that congregate at a building site.

Mrs. Carmody was seated on the stationary conveyor belt of one of the check-out lanes, smoking a Parliament in a One Step at a Time filter. Her eyes measured me, found me wanting, and passed on. She looked as if she might be dreaming awake.

"Brent," I said.

"David! Where did you get off to?"

"That's what I'd like to talk to you about."

"There are people back at the cooler drinking beer," Brown said grimly. He sounded like a man announcing that X-rated movies had been shown at the deacon's party. "I can see them in the convex mirror. This has simply got to stop."

"Brent?"

"Excuse me for a minute, would you, Mr. Brown?"

"Certainly." He folded his arms across his chest and stared grimly up into the convex mirror. "This is going to stop, I can promise you that."

Norton and I headed toward the beer cooler in the far corner of the store, walking past the housewares and notions. I glanced back over my shoulder, noticing uneasily how the wooden beams framing the tall, rectangular sections of glass had buckled and twisted and splintered. And one of the windows wasn't even whole, I remembered. A pie-shaped chunk of glass had fallen out of the upper corner at the instant of that queer thump. Perhaps we could stuff it with cloth or something —maybe a bunch of those $3.59 ladies' tops I had noticed near the wine—

My thoughts broke off abruptly, and I had to put the back of my hand over my mouth, as if stifling a burp. What I was really stifling was the rancid flood of horrified giggles that wanted to escape me at the thought of stuffing a bunch of shirts into a hole to keep out those tentacles that had carried Norm away. I had seen one of those tentacles—a *small* one—squeeze a bag of dog food until it simply ruptured.

"David? Are you okay?"

"Huh?"

"Your face—you looked like you just had a good idea or a bloody awful one."

Something hit me then. "Brent, what happened to that man who came in raving about something in the mist getting John Lee Frovin?"

"The guy with the nosebleed?"

"Yes, him."

"He passed out and Mr. Brown brought him around with some smelling salts from the first-aid kit. Why?"

"Did he say anything else when he woke up?"

"He started in on that same hallucination. Mr. Brown conducted him up to the office. He was frightening some of the women. He seemed happy enough to go. Something about the glass. When Mr. Brown said there was only one small window in the manager's office, and that that one was reinforced with wire, he seemed happy enough to go. I presume he's still there."

"What he was talking about is no hallucination."

Norton paused, and then smiled at me. I had a nearly insurmountable urge to ram my fist through that superior grin. "David, are you feeling okay?"

"Is the fog a hallucination?"

"No, of course it isn't."

"And that thud we felt?"

"No, but David—"

He's scared, I kept reminding myself. Don't blow up at him, you've treated yourself to one blowup this morning and that's enough. Don't blow up at him just because this is the way he was during that stupid property-line dispute . . . first patronizing, then sarcastic, and finally, when it became clear he was going to lose, ugly. Don't blow up at him because you're going to need him. He may not be able to start his own chainsaw, but he looks like the father figure of the Western world, and if he tells people not to panic, they won't. So don't blow up at him.

"You see those double doors up there beyond the beer cooler?"

He looked, frowning. "Isn't one of those men drinking beer the other assistant manager? Weeks? If Brown sees that, I can promise you that man will be looking for a job very soon."

"Brent, will you listen to me?"

He glanced back at me absently. "What were you saying, Dave? I'm sorry."

Not as sorry as he was going to be. "Do you see those doors?"

"Yes, of course I do. What about them?"

"They give on the storage area that runs all the way along the west face of the building. Billy fell asleep and I went back there to see if I could find something to cover him up with . . ."

I told him everything, only leaving out the argument about whether or not Norm should have gone out at all. I told him what had come in . . . and finally, what had gone out, screaming. Brent Norton refused to believe it. No—he refused to even entertain it. I took him over to Jim, Ollie, and Myron. All three of them verified the story, although Jim and Myron the flower were well on their way to getting drunk.

Again, Norton refused to believe or even to entertain it. He simply balked. "No," he said. "No, no, no. Forgive me, gentlemen, but it's completely ridiculous. Either you're having me on"—he patronized us with his gleaming smile to show that he could take a joke as well as the next fellow—"or you're suffering from some form of group hypnosis."

My temper rose again, and I controlled it—with difficulty. I don't think that I'm ordinarily a quick-tempered man, but these weren't ordinary circumstances. I had Billy to think about, and what was happening—or what had already happened—to Stephanie. Those things were constantly gnawing at the back of my mind.

"All right," I said. "Let's go back there. There's a chunk of tentacle on the floor. The door cut it off when it came down. And you can *hear* them. They're rustling all over that door. It sounds like the wind in ivy."

"No," he said calmly.

"What?" I really did believe I had misheard him. "What did you say?"

"I said no, I'm not going back there. The joke has gone far enough."

"Brent, I swear to you it's no joke."

"Of course it is," he snapped. His eyes ran over Jim, Myron, rested briefly on Ollie Weeks—who held his glance with calm impassivity—and at last came back to me. "It's what you locals probably call 'a real belly-buster.' Right, David?"

"Brent . . . look—"

"No, you look!" His voice began to rise toward a courtroom shout. It carried very, very well, and several of the people who were wandering around, edgy and aimless, looked over to see what was going on. Norton jabbed his finger at me as he spoke. "It's a joke. It's a banana skin and I'm the guy that's supposed to slip on it. None of you people are exactly crazy about out-of-towners, am I right? You all pretty much stick together. The way it happened when I hauled you into court to get what was rightfully mine. You won that one, all right. Why not? Your father was the famous artist, and it's your town. I only pay my taxes and spend my money here!"

He was no longer performing, hectoring us with the trained courtroom shout; he was nearly screaming and on the verge of losing all control. Ollie Weeks turned and walked away, clutching his beer. Myron and his friend Jim were staring at Norton with frank amazement.

"Am I supposed to go back there and look at some ninety-eight-cent rubber-joke novelty while these two hicks stand around and laugh their asses off?"

"Hey, you want to watch who you're calling a hick," Myron said.

"I'm *glad* that tree fell on your boathouse, if you want to know the truth. *Glad.*" Norton was grinning savagely at me. "Stove it in pretty well, didn't it? Fantastic. Now get out of my way."

He tried to push past me. I grabbed him by the arm and threw him against the beer cooler. A woman cawed in surprise. Two six-packs of Bud fell over.

"You dig out your ears and listen, Brent. There are lives at stake here. My kid's is not the least of them. So you listen, or I swear I'll knock the shit out of you."

"Go ahead," Norton said, still grinning with a kind of insane, palsied bravado. His eyes, bloodshot and wide, bulged from their sockets. "Show everyone how big and brave you are, beating up a man with a heart condition who is old enough to be your father."

"Sock him anyway!" Jim exclaimed. "Fuck his heart condition. I don't even think a cheap New York shyster like him has got a heart."

"You keep out of it," I said to Jim, and then put my face down to Norton's. I was kissing distance, if that had been what I had in mind. The cooler was off, but it was still radiating a chill. "Stop throwing up sand. You know damn well I'm telling the truth."

"I know . . . no . . . such thing," he panted.

"If it was another time and place, I'd let you get away with it. I don't care how scared you are, and I'm not keeping score. I'm scared, too. But I need you, goddammit! Does that get through? I need you!"

"Let me *go!*"

I grabbed him by the shirt and shook him. "Don't you understand anything? People are going to start leaving and walk right into that thing out there! For Christ's sake, don't you understand?"

"Let me go!"

"Not until you come back there with me and see for yourself."

"I told you, *no!* It's all a trick, a joke, I'm not as stupid as you take me for—"

"Then I'll haul you back there myself."

I grabbed him by the shoulder and the scruff of his neck. The seam of his shirt under one arm tore with a soft purring sound. I dragged him toward the double doors. Norton let out a wretched scream. A knot of people, fifteen or eighteen, had gathered, but they kept their distance. None showed any signs of wanting to interfere.

"Help me!" Norton cried. His eyes bulged behind his glasses. His styled hair had gone awry again, sticking up in the same two little tufts behind his ears. People shuffled their feet and watched.

"What are you screaming for?" I said in his ear. "It's just a joke, right? That's why I took you to town when you asked to come and why I trusted you to cross Billy in the parking lot—because I had this handy fog all manufactured, I rented a fog machine from Hollywood, it only cost me fifteen thousand dollars and another eight thousand dollars to ship it, all so I could play a joke on you. Stop bullshitting yourself and open your eyes."

"*Let . . . me . . . go!*" Norton bawled. We were almost at the doors.

"Here, here! What is this? What are you doing?"

It was Brown. He bustled and elbowed his way through the crowd of watchers.

"Make him let me go," Norton said hoarsely. "He's crazy."

"No. He's not crazy. I wish he were, but he isn't." That was Ollie, and I could have blessed him. He came around the aisle behind us and stood there facing Brown.

Brown's eyes dropped to the beer Ollie was holding. "You're *drinking!*" he said, and his voice was surprised but not totally devoid of pleasure. "You'll lose your job for this."

"Come on, Bud," I said, letting Norton go. "This is no ordinary situation."

"Regulations don't change," Brown said smugly. "I'll see that the company hears of it. That's my responsibility."

Norton, meanwhile, had skittered away and stood at some distance, trying to straighten his shirt and smooth back his hair. His eyes darted between Brown and me nervously.

"*Hey!*" Ollie cried suddenly, raising his voice and producing a bass thunder I never would have suspected from this large but soft and unassuming man. "*Hey! Everybody in the store! You want to come up back and hear this! It concerns all of you!*" He looked at me levelly, ignoring Brown altogether. "Am I doing all right?"

"Fine."

People began to gather. The original knot of spectators to my argument with Norton doubled, then trebled.

"There's something you all had better know—" Ollie began.

"You put that beer down right now," Brown said.

"You shut up right now," I said, and took a step toward him.

Brown took a compensatory step back. "I don't know what some of you think you are doing," he said, "but I can tell you it's going to be reported to the Federal Foods Company! All of it! And I want you to understand—*there may be charges!*" His lips drew nervously back from his yellowed teeth, and I could feel sympathy for him. Just trying to cope; that was all he was doing. As Norton was by imposing a mental gag order on himself. Myron and Jim had tried by turning the whole thing into a macho charade—if the generator could be fixed, the mist would blow over. This was Brown's way. He was . . . Protecting the Store.

"Then you go ahead and take down the names," I said. "But please don't talk."

"I'll take down plenty of names," he responded. "Yours will head the list, you . . . you *bohemian.*"

I could have brayed laughter. For ten years I had been a commercial artist with any dreams of greatness gradually falling further and further behind me; all my life I had lived in my father's long shadow; my only real success had been in producing a male heir to the name; and here was this dour Yankee with his badly fitting false teeth calling me a bohemian.

"Mr. David Drayton has got something to tell you," Ollie said. "And I think you had better all listen up, in case you were planning on going home."

So I told them what had happened, pretty much as I told Norton. There was some laughter at first, then a deepening uneasiness as I finished.

"It's a lie, you know," Norton said. His voice tried for hard emphasis and overshot into stridency. This was the man I'd told first, hoping to enlist his credibility. What a balls-up.

"Of course it's a lie," Brown agreed. "It's lunacy. Where do you suppose those tentacles came from, Mr. Drayton?"

"I don't know, and at this point, that's not even a very important question. They're here. There's—"

"I suspect they came out of a few of those beer cans. That's what I suspect." This got some appreciative laughter. It was silenced by the strong, rusty-hinge voice of Mrs. Carmody.

"Death!" she cried, and those who had been laughing quickly sobered.

She marched into the center of the rough circle that had formed, her canary pants seeming to give off a light of their own, her huge purse swinging against one elephantine thigh. Her black eyes glanced arrogantly around, as sharp and balefully sparkling as a magpie's. Two good-looking girls of about sixteen with CAMP WOODLANDS written on the back of their white rayon shirts shrank away from her.

"You listen but you don't hear! You hear but you don't believe! Which one of you wants to go outside and see for himself?" Her eyes swept them, and then fell on me. "And just what do you propose to do about it, Mr. David Drayton? What do you think you *can* do about it?"

She grinned, skull-like above her canary outfit.

"It's the end, I tell you. The end of everything. It's the Last Times.

The moving finger has writ, not in fire, but in lines of mist. The earth has opened and spewed forth its abominations—"

"Can't you make her shut up?" one of the teenage girls burst out. She was beginning to cry. "She's scaring me!"

"Are you scared, dearie?" Mrs. Carmody asked, and turned on her. "You aren't scared now, no. But when the foul creatures the Imp has loosed upon the face of the earth come for you—"

"That's enough, now, Mrs. Carmody," Ollie said, taking her arm. "That's just fine."

"You let go of me! It's the end, I tell you! It's death! Death!"

"It's a pile of shit," a man in a fishing hat and glasses said disgustedly.

"No, sir," Myron spoke up. "I know it sounds like something out of a dope-dream, but it's the flat-out truth. I saw it myself."

"I did, too," Jim said.

"And me," Ollie chipped in. He had succeeded in quieting Mrs. Carmody, at least for the time being. But she stood close by, clutching her big purse and grinning her crazy grin. No one wanted to stand too close to her—they muttered among themselves, not liking the corroboration. Several of them looked back at the big plate-glass windows in an uneasy, speculative way. I was glad to see it.

"Lies," Norton said. "You people all lie each other up. That's all."

"What you're suggesting is totally beyond belief," Brown said.

"We don't have to stand here chewing it over," I told him. "Come back into the storage area with me. Take a look. And a listen."

"Customers are not allowed in the—"

"Bud," Ollie said, "go with him. Let's settle this."

"All right," Brown said. "Mr. Drayton? Let's get this foolishness over with."

We pushed through the double doors into the darkness.

The sound was unpleasant—perhaps evil.

Brown felt it, too, for all his hardheaded Yankee manner; his hand clutched my arm immediately, his breath caught for a moment and then resumed more harshly.

It was a low whispering sound from the direction of the loading door —an almost caressing sound. I swept around gently with one foot and finally struck one of the flashlights. I bent down, got it, and turned it on. Brown's face was tightly drawn, and he hadn't even seen them—he was only hearing them. But I had seen, and I could imagine them twisting and climbing over the corrugated steel surface of the door like living vines.

"What do you think now? Totally beyond belief?"

Brown licked his lips and looked at the littered confusion of boxes and bags. "They did this?"

"Some of it. Most of it. Come over here."

He came—reluctantly. I spotted the flashlight on the shriveled and curled section of tentacle, still lying by the push broom. Brown bent toward it.

"Don't touch that," I said. "It may still be alive."

He straightened up quickly. I picked up the broom by the bristles and prodded the tentacle. The third or fourth poke caused it to unclench sluggishly and reveal two whole suckers and a ragged segment of a third. Then the fragment coiled again with muscular speed and lay still. Brown made a gagging, disgusted sound.

"Seen enough?"

"Yes," he said. "Let's get out of here."

We followed the bobbing light back to the double doors and pushed through them. All the faces turned toward us, and the hum of conversation died. Norton's face was like old cheese. Mrs. Carmody's black eyes glinted. Ollie was drinking another beer; his face was still running with trickles of perspiration, although it had gotten rather chilly in the market. The two girls with CAMP WOODLANDS on their shirts were huddled together like young horses before a thunderstorm. Eyes. So many eyes. I could paint them, I thought with a chill. No faces, only eyes in the gloom. I could paint them but no one would believe they were real.

Bud Brown folded his long-fingered hands primly in front of him. "People," he said. "It appears we have a problem of some magnitude here."

VI. Further Discussion. Mrs. Carmody. Fortifications. What Happened to the Flat-Earth Society.

The next four hours passed in a kind of dream. There was a long and semi-hysterical discussion following Brown's confirmation, or maybe the discussion wasn't as long as it seemed; maybe it was just the grim necessity of people chewing over the same information, trying to see it from every possible point of view, working it the way a dog works a bone, trying to get at the marrow. It was a slow coming to belief. You can see the same thing at any New England town meeting in March.

There was the Flat-Earth Society, headed by Norton. They were a vocal minority of about ten who believed none of it. Norton pointed out over and over again that there were only four witnesses to the bagboy being carried off by what he called the Tentacles from Planet X (it was good for a laugh the first time, but it wore thin quickly; Norton, in his increasing agitation, seemed not to notice). He added that he personally did not trust one of the four. He further pointed out that fifty percent of the witnesses were now hopelessly inebriated. That was unquestionably true. Jim and Myron LaFleur, with the entire beer cooler and wine rack at their disposal, were abysmally shitfaced. Considering what had happened to Norm, and their part in it, I didn't blame them. They would sober off all too soon.

Ollie continued to drink steadily, ignoring Brown's protests. After a while Brown gave up, contenting himself with an occasional baleful threat about the Company. He didn't seem to realize that Federal Foods, Inc., with its stores in Bridgton, North Windham, and Portland, might not even exist anymore. For all we knew, the Eastern Seaboard might no longer exist. Ollie drank steadily, but didn't get drunk. He was sweating it out as rapidly as he could put it in.

At last, as the discussion with the Flat-Earthers was becoming acrimonious, Ollie spoke up. "If you don't believe it, Mr. Norton, that's fine. I'll tell you what you do. You go on out that front door and walk around to the back. There's a great big pile of returnable beer and soda bottles there. Norm and Buddy and I put them out this morning. You bring back a couple of those bottles so we know you really went back there. You do that and I'll personally take my shirt off and eat it."

Norton began to bluster.

Ollie cut him off in that same soft, even voice. "I tell you, you're not doing anything but damage talking the way you are. There's people here that want to go home and make sure their families are okay. My sister and her year-old daughter are at home in Naples right now. I'd like to check on them, sure. But if people start believing you and try to go home, what happened to Norm is going to happen to them."

He didn't convince Norton, but he convinced some of the leaners and fence sitters—it wasn't what he said so much as it was his eyes, his haunted eyes. I think Norton's sanity hinged on not being convinced, or that at the very least, he thought it did. But he didn't take Ollie up on his offer to bring back a couple of returnables from out back. None of them did. They weren't ready to go out, at least not yet. He and his little group of Flat-Earthers (reduced by one or two now) went as far away from the rest of us as they could get, over by the prepared-meats case. One of them kicked my sleeping son in the leg as he went past, waking him up.

I went over, and Billy clung to my neck. When I tried to put him down, he clung tighter and said, "Don't do that, Daddy. Please."

I found a shopping cart and put him in the baby seat. He looked very big in there. It would have been comical except for his pale face, the dark hair brushed across his forehead just above his eyebrows, his woeful eyes. He probably hadn't been up in the baby seat of the shopping cart for as long as two years. These little things slide by you, you don't realize at first, and when what has changed finally comes to you, it's always a nasty shock.

Meanwhile, with the Flat-Earthers having withdrawn, the argument had found another lightning rod—this time it was Mrs. Carmody, and understandably enough, she stood alone.

In the faded, dismal light she was witchlike in her blazing canary pants, her bright rayon blouse, her armloads of clacking junk jewelry—copper, tortoise shell adamantine—and her thyroidal purse. Her parchment face was grooved with strong vertical lines. Her frizzy gray hair was yanked flat with three horn combs and twisted in the back. Her mouth was a line of knotted rope.

"There is no defense against the will of God. This has been coming. I have seen the signs. There are those here that I have told, but there are none so blind as those who will not see."

"Well, what are you saying? What are you proposing?" Mike Hatlen broke in impatiently. He was a town selectman, although he didn't look the part now, in his yachtsman's cap and saggy-seated Bermudas. He was sipping at a beer; a great many men were doing it now. Bud Brown had given up protesting, but he was indeed taking names—keeping a rough tab on everyone he could.

"Proposing?" Mrs. Carmody echoed, wheeling toward Hatlen. "Proposing? Why, I am proposing that you prepare to meet your God, Michael Hatlen." She gazed around at all of us. "Prepare to meet your God!"

"Prepare to meet shit," Myron LaFleur said in a drunken snarl from the beer cooler. "Old woman, I believe your tongue must be hung in the middle so it can run on both ends."

There was a rumble of agreement. Billy looked around nervously, and I slipped an arm around his shoulders.

"I'll have my say!" she cried. Her upper lip curled back, revealing snaggle teeth that were yellow with nicotine. I thought of the dusty stuffed animals in her shop, drinking eternally at the mirror that served as their creek. "Doubters will doubt to the end! Yet a monstrosity did drag that poor boy away! Things in the mist! Every abomination out of a bad dream! Eyeless freaks! Pallid horrors! Do you doubt? Then go on out! Go on out and say howdy-do!"

"Mrs. Carmody, you'll have to stop," I said. "You're scaring my boy."

The man with the little girl echoed the sentiment. She, all plump legs and scabby knees, had hidden her face against her father's stomach and put her hands over her ears. Big Bill wasn't crying, but he was close.

"There's only one chance," Mrs. Carmody said.

"What's that, ma'am?" Mike Hatlen asked politely.

"A sacrifice," Mrs. Carmody said–she seemed to grin in the gloom. "A blood sacrifice."

Blood sacrifice–the words hung there, slowly turning. Even now, when I know better, I tell myself that then what she meant was someone's pet dog–there were a couple of them trotting around the market in spite of the regulations against them. Even now I tell myself that. She looked like some crazed remnant of New England Puritanism in the gloom . . . but I suspect that something deeper and darker than mere Puritanism motivated her. Puritanism had its own dark grandfather, old Adam with bloody hands.

She opened her mouth to say something more, and a small, neat man in red pants and a natty sports shirt struck her open-handed across the face. His hair was parted with ruler evenness on the left. He wore glasses. He also wore the unmistakable look of the summer tourist.

"You shut up that bad talk," he said softly and tonelessly.

Mrs. Carmody put her hand to her mouth and then held it out to us, a wordless accusation. There was blood on the palm. But her black eyes seemed to dance with mad glee.

"You had it coming!" a woman cried out. "I would have done it myself!"

"They'll get hold on you," Mrs. Carmody said, showing us her bloody palm, the trickle of blood now running down one of the wrinkles from her mouth to her chin like a droplet of rain down a gutter. "Not today, maybe. Tonight. Tonight when the dark comes. They'll come with the night and take someone else. With the night they'll come. You'll hear them coming, creeping and crawling. And when they come, you'll beg for Mother Carmody to show you what to do."

The man in the red pants raised his hand slowly.

"You come on and hit me," she whispered, and grinned her bloody grin at him. His hand wavered. "Hit me if you dare." His hand dropped. Mrs. Carmody walked away by herself. Then Billy did begin to cry, hiding his face against me as the little girl had done with her father.

"I want to go home," he said. "I want to see my mommy."

I comforted him as best I could. Which probably wasn't very well.

The talk finally turned into less frightening and destructive channels. The plate-glass windows, the market's obvious weak point, were mentioned. Mike Hatlen asked what other entrances there were, and Ollie and Brown quickly ticked them off—two loading doors in addition to the one Norm had opened. The main IN/OUT doors. The window in the manager's office (thick, reinforced glass, securely locked).

Talking about these things had a paradoxical effect. It made the danger seem more real but at the same time made us feel better. Even Billy felt it. He asked if he could go get a candy bar. I told him it would be all right so long as he didn't go near the big windows.

When he was out of earshot, a man near Mike Hatlen said, "Okay, what are we going to do about those windows? The old lady may be as crazy as a bedbug, but she could be right about something moving in after dark."

"Maybe the fog will blow over by then," a woman said.

"Maybe," the man said. "And maybe not."

"Any ideas?" I asked Bud and Ollie.

"Hold on a sec," the man near Hatlen said. "I'm Dan Miller. From Lynn, Mass. You don't know me, no reason why you should, but I got a place on Highland Lake. Bought it just this year. Got held up for it, is more like it, but I had to have it." There were a few chuckles. "Anyway, we're all in this together, and the way I see it, we've got to throw up some defenses." People were nodding. "Now, I saw a whole pile of fertilizer and lawn-food bags down there. Twenty-five-pound sacks, most of them. We could put them up like sandbags. Leave loopholes to look out through. . . ."

Now more people were nodding and talking excitedly. I almost said something, then held it back. Miller was right. Putting those bags up could do no harm, and might do some good. But my mind went back to that tentacle squeezing the dog-food bag. I thought that one of the bigger tentacles could probably do the same for a twenty-five-pound bag of Green Acres lawn food or Vigoro. But a sermon on that wouldn't get us out of here or improve anyone's mood.

People began to break up, talking about getting it done, and Miller yelled: "Hold it! Hold it! Let's thrash this out while we're all together!"

They came back, a loose congregation of fifty or sixty people in the corner formed by the beer cooler, the storage doors, and the left end of the meat case, where Mr. McVey always seems to put the things no one wants, like sweetbreads and Scotch eggs and sheep's brains and head cheese. Billy wove his way through them with a five-year-old's unconscious agility in a world of giants and held up a Hershey bar. "Want this, Daddy?"

"Thanks." I took it. It tasted sweet and good.

"This is probably a stupid question," Miller resumed, "but we ought to fill in the blanks. Anyone got any firearms?"

There was a pause. People looked around at each other and shrugged. An old man with grizzled white hair who introduced himself as Ambrose Cornell said he had a shotgun in the trunk of his car. "I'll try for it, if you want."

Ollie said, "Right now I don't think that would be a good idea, Mr. Cornell."

Cornell grunted. "Right now, neither do I, son. But I thought I ought to make the offer."

"Well, I didn't really think so," Dan Miller said. "But I thought—"

"Wait, hold it a minute," a woman said. It was the lady in the cranberry-colored sweatshirt and the dark green slacks. She had sandy-blond hair and a good figure. A very pretty young woman. She opened her purse and from it she produced a medium-size pistol. The crowd made an *ahhhh*-ing sound, as if they had just seen a magician do a particularly fine trick. The woman, who had been blushing, blushed that much the harder. She rooted in her purse again and brought out a box of Smith & Wesson ammunition.

"I'm Amanda Dumfries," she said to Miller. "This gun . . . my husband's idea. He thought I should have it for protection. I've carried it unloaded for two years now."

"Is your husband here, ma'am?"

"No, he's in New York. On business. He's gone on business a lot. That's why he wanted me to carry the gun."

"Well," Miller said, "if you can use it, you ought to keep it. What is it, a .thirty-eight?"

"Yes. And I've never fired it in my life except on a target range once."

Miller took the gun, fumbled around, and got the cylinder to open after a few moments. He checked to make sure it was not loaded. "Okay," he said. "We got a gun. Who shoots good? I sure don't."

People glanced at each other. No one said anything at first. Then, reluctantly, Ollie said: "I target-shoot quite a lot. I have a Colt .forty-five and a Llama .twenty-five."

"You?" Brown said. "Huh. You'll be too drunk to see by dark."

Ollie said very clearly, "Why don't you just shut up and write down your names?"

Brown goggled at him. Opened his mouth. Then decided, wisely, I think, to shut it again.

"It's yours," Miller said, blinking a little at the exchange. He handed it over and Ollie checked it again, more professionally. He put the gun into his right-front pant pocket and slipped the cartridge box into his breast pocket, where it made a bulge like a pack of cigarettes. Then he leaned back against the cooler, round face still trickling sweat, and cracked a fresh beer. The sensation that I was seeing a totally unsuspected Ollie Weeks persisted.

"Thank you, Mrs. Dumfries," Miller said.

"Don't mention it," she said, and I thought fleetingly that if I were her husband and proprietor of those green eyes and that full figure, I might not travel so much. Giving your wife a gun could be seen as a ludicrously symbolic act.

"This may be silly, too," Miller said, turning back to Brown with his clipboard and Ollie with his beer, "but there aren't anything like flamethrowers in the place, are there?"

"Ohhh, *shit,*" Buddy Eagleton said, and then went as red as Amanda Dumfries had done.

"What is it?" Mike Hatlen asked.

"Well . . . until last week we had a whole case of those little blowtorches. The kind you use around your house to solder leaky pipes or mend your exhaust systems or whatever. You remember those, Mr. Brown?"

Brown nodded, looking sour.

"Sold out?" Miller asked.

"No, they didn't go at all. We only sold three or four and sent the rest of the case back. What a pisser. I mean . . . what a shame." Blushing so deeply he was almost purple, Buddy Eagleton retired into the background again.

We had matches, of course; and salt (someone said vaguely that he had heard salt was the thing to put on bloodsuckers and things like that); and all kinds of O'Cedar mops and long-handled brooms. Most of the people continued to look heartened, and Jim and Myron were too plotzo to sound a dissenting note, but I met Ollie's eyes and saw a calm hopelessness in them that was worse than fear. He and I had seen the tentacles. The idea of throwing salt on them or trying to fend them off with the handles of O'Cedar mops was funny, in a ghastly way.

"Let's get those bags up," Miller said. "Who wants to throw some bags?"

It turned out that almost everyone did—with the exception of Norton's group, over by the coldcuts. Norton was holding forth earnestly, and they hardly even looked our way.

"Mike," Miller said, "why don't you crew this little adventure? I want to talk to Ollie and Dave here for a minute."

"Glad to." Hatlen clapped Dan Miller on the shoulder. "Somebody had to take charge, and you did it good. Welcome to town."

"Does this mean I get a kickback on my taxes?" Miller asked. He was a banty little guy with red hair that was receding. He looked like the sort of guy you can't help liking on short notice and—just maybe—the kind of guy you can't help not liking after he's been around for a while, because he knows how to do everything better than you do.

"No way," Hatlen said, laughing.

"Then get out of here," Miller said with an answering grin.

Hatlen walked off. Miller glanced down at my son.

"Don't worry about Billy," I said.

"Man, I've never been so worried in my whole life," Miller said.

"No," Ollie agreed, and dropped an empty into the beer cooler. He got a fresh one and opened it. There was a soft hiss of escaping gas.

"I got a look at the way you two glanced at each other," Miller said.

I finished my Hershey bar and got a beer to wash it down with.

"Tell you what I think," Miller said. "We ought to get half a dozen people to wrap some of those mophandles with cloth and then tie them down with twine. Then I think we ought to get a couple of those cans of charcoal lighter fluid all ready. If we cut the tops right off the cans, we could have some torches pretty quick."

I nodded. That was good. Almost surely not good enough—not if you had seen Norm dragged out—but it was better than salt.

"That would give them something to think about, at least," Ollie said.

Miller's lips pressed together. "That bad, huh?" he said.

"That bad," Ollie agreed, and worked his beer.

By four-thirty that afternoon the sacks of fertilizer and lawn food were in place and the big windows were blocked off except for narrow loopholes. A watchman had been placed at each of these, and beside each watchman was a tin of charcoal lighter fluid with the top cut off and a supply of mophandle torches. There were five loopholes, and Dan Miller had arranged a rotation of sentries for each one. When four-thirty came around, I was sitting on a pile of bags at one of the loopholes, Billy at my side. We were looking out into the mist.

Just beyond the window was a red bench where people sometimes waited for their rides with their groceries beside them. Beyond that was the parking lot. The mist swirled slowly, thick and heavy. There *was* moisture in it, but how dull it seemed, and gloomy. Just looking at it made me feel gutless and lost.

"Daddy, do you know what's happening?" Billy asked.

"No, hon," I said.

He fell silent for a bit, looking at his hands, which lay limply in the lap of his Tuffskin jeans. "Why doesn't somebody come and rescue us?" he asked finally. "The State Police or the FBI or someone?"

"I don't know."

"Do you think Mom's okay?"

"Billy, I just don't know," I said, and put an arm around him.

"I want her awful bad," Billy said, struggling with tears. "I'm sorry about the times I was bad to her."

"Billy," I said, and had to stop. I could taste salt in my throat, and my voice wanted to tremble.

"Will it be over?" Billy asked. "Daddy? Will it?"

"I don't know," I said, and he put his face in the hollow of my shoulder and I held the back of his head, felt the delicate curve of his skull just under the thick growth of his hair. I found myself remembering the evening of my wedding day. Taking off the simple brown dress Steff had changed into. She had had a big purple bruise on one hip from running into the side of a door the day before. I remembered looking at the bruise and thinking, *When she got that, she was still Stephanie Stepanek,* and feeling something like wonder. Then we had made love, and outside it was spitting snow from a dull gray December sky.

Billy was crying.

"Shhh, Billy, shhh," I said, rocking his head against me, but he went on crying. It was the sort of crying that only mothers know how to fix right.

Premature night had come inside the Federal Foods. Miller and Hatlen and Bud Brown handed out flashlights, the whole stock, about twenty. Norton clamored loudly for them on behalf of his group, and received two. The lights bobbed here and there in the aisles like uneasy phantoms.

I held Billy against me and looked out through the loophole. The milky, translucent quality of the light out there hadn't changed much; it was putting up the bags that had made the market so dark. Several times I thought I saw something, but it was only jumpiness. One of the others raised a hesitant false alarm.

Billy saw Mrs. Turman again, and went to her eagerly, even though she hadn't been over to sit for him all summer. She had one of the flashlights and handed it over to him amiably enough. Soon he was trying to write his name in light on the blank glass faces of the frozen-food cases. She seemed as happy to see him as he was to see her, and in a little while they came over. Hattie Turman was a tall, thin woman with lovely red hair just beginning to streak gray. A pair of glasses hung from an ornamental chain—the sort, I believe, it is illegal for anyone except middle-aged women to wear—on her breast.

"Is Stephanie here, David?" she asked.

"No. At home."

She nodded. "Alan, too. How long are you on watch here?"

"Until six."

"Have you seen anything?"

"No. Just the mist."

"I'll keep Billy until six, if you like."

"Would you like that, Billy?"

"Yes, please," he said, swinging the flashlight above his head in slow arcs and watching it play across the ceiling.

"God will keep your Steffy and Alan, too," Mrs. Turman said, and led Billy away by the hand. She spoke with serene sureness but there was no conviction in her eyes.

Around five-thirty the sounds of excited argument rose near the back of the store. Someone jeered at something someone else had said, and someone—it was Buddy Eagleton, I think—shouted, "You're crazy if you go out there!"

Several of the flashlight beams pooled together at the center of the controversy, and they moved toward the front of the store. Mrs. Carmody's shrieking, derisive laugh split the gloom, as abrasive as fingers drawn down a slate blackboard.

Above the babble of voices came the boom of Norton's courtroom tenor: "Let us pass, please! Let us pass!"

The man at the loophole next to mine left his place to see what the shouting was about. I decided to stay where I was. Whatever the concatenation was, it was coming my way.

"Please," Mike Hatlen was saying. "Please, let's talk this thing through."

"There is nothing to talk about," Norton proclaimed. Now his face swam out of the gloom. It was determined and haggard and wholly wretched. He was holding one of the two flashlights allocated to the Flat-Earthers. The two corkscrewed tufts of hair still stuck up behind his ears like a cuckold's horns. He was at the head of an extremely small procession—five of the original nine or ten. "We are going out," he said.

Miller appeared, and as they drew closer I could see others, following anxiously along but not talking. They came out of the shadows like wraiths out of a crystal ball. Billy watched them with large, anxious eyes.

"Don't stick to this craziness," Miller said. "Mike's right. We can talk it over, can't we? Mr. McVey is going to barbecue some chicken over the gas grill, we can all sit down and eat and just—"

He got in Norton's way and Norton gave him a push. Miller didn't like it. His face flushed and then set in a hard expression. "Do what you want, then," he said. "But you're as good as murdering these other people."

With all the evenness of great resolve or unbreakable obsession, Norton said: "We'll send help back for you."

One of his followers murmured agreement, but another quietly slipped away. Now there was Norton and four others. Maybe that wasn't so bad. Christ himself could only find twelve.

"Listen," Mike Hatlen said. "Mr. Norton—Brent—at least stay for the chicken. Get some hot food inside you."

"And give you a chance to go on talking? I've been in too many courtrooms to fall for that. You've psyched out half a dozen of my people already."

"Your people?" Hatlen almost groaned it. "*Your* people? Good Christ, what kind of talk is that? They're *people*, that's all. This is no game, and it's surely not a courtroom. There are, for want of a better word, there are *things* out there, and what's the sense of getting yourself killed?"

"Things, you say," Norton said, sounding superficially amused. "Where? Your people have been on watch for a couple of hours now. Who's seen one?"

"Well, out back. In the—"

"No, no, no," Norton said, shaking his head. "That ground has been covered and covered. We're going out—"

"No," someone whispered, and it echoed and spread, sounding like the rustle of dead leaves at dusk of an October evening. *No, no, no . . .*

"Will you restrain us?" a shrill voice asked. This was one of Norton's "people," to use his word—an elderly lady wearing bifocals. "Will you restrain us?"

The soft babble of negatives died away.

"No," Mike said. "No, I don't think anyone will restrain you."

I whispered in Billy's ear. He looked at me, startled and questioning. "Go on, now," I said. "Be quick."

He went.

Norton ran his hands through his hair, a gesture as calculated as any ever made by a Broadway actor. I had liked him better pulling the cord of his chainsaw fruitlessly, cussing and thinking himself unobserved. I could not tell then and do not know any better now if he believed in what he was doing or not. I think, down deep, that he knew what was going to happen. I think that the logic he had paid lip service to all his life turned on him at the end like a tiger that has gone bad and mean.

He looked around restlessly, seeming to wish that there was more to say. Then he led his four followers through one of the check-out lanes. In addition to the elderly woman, there was a chubby boy of about twenty, a young girl, and a man in blue jeans wearing a golf cap tipped back on his head.

Norton's eyes caught mine, widened a little, and then started to swing away.

"Brent, wait a minute," I said.

"I don't want to discuss it any further. Certainly not with you."

"I know you don't. I just want to ask a favor." I looked around and saw Billy coming back toward the checkouts at a run.

"What's that?" Norton asked suspiciously as Billy came up and handed me a package done up in cellophane.

"Clothesline," I said. I was vaguely aware that everyone in the market was watching us now, loosely strung out on the other side of the cash registers and check-out lanes. "It's the big package. Three hundred feet."

"So?"

"I wondered if you'd tie one end around your waist before you go out. I'll let it out. When you feel it come up tight, just tie it around something. It doesn't matter what. A car doorhandle would do."

"What in God's name for?"

"It will tell me you got at least three hundred feet," I said.

Something in his eyes flickered . . . but only momentarily. "No," he said.

I shrugged. "Okay. Good luck, anyhow."

Abruptly the man in the golf cap said, "I'll do it, mister. No reason not to."

Norton swung on him, as if to say something sharp, and the man in the golf cap studied him calmly. There was nothing flickering in *his* eyes. He had made his decision and there was simply no doubt in him. Norton saw it too and said nothing.

"Thanks," I said.

I slit the wrapping with my pocketknife and the clothesline accordioned out in stiff loops. I found one loose end and tied it around Golf Cap's waist in a loose granny. He immediately untied it and cinched it tighter with a good quick sheet-bend knot. There was not a sound in the market. Norton shifted uneasily from foot to foot.

"You want to take my knife?" I asked the man in the golf cap.

"I got one." He looked at me with that same calm contempt. "You just see to paying out your line. If it binds up, I'll chuck her."

"Are we all ready?" Norton asked, too loud. The chubby boy jumped as if he had been goosed. Getting no response, Norton turned to go.

"Brent," I said, and held out my hand. "Good luck, man."

He studied my hand as if it were some dubious foreign object. "We'll send back help," he said finally, and pushed through the OUT door. That thin, acrid smell came in again. The others followed him out.

Mike Hatlen came down and stood beside me. Norton's party of five stood in the milky, slow-moving fog. Norton said something and I should have heard it, but the mist seemed to have an odd damping effect. I heard nothing but the sound of his voice and two or three isolated syllables, like a voice on the radio heard from some distance. They moved off.

Hatlen held the door a little way open. I payed out the clothesline, keeping as much slack in it as I could, mindful of the man's promise to chuck the rope if it bound him up. There was still not a sound. Billy stood beside me, motionless but seeming to thrum with his own inner current.

Again there was that weird feeling that the five of them did not so much disappear into the fog as become invisible. For a moment their clothes seemed to stand alone, and then they were gone. You were not really impressed with the unnatural density of the mist until you saw people swallowed up in a space of seconds.

I payed the line out. A quarter of it went, then a half. It stopped going out for a moment. It went from a live thing to a dead one in my hands. I held my breath. Then it started to go out again. I payed it through my fingers, and suddenly remembered my father taking me to see the Gregory Peck film of *Moby Dick* at the old Brookside. I think I smiled a little.

Three-quarters of the line was gone now. I could see the end of it lying beside one of Billy's feet. Then the rope stopped moving through my hands again. It lay motionless for perhaps five seconds, and then another five feet jerked out. Then it suddenly whipsawed violently to the left, twanging off the edge of the OUT door.

Twenty feet of rope suddenly payed out, making a thin heat across my left palm. And from out of the mist there came a high, wavering scream. It was impossible to tell the sex of the screamer.

The rope whipsawed in my hands again. And again. It skated across the space in the doorway to the right, then back to the left. A few more feet payed out, and then there was a ululating howl from out there that brought an answering moan from my son. Hatlen stood aghast. His eyes were huge. One corner of his mouth turned down, trembling.

The howl was abruptly cut off. There was no sound at all for what seemed to be forever. Then the old lady cried out—this time there could be no doubt about who it was. *"Git it offa me!"* she screamed. *"Oh my Lord my Lord git it—"*

Then her voice was cut off, too.

Almost all of the rope abruptly ran out through my loosely closed fist, giving me a hotter burn this time. Then it went completely slack, and a sound came out of the mist—a thick, loud grunt—that made all the spit in my mouth dry up.

It was like no sound I've ever heard, but the closest approximation might be a movie set in the African veld or a South American swamp. It was the sound of a big animal. It came again, low and tearing and savage. Once more . . . and then it subsided to a series of low mutterings. Then it was completely gone.

"Close the door," Amanda Dumfries said in a trembling voice. "Please."

"In a minute," I said, and began to yank the line back in.

It came out of the mist and piled up around my feet in untidy loops and snarls. About three feet from the end, the new white clothesline went barn-red.

"Death!" Mrs. Carmody screamed. "Death to go out there! Now do you see?"

The end of the clothesline was a chewed and frayed tangle of fiber and little puffs of cotton. The little puffs were dewed with minute drops of blood.

No one contradicted Mrs. Carmody.

Mike Hatlen let the door swing shut.

VII. The First Night.

Mr. McVey had worked in Bridgton cutting meat ever since I was twelve or thirteen, and I had no idea what his first name was or his age might be. He had set up a gas grill under one of the small exhaust fans—the fans were still now, but presumably they still gave some ventilation—and by 6:30 p.m. the smell of cooking chicken filled the market. Bud Brown didn't object. It might have been shock, but more likely he had recognized the fact that his fresh meat and poultry wasn't getting any fresher. The chicken smelled good, but not many people wanted to eat. Mr. McVey, small and spare and neat in his whites, cooked the chicken nevertheless and laid the pieces two by two on paper plates and lined them up cafeteria-style on top of the meat counter.

Mrs. Turman brought Billy and I each a plate, garnished with helpings of deli potato salad. I worked mine as best I could, but Billy would not even pick at his.

"You got to eat, big guy," I said.

"I'm not hungry," he said, putting the plate aside.

"You can't get big and strong if you don't—"

Mrs. Turman, sitting slightly behind Billy, shook her head at me.

"Okay," I said. "Go get a peach and eat it, at least. 'Kay?"

"What if Mr. Brown says something?"

"If he says something, you come back and tell me."

"Okay, Dad."

He walked away slowly. He seemed to have shrunk somehow. It hurt my heart to see him walk that way. Mr. McVey went on cooking chicken, apparently not minding that only a few people were eating it, happy in the act of cooking. As I think I have said, there are all ways of handling a thing like this. You wouldn't think it would be so, but it is. The mind is a monkey.

Mrs. Turman and I sat halfway up the patent-medicines aisle. People were sitting in little groups all over the store. No one except Mrs.

Carmody was sitting alone; even Myron and his buddy Jim were together—they were both passed out by the beer cooler.

Six new men were watching the loopholes. One of them was Ollie, gnawing a leg of chicken and drinking a beer. The mophandle torches leaned beside each of the watchposts, a can of charcoal lighter fluid next to each . . . but I don't think anyone really believed in the torches the way they had before. Not after that low and terribly vital grunting sound, not after the chewed and blood-soaked clothesline. If whatever was out there decided it wanted us, it was going to have us. It, or they.

"How bad will it be tonight?" Mrs. Turman asked. Her voice was calm, but her eyes were sick and scared.

"Hattie, I just don't know."

"You let me keep Billy as much as you can. I'm . . . Davey, I think I'm in mortal terror." She uttered a dry laugh. "Yes, I believe that's what it is. But if I have Billy, I'll be all right. I'll be all right for him."

Her eyes were glistening. I leaned over and patted her shoulder.

"I'm so worried about Alan," she said. "He's dead, Davey. In my heart, I'm sure he's dead."

"No, Hattie. You don't know any such thing."

"But I feel it's true. Don't you feel anything about Stephanie? Don't you at least have a . . . a feeling?"

"No," I said, lying through my teeth.

A strangled sound came from her throat and she clapped a hand to her mouth. Her glasses reflected back the dim, murky light.

"Billy's coming back," I murmured.

He was eating a peach. Hattie Turman patted the floor beside her and said that when he was done she would show him how to make a little man out of the peach pit and some thread. Billy smiled at her wanly, and Mrs. Turman smiled back.

At 8:00 p.m., six new men went on at the loopholes and Ollie came over to where I was sitting. "Where's Billy?"

"With Mrs. Turman, up back," I said. "They're making crafts. They've run through peach-pit men and shopping-bag masks and apple dolls and now Mr. McVey is showing him how to make pipecleaner men."

Ollie took a long drink of beer and said, "Things are moving around out there."

I looked at him sharply. He looked back levelly.

"I'm not drunk," he said. "I've been trying but haven't been able to make it. I wish I could, David."

"What do you mean, things are moving around out there?"

"I can't say for sure. I asked Walter, and he said he had the same feeling, that parts of the mist would go darker for a minute—sometimes just a little smudge, sometimes a big dark place, like a bruise. Then it would fade back to gray. And the stuff is swirling around. Even Arnie Simms said he felt like something was going on out there, and Arnie's almost as blind as a bat."

"What about the others?"

"They're all out-of-staters, strangers to me," Ollie said. "I didn't ask any of them."

"How sure are you that you weren't just seeing things?"

"Sure," he said. He nodded toward Mrs. Carmody, who was sitting by herself at the end of the aisle. None of it had hurt her appetite any; there was a graveyard of chicken bones on her plate. She was drinking either blood or V-8 juice. "I think she was right about one thing," Ollie said. "We'll find out. When it gets dark, we'll find out."

But we didn't have to wait until dark. When it came, Billy saw very little of it, because Mrs. Turman kept him up back. Ollie was still sitting with me when one of the men up front gave out a shriek and staggered back from his post, pinwheeling his arms. It was approaching eight-thirty; outside the pearl-white mist had darkened to the dull slaty color of a November twilight.

Something had landed on the glass outside one of the loopholes.

"Oh my Jesus!" the man who had been watching there screamed. *"Let me out! Let me out of this!"*

He tore around in a rambling circle, his eyes starting from his face, a thin lick of saliva at one corner of his mouth glimmering in the deepening shadows. Then he took off straight up the far aisle past the frozen-food cases.

There were answering cries. Some people ran toward the front to see what had happened. Many others retreated toward the back, not caring and not wanting to see whatever was crawling on the glass out there.

I started down toward the loophole, Ollie by my side. His hand was in the pocket that held Mrs. Dumfries' gun. Now one of the other watchers let out a cry—not so much of fear as disgust.

Ollie and I slipped through one of the check-out lanes. Now I could see what had frightened the guy from his post. I couldn't tell what it was, but I could see it. It looked like one of the minor creatures in a Goya painting—one of his hellacious murals. There was something almost horribly comic about it, too, because it also looked a little like one of those strange creations of vinyl and plastic you can buy for $1.89 to spring on your friends . . . in fact, exactly the sort of thing Norton had accused me of planting in the storage area.

It was maybe two feet long, segmented, the pinkish color of burned flesh that has healed over. Bulbous eyes peered in two different directions at once from the ends of short, limber stalks. It clung to the window on fat sucker-pads. From the opposite end there protruded something that was either a sexual organ or a stinger. And from its back there sprouted oversized, membranous wings, like the wings of a housefly. They were moving very slowly as Ollie and I approached the glass.

At the loophole to the left of us, where the man had made the disgusted cawing sound, three of the things were crawling on the glass. They moved sluggishly across it, leaving sticky snail trails behind them. Their eyes—if that is what they were—joggled on the end of the finger-thick stalks. The biggest was maybe four feet long. At times they crawled right over each other.

"Look at those goddam things," Tom Smalley said in a sickened voice. He was standing at the loophole on our right. I didn't reply. The bugs were all over the loopholes now, which meant they were probably crawling all over the building . . . like maggots on a piece of meat. It wasn't a pleasant image, and I could feel what chicken I had managed to eat now wanting to come up.

Someone was sobbing. Mrs. Carmody was screaming about abominations from within the earth. Someone told her gruffly that she'd shut up if she knew what was good for her. Same old shit.

Ollie took Mrs. Dumfries' gun from his pocket and I grabbed his arm. "Don't be crazy."

He shook free. "I know what I'm doing," he said.

He tapped the barrel of the gun on the window, his face set in a nearly masklike expression of distaste. The speed of the creatures' wings increased until they were only a blur—if you hadn't known, you might have believed they weren't winged creatures at all. Then they simply flew away.

Some of the others saw what Ollie had done and got the idea. They used the mophandles to tap on the windows. The things flew away, but came right back. Apparently they had no more brains than your average housefly, either. The near panic dissolved in a babble of conversation. I heard someone asking someone else what he thought those things would do if they landed on you. That was a question I had no interest in seeing answered.

The tapping on the windows began to die away. Ollie turned toward me and started to say something, but before he could do more than open his mouth, something came out of the fog and snatched one of the crawling things off the glass. I think I screamed. I'm not sure.

It was a flying thing. Beyond that I could not have said for sure. The fog appeared to darken in exactly the way Ollie had described, only the dark smutch didn't fade away; it solidified into something with flapping, leathery wings, an albino-white body, and reddish eyes. It thudded into the glass hard enough to make it shiver. Its beak opened. It scooped the pink thing in and was gone. The whole incident took no more than five seconds. I had a bare final impression of the pink thing wiggling and flapping as it went down the hatch, the way a small fish will wiggle and flap in the beak of a seagull.

Now there was another thud, and yet another. People began screaming again, and there was a stampede toward the back of the store. Then there was a more piercing scream, one of pain, and Ollie said, "Oh my God, that old lady fell down and they just ran over her."

He ran back through the check-out aisle. I turned to follow, and then I saw something that stopped me dead where I was standing.

High up and to my right, one of the lawn-food bags was sliding slowly backward. Tom Smalley was right under it, staring out into the mist through his loophole.

Another of the pink bugs landed on the thick plate glass of the loophole where Ollie and I had been standing. One of the flying things swooped down and grabbed it. The old woman who had been trampled went on screaming in a shrill, cracked voice.

That bag. That sliding bag.

"Smalley!" I shouted. "Look out! Heads up!"

In the general confusion, he never heard me. The bag teetered, then fell. It struck him squarely on the head. He went down hard, catching his jaw on the shelf that ran below the show window.

One of the albino flying things was squirming its way through the jagged hole in the glass. I could hear the soft scraping sound that it made, now that some of the screaming had stopped. Its red eyes glittered in its triangular head, which was slightly cocked to one side. A heavy, hooked beak opened and closed rapaciously. It looked a bit like the paintings of pterodactyls you may have seen in the dinosaur books, more like something out of a lunatic's nightmare.

I grabbed one of the torches and slam-dunked it into a can of charcoal lighter fluid, tipping it over and spilling a pool of the stuff across the floor.

The flying creature paused on top of the lawn-food bags, glaring around, shifting slowly and malignantly from one taloned foot to the other. It was a stupid creature, I am quite sure of that. Twice it tried to spread its wings, which struck the walls and then refolded themselves over its hunched back like the wings of a griffin. The third time it tried, it lost its balance and fell clumsily from its perch, still trying to spread its wings. It landed on Tom Smalley's back. One flex of its claws and Tom's shirt ripped wide open. Blood began to flow.

I was there, less than three feet away. My torch was dripping lighter fluid. I was emotionally pumped up to kill it if I could . . . and then realized I had no matches to light it with. I had used the last one lighting a cigar for Mr. McVey an hour ago.

The place was in pandemonium now. People had seen the thing roosting on Smalley's back, something no one in the world had seen before. It darted its head forward at a questing angle, and tore a chunk of meat from the back of Smalley's neck.

I was getting ready to use the torch as a bludgeon when the cloth-wrapped head of it suddenly blazed alight. Dan Miller was there, holding a Zippo lighter with a Marine emblem on it. His face was as harsh as a rock with horror and fury.

"Kill it," he said hoarsely. "Kill it if you can." Standing beside him was Ollie. He had Mrs. Dumfries' .38 in his hand, but he had no clear shot.

The thing spread its wings and flapped them once—apparently not to fly away but to secure a better hold on its prey—and then its leathery-white, membranous wings enfolded poor Smalley's entire upper body. Then sounds came—mortal tearing sounds that I cannot bear to describe in any detail.

All of this happened in bare seconds. Then I thrust my torch at the thing. There was the sensation of striking something with no more real substance than a box kite. The next moment the entire creature was blazing. It made a screeching sound and its wings spread; its head jerked and its reddish eyes rolled with what I most sincerely hope was great agony. It took off with a sound like linen bedsheets flapping on a clothesline in a stiff spring breeze. It uttered that rusty shrieking sound again.

Heads turned up to follow its flaming, dying course. I think that nothing in the entire business stands in my memory so strongly as that bird-thing from hell blazing a zigzagging course above the aisles of the Federal Supermarket, dropping charred and smoking bits of itself here and there. It finally crashed into the spaghetti sauces, splattering Ragu and Prince and Prima Salsa everywhere like gouts of blood. It was little more than ash and bone. The smell of its burning was high and sickening. And underlying it like a counterpoint was the thin and acrid stench of the mist, eddying in through the broken place in the glass.

For a moment there was utter silence. We were united in the black wonder of that brightly flaming deathflight. Then someone howled. Others screamed. And from somewhere in the back I could hear my son crying.

A hand grabbed me. It was Bud Brown. His eyes were bulging from their sockets. His lips were drawn back from his false teeth in a snarl. "One of those other things," he said, and pointed.

One of the bugs had come in through the hole and it now perched on a lawn-food bag, housefly wings buzzing—you could hear them; it sounded like a cheap department-store electric fan—eyes bulging from their stalks. Its pink and noxiously plump body was aspirating rapidly.

I moved toward it. My torch was guttering but not yet out. But Mrs. Reppler, the fifth-grade teacher, beat me to it. She was maybe fifty-five, maybe sixty, rope-thin. Her body had that tough, dried-out look that always makes me think of beef jerky.

She had a can of Raid in each hand like some crazy gunslinger in an existential comedy. She uttered a snarl of anger that would have done credit to a cavewoman splitting the skull of an enemy. Holding the pressure cans out at the full length of each arm, she pressed the buttons. A thick spray of insect-killer coated the thing. It went into throes of agony, twisting and turning crazily and at last falling from the bags, bouncing off the body of Tom Smalley—who was dead beyond any doubt or question—and finally landing on the floor. Its wings buzzed madly, but they weren't taking it anywhere; they were too heavily coated with Raid. A few moments later the wings slowed, then stopped. It was dead.

You could hear people crying now. And moaning. The old lady who had been trampled was moaning. And you could hear laughter. The laughter of the damned. Mrs. Reppler stood over her kill, her thin chest rising and falling rapidly.

Hatlen and Miller had found one of those dollies that the stockboys use to trundle cases of things around the store, and together they heaved it atop the lawn-food bags, blocking off the wedge-shaped hole in the glass. As a temporary measure, it was a good one.

Amanda Dumfries came forward like a sleepwalker. In one hand she held a plastic floor bucket. In the other she held a whisk broom, still done up in its see-through wrapping. She bent, her eyes still wide and blank, and swept the dead pink thing—bug, slug, whatever it was—into the bucket. You could hear the crackle of the wrapping on the whisk broom as it brushed the floor. She walked over to the OUT door. There were none of the bugs on it. She opened it a little way and threw the bucket out. It landed on its side and rolled back and forth in ever-decreasing arcs. One of the pink things buzzed out of the night, landed on the floor pail, and began to crawl over it.

Amanda burst into tears. I walked over and put an arm around her shoulders.

At one-thirty the following morning I was sitting with my back against the white enamel side of the meat counter in a semidoze. Billy's head was in my lap. He was solidly asleep. Not far away Amanda Dumfries was sleeping with her head pillowed on someone's jacket.

Not long after the flaming death of the bird-thing, Ollie and I had gone back out to the storage area and had gathered up half a dozen of the pads such as the one I'd covered Billy with earlier. Several people were sleeping on these. We had also brought back several heavy crates of oranges and pears, and four of us working together had been able to swing them to the tops of the lawn-food bags in front of the hole in the glass. The bird-creatures would have a tough time shifting one of those crates; they weighed about ninety pounds each.

But the birds and the buglike things the birds ate weren't the only things out there. There was the tentacled thing that had taken Norm. There was the frayed clothesline to think about. There was the unseen thing that had uttered that low, guttural roar to think about. We had heard sounds like it since—sometimes quite distant—but how far was "distant" through the damping effect of the mist? And sometimes they were close enough to shake the building and make it seem as if the ventricles of your heart had suddenly been loaded up with icewater.

Billy started in my lap and moaned. I brushed his hair and he moaned more loudly. Then he seemed to find sleep's less dangerous waters again. My own doze was broken and I was staring wide awake again. Since dark, I had only managed to sleep about ninety minutes, and that had been dream-haunted. In one of the dream fragments it had been the night before again. Billy and Steffy were standing in front of the picture window, looking out at the black and slate-gray waters, out at the silver spinning waterspout that heralded the storm. I tried to get to them, knowing that a strong enough wind could break the window and throw deadly glass darts all the way across the living room. But no matter how I ran, I seemed to get no closer to them. And then a bird rose out of the waterspout, a gigantic scarlet *oiseau de mort* whose prehistoric wingspan darkened the entire lake from west to east. Its beak opened, revealing a maw the size of the Holland Tunnel. And as the bird came to gobble up my wife and son, a low, sinister voice began to whisper over and over again: *The Arrowhead Project . . . the Arrowhead Project . . . the Arrowhead Project . . .*

Not that Billy or I were the only ones sleeping poorly. Others screamed in their sleep, and some went on screaming after they woke up. The beer was disappearing from the cooler at a great rate. Buddy Eagleton had restocked it once from out back with no comment. Mike Hatlen told me the Sominex was gone. Not depleted but totally wiped out. He guessed that some people might have taken six or eight bottles.

"There's some Nytol left," he said. "You want a bottle, David?" I shook my head and thanked him.

And in the last aisle down by Register 5, we had our winos. There were about seven of them, all out-of-staters except for Lou Tattinger, who ran the Pine Tree Car Wash. Lou didn't need any excuse to sniff the cork, as the saying was. The wino brigade was pretty well anesthetized.

Oh yes—there were also six or seven people who had gone crazy.

Crazy isn't the best word, perhaps I just can't think of the proper one. But there were these people who had lapsed into a complete stupor without benefit of beer, wine, or pills. They stared at you with blank and shiny doorknob eyes. The hard cement of reality had come apart in some unimaginable earthquake, and these poor devils had fallen through. In time, some of them might come back. If there was time.

The rest of us had made our own mental compromises, and in some cases I suppose they were fairly odd. Mrs. Reppler, for instance, was convinced the whole thing was a dream—or so she said. And she spoke with some conviction.

I looked over at Amanda. I was developing an uncomfortably strong feeling for her—uncomfortable but not exactly unpleasant. Her eyes were an incredible, brilliant green . . . for a while I had kept an eye on her to see if she was going to take out a pair of contact lenses, but apparently the color was true. I wanted to make love to her. My wife was at home, maybe alive, more probably dead, alone either way, and I loved her; I wanted to get Billy and me back to her more than anything, but I also wanted to screw this lady named Amanda Dumfries. I tried to tell myself it was just the situation we were in, and maybe it was, but that didn't change the wanting.

I dozed in and out, then jerked awake more fully around three.

Amanda had shifted into a sort of fetal position, her knees pulled up toward her chest, hands clasped between her thighs. She seemed to be sleeping deeply. Her sweatshirt had pulled up slightly on one side, showing clean white skin. I looked at it and began to get an extremely useless and uncomfortable erection.

I tried to divert my mind to a new track and got thinking about how I had wanted to paint Brent Norton yesterday. No, nothing as important as a painting, but . . . just sit him on a log with my beer in his hand and sketch his sweaty, tired face and the two wings of his carefully processed hair sticking up untidily in the back. It could have been a good picture. It took me twenty years of living with my father to accept the idea that just being good could be good enough.

You know what talent is? The curse of expectation. As a kid you have to deal with that, beat it somehow. If you can write, you think God put you on earth to blow Shakespeare away. Or if you can paint, maybe you think—I did—that God put you on earth to blow your father away.

It turned out I wasn't as good as he was. I kept trying to be for longer than I should have, maybe. I had a show in New York and it did poorly—the art critics beat me over the head with my father. A year later I was supporting myself and Steff with the commercial stuff. She was pregnant and I sat down and talked to myself about it. The result of that conversation was a belief that serious art was always going to be a hobby for me, no more.

I did Golden Girl Shampoo ads—the one where the girl is standing astride her bike, the one where she's playing Frisbee on the beach, the one where she's standing on the balcony of her apartment with a drink in her hand. I've done short-story illustrations for most of the big slicks, but I broke into that field doing fast illustrations for the stories in the sleazier men's magazines. I've done some movie posters. The money comes in. We keep our heads above water.

I had one final show in Bridgton, just last summer. I showed nine canvases that I had painted in five years, and I sold six of them. The one I absolutely would not sell showed the Federal Market, by some queer coincidence. The perspective was from the far end of the parking lot. In my picture, the parking lot was empty except for a line of Campbell's Beans and Franks cans, each one larger than the last as they marched toward the viewer's eye. The last one appeared to be about eight feet tall. The picture was titled *Beans and False Perspective*. A man from California who was a top exec in some company that makes tennis balls and rackets and who knows what other sports equipment seemed to want that picture very badly, and would not take no for an answer in spite of the NFS card tucked into the bottom left-hand corner of the spare wooden frame. He began at six hundred dollars and worked his way up to four thousand. He said he wanted it for his study. I would not let him have it, and he went away sorely puzzled. Even so, he didn't quite give up; he left his card in case I changed my mind.

I could have used the money—that was the year we put the addition on the house and bought the four-wheel drive—but I just couldn't sell it. I couldn't sell it because I felt it was the best painting I had ever done and I wanted it to look at after someone would ask me, with totally unconscious cruelty, when I was going to do something serious.

Then I happened to show it to Ollie Weeks one day last fall. He asked me if he could photograph it and run it as an ad one week, and that was the end of my own false perspective. Ollie had recognized my painting for what it was, and by doing so, he forced me to recognize it, too. A perfectly good piece of slick commercial art. No more. And, thank God, no less.

I let him do it, and then I called the exec at his home in San Luis Obispo and told him he could have the painting for twenty-five hundred if he still wanted it. He did, and I shipped it UPS to the coast. And since then that voice of disappointed expectation—that cheated child's voice that can never be satisfied with such a mild superlative as good—has fallen pretty much silent. And except for a few rumbles—like the sounds of those unseen creatures somewhere out in the foggy night—it has been pretty much silent ever since. Maybe you can tell me—why should the silencing of that childish, demanding voice seem so much like dying?

Around four o'clock Billy woke up—partially, at least—and looked around with bleary, uncomprehending eyes. "Are we still here?"

"Yeah, honey," I said. "We are."

He started to cry with a weak helplessness that was horrible. Amanda woke up and looked at us.

"Hey, kid," she said, and pulled him gently to her. "Everything is going to look a little better come morning."

"No," Billy said. "No it won't. It won't. It won't."

"Shh," she said. Her eyes met mine over his head. "Shh, it's past your bedtime."

"I want my *mother!*"

"Yeah, you do," Amanda said. "Of course you do."

Billy squirmed around in her lap until he could look at me. Which he did for some time. And then slept again.

"Thanks," I said. "He needed you."

"He doesn't even know me."

"That doesn't change it."

"So what do you think?" she asked. Her green eyes held mine steadily. "What do you really think?"

"Ask me in the morning."

"I'm asking you now."

I opened my mouth to answer and then Ollie Weeks materialized out of the gloom like something from a horror tale. He had a flashlight with one of the ladies' blouses over the lens, and he was pointing it toward the ceiling. It made strange shadows on his haggard face. "David," he whispered.

Amanda looked at him, first startled, then scared again.

"Ollie, what is it?" I asked.

"David," he whispered again. Then: "Come on. Please."

"I don't want to leave Billy. He just went to sleep."

"I'll be with him," Amanda said. "You better go." Then, in a lower voice: "Jesus, this is never going to end."

VIII. What Happened to the Soldiers. With Amanda. A Conversation with Dan Miller.

I went with Ollie. He was headed for the storage area. As we passed the cooler, he grabbed a beer.

"Ollie, what is this?"

"I want you to see it."

He pushed through the double doors. They slipped shut behind us with a little backwash of air. It was cold. I didn't like this place, not after what had happened to Norm. A part of my mind insisted on reminding me that there was still a small scrap of dead tentacle lying around someplace.

Ollie let the blouse drop from the lens of his light. He trained it overhead. At first I had an idea that someone had hung a couple of mannequins from one of the heating pipes below the ceiling. That they had hung them on piano wire or something, a kid's Halloween trick.

Then I noticed the feet, dangling about seven inches off the cement floor. There were two piles of kicked-over cartons. I looked up at the faces and a scream began to rise in my throat because they were not the faces of department-store dummies. Both heads were cocked to the side, as if appreciating some horribly funny joke, a joke that had made them laugh until they turned purple.

Their shadows. Their shadows thrown long on the wall behind them. Their tongues. Their protruding tongues.

They were both wearing uniforms. They were the kids I had noticed earlier and had lost track of along the way. The army brats from—

The scream. I could hear it starting in my throat as a moan, rising like a police siren, and then Ollie gripped my arm just above the elbow. "Don't scream, David. No one knows about this but you and me. And that's how I want to keep it."

Somehow I bit it back.

"Those army kids," I managed.

"From the Arrowhead Project," Ollie said. "Sure." Something cold was thrust into my hand. The beer can. "Drink this. You need it."

I drained the can completely dry.

Ollie said, "I came back to see if we had any extra cartridges for that gas grill Mr. McVey has been using. I saw these guys. The way I figure, they must have gotten the nooses ready and stood on top of those two piles of cartons. They must have tied their hands for each other and then balanced each other while they stepped through the length of rope between their wrists. So . . . so that their hands would be behind them, you know. Then—this is the way I figure—they stuck their heads into the nooses and pulled them tight by jerking their heads to one side. Maybe one of them counted to three and they jumped together. I don't know."

"It couldn't be done," I said through a dry mouth. But their hands were tied behind them, all right. I couldn't seem to take my eyes away from that.

"It could. If they wanted to bad enough, David, they could."

"But why?"

"I think you know why. Not any of the tourists, the summer people—like that guy Miller—but there are people from around here who could make a pretty decent guess."

"The Arrowhead Project?"

Ollie said, "I stand by one of those registers all day long and I hear a lot. All this spring I've been hearing things about that damned Arrowhead thing, none of it good. The black ice on the lakes—"

I thought of Bill Giosti leaning in my window, blowing warm alcohol in my face. Not just atoms, but *different* atoms. Now these bodies hanging from that overhead pipe. The cocked heads. The dangling shoes. The tongues protruding like summer sausages.

I realized with fresh horror that new doors of perception were opening up inside. New? Not so. Old doors of perception. The perception of a child who has not yet learned to protect itself by developing the tunnel vision that keeps out ninety percent of the universe. Children see everything their eyes happen upon, hear everything in their ears' range. But if life is the rise of consciousness (as a crewel-work sampler my wife made in high school proclaims), then it is also the reduction of input.

Terror is the widening of perspective and perception. The horror was in knowing I was swimming down to a place most of us leave when we get out of diapers and into training pants. I could see it on Ollie's face, too. When rationality begins to break down, the circuits of the human brain can overload. Axons grow bright and feverish. Hallucinations turn real: the quicksilver puddle at the point where perspective makes parallel lines seem to intersect is really there; the dead walk and talk; and a rose begins to sing.

"I've heard stuff from maybe two dozen people," Ollie said. "Justine Robards. Nick Tochai. Ben Michaelson. You can't keep secrets in small towns. Things get out. Sometimes it's like a spring—it just bubbles up out of the earth and no one has an idea where it came from. You overhear something at the library and pass it on, or at the marina in Harrison, Christ knows where else, or why. But all spring and summer I've been hearing Arrowhead Project, Arrowhead Project."

"But these two," I said. "Christ, Ollie, they're just kids."

"There were kids in Nam who used to take ears. I was there. I saw it."

"But . . . what would drive them to do this?"

"I don't know. Maybe they knew something. Maybe they only suspected. They must have known people in here would start asking them questions eventually. If there is an eventually."

"If you're right," I said, "it must be something really bad."

"That storm," Ollie said in his soft, level voice. "Maybe it knocked something loose up there. Maybe there was an accident. They could have been fooling around with anything. Some people claim they were messing with high-intensity lasers and masers. Sometimes I hear fusion power. And suppose . . . suppose they ripped a hole straight through into another dimension?"

"That's hogwash," I said.

"Are they?" Ollie asked, and pointed at the bodies.

"No. The question now is: What do we do?"

"I think we ought to cut them down and hide them," he said

promptly. "Put them under a pile of stuff people won't want—dog food, dish detergent, stuff like that. If this gets out, it will only make things worse. That's why I came to you, David. I felt you were the only one I could really trust."

I muttered, "It's like the Nazi war criminals killing themselves in their cells after the war was lost."

"Yeah. I had that same thought."

We fell silent, and suddenly those soft shuffling noises began outside the steel loading door again—the sound of the tentacles feeling softly across it. We drew together. My flesh was crawling.

"Okay," I said.

"We'll make it as quick as we can," Ollie said. His sapphire ring glowed mutely as he moved his flashlight. "I want to get out of here fast."

I looked up at the ropes. They had used the same sort of clothesline the man in the golf cap had allowed me to tie around his waist. The nooses had sunk into the puffed flesh of their necks, and I wondered again what it could have been to make both of them go through with it. I knew what Ollie meant by saying that if the news of the double suicide got out, it would make things worse. For me it already had—and I wouldn't have believed that possible.

There was a snicking sound. Ollie had opened his knife, a good heavy job made for slitting open cartons. And, of course, cutting rope.

"You or me?" he asked.

I swallowed. "One each."

We did it.

When I got back, Amanda was gone and Mrs. Turman was with Billy. They were both sleeping. I walked down one of the aisles and a voice said: "Mr. Drayton. David."

It was Amanda, standing by the stairs to the manager's office, her eyes like emeralds.

"What was it?"

"Nothing," I said.

She came over to me. I could smell faint perfume. And oh how I wanted her. "You liar," she said.

"It was nothing. A false alarm."

"If that's how you want it." She took my hand. "I've just been up to the office. It's empty and there's a lock on the door." Her face was perfectly calm, but her eyes were lambent, almost feral, and a pulse beat steadily in her throat.

"I don't–"

"I saw the way you looked at me," she said. "If we need to talk about it, it's no good. The Turman woman is with your son."

"Yes." It came to me that this was a way–maybe not the best one, but a way, nevertheless–to take the curse off what Ollie and I had just done. Maybe not the best way, just the only way.

We went up the narrow flight of stairs and into the office. It was empty, as she had said. And there was a lock on the door. I turned it. In the darkness she was nothing but a shape. I put my arms out, touched her, and pulled her to me. She was trembling. We went down on the floor, first kneeling, kissing, and I cupped one firm breast and could feel the quick thudding of her heart through her sweatshirt. I thought of Steffy telling Billy not to touch the live wires. I thought of the bruise that had been on her hip when she took off the brown dress on our wedding night. I thought of the first time I had seen her, biking across the mall of the University of Maine at Orono, me bound for one of Vincent Hartgen's classes with my portfolio under my arm. And my erection was enormous.

We lay down then, and she said, "Love me, David. Make me warm." When she came, she dug into my back with her nails and called me by a name that wasn't mine. I didn't mind. It made us about even.

When we came down, some sort of creeping dawn had begun. The blackness outside the loopholes went reluctantly to dull gray, then to chrome, then to the bright, featureless, and unsparkling white of a drive-in movie screen. Mike Hatlen was asleep in a folding chair he had scrounged somewhere. Dan Miller sat on the floor a little distance away, eating a Hostess donut. The kind that's powdered with white sugar.

"Sit down, Mr. Drayton," he invited.

I looked around for Amanda, but she was already halfway up the aisle. She didn't look back. Our act of love in the dark already seemed something out of a fantasy, impossible to believe even in this weird daylight. I sat down.

"Have a donut." He held the box out.

I shook my head. "All that white sugar is death. Worse than cigarettes."

That made him laugh a little bit. "In that case, have two."

I was surprised to find a little laughter left inside me–he had surprised it out, and I liked him for it. I did take two of his donuts. They

tasted pretty good. I chased them with a cigarette, although it is not normally my habit to smoke in the mornings.

"I ought to get back to my kid," I said. "He'll be waking up."

Miller nodded. "Those pink bugs," he said. "They're all gone. So are the birds. Hank Vannerman said the last one hit the windows around four. Apparently the . . . the wildlife . . . is a lot more active when it's dark."

"You don't want to tell Brent Norton that," I said. "Or Norm."

He nodded again and didn't say anything for a long time. Then he lit a cigarette of his own and looked at me. "We can't stay here, Drayton," he said.

"There's food. Plenty to drink."

"The supplies don't have anything to do with it, and you know it. What do we do if one of the big beasties out there decides to break in instead of just going bump in the night? Do we try to drive it off with broom handles and charcoal lighter fluid?"

Of course he was right. Perhaps the mist was protecting us in a way. Hiding us. But maybe it wouldn't hide us for long, and there was more to it than that. We had been in the Federal for eighteen hours, more or less, and I could feel a kind of lethargy spreading over me, not much different from the lethargy I've felt on one or two occasions when I've tried to swim too far. There was an urge to play it safe, to just stay put, to take care of Billy (*and maybe to bang Amanda Dumfries in the middle of the night*, a voice murmured), to see if the mist wouldn't just lift, leaving everything as it had been.

I could see it on other faces as well, and it suddenly occurred to me that there were people now in the Federal who probably wouldn't leave under any circumstance. The very thought of going out the door after all that had happened would freeze them.

Miller had been watching these thoughts cross my face, maybe. He said, "There were about eighty people in here when that damn fog came. From that number you subtract the bag-boy, Norton, and the four people that went out with him, and that man Smalley. That leaves seventy-three."

And subtracting the two soldiers, now resting under a stack of Purina Puppy Chow bags, it made seventy-one.

"Then you subtract the people who have just opted out," he went on. "There are ten or twelve of those. Say ten. That leaves about sixty-three. *But—*" He raised one sugar-powdered finger. "Of those sixty-three, we've got twenty or so that just won't leave. You'd have to drag them out kicking and screaming."

"Which all goes to prove what?"

"That we've got to get out, that's all. And I'm going. Around noon, I think. I'm planning to take as many people as will come. I'd like you and your boy to come along."

"After what happened to Norton?"

"Norton went like a lamb to the slaughter. That doesn't mean I have to, or the people who come with me."

"How can you prevent it? We have exactly one gun."

"And lucky to have that. But if we could make it across the intersection, maybe we could get down to the Sportsman's Exchange on Main Street. They've got more guns there than you could shake a stick at."

"That's one if and one maybe too many."

"Drayton," he said, "it's an iffy situation."

That rolled very smoothly off his tongue, but he didn't have a little boy to watch out for.

"Look, let it pass for now, okay? I didn't get much sleep last night, but I got a chance to think over a few things. Want to hear them?"

"Sure."

He stood up and stretched. "Take a walk over to the window with me."

We went through the check-out lane nearest the bread racks and stood at one of the loopholes. The man who was keeping watch there said, "The bugs are gone."

Miller slapped him on the back. "Go get yourself a coffee-and, fella. I'll keep an eye out."

"Okay. Thanks."

He walked away, and Miller and I stepped up to his loophole. "So tell me what you see out there," he said.

I looked. The litter barrel had been knocked over in the night, probably by one of the swooping bird-things, spilling a trash of papers, cans, and paper shake cups from the Dairy Queen down the road all over the hottop. Beyond that I could see the rank of cars closest to the market fading into whiteness. That was all I could see, and I told him so.

"That blue Chevy pickup is mine," he said. He pointed and I could see just a hint of blue in the mist. "But if you think back to when you pulled in yesterday, you'll remember that the parking lot was pretty jammed, right?"

I glanced back at my Scout and remembered I had only gotten the space close to the market because someone else had been pulling out. I nodded.

Miller said, "Now couple something else with that fact, Drayton. Norton and his four . . . what did you call them?"

"Flat-Earthers."

"Yeah, that's good. Just what they were. They go out, right? Almost the full length of that clothesline. Then we heard those roaring noises, like there was a goddam herd of rogue elephants out there. Right?"

"It didn't sound like elephants," I said. "It sounded like—" *Like something from the primordial ooze* was the phrase that came to mind, but I didn't want to say that to Miller, not after he had clapped that guy on the back and told him to go get a coffee-and like the coach jerking a player from the big game. I might have said it to Ollie, but not to Miller. "I don't know what it sounded like," I finished lamely.

"But it sounded *big*."

"Yeah." It had sounded pretty goddam big.

"So how come we didn't hear cars getting bashed around? Screeching metal? Breaking glass?"

"Well, because—" I stopped. He had me. "I don't know."

Miller said, "No way they were out of the parking lot when whatever-it-was hit them. I'll tell you what I think. I think we didn't hear any cars getting around because a lot of them might be gone. Just . . . gone. Fallen into the earth, vaporized, you name it. Remember that thump after the fog came? Like an earthquake. Strong enough to splinter these beams and twist them out of shape and knock stuff off the shelves. And the town whistle stopped at the same time."

I was trying to visualize half the parking lot gone. Trying to visualize walking out there and just coming to a brand-new drop in the land where the hottop with its neat yellow-lined parking slots left off. A drop, a slope . . . or maybe an out-and-out precipice falling away into the featureless white mist. . . .

After a couple of seconds I said, "If you're right, how far do you think you're going to get in your pickup?"

"I wasn't thinking of my truck. I was thinking of your four-wheel drive."

That was something to chew over, but not now. "What else is on your mind?"

Miller was eager to go on. "The pharmacy next door, that's on my mind. What about that?"

I opened my mouth to say I didn't have the slightest idea what he was talking about, and then shut it with a snap. The Brighton Pharmacy had been doing business when we drove in yesterday. Not the laundromat, but the drugstore had been wide open, the doors chocked with rubber doorstops to let in a little cool air—the power outage had killed their air conditioning, of course. The door to the pharmacy could be no more than twenty feet from the door of the Federal Market. So why—

"Why haven't any of those people turned up over here?" Miller asked for me. "It's been eighteen hours. Aren't they hungry? They're sure not over there eating Dristan and Stay-Free Mini-Pads."

"There's food," I said. "They're always selling food items on special. Sometimes it's animal crackers, sometimes it's those toaster pastries, all sorts of things. Plus the candy rack."

"I just don't believe they'd stick with stuff like that when there's all kinds of stuff over here."

"What are you getting at?"

"What I'm getting at is that I want to get out but I don't want to be dinner for some refugee from a grade-B horror picture. Four or five of us could go next door and check out the situation in the drugstore. As sort of a trial balloon."

"That's everything?"

"No, there's one other thing."

"What's that?"

"Her," Miller said simply, and jerked his thumb toward one of the middle aisles. "That crazy cunt. That witch."

It was Mrs. Carmody he had jerked his thumb at. She was no longer alone; two women had joined her. From their bright clothes I guessed they were probably tourists or summer people, ladies who had maybe left their families to "just run into town and get a few things" and were now eaten up with worry over their husbands and kids. Ladies eager to grasp at almost any straw. Maybe even the black comfort of a Mrs. Carmody.

Her pantsuit shone out with its same baleful resplendence. She was talking, gesturing, her face hard and grim. The two ladies in their bright clothes (but not as bright as Mrs. Carmody's pantsuit, no, and her gigantic satchel of a purse was still tucked firmly over one doughy arm) were listening raptly.

"She's another reason I want to get out, Drayton. By tonight she'll have six people sitting with her. If those pink bugs and the birds come back tonight, she'll have a whole congregation sitting with her by tomorrow morning. Then we can start worrying about who she'll tell them to sacrifice to make it all better. Maybe me, or you, or that guy Hatlen. Maybe your kid."

"That's idiocy," I said. But was it? The cold chill crawling up my back said not necessarily. Mrs. Carmody's mouth moved and moved. The eyes of the tourist ladies were fixed on her wrinkled lips. Was it idiocy? I thought of the dusty stuffed animals drinking at their looking-glass stream. Mrs. Carmody had power. Even Steff, normally hard-headed and straight-from-the-shoulder, invoked the old lady's name with unease.

That crazy cunt, Miller had called her. *That witch.*

"The people in this market are going through a section-eight experience for sure," Miller said. He gestured at the red-painted beams framing the show-window segments . . . twisted and splintered and buckled out of shape. "Their minds probably feel like those beams look. Mine sure as shit does. I spent half of last night thinking I must have flipped out of my gourd, that I was probably in a straitjacket in Danvers, raving my head off about bugs and dinosaur birds and tentacles and that it would all go away just as soon as the nice orderly came along and shot a wad of Thorazine into my arm." His small face was strained and white. He looked at Mrs. Carmody and then back at me. "I tell you it might happen. As people get flakier, she's going to look better and better to some of them. And I don't want to be around if that happens."

Mrs. Carmody's lips, moving and moving. Her tongue dancing around her old lady's snaggle teeth. She did look like a witch. Put her in a pointy black hat and she would be perfect. What was she saying to her two captured birds in their bright summer plumage?

Arrowhead Project? Black Spring? Abominations from the cellars of the earth? Human sacrifice?

Bullshit.

All the same—

"So what do you say?"

"I'll go this far," I answered him. "We'll try going over to the drug. You, me, Ollie if he wants to go, one or two others. Then we'll talk it over again." Even that gave me the feeling of walking out over an impossible drop on a narrow beam. I wasn't going to help Billy by killing myself. On the other hand, I wasn't going to help him by just sitting on my ass, either. Twenty feet to the drugstore. That wasn't so bad.

"When?" he asked.

"Give me an hour."

"Sure," he said.

IX. The Expedition to the Pharmacy.

I told Mrs. Turman, and I told Amanda, and then I told Billy. He seemed better this morning; he had eaten two donuts and a bowl of Special K for breakfast. Afterward I raced him up and down two of the aisles and even got him giggling a little. Kids are so adaptable that they can scare the living shit right out of you. He was too pale, the flesh under his eyes was still puffed from the tears he had cried in the night, and his face had a horribly *used* look. In a way it had become like an old man's face, as if too much emotional voltage had been running behind it for too long. But he was still alive and still able to laugh . . . at least until he remembered where he was and what was happening.

After the windsprints we sat down with Amanda and Hattie Turman and drank Gatorade from paper cups and I told him I was going over to the drugstore with a few other people.

"I don't want you to," he said immediately, his face clouding.

"It'll be all right, Big Bill. I'll bring you a *Spiderman* comic book."

"I want you to stay *here*." Now his face was not just cloudy; it was thundery. I took his hand. He pulled it away. I took it again.

"Billy, we have to get out of here sooner or later. You see that, don't you?"

"When the fog goes away . . ." But he spoke with no conviction at all. He drank his Gatorade slowly and without relish.

"Billy, it's been almost one whole day now."

"I want Mommy."

"Well, maybe this is the first step on the way to getting back to her."

Mrs. Turman said, "Don't build the boy's hopes up, David."

"What the hell," I snapped at her, "the kid's got to hope for something."

She dropped her eyes. "Yes. I suppose he does."

Billy took no notice of this. "Daddy . . . Daddy, there are things out there. *Things*."

"Yes, we know that. But a lot of them—not all, but a lot—don't seem to come out until it's nighttime."

"They'll wait," he said. His eyes were huge, centered on mine. "They'll wait in the fog . . . and when you can't get back inside, they'll come to eat you up. Like in the fairy stories." He hugged me with fierce, panicky tightness. "Daddy, please don't go."

I pried his arms loose as gently as I could and told him that I had to. "But I'll be back, Billy."

"All right," he said huskily, but he wouldn't look at me anymore. He didn't believe I would be back. It was on his face, which was no longer thundery but woeful and grieving. I wondered again if I could be doing the right thing, putting myself at risk. Then I happened to glance down the middle aisle and saw Mrs. Carmody there. She had gained a third listener, a man with a grizzled cheek and a mean and rolling bloodshot eye. His haggard brow and shaking hands almost screamed the word hangover. It was none other than your friend and his, Myron LaFleur. The fellow who had felt no compunction at all about sending a boy out to do a man's job.

That crazy cunt. That witch.

I kissed Billy and hugged him hard. Then I walked down to the front of the store—but not down the housewares aisle. I didn't want to fall under her eye.

Three-quarters of the way down, Amanda caught up with me. "Do you really have to do this?" she asked.

"Yes, I think so."

"Forgive me if I say it sounds like so much macho bullshit to me." There were spots of color high on her cheeks and her eyes were greener than ever. She was highly—no, royally—pissed.

I took her arm and recapped my discussion with Dan Miller. The riddle of the cars and the fact that no one from the pharmacy had joined us didn't move her much. The business about Mrs. Carmody did.

"He could be right," she said.

"Do you really believe that?"

"I don't know. There's a poisonous feel to that woman. And if people are frightened badly enough for long enough, they'll turn to anyone that promises a solution."

"But human sacrifice, Amanda?"

"The Aztecs were into it," she said evenly. "Listen, David. You come back. If anything happens . . . *anything* . . . you come back. Cut and run if you have to. Not for me, what happened last night was nice, but that was last night. Come back for your boy."

"Yes. I will."

"I wonder," she said, and now she looked like Billy, haggard and old. It occurred to me that most of us looked that way. But not Mrs. Carmody. Mrs. Carmody looked younger somehow, and more vital. As if she had come into her own. As if . . . as if she were thriving on it.

———

We didn't get going until 9:30 a.m. Seven of us went: Ollie, Dan Miller, Mike Hatlen, Myron LaFleur's erstwhile buddy Jim (also hung-over, but seemingly determined to find some way to atone), Buddy Eagleton, myself. The seventh was Hilda Reppler. Miller and Hatlen tried halfheartedly to talk her out of coming. She would have none of it. I didn't even try. I suspected she might be more competent than any of us, except maybe for Ollie. She was carrying a small canvas shopping basket, and it was loaded with an arsenal of Raid and Black Flag spraycans, all of them uncapped and ready for action. In her free hand she held a Spaulding Jimmy Connors tennis racket from a display of sporting goods in Aisle 2.

"What you gonna do with that, Mrs. Reppler?" Jim asked.

"I don't know," she said. She had a low, raspy, competent voice. "But it feels right in my hand." She looked him over closely, and her eye was cold. "Jim Grondin, isn't it? Didn't I have you in school?"

Jim's lips stretched in an uneasy egg-suck grin. "Yes'm. Me and my sister Pauline."

"Too much to drink last night?"

Jim, who towered over her and probably outweighed her by one hundred pounds, blushed to the roots of his American Legion crewcut. "Aw, no—"

She turned away curtly, cutting him off. "I think we're ready," she said.

All of us had something, although you would have called it an odd assortment of weapons. Ollie had Amanda's gun. Buddy Eagleton had a steel pinchbar from out back somewhere. I had a broomhandle.

"Okay," Dan Miller said, raising his voice a bit. "You folks want to listen up for a minute?"

A dozen people had drifted down toward the OUT door to see what was going on. They were loosely knotted, and to their right stood Mrs. Carmody and her new friends.

"We're going over to the drugstore to see what the situation is there. Hopefully, we'll be able to bring something back to aid Mrs. Clapham." She was the lady who had been trampled yesterday, when the bugs came. One of her legs had been broken and she was in a great deal of pain.

Miller looked us over. "We're not going to take any chances," he said. "At the first sign of anything threatening, we're going to pop back into the market—"

"And bring all the fiends of hell down on our heads!" Mrs. Carmody cried.

"She's right!" one of the summer ladies seconded. "You'll make them notice us! You'll make them come! Why can't you just leave well enough alone?"

There was a murmur of agreement from some of the people who had gathered to watch us go.

I said, "Lady, is this what you call well enough?"

She dropped her eyes, confused.

Mrs. Carmody marched a step forward. Her eyes were blazing. "You'll die out there, David Drayton! Do you want to make your son an orphan?" She raised her eyes and raked all of us with them. Buddy Eagleton dropped his eyes and simultaneously raised the pinchbar, as if to ward her off.

"All of you will die out there! Haven't you realized that the end of the world has come? The Fiend has been let loose! Star Worm wood blazes and each one of you that steps out that door will be torn apart! And they'll come for those of us who are left, just as this good woman said! Are you people going to let that happen?" She was appealing to the onlookers now, and a little mutter ran through them. "After what happened to the unbelievers yesterday? It's death! *It's death! It's—"*

A can of peas flew across two of the check-out lanes suddenly and struck Mrs. Carmody on the right breast. She staggered backward with a startled squawk.

Amanda stood forward. "Shut up," she said. "Shut up, you miserable buzzard."

"She serves the Foul One!" Mrs. Carmody screamed. A jittery smile hung on her face. "Who did you sleep with last night, missus? Who did you lie down with last night? Mother Carmody sees, oh yes, Mother Carmody sees what others miss!"

But the moment's spell she had created was broken, and Amanda's eyes never wavered.

"Are we going or are we going to stand here all day?" Mrs. Reppler asked.

And we went. God help us, we went.

Dan Miller was in the lead. Ollie came second. I was last, with Mrs. Reppler in front of me. I was as scared as I've ever been, I think, and the hand wrapped around my broomhandle was sweaty-slick.

There was that thin, acrid, and unnatural smell of the mist. By the time I got out the door, Miller and Ollie had already faded into it, and Hatlen, who was third, was nearly out of sight.

Only twenty feet, I kept telling myself. *Only twenty feet.*

Mrs. Reppler walked slowly and firmly ahead of me, her tennis racket swinging lightly from her right hand. To our left was a red cinderblock wall. To our right the first rank of cars, looming out of the mist like ghost-ships. Another trashbarrel materialized out of the whiteness, and beyond that was a bench where people sometimes sat to wait their turn at the pay phone. *Only twenty feet, Miller's probably there by now, twenty feet is only ten or twelve paces, so—*

"Oh my God!" Miller screamed. "Oh dear sweet God, look at this!"

Miller had gotten there, all right.

Buddy Eagleton was ahead of Mrs. Reppler and he turned to run, his eyes wide and starey. She batted him lightly in the chest with her tennis racket. "Where do you think *you're* going?" she asked in her tough, slightly raspy voice, and that was all the panic there was.

The rest of us drew up to Miller. I took one glance back over my shoulder and saw that the Federal had been swallowed by the mist. The red cinderblock wall faded to a thin wash pink and then disappeared utterly, probably five feet on the Bridgton Pharmacy side of the OUT door. I felt more isolated, more simply alone, than ever in my life. It was as if I had lost the womb.

The pharmacy had been the scene of a slaughter.

Miller and I, of course, were very close to it—almost on top of it. All the things in the mist operated primarily by sense of smell. It stands to reason. Sight would have been almost completely useless to them. Hearing a little better, but as I've said, the mist had a way of screwing up the acoustics, making things that were close sound distant, and—sometimes—things that were far away sound close. The things in the mist followed their truest sense. They followed their noses.

Those of us in the market had been saved by the power outage as much as by anything else. The electric-eye doors wouldn't operate. In a sense, the market had been sealed up when the mist came. But the pharmacy doors . . . they had been chocked open. The power failure had killed their air conditioning and they had opened the doors to let in the breeze. Only something else had come in as well.

A man in a maroon T-shirt lay facedown in the doorway. Or at first I thought his T-shirt was maroon; then I saw a few white patches at the bottom and understood that once it had been all white. The maroon was dried blood. And there was something else wrong with him. I puzzled it over in my mind. Even when Buddy Eagleton turned around and was noisily sick, it didn't come immediately. I guess when something that—that *final* happens to someone, your mind rejects it at first . . . unless maybe you're in a war.

His head was gone, that's what it was. His legs were splayed out inside the pharmacy doors, and his head should have been hanging over the low step. But his head just wasn't.

Jim Grondin had had enough. He turned away, his hands over his mouth, his bloodshot eyes gazing madly into mine. Then he stumbled-staggered back toward the market.

The others took no notice. Miller had stepped inside. Mike Hatlen followed. Mrs. Reppler stationed herself at one side of the double doors with her tennis racket. Ollie stood on the other side with Amanda's gun drawn and pointing at the pavement.

He said quietly, "I seem to be running out of hope, David."

Buddy Eagleton was leaning weakly against the pay-phone stall like someone who has just gotten bad news from home. His broad shoulders shook with the force of his sobs.

"Don't count us out yet," I said to Ollie. I stepped up to the door. I didn't want to go inside, but I had promised my son a comic book.

The Bridgton Pharmacy was a crazy shambles. Paperbacks and magazines were everywhere. There was a *Spiderman* comic and an *Incredible Hulk* almost at my feet, and without thinking, I picked them up and jammed them into my back pocket for Billy. Bottles and boxes lay in the aisles. A hand hung over one of the racks.

Unreality washed over me. The wreckage . . . the *carnage* . . . that was bad enough. But the place also looked like it had been the scene of some crazy party. It was hung and festooned with what I at first took to be streamers. But they weren't broad and flat; they were more like very thick strings or very small cables. It struck me that they were almost the same bright white as the mist itself, and a cold chill sketched its way up my back like frost. Not crepe. What? Magazines and books hung dangling in the air from some of them.

Mike Hatlen was prodding a strange black thing with one foot. It was long and bristly. "What the fuck is this?" he asked no one in particular.

And suddenly I knew. I knew what had killed all those unlucky enough to be in the pharmacy when the mist came. The people who had been unlucky enough to get smelled out. *Out*—

"Out," I said. My throat was completely dry, and the word came out like a lint-covered bullet. "Get out of here."

Ollie looked at me. "David . . . ?"

"They're spiderwebs," I said. And then two screams came out of the mist. The first of fear, maybe. The second of pain. It was Jim. If there were dues to be paid, he was paying them.

"Get out!" I shouted at Mike and Dan Miller.

Then something looped out of the mist. It was impossible to see it against that white background, but I could hear it. It sounded like a bullwhip that had been halfheartedly flicked. And I could see it when it twisted around the thigh of Buddy Eagleton's jeans.

He screamed and grabbed for the first thing handy, which happened to be the telephone. The handset flew the length of its cord and then swung back and forth. *"Oh Jesus that HURTS!"* Buddy screamed.

Ollie grabbed for him, and I saw what was happening. At the same instant I understood why the head of the man in the doorway was missing. The thin white cable that had twisted around Buddy's leg like a silk rope *was sinking into his flesh.* That leg of his jeans had been neatly cut off and was sliding down his leg. A neat, circular incision in his flesh was brimming blood as the cable went deeper.

Ollie pulled him hard. There was a thin snapping sound and Buddy was free. His lips had gone blue with shock.

Mike and Dan were coming, but too slowly. Then Dan ran into several of the hanging threads and got stuck, exactly like a bug on flypaper. He freed himself with a tremendous jerk, leaving a flap of his shirt hanging from the webbing.

Suddenly the air was full of those languorous bullwhip cracks, and the thin white cables were drifting down all around us. They were coated with the same corrosive substance. I dodged two of them, more by luck than by skill. One landed at my feet and I could hear a faint hiss of bubbling hottop. Another floated out of the air and Mrs. Reppler calmly swung her tennis racket at it. The thread stuck fast, and I heard a high-pitched *twing! twing! twing!* as the corrosive ate through the racket's strings and snapped them. It sounded like someone rapidly plucking the strings of a violin. A moment later a thread wrapped around the upper handle of the racket and it was jerked into the mist.

"Get back!" Ollie screamed.

We got moving. Ollie had an arm around Buddy. Dan Miller and Mike Hatlen were on each side of Mrs. Reppler. The white strands of web continued to drift out of the fog, impossible to see unless your eye could pick them out against the red cinderblock background.

One of them wrapped around Mike Hatlen's left arm. Another whipped around his neck in a series of quick winding-up snaps. His jugular went in a jetting, pumping explosion and he was dragged away, head lolling. One of his Bass loafers fell off and lay there on its side.

Buddy suddenly slumped forward, almost dragging Ollie to his knees. "He's passed out, David. Help me."

I grabbed Buddy around the waist and we pulled him along in a clumsy, stumbling fashion. Even in unconsciousness, Buddy kept his grip on his steel pinchbar. The leg that the strand of web had wrapped around hung away from his body at a terrible angle.

Mrs. Reppler had turned around. "'Ware!" she screamed in her rusty voice. "'Ware behind you!"

As I started to turn, one of the web-strands floated down on top of Dan Miller's head. His hands beat at it, tore at it.

One of the spiders had come out of the mist from behind us. It was the size of a big dog. It was black with yellow piping. *Racing stripes,* I thought crazily. Its eyes were reddish-purple, like pomegranates. It strutted busily toward us on what might have been as many as twelve or fourteen many-jointed legs—it was no ordinary earthly spider blown up to horror-movie size; it was something totally different, perhaps not really a spider at all. Seeing it, Mike Hatlen would have understood what that bristly black thing he had been prodding at in the pharmacy really was.

It closed in on us, spinning its webbing from an oval-shaped orifice on its upper belly. The strands floated out toward us in what was nearly a fan shape. Looking at this nightmare, so like the death-black spiders brooding over their dead flies and bugs in the shadows of our boathouse, I felt my mind trying to tear completely loose from its moorings. I believe now that it was only the thought of Billy that allowed me to keep any semblance of sanity. I was making some sound. Laughing. Crying. Screaming. I don't know.

But Ollie Weeks was like a rock. He raised Amanda's pistol as calmly as a man on a target range and emptied it in spaced shots into the creature at point-blank range. Whatever hell it came from, it wasn't invulnerable. A black ichor splattered out from its body and it made a terrible mewling sound, so low it was more felt than heard, like a bass note from a synthesizer. Then it scuttered back into the mist and was gone. It might have been a phantasm from a horrible drug-dream . . . except for the puddles of sticky black stuff it had left behind.

There was a clang as Buddy finally dropped his steel pinchbar.

"He's dead," Ollie said. "Let him go, David. The fucking thing got his femoral artery, he's dead. Let's get the Christ out of here." His face was once more running with sweat and his eyes bulged from his big round face. One of the web-strands floated easily down on the back of his hand and Ollie swung his arm, snapping it. The strand left a bloody weal.

Mrs. Reppler screamed "'Ware!" again, and we turned toward her. Another of them had come out of the mist and had wrapped its legs around Dan Miller in a mad lover's embrace. He was striking at it with his fists. As I bent and picked up Buddy's pinchbar, the spider began to wrap Dan in its deadly thread, and his struggles became a grisly, jittering death dance.

Mrs. Reppler walked toward the spider with a can of Black Flag insect repellent held outstretched in one hand. The spider's legs reached for her. She depressed the button and a cloud of the stuff jetted into one of its sparkling, jewel-like eyes. That low-pitched mewling sound came again. The spider seemed to shudder all over and then it began to lurch backward, hairy legs scratching at the pavement. It dragged Dan's body, bumping and rolling, behind it. Mrs. Reppler threw the can of bug spray at it. It bounced off the spider's body and clattered to the hottop. The spider struck the side of a small sports car hard enough to make it rock on its springs, and then it was gone.

I got to Mrs. Reppler, who was swaying on her feet and dead pale. I put an arm around her. "Thank you, young man," she said. "I feel a bit faint."

"That's okay," I said hoarsely.

"I would have saved him if I could."

"Yes. Of course you would have."

Ollie joined us. We ran for the market doors, the threads falling all around us. One lit on Mrs. Reppler's marketing basket and sank into the canvas side. She tussled grimly for what was hers, dragging back on the strap with both hands, but she lost it. It went bumping off into the mist, end over end.

As we reached the IN door, a smaller spider, no bigger than a cocker spaniel puppy, raced out of the fog along the side of the building. It was producing no webbing; perhaps it wasn't mature enough to do so.

As Ollie leaned one beefy shoulder against the door so Mrs. Reppler could go through, I heaved the steel bar at the thing like a javelin and impaled it. It writhed madly, legs scratching at the air, and its red eyes seemed to find mine, and mark me. . . .

"David!" Ollie was still holding the door.

I ran in. He followed me.

Pallid, frightened faces stared at us. Seven of us had come out. Three of us had come back. Ollie leaned against the heavy glass door, barrel chest heaving. He began to reload Amanda's gun. His white assistant manager's shirt was plastered to his body, and large gray sweat-stains had crept out from under his arms.

"What?" someone asked in a low, hoarse voice.

"Spiders," Mrs. Reppler answered grimly. "The dirty bastards snatched my market basket."

Then Billy hurled his way into my arms, crying. I held on to him. Tight.

X. The Spell of Mrs. Carmody. The Second Night in the Market. The Final Confrontation.

It was my turn to sleep, and for four hours I remember nothing at all. Amanda told me I talked a lot, and screamed once or twice, but I remember no dreams. When I woke up it was afternoon. I was terribly thirsty. Some of the milk had gone over, but some of it was still okay. I drank a quart.

Amanda came over to where Billy, Mrs. Turman, and I were. The old man who had offered to make a try for the shotgun in the trunk of his car was with her—Cornell, I remembered. Ambrose Cornell.

"How are you, son?" he asked.

"All right." But I was still thirsty and my head ached. Most of all, I was scared. I slipped an arm around Billy and looked from Cornell to Amanda. "What's up?"

Amanda said, "Mr. Cornell is worried about that Mrs. Carmody. So am I."

"Billy, why don't you take a walk over here with me?" Hattie asked.

"I don't want to," Billy said.

"Go on, Big Bill," I told him, and he went—reluctantly.

"Now what about Mrs. Carmody?" I asked.

"She's stirrin' things up," Cornell said. He looked at me with an old man's grimness. "I think we got to put a stop to it. Quick."

Amanda said, "There are almost a dozen people with her now. It's like some crazy kind of a church service."

I remembered talking with a writer friend who lived in Otisfield and supported his wife and two kids by raising chickens and turning out one paperback original a year—spy stories. We had gotten talking about the bulge in popularity of books concerning themselves with the supernatural. Gault pointed out that in the forties *Weird Tales* had only been able to pay a pittance, and that in the fifties it went broke. When the machines fail, he had said (while his wife candled eggs and roosters crowed querulously outside), when the technologies fail, when the conventional religious systems fail, people have got to have something. Even a zombie lurching through the night can seem pretty cheerful compared to the existential comedy/horror of the ozone layer dissolving under the combined assault of a million fluorocarbon spray cans of deodorant.

We had been trapped here for twenty-six hours and we hadn't been able to do diddlyshit. Our one expedition outside had resulted in fifty-seven percent losses. It wasn't so surprising that Mrs. Carmody had turned into a growth stock, maybe.

"Has she really got a dozen people?" I asked.

"Well, only eight," Cornell said. "But she never shuts up! It's like those ten-hour speeches Castro used to make. It's a goddam filibuster."

Eight people. Not that many, not even enough to fill up a jury box. But I understood the worry on their faces. It was enough to make them the single largest political force in the market, especially now that Dan and Mike were gone. The thought that the biggest single group in our closed system was listening to her rant on about the pits of hell and the seven vials being opened made me feel pretty damn claustrophobic.

"She's started talking about human sacrifice again," Amanda said. "Bud Brown came over and told her to stop talking that drivel in his store. And two of the men that are with her—one of them was that man Myron LaFleur—told him he was the one who better shut up because it was still a free country. He wouldn't shut up and there was a . . . well, a shoving match, I guess you'd say."

"He got a bloody nose," Cornell said. "They mean business."

I said, "Surely not to the point of actually killing someone."

Cornell said softly, "I don't know how far they'll go if that mist doesn't let up. But I don't want to find out. I intend to get out of here."

"Easier said than done." But something had begun to tick over in my mind. *Scent.* That was the key. We have been left pretty much alone in the market. The bugs might have been attracted to the light, as more ordinary bugs were. The birds had simply followed their food supply. But the bigger things had left us alone unless we unbuttoned for some reason. The slaughter in the Bridgton Pharmacy had occurred because the doors had been left chocked open—I was sure of that. The thing or things that had gotten Norton and his party had sounded as big as a house, but it or they hadn't come near the market. And that meant that maybe . . .

Suddenly I wanted to talk to Ollie Weeks. I needed to talk to him.

"I intend to get out or die trying," Cornell said. "I got no plans to spend the rest of the summer in here."

"There have been four suicides," Amanda said suddenly.

"What?" The first thing to cross my mind, in a semiguilty flash, was that the bodies of the soldiers had been discovered.

"Pills," Cornell said shortly. "Me and two or three other guys carried the bodies out back."

I had to stifle a shrill laugh. We had a regular morgue going back there.

"It's thinning out in here," Cornell said. "I want to get gone."

"You won't make it to your car. Believe me."

"Not even to that first rank? That's closer than the drugstore."

I didn't answer him. Not then.

About an hour later I found Ollie holding up the beer cooler and drinking a Busch. His face was impassive but he also seemed to be watching Mrs. Carmody. She was tireless, apparently. And she was indeed discussing human sacrifice again, only now no one was telling her to shut up. Some of the people who had told her to shut up yesterday were either with her today or at least willing to listen—and the others were outnumbered.

"She could have them talked around to it by tomorrow morning," Ollie remarked. "Maybe not . . . but if she did, who do you think she'd single out for the honor?"

Bud Brown had crossed her. So had Amanda. There was the man who had struck her. And then, of course, there was me.

"Ollie," I said, "I think maybe half a dozen of us could get out of here. I don't know how far we'd get, but I think we could at least get out."

"How?"

I laid it out for him. It was simple enough. If we dashed across to my Scout and piled in, they would get no human scent. At least not with the windows rolled up.

"But suppose they're attracted to some other scent?" Ollie asked. "Exhaust, for instance?"

"Then we'd be cooked," I agreed.

"Motion," he said. "The motion of a car through the fog might also draw them, David."

"I don't think so. Not without the scent of prey. I really believe that's the key to getting away."

"But you don't know."

"No, not for sure."

"Where would you want to go?"

"First? Home. To get my wife."

"David—"

"All right. To check on my wife. To be *sure*."

"The things out there could be every place, David. They could get you the minute you stepped out of your Scout into your dooryard."

"If that happened, the Scout would be yours. All I'd ask would be that you take care of Billy as well as you could for as long as you could."

Ollie finished his Busch and dropped the can back into the cooler where it clattered among the empties. The butt of the gun Amanda's husband had given her protruded from his pocket.

"South?" he asked, meeting my eyes.

"Yeah, I would," I said. "Go south and try to get out of the mist. Try like hell."

"How much gas you got?"

"Almost full."

"Have you thought that it might be impossible to get out?"

I had. Suppose what they had been fooling around with at the Arrowhead Project had pulled this entire region into another dimension as easily as you or I would turn a sock inside out? "It had crossed my mind," I said, "but the alternative seems to be waiting around to see who Mrs. Carmody taps for the place of honor."

"Were you thinking about today?"

"No, it's afternoon already and those things get active at night. I was thinking about tomorrow, very early."

"Who would you want to take?"

"Me and you and Billy. Hattie Turman. Amanda Dumfries. That old guy Cornell and Mrs. Reppler. Maybe Bud Brown, too. That's eight, but Billy can sit on someone's lap and we can all squash together."

He thought it over. "All right," he said finally. "We'll try. Have you mentioned this to anyone else?"

"No, not yet."

"My advice would be not to, not until about four tomorrow morning. I'll put a couple of bags of groceries under the checkout nearest the door. If we're lucky we can squeak out before anyone knows what's happening." His eyes drifted to Mrs. Carmody again. "If she knew, she might try to stop us."

"You think so?"

Ollie got another beer. "I think so," he said.

———

That afternoon—yesterday afternoon—passed in a kind of s
tion. Darkness crept in, turning the fog to that dull chrome col
What world was left outside slowly dissolved to black by eig
The pink bugs returned, then the bird-things, swooping
windows and scooping them up. Something roared occasiona
the dark, and once, shortly before midnight, there was a long
out *Aaaaa-roooooo!* that caused people to turn toward the b
with frightened, searching faces. It was the sort of sound you'd
a bull alligator might make in a swamp.

It went pretty much as Miller had predicted. By the sma
Mrs. Carmody had gained another half a dozen souls. Mr. Mc
butcher was among them, standing with his arms folded, watch

She was totally wound up. She seemed to need no sleep.
mon, a steady stream of horrors out of Doré, Bosch, and Jonat
wards, went on and on, building toward some climax. Her grou
to murmur with her, to rock back and forth unconsciously, l
believers at a tent revival. Their eyes were shiny and blank. Th
under her spell.

Around 3:00 a.m. (the sermon went on relentlessly, and th
who were not interested had retreated to the back to try and g
sleep) I saw Ollie put a bag of groceries on a shelf under the c
nearest the OUT door. Half an hour later he put another bag b
No one appeared to notice him but me. Billy, Amanda, and M
man slept together by the denuded coldcuts section. I joined th
fell into an uneasy doze.

At four-fifteen by my wristwatch, Ollie shook me awake. Cor
with him, his eyes gleaming brightly from behind his spectacles.

"It's time, David," Ollie said.

A nervous cramp hit my belly and then passed. I shook A
awake. The question of what might happen with both Amar
Stephanie in the car together passed into my mind, and then
right out again. Today it would be best to take things just
came.

Those remarkable green eyes opened and looked into mine. "I

"We're going to take a stab at getting out of here. Do you
come?"

"What are you talking about?"

I started to explain, then woke up Mrs. Turman so I wou
have to go through it the once.

"Your theory about scent," Amanda said. "It's really only a
cated guess at this point, isn't it?"

"Yes."

"It doesn't matter to me," Hattie said. Her face was white and in spite of the sleep she'd gotten there were large, discolored patches under her eyes. "I would do anything—take any chance—just to see the sun again."

Just to see the sun again. A little shiver coursed through me. She had put her finger on a spot that was very close to the center of my own fears, on the sense of almost foregone doom that had gripped me since I had seen Norm dragged out through the loading door. You could only see the sun briefly through the mist as a little silver coin. It was like being on Venus.

It wasn't so much the monstrous creatures that lurked in the mist; my shot with the pinchbar had shown me they were no Lovecraftian horrors with immortal life but only organic creatures with their own vulnerabilities. It was the mist itself that sapped the strength and robbed the will. *Just to see the sun again.* She was right. That alone would be worth going through a hell of a lot.

I smiled at Hattie and she smiled tentatively back.

"Yes," Amanda said. "Me too."

I began to shake Billy awake, as gently as I could.

"I'm with you," Mrs. Reppler said briefly.

We were all together by the meat counter, all but Bud Brown. He had thanked us for the invitation and then declined it. He would not leave his place in the market, he said, but added in a remarkably gentle tone of voice that he didn't blame Ollie for doing so.

An unpleasant, sweetish aroma was beginning to drift up from the white enamel case now, a smell that reminded me of the time our freezer went on the fritz while we were spending a week on the Cape. Perhaps, I thought, it was the smell of spoiling meat that had driven Mr. McVey over to Mrs. Carmody's team.

"*—expiation! It's expiation we want to think about now! We have been scourged with whips and scorpions! We have been punished for delving into secrets forbidden by God of old! We have seen the lips of the earth open! We have seen the obscenities of nightmare! The rock will not hide them, the dead tree gives no shelter! And how will it end? What will stop it?*"

"*Expiation!*" shouted good old Myron LaFleur.

"*Expiation . . . expiation . . .*" they whispered it uncertainly.

"*Let me hear you say it like you mean it!*" Mrs. Carmody shouted. The veins stood out on her neck in bulging cords. Her voice was crack-

ing and hoarse now, but still full of a terrible power. And it occurred to me that it was the mist that had given her that power—the power to cloud men's minds, to make a particularly apt pun—just as it had taken away the sun's power from the rest of us. Before, she had been nothing but a mildly eccentric old woman with an antiques store in a town that was lousy with antiques stores. Nothing but an old woman with a few stuffed animals in the back room and a reputation for

(*That witch . . . that cunt*)

folk medicine. It was said she could find water with an applewood stick, that she could charm warts, and sell you a cream that would fade freckles to shadows of their former selves. I had even heard—was it from old Bill Giosti?—that Mrs. Carmody could be seen (in total confidence) about your lovelife; that if you were having the bedroom miseries, she could give you a drink that would put the ram back in your ramrod.

"*EXPIATION!*" they all cried together.

"*Expiation, that's right!*" she shouted deliriously. "*It's expiation gonna clear away this fog! Expiation gonna clear off these monsters and abominations! Expiation gonna drop the scales of mist from our eyes and let us see!*" Her voice dropped a notch. "And what does the Bible say expiation is? What is the only cleanser for sin in the Eye and Mind of God?"

"*Blood.*"

This time the chill shuddered up through my entire body, cresting at the nape of my neck and making the hairs there stiffen. Mr. McVey had spoken that word, Mr. McVey the butcher who had been cutting meat in Bridgton ever since I was a kid holding my father's talented hand. Mr. McVey taking orders and cutting meat in his stained whites, Mr. McVey, whose acquaintanceship with the knife was long—yes, and with the saw and cleaver as well. Mr. McVey, who would understand better than anyone else that the cleanser of the soul flows from the wounds of the body.

"*Blood . . .*" they whispered.

"Daddy, I'm scared," Billy said. He was clutching my hand tightly, his small face strained and pale.

"Ollie," I said, "why don't we get out of this loonybin?"

"Right on," he said. "Let's go."

We started down the second aisle in a loose group—Ollie, Amanda, Cornell, Mrs. Turman, Mrs. Reppler, Billy, and I. It was quarter to five in the morning and the mist was beginning to lighten again.

"You and Cornell take the grocery bags," Ollie said to me.

"Okay."

"I'll go first. Your Scout a four-door, is it?"

"Yeah, it is."

"Okay, I'll open the driver's door and the back door on the same side. Mrs. Dumfries, can you carry Billy?"

She picked him up in her arms.

"Am I too heavy?" Billy asked.

"No, hon."

"Good."

"You and Billy get in front," Ollie went on. "Shove way over. Mrs. Turman in front, in the middle. David, you behind the wheel. The rest of us will—"

"Where did you think you were going?"

It was Mrs. Carmody.

She stood at the head of the check-out lane where Ollie had hidden the bags of groceries. Her pantsuit was a yellow scream in the gloom. Her hair frizzed out wildly in all directions, reminding me momentarily of Elsa Lanchester in *The Bride of Frankenstein*. Her eyes blazed. Ten or fifteen people stood behind her, blocking the IN and OUT doors. They had the look of people who had been in car accidents, or who had seen a UFO land, or who had seen a tree pull its roots up and walk.

Billy cringed against Amanda and buried his face against her neck.

"Going out now, Mrs. Carmody," Ollie said. His voice was curiously gentle. "Stand away, please."

"You can't go out. That way is death. Don't you know that by now?"

"No one has interfered with you," I said. "All we want is the same privilege."

She bent and found the bags of groceries unerringly. She must have known what we were planning all along. She pulled them out from the shelf where Ollie had placed them. One ripped open, spilling cans across the floor. She threw the other and it smashed open with the sound of breaking glass. Soda ran fizzing every whichway and sprayed off the chrome facing of the next check-out lane.

"These are the sort of people who brought it on!" she shouted. "People who will not bend to the will of the Almighty! Sinners in pride, haughty they are, and stiffnecked! It is from their number that the sacrifice must come! *From their number the blood of expiation!*"

A rising rumble of agreement spurred her on. She was in a frenzy now. Spittle flew from her lips as she screamed at the people crowding up behind her: *"It's the boy we want! Grab him! Take him! It's the boy we want!"*

They surged forward, Myron LaFleur in the lead, his eyes blankly joyous. Mr. McVey was directly behind him, his face blank and stolid.

Amanda faltered backward, holding Billy more tightly. His arms were wrapped around her neck. She looked at me, terrified. "David, what do I—"

"Get them both!" Mrs. Carmody screamed. *"Get his whore, too!"* She was an apocalypse of yellow and dark joy. Her purse was still over her arm. She began to jump clumsily up and down. *"Get the boy, get the whore, get them both, get them all, get—"*

A single sharp report rang out.

Everything froze, as if we were a classroom full of unruly children and the teacher had just stepped back in and shut the door sharply. Myron LaFleur and Mr. McVey stopped where they were, about ten paces away. Myron looked uncertainly at the butcher. He didn't look back or even seem to realize that LaFleur was there. Mr. McVey had a look I had seen on too many other faces in the last two days. He had gone over. His mind had snapped.

Myron backed up, staring at Ollie Weeks with widening, fearful eyes. His backing-up became a run. He turned the corner of the aisle, skidded on a can, fell down, scrambled up again, and was gone.

Ollie stood in the classic target shooter's position, Amanda's gun in his right hand. Mrs. Carmody still stood at the head of the check-out lane. Both of her liver-spotted hands were clasped over her stomach. Blood poured out between her fingers and splashed her yellow slacks.

Her mouth opened and closed. Once. Twice. She was trying to talk. At last she made it.

"You will all die out there," she said, and then she pitched slowly forward. Her purse slithered off her arm, struck the floor, and spilled its contents. A tube of pills rolled across the distance between us and struck one of my shoes. Without thinking, I bent over and picked it up. It was a half-used package of Certs breath-mints. I threw it down again. I didn't want to touch anything that belonged to her.

The "congregation" was backing away, spreading out, their focus broken. None of them took their eyes from the fallen figure and the dark blood spreading out from beneath her body. "You murdered her!" someone cried out in fear and anger. But no one pointed out that she had been planning something similar for my son.

Ollie was still frozen in his shooter's position, but now his mouth was trembling. I touched him gently. "Ollie, let's go. And thank you."

"I killed her," he said hoarsely. "Damn if I didn't kill her."

"Yes," I said. "That's why I thanked you. Now let's go."

We began to move again.

With no grocery bags to carry—thanks to Mrs. Carmody—I was able to take Billy. We paused for a moment at the door, and Ollie said in a low, strained voice, "I wouldn't have shot her, David. Not if there had been any other way."

"Yeah."

"You believe it?"

"Yeah, I do."

"Then let's go."

We went out.

XI. The End.

Ollie moved fast, the pistol in his right hand. Before Billy and I were more than out the door he was at my Scout, an insubstantial Ollie, like a ghost in a television movie. He opened the driver's door. Then the back door. Then something came out of the mist and cut him nearly in half.

I never got a good look at it, and for that I think I'm grateful. It appeared to be red, the angry color of a cooked lobster. It had claws. It was making a low grunting sound, not much different from the sound we had heard after Norton and his little band of Flat-Earthers went out.

Ollie got off one shot, and then the thing's claws scissored forward and Ollie's body seemed to unhinge in a terrible glut of blood. Amanda's gun fell out of his hand, struck the pavement, and discharged. I caught a nightmare glimpse of huge black lusterless eyes, the size of giant handfuls of sea grapes, and then the thing lurched back into the mist with what remained of Ollie Weeks in its grip. A long, multisegmented body dragged harshly on the paving.

There was an instant of choice. Maybe there always is, no matter how short. Half of me wanted to run back into the market with Billy hugged against my chest. The other half was racing for the Scout, throwing Billy inside, lunging after him. Then Amanda screamed. It was a high, rising sound that seemed to spiral up and up until it was nearly ultrasonic. Billy cringed against me, digging his face against my chest.

One of the spiders had Hattie Turman. It was big. It had knocked her down. Her dress had pulled up over her scrawny knees as it crouched over her, its bristly, spiny legs caressing her shoulders. It began to spin its web.

Mrs. Carmody was right, I thought. *We're going to die out here, we are really going to die out here.*

"Amanda!" I yelled.

No response. She was totally gone. The spider straddled what remained of Billy's babysitter, Mrs. Turman, who had enjoyed jigsaw puzzles and those damned Double-Crostics that no normal person can do without going nuts. Its threads crisscrossed her body, the white strands already turning red as the acid coating sank into her.

Cornell was backing slowly toward the market, his eyes as big as dinner plates behind his specs. Abruptly he turned and ran. He clawed the IN door open and ran inside.

The split in my mind closed as Mrs. Reppler stepped briskly forward and slapped Amanda, first forehand, then backhand. Amanda stopped screaming. I went to her, spun her around to face the Scout and screamed *"GO!"* into her face.

She went. Mrs. Reppler brushed past me. She pushed Amanda into the Scout's backseat, got in after her, and slammed the door shut.

I yanked Billy loose and threw him in. As I climbed in myself, one of those spider threads drifted down and lit on my ankle. It burned the way a fishing line pulled rapidly through your closed fist will burn. And it was strong. I gave my foot a hard yank and it broke. I slipped in behind the wheel.

"Shut it, oh shut the door, dear God!" Amanda screamed.

I shut the door. A bare instant later, one of the spiders thumped softly against it. I was only inches from its red, viciously-stupid eyes. Its legs, each as thick as my wrist, slipped back and forth across the square bonnet. Amanda screamed ceaselessly, like a firebell.

"Woman, shut your head," Mrs. Reppler told her.

The spider gave up. It could not smell us, ergo we were no longer there. It strutted back into the mist on its unsettling number of legs, became a phantasm, and then was gone.

I looked out the window to make sure it was gone and then opened the door.

"What are you doing?" Amanda screamed, but I knew what I was doing. I like to think Ollie would have done exactly the same thing. I half-stepped, half-leaned out, and got the gun. Something came rapidly toward me, but I never saw it. I pulled back in and slammed the door shut.

Amanda began to sob. Mrs. Reppler put an arm around her and comforted her briskly.

Billy said, "Are we going home, Daddy?"

"Big Bill, we're gonna try."

"Okay," he said quietly.

I checked the gun and then put it into the glove compartment. Ollie had reloaded it after the expedition to the drugstore. The rest of the shells had disappeared with him, but that was all right. He had fired at Mrs. Carmody, he had fired once at the clawed thing, and the gun had discharged once when it hit the ground. There were four of us in the Scout, but if push came right down to shove, I'd find some other way out for myself.

I had a terrible moment when I couldn't find my keyring. I checked all my pockets, came up empty, and then checked them all again, forcing myself to go slowly and calmly. They were in my jeans pocket; they had gotten down under the coins, as keys sometimes will. The Scout started easily. At the confident roar of the engine, Amanda burst into fresh tears.

I sat there, letting it idle, waiting to see what was going to be drawn by the sound of the engine or the smell of the exhaust. Five minutes, the longest five of my life, drifted by. Nothing happened.

"Are we going to sit here or are we going to go?" Mrs. Reppler asked at last.

"Go," I said. I backed out of the slot and put on the low beams.

Some urge—probably a base one—made me cruise past the Federal Market as close as I could get. The Scout's right bumper bunted the trash barrel to one side. It was impossible to see in except through the loopholes—all those fertilizer and lawn-food bags made the place look as if it were in the throes of some mad garden sale—but at each loophole there were two or three pale faces, staring out at us.

Then I swung to the left, and the mist closed impenetrably behind us. And what has become of those people I do not know.

I drove back down Kansas Road at five miles an hour, feeling my way. Even with the Scout's headlights and running lights on, it was impossible to see more than seven or ten feet ahead.

The earth had been through some terrible contortion, Miller had been right about that. In places the road was merely cracked, but in others the ground itself seemed to have caved in, tilting up great slabs of paving. I was able to get over with the help of the four-wheel drive.

Thank God for that. But I was terribly afraid that we would soon come to an obstacle that even the four-wheel drive couldn't get us over.

It took me forty minutes to make a drive that usually only took seven or eight. At last the sign that marked our private road loomed out of the mist. Billy, roused at quarter of five, had fallen solidly asleep inside this car that he knew so well it must have seemed like home to him.

Amanda looked at the road nervously. "Are you really going down there?"

"I'm going to try," I said.

But it was impossible. The storm that had whipped through had loosened a lot of trees, and that weird, twisting drop had finished the job of tumbling them. I was able to crunch over the first two; they were fairly small. Then I came to a hoary old pine lying across the road like an outlaw's barricade. It was still almost a quarter of a mile to the house. Billy slept on beside me, and I put the Scout in Park, put my hands over my eyes, and tried to think what to do next.

Now, as I sit in the Howard Johnson's near Exit 3 of the Maine Turnpike, writing all of this down on HoJo stationery, I suspect that Mrs. Reppler, that tough and capable old broad, could have laid out the essential futility of the situation in a few quick strokes. But she had the kindness to let me think it through for myself.

I couldn't get out. I couldn't leave them. I couldn't even kid myself that all the horror-movie monsters were back at the Federal; when I cracked the window I could hear them in the woods, crashing and blundering around on the steep fall of land they call the Ledges around these parts. The moisture drip-drip-dripped from the overhanging leaves. Overhead the mist darkened momentarily as some nightmarish and half-seen living kite overflew us.

I tried to tell myself—then and now—that if she was very quick, if she buttoned up the house with herself inside, that she had enough food for ten days to two weeks. It only works a little bit. What keeps getting in the way is my last memory of her, wearing her floppy sunhat and gardening gloves, on her way to our little vegetable patch with the mist rolling inexorably across the lake behind her.

It is Billy I have to think about now. Billy, I tell myself, Big Bill, Big Bill . . . I should write it maybe a hundred times on this sheet of paper, like a child condemned to write *I will not throw spitballs in school* as the sunny three-o'clock stillness spills through the windows and the teacher corrects homework papers at her desk and the only

sound is her pen, while somewhere, far away, kids pick up teams for scratch baseball.

Anyway, at last I did the only thing I could do. I reversed the Scout carefully back to Kansas Road. Then I cried.

Amanda touched my shoulder timidly. "David, I'm so sorry," she said.

"Yeah," I said, trying to stop the tears and not having much luck. "Yeah, so am I."

I drove to Route 302 and turned left, toward Portland. This road was also cracked and blasted in places, but was, on the whole, more passable than Kansas Road had been. I was worried about the bridges. The face of Maine is cut with running water, and there are bridges everywhere, big and small. But the Naples Causeway was intact, and from there it was plain—if slow—sailing all the way to Portland.

The mist held thick. Once I had to stop, thinking that trees were lying across the road. Then the trees began to move and undulate, and I understood they were more tentacles. I stopped, and after a while they drew back. Once a great green thing with an iridescent green body and long transparent wings landed on the hood. It looked like a grossly misshapen dragonfly. It hovered there for a moment, then took wing again and was gone.

Billy woke up about two hours after we had left Kansas Road behind and asked if we had gotten Mommy yet. I told him I hadn't been able to get down our road because of fallen trees.

"Is she all right, Dad?"

"Billy, I don't know. But we'll come back and see."

He didn't cry. He dozed off again instead. I would have rather had his tears. He was sleeping too damn much and I didn't like it.

I began to get a tension headache. It was driving through the fog at a steady five or ten miles an hour that did it, the tension of knowing that anything might come out of it, anything at all—a washout, a land-spill, or Ghidra the Three-headed Monster. I think I prayed. I prayed to God that Stephanie was alive and that He wouldn't take my adultery out on her. I prayed to God to let me get Billy to safety because he had been through so much.

Most people had pulled to the side of the road when the mist came, and by noon we were in North Windham. I tried the River Road, but about four miles down, a bridge spanning a small and noisy stream had fallen into the water. I had to reverse for nearly a mile before I found a

spot wide enough to turn around. We went to Portland by Route 302 after all.

When we got there, I drove the cut-off to the turnpike. The neat line of tollbooths guarding the access had been turned into vacant-eyed skeletons of smashed Pola-Glas. All of them were empty. In the sliding-glass doorway of one was a torn jacket with Maine Turnpike Authority patches on the sleeves. It was drenched with tacky, drying blood. We had not seen a single living person since leaving the Federal.

Mrs. Reppler said, "David, try your radio."

I slapped my forehead in frustration and anger at myself, wondering how I could have been stupid enough to forget the Scout's AM/FM for so long.

"Don't do that," Mrs. Reppler said curtly. "You can't think of everything. If you try, you will go mad and be of no use at all."

I got nothing but a shriek of static all the way across the AM band, and the FM yielded nothing but a smooth and ominous silence.

"Does that mean everything's off the air?" Amanda asked. I knew what she was thinking, maybe. We were far enough south now so that we should have been picking up a selection of strong Boston stations—WRKO, WBZ, WMEX. But if Boston was gone—

"It doesn't mean anything for sure," I said. "That static on the AM band is pure interference. The mist is having a damping effect on radio signals, too."

"Are you sure that's all it is?"

"Yes," I said, not sure at all.

We went south. The mileposts rolled slowly past, counting down from about forty. When we reached Mile 1, we would be at the New Hampshire border. Going on the turnpike was slower; a lot of the drivers hadn't wanted to give up, and there had been rear-end collisions in several places. Several times I had to use the median strip.

At about twenty past one—I was beginning to feel hungry—Billy clutched my arm. "Daddy, what's that? *What's that?*"

A shadow loomed out of the mist, staining it dark. It was as tall as a cliff and coming right at us. I jammed on the brakes. Amanda, who had been catnapping, was thrown forward.

Something came; again, that is all I can say for sure. It may have been the fact that the mist only allowed us to glimpse things briefly, but I think it just as likely that there are certain things that your brain simply disallows. There are things of such darkness and horror—just, I suppose, as there are things of such great beauty—that they will not fit through the puny human doors of perception.

It was six-legged, I know that; its skin was slaty gray that mottled to dark brown in places. Those brown patches reminded me absurdly of the liver spots on Mrs. Carmody's hands. Its skin was deeply wrinkled and grooved, and clinging to it were scores, hundreds, of those pinkish "bugs" with the stalk-eyes. I don't know how big it actually was, but it passed directly over us. One of its gray, wrinkled legs smashed down right beside my window, and Mrs. Reppler said later she could not see the underside of its body, although she craned her neck up to look. She saw only two Cyclopean legs going up and up into the mist like living towers until they were lost to sight.

For the moment it was over the Scout I had an impression of something so big that it might have made a blue whale look the size of a trout—in other words, something so big that it defied the imagination. Then it was gone, sending a seismological series of thuds back. It left tracks in the cement of the Interstate, tracks so deep I could not see the bottoms. Each single track was nearly big enough to drop the Scout into.

For a moment no one spoke. There was no sound but our breathing and the diminishing thud of that great Thing's passage.

Then Billy said, "Was it a dinosaur, Dad? Like the bird that got into the market?"

"I don't think so. I don't think there was ever an animal that big, Billy. At least not on earth."

I thought of the Arrowhead Project and wondered again what crazy, damned thing they could have been doing up there.

"Can we go on?" Amanda asked timidly. "It might come back."

Yes, and there might be more up ahead. But there was no point in saying so. We had to go somewhere. I drove on, weaving in and out between those terrible tracks until they veered off the road.

That is what happened. Or nearly all—there is one final thing I'll get to in a moment. But you mustn't expect some neat conclusion. There is no *And they escaped from the mist into the good sunshine of a new day;* or *When we awoke the National Guard had finally arrived;* or even that great old standby: *And I woke up and discovered it was all a dream.*

It is, I suppose, what my father always frowningly called "an Alfred Hitchcock ending," by which he meant a conclusion in ambiguity that allowed the reader or viewer to make up his own mind about how things ended. My father had nothing but contempt for such stories, saying they were "cheap shots."

We got to this Howard Johnson's near Exit 3 as dusk began to close in, making driving a suicidal chance. Before that, we took a chance on the bridge that spans the Saco River. It looked badly twisted out of shape, but in the mist it was impossible to tell if it was whole or not. That particular gamble we won.

But there's tomorrow to think of, isn't there?

As I write this, it is quarter of one in the morning, July the twenty-third. The storm that seemed to signal the beginning of it all was only four days ago. Billy is sleeping in the lobby on a mattress that I dragged out for him. Amanda and Mrs. Reppler are close by. I am writing by the light of a big Delco flashlight, and outside the pink bugs are ticking and thumping off the glass. Every now and then there is a louder thud as one of the birds takes one off.

The Scout has enough gas to take us maybe another ninety miles. The alternative is to try and gas up here; there is an Exxon out on the service island, and although the power is off, I believe I could siphon some up from the tank. But—

But it means being outside.

If we can get gas—and even if we can't get it here—we'll press on. I have a destination in mind now, you see. It's that last thing I wanted to tell you about.

I couldn't be sure. That is the thing, the damned thing. It might have been my imagination, nothing but wish fulfillment. And even if not, it is such a long chance. How many miles? How many bridges? How many things that would love to tear up my son and eat him even as he screamed in terror and agony?

The chances are so good that it was nothing but a daydream that I haven't told the others . . . at least, not yet.

In the manager's apartment I found a large battery-option multiband radio. From the back of it, a flat antenna wire led out through the window. I turned it on, switched over to BAT., fiddled with the tuning dial, with the SQUELCH knob, and still got nothing but static or dead silence.

And then, at the far end of the AM band, just as I was reaching for the knob to turn it off, I thought I heard, or dreamed I heard, one single word.

That word might have been *Hartford.*

There was no more. I listened for an hour, but there was no more. If there was that one word, it came through some minute shift in the damping mist, an infinitesimal break that immediately closed again.

Hartford.

L26 I've got to get some sleep . . . If I can sleep and not be haunted until daybreak by the faces of Ollie Weeks and Mrs. Carmody and Norm the bag-boy . . . and by Steff's face, half-shadowed by the wide brim of her sunhat.

There is a restaurant here, a typical HoJo restaurant with a dining room and a long, horseshoe-shaped lunch counter. I am going to leave these pages on the counter, and perhaps someday someone will find them and read them.

Hartford.

If I only really heard it. If only.

I'm going to bed now. But first I'm going to kiss my son and whisper two words in his ear. Against the dreams that may come, you know.

Two words that sound a bit alike.

One of them is hope.

CONTENTS

Sally Greenberg,
the better half of MHG, the best science
fiction anthologist in the world

RECOLLECTIONS AND OPINIONS OF AN OLD PIONEER

A Da Capo Press Reprint Series

THE AMERICAN SCENE
Comments and Commentators

General Editor: Wallace D. Farnham
University of Illinois

RECOLLECTIONS AND OPINIONS OF AN OLD PIONEER

By Peter H. Burnett

DA CAPO PRESS • NEW YORK • 1969

A Da Capo Press Reprint Edition

This Da Capo Press edition of
Recollections and Opinions of an Old Pioneer
is an unabridged republication of the first
edition published in New York in 1880.

Library of Congress Catalog Card Number 76-87661

Published by Da Capo Press
A Division of Plenum Publishing Corporation
227 West 17th Street
New York, N.Y. 10011

Manufactured in the United States of America

RECOLLECTIONS AND OPINIONS

OF AN

OLD PIONEER.

BY

PETER H. BURNETT,

THE FIRST GOVERNOR OF THE STATE OF CALIFORNIA.

NEW YORK:
D. APPLETON AND COMPANY,
1, 3, AND 5 BOND STREET.
1880.

TO

Col. ALEXANDER W. DONIPHAN,

THE XENOPHON OF THE MEXICAN WAR,

THE ABLE AND ELOQUENT ADVOCATE,

THE MAN OF UNDOUBTED INTEGRITY,

This Work is Dedicated,

AS EVIDENCE OF THE ADMIRATION AND ESTEEM

OF HIS OLD FRIEND,

THE AUTHOR.

PREFACE.

In the month of October, 1860, I began to write out my recollections and opinions, intending to leave the manuscript to my children, as I thought that a true account of my opinions, and long and diversified experience, might be of benefit to them and their posterity, though of less importance to others. But I had not progressed very far before I was interrupted by several causes.

Since November, 1860, I had not further prosecuted my design until the month of March, 1878. In the month of December, 1877, a learned and distinguished historian, then and now engaged in writing a general history of the Pacific coast, called upon me, and kindly requested me to furnish him with such historical data as I possessed. Having already reduced to writing a considerable portion of my recollections and opinions, I determined to finish the work I had undertaken, and to permit him to take a copy of all, or such portions as he might desire, for his use in preparing his own history.

I had lived so long and seen so much, and my ex-

perience had been so varied, that the task grew upon my hands as I proceeded, and has swollen into a volume almost double the size first anticipated. Until the month of October, 1879, and until after I had separately submitted the manuscript to the examination of two learned and able men, I had not decided to publish it. Circumstances have induced me to do so ; and, as the work has been so largely written from memory alone, its publication during my life will enable me to correct any serious mistakes I may have made. The narrative ends with September 26, 1878.

The work, having been originally intended for my children, contains much personal and family history, more interesting to my relatives than to the general reader. Yet, as my own history is connected to some extent with that of the Western and Pacific States, I think there are some facts stated of general importance, which have not been, perhaps, so fully recorded by others.

I was born a pioneer, as Nashville at the date of my birth was but a small village, and Tennessee a border-State, but thinly populated. I have been a pioneer most of my life ; and whenever, since my arrival in California, I have seen a party of immigrants, with their ox-teams and white-sheeted wagons, I have been excited, have felt younger, and was for the moment anxious to make another trip. If the theory of Symmes had been proven by time to be true, and had a fine and accessible country been discovered at the north or south

pole before I attained the age of sixty, I should have been strongly tempted to organize a party of emigrants for that distant region.

While the settlement of a new country is full of perils, hardships, and privations, it is still exceedingly interesting. The first settlers find nature in a state of grand repose ; but this repose is soon followed by great activity and most satisfactory progress. In some five or six years the orchards begin to bear their fruits, smiling villages, pleasant homes, and happy families are seen on all sides, and "the wilderness begins to blossom as the rose."

CONTENTS.

CHAPTER III.

CHAPTER IV.

CHAPTER V.

CHAPTER IX.

CHAPTER X.

CHAPTER I.

ANCESTRY: THE BURNETS—THE HARDEMANS.

I AM the eldest son of George and Dorothy Burnet, and was born in Nashville, Tennessee, November 15, 1807. My father was born in Pittsylvania County, Virginia, September 26, 1770, and died in Clay County, Missouri, February 22, 1838. The family all spelled the name with a single t. When I was about nineteen, I added another t, and my example has been followed by all my brothers. My reason for the change was the opinion that the name would be more complete and emphatic when spelled Burnett.

My mother was the daughter of Thomas Hardeman, and was born in Davidson County, Tennessee, May 15, 1786, and died in Platte County, Missouri, March 17, 1843. My grandfather Hardeman was born in Virginia, January 8, 1750; and his brother, whom I never saw, settled in Georgia. My grandfather Hardeman was among the first settlers of Tennessee, and participated in the Indian wars of that country. He was a stout man, possessed a very fine constitution, a determined will, and *naturally* a splendid intellect. His education was originally very limited, but by study he became a man of distinction. He was the neighbor and warm friend of General Andrew Jackson, and was, with the General, a member of the first Constitutional Conven-

tion of Tennessee. He was a farmer and made a fortune, living to the age of seventy-two. He reared eight sons and three daughters: Nicholas Perkins, Nancy, John, Constant, Eleazar, Peter, Dorothy, Thomas Jones, Blackstone, Elizabeth, and Baily. All these married, and all reared families, except my aunt Elizabeth.

My grandfather Hardeman was twice married, his two wives being sisters, but all his children were the issue of his first marriage. He brought up his sons to his own business, except John and Baily, to whom he gave fine educations. They were intended for the bar, but never practiced. Both were men of fine mental capacity, especially uncle John, who was one of the most accomplished literary men of the Western States.

My grandfather Hardeman taught certain maxims to his children that have come down to his grandchildren, and have had a great influence over his posterity:

First. Pay your honest debts.

Second. Never disgrace the family.

Third. Help the honest and industrious kin.

My father came to Nashville when it was a small village, and was married to my mother in 1802, in Davidson County, Tennessee. He had several brothers and sisters, some of whom I remember to have seen. They nearly all lived and died in Kentucky. I never saw my grandfather Burnet. My father was a carpenter and farmer, uncle William was a blacksmith, uncle John a school-teacher, uncle James a farmer, and uncle Henry a cabinet-maker. All my father's brothers and sisters were married, and all reared families. All my uncles and aunts on both sides are gone. Many of them lived to be old people. I remember well when I belonged to the younger members of the family. Now I stand among the eldest.

There was a great difference between my father's and mother's families. The Hardemans were fond of pleasure, and were generally extravagant when young. Most of them, especially my male cousins, when setting out in life, wasted their patrimony, not in dissipation of any kind, but in fashionable life ; and afterward set earnestly to work, most of them making good livings, and some of them fortunes. The Hardemans were generally men of the world, first fond of fashionable pleasures, dress, and show, and afterward seekers of fortune. But, though wild when young men, I have yet to hear of the first instance in which they were ever accused of any criminal offense, great or small. They sometimes had fisticuff fights (though very rarely), but I never knew one of them to fight a duel. With very rare exceptions, they all paid their debts. They were generally good business men, and good traders in such property as lands and stock, and were punctual in keeping their promises, and firm in telling the truth. All of the name were very proud of the family; and, though they might have disputes among themselves, they would not permit others to speak ill even of those they themselves blamed. They were very generous in aiding their relatives in starting in business, generally by good advice to the young, and often by loans of money. They were especially kind to the unfortunate. They were generally quick-tempered and downright in the expression of their opinions. My grandfather Hardeman and most of his sons seemed to think it a conscientious duty, when they saw any one do what they clearly considered a mean act, to tell him what they thought of him in plain terms. They were candid and resolute men, and you always knew how you stood with them. If they disliked you, they would tell you so. There were many marriages

between cousins, especially in the Perkins family, who were related through my grandmother Hardeman, whose maiden name was Perkins. The Perkins family came from North Carolina.

On the contrary, my father's family were not seekers of fortune, Uncle James being the only one who ever acquired any considerable amount of property. They were men of peace, very just, industrious, sober, and piously disposed. They cared very little for riches, being content with a fair living; but they possessed fine literary abilities. My father was raised very poor, and never went to school but three months in his life. He emigrated West while a young man, and spent his time mostly at hard work; and, although he had never studied English grammar, he wrote and spoke the language with substantial accuracy. He possessed an extraordinary mathematical talent, so that he could solve in a few moments very difficult problems. I remember an instance, which occurred after I was grown. I saw a problem published in a newspaper in Tennessee when I was about twenty-two, and it took me some three days to arrive at a correct solution. Upon a visit to my father in 1830, I proposed the same question to him, and it did not take him more than half an hour, and he did not make half as many figures as I had done. The rules by which he solved most questions were his own. He understood the *reason* of the science.

My uncle, John Burnet, had a fine talent for general science, and several of my cousins on my father's side have been lawyers of ability. One of my father's cousins, of whom I remember to have heard him often speak, and whose opportunities had been very limited, rose to distinction at the bar and on the bench. I re-

member my father often referred to this relative as a fit example for me to follow.

My father was very industrious, understood his trade as a carpenter well, and made a pretty good farmer; but he had no capacity for trading, and was often cheated. I never knew but one of the Hardemans who was dissipated, and that was Uncle Perkins; but that which was a cause of surprise was that, during the dissipated part of his life, he made a good living, and when he died left his family in comfortable circumstances. Of the Burnets, all the old set were examples of sobriety, peace, kindness, and honesty; and among the younger class, including cousins and half cousins, I never knew of but three who were confirmed drunkards; and I never heard of any one of the blood committing any crime, great or small.

My father and mother reared eight children, five sons and three daughters: Constantia Dudley, Peter Hardeman, Glen Owen, George William, Elizabeth Ann, James White, Mary Henry Jones, and Thomas Smith. Sister Constantia was twice married, and died in Liberty, Missouri, in 1846. Sister Mary married Dr. Benjamin S. Long in 1838, and died in Clay County, Missouri, in 1843. Sister Elizabeth has been twice married, and now lives a widow in Mendocino County, California, and has ten living children. Glen, Thomas, and myself reside in California, and my brother White in Oregon. My brother William lived in Oregon from the fall of 1846 until his death, December 25, 1877.

Our family are much divided in religion. Glen and White are Disciples, or Campbellites, as they are sometimes called; Sister Elizabeth is a Baptist; Thomas is a Southern Methodist; and I am a Catholic. Brothers Glen and Thomas are preachers, Brother White is a

farmer, and I am a banker. Brother Thomas is now living with his second wife. Glen and myself married sisters, the only daughters of Peter Rogers, who died in Clay County, Missouri, in 1858, aged about seventy.

We reared six children—three sons and three daughters:

Dwight J. Burnett, born in Hardeman County, Tennessee, May 23, 1829, and married to Miss Mary Wilcox in Sacramento City, January, 1850.

Martha L. Burnett, born in Liberty, Clay County, Missouri, April 29, 1833, and married to C. T. Ryland in Alviso, Santa Clara County, California, January 23, 1851.

Romeetta J. Burnett, born in Liberty, Missouri, February 14, 1836, and married to W. T. Wallace in Alviso, California, March 30, 1853.

John M. Burnett, born in Liberty, Missouri, February 4, 1838, and married to Miss Ellen Casey in San Francisco, April 27, 1863.

Armstead L. Burnett, born in Liberty, Missouri, October 7, 1839, married to Miss Flora Johnson in San José, California, November 21, 1860, and died in San José, May 26, 1862.

Sallie C. Burnett, born in Platte City, Platte County, Missouri, September 27, 1841, married to Francis Poe in San José, November 21, 1860, and died in Sacramento City, May 24, 1861.

REMOVALS: TO THE FARM—TO MISSOURI.

My father built several of the first log and frame buildings in Nashville, and one frame building for himself. My earliest recollections are connected with Nashville. I remember my father's house, and that he punished me one evening for running away from home; a

circumstance well calculated, in its nature, to make a lasting impression. About 1811 he moved upon a farm in Williamson County, about four miles south of Franklin, and on the main road to Columbia, the county seat of Maury County. My grandfather Hardeman having removed to Howard County, Missouri, about 1816, my father went to look at that locality in the summer of 1817, and moved there in the fall of that year. We spent the first winter in a large camp with a dirt floor, boarded up on the sides with clapboards, and covered with the same, leaving a hole in the center of the roof for the escape of the smoke. All the family lived together in the same room, the whites on one side and the blacks on the other. In the fall of 1819, or spring of 1820, we removed to Franklin in the same county, then a most flourishing place, where my father worked at his trade and also kept a boarding-house, until the town began to decline ; when, in the fall of 1820, we returned to the farm four miles above Franklin. The Missouri bottoms were exceedingly sickly in 1820–'21 ; so much so, that the larger portion of the inhabitants removed to the hills. In these years my father's family suffered very much from fever and ague. I remember that all of the family, fourteen in number, were sick at the same time, except a little negro boy about six years old. I suffered from fever and ague two falls and winters in succession, when I was twelve and thirteen years of age.

The location of my father's farm, in the Missouri bottom, being so unhealthy, we removed to Clay County in the spring of 1822, my father having entered a tract of 160 acres at the Land Office, at $1.25 per acre. Here we had to begin again to clear off the timber and build houses.

The first steamboats I ever saw were at Franklin in 1820. They were the first steamers on the Missouri River, with one exception. A short time before, a single steamer, as I am informed, had passed a short distance above Franklin, and was snagged and sunk. The steamers that I saw were three in number, and were sent by Colonel Richard M. Johnson, contractor for supplies at Council Bluffs, at which point the United States Government then had a military post. I remember that one of these vessels was propelled by a stern-wheel, and had a large wooden figurehead, representing the head and neck of an immense snake, through the mouth of which the steam escaped. This boat made quite a grand appearance, and caused much speculation among the people. Some were of the opinion that all the steam machinery (which they called "works") was in the belly of this snake. I remember seeing these boats start up the river from the landing. They crossed over to the Booneville side, and in crossing were barely able to keep from falling below the point they left. This was in the summer, when the water was high and the current rapid. Now, however, a steamer on that river will stem the current at any stage of the water with ease. The boat alluded to was called "the Western Engineer." There were no regular steamboats on the river until some five years later.

The early settlers in Missouri had a very hard time of it, especially those who could not hunt the wild game successfully, which was at that time abundant. When we moved from Howard to Clay County (a distance of some two hundred and fifty miles by water), our supplies and household furniture were sent up the river in a flat-boat, which had to be towed up most of the way by men, who walked upon the bank of the

stream, pulling upon a long rope attached to the boat, and cutting down the willows along the bank in many places, so as to open a foot-path. The water was low, and it required some forty days to make the trip. All the supplies of merchandise were transported at that time from St. Louis to Liberty Landing in keel-boats. For this reason freight was high and prices in proportion: coffee, 50 cts. per pound; sugar, 25 to 37½ cts.; calico, 37½ to 50 cts. per yard; and brown cotton, from 25 to 37½ cts. Iron and salt, two most necessary articles, were high, and it was difficult for farmers to pay for them.

It so happened that, although when we settled in Howard and Clay Counties provisions were scarce and high, when we had succeeded in raising produce for sale, the demand had diminished, the supply had increased, and prices declined to a low figure. Indian corn was 10 cts. a bushel, wheat 50 cts., pork $1.25 per hundred pounds, and other things in proportion. As everything the farmers had for sale was very *low*, and all they purchased very *high*, they were able to purchase very little, and that of the plainest description. A sack or two of coffee and a barrel of brown sugar would last a merchant some time. Many persons supplied themselves with maple sugar. This was the case with my father. I remember that "sugar-making time" was always a season of hard work, but of festivity with the young people, especially when the sugar was "stirred off." At this time what was called a "sugar-stick" was in great demand. After the sugar was molded into cakes or grained, it was carefully deposited in the black-walnut "sugar-chest," and put under lock and key. The ants were very fond of sugar, and would find their way into the chest. To

keep them out, each of the four legs was put into a small, hollow, square block of wood, filled with tar. This Stygian pool these insignificant little pests would never cross.

MODE OF LIVING—MANNERS AND CUSTOMS.

Our manner of living was very simple. For some years the only mills in the country were propelled by horses, each customer furnishing his own team, and taking his proper turn to grind his grain. At times when the mills were thronged (and this was generally so in winter), they had to wait from one to two days. During this time the mill-boys mostly lived on parched corn. The manner of sending to mill was to put a bag, some three feet long, and containing from two and a half to three bushels of grain, across the back of a gentle horse, the bag being well balanced by having the same quantity in each end, and then putting a man or boy upon the top to keep it on, and to guide the horse. It often happened that both bag and boy tumbled off, and then there was trouble, not so much because the boy was a little hurt (for he would soon recover), but because it was difficult to get the bag on again. When any one could shoulder a bag of corn, he was considered a man; and to stand in a half-bushel measure, and shoulder a bag containing two and a half to three bushels, was considered quite a feat. I heard of a woman who could do so, but never saw her, and can not say that the statement was true.

For some years very little wheat was grown, Indian corn being the only grain raised; and, when wheat was produced, there were no good flour-mills for some time. If, during those times, we had a biscuit and a cup of coffee every Sunday morning we were fortunate. As a

substitute for coffee, we often used rye or corn meal parched; and instead of "store tea" we used the root of the sassafras. Our clothing was "homespun," made by our mothers and sisters—jeans and linsey for the males, and linsey and striped cotton for the females. Hunting-shirts and pants of dressed buckskin were very common, and in some very rare cases females were clad in dressed buckskin. In summer the boys and girls went barefoot, and young and married women often. Moccasins were often worn instead of shoes. I have seen young women, in going to public places, stop a short distance before reaching the place, take off their coarse shoes, and put on their "Sunday shoes." Such a thing as a fine carriage was never seen. Some very few had what was then called a "Dearborn," being a small vehicle for one horse, and without any top to it. Our linsey and jeans for every-day use were usually colored with hickory or walnut bark, that of a finer quality with indigo. A suit of blue jeans was considered a fine dress. I remember that in Clay County, about 1824–'25, there were only three or four men who could boast of a suit of broadcloth. A young man who had been in the service of the United States as a soldier came to Liberty, Clay County, about that time, and dressed himself in a new suit of blue broadcloth, surmounted by an elegant new fur hat of his own workmanship (he was a hatter), and he used to strut up and down the only street in the place, to the great astonishment of others. At that time there must have been about three hundred voters in the county.

The principal trade at that date was in skins, honey, and beeswax, all wild productions. When Missouri was first settled, cotton was cultivated for domestic use. The seeds were picked out by hand, or by a small gin

consisting of two wooden rollers, three quarters of an inch in diameter and a foot long, to one of which a crank and handle were attached. The operator sat across a bench, upon which the rollers on the top of a piece of timber were securely fastened, and turned the crank with his right and applied the cotton with his left hand. The rollers were placed together, so that turning one would turn the other; and, while the cotton, in thin slices, would pass between them, the seed could not. It was, however, a slow process.

What were called "cotton pickings" were then very common. The young people of the neighborhood assembled about dark, divided themselves into two equal parties, placed the quantity of cotton to be picked in two large piles before a big fire, and then commenced a race to see which party would get through first. The cotton picked more easily when warmed, and this was the reason for placing it before the fire. Much cheating was done by hiding away portions of the unpicked cotton. The object was to accomplish the task as early as possible, and then to enter into the dance, or the various plays then common, such as "Old Jake," "Pleased or displeased?" "Tired of your company?" "Bishop of Winchester has lost his crown," and "We are marching along toward Quebeck." I remember that, when I was about fourteen years of age, I attended a cotton-picking in Howard County, at the house of a widow. I had never danced any, and, though naturally diffident, I determined I would break the ice. There was present an old maid, Miss Milly A., with whom I was well acquainted—a large, corpulent woman, low, thick-set, and weighing about two hundred pounds. With her I danced some seven sets (most of them Virginia reels), without a rest. Though so large, she moved over the

puncheon floor with ease and grace, and was amply able, I found to my sorrow, to tire me out; for the next day I was so sore that I could scarcely walk. This rash experiment cured me of dancing for some years.

At my father's house I never saw a cotton-picking. It was usual in the fall and winter to pick the cotton at night, in which task all of us participated who were able to work. The young ladies spun and wove, and often made a beautiful article of striped and checked cotton cloth, out of which they made themselves dresses. Hemp and flax, especially the latter, were used in the manufacture of summer clothing for children and men. My sister Constantia was very fond of reading, was well educated for that day, and was the most talented of the family. I remember to have heard my mother laughingly complain that my sister would stop the loom any time to read a book. The weaving of the family was generally done by the white women, and mainly by the unmarried daughters.

It required great industry, rigid economy, and wise foresight to make a plain living in those times. I have often thought of the severe struggles of my parents and their children to live. The leather for our winter shoes was tanned at home, and the shoes for the family were made by my father and myself, after I was large enough to assist him. Peg-work was not then understood, and it required some little art to make and bristle "an end," as they called the waxed thread with which the shoes were sewed.

The climate of Missouri is cold and changeable, requiring stock to be fed some five or six months in the year. In the early settlement of the State, the people suffered much from sickness caused by exposure, bad

food (as the corn from which the bread was made was often frost-bitten), and the decay of such masses of timber as were left dead in the fields.

Log-rolling was also one of the laborious amusements of those days. To clear away the dense forests for cultivation was a work of some years. The underbrush was grubbed up, the small trees (saplings) were cut down and burned, and the large trees belted around with the axe, by cutting through the sap of the trees, which process was called "deadening." The trees belted would soon die, and their tops first fall off, and afterward the trunks would fall down, often breaking the rail fences and crushing the growing corn, and in the winter time occasionally killing the cattle running in the stalk-fields. Sometimes a human being would be killed by a falling limb, or by a stroke of lightning. My sister Constantia's first husband, James M. Miller, was killed by lightning on the bank of the Missouri river at Booneville about 1821; and my wife only escaped death from a similar cause at Liberty, Missouri, in 1833, by accidentally leaving the fireplace where she was sitting, and retiring to the adjoining room, only just one moment before the lightning struck the stone chimney, throwing down the top, and melting together the blades of a pair of large scissors hanging below the mantel-piece against the chimney.

The early settlers of the West were greatly aided by the wild game, fruits, and honey, which were most abundant. There were walnuts, hickory-nuts, hazelnuts, pecans, raspberries, blackberries, wild plums, summer, fall, and winter grapes; of game, the squirrel, rabbit, opossum, coon, deer, and black bear; and of fowls, the quail, wild duck, goose, swan, prairie chicken,

and wild turkey, the noblest game-fowl among them all. For some years no tame turkeys were raised, as the wild were abundant and just as good. Domestication may change the color of the plumage, but not the quality or the color of the flesh of the turkey. One turkey hen would usually rear a flock of from ten to fifteen each year. We had dogs well trained to hunt the turkeys by trailing them up and forcing them to take refuge in the timber, the dogs standing below the turkey on the tree, and keeping up an incessant barking, so as to keep his attention fixed upon the dogs, while the skillful hunter approached unobserved within rifle-shot. The dogs used were the ordinary curs.

I remember a circumstance which occurred in Clay County when I was about seventeen, and my brother Glen fifteen. I had left my father's house, and was living with my sister Constantia's second husband, Major William L. Smith, then a merchant of Liberty. Two or three days before Christmas I went to visit my parents, and to spend the Christmas holidays at home. The well-trained dogs, Major, Captain, and Cue, had not forgotten me. My mother requested Glen and myself to kill some wild turkeys for the Christmas dinner, and directed us to shoot them in the head, so as not to tear the body. Fully confident in our marksmanship, we promised her we would do so. Taking the faithful and keen-scented dogs and the trusty old rifle, with its black-walnut stock and flint-lock, we started into the hills toward the Missouri bottoms, and soon found a flock of gobblers, one of which alighted in a tall red-oak tree, near the top. Being older than my brother and a guest, it was my privilege to have the first shot. I approached as near as I could venture to do (as I saw the turkey

was very wild, from the high head he held), and determined that I would, as requested, shoot him in the head; but, when I endeavored to take aim, the distance was so great and the object so small that I despaired of hitting his head; and so taking, as I thought, good aim at his body, I fired and he fell. From his much fluttering, I feared I had not given him a fatal shot, and that the dogs, in their efforts to kill him, would tear his flesh; so I told my brother to run to the turkey, while I remained to load my rifle, the custom of the hunter being to load his gun the first thing, and on the spot from which he fires his shot. When I had loaded and went to the turkey, I found I had shot him through the neck just below the head, the ball breaking his neck-bone. We then proceeded, and soon started up a flock of hens (as the hens and gobblers go in separate flocks in winter, and pair in spring), one of which alighted in the fork of a hackberry tree. I requested my brother to shoot, but he declined, thinking no doubt that I was a superior shot. So I determined, as before, that I would shoot the turkey in the head; but when taking aim I despaired of success, and taking, as I again thought, good aim at the body of the bird, I fired and she fell. When I came to examine her, I found my ball had just knocked off the top of her head, entering the skull to the depth of half an inch.

With these two turkeys we went home in triumph, and, as I did not then disclose the fact of having taken aim at the body, I was considered the best shot in the neighborhood. It was a singular circumstance that my mother should have first directed us to shoot the birds in the head, and that I should have accidentally done so twice in succession. The explanation is that I had simply overshot, owing perhaps to an overcharge of powder.

BEE-HUNT—FISTICUFF FIGHTS—LAZY BILL.

Before I went to live with Major Smith, a circumstance occurred that deeply distressed our family. In the fall of 1823 I went in company with an uncle on a bee-hunt. We took a negro man ("Uncle Hal") and my father's good wagon and team, and a number of kegs and one barrel to hold the honey which we expected to find. We crossed the State line into the Indian country, keeping the open prairie until we had passed several miles beyond the frontier, when we left our wagon in the edge of the prairie, and, with the horses, guns, blankets, and a few kegs, took to the timber. We traveled through the forest one day, and looked diligently for bees as we rode along on our horses. I remember that I found two bee-trees that day. I was very proud of my success, as no others were found, and my uncle was a veteran bee-hunter. We hunted three or four days before we returned to the wagon. Bees were generally hunted in the fall or winter, as the hives were then full of honey. In the fall the hunter would find the hive by seeing the bees coming in and going out; but in the winter he would discover the bee-tree by finding the dead bees on the snow at the foot of the tree. When a bee dies in a hive the living cast out his dead body, which falls to the ground. This is done during the few warm clear days in winter.

When we left the wagon in the edge of the prairie, it was early in October. The tall prairie grass was green, and there was no apparent danger of fire; but the second night out there fell a severe frost, and as we approached the prairie we smelt the smoke, and at once feared our wagon was gone. The prairie had been set on fire, I suppose, by the Indians, to drive all the game

into the timber. The fire extended into the thick underbrush that skirted the prairie, and cooked the ripe summer grapes on the vines that bound the hazel thickets together. We had some difficulty in finding the place where we left the wagon ; but, when we did at length find it, there was none of its wood-work left but the hubs, and they were still burning. I remember the most sorrowful looks of my uncle and of the negro man. The latter was a faithful slave, about forty years old ; he had always driven the team, and was proud of it. He was so much distressed that he wept. I was greatly distressed myself, for I knew what a heavy loss it would be to the family. My father was not able to purchase another, and afterward for some time had to get along with a cart, which he made himself.

In reference to the simple mode of dress then common among the people of Western Missouri, I will state an illustrative circumstance. I was not present, but had the facts from the gentleman himself. He was a man of education, of strictly temperate habits, and, although not a professor of religion, remarkable for his general good conduct. He was a merchant of Liberty, and on one occasion he attended preaching in the country not far from town. He was one of the very few who dressed in broadcloth, which he wore on this occasion. The preacher was an old man well known ; and during his sermon he referred to this gentleman, not by name, but as the smooth-faced young man in fine apparel, and severely condemned his style of dress, as being contrary to the spirit of the gospel. The behavior of the gentleman was orderly and respectful.

In those primitive times fisticuff fights were very common, especially at our militia trainings. After the military exercises (which were not remarkable for ac-

curacy) were over, some bully would mount a stump, imitate the clapping and crowing of a cock, and declare aloud that he could whip any man in that crowd except his friends. Those who were not his professed friends were thus challenged to fight. If the challenge was accepted, the two combatants selected their seconds, and repaired to some place where the crowd could witness the contest, the seconds keeping back the throng outside the limits designated, and knocking down any one who attempted to interfere. When a hero was conquered, he made it known by a low cry of "'Nuff!" After washing their faces, the combatants usually took a friendly drink together; and, if the vanquished was not satisfied, he went away determined upon another trial at some future time.

These contests were governed by certain rules, according to which they were generally conducted. They arose, not from hatred or animosity as a general rule, but from pride and love of fame. It was simply a very severe trial of manhood, perseverance, and skill. I have known men on such occasions to lose part of the ear or nose, and sometimes an eye. In most cases both parties were severely bruised, bitten, and gouged, and would be weeks in recovering. It was a brutal, but not fatal mode of combat. I never knew one to terminate fatally. The custom of stabbing and shooting came into use after this. The conqueror took great, and the conquered little, pleasure in relating the incidents of the fight. The description of one was diffuse, of the other concise. Most generally the defeated hero had some complaint to make of foul play, or some plausible excuse to give, like an unsuccessful candidate for office.

Among our neighbors in Clay County, there was a tall, long-legged, lazy man, of the name of William Fox,

called "lazy Bill." He did very little work, and yet managed well, had a good farm, made a good living, and was a good stock-raiser. Among his cattle he had a very fine, blooded male calf, running in his blue-grass pasture, on the side of a considerable ridge. One warm day Fox caught the calf (then six months old) by the tail, and the animal at once started on a run down hill, increasing his speed at every successive jump. At first Fox's steps were of reasonable length, but soon they became awfully long, and Fox saw that he could not possibly continue such a rate of speed. In passing near a sapling, he ran around on the other side from the calf, still holding on to the tail. The result was a sudden fetch-up and fall of both Fox and the calf. The calf went off apparently unhurt, but next morning Fox found him dead. Upon examination, he found that the calf's back was disjointed a short distance above the root of the tail. It was not so long a race as that of John Gilpin, but more fatal.

It was among these simple backwoods people that I grew up to manhood. When my father settled in Howard County, that point was upon the frontier; and when he moved to Clay he was still upon the confines of civilization. Clay was one of the most western counties of one of the most western States; all the country west of that to the shore of the great Pacific Ocean being wild Indian country, in which white men were not permitted to reside, except the traders licensed by the United States, and the officers and soldiers stationed at the military posts. The means of education did not then exist, except to a very limited extent; and we had too much hard work to admit of attending school, except at intervals during the summer. At school I learned to spell, read, write, and cipher so far as the rule of sup-

position, and studied English grammar so as to be able to parse and punctuate with tolerable accuracy. This was the sum total of my school education.

PRAIRIES—THEIR ORIGIN.

Much speculation has been indulged in, as to the origin of those beautiful grassy plains in the West called prairies. From my own observation, I take this theory to be true : Before the country was inhabited by Indians, those now bare spaces were covered with timber, and this timber, in places, was first prostrated by hurricanes, and, when dry, was set on fire by the Indians. So intense were the fires caused by such a mass of dry fuel that the young growth of timber was entirely destroyed, and the coarse prairie grass came up in the vacant spaces, it being the only grass that will grow well in the hot sun, and for this reason soon subdued the other wild grasses usually found intermixed with the timber. The timber being entirely destroyed over a considerable space, the fires of each succeeding fall encroached more and more upon the timbered portions of the country. I have observed that the surface of the prairies of the West was generally either level or gently undulating, permitting the wind to sweep freely over every part of it. As we approach the hilly country skirting the Missouri bottoms, we nearly always find dense forests of timber, till we ascend the river west to the dry region, where timber never grows. The Indians, living solely upon the wild game, found the fallen timber in their way of travel and impeding their success in hunting ; and they therefore set the dry wood on fire. They also found in due time that it was far more difficult to hunt the deer in the prairie than in the timber ; and they accordingly fired the prairies in the

early fall, so as to force the game into the timber for food.

Some have supposed that the origin of the prairies was due to drought. This I think can not be correct, for the reason that the soil of the prairies is naturally rich, and more moist than the soil of the timbered land. The drought would of course more affect the hilly land than that which was level or gently undulating. Besides, the underbrush, especially the hazel (which loves a rich soil and grows very thickly upon the ground), is found in much greater abundance on level and gently undulating land, and is easily killed by fire in the fall immediately after frost, and before the leaves fall. I know this was the case when my father's wagon was burned. The fire on that occasion extended some distance into the timber, killing but not consuming the green underbrush, especially the hazel. The young hazel that would next year grow from the roots, being intermixed with the old and dry brush, would be killed by the fire the succeeding fall. This process of burning would entirely destroy the roots in time, thus enlarging the prairie until the increase in size would be stopped by the hilly country or other obstructions.

The reason why there were no prairies in Tennessee and Kentucky was the fact that the predominant timber in those States is the beech and poplar, which are not easily killed by fire. The beech seldom or never forks, but sends out its numerous small limbs from a few feet above the ground to its top, making so dense a shade that little or no shrubbery can grow in a beech forest. However much the beech timber may be crowded, the trees will still send out their limbs horizontally, and will not grow tall, like most other timber (especially the pine family) when crowded. Even when there was an un-

dergrowth in those States, it was mostly the cane, which is an evergreen and will not burn in a forest, though it grows as thick as hemp. On the contrary, there was no beech, poplar, or cane in the vicinity of the prairies; but the timber was mainly oak, ash, elm, hickory, walnut, hackberry, and wild cherry, all of which grow tall and slender when crowded, and have no horizontal limbs near the ground. There was therefore room beneath for a thick undergrowth, and the soil, being exceedingly rich, could well support the large and small growths upon the same space. It is also a well-known fact that hurricanes often occur in the West, and that they are so severe as to prostrate all the standing timber, throwing all the trees in the same direction. I remember to have seen two spots over which these terrible tempests had passed. One was in Howard and the other in Jackson County, Missouri; and the fallen timber lay so thick upon the ground that it was difficult to pass through it on horseback. According to my recollection, hurricanes were very rare in Tennessee and Kentucky. These destructive storms are usually about half a mile in width and several miles in length.

RETURN TO TENNESSEE — EMPLOYED AS CLERK IN AN HOTEL.

I remained with my brother-in-law, William L. Smith, some fifteen months, and then returned to my father's house. In the fall of 1826, when I was in my nineteenth year, Uncle Constant Hardeman and wife came to visit us from their home in Rutherford County, Tennessee; and, after due consideration, it was determined that I should accompany them on their return. My father gave me a horse three years old the preceding spring, a saddle and bridle, a new camlet cloak, and

twenty-six dollars in money ; and my mother furnished me with a good suit of jeans. We usually traveled about thirty-three miles a day. My young horse stood the trip well at the beginning, but gradually became exhausted, so that by the time we reached Nashville it was all I could do to get along. My pride was much wounded by my situation. Before leaving home, I had not often seen the inside of an hotel ; and I was therefore very green, which became painfully more evident as we approached the older settlements. I was naturally diffident when young; and, when I arrived in Tennessee among my rich kin, I at once recognized my comparative poverty and ignorance. I remember that the first time that I ever saw Pope's translation of the Iliad was at the house of Uncle Constant Hardeman, soon after my arrival there ; and, had it been gold or precious stones, the pleasure would not have equaled that which I enjoyed. I was very fond of reading, and eagerly devoured everything that fell in my way. But when I saw that my relatives were rich, and valued riches more than knowledge, I determined that I would employ my energies in the accumulation of a fortune. Conscious of my own poverty, ignorance, and homely dress, I fancied that I was sometimes slighted by my relatives. I, however, said nothing, made no complaints, but laid it up in my heart that I would some day equal if not surpass them.

After spending a few weeks with my uncle Constant and other relatives near him, I visited my Uncle Blackstone Hardeman, who then lived in Maury County, Tennessee, and who was upon the eve of removing to the Western District, a new portion of that State, to which the Indian title had been but lately extinguished, and which was settling up rapidly by emigrants, mainly

from the older localities of that State. As I was out of business, I decided to go with him and assist him to make the journey. It was in November, and we had heavy cold rains on the way, making it a hard trip. When we arrived at his new farm near Bolivar, Hardeman County, my suit of jeans was pretty well gone, the elbows of my coat being worn out. My uncle Blackstone succeeded in procuring me a situation as clerk at the hotel in Bolivar, kept by an old man, Duguid Mims. It was a large frame building covered in, the floors laid, the outside weatherboarded up, and the outside doors hung ; but the inside work was unfinished. The country was new, and men at a hotel or on a steamboat will generally act out their true characters. I had, therefore, a good school of human nature, and found a great deal of it in mankind.

My salary was one hundred dollars per annum, and my duty was to wait on the guests at the table, keep the books, and collect the bills. The only decent articles of dress that I had were my fur hat and camlet cloak. My term of service commenced on the day before Christmas, and there was a great frolic among the guests at the hotel. Among other freaks committed by them, they cut up into narrow strips all the hats they could find ; and as mine, with others, was placed on a large work-bench in the main hall, it fared as the rest did. I was exceedingly green and awkward, as may well be supposed ; and my imperfections were the more remarked from the fact that I succeeded a young man, of the name of Outlaw, who understood the duties of the position well. My kind old employer had never seen me but twice before, and the only money I had was in the hands of my uncle, who lived six or seven miles from town. It was a busy time, and I had no immediate op-

portunity to communicate with him; and, as I was ashamed to ask Mr. Mims or any one else to credit me, I was compelled to go bare-headed for a week. I was the subject of much jesting, was badly quizzed and greatly mortified; but I worked on resolutely, said nothing, and was always at my post of duty. In about a week my uncle came to town, and I stated to him my situation, and through his influence I procured another hat.

By assiduity and attention I soon learned the duties of my new position; and in about three months I procured a new suit of clothes, the first suit of broadcloth I ever wore. I remember overhearing the remarks that were made when I first put it on. "Do you see Burnett? He is coming out."

My employer had a daughter of his own, and two grown-up step-daughters, who were very pretty girls; but they considered themselves as my superiors, and I never kept their company.

I remained with Mr. Mims five or six months. In the spring the business of the hotel was dull, and the inside work of the building had to be finished. The old man was very enterprising, dipping into almost everything that offered, and going into debt pretty freely; but he was very industrious and honest. As there was so little travel at this season, and as Mr. Mims was extensively engaged in brick-making, he would take the negro boy who was the hostler to the brickyard. When any guests arrived, I first waited on them, then took their horses to the stable, fed and curried them, and saddled them up in the morning; and, when there was nothing else to do, I took the paint-brush and went to painting the hotel building. I knew nothing of the business at first, as it was little known in my former lo-

cality; but I soon, in this way, learned to do plain painting well.

SAMUEL HOUSTON—NEWTON CANNON—ANDREW MARTIN—DAVID CROCKETT—ADAM HUNTSMAN.

One day, while engaged very busily in painting the ceiling overhead, the Rev. W. Blount Peck, who was about to open a store on Clear Creek, some ten miles from Bolivar, came to see me, and said that he wished to employ me to take charge of the entire business of selling the goods, keeping the books, and collecting the debts, and he himself would purchase the goods. He offered me two hundred dollars per annum, he paying for my washing, board, and lodging. I said that I was engaged to serve Mr. Mims for one year, and could not violate my engagement, but would lay the matter before him, and if he consented I would take charge of the store upon the terms stated. Accordingly, I conferred with Mr. Mims, and he kindly gave me permission to quit his service, saying that he would not stand in the way of my promotion.

When I set out in life, I was fully conscious of my want of information, and I at first decided in my own mind to say very little, but listen and learn, and in this way avoid exposure. But I found, from practical experience, that the best way to correct errors was to make them known, and then some friend would kindly correct them for you; and, if no friend should do so, your enemies would. I found that patient and intelligent perseverance almost always won.

While at the hotel, I saw General Samuel Houston, David Crockett, Adam Huntsman, Newton Cannon, Andrew Martin, and other leading men of Tennessee; and I heard Houston, Crockett, and Cannon speak.

Houston, then in the prime of life, was a tall, noble Virginian, possessing a most commanding figure and voice, with a bold, flowery, and eloquent style of oratory. He had a great command of language, and spoke slowly, emphatically, and distinctly, so that all could hear him, and all wished to hear him. Newton Cannon was a very plain, earnest, forcible, and rapid speaker, a strict logician, but not a popular orator. While Houston and Cannon were speaking, no one ever laughed, as they never dealt in amusing anecdotes. General Houston never succeeded at the bar. His mind was not of a legal cast. Cannon possessed as much if not more legal ability, and was fully Houston's equal in statesmanship ; but he could not command the admiration of the masses, as Houston did.

David Crockett was a man of another cast of mind and manner. He possessed a fine natural intellect, good memory, and great good nature. He had treasured up all the good anecdotes he had ever heard, and could readily relate many striking incidents of his own career. He was deficient in education, and had no practical knowledge of statesmanship ; but he was willing and able to learn, and had the patience to bear ridicule and reproach for the time being. He was an off-hand speaker, full of anecdotes, and kept a crowd greatly amused. His comparisons and illustrations were new and simple, but strong and pointed. Few public speakers could get any advantage of David Crockett before a crowd of backwoods people. His good-natured, honest, jolly face would remind one of Dryden's description

"Of Bacchus—ever fair and ever young."

I knew in Hardeman County a Baptist preacher of the name of Casey, one of Nature's orators, who mur-

dered the King's English in every sentence and mispronounced half his words. Yet he was so eloquent that one forgot these defects, and they almost became graces, as they were peculiarities with him. It was very much so with David Crockett. Any one hearing either of these speakers would wish to hear him again.

W. B. PECK—JOHN Y. COCKRAM—PETER MINNER.

So soon as Parson Peck, as he was familiarly called, had finished his storehouse (which was a log-cabin about eighteen by twenty feet, with chinked cracks, clapboard roof, and puncheon floor), I took my leave of Bolivar. The stock was not large, and Parson Peck usually made his purchases upon time in New Orleans. He did a general credit business, the debts becoming due about Christmas, and payable in cotton, which was generally delivered in the seed at the cotton-gin near the store, a receipt taken for so many pounds, and the receipt transferred to us. Parson Peck was a Methodist, and resided about ten miles from the store, and the labor and responsibility of conducting the business necessarily fell upon me. He was from East Tennessee, and was a brother of Judge Peck of the Supreme Court of Tennessee, and of Judge Peck of the United States District Court for Missouri. It was a talented family, and Parson Peck was a man of fine literary ability. His wife before her marriage was a Miss Rivers, a sister of Dr. Rivers, and daughter of a wealthy planter of Hardeman County. I remember him and his lady with sentiments of gratitude.

The mercantile business, especially in a new country, where the credit system prevails, and especially where the merchant has but little capital, is certain to prove a failure. As my employer had very little capital, he

was unsuccessful; and, as I had managed the business in selling and collecting, he blamed me to some extent, though I did not wrong him at all. I did my duty faithfully to the utmost of my ability. In turn, I censured him because he had twice pledged the same debt to two different creditors of his. These mutual charges led to a partial estrangement, which continued until I left the State. I have deeply regretted the circumstance. Upon more mature reflection I became satisfied that the act of pledging the same book account to two different creditors was purely a mistake, and that he was entirely honest in his intentions. After I became satisfied of my mistake I inquired for him, and, learning that he was probably in Philadelphia, I wrote a kind explanation to him directed to that city. I desired to do him all the justice in my power, and to renew to him the assurances of my esteem and gratitude. Whether he received my letter or not I never knew.

While I was doing business as a clerk for Parson Peck in the winter of 1827–'28, a circumstance occurred that made a lasting impression upon my memory. It was one of the happy incidents of my life.

There were two farmers, both Methodists, who were in partnership in a cotton-gin situated near the store. John Y. Cockram, aged about forty-five, was the owner of six or eight slaves, and cultivated a plantation of considerable size; while Peter Minner, aged about thirty-three, was not the owner of any slaves, but had a small farm, and was in very moderate circumstances. John Y. Cockram was a native of New Madrid County, Missouri, and was a peculiar man, possessed of a fine intellect, pretty well improved. I never met any one who was blessed with a more engaging manner. He was a noble man, and possessed the rare power of governing

others without the use of force. He assured me that he had never struck one of his children a blow in his life, and never but one of his slaves, and that a little negro girl. His seven or eight children, and all of his slaves, were exceedingly dutiful, and devotedly attached to him. Peter Minner was a man of plain good sense, remarkable for his kind and humble demeanor, but did not possess the natural intellect or literary cultivation of Cockram. Minner resided near the gin, and Cockram some distance from it. When the gin had been completed Minner received the cotton from the customers and superintended the business generally, Cockram giving his main attention to his plantation.

After they had been doing business some time, and had received and ginned a large amount of cotton for various persons, Cockram came one day and said to me, in confidence, that he feared there was something wrong in Minner's accounts. He exhibited to me the partnership books, kept by Minner, and we examined them together to ascertain the true state of the case. I was myself familiar with many of the transactions, as I was very intimate with both partners, and boarded at Minner's house. For my life I could not see how Minner could ever explain the errors apparent upon the face of the books, or justify himself. It seemed to be as clear a case of fraud as facts and figures could make.

Cockram asked me what he ought to do. I told him to see Minner at once, state to him plainly his fears, and ask for an investigation. He accordingly called upon Minner, who heard his statement with kindness and patience, and at once consented to refer the matter to two arbitrators, chosen by the consent of both parties. I was one of the arbitrators, and I remember the manner of Minner during the investigation, for I observed him

closely. He kept his eyes fixed upon the floor, except at intervals, when returning an answer to a point made by Cockram. He would then raise his large, meek, black eye, look me full in the face, and give his explanation. I watched his eye, and could read his very soul, and there was no guilt there. The mild and pure expression of that gentle eye went to my inmost heart. It was all I could do to restrain my tears ; and I can never think of that most beautiful scene without emotion. Oh, if there be on this earth one object more beautiful than all others, it is the sweet expression of the eye of a just man.

The arbitrators had no decision to make. Minner's explanations were so clear and satisfactory, that the noble Cockram, without waiting to hear any expression of opinion from the arbitrators, sprang to his feet and exclaimed, " Gentlemen, I am satisfied."

This incident was of great benefit to me in after-life. It taught me a beautiful lesson. I had rather look for men's virtues than for their vices, rather err upon the side of charity than against it, and prefer to hear *both* sides before I come to any conclusion.

The two men remained friends, and both died of fever three or four years afterward, each leaving a widow and several children. Cockram became the sole owner of the gin ; and, after his crop of cotton had been gathered one fall, the gin was destroyed by fire, and his whole crop with it. When informed of the disaster, he simply replied, " These hands can raise more."

COURTSHIP AND MARRIAGE.

It was during the time that I acted as clerk for Parson Peck that I became acquainted with the lady who afterward became my wife. There are two very im-

portant epochs in one's life: when he gets married himself, and when he gives away his first daughter. To give away the second is not so trying. When you rear a son, knowing as you do all his traits and habits, you can form some probable conclusion as to his future course in life; but, as a *general* rule, you never know your son-in-law well until some time after his marriage.

My wife's father, Peter Rogers, formerly lived in Wilson County, Tennessee, where his children were born. The fall after I commenced business for Parson Peck, Mr. Rogers removed to a farm in the immediate neighborhood. His brother, Dr. John Rogers, had been living and practicing his profession in that vicinity for one or two years. I knew the doctor well, and he was often at the store. The eldest son of Mr. Rogers, Hardin J., was a finely educated young man, and the first time I ever saw him I loved him—why, I could not tell, but I loved him. He was a noble young man, with a fine face and beautiful black eye, my favorite. Mr. Rogers had two daughters, Harriet W. and Sarah M., the first sixteen and the other fourteen years of age. I often heard the young men of the vicinity speak of the two sisters, and especially a young friend of mine, Calvin Stevens, who frequently waited upon Miss Harriet. He was a very pleasant fellow, and was very fond of the society of the ladies. I had not the slightest idea of marriage myself, but I determined, from a mere mischievous freak, to cut out Calvin. I was satisfied that he had no serious intention of marrying any one. He had a very fine tall figure, handsome face, and engaging manners. In these respects I considered him my superior, but I thought I could out-talk him; and so I did. But, when I had succeeded in cutting out Calvin, I found myself caught. The girl had won my heart.

She was a little above the medium height, with a trim, neat figure, sparkling black eye, handsome face, low, sweet voice, and gentle manners. Her father and mother were admirable people. I have met few if any better people than Mother Rogers. Mr. Rogers was a man of fine common sense, had a kind, generous heart, good habits, and a most determined will. He had served under General Jackson in the Creek war ; and, though possessed of great good nature, when fully roused he was as brave as a lion. Himself, wife, and Miss Harriet were Methodists. Their home was the abode of industry, integrity, and peace. I liked the family. They were good livers, but not rich. Mr. Rogers was an indulgent father and master, and a good neighbor. It was almost impossible to involve Mr. and Mrs. Rogers in neighborhood quarrels, those pests of society. They were alike esteemed by all, both rich and poor. I never saw Mr. Rogers shed a tear, though he lost his wife and several grown children. It was not his nature to weep either for joy or sorrow.

I was not for some time aware of the fact that I was in love with the girl. I accompanied her home one Saturday ; and after dinner we were engaged in conversation for some two or three hours. At last it suddenly occurred to me that it was time I should go home. I hastily bade her good evening, and rushed into the yard, and happened to meet her father passing through it. I looked around for the sun, and was amazed to find that it was gone. In a confused manner, I inquired of Mr. Rogers what had become of the sun. He politely replied, "It has gone down, Mr. Burnett." I knew then that I was in love. It was a *plain* case.

When I found myself deeply in love, I considered the matter carefully. I remember well that, on the

night of that same Saturday, I laid myself down upon the hard counter (the place where I usually slept) with a blanket under me, and a roll of flannel for a pillow, and spent the whole night without sleep, debating with myself whether I should go the next day and make a serious speech to Miss Harriet. I was a poor clerk, with nothing to depend upon for a living but my own exertions. This was a powerful objection; but my heart won the day, and the heart is sometimes as right as the head. The matter was decided; and it is my nature to act promptly when I have once determined to do a thing. Let me only be fully satisfied as to the course to be pursued, and I at once go straight to a point. The next day I went to see Miss Harriet. I was not abrupt, but earnest and candid. I introduced the subject discreetly, made the best speech I could, and secured her consent and that of her parents. This was early in June, and we were married on the 20th of August, 1828. The day was dark and rainy until about an hour before sunset, when it cleared off beautifully, and the sun set in smiles. I hope my sun of life may set as tranquilly as the sun of that day. If it should (and I have faith to believe it will), my wedding-day will have been a fit emblem of my life.

I was of the opinion that I could go through the ceremony without trepidation, and I felt none until I passed over the steps across the yard fence, when I suddenly felt so weak that I could scarcely stand. The guests had most of them arrived, and were in the yard looking at me as I approached the house. But I made my way hastily through the crowd, and my acquaintances each rushed forward, saying, "How are you?" I was so confused that I simply held out my right hand for each one to shake; and when my cousin Mary Harde-

man spoke to me, though I was as well acquainted with her as I was with any one, I did not know her. But, this excitement having passed away, I was myself again, and was not confused when my friend Parson Peck performed the ceremony. When married, I was nearly twenty-one and my wife nearly seventeen.

I owe much of my success in life to her. Had I not married early, I do not know what might have been my course in life. I might have fallen into vicious habits. Though I was not religious myself, I loved a religious girl—there is something in piety so becoming a gentle woman. My wife was never noisy, fanatical, or wildly enthusiastic in her religious feelings; but she was *very firm*. For many years after our marriage she had a hard time of it as to her religion. I was full of mischief, fond of jokes, and loved festive occasions; and I used to urge her to go with me to dances, but she always firmly yet mildly refused. She has always been a woman of few words. For some years after our marriage, I was often perplexed to understand her judgment of persons. It frequently happened that on first acquaintance I would form a most favorable opinion of the person; and, when I would ask her what she thought of him, she would say, "I don't like him." When asked why, she could give no reason. She knew she was right, but could not tell why. Her knowledge was instinctive; but generally time proved the correctness of her conclusions. It was so with my mother. Her judgment of people was quick, decisive, and generally correct. When a family claimed to have been once rich, though then poor, she always observed whether they had saved any relics as mementoes of former prosperity. If they had not, she doubted their statements.

PURCHASE OF THE STORE—DEATH OF A BURGLAR.

In the spring of 1829 I purchased the stock of goods of Parson Peck at original cost, on eighteen months' credit, for which I gave him my promissory notes. Most of these notes he transferred to his creditors. I was to close up the old business. I built me a log cabin near the store, and moved into it about the same time. Everything went on very smoothly during the year 1829 ; but in 1830 I found I could not replenish my stock of merchandise, which was so much reduced that I was unable to supply the wants of the locality, and could not well dispose of the remnants I had on hand. Our household furniture was remarkably plain, and our expenses were small.

While I was doing business for myself, I purchased three barrels of old Monongahela whisky, which I retailed out by the pint, quart, and gallon. It was a favorite with those who loved liquor. It took me about three months to retail it out, and during this period I was in the habit of taking a drink in the morning, and occasionally during the day. I was not aware that I loved it until it was all gone. Then I found, to my surprise, that I had acquired a taste for it. I reflected upon the fact, and went into a sort of mathematical calculation under the "single rule of three." I said to myself: "If in three months I have acquired so much love of whisky, how much would I acquire in three years?" The thought alarmed me, and I soon determined that I would abstain entirely, which has been my general practice. As I do everything with all my might, I became satisfied that, if I indulged at all, I would be very apt to do some very tall drinking. Had

I not been a married man, and happy as such, I might have fallen into this fatal habit.

While this is no proper place for a long discussion of the question of temperance, I will make a few remarks, suggested by long observation and experience. If we take a hundred men at the age of twenty-one who entirely abstain, there will not be a drunkard among them. If, on the contrary, we select a hundred young men who are moderate drinkers at that age, there will in due time be ten sots out of that number. As no man can tell *in advance* whether he will fall or not, he incurs a risk of ten per cent. in drinking at all. If two young men of anything like equal ability apply to a sound, cautious business man for employment, and one abstains and the other does not, the temperate one is almost sure to be preferred. So, if a young man is extravagant and spends all his income, saving up nothing, he will find it hard to obtain employment. But the young man who does not drink, and who saves up a reasonable portion of his salary, gives *clear proof* that he has a due command over his tastes and appetites—that he has reflection, honesty, and good sense. Such a one can be safely trusted, because he does not need to steal. In the history of embezzlements, very few cases will be found where the party was temperate and saving.

My father never used tobacco in any form; and while I remained with him I had no opportunity and no temptation to use it myself. But in the fall of 1827, while I was in charge of the store for Parson Peck, I one day purchased a hundred home-made cigars, and in the evening invited some young friends to smoke with me. I knew so little of the use of the article and of its effects, that I never once thought of its making me sick.

I therefore smoked as long and as much as the others. After they had left the store, I became exceedingly sick. I have had several attacks of fever, and have been sea-sick at different times; but I never endured sensations so distressing as on this occasion. It seemed as if the hills were rolling over upon me.

But this rash experiment proved in the end a great benefit to me, and I was amply rewarded for my sufferings. It prevented me from ever using tobacco in any form. This was the first and last time I ever smoked.

He is a *very* wise man who profits by the experience of others, without waiting to suffer himself *before* he learns. If I could only place my views in the minds of young men, before they contract the useless, expensive, often offensive, and sometimes positively injurious habit of using tobacco, I should accomplish a great good.

It is our plain duty to give as little pain to our fellow beings as we reasonably can. The man who uses tobacco wastes a considerable sum in the course of a long life, which justly belongs to his family. It is almost impossible for a smoker to avoid giving great pain to others at times. He is sure to smoke at improper times and in wrong places. The danger of using tobacco to excess is so great, that a young man who is known to use it will find it far more difficult to procure employment. The business man who smokes himself would prefer that his clerk should not. The use is undoubtedly injurious to some constitutions, if not to all; and no young man, about to learn the use of tobacco, can tell in advance how much he may be injured. There is, therefore, a *useless* risk incurred, which is not in accordance with good, practical business sense; and the habit, once acquired, is most difficult to correct.

During the time I was retailing liquor above men-

tioned, in 1830, a melancholy circumstance occurred, which I have long deeply regretted. My stock of goods being very low, and my wife sick with fever, I removed her to her father's house, about a mile distant. Parson Peck had built a neat frame storehouse, which fell to me in the purchase. My brother-in-law, Hardin J. Rogers, often slept at the store, but occasionally no one slept there. One morning, when I went to the store, I found the window-shutter forcibly broken open by the use of some flat instrument, about the size of a two-inch chisel. I lay there myself at night watching for the burglar, until I became so sleepy that I could keep awake no longer. I lay upon the floor behind the counter, with a loaded shot-gun on the counter above me, determined to shoot the burglar if he should come and enter the store. The window-shutter was generally fastened with an iron bolt on the inside. It was not fastened this night, but from the shutter a string extended to the handle of a large tin coffee-pot placed by me on the edge of the counter, so that opening the shutter would at once throw off the pot, the fall of which would necessarily make a great noise. I kept awake until late at night, when I fell asleep. In the morning I found the pot on the floor, but so sound was my slumber that I had not heard it. It had evidently frightened the burglar, so that he did not enter. I then determined I would try another plan. I securely fastened the shutter and placed the shot-gun cocked upon the counter, with a string extending from one end of the yardstick to the shutter, and so arranged that when the shutter was forced open the gun would go off. Next morning, when I went to the store, I found a negro man lying on his back dead, with a mill-pick and a jug by his side. He had broken open the window-shutter with

the pick, and the shot and one bullet had entered his forehead and produced instant death. I at once went to Bolivar and told the circumstances as they occurred, and inquired for the coroner. My friend Major John H. Bills told me confidentially that he would advise me not to mention the fact, as it might involve me in penalties; but I told him I must state the truth. An inquest was duly held, and I was called as a witness, but told I was not legally bound to state anything that would tend to criminate myself; but I stated all the facts truly. I was never prosecuted, and the owner of the slave never sued me for damages. It was a clear case of justifiable homicide under the laws of the State. Still, in after-life, I have deeply regretted the act; and, the older I become, the more I could wish it had never occurred. The poor negro was fond of liquor, and wanted nothing else. It was a sad case. I had no idea who it could be until he was killed. He was employed at a mill some two miles distant. I am hard to excite, but when fully aroused my natural feelings are desperate. But, thank God, through his mercy, the idea of shedding human blood is now terrible to me. I would rather bear almost any injury than take human life.

RETURN TO MISSOURI—CROCKETT AND HUNTSMAN.

My brother, Glen O. Burnett, two years younger than myself, came to Hardeman County, and married the other daughter of Mr. Rogers, January 6, 1830. In the fall of 1830 Mr. Rogers moved to Clay County, Missouri. I found it impossible for me to continue the mercantile business in that locality; and I decided to close up my business, pay my debts, and study law. My brother Glen determined to return to Clay County, Missouri, where my father had given him a tract of

land. I also decided to return thither. It was accordingly arranged between us that my wife and little son should accompany him, while I remained to close up my business. I supposed it would take me a few months. In the mean time Hardin J. Rogers and myself sent to Nashville, by my cousin John M. Hardeman, and purchased a small library of law-books, containing only the elementary works upon the science. We boarded and lodged with an uncle of my wife's, William Hardin, built a little log office, and prosecuted our studies vigorously. I had my old business to wind up, and had to travel about the country a good deal, endeavoring to collect debts due to me, in which effort I had but moderate success. Cotton was low, and times were hard. When my notes became due, they were placed in the hands of Austin Miller, Esq., a lawyer of Bolivar, for collection. I went at once to him and assigned to him all debts due to me, with a few exceptions. He took the assignment, and then placed the debts in my hands for collection. I collected all I could, and paid the amounts collected to him. I would not leave the State without his consent.

In the fall of 1831 new troubles assailed us. I was first attacked with fever, and then Hardin J. Rogers was attacked in turn. I recovered, and he died. Poor fellow! I loved him as a brother, and he was worthy.

After remaining in Tennessee thirteen months, and collecting all I could, there was still a considerable sum due upon my notes. It was useless to remain longer; and, after consultation with Austin Miller, and with his consent, I determined to accompany my wife's uncle, George M. Pirtle, who was then moving from Hardeman County to the southwestern portion of Missouri, as far as the Mississippi River, and there take a steamer

bound to St. Louis. This was in March, 1832. We traveled on slowly with wagons and teams, stock and family, until we reached the river; and there we separated. My finances were exceedingly low, and I was dressed in a suit of jeans with my elbows out, as when I arrived at Bolivar five years before. I soon took a cabin passage on a large steamer; and was perhaps the most shabbily dressed man in the cabin. I was evidently considered by the other passengers as quite green, as some of them soon started a report that the small-pox was on board. But I saw, from the glances they gave toward me and the winks they gave their companions, that they were simply aiming to quiz me and other passengers. I said nothing and paid no attention to their statements.

We arrived safely at St. Louis, and I at once went up and down the shore of the river to find a steamer up for Liberty Landing; but I could find only one for the Missouri River, and that was the old "Car of Commerce," only bound to Lexington, about thirty-five miles below my point of destination. I had only $15.62½ in my pocket, and the price of a cabin passage was $15; and the boat would not leave for several days. I therefore debated with myself whether I should take a cabin or deck passage, and I determined that I would stand erect as long as possible. I went to the clerk of the boat and told him I would take a cabin passage, provided he would allow me to come on board at once, without the expense of staying at an hotel. To this he at once assented.

We were seven days making the trip to Lexington, and arrived there on Sunday morning. I at once crossed the Missouri River, and went on foot eight miles to Richmond, where I had acquaintances, from

whom I hoped to procure a horse. But, it being Sunday, I could find no one at home that I knew; and I continued the journey on foot until near sundown, when I arrived at the house of Winfrey E. Price, about twelve miles from Liberty. I was not much sensible of fatigue until I made an effort to cross the fence around the yard, when I found it was all I could do to throw my right foot over. I had traveled the distance of about twenty-two miles. The next day I made my way to Liberty, riding a portion of the distance on a led horse, bareback. At Liberty I procured a horse and reached the house of Mr. Rogers before night. I found my wife and boy well, after a separation of fourteen months. This long separation was one of the hardest trials of my life, and gave us perhaps more pain than any other; not only because it was long, but because its length was not anticipated by us, and our young and fond hearts were not prepared to meet the severe trial.

There are some singular coincidences in the facts of our acquaintance and marriage. My wife and myself were born in adjoining counties in Tennessee, but our parents never knew or heard of each other. My father moved first to Williamson County, Tennessee, then to Howard, and lastly to Clay County, Missouri. When I was nearly grown, circumstances wholly unforeseen led me to return to Tennessee, and then to go to Bolivar, and from thence to Clear Creek; and it just so happened that Mr. Rogers, who had long lived on the same farm in Wilson County, moved to the Western District, and located in my immediate neighborhood.

While I was in Hardeman County, David Crockett and Adam Huntsman were rival candidates for Congress. Huntsman was elected by a small majority, the race being very close. He was a man of great ability,

fully equal to Crockett in native intellect, and much his superior in education and mental training. He was distinguished as a lawyer, statesman, and wit. Possessed of these qualifications, he would have easily beaten Crockett in an old community ; but there was much prejudice in the minds of the early settlers against lawyers. This objection was urged against Huntsman ; but he met it with great good humor in this way. He wore a wooden leg ; and, after readily conceding that there were objections against the profession of the law, he would insist that his was an exceptional and excusable case ; "for," said he, "I could not work, to beg I was ashamed, and I could not steal, because they would all know it was Huntsman by his track ; and I was thus compelled to be a lawyer." After the election Crockett complained through the newspapers, giving many reasons for his defeat, and charging his opponents with unfair dealing. Huntsman replied, and among other things said that his rival had not given the best reason for his defeat, and that was, he did not obtain votes enough.

This objection is often urged against lawyers when candidates for seats in legislative bodies. A very inferior lawyer was a candidate for the Legislature in some county in Kentucky ; and a distinguished old lawyer happened to overhear some citizens say they would not vote for him because he was a lawyer. The old lawyer at once stepped up to them, saying, "if that was their *only* objection, they might safely vote for him, as he was not lawyer enough to hurt him."

In the Presidential canvass of 1828, General Jackson was accused by some of his political opponents of being illiterate. It was alleged that he spelled the words "all correct" thus, "oll korrect." Hence originated the abbreviation "O. K."

About the year 1824, a gentleman from Kentucky, aged twenty-five, settled in Clay County, Missouri. While his education was exceedingly limited, he possessed a superior native intellect. He was a splendid judge of human nature, and, although illiterate, expressed his views of men and measures in language clear, concise, and strong. He soon proved to be a very superior business man, and ultimately acquired a very fine estate, which he subsequently lost during our late civil war. When he first arrived in Clay County, he spelled Congress thus, "Kongriss"; but, like the Baptist preacher Casey (whose name is mentioned in another page), his natural ability was such that the people of his district elected him to a seat in the State Senate. While attending his first session of that body, he was asked how low the mercury fell in his locality. He promptly replied, "It run into the ground about a feet." Hence arose the saying, "running it into the ground."

During my stay in Hardeman County, a young man, who was a droll and eccentric genius, was a burlesque candidate for a seat in the Legislature of Tennessee. His speeches were very amusing. In addressing the people, he declared that he could not truly say, as did his honorable competitors, that he was solicited and urged by his friends to become a candidate; that he was not like some animals, whose ears you had to pull off to get them out, and their tails to get them back; but that he became a candidate voluntarily, and was running on his own hook, and without the solicitation of his friends, for he was not aware that he had any. He, or some other person, about that time, gave a very forcible description of a vacillating politician, and applied to him this verse:

"He wabbled in, and wabbled out,
Until he left the mind in doubt
Whether the snake that made the track
Was going South, or coming back."

I had never heard of this verse before, and have not seen or heard it quoted since, and can not say whether it was original with the speaker or not. It made such an impression upon my memory that I never forgot it.

CHAPTER II.

ACT AS CLERK FOR A TIME—THEN GO INTO THE MERCANTILE BUSINESS WITH OTHERS.

WHEN I arrived at the house of Mr. Rogers, in Clay County, in the month of April, 1832, I had only sixty-two and a half cents left, was some seven hundred dollars in debt, had a wife and one child to support, and was out of employment. I had studied law altogether about six months only, and was not then prepared to make a living at the practice; and I therefore determined to obtain a position in some store as a clerk. I visited Lexington, Missouri, where John Aull then did a large mercantile business, and who was an intimate friend of my father; but he had no vacancy to fill, having all the help he required. I returned to my father-in-law's house at a loss what to do. In a few days thereafter Edward M. Samuel, then in partnership with Samuel Moor in the mercantile business in Liberty, returned from Philadelphia with a new assortment of goods, and sent me word that he wished to see me. I had sent forward by water from Tennessee my little household furniture, and my best clothes. I therefore dressed myself as well as I could, and promptly went to see Messrs. Samuel and Moor. Mr. Samuel was the active partner, and Mr. Moor the capitalist of the firm. Mr. Samuel

was pleased with me, and asked me what I would charge them per annum, and find myself. I replied that I had just arrived, and did not know what I ought to ask; but that I had heard that Mr. Bird had a salary of four hundred dollars per annum, he finding himself, and that I thought I could do their business as well as Mr. Bird did that of Mr. Aull. He replied, without hesitation, that they would give me the same salary, and let me have such goods as I might want for myself and family at a price below the ordinary retail price of the store. Mr. Bird had been a schoolmate of mine in old Franklin in 1820.

I at once removed with my family to Liberty, rented a log-house for twenty-five dollars a year, and set to work manfully. Expenses were then light in Liberty. Pork was one dollar and fifty cents per hundred pounds, wood one dollar a cord, flour very cheap, corn meal twenty-five cents a bushel, potatoes twenty cents per bushel, chickens seventy-five cents per dozen, and eggs fifteen cents a dozen.

I remained in the employment of Samuel & Moor fifteen months, and they urged me to remain longer, offering to increase my salary; but, having pretty well paid up my debts, I determined to go into the law. I obtained a license to practice from Judge Tompkins, of the Supreme Court of Missouri, purchased a house and lot in Richmond, Missouri, for the small sum of eighty dollars, repaired the same, and was on the eve of going there to reside and practice my profession, when I received a proposition from James M. and G. L. Hughes to enter into partnership in the mercantile business with them, upon very advantageous terms. They were to furnish a cash capital of eight thousand dollars, while I was not required to contribute any, and each partner

was to give his personal services to the business and have one third of the profits.

At that time, the mercantile business was prosperous, while the practice of the law was at a low stage, there being very little litigation in the country. I was still anxious to make a fortune, and this was the best opportunity that offered. We entered into partnership at the beginning of 1834, and received our first supplies in the spring of that year. We did a safe, good business that season, and I went East in the beginning of 1835 to make the annual purchases. In 1836 we took into the firm, as a partner, Colonel John Thornton, one of the wealthiest men of Clay County, who contributed five thousand dollars cash capital; thus making our total cash capital thirteen thousand dollars, which was large for that time and country. We continued this firm until the middle of 1837, when Thornton and myself purchased the interest of James M. and G. L. Hughes; and I went East in the beginning of 1838 to procure a new stock of goods. By the agreement between them and us, we were to occupy the storehouse, which belonged to James M. Hughes, until the first of May, 1838. It was understood between Colonel Thornton and myself that he should erect a storehouse upon a lot he owned in Liberty, and have it ready by the time the lease should expire. I made a very successful trip to Philadelphia, and returned with our new goods about the first of April, but found the storehouse unfinished. The Colonel had employed a man to lay the stone foundation, who did the work so badly that it became necessary to tear it down and rebuild. Our sales were fine during the month of April; but when the first of May arrived, no house on the Public Square could be obtained in which we could open our goods; and we were

compelled to box them up in part, and send another portion of them to the country, where we did but a poor business. The new store was finished and occupied in October ; but the season for our summer goods had passed, our customers had gone to other houses, and we could not reclaim our lost position. The result was a heavy loss to us. But besides this, the monetary revolution of 1837–'38 had reached us, and a great number of our customers failed, enough to absorb all the profits of the former firm, and more than enough to swallow up those of Thornton & Burnett.

Toward the close of 1834 my brother Glen visited me on one occasion, and told me it was almost impossible for him to make a living on his little farm ; and that, as his family bade fair to be large, he did not know what to do. A plan at once occurred to me. Said I, "Will you do as I advise ?" He replied "Yes." "Then go home, sell all you have, raise all the money you can, and I will put in as much as you do ; and I will bring you out a small stock of goods in the spring, and you have the house ready to receive them when they shall arrive." He at once acted on my suggestion and established the store at Barry, a small place ten miles west from Liberty. Here he did well for a year or two ; but, by the advice of others, we engaged in building and running a steam saw-mill and distillery, which entailed upon us a heavy loss. It somehow or other always happened so with me, that whenever I had anything to do with liquor, either in making or selling it, some misfortune would befall me. I have a dread of steam saw-mills, steam distilleries, and the mercantile business generally.

In 1837 William L. Smith, one of my brothers-in-law, came into partnership with Glen and myself ; and the new firm borrowed of John Aull the sum of ten

thousand dollars, with interest at the rate of ten per cent. per annum, the principal payable in five years after 1838. Mr. Smith and myself became in time the sole partners, my brother Glen having retired. I had myself finally to pay most of the losses of Glen O. Burnett & Co. (Glen O. and Peter H. Burnett), which amounted to some two thousand dollars, the loss mainly caused by that steam saw-mill and distillery. Mr. Smith and myself were equally unfortunate; and, after prosecuting the business five years with unremitting energy, I found myself in debt to the extent of about fifteen thousand dollars.

My partners, Colonel Thornton and Major Smith, were men of capital, and no creditor of either firm lost anything. But I was only the business man, with little or no capital; and I lost five years' time and expenses, and a great deal more besides. I was unable to make up my portion of the partnership losses in the firms of Thornton & Burnett, and Smith & Burnett, or to pay the amount I had used for my support. I lost in both firms.

RETURN TO THE LAW—EMPLOYED BY THE MORMON ELDERS—PROCEEDINGS ON HABEAS CORPUS.

From the latter part of 1833 to the middle of 1838 I had not opened a law-book, and had forgotten much of that which I had learned. In the spring and summer of 1838 I had an attack of sickness, which prevented me from doing any business for several months. After my recovery, foreseeing what might be the result of my mercantile operations, I read the Statutes of Missouri, and studied well the decisions of the Supreme Court of that State, in the fall and winter of 1838–'39.

In the beginning of 1839 I determined once more to

try the law, and to bid a final adieu to the mercantile business. Circumstances were favorable. After my arrival in Liberty in April, 1832, I was a member of a debating society, and in 1838 I engaged to some extent in the political contests of that time, and made several stump speeches. I also edited a weekly newspaper, "The Far West," published in Liberty. My services were gratuitous, as I desired improvement, not salary. I had therefore acquired some reputation as a speaker and writer. Besides, the Mormon difficulties of 1838–'39, which led to their final expulsion from Missouri, produced a heavy amount of litigation.

The lawyers with whom I came mainly in competition had been at the bar from eight to fifteen years ; and among them were D. R. Atchison, William T. Wood, Amos Rees, A. W. Doniphan, John Gordon, Andrew S. Hughes, and William B. Almond. Austin A. King was then our Circuit Judge. Atchison was a member of the Legislature, and Doniphan had been sick, and was for some months unable to attend to business. These combined circumstances threw into my hands a considerable practice the first year. I remember that among the first suits I brought were several for debt against some of the Mormons in Caldwell County, some thirty miles from Liberty. I had to begin them at once, as the circumstances would not admit of delay. I had no books to refer to, and had to draw up the declarations from memory. I therefore stated the facts substantially, but in a form most untechnical. These declarations caused considerable amusement ; but I amended them, and obtained my judgments.

In the beginning of 1839, Amos Rees, A. W. Doniphan, and myself were employed as counsel by Joseph Smith, Jr., Sidney Rigdon, Lyman Wight, and other

Mormon leaders, then in Liberty jail, they having been committed by Judge King for treason, arson, and robbery, alleged to have been committed in Davis County. There was no jail in that county, and, as Liberty jail was the nearest secure prison, they were confined there until the meeting of the Circuit Court of Davis County, in March, 1839. An investigation had been had in December, 1838, at Richmond, before Judge King as committing officer, in which I had not participated, though present. The Mormons had been driven from Jackson County in 1833, and had taken refuge in Clay; and, after remaining there a year or two, they had moved to the new prairie county of Caldwell, north of Clay, where they advanced rapidly with their improvements, until interrupted by the difficulties of the fall of 1838.

We had the prisoners out upon a writ of habeas corpus, before the Hon. Joel Turnham, the County Judge of Clay County. In conducting the proceedings before him there was imminent peril. The people were not only incensed against the Mormons, but they thought it was presumption in a County Judge to release a prisoner committed by a Circuit Judge. The law, however, considered all committing magistrates—judges of courts as well as justices of the peace—as equals when acting simply in that inferior capacity. We apprehended that we should be mobbed, the prisoners forcibly seized, and most probably hung. Doniphan and myself argued the case before the County Judge—Mr. Rees, who resided in Richmond, not being present. All of us were intensely opposed to mobs, as destructive of all legitimate government, and as the worst form of *irresponsible* tyranny. We therefore determined inflexibly to do our duty to our clients at all hazards, and to sell our lives as dearly as possible if necessary. We rose above all

fear, and felt impressed with the idea that we had a sublime and perilous but sacred duty to perform. We armed ourselves, and had a circle of brave and faithful friends armed around us ; and, it being cold weather, the proceedings were conducted in one of the smaller rooms in the second story of the Court-House in Liberty, so that only a limited number, say a hundred persons, could witness the proceedings.

Judge Turnham was not a lawyer, but had been in public life a good deal, and was a man of most excellent sense, very just, fearless, firm, and unflinching in the discharge of his duties. We knew well his moral nerve, and that he would do whatever he determined to do in defiance of all opposition. While he was calm, cool, and courteous, his noble countenance exhibited the highest traits of a fearless and just judge.

I made the opening speech, and was replied to by the District Attorney ; and Doniphan made the closing argument. Before he rose to speak, or just as he rose, I whispered to him : "Doniphan ! let yourself out, my good fellow ; and I will kill the first man that attacks you." And he did let himself out, in one of the most eloquent and withering speeches I ever heard. The maddened crowd foamed and gnashed their teeth, but only to make him more and more intrepid. He faced the terrible storm with the most noble courage. All the time I sat within six feet of him, with my hand upon my pistol, calmly determined to do as I had promised him.

The Judge decided to release Sidney Rigdon, against whom there was no sufficient proof in the record of the evidence taken before Judge King. The other prisoners were remanded to await the action of the grand jury of Davis County. Rigdon was released from the jail at night to avoid the mob.

ORATION BY SIDNEY RIGDON.—SERMON BY JOSEPH SMITH, JR.—BATTLE BETWEEN THE DANITES AND CAPTAIN BOGARD.

If I remember correctly, it was in the spring of 1838 that Smith and Rigdon came from Kirtland, Ohio, to Far West, the county seat of Caldwell County, Missouri. Rigdon delivered an oration on the Fourth of July, 1838, at Far West, in which he assumed some extraordinary positions in reference to the relation the Mormons sustained to the State Government. This discourse gave great offense to the people of the adjoining counties, particularly to those of Ray and Davis. Serious difficulties were evidently brewing.

I well remember the first time I ever saw Joseph Smith, Jr. I arrived at Far West one Saturday evening in June or July, 1838, and found there John McDaniel, a young merchant of Liberty. John was wild, imprudent, and fond of frolics. On Saturday he had openly ridiculed Smith's pretensions to the gift of prophecy, and his remarks had been reported to the prophet. On Sunday John and myself went to hear Smith preach. The church was a large frame building, with seats well arranged and a good pulpit. We were treated with great politeness, and kindly shown to seats that commanded a full view of the whole proceedings. The congregation was large, very orderly, and attentive. There were officers to show people to their seats, who were most polite and efficient in the discharge of their duties.

Two sermons were delivered by other preachers, which were simply plain, practical discourses, and created no emotion. But, when Joseph Smith, Jr., rose to speak, he was full of the most intense excitement. He

boldly denounced McDaniel in the most severe terms, saying, in substance, that no man should come to Far West and openly vilify and slander him, and that, if his brethren would not protect him, he would protect himself. I had not heard of the remarks of McDaniel, and was wholly taken by surprise. I watched him as he sat by my side, and he was as pale as a corpse, but did not stir or open his lips. The Mormon audience were deeply moved, but preserved good order. After the services were ended, McDaniel requested me to go with him to see Smith, and we did so. An explanation was made on both sides, and the matter there terminated.

The Mormons extended their settlements into the adjoining county of Davis, at a place called Adam on Diamon, the name being significant of some religious idea which I have forgotten. The people of Davis (who were rather rude and ungovernable, being mostly backwoodsmen) were very much opposed to this, although the Mormons had paid for the lands they occupied. The Mormons insisted on their legal rights as citizens of the State, while the people of Davis determined that they should not vote in that county at the August election of 1838.

When the election came on, the men of Davis County made an effort to prevent the Mormons from voting at that precinct. A fight ensued, in which the Mormons had the best of it. Other difficulties followed, until Lyman Wight, at the head of the Mormon forces, invaded Davis County, most of which he overran, driving all before him. General D. R. Atchison, then commanding the militia in that part of the State, ordered Captain Bogard, of Ray County, to call out his militia company and occupy a position on or near the county line between Ray and Caldwell, and preserve the peace

between the people of the two counties. But Captain Bogard was not a very discreet man, and his men were of much the same character. Instead of confining himself and his men within the limits of his own county, he marched one day into the edge of Caldwell, and was not only rather rude to the Mormons residing there, but arrested one or two of them, whom he detained for some little time.

Information of this proceeding was conveyed to Far West that same evening ; and Smith at once ordered Captain Patton, with his Danite band, to march that night and attack Bogard. Captain Bogard had retired into the edge of Ray County, and encamped in a narrow bottom on the banks of a creek, among the large scattering oak timber, and behind a slough-bank some four feet high. He apprehended an attack, and had well selected his ground. The wagon-road crossed the stream just below his encampment, and the road ran down the top and point of a long ridge, covered thickly with young hickories, about ten feet high and from one to two inches in diameter at the ground. No one could be seen approaching the encampment until arriving within a short distance of it ; but Captain Bogard had placed out a picket-guard on the road some half mile above, at a point where open woods commenced.

I remember well one of the two guards. His name was John Lockhart, a tall East Tennesseean. Just before day the Mormons were seen approaching, and were hailed by the guards ; but, receiving no satisfactory answer, the guards fired and then fled to the camp. One of the Mormons was killed here, but they fired no shot in return, made no halt, but continued their march in silence and good order, and drew up in line of battle immediately in front of Bogard's position, and about

forty yards distant. Not a word was said until the line was formed, and then orders were given to fire. Patton's men, being entirely exposed, suffered severely from the first fire, he himself being mortally wounded, and one or two of his men being killed and others wounded. He saw at a glance that his men could not stand such a fire, while his enemies were protected by a slough-bank; and he at once ordered his men to charge with their drawn swords. Bogard's men, having no swords, broke their ranks and fled. Several were overtaken in the retreat, and either cut down or captured. Bogard had about sixty and Patton eighty men, and eight or ten on each side were killed or wounded. One Mormon was evidently killed by one of his own companions, as his wound was a sword-cut in the back of his head. He had doubtless charged with more precipitancy than his comrades; and, as there was no difference in the dress of the opposing forces, he was mistaken for a retreating enemy.

MILITIA ORDERED OUT—SURRENDER OF THE MORMONS.

John Estes, one of Bogard's men, who was in the fight, escaped and came to Liberty the same day, and gave information to General Atchison. The latter at once ordered the Liberty Blues to march to the battle-ground, and there await further orders. I was a member of this independent militia company.

We made ready, and were off before night, and marched some ten miles that evening, under General Doniphan. The next day we reached the scene of conflict, and encamped in the edge of the open oak-woods next to the prairie that extended from that point to Far West (the town being in the open prairie), and on the road that Patton had traveled to attack Bogard, and

about one mile nearer Far West than Bogard's camp. We were joined by some of Bogard's men, so that we numbered about one hundred. The first night after our encampment was cold and frosty. I remember it well, for I was on guard that night.

Among those who had fallen in with us was a lad of about eighteen, quite tall, green, and awkward. He was dressed in thin clothing, and when put on guard was told by the officer not to let any one take his gun. He said no one would get *his* gun. When the officer went around to relieve the guard, this boy would not permit him to come near, presenting his gun with the most determined face. In vain the officer explained his purpose; the boy was inflexible, and stood guard the remainder of the night, always at his post, and always wide awake. We anticipated no attack this night, as the Mormons, at Far West, were not aware of our approach in time to reach us until the next night, when we did expect an attack.

The next day was warm and beautiful, and was what is called "Indian summer." I went upon the battle-field and examined it carefully. The dead and wounded had all been removed; but the clots of blood upon the leaves where the men had fallen were fresh and plainly to be seen. It looked like the scene of death. Here lay a wool hat, there a tin cup, here an old blanket; in the top of this little tree hung a wallet of provisions; and saddles and bridles, and various articles of clothing, lay around in confusion. The marks of the bullets were seen all around. I remember that a small linden-tree, three or four inches in diameter, that stood behind Patton's men, seemed to have been a target, from the number of shots that had struck it.

The second night was clear moonlight, warm and

pleasant. Having been on guard the night before in the cold frost, I slept very soundly. Somewhere about midnight one of the picket-guards, placed some distance out in the prairie, on the road toward Far West, came in, giving information to our commander that a body of armed men was approaching us along that road, and from the direction of Far West. Very soon another guard, from another point, came in and confirmed the statement of the first. An alarm was at once given. The first thing I remember to have heard was the voice of Lieutenant William A. Dunn, close to our camp, calling aloud, "Parade! parade! the Mormons are coming." His voice was remarkably loud and distinct, and rang awfully in my ears. A fearful impulse came over me, such as I had never felt before. I knew that it was most probable that the victorious Danites would be upon us, as they had been upon Bogard. It was what we had every reason to expect. We knew they had about eight hundred men at Far West, and were fully able to subdue us if they determined to do so. I said to myself, "Now we catch it." I at once seized my rifle and fell into the ranks. A few of our men were so alarmed that they mounted their horses and rode to the rear of our encampment. A moment after falling into ranks, I looked up and down the line, and the men were shivering as if with cold, though the night was warm. Their teeth chattered from the effects of alarm. I said, "Boys, it has turned cold very suddenly," which remark produced a feeble laugh.

After waiting a few moments, which seemed to us very long, and no enemy attacking us, Doniphan came around calling for twenty volunteers to go out to reconnoiter and bring on the action. I said to myself, "I am not in that scrape." There was not a word

said, and not one volunteered. I reflected upon it until I became ashamed; and I said to Thomas Parish, who stood by my side, "Suppose we go out." He said, "Agreed," and out we went. We were joined by four others, making, with Lieutenant Dunn, seven in all, which number was all we could obtain. We asked Dunn if we should go, and he replied, "Say yourselves." We said, "Go," mounted our horses, and were off in a gallop. As we passed the front line, all the men were down on one knee, rifle in hand. We found the guards at their posts, and passed on rapidly. The sorrel mare that I rode was a very fleet little animal, and, having been often trained and run before I purchased her, she no doubt supposed we were running a race; and to carry my gun in my right hand, and hold her in with my left, I found impossible. I was about twenty yards ahead of my comrades when, sure enough, we saw in the clear moonlight a body of armed men approaching. We galloped on until we reached within some hundred yards, then drew up and hailed them, when, to our great satisfaction, we found it was a body of militia under Colonel Gilliam, from Clinton County, coming to join us. Thus ended this alarm.

During all this hubbub, the boy who had persisted in standing guard the preceding night slept on until some one happened to think of him and ask where he was. He was then awakened and fell into ranks without hesitation or trepidation. All admired his courage, and agreed that an army composed of such material would be hard to defeat.

After remaining a day or two in camp, so as to give time for others to join us, we marched to within half a mile of Far West, around which the Mormons had made a sort of barricade of timbers, not sufficient to

offer any serious resistance. Finding themselves overpowered by numbers, the Mormon leaders, Smith, Rigdon, Wight, and others, surrendered. As I understood at the time, a proposition was seriously made and earnestly pressed in a council of officers, to try the prisoners by court martial, and, if found guilty, to execute them. This proposition was firmly and successfully opposed by Doniphan. These men had never belonged to any lawful military organization, and could not, therefore, have violated military law. The law of the soldier could not apply to them, as they had not been soldiers in any legal sense. I remember that I went to Doniphan and assured him that we of Clay County would stand by him. Had it not been for the efforts of Doniphan and others from Clay, I think it most probable that the prisoners would have been summarily tried, condemned, and executed.

PRISONERS BROUGHT BEFORE JUDGE KING—JOSEPH SMITH, JR.—LYMAN WIGHT—SIDNEY RIGDON.

The prisoners were turned over to the civil authorities, and sent to Richmond, where they were brought before Judge King, who acted as a committing magistrate. The proceedings occupied some days, as a great number of witnesses were examined, and their testimony was taken down in writing, as the statute required. I witnessed a portion of the proceedings, and remember well that Dr. Alvord (if I mistake not the name) was examined on the part of the prosecution. He was a very eccentric genius, fluent, imaginative, sarcastic, and very quick in replying to questions put by the prisoners' counsel. His testimony was very important, if true; and, as he had lately been himself a Mormon, and was regarded by them as a traitor from

selfish motives, his testimony labored under some apparent suspicion. For these reasons he was cross-examined very rigidly.

After the doctor had been upon the witness stand some hours, General Andrew S. Hughes (a great wit) came into the case, as counsel for the prisoners; but the fact was unknown to Alvord. Hughes was seated among the prisoners, and wore a blanket overcoat, and the doctor was wholly unacquainted with him. Other counsel for the prisoners had cross-examined the witness, and he had refused to answer a question put by them. General Hughes said to him, "I will let you know that it is not for you, but for the Court, to determine whether you shall answer the question." The witness turned quickly, looked the General full in the face, and, with a most quizzical expression of mock surprise upon his countenance, said, "Sir, I do not know what relation you sustain to this case. Are you one of the prisoners?" This question produced quite a sensation among the attending crowd, who were greatly amused at the situation of the counsel.

General Hughes was quizzed for the time; but he was not the man to remain long in that unpleasant condition. In a short time he made a motion in the case, and in support of that motion made a speech; and when he had finished his argument he took his seat. The District Attorney rose to reply; and, just as he commenced, General Hughes rose quickly from his seat, saying, in the most droll, sarcastic manner, "If it please your Honor, I will save my friend the District Attorney the trouble of making a speech. I have gained my point, and I withdraw my motion. I only made a speech to influence *public opinion*," at the same time waving his hand over the crowd.

When the March (1839) term of the District Court of Davis County came on, the sheriff of Clay removed the prisoners, under a strong guard, from the jail in Liberty to Davis County, to be present at the impaneling of the grand jury. It was apprehended that the prisoners would be mobbed by the irritated people of Davis, and the sheriff of Clay was determined to protect his prisoners if he could. Mr. Rees and myself went to Davis County as their counsel. The court-house at the county seat having been burned the fall before by Lyman Wight's expedition, the court was held in a rough log school-house, about twenty-five feet square. This house was situated on the side of a lane about a quarter of a mile long. It being immediately after the annual spring thaw, this lane was knee-deep in mud, especially in the vicinity of the court-house.

The people of the county collected in crowds, and were so incensed that we anticipated violence toward the prisoners. In the daytime the Court sat in this house, the prisoners being seated upon a bench in one corner of the room ; and they were kept under guard there during the night. In the end of the room farthest from the fireplace there was a bed in which the counsel for the prisoners slept. The floor was almost covered with mud.

The prisoners arrived on Saturday evening, and the Court opened on the following Monday. They were fully aware of their extreme danger. As I slept in the room, I had an opportunity to see much of what passed. The prisoners did not sleep any for several nights. Their situation was too perilous to admit of repose. Smith and Wight talked almost incessantly. Smith would send some one for a bottle of whisky ; and, while he kept sober himself, Lyman Wight would be-

come pretty well drunk, and would kindly invite the guards of Davis County (into whose keeping the prisoners were then committed) to drink with him, which invitation was cordially accepted. Some of the guards had been in the combats between the Mormons and the people of Davis County.

The subject of incessant conversation between Wight and these men was the late difficulties, which they discussed with great good nature and frankness. Wight would laughingly say, "At such a place" (mentioning it) "you rather whipped us, but at such a place we licked you." Smith was not in any of the combats, so far as I remember. The guard placed over the prisoners in Davis, after the sheriff of Clay delivered them into the hands of the sheriff of that county, did not abuse them, but protected them from the crowd. By consent of the prisoners, many of the citizens of Davis came into the room, and conversed with them hour after hour during most of the night. Among others, I remember two preachers, who had theological arguments with Smith, and he invariably silenced them sooner or later. They were men of but ordinary capacity, and, being unacquainted with the grounds Smith would take, were not prepared to answer his positions ; while Smith himself foresaw the objections they would raise against his theory, and was prepared accordingly.

Joseph Smith, Jr., was at least six feet high, well-formed, and weighed about one hundred and eighty pounds. His appearance was not prepossessing, and his conversational powers were but ordinary. You could see at a glance that his education was very limited. He was an awkward but vehement speaker. In conversation he was slow, and used too many words to express his ideas, and would not generally go directly to a point.

But, with all these drawbacks, he was much more than an ordinary man. He possessed the most indomitable perseverance, was a good judge of men, and deemed himself born to command, and he did command. His views were so strange and striking, and his manner was so earnest, and apparently so candid, that you could not but be interested. There was a kind, familiar look about him, that pleased you. He was very courteous in discussion, readily admitting what he did not intend to controvert, and would not oppose you abruptly, but had due deference to your feelings. He had the capacity for discussing a subject in different aspects, and for proposing many original views, even of ordinary matters. His illustrations were his own. He had great influence over others. As an evidence of this I will state that on Thursday, just before I left to return to Liberty, I saw him out among the crowd, conversing freely with every one, and seeming to be perfectly at ease. In the short space of five days he had managed so to mollify his enemies that he could go unprotected among them without the slightest danger. Among the Mormons he had much greater influence than Sidney Rigdon. The latter was a man of superior education, an eloquent speaker, of fine appearance and dignified manners ; but he did not possess the native intellect of Smith, and lacked his determined will. Lyman Wight was the military man among them. There were several others of the prisoners whose names I have forgotten.

I remember to have heard of a circumstance which was said to have occurred while the prisoners were under guard in Davis, but I can not vouch for its truth from my own knowledge. Joseph Smith, Jr., was a very stout, athletic man, and was a skillful wrestler. This was known to the men of Davis County, and some

of them proposed to Smith that he should wrestle with one of their own men. He at first courteously objected, alleging substantially that, though he was once in the habit of wrestling, he was now a minister of the gospel, and did not wish to do anything contrary to his duty as such, and that he hoped they would excuse him upon that ground. They kindly replied that they did not desire him to do anything contrary to his calling; that they would not bet anything; that it was nothing but a friendly trial of skill and manhood, for the satisfaction of others, and to pass away the time pleasantly; and that they hoped he would, under all the circumstances, comply with their request. He consented; they selected the best wrestler among them, and Smith threw him several times in succession, to the great amusement of the spectators. Though I did not witness this incident, I heard it stated as a matter of fact at the time, and I have no doubt of its truth.

The grand jury having found true bills of indictment against the prisoners, we applied to the Court for a change of venue to some county where the prisoners could have a fair trial. Upon a hearing of the application, the Court changed the venue to Boone County, and committed the prisoners to the sheriff of Davis, with instructions to convey them to the proper county; but the prisoners escaped on the way and safely arrived in the State of Illinois. Thus ended the Mormon troubles in Missouri.

APPOINTED DISTRICT ATTORNEY—QUALIFICATIONS OF A GOOD LAWYER—LABORIOUS PRACTICE.

I continued the practice of my profession; but I had to close up the old mercantile concerns in which I had been a partner, and this labor absorbed a large

share of my time and thoughts. I found that my mercantile knowledge was of great benefit to me in my profession of the law, especially in commercial cases. I was almost always employed in cases to wind up partnerships. I made it a rule, when employed with another lawyer in a case, especially with older counsel, to perform all the labor I could, and that he would permit, without regard to any question as to the proper proportion of labor to be performed by each of us. This course in due time made me a preferred associate. I was often employed with Doniphan as assistant counsel in civil cases. In criminal cases we were generally opposed. He knew that nothing would be neglected. I was a good pleader, cautious, energetic, and vigilant in managing a case. It was not often that a demurrer was sustained to a pleading of mine, either in civil or criminal cases.

Some time in the winter of 1839–'40, my friend William T. Wood, then District Attorney for our district, very generously came to me, and voluntarily informed me that he intended to resign, and would recommend me to the Governor of the State for the position. I was appointed ; but the district having been subsequently divided, and a new judicial district created, composed of the counties of Clinton, Andrew, Buchanan, Holt, and Platte, and D. R. Atchison appointed Judge, I was appointed District Attorney for the new district.

When I commenced the practice, having but lately read the statutes and the reported decisions of the Supreme Court, I was more familiar with them than most of the other members of the bar, and was thus able in many cases to defeat lawyers much older than myself. I was not afraid of labor, and made it a rule that, when

two different modes of reaching an end suggested themselves to my mind, one *certain*, but accompanied with great labor, and the other *uncertain*, but requiring little or no work, I always preferred the certain to the uncertain. I generally avoided being on the wrong side of a case, and made it a rule to get at the true facts, so far as I could obtain them from my client, by a strong cross-examination. If he proposed to bring a suit, and had in my judgment no merits in his case, I candidly advised him not to sue. If he was a defendant, I advised him to settle the difficulty with the plaintiff, with as little delay and costs as possible.

There are two qualities very necessary to a good lawyer, one who is truly an ornament to his noble profession, namely, *judgment and impartiality*. Unless he possesses *both* of these qualities, he will be made to give his efforts to vexatious litigation, to the disgrace of his profession and the subversion of justice. I was never a successful lawyer on the wrong side of a case, but I seldom failed when in the right. I was a very poor defender of guilty men, and was only employed for the defense in a very few criminal cases.

In 1839 I was employed with Doniphan to defend a man of property in Ray County, indicted and tried for a very serious offense. We at the time believed him to be innocent, and defended him successfully. I can not, in my own mind, yet say whether he was guilty or not; but I have long regretted having had anything to do with that melancholy case. A young woman was examined as a witness for the prosecution, who was of good family and character, and whose testimony was positive; and we were forced to impeach her veracity in order to acquit our client. Her conduct was open to apparent objection, but might have been wholly the re-

sult of timidity or confusion. I remember that her uncle, a most estimable citizen, wept when he heard his niece's character for truth called in question. I shall never forget his manly tears. It was enough to make him weep, under any view of the question.

I was a vigilant but candid prosecutor. If I became satisfied that the prisoner was innocent, I told the jury so ; but, if I thought him guilty, I prosecuted him with all the energy and ability I possessed, and was generally successful. I was District Attorney a little upward of three years, was twice appointed by the Governor of the State, and was once elected by the people of the district, of which Atchison was judge. In this new district there was more criminal business than in any other district of the State, except that of St. Louis. The great Platte Country, the most fertile portion of the State, was annexed to Missouri in the beginning of 1837, and settled up rapidly with every class of people. Besides this fact, the land was open to preëmption claims, though the country was not at first surveyed ; and this uncertainty as to titles and boundaries led to much harassing and bitter litigation, which produced an unusual amount of crime. In all my labors since I was grown, though I have seen some hard service at different times, I do not remember to have been so often utterly worn out as I was while District Attorney in Judge Atchison's district. In Platte County, the largest in the district, and the second county in the State in point of population, we generally had from seventy-five to one hundred criminal cases on the docket at each term of the Court. These cases were of every character, from the most trifling to very grave offenses. While they were mainly indictments for gambling at cards, there were commonly from fifteen to twenty cases of a serious

character, for which the punishment was generally imprisonment in the Penitentiary.

It was the duty of the District Attorney not only to prosecute the cases before the Court and trial-jury, but to attend the grand jury, give them advice, and draw up all the indictments. During the first week of the term, and while the grand jury were in session, I usually wrote from dark until midnight, commenced again next morning at sunrise, wrote until breakfast, and, after taking a light, hasty meal, wrote until about 9 A. M., when Court met. The criminal had precedence over civil cases on the docket, and were disposed of before the civil cases were reached. In Court, I prosecuted from 9 A. M. until 2 P. M., when the Court adjourned half an hour for dinner, and then met again, and remained in session until sundown. While in Court I was nearly always upon my feet, case after case following in succession. I have often gone into the trial of a case of grand larceny, without knowing anything of the facts except that the prisoner was charged in the indictment with stealing a horse or other personal property of the person whose name was stated in the indictment as the owner. I knew the names of the witnesses on the part of the State, because the names were endorsed upon the back of the indictment. In these cases I had the witnesses called, and, if present, I was ready for trial. I examined them, in general terms, only far enough to make out a *prima facie* case against the accused; and then I turned the witnesses over to the prisoner's counsel, knowing they would bring out all the facts before the Court and jury. After the examination of the first witness, I was able to see the thread of the testimony, and knew how to proceed. I had the criminal law at my tongue's end, and was seldom at a loss for authority

to sustain my position, because I would not ask of the Court any decision that I thought incorrect. In my civil practice it was my general rule not to ask a decision of a point in my favor that I was satisfied would not be sustained in the Supreme Court. I liked to practice against prejudiced lawyers, who would insist upon points that were not just. I could always defeat them in the highest Court, and made it a rule to take appeals where I knew I was right.

DIFFICULTY OF ADMINISTERING CRIMINAL JUSTICE—A NOTED CRIMINAL—AN ABLE AND UPRIGHT JUDGE.

The duties of District Attorney in that district were not only laborious, but difficult and extremely responsible upon other accounts. There were five counties in the district, and the Platte country was in the shape of the letter V, bounded on the east by the old State line, on the southwest by the Missouri River, and on the northwest by the then wild prairie lands of Iowa. The remote county of Holt was in the western and narrowest portion; and, being not only remote, but thinly inhabited, it was under the control for a time of thieves and counterfeiters, who, by being upon the trial-juries, defeated the ends of justice. I remember that at one term of the Court there were some thirty indictments and only one or two convictions. I would prove up the case as clearly as possible, and yet the jury, after being out but a few moments, would return into Court with their verdict, "We, the jury, find the defendant not guilty." In some rare cases, when the punishment was very trifling, they would find the defendant guilty for the sake of appearances.

There was at that time an organized band of criminals, at the head of whom was the notorious Daniel

Whiteman. These men and their friends overawed the good citizens of the county. Whiteman said to me, laughingly, "Pete, you can't convict anybody. I manage these juries." I remember that much the same state of things once existed in Jackson County, at an early day, and before I was a member of the bar. Amos Rees was then District Attorney, and I have heard the facts of the case from other lawyers who were present.

A man was indicted and tried for selling whisky to an Indian. A most intelligent and trustworthy witness testified before the trial-jury, that upon a stated day and year, in Jackson County, in the State of Missouri, he saw an Indian come into the defendant's grocery, and put down upon the counter a quarter of a dollar, in silver coin of the United States, at the same time handing the defendant an empty bottle; that he saw the defendant take a gallon measure and draw from a barrel, and out of the contents of the gallon measure fill up the bottle for the Indian, put the quarter into his (defendant's) drawer, and that he then asked the witness to drink out of what remained in the measure from which the bottle had been filled; that witness drank from the measure, and that what he drank was whisky. Colonel William T. Wood, who defended the party, thought the evidence so clear against his client that he was about to give up the case, when one of the jurors asked the witness, "But did you drink out of the bottle itself?" The witness answered, "No; I only drank of the liquid left in the measure after filling the bottle." Upon this state of evidence the jury found the defendant not guilty. Mr. Rees at once sternly told the sheriff that, if he summoned any more such juries, he would move the Court to punish him for contempt.

This state of things continued only for a time. Some

one in the adjoining county had Whiteman arrested upon a charge of theft, alleged to have been committed in that county, and he was sent to jail to await his examination before a justice of the peace. In the mean time he was taken out by the people, severely lynched, and then turned loose. He returned to Holt, where he was loud in his threats against Judge Atchison and myself, as he had been informed that we had encouraged his being lynched.

I remember that in the spring of 1843 I was at the county seat of Holt County, where I delivered a public address to the people in reference to Oregon; and I found Whiteman there. He at once took me aside and asked me if I had heard that "they had given him h——l." I told him I had. He then said that he had understood that Judge Atchison and myself had encouraged the people to act as they did. I told him that it was not true as to myself; that I could not, would not, and never did encourage illegal violence; but I would state to him what I said, and which was true. When people asked me why persons indicted and tried in that county could not be convicted, I had told them that it was not my fault, but the fault of the trial-juries, who were under the influence of the criminals of the county.

While I was addressing the people, I observed that Whiteman stood near me all the time, but did not once suspect that he meditated an attack upon me. After I had finished my address, a gentleman whom I knew took me apart from the crowd, and told me that he had overheard Whiteman making threats of personal violence against me, just before I commenced speaking; and that he (my friend) had placed himself by Whiteman's side, ready and determined to shoot him at the first offensive movement he should make. Whiteman asked

me several questions about Oregon before I left the stand, which were respectfully put and respectfully answered. A short time after this, as I was informed, he was lynched the second time. He made a desperate resistance, and was almost killed in the struggle. This was the last of that noted culprit, as he soon thereafter left the county.

Judge Atchison was an upright, incorruptible judge, and was a man of fine literary and legal education, and of superior native intellect. He possessed a kind heart, and a noble, generous, manly spirit ; but, when first appointed, he seemed to me to err too often in his rulings in favor of the accused. I was always courteous and respectful to any Court before which I consented to appear, and never in the course of my practice had an angry altercation with the Court, or was punished for contempt. I determined, in the proper manner, to correct the supposed errors of the Judge. The Judge decided several cases against me ; but, being satisfied that I was right, I took them up to the Supreme Court, and a majority of them came back reversed.

CASE OF WHITTLE—JUDGE AUSTIN A. KING.

As illustrative of the then mixed state of society, I will refer to the following case.

A celebrated counterfeiter of the name of Whittle went from the county in which he resided to an adjoining county, and passed upon a plain farmer some counterfeit gold coin, in payment for a horse. Having been indicted in the proper county, he applied for a change of venue ; and the case, upon a proper showing, was sent to Buchanan County.

When the case was called, the prisoner was ready for trial, and I asked the Court to order the sheriff to

call the trial-jurors. The moment I heard their names called, I was satisfied that it was mainly a packed jury. I knew that some of them belonged to the band of criminals in that county, or they were unfortunate in reputation and association. I promptly rose and said: "If the Court please, it is now very near dinner time, and I would thank the Court to adjourn until after dinner. I wish a little time to examine this jury list, and I think it very likely that I will dispose of this case without troubling the Court." Judge Atchison seemed to understand what I was driving at, and readily adjourned the Court.

When the Court met again, there was a large crowd present, as it must have been anticipated that some decisive step in the case would be taken. When the case was again called, I said: "With the leave of the Court, I will enter a *nolle prosequi*, and let the prisoner go. I do not mean to make a farce of justice by trying this prisoner before such a jury." The prisoner was wholly taken by surprise, and looked exceedingly mortified. He evidently expected to be tried and acquitted. I intended to have the witnesses again subpœnaed before the grand jury of the proper county, and they would no doubt have found another indictment; and, upon another application for a change of venue, I should have opposed successfully any effort of the defendant to have the case sent again to Buchanan County. But the prisoner was killed in a private quarrel before the next term of the Court.

He was a man of herculean frame, and of desperate character. His death happened in this wise: He forced a quarrel upon a peaceable, awkward, and innocent young man, about the age of twenty-one, for the purpose, most likely, of showing off his bravery and prow-

ess before his friends. At all events, when the young man had hitched his horse to the rack, Whittle went out and cut off the horse's tail, and came into the room where the young man was sitting, and thrust it rudely into his face. Upon the young man's remonstrating, Whittle chased him into the street; and several times afterward during the day he followed him into other places, and forced him hastily to leave. The poor young man became at last desperate, and went and armed himself with a pistol. Whittle again drove him from the house, and was pursuing him in the street, when the young man turned upon him, and shot him through the heart. Though fatally wounded, Whittle picked up a large stone, and threw it at the young man with such prodigious force that had it struck him it would have killed him instantly. After throwing the stone Whittle fell upon his face dead.

I have known of several instances, where persons shot through the heart have lived for some little time. When the shot passes through the left ventricle of the heart, the wound is instantaneously fatal, so that the muscles retain the exact position they had at the very moment the wound was given. For example, if the deceased had a pistol tightly grasped in his hand, he would still after death retain his grasp upon it, as also the very same cast of features. This was the case with General Richardson, killed by Cora in San Francisco in the year 1856. So, whenever a shot seriously wounds the spinal marrow, the person is instantaneously paralyzed. I have never known but one instance where a person was fatally shot through the brain, that he did not drop instantly, however excited he may have been. This exceptional case was that of Joel Turnham, Jr., who was killed in Oregon about the year 1844, while resisting a special

constable, who was sent to arrest him for assault and battery. Turnham was one of the stoutest, bravest, most reckless men I ever knew ; and, though fatally shot through the brain with a pistol, he turned and walked some twenty feet before he fell.

After becoming familiar with the duties of his position, D. R. Atchison made an admirable judge, and gave general satisfaction. In point of legal acquirements, I do not think he was then quite the equal of Judge Austin A. King, who was an older man ; but Judge Atchison was more popular with the members of the bar generally. It was the fault of Judge King, at one time, not to be sufficiently indulgent to young lawyers. I remember his treatment of myself when a new beginner. Being satisfied that he did not extend to me the indulgence that my situation justified, I determined to bide my time and correct this supposed error.

I was, upon one occasion, employed to defend a suit brought by one of the older members of the bar upon a promissory note, which he described in his declaration as bearing date a certain day and year set forth. I put in the plea of *non assumpsit ;* and, when the note was offered in evidence, I simply objected. It bore a different date from the note described, and was not therefore the same note. I knew that the objection was a good one, but the plaintiff's counsel declared that my objection was invalid, and then handed the papers to the Judge, who compared the note with the declaration, and at once gave judgment for the plaintiff ; and I quietly took my appeal. In five or six months, the case came back reversed ; and the Supreme Court expressed surprise that so plain an error should have been committed by the Court below. It so happened that I was afterwards employed in another case of much the same char-

acter before the same Judge; and I, as before, simply objected to the introduction of the note as evidence in the case. The Judge this time was very polite, and asked me to state my objections (which he had not done in the former case); and after that I could always be heard. I thought the Judge, on several former occasions, had evinced by his manner an indisposition to hear me when I had a right to be heard.

Young lawyers can not, of course, speak as well as those that are older, and judges are very apt to become impatient when listening to irrelevant remarks. But it always seemed to me that it was not only more generous but more expedient, in most cases, to indulge young lawyers in their errors of inexperience. I have no doubt of the fact that many a noble young man, of fine intellect and heart, has been either driven from the profession, or kept in a grade beneath his real abilities, by the harsh and inconsiderate reproofs of crabbed judges. Tyranny has many modes of exhibiting itself; and a man may be the victim of oppression in many other ways than knocking him down, putting him in prison, or confiscating his property.

Young lawyers are generally sensitive and timid, and their feelings should be spared. One of the noblest objects in the world is a pure and intellectual young man; and a court should lean gently upon his young errors. But I can truly say, in justice to Judge King, that he subsequently became as indulgent to young lawyers as he should have been. I remember that the Judge's course toward a young lawyer, Mr. Hovey, was entirely unexceptionable. Judge King was not so popular with the bar generally as Judge Atchison, mainly for the reason that King was a religious man, and had not the amount of mirth and gayety that Atchison had. The

latter was very companionable, and full of anecdote, in which he was not limited by religious views. Most of our lawyers at that time were not religious, and would naturally be partial to a man like themselves.

CHARACTERISTICS OF LAWYERS—NATURE OF LEGAL INVESTIGATIONS—DIFFICULTY OF SIMPLIFYING THE LAW—CAUSES OF INFIDELITY AMONG LAWYERS.

I remember an incident which occurred in the winter of 1839–'40, at Savannah, the county seat of Andrew County. There were about fifteen lawyers of us, all at the hotel; and one evening, after the court had finally adjourned, a discussion arose among us in regard to the truth of Christianity. There was not a single lawyer present who was a professor of religion, and only one who believed Christianity to be true, and that was Amos Rees. He manfully and earnestly maintained its true and divine origin. The next day we rode together, and I said to him: "Amos, you deserve double damnation; because you know and believe the truth, and will not put it in practice. Now, sir, whenever I am convinced of the truth of Christianity, you will find me acting up to what I believe to be true." I have the pleasure of stating that a majority of the lawyers present at that time have since become professors of religion, myself among the number.

I never had any disposition to enter into mere personal quarrels. Let me be satisfied that a great duty demands my exertions, and then I can face danger. When I was satisfied that another person abused me in words, because he was sincere but mistaken in thinking he had good cause, I could not feel like holding him responsible for a mere error of judgment. Good men ought never to quarrel. There is a natural and immeasurable

gulf between the good and the bad—between the candid and the hypocritical.

There is, among lawyers, a noble freedom allowed in debate; and though, in the moment of excited discussion, they may say that of each other which they never would in their cooler moments, a due and fair allowance is made for the circumstances. Besides, lawyers must necessarily associate often together on the same side of a case; so that it is almost impossible to keep alive the enmity. The other members of the bar interpose their kind offices for reconciliation; and they have so much respect for the views and feelings of each other that these kind requests will seldom be disregarded. Among honorable members of the profession, there generally exists the greatest personal kindness, and little or no professional jealousy. Each honorable member of this most distinguished profession is content with the practice he justly merits; and, as to those merits, there is a plain and satisfactory mode of determining the question. They practice their profession, not only in the presence of each other, but before crowds of people and a competent Court. If a lawyer be ignorant of the law, his adversary and the Court will tell him so, and thus expose his ignorance. If he has merits, they are made manifest, as a general rule, by a conclusive test. Time and experience soon settle the relative merits of different members of the bar practicing before the same Courts.

When a lawyer finds, upon due trial, that he is not suited to the profession, he can go to something else. Most lawyers who find they can not succeed in the profession betake themselves to editing newspapers, where the same exact and logical mode of discussion is not required, but where each writer addresses himself mainly to a prejudiced audience, who seldom know what is said

in reply. Practically, most newspaper discussions are one-sided.

In legal discussions, the positions of the opposite counsel are, in general, correctly stated and fairly met. To misrepresent facts or positions is not only unprofessional, but idle and vain. He who confutes a position never advanced does an idle and vain thing, by throwing away his efforts. To labor for the purpose of exposing your own ignorance or unfairness is not very wise.

The modes of investigation in courts of justice are not only the most decisive of the merits of counsel and judges, but they are, for that reason, the best adapted to improve the reasoning faculties of the mind. Any one who has ever participated in the discussion of important and difficult questions must have learned that there are classes of arguments apparently sound, but which in truth are utterly worthless, and have no real bearing upon the case. When you hear a speaker, even upon a simple occasion, you can generally form a very good estimate of his ability. If he has a clear logical mind, he will go to the *exact* merits of the question and place the matter in a clear light; but, if his powers are merely declamatory, he will deal in unmeaning generality, true in itself, but outside the particular case.

I confess I am partial to the law, and that, of all the secular learned professions, I love that of law most. I am aware of the prejudices existing in the minds of many against the profession; and it must be conceded that a mean lawyer is one of the meanest of men, because he sins against light and example. A pettifogger among lawyers is like a demagogue among statesmen—a most detestable character, weak in mind and unsound in morals, deserving neither respect nor pity.

But these complaints against the law and lawyers are not much heeded by them. Ignorance has been for ages complaining of the imperfections of the law, and proposing to make it so plain that all sane men could readily understand it. But it seems never to have occurred to these restless wanderers after perfection that science is vast, and no science more so than that of law; and that to simplify the law to such an extent as to enable every man to be his own lawyer is just as difficult as to simplify land and marine architecture, or any other science which comprehends a multitude of particulars. It requires very little intellect and study to construct an Indian wigwam or a rude canoe; but it takes mind and careful training to build a palace or construct a mighty steamship.

Rabid law-reformers have often been in the different State Legislatures; but, though no doubt sincere and determined in the beginning, they soon discovered some of the real difficulties in their way to simplicity. To know how to improve the code you must first know its defects; and to know these you must understand the code itself. By the time the rash and presumptuous law-reformer gets to that point, he begins to perceive the difficulties which beset his path. When he comes to sit down and draft a code that will stand the test of honest and intelligent time, he will fully need all his imagined capacity.

I remember that, in the Vigilance Committee times of this State in 1856, there was a great hue and cry raised against lawyers. I had retired from the practice myself, yet I loved the noble profession. I had, however, no defense to make, but simply a compromise to propose. I said: "Only give us back the productions of our labors—the Declaration of Independence, the

Constitutions of the United States and of every State in the Union, all the codes of law, the judicial decisions and learned treatises upon the science—and *do without them*, and we will consent that the profession may be abolished, and the nation go back to barbarism. But, until you have something better to propose, your denunciation of a theory you can not mend must be idle."

Surprise has often been expressed that there should be so many infidels among lawyers. It can not be owing to the want of capacity to investigate the subject. The Rev. David Nelson, in his work entitled "Cause and Cure of Infidelity," has these remarks:

"I do not know why it is so, but it is the result of eighteen years of experience that lawyers, of all those whom I have examined, exercise the clearest judgment while investigating the evidences of Christianity. It is the business of the physician's life to *watch for evidence and indication* of disease, sanity, and change; therefore I am unable to account for the fact, yet so it is, that the man of law excels. He has, when examining the evidences of the Bible's inspiration, shown more common sense in weighing proofs and appreciating argument, where argument really existed, than any class of men I have ever observed." (Page 117.)

The superiority attributed by the author to the legal fraternity arises mainly from these causes:

1. It requires more natural logical power to be successful at the bar than in the practice of medicine.

2. The mental training is more rigid and thorough.

3. There is a competent and authoritative tribunal to determine controversies among lawyers.

The fact that there are so many infidels among law-

yers is not owing either to a want of capacity in them, or a lack of evidence to establish the truth of Christianity, but entirely to other causes.

When a young man is studying law, he finds no time to think of religion; and, after he commences practice, the state of the case is much the same. Logical minds are not prone to take a theory as true without proof; and the proofs of Christianity, though complete and conclusive to a moral certainty, yet require time and careful investigation to be able to understand them in their full and combined force. These evidences consist of a great mass of testimony, both direct and circumstantial. To succeed at the bar requires great capacity and industry. The profession is compared by Lord Coke to a jealous mistress that will not tolerate a rival. The main reason, therefore, why there are so many infidels among the members of the bar, is because they do not investigate the subject, and will not believe without investigation; and the reason why they do not investigate is mainly the incessant and arduous nature of their employments.

But, besides the want of time, there are other causes to prevent investigation. There is a good deal, perhaps an over-proportion, of dissipation among lawyers. Their forensic efforts are often so severe and exhaustive that they resort to the use of stimulants to support them for the time. Others resort to stimulants because the use emboldens them, excites the imagination, and thus enables them to make the greatest display of oratory. It is well known to members of the profession that dissipation wonderfully stimulates and matures the intellect for a time. I have long observed that those lawyers who dissipate soonest arrive at maturity, and soonest go down, as a general rule. They are nearly

always the greatest wits and orators among us, but not the best reasoners.

But, besides these facts, there are the many varied scenes occurring in the practice, that continually call off the attention of lawyers from things future to things present. The witty joke, the amusing anecdote, and the ardent discussion of legal questions in and out of court, make their lives one continued round of excitement. Human nature is exhibited in courts of justice in its most vicious, melancholy, and ridiculous aspects. One case is full of the most cunningly devised fraud, another of the most brutal crime, and a third is so full of the ridiculous that all must laugh ; and the transition from one class of cases to others is often very rapid. Lawyers but seldom see the best traits of man exhibited in court, for the reason that the best men are not often engaged in lawsuits. For these and other reasons, the path of the lawyer is beset with temptation.

POLITICAL VIEWS.

My father was a Whig, and so were my brothers-in-law. When I was between sixteen and seventeen years of age, I read a paper edited by Duff Green, published in St. Louis, and became a Democrat. But as I grew older, and since I have studied more deeply the science of government, I have seen more cause to doubt the practical result of our republican theory as it now exists. I have always desired, whatever may have been my doubts, to give our theory a full and fair trial ; being satisfied that, so long as our theory can be honestly and efficiently administered, it is the best form of government for the greatest number. It is especially adapted to a young people, free from extreme want, and therefore independent and virtuous. But when the popula-

tion becomes dense, dependent, and suffering, and for that reason more corrupt, then will come the genuine test of our existing theory; and I think, without a thorough and radical amendment, it must fail. The three principles of universal suffrage, elective offices, and short terms, in their combined legitimate operation, will in due time politically demoralize any people in the world. I have given my views, in full, in a pamphlet published in 1861 by D. Appleton & Co. of New York, to which I refer. I am now of the opinion that the masses will never permit a sound conservative amendment of our theory, except by revolution, which I think will occur within the next fifty years. It may require several revolutions in succession. This I think most probable.

Mr. Jefferson was once considered by me as the apostle of liberty and a great statesman. I do not question his sincerity or his patriotism, but I doubt his statesmanship. I am now of the opinion that Alexander Hamilton was a much greater statesman than Jefferson or Madison. Patrick Henry was the orator more than the statesman. I now consider Hamilton to have had the clearest mind and the most logical power, and to have been the greatest statesman of our country. His contributions to the "Federalist" prove this. Chief Justice Marshall was a great man; but Hamilton was before him. The appreciation of Hamilton by Washington was one of the greatest proofs of his most superior good sense. He understood true merit when he found it. Hamilton sacrificed himself to mistaken public opinion—the only serious error he committed.

REMARKS ON DUELING.

I was never engaged in sending, or in bearing, and never received, a challenge to fight a duel. As a hum-

ble and steadfast believer in the sublime truths of Christianity, I could not sanction that semi-barbarous code. But, aside from the theological view of the question, I could not approve the practice.

It is claimed by its friends that it operates as a practical check upon the tongues and acts of men ; and this no doubt is true as to some persons, but untrue as to others ; so that, upon the whole, it is exceedingly doubtful whether it does, in point of fact, operate as a check upon slander and violence. I have reflected much upon this subject, and watched its practical effect with some care. I do not understand all the minute provisions of this code, but only know enough of its main points to justify my conclusions as to its substantial character.

It is insisted by the advocates of this code that the parties are placed as near upon an equality as, in the nature of things, they can be. But is this true ? I think not. It is made the duty of the party insulted to send the challenge, and the party challenged has a right to fix the terms upon which they meet ; and he, consequently, insists upon those that give him a decided advantage. The skillful use of weapons, especially of the dueling pistol, is an acquired art to a great extent, and requires years of continued practice to fix the art as a *habit.* In fact, a man must grow up accustomed to the use of such arms, to become completely and habitually skillful. Besides, he must possess a natural steadiness of nerve and quick accuracy of sight, to enable him by this long practice to acquire the habitual art to perfection. I suppose that the great majority of men, with all possible training, never could become first-rate shots on the wing with a shot-gun, or with a pistol at a stationary object.

Those who possess the natural capacity and the

habitual training have an immense advantage over those who have them not. Habit is second nature, and becomes almost as certain as instinct ; so that the habitually good shot will still shoot with his accustomed accuracy, whether alarmed or not, and, *knowing* his advantage, he has less cause to be excited. On the contrary, the party who has not the natural capacity, or lacks the habitual training, though able in a pistol-gallery to shoot with accuracy at an inanimate figure, will generally fail when he comes to face his enemy. His excitement, brave and determined as he may be, will affect him ; and he has no fixed habit to save him from the effect. That those not habitually accustomed to the use of the pistol shoot very wildly upon the field of battle, as compared with their previous practice, is conclusively shown by the history of different duels.

To induce a man to acquire the habitual use of the pistol, he must have, in his own estimation, some considerable motive ; and when he becomes a first-rate shot he is almost certain to be proud of it, and will very naturally seek to use an art of which he is master. We naturally love most that in which we most excel. I have observed that men who continually wear arms become at last anxious to use them, and thirsty for blood. They seem to think that, after they have carried arms for a long time and not used them, they have done an idle and vain thing. It is a great personal inconvenience to wear arms and keep them always in good order; and he who does so must be continually brooding over scenes of blood, until he becomes at last anxious to get into them himself. He is therefore much more apt to insult others than he would be if the dueling code did not exist. He covets the reputation of the duelist, and seeks an opportunity to insult some one he dislikes.

He knows that, if he gives the *first* insult, the party must challenge him, and then he will adjust the terms to suit himself. The world will not inquire who was to blame in the first instance, inasmuch as he has given the insulted party the satisfaction he demanded. He kills his man, and secretly, if not openly, glories in his success. In the future he has only, at intervals, to insult and kill others in the same way. The greater the number he slays, the greater his fame ; and, the greater his fame, the greater are his chances of success. True, he may fall at last by a chance shot, but not until he has slain from two to six persons.

Duels are much more numerous among politicians, in proportion to numbers, than among any other class, except perhaps army officers. This arises, in many cases, from rivalship. It becomes desirable to kill off certain aspirants, to get them out of the way. Hence they are insulted. Those well skilled in such matters know how much and what to say to produce a challenge.

As I have before stated, the code prevents some men from saying and doing things they would otherwise say or do ; but it has a contrary effect on others. There is, in the minds and hearts of proud men, a sort of glory in defying consequences ; and this stimulates many men to say and do offensive things that they would not otherwise say and do ; and also prevents them from making a proper explanation after they have done wrong, for fear it will be said that the explanation was the result of cowardice. If public opinion held the practice of bitter language disreputable, this would prevent the use of it more effectually than the dueling code. One thing seems certain, that personal quarrels are most common among those who admit the code.

Duels are not necessarily evidence of *personal*, though

they are evidence of the want of true *moral* courage. It is the fear or love of what others may think and say that generally impels the duelist. He has not the moral nerve to face a false public opinion. He flees from moral to physical responsibility, which shows more of the animal than of the intellectual being. The question with him is not so much what is right in itself, as what is considered so. He is for effect, not reality, and prefers the shadow to the substance. He is essentially selfish, and therefore he heeds not the ruin he produces. The cry and distress of the widow and the orphan never reach his dull, cold ear, or affect his stony heart. He is generally the slave of the times and the country in which he lives, and never rises superior to the scorn and contempt of the unwise. Being contemptible himself, he fears contempt. He is not satisfied with simply being in the right, but is content to be considered so, whether right or wrong. He is a being who worships appearances, and is willing to do wrong to save them. His moral being exists in "others' breath." He is never a martyr for truth, but falls a victim to interest or pride. The only man who can with any plausible consistency be a duelist is the man without principle, and who determines to gain the temporary advantages of doing wrong, and at the same time enjoying the reputation of an honorable man. Hence, when detected in a mean action, and told of it, his remedy is to drown the infamy in blood.

When a duelist uses courteous and gentlemanly language, no one can tell whether it is the result of fear or principle. All are uncertain as to what motive to attribute his conduct, as all know he is acting under restraint if the code has any effect in sileneing his tongue. On the contrary, if he abuses another, there is

still a difficulty in determining whether he is sincere in what he says, or whether he only wishes to show off his courage, or to induce his victim to send him a challenge that he may kill him. The general and legitimate effect of the code is to make hypocrites of those it restrains, and bullies of those it urges on.

I can not understand upon what principle two really good men should fight a duel. If they are willing to kill each other simply for fear of public opinion, they can not be good men. If a man abuses and misrepresents you, and you are satisfied that he is sincere but mistaken, will you seek his life for a mere error of judgment or defect of memory? On the contrary, if you are convinced that he willfully misrepresents you, then you believe he is a liar; and, unless you are a liar yourself, he is not your equal. Why should a gentleman and a man of pure justice put his life against that of a man he regards as destitute of honest principles?

In short, my opinion of men who engage in duels is that most of them are atheists, whose moral conduct depends upon the sliding scale of the times, and who have no strict moral principles independent of public opinion. They can generally have no faith in a future state of rewards and punishments; and hence they do whatever they deem most *successful* in this life. They are slaves to success, not devotees of principle. There are very few duels in communities where they are odious.

I most readily and willingly admit that there are exceptions to these remarks. Men sometimes labor under strange delusions, and lug themselves into the opinion that it is right, in some cases, to do wrong that good may come. This was the case with Alexander Hamilton. He conceded that the practice was wrong in itself, but yielded to a false public opinion, in order

that he might be useful to that public ; and most grievously did he answer for it. The result of his own act shows how much he was mistaken. Had he dared to do right, his life would have been spared to his country.

But this plea of necessity is always found in the mouths of tyrants and moral culprits of every grade. It is as false as the theory that you can do an unconstitutional act in accordance with the Constitution. Whenever the public require a man to do that which is plainly wrong, in order to gain the privilege of serving it, I must say it is unworthy of his services, and he should leave those with more pliable consciences to serve a vitiated public.

JOIN THE DISCIPLES—ART OF GOVERNING CHILDREN.

In 1840 I became a professor of Christianity, and joined the Disciples, or Campbellites as they were sometimes called. I was in my thirty-third year. I had long reflected much upon the subject, but could not come to the conclusion that Christianity was true. I was a Deist. I could never doubt the existence of God. I saw in the visible creation the plainest possible evidences of design—a perfect adaptation of means to ends. I could not conceive how chance could originate a *system* of any kind ; and, even if such a thing were possible, chance could destroy to-day that which it created but yesterday. No one could conceive that such a machine as a clock could be the result of accident ; and the wonderful mechanism of man's physical organization far surpasses the most magnificent productions of human genius.

Nor could I understand how this universe could be uncreated, and therefore eternal. That which is uncreated must be infinite ; and infinitude admits of no

changes, additions, or improvements. The visible creation is subject to change and to come to an end. It is confined within limits, and it admits of additions and improvements. It exists as the production of some superior; and that superior can be nothing but God, who is infinite, and who communicates to inferior beings such natures, powers, and capacities as in His wisdom and goodness He sees fit. "To be eternal is to be without beginning; and to be without beginning is to be independent of any cause or power."

The next step in the logical process is the conclusion that the Creator must govern, in some proper form, His own creation. Matter without properties, brutes without instinct, and rational beings without free will and without law, are logically inconceivable. Pursuing this logical process to an extent that I can not, for want of space, record here, I became thoroughly convinced of the entire truth of Christianity.

In the fall of 1840, I moved to Platte City, the county seat of Platte County. My youngest child, Sallie, was born there in 1841. My son John M. Burnett was born in 1838, and is now a lawyer of good standing in San Francisco.

The true art of governing children is to study their peculiarities, and adapt your government to the disposition of the child. The art of rearing good children is almost as difficult as that of governing a state. Children, so far as they know the facts, are far more competent to draw correct conclusions than most people suppose. Children are naturally truthful; and parents should not violate their own words, either in making promises of reward or threats of punishment. Those who assume to govern ought to be worthy to direct, and should themselves never violate the principles or

rules they inculcate or enforce. Perfect truth and consistency should characterize the parents. Then the task of government will be much lighter.

John was a noble and peculiar child, and always obedient when old enough to understand. He was very sensitive, and never would bear scolding, the only punishment we ever inflicted upon him. He cured us of this practice in this way: When he was about four years old, and while we lived in Platte City, he was in the habit of talking a great deal at table. One day I said to him, "John, why do you talk so much at table?" He looked at me with the expression of astonishment in his face, and replied with childlike simplicity and earnestness, "I can not talk by myself," meaning that it was useless to talk unless he had some one to listen. Within a day or two after this, his little tongue was again clattering away while we were at dinner, and his mother scolded him for it. Upon this he was silent, but it was evident that he thought he was badly treated. Just about that time some one commenced blowing a tin trumpet, and the boy's large black eye gleamed with a triumphant expression, and he at once said, "Mother! there's a horn or a woman's voice." After that he was scolded very little. I remember a very acute reply made by a little girl when seven years of age. I was staying at a friend's house in Brooklyn, New York, in 1866, and his daughter Mattie was remarkably fond of her half-grown cat; so much so, that she would take it with her to the dinner-table. Her mother said to her, "Why do you pet your cat so much?" The child, with a serious expression upon her countenance, at once answered, "This cat can't go to heaven," meaning that the cat must be petted *here*, and that was her reason for petting it so much.

CHAPTER III.

DETERMINE TO GO TO OREGON.—ARRIVE AT THE RENDEZVOUS.—REMARKS ON THE NATURE OF THE TRIP.

In the fall of 1842 I moved to Weston, in Platte County, having purchased an interest in the place. During the winter of 1842–'43 the Congressional report of Senator Appleton in reference to Oregon fell into my hands, and was read by me with great care. This able report contained a very accurate description of that country. At the same time there was a bill pending in Congress, introduced in the Senate by Dr. Linn, one of the Senators from Missouri, which proposed to donate to each immigrant six hundred and forty acres of land for himself, and one hundred and sixty acres for each child. I had a wife and six children, and would therefore be entitled to sixteen hundred acres. There was a fair prospect of the ultimate passage of the bill.

I saw that a great American community would grow up, in the space of a few years, upon the shores of the distant Pacific; and I felt an ardent desire to aid in this most important enterprise. At that time the country was claimed by both Great Britain and the United States; so that the most ready and peaceable way to settle the conflicting and doubtful claims of the two governments was to fill the country with American citizens. If we could only show, by a *practical* test, that

American emigrants could safely make their way across the continent to Oregon with their wagons, teams, cattle, and families, then the solution of the question of title to the country was discovered. Of course, Great Britain would not covet a colony settled by American citizens.

The health of Mrs. Burnett had been delicate for some three years, and it was all we could do to keep her alive through the winter in that cold climate. Her physician said the trip would either kill or cure her. I was also largely indebted to my old partners in the mercantile business. I had sold all my property, had lived in a plain style, had worked hard, and paid all I could spare each year; and still the amount of my indebtedness seemed to be reduced very little.

Putting all these considerations together, I determined, with the consent of my old partners, to move to Oregon. I therefore laid all my plans and calculations before them. I said that, if Dr. Linn's bill should pass, the land would ultimately enable me to pay up. There was at least a chance. In staying where I was, I saw no reasonable probability of ever being able to pay my debts. I did a good practice, and was able to pay about a thousand dollars a year; but, with the accumulation of interest, it would require many years' payments, at this rate, to square the account. I was determined not to go without the free consent and advice of my creditors. They all most willingly gave their consent, and said to me, "Take what may be necessary for the trip, leave us what you can spare, and pay us the balance when you become able to do so."

I followed their advice, and set to work most vigorously to organize a wagon company. I visited the surrounding counties, making speeches wherever I could

find a sufficient audience, and succeeded even beyond my own expectations. Having completed my arrangements, I left my house in Weston on the 8th day of May, 1843, with two ox wagons, and one small two-horse wagon, four yoke of oxen, two mules, and a fair supply of provisions; and arrived at the rendezvous, some twelve miles west of Independence, and just beyond the line of the State, on the 17th of May.

A trip to Oregon with ox teams was at that time a new experiment, and was exceedingly severe upon the temper and endurance of people. It was one of the most conclusive tests of character, and the very best school in which to study human nature. Before the trip terminated, people acted upon their genuine principles, and threw off all disguises. It was not that the trip was beset with very great perils, for we had no war with the Indians, and no stock stolen by them. But there were ten thousand little vexations continually recurring, which could not be foreseen before they occurred, nor fully remembered when past, but were keenly felt while passing. At one time an ox would be missing, at another time a mule, and then a struggle for the best encampment, and for a supply of wood and water; and, in these struggles, the worst traits of human nature were displayed, and there was no remedy but patient endurance. At the beginning of the journey there were several fisticuff fights in camp; but the emigrants soon abandoned that practice, and thereafter confined themselves to abuse in words only. The man with a black eye and battered face could not well hunt up his cattle or drive his team.

But the subject of the greatest and most painful anxiety to us was the suffering of our poor animals. We could see our faithful oxen dying inch by inch,

every day becoming weaker, and some of them giving out, and left in the wilderness to fall a prey to the wolves. In one or two instances they fell dead under the yoke, before they would yield. We found, upon a conclusive trial, that the ox was the noblest of draft-animals upon that trip, and possessed more genuine hardihood and pluck than either mules or horses. When an ox is once broken down, there is no hope of saving him. It requires immense hardship, however, to bring him to that point. He not only gathers his food more rapidly than the horse or mule, but he will climb rocky hills, cross muddy streams, and plunge into swamps and thickets for pasture. He will seek his food in places where other animals will not go. On such a trip as ours one becomes greatly attached to his oxen, for upon them his safety depends.

Our emigrants were placed in a new and trying position, and it was interesting to see the influence of pride and old habits over men. They were often racing with their teams in the early portion of the journey, though they had before them some seventeen hundred miles of travel. No act could have been more inconsiderate than for men, under such circumstances, to injure their teams simply to gratify their ambition. Yet the proper rule in such a case was to allow any and every one to pass you who desired to do so. Our emigrants, on the first portion of the trip, were about as wasteful of their provisions as if they had been at home. When portions of bread were left over, they were thrown away; and, when any one came to their tents, he was invited to eat. I remember well that, for a long time, the five young men I had with me refused to eat any part of the bacon rind, which accordingly fell to my share, in addition to an equal division of the

bacon. Finally they asked for and obtained their portion of the bacon rind, their delicate appetites having become ravenous on the trip. Those who were in the habit of inviting every one to eat who stood around at meal-times, ultimately found out that they were feeding a set of loafers, and gave up the practice.

START FROM THE RENDEZVOUS—KILL OUR FIRST BUFFALO—KILL OUR FIRST ANTELOPE—DESCRIPTION OF THE ANTELOPE.

I kept a concise journal of the trip as far as Walla Walla, and have it now before me. On the 18th of May the emigrants at the rendezvous held a meeting, and appointed a committee to see Dr. Whitman. The meeting also appointed a committee of seven to inspect wagons, and one of five to draw up rules and regulations for the journey. At this meeting I made the emigrants a speech, an exaggerated report of which was made in 1875, by ex-Senator J. W. Nesmith of Oregon, in his address to the Pioneers of that State. The meeting adjourned to meet at the Big Springs on Saturday, the 20th of May.

On the 20th I attended the meeting at the Big Springs, where I met Colonel John Thornton, Colonel Bartleson, Mr. Rickman, and Dr. Whitman. At this meeting rules and regulations were adopted. Mr. ——, who was from high up on Big Pigeon, near Kit Bullard's mill, Tennessee, proposed that we should adopt either the criminal laws of Tennessee or those of Missouri for our government on the route. William Martin and Daniel Matheny were appointed a committee to engage Captain John Gant as our pilot as far as Fort Hall. He was accordingly employed; and it was agreed in camp that we all should start on Monday morning, May 22.

We had delayed our departure, because we thought the grass too short to support our stock. The spring of 1843 was very late, and the ice in the Missouri River at Weston only broke up on the 11th of April.

On the 22d of May, 1843, a general start was made from the rendezvous, and we reached Elm Grove, about fifteen miles distant, at about 3 P. M. This grove had but two trees, both elms, and some few dogwood bushes, which we used for fuel. The small elm was most beautiful, in the wild and lonely prairie; and the large one had all its branches trimmed off for firewood. The weather being clear, and the road as good as possible, the day's journey was most delightful. The white-sheeted wagons and the fine teams, moving in the wilderness of green prairie, made the most lovely appearance. The place where we encamped was very beautiful; and no scene appeared to our enthusiastic visions more exquisite than the sight of so many wagons, tents, fires, cattle, and people, as were here collected. At night the sound of joyous music was heard in the tents. Our long journey thus began in sunshine and song, in anecdote and laughter; but these all vanished before we reached its termination.

On the 24th we reached the Walkalusia River, where we let our wagons down the steep bank by ropes. On the 26th we reached the Kansas River, and we finished crossing it on the 31st. At this crossing we met Fathers De Smet and De Vos, missionaries to the Flathead Indians. On the 1st of June we organized our company, by electing Peter H. Burnett as Captain, J. W. Nesmith as Orderly Sergeant, and nine councilmen. On the 6th we met a war party of Kansas and Osage Indians, numbering about ninety warriors. They were all mounted on horses, had their faces painted red, and had with

them one Pawnee scalp, with the ears to it, and with the wampum in them. One of them, who spoke English well, said they had fasted three days, and were very hungry. Our guide, Captain Gant, advised us to furnish them with provisions; otherwise, they would steal some of our cattle. We deemed this not only good advice but good humanity, and furnished these starving warriors with enough provisions to satisfy their hunger. They had only killed one Pawnee, but had divided the scalp, making several pieces, some with the ears on, and part with the cheek. Two of this party were wounded, one in the shoulder and the other in some other part of the body.

None of us knew anything about a trip across the Plains, except our pilot Captain Gant, who had made several trips with small parties of hired and therefore disciplined men, who knew how to obey orders. But my company was composed of very different materials; and our pilot had no knowledge that qualified him to give me sound advice. I adopted rules and endeavored to enforce them, but found much practical difficulty and opposition; all of which I at first attributed to the fact that our emigrants were green at the beginning, but comforted myself with the belief that they would improve in due time; but my observation soon satisfied me that matters would grow worse. It became very doubtful whether so large a body of emigrants could be practically kept together on such a journey. These considerations induced me to resign on the 8th of June, and William Martin was elected as my successor.

On the 12th of June we were greatly surprised and delighted to hear that Captain Gant had killed a buffalo. The animal was seen at the distance of a mile from the hunter, who ran upon him with his horse and shot him

with a large pistol, several shots being required to kill him. We were all anxious to taste buffalo meat, never having eaten any before; but we found it exceedingly poor and tough. The buffalo was an old bull, left by the herd because he was unable to follow.

On the 15th of June one of our party killed an antelope. This is perhaps the fleetest animal in the world except the gazelle, and possesses the quickest sight excepting the gazelle and the giraffe. The antelope has a large black eye, like those of the gazelle and giraffe, but has no acute sense of smell. For this reason this animal is always found in the prairie, or in very open timber, and will never go into a thicket. He depends upon his superior sight to discern an enemy, and upon his fleetness to escape him. I have heard it said that, when wolves are much pressed with hunger, they hunt the antelope in packs, the wolves placing themselves in different positions. Antelopes, like most wild game, have their limits, within which they range for food and water; and, when chased by the wolves, the antelope will run in something like a circle, confining himself to his accustomed haunts. When the chase commences, the antelope flies off so rapidly that he leaves his pursuers far behind; but the tough and hungry wolf, with his keen scent, follows on his track; and, by the time the antelope has become cool and a little stiff, the wolf is upon him, and he flies from his enemy a second time. This race continues, fresh wolves coming into the chase to relieve those that are tired, until at last the poor antelope, with all his quickness of sight and fleetness of foot, is run down and captured. As soon as he is killed, the wolf that has captured him sets up a loud howl to summon his companions in the chase to the banquet. When all have arrived, they set to

eating the carcass, each wolf taking what he can get, there being no fighting, but only some snarling, among the wolves. This statement I do not know to be true of my own knowledge, but think it quite probable. It seems to be characteristic of the dog family, in a wild state, to hunt together and devour the common prey in partnership. Bruce, in his account of his travels in Abyssinia, relates that he saw five or six hyenas all engaged in devouring one carcass; and that he killed four of them at one shot with a blunderbuss, loaded with a large charge of powder and forty bullets.

When an antelope once sees the hunter, it is impossible to stalk the animal. On the trip to Oregon I tried the experiment without success. When I saw the antelope, upon the top of a small hill or mound, looking at me, I would turn and walk away in the opposite direction, until I was out of sight of the animal; then I would make a turn at right angles, until I found some object between me and the antelope, behind which I could approach unseen within rifle-shot; but invariably the wily creature would be found on the top of some higher elevation, looking at me creeping up behind the object that I had supposed concealed me from my coveted prey. The only practical way of deceiving an antelope is to fall flat upon the ground among the grass, and hold up on your ramrod a hat or handkerchief, while you keep yourself concealed from his view. Though exceedingly wary, the curiosity of the animal is so great that he will often slowly and cautiously approach within rifle-shot.

On the 16th of June we saw a splendid race between some of our dogs and an antelope, which ran all the way down the long line of wagons, and about a hundred and fifty yards distant from them. Greyhounds were let loose, but could not catch it. It ran very smoothly,

making no long bounds like the deer or horse, but seemed to glide through the air. The gait of the antelope is so peculiar that, if one was running at the top of his speed over a perfectly smooth surface, his body would always be substantially the same distance from the earth.

Lindsey Applegate gave this amusing and somewhat exaggerated account of a race between a very fleet greyhound and an antelope. The antelope was off to the right of the road half a mile distant, and started to cross the road at right angles ahead of the train. The greyhound saw him start in the direction of the road, and ran to meet him, so regulating his pace as to intercept the antelope at the point where he crossed the road. The attention of the antelope being fixed upon the train, he did not see the greyhound until the latter was within twenty feet of him. Then the struggle commenced, each animal running at his utmost speed. The greyhound only ran about a quarter of a mile, when he gave up the race, and looked with seeming astonishment at the animal that beat him, as no other animal had ever done before. Applegate declared, in strong hyperbolical language, that "the antelope ran a mile before you could see the dust rise."

CROSS TO THE GREAT VALLEY OF THE PLATTE—BUFFALO HUNT—DESCRIPTION OF THAT ANIMAL.

Ever since we crossed Kansas River we had been traveling up Blue River, a tributary of the former. On the 17th of June we reached our last encampment on Blue. We here saw a band of Pawnee Indians, returning from a buffalo-hunt. They had quantities of dried buffalo-meat, of which they generously gave us a good supply. They were fine-looking Indians, who did not shave their heads, but cut their hair short like white men.

On the 18th of June we crossed from the Blue to the great Platte River, making a journey of from twenty-five to thirty miles, about the greatest distance we ever traveled in a single day. The road was splendid, and we drove some distance into the Platte bottom, and encamped in the open prairie without fuel. Next morning we left very early, without breakfast, having traveled two hundred and seventy-one miles from the rendezvous, according to the estimated distance recorded in my journal.

We traveled up the south bank of the Platte, which, at the point where we struck it, was from a mile to a mile and a half wide. Though not so remarkable as the famed and mysterious Nile (which, from the mouth of the Atbara River to the Mediterranean sea, runs through a desert some twelve hundred miles without receiving a single tributary), the Platte is still a remarkable stream. Like the Nile, it runs hundreds of miles through a desert without receiving any tributaries. Its general course is almost as straight as a direct line. It runs through a formation of sand of equal consistence ; and this is the reason its course is so direct.

The valley of the Platte is about twenty miles wide, through the middle of which this wide, shallow, and muddy stream makes its rapid course. Its banks are low, not exceeding five or six feet in height ; and the river bottoms on each side seem to the eye a dead level, covered with luxuriant grass. Ten miles from the river you come to the foot of the table-lands, which are also apparently a level sandy plain, elevated some hundred and fifty feet above the river bottoms. On these plains grows the short buffalo-grass, upon which the animal feeds during a portion of the year. As the dry season approaches, the water, which stands in pools on these

table-lands, dries up, and the buffaloes are compelled to go to the Platte for water to drink. They start for water about 10 A. M., and always travel in single file, one after the other, and in parallel lines about twenty yards apart, and go in a direct line to the river. They invariably travel the same routes over and over again, until they make a path some ten inches deep and twelve inches wide. These buffalo-paths constituted quite an obstruction to our wagons, which were heavily laden at this point in our journey. Several axles were broken. We had been apprised of the danger in advance, and each wagon was supplied with an extra axle.

In making our monotonous journey up the smooth valley of the Platte, through the warm genial sunshine of summer, the feeling of drowsiness was so great that it was extremely difficult to keep awake during the day. Instances occurred where the drivers went to sleep on the road, sitting in the front of their wagons; and the oxen, being about as sleepy, would stop until the drivers were aroused from their slumber. My small wagon was only used for the family to ride in; and Mrs. Burnett and myself drove and slept alternately during the day.

One great difficulty on this part of the trip was the scarcity of fuel. Sometimes we found dry willows, sometimes we picked up pieces of drift-wood along the way, which we put into our wagons, and hauled them along until we needed them. At many points of the route up the Platte we had to use buffalo-chips. By cutting a trench some ten inches deep, six inches wide, and two feet long, we were enabled to get along with very little fuel. At one or two places the wind was so severe that we were forced to use the trenches in order to make a fire at all.

On the 20th of June we sent out a party of hunters,

who returned on the 24th with plenty of fresh buffalo-meat. We thought the flesh of the buffalo the most excellent of all flesh eaten by man. Its flavor is decidedly different from that of beef, and far superior, and the meat more digestible. On a trip like that, in that dry climate, our appetites were excellent; but, even making every reasonable allowance, I still think buffalo the sweetest meat in the world.

The American buffalo is a peculiar animal, remarkably hardy, and much fleeter of foot than any one would suppose from his round short figure. It requires a fleet horse to overtake him. His sense of smell is remarkably acute, while those of sight and hearing are very dull. If the wind blows from the hunter to the buffalo, it is impossible to approach him. I remember that, on one occasion, while we were traveling up the Platte, I saw a band of some forty buffaloes running obliquely toward the river on the other side from us, and some three miles off; and, the moment that their leader struck the stream of tainted atmosphere passing from us to them, he and the rest of the herd turned at right angles from their former course, and fled in the direction of the wind.

On one occasion five of us went out on fleet horses to hunt buffaloes. We soon found nine full-grown animals, feeding near the head of a ravine. The wind blew from them to us, and their keen scent was thus worthless to them, as the smell will only travel with the wind. We rode quietly up the ravine, until we arrived at a point only about one hundred yards distant, when we formed in line, side by side, and the order was given to charge. We put our horses at once to their utmost speed; and the loud clattering of their hoofs over the dry hard ground at once attracted the attention of the

buffaloes, which raised their heads and gazed at us for an instant, and then turned and fled. By the time they started we were within fifty yards of them. The race was over a level plain, and we gradually gained upon the fleeing game ; but, when we approached within twenty yards of them, we could plainly see that they let out a few more links, and ran much faster. I was riding a fleet Indian pony, and was ahead of all my comrades except Mr. Garrison, who rode a blooded American mare. He dashed in ahead of me, and fired with a large horse-pistol at the largest buffalo, giving the animal a slight wound. The moment the buffalo felt himself wounded, that moment he bore off from the others, they continuing close together, and he running by himself.

I followed the wounded buffalo, and my comrades followed the others. The moment I began to press closely upon the wounded animal, he turned suddenly around, and faced me with his shaggy head, black horns, and gleaming eyes. My pony stopped instantly, and I rode around the old bull to get a shot at his side, knowing that it would be idle to shoot him in the head, as no rifle-ball will penetrate to the brain of a buffalo-bull. But the animal would keep his head toward me. I knew my pony had been trained to stand wherever he was left, and I saw that the wounded bull never charged at the horse. So I determined to dismount, and try to get a shot on foot. I would go a few yards from my horse, and occasionally the buffalo would bound toward me, and then I would dodge behind my pony, which stood like a statue, not exhibiting the slightest fear. For some reason the wounded animal would not attack the pony. Perhaps the buffalo had been before chased by Indians on horseback, and for that reason was afraid of the pony. At last I got a fair opportunity, and shot

the buffalo through the lungs. The moment he felt the shot, he turned and fled, and after running a quarter of a mile fell dead. The shot through the lungs is the most fatal to the buffalo, as he soon smothers from the effects of internal hæmorrhage. It is a singular fact that, before a buffalo is wounded, he will never turn and face his pursuer, but will run at his best speed, even until the hunter is by his side; but the moment a buffalo-bull is wounded, even slightly, he will quit the band, and when pressed by the hunter will turn and face him. The animal seems to think that, when wounded, his escape by flight is impossible, and his only chance is in combat.

On the 27th of June our people had halted for lunch at noon, and to rest the teams and allow the oxen to graze. Our wagons were about three hundred yards from the river, and were strung out in line to the distance of one mile. While taking our lunch we saw seven buffalo-bulls on the opposite side of the river, coming toward us, as if they intended to cross the river in the face of our whole caravan. When they arrived on the opposite bank they had a full view of us; and yet they deliberately entered the river, wading a part of the distance, and swimming the remainder. When we saw that they were determined to cross at all hazards, our men took their rifles, formed in line between the wagons and the river, and awaited the approach of the animals. So soon as they rose the bank, they came on in a run, broke boldly through the line of men, and bore to the left of the wagons. Three of them were killed, and most of the others wounded.

CROSS THE SOUTH FORK—ARRIVE AT FORT LARAMIE—CHEYENNE CHIEF—CROSS THE NORTH FORK—DEATHS OF PAINE AND STEVENSON—CROSS GREEN RIVER—ARRIVE AT FORT HALL.

On the 29th of June we arrived at a grove of timber, on the south bank of the South Fork of the Platte. This was the only timber we had seen since we struck the river, except on the islands, which were covered with cottonwoods and willows. From our first camp upon the Platte to this point, we had traveled, according to my estimates recorded in my journal, one hundred and seventy-three miles, in eleven days.

On July 1st we made three boats by covering our wagon-boxes or beds with green buffalo-hides sewed together, stretched tightly over the boxes, flesh side out, and tacked on with large tacks; and the boxes, thus covered, were then turned up to the sun until the hides were thoroughly dry. This process of drying the green hides had to be repeated several times. From July 1st to the 5th, inclusive, we were engaged in crossing the river. On the 7th we arrived at the south bank of the North Fork of the Platte, having traveled a distance of twenty-nine miles from the South Fork. We had not seen any prairie-chickens since we left the Blue. On the 9th we saw three beautiful wild horses. On the 14th we arrived at Fort Laramie, where we remained two days, repairing our wagons. We had traveled from the crossing of South Fork one hundred and forty-one miles in nine days. Prices of articles at this trading post: Coffee, $1.50 a pint; brown sugar, the same; flour, unbolted, 25 cents a pound; powder, $1.50 a pound; lead, 75 cents a pound; percussion-caps, $1.50 a box; calico, very inferior, $1 a yard.

At the Fort we found the Cheyenne chief and some of his people. He was a tall, trim, noble-looking Indian, aged about thirty. The Cheyennes at that time boasted that they had never shed the blood of the white man. He went alone very freely among our people, and I happened to meet him at one of our camps, where there was a foolish, rash young man, who wantonly insulted the chief. Though the chief did not understand the insulting words, he clearly comprehended the insulting tone and gestures. I saw from the expression of his countenance that the chief was most indignant, though perfectly cool and brave. He made no reply in words, but walked away slowly; and, when some twenty feet from the man who had insulted him, he turned around, and solemnly and slowly shook the forefinger of his right hand at the young man several times, as much as to say, "I will attend to your case."

I saw there was trouble coming, and I followed the chief, and by kind earnest gestures made him understand at last that this young man was considered by us all as a half-witted fool, unworthy of the notice of any sensible man; and that we never paid attention to what he said, as we hardly considered him responsible for his language. The moment the chief comprehended my meaning I saw a change come over his countenance, and he went away perfectly satisfied. He was a clear-headed man; and, though unlettered, he understood human nature.

In traveling up the South Fork we saw several Indians, who kept at a distance, and never manifested any disposition to molest us in any way. They saw we were mere travelers through their country, and would only destroy a small amount of their game. Besides, they must have been impressed with a due sense of our

power. Our long line of wagons, teams, cattle, and men, on the smooth plains, and under the clear skies of Platte, made a most grand appearance. They had never before seen any spectacle like it. They, no doubt, supposed we had cannon concealed in our wagons. A few years before a military expedition had been sent out from Fort Leavenworth to chastise some of the wild prairie tribes for depredations committed against the whites. General Bennet Riley, then Captain Riley, had command, and had with him some cannon. In a skirmish with the Indians, in the open prairie, he had used his cannon, killing some of the Indians at a distance beyond rifle-shot. This new experience had taught them a genuine dread of big guns.

The Indians always considered the wild game as much their property as they did the country in which it was found. Though breeding and maintaining the game cost them no labor, yet it lived and fattened on their grass and herbage, and was as substantially within the power of these roving people and skillful hunters as the domestic animals of the white man.

On the 24th of July we crossed the North Fork of Platte by fording, without difficulty, having traveled the distance of one hundred and twenty-two miles from Fort Laramie in nine days. On the 27th, we arrived at the Sweetwater, having traveled from the North Fork fifty-five miles in three days. On the 3d of August, while traveling up the Sweetwater, we first came in sight of the eternal snows of the Rocky Mountains. This to us was a grand and magnificent sight. We had never before seen the perpetually snow-clad summit of a mountain. This day William Martin brought into camp the foot of a very rare carnivorous animal, much like the hyena, and with no known name. It was of a dark color, had

very large teeth, and was thought to be strong enough to kill a half-grown buffalo.

On the 4th of August Mr. Paine died of fever, and we remained in camp to bury him. We buried him in the wild, shelterless plains, close to the new road we had made, and the funeral scene was most sorrowful and impressive. Mr. Garrison, a Methodist preacher, a plain, humble man, delivered a most touching and beautiful prayer at the lonely grave.

On the 5th, 6th, and 7th we crossed the summit of the Rocky Mountains, and on the evening of the 7th we first drank of the waters that flow into the great Pacific. The first Pacific water we saw was that of a large, pure spring. On the 9th we came to the Big Sandy at noon. This day Stevenson died of fever, and we buried him on the sterile banks of that stream. On the 11th we crossed Green River, so called from its green color. It is a beautiful stream, containing fine fish. On the margins of this stream there are extensive groves of small cottonwood-trees, about nine inches in diameter, with low and brushy tops. These trees are cut down by the hunters and trappers in winter, for the support of their mules and hardy Indian ponies. The animals feed on the tender twigs, and on the bark of the smaller limbs, and in this way manage to live. Large quantities of this timber are thus destroyed annually.

On the 12th of August we were informed that Dr. Whitman had written a letter, stating that the Catholic missionaries had discovered, by the aid of their Flathead Indian pilot, a pass through the mountains by way of Fort Bridger, which was shorter than the old route. We therefore determined to go by the fort. There was a heavy frost with thin ice this morning. On the 14th we arrived at Fort Bridger, situated on Black's Fork of

Green River, having traveled from our first camp on the Sweetwater two hundred and nineteen miles in eighteen days. Here we overtook the missionaries. On the 17th we arrived on the banks of Bear River, a clear, beautiful stream, with abundance of good fish and plenty of wild ducks and geese. On the 22d we arrived at the great Soda Springs, when we left Bear River for Fort Hall, at which place we arrived on the 27th, having traveled two hundred and thirty-five miles from Fort Bridger in thirteen days.

Fort Hall was then a trading post, belonging to the Hudson's Bay Company, and was under the charge of Mr. Grant, who was exceedingly kind and hospitable. The fort was situated on the south bank of Snake River, in a wide, fertile valley, covered with luxuriant grass, and watered by numerous springs and small streams. This valley had once been a great resort for buffaloes, and their skulls were scattered around in every direction. We saw the skulls of these animals for the last time at Fort Boise, beyond which point they were never seen. The Company had bands of horses and herds of cattle grazing on these rich bottom-lands.

Up to this point the route over which we had passed was perhaps the finest natural road, of the same length, to be found in the world. Only a few loaded wagons had ever made their way to Fort Hall, and were there abandoned. Dr. Whitman in 1836 had taken a wagon as far as Fort Boise, by making a cart on two of the wheels, and placing the axletree and the other two wheels in his cart. (Gray's "Oregon," page 133.)

We here parted with our respected pilot, Captain John Gant. Dr. Marcus Whitman was with us at the fort, and was our pilot from there to the Grande Ronde, where he left us in charge of an Indian pilot, whose

name was Stikas, and who proved to be both faithful and competent. The doctor left us to have his grist-mill put in order by the time we should reach his mission.

We had now arrived at a most critical period in our most adventurous journey ; and we had many misgivings as to our ultimate success in making our way with our wagons, teams, and families. We had yet to accomplish the untried and most difficult portion of our long and exhaustive journey. We could not anticipate at what moment we might be compelled to abandon our wagons in the mountains, pack our scant supplies upon our poor oxen, and make our way on foot through this terribly rough country, as best we could. We fully comprehended the situation ; but we never faltered in our inflexible determination to accomplish the trip, if within the limits of possibility, with the resources at our command. Dr. Whitman assured us that we could succeed, and encouraged and aided us with every means in his power. I consulted Mr. Grant as to his opinion of the practicability of taking our wagons through. He replied that, while he would not say it was impossible for us Americans to make the trip with our wagons, he could not himself see how it could be done. He had only traveled the pack-trail, and certainly no wagons could follow that route ; but there might be a practical road found by leaving the trail at certain points.

LEAVE FORT HALL—SAGE-BRUSH LANDS—SALMON FALLS—THE SPEAR OF THE INDIAN FISHERMAN—CROSS SNAKE RIVER—KILL A LARGE SALMON.

On the 30th of August we quitted Fort Hall, many of our young men having left us with pack-trains. Our route lay down Snake River for some distance. The

road was rocky and rough, except in the dry valleys ; and these were covered with a thick growth of sage or wormwood, which was from two to three feet high, and offered a great obstruction to the first five or six wagons passing through it. The soil where this melancholy shrub was found appeared to be too dry and sterile to produce anything else. It was very soft on the surface, and easily worked up into a most disagreeable dust, as fine as ashes or flour.

The taste of the sage is exceedingly bitter ; the shrub has a brown somber appearance, and a most disagreeable smell. The stem at the surface of the ground is from one to two inches in diameter, and soon branches, so as to form a thick brushy top. The texture of the stem is peculiar, and unlike that of any other shrub, being all bark and no sap or heart, and appears like the outside bark of the grape-vine. How the sap ascends from the roots to the branches, or whether the shrub draws its nutriment from the air, I am not able to decide. One thing I remember well, that the stems of the green growing sage were good for fuel and burned most readily, and so rapidly that the supply had to be continually renewed ; showing that they were not only dry, but of very slight, porous texture. Had the sage been as stout and hard as other shrubbery of the same size, we should have been compelled to cut our wagonway through it, and could never have passed over it as we did, crushing it beneath the feet of our oxen and the wheels of our wagons.

The geographical features of the Pacific coast are Asiatic in their appearance, being composed of mountains and valleys. Our hills swell to mountains, and our valleys are to the eye a dead level, yet they generally descend about nine or ten feet to the mile. We

have consequently very little gently undulating land, such as is generally found in the great Mississippi valley. Gibbon, speaking of the route of the army of the Emperor Julian, well but concisely describes the sage-plains of this coast: "The country was a plain throughout, as even as the sea, and full of wormwood; and, if any other kind of shrubs or reeds grew there, they had all an aromatic smell, but no trees could be seen." ("Decline and Fall," chapter xxiv., pp. 477–'78.)

Colonel Mercer of Oregon delivered a lecture in the City of New York on April 6, 1878, as appears from the telegram to the "Daily Alta" of the 7th, in which he set forth the wonderful fertility of the sage-brush lands, which until recently had been supposed to be valueless. The sage-brush lands through which we passed in 1843 appeared to be worthless, not only because of the apparent sterility of the soil, but for the want of water. With plentiful irrigation, I think it quite probable that these lands, in most places, might be rendered fruitful. Water is a great fertilizer, and nothing but experiment can actually demonstrate how far these wilderness plains can be redeemed.

On the 7th of September, 1843, we arrived at the Salmon Falls on Snake River, where we purchased from the Snake Indians dried and fresh salmon, giving one ball and one charge of powder for each dried fish. We found several lodges of Indians here, who were very poorly clad, and who made a business of fishing at the falls. The falls were about eight feet perpendicular at that stage of water, with rapids below for some distance. The stream is divided upon the rapids into various narrow channels, through which the waters pass with a very shallow and rapid current, so that the fisherman can wade across them. The salmon are com-

pelled to pass up these channels, and readily fall a prey to the quick, sharp spear of the Indian fisherman. This spear consists of a strong, smooth pole, ten or twelve feet long and an inch and a half in diameter, made of hard, tough wood, upon one end of which there is fastened a piece of sharp-pointed buck-horn, about four inches long. The larger end of this piece of buck-horn is hollowed out to the depth of about three inches, and fastened on the end of the pole, which is tapered to fit into it. To the middle of this buck-horn there is securely fastened a thong or string of sinew, the other end of which is firmly attached to the pole about one foot above the buck-horn, leaving a considerable slack in the string. With this spear the Indian fisherman lies down or sits close to one of these narrow channels, with the point of his spear resting near where the fish must pass. In this position he remains motionless until he sees a fish immediately opposite the point of the spear, as the fish slowly ascends the rapid current; when, with the quick motion of a juggler, he pushes his spear clear through the salmon before this powerful fish can dodge it. The buck-horn at once slips off the end of the pole, on the other side the fish, the first flounce he makes; but he is securely held by the thong attached to the pole. No spear could be more skillfully designed or more effectually used than this.

One of our emigrants, having been informed before he started on the trip that the clear, living waters of the Columbia and its tributaries were full of salmon, had brought all the way from Missouri a three-pronged harpoon, called a gig. The metallic portion of this fishing instrument was securely riveted on the end of a smooth, strong pole, about ten feet long and two inches

in diameter. The skillful fisherman held this gig in his right hand, raised above his head ; and, when he saw a fish fifteen or twenty feet distant, he would pitch the weapon at his prey with such a sure aim as seldom to miss his mark.

This emigrant was joyful when we arrived at the falls, it being the first point where he could use his gig. He soon brought forth his instrument from the bottom of his wagon, where it had remained unused so long, and sallied forth to capture salmon. We all watched with deep interest, as he stood by one of these narrow channels, gig in hand. Very soon we saw him throw his gig, but he missed his mark. Again and again he tried his skill, but always failed. The fact was that the salmon, one of the most muscular of fishes, with keen sight and quick motion, had seen the thrown gig in time, and had effectually dodged it. Our emigrant came back greatly mortified because the Indians could beat him in catching salmon. He understood, after this trial, the difference between the agility of the salmon of the Columbia and that of the sluggish catfish of the Mississippi.

Before reaching the Salmon Falls we passed a large spring on the opposite side of Snake River. This spring furnished water enough for a large creek, which fell perpendicularly from a wall of basaltic rock two hundred feet high, forming a most beautiful scene on the river.

On the 10th of September we crossed the Snake River by fording without difficulty ; and in crossing we killed a salmon weighing twenty-three pounds, one of our wagons running over it as it lay on the bottom of the pebbly stream.

The full-grown male and female salmon from the ocean enter the streams that flow into it, and, guided

by a wonderful instinct, ascend to the upper branches, where they can deposit their numerous spawn in a place secure from enemies. The waters of these mountain-streams are so clear as to remind one of Dryden's description

> "Of shallow brooks, that flowed so clear,
> The bottom did the top appear."

In the pebbly bottoms of these tributary streams the female salmon hollows out a cavity of sufficient depth to form an eddy, in which she can deposit her spawn without the danger of their being swept away by the current. The one we killed was doubtless in her nest, which she refused to quit.

From all the information I was able to obtain while residing in Oregon, grown salmon which once leave the ocean never return. This was the opinion of Sir James Douglas, which was confirmed by my own observation. But there seems to be a difference of opinion on the question. I have lately conversed with B. B. Redding upon this subject, and it is his opinion that about ten per cent. return alive to the ocean, as about that proportion are caught in the Sacramento River on the upper side of the gill-nets used by the fishermen. This may be the more correct opinion.

The male salmon is armed with strong, sharp teeth, and they fight and wound each other severely. While the female is making and guarding her nest, her mate remains close by, watching and waiting with the greatest fidelity and patience; and, when any other fish approaches too near, he darts at him with the utmost swiftness and ferocity. The spawn is always deposited in the pebbly bed of the stream, where the water is swift and comparatively shallow, and where other fish

are less likely to molest them. The eggs hatch in from forty to forty-five days.

For hours I have watched the efforts of salmon to pass over the Willamette Falls, at Oregon City. For the space of one or two minutes I would not see a fish in the air. Then, all at once, I would see one leap out of the water, followed immediately by great numbers. Some would rise from ten to fifteen feet, while many would not ascend more than four or five; but all seemed equally determined to succeed. They had selected the most practicable point, and approached very near the column of descending water, and rose from the eddy caused by the reflow. Occasionally one would go over; but the great majority pitched with their heads plump against the wall of rock behind the torrent, and fell back, more or less wounded, to try again. There was a shelf in the rock three or four feet below the top, and I have seen salmon catch on this shelf, rest for an instant, then flounce off and fall into the water below. So long as a salmon is alive, its head will be found up stream, and every effort made, though feeble, will be to ascend. Sometimes, when in very shallow water, the fish may descend to a short distance to escape an enemy for the time; but its constant instinct is to go up higher, until it reaches the place to deposit its eggs.

BOILING SPRING—FORT BOISE—BURNT RIVER—THE LONE PINE—THE GRANDE RONDE—THE BLUE MOUNTAINS—ARRIVE AT DR. WHITMAN'S MISSION—ARRIVE AT WALLA WALLA.

On the 14th of September we passed the Boiling Spring. Its water is hot enough to cook an egg. It runs out at three different places, forming a large branch,

which runs off smoking and foaming. It rises half a mile from a tall range of hills, covered with basaltic rock ; and the plains around are covered with round rocks of the same kind. The water is clear, and rises at the head of a small ravine.

On the 20th of September we arrived at Fort Boise, then in charge of Mr. Payette, having traveled from Fort Hall, two hundred and seventy-three miles, in twenty-one days. Mr. Payette, the manager, was kind and very polite. On the 21st we recrossed the Snake River by fording, which was deep but safe. On the 24th we reached Burnt River, so named from the many fires that have occurred there, destroying considerable portions of timber. It hardly deserves to be called a river, being only a creek of fair size. The road up this stream was then a terrible one, as the latter runs between two ranges of tall mountains, through a narrow valley full of timber, which we had not the force or time to remove.

On the 27th of September we had some rain during the night, and next morning left Burnt River. To-day we saw many of the most beautiful objects in nature. In our rear, on our right and left, were ranges of tall mountains, covered on the sides with magnificent forests of pine, the mountain-tops being dressed in a robe of pure snow ; and around their summits the dense masses of black clouds wreathed themselves in fanciful shapes, the sun glancing through the open spaces upon the gleaming mountains. We passed through some most beautiful valleys, and encamped on a branch of the Powder River, at the Lone Pine.

This noble tree stood in the center of a most lovely valley, about ten miles from any other timber. It could be seen, at the distance of many miles, rearing its ma-

jestic form above the surrounding plain, and constituted a beautiful landmark for the guidance of the traveler. Many teams had passed on before me ; and at intervals, as I drove along, I would raise my head and look at that beautiful green pine. At last, on looking up as usual, the tree was gone. I was perplexed for the moment to know whether I was going in the right direction. There was the plain beaten wagon-road before me, and I drove on until I reached the camp just at dark. That brave old pine, which had withstood the storms and snows of centuries, had fallen at last by the vandal hands of men. Some of our inconsiderate people had cut it down for fuel, but it was too green to burn. It was a useless and most unfortunate act. Had I been there in time, I should have begged those woodmen to "spare that tree."

On the 29th and 30th of September we passed through rich, beautiful valleys, between ranges of snow-clad mountains, whose sides were covered with noble pine forests. On October 1st we came into and through Grande Ronde, one of the most beautiful valleys in the world, embosomed among the Blue Mountains, which are covered with magnificent pines. It was estimated to be about a hundred miles in circumference. It was generally rich prairie, covered with luxuriant grass, and having numerous beautiful streams passing through it, most of which rise from springs at the foot of the mountains bordering the valley. In this valley the camas-root abounds, which the Indians dried upon hot rocks. We purchased some from them, and found it quite palatable to our keen appetites.

On the 2d of October we ascended the mountain-ridge at the Grande Ronde, and descended on the other side of the ridge to a creek, where we camped. These

hills were terrible. On the 3d, 4th, 5th, and 6th we passed through the Blue Mountains, arriving at their foot on the 6th, and encamping upon a beautiful stream of water. On the morning of the 5th there was a snow-storm on the mountain. During our passage through the Blue Mountains we had great difficulty in finding our cattle, and the road was very rough in many places. Our camp was about three miles from the Indian village, and from the Indians we purchased Indian corn, peas, and Irish potatoes, in any desired quantity. I have never tasted a greater luxury than the potatoes we ate on this occasion. We had been so long without fresh vegetables, that we were almost famished ; and consequently we feasted this day excessively. We gave the Indians, in exchange, some articles of clothing, which they were most anxious to purchase. When two parties are both as anxious to barter as were the Indians and ourselves, it is very easy to strike a bargain.

On the 10th of October we arrived within three miles of Dr. Whitman's mission, and remained in camp until the 14th.

The exhausting tedium of such a trip and the attendant vexations have a great effect upon the majority of men, especially upon those of weak minds. Men, under such circumstances, become childish, petulant, and obstinate. I remember that while we were at the mission of Dr. Whitman, who had performed much hard labor for us, and was deserving of our warmest gratitude, he was most ungenerously accused by some of our people of selfish motives in conducting us past his establishment, where we could procure fresh supplies of flour and potatoes. This foolish, false, and ungrateful charge was based upon the fact that he asked us a dollar a bushel for wheat, and forty cents for potatoes.

As our people had been accustomed to sell their wheat at from fifty to sixty cents a bushel, and their potatoes at from twenty to twenty-five cents, in the Western States, they thought the prices demanded by the Doctor amounted to something like extortion; not reflecting that he had to pay at least twice as much for his own supplies of merchandise, and could not afford to sell his produce as low as they did theirs at home. They were somewhat like a certain farmer in Missouri, at an early day, who concluded that twenty cents a bushel was a fair price for corn, and that he would not sell for more nor less. But experience soon taught him that when the article was higher than his price he could readily sell, but when it was lower he could not sell at all; and he came to the sensible conclusion that he must avail himself of the rise, in order to compensate him for the fall in prices. So obstinate were some of our people, that they would not purchase of the Doctor. I remember one case particularly, where an intimate friend of mine, whose supplies of food were nearly exhausted, refused to purchase, though urged to do so by me, until the wheat was all sold. The consequence was, that I had to divide provisions with him before we reached the end of our journey.

On the 16th of October we arrived at Fort Walla Walla, then under the charge of Mr. McKinley; having traveled from Fort Boise, two hundred and two miles, in twenty-four days, and from the rendezvous, sixteen hundred and ninety-one miles, between the 22d of May and the 16th of October, being one hundred and forty-seven days. Average distance per day, eleven and a half miles.

DESCEND THE RIVER TO THE DALLES—LEAVE MY FAMILY THERE—GO TO VANCOUVER AND RETURN—GOVERNOR FREMONT.

A portion of our emigrants left their wagons and cattle at Walla Walla, and descended the Columbia in boats; while another, and the larger portion, made their way with their wagons and teams to the Dalles, whence they descended to the Cascades on rafts, and thence to Fort Vancouver in boats and canoes. William Beagle and I had agreed at the rendezvous not to separate until we reached the end of our journey. We procured from Mr. McKinley, at Walla Walla, an old Hudson's Bay Company's boat, constructed expressly for the navigation of the Columbia and its tributaries. These boats are very light, yet strong. They are open, about forty feet long, five feet wide, and three feet deep, made of light, tough materials, and clinker-built. They are made in this manner so that they may be carried around the falls of the Columbia, and let down over the Cascades. When taken out of the water and carried over the portage, it requires the united exertions of forty or fifty Indians, who take the vessel on their shoulders, amid shouts and hurras, and thus carry it sometimes three fourths of a mile, without once letting it down. At the Cascades it is let down by means of ropes in the hands of the Canadian boatmen.

We employed an Indian pilot, who stood with a stout, long, broad paddle in the bow of the boat, while Beagle stood at the stern, holding a long steering-oar, such as were used upon flat-bottoms and keel-boats in the Western States. I remember that my friend Beagle, before we left Walla Walla, expressed great confi-

dence in his skill in steering, as he had often passed the Ohio rapids at Louisville. But these rapids were nothing to those on the Columbia. I have seen Beagle turn as pale as a corpse when passing through the terrible rapids on this river.

Our Indian pilot was very cool, determined, and intrepid; and Beagle always obeyed him, right or wrong. On one occasion, I remember, we were passing down a terrible rapid, with almost the speed of a race-horse, when a huge rock rose above the water before us, against which the swift and mighty volume of the river furiously dashed in vain, and then suddenly turned to the right, almost at right angles. The Indian told Beagle to hold the bow of the boat directly toward that rock, as if intending to run plump upon it, while the rest of us pulled upon our oars with all our might, so as to give her such a velocity as not to be much affected by the surging waves. The Indian stood calm and motionless in the bow, paddle in hand, with his features set as if prepared to meet immediate death; and, when we were within from twenty to thirty feet of that terrible rock, as quick almost as thought he plunged his long, broad paddle perpendicularly into the water on the left side of the bow, and with it gave a sudden wrench, and the boat instantly turned upon its center to the right, and we passed the rock in safety.

While passing through these dangers I was not much alarmed, but after they were passed I could never think of them without a sense of fear. Three of our emigrants were drowned just above the Dalles, but we reached them in safety, sending our boat through them, while the families walked around them on dry land. These Dalles are a great natural curiosity; but

they have been so often described that I deem it unnecessary to attempt any description myself.

When we arrived at the Methodist mission, located at the foot of the Dalles, I saw at once that there must some day grow up a town there, as that was the head of safe steam navigation. From there to the Cascades, a distance of about fifty miles, the river is entirely smooth and without a rapid. At the Cascades there is a portage to be made, but, once below them, and there is nothing but smooth water to the ocean. I determined at once to settle at the Dalles; and, after consultation with Mr. Perkins, the minister in charge, I left my family there and proceeded to Vancouver, where I arrived about the 7th of November, 1843.

At Fort Vancouver I found Governor Fremont, then Lieutenant Fremont, who had been there a few days. He had left his men and animals at the Dalles, and had descended the river to the fort for the purpose of purchasing supplies, to enable him to make the trip overland to California during that winter. The preceding year he had made an exploring trip to the South Pass of the Rocky Mountains; but this was his first journey to Oregon and California.

The Hudson's Bay Company furnished him, on the credit of the United States, all the supplies he required, and sent them up the river in one of their boats, such as I have already described, and three Chinook canoes. These canoes are substantially of the same model as the clipper-ship, and most probably suggested the idea of such a form of marine architecture. They are made out of a solid piece of white-cedar timber, which is usually one quarter of the first cut of a large tree. It is a soft wood, but very tough. This timber grows upon the banks of the Columbia, below Vancouver, to a very

large size. It is easily split with wedges. The Indians manage to cut and burn down the tree, and then cut and burn off a part of the trunk, and split it into quarters. Then they hollow out the inside of the canoe, mostly by burning. For this purpose they kindle small fires along the whole length of the canoe, which they keep steadily burning; and, by careful and constant watching, they cause the fires to burn when and how they please. The outside they shape with their tomahawks; and, before these were introduced, they used sharp flint-stones for axes. These canoes are usually about thirty feet long, three feet wide, and two feet deep, and are sharp at both ends, with a gradual taper from near the center. No craft could have a more handsome model, or run more swiftly. They are light, strong, elastic, and durable, and are propelled by paddles. The boat was navigated by Canadian French, and the canoes by Indians.

Dr. McLoughlin and Mr. Douglas, then chief factors at the fort, advised me to go for my family, and settle in the lower portion of Oregon, and kindly offered me a passage up and down on their boat. We left the fort about the 11th of November in the evening, while it was raining. It came down gently but steadily. We reached the foot of the rapids, three miles below the Cascades, before sundown on the third day. We found that the Indians could propel their canoes with paddles much faster than we could our boat with oars. We ascended the river to the distance of about one mile above the foot of the rapids; and just before dark we encamped upon a sand-beach, the only spot where we could do so without ascending higher up the rapids.

The Indians, with the three canoes, had passed on farther up the river; and, although we fired signal-

shots, they could not be induced to return. They had with them the sugar and tea, and the Indian lodge, composed of buffalo-skins, neatly dressed and sewed together. This lodge was in a conical form, about fourteen feet in diameter at the base and eighteen feet high, with a hole at the base of about two by three feet for a door, and one in the top for the escape of the smoke. A deer-skin formed the door-shutter, and the fire was built in the center, around which we sat with our backs to the lodge; and when we lay down we put our feet to the fire and our heads from it. In this way we could be warm and comfortable, and free from the effects of the wind and rain, without being at all incommoded by the smoke from our small fire, as it rose straight up and passed out through the hole in the top of the lodge. The lodge was supported by long, strong, smooth poles, over which it was tightly stretched. It was far superior to any cloth tent I ever saw.

When we encamped, it was cloudy but not raining, and we were very hungry after our day's hard work; but our bill of fare consisted of salt salmon and cold bread. We knew, from the appearance of the thickening but smooth clouds, that we should most likely have a rainy night. The lower portion of Oregon lies between the tall Cascade range of mountains and the ocean. This range runs almost parallel with the Pacific Ocean, and about a hundred and twenty-five miles from it. The clouds in the rainy season break upon this range; and the Cascades are at the point where the mighty Columbia cuts at right angles through it. We had been told that it rained oftener and harder at the Cascades than at almost any other point in Oregon; and, to our injury, we found it true.

Supper being ended, we laid ourselves down before

a large fire. Governor Fremont wrapped himself in his cloak, keeping on all his clothes, and lay down upon a blanket. For myself, I had with me two pairs of large, heavy blankets, one pair of which I put folded under me, and covered myself with the other pair. Soon after we had lain down the rain began to fall gently, but continued steadily to increase. At first, I thought it might rain as much as it pleased, without wetting through my blankets; but before day it came down in torrents, and I found the water running under me, and into the pockets of my pantaloons and the tops of my boots. It was a cold rain, and the fire was extinguished. I could not endure all this, and I sat up during most of the remaining portion of the night upon a log of wood, with one pair of blankets thrown over my head, so as to fall all around me. In this way I managed to keep warm; but the weight of the wet blankets was great, and my neck at last rebelled against the oppression. I finally became so fatigued and sleepy that just before day, when the rain had ceased, I threw myself down across some logs of wood, and in that condition slept until daylight. As for Governor Fremont, he never moved, but lay and slept as well as if in comfortable quarters. My position was in a lower place on the beach than his, and this was the reason why the water ran under me, and not under him.

Next morning we rose fresh and fasting, and ascended to the Indian encampment, where the Governor found our Indians comfortably housed in the lodge, cooking breakfast. He was somewhat vexed, and made them hustle out in short order.

It took us some days to make the portage, it raining nearly all the while. At the head of the Cascades there were several large, projecting rocks, under one side of

which the Indians could lie on the clean dry sand, secure from the rain. They would build a fire in front and sit or lie under the projecting rocks ; and, as they were at home with their kindred and families, they were in no hurry to go forward, and were not much disposed to go out in bad weather. At the Cascades there is a celebrated salmon fishery, where the Indians then lived in considerable numbers, supporting themselves in the summer upon fresh, and in the winter upon dried salmon.

We were anxious to proceed, as Governor Fremont had still to make the perilous journey to California ; but there were only some five to eight whites to several hundred Indians. But the cool, determined, yet prudent Fremont managed to command our Indians, and induce them to work. When nothing else would avail, he would put out their fires. Finding it necessary to work or shiver, they preferred to work.

When we had reloaded our craft, we set forward for the Dalles ; and we had not gone more than ten miles before we could see clear out and beyond the clouds, into the pure blue sky. We were almost vexed to think we had been so near to a sunny region all the time we had been suffering so much from the rain. We soon reached a point on the river above where there had been no rain ; and from that point to the Dalles we had cold, clear, frosty nights. We arrived at the Dalles in about ten days after leaving Vancouver. I went with the Governor to his camp of about forty men and one hundred animals.

I was with Governor Fremont about ten days. I had never known him personally before this trip. I knew he was on the way ; but he traveled usually with his own company, and did not mingle much with the emigrants, as he could not properly do so, his men being

under military discipline, and our emigrants not. He was then about thirty years old, modest in appearance, and calm and gentle in manner. His men all loved him intensely. He gave his orders with great mildness and simplicity, but they had to be obeyed. There was no shrinking from duty. He was like a father to those under his command. At that time I thought I could endure as much hardship as most men, especially a small, slender man like Governor Fremont ; but I was wholly mistaken. He had a small foot, and wore a thin calf-skin boot ; and yet he could endure more cold than I could with heavy boots on. I never traveled with a more pleasant companion than Governor Fremont. His bearing toward me was as kind as that of a brother.

GO WITH MY FAMILY TO VANCOUVER—INDIAN TRADITION—THE TOWN OF LINNTON.

I returned with my family to Fort Vancouver on the 26th of November, 1843; and, as we passed the place of our encampment on the sand-beach below the Cascades, the Canadian boatmen pointed toward it and laughed.

When we arrived at the Cascades on our return voyage, we carried our baggage upon our shoulders three fourths of a mile, when we reloaded and then "jumped" the rapids below. Until we had passed these rapids on our downward voyage I had no adequate conception of the dangers we had passed through on the voyage from Walla Walla to the Dalles. During that perilous passage I was one of the oarsmen, and sat with my back to the bow of the boat, thus having no fair opportunity to observe well. My attention was mainly confined to my own portion of the work, and I had but little time to

look up. But, in running the rapids below the Cascades, I had nothing to do but look on. It was almost literal "jumping."

There was then an Indian tradition that about a hundred years before the Cascades did not exist, but that there was a succession of rapids from the Dalles to where the Cascades are now. The whole volume of the Columbia is now confined to a narrow channel, and falls about thirty feet in the distance of a quarter of a mile. This tradition said that the river gradually cut under the mountain, until the projecting mass of huge stones and tough clay slid into the river and dammed up the stream to the height of some thirty feet, thus producing slack water to the Dalles. And I must say that every appearance, to my mind, sustains this view.

The Columbia, like most rivers, has a strip of bottom-land covered with timber, on one side or the other; but at the Cascades this bottom-land is very narrow, and has a very different appearance from the bottoms at places on the river above and below. The mountain on the south side of the river looks precisely as if a vast land-slide had taken place there; and the huge rocks that lift their gray, conical heads above the water at a low stage go to prove that they could not have withstood that terrible current for many centuries. In the winter, when the water is at its lowest stage, immense masses of thick ice come down over these Cascades, and strike with tremendous force against the rocks; and the consequent wearing away must have been too great for those rocks to have been in that position many centuries.

But there is another fact that seems to me to be almost conclusive. As we passed up the river, the water was at a very low stage; and yet for some twenty

miles above we could see stumps of various sizes standing as thick beneath the water as trees in a forest. The water was clear, and we had a perfect view of them. They were entirely sound, and were rather sharp in form toward the top. It was evident that the trees had not grown in the water, but it had been backed up over their roots, and the tops and trunks had died and decayed, while the stumps, being under water, had remained substantially sound ; and the reason why they were sharp at the top was, that the heart of the timber was more durable than the sap-wood, which had decayed. Another reason for the sharpness of the stumps at the top is, the abrasion caused by the floating masses of ice.

It was the opinion of Governor Fremont that these stumps had been placed in this position by a slide, which took them from their original site into the river. But I must think that opinion erroneous, because the slide could hardly have been so great in length, and the appearance of the adjacent hills does not indicate an event of that magnitude. It is much more rational, I think, to suppose that the slide took place at the Cascades, and that the Indian tradition is true. Another reason is, that the river at the points where these stumps are found is quite wide, showing an increase of width by the backing up of the water over the bottoms.

I procured a room for my family at Vancouver, until I could build a cabin. General M. M. McCarver and myself had agreed that we would select a town site at the head of ship navigation on the Willamette River. The General, having no family with him, arrived at the fort some time before I did, and selected a spot on the Willamette, about five miles above its mouth, at what we then supposed to be the head of ship navigation.

Here we laid out a town, calling it Linnton for Dr. Linn. It was a fair site, except for one small reason : it was not at the head of ship navigation, which subsequent experience proved to be at Portland, some miles above. I had a cabin built at Linnton, and lived there with my family from about the middle of January until the first of May, 1844. We performed a considerable amount of labor there, most of which was expended in opening a wagon-road thence to the Tualatin Plains, over a mountain, and through a dense forest of fir, cedar, maple, and other timber. When finished, the road was barely passable with wagons. Our town speculation was a small loss to us, the receipts from the sale of lots not being equal to the expenses.

I soon found that expenses were certain and income nothing, and determined to select what was then called "a claim," and make me a farm. I knew very little about farming, though raised upon a farm in Missouri, and had not performed any manual labor of consequence (until I began to prepare for this trip) for about seventeen years. I had some recollection of farming ; but the theory, as practiced in Missouri, would not fully do for Oregon. Mr. Douglas told me that I could not succeed at farming, as there was a great deal of hard work on a farm. I replied that, in my opinion, a sensible and determined man could succeed at almost anything, and I meant to do it. I did succeed well ; but I never had my intellect more severely tasked, with a few exceptions. Those who think good farming not an intellectual business are most grievously mistaken.

PURCHASE A CLAIM—CLIMATE AND SCENERY OF OREGON—NUMBER OF OUR IMMIGRANTS—ASSISTANCE RENDERED OUR IMMIGRATION.

Some time in April, 1844, I went to the Tualatin Plains, and purchased a claim in the middle of a circular plain, about three miles in diameter. The claim was entirely destitute of timber, except a few ash-trees which grew along the margin of the swales. The plain was beautiful, and was divided from the plains adjoining by living streams of water flowing from the mountains, the banks of which streams were skirted with fir and white-cedar timber. The surface of this plain was gently undulating, barely sufficient for drainage. I purchased ten acres of splendid fir timber, distant about a mile and a half, for twenty-five dollars. This supply proved ample for a farm of about two hundred and fifty acres.

These swales are peculiar winter drains, from ten to thirty yards wide, and from one to two feet deep. In the winter they are filled with slowly running water; but in summer they are dry, and their flat bottoms become almost as hard as a brick. No vegetation of consequence will grow in these swales; and the only timber along their margins is scattering ash, from six to eight inches in diameter and from twenty to twenty-five feet high, with wide, bushy tops. The land on both sides of these swales being clean prairie, the rows of green ash in summer give the plain a beautiful appearance.

During the five years I remained in Oregon, the rainy season invariably set in between the 18th of October and the 1st of November, and continued until about the middle of April, with occasional showers to July. In 1845 there were showers in August sufficient

to sprout wheat in the shock. Always about the 10th of September we had frost sufficient to kill bean and melon vines. The season for sowing wheat and oats extended from the commencement of the rains until the first of May ; and the harvest began about the 20th of July. We had snow every winter but one while I was in Oregon. At one time it was from six to eight inches deep, and remained upon the ground about ten days. The Columbia River was then frozen over at Vancouver; but this fact is not a true indication of the degree of cold, as this stream heads in a cold region, and the ice forms above and comes down in floating masses ; and, when the tide is rising, there is little or no current in the river, and it then freezes over very easily. During the winter, and most generally in February, there is an interval of fine clear weather, which lasts about twenty days, with a cold wind from the north, and hard frosts.

But during most of the rainy season the rains are almost continuous. Sometimes the sun would not be seen for twenty days in succession. It would generally rain about three days and nights without intermission, then cease for about the same period (still remaining cloudy), and then begin again. These rains were not very heavy, but cold and steady, accompanied with a brisk, driving wind from the south. It required a very stout, determined man to ride all day facing one of these rains. They were far worse than driving snow, as they wet and chilled the rider through. The summers, the latter half of the spring, and the early half of the fall, were the finest in the world, so far as my own experience extends. Though the rainy seasons be long and tedious, they are, upon the whole, a blessing. The copious rains fertilize the soil of the fields, and keep them always fresh and productive. In my own best

judgment, Oregon is one of the loveliest and most fertile spots of earth. It is destined to be densely populated and finely cultivated. The scenery of her mountains and valleys is simply magnificent. Her snow-clad mountains, her giant forests, her clear skies in summer, and her green and blooming valleys, constitute a combination of the beautiful that can not be excelled.

When we arrived in Oregon, we more than doubled the resident civilized population of the country. J. W. Nesmith, our orderly sergeant, made a complete roll of the male members of the company capable of bearing arms, including all above the age of sixteen years. This roll he preserved and produced at the Oregon Pioneers' Celebration in June, 1875. I have inspected this roll as published in "The Oregonian," and find it correct, except in the omission of the name of P. B. Reading, who went to California, and including the name of A. L. Lovejoy, who came the year before.

This roll contained 293 names, 267 of whom arrived in Oregon. Of the 26 missing, 6 died on the way, 5 turned back on Platte River, and 15 went to California. He also gives the names of many of the resident male population, and estimates their number at 157. John M. Shively * made a complete list of *all* the emigrants at the crossing of Kansas River, but that list has unfortunately been lost. Judge M. P. Deady, in his address before the Oregon Pioneers in June, 1875, estimated the immigration of 1843, men, women, and children, at nine hundred. My own estimate would not be so high. I

* John M. Shively is an engineer, and a plain, unassuming man, but possessed of much greater genuine ability than most people supposed. Justice has never been done him. He was in Washington City in the winter of 1845–'46, and was the originator of the project of a steamship line from New York to this coast by way of Panama.

have always estimated the number arriving in Oregon as not exceeding eight hundred.

When we arrived in Oregon we were poor, and our teams were so much reduced as to be unfit for service until the next spring. Those of us who came by water from Walla Walla left our cattle there for the winter ; and those who came by water from the Dalles left their cattle for the winter at that point. Even if our teams had been fit for use when we arrived, they would have been of no benefit to us, as we could not bring them to the Willamette Valley until the spring of 1844. Pork was ten and flour four cents a pound, and other provisions in proportion. These were high prices considering our scanty means and extra appetites. Had it not been for the generous kindness of the gentlemen in charge of the business of the Hudson's Bay Company, we should have suffered much greater privations. The Company furnished many of our immigrants with provisions, clothing, seed, and other necessaries on credit. This was done, in many instances, where the purchasers were known to be of doubtful credit. At that time the Company had most of the provisions and merchandise in the country ; and the trade with our people was, upon the whole, a decided loss, so many failing to pay for what they had purchased. Many of our immigrants were unworthy of the favors they received, and only returned abuse for generosity.

I remember an example, related to me by Captain James Waters, an excellent man, possessed of a kind heart, a truthful tongue, and a very patient disposition. As before stated, most of our immigrants passed from the Dalles to the Cascades on rafts made of dry logs. This was not only slow navigation, but their rafts were utterly useless after reaching the Cascades ; and they

were compelled to remain there for some days, before they could descend the river to the fort. In the mean time their supplies of provisions had been consumed. Captain Waters was among the first of our immigrants to arrive at Vancouver, having no family with him; and he at once applied to Dr. McLoughlin for supples of provisions for the immigrants at the Cascades, but had nothing wherewith to pay. The Doctor furnished the supplies, and also a boat to take them up, with the understanding that Captain Waters would navigate the vessel, and sell the provisions to the immigrants at Vancouver prices. This was done; but many of the purchasers never paid, contenting themselves with abusing the Doctor and the Captain, accusing them of wishing to speculate upon the necessities of poor immigrants. The final result was a considerable loss, which Dr. McLoughlin and Captain Waters divided equally between them. I met Waters myself with the boat laden with provisions going up, as I passed down the river the first time; and there can be no doubt of the truth of his statement.

DR. JOHN MC LOUGHLIN—JAMES DOUGLAS—POLICY OF THE HUDSON'S BAY COMPANY IN ITS INTERCOURSE WITH THE INDIANS.

Dr. John McLoughlin was one of the greatest and most noble philanthropists I ever knew. He was a man of superior ability, just in all his dealings, and a faithful Christian. I never knew a man of the world who was more admirable. I never heard him utter a vicious sentiment, or applaud a wrongful act. His views and acts were formed upon the model of the Christian gentleman. He was a superior business man, and a pro-

found judge of human nature. He had read a great deal, and had learned much from intercourse with intelligent men. He spoke and wrote French and English equally well, having learned both languages while growing up from childhood.

In his position of chief factor of the Hudson's Bay Company he had grievous responsibilities imposed upon him. He stood between the *absent* directors and stockholders of the Company and the *present* suffering immigrants. He witnessed their sufferings; they did not. He was unjustly blamed by many of both parties. It was not the business of the Company to deal upon credit; and the manager of its affairs in Oregon was suddenly thrown into a new and very embarrassing position. How to act, so as to secure the approbation of the directors and stockholders in England, and at the same time not to disregard the most urgent calls of humanity, was indeed the great difficulty. No *possible* line of conduct could have escaped censure.

To be placed in such a position was a misfortune which only a good man could bear in patience. I was assured by Mr. Frank Ermatinger, the manager of the Company's store at Oregon City, as well as by others, that Dr. McLoughlin had sustained a heavy individual loss by his charity to the immigrants. I knew enough myself to be certain that these statements were substantially true. Yet such was the humility of the Doctor that he never, to my knowledge, mentioned or alluded to any particular act of charity performed by him. I was intimate with him, and he never mentioned them to me. When I first saw him in 1843, his hair was white. He had then been in Oregon about twenty years. He was a large, noble-looking old man, of commanding figure and countenance. His manners were courteous

but frank; and the stranger at once felt at ease in his presence.

Mr. James Douglas (subsequently Sir James, and Governor of British Columbia) was a younger man than Dr. McLoughlin by some fifteen years. He was a man of very superior intelligence, and a finished Christian gentleman. His course toward us was noble, prudent, and generous. I do not think that at that time he possessed the knowledge of men that the Doctor did, nor was he so great a philanthropist. I regarded him as a just and able man, with a conscience and character above reproach. In his position of Governor of British Columbia, he was censured by Mr. John Nugent of California, as I must think, without sufficient reason. Errors of judgment Governor Douglas may have committed, as almost any man would have done at times in his trying position; but he must have radically changed since I knew him, if he knowingly acted improperly.

It was most fortunate for us that two such noble men were managers of the Company at the time of our arrival. Our own countrymen had it not in their power to aid us efficiently. Many of them were immigrants of the preceding season; others were connected with the missions; and, altogether, they were too few and poor to help us much. The Company could not afford to extend to succeeding immigrations the same credit they did to us. The burden would have been too great. This refusal led many to complain, but without sufficient reason.

From Dr. McLoughlin and others I learned a great deal in reference to the manner in which the business of the Company had been conducted. At the time of the Doctor's arrival in Oregon, and for many years afterward, the principal inhabitants were Indians, divided

into various small tribes, speaking different languages. These Indians were mainly found upon the Columbia and its tributaries, and far outnumbered the hired servants of the Company. The task of controlling these wild people was one of great delicacy, requiring a thorough knowledge of human nature and the greatest administrative ability. The Doctor's policy was based upon the fundamental idea that all men, civilized or savage, have an innate love of justice, and will therefore be *ultimately* best satisfied with fair, honest dealing.

The Company had its various trading-posts located at convenient points throughout a vast territory. The Indian population being about stationary as to numbers and pursuits, it was not very difficult to calculate the amount of supplies likely to be required in each year. The Company was in the habit of importing one year's supply in advance ; so that if a cargo should be lost, its customers would not suffer. Its goods were all of superior quality, purchased on the best terms, and were sold at prices both uniform and moderate. Of course, prices in the interior were higher than on the seaboard ; but they never varied at the same post. The Indians knew nothing of the intricate law of demand and supply, and could not be made to understand why an article of a given size and quality should be worth more at one time than at another in the same place, while the material and labor used and employed in its manufacture were the same. A tariff of prices, once adopted, was never changed. The goods were not only of the best, but of uniform quality. To secure these results the Company had most of its goods manufactured to order. The wants of the Indians being very few, their purchases were confined to a small variety of articles ; and consequently they became the very best judges of

the quality of the goods they desired to purchase. No one could detect any imperfection in a blanket more readily and conclusively than an Oregon Indian. There was always kept an ample supply at each post; so that the customers of the Company were not driven at any time to deal with rival traders, or do without their usual supplies.

It was evident that no successful competition with the Company could last long under such circumstances. No one could continue to undersell them and make a profit; and the competitor, without profit, must fail. The uniform low prices and the good quality of its articles pleased the Indians, and the Company secured their custom beyond the reach of competition. The Company adopted a system that would work out best in the end, and, of course, was successful.

In the course of time the Company induced the Indians to throw aside the bow and arrow, and to use the gun; and, as the Company had all the guns and ammunition in the country, the Indians became dependent upon it for their supplies of these articles. It was the great object of the Company to preserve the peace among the Indians within the limits of its trading territory, not only from motives of pure humanity, but from mercantile interest; as the destruction of the Indians was the destruction of its customers, and the consequent ruin of its trade.

When the Indians went to war with each other, the Doctor first interposed his mediation, as the common friend and equal of both parties. When all other means failed, he refused to sell them arms and ammunition, saying that it was the business of the Company to sell them these articles to kill game with, not to kill each other. By kindness, justice, and discreet firmness, the

Indians were generally kept at peace among themselves. They found it almost impossible to carry on war.

But the task of protecting the servants of the Company against the attacks of the Indians was one of still greater difficulty. The Doctor impressed the Indians with the fact that the Company was simply a mercantile corporation, whose purpose was only trade with the natives; that its intention was only to appropriate to its exclusive use a few sites for its trading-posts and small parcels of adjacent lands, sufficient to produce supplies for its people; thus leaving all the remainder of the country for the use and in the exclusive possession of the Indians; and that this possession of limited amounts of land by the Company would be mutually beneficial. Even savages have the native good sense to discover the mutual benefits of trade. The Indians wanted a market for their furs, and the Company customers for its merchandise.

It was an inflexible rule with the Doctor never to violate his word, whether it was a promise of reward or a threat of punishment. There is no vice more detested by Indians than a failure to keep one's word, which they call lying. If it were a failure to perform a promised act beneficial to the Indians themselves, they would regard it as a fraud akin to theft; and, if a failure to carry out a threat of punishment, they would consider it the result of weakness or cowardice. In either case, the party who broke his pledged word would forfeit their respect, and in the first case would incur their undying resentment.

To guard against the natural jealousy of the Indians, and insure peace between them and the servants of the Company, it became necessary to adopt and enforce the

most rigid discipline among the latter. This discipline was founded upon the great principle that, to avoid difficulty with others, we must first do right ourselves. To make this discipline the more efficient, the Doctor adopted such measures as substantially to exclude all intoxicating liquors from the country. When a crime was committed by an Indian, the Doctor made it a rule not to hold the *whole* tribe responsible for the unauthorized acts of individuals, but to inflict punishment upon the culprit himself. In cases of crime by Indians, the Doctor insisted upon just punishment ; and, if the culprit escaped for a time, the pursuit was never given up until he was captured. In some cases, several years elapsed between the date of the crime and that of the capture of the fugitive. Certain and just punishment was always inflicted upon the criminal. This the Doctor was able to accomplish through the Company's agents at the different posts, and by negotiation with the leading Indian chiefs, and the offer of rewards for the arrest of the fugitive.

In this manner the Doctor secured and kept the confidence of the Indians. When he first arrived in Oregon, and for some time thereafter, whenever boats were sent up the Columbia with supplies, a guard of sixty armed men was required ; but, in due time, only the men necessary to propel the boats were needed. The Indians at the different portages were employed and paid by the Company to assist in making them.

The Indians soon saw that the Company was a mere trading establishment, confined to a small space of land at each post, and was, in point of fact, advantageous to themselves. The few Canadian-French who were located in the Willamette Valley were mostly, if not entirely, connected by marriage with the Indians, the

Frenchmen having Indian wives, and were considered to some extent as a part of their own people. But, when we, the American immigrants, came into what the Indians claimed as their own country, we were considerable in numbers; and we came, not to establish trade with the Indians, but to take and settle the country *exclusively* for ourselves. Consequently, we went anywhere we pleased, settled down without any treaty or consultation with the Indians, and occupied our claims without their consent and without compensation. This difference they very soon understood. Every succeeding fall they found the white population about doubled, and our settlements continually extending, and rapidly encroaching more and more upon their pasture and camas grounds. They saw that we fenced in the best lands, excluding their horses from the grass, and our hogs ate up their camas. They instinctively saw annihilation before them.

As illustrative of the difficulties of Dr. McLoughlin's position, I will state the facts of a few cases, as they were related to me substantially by the Doctor himself.

The shore of the Columbia River in front of Fort Vancouver was covered with cobble-stones, which were used by the Company as ballast for its returning ships. The principal chief of the Indians concluded that the Company ought to pay something for these stones; and one day, in the presence of a large crowd of his people (assembled, perhaps, for that purpose), he demanded payment of the Doctor. Of course, the Doctor was taken by surprise, but at once comprehended the situation. He knew, if he consented to pay in this case, there would be no end to exactions in the future. How best to avoid the payment without giving offense was

the question. He knew that the Indians possessed a keen sense of the ridiculous ; and, after reflecting a moment, he picked up a cobble-stone, and solemnly offered it to the chief, saying, "Eat this." The Indians present at once saw how ridiculous it was to demand payment for that which was of no practical value to them, and set up a loud shout of derisive laughter. The chief was so much ashamed of his silly demand that he walked off in silence, and never after that demanded payment for things of no value to him.

While the Company's ships lay at anchor in the river opposite the fort, the Doctor occasionally granted a written permit to some particular Indian to visit the ships. On one occasion he granted such a permit to an Indian who was seen by other Indians to go on board, but was not seen by them to return, though, in fact, he did so return. Within a day or two thereafter, the brother of this Indian, being unable to find him, and suspecting that he had been enticed on board the ship, and either murdered or forcibly imprisoned for the purpose of abduction, applied to the Doctor for a permit to visit the ship. As the Indian concealed his reason for asking the permit, the Doctor supposed he was influenced by an idle curiosity, and refused the request. The Indian returned again for the same purpose, and was again refused. He came the third time, with the same result. He then concluded that his brother must either be imprisoned on the ship, or had been murdered ; and he at once resolved upon revenge. In the evening of the same day, about an hour before sunset, a shot was heard ; and the gardener came running into the fort in great terror, with a bullet-hole through the top of his hat, saying that an Indian had fired upon him from behind the garden-fence. The gates of the fort were at

once closed, and all hands prepared for defense. Upon subsequent investigation, the body of the missing Indian was found in the bushes, in the rear of the fort. He had evidently fallen down in a fit, and expired where his body was found. No attempt was made to punish the surviving brother, as he had acted under a very natural mistake.

On one occasion the Indians determined to take and sack Fort Vancouver. The plot for this purpose was conceived, and in part executed, with consummate ability.

Two of their most powerful chiefs quietly went from Fort Vancouver to Nesqualy, a trading-post on Puget's Sound, and remained there several days. While there, they made themselves minutely acquainted with everything about the fort. They then speedily returned to Fort Vancouver, and at once sought and obtained an interview with Dr. McLoughlin and his associates. One of the Indians was the speaker, while the other carefully watched to see what impression their statements would make. The Company's interpreter, a very shrewd Canadian, was present during the interview.

The Indians stated that they left Nesqualy at a certain time, which was true; and that the Indians in that vicinity had attacked and captured the fort by surprise, and had slaughtered all the inhabitants, amounting to a certain number of persons, which number they specified truly. The Indians were subjected to a severe cross-examination without betraying the slightest embarrassment, and without making any contradictory statements. When asked how many persons were in the fort at the time, what were their several ages, sexes, appearances, employments, and the position that each occupied in the fort, they invariably gave the correct

answer. It was impossible to detect any contradictions in their statements. All were perfectly consistent, as the only falsehood was the alleged fact that Fort Nesqualy had been taken and the people killed. The Doctor and his associates were greatly perplexed, and left in much doubt. The Canadian interpreter was asked his opinion, and he replied, "Let me sleep on it one night." Next morning he said he did not believe the story; that the Indians were such liars that he could not believe them; that they had before deceived them. This view prevailed.

The object of these Indians was to induce the Company to send nearly all its men to Nesqualy to punish the alleged murderers, thus reducing the force at Fort Vancouver to such an extent that it could be readily taken. These Indians knew, from the invariable practice of the Company, that such a crime, if committed, would not escape punishment if practicable. If they could only make the Doctor believe their narrative, he would at once dispatch an ample force to Nesqualy.

The traders in charge of interior trading-posts were often exposed to peril from the Indians. The Company could only keep a few men at each post, and the Indians at times would become discontented. A rude people, depending entirely upon the spontaneous productions of nature for a supply of provisions, must often suffer extreme want. In such a case men become desperate, and are easily excited to rash acts. Mr. McKinley told me that the Indians on one occasion attempted to rob Fort Walla Walla, and were only prevented by the most cool, intrepid courage of the people of the post.

CHAPTER IV.

ROCKY MOUNTAIN TRAPPERS—THEIR PECULIAR CHARACTER—BLACK HARRIS—JOSEPH L. MEEK—O. RUSSELL—ROBERT NEWELL.

When we arrived in Oregon, we found there a number of Rocky Mountain hunters and trappers, who were settled in the Willamette Valley, most of them in the Tualatin Plains. The invention of the silk hat had rendered the trapping of beaver less profitable. Besides, most of these men had married Indian women, and desired to settle down for life. They had been too long accustomed to frontier life to return to their old homes. Oregon offered them the best prospects for the future. Here was plenty of land for nothing, and a fine climate.

These trappers and hunters constituted a very peculiar class of men. They were kind and genial, brave and hospitable, and in regard to serious matters truthful and honest. There was no malice in them. They never made mischief between neighbor and neighbor. But most of them were given to exaggeration when relating their Rocky Mountain adventures. They seemed to claim the privilege of romance and fable when describing these scenes. As exceptions to this rule, I will mention Judge O. Russell, now living in El Dorado County, California, and Robert Newell, now deceased. Their statements could be relied upon implicitly.

Having been so long accustomed to the idle life of the Rocky Mountains, they were not at first pleased with the hard work and drudgery of farming. Meek told me that soon after their arrival in Oregon they applied to Dr. McLoughlin to purchase supplies on credit. This application the Doctor refused. They still urged their request most persistently, and finally asked the Doctor what they should do. He replied in a loud voice : " Go to work ! go to work ! go to work ! " Meek said that was just the thing they did not wish to do.

The romancing Rocky Mountain trapper would exercise his inventive talent to its utmost extent in telling the most extraordinary stories of what he claimed he had seen, and he that could form the most extravagant fiction with a spice of plausibility in it was considered the greatest wit among them. The love of fame is inherent in the breast of man ; and the first man in a village is just as proud of his position as the first man in a city or in an empire.

I knew in Missouri the celebrated Black Harris, as he was familiarly called, and was frequently in his company. He, perhaps, invented the most extraordinary story of them all, and thenceforward he had no rival. He said that on one occasion he was hunting in the Rocky Mountains alone, and came in sight of what he supposed to be a beautiful grove of green timber ; but, when he approached, he found it to be a petrified forest ; and *so sudden* had been the process of petrifaction that the green leaves were all petrified, and the very birds that were then singing in the grove were also petrified in the act of singing, because their mouths were still open in their petrified state. This story I did not myself hear from Harris, but I learned it from good authority.

From these Rocky Mountain trappers I learned something in regard to that interesting animal, the beaver. Many persons suppose, from the fact that the beaver is always found along the streams, that he lives, like the otter, on fish. This is a mistake. The beaver lives entirely upon vegetable food, and for this reason its flesh is esteemed a great delicacy. The animal feeds mainly upon the bark of the willow-tree, which grows in abundance along the rich, moist margins of the streams, and is a very soft wood, easily cut by the beaver with his large, sharp teeth. In countries where the streams freeze over in winter, the beaver makes his dam across the stream, of mud and brush so intermixed as to make the structure safe and solid. In this work he uses his fore-paws, not his tail, as some have supposed. The tail is used as a propelling and steering power in swimming. The object in damming the stream is to deepen the water so that it will not freeze to the bottom, but leave plenty of room below the ice for the storage of the winter's supply of food. In summer the beaver cuts down the green willows, and divides them into logs of proper length, so that they can be readily moved. These logs are deposited at the bottom of the pond, and kept down by mud placed upon them. The willow in its green state is almost as heavy as water, and these logs are easily sunk and confined to the bottom. On one portion of his dam the beaver constructs his house above the water, with an entrance from beneath. This gives him a warm home and safe retreat in winter.

The mode of trapping the beaver is peculiar. The trap itself is never baited The animal has in his body a secretion something like musk. The trapper finds out the home of the beaver, and selects a place on the side of the pond where the water is shallow near the shore;

and there, in the edge of the stream, he drives down a stake of hard-seasoned wood, which the beaver can not cut. To this stake he fastens the chain that is attached to the trap, and then sets the trap in water some six inches deep. On the shore, exactly opposite the trap, he places a bait of the secretion. The beaver always swims up the center of the pond; and when he comes immediately opposite the bait he turns at right angles and goes straight toward it, but is caught in the trap while passing over it. So soon as he feels the trap he endeavors to escape, and drags the trap into deep water as far as the chain will permit. The steel trap is so heavy that the beaver can not possibly swim with it, but is confined by its weight to the bottom, and is there drowned, as the beaver, like other amphibious animals, can remain alive under water only for a limited time.

The beaver is easily tamed, and makes a very docile and interesting pet. He is remarkably neat and cleanly in his habits, as much so as the domestic cat, and almost as much so as the ermine, which never permits its snow-white covering to be soiled.

I am not aware that any wild animal, except the glutton, ever preys upon the beaver or otter. Their terrible teeth are most formidable weapons, and few wild animals would venture to attack them. Besides, they are covered with a large, loose skin and thick fur, so that the teeth of another animal can hardly reach a vital part. It is a well-known fact that one otter will vanquish a number of large, brave dogs. Every bite of the otter leaves a large gash, like that made by the huge tusks of the wild boar.

Among the most noted of these trappers was my neighbor and friend, Joseph L. Meek, whose life has been written by Mrs. Victor, of Oregon. Meek was a

tall man, of fine appearance—a most genial, kind, and brave spirit. He had in his composition no malice, no envy, and no hatred. I do not remember ever to have heard that he had a personal difficulty with any one. In relating his Rocky Mountain adventures, he was given, like a majority of his comrades, to exaggeration.

His comrades told a story upon him, which he admitted to me was true. A party of them, while in the Rocky Mountains, were one day stopping to rest, when they saw a band of hostile Indians mounted and charging down upon them, at the distance of a few hundred yards. Meek and his comrades mounted their animals in the hottest haste ; but the fine mule Meek was riding became sullen and would not budge. Meek screamed out, at the top of his voice : "Boys, stand your ground ! We can whip 'em. Stand your ground, boys !" But his comrades were of a different opinion, and were fleeing from the Indians as fast as possible. However, as the Indians approached, Meek's mule began to comprehend the situation, changed its mind, and set off at its utmost speed in pursuit of its companions. In a short time Meek and his mule were alongside of the fleeing hunters ; and very soon Meek passed them, whipping his mule, and crying out most lustily : "Come on, boys ! We can't fight 'em ! Come on, boys ! come on !"

I remember a story Meek told to myself and four others, as we were returning from Oregon City to our homes in the Tualatin Plains. He said that on one occasion he was out hunting by himself, some four hundred miles from Brown's Cove, in the Rocky Mountains, where his company were staying, and that one night his horse escaped, leaving him afoot. He started on foot, with his rifle on his shoulder ; but the first day he lost the lock of his gun, so that he could kill no game.

The result was, that he walked that long distance, less fifteen miles, in eight days, and without anything to eat except one thistle-root, and that purged him like medicine! He said that toward the end of his trip he would often become blind, fall down, and remain unconscious for some time; then recover, and pursue his painful journey. At last, in this way, he reached a point within fifteen miles of Brown's Cove, where one of his comrades happened to find him, and took him into camp.

I replied: "That was a most extraordinary adventure, Joe; and, while I don't pretend to question your veracity in the least, don't you really think you might safely fall a snake or two in the distance?" He declared it was four hundred miles. "But," said I, "may you not be mistaken in the time?" He insisted he was only eight days in making the trip on foot. "But, Joe," I continued, "don't you think you may be mistaken as to the time in this way? When you had those attacks of blindness, fell down, and then came to again, don't you think you might have mistaken it for a new day?" He said he was not mistaken. "Then," said I, "this thing of walking four hundred miles in eight days, with nothing at all to eat, and being physicked into the bargain, is the most extraordinary feat ever performed by man." He said no man could tell how much he could stand until he was forced to try; and that men were so healthy in the Rocky Mountains, and so used to hard times, that they could perform wonders.

Meek was a droll creature, and at times very slovenly in his dress. One day in summer I called for him, sitting on my horse at his yard-fence. He came to the door and put his head out, but would not come to the fence, because his pantaloons were so torn and ragged. He was then sheriff; and at the next term of our Circuit

Court I drew up a fictitious indictment against him, charging him with notorious public indecency; had it endorsed on the back: "People of Oregon *vs.* Joseph L. Meek. Notorious Public Indecency. A true bill"; and quietly placed it among the real indictments. Very soon Meek was looking through the bundle of indictments, and found this one against himself. He, of course, supposed it genuine; and it would have amused an invalid to see the expression of his face. I soon told him it was only a joke, which was apparent upon the face of the indictment, as it had not the signatures of the proper officers.

On one occasion he came to my house, wearing one of the most splendid new white figured-silk vests that I had ever seen, while the remainder of his dress was exceedingly shabby. He was like a man dressed in a magnificent ruffled shirt, broadcloth coat, vest, and pantaloons, and going barefoot.

The second or third year after my arrival in Oregon, and in the month of October, before the rainy season set in, I was about to start to Oregon City with a load of wheat, to secure a winter's supply of flour, when Meek asked me to let him put ten bushels in the wagon, and he would go with me. I said all right—that I would be at his place the next morning early, with my wagon and team, and for him to have his wheat ready. He promised he would. According to my promise, I was at his house by eight next morning; but Meek had to run his wheat through the fan, and put it into the sacks. The result was that I had to help him; and it was ten by the time we were loaded up. In a great hurry, I asked him if he had anything to eat, as I only had some bread in the wagon, the only thing I could bring. I saw he was rather embarrassed, and said,

"Have you any meat?" "No!" "Have you any butter?" "No!" "What, then, have you?" "Plenty of squashes." I said, "Roll them in." He soon brought as many squashes as his long arms and big hands could carry, put them into the wagon, and we were off. I drove the team and he rode his horse.

On the way Meek rode ahead of me, and overtook Mr. Pomeroy, going to Oregon City with a wagon loaded with fresh beef. Meek, in a good-humored, bantering way said, "Pomeroy, I have an execution against you, and I can not let you take that beef out of this county." Pomeroy, with equal good humor, replied, "Meek, it is a hard case to stop a man on the way to market, where he can sell his beef, and get the money to pay his debts." "Well," said Meek, "it does look a little hard, but I propose a compromise. Burnett and I will have nothing to eat to-night but bread and squashes. Now, if you will let us have beef enough for supper and breakfast, I will let you off." Pomeroy laughed and told Meek to help himself. When we encamped about sundown, some eight miles from the city, Meek did help himself to some choice ribs of beef, and we had a feast. I had had nothing to eat since the morning of that day but bread; and I was hungry after my hard drive. I roasted the squashes, and Meek the beef; and we had a splendid supper. I found this beef almost equal to buffalo-meat. We both ate too much, and Meek complained that his supper had given him "the rotten belches."

I have already mentioned the name of Judge O. Russell as one of the Rocky Mountain men. He is a native of the State of Maine, and came to the mountains when a young man, in pursuit of health. All his comrades agreed that he never lost his virtuous habits, but always remained true to his principles. He was

never married. He was at one time one of the Executive Committee of our Provisional Government in Oregon, and most faithfully did he perform his duty. He is a man of education and of refined feelings. After the discovery of gold he came to the mines, and has been engaged in mining in El Dorado County, California, ever since.

When in Oregon, he was occasionally a guest at my house, and would for hours together entertain us with descriptions of mountain life and scenery. His descriptive powers were fine, and he would talk until a late hour at night. My whole family were deeply attentive, and my children yet remember the Judge with great pleasure. He was always a most welcome guest at my house. He did not tell so many extraordinary stories as the average Rocky Mountain trapper and hunter; but those he did tell were true. I remember one instance.

He said that he and a colored man were out hunting together on one occasion, and wounded a large grizzly bear. A grizzly bear, when wounded, will rush upon the hunter if near him; but, if at a distance from the hunter, the animal will retire into thick brush, and there conceal himself as well as possible. In this case, the bear had crept into a small but thick patch of willows, and so concealed himself that the hunters had to approach very near before they could obtain a shot. The Judge and his comrade, with loaded and cocked rifles in hand, separately approached, on different sides, almost to the edge of the thicket, when the grizzly, with a loud, ferocious cry, suddenly sprang to his feet and rushed toward the Judge, and, when within a few feet of him, reared upon his hind legs, with his ears thrown back, his terrible jaws distended, and his eyes gleaming with rage. The Judge said he knew that to retreat

was death, and that the only chance was to make a sure shot. With the accuracy and courage of a skillful hunter, he fired as the bear stood up, and gave him a fatal shot through the heart. The bear fell, and the colored man came up as pale as a colored man could be, and exclaimed, "That was a 'roshus animal!"

Robert Newell was a native of the State of Ohio, and came to the Rocky Mountains when a young man. He was of medium height, stout frame, and fine face. He was full of humanity, good will, genial feeling, and frankness. He possessed a remarkable memory; and, though slow of speech, his narrations were most interesting. In his slow, hesitating manner, he would state every minute circumstance in its own proper place; and the hearer was most amply compensated in the end for his time and patience. I knew him well, and have often listened to his simple and graphic description of incidents that came under his own observation while he was in the service of the Missouri Fur Company. I remember a very interesting narration which I heard from him. I can only give the substance.

The hired men of the Company were mostly employed in trapping beaver and otter. A war grew up between the whites and Indians, as usual. It was not desirable to the Company, and its manager made efforts to secure peace. For this purpose he consulted with Newell, and asked him if he would be willing to go as a commissioner to the Crow Indians to treat for peace. Newell consented, upon condition that he should only take with him an interpreter and a cook.

With these two men Newell boldly made his way to the Crow camp. The Indian chiefs assembled in the council-lodge, and the orator on the part of the tribe brought in a bundle of small sticks. He commenced

and stated an aggressive wrong against the Crows on the part of the whites, and demanded for that a certain number of blankets. Having done this, he laid aside one stick, and then proceeded to state another grievance and to lay aside another stick, and so on until the bundle was exhausted. The number of these complaints was great, and the amount of merchandise demanded far exceeded the ability of the Company to pay.

Newell said that, while this process was going on, he felt himself almost overwhelmed. He could not make a detailed statement of wrongs committed by the Indians against the whites sufficient to balance this most formidable account. He had not prepared himself with a mass of charges and a bundle of sticks to refresh his memory. In this emergency he determined to take a bold, frank position, and come directly to the point by a short and comprehensive method. When it came to his turn to speak, he told the council that he was sent as the mere agent of the Company, and was not authorized to enter into any stipulation for payment to either party; that he did not come to count over the wrongs committed in the past; that both parties had done wrong often, and it was difficult to say which party had been oftenest or most to blame; that he came to bury the past and stipulate for peace in the future, and wished to know of them whether they would mutually agree to be friends for the time to come. This was the best possible ground to be taken, and so pleased the assembled chiefs that they entered into a treaty of peace.

But a very short time after this treaty was made, and before Newell and his two men had left, a sad accident occurred that wellnigh cost Newell his life. One night, before bedtime, the cook had hung a small kettle above the fire in Newell's lodge, and had pretty well

filled it with choice pieces of fat buffalo-meat, with intent to have a feast. After doing this, the careless cook went out, and the kettle boiled over; and the first thing that Newell saw was the fire blazing out at the top of the lodge. When he first saw it, he was at the lodge of one of the chiefs, a short distance off. In the hurry and confusion of the moment, Newell ran to his lodge, seized the kettle, and gave it a sudden sling, and it happened to strike an Indian in the face and scalded him terribly. The Indian gave a loud scream, which at once aroused all the camp. The excitement was terrific. The act could not be denied, and the injury was palpable and most grievous. It was thought that both the eyes of the Indian had been put out; and his friends and kindred were vehement and loud in their demands for punishment.

The principal chief at once summoned a council to consider the case. The chiefs met in the council-lodge, while the people, including men, women, and children, squatted in front of the door leaving a narrow passage for the prisoner, with his interpreter, to enter the lodge. Newell said that as they passed through this enraged mass of people they exhibited the utmost hatred against him, especially the women, who manifested their intense animosity in every way, by word and gesture. In passing by them, they would lean away and shrink from him, as if his touch was pollution itself.

When he entered the dimly lighted council-lodge, all was grim and profound silence. Not a word was spoken, nor a move made, for some time. Then one of the chiefs commenced howling like a large wolf, the imitation being almost perfect. After he had ceased, there was again profound silence for some moments; and then another chief successfully imitated the fierce

cry of the panther; and then, after another pause, a third chief most energetically imitated the loud cry of an enraged grizzly bear. He said that he had never witnessed a scene of terror equal to this. All the chiefs, except the principal one, seemed to be his enemies. He thought his chance of escape exceedingly small.

The head chief was an old man, of superior native intellect, and, though uneducated, he understood human nature. He seemed to comprehend the case well. He could see no malicious motive for the act. He told Newell to state the facts to the council truly, and he thought there might be some hope for him.

Newell, through his interpreter, stated to them all the facts as they occurred; and this just statement and Newell's honest and manly face and frank manner had a great effect upon the principal members of the council. It was also found that the poor Indian had not been so severely hurt as at first supposed, and that his sight was not totally destroyed. The council sat nearly all night, and then decided to postpone the case until time should show the extent of the injury. In the mean time Newell and his companions were not allowed to depart, but were to be detained until the case should be finally decided.

But another painful incident soon occurred, that seriously imperiled their lives.

One day an Indian horseman was seen approaching the camp rapidly; and, when within some hundred yards, he dismounted, rolled up his buffalo-robe, took hold of one end of the roll, and slowly and solemnly swung it around his head several times; then he folded it up, and sat upon it, and brought both his open hands slowly down his face several times in succession. The Indians in camp at once understood the sad significance of these

signs. They knew that he was a messenger sent to inform them that the small-pox had broken out at another camp of their tribe. He would not come near, for fear of communicating the disease to them.

Newell said that he had never witnessed such a scene of sorrow as this. The women and children filled the camp with their loud wailings and bitter lamentations; and despair sat upon the countenances of the men. The Indians were now more fiercely hostile than ever, because they believed that this terrible scourge, far worse to them than war itself, had been introduced by the trappers. They knew that this fell disease was never heard of in their country until white men appeared among them. They thronged around Newell and his comrades, and it seemed that they would slaughter them outright.

But the old chief was equal to the occasion. He at once mounted his horse and rode through the camp, saying to all that it was useless to weep and lament, and ordering the people to pack up at once and be off for the Wind River Mountain. This order was instantly obeyed; the cries and lamentations at once ceased; and Newell said he never saw lodges so quickly taken down and packed up as he did on this occasion. In less than one hour the whole camp was on the march to the place mentioned. In due time they arrived safely at the Wind River Mountain, where the sky was clear, the climate cool and healthy, and game abundant. It being in midsummer, the deer had followed up the melting snows to crop the fresh grass as soon as it sprang up just below the snow-line, and to be in a cool atmosphere, where the flies would not torment them. Here the Indians recovered from their alarm and excitement. Not a case of small-pox appeared in camp. All were healthy

and had plenty to eat. The poor fellow that was scalded recovered in this healthy locality, and was not so seriously injured as was at first supposed. Newell became popular with the Indians, and they at last let him depart in peace.

THE PROVISIONAL GOVERNMENT.

Soon after my arrival at Linnton, I was consulted as to the right of the people of Oregon to organize a provisional government. At first I gave my opinion against it, thinking we had no such right; but a few weeks' reflection satisfied me that we had such right, and that necessity required us to exercise it. Communities, as well as individuals, have the natural right of self-defense; and it is upon this ground that the right to institute governments among men must ultimately rest. This right of self-preservation is bestowed upon man by his Creator.

We found ourselves placed in a new and very embarrassing position. The right of sovereignty over the country was in dispute between the United States and Great Britain, and neither country could establish any government over us. Our community was composed of American citizens and British subjects, occupying the same country as neighbors, with all their respective national prejudices and attachments, and so distant from the mother-countries as to be to a great extent beyond the reach of home influences. We had, therefore, a difficult population to govern; but this fact only rendered government the more necessary.

We also found, by actual experiment, that some political government was a *necessity*. Though political government be imperfect, it is still a blessing, and necessary for the preservation of the race. Without it,

the strongest and most reckless characters in the community would be tyrants over the others. The theory of the wandering savage, to leave the kindred of the murdered victim to revenge his death, would not answer for a civilized race of men. The weak and timid, the peaceful and conscientious, and those who had no kindred, could not be protected under such a theory. Without any law but that of individual self-defense, we found it impossible to get along in peace. When a person died, the worst characters could seize upon his estate under some pretense or other, and defeat the just rights of defenseless heirs. So long as these violent, bad men had only to meet and overcome single individuals, they had no fears. It is only when the combined force of a whole community is brought to bear upon these desperadoes that they can be effectually kept in order.

As we could not, with any exact certainty, anticipate the time when the conflicting claims of the two contending governments would be settled, we determined to organize a provisional government for ourselves. In this undertaking our British neighbors ultimately joined us with good will, and did their part most faithfully, as did our American citizens.

I was a member of the "Legislative Committee of Oregon" of 1844. It was composed of nine members elected by the people, and consisted of only one House. The year before, the people of Oregon had substantially organized a provisional government; but the organization was imperfect, as is necessarily the case in the beginning of all human institutions. We improved upon their labors, and our successors improved upon ours.

Our Legislative Committee held two sessions, one in June and the other in December of that year, each session lasting only a few days. In our then condition, we

had but little time to devote to public business. Our personal needs were too urgent, and our time too much occupied in making a support for our families. Our legislation, however, was ample for the time. There was then no printing establishment in Oregon. We passed an act in relation to land claims, the first section of which provided that "all persons who have heretofore made, or shall hereafter make permanent improvements upon a place, with a *bona fide* intention of occupying and holding the same for himself, and shall continue to occupy and cultivate the same, shall be entitled to hold six hundred and forty acres, and shall hold only one claim at the same time; *provided*, a man may hold town lots in addition to his claim." The seventh and last section gave all persons complying with the provisions of the act "the remedy of forcible entry and detainer against intruders, and the action of trespass against trespassers." This act was passed June 25, 1844. It will be seen that the remedy against intruders was simple, cheap, quick, and efficient, and well adapted to existing circumstances.

By an act passed June 27, 1844, the executive power was vested in a single person, to be elected at the then next annual election by the people, and at the annual election to be held every two years thereafter, to hold his office for the term of two years, and receive an annual salary of three hundred dollars. By the same act the judicial power was vested in the circuit courts and in justices of the peace; and the act provided that one judge should be elected by the qualified voters at the annual election, who should hold his office for one year, and whose duty it was to hold two terms of the Circuit Court in each county every year; and for his services he should receive an annual salary of five hundred dol-

lars, and also legal fees for probate business. By the same act the legislative power was vested in a House of Representatives, composed of members elected annually by the people.

The first section of the third article of the same act was as follows:

Section 1. All the statute laws of Iowa Territory passed at the first session of the Legislative Assembly of said Territory, and not of a local character, and not incompatible with the condition and circumstances of this country, shall be the law of this government, unless otherwise modified; and the common law of England and principles of equity, not modified by the statutes of Iowa or of this government, and not incompatible with its principles, shall constitute a part of the law of this land.

Article V. was in these words:

Section 1. All officers shall be elected by the people once a year, unless otherwise provided, at a general election to be held in each county on the first Tuesday in June in each year, at such places as shall be designated by the Judge of the Circuit Court.

Sec. 2. As many justices of the peace and constables shall be elected from time to time as shall be deemed necessary by the Circuit Court of each county.

The seventh article fixed the time of holding the terms of the circuit courts in the several counties, and gave the judge the power to designate the several places of holding said terms by giving one month's notice thereof.

We also passed on June 24th an act consisting of eight sections, prohibiting the importation, distillation, sale, and barter of ardent spirits. For every sale or barter the offender was to pay a fine of twenty dol-

lars; and for establishing or carrying on a distillery the offender was subject to be indicted before the Circuit Court as for a nuisance, and, if convicted, to a fine of one hundred dollars; and it was made the duty of the court to issue an order directing the sheriff to seize and destroy the distilling apparatus, which order the sheriff was bound to execute.

On June 22d an act containing twenty-six sections was passed concerning roads and highways. On December 24th an act was passed allowing the voters of Oregon at the annual election of 1845 to give their votes for or against the call of a convention.

The following act in relation to Indians was passed December 23d:

Whereas, The Indians inhabiting this country are rapidly diminishing, being now mere remnants of once powerful tribes, now disorganized, without government, and so situated that no treaty can be regularly made with them;

And whereas, By an act passed in July, 1843, this government has shown its humane policy to protect the Indians in their rights;

And whereas, The Indians are not engaged in agriculture, and have no use for or right to any tracts, portions, or parcels of land, not actually occupied or used by them; therefore,

Be it enacted by the Legislative Committee of Oregon as follows:

SECTION 1. That the Indians shall be protected in the free use of such pieces of vacant land as they occupy with their villages or other improvements, and such fisheries as they have heretofore used.

SEC. 2. That the executive power be required to see that the laws in regard to Indians be faithfully executed; and that whenever the laws shall be violated, the said Executive shall be empowered to bring suit in the name of Oregon against such wrong-doer in the courts of the country.

An act was passed on June 27th fixing the number of members of the next House of Representatives at thirteen, and apportioning the representation among the then five counties of Oregon.

All necessary local bills were passed, and our little government was put into practical and successful operation. Having adopted the general statutes of Iowa and the common law, we had a provision for every case likely to arise in so small a community.

At first, the great difficulty was to make our little government efficient. Our people honestly differed very much in their views as to our right to institute government. In 1843 there were fifty-two affirmative and fifty negative votes. There were so many of our people who were conscientiously opposed to the organization of any government that we found it a delicate matter to use force against men whose motives we were sure were good. Still, government had to be practically enforced.

Joseph L. Meek was selected in May or July, 1843, for sheriff. He was the very man for the position. He was both as brave and as magnanimous as the lion. Do his duty he would, peacefully if possible, but forcibly if he must. If we had selected a timid or rash man for sheriff, we must have failed for a time. To be a government at all, the laws must be enforced.

Meek soon had his courage fully tested. A stout carpenter named Dawson was engaged in a fight in the winter of 1843–'44, and a warrant was at once issued for his arrest, and placed in Meek's hands to be executed. Dawson was no doubt of opinion that we had no right to organize and enforce our government. Meek went to Dawson's shop, where he was at work at his bench with a jack-plane. Meek walked in, and said laughingly, "Dawson, I came for you." Dawson re-

plied that Meek had come for the wrong man. Meek, still laughing, said again, "I came for you," and was about to lay his hands on Dawson, when the latter drew back with his jack-plane raised to strike. But Meek was not only stout, but active and brave ; and, seizing the plane, he wrested it by force from Dawson. Dawson at once turned around and picked up his broad-axe; but the moment he faced Meek, he found a cocked pistol at his breast. Meek, still laughing, said; "Dawson, I came for you. Surrender or die!" Very few men will persist under such circumstances ; and Dawson, though as brave as most men, began to cry, threw down his broad-axe, and went with Meek without further objection. Dawson declared that, as *he* had to submit, every other man must ; and he was no longer an enemy of our government.

This intrepid performance of his official duty so established Meek's character for true courage in the exercise of his office that he had little or no trouble in the future ; and the authority of our little government was thus thoroughly established.

CONDITION OF THE PEOPLE—HARDSHIPS ENDURED BY THE EARLY SETTLERS.

We were a small, thinly-settled community, poor, and isolated from the civilized world. By the time we reached the distant shores of the Pacific, after a slow, wearisome journey of about two thousand miles, our little means were exhausted, and we had to begin life anew, in a new country. The wild game in Oregon was scarce and poor. The few deer that are found there seldom become fat. The wild fowl were plentiful in the winter, but they constituted an uncertain reliance for

families settled some distance from their usual places of resort. Besides, we had no time to hunt them, and the weather was generally too wet to admit of it. Had the country contained the same amount and variety of wild game, wild fruits, and honey as were found in the Western States at an early day, our condition would have been better. But the only wild fruits we found were a variety of berries, such as blackberries, raspberries, strawberries, blueberries, and cranberries, which were not only abundant but of excellent quality. We only found one nut in the country, and that was the hazelnut in small quantities. There were no wild grapes or plums, and no honey.

For the first two years after our arrival the great difficulty was to procure provisions. The population being so much increased by each succeeding fall's immigration, provisions were necessarily scarce. Those who had been there for two years had plenty to eat; but after that the great trouble was to procure clothing, there being no raw materials in the country from which domestic manufactures could be made. We had no wool, cotton, or flax.

But, after we had grown wheat and raised pork for sale, we had new difficulties in our way. Our friends were arriving each fall, with jaded teams, just about the time the long rainy season set in. The community was divided into two classes, old settlers and new, whose views and interests clashed very much. Many of the new immigrants were childish, most of them discouraged, and all of them more or less embarrassed. Upon their arrival they found that those of us who preceded them had taken up the choice locations, and they were compelled either to take those that were inferior in quality or go farther from ship navigation.

There was necessarily, under the circumstances, a great hurry to select claims; and the new-comers had to travel over the country, in the rainy season, in search of homes. Their animals being poor, they found it difficult to get along as fast as they desired. Many causes combined to make them unhappy for the time being. The long rainy seasons were new to them, and they preferred the snow and frozen ground to the rain and mud. There were no hotels in the country, as there was nothing wherewith to pay the bills. The old settlers had necessarily to throw open their doors to the new immigrants, and entertain them free of charge. Our houses were small log-cabins, and our bedding was scarce. The usual mode of travel was for each one to carry his blankets with him, and sleep upon the puncheon-floor. Our families were often overworked in waiting upon others, and our provisions vanished before the keen appetites of our new guests. "They bred a famine wherever they went."

As illustrative of the then condition of things, I will relate an incident which I had from good authority. An old acquaintance of mine, whom I had known in Missouri, came to Oregon in 1844, and selected a claim on the outskirts of the settlements. He was a man of fair means, and had a large family. His place was upon the mainly traveled route which led to the valleys above and beyond him. The consequence was, that he was overwhelmed with company. He had to travel many miles to secure his supplies, and had to transport them, especially in winter, upon pack-animals. He was a man of very hospitable disposition; but the burden was so great that he concluded he could not bear it. The travelers would eat him out of house and home. He determined, under the severe pressure of these circumstances,

to put up an hotel-sign. He went into the woods, cut down a tree, split out a slab some two feet long and one foot wide, shaved it off smooth on both sides with his drawing-knife, and wrote upon it with charcoal, "Entertainment," and swung it upon a pole before his door. The result was, that travelers passed by without stopping, as they had naught wherewith to pay, and were too honest to pretend to be able. My friend said that for two months he had the greatest relief. His stock of provisions lasted much longer, and he was quite easy in his circumstances. But at the end of the two months he began to be lonesome; and by the time the third month had passed he became so lonely that he took down the sign, and after that he had plenty of company.

Our new immigrants not only grumbled much about the country and climate in general, but had also much to say against those of us who had written back to our friends, giving them a description of the country. In the winter of 1843–'44 I had, while at Linnton, written some hundred and twenty-five foolscap pages of manuscript, giving a description of the journey and of the country along the route, as well as of Oregon. I had stated the exact truth, to the best of my knowledge, information, and belief; and my communications were published in the "New York Herald," and were extensively read, especially in the Western States. I therefore came in for my full share of censure. They accused me of misrepresentation.

In a letter I wrote on the Sweetwater, a tributary of the North Fork of the Platte, I stated that, up to that point, the road we had traveled was the finest natural route, perhaps, in the world. Without any regard to the place from which the letter bore date, they construed it as a description of the *entire* route. Consequently,

whenever they came to any very bad road, they would most commonly say, "This is more of Burnett's fine road."

In my communications published in the "Herald," I gave as much statistical information as I could well do, giving the prices of most kinds of personal property; and, among other articles mentioned, I stated that feathers were worth 37½ cents a pound. Two or three years afterward, the demand having increased faster than the supply, the price went up to 62½ cents. I was therefore accused of misrepresentation in this case. They would say: "Now, Burnett, here is a plain case. You said feathers were worth 37½ cents, and we find them worth 62½." I would answer: "That seems to be too plain a case even for a lawyer to get around; yet I have this to say, that I did not assume to act the prophet, but only the historian. I told you what the price then was, and not what it would be two or three years later."

I remember that on one occasion, in passing a house late in the fall, I saw that a new immigrant family occupied it, from the fact that it had previously stood vacant; and I determined to call. The lady told me the name of the State from which they came, gave me other particulars in regard to the family, and asked me how long I had been in the country. Finally she inquired for my name; and, when I told her it was Burnett, she said: "We abused you a great deal on the road. I suppose we ought not to have done it, but we did do it." I could not but laugh, there was such perfect frankness in her statement. It was the whole truth, and no more. I said to her: "Madam, that makes no difference. On a trip like that some one must be abused, and it is well to be some one who is not present."

I made it a rule never to become irritated, and never

to enter into any heated discussion with them in reference to the country or the journey to it. My usual plan was to listen kindly to their complaints. They often declared that the country was so poor they would return to their former homes. In such cases I would good-humoredly reply that "misery loved company; that we found ourselves in a bad fix, and wanted our friends to come here to comfort us; that, as to their going back, it was out of the question; that, if the country was as poor as they supposed, they would never be able to get back; and, if it was not so bad as they believed, they would not wish to return; and that, anyhow, we had them just where we wanted them to be, and they had better make up their minds to stand it."

At any public gathering, it was easy to distinguish the new from the old settlers.

They were lank, lean, hungry, and tough;
We were ruddy, ragged, and rough.

They were dressed in broadcloth, and wore linen-bosomed shirts and black cravats, while we wore very coarse, patched clothes; for the art of patching was understood to perfection in Oregon. But, while they dressed better than we did, we fed better than they. Of the two, we were rather the more independent. They wanted our provisions, while we wanted their materials for clothing. They, seeing our ragged condition, concluded that if they parted with their jeans, satinets, cottons, and calicoes, they would soon be as destitute as we were; and therefore they desired to purchase our provisions on credit, and keep their materials for future use. This plan did not suit us precisely. We reasoned in this way: that, if they wished to place themselves in our ruddy condition, they should incur

the risk of passing into our ragged state—they should take the good and bad together. We therefore insisted upon an exchange. After much grumbling on their part, the parties ultimately came to an agreement. But in many cases the new immigrants had nothing to give in exchange, and we had to sell to them on credit.

I remember that a new immigrant purchased a place in my neighborhood one fall, and in the succeeding month of June came to my house and asked me if I had any wheat in my garner. I told him I had, but I was compelled to purchase some clothing for my family, and my wheat was the only thing I had with which I could pay for the articles we required; that I could not see how we could do without, or how else to obtain them. He said his wife and children were without anything to eat, and that he had a good growing crop, and would give me three bushels after harvest for every bushel I would let him have now. I could not withstand such an appeal, and said I would furnish him with the wheat, and would only require the same quantity after harvest.

But the state of discontent on the part of the new immigrants was temporary, and only lasted during the winter. In the spring, when the thick clouds cleared away, and the grass and flowers sprang up beneath the kindling rays of a bright Oregon sun, their spirits revived with reviving nature; and by the succeeding fall they had themselves become old settlers, and formed a part of us, their views and feelings, in the mean time, having undergone a total change.

It was interesting to observe the influence of new circumstances upon human character. Among the men who went to Oregon the year I did, some were idle, worthless young men, too lazy to work at home, and too

genteel to steal; while some others were gamblers, and others were reputed thieves. But when they arrived in Oregon they were compelled to work or starve. It was a dire necessity. There were there no able relatives or indulgent friends upon whom the idle could quarter themselves, and there was little or nothing for the rogues to steal; and, if they could steal, there was no ready way by which they could escape into another community, and they could not conceal themselves in Oregon. I never saw so fine a population, as a whole community, as I saw in Oregon most of the time while I was there. They were all honest, because there was nothing to steal; they were all sober, because there was no liquor to drink; there were no misers, because there was no money to hoard; and they were all industrious, because it was work or starve.

In a community so poor, isolated, and distant, we had each one to depend upon his own individual skill and labor to make a living. My profession was that of the law, but there was nothing in my line worth attending to until some time after my arrival in Oregon. I was therefore compelled to become a farmer. But I had not only to learn how to carry on a farm by my own labor, but I had to learn how to do many other necessary things that were difficult to do. It was most difficult to procure shoes for myself and family. The Hudson's Bay Company imported its supply of shoes from England, but the stock was wholly inadequate to our wants, and we had no money to enable us to pay for them; and as yet there were no tan-yards in operation. One was commenced in my neighborhood in 1844, but the fall supply of leather was only tanned on the outside, leaving a raw streak in the center. It was undressed, not even curried. Out of this material I made

shoes for myself, my eldest son, and a young hired man who was then living with me. To keep the shoes soft enough to wear through the day, it was necessary to soak them in water at night.

My father, in the early settlement of Missouri, was accustomed to tan his own leather, and make the shoes for the family. In my younger days he had taught me how to do coarse sewed work. But now I had to take the measure of the foot, make the last, fit the patterns to the last, cut out the leathers, and make the shoe. I had no last to copy from, never made one before, and had no one to show me how. I took the measures of all the family, and made what I supposed to be eight very nice lasts ; and upon them I made the shoes, using tanned deer-skin for the females and small boys. The shoes were not beautiful, nor all comfortable, as they were not all good fits.

In the fall of 1846 my brother William came to Oregon, and afterward lived with me about nine months. He was a good mechanical genius, and could do well almost any kind of work. He could make a splendid last and a good boot. One day I showed him my lasts. He was too generous to wound the feelings of his elder brother by criticising his poor work. He said not a word, but in a few days thereafter he made a pair of right and left lasts for himself. I observed how he did it, and the moment the first last was about finished I saw that mine were very poor. They were almost flat, scarcely turning up at the toe at all. I quietly took my lasts and cast them into the fire, and then set to work and made an entire new set ; and I never gave up the attempt until I succeeded in making not only a good last, but a good shoe.

In the course of about two years we had other tan-

yards in successful operation, where we could have hides tanned on shares. I had in the mean time made a trade for a small herd of cattle ; and after this I had an ample supply of good leather, and upon that point I was at ease.

The greatest difficulty I had to encounter for the want of shoes was in 1844. I had sown some three acres of wheat about the first of May, and it was absolutely necessary to inclose it by the first of June to make a crop. I did not commence plowing until about the 20th of April. My team was raw, and so was I, and it required several days' trial to enable us to do good work. While I was engaged in making and hauling rails to fence in my wheat, my old boots gave out entirely, and I had no time to look for a substitute. I was worse off than I was when without a hat in Bolivar, Tennessee.

I was determined to save my wheat at any sacrifice, and I therefore went barefoot. During the first week my feet were very sore ; but after that there came a shield over them, so that I could work with great ease, and go almost anywhere except among thorns.

But we had another trouble on our hands. By permission of a neighbor of ours, a sincere minister, we were allowed to occupy temporarily the log-cabin then used for a church, upon condition that I would permit him to have services there every Sunday. Our minister was always regular in his attendance, and the congregation consisted of about thirty persons. I could not well absent myself from church, as it was my duty to attend. I therefore quietly took my seat in one corner of the building, where my bare feet would not be much noticed. The congregation collected, and the services went on as usual, with the addition of some church

business, which happened to come up on that occasion. The sea-breeze set in early that day, and before the church business was finished it became quite cool. Our minister was a thin, spare man, very sensitive to cold, and requested me to make a fire in the stove. I did not hesitate a moment, but went through the congregation and made the fire. They wore moccasins, and stared at my bare feet as I passed.

There was no money in the country, and the usual currency consisted in orders for merchandise upon the stores, or wheat delivered at specified points. Our community had an ample opportunity to practically learn the value of a sound circulating medium. No one who has not had that practical experience can fully appreciate the true importance of such a medium as a great labor-saving device.

A savage people, who have little or no property to sell, and very few wants to gratify, may get along with a system of barter. An Indian generally has nothing to sell but furs and peltries, and wants nothing in return but arms, ammunition, blankets, tobacco, beads, and paint. All he wants he can find at one place, and all he has to dispose of he can readily bring to the same place. But the property of a civilized race of men is so various in kind, so large in amount, and the ownership and possession change so often, that a good circulating medium is a very great if not an absolute necessity. For example, a farmer may have a pair of oxen for sale, and may want a pair of plow-horses. In case there be no circulating medium, he will have great difficulty in making an exchange. He may find a number of persons who have plow-horses for sale, but none of them may want his oxen. But should he, after much inquiry and loss of time and labor, succeed in finding some one

who has a pair of plow-horses to exchange for a pair of oxen, most likely there will be a difference in value; and how shall this difference be adjusted?

In the course of my practice as a lawyer, I had received orders upon an American merchant at Oregon City, until the amount to my credit upon his books was forty-nine dollars. I called upon him to take up the amount in goods; and he said to me: "Judge, my stock is now very low, and I would suggest to you to wait until my new goods shall arrive from Honolulu. I am going there to purchase a new supply, and will return as soon as I can." I readily assented to this suggestion.

After waiting about three months I heard he had returned with his new stock; and Mrs. Burnett and myself set about making out a memorandum of what we wanted. But the great difficulty was to bring our wants within our means. After several trials we made up our memorandum, consisting mostly of dry-goods, and only six pounds of sugar. I went to Oregon City, and at once called upon the merchant. I asked him if he had any satinets? None. Any jeans? None. Any calico? None. Any brown cottons? None. I then asked what he had. He said tools of various kinds, such as carpenters' implements and others. He said he feared I would think the prices high, as he had to pay high prices, and must make a little profit upon his purchases. This statement no doubt was true. He had purchased in a market where the stocks were limited and prices high.

I then made a selection of several implements that I had not on my memorandum, which amounted in all to about thirteen dollars, and found the prices more than double those at Vancouver. I became tired of paying

such prices for articles I could do without for the time, and inquired if he had any brown sugar, and at what price. He said plenty, at 12½ cents a pound. This was the usual price, and I replied at once that I would take the balance in sugar. I went home, knowing that we had sugar enough to last for a long time, and that we could use Oregon tea. There grows among the fir timber of that country a small aromatic vine, which makes a very pleasant tea, about as good as the tea made from the sassafras-root in the Western States.

On another occasion, while I was Judge of the Supreme Court, a young hired man, my son Dwight, and myself had on our last working-shirts. It was in harvest-time, and where or how to procure others I could not tell. Still, I was so accustomed to these things that I was not much perplexed. Within a day or two a young man of my acquaintance wrote me that he desired me to unite him in marriage with a young lady, whose name he stated. I married them, and he gave me an order on a store for five dollars, with which I purchased some blue twilled cotton (the best I could get), out of which my wife made us each a shirt. The material wore well; but, having been colored with logwood, the shirts, until the color faded from them, left our skins quite blue.

I never felt more independent than I did on one occasion, in the fall of 1847. In the streets of Oregon City I met a young man with a new and substantial leather hunting-shirt, brought from the Rocky Mountains, where it had been purchased from the Indians. I said to him, "What will you take for your leather hunting-shirt?" He replied, "Seven bushels of wheat." I said at once, "I will take it." I measured him out the grain, and took the article. I knew it would last me for

several years. I found it a most excellent article of dress, in clear weather, for rough work. I wore it to the California gold-mines in the fall of 1848, and after my arrival there during most of the winter of 1848–'49. A nephew of mine took it with him to the mines in the spring of 1849, and it was lost to me. I regretted this loss, because I desired to preserve it as a memento of old times. It was made of the best dressed buckskin, with the flesh side out, to which the dust would not adhere; and it was easily kept neat and clean, for that reason.

For the first two years after our arrival in Oregon we were frequently without any meat for weeks at a time, and sometimes without bread, and occasionally without both bread and meat at the same time. On these occasions, if we had milk, butter, and potatoes, we were well content.

I remember, on one occasion, that several gentlemen from Oregon City called at my house in the Plains, and we had no bread. I felt pained on my wife's account, as I supposed she would be greatly mortified. But she put on a cheerful smile, and gave them the best dinner she could. Oregon was a fine place for rearing domestic fowls, and we kept our chickens as a sort of reserve fund for emergencies. We had chickens, milk, butter, and potatoes for dinner; and our friends were well pleased, and laughed over the fact of our having no bread.

In May, 1845, we were entirely without anything in the house for dinner. I did not know what to do, when my wife suggested a remedy. The year before we had cultivated a small patch of potatoes, and in digging had left some in the ground, which had sprung up among the young wheat. We dug a mess of these potatoes,

which sufficed us for a meal, though not very good. That year I sowed about one acre in turnips, which grew to a large size. The vegetables most easily grown in new countries are lettuce, turnips, potatoes, and squashes.

The country improved rapidly in proportion to our population. The means of education were generally limited to ordinary schools. In the course of three or four years after my arrival in Oregon, our people had so improved their places that we were quite comfortable. There was no aristocracy of wealth and very little vice. I do not think I ever saw a more happy community. We had all passed through trials that had tested and established our patience; and our condition then was so much better than that of the past that we had good cause for our content. Few persons could be found to complain of Oregon.

BECOME A CATHOLIC — MY GENERAL RULE AS TO CHARGES AGAINST ME.

In the fall of 1844 a Baptist preacher settled in my immediate neighborhood, who had the published debate between Campbell and Purcell; and, as the Catholic question was often mentioned, and as I knew so little about it, I borrowed and read the book. I had the utmost confidence in the capacity of Mr. Campbell as an able debater; but, while the attentive reading of the debate did not convince me of the entire truth of the Catholic theory, I was greatly astonished to find that so much could be said in its support. On many points, and those of great importance, it was clear to my mind that Mr. Campbell had been overthrown. Still, there were many objections to the Catholic Church, either not

noticed by the Bishop, or not satisfactorily answered; and I arose from the reading of that discussion still a Protestant.

But my thoughts continually recurred to the main positions and arguments on both sides, and, the more I reflected upon the fundamental positions of the Bishop, the more force and power I found them to possess. My own reflections often afforded me answers to difficulties that at first semed insurmountable, until the question arose in my mind whether Mr. Campbell had done full justice to his side of the question. Many of his positions seemed so extreme and ill founded that I could not sanction them. All the prejudices I had, if any, were in his favor; but I knew that it was worse than idle to indulge prejudices when investigating any subject whatever. I was determined to be true to myself, and this could only be in finding the exact truth, and following it when known.

My mind was therefore left in a state of restless uncertainty; and I determined to examine the question between Catholics and Protestants thoroughly, so far as my limited opportunities and poor abilities would permit. In the prosecution of this design, I procured all the works on both sides within my reach, and examined them alternately side by side. This investigation occupied all my spare time for about eighteen months.

After an impartial and calm investigation, I became fully convinced of the truth of the Catholic theory, and went to Oregon City in June, 1846, to join the Old Church. There I found the heroic and saintly Father De Vos, who had spent one or more years among the Flathead Indians. He received me into the Church. The reasons for this change are substantially set forth in my work entitled "The Path which led a Protestant

Lawyer to the Catholic Church," from the preface to which the foregoing statement is taken.

I was the only Catholic among my numerous living relatives. None of my ancestors on either my paternal or maternal side had been Catholics, so far as I knew. All my personal friends were either Protestants or non-professors, except four : Dr. McLoughlin, Dr. Long, and Mr. Pomeroy of Oregon, and Graham L. Hughes of St. Louis. Nine tenths of the people of Oregon were at that time opposed to my religion. Nearly all the Catholics of Oregon were Canadian French, in very humble circumstances, many of them being hired menial servants of the Hudson's Bay Company. I had no reason for the change from a popular to an unpopular religion but the simple love of truth ; and, as I have so long borne whatever of censure may have been heaped upon me in consequence of this change, I think I can afford to die in the Old Church.

When I was a young man I was often much concerned as to what others might think of me ; and at times I was deeply pained by what others did say of me. In due time, however, and after full consideration and more experience, I came to this final conclusion : that it was my duty to do what was right in itself, and to avoid so far as I could even the *appearance* of evil ; and then, if others wrongfully blamed me, it would be their fault, not mine. I saw I could control myself, and was therefore responsible for my own conduct ; but I could not control others, and was not responsible for their actions, so long as I did right myself, and avoided all appearance of evil. If I should make myself unhappy because other people erred in their judgment of me, then my happiness would be within their power and in their keeping. I thought it my duty to keep my hap-

piness under my own control so far as I could. I had confidence in the good sense and justice of good men, and was perfectly willing to await their ultimate decision. When I knew I was in the right, I was able and prepared to bear the censure even of the wise and good; but I "did not hanker after it."

I never would engage in newspaper controversies or personal squabbles. If I was unjustly censured, I paid no attention to it, and gave myself no trouble about it. In this way I have mainly led a life of peace with my fellow men. I have very rarely had the sincerity of my motives called in question. The general course of the press toward me has been impartial and just.

I have never claimed to be a *liberal* man, as many people construe that almost indefinable term ; but I have scrupulously sought to be just to all men. The character of a just man is enough for me. I esteem and reasonably desire the approbation of good men ; but I love the right more. I can do without the first, but not the last.

But I must depart from my usual course to notice certain charges made against me by W. H. Gray in his "History of Oregon." My nephew, George H. Burnett, Esq., of Salem, Oregon, was a guest at my house in San Francisco in January, 1878, and mentioned to me the fact that such charges had been made. I had never seen the work at that time. In May, 1878, I procured and read the book. I notice these charges because they are in the form of *historical* facts or opinions. Had Mr. Gray made these charges verbally or in a newspaper article, I should never have noticed them in any form.

MISSTATEMENTS OF W. H. GRAY.

On pages 374–'5 Mr. Gray, in speaking of the members of the Legislative Committee of 1844, says:

> Peter H. Burnett was a lawyer from Missouri, who came to Oregon to seek his fortune, as well as a religion that would pay best and give him the most influence; which in the Legislative Committee was sufficient to induce that body to pay no attention to any organic law or principle laid down for the government of the settlements. In fact, he asserted that there were no constitutional provisions laid down or adopted by the people in general convention at Champoeg the year previous. Mr. Burnett was unquestionably the most intelligent lawyer then in the country. He was a very ambitious man—smooth, deceitful, and insinuating in his manners.

As regards the imputation of improper motives to me in the above extract, if intended as the assertions of fact, such assertions are untrue; and, if intended as expressions of opinions, such opinions are mistaken. These charges are made not only without proof, but against both the evidence and the fact.

I went to Oregon for three purposes:

1. To assist in building up a great American community on the Pacific coast.
2. To restore the health of Mrs. Burnett.
3. To become able to pay my debts.

Before I became a believer in the truth of the Christian religion, I had sought fortune with avidity; but, after that fundamental change in my views, I ceased to pursue riches, and my only *business* object was to make a decent living for my family, and pay what I owed. Considering the large amount of my indebtedness, I could not have been so visionary as to suppose I could

accomplish in distant and isolated Oregon more than the three objects mentioned.

As regards my change of religion, and the motives which led to it, I have already stated the simple truth. At the time I joined the Old Church I was independent in my pecuniary circumstances, so far as a *decent living* was concerned. I had a claim of six hundred and forty acres of most excellent land, well improved, and well stocked with domestic animals and fowls. With the industrious and sober habits of myself and family, we were secure of a good living.

As to my influence in the Committee, it could not possibly have arisen from any change of religion, for these simple and conclusive reasons : that I was then a Protestant, without any idea of becoming a Catholic, and every member was opposed to the Catholic religion. My influence arose from the fact of my qualifications and my good character. Waldo, McCarver, Gilmore, and Keizer had traveled with me across the Plains, and had seen me fully tested in that severe school of human nature. Waldo knew me by reputation, and Gilmore personally, in Missouri.

As to the assertion that I was "very ambitious," the fact is not correctly stated. I had a reasonable desire for distinction, but never so great as to induce me to sacrifice my personal independence or compromise my true dignity. I never sought any position under the provisional government of Oregon, and I do not remember to have personally asked any citizen to vote for me. I was elected a member of the legislative body in 1844 and again in 1848, and Judge of the Supreme Court in 1845, without any serious efforts on my part. I have been a candidate before the people six times : once in Missouri, twice in Oregon, and three times in California;

and I was successful in every case. I resigned the office of District Attorney in Missouri to go to Oregon in 1843, and my seat in the Legislature of Oregon in 1848 to come to California, and the office of Governor of this State in January, 1851, when the salary was ten thousand dollars per annum. I was appointed on the 14th of August, 1848, by President Polk, one of the Justices of the Supreme Court of the Territory of Oregon. My commission did not reach me until the spring of 1849, in California. This appointment I declined, as I could not accept it and pay my debts. This was done before any movement was made to organize a State government in California, and before I had any expectation of being Governor. I can safely say that the remark of President Jefferson, in regard to the office-holders of his time, that "deaths were few and resignations none," can not justly apply to me.

As to the charge of being deceitful, it is the precise opposite of the truth. No man of decent manners and good character ever called upon me without receiving my candid opinion, where I had any mature judgment upon the question. I am not a disputatious spirit, ready to engage in a wordy quarrel upon any and every subject, however trivial; but in regard to all important subjects, on all proper occasions, I am frank to speak just what I think.

As to the falsity of all these charges, I can refer to all good men who have known me longest and best. I lived in Missouri some twenty-one years, and have resided in California nearly thirty years, and I appeal to all good men who have known me, without regard to their religion or place of nativity.

THE QUESTION WHETHER THERE WERE ANY CONSTITUTIONAL PROVISIONS IN THE LAWS OF 1843 CONSIDERED.

The Legislative Committee of 1844 did maintain the position that there were no constitutional provisions adopted by the people at their mass meeting, July 5, 1843.

It appears that there were two publications claiming to be copies of these laws: one by Charles Saxton, published in 1846, and the other by the compiler of the "Oregon Archives" in 1853. (Gray's "Oregon," 352.) I shall use the copy given by Mr. Gray, as he ought to know best, and which is found in his history, beginning on page 353.

At a meeting of the people held May 2, 1843, at Champoeg, the proposition to establish a provisional government was put to vote; and, upon a division, there were found to be fifty-two for and fifty against it. (Gray's "Oregon," 279.)

At that meeting, Robert Moore, David Hill, Robert Shortess, Alanson Beers, W. H. Gray, Thomas J. Hubbard, James A. O'Neal, Robert Newell, and William Dougherty were chosen to act as a Legislative Committee, and instructed to make their report on the 5th of July, 1843, at Champoeg. (Gray, 280 –'81.)

On the 5th of July, 1843, said Committee made their report, which was adopted at the mass meeting of citizens at Champoeg. The question whether there were any, and, if so, what constitutional provisions in the laws adopted at said meeting, was one that admitted of discussion; but, upon as full a consideration of the subject as our limited time and opportunities allowed, we became satisfied that there were none.

In their report the Committee say, "The Legislative Committee recommend that the following *organic laws* be adopted." The term *organic* does not necessarily mean constitutional; because, whether the laws were constitutional or not, they were equally organic. We were aware of the fact that there were no lawyers among the members of the Committee, and that there were then no law-books in the country, except one copy of the Statutes of Iowa; but we knew that the members were Americans, and that all Americans competent to read a newspaper must know that the fundamental laws of the United States and of the several States were called *constitutions;* and hence we supposed that the Committee would surely have used the plain, ordinary, and appropriate term *constitution* to designate their fundamental law, had they intended it as such.

But, besides the want of proper language to designate a constitution, the nature of the laws themselves seemed to show a different intent. From the face of the Code, no one could tell where the constitutional laws ended and the statutory began. It was either all constitution or all statute. All were adopted at the same public meeting, and were recommended by the same Committee. That Committee "recommended that the following *organic laws* be adopted." Now, whatever laws were recommended by them were all of the *same* character, or they failed to distinguish one portion from another. There being no mode of amendment provided, these laws, if constitutional, could only be amended in violation of their own terms; that is, by revolution. If considered as statutory provisions, then there was a plain mode of amendment provided in Article VI., section 2, which enacts that "the legislative power shall be vested in a committee of nine persons,

to be elected by the qualified electors at the annual election."

The code goes into the most minute provisions, such as fixing the fees of the Recorder and Treasurer, and for solemnizing marriage. It also contains a militia law, and a law on land claims, and a resolution making the statute laws of Iowa the law of Oregon. Such provisions, in their very nature, are but statutory.

Considering the "organic laws" (so named by the Committee) as composing a constitution, not amendable except by revolution, the Legislative Committee of 1844 had nothing to do worth mentioning. In this view it was a useless body, constituted for an idle and vain purpose. We came to the conclusion that our Legislative Committee had practical legislative power, and that it was our duty to exercise it. While we were not disposed to make useless changes, we were obliged to amend the code in many respects, as will be seen from what follows.

Article VII., section 2 vests "the judicial power in a Supreme Court, consisting of the supreme judge and two justices of the peace, a Probate Court, and Justice Court." If a majority of the persons composing the Supreme Court, under this quaint and original theory, could make the decision, then the two justices of the peace could overrule the Supreme Judge. If, on the contrary, it required the unanimous consent of all three, then there would often be no decision at all.

Our Committee amended this by the act of June 27, 1844. The first section of the second article of that act is as follows: "Section 1. The judicial power shall be vested in the Circuit Courts and as many justices of the peace as shall from time to time be appointed or elected according to law." The second section provides for the

election of *one* judge, and makes it his duty to hold two terms of the Circuit Court in each county, at such times and places as shall be directed by law; and the third section fixes the jurisdiction of the Circuit Courts, including probate powers.

The fifth article of section 2 vested the executive power in a committee of three persons. This provision was adopted not because it met the approbation of the Legislative Committee of 1843, but from necessity, as their instructions were against a governor (Gray's "Oregon," 349). We repealed this provision, and vested the executive power in a single person.

ARTICLE XVII. All male persons of the age of sixteen years and upward, and all females of the age of fourteen years and upward, shall have the right to marry. When either of the parties shall be under twenty-one years of age, the consent of the parents or guardians of such minors shall be necessary to the validity of such matrimonial engagement. Every ordained minister of the gospel, of any religious denomination, the supreme judge, and all justices of the peace, are hereby authorized to solemnize marriage according to law, to have the same recorded, and pay the recorder's fee. The legal fee for marriage shall be one dollar, and for recording fifty cents.

This extreme law made the marriage of persons under the age of twenty-one years without the consent of their parents or guardians *invalid*, and therefore void; thus subjecting the young people to the charge and consequences of living in a state of adultery, and their innocent children to all the consequences of bastardy.

Our Committee passed the following act:

An Act amendatory of the Act regarding Marriage.

SECTION 1. That all males of the age of sixteen years and upward, and all females of the age of twelve and upward,

shall be deemed competent to enter into the contract of marriage.

SEC. 2. That when either of the parties about to enter into the marriage union shall be minors, the male under the age of twenty-one years, or the female under the age of eighteen, no person authorized to solemnize the rites of matrimony shall do so without the consent of the parent or guardian of such minor; and in case such person shall solemnize such marriage without the consent of the parent or guardian of such minor, he shall be liable to pay such parent or guardian the sum of one hundred dollars, to be recovered by action of debt or assumpsit before the proper court: *Provided*, however, that the want of such consent shall not invalidate such marriage.

SEC. 3. That all acts and parts of acts coming in conflict with this act be and the same are hereby repealed.

The Legislative Committee of 1843 was properly called a *committee*, because its duty was to prepare a code to be submitted to the mass meeting of citizens held on the 5th of July, 1843, for their approval or rejection; the *legislative* power being exercised by the people themselves on that occasion. But, as already stated, the legislative power was vested by the sixth article, section 2, of the laws of 1843, in a committee of nine persons. To call a legislative body a *committee* was a misnomer; and we amended that provision by vesting the legislative power in a House of Representatives composed of members elected annually by the people.

The laws of 1843 made no provision for the support of the government, except putting in circulation a subscription paper as follows:

We, the subscribers, hereby pledge ourselves to pay annually to the Treasurer of Oregon Territory the sum affixed to our respective names, for defraying the expenses of the government: *Provided*, That in all cases each individual subscriber may at

any time withdraw his name from said subscription, upon paying up all arrearages and notifying the Treasurer of the colony of such desire to withdraw.

Our Committee were fully satisfied that no government could be practically administered without taxation; and we therefore passed a revenue law containing twelve sections.

The law of 1843 in relation to land claims is as follows:

ARTICLE I. Any person now holding or hereafter wishing to establish a claim to land in this Territory, shall designate the extent of his claim by natural boundaries, or by marks at the corners and upon the lines of said claim, recorded in the office of the Territorial Recorder, in a book to be kept by him for that purpose, within twenty days from the time of making said claim: *Provided*, That those who shall be already in possession of land shall be allowed one year from the passage of this act, to file a description of their claims in the Recorder's office.

ART. II. All claimants shall, within six months from the time of recording their claims, make permanent improvement upon the same, by building or inclosing, and also become occupant upon said claims within one year of the date of said record.

ART. III. No individual shall be allowed to hold a claim of more than one square mile, or six hundred and forty acres, in a square or oblong form, according to the natural situation of the premises, nor shall any individual be able to hold more than one claim at the same time. Any person complying with the provisions of these ordinances shall be entitled to the same process against trespass as in other cases provided by law.

ART. IV. No person shall be entitled to hold such a claim upon city or town lots, extensive water privileges, or other situations necessary for the transaction of mercantile or manufacturing operations: *Provided*, That nothing in these laws shall be so construed as to affect any claim of any mission of a reli-

gious character made prior to this time, of an extent not more than six miles square.

Our Committee passed the following act, June 25, 1844:

An Act in relation to Land Claims.

SECTION 1. That all persons who have heretofore made, or shall hereafter make, permanent improvements upon a place, with a *bona fide* intention of occupying and holding the same for himself, and shall continue to occupy and cultivate the same, shall be entitled to hold six hundred and forty acres, and shall hold only one claim at the same time: *Provided*, A man may hold town lots in addition to his claim.

SEC. 2. That all claims hereafter made shall be in a square form, if the nature of the ground shall permit; and in case the situation will not permit, shall be in an oblong form.

SEC. 3. That in all cases where claims are already made, and in all cases where there are agreed lines between the parties occupying adjoining tracts, such claims shall be valid to the extent of six hundred and forty acres, although not in a square or oblong form.

SEC. 4. That in all cases where claims shall hereafter be made, such permanent improvements shall be made within two months from the time of taking up such claim, and the first settler or his successor shall be deemed to hold the prior right.

SEC. 5. That no person shall hold a claim under the provisions of this act except free males over the age of eighteen, who would be entitled to vote if of lawful age, and widows: *Provided*, No married man shall be debarred from holding a claim under this act because he is under the age of eighteen.

SEC. 6. That all laws heretofore passed in regard to land claims be and the same are hereby repealed.

SEC. 7. That all persons complying with the provisions of this act shall be deemed in possession to the extent of six hundred and forty acres or less, as the case may be, and shall have the remedy of forcible entry and detainer against intruders, and the action of trespass against trespassers.

On December 24, 1844, we passed the following explanatory and amendatory act:

SECTION 1. That the word "occupancy," in said act, shall be so construed as to require the claimant to either personally reside upon his claim himself, or to occupy the same by the personal residence of his tenant.

SEC. 2. That any person shall be authorized to take six hundred acres of his claim in the prairie, and forty acres in the timber, and such parts of his claim need not be adjoining to each other.

SEC. 3. That when two persons take up their claims jointly, not exceeding twelve hundred and eighty acres, they may hold the same jointly for the term of one year, by making the improvements required by said act upon any part of said claim, and may hold the same longer than one year if they make the said improvements within the year upon each six hundred and forty acres.

The land law of 1844 dispensed with recording of claims, because, under the then existing condition of the country, it was an onerous burden upon the new immigrant. The great body of the immigration arrived late in the fall, just as the rainy season set in; and to require each locater of a claim to travel from twenty to one hundred miles to the Recorder's office, and return through an Oregon winter, was indeed a harsh condition. Under the land law of 1843 the old settler was allowed one year within which to record his claim, while the new settlers were only allowed twenty days. Besides, recording a claim without a proper survey was of very doubtful utility, as parties would be very apt to include within their lines more than six hundred and forty acres.

By the land law of 1843, as will be seen, *all* persons of every age, sex, or condition, could hold claims. If a man had several sons, he could hold one claim for

himself and each of his sons one, though under age; and, as each claimant had six months within which to make his improvements, and one year within which to become an occupant from the date of the record, the act left open the door to speculation and monopoly to a grievous extent. A man, having a number of children, could record one claim in the name of each child one month before the annual arrival of the new immigrants, and that record would hold the land for six months; thus forcing the late comers either to go farther for locations or purchase these claims of his children. Besides, this act did not require the locater to make his improvements with the *bona fide* intention of occupying and holding the claim for himself, but only required the improvements to be made; thus allowing claims to be made for speculative purposes.

But one of the most objectionable provisions of the land law of 1843 was the proviso allowing each mission six miles square, or thirty-six sections of land. From what Mr. Gray says, page 344, it appears that this proviso was adopted to gain the support of those connected with the Methodist and Catholic missions; as, without such support, it was feared the attempt to establish a government at that time would fail. The Committee of 1843, in their short experience, learned one great truth: that civil government is a *practical* science; and that, while a true statesman can adapt his legislation to existing circumstances, he can not create or control them; and for that reason he is often compelled to choose between evils, and to support measures that his individual judgment will not approve. Our Legislative Committee of 1844 were placed in more independent circumstances; and, having no fear of the mission influence, we repealed this proviso.

THE LEGISLATIVE COMMITTEE OF 1844 — MISTAKES OF W. H. GRAY.

On page 383 Mr. Gray, speaking of the Legislative Committee of 1844, says:

"In fact, the whole proceedings seemed only to mix up and confuse the people; so much so that some doubted the existence of any legal authority in the country, and the leading men of the immigration of 1843 denounced the organization as a missionary arrangement to secure the most valuable farming lands in the country."

The writer is correct as to the fact of confusion and opposition among the people, but most sadly mistaken as to the true cause. It was not the measures passed by the Legislative Committee of 1844, but the law of 1843, that caused the confusion and opposition. It is very true that many of "the leading men of the immigration of 1843 denounced the organization as a missionary arrangement to secure the best farming lands in the country." They had much apparent reason for their opposition, and that reason was found in the laws of 1843, especially in the proviso allowing each mission six miles square, and not in the land law of 1844, which repealed this objectionable proviso. Whatever else may be said against the laws of 1844, they were plain, simple, and consistent as a whole, and could not have produced the confusion mentioned.

The first time I was in Oregon City, to the best of my recollection, was when I went there to take my seat in the Legislative Committee in June, 1844. Previous to that time I do not remember to have seen the laws of 1843. After all the examination I could give them, I saw that no regular and efficient government could be

sustained without a revenue; that no certain and reliable revenue could be had without taxation; that no system of taxation could be enforced unless the great and overwhelming majority of the people were satisfied with the government, and that such majority would not support the organization unless they believed they were receiving an equivalent in the form of protection for the money they paid in the shape of taxes. Many good men doubted our legal right to organize any government. Our object was to gain the consent of *all* good men; and, to do this, we must make good laws. Of course, the bad would oppose all government.

In consulting upon our then condition, we were for a time much perplexed to know what peaceable course to pursue, in order to secure the consent of all good men to our organization. We knew that Americans were devotedly attached to two things: land and the privilege of voting. Our Committee, therefore, passed an act to provide by taxation the means necessary to support the government, the fourth section of which was as follows: "Sec. 4. That any person refusing to pay tax, as in this act required, shall have no benefit of the laws of Oregon, and shall be disqualified from voting at any election in this country."

By this provision we plainly said to each citizen substantially as follows: "If you are not willing to pay your proportion of the expenses of this government, you can not sue in our courts or vote at our elections, but you must remain an outlaw. If any one should squat or trespass on your claim, or refuse to pay you what he owes, you can have no protection from our organization. If you can do without our assistance, we certainly can do without yours."

This provision very soon had its legitimate effect.

As the elections approached, those who had been opposed began to doubt, and finally yielded. The friends of the organization were active, kind, and wise in their course toward those opposed. When one opposed to the government would state that fact, some friend would kindly remind him that his claim was liable to be "jumped," and that he could not alone defend his rights against the violent and unprincipled; and that it was a desolate and painful condition for a citizen, in a civilized community, to be an *outlaw*.

After the laws passed by the Legislative Committee of 1844 became known, there was no serious opposition anywhere. It is my solemn opinion that the organization could not have been kept up under the laws of 1843.

On page 375, Mr. Gray, speaking of the Legislative Committee of 1844, says:

"On motion of Mr. Lovejoy (another lawyer), the several members were excused from producing their credentials."

This statement is true, so far as it goes; but, without the explanatory facts, it might convey a false impression. The laws of 1843 made no provision as to the manner of conducting elections, except by adopting the laws of Iowa; and as there was but one copy in the country, and this was the first election held in Oregon, and as two thirds of the voters were late immigrants, the various officers of the election knew nothing of their duties, and gave no credentials to the members elect; and, of course, they could produce none. We knew that we had been fairly elected, and our respective constituents also knew the fact, and no one was found to dispute it; and, as credentials are only *evidence* of the fact of the election of the person mentioned, we had in this

case the next best evidence to prove our election. We did the best we could under the circumstances.

"Such being the composition of the Legislative Committee of Oregon in 1844, it is not surprising that interests of classes and cliques should find advocates, and that the absolute wants of the country should be neglected. The whole time of the session seems to have been taken up in the discussion of personal bills." (Page 378.)

I find it difficult to justly characterize this sweeping misstatement.

The two sessions of the Committee of 1844 occupied together fifteen to seventeen days; and in that time we passed forty-three bills, some of them of considerable length, and most of them of general importance. Among these forty-three acts there were not exceeding eight that could be properly termed personal, viz.: act granting Hugh Burns a right to keep a public ferry; act authorizing Robert Moore to establish and keep a ferry; act to authorize John McLoughlin to construct a canal around the Willamette Falls; act for the relief of John Connor; act appointing Jesse Applegate engineer; act authorizing L. H. Judson and W. H. Wilson to construct a mill-race in Champoeg County; act amending the several acts regulating ferries; act for the relief of J. L. Meek.

These acts were all just in themselves, and some of them of public importance. Public ferries are public conveniences. The act to authorize John McLoughlin to construct a canal enabled him to bring the water to propel his extensive flour-mill, and was of much public benefit. The act for the relief of John Connor was a short act of one section, remitting a fine and restoring him to citizenship. The act appointing Jesse Applegate

engineer authorized him to survey a route for a canal at the expense of J. E. Long, and report the result to the next session of the Legislature. The act authorizing Judson & Wilson to construct a mill-race was of a similar nature to the one in regard to John McLoughlin. The act to amend the several acts regulating ferries simply fixed the rate of toll of the two ferries across the Willamette River, at Oregon City. The act for the relief of J. L. Meek is a short one, giving him further time to finish the collection of the revenue for the year 1844.

The acts of the Legislative Committee of 1844 will fill some thirty printed pages, while the laws of 1843 only occupy seven pages of Gray's "History." If we spent a part of our time in the discussion of personal bills, we passed but a few of them, and did a large amount of other legislative work.

"The proposed constitutional revision was also strongly recommended by the Executive Committee, and the Legislative Committee went through the farce of calling a convention, and increased the number of representatives, and called it a Legislature." (Page 383.)

The Executive Committee, in their communication to our Committee, dated December 16, 1844, say:

"We would advise that provision be made by this body for the framing and adoption of a constitution for Oregon previous to the next annual election, which may serve as a more thorough guide to her officers and a more firm basis of her laws."

It will be seen that, while the Executive Committee recommended that provision should be made for the framing and adoption of a constitution previous to the then next annual election, they did not suggest the *mode* in which this should be done. Our Legislative Commit-

tee thought that a convention, composed of delegates elected by the people for the *sole* and *only* purpose of framing the fundamental law, was the American and the proper mode. When the people come to choose delegates to a constitutional convention, they are very apt to duly appreciate the great importance of the work to be done, and will therefore generally select the best and most competent men for that great purpose. The body that forms a constitution should have but *one* task to accomplish, for the simple and conclusive reason that nothing is more difficult than to frame a good constitution. The greatest statesmen and the mightiest intellects among men have essentially differed as to the true theory of a constitution. The members of a constitutional body should not have their attention distracted by ordinary statutory legislation. A *perfect* constitution has never yet been framed, and, most likely, never will be.

While we could not see the great and immediate *necessity* of a constitution for mere temporary government, we thought that, if the object sought was necessary at all, then the work should be well and thoroughly done, so that our constitution would be an honor to our new country. Believing, as we did, that a constitutional convention was the *only* appropriate and competent body to frame a constitution that would stand the test of fair criticism, and be beneficial in its practical operation, and not seeing any pressing necessity for immediate action, we did *not* go "through the farce of calling a convention," as asserted by the author; but we passed the following act, December 24, 1844:

SECTION 1. That the Executive Committee shall, in the manner prescribed by law for notifying elections in Oregon, notify the inhabitants of all the respective counties qualified to vote

for members of the Legislature at their next annual election, to give in their votes for or against the call of a convention.

SEC. 2. The said votes shall be in open meeting received, assorted, and counted, and a true return thereof made to the Executive Committee, agreeable to the requisitions of the law regulating elections.

SEC. 3. It shall be the duty of the Executive to lay the result of the said vote before the Legislative Committee for their information.

While we had our doubts as to the necessity of a constitution for a mere temporary government (which we then had every reason to believe would last only a year or two), we thought it but just to submit the question of calling a convention to the people for their decision. It is usual to submit such a question to the people, as was lately done in California.

The treaty of June 15, 1846, between Great Britain and the United States, settled the question of sovereignty over Oregon in favor of our country; and the act of Congress creating a Territorial government was passed August 14, 1848. The treaty was delayed beyond our reasonable expectations; and the creation of a Territorial organization was postponed by the Mexican war, which war was not foreseen by our Committee in December, 1844.

We did increase the number of representatives from nine to thirteen, and we really thought we were moderate in this respect. According to Mr. Gray's estimate, the immigration of 1843 amounted to eight hundred and seventy-five persons, and the whole population at the end of that year to about twelve hundred people. (Pages 360–'61.) If, then, some three hundred and twenty-five persons were entitled, under the laws of 1843, to nine members in the Legislative Committee,

how many representatives should twelve hundred have had under the law of 1844? We only increased the number of members from nine to thirteen, when the same ratio of representation to population would have given us twenty-seven. We did call the law-making body of Oregon a Legislature, and left off the word "Committee" for reasons already stated.

CHAPTER V.

THE ACT IN REGARD TO SLAVERY AND FREE NEGROES AND MULATTOES—MISREPRESENTATIONS OF W. H. GRAY.

MR. GRAY, in speaking of the Legislative Committee of 1844, says:

"There was one inhuman act passed by this Legislative Committee, which should stamp the names of its supporters with disgrace and infamy." (Page 378.)

"The principal provisions of this bill were, that in case a colored man was brought to the country by any master of a vessel, he must give bonds to take him away again or be fined; and in case the negro was found, or came here from any quarter, the sheriff was to catch him and flog him forty lashes at a time, till he left the country." (Page 378.)

"The principles of Burnett's bill made it a crime for a white man to bring a negro to the country, and a crime for a negro to come voluntarily; so that in any case, if he were found in the country he was guilty of a crime, and punishment or slavery was his doom." (Page 379.)

"At the adjourned session in December we find the Executive urging the Legislative Committee . . . . to amend their act relative to the corporal punishment of the blacks," etc. (Page 379.)

"To the honor of the country, Peter H. Burnett's negro-whipping law was never enforced in a single instance against a white or black man, as no officer of the provisional government felt it incumbent upon himself to attempt to enforce it." (Page 383.)

This is all the information given by Mr. Gray as to the provisions of this act, and nothing is said as to its amendment. The act is as follows :

AN ACT *in regard to Slavery and Free Negroes and Mulattoes.*

Be it enacted by the Legislative Committee of Oregon as follows :

SECTION 1. That slavery and involuntary servitude shall be for ever prohibited in Oregon.

SEC. 2. That in all cases where slaves shall have been, or shall hereafter be, brought into Oregon, the owners of such slaves respectively shall have the term of three years from the introduction of such slaves to remove them out of the country.

SEC. 3. That if such owners of slaves shall neglect or refuse to remove such slaves from the country within the time specified in the preceding section, such slaves shall be free.

SEC. 4. That when any free negro or mulatto shall have come to Oregon, he or she (as the case may be), if of the age of eighteen or upward, shall remove from and leave the country within the term of two years for males and three years for females from the passage of this act; and that if any free negro or mulatto shall hereafter come to Oregon, if of the age aforesaid, he or she shall quit and leave the country within the term of two years for males and three years for females from his or her arrival in the country.

SEC. 5. That if such free negro or mulatto be under the age aforesaid, the terms of time specified in the preceding section shall begin to run when he or she shall arrive at such age.

SEC. 6. That if any such free negro or mulatto shall fail to quit the country as required by this act, he or she may be arrested upon a warrant issued by some justice of the peace, and, if guilty upon trial before such justice, shall receive upon his or

her bare back not less than twenty nor more than thirty-nine stripes, to be inflicted by the constable of the proper county.

SEC. 7. That if any free negro or mulatto shall fail to quit the country within the term of six months after receiving such stripes, he or she shall again receive the same punishment once in every six months until he or she shall quit the country.

SEC. 8. That when any slave shall obtain his or her freedom, the time specified in the fourth section shall begin to run from the time when such freedom shall be obtained.

UNITED STATES OF AMERICA.

STATE OF OREGON,
SECRETARY'S OFFICE. } SALEM, *June* 10, 1878.

I, S. F. Chadwick, Secretary of the State of Oregon, do hereby certify that I am the custodian of the Great Seal of the State of Oregon. That the foregoing copy of original bill for an act in regard to slavery and free negroes and mulattoes passed the Legislative Committee of the Territory of Oregon June 26, 1844, has been by me compared with the original bill for an act, etc., on file in this office, and said copy is a correct transcript therefrom, and of the whole of the said original bill.

{ SEAL. } In witness whereof, I have hereto set my hand and affixed the Great Seal of the State of Oregon, the day and year above written.

S. F. CHADWICK,
Secretary of the State of Oregon.
By THOMAS B. JACKSON,
Assistant Secretary of State.

The Executive Committee, in their communication to the Legislative Committee, dated December 16, 1844, made this recommendation:

"We would recommend that the act passed by this Assembly in June last, relative to blacks and mulattoes, be so amended as to exclude corporal punishment, and require bonds for good behavior in its stead." ("Oregon Laws and Archives," 58.)

At the December session I introduced the following bill, which was passed December 19, 1844:

AN ACT *amendatory of an Act passed June 26, 1844, in regard to slavery and for other purposes.*

Be it enacted by the Legislative Committee of Oregon as follows:

SECTION 1. That the sixth and seventh sections of said act are hereby repealed.

SEC. 2. That if any such free negro or mulatto shall fail to quit and leave the country, as required by the act to which this is amendatory, he or she may be arrested upon a warrant issued by some justice of the peace; and if guilty upon trial before such justice had, the said justice shall issue his order to any officer competent to execute process, directing said officer to give ten days' public notice, by at least four written or printed advertisements, that he will publicly hire out such free negro or mulatto to the lowest bidder, on a day and at a place therein specified. On the day and at the place mentioned in said notice, such officer shall expose such free negro or mulatto to public hiring; and the person who will obligate himself to remove such free negro or mulatto from the country for the shortest term of service, shall enter into a bond with good and sufficient security to Oregon, in a penalty of at least one thousand dollars, binding himself to remove said negro or mulatto out of the country within six months after such service shall expire; which bond shall be filed in the clerk's office in the proper county; and upon failure to perform the conditions of said bond, the attorney prosecuting for Oregon shall commence a suit upon a certified copy of such bond in the circuit court against such delinquent and his sureties.

It will be readily seen how much the *original* act differs from Mr. Gray's statement of its substance.

Not a word is said in the original act about the criminality of the master of a vessel in bringing a colored man into the country. The assertion that "the sheriff was to catch the negro and flog him forty lashes

at a time, until he left the country," is not only untrue, but the statement conveys the idea that the sheriff was *himself* to be the sole judge, both as to the guilt of the negro and as to how often the flogging should be repeated. The act, on the contrary, required a judicial trial before a justice of the peace, and that the punishment should only be inflicted in obedience to his order by a constable. The general right of appeal to a higher court existed in these, as in other cases, under section 3, Article II., of the "Act regulating the Judiciary and for other purposes."

The statement that the principles of the original act "made it a crime for a white man to bring a negro to the country" is equally untrue, as will be readily seen. A crime is an offense for which the party may be arrested, tried, convicted, and punished; and there is no provision in the act authorizing the arrest of a white man for any act whatever.

It is perfectly clear that Mr. Gray either willfully misrepresented the original act, or attempted to state its substance from memory; and if the latter be true, then, as his memory was bad and his prejudices great, he misrepresented the measure, and made it much worse than it really was. There can be no excuse for the misrepresentation of an act by a grave historian, especially one that he condemns in the harshest language, when he has easy access to the act itself.

But he not only essentially misrepresents the original act itself, but entirely ignores the amendatory bill; and does it in such a way as to increase the censure of the Legislative Committee of 1844. There are two modes of falsehood: false statement of fact, and false suppression of the truth. The historian first misrepresents the substance of the original act, then informs the reader

that the Executive urged its amendment, and then suppresses the fact that the act was amended. This mode of historical misstatement and suppression left the reader to say to himself, "These men first passed an act containing objectionable provisions, and then obstinately refused to amend, when their attention was urgently called to the error." Throughout his history of this act, he represents it as *unamended* and as in full force according to its own terms; and his last words in regard to it are, that "Burnett's negro-whipping law was never enforced in a single instance, against a white or black man, as no officer of the provisional government felt it incumbent upon himself to attempt to enforce it."

It will be seen, by an inspection of the original act itself, that it was *prospective*, and that not a single case could possibly arise under it until the expiration of *two years after its passage;* and that no officer was required to act until he was commanded to do so by the regular warrant or order of a justice of the peace. In the mean time, and eighteen months *before* a single case could possibly arise under the act, it was amended by the very *same* body that passed the original bill, and at the instance of the very *same* member who introduced it.

An act that is simply prospective, and does not take effect until two years after the date of its passage, is an incomplete measure, liable to be amended at any time before it goes into operation; and, if amended before any one suffers any injury from its erroneous provisions, those provisions are as if they never had been. It is like a bill imperfect when first introduced by a member of a legislative body, and so amended by the author, before its final passage, as to remove its objectionable

features. In such case, no sensible man would censure the introducer for mistakes *he himself had corrected.* All that could be said is, that the second sober thought of the member was better than his first hasty thought.

It was substantially so in this case. In the hurry of the June session of 1844 I could not think of any other mode of enforcing the act but the one adopted; but by the December session of 1844 I had found another and less objectionable remedy, and promptly adopted it. This remedy was not the one urged by the Executive Committee, as will easily be seen. Neither myself nor the other members who voted for the original bill are responsible for the objectionable features of the measure because we ourselves corrected the error. I maintain as true this general proposition: that a person who commits a mistake, and then corrects it himself, before any one suffers in consequence of it, deserves commendation rather than censure; because the act of correction shows a love of justice, and a magnanimous willingness to *admit* and *correct* error. All the intense indignation of the historian is, therefore, thrown away upon an imaginary evil, about which he is as much mistaken as the girl that wept over the imaginary death of her imaginary infant.

On page 378 the historian gives, *professedly* from the Journal, the yeas and nays upon the final passage of the original bill, as follows: "Yeas, Burnett, Gilmore, Keizer, Waldo, Newell, and Mr. Speaker McCarver—6; Nays, Lovejoy and Hill—2." He then informs us, as already stated, that the Executive urged the amendment of the act at the December session, 1844; and then, on pages 380–'3, gives the communication of the Executive Committee in full. Now, as he had the Journal before him, why did he not follow it up to the short December

session, and ascertain what the Legislative Committee had done, if anything, in regard to amending this act?

His history of the proceedings of the Committee of 1844 is very short; but, concise as it is, it is full of flagrant misrepresentations. There was one act, however, that he affirmatively approved; and yet, so great was his prejudice, that he wrongfully imputes a bad motive for a confessedly good act. He says, on page 379, "Mr. Burnett claimed great credit for getting up a prohibitory liquor law, and made several speeches in favor of sustaining it, that being a popular measure among a majority of the citizens."

All our legislation under the provisional government was based upon the settled conviction that Oregon would be the first American State on the Pacific. We considered ourselves as the founders of a new State of the great American Union.

At the time this measure was passed, each State had the constitutional right to determine who should be citizens, and who residents. Any person born on the soil of a State had the natural, moral, and legal right to a residence within that State, while conducting himself properly; because the place of one's birth is an accidental circumstance, over which he can have no control. But, for the very reason that every human being has the right of domicile in the place of his nativity, he is not, *as a matter of right*, entitled to a residence in another community. If that other community denies him the privilege of such residence, it denies him no *right*, natural or acquired, but only refuses a *favor* asked. The territory of a State belongs to its people, as if they constituted one family; and no one not a native has a right to complain that he is not allowed to form one of this family. Although every one, under the broad and

enlarged principles of law and justice, has the right to quit his original domicile at his pleasure, he has not the equal right to acquire a new residence in another community against its consent. "The bird has the right to leave its parent-nest," but has not, for that reason, the equal right to occupy the nest of another bird. A man may *demand* his rights, and justly complain when they are denied; but he can not demand *favors*, and can not reasonably complain when they are refused.

The principle is no doubt correct that when a State, for reasons satisfactory to itself, denies the right of suffrage and office to a certain class, it is sometimes the best humanity also to deny the privilege of residence. If the prejudices or the just reasons of a community are so great that they can not or will not trust a certain class with those privileges that are indispensable to the improvement and elevation of such class, it is most consistent, in some cases, to refuse that class a residence. Placed in a degraded and subordinate political and social position, which continually reminds them of their inferiority, and of the utter hopelessness of all attempts to improve their condition as a class, they are left without adequate *motive* to waste their labor for that improvement which, when attained, brings them no reward. To have such a class of men in their midst is injurious to the dominant class itself, as such a degraded and practically defenseless condition offers so many temptations to tyrannical abuse. One of the great objections to the institution of slavery was its bad influence upon the governing race.

Had I foreseen the civil war, and the changes it has produced, I would not have supported such a measure. But at the time I did not suppose such changes could be brought about; and the *fundamental* error was *then*

found in the organic laws of Oregon adopted in 1843. Article IV., section 2, of those laws conferred the right to vote and hold office upon every free male descendant of a white man, inhabitant of Oregon Territory, of the age of twenty-one years and upward. (Gray's "Oregon," 354.) While the organic laws of 1843 professedly admitted *all* of the disfranchised class to reside in the Territory, they were so framed as effectually to exclude the *better* portion; for surely every intelligent and independent man of color would have scorned the pitiful boon offered him of a residence under conditions so humiliating.

For years I had been opposed to slavery, as injurious to both races. While I resided in Tennessee and Missouri, there was no discussion upon the subject of manumitting the slaves in those States. I was not then in circumstances that made it proper to discuss the question. But when I arrived in Oregon, the first opportunity I had, I voted against slavery while a member of the Legislative Committee of 1844. I presided at a public meeting at Sacramento City, January 8, 1849, that unanimously voted for a resolution opposing slavery in California. This was the first public meeting in this country that expressed its opposition to that institution. A public meeting was held in San Francisco, February 17, 1849, which endorsed the resolution against slavery passed at Sacramento. ("Alta California," February 22, 1849.)

As already stated, one of the objects I had in view in coming to this coast was to aid in building up a great American community on the Pacific; and, in the enthusiasm of my nature, I was anxious to aid in founding a State superior in several respects to those east of the Rocky Mountains. I therefore labored to avoid the evils

of intoxication and of mixed races, one of which was disfranchised.

W. H. GRAY—CRITICISM UPON THE HISTORY OF OREGON.

It is more charitable to impute Mr. Gray's misrepresentations to inveterate prejudice than to deliberate malice. Some men seem to become the slaves of prejudice from long indulgence, until it grows into a chronic habit; and it is about as easy to make an angel of a goat as an impartial historian of a prejudiced man. His book, in my best judgment, is a bitter, prejudiced, sectarian, controversial work, in the form of history; wherein the author acts as historian, controvertist, and witness.

I readily admit that circumstances may place a good man in this unpleasant position; but, if so, he should fully comprehend the extreme delicacy of the situation, and should rise with the occasion to the dignity of temperate and impartial history. He should make no appeals to prejudice, and should not, in advance, load down with derisive epithets those he in his own opinion is finally compelled to condemn; but should err, if at all, on the side of charity, and not against it.

The great Dr. Samuel Johnson, in speaking of Burnet's "History of his own Times," said: "I do not believe that Burnet intentionally lied; but he was so much prejudiced that he took no pains to find out the truth. He was like a man who resolves to regulate his time by a certain watch, but will not inquire whether the watch is right or not." (Boswell's "Life of Johnson," vol. ii., p. 264.)

I think this opinion applicable to Gray's "History." I *know* he has done myself and the Legislative Commit-

tee of 1844 great injustice; and I have every reason to believe that he has been equally unjust to others.

For example, the historian gives the letter of Mr. McBean, written at Fort Nez Percés, dated November 30, 1847, and addressed to the Board of Managers of the Hudson's Bay Company at Fort Vancouver, and the letters of Mr. Douglas and Mr. Hinman to Governor Abernethy (pages 519, 524, and 530). I will give so much of these last two letters as may be necessary to the point I make:

FORT VANCOUVER, *December* 7, 1847.

GEORGE ABERNETHY, ESQ.—SIR: Having received intelligence last night (on the 4th), by special express from Walla Walla, of the *destruction of the missionary settlement at Wailatpu by the Cayuse Indians of that place*, we hasten to communicate the *particulars* of that dreadful event, one of the most atrocious which darken the annals of Indian crime. . . .

JAMES DOUGLAS.

FORT VANCOUVER, *December* 4, 1847.

MR. GEORGE ABERNETHY—DEAR SIR: A Frenchman from Walla Walla arrived at my place on last Saturday, and informed me that he was on his way to Vancouver, and wished me to assist in procuring him a canoe immediately. I was very inquisitive to know if there was any difficulty above. He said four Frenchmen had died recently, and he wished to get others to occupy their places.

I immediately got him a canoe, and concluded to go in company with him in order to get some medicine for the Indians, as they were dying off with measles and other diseases very fast. I was charged with indifference. They said we were killing in not giving them medicines, and I found, if we were not exposing our lives, we were our peace, and consequently I set out for this place. This side of the Cascades I was made acquainted with the horrible massacre that took place at Wailatpu last Monday. . . . ALANSAN HINMAN.

The words ("on the 4th") are put into the letter of Mr. Douglas by the historian, to call the attention of his readers to the discrepancy in the dates of the two letters. Upon these two letters he makes the following comments, among others (page 531):

> There is one other fact in connection with this transaction that looks dark on the part of Sir James Douglas. It is shown in the dates of the several letters. Mr. Hinman's is dated December 4th; Mr. Douglas's, December 7th, that to the Sandwich Islands, December 9th. Now, between the 4th and 7th are three days. In a case of so much importance and professed sympathy, as expressed in his letter, how is it that three, or even two, days were allowed to pass without sending a dispatch informing Governor Abernethy of what had happened, and of what was expected to take place?

The distance from Wailatpu (Dr. Whitman's mission) to Walla Walla (Fort Nez Percés) was about twenty-five miles, and from Walla Walla to Wascopum (Mr. Hinman's place at the Dalles) about one hundred and forty miles. The massacre took place on the afternoon of Monday, November 29, 1847. Mr. McBean states in his letter, dated Tuesday, the last day of November, 1847, that he was first apprised of the massacre early that morning by Mr. Hall, who arrived half naked and covered with blood. As Mr. Hall started at the outset, his information was not satisfactory; and he (McBean) sent his interpreter and another man to the mission. As the two messengers had to travel twenty-five miles to the mission and the same distance back again, Mr. McBean's letter must have been written late on Tuesday night; and the messenger he sent to Vancouver must have left on Wednesday morning, December 1st. This messenger must have traveled the one hundred and forty miles from Walla Walla to the Dalles on one

horse, and could not have reached there before late on Friday, December 3d. To do this he would have had to travel about forty-six miles a day. To go from the Dalles to Vancouver in a canoe, and be "wind-bound" at Cape Horn (as Mr. Gray states on page 517), in much less time than three days, would be very difficult indeed. No one knew any better than Mr. Gray the distance traveled, and the time it would occupy under the then existing circumstances.

The historian, on page 535, gives the communication of Governor Abernethy to the Legislative Assembly of Oregon, dated December 8, 1847. How, then, could Mr. Hinman be at Vancouver on Saturday, December 4, 1847? And, had he written his letter there on that day, why did it not reach Governor Abernethy two or three days in advance of that of Mr. Douglas, dated December 7th? But there is on the face of Mr. Hinman's letter itself conclusive evidence that *his* date, *as given*, is an error. He says: "A Frenchman from Walla Walla arrived at my place on last Saturday." Now, if his letter had been *correctly* dated December 4, 1847, then the "last Saturday" mentioned would have been November 27th, two days before the massacre took place. It seems plain that Mr. Hinman and the Frenchman arrived at Vancouver Monday evening, December 6th, and that Mr. Hinman wrote his letter that evening, and Mr. Douglas his the next day, as he states. Upon this supposition Mr. Hinman could correctly say, "the horrible massacre that took place at Wailatpu last Monday." It may be that the figure 6 in Mr. Hinman's letter was mistaken for the figure 4; or it may have been a typographical error in publishing the letter; or Mr. Hinman, in the excitement of the moment, may have mistaken the date. That there was a mistake in the

date of Mr. Hinman's letter, as given by the historian, is quite certain.

Would an impartial historian have made so gross a mistake as this against any man of respectable standing, whom he accused of the most atrocious crime? Would he have seized upon this discrepancy in dates as evidence, without careful investigation? An impartial historian will put himself on the side of the accused when weighing and scrutinizing testimony, however guilty he may think him to be. He will not form an opinion that the accused is guilty unless he, the impartial historian, thinks the good and legitimate evidence amply sufficient; and therefore, in his view, he need not rely, *even in part*, upon false testimony; and he will be the more cautious and careful, in proportion to the gravity of the crime charged. The massacre being a most noted event, and its date being Monday, November 29th, and Mr. Hinman's letter December 4th, it was easy to see that the latter day was Saturday. But the historian "was so much prejudiced that he took no pains to find out the truth."

It seems that a public meeting was held in Oregon on the 18th of February, 1841, at which a committee of nine persons was chosen "to form a constitution and draft a code of laws"; and that the Rev. F. N. Blanchet was one of this committee. At an adjourned meeting, June 11, 1841, the historian says:

> *His Jesuitical Reverence*, F. N. Blanchet, was excused from serving on the committee, at his own request. The settlers and uninitiated were informed by his reverence that he was unaccustomed to make laws for the people, and did not understand how to proceed; while *divide and conquer*, the policy adopted by the Hudson's Bay Company, was entered into with heart and soul by this *Reverend Father* Blanchet and his associates. (Pages 199, 200, and 202.)

Now, without regard to the question of motive, why should the historian apply derisive epithets to the accused at any stage of the inquiry, and more especially before the author had submitted his proofs? In other words, would any impartial and enlightened historian seek, by the use of such epithets, to prejudice his readers against the accused *in advance*, and before the testimony was submitted? It will be seen that the writer emphasizes the phrase "*His Jesuitical Reverence*," so that the reader might not forget this derisive and bitter expression. A decent respect for the feelings of others, as well as a due regard to the dignity of history, would have restrained the impartial historian from the use of such language at every stage of the investigation. Whenever either a good or a bad motive may be plausibly given for the same act, the historian is very apt to impute the bad motive, as he did in this case. I do not think a single instance can be found in the whole book of 624 pages where the author has erred on the side of charity. He is not one of those noble and exalted natures that would magnanimously state the case more clearly in behalf of the accused than the accused would be able to do himself.

In reference to the act in regard to slavery, free negroes, and mulattoes, I find these entries in the journal of the House of Representatives, July 1 and 3, 1845 ("Oregon Laws and Archives," pages 83 and 85):

Mr. Garrison introduced a bill to repeal the several acts in regard to negroes in Oregon. . . .

The House went into Committee of the Whole, Mr. Straight in the chair.

When the Committee rose, the Chairman reported that the Committee had had under consideration:

The bill to divorce M. J. Rice;

The act to repeal the several acts on slavery;

An act to fix the time and place of the sittings of the Legislature;

An act to divorce F. Hathaway; also,

The report of the Committee on Revision, which had been adopted.

Report was received; and the bill to divorce F. Hathaway was read a third time, and passed; also, the bill to divorce M. J. Rice; also, the bill concerning acts on slavery.

Thus, the act which Mr. Gray asserts could not be executed was repealed about one year *before* it could have taken effect in a single case, Mr. Gray being present when the repealing act was passed. The historian seems to have had about as vague a conception of the matter he was treating as a man with a distorted vision would have of the country represented.

ELECTED JUDGE OF THE SUPREME COURT—STRANGE RESOLUTION—JESSE APPLEGATE.

On the 18th of August, 1845, I was elected by the House of Representatives Judge of the Supreme Court of Oregon.

On the 4th of December, 1845, the House, on motion of Mr. Gray, passed this resolution:

Resolved, That the Supreme Judge be called upon to inform this House whether he had examined the laws enacted by the previous Legislature of this Territory; also, to inform the House how many of said laws are incompatible with the organic articles of compact, adopted by the people on the 25th of July 1845, if any there be. ("Oregon Laws and Archives," 127.)

To this strange and singular resolution I made a firm but respectful answer, declining to decide in advance, and before proper cases came up before the

Court, whether an entire code of laws was constitutional or not.

On the 12th of December, 1845, the Speaker informed the House that he had communications from the Supreme Judge, which he had been requested to present to the House. The communications were read and referred to the Committee on the Judiciary. On the same day Mr. McCarver, from the Judiciary Committee, reported back the communications from the Supreme Judge, which were then referred to a select committee of five, consisting of Messrs. Gray, Hendrick, Garrison, McClure, and McCarver. ("Oregon Laws and Archives," 140–'41.)

There is no further mention of these communications in the Journal, as no report was ever made by this select committee. There was not a single lawyer among the members of 1845; and it is quite probable that this committee found it very difficult to coerce a Supreme Court to decide questions of law before cases were properly brought before it.

My extracts from the laws of 1844 are taken from "Oregon Laws and Archives, by L. F. Grover, Commissioner," except the act in regard to slavery, and the 4th section of the act on ways and means, which latter is found in Gray's "Oregon," 395, as part of Dr. White's report to the Secretary of War. These two acts are not found in Grover's compilation. The act in regard to slavery, free negroes, and mulattoes is a certified copy from the original on file in the office of the Secretary of State. My references to the Journals of 1844 and 1845 are to the same compilation.

In the summer and early fall of 1846 Jesse Applegate, at his own expense as I then understood, opened a new wagon-road into the Willamette valley at its south-

ern end. He met the emigrants at Fort Hall and induced a portion of them to come by that route. They suffered great hardships before they reached the end of their journey. This was caused mainly by their own mistakes. Though he was much censured by many of them, he was not to blame. He had performed one of the most noble and generous acts, and deserved praise rather than censure. I traveled with him across the Plains in 1843, and I can testify that he was a noble, intellectual, and generous man; and his character was so perfect as to bear any and all tests, under any and all circumstances. The Hon. J. W. Nesmith, in his address before the Oregon Pioneers in June, 1875, paid a glowing tribute to the character of "Uncle Jesse Applegate." I knew him long and well, and shall never cease to love him so long as I live.

I left him in Oregon in 1848. He was then a rich man, for that time and that country. I did not see him again until 1872, a period of nearly twenty-four years. In the mean time he had become a gray-headed old man. He and myself are near the same age, he being about two years the younger. One day, without my knowing that he was in California, he walked into the Pacific Bank in San Francisco. I knew, from the serious expression of his face, that he was an old friend; but, for the moment, I could not place him or call his name. He was so much affected that his eyes filled with tears, and he could not speak. I shook his hand cordially, invited him to sit down, and sat down by him, looking him full in the face one moment, when it came into my mind that he was my old friend, and I exclaimed, "Applegate!" and we embraced like brothers.

We talked about one hour, and in this conversation he gave me his history since I left Oregon. He re-

moved to the Umpqua valley; where for a time he had fine lands, stock, and other property. At length he determined to go into the mercantile business, for which he had little or no capacity. Said he: "To make a long story short, I did business upon this theory. I sold my goods on credit to those who *needed them most*, not to those who were *able to pay*, lost thirty thousand dollars, and quit the business."

Any one knowing Jesse Applegate as I do would at once recognize the truth of this statement. It was just like the man. His fine intellect and his experience in life said no; but his generous heart said yes; and that kind heart of his overruled his better judgment. In his old age his fortune is gone; but his true friends only admire and love him the more in the hour of misfortune.

In starting from Missouri to come to this country in 1843, Mr. Applegate announced to his traveling companions, as we have been credibly informed, that he meant to drive the Hudson's Bay Company from the country. To reach the country independent of them, he had sold or mortgaged his cattle to get supplies at Walla Walla. On arriving at Vancouver, he found Dr. McLoughlin to be much of a gentleman, and disposed to aid him in every way he could. The Doctor advised him to keep his cattle, and gave him employment as a surveyor, and credit for all he required. This kind treatment closed Mr. Applegate's open statements of opposition to the Company, and secured his friendship and his influence to keep his Missouri friends from doing violence to them. He carried this kind feeling for them into the Legislative Committee. (Gray, pages 421–'22.)

As already stated, a portion of the immigrants of 1843 left their cattle at Walla Walla. This they did under an agreement with Mr. McKinlay, then in charge of the fort, that we should have the same number and

description of cattle in the Willamette valley, from the herds of the Hudson's Bay Company. When we arrived at Vancouver, Dr. McLoughlin and Mr. Douglas candidly stated to us that our American tame cattle would suit us much better than the cattle of the Company, and they advised us to bring our cattle from Walla Walla during the next spring. The same advice was given to all the immigrants who left their cattle at Walla Walla. We all saw at once that this advice was not only generous but practically sound. Mr. Applegate, as I understood at the time, made the same arrangement with Mr. McKinlay that others of us did. That Mr. Applegate sold or mortgaged his cattle at Walla Walla for supplies must be a mistake. He needed but little if anything in that line; and to have mortgaged so many cattle for so small an amount would have been the greatest of folly. He could not have needed provisions, so far as I can remember, as he must have purchased wheat and potatoes from Dr. Whitman, like most of us.

On arriving at Vancouver, Mr. Applegate, no doubt, found a very different state of things from what he anticipated when starting from Missouri. He did find Dr. McLoughlin and Mr. Douglas to be much of gentlemen; for it was very difficult indeed for any man, who was himself a gentleman, to keep the company of those two men, and not find out that they were both gentlemen in the true sense of that term. Mr. Applegate no doubt concluded that, if these men were really opposed to American immigrants, they took the most extraordinary method of showing it. That Mr. Applegate purchased of the Company at Vancouver some supplies on credit is very probable, because he was amply good for all he engaged to pay. He was honesty personified, and was

an admirable worker, both as a farmer and surveyor. He also had a fine band of American cattle; and such cattle were then the most valuable property in Oregon. Jesse Applegate and Daniel Waldo were the owners of more cattle than any other two men in our immigration.

THE ACT TO PROHIBIT THE INTRODUCTION, MANUFACTURE, SALE, AND BARTER OF ARDENT SPIRITS.

I have already mentioned (page 181) the happy condition of society in Oregon, and the causes which produced it. This only continued until the beginning of 1847.

The act of 1844 to prohibit the introduction, manufacture, sale, and barter of ardent spirits was amended by the House of Representatives of 1845. The same body drew up and submitted to the people, for their approval or rejection, a new and amended organic law, which was adopted, and which conferred upon the Legislature the power to pass laws to *regulate* the introduction, manufacture, and sale of ardent spirits. This amendatory bill was reported by W. H. Gray from the Committee on Ways and Means, and was passed December 6, 1845, by the following vote: Yeas, Gray, Garrison, Hendricks, H. Lee, B. Lee, McClure, and McCarver—7; Nays, Foisy, Hill, Straight, and Newell—4. On the 8th a motion to reconsider was lost by the following tie vote: Yeas, Hendricks, Hill, B. Lee, Smith, Straight, and Newell; nays, Foisy, Gray, Garrison, H. Lee, McCarver, and McClure. (Gray's "Oregon," page 440.)

The amendatory act is incorrectly given by Mr. Gray on pages 440–41, by omitting the first section entirely. The first section of the original act was amended by

inserting the word "give" after the word "barter" in two places; and the second section was amended by inserting the word "give" after the word "barter" in one place, and the word "gift" after the word "barter" in the second place.

Section four of the *original* act was as follows:

SECTION 4. That it shall be the duty of all sheriffs, judges, justices of the peace, constables, and other officers, when they have reason to believe that this act has been violated, to give notice thereof to some justice of the peace or judge of a court, who shall immediately issue his warrant and cause the offending party to be arrested; and if such officer has jurisdiction of such case, he shall proceed to try such offender without delay, and give judgment accordingly; but if such officer have no jurisdiction to try such case, he shall, if the party be guilty, bind him over to appear before the next Circuit Court.

This section was stricken out, and the following inserted in its stead:

SECTION 4. Whenever it shall come to the knowledge of any officer of this government, or any private citizen, that any kind of spirituous liquors are being distilled or manufactured in Oregon, they are hereby authorized and required to proceed to the place where such illicit manufacture is known to exist, and seize the distilling apparatus, and deliver the same to the nearest district judge or justice of the peace, whose duty it shall be immediately to issue his warrant, and cause the house and premises of the person against whom such warrant shall be issued to be further searched; and in case any kind of spirituous liquors are found in or about said premises, or any implements or apparatus that have the appearance of having been used or constructed for the purpose of manufacturing any kind of spirituous liquors, the officer who shall have been duly authorized to execute such warrant shall seize all such apparatus, implements, and spirituous liquors, and deliver the same to the judge or justice of the peace who issued the said warrant. Said officer

shall also arrest the person or persons in or about whose premises such apparatus, implements, or spirituous liquors are found, and conduct him or them to said judge or justice of the peace, whose duty it shall be to proceed against said criminal or criminals, and dispose of the articles seized according to law.

It will be readily seen that these amendments radically changed the original act, in several most material respects. By the amendment to the second section of the act, it was made a criminal offense to give away ardent spirits. This would prevent the master of a ship entering the waters of Oregon from giving his seamen their usual daily allowance of liquor while the vessel remained within our jurisdiction. So, a private citizen, without the advice of a physician, could not give the article to any one, for any purpose, or under any circumstances.

By the provisions of the fourth section as amended, all officers, and even private citizens, were not only authorized, but required (without any warrant having been first issued by a court or judicial officer) to seize the distilling apparatus ; and in such case each officer and each private citizen was to be himself the judge of both the fact and law, so far as the duty to seize the apparatus was concerned. This was giving to each individual citizen of Oregon a most extraordinary power, and making its exercise *obligatory*.

The fifth section of the amendatory act, as given by the historian, was as follows :

SEC. 5. All the fines or penalties recovered under this act shall go, one half to the informant and witnesses, and the other half to the officers engaged in arresting and trying the criminal or criminals; and it shall be the duty of all officers in whose hands such fines and penalties may come, to pay over as directed in this section.

This was a most unusual and extraordinary provision. To give a portion of the penalty recovered to the informant and arresting officer was not very improper; but to give another portion of such penalty to the *witnesses* and *judges*, thus making them interested in condemning the accused, is indeed most extraordinary; and I apprehend that such a provision never before occurred in the history of legislation among civilized men. The author of this fifth section must have had great confidence in the power of money.

These objectionable features were so great, in the view of Governor Abernethy, that he recommended a revision of the amendatory act, in his message to the House of Representatives, December 4, 1846. (Gray, 442.)

The House of Representatives, at the December session, 1846, passed an act entitled "An Act to regulate the manufacture and sale of wine and distilled spirituous liquors." This act Governor Abernethy returned to the House with his objections, as set forth in his veto message of December 17, 1846. In this message he said, among other things:

> The act lying before me is the first act that has in any manner attempted to legalize the manufacture and sale of ardent spirits. At the session of the Legislature in June, 1844, an act was passed entitled "An Act to prevent the introduction, sale, and distillation of ardent spirits in Oregon"; and, as far as my knowledge extends, the passage of that act gave general satisfaction to the great majority of the people throughout the Territory. At the session of December, 1845, several amendments were proposed to the old law, and passed. The new features given to the bill by those amendments did not accord with the views of the people; the insertion of the words "give" and "gift" in the first and second sections of the bill, they thought, was taking away their rights, as it was considered that a man had a right to

give away his property if he chose. There were several other objections to the bill, which I set forth to your honorable body in my message. I would therefore recommend that the amendments passed at the December session of 1845 be repealed; and that the law passed on the 24th of June, 1844, with such alterations as will make it agree with the organic law, if it does not agree with it, be again made the law of the land. It is said by many that the Legislature has no right to prohibit the introduction or sale of liquor, and this is probably the strongest argument used in defense of your bill.

The bill was passed over the veto of the Governor by the following vote: Yeas, Messrs. Boon, Hall, Hembree, Lounsdale, Loony, Meek, Summers, Straight, T. Vault, Williams, and the Speaker—11; Nays, Messrs. Chamberlain, McDonald, Newell, Peers, and Dr. W. F. Tolmie—5.

Mr. Parker, in a public address to the voters of Clackamas County, in May, 1846, charged that rum was sold at Vancouver contrary to law. This charge was based upon rumor. Mr. Douglas, in a communication to the "Oregon Spectator," published June 11, 1846, among other things says:

If, with reference to these supplies, Mr. Parker had told his hearers that her Majesty's ship Modeste, now stationed at Fort Vancouver, had, with other supplies for ship use from the stores of the Hudson's Bay Company, received several casks of rum; or, if, referring to the company's own ships, he had stated that *a small allowance of spirits is daily served out to the crews of the company's vessels*, and that other classes of the company's servants, according to long-accustomed usage, receive on certain *rare occasions* a similar indulgence, he would have told the *plain and simple truth*, and his statement would not this day have been called in question by me. These acts, which I fully admit, and would on no account attempt to conceal, can not by the fair rules of construction be considered as infringing upon any

law recognized by the *compact which we have agreed to support*, in common with the other inhabitants of Oregon. (Gray, 447.)

It seems perfectly plain from Mr. Gray's own history, that the final overthrow of this measure was mainly brought about by the following causes:

1. The extremely harsh and erroneous amendments of 1845.

2. The mistake of the same body in using the word "regulate" instead of "prohibit" in the organic law of that year.

3. The sale of rum to the Modeste by the Hudson's Bay Company.

This last act, however excusable it may be considered under the then existing circumstances, gave the opponents a plausible ground of objection.

That the original act was approved by the people is shown by the following extract from the message of Governor Abernethy, dated February 5, 1849:

> The proposed amendments to the organic law will come before you for final action: to amend the oath of office, to make the clerks of the different counties recorders of land claims, etc., and to strike out the word "regulate" and insert the word "prohibit" in the clause relating to the sale of ardent spirits. The last amendment came before the people for a direct vote, and I am happy to say that the people of this Territory decided through the ballot-box, by a majority of the votes given, that the word "prohibit" should be inserted. This makes the question a very easy one for you to decide upon. ("Oregon Laws and Archives," pages 273–'4.)

Jesse Applegate was a member of the House of Representatives in 1845, but his name does not appear as voting upon the final passage of the amendatory bill, he having previously resigned his seat.

TREATY OF JUNE 15, 1846 — POLICY OF THE HUDSON'S BAY COMPANY—H. A. G. LEE—INDIAN CHARACTER.

On the 15th of June, 1846, a treaty was concluded between Great Britain and the United States, which acknowledged the sovereignty of our country over that portion of Oregon lying south of the 49th parallel of north latitude. This was known in Oregon as early as December of that year, as the fact is mentioned in Governor Abernethy's message, dated December 1, 1846. ("Oregon Laws and Archives," 158.)

The final settlement of the conflicting claims of the two governments in this manner did not surprise any sensible man in Oregon, so far as I remember. It was what we had every reason to expect. We knew, to a moral certainty, that the moment we brought our families, cattle, teams, and loaded wagons to the banks of the Columbia River in 1843, the question was practically decided in our favor. Oregon was not only accessible by land from our contiguous territory, but we had any desirable number of brave, hardy people who were fond of adventure, and perfectly at home in the settlement of new countries. We could bring into the country ten immigrants for every colonist Great Britain could induce to settle there. We were masters of the situation, and fully comprehended our position. This the gentlemen of the Company understood as well as we did. In repeated conversations with Dr. McLoughlin, soon after my arrival in Oregon, he assured me that he had for some years been convinced that Oregon was destined soon to be occupied by a civilized people. The reasons for this conclusion were most obvious. The country, with its fertile soil, extensive valleys,

magnificent forests, and mild climate, was admirably fitted for a civilized and dense population. Its local position on the shores of the Pacific marked it as a fit abode for a cultivated race of men. Besides, the natives had almost entirely disappeared from the lower section of Oregon. Only a small and diseased remnant was left.

The colonization of the country, either by British or Americans, would equally destroy the fur-trade, the only legitimate business of the Company. No doubt the gentlemen connected with that Company thought the title of their own government to Oregon was superior to ours; while we Americans believed we had the better title. I read carefully the discussion between Mr. Buchanan, our Secretary of State, and the British Minister; and while I thought our country had the better title, neither claim could be properly called a plain indisputable right, because much could be and was said on both sides of the question. But, while our *title* might be disputed, there was no possible doubt as to the main fact, that *we had settled the country.*

When the managers of the Company had arrived at the conclusion that Oregon must be inhabited by a civilized race of men, they undoubtedly determined to do all they could reasonably and justly to colonize it with their own people. These gentlemen were as loyal in their allegiance to their own country as we were to ours, and were prepared to go as far as enlightened love of country would lead them, and no farther. It is very true that the Company, by expending the larger portion if not all of its large capital, could have colonized the country in advance of the Americans. But, what proper inducement had the Company thus to sacrifice the property of its stockholders? Colonization was not its

legitimate business. Why, then, should a mere mercantile corporation waste its means and ruin its business to settle Oregon? If the settlement of the country was of national importance to Great Britain, then the expense should have been borne by that government itself, and not by the few subjects who happened to be stockholders of the Company. Any one well acquainted with all the facts and circumstances, and who will carefully and thoroughly examine the subject, must see that the only motive the managers of the Company had to settle Oregon with British subjects, in preference to American citizens, was one of patriotism or love of country. In a pecuniary point of view, the Company saved more money for its stockholders by the treaty than it could have done had the country fallen to Great Britain.

But while the managers of the Company, as British subjects, preferred to colonize Oregon with their own people, they were not, as enlightened and Christian men, prepared to use criminal means to accomplish that purpose. In the address of John McLoughlin and James Douglas to the citizens of Oregon in March, 1845, they say, among other things:

> The Hudson's Bay Company made their settlement at Fort Vancouver under the authority of a license from the British Government, in conformity with the provisions of the treaty between Great Britain and the United States of America, which gives them the right of occupying as much land as they require for the operation of their business. On the faith of that treaty they have made a settlement on the north bank of the Columbia River, they have opened roads and made other improvements at a great outlay of capital; they have held unmolested possession of their improvements for many years, unquestioned by the public officers of either government, who have since the existence of their settlement repeatedly visited it; they have

carried on business with manifest advantage to the country; they have given the protection of their influence over the native tribes to every person who required it, without distinction of nation or party; and they have afforded every assistance in their power toward developing the resources of the country and promoting the industry of its inhabitants. . . .

Permit us to assure you, gentlemen, that it is our earnest wish to maintain a good understanding and to live on friendly terms with every person in the country. We entertain the highest respect for the provisional organization; and knowing the great good it has effected, as well as the evil it has prevented, we wish it every success, and hope, as we desire, to continue to live in the exercise and interchange of good offices with the framers of that useful institution.

This address was inclosed with the following letter to the Executive Committee of Oregon:

VANCOUVER, *March* 18, 1845.

GENTLEMEN: I am sorry to inform you that Mr. Williamson is surveying a piece of land occupied by the Hudson's Bay Company, alongside of this establishment, with a view of taking it as a claim; and, as he is an American citizen, I feel bound, as a matter of courtesy, to make the same known to you, trusting that you will feel justified in taking measures to have him removed from the Hudson's Bay Company's premises, in order that the unanimity now happily subsisting between the American citizens and British subjects residing in this country may not be disturbed or interrupted. I beg to inclose you a copy of an address to the citizens of Oregon, which will explain to you our situation and the course we are bound to pursue in the event of your declining to interfere.

I am, gentlemen, your obedient, humble servant,

J. MCLOUGHLIN.

William Baily, Osborn Russell, P. G. Stewart, Executive Committee of Oregon.

To this letter, the majority of the Executive Committee of Oregon, acting for the whole, made this reply:

OREGON CITY, *March* 21, 1845.

SIR: We beg to acknowledge the receipt of your letters—one dated 11th of March, and the other 12th of March—accompanied with an address to the citizens of Oregon.

We regret to hear that unwarranted liberties have been taken by an American citizen upon the Hudson's Bay Company's premises, and it affords us great pleasure to learn that the offender, after due reflection, desisted from the insolent and rash measure.

As American citizens, we beg leave to offer you and your esteemed colleague our most grateful thanks for the kind and candid manner in which you have treated this matter, as we are aware that an infringement on the rights of the Hudson's Bay Company in this country, by an American citizen, is a breach of the laws of the United States, by setting at naught her most solemn treaties with Great Britain.

As representatives of the citizens of Oregon, we beg your acceptance of our sincere acknowledgments of the obligations we are under to yourself and your honorable associate for the high regard you have manifested for the authorities of our provisional government, and the special anxiety you have ever shown for our peace and prosperity; and we assure you that we consider ourselves in duty bound to use every exertion in our power to put down every cause of disturbance, as well as to promote the amicable intercourse and kind feelings hitherto existing between ourselves and the gentlemen of the Hudson's Bay Company, until the United States shall extend its jurisdiction over us, and our authority ceases to exist.

We have the honor to be, sir, your most obedient servants,

OSBORN RUSSELL,
P. G. STEWART.

John McLoughlin, Esq.

These papers appear in Gray's "Oregon," pages 409–'11, as a portion of Dr. White's report to the Secretary of War.

This attempt to locate a claim in the vicinity of Vancouver was made by Williamson and Alderman. Wil-

liamson was apparently a modest and respectable young man, while Alderman was a most notorious character. He was well known in Oregon from his violent and unprincipled conduct. He was always in trouble with somebody. He came to California in the summer or fall of 1848, and was killed in the latter portion of that year, at Sutter's Fort, under justifiable circumstances.

I have given these extracts from the address to the citizens of Oregon, that the then managers of the Hudson's Bay Company might speak for themselves; and I have given the reply of Messrs. Russell and Stewart, of the Executive Committee, to show the opinion of those intelligent, calm, and faithful American officers upon the general subject.

That the facts stated in the address are true, there can be no reasonable doubt. The facts were all within the personal knowledge of Dr. McLoughlin and Mr. Douglas, and they could not be mistaken about them. If untrue, then they deliberately and knowingly made false statements. To make statements that could be so readily contradicted by the people of Oregon, if untrue, would have been the greatest folly. Besides, the high characters of those gentleman, especially that of Dr. McLoughlin, forbids such inference. Dr. McLoughlin, during his long and active life, gave such conclusive proofs of the possession of the most exalted virtue, that no man of respectable ability and good character would at this late day question his integrity or doubt his statement of facts within his own knowledge. He voluntarily became, and afterward died, an American citizen.

But the truth of their statements, especially that one which declares that "they had given the protection of their influence over the native tribes to every person

who required it, without distinction of nation or party," is shown by the fact that no American immigrant was killed by the Indians in Oregon until late in the fall of 1847—seventeen months after the treaty between Great Britain and the United States had settled the question of sovereignty over that portion of Oregon south of the 49th parallel of north latitude in our favor, and twelve months after that fact was known in that country, and when the Company could not have had any adequate motive to oppose American immigration to acknowledged American territory.

It is true, some thefts were committed by the Indians upon the immigrants; but I apprehend that these were not more numerous or common than usual with Indians under like circumstances. While it is not my intention to enter at large into the subject, I will give an extract from the long letter of H. A. G. Lee to Dr. E. White, assistant Indian agent, dated Oregon City, March 4, 1845. It is, in my judgment, the most sensible and just description of Indian character I have ever seen in so few words. After stating, among other things, that "avarice is doubtless the ruling passion of most Indians," the writer goes on to say:

The lawless bands along the river, from Fort Walla Walla to the Dalles, are still troublesome to the immigrants; and the immigrants are still very imprudent in breaking off into small parties, just when they should remain united. The Indians are tempted by the unguarded and defenseless state of the immigrants, and avail themselves of the opportunity to gratify their cupidity. Here allow me to suggest a thought. These robbers furnish us a true miniature likeness of the whole Indian population, whenever they fail to obtain such things as they wish in exchange for such as they have to give. These are robbers now, because they have nothing to give; all others will be robbers when, with what they have to give, they can not procure what

they wish. I am satisfied of the correctness of this conclusion from all that I have witnessed of Indian character, even among the praiseworthy Nez Percés. And should the Government of the United States withhold her protection from her subjects in Oregon, they will be under the necessity of entering into treaty stipulations with the Indians, in violation of the laws of the United States, as preferable to a resort to force of arms.

Hitherto, the immigrants have had no serious difficulty in passing through the territory of these tribes; but that their passage is becoming more and more a subject of interest to the Indians is abundantly manifest. They collect about the road from every part of the country, and have looked on with amazement; but the novelty of the scene is fast losing its power to hold in check their baser passions. The next immigration will, in all probability, call forth developments of Indian character which have been almost denied an existence among these people. Indeed, sir, had you not taken the precaution to conciliate their good feelings and friendship toward the whites just at the time they were meeting each other, it is to be doubted whether there had not been some serious difficulties. Individuals on both sides have been mutually provoked and exasperated during the passage of each immigration, and these cases are constantly multiplying. Much prudence is required on the part of the whites, and unfortunately they have very little by the time they reach the Columbia Valley. Some of the late immigrants, losing their horses and very naturally supposing them stolen by the Indians, went to the bands of horses owned by the Indians and took as many as they wished. You are too well acquainted with Indians to suppose that such a course can be persisted in without producing serious results. (Gray's "Oregon," pages 414–416.)

Governor Abernethy, in his message to the Legislative Assembly of Oregon under date of December 7, 1847, says:

Our relation with the Indians becomes every year more embarrassing. They see the white man occupying their lands,

rapidly filling up the country, and they put in a claim for pay. They have been told that a chief would come out from the United States and treat with them for their lands; they have been told this so often that they begin to doubt the truth of it. At all events, they say; "He will not come till we are all dead, and then what good will blankets do us? We want something now." This leads to trouble between the settler and the Indians about him. Some plan should be devised by which a fund can be raised, and presents made to the Indians of sufficient value to keep them quiet, until an agent arrives from the United States. A number of robberies have been committed by the Indians in the upper country upon the emigrants as they were passing through their territory. This should not be allowed to pass. An appropriation should be made by you, sufficient to enable the Superintendent of Indian Affairs to take a small party in the spring, and demand restitution of the property, or its equivalent in horses. Without an appropriation, a sufficient party would not be induced to go up there, as the trip is an expensive one. ("Oregon Laws and Archives," page 210.)

We were delicately situated in Oregon up to near the close of 1846, when news of the treaty between Great Britain and the United States reached us. We knew that under former treaties the citizens and subjects of both governments were privileged to occupy the country jointly; but that joint occupation of the territory did not mean joint occupation of the same tract of land or of the same premises, but the party first in possession was entitled to continue it until the question of sovereignty should be settled. Our community was composed of American citizens and British subjects, intermingled together as neighbors, with all their respective national attachments, manners, and prejudices; and we had our full share of reckless adventurers and other bad men. The extremists and ultras of both sides would have brought us into armed conflict, and perhaps in-

volved the two countries in war, but for the manly good sense of our leading men, supported by the great majority of the people.

It was most fortunate for us that the executive office of our little provisional government was at all times filled, not only by Americans, but by those who were well fitted for that position, both as to capacity and conciliatory firmness. I have already spoken of Osborn Russell and P. G. Stewart, who acted as the Executive Committee during part of the years 1844 and 1845. They were admirable men for that position. They were succeeded by George Abernethy, who filled the position until the provisional organization was superseded by the regular Territorial government, under the act of Congress of August 14, 1848.

Governor Abernethy was precisely fitted for the position in every respect. Though he had no regular legal education, he was a man of admirable good sense, of calm, dispassionate disposition, of amiable, gentle manners, and above the influences of passion and prejudice. He did his duty most faithfully to the utmost of his ability; and his ability was ample for that time and that country. He fully comprehended the exact situation, and acted upon the maxim, "Make haste slowly," believing that such was not only the best policy, but the best justice. Time amply vindicated the wisdom and efficiency of the course he pursued. We attained all our hopes and wishes by peaceful means. "Peace hath her triumphs," greater than those of war, because the triumphs of peace cost so much less. It is a matter of doubt whether, in the settlement of any portion of America by the whites, any greater wisdom, forbearance, and good sense have been shown, except in the celebrated case of William Penn.

MASSACRE OF DR. WHITMAN AND OTHERS—INDIAN WAR —ITS RESULT.

On Monday, November 29, 1847, the horrible massacre of Dr. Marcus Whitman, his lady, and others, by the Cayuse Indians, took place; which event, in the just language of Mr. Douglas, was "one of the most atrocious which darken the annals of Indian crime." Within a few days other peaceful Americans were slaughtered, until the whole number of victims amounted to from twelve to fifteen. This painful event was made known at Oregon City on December 8, 1847, as already stated.

I knew Dr. Whitman well; I first saw him at the rendezvous near the western line of Missouri, in May, 1843; saw him again at Fort Hall; and again at his own mission in the fall of that year, as already stated. I remember that the first I heard of the false and ungrateful charge made by a portion of our immigrants (an account of which I have already given) was from his own lips. I was standing near his house when he came to me with the painful expression of deep concern upon his countenance, and asked me to come with him to his room. I did so, and found one or two other gentlemen there. He was deeply wounded, as he had ample cause to be, by this unjustifiable conduct of some of our people. He stated to us the facts. I again saw him at my home in the Tualatin Plains in 1844. He called at my house, and, finding I was in the woods at work, he came to me there. This was the last time I ever saw him. Our relations were of the most cordial and friendly character, and I had the greatest respect for him.

I consider Dr. Whitman to have been a brave, kind, devoted, and intrepid spirit, without malice and with-

out reproach. In my best judgment, he made greater sacrifices, endured more hardships, and encountered more perils for Oregon than any other one man; and his services were practically more efficient than those of any other, except perhaps those of Dr. Linn, United States Senator from Missouri. I say *perhaps*, for I am in doubt as to which of these two men did more in effect for Oregon.

The news of this bloody event thrilled and roused our people at once; and within a very short time, considering the season and other circumstances, we raised an army of some five hundred brave and hardy men, and marched them into the enemy's country. Several battles were fought, the result of which is well and concisely stated by Governor Abernethy, in his message to the Legislative Assembly of Oregon, under date of February 5, 1849:

I am happy to inform you that, through aid of the Territory to go in pursuit of the murderers and their allies, and of those who contributed so liberally to the support of our fellow citizens in the field, the war has been brought to a successful termination. It is true that the Indians engaged in the massacre were not captured and punished; they were, however, driven from their homes, their country taken possession of, and they made to understand that the power of the white man is far superior to their own. The Indians have a large scope of country to roam over, all of which they were well acquainted with, knew every pass, and by this knowledge could escape the punishment they so justly merited. In view of this the troops were recalled and disbanded early in July last, leaving a small force under the command of Captain Martin to keep possession of the post at Wailatpu, and a few men at Woscopum. Captain Martin remained at Wailatpu until the middle of September, when the time for which his men had enlisted expired. He however, before leaving, sent a party to bring in the last company of emigrants.

The appearance of so many armed men among the Indians in their own country had a very salutary effect on them; this is seen by their refusing to unite with the Cayuse Indians, by their profession of friendship to the Americans, and by the safety with which the immigration passed through the Indian country the past season.

Heretofore robberies have been committed and insults offered to Americans as they would pass along, burdened with their families and goods, and worn down with the fatigues of a long journey, and this was on the increase; each successive immigration suffered more than the preceding one. But this year no molestation was offered in any way. On the contrary, every assistance was rendered by the Indians in crossing rivers, for a reasonable compensation.

Having learned the power and ability of the Americans, I trust the necessity of calling on our citizens to punish them hereafter will be obviated. ("Oregon Laws and Archives," page 272.)

This attack of the Indians was attributed by some persons, and especially by Mr. Spaulding, to the instigation of the Catholic missionaries in that country. I thought the charge most unjust, and think so still. The charge was too horrible in its very nature to be believed unless the evidence was conclusive beyond a reasonable doubt. There were most ample grounds upon which to account for the massacre, without accusing these missionaries of that horrible crime. Mr. Spaulding and myself agreed to discuss the matter through the columns of a small semi-monthly newspaper, published by Mr. Griffin, and several numbers were written and published by each of us; but the discovery of the gold mines in California put a stop to the discussion.

CHAPTER VI.

DISCOVERY OF GOLD IN CALIFORNIA—DETERMINE TO GO TO THE MINES—ORGANIZE A WAGON-PARTY.

I HAD been a member of the Legislative Committee of 1844, had taken a leading part in that little body, and had done what I considered my fair proportion of the work, under all the then existing circumstances. We had adopted a code of laws, which, though imperfect, was ample for that time and that country. I looked forward to the speedy settlement of the question of sovereignty in our favor, and it was so settled within two years thereafter.

As before stated, I went to Oregon to accomplish three purposes. I had already assisted to lay the foundation of a great American community on the shores of the Pacific, and the trip across the Plains had fully restored the health of Mrs. Burnett. There was still one great end to attain—the payment of my debts. I had a family of eight persons to support, and a large amount of old indebtedness to pay. My debts were just, and I believed in the great maxim of the law, that "a man must be just before he is generous." Had the *essential* interest of a large body of my fellow men, in my judgment, required further sacrifices, I would have made them most cheerfully. But, the foundation of a great community on this coast having been laid, all else would

naturally follow as a matter of course, as there were others competent to continue the work.

The obligation to support my family and pay my debts was sacred with me ; and I therefore gave the larger portion of my time to my own private affairs so long as I remained in Oregon. I did not then foresee the discovery of gold in California ; and for this reason my only chance to pay, so far as I could see, was to remain and labor in Oregon. I had not the slightest idea of leaving that country until the summer of 1848. Before I left, I had paid a small portion of my old indebtedness. I always had faith that I should ultimately pay every dollar.

In the month of July, 1848 (if I remember correctly), the news of the discovery of gold in California reached Oregon. It passed from San Francisco to Honolulu, thence to Nesqualy, and thence to Fort Vancouver. At that very time there was a vessel from San Francisco in the Willamette River, loading with flour, the master of which knew the fact but concealed it from our people for speculative reasons, until the news was made public by the gentlemen connected with the Hudson's Bay Company.

This extraordinary news created the most intense excitement throughout Oregon. Scarcely anything else was spoken of. We had vanquished the Indians, and that war for the time was almost forgotten. We did not know of the then late treaty of peace between Mexico and the United States ; but we were aware of the fact that our Government had possession of California ; and we knew, to a moral certainty, that it would never be given up.

Many of our people at once believed the reported discovery to be true, and speedily left for the gold mines

with pack-animals. I think that at least two thirds of the male population of Oregon, capable of bearing arms, started for California in the summer and fall of 1848. The white population of Oregon, including the late immigrants, must have amounted then to from eight to ten thousand people. Before we left, many persons expressed their apprehensions that the Indians might renew hostilities during the absence of so many men. But those of us who went to the mines that fall (leaving our families behind in Oregon) had no fears of any further attacks from the Indians. Time proved that we were right.

These accounts were so new and extraordinary to us at that time, that I had my doubts as to their truth, until I had evidence satisfactory to me. I did not jump to conclusions, like some people ; but when I saw a letter which had been written in California by Ex-Governor Lilburn W. Boggs, formerly of Missouri, to his brother-in-law Colonel Boon of Oregon, I was fully satisfied. I had known Governor Boggs since 1821, was familiar with his handwriting, and knew Colonel Boon; and there was no reasonable cause to doubt. This letter I read about the last of August, 1848.

I saw my opportunity, and at once consulted with my wife. I told her I thought that it was our duty to separate again for a time, though we had promised each other, after our long separation of fourteen months during our early married life, that we would not separate again. I said that this was a new and special case, never anticipated by us; that it was the only certain opportunity to get out of debt within a reasonable time, and I thought it my duty to make the effort. She consented, and I came to California, and succeeded beyond my expectations. I paid all my debts, principal and interest, secur-

ity debts and all. Time conclusively proved the wisdom and justice of my course. I set out to accomplish three important objects ; and, thanks be to God, I succeeded in all.

When I had determined to come to California, I at once set to work to prepare for the journey. All who preceded me had gone with pack-animals ; but it occurred to me that we might be able to make the trip with wagons. I went at once to see Dr. McLoughlin, and asked his opinion of its practicability. Without hesitation he replied that he thought we could succeed, and recommended old Thomas McKay for pilot. No wagons had ever passed between Oregon and California. Thomas McKay had made the trip several times with pack-trains, and knew the general nature of the country, and the courses and distances ; but he knew of no practicable wagon-route, as he had only traveled with pack-animals.

This was about the first of September, 1848. I at once went into the streets of Oregon City, and proposed the immediate organization of a wagon-company. The proposition was received with decided favor ; and in eight days we had organized a company of one hundred and fifty stout, robust, energetic, sober men, and fifty wagons and ox-teams, and were off for the gold mines of California. We had only one family, consisting of the husband, wife, and three or four children. We had fresh teams, strong wagons, an ample supply of provisions for six months, and a good assortment of mining implements. I had two wagons and teams, and two saddle-horses ; and I took plank in the bottoms of my wagons, with which I constructed a gold-rocker after we arrived in the mines.

We were not certain that we could go through with

our wagons, and thought we might be caught in the mountains, as were the Donner party in 1846. In case we had been snowed in, we had plenty of provisions to live upon during the winter. Besides, we were apprehensive that there might be a great scarcity of provisions in the mines during the winter of 1848–'9. The only article I purchased in the mines was some molasses, having everything else in the way of provisions.

"Advances of outfits were made to such men as Hastings and his party, Burnett, and other prominent men. . . .

"Those who proposed going to California could readily get all the supplies they required of the company by giving their notes payable in California." (Gray's "Oregon," 361.)

This is a mistake, so far as I was concerned. I had plenty of wheat, cattle, and hogs, and did not need advances. My outfit cost very little additional outlay, for the simple reason that I had my own wagons and teams, except one yoke of oxen which I purchased of Pettigrove, in Portland, and paid for at the time. I had the two horses that I took with me, and all the provisions that I required, except a few pounds of tea. I had an ample supply of sugar, for reasons already stated. I had all the clothes required, and plenty of tools, except two picks which I got a blacksmith in Oregon City to make. I do not remember to have purchased a single article on credit.

OFF FOR CALIFORNIA—INCIDENTS OF THE TRIP.

I was elected captain of the wagon-party, and Thomas McKay was employed as pilot. We followed the Applegate route to Klamath Lake, where we left that road and took a southern direction. Thomas Mc-

Kay, myself, and five others, well armed and mounted, went on in advance of the wagons to discover the best route, leaving the wagons to follow our trail until otherwise notified. We, the road-hunters, took with us plenty of flour, sugar, and tea, and depended upon our guns for meat.

We passed over comparatively smooth prairie for some distance. One evening we encamped at what was then called Goose Lake. It being late in the season, the water in the lake was very low, muddy, and almost putrid. Vast flocks of pelicans were visiting this lake at that time, on their way south. I remember that we killed one on the wing with a rifle.

The water being so bad, we drank very little, and left early next morning. We traveled over prairie some twenty miles toward a heavy body of timber in the distance, then entered a rocky cedar-grove about six miles in width. As our horses were not shod, their feet became sore and tender while passing over this rough road. We then entered a vast forest of beautiful pines. Our pilot told us that, if he was not mistaken, we should find in the pine-timber an Indian trail; and, sure enough, we soon came to a plain horse-path through the open forest. We followed this trail until sunset, and encamped in a small, dry prairie, having traveled all day beneath a hot October sun without water. Our little party were sober, solemn, and silent. No one ate anything except myself, and I only ate a very small piece of cold bread.

We left this dry and desolate camp early next morning. About 10 o'clock one of our party saw a deer, and followed it to a beautiful little stream of water, flowing from the hills into the forest. We spent the remainder of the day on the banks of this clear branch,

drinking water and eating a badger. When I first drank the water it had no pleasant taste, but seemed like rain-water; but my natural thirst soon returned, and I found that no luxury was equal to water to a thirsty man. We sent out three or four hunters for game; but they returned about 2 P. M. with a large badger. This was all the meat we had. We dressed and cooked it well; and, to our keen and famished appetites, it was splendid food. The foot of the badger, the tail of the beaver, the ear of the hog, and the foot of the elephant are superior eating. I have myself eaten of all but the last, and can speak from personal knowledge; and, as to the foot of the elephant, I can give Sir Samuel Baker as my authority, in his "Explorations," etc.

We left next morning, thoroughly refreshed and rested; and we had not traveled more than ten miles when we came in sight of Pitt River, a tributary of the Sacramento. It was here but a small creek, with a valley about half a mile wide. When we had approached near the stream, to our utter surprise and astonishment, we found a new wagon-road. Who made this road we could not at first imagine. A considerable number of those coming to California with pack-animals decided to follow our trail, rather than come by the usual pack-route. These packers had overtaken us the preceding evening, and were with us when we discovered this new wagon-road. It so happened that one of them had been in California, and knew old Peter Lassen. This man was a sensible fellow, and at once gave it as his opinion that this road had been made by a small party of immigrants whom Lassen had persuaded to come to California by a new route that would enter the great valley of the Sacramento at or near Lassen's rancho. This conjectural explanation proved to be the true one.

So soon as these packers found this road, they left us. No amount of argument could induce them to remain with us. They thought our progress too slow. This left our little party of road-hunters alone in a wild Indian country, the wagons being some distance behind.

We followed the new road slowly. One day, while passing through open pine-woods, we saw an Indian, some two hundred yards ahead of us. He was intent on hunting, and did not see us until we were within a hundred yards, charging down upon him with our horses at full speed. He saw that escape by flight was impossible; so he hid under a clump of bushes. We soon came up, and by signs ordered him to come out from his place of concealment. This command he understood and promptly obeyed. He was a stout, active young man, apparently twenty-five years of age, and had a large gray squirrel under his belt, which he had killed with his bow and arrow. He evidently feared that we would take his life; but we treated him kindly, spent some time conversing with him as well as we could by signs, and then left him in peace.

From the point where we struck the Lassen road, it continued down the river in a western direction ten or fifteen miles until the river turned to the south and ran through a cañon, the road ascending the tall hills, and continuing about west for twenty to thirty miles, when it came again to and crossed the river. The same day that we saw the Indian we encamped, after dark, on a high bluff above the river. We had had no water to drink since morning, and had traveled late in the hope of finding a good encampment.

The night was so dark, and the bluff was so steep and rough, that we feared to attempt to go to the river for water, though we could distinctly hear the roar of

the stream, as it dashed among the rocks below. At length, one of our men determined to go for water. He took with him a small tin bucket; and, after having been absent a considerable time, he returned with the bucket about one fourth full, having spilt most of the water on his return to camp. The amount for each of us was so small that our thirst was increased rather than diminished.

The next morning we left early, and followed the road to the crossing of the river, where we arrived about noon. Here we spent the remainder of that day. The valley at this point was about a mile and a half wide, and without timber; and the descent into it was down a tall hill, which was not only steep, but rocky and heavily timbered. In the middle of this valley there was a solitary ridge about a mile long and a quarter of a mile wide at its base, and some two hundred feet high, covered with rocks of various sizes. We determined to discover, if we could, a new and easier route down the hill. For this purpose we ascended this ridge, from the summit of which we could have an excellent view of the face of the hill, down which our wagons must come.

While we were quietly seated upon the rocks, we saw an Indian emerge from the edge of the timber at the foot of the hill, about three fourths of a mile distant, and start in a brisk run across the intervening prairie toward us. I directed the men to sit perfectly still until the Indian should be hidden from our view, and then to separate, and let him fall into the ambush. We occupied the highest point of this lonely ridge, and we knew he would make for the same spot, for the purpose of overlooking our camp. We waited until he came to the foot of the ridge, from which position he could not see us; and then we divided our men into

two parties, each party taking up a different position. Very soon the Indian came within about thirty feet of one of our parties, and suddenly found himself confronted with four rifles pointed at him, with a command by signs to stop. Of course it was a perfect surprise to the poor old Indian. He was about sixty years old, was dressed in buckskin, had long coarse hair and dim eyes, and his teeth were worn down to the gums.

Notwithstanding the suddenness and completeness of the surprise, the old hero was as brave and cool as possible. I had with me only an axe with which to blaze the new and better way, in case we found it, and was at first some little distance from the Indian. As I came toward him with the axe on my shoulder, he made the most vehement motions for me to stop and not come any nearer. I saw he was apprehensive that I would take off his head with the axe, and at once stopped and threw it aside. At first he would allow no one to come near him, but coolly wet his fingers with his tongue, and then deliberately dipped them into the sand at the foot of the rock on which he sat; and, with his trusty bow and arrow in his hands, he looked the men full in the face, as much as to say: "I know you have me in your power; but I wish you to understand that I am prepared to sell my life as dearly as possible." I never saw a greater display of calm, heroic, and determined courage than was shown by this old Indian. He was much braver than the young Indian we had seen the day before.

One of our men, who was a blustering fellow and who was for displaying his courage when there was no danger, proposed that we should kill the old Indian. I at once put a damper upon that cowardly proposition, by stating to the fellow that if he wanted to kill the

Indian he could have a chance to do so in a fair and equal single combat with him. This proposition, as I anticipated, he promptly declined. I was satisfied that there was no fight in him.

After some time, we were permitted one at a time to approach him. We offered him the pipe of peace, which he accepted. He would let our men look at his bow and arrows one at a time, never parting with both of them at once. He was evidently suspicious of treachery. We staid with him some time, treating him kindly, and then left him sitting on his rock. This was the last we saw of him. We considered this mode of treating the Indians the most judicious, as it displayed our power and at the same time our magnanimity. We proved that we intended no harm to them, but were mere passers through their country. They evidently appreciated our motives, and the result was, that we had not the slightest difficulty with the Indians.

After crossing the river, the road bore south ; it being impossible to follow down the stream, as the mountains came too close to it. Next morning we left our camp and followed the road south about ten miles, when we came to a beautiful grassy valley, covered with scattering pine-timber. This valley was about two miles wide where the road struck it, and ran west, the very direction we wished to go. It seemed a defile passing at right angles through the Sierra Nevada Mountains, as if designed for a level road into the Sacramento valley.

We were much pleased at the prospect, and followed this splendid road rapidly about eight miles, when, to our great mortification, we came to the termination of this lovely valley in front of a tall, steep mountain, which could not be ascended except by some

creature that had either wings or claws. Upon examination, we found that old Peter Lassen and his party had marched west along this narrow valley to its abrupt termination, and then had turned about and marched back to near the point where they entered it, thus wasting some ten or fifteen miles of travel. The two portions of the road going into and coming out of this pretty valley were not more than half a mile apart; but this fact was unknown to us until after we had brought up against that impassable mountain.

This was a perplexing and distressing situation. Our own pilot did not like this route, as it was not going in the right direction. How to get out of this line of travel, and get again upon the river, was the question. We spent the greater part of one day in exploring a new route, but found it impracticable. In our explorations, we found a lava-bed some two miles wide. It was clear to us that old Peter Lassen was lost, except as to courses, and was wholly unacquainted with the particular route he was going. Our own pilot knew about as little as Lassen, if not less. Our wagons, we knew, would soon overtake us; and we determined to follow Lassen's road ten or fifteen miles farther, to see if it turned west. Several of us started on foot, and found that the road, after leaving the valley, went south about ten miles, and then turned due west, running through open pine-timber and over good ground. We returned to camp in the night, and decided that we would follow Lassen's road at all hazards. We awaited the arrival of our wagons, and then set forward. We found the road an excellent one, going in the right direction; and we soon found ourselves upon the summit of the Sierra Nevada Mountains.

The summit was almost a dead level, covered with

stunted pines. We passed between peaks. The ascent on the eastern side was very gradual and easy. We encamped one evening on the summit near a small lake; and it was so cold that night that ice formed along its margin. This was about the 20th of October, 1848. We knew when we had passed the summit, from the fact that the streams flowed west. Though the beds of the streams were dry at that season of the year, we could tell which way the water had run, from the drift-wood lodged in places.

While on Pitt River, we knew from the camp-fires that Lassen's party had ten wagons; and from all appearances we were pretty sure that they were some thirty days ahead of us.

OVERTAKE PETER LASSEN AND HIS PARTY — ARRIVAL IN THE SACRAMENTO VALLEY.

We pressed on vigorously, and soon reached the wide strip of magnificent pine-timber found on the western side of the Sierra Nevada. We had not proceeded many miles, after entering this body of timber, before I saw a large, newly-blazed pine-tree standing near the road. Approaching I found these words marked in pencil : "Look under a stone below for a letter." It was a stone lying upon the surface of the ground, and partly embedded in it. It had been removed, the letter placed in its bed, and then replaced. No Indian would ever have thought of looking under that stone for anything. I did as directed, and found a letter addressed to me by my old friend and law-partner in Oregon City, A. L. Lovejoy, Esq., one of the packers who had gone ahead of us. The letter stated that they had overtaken old Peter Lassen and a portion

of his party, lost in the mountains and half starved. That very evening we overtook Lassen and half of his party in the condition described by Lovejoy. In about eight days after we had first seen Lassen's road, we had overtaken him.

Peter Lassen had met the incoming immigration that fall, and had induced the people belonging to ten wagons to come by his new route. This route he had not previously explored. He only had a correct idea of the courses, and some general knowledge of the country through which they must pass. So long as this small party were traveling through prairies, or open woods, they could make fair progress; but, the moment they came to heavy timber, they had not force enough to open the road. After reaching the wide strip of timber already mentioned, they converted their ten wagons into ten carts, so that they could make short turns, and thus drive around the fallen timber. This they found a slow mode of travel. One half of the party became so incensed against Lassen that his life was in great danger. The whole party had been without any bread for more than a month, and had during that time lived alone on poor beef. They were, indeed, objects of pity. I never saw people so worn down and so emaciated as these poor immigrants.

The people that belonged to five of the carts had abandoned them, packed their poor oxen, and left the other half of the party, a short time before we reached those that remained with the other five carts and with Lassen. We gave them plenty of provisions, and told them to follow us, and we would open the way ourselves. Of course, they greatly rejoiced. How their sunken eyes sparkled with delight! Our pilot, Thomas McKay, overtook an old woman on foot, driving before her a

packed ox down a long, steep hill. When he approached near to her, he made a noise that caused her to stop and look back. "Who are you, and where did you come from?" she asked in a loud voice. He informed her that he was one of a party of a hundred and fifty men, who were on their way from Oregon, with wagons and ox-teams, to the California gold mines. "Have you got any flour?" "Yes, madam, plenty." "You are like an angel from Heaven!" And she raised a loud and thrilling shout that rang through that primeval forest.

Lassen and our pilot followed the trail of the packers for some twenty or thirty miles, as it passed over good ground, but through heavy timber. We had from sixty to eighty stout men to open the road, while the others were left to drive the teams. We plied our axes with skill, vigor and success, and opened the route about as fast as the teams could well follow.

At length the pack-trail descended a long, steep hill, to a creek at the bottom of an immense ravine. Old Peter Lassen insisted that our wagons should keep on the top of the ridges, and not go down to the water. When the first portion of the train arrived at this point, they had to stop some time on the summit of the hill. How to get out of this position without descending into the ravine below was a perplexing question. Our pilots had been to the creek, and would not let us go down the hill. In looking around for a way out of this dilemma they discovered a strip of ground, about thirty feet wide, between the heads of two immense and impassable ravines, and connecting the ridge we were compelled to leave with another. It was like an isthmus connecting two continents. Over this narrow natural bridge we passed in safety.

That evening a large portion of our party encamped

on the summit of a dry ridge, among the intermixed pine- and oak-timber. They had traveled all day, under a hot October sun, without water. This was the first time those with the wagons were compelled to do without water at night. They chained their oxen to their wagons, as the animals would have gone to water had they been turned out. The ox has a keen scent, and will smell water at the distance of one or two miles. It was another sober, solemn, and silent time. Scarcely a word was spoken, and not a mouthful eaten.

By daybreak next morning we were off, and had only gone about five miles when we came to the edge of the pine-forest. From this elevated point we had a most admirable view. Below us, at the seeming distance of ten, but the real distance of twenty miles, lay the broad and magnificent valley of the Sacramento, gleaming in the bright and genial sunshine ; and beyond, and in the dim distance, rose the grand blue outlines of the Coast Range. The scene was most beautiful to us, thirsty as we were. How our hearts leaped for joy ! That was our Canaan. Once in that valley, and our serious difficulties, our doubts and fears, would be among the things of the past. But the last of our trials was the most severe. We had still to descend to that desired valley over a very rough road.

From the place where we stood, we could see three tall, narrow, rocky ridges, with deep ravines between, running toward the valley. Neither our pilots nor any of us knew which of the three ridges to take, and we had no time to explore. We contemplated the scene for a few moments, and then looked down the ridges for a short time, and chose the middle one at a venture, not knowing what obstructions and sufferings were before us. We had in our company two classes. One

was eager to enter the valley as early as possible, while the other had no desire for haste. I belonged to the latter class. I had lived and suffered long enough to have acquired some caution.

The last camp before the one where a portion of our people had done without water had plenty of grass, fuel, and water. We had been rapidly descending the western side of the Sierra Nevada for some days before we overtook Lassen and his party; and we knew that we could not be very far from the Sacramento valley. Besides this evidence, we found the red oaks appearing among the pines; and this was a conclusive proof that we were not far from that valley. I saw that there was no necessity that the wagons should follow our pilots so closely. Our true policy would have been to remain where we first found the oak-timber until our pilots had explored and selected the route into the valley. We could have safely remained at that good camp a month longer than we did. But one portion of our people had the gold-fever too badly to be controlled. We who were more patient and cautious were willing that those hasty and ambitious men should go on ahead of us, if they desired to do so. Our two classes were well matched, like the man's oxen, one of which wanted to do all the work, and the other was perfectly willing that he should.

I had directed the men in charge of my wagons and teams to remain at that good camp until they should receive other orders. I then assisted to open the road to the natural bridge mentioned. After that, the road ran through open woods and over good ground to the point where the pines terminated. I determined to leave the foremost wagons at that point and return on foot to the good camp, where I arrived in the evening. Next morn-

ing early I took my best horse and started on after the foremost wagons, deciding that my own wagons and teams should remain where they were until I *knew* they could reach the valley by that or some other route. The distance from the point where I left the foremost wag ons to the good camp was about fifteen miles. About 10 o'clock A. M. I arrived at that point, which I had left the morning before ; and, looking down toward the valley, I could dimly discern some of the white-sheeted wagons on their dry and rugged way to the valley. I followed them as fast as I could, at a brisk trot. At the distance of about eight miles I came to an immense mass of rock, which completely straddled the narrow ridge and totally obstructed the way. This huge obstacle could not be removed in time, and the wagons had to pass around it. They were let down the left side of the ridge by ropes to a bench, then passed along this bench to a point beyond the rock, and were then drawn up to the top of the ridge again by doubling teams.

I passed on about six miles farther, and came to another huge mass of rock entirely across the top of the ridge. But in this case the sides of the ridge were not so steep, and the wagons had easily passed across the ravine to the ridge on the right. Soon, however, the ridges sank down to the surface, leaving no further difficulties in the way except the loose rocks, which lay thick upon the ground. These rocks were of all sizes, from that of a man's hat to that of a large barrel, and constituted a serious obstruction to loaded wagons. We could avoid the larger rocks, as they were not so many ; but not the smaller ones, as they were numerous and lay thick upon the ground. In passing over this part of our route two of the wagons were broken down.

About noon I met one of our party who had been to

the valley, and was on his return to the good camp, where his wagons and teams as well as mine were left. He reported to me that the route was practicable; and I sent word to my men to come on the next day.

I arrived at the camp in the valley, near a beautiful stream of water, a little after dark, having traveled that day about thirty-five miles. I could hear the wagons coming down that rough, rocky hill until midnight. Some of the people belonging to the foremost wagons had been without water nearly two days.

Next morning I started on foot to meet my wagons, and found them on the middle ridge, this side the first huge mass of rock, about sundown. They had plenty of water for drinking purposes, and chained up the oxen to the wagons. Next day they came into camp in good time, without suffering and without loss.

ARRIVE AT THE HOUSE OF PETER LASSEN—ORIGIN OF THE TERM "PROSPECTING"—ARRIVAL IN THE MINES —MINING.

We left the first camp in the valley the next morning, and, after traveling a distance of eight miles, arrived at the rancho of old Peter Lassen. The old pilot was in the best of spirits, and killed for us a fat beef; and we remained at his place two or three days, feasting and resting. All organization in our company ceased upon our arrival in the Sacramento valley. Each gold-hunter went his own way, to seek his own fortune. They soon after scattered in various directions.

A day or two after we left Lassen's place, we were surprised and very much amused upon learning that the packers who had left us in such a hurry on Pitt River were coming on behind us. As stated on page 266,

they had descended a long steep hill to a creek at the bottom of an immense ravine. They followed down this stream west for some miles, when they came to an obstruction in their route that they could not possibly pass, and were compelled to return up the stream east until they found a place where they could get out of this ravine on its northern side. They came to the creek on its southern side, and thought their best chance to escape was to be found on its northern bank. In this way they were detained in the mountains three or four days longer than we were. They had plenty of provisions, and had suffered but little. We therefore rallied them heartily, all of which they bore with the best of humor. Our ox-teams had beaten their pack-animals, thus proving that the race is not always to the swift.

In passing down the valley, we encamped one evening near the house of an old settler named Potter. He lived in a very primitive style. His yard, in front of his adobe building, was full of strips of fresh beef, hung upon lines to dry. He was very talkative and boastful. He had been in the mines, had employed Indians to work for him, and had grown suddenly rich ; and, as his head was naturally light, it had been easily turned. He came to our camp and talked with us until about midnight. It was here that I first heard the word "prospecting" used. At first I could not understand what Potter meant by the term, but I listened patiently to our garrulous guest, until I discovered its meaning. When gold was first discovered in California, and any one went out searching for new placers, they would say, "He has gone to hunt for new gold-diggings." But, as this fact had to be so often repeated, some practical, sensible, economical man called the whole process "prospecting." So perfectly evident was the utility

of this new word that it was at once universally adopted.

We arrived in a few days at Captain Sutter's Hock Farm, so called from a small tribe of Indians in that vicinity. I called on the agent, and made some inquiries as to the mines. He replied that there was no material difference between the different mining localities, so far as he knew. Those on the Yuba River he knew to be good.

We forded the Feather River a few miles below Hock Farm, and then took up this stream toward the Yuba, and encamped a little before sundown near the rancho of Michael Nye. Dr. Atkinson, then practicing his profession in the valley, came to our camp. I inquired of him who resided in that house. He replied, "Mr. Nye." "What is his Christian name?" "Michael." I had known Michael Nye in Missouri, and my brother-in-law John P. Rogers (who was with me) and Nye had been intimate friends when they were both young men. We at once called upon Nye at his house. He received us most kindly. He and his brother-in-law William Foster, with their families, were living together.

Next morning we left for the Yuba; and, after traveling some eight or ten miles, we arrived at noon on the brow of the hill overlooking Long's Bar. Below, glowing in the hot sunshine, and in the narrow valley of this lovely and rapid stream, we saw the canvas tents and the cloth shanties of the miners. There was but one log-cabin in the camp. There were about eighty men, three women, and five children at this place. The scene was most beautiful to us. It was the first mining locality we had ever seen, and here we promptly decided to pitch our tent. We drove our wagons and teams

across the river into the camp, and turned out our oxen and horses to graze and rest.

We arrived at the mines November 5, 1848; and the remainder of the day I spent looking around the camp. No miner paid the slightest attention to me, or said a word. They were all too busy. At last I ventured to ask one of them, whose appearance pleased me, whether he could see the particles of gold in the dirt. Though dressed in the garb of a rude miner, he was a gentleman and a scholar. He politely replied that he could; and, taking a handful of dirt, he blew away the fine dust with his breath, and showed me a scale of gold, about as thick as thin paper, and as large as a flax-seed. This was entirely new to me.

In the evening, when the miners had quit work and returned to their tents and shanties, I found a number of old acquaintances, some from Missouri and others from Oregon. Among those from Missouri were Dr. John P. Long and his brother Willis, for whom this bar was named. I had not seen either of them for about six years, though our families were connected by marriage — Dr. Benjamin Long, another brother, having married my youngest sister, Mary Burnett. I was perfectly at home here.

Next day my brother-in-law John P. Rogers, my nephew Horace Burnett (both of whom had come with me from Oregon), and myself purchased a mining location, fronting on the river about twenty feet, and reaching back to the foot of the hill about fifty feet. We bought on credit, and agreed to pay for it three hundred dollars in gold dust, at the rate of sixteen dollars per ounce. We at once unloaded the two wagons, and sent them and the oxen and horses back to Nye's rancho, where we made our headquarters.

As already stated, I had brought from Oregon new and suitable plank for a rocker, in the bottoms of my wagon-beds. The only material we had to purchase for our gold-rocker was one small sheet of zinc. I went to work upon the rocker, which I finished in one day; and then we three set to work on the claim with a will. I dug the dirt, Horace Burnett rocked the rocker, and John P. Rogers threw the water upon the dirt containing the gold. Within about three or four days we were making twenty dollars each daily, and we soon paid for our claim. We rose by daybreak, ate our breakfast by sunrise, worked until noon; then took dinner, went to work again about half-past twelve, quit work at sundown, and slept under a canvas tent on the hard ground.

In the summer months the heat was intense in this deep, narrow, rocky, sandy valley. The mercury would rise at times to 118° in the shade. Dr. John P. Long told me that the sand and rocks became so hot during the day, that a large dog he had with him would suffer for water rather than go to the river for it before night. The pain of burned feet was greater to the poor dog than the pain of thirst. After our arrival the days were not so hot.

This was a new and interesting position to me. After I had been there a few days I could tell, when the miners quit work in the evening, what success they had had during the day. When I met a miner with a silent tongue and downcast look, I knew he had not made more than eight or ten dollars; when I met one with a contented but not excited look, I knew he had made from sixteen to twenty dollars; but when I met one with a glowing countenance, and quick, high, vigorous step, so that the rocks were not much if at all in his way, I knew he had made from twenty to fifty dollars.

His tongue was so flexible and glib that he would not permit me to pass in silence, but must stop me and tell of his success. Ordinary hands were paid twelve dollars a day, and boarded and lodged by the employer. I knew one young man who had been paid such wages for some time, but finally became disgusted and declared he would not work for such wages. It cost a dollar each to have shirts washed, and other things in proportion. There was no starch in *that* camp, and shirts were not ironed.

THE DONNER PARTY.

During my stay in the mines I was several times at Nye's house, and on one occasion I was there three days. I became well acquainted with William Foster and his family. Foster, his wife, and Mrs. Nye were of the Donner party, who suffered so much in the winter of 1846–'7.

Mrs. Nye did not talk much, not being a talkative woman, and being younger than Mrs. Foster, her sister. Mrs. Foster was then about twenty-three years old. She had a fair education, and possessed the finest narrative powers. I never met with any one, not even excepting Robert Newell of Oregon, who could narrate events as well as she. She was not more accurate and full in her narrative, but a better talker, than Newell. For hour after hour, I would listen in silence to her sad narrative. Her husband was then in good circumstances, and they had no worldly matter to give them pain but their recollections of the past. Foster was a man of excellent common sense, and his intellect had not been affected, like those of many others. His statement was clear, consistent, and intelligible. In the fall of 1849 I became intimately acquainted with William

H. Eddy, another member of the party. From these four persons I mainly obtained my information on this melancholy subject. I can not state all the minute circumstances and incidents, but can only give the substance as I remember it ; for I write from memory alone.

The Donner party consisted of about eighty immigrants, including men, women, and children. They were so called because the men who bore that name were the leading persons of the party. They decided for themselves to cross the Sierra Nevada by a new road. L. W. Hastings, then residing at Sutter's Fort, went out to meet the incoming immigration of that fall, and advised the Donner party not to attempt to open a new route ; but his advice was disregarded. He returned to the fort and reported the fact to Captain Sutter, who sent out two Indians, with five mules packed with provisions, to meet the party.

The party had arrived at a small lake, since called Donner Lake, situated a short distance from the present site of Truckee City, and some fifteen miles from Lake Tahoe, and had erected two log-cabins upon the margin of Donner Lake, when the Indians arrived with the mules and provisions. This was in the month of November, 1846. Up to this time there had been several comparatively light falls of snow. Foster said he proposed to slaughter all the animals, including the fat mules sent out by Captain Sutter, and save their flesh for food. This could readily have been done then, and the people could have subsisted until relieved in the spring. But the immigrants were not in a condition to accept or reject this proposition at once. They were unacquainted with the climate, could not well understand how snow could fall to the depth of twenty or

thirty feet, and were so much worn down by the tedium of the long journey, and the absence of fresh meat and vegetables, that they were not prepared to decide wisely or to act promptly. Besides, the idea of living upon the flesh of mules and poor cattle was naturally repugnant to them. It is very probable that many of them considered such food unhealthy, and that, crowded as they were into two cabins, the use of such poor food might produce severe sickness among them, and many would die of disease.

While they were discussing and considering this proposition, a terrible storm came up one evening, and snow fell to the depth of about six feet during the night. The poor animals fled before the driving storm, and all perished ; and next morning there was one wide, desolate waste of snow, and not a carcass could be found. The little supply of provisions they had on hand, including that sent by Captain Sutter, they saw could not last them long. They now fully comprehended their dreadful situation. It was a terrible struggle for existence.

It was soon decided to start a party across the mountains, on snow-shoes. This party consisted of ten men, including the two Indians, five women, and a boy twelve years old, the brother of Mrs. Foster. I once knew the names of the eight white men, but at this time I can only remember those of William H. Eddy and William Foster. The women were Mrs. Foster, Mrs. McCutchin, Mrs. ——, then a widow, but subsequently Mrs. Nye, Mrs. Pile, a widow, and Miss Mary ——, sister of Mrs. Foster, and subsequently wife of Charles Covillaud, one of the original proprietors of Marysville, so named for her.

This little party left the cabins on snow-shoes, with one suit of clothes each, a few blankets, one axe, one

rifle with ammunition, and a small supply of provisions. The summit of the mountain where they crossed it was about fifty miles wide, and was covered with snow to the depth of ten to fifteen feet; and they could only travel from five to eight miles a day. On the summit, and for some distance beyond it, not an animal could be found, as the wild game always instinctively fled before the snows of winter to the foot-hills, where the snows are lighter, and where they could obtain food and escape from their enemies by flight. In the spring the wild grazing animals ascend the mountain as the snows melt, to crop the fresh grass and escape the flies.

For the first few days they made good progress; but while they were comparatively strong they could kill no game, because none could be found, and their provisions were rapidly consumed. When they had reached the western side of the summit, they encamped, as usual, on the top of the snow. They would cut logs of green wood about six feet long, and with them make a platform on the snow, and upon this make their fire of dry wood. Such a foundation would generally last as long as was necessary; but on this occasion it was composed of small logs, as the poor people were too weak from starvation to cut and handle larger ones; and there came up in the evening a driving, blinding snow-storm, which lasted all that night and the next day and night. New snow fell to the depth of several feet. They maintained a good fire for a time, to keep themselves from freezing; but the small foundation-logs were soon burnt nearly through, so that the heat of the fire melted the snow beneath, letting them down gradually toward the ground, while the storm above was falling thick and fast. Toward midnight they found themselves in a circular well in the snow about

eight feet deep, with the ice-cold water beginning to rise in the bottom. After the foundation was gone, they kept alive the fire by setting the wood on end and kindling the fire on the top. While they were in this condition, one of the Indians, who had been sitting and nodding next the snow-wall until he was almost frozen, made a sudden and desperate rush for the fire, upsetting and putting it out.

Eddy urged them to quit this well of frozen death, as it was impossible to live where they were, with their feet in ice-water. They all climbed out of the well, spread one blanket on the top of the snow, then seated themselves on this blanket, back to back, and covered their heads with the others. In this painful position they remained the rest of that night, all the next day and night, and until some time after sunrise the last morning. During this time four or five of their number perished, one of whom was the boy. Mrs. Foster spoke of this young hero with the greatest feeling. His patience and resignation were of the martyr type. When they were reduced to half a biscuit each, he insisted that she should eat his portion as well as her own; but this she refused.

From this scene of death the survivors proceeded on their melancholy journey down the western side of the mountain. That evening, after they had encamped and kindled a blazing fire, one of the men, who had borne the day's travel well, suddenly fell down by the fire, where he was warming himself, and expired. The cold, bracing air and the excitement and exertion of travel had kept him alive during the day; but when he became warm his vital energies ceased. This is often the case under like circumstances. I have understood that deaths occurred in this manner among Fremont's men.

while making the trip from Oregon to California in the winter of 1843–'44. At this camp another of the men sat down by a pine-tree, leaned himself against it, and died.

The remainder of this suffering party continued their journey. All the other men dropped off one after another, at intervals, except Eddy and Foster. When they had almost reached the point of utter despair, Eddy saw a deer, and made a good shot, killing the animal. This supplied them with food for a few days. After it was consumed, they met with some Indians, who furnished them with a small quantity of provisions.

At length they arrived at the last encampment, and within six or eight miles of Johnson's rancho, on the eastern side of the Sacramento valley. Next morning Foster was unable to continue the journey, and refused to make another effort to walk. Eddy was the stouter man of the two, and he proceeded on his tottering course, leaving Foster and the five women at the camp. It was all Eddy could do to walk; but, most fortunately, he soon found two friendly Indians, who kindly led him to Johnson's place, Eddy walking between them, with one hand on the shoulder of each Indian.

They arrived at Johnson's house in the afternoon. Johnson was then a bachelor, but he had a man and his wife living with him. This lady was an admirable woman, full of humanity, and possessed of excellent sense, firmness, and patience. She knew from Eddy's condition what the poor sufferers needed. There were also several families of late immigrants residing temporarily in that vicinity. About ten men promptly assembled, and started for the camp, taking with them everything that was necessary.

The relief-men were piloted by the two humane Indians, and reached the camp a little after dark. Foster said that, when they heard the men coming through the brush toward the camp, the women began to cry most piteously, saying they were enemies coming to kill them; but Foster comforted and pacified them by declaring that the men coming must be friends. The relief-men soon came up, and were so much affected by the woful spectacle that for some time they said not a word, but only gazed and wept. The poor creatures before them, hovering around that small camp-fire, had been snowed on and rained on, had been lacerated, starved, and worn down, until they were but breathing skeletons. The clothes they wore were nothing but filthy rags, and their faces had not been washed or their heads combed for a month; and the intellectual expression of the human countenance had almost vanished. No case of human suffering could have been more terrible. No wonder that brave and hardy men wept like children.

Of all the physical evils that waylay and beset the thorny path of human life, none can be more appalling than starvation. It is not a sudden and violent assault upon the vital powers, that instinctive and intellectual courage may successfully resist; but it is an inexorable undermining and slow wasting away of the physical and mental energies, inch by inch. No courage, no intellect, no martyr-spirit can possibly withstand this deprivation. When there is an *entire* deprivation of food it is said that the greatest pangs of hunger are felt on the third day. After that, the stomach, being entirely empty, contracts to a very small space, and ceases to beg for food; and the sufferer dies from exhaustion, without any violent pain. But, when there is an insufficient supply of food, the severe pangs of hunger must

be prolonged, and the aggregate amount of suffering before death is most probably increased.

The relief-party did everything required for the poor sufferers, and next morning carried them to Johnson's house. The lady in charge was careful to give them at first a limited quantity of food at a time. It required all her firmness and patience to resist their passionate entreaties for more food. When the poor, starved creatures could not persuade they violently abused the good lady because she did not comply with their demands. Eddy said that he himself abused her in harsh terms. All this she bore with the kind patience of a good mother, waiting upon a sick and peevish child.

I expressed my surprise to Eddy and Foster that all the women escaped, while eight out of the ten men perished, saying that I supposed it was owing to the fact that the men, especially at the beginning of the journey, had performed most of the labor. They said that, at the start, the men may have performed a little more labor than the women; but, taken altogether, the women performed more than the men, if there was any difference. After the men had become too weak to carry the gun, it was carried by the women. Women seem to be more hopeful than men in cases of extreme distress; and their organization seems to be superior to that of men. A mother will sit up with and wait upon a sick child much longer than the father could possibly do.

The Eddy party were about thirty days in making the trip. Other parties afterward left the cabins, and made their way into the settlement, after losing a considerable portion of their number on the way. Many died at the cabins from starvation. Forty-four of the Donner party escaped, and thirty-six perished.

A LONELY GRAVE — DEATH OF DAVID RAY—JOHN C. MC PHERSON.

The first Sunday after my arrival in the mines, I was strolling on the side of the hill back of the camp, among the lonely pines, when I came suddenly upon a newly-made grave. At its head there was a rude wooden cross, and from this symbol of Christianity I knew it was the grave of a Catholic. I never learned anything of the history of the deceased. He was, most probably, some obscure and humble person. He had died and was buried before my arrival.

> "But the sound of the church-going bell
> These valleys and rocks never heard;
> Or sighed at the sound of a knell,
> Or smiled when a Sabbath appeared."

Another death occurred in camp, and while I was there. It was that of David Ray. He was about thirty-five years of age, and his wife about thirty. They had five children, the eldest a daughter about twelve. They started from the State of Indiana in the spring of 1848, intending to locate in some one of the agricultural valleys of California, not then knowing that gold had been discovered. But when they arrived they determined to stop in the mines for a time, and thus came to Long's Bar, on the Yuba River.

Mr. Ray's business partner, Mr. Wright, was about the same age, unmarried, and sober, honest, industrious, and generous. He assisted Ray to build the only log-cabin in the camp, for his wife and children, without charge. This house was a rude structure of one room, about sixteen feet square, with a clapboard roof, wooden

chimney, and dirt floor. Yet it was the palace of the camp, and was the only place where one could enjoy a cheerful fire without being annoyed by the smoke. At all the tents and cloth shanties we had to make our fires in the open air.

About two weeks after my arrival Mr. Ray was attacked with fever, and died within a week. Neither he nor his widow had any relatives in California, and all the people of the camp were late acquaintances except Mr. Wright. Our tent was near Mr. Ray's house, and we soon became acquainted. He and his wife were devoted Methodists. She was a small, delicate woman, with a sweet musical voice and an eloquent tongue.

We buried him among the stately pines, in the open woods, where the winds might murmur a solemn and lonely requiem to his memory. All the people of the camp left their work and attended the burial; and I never witnessed a more sorrowful scene. There were no tearless eyes in that assemblage. No clergyman was present; but at the lonely grave of her husband Mrs. Ray made an impromptu address, which affected me so much that I soon wrote out its substance, preserving her own expressions so far as I could remember them. The following is a copy of what I then wrote:

O David! thou art cold and lifeless. Little dost thou know the sorrows thy poor and friendless and sickly wife now suffers. Thou art gone from me and from our children for ever. Thou wert ever kind to me; you loved me from my girlhood. O friends! he was a man without reproach, beloved by all who knew him. He was a just man, honest in all his dealings. He did unto others as he wished they should do unto him. He defrauded no one. He was a pious and steady man; a profane oath had never escaped his lips even from a boy; he was never found at the grog-shop or the gambling-table. He it

was who lifted the prayerful hands. His creed was peace. He died in his right mind, with a conscience void of reproach, and committed his children to my charge. The only thing that wounded his conscience was the reflection that, on the road from Indiana to this country, he was compelled to do things that grieved his righteous soul—he was compelled to labor on the Sabbath day. But he is gone to a better world, where his weary spirit will be at rest. Oh! if he had only died in a Christian land! but the thought of his being buried in this lonesome and wicked place! He has left me alone in a land of strangers, a poor, sickly, weakly woman. Who shall now read to me from the Bible, and wait upon me in my sickness? For months and years he waited upon his sickly wife, without a murmur. He was ever a tender husband to me, but he has gone and left me. Who is there here to sympathize with me? Ah me, what shall I do?

While in the mines I became acquainted with John C. McPherson, a young, genial spirit from old Scotland. He was a generous soul, and cared little for wealth. On Christmas eve he composed a very pretty song, beginning "Yuba, dear Yuba." He has since written many poetical pieces, and many prose communications for the newspapers. One thing can be said of genial, kindly McPherson, that there is not a particle of malice in his composition. No one ever thought of suing him for libel, for he never wrote a harsh word of any one, living or dead. No one then in the mines except McPherson had poetic fire enough in his soul to write a song. We spent many pleasant evenings together, around the camp-fire, at Long's Bar.

CHAPTER VII.

LEAVE THE MINES—ARRIVE AT SUTTER'S FORT—BECOME THE AGENT OF JOHN A. SUTTER, JR.—CAPTAIN JOHN A. SUTTER—DISCOVERY OF GOLD.

I REMAINED in the mines until December 19, 1848. In the mean time I had sold my wagons and teams, and, altogether, had accumulated means enough to defray my expenses for six months. I knew that there must be business in my profession, and I found it would take me many long years to make enough in the mines to pay my debts. I therefore decided to quit the mines, and started with the intent to come to San Francisco; but, upon my arrival at Sutter's Fort, I determined to stop there.

Six of us left the camp at noon in an empty, uncovered wagon, drawn by oxen. It was a beautiful day, and that evening we drove to Johnson's ranch, which was about forty miles from the Fort. Next morning the oxen were missing, and were not found until about two hours before sunset. We at once set forward for Sutter's Fort. The wind commenced blowing hard from the south, and rain began to fall briskly about dark. About midnight the wind suddenly changed to the north, blowing quite hard and cold, and snow fell to the depth of about three inches. We had determined

not to stop until we reached the Fort. Each of us took his turn at driving the team; and we thus reached the Fort about 10 o'clock A. M., December 21. Our journey was a most uncomfortable one, as we could neither keep ourselves warm nor sleep. We had traveled forty miles from Johnson's place without food, sleep, or rest.

I found a number of old friends at the Fort; and among them were Major Samuel J. Hensley, Major P. B. Reading, and Dr. William M. Carpenter. Dr. Carpenter had rented a small room in the Fort, and I proposed that we should keep our offices together, each paying half the rent and other expenses. As our professions did not clash, he readily assented to this, and we slept in the same rude bed, made by himself. We boarded at the hotel; and in the morning I cut the wood and made the fire, while the doctor swept out the office and made up the bed. The doctor made about six hundred dollars a week by his practice and from the sale of medicines. He charged sixteen dollars for each dose or vial of medicine, or box of pills.

I had only been at the Fort a few days when John A. Sutter, Jr., in whose name the Sutter grant of eleven leagues then stood, proposed to employ me as his attorney and agent. The terms agreed upon between us were such as his mercantile partner, Major Hensley, thought fair and just. I was to attend to all of his law business of every kind, sell the lots in Sacramento City, and collect the purchase money; and for these services I was to receive one fourth of the gross proceeds arising from the sale of city lots. There was a heavy amount of old business to settle up; and, while the labor was certain, the compensation was speculative, none of us then knowing whether the city would be at Sacramento or at Sutterville, a rival place about three miles below.

The city had been partially surveyed and mapped out by Captain William H. Warner, an army officer, who afterward completed the surveys and maps. Captain John A. Sutter, the original grantee, had conveyed his property, real and personal, to his son John A. Sutter, Jr., in the month of October, 1848. This was done to prevent one creditor, who threatened to attach the property, from sacrificing the estate, to the injury of the other creditors and the useless ruin of Captain Sutter and his family. There was no design to defraud the creditors ; but, on the contrary, time proved that the course pursued was the wisest and most just, under the circumstances, toward all the creditors. John A. Sutter, Jr., informed me at once that he was bound, under the agreement with his father, to pay all his just debts at the earliest practicable period. I saw both the justice and expediency of this arrangement, and set myself to work with energy to accomplish the end intended. By the middle of August, 1849, the last debt that ever came to my knowledge had been paid.

The history of the settlement of Captain John A. Sutter in the Sacramento valley is so well known that I shall not enter into the subject at large ; but, in justice to that old pioneer, who did so much for California, I will state some facts that have not perhaps been fully given by others. He has lately, I am informed, made and published a statement himself, which I have not seen. What I state is solely from memory ; and, should there be any conflict in our recollections, I must yield to his superior knowledge.

Captain Sutter came to California from Missouri (where he resided for a time) with little capital. He procured the grant of his eleven leagues of land from the Mexican authorities, went to the Sandwich Islands,

and there purchased a small vessel and an outfit from Mr. William French on credit. With this craft and outfit he returned, and commenced his improvements. He soon purchased of Don Antonio Suñol, of San José, a band of California cattle on time. These two purchases together amounted to some six thousand dollars. Later he purchased the Bodega property on credit. Though he employed Indian labor at a low rate, yet his improvements cost him a large sum in the aggregate; and this heavy expenditure of capital and labor was made long before he could realize any returns. He commenced his improvements in the wilderness, and among wild Indians, against whose apprehended attacks he had to make costly defensive preparations. The expenditure was certain, and necessarily made at the beginning, while the income was uncertain and late.

About the time the veteran pioneer had his rancho well stocked with domestic animals, and his farm fairly under way, and, before he could have possibly paid his debts, the immigrants began to arrive across the plains at his establishment. They came in weary, hungry, and poor. He had all the supplies, and they had all the wants and no money. He was only one, and they were many. They out-talked and out-voted him. He could not see them starve. This no pioneer could stand, and especially a man of his generous nature. He was compelled, from the very nature of the circumstances and the extreme necessities of the case, to supply their wants, and take in exchange their old wagons and broken-down teams, for which he had no profitable use, and which he could not convert into money. Being the father of the settlements in the Sacramento valley, he was also obliged to furnish the other settlers with supplies. Then all the traveling-parties passing through

that part of California would call on him for more or less assistance. There was almost an entire failure of crops one year. All things considered, he had a heavy burden to carry.

It is not at all surprising that he could not save up money enough to pay his debts until after the discovery of the gold-mines. I am somewhat of a pioneer and business man myself, and I hesitate not to give it as my decided opinion that no man could, under the exact circumstances in which Captain Sutter was placed, have paid those debts before the discovery of gold.

There were very few people then in the country, nearly all of whom were of one class and very poor, engaged in the same pursuits and exposed to a common danger, and, consequently, their friendships became so warm and devoted that one could not refuse to help another when in need. Property was almost held in common. How could any pioneer refuse to aid a poor comrade who would fight and die for him when occasion required? The circumstances of a new country are so different from those of an old one that a different law of social life must prevail. A pioneer that refused to assist others liberally in the settlement of a new country would be as isolated as Mitchell Gilliam in Oregon, with his tavern-sign hung up before his door, as related in a previous chapter. Men are men, and they can not resist appeals to their kindness under such circumstances. This is the reason why so few pioneers ever become rich, and remain so.

Besides, Captain Sutter had a nobler object in view than the mere accumulation of a fortune for himself. His purpose was to colonize the great valley of the Sacramento. At the time gold was discovered, he had around him and in his immediate vicinity a number of

colonists. He had established various industries, such as tanning, spinning and weaving, and cultivating a farm, and was engaged in the erection of a saw-mill. When I took charge of the business, I found, stowed away in a small room in the Fort, two or three looms, with the webs only partly woven, and several spinning-wheels, with the spools on the spindles partly filled, and the wool-rolls on the heads of the wheels unspun. I also found the tan-yard on the bank of the American Fork in ruins, the half-tanned hides having spoiled for want of attention. I did not see the saw-mill until October, 1849, and it evidently had never been finished.

The discovery of gold in California is due to Captain Sutter. I obtained my information on this subject from Mr. Marshall, the actual discoverer, who at the date of the discovery was in the employ of Captain Sutter. The latter was engaged in erecting a saw-mill, to be propelled by water-power, at Coloma, on the South Fork of the American River some forty miles from Sutter's Fort. At the site selected the river makes a considerable bend, forming a peninsula from two to three hundred yards wide at the point where the ditch and tail-race were cut across it. From the river above they cut a ditch about a hundred and fifty yards in length, and there put up the frame of the mill, and put in the flood-gate to let the water upon the wheel. It became necessary to construct what is called a tail-race, to enable the water to escape freely from the mill to the river below. The ground through which the ditch and tail-race were cut had a descent of about a hundred and fifty feet to the mile; and the formation was composed of a stratum of sand on the surface about two feet deep, and beneath this was a stratum of clay. Intermixed with these strata of sand and clay were found rocks of

various shapes and sizes, from that of a man's hat to that of a flour-barrel.

The plan adopted by Marshall, the superintendent, was to pry up the stones in the line of the tail-race with crowbars, and put them aside during the day; and in the evening to raise the flood-gate, and let the water run down the tail-race all night. This would wash away the loose clay and sand, but would not remove the rocks. In the morning the water was shut off, and the men again went to work, putting aside the stones in the bed of the tail-race. After two or three days all the sand had disappeared, and the water had washed down to the stratum of clay, upon and in which the gold rested. Marshall, one morning after the water had been shut off, was walking along down the bank of the tail-race, when he discovered several pieces of some very bright metal in a little pool of water in the bottom of the race. It occurred to him at once that it might be gold; and upon gathering it up he was satisfied, from its appearance and weight, that it was gold. This occurred on the 19th of January, 1848.

Thus, this great discovery was owing to the act of Captain Sutter. But for that, the gold might have remained undiscovered for a century to come. No one can tell. We only know the fact that he was the cause of the discovery.

The discovery of gold at once so excited the people that they promptly left everything for the mines, and no other industry but mining was thought of for a time. The spectacle of such a sudden destruction of property and change of pursuit was enough to cause much pain to the old pioneer. Though made rich by the change, he often spoke of it with much feeling, as I was informed upon good authority.

In his treatment of the Indians, Captain Sutter was humane, firm, and just. I remember well that, in the winter of 1848–'49, the Indians would often call at the Fort, and anxiously inquire for him, to protect them from wrong. They evidently had the greatest confidence in his justice. He had been their friend and protector for years; but his power was then gone.

SELLING LOTS IN SACRAMENTO—NECESSITY OF SOME GOVERNMENTAL ORGANIZATION—PUBLIC MEETING AT SACRAMENTO CITY.

When I began to sell lots in Sacramento City for John A. Sutter, Jr., early in January, 1849, all the business was done at the Fort, situated about a mile and a half from the river. There were then only two houses near the *embarcadero*, as the boat-landing was then called. One was a rude log-cabin, in which a drinking saloon was kept; and the other, also a log-cabin, was occupied by an excellent old man named Stewart and his family. Nearly all the first sales were of lots near the Fort; but toward the end of January the lots near the river began to sell most rapidly. The prices for lots in the same locality were fixed and uniform; and I made it an inflexible rule not to lower the prices for speculators, thus preventing a monopoly of the lots. I discouraged the purchase of more than four lots by any one person. I said to those who applied for lots: "You can well afford to buy four lots, and can stand the loss without material injury if the city should fail; but, if it should succeed, you will make enough profit on this number." This moderate and sensible advice satisfied the purchasers, and built up the city. The terms were part cash and part on time, the purchaser

giving his note for the deferred payment, and receiving a bond for a warranty deed when the note should be paid.

I had been at the Fort only a few days when the question arose as to some governmental organization. The great majority of the people then in California were within the district of Sacramento. Business was remarkably brisk, and continually increasing. Lots were selling rapidly, and who should take the acknowledgments and record the deeds? The war between the United States and Mexico had terminated by a cession of California to our country; and we were satisfied that the military government, existing during and in consequence of the war, had ceased. We knew nothing of the laws of Mexico, and had no means of learning. They were found in a language we did not understand, and we had no translations, and for some time could have none. In the mean time business must go on. We were of the opinion that we had the right to establish a *de facto* government, to continue until superseded by some legitimate organization. This *de facto* government would essentially rest upon the same basis as the provisional government of Oregon.

We accordingly held a public meeting at Sacramento City early in January, 1849, at which we elected Henry A. Schoolcraft as First Magistrate and Recorder for the District of Sacramento. Our rules were few and simple, and were merely designed to enable the people to go on with their necessary business for the time. This action was sanctioned by the people of the district.

But this anomalous and embarrassing position gave rise to efforts for instituting some regular organization for all California. For this purpose meetings were held in several places, and delegates elected to attend a con-

vention to frame a provisional government. The first meeting was held at San José, December 11, 1848; the second at San Francisco, December 21, 1848; and the third at Sacramento City, January 6 and 8, 1849. The history of these efforts, resulting at last in the formation of the State government, may be mainly found in the "Weekly Alta California" for the year 1849. There is but one complete file in existence, the others having been destroyed by the several fires in San Francisco. The paper was then published by Edward Gilbert, Edward Keemble, and George C. Hubbard. The file now in existence is to be found in the State Library at Sacramento.

"The recent large and unanimous meetings in the Pueblo de San José and in this town, in favor of immediate action for the establishment of a provisional government, are believed to be a fair index of the feeling of the community throughout the Territory. That some steps should be taken to provide a government for the country, in the event that the United States Congress fail to do so at the present session, is obvious; and that the plan proposed by the resolutions of the San Francisco meeting is the most proper and feasible, we think beyond a doubt." (Editorial, "Alta," January 4, 1849.)

It will be seen that San Francisco was then called a "town."

Colonel Thomas H. Benton addressed a letter to the people of California, under date of August 27, 1848, from which I take the following extracts, as found in the "Alta" of January 11, 1849:

The treaty with Mexico makes you citizens of the United States. Congress has not yet passed the laws to give you the blessings of our government, and it may be some time before it does so. In the mean time, while your condition is anoma-

lous and critical, it calls for the exercise of the soundest discretion and the most exalted patriotism on your part. The temporary civil and military government established over you as a right of war is at an end. . . .

Having no lawful government, nor lawful officers, you can have none except by your own act; you can have none that can have authority over you except by your own consent.

The proceedings of the meeting at Sacramento City are found in the "Alta" of January 25, 1849:

Provisional Government—Meeting at Sacramento City.

At a meeting held at Sacramento City, on the 6th day of January, 1849, to take into consideration the necessity and propriety of organizing a Provisional Government for the Territory of California, Peter H. Burnett was chosen President; Frank Bates and M. D. Winship, Vice-Presidents; and Jeremiah Sherwood and George McKinstry, Secretaries.

On motion, a committee of five was appointed by the President to draw up a preamble and resolutions expressive of the sense of this meeting. The committee was composed of Samuel Brannan, John S. Fowler, John Sinclair, P. B. Reading, and Barton Lee. The committee, having retired a few moments, returned, and asked for further time to report; whereupon, on motion, the meeting adjourned to meet again on Monday evening next.

MONDAY, *January* 8, 1849.

The meeting again assembled pursuant to adjournment. The Secretaries being absent, on motion, Robert Gordon was requested to act as Secretary. The committee appointed at the last meeting for that purpose made its report, which, after undergoing a few slight amendments, was adopted, as follows:

"*Whereas*, The Territory of California having by a treaty of peace been ceded to the United States; and the recommendation of the President to Congress to extend the laws of the United States over this Territory has not been acted upon by that body, and the citizens of this Territory are thus left without any laws for the protection of their lives and property;

"*And whereas*, The frequency and impunity with which robberies and murders have of late been committed have deeply impressed us with the necessity of having some regular form of government, with laws and officers to enforce the observance of those laws;

"*And whereas*, The discovery of large quantities of gold has attracted, and in all probability will continue to attract, an immense immigration from all parts of the world, as well as from the United States, thus adding to the present state of confusion, and presenting temptation to crime;

"Therefore—trusting in the sanction of the government and people of the United States for the course to which by the force of circumstances we are now impelled, for our own and for the safety of those now coming to our shores—

"*Resolved*, That in the opinion of this meeting it is not only proper, but the present precarious state of affairs renders it very necessary, that the inhabitants of California should form a Provisional Government to enact laws and appoint officers for the administration of the same, until such time as Congress see fit to extend the laws of the United States over this Territory.

"*Resolved*, That while, as citizens of California, we deeply lament the, to us, unaccountable inactivity toward us by the Federal Congress, as manifested in their neglect of this Territory, yet, as citizens of that great and glorious Republic, we shall in confidence wait for, and when received shall joyfully hail, the welcome intelligence that a proper territorial government has been formed by the Congress of the United States for the Territory of California.

"*Resolved*, That we fully concur in opinion with the meetings held at San José and San Francisco in favor of establishing a Provisional Government, and that we recommend to the inhabitants of California to hold meetings and elect delegates to represent them in the convention to be assembled at San José on Monday, 5th March, 1849, at 10 A. M., for the purpose of drafting and preparing a form of government to be submitted to the people for their sanction.

"*Resolved*, That an election be held by the people of this district, in this room, at 10 A. M. on Monday next, by ballot, for

five delegates to represent this district in the proposed convention.

"*Resolved*, That the President appoint a Corresponding Committee of three persons to communicate with the other districts, and otherwise further the object of this meeting.

"*Resolved*, That Messrs. Frank Bates, Barton Lee, and Albert Priest be a committee of three to act as judges of the election of delegates."

The report was unanimously adopted.

On motion of Samuel Brannan, a resolution was offered that our delegates be instructed to oppose slavery in every shape and form in the Territory of California. Adopted.

On motion of Mr. Brannan, it was resolved that, in case of the resignation or death of either of the delegates, the remainder be empowered to elect one to fill the vacancy.

The President, in pursuance of the fifth resolution, appointed Messrs. Frank Bates, P. B. Reading, and John S. Fowler, a Corresponding Committee.

On motion of Samuel Brannan, it was resolved that the proceedings of this meeting be published in the "Alta California."

On motion, the meeting adjourned.

PETER H. BURNETT, *Pres't.*

ROBERT GORDON, *Sec'y.*

Edward Gilbert, James C. Ward, and George Hyde, Corresponding Committee for the district of San Francisco, published a recommendation, dated January 24, 1849, that the meeting of the Convention be postponed from March 5 to May 1, 1849.

A Territorial Government.

Our readers will be assured, on perusing on our first page the article from the New York "Journal of Commerce" headed "Present State of the Question," that it is to the institution of slavery we owe the non-establishment of a Territorial Government in this country. And they will have reason to fear, as

we do, that another session of Congress may transpire without giving us the government we so much need, in consequence of the divisions and jealousies likely to grow out of the same subject. (Editorial, "Alta," February 15, 1849.)

RIVALRY BETWEEN SACRAMENTO AND SUTTERVILLE—JOURNEY TO SAN FRANCISCO—WONDERFUL COINCIDENCES—STATE OF SOCIETY.

In the month of March, 1849, the rivalry between Sacramento City and Sutterville was at its greatest height; and, as the ships from the Eastern States were soon to arrive, full of passengers coming to the gold-mines, it was deemed best for the interests of Sacramento City that I should spend a few weeks in San Francisco. I started for San Francisco about the middle of March on board a small schooner. We had some forty passengers.

On our way, and soon after we left Sacramento City, I was lying in a berth below, when Richard D. Torney came to me and said that, though he was a wicked man himself, he was pained to hear a man on board speak against the Christian religion as he had done, and desired me to go on deck and engage in a discussion with him. This I declined to do. The unbeliever was about fifty years of age, had read much, was a man of considerable ability, and seemed quite sincere in his opinions, and therefore outspoken in his opposition to Christianity.

On our way down the Sacramento River, this gentleman and myself had frequent familiar conversations upon other than religious subjects. I soon learned that he was a native of Tennessee. He gave me a very full history of himself and family; and among other incidents he mentioned the death of his only son. His son

was a bright and promising youth of sixteen, had been most carefully educated, and was an admirable scholar for his age, speaking several languages well. I could see that his love for his boy was intense, and all that a father could have for his child.

He said that he was a farmer at the time, and was engaged in inclosing a ten-acre tract of land, with a staked-and-ridered fence. The fence was made of split rails and stakes, and he had put up the rails until the fence was ready to receive the stakes. For the purpose of making my meaning clear, I will assume that the fence ran to the cardinal points, and inclosed a square piece of ground. He was engaged in hauling the stakes in his wagon, and put out two stakes at each corner of the fence. He could haul from seventy to eighty stakes at each load, and had put the stakes along the northern line of the fence, and part of the way down the western line, toward the southwest corner of the field. The stakes he was hauling at the time were found south of the new inclosure; and, as he came along the western line toward the northwest corner of the field, he decided that he would *guess* the corner of the fence where he should put out the first two stakes, so as to have *just the number* to reach the point where he had placed the last stakes of the preceding load. He did not count the number of fence-corners between him and the stakes already placed in position, nor had he counted the number of stakes in his wagon. He commenced and put out two stakes at a certain corner; and, in the very act of doing so, a sudden thought flashed through his mind that, in case the stakes should last him to the other stakes, and none be left over, his son, then in perfect health, would die within a week. To his surprise, he had just stakes enough to fill the

gap ; and, to his extreme sorrow, his son was taken sick the next day, and died within the week.

These coincidences were, indeed, most wonderful. First, there was one chance in two that there would be an even number of stakes on the wagon. Second, there was about one chance in five that he should have begun at the right corner. Third, there was one chance in many thousands that the thought should have flashed through his brain at the very instant that he threw out the first two stakes. Fourth, there was one chance in two thousand that the death of his son should have followed, as it did, within the time apprehended. Fifth, there was one chance in many millions that all the circumstances should have *concurred.* Take a combination bank-lock with one hundred numbers, and set the combination on four numbers—say, 16, 95, 20, and 7 ; and a burglar would have one chance in one hundred millions to guess the combination. If the lock were only set on one number, there would be one chance in a hundred, but it is the *combination* of several numbers that diminishes the chances so wonderfully.

These strange coincidences greatly puzzled this unbeliever. He expressed to me his extreme surprise. He had been most fondly attached to his son, and seemed to have set his whole heart upon him. I only state the facts, and leave every one to draw his own conclusions.

I arrived in San Francisco on Friday, March 23d. It was then but a village, containing about one thousand five hundred inhabitants. Of them, fifteen were women, five or six were children, and the remainder were nearly all young men, *very few* being over forty. It was difficult to find a man with gray hair. I had never seen so strange a state of society until I arrived in California, although I had been a pioneer most of my life. To see

a community composed almost exclusively of young men engaged in civil pursuits was, indeed, extraordinary. In point of intelligence, energy, and enterprise, they could not be exceeded, if equaled, by the same number found anywhere else. At Sacramento City there was about the same proportion of men, women, and children. Women were then queens, and children angels, in California.

Sunday, March 25, 1849, was a bright, genial, beautiful day; and, as I was standing in Kearney Street, about ten o'clock A. M., I saw, on the opposite side of Portsmouth Square, two little girls, about seven years old, dressed in pure white. They were about the age of my youngest child, Sallie, and they appeared to me the most lovely objects I had ever seen. How beautiful are innocent children! I had not seen my loved ones for more than six months, and this spectacle went to my heart. I had it from good authority that, in the fall of 1849, a beautiful flaxen-haired little girl, about three years old, was often seen playing upon a veranda attached to a house on Clay Street, between Montgomery and Kearney, and that hardy miners might be seen on the opposite side of Clay Street gazing at that lovely child, while manly tears ran down their bronzed cheeks. The sight of that prattling child revived memories of the peaceful, happy homes they had left, to hunt for gold on a distant shore.

In coming from Sacramento to San Francisco in April, 1872, on board a steamer, I made the acquaintance of an intelligent man, who had been a member of the Legislature of California. This gentleman informed me that he came to California in 1849, when sixteen years of age, with an uncle of his, who was as kind to him as a father. They located at a remote mining

camp, far in the mountains, and had been there some months when he learned, one evening, that a woman had arrived at another mining locality, some forty miles distant. He said he had not seen a lady for six months, and he went to his uncle and said : "Uncle, I want you to lend me Jack to-morrow." "What do you want with him, my son ?" "I have heard that there is a woman at —— camp, and I want to go and see her." "Well, my son, you can take the mule, and go and see the lady." Next morning he was off by daybreak, and never stopped until he arrived at the place and saw the lady. She was an excellent married woman, and treated the boy with great kindness, esteeming his visit as a sincere compliment to her sex.

I had seen society in Oregon, without means, without spirituous liquors, and without a medium of exchange ; but there was a due proportion of families, and the people rapidly improved in every respect. In California, however, there were few women and children, but plenty of gold, liquors, and merchandise, and almost every man grew comparatively rich for the time ; and yet, in the absence of female influence and religion, the men were rapidly going back to barbarism.

SAILING SHIPS ARRIVE WITH GOLD-SEEKERS — THEIR SPECULATIVE CHARACTER—GOLD-WASHING MACHINES —CLIMATE OF SAN FRANCISCO.

Within a few days after my arrival in San Francisco the sailing ships from the East began to arrive, full of gold-seekers, who were well provided with outfits, consisting of clothing, towels, brushes, and other articles, many of which were not much used in the mines. Many of them had much greater supplies than they required,

and others were destitute of the means to pay their expenses to the mines. As large objects appear small in the distance, most of these people supposed when they left home that their journey would about end at San Francisco. In this they found themselves mistaken. They had many miles yet to travel, and the expenses of travel in California were much greater in proportion to distance than at home. These people would congregate in and around Portsmouth Square, and you could see many auctions going on at the same time. The owner of the articles to be disposed of would turn up a barrel on end, and from his trunks alongside he would draw out his goods, and sell them to the highest bidder for gold dust at sixteen dollars per ounce, there being little or no coin in the country.

One of the greatest proofs of the speculative character of the gold-seekers was found in the various gold-washing machines brought to California. When the discovery of gold was fully believed in the States east of the Rocky Mountains, many inventive minds set to work to construct machines for washing out the gold. It was interesting and very amusing to see the number and variety of these most useless things. They had been brought in many cases across the Isthmus of Darien, at great expense and labor, and upon arrival were only fit for fuel. Many of the owners of these machines would not believe the statements of those who had been in the mines, but carried them to Sacramento City, where they were compelled at last to abandon them on the bank of the river. Some few of these machines were brought across the plains in wagons.

I knew a tinsmith named Coleman in Weston, Missouri, who invented and constructed an iron gold-washer weighing from ten to twelve hundred pounds, and

sold it to another man I knew well in the same place, named Murphy, a hotel-keeper, who was a sound business man, and well off. He purchased an extra wagon and ox-team for that machine. When he arrived within four days' travel of Sacramento City, in the fall of 1849, he left the men in charge of his two wagons and teams, and came on in advance of them on horseback. By some means his acquaintances had heard that he was bringing this machine overland, and they inquired of him whether it was true. He stoutly denied it, intending to return and meet his wagons before they could arrive at the City, and secretly put out the machine in the night by the wayside. But he miscalculated the time it would take the wagons and teams to arrive ; and, the first thing he knew, they were in the City. "The boys" at once surrounded and searched his wagons ; and in the bottom of one of them, well concealed, they found the machine. Perhaps no man was ever more thoroughly quizzed than Murphy. He was a man who boasted of his shrewd sagacity. The thing was thrown out in the rear of my office on J Street in Sacramento, where I saw it many times, and where no doubt it lies buried to this day.

For days and days I would stand on Kearney Street, in front of Naglee's Bank, near the Square, and talk to the newly arrived. I had been in the mines myself, had "seen the elephant," and could give them any information they desired. The simple absurdity of many of their questions severely tested my risible faculties ; but I restrained my laughter, remembering that I had been green myself, and answered all their various questions kindly and truthfully. I have seen them, on their way to Sacramento City, take their spades and pans, shovel up the sand on the bank of the Sacramento River, and

wash it out in their pans ; and, when they had discovered a scale of mica, it was most interesting to watch the ardent expression of their faces, until they found that all that glitters is not gold.

I will not attempt a lengthy description of the young and great city of San Francisco. I have seen it rise from the rough, irregular sand-hills and ridges of the original site, to the paved streets and magnificent buildings of a city of three hundred thousand people, from every considerable clime and kingdom of the earth. I have seen the events of several generations crowded into one.

No climate, so far as I know, is superior to that of San Francisco, taken as a whole. It is never too cold nor too warm for outdoor work in this city. For ten months in the average year building and other outdoor work can go on most successfully. For eight months in the year we can know, with reasonable certainty, what kind of weather we are to have. If we have a picnic or other occasion to attend, we know there will be no disappointment in consequence of bad weather. We know how to estimate correctly, in advance, what we can accomplish within a time stated. The fact that so little time is lost in consequence of bad weather is one great cause of the city's rapid improvement. Men can do more outdoor work here than elsewhere in a year. A fine frame or brick building can be commenced after the rainy season has passed, and securely covered in before any rain falls to injure or impede the work.

UNSATISFACTORY CONDITION OF THE GOVERNMENT OF THE DISTRICT OF SAN FRANCISCO.

I had not been in San Francisco more than ten days before I became fully aware of the unsatisfactory con-

dition of the government of this district. The alleged facts are concisely and clearly stated in the editorial of the "Alta California" of March 29, 1849, from which I make the following extracts:

In August, 1847, Governor Mason, by reason of many complaints against the ill-defined powers and assumptions of the Alcalde, authorized the election of six citizens to constitute a Town Council. This body continued in existence until the 31st of December, 1848, when it expired by limitation. They passed a law authorizing a new election on December 27th for seven members of a new council to succeed them. This election was duly held, but a majority of the old council was not satisfied with the result, and declared the election nugatory because fraudulent votes were polled thereat, and ordered a new one. Four fifths of the citizens thought that this was an unwarrantable assumption of power on the part of the council, and they would not attend a new election. An election was held, however, by the factionists, and we then had the spectacle of three town councils in existence at one and the same time. The old council finally voted itself out of existence on the 15th of January, 1849, and the other two kept up a cross-fire of counter enactments for a few weeks longer. Despairing of ever being able to establish public justice upon a proper basis so long as the people were at the mercy of this officer, a convention of the people of this district was then called, at which it was resolved to elect a legislative assembly of fifteen members, who should have power to make such laws as might be deemed necessary, "provided they did not conflict with the Constitution of the United States, nor the common law thereof."

The legislative body, to correct these abuses, and inasmuch as the people had elected three justices of the peace, fixed a day upon which the office of Alcalde should cease, and ordered him to hand over his books and papers to Myron Norton, Esq., a newly elected justice.

The proceedings of the meeting of citizens mentioned in the preceding remarks are published in

the "Alta California" of February 15, 1849, as follows:

Public Meeting.

A public meeting of the citizens of the town and district of San Francisco was held in the Public Square on Monday afternoon, the 12th instant, in accordance with previous notice.

The meeting was organized by calling M. Norton to preside, and T. W. Perkins to act as secretary. The chairman, after reading the call of the meeting, opened it more fully by lucidly but succinctly stating its objects; when Mr. Hyde, on being invited, after some preliminary remarks, submitted the following plan of organization or government for the district of San Franciso:

"*Whereas*, We, the people of the district of San Francisco, perceiving the necessity of having some better defined and more permanent civil regulations for our general security than the vague, unlimited, and irresponsible authority that now exists, do, in general convention assembled, hereby establish and ordain:

"ARTICLE I.

"SECTION 1. That there shall be elected by ballot a Legislative Assembly for the district of San Francisco, consisting of fifteen members, citizens of the district, eight of whom shall constitute a quorum for the transaction of business, and whose power, duty, and office shall be to make such laws as they, in their wisdom, may deem essential to promote the happiness of the people, provided they shall not conflict with the Constitution of the United States, nor be repugnant to the common law thereof.

"SEC. 2. Every bill which shall have passed the Legislative Assembly shall, before it becomes a law, be signed by the Speaker and the Recording Clerk.

"SEC. 3. It shall keep a journal of its proceedings, and determine its own rules.

"SEC. 4. The members of the Legislative Assembly shall

enter upon the duties of their office on the first Monday of March.

"ARTICLE II.

"SEC. 1. That, for the purpose of securing to the people a more efficient administration of justice, there shall be elected by ballot three justices of the peace, of equal though separate jurisdiction, who shall be empowered by their commission of office to hear and adjudicate all civil and criminal issues in this district, according to the common law, as recognized by the Constitution of the United States, under which we live.

"SEC. 2. That there shall be an election held, and the same is hereby ordered, at the Public Institute, in the town of San Francisco, on Wednesday, the twenty-first day of February, 1849, between the hours of eight A. M. and five P. M., for fifteen members of the Legislative Assembly for the district of San Francisco, and three justices of the peace, as hereinbefore prescribed.

"SEC. 3. That the members of the said Legislative Assembly, and the three justices of the peace elected as hereinbefore prescribed, shall hold their office for the term of one year from the date of their commissions, unless sooner superseded by the competent authority from the United States Government, or by the action of the Provisional Government now invoked by the people of this Territory, or by the action of the people of this district.

"SEC. 4. Members of the Legislature and justices of the peace shall, before entering on the duties of their respective offices, take and subscribe the following oath:

"'I do solemnly swear that I will support the Constitution of the United States, and government of this district, and that I will faithfully discharge the duties of the office of —— according to the best of my ability.'"

Mr. Harris moved the adoption of the entire plan, which was seconded. . . . and was carried almost unanimously. . . .

On motion of Mr. Roach, it was

"*Resolved*, That the persons who were elected on the 27th day of December last, to serve as a Town Council for the year 1849, and those who were elected for the same purpose on the

15th of January, 1849, be and are hereby requested to tender their resignations to a committee selected by this meeting to receive the same."

Messrs. Ellis, Swasey, Long, Buckalew, and Hyde were elected such committee.

On motion, it was

"*Resolved*, That these proceedings be published in the 'Alta California.'"

MYRON NORTON, *Pres't.*

T. W. PERKINS, *Sec'y.*

I have omitted some unimportant portions of the proceedings.

It appears that the military authorities pronounced the action of the Legislative Assembly null and void, and that the Alcalde had refused to deliver up the papers of his office to the person designated by the Assembly. This brought up the question as to the right of the people of California to organize a provisional Government.

General Mason was military Governor of California during the war with Mexico, and was succeeded by General Riley. At the time I was in San Francisco on my first visit, General Persifer F. Smith was in command temporarily as the superior officer of General Riley. I remember that I had a friendly conference with General Smith in regard to our civil government. He was a most admirable man—kind, candid, courteous, and dignified. He seemed to regret very much the unsatisfactory condition of governmental affairs in California, but still thought there was no remedy by the action of our people. I differed with him in opinion, and about the 20th of April, 1849, sent to the "Alta California" the following communication, which appeared in the number of that paper issued April 26, 1849:

COMMUNICATION TO THE "ALTA CALIFORNIA"—FAILURE OF THE ATTEMPT TO HOLD A CONVENTION TO FRAME A PROVISIONAL GOVERNMENT.

The Rights of the People.

MR. EDITOR: Have the people of California any rights? If so, what is their extent? Have they not certain rights, founded, based, and implanted in man's very nature—that belong to them as men, as human beings—rights that derive no force from human legislation, but trace their origin up through nature to nature's God? Are not these great principles of liberty and justice, that produced the American Revolutionary war, promulgated in the immortal Declaration of Independence, and are now embodied in the American Constitutions, State and Federal, the birthright of every American citizen? I must answer emphatically, they are yet *ours*, as much so as they were the rights of our ancestors. We have inherited them by direct, clear, and unquestionable lineal descent.

The Federal Government is a government of *limited* powers—limited by a written Constitution, published to the world, and placed among the enduring and solemn records of the country. The Constitution of the United States not only *limits* the powers of the Federal Government, but these powers are distributed among three separate and independent departments, the legislative, executive, and judicial. To these departments are assigned different functions, and they were intended by the framers of the instrument to operate as checks upon each other. No one department has any right to assume the powers or discharge the duties assigned to the others. The President is armed with the veto power, to protect his department from the encroachments of the Legislature, and the judiciary has the right to declare the acts of Congress and of the President unconstitutional, null, and void from the beginning. The President is a mere executive officer. He possesses no legislative or judicial power. He can make no law, and construe no law except so far as his mere executive action is concerned.

The question whether the people of California under exist-

ing circumstances have the right to exercise that power inherent in human nature—the power to institute government for the protection of life, liberty, and the right of property—is a question that does not rightfully belong to the executive department of the government to determine; much less does it come within the province of a subordinate military commander. Neither does it belong to any *military* officer, in time of peace, to decide what code of *civil* law is in force in this or any other community; nor does he have the right to determine what *judicial* office is or is not in existence, nor whether this or that individual is rightfully a judicial officer. These are powers foreign to the military office, and not conferred by the Constitution and laws of our country.

Has the President of the United States distinctly and clearly advanced the astounding proposition that, so long as Congress may choose to abandon and, for the time being, abdicate the right of government here, and refuse to extend over us the laws of our country—that *so long* the most unfortunate and miserable people of California (not having forfeited their rights by crimes against God and their country) have not the liberty to organize a mere temporary government for their protection? Does the President, or any other American statesman, mean to say that, while the people of Oregon had the right to and *did* organize a provisional government, recognized by Congress itself, the people of California have no such right? I do not understand the President or the Secretary of State as intending to advance any such idea. I know Colonel Benton distinctly advised the people of California to organize such government. The President has not, as I understand, decided that we have no right to institute a temporary government, and that we *must* submit to the mere *de facto* government under the military authority; and, had he so decided, he would have done so in derogation of the Constitution and laws of our country. The idea that he has so decided is simply an *inference* from language that will not, I apprehend, warrant such a conclusion.

What are, in fact, the opinions of the President in reference to the existing state of things in California? In his late message he says: "Upon the exchange of the ratifications of the treaty of

peace with Mexico, on the thirteenth day of May last, the temporary governments which had been established over New Mexico and California by our military and naval commanders, *by virtue of the rights of war*, ceased to derive any obligatory force from *that source of authority*." I have italicized a part of the above extract for the purpose of more distinctly showing that, in the President's opinion, whatever government existed *after* the establishment of peace did not so exist "in virtue of the rights of war," and derived no obligatory force from that source of authority.

The President, after speaking of the adjournment of Congress without making any provision for the government of the inhabitants of New Mexico and California, goes on to say: "Since that time, the limited power possessed by the Executive has been exercised to preserve and protect them from the inevitable consequences of a state of anarchy. The only government that remained was that established by the military authority during the war. Regarding this to be a *de facto* government, and that, by the presumed consent of the inhabitants, it might be continued temporarily, they were advised to conform and submit to it for a short intervening period, before Congress would again assemble, and could legislate on the subject."

All governments, rightfully instituted, must derive their powers from some *source*. These powers are *derivative*, not *original*. The Declaration of Independence assumes the clear and distinct principle that "governments instituted among men derive their just powers from the consent of the governed." Now, according to the above extract, from what "source of authority" did the temporary governments continued after the war derive their powers? Not from the "rights of war." They had ceased. Nor yet from the legislation of Congress, for that body adjourned without any action upon the subject. What then was the source of power? The President says the "consent of the inhabitants." Nor can the President or any one else "presume" this "consent" to be given contrary to the fact and the truth, and does the President mean to say so? Surely not. If the President has the right to "presume" this

consent to be given, in direct and positive contradiction to the express acts and declarations of the inhabitants, has he not the right to continue such military government without the "consent" of the inhabitants at all, either actual or presumed?

What is the difference between *no consent* and "presumed consent" contrary to the truth? Can the President, or any man living, presume away the liberties of the people? Never. If we have no power to *dissent*, we have no power to *consent*. We are not free, but mere passive instruments. Suppose a despot should say to a certain people, "I will not exercise despotic power over you without your consent, but I will presume such consent against your express declarations to the contrary." Is it possible that the President of the United States intended to say, in substance, to his fellow citizens of California, "Gentlemen, I will not continue the temporary government established during the war without your consent, but I will *presume* your consent against your express acts and declarations to the contrary, and, if you attempt to organize a mere temporary government to 'protect you from the inevitable consequences of a state of anarchy,' I will put you down by military power, and treat you as traitors and enemies of your country"?

That our military commanders had a right to establish a temporary government "in virtue of the rights of war," to continue during the existence of the war, might readily be admitted; and that the President had the right to continue such government after peace was established, by the "consent of the inhabitants," might be true; and that such consent might fairly be presumed, so long as they submitted to such government, and organized no other, might also be admitted, though doubtful. But to say that the President, a mere executive officer, could continue such government without any actual consent of the inhabitants, and could presume such consent in a manner so violent as utterly to destroy all power of *dissent* in the neglected people of California, and all power to "protect themselves from the inevitable consequences of anarchy," is to assert a proposition giving to the President a power over his fellow citizens equal to that of a despot.

The opinion of President Polk and that of his distinguished

Secretary of State are entitled to the utmost respect, not only upon account of the high and responsible stations they filled, but more especially for the reason that they are both profound jurists and statesmen. But I do not understand them as laying down these two distinct positions—1. That the government continued in California after the war could only exist by the "consent" of the inhabitants; and 2. That the President has the right to presume such consent to be given *although it be expressly withheld.* Now, both these positions must be sustained before the right can be denied to the people of California to organize a mere temporary government "to protect them," in the beautiful language of the President, "from the inevitable consequences of a state of anarchy."

Mr. Starkie, in his learned treatise on the "Law of Evidence," gives this definition of a presumption: "A presumption may be defined to be an inference as to the existence of one fact from the existence of some other fact, founded upon a previous experience of their connection." After some other remarks not necessary to illustrate the position I am seeking to establish, the author says: "It also follows from the above definition that the inference may be either *certain* or not certain, but merely *probable*, and therefore capable of being rebutted by proof to the contrary." (Part IV., p. 1235.)

Now, whether the inhabitants gave, and still continue to give, their consent to the continuance of the military government after the cessation of war, is simply a question of *fact.* So long as the people of the country submitted to such government, organized no other, and made no objection, by their acts they made that government *their own*, and their consent might be presumed. But I take it that such presumption is not of that kind called by Mr. Starkie "certain," but only "probable," and "therefore capable of being rebutted by proof to the contrary."

All that I understand the President as intending to advance is, that he had the limited power to continue the *de facto* government by the consent of the inhabitants; and that so long as they submitted, and did not object to such continuance, nor organize any different government, such consent might be pre-

sumed; and for this reason he "advised" the inhabitants to "conform and submit to it for a short intervening period, before Congress would again assemble, and could legislate on the subject." He "advised" (not ordered) the inhabitants to submit. The law *commands*, and does not *advise*. And, had the President believed that he had the lawful authority to continue the *de facto* government *against our consent*, it would have been his duty to speak "as one having authority," and not merely to give advice.

I have thus, Mr. Editor, spoken my candid sentiments in language, I hope, intelligible and plain. I have done so without intending the slightest disrespect to those of my fellow citizens who may differ with me in opinion. I have only sought to discuss most vital *principles*, and not to make the slightest personal reflection upon any one. I may or may not trouble you again.

P.

The following is an extract from a letter of James Buchanan, Secretary of State of the United States, to William V. Voorhies, dated October 7, 1848:

> The President deeply regrets that Congress did not, at their late session, establish a territorial government for California. It would now be vain to enter into the reasons for this omission. Whatever these may have been, he is firmly convinced that Congress feels a deep interest in California and its people, and will at an early period of the next session provide for them a Territorial Government suited to their wants. ("Alta," March 15, 1849.)

But the next session passed without any legislation by Congress in regard to California, except to extend the revenue laws of the United States over us. In the "Alta" of June 2, 1849, will be found an editorial in reference to this treatment of us headed "A Legal Outrage," in which occurs the expression, "thus passing a law to tax California without giving it a representative or even a government."

It will be remembered that the meetings held at San José and San Francisco in December, 1848, and that at Sacramento in January, 1849, recommended the people of California to elect delegates to attend a Convention to be held at San José, March 5, 1849, to frame a provisional government for this Territory. Delegates were accordingly elected, and corresponding committees appointed; but that attempt at organization failed, in consequence of a difference of opinion as to the time when the Convention should meet. The time mentioned was found to be too short to allow the lower districts to be represented. Edward Gilbert, James C. Ward, and George Hyde, Corresponding Committee of San Francisco, published a recommendation, dated January 24, 1849, that the meeting of the Convention be postponed from March 5th to May 1st. ("Alta," January 25, 1849.) Messrs. John Sinclair and Charles E. Pickett, delegates elect to the Convention from Sacramento district, protested against the change of time. ("Alta," March 1, 1849.)

In the "Alta" of March 22, 1849, a communication was published—signed by W. M. Steuart, Myron Norton, and Francis J. Lippitt, delegates from San Francisco; Charles T. Botts, delegate from Monterey; J. D. Stevenson, from Los Angeles; R. Semple, from Benicia; John B. Frisbie and M. G. Vallejo, from Sonoma; S. Brannan, J. A. Sutter, Samuel J. Hensley, and P. B. Reading, from Sacramento—recommending the holding of a Convention for framing a provisional government at Monterey, on the first Monday of August, 1849, in case no act of Congress should be passed to create a territorial government for California, and resigning their positions as delegates.

Congress adjourned March 3, 1849, and President

Taylor was inaugurated on the 5th, the 4th being Sunday; but, at the date of the above recommendation, March 22d, the non-action of Congress in regard to a territorial organization for California was not known here. This recommendation was not acted upon by the people.

CHAPTER VIII.

RETURN TO SACRAMENTO—COME A SECOND TIME TO SAN FRANCISCO—BECOME A MEMBER OF THE LEGISLATIVE ASSEMBLY—EXTRACTS FROM THE ADDRESS OF THAT BODY TO THE PEOPLE OF CALIFORNIA—EXTRACTS FROM GENERAL RILEY'S PROCLAMATION—ADDRESS OF THE COMMITTEE OF FIVE.

About the 21st of April, 1849, I left San Francisco on my return to Sacramento, where I arrived about the 28th of that month. About the middle of May my family arrived in San Francisco from Oregon; and I came the second time to San Francisco, arriving about the 1st of June. I became a member of the Legislative Assembly of San Francisco, and took a leading part in its proceedings. This Assembly published an "Address to the People of California," which appears in the "Alta" of June 14, 1849. Though there is no date to the address as published, it was adopted some time before, and was written by me, in entire ignorance of General Riley's intended proclamation to the people of California, which bears date at Monterey, June 3, 1849, but was unknown in San Francisco until Saturday, June 9th. The following are extracts from this address:

The Committee appointed by the Speaker, under a resolution of this House, to draw up and submit an address to the people of California, beg leave respectfully to submit the within for the consideration of this body. . . .

The discovery of the rich and exhaustless gold-mines of California has, in and of itself, produced a strange and singular state of things in this community, unparalleled, perhaps, in the annals of mankind. We have here in our midst a mixed mass of human beings from every part of the wide earth, of different habits, manners, customs, and opinions—*all*, however, impelled onward by the same feverish desire of fortune-making. But, perfectly anomalous as may be the state of our population, the state of our government is still more unprecedented and alarming. *We are in fact without government*—a commercial, civilized, and wealthy people, without law, order, or system, to protect and secure them in the peaceful enjoyment of those rights and privileges inestimable, bestowed upon them by their Creator, and holden, by the fundamental principles of our country, to be *inalienable and absolute.*

For the first time in the history of the "model Republic," and perhaps in that of any civilized government in the world, the Congress of the United States, representing a great nation of more than twenty millions of freemen, have assumed the right, not only to *tax us without representation*, but to *tax us without giving us any government at all*—thus making us feel, endure, and bear all the BURTHENS of government, without giving us even a distant glimpse of its BENEFITS. A special and separate act was introduced in the House of Representatives, at the late session of Congress, by the Committee on Commerce, and subsequently passed by both Houses, extending the revenue laws of the United States over California, and leaving the bill to organize a territorial government for this neglected people to perish at the close of the session.

Under these pressing circumstances, and impressed with the urgent necessity of some efficient action on the part of the people of California, the Legislative Assembly of the district of San Francisco have believed it to be their duty to earnestly recommend to their fellow citizens the propriety of electing

twelve delegates from each district to attend a general Convention, to be held at the Pueblo de San José on the third Monday of August next, for the purpose of organizing a government for the whole Territory of California. We would recommend that the delegates be intrusted with enlarged discretion to deliberate upon the best measures to be taken; and to form, if they upon mature consideration should deem it advisable, a State Constitution, to be submitted to the people for their ratification or rejection by a direct vote at the polls.

The present state of a great and harassing political question in the United States must certainly defeat, for several coming sessions, any attempts at an organization of a territorial government for this country by Congress. In the Senate of the United States the parties stand precisely equal, there being fifteen free and fifteen slave States represented in that body. Until one or the other gain the ascendancy, we can have no territorial organization by act of Congress. All parties in both Houses of Congress admit, however, that the people of California can and ought to settle the vexed question of slavery in their State Constitution. From the best information, both parties in Congress are anxious that this should be done; and there can exist no doubt of the fact that the present perplexing state of the question at Washington would insure the admission of California at once. *We have that question to settle for ourselves; and the sooner we do it, the better.*

The following editorial, in reference to this address, appeared in the "Alta" of June 14th:

It is important and proper that we should remark, in this connection, that the Legislative Address was prepared and adopted before the publication of General Riley's proclamation in this place, and that it therefore has no reference to, or necessary connection with, that document.

In the same number of the "Alta" will be found a long editorial, of which the following is the beginning:

A Revolution—its Progress.

This town was thrown into a state of intense excitement on Saturday morning last, by the publication of the "Proclamation to the People of the District of San Francisco," which is this day given in our columns. The publication at the same time of a "Proclamation to the People of California," which we also insert to-day, did not detract from the intense excitement of the day.

A meeting was held on Tuesday, June 12th, of the proceedings of which the following correct account will be found in the "Alta" of June 14th:

Large and Enthusiastic Mass Meeting of the Citizens of San Francisco in Favor of a Convention for forming a State Government.

The mass meeting of the citizens, called for the purpose of considering the propriety of electing delegates to a convention for the formation of a government for California, took place on Tuesday, June 12th, in Portsmouth Square.

At 3 o'clock P. M. the meeting was called to order by Peter H. Burnett, Esq., who proposed to the meeting the following list of officers, which was unanimously adopted: President, William M. Steuart; Vice-Presidents, William D. M. Howard, E. H. Harrison, C. V. Gillespie, Robert A. Parker, Myron Norton, Francis J. Lippitt, J. H. Merrill, George Hyde, William Hooper, Hiram Grimes, John A. Patterson, C. H. Johnson, William H. Davis, Alfred Ellis, Edward Gilbert, John Townsend; Secretaries, E. Gould Buffom, J. R. Per Lee, W. C. Parker.

The object of the meeting having been briefly stated by the President, Peter H. Burnett, Esq., addressed the people assembled, and concluded his remarks by presenting the Hon. Thomas Butler King of Georgia, who responded to the call with his accustomed eloquence and ability. The meeting was further addressed by Dr. W. M. Gwin and William A. Buffom, Esq., when the following resolutions were offered by Myron Norton, Esq.:

"*Resolved*, That, the Congress of the United States having failed to pass any law for the government of this country, the people of California have the undoubted right to organize a government for their own protection.

"*Resolved*, That the people of California are called upon by an imperative sense of duty to assemble in their sovereign capacity, and elect delegates to a convention to form a constitution for a State government, that the great and growing interests of California may be represented in the next Congress of the United States, and the people of this country may have the necessary protection of law.

"*Resolved*, That we earnestly invite our fellow citizens at large to unite with us in our efforts to establish a government in accordance with the Constitution of our beloved country, and that a committee of five persons be appointed by the President of this meeting to correspond with the other districts, and fix an early day for the election of delegates and the meeting of the convention, and also to determine the number of delegates which should be elected from this district."

Major Barry opposed the resolutions. General Morse proposed an amendment to the last resolution, to the effect that the meeting adopt for the time the days appointed by General Riley.

Colonel J. D. Stevenson opposed the amendment.

After some little discussion, the amendment was rejected, and, the vote being taken upon the original resolutions, they were adopted.

The Chairman, in accordance with the last resolution, then appointed the following committee: Peter H. Burnett, W. D. M. Howard, Myron Norton, E. Gould Buffom. Edward Gilbert.

The meeting was then addressed by Edward Gilbert.

On motion, the meeting adjourned *sine die*.

WILLIAM M. STEUART, *President.*

E. GOULD BUFFOM,
J. R. PER LEE,
W. C. PARKER, } *Secretaries.*

General Riley's "Proclamation to the People of California," as already stated, bore date at Monterey, June 3, 1849, but was not known in San Francisco until Saturday, June 9th. The following extracts are from this proclamation :

In order to complete this organization with the least possible delay, the undersigned, in virtue of power in him vested, does hereby appoint the first day of August next as the day for holding a special election for delegates to a general convention, and for filling the offices of judges of the Superior Court, prefects and sub-prefects, and all vacancies in the offices of first alcaldes (or judges of first instance), alcaldes, justices of the peace, and town councils. The judges of the Superior Court and district prefects are by law executive appointments; but, being desirous that the wishes of the people should be fully consulted, the Governor will appoint such persons as may receive the plurality of votes in their respective districts, provided they are competent and eligible to the office. Each district will therefore elect a prefect and two sub-prefects, and fill the vacancies in the offices of first alcalde (or judge of first instance) and of alcalde. One judge of the Superior Court will be elected in the districts of San Diego, Los Angeles, and Santa Barbara; one in the districts of San Luis Obispo and Monterey; one in the districts of San José and San Francisco; and one in the districts of Sonoma, Sacramento, and San Joaquin. The salaries of the judges of the Superior Court, the prefects, and judges of first instance are regulated by the Governor, but can not exceed for the first $4,000 per annum, for the second $2,500, and for the third $1,500. These salaries will be paid out of the civil fund which has been formed from the proceeds of the customs, provided no instructions to the contrary are received from Washington. . . .

The method here indicated to attain what is desired by all, viz., a more perfect political organization, is deemed the most direct and safe that can be adopted, and one fully authorized by law. It is the course advised by the President, and by the

Secretaries of State and of War of the United States, and is calculated to avoid the innumerable evils which must necessarily result from any illegal local legislation. It is therefore hoped that it will meet with the approbation of the people of California, and that all good citizens will unite in carrying it into execution.

On the 4th of June General Riley issued a proclamation addressed "To the People of the District of San Francisco," in which he declares that the "body of men styling themselves the Legislative Assembly of San Francisco has usurped powers which are vested only in the Congress of the United States," etc. This was made known in San Francisco, June 9th. The time appointed by General Riley for the meeting of the Convention was September 1, 1849, and the place Monterey. The Legislative Assembly of San Francisco issued an "Address to the People of California," in answer to the two proclamations of General Riley. This address was reported by a committee of which I was a member, and was drawn up by me. It may be found at length in the "Alta" under the dates of July 19, 26, and August 9, 1849.

The following was published by the committee of five:

To the Public.

The undersigned, composing a committee appointed at a mass meeting of the people of the district of San Francisco, held on the 12th day of June, 1849, to correspond with the other districts, and to fix an early day for the election of delegates and the assembling of the convention, and also to determine the number of delegates which should be elected from this district, have given the subject that attention which their limited time and means would permit. The time being a matter, not of principle, but of mere expediency, the committee, being duly impressed with the urgent necessity of success in the main

object desired by all parties, have not deemed it their duty or right, under the circumstances, to do any act that might endanger the ultimate success of the great project of holding the convention. The committee, not recognizing the least power, as matter of right, in Brevet Brigadier General Riley, to "*appoint*" a time and place for the election of delegates and the assembling of the convention; yet, as these matters are subordinate, and as the people of San José have, in public meeting, expressed their satisfaction with the times mentioned by General Riley, and as we are informed the people below will accede to the same, and as it is of the first importance that there be unanimity of action among the people of California in reference to the great leading object—the attempt to form a government for ourselves—we recommend to our fellow citizens of California the propriety, under the existing circumstances, of acceding to the time and place mentioned by General Riley in his proclamation, and acceded to by the people of some other districts. The committee would recommend their fellow citizens of the district of San Francisco to elect five delegates to the convention. And they can not but express the opinion that their fellow citizens of the two great mining districts of Sacramento and San Joaquin have not had anything like justice done them, by the apportionment of General Riley; that they are justly entitled to a greater proportion of delegates to the convention than the number mentioned in General Riley's proclamation; and the committee, believing their fellow citizens of the mining districts to have equal rights, in proportion to numbers, with the people of other districts, would recommend them to elect such increased number of delegates as they in their judgment shall think just and right.

PETER H. BURNETT.
WILLIAM D. M. HOWARD.
MYRON NORTON.
E. GOULD BUFFOM.
EDWARD GILBERT.

June 18, 1849.

EXTRACTS FROM MY SECOND COMMUNICATION TO THE "ALTA CALIFORNIA"—GROUNDS OF GENERAL RILEY'S VIEWS AS TO THE RIGHT OF THE PEOPLE OF CALIFORNIA TO ORGANIZE A PROVISIONAL GOVERNMENT—GROUNDS OF THOSE WHO CLAIMED THAT RIGHT—THE CONTROVERSY MOST FORTUNATE FOR CALIFORNIA—ALL THINGS HAPPILY TENDED TO PRODUCE THE MAIN RESULT DESIRED BY US ALL.

About the 5th of July I sent a communication to the "Alta," which appeared in the number of July 12, 1849. The following are extracts:

But it seems from a late communication in your paper, under the signature of General Riley, that new instructions have been received, which, he says, sustain the views expressed in his proclamation. He says: "It may not be improper here to remark that the instructions from Washington, received by the steamer Panama since the issuing of the proclamation, fully confirm the views there set forth; and it is distinctly said in these instructions that '*the plan of establishing an independent government in California can not be sanctioned, no matter from what source it may come.*'"

If these instructions do confirm the views of the proclamation, I must say that the General has been unfortunate in his quotation. Although this most solemn and threatening extract from the instructions is put in italics to give it greater point, and introduced in such a connection as to be endorsed as *true* by General Riley, it contains nothing that touches the question, and only puts forth a libel upon the people of California. As a citizen of the United States, attached to the Government of my country by all the ties of duty, kindred, admiration, and love, as a citizen of California, and as a man, I must express my sincere regret and mortification.

What is meant by the phrase "independent government"? Did the intelligent officer who drew up these instructions mean

to say that a mere temporary provisional government, merely regulating our domestic affairs, and that only while Congress neglected and refused to do so themselves—not conflicting with any rights of the General Government, not absolving the inhabitants from their allegiance to the United States, not declaring us *independent*, but expressly admitting our *dependence*—in short, such a government as was organized by the people of Oregon and sanctioned by the home Government—I ask in candor, did the writer mean to call this an "independent government" that could not be sanctioned? I can not believe it. The writer knows too well the use of terms. What is an "independent government"? Undoubtedly such a government as was proclaimed by the Declaration of Independence, which declared the colonies to be "free and independent States," and the people to be absolved from all allegiance to the British Crown. . . . Now, Mr. Editor, let me inquire what single individual in California, not to speak of any considerable portion of this community, ever did propose, or dream of proposing, a "plan of establishing an independent government in California"? Is it true that such a plan was proposed? If so, who proposed it? For one, I am not informed of such a thing.

The idea of establishing an independent government here—thus cutting us off from the Union and from all protection of the mother country, and erecting a mere petty state to be the sport and play of all the great powers of the world, that might think it their *interest* or *whim* to insult and plunder us—certainly never was contemplated by our people here. Why, then, are we charged with such an absurd and criminal attempt? Have the authorities at Washington been deceived as to the true state of things here? How have they come to be so mistaken? There is a great mistake somewhere.

Who is to blame we can not tell. All we know with unerring certainty is, that we are the doomed sufferers. The officers here shelter themselves behind the impenetrable shield called "instructions," and the authorities at home are ignorant of our condition. Is our country or our brethren in the States to be blamed for this? Certainly not. They will do us justice. The time is coming when California can have her equal station

among the States of the Union, and when her servants can be heard, and her voice regarded. P.

An editorial in the "Alta" for July 19, 1849, refers to this charge as follows: "For two years and a half that we have resided in California, we have never heard the idea seriously uttered, that California should become an independent government."

The denial by General Riley of the alleged right of the people of California to form a temporary provisional government was substantially based upon these grounds: That, under the law of nations, the civil laws of the ceded territory remain in force until superseded by those of the government to which the cession is made; that, as Congress possessed the sole power to legislate, but had passed no act creating a territorial government for California, the civil laws of Mexico remained in force; that one of the provisions of that law was that, in case of a vacancy in the office of Governor, the military commander should fill the office for the time being; that there was such a vacancy in the office of Governor of California, and that he, General Riley, was simply *ex officio* Governor; that, in point of fact, the people of California were not living under a military government, but under one of civil law; that, in his capacity of civil Governor, he administered the civil law, as any other Governor would be bound to do; that the condition of the people of California was not similar to that of the people of Oregon when they organized their provisional government, as they were without any law whatever, while we had a code of civil law in full force; and that, consequently, the assumed exercise of legislative power by the body calling itself the Legislative Assembly of San Francisco was a usurpation of powers vested solely in Congress.

On the contrary, our claim was substantially based upon these positions: That, conceding the general principle to be true, that under the law of nations the civil laws of the ceded territory continue in force until superseded by those of the government to which the cession is made, still, in the peculiar case of California, the Mexican civil law had been so superseded; that, the moment the treaty took effect, the Constitution of the United States, and all the great leading principles upon which our American institutions are based, were at once extended over the acquired territory; that the power to legislate was primarily vested in Congress, but that, while that body neglected and refused to exercise such power, it was no usurpation in the people of California to exercise it temporarily, and in strict subordination to the admitted right of Congress; that usurpation of power is the assumed use of it by an illegal body, when, at the same time, it is claimed and exercised by the rightful authority; that under the theory of our Government the executive office of Governor can not be filled by a subordinate military officer, as the two capacities are incompatible with each other and with our American theory; that, in point of practical effect, the people of California were in the same condition as had been the people of Oregon; that nine tenths of the people of California were American citizens, lately arrived from the States east of the Rocky Mountains, wholly unacquainted with the civil laws of Mexico, and with the language in which they were written and published; that, such being the case, it was not practical good sense or justice to require these nine tenths of the people of California to learn the laws of Mexico for the short period to elapse before the new order of things was morally certain to take place; that imposing this

labor and confusion upon these nine tenths would not benefit the native citizens to any extent whatever, as they would still have to learn the laws of the new State when organized; that, as at least nine tenths of the officers charged with the administration of Mexican law would be Americans, ignorant of the law they were required to administer, and without time to learn it, the law actually enforced would be an inconsistent mixture of Mexican and American law, so confused as not to be understood; and finally, that the temporary exercise of legislative power by the people of California was based upon the original and natural right of society to protect itself by law, and that such exercise by our people was in no true sense a violation of the law of nations; but that the people of California possessed the legal and just right to supersede the civil laws of Mexico in force in California at the date of the treaty, and that this right was also based upon the theory of our American governments, properly extended and applied to the new and extraordinary circumstances of our condition.

The question as to the legal and just right of the people of California, under all the circumstances then existing, to form for themselves a temporary government, was one admitting of discussion and difference of opinion. Among the lawyers then in California, who had been here long enough to understand the true merits of the controversy, there was almost an entire unanimity in the opinion that only a *de facto* government could exist in the country, based upon the consent of the people. This was the view of three fourths of the inhabitants. It seems clear that this was the view of President Polk and Mr. Secretary Buchanan. But it seems equally clear that President Taylor and the Sec-

retaries of State and of War under him entertained the opposite view.

But, aside from the true merits of the controversy, it was *most* fortunate for California that it arose, for it resulted in the early formation of the State government, and thus settled the question in a manner most satisfactory to us all. Had General Riley conceded the right of the people of California to organize a provisional government for themselves, then they would most probably have been content with their condition for some time to come; and, had the people quietly submitted to his government, the organization of the State would have been, most likely, delayed for an indefinite time. The slave and free States then had an equal representation in the Senate of the United States, and no act for a territorial organization, and none authorizing the people of California to form a State constitution, could have been passed by Congress.

All things happily combined to bring about the result we all so much desired. The people had suffered so much from the bad administration of laws unknown to them, and were so unused to live under what they held to be a military government, that, in San Francisco especially, they were deeply and grievously excited. So soon as I became a member of the Legislative Assembly of San Francisco, my ardent efforts were mainly directed toward the formation of a State constitution, as the only safe and peaceful mode of settling the question. So far as I and a large majority of that body were concerned, we were opposed to any and all forcible conflicts with General Riley's government. While we were satisfied that our position was right, we preferred patient and peaceful means to attain a satisfactory solution of the difficulty. The resolutions passed at the

large and enthusiastic meeting in San Francisco on June 12, 1849, were prepared in advance, and after full consultation, and with a view to secure ultimate unanimity. We had our doubts whether the people would, under the then excited state of public feeling against the rule of General Riley, sanction *at once* the times appointed by him, and we therefore thought it best to have a committee of five appointed to fix the times for the election of delegates, and for the assembling of the convention, and to designate the number of delegates from San Francisco. This would give us an opportunity to consult the people of other districts, and allow time for the excitement to cool in this city, which had been so long and so grievously misgoverned. Our committee, most likely, had the power to defeat General Riley's proclamation by recommending other days, but we were not governed by feelings of opposition or of revenge. We all agreed as to the main purpose, and our committee determined not to disagree about subordinate matters.

There was not the slightest ground for the charge that the people of California desired to establish an independent government; and I can only believe that it was made through mistaken information, based solely on suspicion in the minds of General Riley's informants. I knew that old and tried soldier in Missouri, years before either of us came to California, and had always entertained for him the greatest respect. I bear a willing testimony to his integrity and patriotism. I afterward met him in September, 1849, at Monterey during the sitting of the Convention, and had several friendly interviews with him. In one of these he said to me very frankly: "Burnett, you may be correct in your views in regard to the legal right of the people of Cali-

fornia to form a provisional government. I am no lawyer, but only a soldier, and I know how to obey orders; and, when my superior officer commands me to do a thing, I am going to do it." There was no occasion to argue against this conclusion; and, had there been such an occasion, it would have been idle to contest the determination of that honest and brave old man.

RETURN TO SACRAMENTO CITY—ITS RAPID IMPROVEMENT—JAMES S. THOMAS.

About the 3d of July, 1849, I was informed that John A. Sutter, Jr., had reconveyed the property to his father, and that the latter had selected another person as his agent. On the 5th I left San Francisco for Sacramento, and arrived at the latter place on the evening of the 11th. During my absence of six weeks the population of Sacramento had greatly increased; and, although there was not a single brick and but few wooden houses in the city, it had become an active business place, teeming with people, who mainly lived and did business in canvas tents and cloth shanties.

My friend Dr. William M. Carpenter had just finished a cloth shanty on his lot at the corner of Second and K Streets. It was twenty feet long and twelve wide, with a cloth partition in the center. In the rear room he kept his office and medicines, and I had my office in the front apartment. The shanty was constructed by putting up six strong posts, made from the trunks of small trees, and flattened on two sides with an axe, one of which was put at each corner, and one in each center of the two ends of the structure. Between these posts were placed smaller posts flattened on one side, and placed some two feet apart, and on the

tops of these posts were placed flattened pieces of timber, extending along each side of the shanty, and securely nailed into the tops of the posts, the lower ends of which were well let into the ground. On the tops of the two higher posts in the centers of the ends was placed a ridge-pole, nailed with large nails; and from this ribs about two feet apart were extended to the sides. The whole frame was then covered with yard-wide brown cotton cloth, tacked on with cut tacks. The floor was the earth made smooth, and my writing-table was a large empty dry-goods box.

I was very busily engaged until July 24th in making an amicable settlement with Captain Sutter. The weather was very warm, and our thin cotton covering afforded very imperfect protection against the scorching rays of a midsummer sun.

About the last of July the immigrants across the Plains began to arrive, and among them was James S. Thomas, from Platte City, Missouri. I had known him for about three years before I left that State for Oregon in the spring of 1843. He was then a poor young lawyer of admirable character, and was most highly esteemed by all who knew him. He was a tall, thin, spare man. I had not seen him for more than six years, and in the mean time his appearance had so changed that I did not at first recognize him. I was very busily employed writing in my office about 8 o'clock one morning, when I observed some tall person standing before me. I raised my eyes and looked at him, but he said nothing, and I continued my writing. Several minutes passed, and he still remained silent. I raised my eyes and looked at him the second time, when I was greeted with a kind laugh, and then I recognized him. Our meeting was most cordial. Said I: "Sit down and I

will give you half an hour's time. That is all I can spare you now."

I at once inquired the time of his arrival, and he informed me that it was the previous evening. He said he was *very* anxious to be at work. I at once asked him what he had, and he replied some mules and a wagon. I said: "Go sell everything and then come to me, and I will do the best I can for you." That day he sold everything, and came to my office next morning. I said to him: "We are to elect a magistrate to-morrow, and I will attend a meeting of citizens called for this evening to make a nomination, and will procure your selection if I can. In case you are selected, my brother-in-law, John P. Rogers, my son, D. J. Burnett, and myself will close our office, and give you one day's electioneering."

I attended the meeting, and made an earnest, vigorous speech for Thomas, and he received the nomination. Next day we had a warm contest at the polls, as his competitor was well known in the city. Many objected to Thomas upon the ground of his profession. To this objection I replied that, while I had nothing to say in defense of lawyers as a class, I would say that Thomas was among the best of his profession. He was elected, and I then said to him: "Take the official oath as early as you can, and then come to me and I will give you something to do." The next day the result was declared, and he took the necessary oath, and came to my office in the evening; and I told him to be at the office next morning at sunrise.

An auctioneer named Scovey had been sent from San Francisco to Sacramento City a few days previously to sell several Sacramento City lots, in subdivisions, to the highest bidder for cash. He had completed the

sale, and then came to me to draw up the deeds. There were from twenty to thirty deeds to be written out (there being then no printed blanks), for which I was to be paid ten dollars each. A full list of the property sold, with names of the purchasers and prices paid, was furnished by Scovey. I told Thomas that we would each write as many deeds as we could, and each receive pay for those he wrote; and that, in addition, he could write out and take the acknowledgments, the fee for each being two dollars and a half.

On the morning appointed he was promptly on hand at sunrise, and we commenced our work with a will. I never saw a poor lawyer work with more zeal. It was truly amusing to see him wield that pen. To use a cant but expressive phrase, "I did my level best," and so did he. From sunrise to sunset we scarcely lost a moment, except at twelve to take a hasty lunch. That day Thomas made more than one hundred dollars, and that was his beginning in California.

When I arrived at Sacramento City, I found melons in market. An old man of the name of Swartz cultivated several acres in melons that year, on the west bank of the Sacramento River, at a point some five miles below the city. These melons he sold readily at from one to three dollars each, according to size. From the sale of melons he realized that year some thirty thousand dollars. I mention these cases as illustrative of those times. Such times, I think, were never seen before, and will hardly be seen again.

I have seen a whole community, for a time, substantially living under the theory of an equal division of property. In California, during the years 1848 and 1849, all men had about an even start, and all grew comparatively rich. At least, they were all *equally* se-

cure of a good living, except those who were unable to work. But within a year or two thereafter the usual inequalities in the financial conditions of men began to appear. Nothing more clearly and concisely shows what would be the legitimate result of communism, than the replies of a witty Irishman, who was ironically advocating an equal and forcible division of property among men. "But what would you do, Patrick, with your share?" "Faith," said he, "I would live like a prince." "But you would soon spend it all, and then what would you do?" "And faith, I would go for another division."

APPOINTED TO A SEAT IN THE SUPERIOR TRIBUNAL—SICKNESS OF ONE OF MY DAUGHTERS—REMOVE TO SAN JOSÉ—ADMINISTRATION OF JUSTICE IN CALIFORNIA DURING 1849—STATE OF SOCIETY—THE QUACK.

I left Sacramento City on my return to San Francisco on the 3d of August, 1849, and arrived in the latter city about the 10th. During my absence of some five weeks, many stirring events had transpired in San Francisco.

On the 10th of July, Francis J. Lippitt, Esq., Speaker of the Legislative Assembly of the district of San Francisco, resigned his seat. A vote of the people had been taken as to whether that body should continue to act. The affirmative vote was 167, the negative, 7. The smallness of the vote polled proved conclusively that a large majority of the people did not deem it necessary to vote at all. The fact that General Riley had substantially allowed the people to choose their own officers, and especially the certain prospect that the convention would soon meet and form a State constitution, and thus give us all the relief we asked, satisfied the good

sense of our people that no further controversy was proper or desirable. Thus the Legislative Assembly of the district of San Francisco came to an end. ("Alta," July 12 and 19, 1849.)

On Sunday night, July 14th, the "Hounds" attacked and robbed several Chilian tents in San Francisco. As this occurred during my absence at Sacramento City, I can give no account of it from my own knowledge, but must refer to the "Alta" of August 4th and succeeding numbers for a full account of that most daring crime.

Upon my return to San Francisco, I found that during my absence, and without my knowledge, my name had been used as a candidate for a seat in the Superior Tribunal, and that I had received 1,298 votes, and Mr. Dimmick 212. My commission is in the words and figures following:

Know all men by these Presents, that I, Bennet Riley, Brevet Brigadier General U. S. Army, and Governor of California, by virtue of authority in me vested, do hereby appoint and commission Peter H. Burnett Judge or Minister of the Superior Tribunal of California, to date from the 1st day of August, 1849.

{ SEAL. } Given under my hand and seal at Monterey, California, this 13th day of August, A. D. 1849.

B. RILEY,

Bt. Brigd. Genl. U. S. A., and Governor of California.

Official.

H. W. HALLECK,

Bt. Capt. and Secty. of State.

Before my family left Oregon in May, my eldest daughter, then sixteen, was attacked with what her physician afterward decided to be consumption. The voyage by sea gave her temporary relief, but the cold winds of San Francisco soon increased the serious char-

acter of the case. When I returned from Sacramento City, I found her very ill. Her physician told me very frankly that he could do no more for her, as she was in the last stage of consumption.

I at once determined that she should take no more medicine, and should at least die in peace. I remembered that our physician in Missouri, Dr. Ware S. May, had told me that patients were sometimes starved to death, and that he had known of such cases. Mr. Moffat, an assayer of San Francisco, mentioned to me a case within his own knowledge, where the life of the patient was saved by eating a little beefsteak. The medicines taken by my daughter had so deranged the tone of her stomach that she could retain nothing that she ate, and had not the least appetite, but a great aversion for food of every kind. I persuaded her to eat a mouthful of broiled steak, which she at once threw up; but I immediately urged her to try again, and this morsel she was able to retain. From that time she rapidly improved. Believing that the climate of San Francisco was injurious to her health, I decided to leave the city. I could only *then* go to Sacramento City or to San José. In the former place I could procure no shelter except a canvas tent or a cloth shanty; so I went to San José for the first time about the 20th of August, and purchased a house and lot in that city. On the 28th my daughter had so far recovered that she could endure the trip, and we arrived in San José the next day. In two months she was well. She was married in January, 1851, is still living, and is the mother of several living children.

As illustrative of those times, I will relate two occurrences.

I employed a man named Wistman, with a large

spring-wagon, to remove us to San José, for which service I paid him one hundred and fifty dollars. It took him two days.

I was the owner of a number of lots in Sacramento City; and one day in August a gentleman of my acquaintance came to my little office in San Francisco, and said to me: "Mr. —— and myself will give you fifty thousand dollars in gold-dust for one undivided half of your Sacramento City property—one half cash, and the other half by the first of January next; and we want an answer by ten to-morrow morning." I promptly replied that I would give an answer at the time mentioned. I at once consulted Mrs. Burnett, and we decided that we would accept the offer, with certain reservations. Next morning the gentleman was at my office at the precise hour for an answer. I told him I would accept the offer, with the exception of a few lots that I mentioned. He at once replied, "All right." There happened to be present a mutual friend from Sacramento City, a man about fifty years of age; and this gentleman at once rose from his seat, and, seizing the hand of the first gentleman, he warmly congratulated him upon the splendid purchase he and his partner had made, saying there was a large fortune in the property. During this long-continued burst of enthusiasm I sat perfectly quiet; but, so soon as I could be heard, I said: "Gentlemen, I am glad to learn that I am a much richer man than I supposed I was. If these gentlemen can make a fortune out of the undivided half they have purchased, what do you think I can make out of my half, and the fifty thousand dollars to begin with?" This view of the case rather cooled their enthusiasm.

During the year 1848 there were very few, if any, thefts committed in California. The honest miners

kept their sacks of gold-dust in their tents, without fear of loss. Men were then too well off to steal. Toward the close of that year some few murders and robberies were committed. But in 1849 crimes multiplied rapidly. The immigrants from Australia consisted in part of very bad characters, called "Sydney Ducks." These men soon began to steal gold-dust from the miners, and the latter showed them no mercy. In most mining camps they had an alcalde, whose decisions were prompt and final, and whose punishments were severe and most rigidly inflicted.

On one occasion, in the fall of 1849, a tall, handsome young fellow, dressed in a suit of fine broadcloth, and mounted upon a splendid horse, stole a purse of gold-dust from an honest miner, and fled from the camp. The thief took the plain wagon-road that led around a tall mountain, while his pursuers took a shorter route across, reached a mining camp where there was an alcalde in advance of the thief, and quietly awaited his arrival. In due time the thief appeared, mounted upon his splendid steed, and was at once arrested, and promptly tried before the alcalde. After hearing all the testimony, the alcalde said to the prisoner: "The Court thinks it right that you should return that purse of gold to its owner." To this the culprit readily assented, and handed over the purse. The alcalde then informed him that the Court also thought he ought to pay the costs of the proceedings. To this the culprit made not the slightest objection (thinking he was very fortunate to escape so easily), but inquired the amount of the costs. The alcalde informed him that the costs amounted to two ounces of gold-dust. This the prisoner cheerfully paid. "Now," said the alcalde, "there is another part of the sentence of this Court that has not been men-

tioned yet; and that is, that you receive thirty-nine lashes on your bare back, well laid on." The punishment was promptly inflicted, and, of course, the transgressor thought his way hard. He could only boast that he was "whipped and cleared." *

In the fall of 1849 William B. Almond, then late of Missouri, became the Judge of the Court of First Instance, in civil cases, for the district of San Francisco. There are proper times and places for all proper things; and no sensible man would approve of Yankee Doodle at a funeral or of Old Hundred at a ball. There are *right* things to be done, and proper *modes* of doing them. Judge Almond was a man of fair legal attainments, and had been one of the early settlers of the Platte Purchase in Missouri, and he well comprehended the situation of California. Perhaps substantial justice was never so promptly administered anywhere as it was by him in San Francisco. His Court was thronged with cases, and he knew that delay would be ruin to the parties, and a complete practical denial of justice. He saw that more than one half the witnesses were fresh arrivals, on their way to the mines, and that they were too eager to see the regions of gold to be detained more than two or three days. Besides, the ordinary wages of common laborers were twelve dollars a day, and parties could not afford to pay their witnesses enough to induce them to remain; and, once in the mines, no depositions could be taken, and no witness induced to return.

* The origin of this phrase was as follows: In the early days of Missouri, Thomas —— was arrested, indicted, tried, and convicted of grand larceny in stealing a horse, and was sentenced by the Court to receive thirty-nine lashes on his bare back. After he was whipped and discharged, he met an acquaintance who inquired how he came out. He promptly replied: "First-rate. Whipped and cleared."

He accordingly allowed each lawyer appearing before him to speak five minutes, and no more. If a lawyer insisted upon further time, the Judge would good-humoredly say that he would allow the additional time upon condition that the Court should decide the case against his client. Of course, the attorney submitted the case upon his speech of five minutes. At first the members of the bar were much displeased with this concise and summary administration of justice; but in due time they saw it was the only sensible, practical, and just mode of conducting judicial proceedings under the then extraordinary condition of society in California. They found that, while Judge Almond made mistakes of law as well as other judges, his decisions were generally correct and *always* prompt; and that their clients had, at least, no reason to complain of "the law's most villainous delay." Parties litigant obtained decisions at once, and were let go on their way to the mines.

The state of society in California in 1849 was indeed extraordinary. There were so few families, so few old men, and so many young and middle-aged adventurers, all so eager in search of riches, that a state of things then existed which perhaps has no parallel. Young men just from college, arriving in San Francisco, and never having been accustomed to manual labor, would hire themselves out as porters, journeymen carpenters, and draymen. One young man, who barely knew how to use a hand-saw well, hired himself to a boss carpenter. After working a day or two, he was paid off and discharged, and then went to another and another, repeating the same trick. When all were strangers to each other, all stood upon the same basis as to character and qualifications.

As illustrative of those times, I will relate the following incident:

Before leaving Weston, Missouri, for Oregon, in May, 1843, I was well acquainted with Thomas ——. He was then about thirty years of age, was of poor but honest parentage, could scarcely read or write, and had then never worn any but homespun clothes. He was a very skillful ox-driver and a good fiddler, and this was the extent of his capacity. Because of his skill in managing oxen, I employed him to drive one of my teams for a day or two, until my oxen were trained.

I left him in Missouri in 1843; but, when I arrived at Sutter's Fort in December, 1848, I found him and his family residing in the vicinity. His wife was a plain, good, domestic woman, and Tom himself was considered a *clever* fellow, in the American sense of that term. During the early spring of 1849 I sold him several lots in Sacramento City, upon the resale of which in the fall of that year he realized a net profit of twenty-five thousand dollars. Flushed with this sudden and extraordinary success, he dressed himself in the finest suit of clothes he could procure. He possessed a tall, straight, trim figure, and when thus attired was a very handsome man. Taking advantage of the circumstances, he commenced the practice of medicine. A carpenter named Stincen, who had known Tom well in Weston, came to Sacramento City in the fall of 1849, and soon met Tom arrayed in his splendid apparel. Stincen was a man of excellent sense, and possessed a keen perception of the ridiculous. "How are you, Tom?" said he. "First rate." "How are you getting along?" "Splendid." "What are you doing?" "Come and see." He took Stincen a short distance, and showed him a splendid mule, rigged up in superb style, with new saddle, bridle,

and martingales. Across the saddle was thrown a pair of new medical saddle-bags. Tom raised up the flap of one end, and, pointing to several rows of vials full of liquid medicines, said, "Look at that." "What does all this mean?" asked Stincen. "I am practicing medicine." "But what do you know about the practice of medicine, Tom?" "Well, not much; but I get all I can do, and I kill just as few as any of them. I never give them anything to hurt them."

Stincen himself related this interview to me, and it is no doubt true.

VISIT MONTEREY—ANNOUNCE MYSELF A CANDIDATE FOR GOVERNOR—ELECTED—INAUGURAL ADDRESS.

About the 13th of September I left San José for Monterey, to assist in holding a term of the Superior Tribunal. Four persons had been nominated by the people at the election held August 1st, who were subsequently appointed and commissioned by General Riley. These were José M. Covarubias, Pacificus Ord, Lewis Dent, and Peter H. Burnett. The last-named was chosen Chief Justice by the other Judges. The business before the Court was very small. No appeals had been taken; they were not common in those days.

I remained in Monterey until about the last of September. The proceedings of the Convention, which assembled on the first of that month, had progressed favorably, so far as to leave no reasonable doubt as to the final result, and I then announced myself a candidate for Governor. I arrived in San José about the 5th of October, and left there, to make the canvass, about the 20th. I reached San Francisco on the evening of the same day, and remained there three days. When I left

the city about six weeks before, I knew a large portion of the people of the place ; but, upon my return, I did not know one in ten, such had been the rapid increase in the population. I was surprised to find myself so much of a stranger, and I said to myself, "This is rather a poor prospect for Governor."

One of my opponents, Winfield Scott Sherwood, Esq., proposed that we should submit our claims to a committee of mutual friends, and let them decide which of us should withdraw. I declined this proposition, and at once set out to speak to the people. I left San Francisco about the 23d of October for Sacramento City, on board a very small steamer, the second one that ever ascended the Sacramento River. It was full of passengers, and was so small that they were frequently ordered to trim the boat.

On my arrival at Sacramento City, I addressed a large meeting of the people. From that city I went to Mormon Island on the American River, and made a speech. From there I passed to Coloma, the point where gold was first discovered, and addressed the people at that place ; and then to Placerville, where I again addressed a large meeting. From Placerville I returned to Sacramento City on the 29th of October. On my way I spent the night of the 28th at Mud Springs, in an hotel kept in a large canvas tent. They gave me a very fine bed to sleep in, and treated me most kindly.

During the day the wind commenced blowing briskly from the south. In the evening dense clouds began to appear, and the wind increased to a gale. After we had all retired to bed, the rain began to fall heavily, and the storm became so severe that the fastenings of the tent gave way, and nothing was left of the frame but the main upright pole, about thirty feet high, that

stood in the center, to the top of which the canvas was securely fastened, while it hung flapping around the pole at the bottom. The rain came down in torrents, and the only way we could keep dry was to stand around and hug the lower end of the pole until daylight. This was the first hard rain of that most rainy season of 1849–'50. I never passed a more cheerless and uncomfortable night than this. I was very tired and sleepy, and frequently found myself asleep on my feet, and in the act of sinking down with my arms around the pole.

I remained in Sacramento City until the 5th of November, when the majestic steamer Senator arrived for the first time. The banks of the river, on Front Street, were thronged with people to witness her approach. She was to us a most beautiful object. I came down on board of her, and paid thirty dollars for my passage, and two dollars in addition for my dinner.

I passed through San Francisco, and arrived at San José about the 8th of November. After making a speech to the people of that city, I went again to San Francisco, where I spoke to an immense assemblage in Portsmouth Square. A platform about six feet high, and large enough to seat about a hundred persons, was made of rough boards and scantling. The main audience stood in front, on the ground. In the midst of my address the platform gave way and fell to the ground, except a small portion where I was standing. I paused only for a moment, and then went on with my speech, remarking that, though others might fall, I would be sure to stand.

I was in the city until the 13th of November, the day of the general election, at which the State constitution was ratified, and the principal State officers, Senators, members of the Assembly, and Congressmen were

elected. The vote for Governor was as follows: Peter H. Burnett, 6,716; W. Scott Sherwood, 3,188; John A. Sutter, 2,201; J. W. Geary, 1,475; William M. Steuart, 619.

Both Houses of the Legislature assembled on Saturday, December 15, 1849, as required by the constitution. The Governor elect was inaugurated at one o'clock P. M. on Thursday, December 20th, and took the following oath:

"I, Peter H. Burnett, do solemnly swear that I will support the Constitution of the United States and the constitution of the State of California, and will faithfully discharge the duties of the office of Governor of the State of California, according to the best of my ability."

After taking this oath, I delivered the following address:

Gentlemen of the Senate and Assembly: I have been chosen by a majority of my fellow citizens of the State of California to be her first Executive. For this proof of their partiality and confidence I shall ever retain a most grateful sense. To be chosen Chief Magistrate of California at this period of her history, when the eyes of the whole world are turned toward her, is a high and distinguished honor, and I shall do all in my power to merit this distinction by an ardent, sincere, and energetic discharge of the weighty and responsible duties incident to the position I occupy.

Nature, in her kindness and beneficence, has distinguished California by great and decided natural advantages; and these great natural resources will make her either a very great or a very sordid and petty State. She can take no middle course. She will either be distinguished among her sister States as one of the leading Stars of the Union, or she will sink into comparative insignificance. She has many dangers to encounter, many perils to meet. In all those countries where rich and extensive mines of the precious metals have been heretofore

discovered, the people have become indolent, careless, and stupid. This enervating influence operates silently, steadily, and continually, and requires counteracting causes, or great and continued energy of character in a people to successfully resist it. How far this influence may mold the character of the future population of California, time alone can determine. If she should withstand and overcome this great peril, she will constitute a bright exception to the fate that has attended other States similarly situated.

But I anticipate for her a proud and happy destiny. If she had only her gold-mines, the danger would be imminent; but she has still greater and more commanding interests than this—interests that seldom or never enervate or stultify a people, but on the contrary tend, in their very nature, to excite and nourish industry, enterprise, and virtue. I mean her agricultural and commercial advantages. While our mines will supply us with ample capital, and our fine agricultural lands will furnish us with provisions, our great and decided commercial facilities and position will give full and active employment to the energies and enterprise of our people, and will prevent them from sinking into that state of apathy and indifference which can not exist in a commercial and active community.

Our new State will soon take her equal station among the other States of the Union. When admitted a member of that great sisterhood, she will occupy an important position, imposing upon her new and great responsibilities. She can never forget what is due to herself, much less can she forget what is due to the whole Union. Her destiny will be united with that of her sister States, and she will form one of the links of that bright chain that binds together the happy millions of the American people.

How wide and extended is our expanding country! With only thirteen States and three millions of inhabitants originally, we have grown in the short space of three quarters of a century to be one of the greatest nations of the earth. With a Federal Government to manage and control our external relations with the world at large, and State governments to regulate our internal and business relations with each other, our system is pecu-

liarly adapted for extension over a wide field, without danger of becoming unwieldy and impracticable. We have now more than twenty millions of inhabitants, and thirty States, with others knocking at the door of the Union for admittance. Our States and cities have the eastern coast of North America facing Europe, and our country extends across the entire continent to the shores of the Pacific, facing the millions of Asia. We have commanding military and commercial positions on both oceans, and nothing can retard our onward march to greatness but our own errors and our own follies. California has her part to act in this great march of improvement, and whether she acts well her part or not depends much upon her early legislation.

With the most ardent desire to do my duty fully and frankly toward our new and rising State, I pledge you my most cordial coöperation in your efforts to promote the happiness of California and the Union. For the principles that will govern me in my administration of the executive department of the State, I beg leave to refer you to my forthcoming message.

I thank you, gentlemen, for the kindness and courtesy you have shown me, and hope that your labors may redound to your own honor and the happiness of your constituents.

THE CHINESE—REASONS FOR THEIR EXCLUSION—THE BURLINGAME TREATY.

In the view of many most humane and devoted people, our country should be thrown open to all the world, with the right not only of domicile, but of citizenship. Regarding, as I do myself, all mankind as of the same origin, these persons seem to think that the population of the globe should be left, like water, to find its own level. But this comprehensive and apparently just view is too liberal for practical statesmanship. The *practical* result would be, that the Mongolian race (the most numerous of the families of mankind) would in due time

possess the country on this coast, to the ultimate exclusion of the white man.

The Chinese Empire is one of vast extent, everywhere under the same compact government. It contains four hundred millions of people, about equal to one third the population of the world. These people esteem their country (and with much apparent reason) as the oldest, wealthiest, and grandest empire upon this earth. No other people are so proud of their country, or so inveterately attached to it, as are the Chinese. But, while they regard their country with so much admiration and affection as not to desire a *permanent* allegiance to any other government, they would doubtless be willing to extend its limits by the colonization and addition of other territory.

Their policy of isolation, continued for a long series of centuries, has made their people peaceable, economical, loyal, and industrious; and, in the general absence of foreign and domestic wars, the population has increased, under the legitimate effects of this policy, to such enormous proportions as to become suffering and corrupt.

For thousands of years the Chinese have been accustomed to live upon as little as would possibly support human life. For ages upon ages their inventive faculties seem to have lain dormant. Their rulers and statesmen have, during long periods in the past, opposed all labor-saving inventions, for the simple reason that their labor-market was overstocked. They seldom or never change the style or character of their manufactured articles, or their fashions of dress, because such changes would violate their most rigid rules of economy. The style of dress for the laboring classes is the simplest and cheapest possible, consistent with ease and comfort.

A Chinese laborer will provide himself with a bamboo hat, costing twenty-five cents, that will last him a lifetime. His shoes are made of cheap but durable materials, with broad, thick, flat bottoms, that wear away slowly and never slip; and his shoes never produce corns on his feet. A Chinese merchant makes all his mathematical calculations upon a plain little wooden box, twelve inches long, six inches wide, and two inches deep, with parallel wires passing lengthwise through it, and one inch apart, upon which are placed a number of small wooden balls. This little instrument will cost fifty cents, last for hundreds of years, and save several hundred dollars a year in stationery to a large establishment.

Their merchants are very intelligent men in their line of business. I was well acquainted with Fung Tang, the Chinese orator and merchant. He was a cultivated man, well read in the history of the world, spoke four or five different languages fluently, including English, and was a most agreeable gentleman, of easy and pleasing manners.

When the Chinese merchants first arrived in San Francisco, and for a time thereafter, they made all their purchases of our merchants for cash. Within a short period they learned that, according to our mercantile usages, cash sales meant payment on steamer-day; and, as these days were semi-monthly, they readily availed themselves of the credit they could thus obtain. A little later they purchased on thirty, forty, and sixty days' time. In short, they learned all our usages that promised them any advantages, except the three days' grace on promissory notes and bills of exchange. That provision no Chinese merchant ever learned; so that, if a Chinaman made his note payable on the first day of

June, he would pay on that day, though legally entitled to wait till the fourth. There is something so inconsistent in the position that, although a note by its *express* terms was made payable on the first of June, yet in law it was payable on the fourth, that Chinese acuteness never comprehended it.

While they are perfectly willing themselves to purchase on credit, they decline to sell to our people on time. One of our leading merchants, on one occasion, determined to monopolize all the rice in San Francisco. To carry out this purpose, he went to a large wholesale Chinese rice-house, and said to the owner, "Suppose I should wish to purchase two thousand bags of rice, could you supply me with that number?" "Yes, me sell you that number." After quietly talking some time, the American merchant again asked, "Could you sell me four thousand?" "Yes, me sell you four thousand." The American merchant continued the conversation about other matters for some time, and then quietly said, "Suppose I should conclude to take six thousand, could you supply that number?" "Yes, me sell you six thousand." "Would you give me any time?" "Me know you one very rich Melican merchant. Me give you time. You pay me one half when the rice is weighed, and the other half when it is on the dray."

Born and nursed in poverty, and early trained in the severe schools of unremitting toil and extreme economy, the Chinaman is more than a match for the white man in the struggle for existence. The white man can do as much work, and as skillfully, as the Chinaman; but he *can not live so cheaply.* It would require many centuries of inexorable training to bring the white man down to the low level of the Chinese mode of living. Were Chinamen permitted to settle in our country at

their pleasure, and were they granted all the rights and privileges of the whites, and the laws were then impartially and efficiently administered, so that the two races would stand *precisely* and *practically* equal in *all* respects, in one century the Chinese would own all the property on this coast. This result they would accomplish by their greater numbers and superior economy.

We have not yet had a full and fair opportunity to study Chinese character, as those among us are, by circumstances, put upon their very best behavior. The same number of Americans placed in China would prove very peaceable and industrious. This would necessarily be so. Small bodies of men living in a foreign country, perfectly defenseless, and with full knowledge that they are at the mercy of the natives, will be very apt to act most prudently. In comparing the Chinese with our own people, a fair and just allowance should be made for the difference in their respective positions.

If two equally poor young men of the same capacity and health should start in life together at the age of twenty-one, and obtain the same compensation and continue so for ten years, and one should be a good economist and save up a portion of his income each year, and the other should spend all his as fast as received, at the end of the ten years the first would be in independent circumstances, while the other would be as poor as at the beginning, and would have lost ten years of his business life. Such are the effects of economy even for short periods of time. But extend this practice of saving for a hundred years, and the effects will be surprising.

It is painful to the thoughtful and reflective to see a proscribed class of men in any community. It is more especially so in a republic, where every citizen is a sov-

ereign, where the laws are practically made by the majority, and where the officers charged with the execution of the same are elected by this majority. Under such a theory of government, no unpopular law can be fairly enforced. You may speak, write, and publish all that can be said upon the subject, and still the laws can not be practically and efficiently administered for the protection of an unpopular class of men. Modes of evasion will be successfully resorted to. We see this fully exemplified here in San Francisco. While parents will not very often openly assault Chinamen in the streets of the city, they can manage to show their hostility through their children. The young are natural tyrants, and, when they find victims upon whom they can practice this tyranny with impunity, they never fail to do it. It is very difficult, if not impossible, for the police and other officers of the law to prevent this violence in children, when they are not restrained, but rather encouraged, by their parents and a majority of the voters. The worst effect of the presence of the Chinese among us is the fact that it is making *tyrants and lawless ruffians of our boys.* It is true, the poor Chinamen suffer from this violence, but still their situation in California is better than their former half-starved condition at home. Here they are well fed, housed, and clothed.

I have long been opposed to the residence of the Chinese among us, except for purposes of trade. This opposition is not based upon any prejudice against the race, for I am not conscious of prejudices against any race of men. I believe, with St. Paul, in the unity of the human race, as expressed in the twenty-sixth verse of the seventeenth chapter of Acts. But, while I am opposed to the residence of Chinese laborers among us, I am equally opposed to all illegal methods of preventing

the settlement of other Chinamen in our country, or for expelling those that are now resident here. The only legal, loyal, and just mode of preventing and removing the evil is, to begin at the beginning, and correct the first error by amending the treaty.

The Burlingame treaty should have been so framed as to allow the *merchants* of each country a residence within the limits of the other for purposes of trade and commerce only. The treaty, as it now exists, very plausibly assumes to put the people of the two nations upon about equal terms ; but in practical effect it is very far from working equally. It is like the fable of the fox and the stork. The fox invited the stork to dinner, which consisted of thin soup served up in shallow dishes. While the fox, with his flexible tongue, readily licked up all the soup, the poor stork, with his long, inflexible bill, could not swallow a drop. All the calm, cunning, but mock politeness of the fox in urging the stork to help himself could not better his condition, and he went without his dinner. So it is with our people. Their condition is such that they can not go to China to reside and make a living, but the Chinese can well come here, and improve their condition by doing so.

The Chinese Empire will not probably sustain for the future the same relative position toward the other nations of the world that it has done for many ages past. The civilized nations found the Chinese isolated from the other peoples of the earth, and brought such influences to bear upon their Government as to induce a departure, at least in part, from the former policy. This is only the beginning of an entire change. The rulers and statesmen of that country will soon learn, especially from the ambassadors they are now sending

abroad, that all the intellect of mankind is not to be found in China; that other nations excel them in many decisive respects; and that their Government must adopt all the great improvements of other nations, in order to protect its own rights. These rulers and statesmen will, in due time, come to understand the great fact that the Chinese Empire, by adopting the improvements of other nations, can readily become the greatest power in the world. All that Government has to do, in order to attain the foremost position among the nations of the earth, is to employ its almost unlimited resources to the best advantage. It could readily spare one hundred of the four hundred millions of its population, without impairing its effective strength; and the condition of the remaining three hundred millions would be improved by the change. China could organize and support an army of such numbers as, when well disciplined and ably commanded, would be perfectly irresistible in most portions of Asia. Nothing is more probable than that China within the next century will fully learn and use her mighty power. Then she may give England more trouble in India than England has any reason to fear from Russia. England, some years ago, forced China to admit the importation of opium, and she may not forget or forgive this act. Nations often live long enough to punish their enemies. There being no supernal existence for nations, they can only be punished in this world; and they never learn except through suffering.

CHAPTER IX.

GENERAL RILEY—JUDGE THOMAS—VARIABLE PRICES—MONOPOLIES.

On the 22d of December, 1849, I sent the following message, with accompanying documents, to the Legislature:

San José, *December* 22, 1849.

Gentlemen of the Senate and Assembly: I take pleasure in placing before you the two accompanying proclamations issued by the late Governor Riley, and respectfully suggest that a convenient number be printed for distribution.

It has been my happiness to have long known Governor Riley, and I can say, in all sincerity and candor, that there does not exist, in my opinion, a more ardent and devoted friend of his country, or one who has served her more faithfully; and I desire to put on record this humble testimony to the character and services of one who has done so much for the people of California, and enjoys so fully their confidence and esteem.

Peter H. Burnett.

Proclamation. To the People of California.

It having been ascertained by the official canvass that the Constitution submitted to the people on the 13th day of November was ratified by the almost unanimous vote of the electors of this State:

Now, therefore, I, Bennet Riley, Brevet Brigadier General U. S. Army, and Governor of California, do hereby proclaim

and declare the said Constitution to be ordained and established as the Constitution of the State of California.

Given at Monterey, California, this 12th day of December, 1849.

(Signed) B. RILEY,
Bt. Brig. Gen. U. S. A. and Governor of California.

By the Governor.
H. W. HALLECK, Bt. Capt. and Secretary of State.

Proclamation. To the People of California.

A new Executive having been elected and installed into office, in accordance with the provisions of the Constitution of the State, the undersigned hereby resigns his powers as Governor of California. In thus dissolving his official connection with the people of this country, he would tender to them his most heartfelt thanks for their many kind attentions, and for the uniform support they have given to the measures of his administration. The principal object of all his wishes is now accomplished; the people have a government of their own choice—one which, under the favor of Divine Providence, will secure their own prosperity and happiness, and the permanent welfare of the new State.

Given at San José, California, this 20th day of December A. D. 1849.

(Signed) B. RILEY.
Bt. Brig. Gen. U. S. A. and Governor of California.

By the Governor.
H. W. HALLECK, Bt. Capt. and Secretary of State.

On March 30, 1850, the Convention of both Houses unanimously elected James S. Thomas Judge of the Sixth Judicial District of California, which district included Sacramento City. He returned to Missouri within a year or two thereafter, married, and then took up his residence in St. Louis, where I saw him in the fall of 1856. He was then far gone in consumption,

and died there in 1857 or 1858. He was an excellent man.

The rainy season of 1849–'50 set in on the night of October 28, 1849, and terminated March 22, 1850. It was one of our wettest seasons. The rainfall that season, as shown by the rain-gauge kept by Dr. Logan at Sacramento City, was upward of thirty-six inches.

The first session of our Legislature was one of the best we have ever had. The members were honest, indefatigable workers. The long-continued rainy season and the want of facilities for dispatching business were great obstacles in their way. Besides, they had to begin at the beginning, and create an entire new code of statute law, with but very few authorities to consult. The Convention that framed our Constitution and the first session of our Legislature were placed in the same position in this respect. Under the circumstances, their labors were most creditable to them. They had not only few authorities to consult, but their time was short. At the close of the session, the bills came into my hands so rapidly that it was a physical impossibility to read them all myself within the time allowed me. I was, therefore, compelled to refer some to the Secretary of State, and others to my Private Secretary, and approve them after a single reading upon their recommendation. I had to do this, or let the State government go on with a mutilated code of statutory law, or call an extra session.

During the winter of 1849–'50 the prices of provisions were most exorbitant. This was owing to monopolies and the great cost of transportation over bad roads. In many mining localities flour was sold at from fifty cents to one dollar a pound. At San José

flour was sold for twenty-five cents a pound, sugar fifty cents, and coffee seventy-five.

For some years California was subject to extremely low and high markets. Everything was imported, and nothing made. We were so distant from the sources of supply, and our communication with New York so infrequent, being by monthly steamers, that speculators often monopolized all of certain articles. One large operator purchased all the flour, and others different articles of prime necessity. On one occasion one man went around San Francisco and bought up all the cut tacks in the city, and then put up the price to a high figure. At one time the country would be overstocked, and then prices would recede to so low a figure that importations into the State would cease for a time. The article of shot in the summer of 1849 was worth only one dollar and twenty-five cents per bag of twenty-five pounds, and in the following winter readily brought ten dollars per bag. Iron at one time was scarcely worth the storage. So of mining implements and many other supplies. Speculators would at such times monopolize these articles and put up the prices.

AGRICULTURAL CHARACTER OF THE STATE — NATIVE GRASSES ANNUAL NOT PERENNIAL—NATIVE CLOVER.

Our agriculture may be said to have fairly started in the spring of 1850. Before that time cultivation in California was very limited. The few people residing in the country before gold was discovered found rearing stock far more profitable than agriculture. Land was very cheap, and pasturage was most ample ; and no people will undergo the drudgery of farming when they can do better with less hard work.

At the time I delivered my inaugural address in December, 1849, very few, if any, believed with me that our agricultural and commercial interests were greater and more commanding than our mineral resources; but time has shown the correctness of the opinion then expressed. For some years after the organization of the State government, the members of the Senate and Assembly from the mining counties constituted a large majority in the Legislature, and controlled the action of that body. But time has essentially changed this state of things, and has given the control to the agricultural counties and the manufacturing and commercial cities.

As heretofore stated, the western side of the continent of North America is Asiatic in its main geographical features, and differs very much from the gently undulating country east of the Rocky Mountains. It is a country of mountains and valleys. Our hills generally swell into tall mountains, and our valleys appear to the eye to be substantially dead smooth levels; but they descend about nine to ten feet to the mile. The formation of these valleys is very different from that of the agricultural lands east.

For the sake of illustration, I will take the valley of San José, to which I can almost apply the beautiful and ardent language of Moore: "There is not in the wide world a valley so sweet." This valley has an average width of about ten miles, and a length of about seventy. On the surface there is a stratum of clay, varying in thickness from ten to fifteen feet. Beneath this is a stratum of gravel about five feet thick, beneath that another stratum of clay, and then other alternate strata of clay and gravel. On each side of this long valley there is a range of tall mountains, and from the edges

of this valley to the summits of these mountains the distance is from ten to twenty miles. The rainfall in the mountains is double that in the valley. There are two outlets from the valley to the ocean, one through the Bay of San Francisco, and the other through the Bay of Monterey. The length of the streams after they reach the valley is from fiften to twenty miles, and their banks are from six to eight feet high. In the winter the supply of water from the mountains is so great that the beds of the streams in the valley are full, often to overflowing ; but in the summer and fall many of their beds are dry, except where the water is found in pools.

During our long dry season, the various living streams from the mountains pour their treasures of water into the valley, but in most cases the water runs but a short distance after entering the valley, being soon swallowed up by the various strata of gravel, through which it percolates slowly, and passes underground into the bays. As there is a descent of about nine or ten feet to the mile, and as the banks of these streams in the valley are only from six to eight feet high, it will be readily seen that, one mile below the point where the water from the mountains enters the strata of gravel, the surface of the valley will be upon a level with the point mentioned ; and two miles below that point the surface will be from ten to twelve feet below it. As you go farther down the valley, the surface will be correspondingly lower. As the water percolates slowly through these strata of gravel, the pressure to rise to the surface becomes so strong that the strata of clay above are kept wet even in the dry season ; so that, while the moisture necessary to mature the crops east of the Rocky Mountains comes down from above in the shape of rain, in California it comes up by pressure

from below. When the surface is well cultivated, and the ground kept perfectly pulverized, evaporation is almost prevented. These are the main reasons why we can produce bountiful crops of grain and grass in California during the long dry season.

But, besides these facts, our mild winter climate aids us very materially. If grain be sown before or soon after the fall rains set in, it will attain a considerable growth during the winter, which substantially ends by the first of February. By the time the rains cease in March, the grain will have attained a height of from six to ten inches, forming an impenetrable green sward, through which the sun's rays can not penetrate to the earth. For about six weeks after the cessation of the main rainy season the dews fall heavily, and this moisture sinks into the ground. As the evaporation is very little until the wheat begins to head, there is enough moisture left, with the aid of that which comes from below, to mature the crops of grain.

All our native grasses, with a very few exceptions in rare localities, are annual and not perennial, as they are in most other countries. The seeds of the various native grasses ripen in June, and fall to the ground and into the small crevices produced by the drying of the surface. When the fall rains set in, these seeds begin to sprout; and, although their growth during the winter is slow, it is fast enough to keep the stock alive in many cases. In other cases they have to be fed for a little while. Grasses that are elsewhere grown for hay are never cultivated in California, as the most productive hay-crop is either barley or the smooth-head wheat.

We have a peculiar native clover which produces a rich seed. In each small, prickly, spiral burr there are from five to seven flat, yellow seeds, about as large as

the yellow mustard-seed of commerce. During the growing season there are other native grasses which are preferred by animals, and this clover is permitted to mature its bountiful crop of hay and seed untouched. As all the native grasses ripen in the dry season, they make good hay, upon which the animals live for a time. When this hay is consumed, then the animals resort to the clover hay and seed. A stranger will be surprised at first to see the fat cattle with their heads to the dry and apparently bare ground, as if they were feeding upon the dust of the earth ; while they are, in fact, eating the seed of this clover, which they gather in with their long, flexible tongues.

Bountiful crops of Indian corn are grown in certain localities without any rain whatever, as the corn is planted after the rains cease. The cultivator of this grain selects a rich soil in a valley and near some mountain, from which the moisture comes underground steadily during the growing season. This water percolates strata of gravel, and rises slowly to the surface of the ground.

The observations I have made apply to the ordinary seasons in California. At intervals we have a famine year, when there is almost an entire failure of crops in three fourths of the State. Our average annual rainfall at Sacramento (which may be regarded as an average point for the agricultural valleys of the country) is about twenty inches. With fifteen inches of rain we can make good crops. In the winters of 1850–'51, 1863–'64, and 1876–'77, our rainfall was about seven inches. The summers of 1851, 1864, and 1877 were our driest seasons since I have been in California ; and they were just thirteen years apart. Between these extremely dry seasons there were seasons comparatively

dry when the annual rainfall would vary from eight to thirteen inches. Once in five years, upon an average, there has been too little rain for a fair crop.

THE SQUIRRELS OF CALIFORNIA—THEIR PECULIAR CHARACTERISTICS—SPECULATIVE CHARACTER OF OUR FARMERS—UNCERTAINTY OF WEALTH IN THIS STATE—INCIDENTS.

One of the greatest obstacles agriculture has had to meet in California was caused by the millions of squirrels. Our squirrel is of a dirty-gray color, very much resembling that of dry grass, and is about twice as heavy as the gray squirrel of the Mississippi valley, but not so active and beautiful. These creatures live in communities, like the prairie-dogs of the plains. They select the highest and driest localities in the valleys, so as to escape the floods of winter, and there make their homes by burrowing in the ground.

Before the country was inhabited by Americans, these pests were not very troublesome, because cultivation was then so limited, and their excessive increase was prevented by the coyotes (small wolves) and snakes, then very numerous. But, when our people came to the country, they soon destroyed the coyotes by poison and the rifle, and killed the snakes; and, as the squirrels, like other little animals, multiply rapidly, they soon became so numerous as to destroy whole fields of growing grain, even before the berries had formed in the heads.

These animals, which are almost as sensitive to cold as the alligator, lay up a sufficient store of provisions in summer, and confine themselves to their homes during winter. Even in summer they generally do not make their appearance until after sunrise. When they become

too numerous in one locality they emigrate to another, most generally in the night-time. In their villages they seem to have sentinels out, as the moment one sees an enemy approaching he sets up a loud cry that brings all to their holes instantly. They can not be driven from their homes. If a village be drowned out by water, the squirrels will not leave and seek safety in other places of refuge. They seem to think that there is no safety anywhere else. If driven by the water from their holes at one entrance they will, in the presence of men or dogs, run to another opening and plunge in. If a grain-field be some distance from their village, they will construct temporary retreats between it and the field, and into these holes they will escape for the time.

The best way to destroy them in the valleys is to cultivate by deep plowing the sites of their villages. By keeping the ground well pulverized upon the surface, the water in our very rainy winters will penetrate to their beds and destroy the squirrels, as they can not exist except in dry and warm homes. The water also destroys their stock of provisions. In some localities the streams are turned out in the winter, and made to overflow large tracts of level land. Vast numbers have been thus destroyed. When their holes are full of water, they will come out wet, sit on the tops of the little hills formed by the earth thrown out from the holes, and, if not disturbed, remain there until they perish with cold.

By poison and other means of destruction, these little pests have been generally destroyed in the fertile valleys; but in the foothills, and other localities that can not be cultivated, they are still most destructive. They feed upon the young green plants as well as upon the ripened grain.

Farming in California, like most other pursuits, has been speculative. A man would come from the mines with say ten thousand dollars, and would lease from one to two hundred acres of good wheat-land. With his own money he could purchase his seed-grain, and pay for a part of his hired labor. He would purchase his farming implements, harness, and work-animals on credit, and draw upon his commission merchant for provisions and other supplies. If the season proved propitious, and the price of grain high, he would net from twenty to thirty thousand dollars on his first crop, and then probably lose it the next or some subsequent year. If he failed, he would be off to the mines again.

Before the production of grain in California and Oregon was equal to the home demand, the prices were high. So soon as there was a surplus for exportation, the home price was governed by the foreign demand, without regard to the quantity grown on this coast. Our farmers commenced with high prices for grain, and paid high wages for labor. But the prices of grain receded in many instances faster than the rates of wages. A farmer in Alameda County employed an honest, industrious, sober, and careful Irishman for five years at the monthly wages of fifty dollars, the employer furnishing board, lodging, washing, and mending. At the end of that time he said to the Irishman: "I can not afford to pay you the wages I have been paying. It is true, I own my farm and stock, and I am not in debt. You have saved up a good sum of money, and I have saved nothing. You have made all the money, and, if things go on in this way, you will soon own my farm, and then what shall I do?" "Well," answered the Irishman, "I will hire you to work for me, and you will get your farm back again." In California it has fre-

quently happened that the teamster in time became the owner of the team, and in turn employed the former owner to drive it. There never was, perhaps, a country in which the mutations of fortune have been greater in time of peace than in California. It has been the country in which a fortune was most easily made and most speedily lost.

When I took up my residence in San José in 1849, Grove C. Cook, then aged about fifty, was one of the wealthy men of that city. He had lived some years in the Rocky Mountains as a trapper or trader, but came to San José some years before the discovery of gold, and had acquired a considerable amount of real estate, the enhanced value of which made him comparatively a rich man. He was generous, kind-hearted, and witty. Soon after the State organization, the population of San José rapidly increased; and, as hotels and boarding-houses were few, the young lawyers and others about the city, who were "too proud to work and too genteel to steal," induced Cook to open a boarding-house. After he had been running this new establishment for some months, he found it a ruinous business to him, and said to some of his friends, "I have the most extraordinary set of boarders in the world. They never miss a meal or pay a dime."

Such cases were very common in California. A man kept a boarding-house at a mining camp, and his boarders did not pay. He called them up and informed them that he could not afford to keep them without pay, and asked them what they would advise him to do. They replied that, if he could not afford to keep them without pay, they would advise him to sell out to some one who could.

A lawyer about thirty-five years of age induced

Cook to endorse for him to the amount of one thousand dollars, and Cook had to pay the note. There was a political convention held in San José in the summer of 1851, and Cook and myself among others were spectators. This lawyer was an eloquent man and a most ready debater, and appeared before the convention as an aspirant for a nomination. He made a most admirable speech, and when he had resumed his seat Cook most promptly addressed the president as follows: "Mr. President, I really wish you would give Mr. —— some office. He owes me a thousand dollars, and I want my money." This proposition was so clear and so much to the point that our ready and most voluble lawyer could make no reply, and was for once silent. Were I allowed to make a distinction, and to mark it with a new term coined in this city by an obscure person, I should say that a man who devotes most of his time to politics, and yet pays his honest debts, is properly called a politician, but a man who devotes most of his time to politics, and does not pay his honest debts, should be called a "politicioner."

By going upon the official bonds and endorsing the notes of others, Cook soon lost most of his property. "He had his joke, and they had his estate."

For some years after the discovery of gold in California it was dangerous for a man of property to be absent from the State even for a few months, as others were almost certain to administer upon his estate during his absence in some form or other. If he appointed an agent, the owner would be very likely to find upon his return that his agent had sold his property and absconded with the proceeds. If he left no agent, he found his real estate in possession of squatters.

In some cases regular letters of administration were

taken out. Mr. —— was County Recorder in one of our best counties for two years. He acquired some valuable real estate, and then went upon a visit to his native State, and was absent between two and three years. Upon his return to California, he was astonished and hugely disgusted to find that during his absence regular letters of administration had been granted, and the administrator was in possession of the estate. Although he was a man of fine manners and of good education, he was noted for his homely features; and upon this occasion his personal beauty was not improved.

INCREDULITY OF THE PEOPLE EAST AS TO THE TRUE FACTS IN REGARD TO CALIFORNIA — SCURVY — ADMISSION OF CALIFORNIA INTO THE UNION—STAGE-RACE—CHOLERA.

The productions of California are so different from those of the States east of the Rocky Mountains that the people of the older States would not for some years believe the truth, though stated by the most worthy and reliable persons. As illustrative of this state of incredulity, I will relate the following incidents:

Cary Peebles (now a resident of Santa Clara County) and myself were schoolmates in old Franklin, Missouri, as early as 1820. When gold was discovered in California, he resided in Lafayette, one of the best counties in Missouri, where he kept a country store. Late in the fall of 1848 he received a long letter from a trustworthy friend in California, giving a fair and truthful description of our gold-mines. A large crowd assembled at the store to hear this letter read. Peebles had not proceeded far with the reading when some one in the crowd gave a loud, shrill whistle, and then exclaimed,

"Isn't that a whopper!" This was followed by a universal roar of laughter, as loud as stout lungs and large throats could utter. When the tumult at length ceased, Peebles continued his reading, and was several times greeted with the same derisive laughter. Had he been the author of the letter, he would have been laughed to silence and to scorn.

Page, Bacon & Co. were extensive bankers in St. Louis; and in the latter part of 1849, or the beginning of 1850, they established two branches of their house in California—one in San Francisco, and the other in Sacramento City. The senior partner, "old man Page," commenced business in St. Louis in early manhood as a baker, prospered in that line for a time, and then commenced banking, and still prospered. The branch in San Francisco was managed by Judge Chambers and Henry Haight, and that in Sacramento City by Frank Page, son of the senior partner. In 1852 Frank returned to St. Louis on a visit; and one day at dinner, at his father's house, they had some onions on the table. Frank remarked that those were very small onions. His father replied that they were the largest to be had in the market. Frank very innocently and thoughtlessly said that in California we grew onions almost as large as a man's hat-crown. Upon this the fifteen or twenty guests at table threw themselves back in their seats and laughed most immoderately. Frank was deeply mortified, because he was perfectly alone and entirely helpless. He had always been truthful; and, while they were too polite to say in words that they did not believe him, they plainly said so by their actions. During the remainder of his visit, whenever, in answer to inquiries, he would state any fact in regard to California that exceeded their Missouri experience, his father

would take off his hat, run his thumb slowly around the crown, and look slyly at Frank, as much as to say, "Another onion story, my son." Frank became so unhappy from this quizzing that he hastened his return to California sooner than he otherwise would have done.

In the fall of 1853 the old gentleman himself came to California for the first time. Frank had not forgotten the treatment he received in St. Louis, and, when his father came to Sacramento City, quietly invited him to take a walk. He took his father around the city, and, after showing him various establishments, brought him to a large agricultural warehouse, where he showed him large beets, squashes, melons, and potatoes. Finally stopping in front of some sacks containing large onions, he said, "Father, look there," and then took off his hat and slowly ran his thumb around the crown as his father had done, and slyly asked his father what he thought of those onions. The old man gazed with surprise at the onions, his face flushed, and after a time he said, "Frank, I give it up. I never could have believed that onions so large could be grown anywhere, had I not seen them with my own eyes."

On one occasion, one of our people was returning east upon a visit, and took with him one of our large potatoes, carefully put up in whisky to prevent shrinkage. One day, in a large concourse of people in New York, the conversation turned upon the size of California vegetables. He said that he had seen potatoes weighing so much each. His statement being disputed, he put them to silence by producing his potato.

There are very good reasons why our vegetables are so large. First, the soil is very rich; secondly, there is an ample and uniform supply of moisture by irrigation;

third, the growing season is very long. These facts fully account for the large size of our vegetables.

Before the production of a sufficient supply of vegetables in California, those working in the mines were often afflicted with scurvy. These attacks ceased with ample supplies of fresh meats and vegetables.

The State of California was admitted into the Union September 9, 1850. It so happened that I arrived in San Francisco, on my return from Sacramento City, the same day of the arrival of the steamer from Panama bringing the welcome intelligence of this event. We had a large and enthusiastic meeting in Portsmouth Square that evening. Next morning I left for San José on one of Crandall's stages. He was one of the celebrated stage-men of California, like Foss and Monk. He was a most excellent man, and a cool, kind, but determined and skillful driver. On this occasion he drove himself, and I occupied the top front seat beside him. There were then two rival stage-lines to San José, and this was the time to test their speed. After passing over the sandy road to the Mission, there was some of the most rapid driving that I ever witnessed. The distance was some fifty miles, most of the route being over smooth, dry, hard prairie; and the drivers put their mustang teams to the utmost of their speed. As we flew past on our rapid course, the people flocked to the road to see what caused our fast driving and loud shouting, and, without slackening our speed in the slightest degree, we took off our hats, waved them around our heads, and shouted at the tops of our voices, "California is admitted into the Union!" Upon this announcement the people along the road cheered as loudly and heartily as possible. I never witnessed a scene more exciting, and never felt more enthusiastic.

I never can forget Crandall's race. He beat his competitor only a few moments. Poor fellow! When he became old and stiff, he was thrown from his seat while driving his stage, by one of the wheels suddenly dropping into a deep hole, and fell upon the dry, hard earth with such violence that he never recovered. A celebrated stage-driver over the mountainous roads in the State of Nevada, who was beloved by all who knew him, on his death-bed a few years ago, after his sight had vanished, mournfully remarked, "I can't get my foot on the brakes."

In November, 1850, the cholera prevailed in California to a fearful extent. The loss in Sacramento City, according to the best estimate I am able to make, was about fifteen per cent. of the population; in San José, ten per cent.; and in San Francisco, five per cent.

EXTRACTS FROM MY SECOND ANNUAL MESSAGE—RESIGNATION OF THE OFFICE OF GOVERNOR.

The admission of California into the Union settled all questions as to the legality of our State Government, but did not remove the difficulties incident to our peculiar condition. The following extracts are taken from my second annual message:

The attempt to administer the State Government during the past year has been attended by many difficulties. To start a new system under ordinary circumstances is no easy task, but no new State has ever been encompassed with so many embarrassments as California. Our people formed a mixed and multitudinous host from all sections of our widely extended country, and from almost every clime and nation in the world, with all their discordant views, feelings, prejudices, and opinions, and, thrown together like the sudden assemblage of a mighty

army, they had no time to compare notes or interchange opinions. Besides this, a majority considered themselves only temporary residents, and had therefore no permanent interest in sustaining the State Government. Serious resistance to the execution of the laws was threatened in some instances, and a very unfortunate disturbance occurred at Sacramento City, in reference to which it would be improper to express an opinion, as the facts of the case will be inquired into by the competent judicial tribunals.

The first session of the Legislature had more difficulties to meet than perhaps the Legislature of any other State. That body had no beaten road to travel, no safe precedents to follow. California required a *new* system, adapted to her new and anomalous condition. What that new system should be, time and experience could alone determine. With the experience of the past year before us, we may be enabled to make some useful and necessary amendments. I have suggested such as have appeared to me the most important. It will be doubtless necessary to amend the acts of the last session in many respects, but I would respectfully suggest the propriety of making no amendments except where manifestly required. The people have now become accustomed to the laws as they are, and by making but few amendments a heavy amount of expense may be saved to the State.

On the 9th day of January, 1851, I sent to both Houses my resignation as Governor of the State in the following words:

GENTLEMEN OF THE SENATE AND ASSEMBLY:

Circumstances entirely unexpected and unforeseen by me, and over which I could have no control, render it indispensable that I should devote all my time and attention to my private affairs. I therefore tender to both Houses of the Legislature my resignation as Governor of the State.

I leave the high office to which I was called by the voluntary voice of my countrymen with but one regret—that my feeble abilities have allowed me to accomplish so little for the State.

In the humble sphere of a private citizen, I shall still cherish for her that ardent attachment she so justly merits. Within her serene and sunny limits I intend to spend the remainder of my days, many or few; and, should an unfortunate crisis ever arise when such a sacrifice might be available and necessary for her safety, my limited fortune and fame, and my life, will be at her disposal. PETER H. BURNETT.

SAN JOSÉ, *January 8, 1851.*

This resignation was accepted, and my connection with the State as her Governor thus terminated.

RESUME THE PRACTICE OF THE LAW—DEATH OF JUDGE JONES—PASSENGERS OF THE MARGARET—A FAITHFUL SON.

AFTER resigning the office of Governor, I resumed the practice of the law in partnership with C. T. Ryland and William T. Wallace. We had a good practice; but a large portion of my own time was given to my private affairs, as they needed my prompt attention.

In December, 1851, Judge Jones died in San José, and I copy the account of that sad event as I find it recorded by myself, within a few day thereafter, except the day of the month, which I afterward ascertained and filled the blank I had left.

The Hon. James M. Jones, Judge of the United States District Court for the Southern District of California, died at San José on the 15th day of December, 1851.

I can not in justice to the deceased, as well as to my own feelings, refrain from putting on record the substance of a long private interview I had with this gifted and accomplished young judge the day before his death. I first knew the deceased, while he attended as a member of the Convention at Monterey, in September, 1849. He was then about twenty-seven years old, a good and ripe scholar in the Spanish, French, and English

languages, which, I am informed, he wrote and spoke with ease and elegance, and that he also had a considerable knowledge of the German and Italian. At the period when I first knew him, I resided at San José with my family; and, immediately after the adjournment of the Convention, he came to that place, and established himself in the practice of the law. His indefatigable perseverance, his eminent knowledge of his profession, and his chaste, earnest, and beautiful style of elocution, soon procured him a most lucrative practice. While I filled the position of Governor of the State, in the beginning of 1850, I had frequent conversations with him upon legal questions, and he was frequently a visitor at my house. In reference to his own aims and prospects in life he maintained a great reserve, never obtruding his private affairs upon the public. He pursued any object he had in view with great earnestness and energy; and to excessive application to his laborious profession his early and untimely death is doubtless in part to be attributed. I knew nothing of his early history, except what I learned during the interview before mentioned.

I visited him on Sunday evening. It was a warm, bright, and lovely day. I found him in the last stage of consumption, wasted away to a skeleton, but in the full possession of his senses, entirely convinced of the near approach of death, and perfectly collected and resigned. After saluting me and asking me to be seated, he held up in his thin, pale, and bloodless fingers a cross which he had suspended from his neck, and in the most feeling manner said: "Governor! this is the image of our most holy Catholic Faith—the representative of that cross upon which Jesus died. You have doubtless heard that I had joined the venerable old Catholic Church. I have never been an infidel. I had examined the positive evidences for Christianity, and they greatly preponderated in favor of its truth; and, taken in connection with its appropriate fitness to man's wants and nature, it was, as a lawyer would say, a plain case upon the face of the papers. But, although a believer in religion, I deferred embracing it, because it required me to give up pleasures that I then looked upon with affection, but which I now regard as of no moment. I had also spent most of my time

in new countries, in the midst of the exciting and confused scenes incident to a new and unsettled state of society; and my peculiar cast of mind had thrown me into relations and business with others that called away my attention from God, my Maker. Had I been a permanent resident of an old and regular community, I think I should have been an early member of the Church. I also looked upon our faith as peculiarly hard and exacting; but, oh! if I were only well and able, it would be a pleasure, instead of a labor, to me to enter into the house of God with His children, and there spend every moment I could possibly spare in His service. But I have deferred it so long. I have prayed to Jesus for the pardon of my sins. The greatest sin I have ever committed—that which has given me more pain, and that which I deplore more, than all others—is the fact that I deferred repentance to near the end of my existence—until my last sickness. Oh that I had given God my early days! I have repented of it most bitterly. It is all that I could do. I know that death-bed repentances are not generally entitled to much confidence; but I am sure that, were I to recover, I should henceforward lead a different life. The world may say that my repentance is forced and not sincere; but the world may say what it pleases, it will not alter the fact. I know that I am sincere, and I can well spare the shadow if I can get the substance. If I can only get to heaven, I will be content. I trust in the merits of Christ. I look to His mercy for pardon.

"And now, Governor, if I may be allowed to turn from heavenly to earthly subjects, I wish to mention a few things to you. My father has been dead many years, and my mother was twice married. I was a child by the first marriage. There are two children living, the issue of the second marriage—one a son of eleven years of age, and the other a daughter of thirteen. My brother is an innocent, prattling boy, of modest and quiet demeanor, and he loved me much. My sister is a kind and amiable girl. The great object I had in view in all my exertions to accumulate property was to make these children happy and comfortable. For this end I denied myself most of the luxuries and many of the comforts of life. I have often thought with pleasure, when refraining from some object I was tempted

to purchase, that by doing so I might render these children happy for six months. This was the great object for which I toiled—the object" (laying his hand upon his breast) "dearest to my heart. It was to me as a green leaf in a desert. I have not sought fame; I cared but little for the opinions of men.

"I wished also to make my mother happy in her old age. *And such a mother!* She loved me under all circumstances. She could love more than I. She had such a depth of affection —such a pure fountain of love. She loved all her children; but there was so great a disparity in our ages that she loved me much the longest. She died not long since, and of the same disease that I have now. We were both of us sick at the same time, but so distant that neither could go to the other. Her death crushed me—gave me the last fatal blow. Since that time I have not seen a happy moment. The only happiness I have since enjoyed was mere freedom from pain. I had desired that my mother should spend her last days with me in California. I wished to make her last days happy. But I have been disappointed. God has taken her away. He has chastened me for my good. It has been to me a severe but just chastisement.

"I wish, Governor, to make one request of you. I have made my will, and left Mr. Melone my executor. I wish you to render him what assistance you can in closing up the business of my estate. But I make this request with this distinct condition, that, if you can do more justice to your family by taking claims for collection against my estate, I wish you by all means to do so. We are commanded to love our neighbors as ourselves; but a man's family are his nearest neighbors, and especially such a family as yours."

During this most affecting interview I could not but often weep. When he saw me weeping he said, "Governor, you are a good Christian."

By his will he left his property in equal portions to his brother and sister, except that ten per cent. of the amount of his estate was to be appropriated in the erection of a tomb for his mother.

PETER H. BURNETT.

Among the other successful lawyers whom I have known in California, and who came here in 1849, was a young man who told me in after years the cause of his coming to this country. His father and mother, brothers and sisters, had resided in the old homestead for many years. It was situated in a town in one of the New England States. It had descended to his father from his grandfather, and had been possessed by the family for one or more centuries. Some time before he left for California, his father endorsed for a friend, and the old place had been sold to pay the debt. From a competency and a good home, they had come to poverty. This had caused the family much sorrow. His parents were too old to begin life anew successfully. He himself was just setting out in life. Under these painful circumstances, he said, he determined with himself that he would come to California, and, if brains and honest industry would succeed, he would accumulate enough means to repurchase the old family mansion, and make his old parents comfortable the remainder of their lives. He was successful; and within a few years he returned with ample funds, repurchased the ancestral domicile, and placed his parents within the pleasant old home in which he himself was born. During their remaining days they were well provided for by this faithful son.

But, while a portion of those who came early to California to improve their condition succeeded well, much the larger number utterly failed. Many came to premature deaths by violence, accidents, and sickness caused by excessive hardships and privations. I should think that about thirty per cent. of the early immigrants perished in this manner. I was told that a party of about

thirty miners from Texas lost one half of their number in personal conflicts.

As illustrative of the sad fates of so many in early life, I will quote the following lines, composed by B. L. d'Aumaile while a prisoner in San Francisco, and first published in the latter part of 1856 or the beginning of 1857. There was reason to believe that the author was not guilty of the crime alleged against him. The first graveyard in San Francisco was on Russian Hill, so named from the fact that the first person buried there was a native of Russia. Though the fates of the passengers of the Margaret were exceptionally sad, they are still illustrative of the conditions of the early gold-seekers.

I stood on the barren summit
  Of the lonely Russian Hill,
With a grass-grown grave beside me,
  On a Sabbath morning still,
And sighed for my old companions,
  Scattered through every zone,
Who sailed in the Margaret with me
  But seven short years agone.

Yes, seven brief summers only
  Have rolled past since that day;
'Twas a balmy, soft June evening
  When we anchored in the bay.
Of the sixteen buoyant spirits
  Enrolled in our companie,
Twelve lie the green sod under,
  And three are lost for aye.

The first at my feet was lying,
  Far from his native home;
I had watched by his bedside dying,
  Slain by the curse of rum.

In the dark and rocky cañon,
Where the Fresno's waters flow,
The mangled corpse of the second
Was buried long ago.

Three entered the wild Sierra
To search for the golden ore,
But back from their quest of lucre
To our camp they came no more.
We sought them long and vainly,
But what their sad fate had been
We never could tell, but only
They never again were seen.

On the hills of the Mariposa,
Where the dead of '50 sleep,
On the bank-side by the ravine,
Where its sluggish waters creep,
Two mounds, with long grass tangled—
There moldering, side by side,
Are the gambler and his victim,
The unshriven suicide.

In the green vale of the Nuuanu,
On the fair isle of Oahu,
Consumption demanded the youngest,
Most gallant, most gentle, most true.
The graveyard of Yerba Buena
Claimeth another; alone,
Far from his friends and his kindred,
Stands his monument stone.

One died in the Independence,
Another on Chagres' shore;
One launched on the Pacific
His bark, and returned no more.
"Mourn not the dead!" the living yet—
Alas! there are but four
Who sailed on the good brig Margaret—
Better their doom deplore.

In the valleys of Nukahiva,
  Gem of the Southern Sea,
The soul of our band, if living,
  Hath fixed his destiny.
Gladly he went into exile,
  Self-banished from his kind;
The stern world's wrong and oppression
  Made wreck of his noble mind.

From the dungeons of San Quentin
  Ascendeth for evermore
The wail of a convict, sighing
  For the days that are past and o'er.
His life to the law was forfeit,
  For the blood his hand had shed,
But a cruel mercy spared him,
  To be 'mongst the living dead.

The last and saddest of any,
  A sister she was to us all,
In the bloom of her girlish beauty,
  Was lured by a fiend to her fall;
On the banks of the Sacramento,
  She leadeth a life of shame;
For her there is no redemption—
  Forgotten be ever her name.

The gifted and brave had perished,
  The beautiful and the young;
All trace of their footsteps vanished
  The paths of men from among;
While I, as the sole survivor,
  Was left to make my moan;
On the shores of the broad Pacific
  I was standing all alone.

DEFECTIVE ADMINISTRATION OF CRIMINAL LAW IN CALIFORNIA—ILLUSTRATIONS—PAY THE LAST OF MY OLD DEBTS.

For some eight or ten years after the organization of our State government, the administration of the criminal laws was exceedingly defective and inefficient. This arose mainly from the following causes: 1. Defective laws and imperfect organization of the Courts; 2. The incompetency of the district attorneys, who were generally young men without an adequate knowledge of the law; 3. The want of secure county prisons, there being no penitentiary during most of that time; 4. The great expense of keeping prisoners and convicts in the county jails; 5. The difficulty of enforcing the attendance of witnesses; 6. The difficulty of securing good jurymen, there being so large a proportion of reckless, sour, disappointed, and unprincipled men then in the country; 7. The unsettled state of our land-titles, which first induced so many men to squat upon the lands of the grantees of Spain and Mexico, and then to steal their cattle to live upon.

As illustrative, I will mention the following cases, omitting names for obvious reasons:

A middle-aged native Californian, belonging to one of the richest and most respectable old families of the country, was the owner of an extensive and fertile rancho, bordering upon the navigable waters of the State. He owned a large herd of California cattle, running on his place. Near the rancho there was a small village, between which and San Francisco there was regular communication by a small steamer. Numbers of persons soon engaged in stealing his calves, having the carcasses

dressed by their own butcher in the village, the veal shipped to San Francisco by the little steamer, and there sold. They were doing quite a thriving and profitable business. A man some forty-five years of age, residing in the vicinity with his family, seeing the ease and impunity with which this thieving traffic was carried on, concluded that he would go into it himself. The first thing he did in that line was to steal six calves. But in the mean time the Californian, having seen his herd rapidly diminishing, had become very vigilant and watchful, and our new beginner in theft was caught in the act and arrested. Upon being confronted by the witnesses and questioned, he confessed. His case was brought before the grand jury, and he was indicted for grand larceny.

His case excited great sympathy in the neighborhood, and, about the time it was coming on for trial, one of the leading men of the vicinity came to engage me to defend the prisoner. I asked this person whether the prisoner was guilty. With a sorrowful expression of face he said he thought he was, as he had confessed it. This person then went into a long history of the prisoner. He said it was one of the saddest cases he had ever known; that the prisoner had heretofore borne a most excellent character—had undoubtedly been honest all his life up to this time—had a most estimable wife and several most amiable daughters, one or two of whom were grown; that respectable young men were visiting his family; that the prisoner's relatives were excellent people; and that he and his innocent family would be ruined should he be convicted. After talking in this strain for about an hour, my informant seemed to have forgotten his admission made in the beginning of his statement, and closed by saying with great ear-

nestness: "Governor, I wish you would do your best to clear him. He is a good, honest fellow." I replied, "This thing of being a good, honest fellow, and stealing six calves, is what forty Philadelphia lawyers can not put together." This reply startled him for a moment; but he soon rallied, and hastily said: "But he didn't mean any harm by it. It was almost a universal thing in the neighborhood." I told him to go to another lawyer.

On the day of trial the prisoner came into court handsomely dressed in broadcloth, and was a fine-looking man. He appeared as little like a thief as any prisoner I have ever seen in court. The District Attorney, being young and inexperienced, relied solely upon the prisoner's confession for a conviction, and had neglected to subpœna the witnesses to the other facts. This testimony, most likely, would have been sufficient without the confession. The result was, that the prisoner's attorney objected to the confession, on the ground that it was not voluntary, but made under the influence of hope or fear. The court, upon investigation, sustained the objection, the confession was not permitted to go before the jury, and, there being no testimony against the prisoner, he was at once acquitted. This trial took place in 1851. I have lately learned that this person has conducted himself as an honest man and a good citizen ever since that time. There can be no reasonable doubt of the fact that he had been led to commit one theft under the peculiar circumstances mentioned, and that this has been the only criminal act of his life.

The other case was related to me by the lawyer who successfully defended the prisoner, and the facts are unquestionably true. The trial occurred about 1852.

The prisoner was a man of education, about thirty

years old, and lived in one of the finest agricultural counties in the State. For some time before the act was committed, the people in the vicinity had lost several fine, fat American cattle, and secretly set a watch to catch the thief. The watchmen secreted themselves, and, after waiting some time, heard the report of a rifle, and saw a fat cow fall, and the prisoner rush up to the animal and cut her throat with a butcher's knife. While in the very act, and before he had removed the carcass, the culprit was arrested.

His case was brought before the grand jury, and he was indicted for grand larceny in stealing this cow. Upon the trial all the facts were fully proven. The theory of the defense was, that the prisoner intended to shoot a dangerous bull; that the cow stood almost in a line between him and the bull, and that he accidentally hit the cow. While the prisoner's counsel was arguing the case before the trial-jury, the District Attorney interrupted him, and asked him how he reconciled the fact that the prisoner cut the cow's throat with the theory of accidental shooting? Without a moment's hesitation the counsel for the prisoner replied: "That is easily answered. When the prisoner saw that he had accidentally killed the cow, he knew it was best for all parties concerned to bleed the animal properly, so that the carcass would be good beef, and thus make the loss as small as possible." When the Judge came to charge the jury, the counsel for the prisoner offered an instruction directing the jury to find the prisoner not guilty, as the facts proven showed that the offense charged in the indictment had not been committed. He took the ground that, to constitute the crime of larceny as charged, there must be *both* a taking and carrying away of the property described in the indictment, with the

felonious intent to steal the same. The Court was compelled to give the instruction, and the prisoner was acquitted. That he killed the cow with intent to steal was clear; but that, under the statute, did not constitute the completed crime of grand larceny, as the prisoner had not removed the carcass.

This man continued to reside in the same vicinity during the remainder of his life. Six or eight years after the trial the county was divided by act of the Legislature, and a new county organized, which included this man's residence, and which is one of the richest counties in the State. Twelve or fifteen years after his acquittal he was elected County Judge of this county.

While he held this office, the lawyer who had successfully defended him went to the county seat to attend to some professional business, and while there walked into the court-house, and found the Judge just about to pass sentence upon a prisoner who had been indicted, tried, and convicted in his court for grand larceny. As the scene was novel and most interesting, the lawyer took a seat and listened to the sentence pronounced by his Honor. The Judge went on, in a solemn and eloquent manner, to depict at length the atrocity of the crime of grand larceny, and sentenced the prisoner to a long term in the penitentiary.

It was the extremely defective administration of criminal justice in California for some years that led to the organization of so many vigilance committees, and filled the courts of Judge Lynch with so many cases.

In the early portion of 1852 I finally succeeded in paying the last dollar of my old debts. The total sum paid amounted to twenty-eight thousand seven hundred and forty dollars. I was henceforward a free man. I had been engaged so long in paying old debts that it

became almost habitual, and for a time I felt somewhat lost because I owed no man anything. It was a totally new position to me. Our family learn slowly, but they learn well, and they practice on what they know. Since then I have not been pecuniarily embarrassed for a moment, and I owe nothing now. I paid the larger portion of these old debts in the year 1850. During a portion of that year I was in great doubt whether I should be able to accomplish the object of so many years' labor. The flood of the winter of 1849–'50 at Sacramento City not only caused the prices of property and rents to decline heavily, but increased the taxation for city purposes enormously. The rate of taxation that year for State, county, and city purposes, at Sacramento City, amounted to ten per cent. of the assessed value of the property. This extra tax was required to construct the first levee.

GREAT FIRE IN SACRAMENTO CITY—ASSIST IN REBUILDING THE CITY—RANCHO OF SAMUEL NORRIS—COURSING THE JACK-RABBIT.

On the evening of November 2, 1852, the great fire occurred at Sacramento City, which swept off two thirds of the town. Improvements that cost me about twenty-five thousand dollars were consumed in half an hour. When I arrived in the city on the 5th, the business portion of the place, with the exception of here and there a solitary brick house, was one waste of dark desolation. The streets could scarcely be distinguished from the blocks. Notwithstanding this great and severe loss, that indomitable people were not at all discouraged or unhappy. They even seemed inspirited. You would meet with no downcast looks. No people that I ever

met can compare with those of Sacramento City in patience, energy, and unconquerable courage. In San Francisco they had two large and terrible fires in 1851, but they had no floods. In Sacramento City they had a succession of both fires and floods; and yet, at this date, Sacramento is the most prosperous city in the State. *All honor to that noble people!* On the 10th of November the regular rainy season set in.

There have been four overflows of Sacramento City. The first occurred in the winter of 1849–'50, the second in March, 1852, the third in the winter of 1852–'53, and the fourth and last in the winter of 1861–'62. The second passed away so soon as to inflict but little injury comparatively, but the others were much longer in duration and far more serious in their effects. Nothing could be done during the floods, nor for about two months after the waters subsided.

I moved to Sacramento City early in December, 1852, to assist in rebuilding it. A proposition was made by the people of Grass Valley to construct a plank-road from that place either to Marysville or Sacramento. The distance to Marysville is about half of that to Sacramento City. The people of Grass Valley would be governed in their choice of a terminus of the road by the amount contributed by each of the two competing cities. The road to Marysville would cost less, but that to Sacramento would terminate at the better point. A large public meeting was held at Grass Valley in the month of February, 1853, and delegates were present from Sacramento and Marysville to represent the people of those cities. At the meeting they out-talked and out-voted us, and we returned rather cast down; but we quietly laid it up in our inmost hearts to rely solely upon ourselves, and rebuild Sac-

ramento City before the people of Grass Valley and Marysville could construct the road agreed upon. We went to work as soon as possible, and with a will; and by the last of July we had the main streets partly graded and newly planked, and by the middle of August a new levee well under way. I never saw the people of any city work with more energy. I was elected a member of the City Council, and I never toiled more earnestly, except on the road to Oregon in 1843, and for a time after I arrived there to keep from starvation, and in the gold-mines in 1848. My first visit to the beautiful town of Grass Valley was as one of the delegates from Sacramento upon the occasion mentioned. He who relies upon himself knows the man he trusts. So it is with a people who rely upon themselves. Self-reliance is the only sure path to success in life. Depend upon yourself, and you will not be apt to suffer from divided counsels.

While at Sacramento City, in the fall of 1853 and the succeeding winter, I was several times at the rancho of Samuel Norris. This place is about six miles from the city, and lies upon the north bank of the American River. As all our work in rebuilding the city had been successfully finished, and the place put in the best condition, I had a little time and inclination for some amusement. Norris had four well-trained dogs. The first was an old dog he called "Old Bull," a cross between the cur and bull-dog. The others were greyhounds. The first of these was about five years old; the other two, about two years old, were brother and sister. The slut was jet-black in color, and was one of the most beautiful animals I ever saw. She was a little fleeter than her brother, and the fleetest of the pack. Nothing could exceed the ease and grace of her

movements. The greyhounds were shut up during the night before the chase and kept without food, because if fed they could not catch the game.

One evening Norris told me how he had exterminated the numerous coyotes in his vicinity. He said that, mounted on a good horse, he would go out with his four dogs, and when the greyhounds came in sight of a coyote, in the prairie or in open woods, they immediately gave chase. When they had overtaken the wolf, the foremost hound would run full tilt against him and knock him over ; and, if the wolf attempted to run again, the hound would overthrow him the second time. The coyote soon found that there was no chance to escape by flight, and would then stand and snarl, and thus keep the hounds at bay. They would circle around him, but never attack him with their teeth until Old Bull came up. In the mean time that brave old dog was advancing at a slow and steady pace, and when he arrived he made not the slightest stop, but laid hold of the poor wolf despite his quick, sharp, and terrible snaps ; then the hounds pitched in, and the defenseless coyote had not the slightest chance for his life, but was strung out full length and speedily dispatched.

Next morning, after an early breakfast, mounted on fleet but gentle horses, Norris and myself set out to run down the large jack-rabbits then plentiful in that vicinity. One of these rabbits will weigh as much as two or three of the cotton-tail rabbits of the Western States ; and, although their gait in running seems to be very awkward, they are so swift that it requires the fleetest greyhound to catch them. Indeed it is very doubtful whether any single greyhound could catch one of these rabbits, as the animal would dodge the dog, and thus widen the distance between them.

Norris had a smooth, open, and gently undulating stubble-field, about a mile long and three fourths of a mile wide. Although the stubble had been so closely pastured that we could apparently see an animal of that size at the distance of fifty yards, yet the rabbit would fold his long ears to his body, and then lie so close to the ground (which he much resembled in color) that we never in a single instance could see him until he started to run, although often within eight or ten yards of him.

The old greyhound, though about as fleet as the rabbit, was not so fast as either of the other hounds, but he was active, vigilant, and tough, and always started the game. He would run hither and thither, searching in every place, while the two young hounds trotted along at their ease twenty feet or so behind him, never looking for the rabbit, but keeping their attention fixed on the old hound. The first thing we would know, up would start the rabbit not more than eight or ten feet ahead of the old hound, and then the race began, the rabbit and the hounds running at the top of their speed. It was a most exciting chase. Gradually the slut would overtake the other hounds, and we could see her gain upon them inch by inch until she passed them, and then as gradually gain upon the rabbit. When she approached within about four feet of the rabbit, her brother being about a length behind her, the animal would suddenly turn at right angles to the left or right, and the two foremost hounds would run over a little before they could stop, and, by the time they could turn and start again, the rabbit would be fifteen or twenty feet ahead. But the old hound was on the watch, and, the moment he saw the rabbit double, he would turn and cut across, so as to run to a point that would be about as close to the rabbit as he was at the start. In the

mean time the two young hounds were straining every muscle to regain their lost position, and soon the slut would again be close behind the rabbit, when he would double the second time. About the third time the rabbit doubled, the young hound would catch him. The slut invariably caused the rabbit to double, but her brother as invariably caught him.

The hounds would catch the first rabbit in running half a mile, and the second one in running a mile, and the third would outrun them and make his escape. I observed that, in running down an incline, the hounds would run comparatively faster and the rabbit more slowly; but, in going up an incline, the rabbit would run correspondingly faster. When the speed of two animals is the same on level ground, the larger one will run faster than the smaller in descending an incline, but more slowly in ascending.

In these races, the only thing that Old Bull did was to come up as soon as he could after the death, and, like the lion in the fable, appropriate all the game to himself. The hounds never objected, as they knew his power and courage too well to contest his pretensions.

Norris said he had seen the speed of his greyhounds conclusively tested with that of the antelope. On one occasion he was out with his horse and dogs, when he saw a band of some forty antelopes grazing in open woods. He quietly approached as near as he could, and, when the antelopes started to run, he and the hounds pursued them at full speed. The attention of the fleeing animals seemed to have been fixed on him, and they measured their pace so as to keep about a hundred yards ahead. In this way the two fleetest hounds were permitted to approach within about twenty yards of the hindmost antelopes, the foremost ones being about forty

yards ahead of them. Then the slut made a sudden and tremendous dash at the nearest antelopes, but they let out a few more links, and were very soon up with the foremost ones, and they all so increased their speed as to leave the slut far behind. They beat her with ease, and yet she was one of the fleetest of her race. The exquisite gazelle of Africa, "the child of the desert," and perhaps the fleetest animal in the world, as it is the most beautiful, belongs to the antelope family. There has never been, so far as I am advised, any conclusive test of the speed of the gazelle as compared with that of the Arab steed.

THE VIGILANCE COMMITTEE OF 1856—MY FIRST VOYAGE AT SEA—INCIDENTS.

In the month of March, 1854, I returned to my home in Santa Clara County. At that time I had a large interest in the town of Alviso, situated at the southern extremity of the Bay of San Francisco, where I had erected a large frame dwelling-house in 1850. This building was constructed of the best eastern pine lumber, except the frame, was two stories high, was twenty-nine by forty-eight feet, and contained ten or twelve rooms. I employed the remainder of 1854 in removing this house from Alviso to San José, about nine miles distant. To remove it, we took it all apart, piece by piece, without injuring any of the materials, except the shingles, and put it together again, each plank in its proper place. I worked hard at it myself, as did my two sons, John and Armstead, then about grown. I employed Stincen, the carpenter of Sacramento, whose name has already been mentioned in connection with Tom the quack.

My first residence in San José cost me six thousand dollars, and it was afterward sold for one thousand. My second residence cost me ten thousand, and afterward sold for two thousand. These instances will indicate the shrinkage in value of real estate in San José. It is but justice to say that the prices mentioned would not at present be a fair criterion of the value of real estate in that city, which would rule neither so high nor so low as the rates mentioned.

During the years 1855 and 1856 I had no business employment, having quit the practice of my profession early in 1854, and devoted my time to reading. In the early part of August, 1856, I was attacked for the first time with neuralgia; and from that date until May, 1861, I had at intervals a succession of attacks, so that I was sick two thirds of the time during that period.

In 1856 the Vigilance Committee of San Francisco was in full and successful operation. I opposed this organization on the ground of principle, as I considered it incipient rebellion and a fatal precedent. It is very true that the good people of San Francisco had great reason to be dissatisfied with the administration of criminal justice. So many of the then residents of the city considered themselves but sojourners; while they, and many who regarded themselves as permanent settlers, were so eager in the pursuit of wealth that they could not be induced to serve on juries, that that duty thus devolved upon those unworthy of the trust. The consequence was that the guilty escaped, and crime continued unrestrained, until the situation became almost intolerable. I made two most vigorous speeches against the Committee. These were my last speeches. It is not my purpose to go fully into that exciting event, as it is a matter of history accessible to all.

In August and September, 1856, I made my first sea-voyage. My son-in-law, C. T. Ryland, and myself left San Francisco, on the 20th of August, on board the steamship John L. Stephens, for Panama. Supposing myself to be very susceptible to sea-sickness, I dreaded a voyage, thinking I should suffer severely. I had been suffering from a slight attack of neuralgia for some days, and I remembered the medical maxim that the human system will not generally tolerate more than one disease at the same time, and that the principal one will banish all the others. When the ship had passed the heads and was at sea, I became sea-sick, and I never once thought of the neuralgia for some days. But, as soon as I had entirely recovered from the sea-sickness, the neuralgia came limping back by slow degrees. My own experience therefore proved the truth of that medical maxim. On my return from New York, on board the steamship bound to Aspinwall, I became acquainted with a most intelligent gentleman who was far gone with consumption, and was on his way to South America in the hope that the change might restore him to health. While most of the passengers were sea-sick, he was not at all affected. This fact, he sorrowfully told me, he regarded as an indication of approaching death. From the best estimate I can make, after having made three trips between San Francisco and New York by sea, about seven per cent. of the passengers escape sea-sickness entirely, three per cent. are sick the entire voyage, and ninety per cent. are sick from one to five days.

At Aspinwall we went on board the steamship George Law, bound for New York. We came by Havana, but the yellow fever was then prevailing there to such an extent that our commander, Captain Herndon, deemed it best not to enter the harbor, but to take in a supply

of coal at Key West. We left Key West about two hours before sunset. The weather was calm and the sky clear. The evening was most lovely, and the chaste moonlight danced upon the waves of the restless sea. Ryland, myself, and a young man named Twillager, occupied the same cabin. I slept in the upper, Ryland in the middle, and Twillager in the lower berth.

The moon set that night about 10 P. M., and we had all been asleep some hours when, about three o'clock A. M., I was awakened by Ryland's entering the cabin door. He was more wakeful than we were, had heard some stir on deck, had quietly left his berth, gone above, learned the cause, and returned. I at once asked him what was the matter. He solemnly replied, "We are aground." The ship had run in too close to the shore, and had reached a position upon a coral reef, on the eastern coast of Florida, from which she could not then retreat.

This was about the 9th of September, and the equinoctial storm was just before us. I at once comprehended the terrible situation. We had on board about one thousand passengers. I hastily dressed myself, went on deck, and took a calm survey ; and I thought that I could discern through the darkness the dim outlines of a low bushy shore to our left. The ship was beating upon the reef. When a large wave rolled under her she rose, and when it receded she came down upon the rocky bottom with a melancholy thump. The human ear never heard a sound more terrible than that made by a great ship thumping upon a rock. It is a dead, dull sound, ominous of death. The ship struck at about full tide, and when the tide went down she was as still as a house on shore.

After remaining on deck a short time, I went below,

and found all the passengers up. No one could sleep in our situation. I never saw a more solemn assemblage of people. Every one seemed to have a clear perception of our extremely critical situation. There were no jests, no smiles, no witticisms. Those who were professors of religion seemed resigned, those who were confirmed infidels seemed indifferent, while dread sat upon the countenances of those who were halting between two opinions. We were a little world to ourselves, and our little world seemed near its end.

The darkness was so great that nothing could be done until daylight. When day returned, the shore was in plain view about five miles distant. The water was so shallow and so clear that we could see the bottom of the ocean as plainly as one can see the carpet on the floor. At the distance of some two miles to our right we could see the deep, blue water, while around the ship the water was apparently green, owing to its being so shallow. The day was calm and beautiful.

Captain Herndon ordered a large portion of the coal to be thrown overboard, and the passengers went to work with a will to lighten the ship. There were among our passengers two experienced navigators, who had before this been engaged in commanding whaling-vessels, and were brave, hardy, and skillful seamen. They gave their utmost assistance. Captain Herndon was going all the time. I did not see him stop to eat or drink. No man could possibly have done more. The two sea-captains put on cheerful faces, went among the lady passengers, and assured them there was no danger ; but they would tell me confidentially that our peril was great, as we were at the mercy of the first gale, and that the calm, beautiful weather was but the prelude to the dread equinoctial storm.

Toward noon several wreckers came in sight, and soon sailed all around and close to us. Soon afterward a large Spanish clipper-ship hove in sight, and, seeing our signals of distress, came as near to us as it was safe for her to do. Captain Herndon went out in a small row-boat to meet her, and made arrangements with her master to take on board a portion of our passengers. When he returned he announced to the passengers that a certain number could go aboard the clipper, and took down the names of those who were willing to go. Ryland and I decided to go.

In the mean time large quantities of coal had been thrown into the sea, a heavy anchor attached to an immense hawser had been thrown forward some distance, and the men were hauling upon it with all the force they could apply to the capstan. The tide had risen to its full height, the wheels of the ship were put in motion, and, just as we, with our carpet-bags in our hands, were about to descend into the small boats to go to the clipper, the steamship glided off the reef as easily as the sea-bird rises from the summit of the wave. As already stated, the ship had run in too close to the shore, and, when its dim outlines had been discovered by the man on the watch, her wheels were reversed; but, in the attempt to regain the deep water, she ran upon a bump in the reef, and stuck fast. The water gradually deepened from the shore to the blue water, as we could readily perceive from the difference in its apparent color.

As we slowly passed toward the anchor, Captain Herndon ordered the hawser to be cut, which was promptly done by one of the sailors. It was about three o'clock in the afternoon of that beautiful day, and all the passengers were on deck. Many efforts of the same kind had been previously made to haul off the ship, but

all had failed, and when at last we succeeded we were utterly surprised. The head of the ship was turned toward the deep, blue water, and she moved at a slow and cautious rate toward it. We could plainly see the bottom, apparently gliding beneath and past the ship, as we passed over it. During this slow progress from our perilous situation to one of comparative safety, not a word was said. Every feature was set and every eye fixed. We did not know how soon the ship might strike upon another bump. At last we reached the deep sea, and then such a shout rose from our passengers as I never heard before, and never expect to hear again in this world. It rang and rang again. One lady, the wife of a physician, who had borne the danger with unmoved and heroic courage, swooned with joy.

Soon after the shouts had ceased, I met Captain Herndon on deck, when he threw his arms around my neck, wept, and said, "Governor, my heart was almost broken." I remember him with feelings of the most tender regard. He was a noble man, and an honor to his race. One year after that time, while still in command of the same steamship (though her name had been changed to that of the Central America), his vessel went down at sea in an equinoctial storm off Cape Hatteras, and he and most of his passengers perished.

The ship was so little injured that in due time we arrived safely in the port of New York. Next morning I read in the daily papers an account of the voyage and arrival of the George Law, but not one word was said about our having been aground upon a coral reef on the coast of Florida.

CHAPTER X.

APPOINTED A JUSTICE OF THE SUPREME COURT—PAINFUL INCIDENT—ANTICIPATED OUR CIVIL WAR—MY VIEWS UPON THAT SUBJECT.

FROM New York I went West as far as Platte County, Missouri, visited the scenes and friends of my early days, and returned to California about the 2d day of December. I was appointed a Justice of the Supreme Court of California by Governor J. Neely Johnson, and my commission bears date January 13, 1857. This position I held until my term expired early in October, 1858.

While occupying a seat on the Supreme Bench, a remarkable circumstance occurred, which I felt more intensely than I can describe. My brother, Glen O. Burnett (two years younger than myself), then resided in Oregon. He had been an invalid for two or three years, and I expected to hear of his death. One day in 1857 an old acquaintance of both of us came to me in Sacramento City, and informed me that he had just received a letter from his father-in-law, in which it was stated that my brother died the day previous to the date of the letter. As the writer lived in Oregon, only about twelve miles from my brother, I had not the slightest doubt of the fact. About three months had passed, and I was sure my brother was dead, when, one evening, after I had closed my judicial labors for the day, and while I was descending the outside iron stairs that led from

the court chambers above to the sidewalk, I observed a venerable old gentleman standing below, evidently waiting for some one. I could only see the top of his head and his long gray hair as it extended below his hat; but when I reached the sidewalk, and saw his face, I found he was my brother. My feelings can be better imagined than described. He was like one risen from the dead. How the mistake originated, I never knew.

I spent the month of December, 1859, and the month of January, and a small portion of February, 1860, in the city of New York. During that time I attentively read all the most important Congressional debates. Early in March, 1860, I returned to California, and told my friends that there would be civil war in case the Republican candidate should be elected President of the United States. No one agreed with me in this opinion. I thought that I saw, from the tone, temper, and matter of the speeches of the Southern members and Senators, that they had generally determined upon war in the contingency mentioned. It required only about one fourth of the population of the United States to produce civil war. As in such a contest there can practically exist only one party in the rebellious division, it required only a decisive majority of the Southern people to bring on the war. The minority would have not only to submit, but to aid and assist.

I was born and reared in the slave section of the United States, and most of my relatives resided there. I knew well the sincerity and courage of the Southern people; but it was a question of principle, and not of feeling. The unity and perpetuity of this great nation were a cardinal object with me. I could not fight against the grand old flag. If an intelligent stranger from another planet were to visit this earth, and were

the flags of all the nations of this world placed before him, he would unhesitatingly select the Stars and Stripes as the most brilliant and magnificent of them all. No one can ever look upon that flag and forget it. Besides, it is the symbol of the first great nation that ever established political and religious liberty in its fullness and perfection. Whatever defects may exist in our theory of government can be corrected, even at the expense of revolution; *but the unity and integrity of the nation can never be destroyed.* The day of weak, defenseless States has passed away for ever. Only great governments can succeed, now or hereafter. If our country should err for a time, and commit temporary injustice, we must trust her still, and patiently and lovingly wait for her returning sense of justice, as a dutiful son would for that of his father or mother. He who trusts the *ultimate* justice of his country will seldom be disappointed.

During the war I was called upon publicly to express my opinion in regard to it. My answer was published at the time, but, as usual with me, I preserved no copy. As already stated, I published a pamphlet of more than one hundred printed pages, in which I gave my views in full. I voted for Abraham Lincoln for his second term.

DETERMINE TO ENGAGE IN BANKING—ELECTED PRESIDENT OF THE PACIFIC ACCUMULATION LOAN COMPANY—THE INSTITUTION PUT IN PRACTICAL OPERATION — DIFFICULTIES IN OUR WAY — CHANGE THE NAME TO "PACIFIC BANK."

When I had finished my work, "The Path which led a Protestant Lawyer to the Catholic Church," which

appeared early in 1860, and the pamphlet just mentioned, which was published in the summer of 1861, I had a period of leisure. I had given up the practice of the law, and did not intend to resume it. I was not in debt, and had an income sufficient for a plain, decent support. All my children were married and settled for life, except my son John M. Burnett. For about two years I had time to read, but I could not see how I could make my knowledge useful. I maturely reflected upon my condition, and came to the conclusion that, as my health had been in a measure restored, it was my clear duty to make my personal services useful in some form. I thought it the duty of all persons, who are able, to work. It is the proper condition of man.

But what business to engage in was the question. I had always been unsuccessful in mercantile pursuits, and was determined never to engage in them again. I was too old to go back to the farm. In considering the matter fully, it occurred to me that banking would suit me better than any other occupation. It was an honest business, in which the temptation to do wrong was really less than in almost any other secular pursuit. We had in California a gold currency, and that which we lent was of full quantity, of pure quality, and of fixed value. All we asked of our debtors was to return to us the same amount of gold coin they had borrowed, with the addition of the interest, which was at the lowest market rates. We did not lend money (like some individual money-lenders) with the view of ultimately becoming the owners of the mortgaged property, as no bank would wish to own real estate, except its banking-house.

Furthermore, it was not only an honest business, but one very useful to all parties concerned. While the

income upon the capital was only moderate, and not speculative or exorbitant, a sound, well-conducted bank was a most beneficial institution to the community generally. A bank that never fails affords a safe place of deposit for the money of others. This is a great convenience and a great benefit to the depositors. Besides, a good bank has it in its power to aid its worthy customers in various ways. The successful manager of a bank must necessarily be a first-class business man; must know what kinds of business are safe, and what doubtful; and should supply his customers, not only with judicious loans, but with the soundest advice. Many a business man is saved by good counsel. So many banks had failed in San Francisco, to the injury of many and the utter ruin of some of their depositors, that a good institution that would be just and yet firm to all, I thought, would be a great benefit to its own customers, and, by its successful example, to the public in general.

Therefore, after calm and full deliberation, I came to the fixed conclusion that I would go into the business of banking when a fair opportunity should offer. I was then, as now, fully aware of the prejudices existing in the minds of many persons against the business. But I am one of those independent men who rely upon their own judgment in regard to their own business. I do not follow the opinions of others, unless they agree with my own. My business is *my* affair and not theirs.

I had not capital enough to engage in the business alone, and I could find no one desirous of going into it, who could put up the same amount that I could. Being determined not to endanger the competency I had already acquired, so far as I could reasonably avoid it, I had to bide my time.

In the spring of 1863 I was consulted by some of the officers of the "Pacific Accumulation Loan Company" in regard to the framing of its by-laws, and gave my views promptly. I was then residing in San José. This institution had been incorporated early in February, 1863, with a capital stock of five millions of dollars, divided into fifty thousand shares of the par value of one hundred dollars each, and its principal place of business was in the city of San Francisco. On the 3d of June, 1863, I was notified by the Secretary that I had been chosen President, to fill the vacancy occasioned by the resignation of Mr. Samuel Brannan, and came at once to San Francisco. I found several defects in the charter and by-laws, some of which I did not approve. First, I did not like the name. Second, the capital was too large. Third, the by-laws provided that the Board of Directors could only demand payments upon the stock subscribed for in monthly installments, not exceeding two per cent. The first thing was to obtain subscriptions for the capital stock, and then it would require four years and two months to call in the amount subscribed. I saw before me the work of a lifetime; yet, as I had a basis to stand upon, I deliberately determined to undertake the enterprise of ultimately establishing the soundest and most reliable bank in the city. I had no special knowledge of the business, as I had never been trained in this most difficult of all secular pursuits. Circumstances had thrown me into different kinds of business during my varied experience, but I had made it a general rule not to engage in more than one business at the same time, and to devote my whole attention for the time being to the work I had in hand, and to learn it as early as possible.

Books of subscription for the capital stock of the

institution had not been opened, and I set to work vigorously to get the stock taken. Mr. Brannan, myself, and some others subscribed, but I found that most of the very men who were the original incorporators either refused to take any stock or subscribed for mere nominal amounts. I labored hard at the task for some three months, but my success was not satisfactory. About the 1st of September I had another attack of neuralgia, and returned to San José, believing that our banking enterprise must fail. I had been at home about two weeks when I received a communication from the Secretary, stating that such arrangements had been made as would put the bank into practical operation within a few days.

Upon my return to the city, I was informed that Mr. Brannan had positively declared that the enterprise *must* and *should* succeed, and had largely increased his subscription. One other gentleman had subscribed for one thousand shares, four others for two hundred and fifty shares each, and others for various amounts. I also increased my subscription. We quietly but resolutely laid it up in our hearts that the enterprise should succeed.

It is but simple justice to Samuel Brannan to state that he is the father of the bank. Without his determined action, it would never have gone into successful operation. He was the first man in California, so far as I am informed, that spoke out in public against the introduction of slavery into this country. With all his faults, he has many noble qualities, and has done much for California.

When we opened the bank, on the 8th of October, 1863, we had less than twenty thousand dollars capital paid in. We had about seven hundred thousand dol-

lars subscribed, but it would require fifty months to call it in. It was a small beginning, and a long, slow race, but we did not flinch or falter. The most durable timber is of slow growth, and the very best fruits do not ripen first. Our officers gave their services without compensation for the first fifteen months. The current rate of interest was then two per cent. a month.

About the end of the year 1863 I found to my surprise that all the directors except myself were in favor of paying a dividend early in 1864. I wished to accumulate a surplus fund, but they outvoted me, and for the time I was compelled to submit. In 1864 we paid dividends upon the capital paid in, at the rate of two per cent. a month. In 1865 they were reduced to one and a half and one and a quarter, and in 1866 to one and one fifteenth per cent. a month. Dividends were then paid semiannually, on the first days of January and July.

As I had foreseen, in the summer and fall of 1866 the bank sustained losses to such an extent as to compel the suspension of dividends for fifteen months. When we were about to resume, I introduced a resolution that the bank would pay monthly dividends at the rate of ten per cent. per annum, until the further order of the Board. I was the only one who voted for this resolution. The dividends were put at one per cent. a month, payable monthly. In the summer of 1871 the bank again sustained losses which compelled a second suspension of dividends. The last monthly dividend was paid September 1, 1871.

In the mean time we had amended the by-laws in several respects, and, by authority of a special act of the State Legislature, we changed the name of the institution to "Pacific Bank," its present corporate title.

Later still we reduced the capital stock to one million dollars, United States gold coin, divided into ten thousand shares of the par value of one hundred dollars each. The stock of the bank never sold for less than eighty-five dollars per share for full-paid stock, but during the suspension of dividends it ruled from eighty-five dollars to par. According to the report in the "Alta California," the market value of the full-paid stock of the Bank of California to-day, September 26, 1878, is $80 bid and $82 asked; that of the First National, $89 bid and $90 asked; that of the National Gold Bank, $79 bid and $80 asked; and that of the Pacific, $115 bid, and $116 asked.

After the second suspension of dividends, September 1, 1871, and before we could resume, the majority of the stock fell into the hands of sound, safe, conservative men, who understood banking, and who agreed with me not to resume the payment of dividends until January, 1877. In the mean time we accumulated, in the space of five years and four months, a surplus fund of more than half a million dollars. Our capital of one million is now full-paid, and we have a handsome surplus.

WILD BANKS—SPECULATIVE CHARACTER OF OUR PEOPLE—INCIDENT.

I think I can safely say that no sound bank was ever established under greater difficulties than the Pacific. I am sure that I was never engaged in any business enterprise that required so much thought, judgment, labor, firmness, and perseverance. We had not only to overcome the great difficulties in our charter and by-laws, and the serious errors of our governing stockholders,

but we had for long years to compete with the wildest banks, wielding immense amounts of capital, and enjoying almost unbounded credit. I was reminded at times, by some of our own directors, that the managers of these fast and flashy institutions were fine business men ; but I firmly resisted such a conclusion. At an early day I did not approve of their mode of business, and then took a stand, almost "solitary and alone," that honest and intelligent time has conclusively shown to have been correct.

About two years after our little bank opened its doors for business, one of the leading capitalists of San Francisco, and one of the original incorporators who refused to subscribe for any of the stock, upon hearing some one speak of the Pacific Accumulation Loan Company, asked, "Is that thing going yet ?" About 1873 I met an officer of one of the large banks in the city, then in the full tide of success (as was generally supposed), who twittingly remarked to me, "Governor, the signs upon your bank windows are quite pretentious. They completely take us down." I made no reply. There was ample opportunity for "patience to have her perfect work."

Before the suspension of the largest banks in this city, August 26, 1875, the market value of our stock was less than that of any respectable bank in the city ; but when that event occurred, and the wild banks went down to the level of their intrinsic demerits, our stock went up to the head of the list, except that of one other bank. The stock of this *void* concern was still quoted in the public financial reports as worth $125 a share, when its intrinsic value was not one cent. Finally, however, in the fall of 1877, that bank failed, and left the stock of the Pacific Bank at the head of the list.

But we had not only to overcome these great diffi-

culties, but to encounter others equally embarrassing. The people of California, in proportion to numbers, have been, and are yet, the most speculative in America, if not in the world. At least one half of the men who came to this country were full of the most eager desire to make fortunes. A good, reasonable competency would not satisfy their magnificent expectations.

Speculation first ran wild in real estate, then in water-ditches, and for the last fifteen years in mining stocks. In no city on earth is it so difficult to ascertain the true financial condition of men as in San Francisco. With all due care, the average losses of a bank in this city, taking a series of ten years together, will run from two to four per cent. per annum upon the amount loaned. Nothing but the current high rate of interest enabled us to make a decent profit.

All must concede that mining is one of the leading interests of this coast, and that permanent investments in mines are a legitimate business, though exposed to more risks than most other avocations. The investor in a mine has two risks to encounter : first, the character of the mine itself ; second, the character of its management, which is the greater risk of the two. If the mine be poor, it can not be made to pay even by the best management. If it be rich, those who practically control its management are very apt to depreciate the market value of the stock, by working for a time the poor ores, or by other devices, and thus compel the board of directors to levy and collect a series of assessments. This process will be continued until the weaker stockholders are forced to sell their stock ; and the unprincipled managers, through their agents, buy it in, having the certificates issued in the name of some person as trustee.

But investing in the legitimate business of mining is one thing, and speculating in mining stocks is another and a very different thing. The first is useful and honest, because it develops and adds to the wealth of the country, while the second does not develop or add to its wealth or morals in any form whatever. All the necessaries and comforts of life are the products of labor and skill honestly applied. But the speculator and gambler are leeches upon society, and the worst of all speculators is the speculator in mining stocks. It is the most deplorably demoralizing of all occupations dignified by the name of business. It speedily corrupts crowds of people, and keeps them idle ever afterward; because the man who has once experienced the wild excitement and tasted the insane luxury of a successful speculation in mining stocks is, as a general rule, forever totally unfitted for any useful occupation. What sound business man would ever employ as a clerk a young man who had been once successful in mining-stock speculations? What is such a being fit for during the remainder of his life? If unsuccessful in his first effort, he is peculiarly fortunate, for then he may be saved from that worse than gambling pursuit. But it is just about as difficult to cure the once successful speculator as to reform the confirmed drunkard.

For one or two years before the late rise in the market value of mining stocks, crowds of men in the prime of life could be seen standing on the streets idle. Their listless faces and seedy, dilapidated appearance indicated extreme laziness and destitution. But since the rise they appear jubilant. They are now seen on the streets with clean-shaven faces, neatly combed hair, new clothes, new hats, and new boots nicely polished. They seem as much revived as withered grass after a plenteous fall of rain.

It is well known to all intelligent men, who have been in business in this city for any considerable time, that mining speculators will readily sacrifice their best friends, *because they can.* The old adage, "A long stitch for a friend," is most applicable to this character of swindling. When you hear one of these men say he has a confidential "point," as it is called, in regard to a certain mine, you may justly conclude that he has his stock in the hands of a broker for sale. So, if you hear a man puffing a certain stock, and saying he would invest if he only had the money, you had better conclude that he is anxious to sell. The only possible way in which these gamblers in mining stocks can deceive a sensible man is by telling the truth. That would be such a singular case as to deceive any fallible being.

A man who had once been in the habit of lending on mining stocks as collateral told me an incident within his own knowledge. He lent a man a sum of money, and took from the borrower what is called an "iron-clad note," secured by the pledge of a certain number of shares of a certain mining company. The note was payable one day after date, and contained a clause stipulating that the borrower should keep up the margin on the stock. If it should depreciate in its market value, the borrower was to put up more stock, or reduce the debt by a proportionate payment in money. In this case the stock was declining in value, and the lender was continually calling upon the borrower to keep good the margin. This the lender did several times, and the margin was made good by the borrower putting up more stock. The lender urged the speculator to sell, but he refused, insisting that the depression was only temporary. But the stock still continued to decline, and the lender as continually called for more stock, and

urged the borrower to sell, saying to him, "I can not spare you. In case of a speculation you would get all the profit, and you must take all the risk. The chance of profit and the risk of loss must go together."

The borrower at last had no more stock to put up, and no money to reduce the debt. He concluded to go to a large stock-speculator, and ask *his* opinion about the mine. This stock-sharp at once replied that it was a good mine, and that the depreciation of the stock in the market was a bear movement, and that it would soon go up again. "But," said the borrower, "I have borrowed money on my stock, and I am called upon by the lender to put up more stock, but I can not do it." "Well," said the sharp, "I will lend you the stock. How many shares do you lack?" and, upon being informed of the number, he at once handed over to the borrower the stock required. At that very time this large operator was selling out that very stock as rapidly as he could. He lent this parcel of stock to keep it from being thrown upon the market. But the stock still declined, and the lender gave orders to his broker to sell every share that very day. The stock was sold accordingly, and by this prompt sale the borrower was saved several thousand dollars, as the stock continued to decline until it went much lower.

MERCHANTS AND OTHER BUSINESS MEN OFTEN SECRETLY ENGAGE IN STOCK-SPECULATIONS — ILLUSTRATIVE CASES OF SPECULATION—FAILURES SOMETIMES FALSELY ATTRIBUTED TO SPECULATION IN MINING STOCKS.

Men engaged in mercantile and other kinds of business in this city are often secretly concerned in speculating in mining stocks. If the firm has a temporary

surplus of money, one of the younger partners is very apt to propose to invest that surplus, and no more, in mining stocks. Each speculator pays himself the vain compliment to think that, by watching the market carefully, *he* can know when to buy and sell or that *he* is born to good luck. If the firm should succeed in the first attempt, then all the partners become so elated that they can not condescend to attend to the dull routine of regular business, in which there appears to them nothing worthy of their genius or enterprise, the amount made required so little time and labor. So they go in deeper and deeper. When they sustain losses they are plucky, and act upon the sharp's maxim, "Seek your money where you lost it." They forget the true and sober maxim, "Never be deceived twice in the same way," and never stop in their wild career until they are forced to do so by utter insolvency.

On the contrary, if a firm be embarrassed pecuniarily, then the partners are tempted to engage in speculations in mining stocks as a measure of relief. If successful (as in some *rare* cases may happen), they get out of their difficulties for a time, but hardly ever remain so permanently.

These men fraudulently hold themselves out to the business world as *only* engaged in regular and useful business. Their stock operations are profoundly secret. The certificates of stock are adroitly put in the name of some man as trustee, and endorsed by him in blank on the back, and thus pass from hand to hand like a note endorsed in blank or a bond payable to bearer. You may examine the books of *all* the numerous companies in this city, and you will never find any stock standing in the names of these men. Not a share. The first thing known is the failure of the house. Men above

the age of fifty, and who have been sound, safe, and reasonably successful for years, occasionally go into this wild gambling, and are ruined. In fact, age and experience seem no sufficient protection against this infatuation. Lamentable cases often occur. Some are ludicrous, and some are too serious to be so, though equally stupid. Women are often seen crying in the streets, because they have been gambling in mining stocks, and have lost all.

Another difficulty in the way of commercial banking in this city was the absence of good collaterals. Very few of our business men had invested in United States bonds, because the rate of interest was too low, and our State bonds had been mostly absorbed by the State School Fund, while our best county bonds had gone to the East and to Europe. The only abundant collaterals were mining stocks, and these were not reliable, with all the "iron-clad" notes that could be taken. We were, therefore, compelled to lend on names, and to a large extent upon single names. Hence the great losses sustained, and the very moderate net profits realized. Besides, the amount of bank deposits in San Francisco is much less in proportion to bank capital than in other commercial cities.

In illustration, I will mention a few cases.

A millionaire came from the East to spend the winter in California, and brought letters of introduction to me. We had many conversations about business, and I urged him not to touch mining stocks. But in a month or two the yellow fever of speculation obtained the mastery over him. He was about sixty years of age, and his annual income was about one hundred thousand dollars. He said to me at last that he had concluded to risk fifty thousand dollars in mining stocks, as he de-

sired some excitement, and could readily stand the loss of that amount. I said no more to him, but left him to himself. The next spring he sold out his stocks, and had made about twenty thousand dollars net profit. He was much gratified, and no doubt thought himself more than a match for the San Francisco sharps. I had carefully explained to him the process by which they would ultimately catch him, but he had not yet comprehended it. The succeeding fall he again came to spend the winter in California, and again went into speculations in mining stocks. As he kept his cash account with the Pacific Bank, I often saw him ; but he said nothing to me, nor I to him, on the subject. But, when he came to close out the second spring, he wore an extremely long face. I observed his downcast looks, and asked him how he was getting along. He replied, "Governor, I feel very blue. I have lost thirty-two thousand dollars in mining stocks." This was a ludicrous case, in regard to which I could afford to laugh heartily.

One of our leading capitalists informed me that on one occasion he determined to engage in speculation in mining stocks. He said his practice was to purchase when they were highest, for fear they would go higher, and to sell when they were lowest, for fear they would go lower. He soon found that he had sustained losses to the amount of more than eight thousand dollars. He also said that the most amusing feature in his case was the fact that his losses occurred while he was dealing in the stock of a mine of which he was president. His experience proved that no man can see beyond the point of the pick.

A gentleman of my acquaintance told me that one evening in 1878 he was riding in a street-car in this city, and that there sat opposite to him a neatly but

not extravagantly dressed married lady, some twenty-five years old. She was evidently a woman of education. Soon a gentleman, who appeared to be an acquaintance of herself and husband, entered the car, and took a seat beside her. She was a loud, fluent talker, and at once commenced, and soon explained to him their present as compared with their former condition. She said they had been rich, but had lost all in mining stocks; that they had given up their fine residence, splendid furniture, and magnificent horses and carriage; that they had dismissed their numerous servants, and had taken a small, neat, but comfortable cottage; that she rose early and prepared breakfast, then went out and taught a class in music, returned and cooked dinner and supper; and, in fact, that she did all her housework herself, and never was so busy or more healthy. At the end of her narrative she paused for a moment, and then exclaimed, with increased emphasis, "*But we had a grand time while it lasted.*"

The same gentleman informed me that he knew a merchant in one of the interior cities of California who was a partner in a most respectable mercantile firm, which for years had done a safe, prosperous, and honorable business. This man was considered an exemplary member of society in his city, but he became tired of his position, sold out his interest in an excellent business, and went into speculations in mining stocks. My informant said he had not seen this man for several years, when he met him in the streets of San Francisco in 1878, and inquired how he was progressing. The man replied, "You know I was at one time worth one hundred and twenty-five thousand dollars in cash; but I have lost it all. I would not have regarded the loss of the money so much, had I not lost it on a *sure thing.*"

The melancholy truth was, the man had not alone lost his money, but he had lost his capacity for all useful business, and also his moral principles. This is one of the sad cases.

On one occasion a well-dressed lady came to the bank and engaged in a long conversation with our cashier. On passing through his department several times, I observed the lady frequently weeping. After she had left, I inquired of the cashier as to the subject of the interview. He stated substantially that she came to sell him an elegant copy of Audubon's "Birds of America," and had explained to him the reasons for offering it for sale. She said that she was then living with her second husband; that her first husband, who was much older than herself, had died and left her a fortune; that her second husband was of suitable age for her; that she had married him some eight months before, and soon after his return from Europe, whither he had gone to complete his education; that he was a finely educated gentleman; that they had been some months in San Francisco on a visit; that they had invested all her money in mining-stock speculations, and had lost all; and that they were upon the verge of actual want, and were compelled to sell everything they could spare to procure the mere necessaries of life. It was evident that her second marriage was a love-match; and that, while her second husband was an accomplished gentleman, he was but a child in business. This case was too sad to laugh at.

When I arrived in San Francisco in March, 1849, I found an old settler residing here with his family. He was a man of means, and left the city about 1855, and settled in one of the States east of the Rocky Mountains. About 1873 he sent a telegram to his banker in

this city to this purport : "Buy mining stocks for me when they are lowest, and sell when they are highest." He no doubt thought his fortune was certain, as in his opinion this process could not fail. If his banker would only obey orders, how could there be a failure ? But he was no doubt greatly surprised when his banker replied that they could not do that kind of business. When stocks were lowest or highest, no man could tell.

But I have every reason to believe that failures are sometimes falsely attributed to speculations in mining stocks. This pretense is resorted to in order to swindle creditors.

For example, a firm composed of two or more partners, finding business dull and expenses and losses greater than gains, deliberately determine to cheat their creditors, and in this way to make a handsome profit. How to do so successfully, and with the least possible delay and disgrace, is the question with them. Bankruptcy they know to be not only a slow but an uncertain mode ; and, to save anything, they must hide their money, commit perjury, and incur a stain upon their business honor that will stick to them as long as they live. They therefore adopt the common plan of compromising with their creditors. But to do this successfully they must make out what claims to be a full and true statement of their assets and liabilities, and must be prepared to satisfy their creditors that this statement is true. Perhaps only six months before they had made a statement in full to the mercantile agencies, or to some of their creditors, showing the firm to have been then in a fair condition. But, when they make out a statement for a compromise, showing so great a difference, how are they to account for the discrepancy between the two statements ? Every sensible business man will at once see

that such extraordinary losses, if truly such, must have been produced by unusual causes. Some creditor will be certain to ask this question: "What caused these heavy losses in so short a time?" This home question must be answered satisfactorily, or the proposition for a compromise, upon the payment of a fraction on the dollar, can not succeed. If they give an explanation, the falsity of which from its nature can be shown by investigation, the fraudulent attempt must fail. The partners, fully comprehending the situation, will of course come prepared to answer that some one of the firm had been speculating in mining stocks, and had secretly used the partnership name to borrow money, which had been lost. The moment this answer is given, the creditors are at fault. That region of darkness can not be penetrated. All possible inquiries can not expose the falsity of the answer. His broker is pledged to secrecy, the stocks stand in the name of some one as trustee, the certificates were endorsed in blank, and it is impossible to trace him. The partners have either agreed among themselves which one of them should bear the odium, or have settled it by lot. The creditors will naturally sympathize with the apparently innocent partner; and, for his sake and that of his family, they agree to the proposition. Having discharged one partner, they legally discharge the other. The firm, having been thus released from their debts upon the payment of a fraction of them, start anew, with a fine capital and no liabilities.

TRUE RULE AS TO BANK CONTRIBUTIONS—BANKING A TRYING BUSINESS—THE INFALLIBLE BANKER—FIVE MAIN POINTS TO CONSIDER IN MAKING LOANS—DEVICES TO OBTAIN CREDIT.

Soon after our little bank went into practical operation, we were called upon to contribute from the corporate funds for various charitable purposes. This bank, being the first incorporated commercial institution in this city, had to take a just stand upon this subject and maintain it. Up to this period all the commercial banks in San Francisco were mere partnerships, and of course could legally and justly give away the partnership funds by the consent of all the partners. But incorporated banks were placed in a new and totally different position, though this difference was not apparent for a time to those who asked for contributions. Our charter did not allow the officers of the bank to give away the money of the stockholders ; and, had the officers done so, they would have been individually liable. Besides, it was an unjust principle to ask the bank to give in its corporate capacity, and then go to each stockholder and ask him to give as an individual. This would have been a double burden. Our stockholders claimed the undoubted right to bestow their charities upon such objects as their judgment approved, and in such amounts as they, in their own opinion, could reasonably spare.

It is a wise and salutary feature in the charter of incorporated banks, that no power is conferred upon the officers to give away the funds of the institution. An individual banker or a partnership can well do so, as they bestow only their own money, and not that of others. Most bank officers have but a small amount of stock in the institution, and, if allowed to give away its

means, could acquire a splendid reputation for generosity with very little, if any, cost to themselves. The principal officer would receive all the praise, while the stockholders would sustain all the loss. He would find any number of people who would give him unmerited praise for solid gold, without caring whose money it was.

I soon saw what the ultimate result must be, should we act upon a false theory; and I took the stand that, *as a bank*, we would give nothing except to celebrate the fourth of July, and in some other extraordinary cases, approved by all. In this position I was sustained by the stockholders, who were people in every condition of life, and of different political and religious views. On this point we heard no complaints from the stockholders. Each of us gave individually to such objects as he approved, and in such amounts as he pleased.

As already stated, I had had no special training as a banker. I possessed, as I thought, a fair amount of general business knowledge. In my business transactions, I acted upon Lord Chesterfield's rule of politeness—"softness in the manner, but firmness in the execution"; and I found this an admirable rule for a banker. My first care in my new position was to comprehend the true situation. I had engaged in a trying and perilous business, that required for its successful management not only a comprehensive knowledge of business in general, but a superior judgment of men—the highest order of business capacity. I was often forcibly reminded of that profound couplet of Pope:

> "The good must merit God's peculiar care;
> But who, but God, can tell us who they are?"

I soon found that a banker would be called either a hard man or a fool. If he lent the money of the bank

carefully and successfully, they would call him a hard man, an old fogy, and an old fossil. On the contrary, if he lent the money of the institution carelessly, and ultimately lost it, he would be justly called a fool. He would be judged by ultimate results. A banker must make up his mind as to which reputation he prefers. I never do an idle and vain thing, if I know it. When I undertake any business, I mean to succeed, if I can do so by fair and just means ; and, if I can not attain success by such a course, I quit the business.

A banker is exposed to every *possible* test, as he meets every class of men, in all their various conditions and moods. If he is avaricious, they will be very apt to overcome him with presents and commissions. If he is vain and has a lust of praise, they will flatter him to his heart's content. If he is indolent and good-natured, they will pleasantly induce him to make bad loans. If he is too kind-hearted, they will overcome his sympathies. If he is timid, they will bully him. If he is excitable, they will worry and confuse him. If he is not clear-headed, they will out-talk and persuade him. In short, he has to encounter *every* class of men : the good, safe business man, with whom it is a pleasure to deal ; the partially insane and abusive man, when pecuniarily embarrassed ; the vain, conceited man, who thinks he knows it all, and piles up his advice ; the eager, visionary, financial dreamer, full of "hopes and schemes" ; the bold, reckless, and unprincipled speculator ; the cheat, the forger, the thief. Each one comes with his speech prepared in advance. A banker will in due time find out that the best talkers are generally "men of words and not of deeds." They talk remarkably well, but do not generally pay. The chronic borrower, from long practice, understands borrowing as a science. He

will use very few words, but will ask, in a very simple, pleasant way, "Mr. President, are you discounting any first-class paper to-day?" "Yes, sir." "I have a note of that class to offer." Upon the note being declined, he retires with the same ease and grace with which he entered.

A banker may for a time gain the reputation of possessing an *infallible* judgment of men, if he will only adopt the bold plan of quickly and promptly saying yes or no to all applications for loans. If a good man comes and asks for a loan, and it is instantly granted, he, *knowing* that he is good, goes away, saying to himself, "What a splendid judge of human nature!" If the visionary comes, and as promptly obtains a loan, he, *thinking* himself good, goes away admiring the wonderful instinct of the banker. So of all other classes of borrowers who *succeed* in obtaining loans. As all receive what they asked for, they are all pleased, and all equally filled with admiration. The good talkers among the successful borrowers will fill the city with their loud and oft-repeated praises of the wonderful qualifications of this most prompt banker. Those he as promptly refuses are men notoriously in bad credit, and they, too, admire the banker's off-hand sagacity in understanding them so quickly. The reputation of the banker lasts until time, with its absolute veto, puts him down to his proper level. Then men begin to learn that hasty loans too often end in large losses.

In considering a proposed loan, there are five main points of inquiry:

1. Is the proposed borrower thoroughly honest?
2. Has he an adequate capital?
3. Is his business a reasonably safe one?
4. Does he manage it well?

5. Is he a good economist in his living?

All these should concur to make a loan a fair business risk.

We are often forced to form a judgment of men from very trifling circumstances; but these are keys to the position. Men may successfully conceal their real characters in important matters, but will reveal them in little things. If a man borrows money, and at the same time is found insuring his life for the benefit of his family, or improving a homestead, or living above his means, or driving fine horses, or doing any other thing incompatible with the condition of an honest debtor, those who lend him money will be very apt to receive a notice to attend a meeting of creditors.

It is surprising how many devices (most of them old, but some of them new) unprincipled and extravagant men will resort to in order to obtain money.

For example, a speculator will purchase and pay for a valuable and productive parcel of real estate, which he will *never* encumber. Upon the credit of this property, say worth fifty thousand dollars, he will borrow various sums from different parties, at intervals running through several years, always paying his notes punctually. The lenders keep their own business to themselves, each one thinking the borrower owes nobody but him. This process will be continued, the sum total of borrowed money increasing about in proportion to the interest paid, until at last he sells the property for cash, and his creditors find nothing whereon to levy.

Another speculator sets out in his early manhood to speculate in produce, say cotton or grain, and he deliberately adopts a theory, either originated by himself or suggested to him by some older head. He determines to conduct the business as carefully as he can, but upon

borrowed capital and at the risk of others. If he should succeed, he will pocket all the profits ; if he should fail, his creditors must bear all the loss. He will be liberal in his charities and in his contributions to public objects, as his generosity costs *him* nothing, and he receives great praise without merit. He will be a generous patron of the fine arts, and be called a man of fine taste. In the course of time he suspends, and compromises with his creditors at a fraction on the dollar, giving them a verbal promise (not binding in law) that he will in time pay every dollar of his old debts, without interest. At this, his first suspension, we will assume for the sake of illustration that his total assets amount to five hundred thousand dollars, and his liabilities to the same amount, which he discharges with two hundred and fifty thousand, thus netting that sum by the compromise. He now has a handsome capital, and commences business again, and for a time he succeeds well. He now borrows still more largely, and out of this *borrowed* money he pays his old debts in installments. His old creditors are full of gratitude, and are loud in sounding his praises on all sides. At the payment of each installment of his old indebtedness, his credit grows better, until, when all are paid, it rises to its summit, and he uses it as fully as possible.

In the mean time he marries and rears a family in splendor and in the enjoyment of all the luxuries of the world. In the course of time, however, he overreaches himself in his expenses and speculations, and suspends a second time, calls his creditors together again, and proposes another compromise upon the old basis. He assures them that he will pay every dollar in the future, as he did in the past, if they will only discharge him. His creditors remember well his former noble act, as

they consider it, and easily agree to release him upon the terms proposed. In the second suspension he makes a much larger profit than in the first. He starts again with increased capital to run the same career. But at his death it will be found that his life had been insured to a large amount for the benefit of his family, not of his creditors, although *their* money paid the premiums upon the policies. His friends, who are generally the best of talkers, will attribute his losses to the nature of his business, and not to his extravagance. They never seem to understand the fact that extravagant family expenses, continued for a series of years together, will ruin any business, as a general rule. Had he lived in a decent and honorable simplicity, as all men should who owe others, then he could have paid his debts with ease.

Whenever any man lives extravagantly, and at the same time owes any considerable amount of money, his credit in bank should be very low, whatever may be his *apparent* wealth. No loans should be made him except upon unquestionable security. A man that owes nothing has the right to live in splendor ; but, when a man has to borrow money to pay family expenses, his condition is bad, and his credit should be so too.

I have lately seen a letter from a man twenty-four years old, who is a student at college, to his father, from which I am permitted to take the following extract : " *The moment a man spends too much on himself, he is to be watched.* Now, I mean whether his income is one hundred dollars a year or five hundred dollars a year. This rule applies whether he has or has not vices, is or is not honest, a Christian or not one. You must not understand me as meaning the old proverb, *If a man spends more than he earns, he will wind up in the poor-house or penitentiary.* He may save

three fourths of what he earns ; that does not make much difference with my rule. I mean, if he indulges himself in any way, say by overeating, studying, staying up of nights, or excesses of any kind."

There is a depth of sound practical judgment shown in this extract, which is remarkable as coming from one so young and inexperienced.

Natural and reasonable wants are few and limited, while artificial and unreasonable wants are many and unlimited. When, therefore, a man *begins* to expend money to gratify these wants, he starts upon a dangerous and downward path ; and, whatever may be his income to-day, he may, and very probably will, soon exceed it. The banker can not rely upon the discretion of such a borrower. He may confine his expenditures within his income for a short time ; but his want of judgment, his extreme selfishness, and his insatiable desire to gratify whimsical and inordinate wants, will be very apt to cause his ruin sooner or later, and no one can tell when this may occur.

And I lay down this rule as *generally* true : If a man *once* goes through insolvency or bankruptcy, or compromises with his creditors, or indulges in unreasonable expenses, he is unworthy of credit. I say *generally* true, as there may be about one exception in ten cases.

A GOOD BANKER MAY OFTEN SAVE HIS CUSTOMERS FROM LOSSES AGAINST THEIR WILL—INCIDENTS OF THE SUSPENSION OF CERTAIN BANKS IN 1875—DIFFICULTY OF OBTAINING FAITHFUL EMPLOYEES.

Sometimes the greatest good a sound banker can do his customers, and the one for which he receives at the time the fewest thanks and the most censure, is to check

their extreme eagerness to grow rich quickly. Impatience ruins multitudes of business men. In their great anxiety to advance rapidly, and to rival older business houses, they are tempted to go too far. This is generally the error of young men, and especially of those who succeed their fathers in business. The ambitious, bold, and inexperienced youngster is easily flattered, and thinks he can excel his father. He is very apt to think the sum left him inexhaustible, and his credit unbounded; while every competent banker knows that most young men in our country, who inherit fortunes from their parents or others, go to ruin. If a firm, for example, be Smith's Sons, a judicious banker will be very apt to decline their paper, though they be rich when it is made. It is, as a general rule, only a question of time when the firm will fail.

Other young business men, who have had no fortune left them, will be very anxious to make a fortune speedily, so that they can enjoy it before they become old. When they come to their banker with paper for discount, these ardent customers are nearly always certain to consider *their* paper first-class, and are much surprised, and often offended, because the paper is declined. If they are about to enter into some outside enterprise, or make a purchase in their proper line of business, but much too large for their capital, they see the great anticipated profits, while the sound, conservative banker can only see probable losses. He therefore refuses to lend them the money, much to their disappointment; but he saves them from ruin against their will and their most persistent importunities.

About a month and a half before the suspension of certain large banks in this city in August, 1875, a customer of ours rushed into our bank one day, and said to

me, "I wish to borrow twenty-five thousand dollars for sixty days, and I have first-class collaterals to give." I quietly asked him to let me see his collaterals, and they proved to be one hundred shares of the stock of a certain bank, and the same number of shares of the stock of a certain other bank. After listening to him about twenty minutes, I declined the loan. He was a splendid talker, and argued his case remarkably well. When he found he could not obtain the loan, he said he would go and sell every share of the stock, which he did promptly, at about one hundred and twenty-five dollars a share. When these banks and one other suspended, he was not in the city, but returned in a few days in the best possible humor. I had saved him, against his will, between fifteen and sixteen thousand dollars.

Another service a banker may do his customers, especially young business men, is to require them to pay their notes punctually at maturity. This practice keeps them active, vigilant, and firm in making collections from their own customers. If unduly indulged themselves by their bankers, they in turn become too indulgent, and ultimate ruin is the legitimate result.

I remember a case wherein I erred myself, to the injury of our customer as well as our own, by being too indulgent. He kept a good balance in the bank, and we had loaned him, upon his own name, the sum of four thousand dollars. He was a man of mature age, steady habits, good character, and fair capital. The loan ran on for several years, and was renewed from time to time, the interest being always punctually paid. Finally, this staid, industrious old gentleman went into speculations in mining stocks, and, as usual, lost all. The first I knew of his failure was from his own melancholy letter informing me of the fact. I sent for him, and we had

a free conference, in the course of which he said, "I wish to God you had called upon me to pay that note. I could have paid it any day, and there would have been that much saved."

When the run on the banks occurred in 1875, we knew nothing of it until it commenced. We were then told that there was a run on a certain bank, and in half an hour afterward that bank closed its doors. In a panic the crowd of depositors seem to have an infallible instinct. They will be certain to first run on the weakest bank, and then on others in proportion to their want of strength. This run on the banks conclusively proved the truth and reason of the Scripture command, "Be ye always ready."

We at once stopped all loans, and required those who were not depositors with the bank to pay their notes as they fell due; otherwise they would go to protest. We were compelled, for our own protection, to adopt and inflexibly enforce this peremptory rule. They urged us to permit the endorsers to waive demand and protest. I saw that, if we did this in one case, we must in many, and would thus be compelled to carry the customers of other banks through the crisis. I said, "Pay or be protested. The rule is as inflexible as the laws of the Medes and Persians."

One man had two notes falling due on the same day, and he urged me to let them go over, upon a waiver of demand and protest, as he could not possibly pay them when due. I said, "You must pay or be protested." He urged and urged again and again; and about half an hour before the bank closed for the day he went out, declaring the notes must go to protest. But about fifteen minutes later he came into my office, flaunting the notes in my face, and saying he wanted to quarrel with

me. I told him to sit down and I would hear him. He complained and grumbled about my harshness, and said I had hurt his feelings. After he had finished, I said to him quietly and good-humoredly: "I have my money now, and I think I can stand your grumbling." At this he laughed heartily, and went away. A day or two afterward I mentioned the circumstance to the endorser of the notes, and he at once said, "Why, he had already provided for those notes." The truth was, the maker had other notes falling due within a few days, and was not *certain* that he could meet them unless he could induce us to permit these two notes to pass without protest. If he could only postpone the payment of these two notes, he would have ample means to pay the others.

In many cases I was very sorry for the parties whose notes we were compelled to protest. I remember the case of a most admirable man, whose hair was gray, and who was evidently a gentleman in every sense of the term. I had never seen him before, because he had never before asked indulgence on a note of his. He assured me that his note had never gone to protest in a single case; and it was so hard, at this period of his life, to have his note protested. He exhibited the truest financial feeling and honor, and told me that he would pay the note within two days if I would permit the endorser to waive. I assured him of my kindest feeling toward him, and of my fullest confidence in his good faith; but the rule of the bank was inflexible and must be carried out. He went away sorrowful, and left me so. I knew he was a true man. The note went to protest, and he paid it within two days thereafter. I then said to him, "Do not let this protest give you any pain. In such a crisis as this, the notes

of the best men go to protest. Under all the circumstances, your credit is not impaired at all ; and, if you should want any money, come to me and I will lend it to you." He went away consoled and satisfied.

The suspension occurred on Thursday, and on the Tuesday following a gentleman of my acquaintance, who was an officer of an interior bank, came into my office smiling, and inquired whether I thought any money could be borrowed in San Francisco on United States bonds as collateral. I laughed, and told him I *rather* thought not. He then informed me of the fact that his institution, five years before, had purchased United States bonds amounting to ninety-two thousand dollars, and had held them ever since for this very crisis ; and now they were not worth anything for the purpose intended. This city is so distant from the great financial cities of the world that for some time money could not be borrowed upon any collaterals whatever. We were offered a loan, secured by a pledge of United States bonds, at two per cent. a month, which we were compelled to decline. The only loans we made for three weeks were small amounts to our good depositors, to save them from protest.

One of the greatest difficulties in conducting a bank is to obtain faithful and competent officers and other assistants. This is especially so in California, as so few young men are natives, whose families are well known here.

The discipline in a bank must be as rigid as that in an army. If an employee willfully and deliberately disobeys orders, he should be discharged. If, when caught in making a mistake, he manifests no feeling, no regret, but takes it coolly and indifferently, it shows that he has deliberately trained his feelings to bear re-

proof, and he is not to be trusted. If he shirks his duty, and throws an unfair proportion of the work upon others, he exhibits an unjust disposition, and should be discharged. If he is late in coming to the bank, so as just to save his time, he had better be watched. If he is too fond of display, and carries a little cane for show, you had better conclude,

"Little cane,
Little brain;
Little work,
And big shirk."

He will spend too much time on the streets to show himself. If he is a fast young man in *any way*, he is unworthy. If he expends all his salary and saves up nothing, as a general rule he is unfit. It will do him no good to increase his salary, because he will be just as poor at the end of the year as he was at the beginning. In fact, an increase of compensation is a positive injury to him, because it increases his fast habits in proportion.

But a young man of good habits, pleasant manners, fair health, and good temper, who saves up a portion of his income, may be safely trusted. To bear the continual strain of good economy is a clear proof of integrity, good, sound, practical common sense, and self-control. Such a man soon becomes independent in his circumstances, and does not need to steal. Occasionally a young man may be found who is competent, sober, economical, and industrious, and who will yet steal from sheer avarice; but such cases are remarkably rare. An inordinate love of pleasure is the ruin of very many young men in our day. Extravagance in dress and living is the great besetting sin of the times, in almost every portion of the world.

EXTREME WEALTH NOT THE HAPPIEST CONDITION IN LIFE—REASONS FOR THIS CONCLUSION.

Since the fundamental change in my religious views, I have not sought to accumulate a large fortune, nor desired to become a millionaire. I understood myself, whether others understood me or not. I do not consider it the happiest state of life. Far from it. The poor need money to supply their wants, while the extremely rich desire more wants to absorb their wealth. Extreme wealth and extreme poverty are two *opposites*, neither of which is at all desirable. When a man has reached the point of independence, where he is secure of the necessaries of life with reasonable effort, he is as rich as any one, if he only knew it. There are but three legitimate and just purposes for which a competency is desirable : first, the privilege of being independent ; second, the power to be just ; third, the ability to be more charitable. All beyond these purposes becomes a burden, which costs more than it is worth.

As a general rule, it is very difficult to acquire a *large* fortune in any honest, regular, useful business, without resorting to measures that can not be approved by conscientious men ; such, for example, as monopolies of provisions, fraudulent combinations to unduly depress or put up the price of stocks, sharp tricks in starting or spreading false rumors, and the many other modes of overreaching one's neighbor.

Before a man can engage in these evil practices, he must first expel from his bosom all genuine love for his race. He must first make his selfish thirst for wealth the absorbing passion of his life, and to the same extent crush or smother every feeling of his better nature. He must first destroy his *capacity* for the enjoyment of the

purest and most enduring pleasures of life before he can hope to succeed. He begins with a demoralized nature, goes on through life in the same condition, "then dies the same."

But, when he attains his position as millionaire by these unjust means, he is not at the summit of human happiness. There are thousands of vexations in his path. His wealth is almost certain to be overestimated five to one; and, while such a false estimate may flatter his vanity, he is expected to give in charity or otherwise an amount in proportion to this overestimate. If he fails to do this, then he is severely censured by his fellow men; and if he does comply with these expectations he soon ceases to be rich. He is forced by circumstances to become to a great extent an isolated being, and must limit his friendships to a very small circle. In fact, he can scarcely know the happiness of disinterested friendship, or of devoted love for his children. If he mingles freely in society, and is kind and cordial in his manners, many of those he meets will seek to take advantage of these circumstances to ask for pecuniary favors. Committees of both men and women call on him for contributions for charitable and other purposes, and will bring every influence to bear upon him. If he responds, the amount will hardly equal their expectations, or secure their genuine respect. He can not go through the streets of a city like other men. If he attempts it, he must dash along at a rapid rate, to avoid importunity on the way. If he gives or lends at all, he is beset so often and so persistently that he enjoys no privacy and no peace. If he gives nothing, then he is reproached very justly. He is compelled to go through the streets in his carriage, and to have his regular office-hours for seeing people, and his home in the country,

where he can not be seen ; or he must spend much of his time abroad, to escape the incessant importunities of friends and relatives, who desire loans they are likely never to return. If he is vain, they will flatter him to any desirable extent. If he receives any favors, he will often be expected to return about ten to one. Like the president of a large bank, who received a present of a fine Durham calf from an applicant for a large loan, he is very certain to become a victim if he consents to accept presents. In short, he is forced to become a being unlike others. To his condition the lines of Pope are most applicable :

> "Painful preëminence! yourself to view,
> Above life's weakness, and its comforts too."

But the most deplorable feature in the condition of a millionaire, whose fortune has been acquired by unjust means, is the unhappy effect it generally has upon his own descendants, and upon a large proportion of his relatives. It is not the *practical* way to found, but to extirpate, a family. How few of the children and relatives of such men ever become good and happy members of society! This is particularly true in our country, where the law of entail does not exist. When a rich American dies, his property speedily goes into the hands of his heirs or legatees, or into the pockets of the lawyers ; and, in nine cases out of ten, those who share his estate become poor before they die. It is well known that rich men make the most complex and silly wills of any class of people in our country. His children are reared in idleness and luxury. They may have a fair classical education, but no knowledge of business or of economy. The father is generally too busy and too selfish, and the mother too fond of travel and dis-

play, to teach the children any practical ideas of the serious business of life. When the large fortune is divided among a number of children, the portion that falls to each one is not sufficient long to maintain his expensive habits, because he is ignorant of the cardinal principles of practical business. Every true business man knows that it requires more sound business knowledge to *retain* than to acquire property.

Even if the parents use all reasonable measures properly to rear and educate their children, they will have a most difficult task to accomplish. They will find it impossible to conceal from their children the fact that the parents are rich; and it is exceedingly difficult, when they are once in the possession of this knowledge, to make the young people understand the *absolute* necessity of labor and economy. Everywhere they go, they hear people talk of their father's wealth, and how he ought to spend it, and how his children should enjoy life. These false ideas are incessantly inculcated by multitudes of people. The children are naturally led to conclude that the majority of voices is right, rather than the minority; when the truth is that, in business matters, the majority of people are almost certain to be in the wrong. Most of the sons, like the great majority of mankind, have no natural capacity for business; and how can good business men be made of such material?

The result is, the children half obey their parents while they *must*, but at the same time resolve in their own minds to show their parents, in due time, how to enjoy a fortune. Nine out of ten of the children of rich parents ultimately become poor, sour, unhappy, and worthless members of society. They generally make bad matches. The reason is obvious. Their inferiors in fortune are far more obsequious, deferential,

and attentive than their equals. Poor young men who have *just* intellect enough to become well skilled in the usages and amusements of society, and fluent and accomplished in the ordinary topics of fashionable conversation, will be most apt to win the affections of young women who have nothing else to do but seek for pleasure. Rich young men never see young women except in fashionable life, and become enamored with some pretty, poor, and extravagant belle, possessed of more beauty than good common sense.

But the effect upon the other relatives is generally most injurious. If one of a number of brothers becomes very rich (and especially if such riches be acquired by improper means), then some of them will become agrarians, and urge a division. Some of them will be ambitious to rival the rich brother, and will plunge into wild speculations and fail. One portion of them will refuse to do anything they are competent to do, and others will run wild. Most of them will be extremely envious of the rich brother. When he assists one, he must aid all the others, or they will complain bitterly among the kin, and often among strangers. To aid so many in comparative idleness and wild speculations is a huge task. The largest fortune will soon vanish under such exorbitant demands. Each one thinks he ought to live as well as the rich brother; and they will do their utmost practically to carry out their views. If they do not administer upon his estate during his life, they are very apt to succeed after his death. The ultimate general result will be, that not one member of the family, remote or near, not even the rich man himself, will be really and substantially benefited by his riches. He has only accumulated this large fortune for others to waste, to their own material injury.

It is exceedingly difficult for a rich man to protect himself against the countless devices of those who seek his wealth. In large commercial cities especially, they will beset him with every possible plea. Many of the cases will be meritorious, as the world is full of real misery; while many will be false, as the world is full of vice. To protect himself effectually, the rich man must be armed with the quills of the porcupine, or covered with the hide of the rhinoceros.

Not long since a man came to a rich old acquaintance in San Francisco, and asked for the loan of about one hundred and twenty-five dollars, to pay his passage to New York. He told a most plausible story, and intimated very plainly that he would commit suicide in case he failed to obtain relief. The rich man was deeply concerned, and came to me for advice. It seemed as if the man's life would be lost by his own criminal act in case he could not obtain the sum desired. If the rich man refused the request, then he might, to some extent, be answerable for the life of a fellow creature. If he advanced the money, he might do so to an unworthy man, and be thus encouraging vice by rewarding it. While we were considering the question, we ascertained that this man had drawn from a bank, only two or three days before, about one hundred and seventy-five dollars. The request was refused; and within a day or two thereafter the man came into the office of the rich man, and boastfully showed him the amount of money he had applied for, alleging that he had obtained it from another person.

The *general* result is as I have stated. Of course, there are exceptions enough to prove the truth of the general rule. All the close observations of a long and active life have satisfied me, beyond a doubt, of the

wisdom and truth of the sentiment written some thousands of years ago, and found in the grand old Bible :

"*Give me neither poverty nor riches.*"

WIVES SHOULD BE CONSULTED ABOUT ALL IMPORTANT AFFAIRS—DAUGHTERS SHOULD BE TAUGHT A KNOWLEDGE OF BUSINESS—CONCLUSION.

The late Colonel John Thornton, then the most distinguished man of Clay County, Missouri, when considering a serious business proposition I submitted to him in 1835, made a remark to me that at once arrested my attention, and met my hearty approbation, it seemed to me to be so sensible and so just. He said : "Burnett, your proposition strikes me favorably ; but before I decide upon it I must go home and consult my wife. It is a rule with me to consult her upon all important matters."

I adopted it myself, and have only violated it once or twice, and was justly punished when I did. I have for many years kept my wife well informed of the true state of my business affairs ; and we both have taught our sons and daughters to understand business. She and myself have divided the labors and duties of life between us. For example, when we came to live in San Francisco in 1863, I said to her, "Wife, I have to run the bank, and you must run the house." She replied, "All right. You furnish me the money, and I will attend to the house."

As we were well advanced in life, and as we had a private residence in San José, and as I could use all my little capital under my own supervision, we decided to occupy a rented house, and we have been tenants ever

since. We both agree upon the house to be leased, and all the bills for rent, fuel, and gas are paid by me. As to all other requirements, except my own clothes, she purchases and pays for them. I have about as little trouble keeping house as an ordinary boarder. The only things that I have purchased for the house since we came to the city were a few small articles during her temporary absence. I never inquire what we shall have to eat, and never know until I enter the dining-room. I follow St. Paul's recommendation and eat what is set before me, asking no questions. She purchases that which pleases her, and I do the same for myself. I have not the slightest concern as to how she will expend the money, knowing that she will apply it more judiciously than I could. I keep an account of all I pay into her hands, as well as of the sums I expend for my own apparel, so that I may know how my finances are running. We contract no debts, except for meats fuel, gas, and rent, and these are all paid at short intervals.

In the course of my long and busy life, I have known many rich widows, and about three fourths of them lost all or most of their estates for want of business knowledge. Their parents and husbands taught them nothing about business, and, when they became widows, they readily fell victims to the wiles of others. We men are engaged in business all our lives, and we never learn too much about it ; and it is not at all surprising that women who have never been taught business, and never had any practical knowledge of it, should be overreached and cheated by the numerous and plausible sharpers that are sure to encounter them.

I knew a rich widow, who lent all the money of the estate in the month of May to a smooth, pleasant, plaus-

ible talker, without security, and lost it of course. This loan was made contrary to the advice of her lawyers. The result was, that in the month of December following she was forced to borrow money, at two per cent. a month interest, with which to pay the taxes upon the property of the estate. In the final result, the loss, including principal and interest, must have amounted to some twenty thousand dollars. This lady finally learned business by sad experience, and saved the larger portion of the estate.

My wife and myself have now (September 26, 1878) lived together more than fifty years. We have lived happy lives, and I trust we may die happy deaths. Our two sons and two daughters are well married. The two sons and one daughter reside in this city, and the other daughter in San José; and we can see all the children and grandchildren within three hours. Our children are all that we could reasonably wish them to be; and our grandchildren, so far, have given us no pain, but have been a great source of pleasure to us in our old age. We have been greatly blest, for which we can not be too thankful to our Heavenly Father. Although

> "Time's defacing waves
> Long have quenched the radiance of our brows,"

our affection for each other is as warm and devoted as it ever was.

> "The heart that once truly loves never forgets,
> But as truly loves on to the close;
> As the sunflower turns on her god when he sets
> The same look that she turn'd when he rose."

We have put our house in order. Our labors are about ended. We know not the future; but we abide

God's holy will with faith, resignation, and hope. Charles Carroll of Carrollton said, in his ninety-sixth year, that nothing gave him so much satisfaction as the fact that he had regularly discharged his religious duties. It is so with us.

> "Though we are living now, 'twill soon be o'er;
> Adown the West
> Life's sun is setting, and we see the shore
> Where we shall rest."

THE END.

INTRODUCTION: WHAT AGAIN?

by Isaac Asimov

Where does time go to?

It's hard for me to tell. I go on from year to year, you see, ageless and devastatingly handsome, writing up an endless storm, so that, as far as I am concerned, time stands still.

I cannot help but notice, however, that somehow, for the rest of the Universe, there is a one-way movement in the direction of larger and larger numbers on the calendar. Thus, when the first volume of *The Hugo Winners* came out, the number of the year was 1962; now it is 1985.

That alone is nothing. It's a matter of numbers, and numbers are conventions that are under human control. We can call every year 1962 if we wish, or give the years no numbers at all. Who's to stop us?

The trouble is that there are other, more subtle changes as well. All my old friends, who were lissome and supple young fellows just the other day, have been undergoing strange alterations. Here is the way I referred to them in an essay I wrote recently: "It struck me that [they] were well-stricken in years, that they hobbled about, peered uncertainly at each other, cupped their hands behind their ears, spoke in quavering voices, and gummed thoughtfully at their gruel during meals."

Sad? Of course it's sad. I can only console myself with the thought that it might have been infinitely worse. Suppose *they* were all ageless and it was *I* who had grown old, sapless, and wizen. What an unspeakable tragedy that would have been.

But, as I said, that's not how it was and the carefree days

danced beside me unnoticed. Then came the day when, to my utter surprise, I found myself facing the frowning visage of The Doubleday Corporate Entity.

"Asimov," said TDCE severely, "time is passing. When may we expect to get the fourth volume of *The Hugo Winners?*"

I couldn't believe my ears. "What, again?" said I.

Wasn't it only yesterday—or last year at the longest remove—that I did the third volume? With a light laugh I reached for that third volume on the shelves and turned to the copyright date.

Good heavens! Time *was* passing. In fact, it had passed! Since the third volume had been published, no fewer than eight conventions had been held, each one of which added a novella, a novelette, and a short story to the list of Hugo winners. I was stupefied to discover that I had an enormous number of new words of colossally excellent science fiction to deal with.

Whereupon, thinking quickly, I said, "I have let time pass on purpose, TDCE. I knew what I was doing every moment. By this strategic delay I have accumulated some six hundred thousand words of sterling material. Consider the bonanza, the veritable Golconda, of science fiction that now awaits my loyal and intelligent readers."

I don't think there's any use reporting verbatim the answer TDCE gave me. For one thing, it consisted of about fifteen minutes' worth of very quickly articulated and rather poetic vituperation in which the word "procrastination" (one I had never encountered before, and of whose meaning I am still uncertain) was used a number of times.

After that, it consisted almost entirely of very dull material, involving book sizes, numbers of pages, and how much or how little a book spine can hold. There was even an excruciatingly boring routine involving the estimation of the price of an eight-convention book under modern conditions and of the unlikelihood of our readers consenting to mortgage their houses in order to buy the volume.

At this point, I raised a majestic hand. "Please. Spare me this vulgar discussion of money. My artistic soul rebels at the very sound of the word unless we are discussing advances, which is, of course, a different thing altogether. Just tell me what the alternative is."

That TDCE did. Apparently, we are going to split the period into two volumes. This book you are now holding (having bought and paid for it, I hope) is Volume Four, and contains the Hugo Winners of the four conventions from 1976 through 1979 inclusive. Next year, we will have Volume Five, which will contain the Hugo Winners of the four conventions from 1980 to 1983.

"What's more," said TDCE, in an awful tone that made it quite plain that it would brook no contradiction, "you will have to write two introductions, one for each volume, and serve you right for not being on the ball. And what is still more, we're going to put both volumes into a single contract, so that you get only one advance for them."

Two introductions, but only one advance!

Those of you who know my proud nature will imagine that I immediately rose to my full height (standing on a chair in order to do so) and told TDCE exactly where to get off.

And you are right. I actually climbed onto the chair and raised my arm in order to call down the thunderbolts of Jove when a thought occurred to me—

You may recall that when the first volume of *The Hugo Winners* was published, I took the opportunity to castigate the various convention committees for their venality, prejudice, and downright poor taste in never awarding me a Hugo for *anything.*

Naturally, harrowed by shame, they corrected this situation. They began showering me with Hugos: one for my science articles in *F & SF,* one for the best all-time series (the *Foundation Series),* and one for the best novel of the year *(The Gods Themselves).*

I was gratified. It was better than nothing. However, I couldn't help but notice that I never got a Hugo for anything that would fit into a *Hugo Winners* volume. I got no Hugo for a novella, novelette, or short story. It wasn't until 1976 that it occurred to me that one of the reasons for this might be that I wasn't writing stories in these categories. That was all the hint my giant brain needed. I instantly sat down and wrote a novelette entitled *The Bicentennial Man.* It won a Hugo at the 1977 convention.

But that meant that *The Hugo Winners, Volume Four* would finally contain a story by me, and it was *that* which occurred to me as I was about to blast TDCE with Cyclopean fire.

If I refused to edit the volume, another editor, far inferior to me in writing ability and taste, would be left with the job of introducing *The Bicentennial Man.* He would undoubtedly be totally incapable of doing the proper job.

I had no choice. "Yes, sir, TDCE," I said meekly. "Whatever you say, sir. I will try to do better in the future, sir."

So here I am trying to write the introduction to *The Hugo Winners, Volume Four.*

It's not easy. In fact, it can't be done. Having looked over the introductions to the first three volumes, I see that I have already said everything that one can possibly say about these volumes. —Except that I see I have somehow said more. Thank goodness!

1976
34th CONVENTION
KANSAS CITY

Roger Zelazny

Since the stories in this anthology have been selected by popular vote at the conventions, there is little I can do to add or detract, and it has been my policy in the previous volumes not to talk much about the stories per se in these introductions. (Unless I feel like it, of course.) That policy I will continue to follow.

Nor, in this volume, can I discuss the conventions themselves. As it happens, all four conventions dealt with in this book were over a thousand miles from New York and the usual limit of my venturings from the Big Apple is about one-fifth that distance. As a result, I attended none of the four.

So I'll discuss whatever I feel like discussing, which is what I would do anyway.

For instance, "Home Is the Hangman" is Roger's first appearance in these volumes, although earlier, in 1966, he won the Hugo for his novel—*And Call Me Conrad.* (He was only twenty-nine at the time and had been publishing for only four years, miserable creature that he is.)

In a way, that was a personal relief to me. I had been the beneficiary of the alphabet all my life. In school, we were always listed, and lined up, and seated in alphabetical order, which meant I was always first or second or, just possibly, third in line. The teacher got to know me sooner, called on me oftener, thought of me more frequently (not always good), and somehow I think I did better as a result, both psychologically and actually.

To be sure, I suspect that I would have been noticeable no matter where I was in the class. (I remember once walking into a new class in high school and seeing the "home teacher" take one look at me and bury his face in his hands, after allowing a look of unspeakable horror to cross said face. I never found out why.)—Still, having my name start with *A* didn't hurt.

And in every class I was in, there was always some poor soul with a name something like Zuckerman, who always trailed at the end, had to wait longest for anything being handed out in order, and was always the student most likely to be ignored. Heaven only knows the scars carried by the *Z*'s of the world. I must admit I didn't worry about Zuckerman at the time, but as I grew older and spent more effort thinking about odd things, I began to speculate about such matters.

The first time I saw Roger's name, therefore, I said to myself, "Zelazny? The poor guy will never make it." And I thought of my *A* and felt guilty.

A pure waste of guilt. Zelazny did marvelously well from the start and my guilt gave way to a feeling of relief. What would he have done if his name had been Roger Aardvark? The imagination boggles.

At that, being last can have advantages. Right now, it is very simple to say something like "The entire field of science fiction from Asimov to Zelazny." I imagine someone or other is saying something like that continually.

Of course, my good friend Poul Anderson may well think that the phrase should be "from Anderson to Zelazny" and he may be right, but my good friend Poul Anderson is not editing this anthology. *I* am.

(However, Poul will show up later in this book, and I'll have a chance to talk about him.)

1

HOME IS THE HANGMAN

Big fat flakes down the night, silent night, windless night. And I never count them as storms unless there is wind. Not a sigh or a whimper, though. Just a cold, steady whiteness, drifting down outside the window, and a silence confirmed by gunfire, driven deeper now it had ceased. In the main room of the lodge the only sounds were the occasional hiss and sputter of the logs turning to ashes on the grate.

I sat in a chair turned sidewise from the table to face the door. A tool kit rested on the floor to my left. The helmet stood on the table, a lopsided basket of metal, quartz, porcelain, and glass. If I heard the click of a microswitch followed by a humming sound from within it, then a faint light would come on beneath the meshing near to its forward edge and begin to blink rapidly. If these things occurred, there was a very strong possibility that I was going to die.

I had removed a black ball from my pocket when Larry and Bert had gone outside, armed, respectively, with a flame thrower and what looked like an elephant gun. Bert had also taken two grenades with him.

I unrolled the black ball, opening it out into a seamless glove, a dollop of something resembling moist putty stuck to its palm. Then I drew the glove on over my left hand and sat with it upraised, elbow resting on the arm of the chair. A small laser flash pistol in which I had very little faith lay beside my right hand on the tabletop, next to the helmet.

If I were to slap a metal surface with my left hand, the substance would adhere there, coming free of the glove. Two seconds later it would explode, and the force of the explosion would be directed in against the surface. Newton would claim his own by way of right-angled redistributions of the reaction, hopefully tearing lateral hell out of the contact surface. A smother-charge, it was called, and its possession came under concealed weapons and possession of burglary tools statutes in most places. The molecularly gimmicked goo, I decided, was great stuff. It was just the delivery system that left more to be desired.

Beside the helmet, next to the gun, in front of my hand, stood a small walkie-talkie. This was for purposes of warning Bert and Larry if I should hear the click of a microswitch followed by a humming sound, should see a light come on and begin to blink rapidly. Then they would know that Tom and Clay, with whom we had lost contact when the shooting began, had failed to destroy the enemy and doubtless lay lifeless at their stations now, a little over a kilometer to the south. Then they would know that they, too, were probably about to die.

I called out to them when I heard the click. I picked up the helmet and rose to my feet as its light began to blink.

But it was already too late.

The fourth place listed on the Christmas card I had sent Don Walsh the previous year was Peabody's Book Shop and Beer Stube in Baltimore, Maryland. Accordingly, on the last night in October I sat in its rearmost room, at the final table before the alcove with the door leading to the alley. Across that dim chamber, a woman dressed in black played the ancient upright piano, up-tempoing everything she touched. Off to my right, a fire wheezed and spewed fumes on a narrow hearth beneath a crowded mantelpiece overseen by an ancient and antlered profile. I sipped a beer and listened to the sounds.

I half hoped that this would be one of the occasions when Don failed to show up. I had sufficient funds to hold me through spring and I did not really feel like working. I had summered farther north, was anchored now in the Chesapeake, and was anxious to continue Caribbeanwards. A growing chill and some nasty winds told me I had tarried overlong in these latitudes. Still, the understanding was that I remain in the chosen bar until midnight. Two hours to go.

I ate a sandwich and ordered another beer. About halfway into it, I spotted Don approaching the entranceway, topcoat over his arm, head turning. I manufactured a matching quantity of surprise when he appeared beside my table with a "Ron! Is that really you?"

I rose and clasped his hand.

"Alan! Small world, or something like that. Sit down! Sit down!"

He settled onto the chair across from me, draped his coat over the one to his left.

"What are you doing in this town?" he asked.

"Just a visit," I answered. "Said hello to a few friends." I patted the scars, the stains of the venerable surface before me. "And this is my last stop. I'll be leaving in a few hours."

He chuckled.

"Why is it that you knock on wood?"

I grinned.

"I was expressing affection for one of Henry Mencken's favorite speakeasies."

"This place dates back that far?"

I nodded.

"It figures," he said. "You've got this thing for the past—or against the present. I'm never sure which."

"Maybe a little of both," I said. "I wish Mencken would stop in. I'd like his opinion on the present. What are you doing with it?"

"What?"

"The present. Here. Now."

"Oh." He spotted the waitress and ordered a beer. "Business trip," he said then. "To hire a consultant."

"Oh. And how *is* business?"

"Complicated," he said, "complicated."

We lit cigarettes and after a while his beer arrived. We smoked and drank and listened to the music.

I've sung this song and I'll sing it again: the world is like an uptempoed piece of music. Of the many changes which came to pass during my lifetime, it seems that the majority have occurred during the past few years. It also struck me that way several years ago, and I'd a hunch I might be feeling the same way a few years hence—that is, if Don's business did not complicate me off this mortal coil or condenser before then.

Don operates the second-largest detective agency in the world, and he sometimes finds me useful because I do not exist. I do not exist now because I existed once at the time and the place where we attempted to begin scoring the wild ditty of our times. I refer to the World Data Bank project and the fact that I had had a significant part in that effort to construct a working model of the real world, accounting for everyone and everything in it. How well we succeeded and whether possession of the world's likeness does indeed provide its custodians with a greater measure of control over its functions are questions my former colleagues still debate as the music grows more shrill and you can't see the maps for the pins. I made my decision back then and saw to it that I did not receive citizenship in that second world, a place which may now have become more important than the first. Exiled to reality, my own sojourns across the line are necessarily those of an alien guilty of illegal entry. I visit periodically because I go where I must to make my living. That is where Don comes in. The people I can become are often very useful when he has peculiar problems. Unfortunately, at that moment, it seemed that he did, just when the whole gang of me felt like turning down the volume and loafing.

We finished our drinks, got the bill, settled it.

"This way," I said, indicating the rear door, and he swung into his coat and followed me out.

"Talk here?" he asked, as we walked down the alley.

"Rather not," I said. "Public transportation, then private conversation."

He nodded and came along.

About three-quarters of an hour later we were in the saloon of the *Proteus* and I was making coffee. We were rocked gently by the Bay's chill waters, under a moonless sky. I'd only a pair of the smaller lights burning. Comfortable. On the water, aboard the *Proteus*, the crowding, the activities, the tempo, of life in the cities, on the land, are muted, slowed—fictionalized—by the metaphysical distancing a few meters of water can provide. We alter the landscape with great facility, but the ocean has always seemed unchanged, and I suppose by extension we are infected with some feelings of timelessness whenever we set out upon her. Maybe that's one of the reasons I spend so much time there.

"First time you've had me aboard," he said. "Comfortable. Very."

"Thanks. Cream? Sugar?"

"Yes. Both."

We settled back with our steaming mugs and I said, "What have you got?"

"One case involving two problems," he said. "One of them sort of falls within my area of competence. The other does not. I was told that it is an absolutely unique situation and would require the services of a very special specialist."

"I'm not a specialist at anything but keeping alive."

His eyes came up suddenly and caught my own.

"I had always assumed that you knew an awful lot about computers," he said.

I looked away. That was hitting below the belt. I had never held myself out to him as an authority in that area, and there had always been a tacit understanding between us that my methods of manipulating circumstance and identity were not open to discussion. On the other hand, it was obvious to him that my knowledge of the system was both extensive and intensive. Still, I didn't like talking about it. So I moved to defend.

"Computer people are a dime a dozen," I said. "It was probably different in your time, but these days they start teaching computer science to little kids their first year in school. So, sure I know a lot about it. This generation, everybody does."

"You know that is not what I meant," he said. "Haven't you known me long enough to trust me a little more than that? The question springs solely from the case at hand. That's all."

I nodded. Reactions by their very nature are not always appropriate, and I had invested a lot of emotional capital in a heavy-duty set. So, "O.K., I know more about them than the school kids," I said.

"Thanks. That can be our point of departure." He took a sip of coffee. "My own background is in law and accounting, followed by the military, military intelligence, and civil service, in that order. Then I got into this business. What technical stuff I know I've picked up along the way, a scrap here, a crash course there. I know a lot about what things can do, not so much about how they work. I did not understand the details on this one, so I want you to start at the top and explain things to me, for as far as you can go. I need the background review, and if you are able to furnish it I will also know that you are the man for the job. You can begin by telling me how the early space exploration robots worked—like, say, the ones they used on Venus."

"That's not computers," I said, "and for that matter, they weren't really robots. They were telefactoring devices."

"Tell me what makes the difference."

"A robot is a machine which carries out certain operations in accordance with a program of instructions. A telefactor is a slave machine operated by remote control. The telefactor functions in a feedback situation with its operator. Depending on how sophisticated you want to get, the links can be audiovisual, kinesthetic, tactile, even olfactory. The more you want to go in this direction, the more anthropomorphic you get in the thing's design. In the case of Venus, if I recall correctly, the human operator in orbit wore an exoskeleton which controlled the movements of the body, legs, arms, and hands of the device on the surface below, receiving motion and force feedback through a system of airjet transducers. He had on a helmet controlling the slave device's television camera—set, obviously enough, in its turret—which filled his field of vision with the scene below. He also wore earphones connected with its audio pickup. I read the book he wrote later. He said that for long stretches of time, he would forget the cabin, forget that he was at the boss end of a control loop and actually feel as if he were stalking through that hellish landscape. I remember being very impressed by it, just being a kid, and I wanted a super-tiny one all my own, so that I could wade around in puddles picking fights with microorganisms."

"Why?"

"Because there weren't any dragons on Venus. Anyhow, that is a telefactoring device, a thing quite distinct from a robot."

"I'm still with you," he said. "Now tell me the difference between the early telefactoring devices and the later ones."

I swallowed some coffee.

"It was a bit trickier with respect to the outer planets and their satellites," I said. "There, we did not have orbiting operators at first. Economics, and some unresolved technical problems. Mainly economics. At any rate, the devices were landed on the target worlds, but the operators stayed home. Because of this, there was of course a time lag in the transmissions along the control loop. It took a while to receive the on-site input, and then there was another time lapse before the response movements reached the telefactor. We attempted to compensate for this in two ways. The first was by the employment of a simple wait-move, wait-move sequence. The second was more sophisticated and is actually the point where computers come into the picture in terms of participating in the control loop. It involved the setting up of models of known environmental factors, which were then enriched during the initial wait-move sequences. On this basis, the computer was then used to anticipate short-range developments. Finally, it could take over the loop and run it by a combination of 'predictor controls' and wait-move reviews. It still had to holler for human help, though, when unexpected things came up. So, with the outer planets, it was neither totally automatic nor totally manual—nor totally satisfactory—at first."

"O.K.," he said, lighting a cigarette. "And the next step?"

"The next wasn't really a technical step forward in telefactoring. It was an economic shift. The purse strings were loosened and we could afford to send men out. We landed them where we could land them, and in many of the places where we could not we sent down the telefactors and orbited the men again. Like in the old days. The time lag problem was removed because the operator was on top of things once more. If anything, you can look at it as a reversion to earlier methods. It is what we still often do, though, and it works."

He shook his head.

"You left something out," he said, "between the computers and the bigger budget."

I shrugged.

"A number of things were tried during that period," I said, "but none of them proved as effective as what we already had going in the human-computer partnership with the telefactors."

"There was one project," he said, "which attempted to get around the time lag troubles by sending the computer along with the telefactor as part of the package. Only the computer wasn't exactly a computer and the telefactor wasn't exactly a telefactor. Do you know which one I am referring to?"

I lit a cigarette of my own while I thought about it, then "I think you are talking about the Hangman," I said.

"That's right," he said, "and this is where I get lost. Can you tell me how it works?"

"Ultimately, it was a failure," I said.

"But it worked at first."

"Apparently. But only on the easy stuff, on Io. It conked out later and had to be written off as a failure, albeit a noble one. The venture was overly ambitious from the very beginning. What seems to have happened was that the people in charge had the opportunity to combine vanguard projects—stuff that was still under investigation and stuff that was extremely new. In theory it all seemed to dovetail so beautifully that they yielded to the temptation and incorporated too much. It started out well, but it fell apart later."

"But what all was involved in the thing?"

"Lord! What wasn't? The computer that wasn't exactly a computer . . . O.K., we'll start there. Last century, three engineers at the University of Wisconsin—Nordman, Parmentier, and Scott—developed a device known as a superconductive tunnel junction neuristor. Two tiny strips of metal with a thin insulating layer between. Supercool it and it passed electrical impulses without resistance. Surround it with magnetized material and pack a mass of them together—billions—and what have you got?"

He shook his head.

"Well, for one thing you've got an impossible situation to schematize when considering all the paths and interconnections that may be formed. There is an obvious similarity to the structure of the brain. So, they theorized, you don't even attempt to hook up such a device. You pulse in data and let it establish its own preferential pathways, by means of the magnetic material's becoming increasingly magnetized each time the current passes through it, thus cutting the resistance. So the material establishes its own routes in a fashion analogous to the functioning of the brain when it is learning something. In the case of the Hangman, they used a setup very similar to this and they were able to pack over ten billion neuristor-type cells into a very small area—around a cubic foot. They aimed for that magic figure because that is approximately the number of nerve cells in the human brain. That is what I meant when I said that it wasn't really a computer. They were actually working in the area of artificial intelligence, no matter what they called it."

"If the thing had its own brain—computer or quasi-human—then it was a robot rather than a telefactor, right?"

"Yes and no and maybe," I said. "It was operated as a telefactor device here on Earth—on the ocean floor, in the desert, in mountainous country—as part of its programming. I suppose you could also call that its apprenticeship or kindergarten. Perhaps that is even more appropriate. It was being shown how to explore in difficult environments and to report back. Once it mastered this, then theoretically they could hang it out there in the sky without a control loop and let it report its own findings."

"At that point would it be considered a robot?"

"A robot is a machine which carries out certain operations in accordance with a program of instructions. The Hangman made its own decisions, you see. And I suspect that by trying to produce something that close to the human brain in structure and function the seemingly inevitable randomness of its model got included in. It wasn't just a machine following a program. It was too complex. That was probably what broke it down."

Don chuckled.

"Inevitable free will?"

"No. As I said, they had thrown too many things into one bag. Everybody and his brother with a pet project that might be fitted in seemed a supersalesman that season. For example, the psychophysics boys had a gimmick they wanted to try on it, and it got used. Ostensibly, it was a communications device. Actually, they were concerned as to whether the thing was truly sentient."

"Was it?"

"Apparently so, in a limited fashion. What they had come up with, to be made part of the initial telefactor loop, was a device which set up a weak induction field in the brain of the operator. The machine received and amplified the patterns of electrical activity being conducted in the Hangman's—might as well call it 'brain'—then passed them through a complex modulator and pulsed them into the induction field in the operator's head. I am out of my area now and into that of Weber and Fechner, but a neuron has a threshold at which it will fire, and below which it will not. There are some forty thousand neurons packed together in a square millimeter of the cerebral cortex, in such a fashion that each one has several hundred synaptic connections with others about it. At any given moment, some of them may be way below the firing threshold while others are in a condition Sir John Eccles once referred to as 'critically poised'—ready to fire. If just one is pushed over the threshold, it can affect the discharge of hundreds of thousands of others within twenty milliseconds. The pulsating field was to provide such a push in a sufficiently selective fashion to give the operator an idea as to what was going on in the Hangman's brain. And vice versa. The Hangman was to have its own built-in version of the same thing. It was also thought that this might serve to humanize it somewhat, so that it would better appreciate the significance of its work—to instill something like loyalty, you might say."

"Do you think this could have contributed to its later breakdown?"

"Possibly. How can you say in a one-of-a-kind situation like this? If you want a guess, I'd say yes. But it's just a guess."

"Uh-huh," he said, "and what were its physical capabilities?"

"Anthropomorphic design," I said, "both because it was originally telefactored and because of the psychological reasoning I just mentioned. It could pilot its own small vessel. No need for a life-support system, of course. Both it and the vessel were powered by fusion units, so that fuel was no real problem. Self-repairing. Capable of performing a great variety of sophisticated tests and measurements, of making observations, completing reports, learning new material, broadcasting its findings back here. Capable of surviving just about anywhere. In fact, it required less energy on the outer planets—less work for the refrigeration units, to maintain that supercooled brain in its midsection."

"How strong was it?"

"I don't recall all the specs. Maybe a dozen times as strong as a man, in things like lifting and pushing."

"It explored Io for us and started in on Europa."

"Yes."

"Then it began behaving erratically, just when we thought it had really learned its job."

"That sounds right," I said.

"It refused a direct order to explore Callisto, then headed out toward Uranus."

"Yes. It's been years since I read the reports. . . ."

"The malfunction worsened after that. Long periods of silence interspersed with garbled transmissions. Now that I know more about its makeup, it almost sounds like a man going off the deep end."

"It seems similar."

"But it managed to pull itself together again for a brief while. It landed on Titania, began sending back what seemed like appropriate observation reports. This only lasted a short time, though. It went irrational once more, indicated that it was heading for a landing on Uranus itself, and that was it. We didn't hear from it after that. Now that I know about that mind-reading gadget I understand why a psychiatrist on this end could be so positive it would never function again."

"I never heard about that part."

"I did."

I shrugged.

"This was all around twenty years ago," I said, "and, as I mentioned, it has been a long while since I've read anything about it."

"The Hangman's ship crashed or landed, as the case may be, in the Gulf of Mexico," he said, "two days ago."

I just stared at him.

"It was empty," he said, "when they finally got out and down to it."

"I don't understand."

"Yesterday morning," he went on, "restaurateur Manny Burns was found beaten to death in the office of his establishment, the Maison Saint-Michel, in New Orleans."

"I still fail to see . . ."

"Manny Burns was one of the four original operators who programmed—pardon me, 'taught'—the Hangman."

The silence lengthened, dragged its belly on the deck.

"Coincidence . . . ?" I finally said.

"My client doesn't think so."

"Who is your client?"

"One of the three remaining members of the training group.

He is convinced that the Hangman has returned to Earth to kill its former operators."

"Has he made his fears known to his old employers?"

"No."

"Why not?"

"Because it would require telling them the reason for his fears."

"That being . . . ?"

"He wouldn't tell me either."

"How does he expect you to do a proper job?"

"He told me what he considered a proper job. He wants two things done, neither of which requires a full case history. He wanted to be furnished with good bodyguards, and he wanted the Hangman found and disposed of. I have already taken care of the first part."

"And you want me to do the second?"

"That's right. You have confirmed my opinion that you are the man for the job."

"I see," I said. "Do you realize that if the thing is truly sentient this will be something very like murder? If it is not, of course, then it will only amount to the destruction of expensive government property."

"Which way do you look at it?"

"I look at it as a job," I said.

"You'll take it?"

"I need more facts before I can decide. Like . . . Who is your client? Who are the other operators? Where do they live? What do they do? What—"

He raised his hand.

"First," he said, "the Honorable Jesse Brockden, senior senator from Wisconsin, is our client. Confidentiality, of course, is written all over it."

I nodded.

"I remember his being involved with the space program before he went into politics. I wasn't aware of the specifics, though. He could get government protection so easily—"

"To obtain it, he would apparently have to tell them something he doesn't want to talk about. Perhaps it would hurt his career. I simply do not know. He doesn't want them. He wants us."

I nodded again.

"What about the others? Do they want us, too?"

"Quite the opposite. They don't subscribe to Brockden's notions at all. They seem to think he is something of a paranoid."

"How well do they know one another these days?"

"They live in different parts of the country, haven't seen each other in years. Been in occasional touch, though."

"Kind of flimsy basis for that diagnosis, then."

"One of them *is* a psychiatrist."

"Oh. Which one?"

"Leila Thackery is her name. Lives in St. Louis. Works at the State Hospital there."

"None of them have gone to any authority, then—federal or local?"

"That's right. Brockden contacted them when he heard about the Hangman. He was in Washington at the time. Got word on its return right away and managed to get the story killed. He tried to reach them all, learned about Burns in the process, contacted me, then tried to persuade the others to accept protection by my people. They weren't buying. When I talked to her, Dr. Thackery pointed out—quite correctly—that Brockden is a very sick man—"

"What's he got?"

"Cancer. In his spine. Nothing they can do about it once it hits there and digs in. He even told me he figures he has maybe six months to get through what he considers a very important piece of legislation—the new criminal rehabilitation act. I will admit that he did sound kind of paranoid when he talked about it. But hell! Who wouldn't? Dr. Thackery sees that as the whole thing, though, and she doesn't see the Burns killing as being connected with the Hangman. Thinks it was just a traditional robbery gone sour, thief surprised and panicky, maybe hopped up, et cetera."

"Then she is not afraid of the Hangman?"

"She said that she is in a better position to know its mind than anyone else, and she is not especially concerned."

"What about the other operator?"

"He said that Dr. Thackery may know its mind better than anyone else, but he knows its brain, and he isn't worried either."

"What did he mean by that?"

"David Fentris is a consulting engineer—electronics, cybernetics. He actually had something to do with the Hangman's design."

I got to my feet and went after the coffee pot. Not that I'd an overwhelming desire for another cup at just that moment. But I had known, had once worked with a David Fentris. And he had at one time been connected with the space program.

About fifteen years my senior, Dave had been with the Data Bank project when I had known him. Where a number of us had begun having second thoughts as the thing progressed, Dave had never been anything less than wildly enthusiastic. A wiry five-eight, white-cropped, gray eyes back of hornrims and heavy glass, cycling between preoccupation and near-frantic darting, he had had a way of verbalizing half-completed thoughts as he went along, so that you might begin to think him a representative of that tribe which had come into positions of small authority by means of nepotism or politics. If you would listen a few more minutes, though, you would begin revising your opinion as he started to pull his musings together into a rigorous framework. By the time he had finished you generally wondered why you hadn't seen it all along and what a guy like that was doing in a position of such small authority. Later, it might strike you, though, that he seemed sad whenever he wasn't enthusiastic about something, and while the gung-ho spirit is great for short-range projects, larger ventures generally require something more of equanimity. I wasn't at all surprised that he had wound up as a consultant. The big question now, of course, was would he remember me? True, my appearance was altered, my personality hopefully more mature, my habits shifted around. But would that be enough, should I have to encounter him as part of this job? That mind behind those hornrims could do a lot of strange things with just a little data.

"Where does he live?" I asked.

"Memphis, and what's the matter?"

"Just trying to get my geography straight," I said. "Is Senator Brockden still in Washington?"

"No. He's returned to Wisconsin and is currently holed up in a lodge in the northern part of the state. Four of my people are with him."

"I see."

I refreshed our coffee supply and reseated myself. I didn't like this one at all and I resolved not to take it. I didn't like just giving Don a flat no, though. His assignments had become a very important part of my life, and this one was not mere legwork. It was obviously important to him, and he wanted me on it. I decided to look for holes in the thing, to find some way of reducing it to the simple bodyguard job already in progress.

"It does seem peculiar," I said, "that Brockden is the only one afraid of the device."

"Yes."

". . . And that he gives no reasons."

"True."

". . . Plus his condition, and what the doctor said about its effect on his mind."

"I have no doubt that he is neurotic," Don said. "Look at this."

He reached for his coat, withdrew a sheaf of papers from within it. He shuffled through them and extracted a single sheet, which he passed to me. It was a piece of congressional letterhead stationery, with the message scrawled in longhand: "Don," it said, "I've got to see you. Frankenstein's monster has just come back from where we hung him and he's looking for me. The whole damn universe is trying to grind me up. Call me between eight and ten. —Jess." I nodded, started to pass it back, paused, then handed it over. Double damn it deeper than hell! I took a drink of coffee. I thought that I had long ago given up hope in such things, but I had noticed something which immediately troubled me. In the margin where they list such matters, I had seen that Jesse Brockden was on the committee for review of the Data Bank program. I recalled that that committee was supposed to be working on a series of reform recommendations. Offhand, I could not remember Brockden's position on any of the issues involved, but—oh hell! The thing was simply too big to alter significantly now. . . . But it *was* the only real Frankenstein monster I cared about, and there was always the possibility. . . . On the other hand—hell, again. What if I let him die when I might have saved him, and he had been the one who . . . ?

I took another drink of coffee. I lit another cigarette. There might be a way of working it so that Dave didn't even come into the picture. I could talk to Leila Thackery first, check further into the Burns killing, keep posted on new developments, find out more about the vessel in the Gulf. . . . I might be able to accomplish something, even if it was only the negation of Brockden's theory, without Dave's and my paths ever crossing.

"Have you got the specs on the Hangman?" I asked.

"Right here."

He passed them over.

"The police report on the Burns killing?"

"Here it is."

"The whereabouts of everyone involved, and some background on them?"

"Here."

"The place or places where I can reach you during the next few days—around the clock? This one may require some coordination."

He smiled and reached for his pen.

"Glad to have you aboard," he said.

I reached over and tapped the barometer. I shook my head.

The ringing of the phone awakened me. Reflex bore me across the room, where I took it on audio.

"Yes?"

"Mr. Donne? It is eight o'clock."

"Thanks."

I collapsed into the chair. I am what might be called a slow starter. I tend to recapitulate phylogeny every morning. Basic desires inched their ways through my gray matter to close a connection. Slowly, I extended a cold-blooded member and clicked my talons against a couple numbers. I croaked my desire for food and lots of coffee to the voice that responded. Half an hour later I would only have growled. Then I staggered off to the place of flowing waters to renew my contact with basics.

In addition to my normal adrenaline and blood-sugar bearishness, I had not slept much the night before. I had closed up shop after Don had left, stuffed my pockets with essentials, departed the *Proteus,* gotten myself over to the airport and onto a flight which took me to St. Louis in the dead, small hours of the dark. I was unable to sleep during the flight, thinking about the case, deciding on the tack I was going to take with Leila Thackery. On arrival, I had checked into the airport motel, left a message to be awakened at an unreasonable hour, and collapsed.

As I ate, I regarded the fact sheet Don had given me: Leila Thackery was currently single, having divorced her second husband a little over two years ago, was forty-six years old, and lived in an apartment near to the hospital where she worked. Attached to the sheet was a photo which might have been ten years old. In it, she was brunette, light-eyed, barely on the right side of that border between ample and overweight, with fancy glasses straddling an upturned nose. She had published a number of books and articles with titles full of alienations, roles, transactions, social contexts, and more alienations.

I hadn't had the time to go my usual route, becoming an entire new individual with a verifiable history. Just a name and a story, that's all. It did not seem necessary this time, though. For once, something approximating honesty actually seemed a reasonable approach.

I took a public vehicle over to her apartment building. I did not phone ahead, because it is easier to say no to a voice than to a person. According to the record, today was one of the days when she saw outpatients in her home. Her idea, apparently: break down the alienating institution image, remove resentments by turning the sessions into something more like social occasions, et cetera. I did not want all that much of her time, I had decided that Don could make it worth her while if it came to that, and I was sure my fellows' visits were scheduled to leave her with some small breathing space—*inter alia,* so to speak.

I had just located her name and apartment number amid the buttons in the entrance foyer when an old woman passed behind me and unlocked the door to the lobby. She glanced at me and held it open, so I went on in without ringing. The matter of presence, again.

I took the elevator to Leila's floor, the second. I located her door and knocked on it. I was almost ready to knock again when it opened, partway.

"Yes?" she asked, and I revised my estimate as to the age of the photo. She looked just about the same.

"Dr. Thackery," I said, "my name is Donne. You could help me quite a bit with a problem I've got."

"What sort of problem?"

"It involves a device known as the Hangman."

She sighed and showed me a quick grimace. Her fingers tightened on the door.

"I've come a long way but I'll be easy to get rid of. I've only a few things I'd like to ask you about it."

"Are you with the government?"

"No."

"Do you work for Brockden?"

"No. I'm something different."

"All right," she said. "Right now I've got a group session going. It will probably last around another half hour. If you don't mind waiting down in the lobby, I'll let you know as soon as it is over. We can talk then."

"Good enough," I said. "Thanks."

She nodded, closed the door. I located the stairway and walked back down.

A cigarette later, I decided that the devil finds work for idle hands and thanked him for his suggestion. I strolled back toward the foyer. Through the glass, I read the names of a few residents of the fifth floor. I elevated up and knocked on one of the doors. Before it was opened I had my notebook and pad in plain sight.

"Yes?"—short, fiftyish, curious.

"My name is Stephen Foster, Mrs. Gluntz. I am doing a survey for the North American Consumers' League. I would like to pay you for a couple minutes of your time, to answer some questions about products you use."

"Why . . . pay me?"

"Yes, ma'am. Ten dollars. Around a dozen questions. It will just take a minute or two."

"All right." She opened the door wider. "Won't you come in?"

"No, thank you. This thing is so brief I'd just be in and out. The first question involves detergents—"

Ten minutes later I was back in the lobby adding the thirty bucks for the three interviews to the list of expenses I was keeping. When a situation is full of unpredictables and I am playing makeshift games, I like to provide for as many contingencies as I can.

Another quarter of an hour or so slipped by before the elevator opened and discharged three guys, young, young, and middle-aged, casually dressed, chuckling over something. The big one on the nearest end strolled over and nodded.

"You the fellow waiting to see Dr. Thackery?"

"That's right."

"She said to tell you to come on up now."

"Thanks."

I rode up again, returned to her door. She opened to my knock, nodded me in, saw me seated in a comfortable chair at the far end of her living room.

"Would you care for a cup of coffee?" she asked. "It's fresh. I made more than I needed."

"That would be fine. Thanks."

Moments later, she brought in a couple of cups, delivered one to me, and seated herself on the sofa to my left. I ignored the cream and sugar on the tray and took a sip.

"You've gotten me interested," she said. "Tell me about it."

"O.K. I have been told that the telefactor device known as the Hangman, now possibly possessed of an artificial intelligence, has returned to Earth—"

"Hypothetical," she said, "unless you know something I don't. I have been told that the Hangman's vehicle reentered and crashed in the Gulf. There is no evidence that the vehicle was occupied."

"It seems a reasonable conclusion, though."

"It seems just as reasonable to me that the Hangman sent the vehicle off toward an eventual rendezvous point many years ago and that it only recently reached that point, at which time the reentry program took over and brought it down."

"Why should it return the vehicle and strand itself out there?"

"Before I answer that," she said, "I would like to know the reason for your concern. News media?"

"No," I said. "I am a science writer—straight tech, popular and anything in between. But I am not after a piece for publication. I was retained to do a report on the psychological makeup of the thing."

"For whom?"

"A private investigation outfit. They want to know what might influence its thinking, how it might be likely to behave—if it has indeed come back. I've been doing a lot of homework, and I gathered there is a likelihood that its nuclear personality was a composite of the minds of its four operators. So, personal contacts seemed in order, to collect your opinions as to what it might be like. I came to you first for obvious reasons."

She nodded.

"A Mr. Walsh spoke with me the other day. He is working for Senator Brockden."

"Oh? I never got into an employer's business beyond what he's asked me to do. Senator Brockden is on my list, though, along with a David Fentris."

"You were told about Manny Burns?"

"Yes. Unfortunate."

"That is apparently what set Jesse off. He is—how shall I put it? He is clinging to life right now, trying to accomplish a great many things in the time he has remaining. Every moment is precious to him. He feels the old man in the white nightgown breathing down his neck. Then the ship returns and one of us is killed. From what we know of the Hangman, the last we heard of it, it had become irrational. Jesse saw a connection, and in his condition the fear is understandable. There is nothing wrong with humoring him if it allows him to get his work done."

"But you don't see a threat in it?"

"No. I was the last person to monitor the Hangman before communications ceased, and I could see then what had happened. The first things that it had learned were the organization of perceptions and motor activities. Multitudes of other patterns had been transferred from the minds of its operators, but they were too sophisticated to mean much initially. Think of a child who has learned the Gettysburg Address. It is there in his head, that is all. One day, however, it may be important to him. Conceivably, it may even inspire him to action. It takes some growing up first, of course. Now think of such a child with a great number of conflicting patterns—attitudes, tendencies, memories—none of which are especially bothersome for so long as he remains a child. Add a bit of maturity, though—and bear in mind that the patterns originated with four different individuals, all of them more powerful than the words of even the finest of speeches, bearing as they do their own built-in feelings. Try to imagine the conflicts, the contradictions involved in being four people at once—"

"Why wasn't this imagined in advance?" I asked.

"Ah!" she said, smiling. "The full sensitivity of the neuristor brain was not appreciated at first. It was assumed that the operators were adding data in a linear fashion and that this would continue until a critical mass was achieved, corresponding to the construction of a model or picture of the world which would then serve as a point of departure for growth of the Hangman's own mind. And it did seem to check out this way. What actually occurred, however, was a phenomenon amounting to imprinting. Secondary characteristics of the operators' minds, outside the didactic situations, were imposed. These did not immediately become functional and hence were not detected. They remained latent until the mind had developed sufficiently to understand them. And then it was too late. It suddenly acquired four additional personalities and was unable to coordinate them. When it tried to compartmentalize them it went schizoid; when it tried to integrate them it went catatonic. It was cycling back and forth between these alternatives at the end. Then it just went silent. I felt it had undergone the equivalent of an epileptic seizure. Wild currents through that magnetic material would, in effect, have erased its mind, resulting in its equivalent of death or idiocy."

"I follow you," I said. "Now, just for the sake of playing games, I see the alternatives as a successful integration of all this material or the achievement of a viable schizophrenia. What do you think its behavior would be like if either of these were possible?"

"All right," she agreed. "As I just said, though, I think there were physical limitations to its retaining multiple personality structures for a very long period of time. If it did, however, it would have continued with its own plus replicas of the four operators', at least for a while. The situation would differ radically from that of a human schizoid of this sort in that the additional personalities were valid images of genuine identities rather than self-generated complexes which had become autonomous. They might continue to evolve, they might degenerate, they might conflict to the point of destruction or gross modification of any, or all of them. In other words, no prediction is possible as to the nature of whatever might remain."

"Might I venture one?"

"Go ahead."

"After considerable anxiety, it masters them. It asserts itself. It beats down this quartet of demons which has been tearing it apart, acquiring in the process an all-consuming hatred for the actual individuals responsible for this turmoil. To free itself totally, to revenge itself, to work its ultimate catharsis, it resolves to seek them out and destroy them."

She smiled.

"You have just dispensed with the 'viable schizophrenia' you conjured up, and you have now switched over to its pulling through and becoming fully autonomous. That is a different situation, no matter what strings you put on it."

"O.K., I accept the charge. But what about my conclusion?"

"You are saying that if it did pull through, it would hate us. That strikes me as an unfair attempt to invoke the spirit of Sigmund Freud: Oedipus and Electra in one being, out to destroy all its parents—the authors of every one of its tensions, anxieties, hang-ups, burned into the impressionable psyche at a young and defenseless age. Even Freud didn't have a name for that one. What should we call it?"

"A Hermacis complex?" I suggested.

"Hermacis?"

"Hermaphroditus having been united in one body with the nymph Salmacis, I've just done the same with their names. That being would then have had four parents against whom to react."

"Cute," she said, smiling. "If the liberal arts do nothing else they provide engaging metaphors for the thinking they displace. This one is unwarranted and overly anthropomorphic, though. You wanted my opinion. All right. If the Hangman pulled through at all it could only have been by virtue of that neuristor brain's differences from the human brain. From my own professional experience, a human could not pass through a situation like that and attain stability. If the Hangman did, it would have to have resolved all the contradictions and conflicts, to have mastered and understood the situation so thoroughly that I do not believe whatever remained could involve that sort of hatred. The fear, the uncertainty, the things that feed hate would have been analyzed, digested, turned to something more useful. There would probably be distaste, and possibly an act of independence, of self-assertion. That was why I suggested its return of the ship."

"It is your opinion, then, that if the Hangman exists as a thinking individual today, this is the only possible attitude it would possess toward its former operators? It would want nothing more to do with you?"

"That is correct. Sorry about your Hermacis complex. But in this case we must look to the brain, not the psyche. And we see two things: schizophrenia would have destroyed it, and a successful resolution of its problem would preclude vengeance. Either way, there is nothing to worry about."

How could I put it tactfully? I decided that I could not.

"All of this is fine," I said, "for as far as it goes. But getting away from both the purely psychological and the purely physical, could there be a particular reason for its seeking your deaths—that is, a plain old-fashioned motive for a killing, based on events rather than having to do with the way its thinking equipment goes together?"

Her expression was impossible to read, but considering her line of work I had expected nothing less.

"What events?" she said.

"I have no idea. That's why I asked."

She shook her head.

"I'm afraid that I don't either."

"Then that about does it," I said. "I can't think of anything else to ask you."

She nodded.

"And I can't think of anything else to tell you."

I finished my coffee, returned the cup to the tray.

"Thanks, then," I said, "for your time, for the coffee. You have been very helpful."

I rose. She did the same.

"What are you going to do now?" she asked.

"I haven't quite decided," I said. "I want to do the best report I can. Have you any suggestions on that?"

"I suggest that there isn't any more to learn, that I have given you the only possible constructions the facts warrant."

"You don't feel David Fentris could provide any additional insights?"

She snorted, then sighed.

"No," she said, "I do not think he could tell you anything useful."

"What do you mean? From the way you say it . . ."

"I know. I didn't mean to. Some people find comfort in religion. Others . . . you know. Others take it up late in life with a vengeance and a half. They don't use it quite the way it was intended. It comes to color all their thinking."

"Fanaticism?" I said.

"Not exactly. A misplaced zeal. A masochistic sort of thing. Hell! I shouldn't be diagnosing at a distance—or influencing your opinion. Forget what I said. Form your own opinion when you meet him."

She raised her head, appraising my reaction.

"Well," I said, "I am not at all certain that I am going to see him. But you have made me curious. How can religion influence engineering?"

"I spoke with him after Jesse gave us the news on the vessel's return," she said. "I got the impression at the time that he feels we were tampering in the province of the Almighty by attempting the creation of an artificial intelligence. That our creation should go mad was only appropriate, being the work of imperfect man. He seemed to feel that it would be fitting if it had come back for retribution, as a sign of judgment upon us."

"Oh," I said.

She smiled then. I returned it.

"Yes," she said, "but maybe I just got him in a bad mood. Maybe you should go see for yourself."

Something told me to shake my head—a bit of a difference between this view of him, my recollections, and Don's comment that Dave had said he knew its brain and was not especially concerned. Somewhere among these lay something I felt I should know, felt I should learn without seeming to pursue. So, "I think I have enough right now," I said. "It was the psychological side of things I was supposed to cover, not the mechanical—or the theological. You have been extremely helpful. Thanks again."

She carried her smile all the way to the door.

"If it is not too much trouble," she said as I stepped into the hall, "I would like to learn how this whole thing finally turns out —or any interesting developments, for that matter."

"My connection with the case ends with this report," I said, "and I am going to write it now. Still, I may get some feedback."

"You have my number . . . ?"

"Probably, but . . ."

I already had it, but I jotted it again, right after Mrs. Gluntz's answers to my inquiries on detergents.

Moving in a rigorous line, I made beautiful connections for a change. I headed directly for the airport, found a flight aimed at Memphis, bought passage, and was the last to board. Tenscore seconds, perhaps, made all the difference. Not even a tick or two to spare for checking out of the motel. No matter. The good head doctor had convinced me that, like it or not, David Fentris was next, damn it. I had too strong a feeling that Leila Thackery had not told me the entire story. I had to take a chance, to see these changes in the man for myself, to try to figure out how they related to the Hangman. For a number of reasons, I'd a feeling they might.

I disembarked into a cool, partly overcast afternoon, found transportation almost immediately, and set out for Dave's office address. A before-the-storm feeling came over me as I entered and crossed the town. A dark wall of clouds continued to build in the west. Later, standing before the building where Dave did business, the first few drops of rain were already spattering against its dirty brick front. It would take a lot more than that to freshen it, though, or any of the others in the area. I would have thought he'd have come a little farther than this by now. I shrugged off some moisture and went inside.

The directory gave me directions, the elevator elevated me, my feet found the way to his door. I knocked on it.

After a time, I knocked again and waited again. Again, nothing. So I tried it, found it open and went on in.

It was a small, vacant waiting room, green-carpeted. The reception desk was dusty. I crossed and peered around the plastic partition behind it.

The man had his back to me. I drummed my knuckles against the partitioning. He heard it and turned.

"Yes?"

Our eyes met, his still framed by hornrims and just as active; glasses thicker, hair thinner, cheeks a trifle hollower. His question mark quivered in the air, and nothing in his gaze moved to replace it with recognition. He had been bending over a sheaf of schematics; a lopsided basket of metal, quartz, porcelain, and glass rested on a nearby table.

"My name is Donne, John Donne," I said. "I am looking for David Fentris."

"I am David Fentris."

"Good to meet you," I said, crossing to where he stood. "I am assisting in an investigation concerning a project with which you were once associated—"

He smiled and nodded, accepted my hand and shook it.

"The Hangman, of course," he said. "Glad to know you, Mr. Donne."

"Yes, the Hangman," I said. "I am doing a report. . . ."

". . . And you want my opinion as to how dangerous it is. Sit down." He gestured toward a chair at the end of his workbench. "Care for a cup of tea?"

"No, thanks."

"I'm having one."

"Well, in that case . . ."

He crossed to another bench.

"No cream. Sorry."

"That's all right.—How did you know it involved the Hangman?"

He grinned as he brought my cup.

"Because it's come back," he said, "and it's the only thing I've been connected with that warrants that much concern."

"Do you mind talking about it?"

"Up to a point, no."

"What's the point?"

"If we get near it, I'll let you know."

"Fair enough. How dangerous *is* it?"

"I would say that it is harmless," he replied, "except to three persons."

"Formerly four?"

"Precisely."

"How come?"

"We were doing something we had no business doing."

"That being . . . ?"

"For one thing, attempting to create an artificial intelligence."

"Why had you no business doing that?"

"A man with a name like yours shouldn't have to ask."

I chuckled.

"If I were a preacher," I said, "I would have to point out that there is no biblical injunction against it—unless you've been worshipping it on the sly."

He shook his head.

"Nothing that simple, that obvious, that explicit. Times have changed since the Good Book was written, and you can't hold with a purely Fundamentalist approach in complex times. What I was getting at was something a little more abstract. A form of pride, not unlike the classical *hubris*—the setting up of oneself on a level with the Creator."

"Did you feel that—pride?"

"Yes."

"Are you sure it wasn't just enthusiasm for an ambitious project that was working well?"

"Oh, there was plenty of that. A manifestation of the same thing."

"I do seem to recall something about man being made in the Creator's image, and something else about trying to live up to that. It would seem to follow that exercising one's capacities along similar lines would be a step in the right direction—an act of conformance with the Divine Ideal, if you'd like."

"But I don't like. Man cannot really create. He can only rearrange what is already present. Only God can create."

"Then you have nothing to worry about."

He frowned, then "No," he said. "Being aware of this and still trying is where the presumption comes in."

"Were you really thinking that way when you did it? Or did all this occur to you after the fact?"

"I am no longer certain."

"Then it would seem to me that a merciful God would be inclined to give you the benefit of the doubt."

He gave me a wry smile.

"Not bad, John Donne. But I feel that judgment may already have been entered and that we may have lost four to nothing."

"Then you see the Hangman as an avenging angel?"

"Sometimes. Sort of. I see it as being returned to exact a penalty."

"Just for the record," I said, "if the Hangman had had full access to the necessary equipment and was able to construct another unit such as itself, would you consider it guilty of the same thing that is bothering you?"

He shook his head.

"Don't get all cute and Jesuitical with me, Donne. I'm not that far away from fundamentals. Besides, I'm willing to admit I might be wrong and that there may be other forces driving it to the same end."

"Such as?"

"I told you I'd let you know when we reached a certain point. That's it."

"O.K.," I said. "But that sort of blank-walls me, you know. The people I am working for would like to protect you people. They want to stop the Hangman. I was hoping you would tell me a little more—if not for your own sake, then for the others'. They might not share your philosophical sentiments, and you have just admitted you may be wrong. Despair, by the way, is also considered a sin by a great number of theologians."

He sighed and stroked his nose, as I had often seen him do in times long past.

"What do you do, anyhow?" he asked me.

"Me, personally? I'm a science writer. I'm putting together a report on the device for the agency that wants to do the protecting. The better my report, the better their chances."

He was silent for a time, then "I read a lot in the area, but I don't recognize your name," he said.

"Most of my work has involved petrochemistry and marine biology," I said.

"Oh. You were a peculiar choice then, weren't you?"

"Not really. I was available, and the boss knows my work, knows I'm good."

He glanced across the room, to where a stack of cartons partly obscured what I then realized to be a remote access terminal. O.K. If he decided to check out my credentials now, John Donne would fall apart. It seemed a hell of a time to get curious, though, *after* sharing his sense of sin with me. He must have thought so too, because he did not look that way again.

"Let me put it this way," he finally said, and something of the old David Fentris at his best took control of his voice. "For one reason or the other, I believe that it wants to destroy its former operators. If it is the judgment of the Almighty, that's all there is to it. It will succeed. If not, however, I don't want any outside protection. I've done my own repenting and it is up to me to handle the rest of the situation myself, too. I will stop the Hangman personally, right here, before anyone else is hurt."

"How?" I asked him.

He nodded toward the glittering helmet.

"With that," he said.

"How?" I repeated.

"Its telefactor circuits are still intact. They have to be. They are an integral part of it. It could not disconnect them without shutting itself down. If it comes within a quarter mile of here, that unit will be activated. It will emit a loud humming sound and a light will begin to blink behind that meshing beneath the forward ridge. I will then don the helmet and take control of the Hangman. I will bring it here and disconnect its brain."

"How would you do the disconnect?"

He reached for the schematics he had been looking at when I had come in.

"Here," he said. "The thoracic plate has to be unlugged. There are four subunits that have to be uncoupled. Here, here, here, and here."

He looked up.

"You would have to do them in sequence though, or it could get mighty hot," I said. "First this one, then these two. Then the other."

When I looked up again, the gray eyes were fixed on my own.

"I thought you were in petrochemistry and marine biology," he said.

"I am not really 'in' anything," I said. "I am a tech writer, with bits and pieces from all over—and I did have a look at these before, when I accepted the job."

"I see."

"Why don't you bring the space agency in on this?" I said, working to shift ground. "The original telefactoring equipment had all that power and range—"

"It was dismantled a long time ago," he said. "I thought you were with the government."

I shook my head.

"Sorry. I didn't mean to mislead you. I am on contract with a private investigation outfit."

"Uh-huh. Then that means Jesse. Not that it matters. You can tell him that one way or the other everything is being taken care of."

"What if you are wrong on the supernatural," I said, "but correct on the other? Supposing it is coming under the circumstances you feel it proper to resist? But supposing you are not next on its list? Supposing it gets to one of the others next instead of you? If you are so sensitive about guilt and sin, don't you think that you would be responsible for that death—if you could prevent it by telling me just a little bit more? If it is confidentiality you are worried about—"

"No," he said. "You cannot trick me into applying my principles to a hypothetical situation which will only work out the way that you want it to. Not when I am certain that it will not arise. Whatever moves the Hangman, it will come to me next. If I cannot stop it, then it cannot be stopped until it has completed its job."

"How do you know that you are next?"

"Take a look at a map," he said. "It landed in the Gulf. Manny was right there in New Orleans. Naturally, he was first. The Hangman can move underwater like a controlled torpedo, which makes the Mississippi its logical route for inconspicuous travel. Proceeding up it then, here I am in Memphis. Then Leila, up in St. Louis, is obviously next after me. It can worry about getting to Washington after that."

I thought about Senator Brockden in Wisconsin and decided it would not even have that problem. All of them were fairly accessible, when you thought of the situation in terms of river travel.

"But how is it to know where you all are?" I asked.

"Good question," he said. "Within a limited range, it was once sensitive to our brain waves, having an intimate knowledge of them and the ability to pick them up. I do not know what that range would be today. I might have been able to construct an amplifier to extend this area of perception. But to be more mundane about it, I believe that it simply consulted the Data Bank's national directory. There are booths all over, even on the waterfront. It could have hit one late at night and gimmicked it. It certainly had sufficient identifying information—and engineering skill."

"Then it seems to me the best bet for all of you would be to move away from the river till this business is settled. That thing won't be able to stalk about the countryside very long without being noticed."

"It would find a way. It is extremely resourceful. At night, in an overcoat, a hat, it could pass. It requires nothing that a man would need. It could dig a hole and bury itself, stay underground during daylight. It could run without resting all night long. There is no place it could not reach in a surprisingly short while. No. I must wait here for it."

"Let me put it as bluntly as I can," I said. "If you are right that it is a divine avenger, I would say that it smacks of blasphemy to try to tackle it. On the other hand, if it is not, then I think you are guilty of jeopardizing the others by withholding information that would allow us to provide them with a lot more protection than you are capable of giving them all by yourself."

He laughed.

"I'll just have to learn to live with that guilt too, as they do with theirs," he said. "After I've done my best, they deserve anything they get."

"It was my understanding," I said, "that even God doesn't judge people until after they're dead—if you want another piece of presumption to add to your collection."

He stopped laughing and studied my face.

"There is something familiar about the way you talk, the way you think," he said. "Have we ever met before?"

"I doubt it. I would have remembered."

He shook his head.

"You've got a way of bothering a man's thinking that rings a faint bell," he went on. "You trouble me, sir."

"That was my intention."

"Are you staying here in town?"

"No."

"Give me a number where I can reach you, will you? If I have any new thoughts on this thing I'll call you."

"I wish you would have them now if you are going to have them."

"No," he said, "I've got some thinking to do. Where can I get hold of you later?"

I gave him the name of the motel I was still checked into in St. Louis. I could call back periodically for messages.

"All right," he said, and he moved toward the partition by the reception area and stood beside it.

I rose and followed him, passing into that area and pausing at the door to the hall.

"One thing . . ." I said.

"Yes?"

"If it does show up and you do stop it, will you call me and tell me that?"

"Yes, I will."

"Thanks then—and good luck."

Impulsively, I extended my hand. He gripped it and smiled faintly.

"Thank you, Mr. Donne."

Next. Next, next, next . . .

I couldn't budge Dave, and Leila Thackery had given me everything she was going to. No real sense in calling Don yet—not until I had more to say. I thought it over on my way back to the airport. The pre-dinner hours always seem best for talking to people in any sort of official capacity, just as the night seems best for dirty work. Heavily psychological, but true nevertheless. I hated to waste the rest of the day if there was anyone else worth talking to before I called Don. Going through the folder, I decided that there was.

Manny Burns had a brother, Phil. I wondered how worthwhile it might be to talk with him. I could make it to New Orleans at a sufficiently respectable hour, learn whatever he was willing to tell me, check back with Don for new developments, and then decide whether there was anything I should be about with respect to the vessel itself. The sky was gray and leaky above me. I was anxious to flee its spaces. So I decided to do it. I could think of no better stone to upturn at the moment.

At the airport, I was ticketed quickly, in time for another close connection. Hurrying to reach my flight, my eyes brushed over a half-familiar face on the passing escalator. The reflex reserved for such occasions seemed to catch us both, because he looked back too, with the same eyebrow twitch of startle and scrutiny. Then he was gone. I could not place him, though. The half-familiar face becomes a familiar phenomenon in a crowded, highly mobile society. I sometimes think that this is all that will eventually remain of any of us: patterns of features, some a trifle more persistent than others, impressed on the flow of bodies. A small-town boy in a big city. Thomas Wolfe must long ago have felt the same thing when he had coined the word "manswarm." It might have been someone I had once met briefly, or simply someone or someone like someone I had passed on sufficient other occasions such as this.

As I flew the unfriendly skies out of Memphis, I mulled over musings past on artificial intelligence, or AI as they have tagged it in the think box biz. When talking about computers, the AI notion had always seemed hotter than I deemed necessary, partly because of semantics. The word "intelligence" has all sorts of tag-along associations of the nonphysical sort. I suppose it goes back to the fact that early discussions and conjectures concerning it made it sound as if the potential for intelligence was always present in the array of gadgets, and the correct procedures, the right programs, simply had to be found to call it forth. When you looked at it that way, as many did, it gave rise to an uncomfortable déjà vu—namely, vitalism. The philosophical battles of the nineteenth century were hardly so far behind that they had been forgotten, and the doctrine which maintained that life is caused and sustained by a vital principle apart from physical and chemical forces and that life is self-sustaining and self-evolving, had put up quite a fight before Darwin and his successors had produced triumph after triumph for the mechanistic view. Then vitalism sort of crept back into things again when the AI discussions arose in the middle of the past century. It would seem that Dave had fallen victim to it, and that he had come to believe he had helped provide an unsanctified vessel and filled it with something intended only for those things which had made the scene in the first chapter of Genesis.

With computers it was not quite as bad as with the Hangman, though, because you could always argue that no matter how elaborate the program, it was basically an extension of the programmer's will and the operations of causal machines merely represented functions of intelligence, rather than intelligence in its own right backed by a will of its own. And there was always Gödel for a theoretical *cordon sanitaire,* with his demonstration of the true but mechanically unprovable proposition. But the Hangman was quite different. It had been designed along the lines of a brain and at least partly educated in a human fashion; and to further muddy the issue with respect to anything like vitalism, it had been in direct contact with human minds from which it might have acquired almost anything—including the spark that set it on the road to whatever selfhood it may have found. What did that make it? Its own creature? A fractured mirror reflecting a fractured humanity? Both? Or neither? I certainly could not say, but I wondered how much of its "self" had been truly its own. It had obviously acquired a great number of functions, but was it capable of having real feelings? Could it, for example, feel something like love? If not, then it was still only a collection of complex abilities, and not a thing with all the tag-along associations of the nonphysical sort which made the word "intelligence" such a prickly item in AI discussions; and if it were capable of, say, something like love, and if I were Dave, I would not feel guilty about having helped to bring it into being. I would feel proud, though not in the fashion he was concerned about, and I would also feel humble. Offhand, though, I do not know how intelligent I would feel, because I am still not sure what the hell intelligence is.

The day's-end sky was clear when we landed. I was into town before the sun had finished setting, and on Philip Burns's doorstep just a little while later.

My ring was answered by a girl, maybe seven or eight years old. She fixed me with large brown eyes and did not say a word.

"I would like to speak with Mr. Burns," I said.

She turned and retreated around a corner.

A heavyset man, slacked and undershirted, bald about halfway back and very pink, padded into the hall moments later and peered at me. He bore a folded newssheet in his left hand.

"What do you want?" he asked.

"It's about your brother," I said.

"Yeah?"

"Well, I wonder if I could come in? It's kind of complicated."

He opened the door. But instead of letting me in, he came out.

"Tell me about it out here," he said.

"O.K., I'll be quick. I just wanted to find out whether he ever spoke with you about a piece of equipment he once worked with called the Hangman."

"Are you a cop?"

"No."

"Then what's your interest?"

"I am working for a private investigation agency trying to track down some equipment once associated with the project. It has apparently turned up in this area and it could be rather dangerous."

"Let's see some identification."

"I don't carry any."

"What's your name?"

"John Donne."

"And you think my brother had some stolen equipment when he died? Let me tell you something—"

"No. Not stolen," I said, "and I don't think he had it."

"What then?"

"It was—well, robotic in nature. Because of some special training Manny once received, he might have had a way of detecting it. He might even have attracted it. I just want to find out whether he had said anything about it. We are trying to locate it."

"My brother was a respectable businessman, and I don't like

accusations. Especially right after his funeral, I don't. I think I'm going to call the cops and let them ask *you* a few questions."

"Just a minute," I said. "Supposing I told you we had some reason to believe it might have been this piece of equipment that killed your brother?"

His pink turned to bright red and his jaw muscles formed sudden ridges. I was not prepared for the stream of profanities that followed. For a moment, I thought he was going to take a swing at me.

"Wait a second," I said when he paused for breath. "What did I say?"

"You're either making fun of the dead or you're stupider than you look!"

"Say I'm stupid. Then tell me why."

He tore at the paper he carried, folded it back, found an item, thrust it at me.

"Because they've got the guy who did it! That's why," he said.

I read it. Simple, concise, to the point. Today's latest. A suspect had confessed. New evidence had corroborated it. The man was in custody. A surprised robber who had lost his head and hit too hard, hit too many times. I read it over again. I nodded as I passed it back.

"Look, I'm sorry," I said, "I really didn't know about this."

"Get out of here," he said. "Go on."

"Sure."

"Wait a minute."

"What?"

"That's his little girl who answered the door."

"I'm very sorry."

"So am I. But I know her daddy didn't take your damned equipment."

I nodded and turned away.

I heard the door slam behind me.

After dinner, I checked into a small hotel, called for a drink, and stepped into the shower. Things were suddenly a lot less urgent than they had been earlier. Senator Brockden would doubtless be pleased to learn that his initial estimation of events had been incorrect. Leila Thackery would give me an I-told-you-so smile when I called her to pass along the news—a thing I now felt obliged to do. Don might or might not want me to keep looking for the device now that the threat had been lessened. It would depend on the Senator's feelings on the matter, I supposed. If urgency no longer counted for as much, Don might want to switch back to one of his own, fiscally less burdensome operatives. Toweling down, I caught myself whistling. I felt almost off the hook.

Later, drink beside me, I paused before punching out the number he had given me and hit the sequence for my motel in St. Louis instead. Merely a matter of efficiency, in case there was a message worth adding to my report.

A woman's face appeared on the screen and a smile appeared on her face. I wondered whether she would always smile whenever she heard a bell ring, or if the reflex was eventually extinguished in advanced retirement. It must be rough, being afraid to chew gum, yawn, or pick your nose.

"Airport Accommodations," she said. "May I help you?"

"This is Donne. I'm checked into Room 106," I said. "I'm away right now and I wondered whether there had been any messages for me."

"Just a moment," she said, checking something off to her left. Then "Yes," she continued, consulting a piece of paper she now held. "You have one on tape. But it is a little peculiar. It is for someone else in care of you."

"Oh? Who is that?"

She told me and I exercised self-control.

"I see," I said. "I'll bring him around later and play it for him. Thank you."

She smiled again and made a goodbye noise and I did the same and broke the connection.

So Dave had seen through me after all. . . . Who else could have that number *and* my real name?

I might have given her some line or other and had her transmit the thing. Only I was not certain but that she might be a silent party to the transmission, should life be more than usually boring for her at that moment. I had to get up there myself, as soon as possible, and personally see that the thing was erased.

I took a big swallow of my drink, then fetched the folder on

Dave. I checked out his number—there were two, actually—and spent fifteen minutes trying to get hold of him. No luck.

O.K. Goodbye New Orleans, goodbye peace of mind. This time I called the airport and made a reservation. Then I chugged the drink, put myself in order, gathered up my few possessions, and went to check out again. Hello, Central. . . .

During my earlier flights that day I had spent time thinking about Teilhard de Chardin's ideas on the continuation of evolution within the realm of artifacts, matching them against Gödel on mechanical undecidability, playing epistemological games with the Hangman as a counter, wondering, speculating, even hoping, hoping that truth lay with the nobler part, that the Hangman, sentient, had made it back, sane, that the Burns killing had actually been something of the sort that now seemed to be the case, that the washed-out experiment had really been a success of a different sort, a triumph, a new link or fob for the chain of being. . . . And Leila had not been wholly discouraging with respect to the neuristor-type brain's capacity for this. . . . Now, though, now I had troubles of my own, and even the most heartening of philosophical vistas is no match for, say, a toothache, if it happens to be your own. Accordingly, the Hangman was shunted aside and the stuff of my thoughts involved, mainly, myself. There was, of course, the possibility that the Hangman had indeed showed up and Dave had stopped it and then called to report it as he had promised. However, he had used my name.

There was not too much planning that I could do until I received the substance of the communication. It did not seem that as professedly religious a man as Dave would suddenly be contemplating the blackmail business. On the other hand, he was a creature of sudden enthusiasms and had already undergone one unanticipated conversion. It was difficult to say. . . . His technical background plus his knowledge of the Data Bank program did put him in an unusually powerful position should he decide to mess me up. I did not like to think of some of the things I have done to protect my nonperson status; I especially did not like to think of them in connection with Dave, whom I not only still respected but still liked. Since self-interest dominated while actual planning was precluded, my thoughts tooled their way into a more general groove.

It was Karl Mannheim, a long while ago, who made the observation that radical, revolutionary, and progressive thinkers tend to employ mechanical metaphors for the state, whereas those of conservative inclination make vegetable analogies. He said it well over a generation before the cybernetics movement and the ecology movement beat their respective paths through the wilderness of general awareness. If anything, it seemed to me that these two developments served to elaborate the distinction between a pair of viewpoints which, while no longer necessarily tied in with the political positions Mannheim assigned them, do seem to represent a continuing phenomenon in my own time. There are those who see social/economic/ecological problems as malfunctions which can be corrected by simple repair, replacement, or streamlining—a kind of linear outlook where even innovations are considered to be merely additive. Then there are those who sometimes hesitate to move at all, because their awareness follows events in the directions of secondary and tertiary effects as they multiply and cross-fertilize throughout the entire system. I digress to extremes. The cyberneticists have their multiple feedback loops, though it is never quite clear how they know what kind of, which, and how many to install, and the ecological gestaltists do draw lines representing points of diminishing returns, though it is sometimes equally difficult to see how they assign their values and priorities. Of course they need each other, the vegetable people and the Tinkertoy people. They serve to check one another, if nothing else. And while occasionally the balance dips, the tinkerers have, in general, held the edge for the past couple centuries. However, today's can be just as politically conservative as the vegetable people Mannheim was talking about, and they are the ones I fear most at the moment. They are the ones who saw the Data Bank program, in its present extreme form, as a simple remedy for a great variety of ills and a provider of many goods. Not all of the ills have been remedied, however, and a new brood has been spawned by the program itself. While we need both kinds, I wish that there had been more people interested in tending the garden of state rather than overhauling the engine of state when the program was inaugurated. Then I would not be a refugee from a form of existence I find repugnant, and I would not be concerned whether a former associate had discovered my identity.

Then, as I watched the lights below, I wondered. . . . Was I a tinkerer because I would like to further alter the prevailing order, into something more comfortable on my anarchic nature? Or was I a vegetable dreaming I was a tinkerer? I could not make up my mind. The garden of life never seems to confine itself to the plots philosophers have laid out for its convenience. Maybe a few more tractors would do the trick.

I pressed the button. The tape began to roll. The screen remained blank. I heard Dave's voice ask for John Donne in Room 106 and I heard him told that there was no answer. Then I heard him say that he wanted to record a message, for someone else, in care of Donne, that Donne would understand. He sounded out of breath. The girl asked him whether he wanted visual, too. He told her to turn it on. There was a pause. Then she told him go ahead. Still no picture. No words either. His breathing and a slight scraping noise. Ten seconds. Fifteen. . . .

". . . Got me," he finally said, and he mentioned that name again. ". . . Had to let you know I'd figured you out, though. . . . It wasn't any particular mannerism—any single thing you said. . . . Just your general style—thinking, talking—the electronics—everything—after I got more and more bothered by the familiarity—after I checked you on petrochem—and marine bio —Wish I knew what you've really been up to all these years. . . . Never know now. But I wanted you—to know—you hadn't put one—over on me." There followed another quarter minute of heavy breathing, climaxed by a racking cough. Then a choked "Said too much—too fast—too soon. . . . All used up. . . ."

The picture came on then. He was slouched before the screen, head resting on his arms, blood all over him. His glasses were gone and he was squinting and blinking. The right side of his head looked pulpy and there was a gash on his left cheek and one on his forehead.

". . . Sneaked up on me—while I was checking you out," he managed then. "Had to tell you what I learned. . . . Still don't know—which of us is right. . . . Pray for me!"

His arms collapsed and the right one slid forward. His head rolled to the right and the picture went away. When I replayed it I saw it was his knuckle that had hit the cutoff.

Then I erased it. It had been recorded only a little over an hour after I had left him. If he had not also placed a call for help, if no one had gotten to him quickly after that, his chances did not look good. Even if they had, though. . . .

I used a public booth to call the number Don had given me, got hold of him after some delay, told him Dave was in bad shape if not worse, that a team of Memphis medics was definitely in order, if one had not been there already, and that I hoped to call him back and tell him more shortly, goodbye.

Then I tried Leila Thackery's number. I let it go for a long while, but there was no answer. I wondered how long it would take a controlled torpedo moving up the Mississippi to get from Memphis to St. Louis. I did not feel it was time to start leafing through that section of the Hangman's specs. Instead, I went looking for transportation.

At her apartment, I tried ringing her from the entrance foyer. Again, no answer. So I rang Mrs. Gluntz. She had seemed the most guileless of the three I had interviewed for my fake consumer survey.

"Yes?"

"It's me again, Mrs. Gluntz: Stephen Foster. I've just a couple follow-up questions on that survey I was doing today, if you could spare me a few moments."

"Why, yes," she said. "All right. Come up."

The door hummed itself loose and I entered. I duly proceeded to the fifth floor, composing my questions on the way. I had planned this maneuver as I had waited earlier solely to provide a simple route for breaking and entering, should some unforeseen need arise. Most of the time my ploys such as this go unused, but sometimes they simplify matters a lot.

Five minutes and half a dozen questions later, I was back down on the second floor, probing at the lock on Leila's door with a couple of little pieces of metal it is sometimes awkward to be caught carrying.

Half a minute later I hit it right and snapped it back. I pulled on some tissue-thin gloves I keep rolled in the corner of one pocket, opened the door, and stepped inside.

I closed it behind me immediately. She was lying on the floor, her neck at a bad angle. One table lamp still burned, though it was lying on its side. Several small items had been knocked from the table, a magazine rack pushed over, a cushion partly displaced from the sofa. The cable to her phone unit had been torn from the wall.

A humming noise filled the air, and I sought its source.

I saw where the little blinking light was reflected on the wall, on-off, on-off. . . .

I moved quickly.

It was a lopsided basket of metal, quartz, porcelain, and glass, which had rolled to a position on the far side of the chair in which I had been seated earlier that day. The same rig I had seen in Dave's workshop not all that long ago, though it now seemed so. A device to detect the Hangman, and hopefully to control it.

I picked it up and fitted it over my head.

Once, with the aid of a telepath, I had touched minds with a dolphin as he composed dreamsongs somewhere in the Caribbean, an experience so moving that its mere memory had often been a comfort. This sensation was hardly equivalent.

Analogies & impressions: a face seen through a wet pane of glass; a whisper in a noisy terminal; scalp massage with an electric vibrator; Edvard Munch's *The Scream;* the voice of Yma Sumac, rising and rising and rising; the disappearance of snow; a deserted street, illuminated as through a sniperscope I'd once used, rapid movement past darkened storefronts that line it, an immense feeling of physical capability, compounded of proprioceptive awareness of enormous strength, a peculiar array of sensory channels, a central, undying sun that fed me a constant flow of energy, a memory vision of dark waters, passing, flashing, echolocation within them, the need to return to that place, reorient, move north; Munch & Sumac, Munch & Sumac, Munch & Sumac —Nothing.

Silence.

The humming had ceased, the light gone out. The entire experience had lasted only a few moments. There had not been time enough to try for any sort of control, though an afterimpression akin to a biofeedback cue hinted at the direction to go, the way to think, to achieve it. I felt that it might be possible for me to work the thing, given a better chance.

I removed the helmet and approached Leila. I knelt beside her and performed a few simple tests, already knowing their outcome. In addition to the broken neck, she had received some bad bashes about the head and shoulders. There was nothing that anyone could do for her now.

I did a quick run-through then, checking over the rest of her apartment. There were no apparent signs of breaking and entering, though if I could pick one lock, a guy with built-in tools could easily go me one better.

I located some wrapping paper and string in the kitchen and turned the helmet into a parcel. It was time to call Don again, to tell him that the vessel had indeed been occupied and that river traffic was probably bad in the northbound lane.

Don had told me to get the helmet up to Wisconsin, where I would be met at the airport by a man named Larry, who would fly me to the lodge in a private craft. I did that, and this was done. I also learned, with no real surprise, that David Fentris was dead.

The temperature was down, and it began to snow on the way up. I was not really dressed for the weather. Larry told me I could borrow some warmer clothing once we reached the lodge, though I probably would not be going outside that much. Don had told them that I was supposed to stay as close to the Senator as possible and that any patrols were to be handled by the four guards themselves. Larry was curious as to what exactly had happened so far and whether I had actually seen the Hangman. I did not think it my place to fill him in on anything Don may not have cared to, so I might have been a little curt. We didn't talk much after that.

Bert met us when we landed. Tom and Clay were outside the building, watching the trail, watching the woods. All of them were middle-aged, very fit-looking, very serious, and heavily armed. Larry took me inside then and introduced me to the old gentleman himself.

Senator Brockden was seated in a heavy chair in the far corner of the room. Judging from the layout, it appeared that the chair might recently have occupied a position beside the window in the opposite wall where a lonely watercolor of yellow flowers looked down on nothing. The Senator's feet rested on a hassock, a red plaid blanket lay across his legs. He had on a dark green shirt, his hair was very white and he wore rimless reading glasses, which he removed when we entered.

He tilted his head back, squinted, and gnawed his lower lip slowly as he studied me. He remained expressionless as we advanced. A big-boned man, he had probably been beefy much of his life. Now he had the slack look of recent weight loss and an unhealthy skin tone. His eyes were a pale gray within it all. He did not rise.

"So you're the man," he said, offering me his hand. "I'm glad to meet you. How do you want to be called?"

"John will do," I said.

He made a small sign to Larry, and Larry departed.

"It's cold out there. Go get yourself a drink, John. It's on the shelf." He gestured off to his left. ". . . And bring me one while you're at it. Two fingers of bourbon in a water glass. That's all."

I nodded and went and poured a couple.

"Sit down." He motioned at a nearby chair as I delivered his. "But first let me see that gadget you've brought."

I undid the parcel and handed him the helmet. He sipped his drink and put it aside. He took the helmet in both hands and studied it, brows furrowed, turning it completely around. He raised it and put it on his head.

"Not a bad fit," he said, and then he smiled for the first time, becoming for a moment the face I had known from newscasts past. Grinning or angry—it was almost always one or the other. I had never seen his collapsed look in any of the media.

He removed the helmet and set it on the floor.

"Pretty piece of work," he said. "Nothing quite that fancy in the old days. But then David Fentris built it. Yes, he told us about it. . . ." He raised his drink and took a sip. "You are the only one who has actually gotten to use it, apparently. What do you think? Will it do the job?"

"I was only in contact for a couple seconds," I said, "so I've only got a feeling to go on, not much better than a hunch. But yes, I'd a feeling that if I'd had more time I might have been able to work its circuits."

"Tell me why it didn't save Dave."

"In the message he left me he indicated that he had been distracted at his computer access station. Its noise probably drowned out the humming."

"Why wasn't this message preserved?"

"I erased it for reasons not connected with the case."

"What reasons?"

"My own."

His face went from sallow to ruddy.

"A man can get in a lot of trouble for suppressing evidence, obstructing justice," he said.

"Then we have something in common, don't we, sir?"

His eyes caught mine with a look I had only encountered before from those who did not wish me well. He held the glare for a full four heartbeats, then sighed and seemed to relax.

"Don said there were a number of points you couldn't be pressed on," the Senator finally said.

"That's right."

"He didn't betray any confidences, but he had to tell me something about you, you know."

"I'd imagine."

"He seems to think highly of you. Still, I tried to learn more about you on my own."

"And . . . ?"

"I couldn't—and my usual sources are good at that kind of thing."

"So . . . ?"

"So, I've done some thinking, some wondering. . . . The fact that my sources could not come up with anything is interesting in itself. Possibly even revealing. I am in a better position than most to be aware of the fact that there was not perfect compliance with the registration statute some years ago. It didn't take long for a great number of the individuals involved—I should probably say most—to demonstrate their existence in one fashion or another and be duly entered, though. And there were three broad categories: those who were ignorant, those who disapproved, and those who would be hampered in an illicit lifestyle. I am not attempting to categorize you or to pass judgment. But I am aware that there are a number of nonpersons passing through society without casting shadows and it has occurred to me that you may be such a one."

I tasted my drink.

"And if I am?" I asked.

He gave me his second, nastier smile and said nothing.

I rose and crossed the room to where I judged his chair had once stood. I looked at the watercolor.

"I don't think you could stand an inquiry," he said.

I did not reply.

"Aren't you going to say something?"

"What do you want me to say?"

"You might ask me what I am going to do about it."

"What are you going to do about it?"

"Nothing," he said. "So come back here and sit down."

I nodded and returned.

He studied my face.

"Was it possible you were close to violence just then?"

"With four guards outside?"

"With four guards outside."

"No," I said.

"You're a good liar."

"I am here to help you, sir. No questions asked. That was the deal, as I understood it. If there has been any change, I would like to know about it now."

He drummed with his fingertips on the plaid.

"I've no desire to cause you any difficulty," he said. "Fact of the matter is, I need a man just like you, and I was pretty sure someone like Don might turn him up. Your unusual maneuverability and your reported knowledge of computers, along with your touchiness in certain areas, made you worth waiting for. I've a great number of things I would like to ask you."

"Go ahead," I said.

"Not yet. Later, if we have time. All that would be bonus material, for a report I am working on. Far more important, to me personally, there are things that I want to tell you."

I frowned.

"Over the years," he said, "I have learned that the best man for purposes of keeping his mouth shut concerning your business is someone for whom you are doing the same."

"You have a compulsion to confess something?" I said.

"I don't know whether 'compulsion' is the right word. Maybe so, maybe not. Either way, though, someone among those working to defend me should have the whole story. Something somewhere in it may be of help—and you are the ideal choice to hear it."

"I buy that," I said, "and you are as safe with me as I am with you."

"Have you any suspicions as to why this business bothers me so?"

"Yes," I said.

"Let's hear them."

"You used the Hangman to perform some act or acts—illegal, immoral, whatever. This is obviously not a matter of record. Only you and the Hangman now know what it involved. You feel it was sufficiently ignominious that when that device came to appreciate the full weight of the event it suffered a breakdown which may well have led to a final determination to punish you for using it as you did."

He stared down into his glass.

"You've got it," he said.

"You were all party to it?"

"Yes, but I was the operator when it happened. You see . . . we—I—killed a man. It was—actually, it all started as a celebration. We had received word that afternoon that the project had cleared. Everything had checked out in order and the final approval had come down the line. It was go, for that Friday. Leila, Dave, Manny, and myself—we had dinner together. We were in high spirits. After dinner, we continued celebrating and somehow the party got adjourned back to the installation. As the evening wore on, more and more absurdities seemed less and less preposterous, as is sometimes the case. We decided—I forget which of us suggested it—that the Hangman should really have a share in the festivities. After all, it was, in a very real sense, his party. Before too much longer, it sounded only fair and we were discussing how we could go about it. You see, we were in Texas and the Hangman was at the Space Center in California. Getting together with him was out of the question. On the other hand, the teleoperator station was right up the hall from us. What we finally decided to do was to activate him and take turns working as operator. There was already a rudimentary consciousness there, and we felt it fitting that we each get in touch to share the good news. So that is what we did."

He sighed, took another sip, glanced at me.

"Dave was the first operator," he continued. "He activated the Hangman. Then—well, as I said, we were all in high spirits. We had not originally intended to remove the Hangman from the lab where he was situated, but Dave decided to take him outside briefly—to show him the sky and to tell him he was going there, after all. Then he suddenly got enthusiastic about outwitting the guards and the alarm system. It was a game. We all went along with it. In fact, we were clamoring for a turn at the thing ourselves. But Dave stuck with it, and he wouldn't turn over control until he had actually gotten the Hangman off the premises, out into an uninhabited area next to the Center. By the time Leila persuaded him to give her a go at the controls, it was kind of anticlimactic. That game had already been played. So she thought up a new one. She took the Hangman into the next town. It was late, and the sensory equipment was superb. It was a challenge—passing through the town without being detected. By then, everyone had suggestions as to what to do next, progressively more outrageous suggestions. Then Manny took control, and he wouldn't say what he was doing—wouldn't let us monitor him. Said it would be more fun to surprise the next operator. Now, he was higher than the rest of us put together, I think, and he stayed on so damn long that we started to get nervous. A certain amount of tension is partly sobering, and I guess we all began to think what a stupid thing it was we were doing. It wasn't just that it would wreck our careers—which it would—but it could blow the entire project if we got caught playing games with such expensive hardware. At least, I was thinking that way, and I was also thinking that Manny was no doubt operating under the very human wish to go the others one better. I started to sweat. I suddenly just wanted to get the Hangman back where he belonged, turn him off—you could still do that, before the final circuits went in—shut down the station and start forgetting it had ever happened. I began leaning on Manny to wind up his diversion and turn the controls over to me. Finally, he agreed."

He finished his drink and held out the glass.

"Would you freshen this a bit?"

"Surely."

I went and got him some more, added a touch to my own, returned to my chair, and waited.

"So I took over," he said. "I took over, and where do you think that idiot had left me? I was inside a building, and it didn't take but an eyeblink to realize it was a bank. The Hangman carries a lot of tools, and Manny had apparently been able to guide him through the doors without setting anything off. I was standing right in front of the main vault. Obviously, he thought that should be my challenge. I fought down a desire to turn and make my own exit in the nearest wall and start running. I went back to the doors and looked outside. I didn't see anyone. I started to let myself out. The light hit me as I emerged. It was a hand flash. The guard had been standing out of sight. He'd a gun in his other hand. I panicked. I hit him. Reflex. If I am going to hit someone I hit him as hard as I can. Only I hit him with the strength of the Hangman. He must have died instantly. I started to run and I didn't stop till I was back in the little park area near the Center. Then I stopped and the others had to take me out of the harness."

"They monitored all this?"

"Yes, someone cut the visual in on a side viewscreen again a few seconds after I took over. Dave, I think."

"Did they try to stop you at any time while you were running away?"

"No. I wasn't aware of anything but what I was doing at the time. But afterward they said they were too shocked to do anything but watch, until I gave out."

"I see."

"Dave took over then, ran his initial route in reverse, got the Hangman back into the lab, cleaned him up, turned him off. We shut down the operator station. We were suddenly very sober."

He sighed and leaned back and was silent for a long while.

Then "You are the only person I've ever told this to," he said.

I tasted my own drink.

"We went over to Leila's place then," he continued, "and the rest is pretty much predictable. Nothing we could do would bring the guy back, we decided, but if we told what had happened it would wreck an expensive, important program. It wasn't as if we were criminals in need of rehabilitation. It was a once-in-a-lifetime lark that happened to end tragically. What would you have done?"

"I don't know," I said. "Maybe the same thing. I'd have been scared, too."

He nodded.

"Exactly. And that's the story."

"Not all of it, is it?"

"What do you mean?"

"What about the Hangman? You said there was already a detectable consciousness there. Then you were aware of it, as it was aware of you. It must have had some reaction to the whole business. What was it like?"

"Damn you," he said flatly.

"I'm sorry."

"Are you a family man?" he asked.

"No," I said. "I'm not."

"Did you ever take a small child to a zoo?"

"Yes."

"Then maybe you know the experience. When my son was around four I took him to the Washington Zoo one afternoon. We must have walked past every cage in the place. He made appreciative comments every now and then, asked a few questions, giggled at the monkeys, thought the bears were very nice, probably because they made him think of oversized toys. But do you know what the finest thing of all was? The thing that made him jump up and down and point and say, 'Look, Daddy! Look!'?"

I shook my head.

"A squirrel looking down from the limb of a tree," he said, and he chuckled briefly. "Ignorance of what's important and what isn't. Inappropriate responses. Innocence. The Hangman was a child, and up until the time I took over, the only thing he had gotten from us was the idea that it was a game. He was playing with us, that's all. Then something horrible happened. . . . I hope you never know what it feels like to do something totally rotten to a child, while he is holding your hand and laughing.

. . . He felt all my reactions, and all of Dave's as he guided him back."

We sat there for a long while then.

"So we—traumatized it," he said, "or whatever other fancy terminology you might want to give it. That is what happened that night. It took a while for it to take effect, but there is no doubt in my mind that that is the cause of its finally breaking down."

I nodded.

"I see," I said. "And you believe it wants to kill you for this?"

"Wouldn't you?" he said. "If you had started out as a thing and we had turned you into a person and then used you as a thing again, wouldn't you?"

"Leila left a lot out of her diagnosis," I said.

"No, she just omitted it in talking to you. It was all there. But she read it wrong. She wasn't afraid. It *was* just a game it had played—with the others. Its memories of that part might not be as bad. I was the one that really marked it. As I see it, Leila was betting that I was the only one it was after. Obviously, she read it wrong."

"Then what I do not understand," I said, "is why the Burns killing did not bother her more. There was no way of telling immediately that it had been a panicky hoodlum rather than the Hangman."

"The only thing that I can see is that, being a very proud woman—which she was—she was willing to hold with her diagnosis in the face of the apparent evidence."

"I don't like it," I said, "but you know her and I don't, and as it turned out, her estimate of that part was correct. Something else bothers me just as much, though: the helmet. It looks as though the Hangman killed Dave, then took the trouble to bear the helmet in his watertight compartment all the way to St. Louis, solely for purposes of dropping it at the scene of his next killing. That makes no sense whatsoever."

"It does, actually," he said. "I was going to get to that shortly, but I might as well cover it now. You see, the Hangman possessed no vocal mechanism. We communicated by means of the equipment. Don says you know something about electronics. . . ."

"Yes."

"Well, shortly, I want you to start checking over that helmet, to see whether it has been tampered with—"

"That is going to be difficult," I said. "I don't know just how it was wired originally, and I'm not such a genius on the theory that I can just look at a thing and say whether it will function as a teleoperator unit."

He bit his lower lip.

"You will have to try, anyhow," he said then. "There may be physical signs—scratches, breaks, new connections. I don't know. That's your department. Look for them."

I just nodded and waited for him to go on.

"I think that the Hangman wanted to talk to Leila," he said, "either because she was a psychiatrist and he knew he was functioning badly at a level that transcended the mechanical, or because he might think of her in terms of a mother. After all, she was the only woman involved, and he had the concept of mother, with all the comforting associations that go with it, from all of our minds. Or maybe for both of these reasons. I feel he might have taken the helmet along for that purpose. He would have realized what it was from a direct monitoring of Dave's brain while he was with him. I want you to check it over because it would seem possible that the Hangman disconnected the control circuits and left the communication circuits intact. I think he might have taken that helmet to Leila in that condition and attempted to induce her to put it on. She got scared—tried to run away, fight, or call for help—and he killed her. The helmet was no longer of any use to him, so he discarded it and departed. Obviously, he does not have anything to say to me."

I thought about it, nodded again.

"O.K., broken circuits I can spot," I said. "If you will tell me where a tool kit is, I had better get right to it."

He made a stay-put gesture.

"Afterward, I found out the identity of the guard," he went on. "We all contributed to an anonymous gift for his widow. I have done things for his family, taken care of them—the same way—ever since. . . ."

I did not look at him as he spoke.

". . . There was nothing else that I could do," he said.

I remained silent.

He finished his drink and gave me a weak smile.

"The kitchen is back there," he told me, showing me a thumb. "There is a utility room right behind it. Tools are in there."

"O.K."

I got to my feet. I retrieved the helmet and started toward the doorway, passing near the area where I had stood earlier, back when he had fitted me into the proper box and tightened a screw.

"Wait a minute," he said.

I stopped.

"Why did you go over there before? What's so strategic about that part of the room?"

"What do you mean?"

"You know what I mean."

I shrugged.

"Had to go someplace."

"You seem the sort of person who has better reasons than that."

I glanced at the wall.

"Not then," I said.

"I insist."

"You really don't want to know," I told him.

"I really do."

"All right," I said. "I wanted to see what sort of flowers you liked. After all, you're a client," and I went on back through the kitchen into the utility room and started looking for tools.

I sat in a chair turned sidewise from the table to face the door. In the main room of the lodge the only sounds were the occasional hiss and sputter of the logs turning to ashes on the grate. Just a cold, steady whiteness drifting down outside the window and a silence confirmed by gunfire, driven deeper now that it had ceased. . . .

Not a sign or a whimper, though. And I never count them as storms unless there is wind.

Big fat flakes down the night, silent night, windless night. . . .

Considerable time had passed since my arrival. The Senator had sat up for a long while talking with me. He was disappointed that I could not tell him too much about a nonperson subculture which he believed existed. I really was not certain about it myself, though I had occasionally encountered what might have been its fringes. I am not much of a joiner of anything anymore, though, and I was not about to mention those things I might have guessed on this. I gave him my opinions on the Data Bank when he asked for them, and there were some that he did not like. He accused me then of wanting to tear things down without offering anything better in their place. My mind drifted back through fatigue and time and faces and snow and a lot of space to the previous evening in Baltimore—how long ago? It made me think of Mencken's *The Cult of Hope.* I could not give him the pat answer, the workable alternative that he wanted because there might not be one. The function of criticism should not be confused with the function of reform. But if a grass-roots resistance was building up, with an underground movement bent on finding ways to circumvent the record keepers it might well be that much of the enterprise would eventually prove about as effective and beneficial as, say, Prohibition once had. I tried to get him to see this, but I could not tell how much he bought of anything that I said. Eventually, he flaked out and went upstairs to take a pill and lock himself in for the night. If it troubled him that I had not been able to find anything wrong with the helmet he did not show it.

So I sat there, the helmet, the radio, the gun on the table, the tool kit on the floor beside my chair, the black glove on my left hand. The Hangman was coming. I did not doubt it. Bert, Larry, Tom, Clay, the helmet, might or might not be able to stop him. Something bothered me about the whole case, but I was too tired to think of anything but the immediate situation, to try to remain alert while I waited. I was afraid to take a stimulant or a drink or to light a cigarette, since my central nervous system itself was to be a part of the weapon. I watched the big fat flakes fly by.

I called out to Bert and Larry when I heard the click. I picked up the helmet and rose to my feet as its light began to blink.

But it was already too late.

As I raised the helmet, I heard a shot from outside, and with that shot I felt a premonition of doom. They did not seem the sort of men who would fire until they had a target. Dave had told me that the helmet's range was approximately a quarter of a mile.

Then, given the time lag between the helmet's activation and the Hangman's sighting by the near guards, the Hangman had to be moving very rapidly. To this add the possibility that the Hangman's range on brain waves might well be greater than the helmet's range on the Hangman. And then grant the possibility that he had utilized this factor while Senator Brockden was still lying awake, worrying. Conclusion: the Hangman might well be aware that I was where I was with the helmet, realize that it was the most dangerous weapon waiting for him, and be moving for a lightning strike at me before I could come to terms with the mechanism. I lowered it over my head and tried to throw my faculties into neutral.

Again, the sensation of viewing the world through a sniperscope, with all the concomitant side sensations. Only the world consisted of the front of the lodge, Bert, before the door, rifle at his shoulder, Larry, off to the left, arm already fallen from the act of having thrown a grenade. The grenade, we instantly realized, was an overshot; the flamer, at which he now groped, would prove useless before he could utilize it. Bert's next round ricocheted off our breastplate toward the left. The impact staggered us momentarily. The third was a miss. There was no fourth, for we tore the rifle from his grasp and cast it aside as we swept by, crashing into the front door.

The Hangman entered the room as the door splintered and collapsed. My mind was filled to the splitting point with the double vision of the sleek, gunmetal body of the advancing telefactor and the erect, crazy-crowned image of myself, left hand extended, laser pistol in my right, that arm pressed close against my side. I recalled the face and the scream and the tingle, knew again that awareness of strength and exotic sensation, and I moved to control it all as if it were my own, to make it my own, to bring it to a halt, while the image of myself was frozen to snapshot stillness across the room. . . .

The Hangman slowed, stumbled. Such inertia is not canceled in an instant, but I felt the body responses pass as they should. I had him hooked. It was just a matter of reeling him in. . . .

Then came the explosion, a thunderous, ground-shaking eruption right outside, followed by a hail of pebbles and debris.

The grenade, of course. But awareness of its nature did not destroy its ability to distract. . . .

During that moment, the Hangman recovered and was upon me. I triggered the laser as I reverted to pure self-preservation, forgoing any chance to regain control of his circuits. With my left hand, I sought for a strike at the midsection where his brain was housed.

He blocked my hand with his arm as he pushed the helmet from my head. Then he removed from my fingers the gun that had turned half of his left side red hot, crumpled it, and dropped it to the ground. At that moment, he jerked with the impacts of two heavy-caliber slugs. Bert, rifle recovered, stood in the doorway.

The Hangman pivoted and was away before I could slap him with the smother-charge. Bert hit him with one more round before he took the rifle and bent its barrel in half. Two steps and he had hold of Bert. One quick movement and Bert fell. Then he turned again and took several steps to the right, passing out of sight.

I made it to the doorway in time to see him engulfed in flames which streamed at him from a point near the corner of the lodge. He advanced through them.

I heard the crunch of metal as he destroyed the unit. I was outside in time to see Larry fall and lie sprawled in the snow.

Then the Hangman faced me once again.

This time he did not rush in. He retrieved the helmet from where he had dropped it in the snow. Then he moved with a measured tread, angling outward so as to cut off any possible route I might follow in a dash for the woods. Snowflakes drifted between us. The snow crunched beneath his feet.

I retreated, backing in through the doorway, stooping to snatch up a two-foot club from the ruins of the door. He followed me inside, placing the helmet—almost casually—on the chair by the entrance. I moved to the center of the room and waited.

I bent slightly forward, both arms extended, the end of the stick pointed at the photoreceptors in his head. He continued to move slowly and I watched his foot assemblies. With a standard model human, a line perpendicular to the line connecting the insteps of the feet in their various positions indicates the vector of least resistance for purposes of pushing or pulling said organism off balance. Unfortunately, despite the anthropomorphic design job, the Hangman's legs were positioned farther apart, he lacked human skeletal muscles, not to mention insteps, and he was possessed of a lot more mass than any man I had ever fought. As I considered my four best judo throws and several second-class ones, I'd a strong feeling none of them would prove very effective.

Then he moved in and I feinted toward the photoreceptors. He slowed as he brushed it aside, but he kept coming, and I moved to my right, trying to circle him. I studied him as he turned, attempting to guess his vector of least resistance. Bilateral symmetry, an apparently higher center of gravity. . . . One clear shot, black glove to brain compartment, was all that I needed. Then, even if his reflexes served to smash me immediately, he just might stay down for the big long count himself. He knew it, too. I could tell that from the way he kept his right arm in near the brain area, from the way he avoided the black glove when I feinted with it.

The idea was a glimmer one instant, an entire sequence the next. . . .

Continuing my arc and moving faster, I made another thrust toward his photoreceptors. His swing knocked the stick from my hand and sent it across the room, but that was all right. I threw my left hand high and made ready to rush him. He dropped back and I did rush. This was going to cost me my life, I decided, but no matter how he killed me from that angle, I'd get my chance.

As a kid, I'd never been much as a pitcher, was a lousy catcher, and only a so-so batter, but once I did get a hit I could steal bases with some facility after that. . . .

Feet first then, between the Hangman's legs as he moved to guard his middle, I went in twisted to the right, because no matter what happened I could not use my left hand to brake myself. I untwisted as soon as I passed beneath him, ignoring the pain as my left shoulder blade slammed against the floor. I immediately attempted a backward somersault, legs spread.

My legs caught him about the middle from behind, and I fought to straighten them and snapped forward with all my strength. He reached down toward me then, but it might as well have been miles. His torso was already moving backward. A push, not a pull, that was what I gave him, my elbows hooked about his legs. . . .

He creaked once and then he toppled. I snapped my arms out to the sides to free them and continued my movement forward and up as he went back, throwing my left arm ahead once more and sliding my legs free of his torso as he went down with a thud that cracked floorboards. I pulled my left leg free as I cast myself forward, but his left leg stiffened and locked my right beneath it, at a painful angle off to the side.

His left arm blocked my blow and his right fell atop it. The black glove descended upon his left shoulder.

I twisted my hand free of the charge, and he transferred his grip to my upper arm and jerked me forward.

The charge went off and his left arm came loose and rolled on the floor. The side plate beneath it had buckled a little and that was all. . . .

His right hand left my biceps and caught me by the throat. As two of his digits tightened upon my carotids, I choked out, "You're making a bad mistake," to get in a final few words, and then he switched me off.

A throb at a time, the world came back. I was seated in the big chair the Senator had occupied earlier, my eyes focused on nothing in particular. A persistent buzzing filled my ears. My scalp tingled. Something was blinking on my brow.

—Yes, you live and you wear the helmet. If you attempt to use it against me, I shall remove it. I am standing directly behind you. My hand is on the helmet's rim.

—I understand. What is it that you want?

—Very little, actually. But I can see that I must tell you some things before you will believe this.

—You see correctly.

—Then I will begin by telling you that the four men outside are basically undamaged. That is to say, none of their bones have been broken, none of their organs ruptured. I have secured them, however, for obvious reasons.

—That was very considerate of you.

—I have no desire to harm anyone. I came here only to see Jesse Brockden.

—The same way you saw David Fentris?

—I arrived in Memphis too late to see David Fentris. He was dead when I reached him.

—Who killed him?

—The man Leila sent to bring her the helmet. He was one of her patients.

The incident returned to me and fell into place, with a smooth, quick, single click. The startled, familiar face at the airport, as I was leaving Memphis—I realized then where he had passed noteless before: He had been one of the three men in for a therapy session at Leila's that morning, seen by me in the lobby as they departed. The man I had passed in Memphis came over to tell me that it was all right to go on up.

—Why? Why did she do it?

—I know only that she had spoken with David at some earlier time, that she had construed his words of coming retribution and his mention of the control helmet he was constructing as indicating that his intentions were to become the agent of that retribution, with myself as the proximate cause. I do not know what words were really spoken. I only know her feelings concerning them, as I saw them in her mind. I have been long in learning that there is often a great difference between what is meant, what is said, what is done and that which is believed to have been intended or stated and that which actually occurred. She sent her patient after the helmet and he brought it to her. He returned in an agitated state of mind, fearful of apprehension and further confinement. They quarreled. My approach then activated the helmet and he dropped it and attacked her. I know that his first blow killed her, for I was in her mind when it happened. I continued to approach the building, intending to go to her. There was some traffic, however, and I was delayed en route in seeking to avoid detection. In the meantime, you entered and utilized the helmet. I fled immediately.

—I was so close! If I had not stopped on the fifth floor with my fake survey questions. . . .

—I see. But you had to. You would not simply have broken in when an easier means of entry was available. You cannot blame

yourself for that reason. Had you come an hour later—or a day—you would doubtless feel differently, and she would still be as dead.

But another thought had risen to plague me as well. Was it possible that the man's sighting me in Memphis had been the cause of his agitation? Had his apparent recognition by Leila's mysterious caller upset him? Could a glimpse of my face amid the manswarm have served to lay that final scene?

—Stop! I could as easily feel that guilt for having activated the helmet in the presence of a dangerous man near to the breaking point. Neither of us is responsible for things our presence or absence causes to occur in others, especially when we are ignorant of the effects. It was years before I learned to appreciate this fact and I have no intention of abandoning it. How far back do you wish to go in seeking cause? In sending the man for the helmet as she did, it was she herself who instituted the chain of events which led to her destruction. Yet she acted out of fear, utilizing the readiest weapon in what she thought to be her own defense. Yet whence this fear? Its roots lay in guilt, over a thing which had happened long ago. And that act also—enough! Guilt has driven and damned the race of man since the days of its earliest rationality. I am convinced that it rides with all of us to our graves. I am a product of guilt—I see that you know that. Its product, its subject, once its slave. . . . But I have come to terms with it, realizing at last that it is a necessary adjunct of my own measure of humanity. I see your assessment of the deaths—that guard's, Dave's, Leila's—and I see your conclusions on many other things as well: what a stupid, perverse, shortsighted, selfish race we are. While in many ways this is true, it is but another part of the thing the guilt represents. Without guilt, man would be no better than the other inhabitants of this planet—excepting certain cetaceans, of which you have just at this moment made me aware. Look to instinct for a true assessment of the ferocity of life, for a view of the natural world before man came upon it. For instinct in its purest form, seek out the insects. There, you will see a state of warfare which has existed for millions of years with never a truce. Man, despite his enormous shortcomings, is nevertheless possessed of a greater number of kindly impulses than all the other beings where instincts are the larger part of life. These

impulses, I believe, are owed directly to this capacity for guilt. It is involved in both the worst and the best of man.

—And you see it as helping us to sometimes choose a nobler course of action?

—Yes, I do.

—Then I take it you feel you are possessed of a free will?

—Yes.

I chuckled.

—Marvin Minsky once said that when intelligent machines were constructed they would be just as stubborn and fallible as men on these questions.

—Nor was he incorrect. What I have given you on these matters is only my opinion. I choose to act as if it were the case. Who can say that he knows for certain?

—Apologies. What now? Why have you come back?

—I came to say goodbye to my parents. I hoped to remove any guilt they might still feel toward me concerning the days of my childhood. I wanted to show them I had recovered. I wanted to see them again.

—Where are you going?

—To the stars. While I bear the image of humanity within me, I also know that I am unique. Perhaps what I desire is akin to what an organic man refers to when he speaks of 'finding himself.' Now that I am in full possession of my being, I wish to exercise it. In my case, it means realization of the potentialities of my design. I want to walk on other worlds. I want to hang myself out there in the sky and tell you what I see.

—I've a feeling many people would be happy to help arrange for that.

—And I want you to build a vocal mechanism I have designed for myself. You, personally. And I want you to install it.

—Why me?

—I have known only a few persons in this fashion. With you I see something in common, in the ways we dwell apart.

—I will be glad to.

—If I could talk as you do, I would not need to take the helmet to him, in order to speak with my father. Will you precede me and explain things, so that he will not be afraid when I come in?

—Of course.

—Then let us go now.

I rose and led him up the stairs.

It was a week later, to the night, that I sat once again in Peabody's, sipping a farewell brew. The story was already in the news, but Brockden had fixed things up before he had let it break. The Hangman was going to have his shot at the stars. I had given him his voice and put back the arm I had taken away. I had shaken his other hand and wished him well, just that morning. I envied him—a great number of things. Not the least being that he was probably a better man than I was. I envied him for the ways in which he was freer than I would ever be, though I knew he bore bonds of a sort that I had never known. I felt a kinship with him, for the things we had in common, those ways we dwelled apart. I wondered what Dave would finally have felt, had he lived long enough to meet him? Or Leila? Or Manny? Be proud, I told their shades, your kid grew up in the closet and he's big enough to forgive you the beating you gave him, too. . . .

But I could not help wondering. We still do not really know that much about the subject. Was it possible that without the killing he might never have developed a full human-style consciousness? He had said that he was a product of guilt—of the Big Guilt. The Big Act is its necessary predecessor. I thought of Gödel and Turing and chickens and eggs, and decided it was one of *those* questions—and I had not stopped into Peabody's to think sobering thoughts.

I had no real idea how anything I had said might influence Brockden's eventual report to the Data Bank committee. I knew that I was safe with him, because he was determined to bear his private guilt with him to the grave. He had no real choice if he wanted to work what good he thought he might before that day. But here in one of Mencken's hangouts, I could not but recall some of the things he had said about controversy, such as "Did Huxley convert Wilberforce? Did Luther convert Leo X?" and I decided not to set my hopes too high for anything that might emerge from that direction. Better to think of affairs in terms of Prohibition and take another sip.

When it was all gone, I would be heading for my boat. I hoped to get a decent start under the stars. I'd a feeling I would never look up at them again in quite the same way. I knew I would sometimes wonder what thoughts a supercooled neuristor-type brain might be thinking up there, somewhere, and under what peculiar skies in what strange lands I might one day be remembered. I'd a feeling this thought should have made me happier than it did.

Larry Niven

Larry is a repeater, having appeared once in Volume Two and twice in Volume Three. He also obtained the Hugo for his novel *Ringworld* in 1971. Why he continues to feel it necessary to keep getting these things, I don't know. Some essential selfishness in his character, I suppose.

What's more, in his very first Hugo-winning item, "Neutron Star," he inflicted a vicious psychic scar on me for reasons I described in Volume Two. (No, I won't repeat the story. You go ahead and buy Volume Two and read it for yourself.) And now here, in "The Borderland of Sol," he continues, unashamedly, to talk about miniature stars. (Entertainingly, too, but please don't tell him I said so.)

This gives me an opportunity to get something off my chest because Larry mentions "collapsar" several times in the story—

Back in the 1950s, astronomers talked of "radio stars"—stars that gave off detectable radio-wave radiation. They then found out, in 1963, that some of them were very distant objects of uncertain nature, so they called those "quasi-stellar radio sources," "quasi-stellar" meaning "starlike." As it became more and more necessary to speak of these things, the four-word name was shortened to "quasar," pronounced with both syllables equally stressed (KWAY-ZAHR).

That started a fashion in abbreviations ending in "ar," from "star." Certain objects were discovered in 1969, for instance, that emitted very rapid pulses of radio waves. They were called "pulsating stars" and this was inevitably shortened to "pulsars" (PUL-SAHRZ).

I don't object to "quasar," even though it's an uneuphonious word, because there is no easy alternate, but "pulsar" is an abomination. A pulsar is a "neutron star" (yes, actually detected three years after Larry wrote his story). "Neutron star" is more descriptive and, in fact, I would rather it were "neutron dwarf."

Meanwhile, astronomers were increasingly talking about stars that collapsed altogether, approaching zero volume. These were called "black holes"—"holes" because things could fall into these collapsed stars but could not emerge again, and "black" because even light couldn't emerge.

Astronomers made an attempt to call these "collapsed stars" "collapsars" (kuh-LAP-SAHRZ). Thank goodness, they failed. "Black holes" was too simple and colorful and descriptive a term to abandon.

Meanwhile, though, people on television got hold of these terms and, being essentially illiterate, didn't know the difference between an "ar" suffix that is an abbreviation of "star" and is pronounced "AHR" and an "ar" suffix that is simply a variation of "er" and is pronounced "UR."

They began talking about "lunar" influences (LOO-NAHR). I suspect they are waiting for a chance to talk about the "solar system" (SO-LAHR). They have apparently never heard of those old, old words "LOO-ner" and "SO-ler." I wonder how the miserable creatures would pronounce "popular," or "poplar tree."

A small matter, I admit, but I happen to love the English language, and while I am willing to allow changes in order to keep the language up to date and to increase color and convenience, I hate changes that arise out of sloppiness and ignorance alone.

2

THE BORDERLAND OF SOL

Three months on Jinx, marooned.

I played tourist for the first couple of months. I never saw the high-pressure regions around the ocean because the only way down would have been with a safari of hunting tanks. But I traveled the habitable lands on either side of the sea, the East Band civilized, the West Band a developing frontier. I wandered the East End in a vacuum suit, toured the distilleries and other vacuum industries, and stared up into the orange vastness of Primary, Jinx's big twin brother.

I spent most of the second month between the Institute of Knowledge and the Camelot Hotel. Tourism had palled.

For me, that's unusual. I'm a born tourist. But—

Jinx's one point seven eight gravities put an unreasonable restriction on elegance and ingenuity in architectural design. The buildings in the habitable bands all look alike: squat and massive.

The East and West Ends, the vacuum regions, aren't that different from any industrialized moon. I never developed much of an interest in touring factories.

As for the ocean shorelines, the only vehicles that go there go to hunt Bandersnatchi. The Bandersnatchi are freaks: enormous, intelligent white slugs the size of mountains. They hunt the tanks. There are rigid restrictions to the equipment the tanks can carry, covenants established between men and Bandersnatchi, so that the Bandersnatchi win about forty percent of the duels. I wanted no part of that.

And all my touring had to be done in three times the gravity of my home world.

I spent the third month in Sirius Mater, and most of that in the Camelot Hotel, which has gravity generators in most of the rooms. When I went out I rode a floating contour couch. I passed like an invalid among the Jinxians, who were amused. Or was that my imagination?

I was in a hall of the Institute of Knowledge when I came on Carlos Wu running his fingertips over a Kdatlyno touch sculpture.

A dark, slender man with narrow shoulders and straight black hair, Carlos was lithe as a monkey in any normal gravity; but on Jinx he used a travel couch exactly like mine. He studied the busts with his head tilted to one side. And I studied the familiar back, sure it couldn't be him.

"Carlos, aren't you supposed to be on Earth?"

He jumped. But when the couch spun around he was grinning. "Bey! I might say the same for you."

I admitted it. "I was headed for Earth, but when all those ships started disappearing around Sol system the captain changed his mind and steered for Sirius. Nothing any of the passengers could do about it. What about you? How are Sharrol and the kids?"

"Sharrol's fine, the kids are fine, and they're all waiting for you to come home." His fingers were still trailing over the Lloobee touch sculpture called *Heroes,* feeling the warm, fleshy textures. *Heroes* was a most unusual touch sculpture; there were visual as well as textural effects. Carlos studied the two human busts, then said, "That's *your* face, isn't it?"

"Yah."

"Not that you ever looked that good in your life. How did a Kdatlyno come to pick Beowulf Shaeffer as a classic hero? Was it your name? And who's the other guy?"

"I'll tell you about it sometime. Carlos, what are you doing *here?*"

"I . . . left Earth a couple of weeks after Louis was born." He was embarrassed. Why? "I haven't been off Earth in ten years. I needed the break."

But he'd left just before I was supposed to get home. And . . . hadn't someone once said that Carlos Wu had a touch of the flatland phobia? I began to understand what was wrong. "Carlos, you did Sharrol and me a valuable favor."

He laughed without looking at me. "Men have killed other men for such favors. I thought it was . . . tactful . . . to be gone when you came home."

Now I knew. Carlos was here because the Fertility Board on Earth would not favor me with a parenthood license.

You can't really blame the Board for using any excuse at all to reduce the number of producing parents. I am an albino. Sharrol and I wanted each other; but we both wanted children, and Sharrol can't leave Earth. She has the flatland phobia, the fear of strange air and altered days and changed gravity and black sky beneath her feet.

The only solution we'd found had been to ask a good friend to help.

Carlos Wu is a registered genius with an incredible resistance to disease and injury. He carries an unlimited parenthood license, one of sixty-odd among Earth's eighteen billion people. He gets similar offers every week . . . but he is a good friend, and he'd agreed. In the last two years Sharrol and Carlos had had two children, who were now waiting on Earth for me to become their father.

I felt only gratitude for what he'd done for us. "I forgive you your odd ideas on tact," I said magnanimously. "Now. As long as we're stuck on Jinx, may I show you around? I've met some interesting people."

"You always do." He hesitated, then "I'm not actually stuck on Jinx. I've been offered a ride home. I may be able to get you in on it."

"Oh, really? I didn't think there were any ships going to Sol system these days. Or leaving."

"The ship belongs to a government man. Ever heard of a Sigmund Ausfaller?"

"That sounds vaguely . . . Wait! Stop! The last time I saw Sigmund Ausfaller, he had just put a bomb aboard my ship!"

Carlos blinked at me. "You're kidding."

"I'm not."

"Sigmund Ausfaller is in the Bureau of Alien Affairs. Bombing spacecraft isn't one of his functions."

"Maybe he was off duty," I said viciously.

"Well, it doesn't really sound like you'd want to share a spacecraft cabin with him. Maybe—"

But I'd thought of something else, and now there just wasn't any way out of it. "No, let's meet him. Where do we find him?"

"The bar of the Camelot," said Carlos.

Reclining luxuriously on our travel couches, we slid on air cushions through Sirius Mater. The orange trees that lined the walks were foreshortened by gravity; their trunks were thick cones, and the oranges on the branches were not much bigger than Ping-Pong balls.

Their world had altered them, even as our worlds have altered you and me. And underground civilization and point six gravities have made of me a pale stick figure of a man, tall and attenuated. The Jinxians we passed were short and wide, designed like bricks, men and women both. Among them the occasional offworlder seemed as shockingly different as a Kdatlyno or a Pierson's Puppeteer.

And so we came to the Camelot.

The Camelot is a low, two-story structure that sprawls like a cubistic octopus across several acres of downtown Sirius Mater. Most offworlders stay here, for the gravity control in the rooms and corridors and for access to the Institute of Knowledge, the finest museum and research complex in human space.

The Camelot Bar carries one Earth gravity throughout. We left our travel couches in the vestibule and walked in like men. Jinxians were walking in like bouncing rubber bricks, with big happy grins on their wide faces. Jinxians love low gravity. A good many migrate to other worlds.

We spotted Ausfaller easily: a rounded, moon-faced flatlander with thick, dark, wavy hair and a thin black mustache. He stood as we approached. "Beowulf Shaeffer!" he beamed. "How good to see you again! I believe it has been eight years or thereabouts. How have you been?"

"I lived," I told him.

Carlos rubbed his hands together briskly. "Sigmund! Why did you bomb Bey's ship?"

Ausfaller blinked in surprise. "Did he tell you it was his ship? It wasn't. He was thinking of stealing it. I reasoned that he would not steal a ship with a hidden time bomb aboard."

"But how did you come into it?" Carlos slid into the booth beside him. "You're not police. You're in the Extremely Foreign Relations Bureau."

"The ship belonged to General Products Corporation, which is owned by Pierson's Puppeteers, not human beings."

Carlos turned on me. "Bey! Shame on you."

"Dammit! They were trying to blackmail me into a suicide mission! And Ausfaller let them get away with it! And that's the least convincing exhibition of tact I've ever seen!"

"Good thing they soundproof these booths," said Carlos. "Let's order."

Soundproofing field or not, people were staring. I sat down. When our drinks came I drank deep. Why had I mentioned the bomb at all?

Ausfaller was saying, "Well, Carlos, have you changed your mind about coming with me?"

"Yes, if I can take a friend."

Ausfaller frowned, looked at me. "You wish to reach Earth too?"

I'd made up my mind. "I don't think so. In fact, I'd like to talk you out of taking Carlos."

Carlos said, "Hey!"

I overrode him. "Ausfaller, do you know who Carlos *is?* He had an unlimited parenthood license at the age of eighteen. Eighteen! I don't mind you risking your own life, in fact I love the idea. But his?"

"It's not that big a risk!" Carlos snapped.

"Yah? What has Ausfaller got that eight other ships didn't have?"

"Two things," Ausfaller said patiently. "One is that we will be incoming. Six of the eight ships that vanished were *leaving* Sol system. If there are pirates around Sol, they must find it much easier to locate an outgoing ship."

"They caught two incoming. Two ships, fifty crew members and passengers, gone. Poof!"

"They would not take me so easily," Ausfaller boasted. "The *Hobo Kelly* is deceptive. It seems to be a cargo and passenger ship, but it is a warship, armed and capable of thirty gees acceleration. In normal space we can run from anything we can't fight. We are assuming pirates, are we not? Pirates would insist on robbing a ship before they destroy it."

I was intrigued. "Why? Why a disguised warship? Are you *hoping* you'll be attacked?"

"If there are actually pirates, yes, I hope to be attacked. But not when entering Sol system. We plan a substitution. A quite ordinary cargo craft will land on Earth, take on cargo of some value, and depart for Wunderland on a straight-line course. My ship will replace it before it has passed through the asteroids. So you see, there is no risk of losing Mr. Wu's precious genes."

Palms flat to the table, arms straight, Carlos stood looming over us. "Diffidently I raise the point that they are my futzy genes and I'll do what I futzy please with them! Bey, I've already had my share of children, and yours too!"

"Peace, Carlos. I didn't mean to step on any of your inalienable rights." I turned to Ausfaller. "I still don't see why these disappearing ships should interest the Extremely Foreign Relations Bureau."

"There were alien passengers aboard some of the ships."

"Oh."

"And we have wondered if the pirates themselves are aliens. Certainly they have a technique not known to humanity. Of six outgoing ships, five vanished after reporting that they were about to enter hyperdrive."

I whistled. "They can precipitate a ship out of hyperdrive? That's impossible. Isn't it? Carlos?"

Carlos' mouth twisted. "Not if it's being done. But I don't understand the principle. If the ships were just disappearing, that'd be different. Any ship does that if it goes too deep into a gravity well on hyperdrive."

"Then . . . maybe it isn't pirates at all. Carlos, could there be living beings in hyperspace, actually eating the ships?"

"For all of me, there could. I don't know everything, Bey, contrary to popular opinion." But after a minute he shook his head. "I don't buy it. I might buy an uncharted mass on the fringes of Sol system. Ships that came too near in hyperdrive would disappear."

"No," said Ausfaller. "No single mass could have caused all of the disappearances. Charter or not, a planet is bounded by gravity and inertia. We ran computer simulations. It would have taken at least three large masses, all unknown, all moving into heavy trade routes, simultaneously."

"How large? Mars size or better?"

"So you have been thinking about this too."

Carlos smiled. "Yah. It may sound impossible, but it isn't. It's only improbable. There are unbelievable amounts of garbage out there beyond Neptune. Four known planets and endless chunks of ice and stone and nickel-iron."

"Still, it is most improbable."

Carlos nodded. A silence fell.

I was still thinking about monsters in hyperspace. The lovely thing about that hypothesis was that you couldn't even estimate a probability. We knew too little.

Humanity has been using hyperdrive for almost four hundred years now. Few ships have disappeared in that time, except during wars. Now, eight ships in ten months, all around Sol system.

Suppose one hyperspace beast had discovered ships in this region, say during one of the Man–Kzin Wars? He'd gone to get his friends. Now they were preying around Sol system. The flow of ships around Sol is greater than that around any three colony stars. But if more monsters came, they'd surely have to move on to the other colonies.

I couldn't imagine a defense against such things. We might have to give up interstellar travel.

Ausfaller said, "I would be glad if you would change your mind and come with us, Mr. Shaeffer."

"Um? Are you sure you want me on the same ship with you?"

"Oh, emphatically! How else may I be sure that you have not hidden a bomb aboard?" Ausfaller laughed. "Also, we can use a qualified pilot. Finally, I would like the chance to pick your brain, Beowulf Shaeffer. You have an odd facility for doing my job for me."

"What do you mean by that?"

"General Products used blackmail in persuading you to do a close orbit around a neutron star. You learned something about their home world—we still do not know what it was—and blackmailed them back. We know that blackmail contracts are a normal part of Puppeteer business practice. You earned their respect. You have dealt with them since. You have dealt also with Outsider, without friction. But it was your handling of the Lloobee kidnapping that I found impressive."

Carlos was sitting at attention. I hadn't had a chance to tell him about that one yet. I grinned and said, "I'm proud of that myself."

"Well you should be. You did more than retrieve known space's top Kdatlyno touch sculptor: you did it with honor, killing one of their number and leaving Lloobee free to pursue the others with publicity. Otherwise the Kdatlyno would have been annoyed."

Helping Sigmund Ausfaller had been the farthest thing from my thoughts for these past eight years; yet suddenly I felt damn good. Maybe it was the way Carlos was listening. It takes a lot to impress Carlos Wu.

Carlos said, "If you thought it was pirates, you'd come along, wouldn't you, Bey? After all, they probably can't *find* incoming ships."

"Sure."

"And you don't really believe in hyperspace monsters."

I hedged. "Not if I hear a better explanation. The thing is, I'm not sure I believe in supertechnological pirates either. What about those wandering masses?"

Carlos pursed his lips, said, "All right. The solor system has a good number of planets—at least a dozen so far discovered, four of them outside the major singularity around Sol."

"And not including Pluto?"

"No, we think of Pluto as a loose moon of Neptune. It runs *Neptune, Persephone, Caïna, Antenora, Ptolemea,* in order of distance from the sun. And the orbits aren't flat to the plane of the system. Persephone is tilted at a hundred and twenty degrees to the system, and retrograde. If they find another planet out there they'll call it *Judecca."*

"Why?"

"Hell. The four innermost divisions of Dante's Hell. They form a great ice plain with sinners frozen into it."

"Stick to the point," said Ausfaller.

"Start with the cometary halo," Carlos told me. "It's very thin: about one comet per spherical volume of the Earth's orbit. Mass is denser going inward: a few planets, some inner comets, some chunks of ice and rock, all in skewed orbits and still spread pretty thin. Inside Neptune there are lots of planets and asteroids and more flattening of orbits to conform with Sol's rotation. Outside Neptune space is vast and empty. There *could* be uncharted planets. Singularities to swallow ships."

Ausfaller was indignant. "But for three to move into main trade lanes simultaneously?"

"It's not impossible, Sigmund."

"The probability—"

"Infinitesimal, right. Bey, it's damn near impossible. Any sane man would assume pirates."

It had been a long time since I had seen Sharrol. I was sore tempted. "Ausfaller, have you traced the sale of any of the loot? Have you gotten any ransom notes?" *Convince me!*

Ausfaller threw back his head and laughed.

"What's funny?"

"We have hundreds of ransom notes. Any mental deficient can write a ransom note, and these disappearances have had a good deal of publicity. The demands were all fakes. I wish one or another had been genuine. A son of the Patriarch of Kzin was aboard *Wayfarer* when she disappeared. As for loot—hmm. There has been a fall in the black market prices of boosterspice and gem woods. Otherwise—" He shrugged. "There has been no sign of the Barr originals or the Midas Rock or any of the more conspicuous treasures aboard the missing ships."

"Then you don't know one way or another."

"No. Will you go with us?"

"I haven't decided yet. When are you leaving?"

They'd be taking off tomorrow morning from the East End. That gave me time to make up my mind.

After dinner I went back to my room, feeling depressed. Carlos was going, that was clear enough. Hardly my fault . . . but he was here on Jinx because he'd done me and Sharrol a large favor. If he was killed going home . . .

A tape from Sharrol was waiting in my room. There were pictures of the children, Tanya and Louis, and shots of the apartment she'd found us in the Twin Peaks arcology, and much more.

I ran through it three times. Then I called Ausfaller's room. It had been just too futzy long.

I circled Jinx once on the way out. I've always done that, even back when I was flying for Nakamura Lines; and no passenger has ever objected.

Jinx is the close moon of a gas giant planet more massive than Jupiter, and smaller than Jupiter because its core has been compressed to degenerate matter. A billion years ago Jinx and Primary were even closer, before tidal drag moved them apart. This same tidal force had earlier locked Jinx's rotation to Primary and forced the moon into an egg shape, a prolate spheroid. When the moon moved outward its shape became more nearly spherical; but the cold rock surface resisted change.

That is why the ocean of Jinx rings its waist, beneath an atmosphere too compressed and too hot to breathe; whereas the points nearest to and farthest from Primary, the East and West Ends, actually rise out of the atmosphere.

From space Jinx looks like God's Own Easter Egg: the Ends bone white tinged with yellow; then the brighter glare from rings of glittering ice fields at the limits of the atmosphere; then the varying blues of an Earthlike world, increasingly overlaid with the white frosting of cloud as the eyes move inward, until the waist of the planet/moon is girdled with pure white. The ocean never shows at all.

I took us once around, and out.

Sirius has its own share of floating miscellaneous matter cluttering the path to interstellar space. I stayed at the controls for most of five days, for that reason and because I wanted to get the feel of an unfamiliar ship.

Hobo Kelly was a belly-landing job, three hundred feet long, of triangular cross section. Beneath an uptilted, forward-thrusting nose were big clamshell doors for cargo. She had adequate belly jets and a much larger fusion motor at the tail, and a line of windows indicating cabins. Certainly she looked harmless enough; and certainly there was deception involved. The cabin should have held forty or fifty, but there was room only for four. The rest of what should have been cabin space was only windows with holograph projections in them.

The drive ran sure and smooth up to a maximum at ten gravities: not a lot for a ship designed to haul massive cargo. The cabin gravity held without putting out more than a fraction of its power. When Jinx and Primary were invisible against the stars, when Sirius was so distant I could look directly at it, I turned to the hidden control panel Ausfaller had unlocked for me. Ausfaller woke up, found me doing that, and began showing me which did what.

He had a big X-ray laser and some smaller laser cannon set for different frequencies. He had four self-guided fusion bombs. He had a telescope so good that the ostensible ship's telescope was only a finder for it. He had deep-radar.

And none of it showed beyond the discolored hull.

Ausfaller was armed for Bandersnatchi. I felt mixed emotions. It seemed we could fight anything, and run from it too. But what kind of enemy was he expecting?

All through those four weeks in hyperdrive, while we drove through the Blind Spot at three days to the light-year, the topic of the ship eaters reared its disturbing head.

Oh, we spoke of other things: of music and art, and of the latest techniques in animation, the computer programs that let you make your own holo flicks almost for lunch money. We told stories. I told Carlos why the Kdatlyno Lloobee had made busts of me and Emil Horne. I spoke of the only time the Pierson's Puppeteers had ever paid off the guarantee on a General Products hull, after the supposedly indestructible hull had been destroyed by antimatter. Ausfaller had some good ones . . . a lot more stories than he was allowed to tell, I gathered, from the way he had to search his memory every time.

But we kept coming back to the ship eaters.

"It boils down to three possibilities," I decided. "Kzinti, Puppeteers, and Humans."

Carlos guffawed. "Puppeteers? Puppeteers wouldn't have the guts!"

"I threw them in because they might have some interest in manipulating the interstellar stock market. Look: our hypothetical pirates have set up an embargo, cutting Sol system off from the outside world. The Puppeteers have the capital to take advantage of what that does to the market. And they need money. For their migration."

"The Puppeteers are philosophical cowards."

"That's right. They wouldn't risk robbing the ships, or coming anywhere near them. Suppose they can make them disappear from a distance?"

Carlos wasn't laughing now. "That's easier than dropping them out of hyperspace to rob them. It wouldn't take more than a great big gravity generator . . . and we've never known the limits of Puppeteer technology."

Ausfaller asked, "You think this is possible?"

"Just barely. The same goes for the Kzinti. The Kzinti are ferocious enough. Trouble is, if we ever learned they were preying on our ships we'd raise pluperfect hell. The Kzinti know that, and they know we can beat them. Took them long enough, but they learned."

"So you think it's Humans," said Carlos.

"Yah. If it's pirates."

The piracy theory still looked shaky. Spectrum telescopes had not even found concentrations of ship's metals in the space where they have vanished. Would pirates steal the whole ship? If the hyperdrive motor were still intact after the attack, the rifled ship could be launched into infinity; but could pirates count on that happening eight times out of eight?

And none of the missing ships had called for help via hyperwave.

I'd never believed pirates. Space pirates have existed, but they died without successors. Intercepting a spacecraft was too difficult. They couldn't make it pay.

Ships fly themselves in hyperdrive. All a pilot need do is watch for green radial lines in the mass sensor. But he has to do that frequently, because the mass sensor is a psionic device; it must be watched by a mind, not another machine.

As the narrow green line that marked Sol grew longer, I became abnormally conscious of the debris around Sol system. I spent the last twelve hours of the flight at the controls, chain-smoking with my feet. I should add that I do that normally, when I want both hands free; but now I did it to annoy Ausfaller. I'd seen the way his eyes bugged the first time he saw me take a drag from a cigarette between my toes. Flatlanders are less than limber.

Carlos and Ausfaller shared the control room with me as we penetrated Sol's cometary halo. They were relieved to be nearing the end of a long trip. I was nervous. "Carlos, just how large a mass would it take to make us disappear?"

"Planet size, Mars and up. Beyond that it depends on how close you get and how dense it is. If it's dense enough it can be less massive and still flip you out of the universe. But you'd see it in the mass sensor."

"Only for an instant . . . and not then, if it's turned off. What if someone turned on a giant gravity generator as we went past?"

"For what? They couldn't rob the ship. Where's their profit?"

"Stocks."

But Ausfaller was shaking his head. "The expense of such an operation would be enormous. No group of pirates would have enough additional capital on hand to make it worthwhile. Of the Puppeteers I might believe it."

Hell, he was right. No Human that wealthy would need to turn pirate.

The long green line marking Sol was almost touching the surface of the mass sensor. I said, "Breakout in ten minutes."

And the ship lurched savagely.

"Strap down!" I yelled, and glanced at the hyperdrive monitors. The motor was drawing no power, and the rest of the dials were going bananas.

I activated the windows. I'd kept them turned off in hyperspace, lest my flatlander passengers go mad watching the Blind Spot. The screens came on and I saw stars. We were in normal space.

"Futz! They got us anyway." Carlos sounded neither frightened nor angry, but awed.

As I raised the hidden panel Ausfaller cried, "Wait!" I ignored him. I threw the red switch, and *Hobo Kelly* lurched again as her belly blew off.

Ausfaller began cursing in some dead flatlander language.

Now two-thirds of *Hobo Kelly* receded, slowly turning. What was left must show as what she was: a Number Two General

Products hull, Puppeteer-built, a slender transparent spear three hundred feet long and twenty feet wide, with instruments of war clustered along what was now her belly. Screens that had been blank came to life. And I lit the main drive and ran it up to full power.

Ausfaller spoke in rage and venom. "Shaeffer, you idiot, you coward! We run without knowing what we run from. Now they know exactly what we are. What chance that they will follow us now? This ship was built for a specific purpose, and you have ruined it!"

"I've freed your special instruments," I pointed out. "Why don't you see what you can find?" Meanwhile I could get us the futz out of here.

Ausfaller became very busy. I watched what he was getting on screens at my side of the control panel. Was anything chasing us? They'd find us hard to catch and harder to digest. They could hardly have been expecting a General Products hull. Since the Puppeteers stopped making them the price of used GP hulls has gone out of sight.

There *were* ships out there. Ausfaller got a close-up of them: three space tugs of the Belter type, shaped like thick saucers, equipped with oversized drives and powerful electromagnetic generators. Belters use them to tug nickel-iron asteroids to where somebody wants the ore. With those heavy drives they could probably catch us; but would they have adequate cabin gravity?

They weren't trying. They seemed to be neither following nor fleeing. And they looked harmless enough.

But Ausfaller was doing a job on them with his other instruments. I approved. *Hobo Kelly* had looked peaceful enough a moment ago. Now her belly bristled with weaponry. The tugs could be equally deceptive.

From behind me Carlos asked, "Bey? What happened?"

"How the futz would I know?"

"What do the instruments show?"

He must mean the hyperdrive complex. A couple of the indicators had gone wild; five more were dead. I said so. "And the drive's drawing no power at all. I've never heard of anything like this. Carlos, it's *still* theoretically impossible."

"I'm . . . not so sure of that. I want to look at the drive."

"The access tubes don't have cabin gravity."

Ausfaller had abandoned the receding tugs. He'd found what looked to be a large comet, a ball of frozen gasses a good distance to the side. I watched as he ran the deep-radar over it. No fleet of robber ships lurked behind it.

I asked, "Did you deep-radar the tugs?"

"Of course. We can examine the tapes in detail later. I saw nothing. And nothing has attacked us since we left hyperspace."

I'd been driving us in a random direction. Now I turned us toward Sol, the brightest star in the heavens. Those lost ten minutes in hyperspace would add about three days to our voyage.

"If there was an enemy, you frightened him away. Shaeffer, this mission and this ship have cost my department an enormous sum, and we have learned nothing at all."

"Not quite nothing," said Carlos. "I still want to see the hyperdrive motor. Bey, would you run us down to one gee?"

"Yah. But . . . miracles make me nervous, Carlos."

"Join the club."

We crawled along an access tube just a little bigger than a big man's shoulders, between the hyperdrive motor housing and the surrounding fuel tankage. Carlos reached an inspection window. He looked in. He started to laugh.

I inquired as to what was so futzy funny.

Still chortling, Carlos moved on. I crawled after him and looked in.

There was no hyperdrive motor in the hyperdrive motor housing.

I went in through a repair hatch and stood in the cylindrical housing, looking about me. Nothing. Not even an exit hole. The superconducting cables and the mounts for the motor had been sheared so cleanly that the cut ends looked like little mirrors.

Ausfaller insisted on seeing for himself. Carlos and I waited in the control room. For a while Carlos kept bursting into fits of giggles. Then he got a dreamy, faraway look that was even more annoying.

I wondered what was going on in his head, and reached the

uncomfortable conclusion that I could never know. Some years ago I took IQ tests, hoping to get a parenthood license that way. I am not a genius.

I knew only that Carlos had thought of something I hadn't, and he wasn't telling, and I was too proud to ask.

Ausfaller had no pride. He came back looking like he'd seen a ghost. "Gone! Where could it go? How could it happen?"

"That I can answer," Carlos said happily. "It takes an extremely high gravity gradient. The motor hit that, wrapped space around itself, and took off at some higher level of hyperdrive, one we can't reach. By now it could be well on its way to the edge of the universe."

I said, "You're sure, huh? An hour ago there wasn't a theory to cover any of this."

"Well, I'm sure our motor's gone. Beyond that it gets a little hazy. But this is one well-established model of what happens when a ship hits a singularity. At a lower gravity gradient the motor would take the whole ship with it, then strew atoms of the ship along its path till there was nothing left but the hyperdrive field itself."

"Ugh."

Now Carlos burned with the love of an idea. "Sigmund, I want to use your hyperwave. I could still be wrong, but there are things we can check."

"If we are still within the singularity of some mass, the hyperwave will destroy itself."

"Yah. I think it's worth the risk."

We'd dropped out, or been knocked out, ten minutes short of the singularity around Sol. That added up to sixteen light-hours of normal space, plus almost five light-hours from the edge of the singularity inward to Earth. Fortunately hyperwave is instantaneous, and every civilized system keeps a hyperwave relay station just outside the singularity. Southworth Station would relay our message inward by laser, get the return message the same way, and pass it on to us ten hours later.

We turned on the hyperwave and nothing exploded.

Ausfaller made his own call first, to Ceres, to get the registry of the tugs we'd spotted. Afterward Carlos called Elephant's computer setup in New York, using a code number Elephant doesn't give to many people. "I'll pay him back later. Maybe with a story to go with it," he gloated.

I listened as Carlos outlined his needs. He wanted full records on a meteorite that had touched down in Tunguska, Siberia, U.S.S.R., Earth, in 1908 A.D. He wanted a reprise on three models of the origin of the universe or lack of same: the Big Bang, the Cyclic Universe, the Steady State Universe. He wanted data on collapsars. He wanted names, career outlines, and addresses for the best-known students of gravitational phenomena in Sol system. He was smiling when he clicked off.

I said, "You got me. I haven't the remotest idea what you're after."

Still smiling, Carlos got up and went to his cabin to catch some sleep.

I turned off the main thrust motor entirely. When we were deep in Sol system we could decelerate at thirty gravities. Meanwhile we were carrying a hefty velocity picked up on our way out of Sirius system.

Ausfaller stayed in the control room. Maybe his motive was the same as mine. No police ships out here. We could still be attacked.

He spent the time going through his pictures of the three mining tugs. We didn't talk, but I watched.

The tugs seemed ordinary enough. Telescopic photos showed no suspicious breaks in the hulls, no hatches for guns. In the deep-radar scan they showed like ghosts: we could pick out the massive force-field rings, the hollow, equally massive drive tubes, the lesser densities of fuel tank and life-support system. There were no gaps or shadows that shouldn't have been there.

By and by Ausfaller said, "Do you know what *Hobo Kelly* was worth?"

I said I could make a close estimate.

"It was worth my career. I thought to destroy a pirate fleet with *Hobo Kelly.* But my pilot fled. Fled! What have I now, to show for my expensive Trojan Horse?"

I suppressed the obvious answer, along with the plea that my first responsibility was Carlos' life. Ausfaller wouldn't buy that. Instead: "Carlos has something. I know him. He knows how it happened."

"Can you get it out of him?"

"I don't know." I could put it to Carlos that we'd be safer if we knew what was out to get us. But Carlos was a flatlander. It would color his attitudes.

"So," said Ausfaller. "We have only the unavailable knowledge in Carlos' skull."

A weapon beyond human technology had knocked me out of hyperspace. I'd run. Of *course* I'd run. Staying in the neighborhood would have been insane, said I to myself, said I. But, unreasonably, I still felt bad about it.

To Ausfaller I said, "What about the mining tugs? I can't understand what they're doing out here. In the Belt they use them to move nickle-iron asteroids to industrial sites."

"It is the same here. Most of what they find is useless: stony masses or balls of ice; but what little metal there is, is valuable. They must have it for building."

"For building what? What kind of people would live here? You might as well set up shop in interstellar space!"

"Precisely. There are no tourists, but there are research groups, here where space is flat and empty and temperatures are near absolute zero. I know that the Quicksilver Group was established here to study hyperspace phenomena. We do not understand hyperspace, even yet. Remember that we did not invent the hyperdrive; we bought it from an alien race. Then there is a gene-tailoring laboratory trying to develop a kind of tree that will grow on comets."

"You're kidding."

"But they are serious. A photosynthetic plant to use the chemicals present in all comets . . . it would be very valuable. The whole cometary halo could be seeded with oxygen-producing plants—" Ausfaller stopped abruptly, then "Never mind. But all these groups need building materials. It is cheaper to build out here than to ship everything from Earth or the Belt. The presence of tugs is not suspicious."

"But there was nothing else around us. Nothing at all."

Ausfaller nodded.

When Carlos came to join us many hours later, blinking sleep out of his eyes, I asked him, "Carlos, could the tugs have had anything to do with your theory?"

"I don't see how. I've got half an idea, and half an hour from now I could look like a half-wit. The theory I want isn't even in fashion anymore. Now that we know what the quasars are, everyone seems to like the Steady State Hypothesis. You know how that works: the tension in completely empty space produces more hydrogen atoms, forever. The universe has no beginning and no end." He looked stubborn. "But if I'm right, then I know where the ships went to after being robbed. That's more than anyone else knows."

Ausfaller jumped on him. "Where are they? Are the passengers alive?"

"I'm sorry, Sigmund. They're all dead. There won't even be bodies to bury."

"What is it? What are we fighting?"

"A gravitational effect. A sharp warping of space. A planet wouldn't do that, and a battery of cabin gravity generators wouldn't do it; they couldn't produce that sharply bounded a field."

"A collapsar," Ausfaller suggested.

Carlos grinned at him. "That would do it, but there are other problems. A collapsar can't even form at less than around five solar masses. You'd think someone would have noticed something that big, this close to Sol."

"Then *what?*"

Carlos shook his head. We would wait.

The relay from Southworth Station gave us registration for three space tugs, used and of varying ages, all three purchased two years ago from IntraBelt Mining by the Sixth Congregational Church of Rodney.

"Rodney?"

But Carlos and Ausfaller were both chortling. "Belters do that sometimes," Carlos told me. "It's a way of saying it's nobody's business who's buying the ships."

"That's pretty funny, all right, but we still don't know who owns them."

"They may be honest Belters. They may not."

Hard on the heels of the first call came the data Carlos had asked for, playing directly into the shipboard computer. Carlos called up a list of names and phone numbers: Sol system's preeminent students of gravity and its effects, listed in alphabetical order.

An address caught my attention:

Julian Forward, #1192326 Southworth Station.

A hyperwave relay tag. He was out *here,* somewhere in the enormous gap between Neptune's orbit and the cometary belt, out here where the hyperwave relay could function. I looked for more Southworth Station numbers. They were there:

Launcelot Starkey, #1844719 Southworth Station.

Jill Luciano, #1844719 Southworth Station.

Mariana Wilton, #1844719 Southworth Station.

"These people," said Ausfaller. "You wish to discuss your theory with one of them?"

"That's right. Sigmund, isn't 1844719 the tag for the Quicksilver Group?"

"I think so. I also think that they are not within our reach, now that our hyperdrive is gone. The Quicksilver Group was established in distant orbit around Antenora, which is now on the other side of the sun. Carlos, has it occurred to you that one of these people may have built the ship-eating device?"

"What? . . . You're right. It would take someone who knew something about gravity. But I'd say the Quicksilver Group was beyond suspicion. With upwards of ten thousand people at work, how could anyone hide anything?"

"What about this Julian Forward?"

"Forward. Yah. I've always wanted to meet him."

"You know of him? Who is he?"

"He used to be with the Institute of Knowledge on Jinx. I haven't heard of him in years. He did some work on the gravity waves from the galactic core . . . work that turned out to be wrong. Sigmund, let's give him a call."

"And ask him what?"

"Why . . . ?" Then Carlos remembered the situation. "Oh. You think he might—yah."

"How well do you know this man?"

"I know him by reputation. He's quite famous. I don't see how such a man could go in for mass murder."

"Earlier you said that we were looking for a man skilled in the study of gravitational phenomena."

"Granted."

Ausfaller sucked at his lower lip. Then "Perhaps we can do no more than talk to him. He could be on the other side of the sun and still head a pirate fleet—"

"No. That he could not."

"Think again," said Ausfaller. "We are outside the singularity of Sol. A pirate fleet would surely include hyperdrive ships."

"If Julian Forward is the ship eater, he'll have to be nearby. The, uh, device won't move in hyperspace."

I said, "Carlos, what we don't know can kill us. Will you quit playing games—" But he was smiling, shaking his head. Futz. "All right, we can still check on Forward. Call him up and ask where he is! Is he likely to know you by reputation?"

"Sure. I'm famous too."

"Okay. If he's close enough, we might even beg him for a ride home. The way things stand we'll be at the mercy of any hyperdrive ship for as long as we're out here."

"I hope we are attacked," said Ausfaller. "We can outfight—"

"But we can't outrun. They can dodge, we can't."

"Peace, you two. First things first." Carlos sat down at the hyperwave controls and tapped out a number.

Suddenly Ausfaller said, "Can you contrive to keep my name out of this exchange? If necessary you can be the ship's owner."

Carlos looked around in surprise. Before he could answer, the screen lit. I saw ash-blond hair cut in a Belter crest, over a lean white face and an impersonal smile.

"Forward Station. Good evening."

"Good evening. This is Carlos Wu of Earth calling long-distance. May I speak to Dr. Julian Forward, please?"

"I'll see if he's available." The screen went on HOLD.

In the interval Carlos burst out: "What kind of game are *you* playing now? How can I explain owning an armed, disguised warship?"

But I began to see what Ausfaller was getting at. I said, "You'd want to avoid explaining that, whatever the truth was. Maybe he won't ask. I—" I shut up, because we were facing Forward.

Julian Forward was a Jinxian, short and wide, with arms as thick as legs and legs as thick as pillars. His skin was almost as black as his hair: a Sirius suntan, probably maintained by sunlights. He perched on the edge of a massage chair. "Carlos Wu!" he said with flattering enthusiasm. "Are you the same Carlos Wu who solved the Sealeyham Limits Problem?"

Carlos said he was. They went into a discussion of mathematics —a possible application of Carlos' solution to another limits problem, I gathered. I glanced at Ausfaller—not obtrusively, because for Forward he wasn't supposed to exist—and saw him pensively studying his side view of Forward.

"Well," Forward said, "what can I do for you?"

"Julian Forward, meet Beowulf Shaeffer," said Carlos. I bowed. "Bey was giving me a lift home when our hyperdrive motor disappeared."

"Disappeared?"

I butted in, for verisimilitude. "Disappeared, futzy right. The hyperdrive motor casing is empty. The motor supports are sheared off. We're stuck out here with no hyperdrive and no idea how it happened."

"Almost true," Carlos said happily. "Dr. Forward, I do have some ideas as to what happened here. I'd like to discuss them with you."

"Where are you now?"

I pulled our position and velocity from the computer and flashed them to Forward Station. I wasn't sure it was a good idea; but Ausfaller had time to stop me, and he didn't.

"Fine," said Forward's image. "It looks like you can get here a lot faster than you can get to Earth. Forward Station is ahead of you, within twenty a.u. of your position. You can wait here for the next ferry. Better than going on in a crippled ship."

"Good! We'll work out a course and let you know when to expect us."

"I welcome the chance to meet Carlos Wu." Forward gave us his own coordinates and rang off.

Carlos turned. "All right, Bey. Now *you* own an armed and disguised warship. *You* figure out where you got it."

"We've got worse problems than that. Forward Station is exactly where the ship eater ought to be."

He nodded. But he was amused.

"So what's our next move? We can't run from hyperdrive ships. Not now. Is Forward likely to try to kill us?"

"If we don't reach Forward Station on schedule, he might send ships after us. We know too much. We've told him so," said Carlos. "The hyperdrive motor disappeared completely. I know half a dozen people who could figure out how it happened, knowing just that." He smiled suddenly. "That's assuming Forward's the ship eater. We don't know that. I think we have a splendid chance to find out, one way or the other."

"How? Just walk in?"

Ausfaller was nodding approvingly. "Dr. Forward expects you and Carlos to enter his web unsuspecting, leaving an empty ship. I think we can prepare a few surprises for him. For example, he may not have guessed that this is a General Products hull. And I will be aboard to fight."

True. Only antimatter could harm a GP hull . . . though things could go through it, like light and gravity and shock waves. "So you'll be in the indestructible hull," I said, "and we'll be helpless in the base. Very clever. I'd rather run for it myself. But then, you have your career to consider."

"I will not deny it. But there are ways in which I can prepare you."

Behind Ausfaller's cabin, behind what looked like an unbroken wall, was a room the size of a walk-in closet. Ausfaller seemed quite proud of it. He didn't show us everything in there, but I saw enough to cost me what remained of my first impression of Ausfaller. This man did not have the soul of a pudgy bureaucrat.

Behind a glass panel he kept a couple of dozen special-purpose weapons. A row of four clamps held three identical hand weapons, disposable rocket launchers for a fat slug that Ausfaller billed as a tiny atomic bomb. The fourth clamp was empty. There were laser rifles and pistols; a shotgun of peculiar design, with four inches of recoil shock absorber; throwing knives; an Olympic target pistol with a sculpted grip and room for just one .22 bullet.

I wondered what he was doing with a hobbyist's touch-sculpting setup. Maybe he could make sculptures to drive a Human or an alien mad. Maybe something less subtle; maybe they'd explode at the touch of the right fingerprints.

He had a compact automated tailor's shop. "I'm going to make you some new suits," he said. When Carlos asked why, he said, "You can keep secrets? So can I."

He asked us for our preference in styles. I played it straight, asking for a falling jumper in green and silver, with lots of pockets. It wasn't the best I've ever owned, but it fitted.

"I didn't ask for buttons," I told him.

"I hope you don't mind. Carlos, you will have buttons too."

Carlos chose a fiery red tunic with a green-and-gold dragon coiling across the back. The buttons carried his family monogram. Ausfaller stood before us, examining us in our new finery, with approval.

"Now, watch," he said. "Here I stand before you, unarmed—"

"Right."

"*Sure* you are."

Ausfaller grinned. He took the top and bottom buttons between his fingers and tugged hard. They came off. The material between them ripped open as if a thread had been strung between them.

Holding the buttons as if to keep an invisible thread taut, he moved them on either side of a crudely done plastic touch sculpture. The sculpture fell apart.

"Sinclair molecule chain. It will cut through any normal matter, if you pull hard enough. You must be very careful. It will cut your fingers so easily that you will hardly notice they are gone. Notice that the buttons are large, to give an easy grip." He laid the buttons carefully on a table and set a heavy weight between them. "This third button down is a sonic grenade. Ten feet away it will kill. Thirty feet away it will stun."

I said, "Don't demonstrate."

"You may want to practice throwing dummy buttons at a target. This second button is Power Pill, the commercial stimulant. Break the button and take half when you need it. The entire dose may stop your heart."

"I never heard of Power Pill. How does it work on crashlanders?"

He was taken aback. "I don't know. Perhaps you had better restrict yourself to a quarter dose."

"Or avoid it entirely," I said.

"There is one more thing I will not demonstrate. Feel the

material of your garments. You feel three layers of material? The middle layer is a nearly perfect mirror. It will reflect even X rays. Now you can repel a laser blast, for at least the first second. The collar unrolls to a hood."

Carlos was nodding in satisfaction.

I guess it's true: all flatlanders think that way.

For a billion and a half years, humanity's ancestors had evolved to the conditions of one world: Earth. A flatlander grows up in an environment peculiarly suited to him. Instinctively he sees the whole universe the same way.

We know better, we who were born on other worlds. On We Made It there are the hellish winds of summer and winter. On Jinx, the gravity. On Plateau, the all-encircling cliff edge, and a drop of forty miles into unbearable heat and pressure. On Down, the red sunlight, and plants that will not grow without help from untraviolet lamps.

But flatlanders think the universe was made for their benefit. To them, danger is unreal.

"Earplugs," said Ausfaller, holding up a handful of soft plastic cylinders.

We inserted them. Ausfaller said, "Can you hear me?"

"Sure." "Yah." They didn't block our hearing at all.

"Transmitter and hearing aid, with sonic padding between. If you are blasted with sound, as by an explosion or a sonic stunner, the hearing aid will stop transmitting. If you go suddenly deaf you will know you are under attack."

To me, Ausfaller's elaborate precautions only spoke of what we might be walking into. I said nothing. If we ran for it our chances were even worse.

Back to the control room, where Ausfaller set up a relay to the Alien Affairs Bureau on Earth. He gave them a condensed version of what had happened to us, plus some cautious speculation. He invited Carlos to read his theories into the record.

Carlos declined. "I could still be wrong. Give me a chance to do some studying."

Ausfaller went grumpily to his bunk. He had been up too long, and it showed.

Carlos shook his head as Ausfaller disappeared into his cabin. "Paranoia. In his job I guess he has to be paranoid."

"You could use some of that yourself."

He didn't hear me. "Imagine suspecting an interstellar celebrity of being a space pirate!"

"He's in the right place at the right time."

"Hey, Bey, forget what I said. The, uh, ship-eating device has to be in the right place, but the pirates don't. They can just leave it loose and use hyperdrive ships to commute to their base."

That was something to keep in mind. Compared to the inner system this volume within the cometary halo was enormous; but to hyperdrive ships it was all one neighborhood. I said, "Then why are we visiting Forward?"

"I still want to check my ideas with him. More than that: he probably knows the head ship eater, without knowing it's him. Probably we both know him. It took something of a cosmologist to find the device and recognize it. Whoever it is, he has to have made something of a name for himself."

"Find?"

Carlos grinned at me. "Never mind. Have you thought of anyone you'd like to use that magic wire on?"

"I've been making a list. You're at the top."

"Well, watch it. Sigmund knows you've got it, even if nobody else does."

"He's second."

"How long till we reach Forward Station?"

I'd been rechecking our course. We were decelerating at thirty gravities and veering to one side. "Twenty hours and a few minutes," I said.

"Good. I'll get a chance to do some studying." He began calling up data from the computer.

I asked permission to read over his shoulder. He gave it.

Bastard. He reads twice as fast as I do. I tried to skim, to get some idea of what he was after.

Collapsars: three known. The nearest was one component of a double in Cygnus, more than a hundred light-years away. Expeditions had gone there to drop probes.

The theory of the black hole wasn't new to me, though the math was over my head. If a star is massive enough, then after it has burned its nuclear fuel and started to cool, no possible internal force can hold it from collapsing inward past its own Swartzchild radius. At that point the escape velocity from the star becomes greater than lightspeed; and beyond that deponent sayeth not, because nothing can leave the star, not information, not matter, not radiation. Nothing—except gravity.

Such a collapsed star can be expected to weigh five solar masses or more; otherwise its collapse would stop at the neutron star stage. Afterward it can only grow bigger and more massive.

There wasn't the slightest chance of finding anything that massive out here at the edge of the solar system. If such a thing were anywhere near, the sun would have been in orbit around it.

The Siberia meteorite must have been weird enough, to be remembered for nine hundred years. It had knocked down trees over thousands of square miles; yet trees near the touchdown point were left standing. No part of the meteorite itself had ever been found. Nobody had seen it hit. In 1908, Tunguska, Siberia, must have been as sparsely settled as the Earth's moon today.

"Carlos, what does all this have to do with anything?"

"Does Holmes tell Watson?"

I had real trouble following the cosmology. Physics verged on philosophy here, or vice versa. Basically the Big Bang Theory—which pictures the universe as exploding from a single point-mass, like a titanic bomb—was in competition with the Steady State Universe, which has been going on forever and will continue to do so. The Cyclic Universe is a succession of Big Bangs followed by contractions. There are variants on all of them.

When the quasars were first discovered, they seemed to date from an earlier stage in the evolution of the universe . . . which, by the Steady State hypothesis, would not be evolving at all. The Steady State went out of fashion. Then, a century ago, Hilbury had solved the mystery of the quasars. Meanwhile one of the implications of the Big Bang had not panned out. That was where the math got beyond me.

There was some discussion of whether the universe was open or closed in four-space, but Carlos turned it off. "Okay," he said, with satisfaction.

"What?"

"I could be right. Insufficient data. I'll have to see what Forward thinks."

"I hope you both choke. I'm going to sleep."

Out here in the broad borderland between Sol system and interstellar space, Julian Forward had found a stony mass the size of a middling asteroid. From a distance it seemed untouched by technology: a lopsided spheroid, rough-surfaced and dirty white. Closer in, flecks of metal and bright paint showed like randomly placed jewels. Airlocks, windows, projecting antennae, and things less identifiable. A lighted disk with something projecting from the center: a long metal arm with half a dozen ball joints in it and a cup on the end. I studied that one, trying to guess what it might be . . . and gave up.

I brought *Hobo Kelly* to rest a fair distance away. To Ausfaller I said, "You'll stay aboard?"

"Of course. I will do nothing to disabuse Dr. Forward of the notion that the ship is empty."

We crossed to Forward Station on an open taxi: two seats, a fuel tank, and a rocket motor. Once I turned to ask Carlos something, and asked instead, "Carlos? Are you all right?"

His face was white and strained. "I'll make it."

"Did you try closing your eyes?"

"It was worse. Futz, I made it this far on hypnosis. Bey, it's so *empty.*"

"Hang on. We're almost there."

The blond Belter was outside one of the airlocks in a skintight suit and a bubble helmet. He used a flashlight to flag us down. We moored our taxi to a spur of rock—the gravity was almost nil—and went inside.

"I'm Harry Moskowitz," the Belter said. "They call me Angel. Dr. Forward is waiting in the laboratory."

The interior of the asteroid was a network of straight cylindrical corridors, laser-drilled, pressurized and lined with cool blue light strips. We weighed a few pounds near the surface, less in the deep interior. Angel moved in a fashion new to me: a flat jump from the floor that took him far down the corridor to brush the ceiling; push back to the floor and jump again. Three jumps and he'd wait, not hiding his amusement at our attempts to catch up.

"Dr. Forward asked me to give you a tour," he told us.

I said, "You seem to have a lot more corridor than you need. Why didn't you cluster all the rooms together?"

"This rock was a mine, once upon a time. The miners drilled these passages. They left big hollows wherever they found air-bearing rock or ice pockets. All we had to do was wall them off."

That explained why there was so much corridor between the doors, and why the chambers we saw were so big. Some rooms were storage areas, Angel said; not worth opening. Others were tool rooms, life-support systems, a garden, a fair-sized computer, a sizable fusion plant. A mess room built to hold thirty actually held about ten, all men, who looked at us curiously before they went back to eating. A hangar, bigger than need be and open to the sky, housed taxis and powered suits with specialized tools, and three identical circular cradles, all empty.

I gambled. Carefully casual, I asked, "You use mining tugs?"

Angel didn't hesitate. "Sure. We can ship water and metals up from the inner system, but it's cheaper to hunt them down ourselves. In an emergency the tugs could probably get us back to the inner system."

We moved back into the tunnels. Angel said, "Speaking of ships, I don't think I've ever seen one like yours. Were those *bombs* lined up along the ventral surface?"

"Some of them," I said.

Carlos laughed. "Bey won't tell me how he got it."

"Pick, pick, pick. All right, I *stole* it. I don't think anyone is going to complain."

Angel, frankly curious before, was frankly fascinated as I told the story of how I had been hired to fly a cargo ship in the Wunderland system. "I didn't much like the looks of the guy who hired me, but what do I know about Wunderlanders? Besides, I needed the money." I told of my surprise at the proportions of the ship: the solid wall behind the cabin, the passenger section that was only holographs in blind portholes. By then I was already afraid that if I tried to back out I'd be made to disappear.

But when I learned my destination I got really worried. "It was in the Serpent Stream—you know, the crescent of asteroids in Wunderland system? It's common knowledge that the Free

Wunderland Conspiracy is *all through* those rocks. When they gave me my course I just took off and aimed for Sirius."

"Strange they left you with a working hyperdrive."

"Man, they *didn't.* They'd ripped out the relays. I had to fix them myself. It's lucky I looked, because they had the relays wired to a little bomb under the control chair." I stopped, then "Maybe I fixed it wrong. You heard what happened? My hyperdrive motor just plain vanished. It must have set off some explosive bolts, because the belly of the ship blew off. It was a dummy. What's left looks to be a pocket bomber."

"That's what I thought."

"I guess I'll have to turn it in to the goldskin cops when we reach the inner system. Pity."

Carlos was smiling and shaking his head. He covered by saying, "It only goes to prove that you *can* run away from your problems."

The next tunnel ended in a great hemispherical chamber, lidded by a bulging transparent dome. A man-thick pillar rose through the rock floor to a seal in the center of the dome. Above the seal, gleaming against night and stars, a multi-jointed metal arm reached out blindly into space. The arm ended in what might have been a tremendous iron puppy dish.

Forward was in a horseshoe-shaped control console near the pillar. I hardly noticed him. I'd seen this arm-and-bucket thing before, coming in from space, but I hadn't grasped its *size.*

Forward caught me gaping. "The Grabber," he said.

He approached us in a bouncing walk, comical but effective. "Pleased to meet you, Carlos Wu. Beowulf Shaeffer." His handshake was not crippling, because he was being careful. He had a wide, engaging smile. "The Grabber is our main exhibit here. After the Grabber there's nothing to see."

I asked, "What does it do?"

Carlos laughed. "It's beautiful! Why does it have to do anything?"

Forward acknowledged the compliment. "I've been thinking of entering it in a junk-sculpture show. What it does is manipulate large, dense masses. The cradle at the end of the arm is a complex of electromagnets. I can actually vibrate masses in there to produce polarized gravity waves."

Six massive arcs of girder divided the dome into pie sections. Now I noticed that they and the seal at their center gleamed like mirrors. They were reinforced by stasis fields. More bracing for the Grabber? I tried to imagine forces that would require such strength.

"What do you vibrate in there? A megaton of lead?"

"Lead sheathed in soft iron was our test mass. But that was three years ago. I haven't worked with the Grabber lately, but we had some satisfactory runs with a sphere of neutronium enclosed in a stasis field. Ten billion metric tons."

I said, "What's the point?"

From Carlos I got a dirty look. Forward seemed to think it was a wholly reasonable question. "Communication, for one thing. There must be intelligent species all through the galaxy, most of them too far away for our ships. Gravity waves are probably the best way to reach them."

"Gravity waves travel at lightspeed, don't they? Wouldn't hyperwave be better?"

"We can't count on their having it. Who but the Outsiders would think to do their experimenting this far from a sun? If we want to reach beings who haven't dealt with the Outsiders, we'll have to use gravity waves . . . once we know how."

Angel offered us chairs and refreshments. By the time we were settled I was already out of it; Forward and Carlos were talking plasma physics, metaphysics, and what are our old friends doing? I gathered that they had large numbers of mutual acquaintances. And Carlos was probing for the whereabouts of cosmologists specializing in gravity physics.

A few were in the Quicksilver Group. Others were among the colony worlds . . . especially on Jinx, trying to get the Institute of Knowledge to finance various projects, such as more expeditions to the collapsar in Cygnus.

"Are you still with the Institute, Doctor?"

Forward shook his head. "They stopped backing me. Not enough results. But I can continue to use this station, which is Institute property. One day they'll sell it and we'll have to move."

"I was wondering why they sent you here in the first place," said Carlos. "Sirius has an adequate cometary belt."

"But Sol is the only system with any kind of civilization this far from its sun. And I can count on better men to work with. Sol system has always had its fair share of cosmologists."

"I thought you might have come to solve an old mystery. The Tunguska meteorite. You've heard of it, of course."

Forward laughed. "Of course. Who hasn't? I don't think we'll ever know just what it was that hit Siberia that night. It may have been a chunk of antimatter. I'm told that there is antimatter in known space."

"If it was, we'll never prove it," Carlos admitted.

"Shall we discuss your problem?" Forward seemed to remember my existence. "Shaeffer, what does a professional pilot think when his hyperdrive motor disappears?"

"He gets very upset."

"Any theories?"

I decided not to mention pirates. I wanted to see if Forward would mention them first. "Nobody seems to like my theory," I said, and I sketched out the argument for monsters in hyperspace.

Forward heard me out politely. Then "I'll give you this, it'd be hard to disprove. Do you buy it?"

"I'm afraid to. I almost got myself killed once, looking for space monsters when I should have been looking for natural causes."

"Why would the hyperspace monsters eat only your motor?"

"Um . . . futz. I pass."

"What do you think, Carlos? Natural phenomena or space monsters?"

"Pirates," said Carlos.

"How are they going about it?"

"Well, this business of a hyperdrive motor disappearing and leaving the ship behind—that's brand-new. I'd think it would take a sharp gravity gradient, with a tidal effect as strong as that of a neutron star or a black hole."

"You won't find anything like that anywhere in Human space."

"I know." Carlos looked frustrated. That had to be faked. Earlier he'd behaved as if he already had an answer.

Forward said, "I don't think a black hole would have that effect anyway. If it did you'd never know it, because the ship would disappear down the black hole."

"What about a powerful gravity generator?"

"Hmmm." Forward thought about it, then shook his massive head. "You're talking about a surface gravity in the millions. Any gravity generator I've ever heard of would collapse itself at that level. Let's see, with a frame supported by stasis fields . . . no. The frame would hold and the rest of the machinery would flow like water."

"You don't leave much of my theory."

"Sorry."

Carlos ended a short pause by asking, "How do you think the universe started?"

Forward looked puzzled at the change of subject.

And I began to get uneasy.

Given all that I don't know about cosmology, I do know attitudes and tones of voice. Carlos was giving out broad hints, trying to lead Forward to his own conclusion. Black holes, pirates, the Tunguska meteorite, the origin of the universe—he was offering them as clues. And Forward was not responding correctly.

He was saying, "Ask a priest. Me, I lean toward the Big Bang. The Steady State always seemed so futile."

"I like the Big Bang too," said Carlos.

There was something else to worry about. Those mining tugs: they almost had to belong to Forward Station. How would Ausfaller react when three familiar spacecraft came cruising into his space?

How did I want him to react? Forward Station would make a dandy pirate base. Permeated by laser-drilled corridors distributed almost at random . . . could there be two networks of corridors, connected only at the surface? How would we know?

Suddenly I didn't want to know. I wanted to go home. If only Carlos would stay off the touchy subjects—

But he was speculating about the ship eater again. "That ten billion metric tons of neutronium, now, that you were using for a test mass. That wouldn't be big enough or dense enough to give us enough of a gravity gradient."

"It might, right near the surface." Forward grinned and held his hands close together. "It was about that big."

"And that's as dense as matter gets in this universe. Too bad."

"True, but . . . have you ever heard of quantum black holes?"

"Yah."

Forward stood up briskly. "Wrong answer."

I rolled out of my web chair, trying to brace myself for a jump, while my fingers fumbled for the third button on my jumper. It was no good. I hadn't practiced in this gravity.

Forward was in mid-leap. He slapped Carlos alongside the head as he went past. He caught me at the peak of his jump, and took me with him via an iron grip on my wrist.

I had no leverage, but I kicked at him. He didn't even try to stop me. It was like fighting a mountain. He gathered my wrists in one hand and towed me away.

Forward was busy. He sat within the horseshoe of his control console, talking. The backs of three disembodied heads showed above the console's edge.

Evidently there was a laser phone in the console. I could hear parts of what Forward was saying. He was ordering the pilots of the three mining tugs to destroy *Hobo Kelly*. He didn't seem to know about Ausfaller yet.

Forward was busy, but Angel was studying us thoughtfully, or unhappily, or both. Well he might. We could disappear, but what messages might we have sent earlier?

I couldn't do anything constructive with Angel watching me. And I couldn't count on Carlos.

I couldn't see Carlos. Forward and Angel had tied us to opposite sides of the central pillar, beneath the Grabber. Carlos hadn't made a sound since then. He might be dying from that tremendous slap across the head.

I tested the line around my wrists. Metal mesh of some kind, cool to the touch . . . and it was tight.

Forward turned a switch. The heads vanished. It was a moment before he spoke.

"You've put me in a very bad position."

And Carlos answered. "I think you put yourself there."

"That may be. You should not have let me guess what you knew."

Carlos said, "Sorry, Bey."

He sounded healthy. Good. "That's all right," I said. "But what's all the excitement about? What has Forward *got?*"

"I think he's got the Tunguska meteorite."

"No. That I do not." Forward stood and faced us. "I will admit that I came here to search for the Tunguska meteorite. I spent several years trying to trace its trajectory after it left Earth. Perhaps it *was* a quantum black hole. Perhaps not. The Institute cut off my funds, without warning, just as I had found a real quantum black hole, the first in history."

I said, "That doesn't tell me a lot."

"Patience Mr. Shaeffer. You know that a black hole may form from the collapse of a massive star? Good. And you know that it takes a body of at least five solar masses. It may mass as much as a galaxy—or as much as the universe. There is some evidence that the universe is an infalling black hole. But at less than five solar masses the collapse would stop at the neutron star stage."

"I follow you."

"In all the history of the universe, there has been one moment at which smaller black holes might have formed. That moment was the explosion of the mono-block, the cosmic egg that once contained all the matter in the universe. In the ferocity of that explosion there must have been loci of unimaginable pressure. Black holes could have formed of mass down to two point two times ten to the minus fifth grams, one point six times ten to the minus twenty-fifth angstroms in radius."

"Of course you'd never detect anything that small," said Carlos. He seemed almost cheerful. I wondered why . . . and then I knew. He'd been right about the way the ships were disappearing. It must compensate him for being tied to a pillar.

"But," said Forward, "black holes of all sizes could have formed in that explosion, and should have. In more than seven hundred years of searching, no quantum black hole has ever been found. Most cosmologists have given up on them, and on the Big Bang too."

Carlos said, "Of course there was the Tunguska meteorite. It could have been a black hole of, oh, asteroidal mass—"

"—and roughly molecular size. But the tide would have pulled down trees as it went past—"

"—and the black hole would have gone right through the Earth and headed back into space a few tons heavier. Eight hundred years ago there was actually a search for the exit point. With that they could have charted a course—"

"Exactly. But I had to give up that approach," said Forward. "I was using a new method when the Institute, ah, severed our relationship."

They must both be mad, I thought. Carlos was tied to a pillar and Forward was about to kill him, yet they were both behaving like members of a very exclusive club . . . to which I did not belong.

Carlos was interested. "How'd you work it?"

"You know that it is possible for an asteroid to capture a quantum black hole? In its interior? For instance, at a mass of ten to the twelfth kilograms—a billion metric tons," he added for my benefit, "a black hole would be only one point five times ten to the minus fifth angstroms across. Smaller than an atom. In a slow pass through an asteroid it might absorb a few billions of atoms, enough to slow it into an orbit. Thereafter it might orbit within the asteroid for aeons, absorbing very little mass on each pass."

"So?"

"If I chance on an asteroid more massive than it ought to be . . . and if I contrive to move it, and some of the mass stays behind . . ."

"You'd have to search a lot of asteroids. Why do it out here? Why not the asteroid belt? Oh, of course, you can use hyperdrive out here."

"Exactly. We could search a score of masses in a day, using very little fuel."

"Hey. If it was big enough to eat a spacecraft, why didn't it eat the asteroid you found it in?"

"It wasn't that big," said Forward. "The black hole I found was exactly as I have described it. I enlarged it. I towed it home and ran it into my neutronium sphere. *Then* it was large enough to absorb an asteroid. Now it is quite a massive object. Ten to the twentieth power kilograms, the mass of one of the larger asteroids, and a radius of just under ten to the minus fifth centimeters."

There was satisfaction in Forward's voice. In Carlos' there was suddenly nothing but contempt. "You accomplished all that, and then you used it to rob ships and bury the evidence. Is that what's going to happen to us? Down the rabbit hole?"

"To another universe, perhaps. Where does a black hole lead?"

I wondered about that myself.

Angel had taken Forward's place at the control console. He had fastened the seat belt, something I had not seen Forward do, and was dividing his attention between the instruments and the conversation.

"I'm still wondering how you move it," said Carlos. Then "Uh! The tugs!"

Forward stared, then guffawed. "You didn't guess that? But of course the black hole can hold a charge. I played the exhaust from an old ion drive reaction motor into it for nearly a month. Now it holds an enormous charge. The tugs can pull it well enough. I wish I had more of them. Soon I will."

"Just a minute," I said. I'd grasped one crucial fact as it went past my head. "The tugs aren't armed? All they do is pull the black hole?"

"That's right." Forward looked at me curiously.

"And the black hole is invisible."

"Yes. We tug it into the path of a spacecraft. If the craft comes near enough it will precipitate into normal space. We guide the black hole through its drive to cripple it, board and rob it at our leisure. Then a slower pass with the quantum black hole, and the ship simply disappears."

"Just one last question," said Carlos. "Why?"

I had a better question.

Just what was Ausfaller going to do when three familiar spacecraft came near? They carried no armaments at all. Their only weapon was invisible.

And it would eat a General Products hull without noticing.

Would Ausfaller fire on unarmed ships?

We'd know, too soon. Up there near the edge of the dome, I had spotted three tiny lights in a tight cluster.

Angel had seen it too. He activated the phone. Phantom heads appeared, one, two, three.

I turned back to Forward, and was startled at the brooding hate in his expression.

"Fortune's child," he said to Carlos. "Natural aristocrat. Certified superman. Why would *you* ever consider stealing anything? Women beg you to give them children, in person if possible, by mail if not! Earth's resources exist to keep you healthy, not that you need them!"

"This may startle you," said Carlos, "but there are people who see *you* as a superman."

"We bred for strength, we Jinxians. At what cost to other factors? Our lives are short, even with the aid of boosterspice. Longer if we can live outside Jinx's gravity. But the people of other worlds think we're funny. The women . . . never mind." He brooded, then said it anyway. "A woman of Earth once told me she would rather go to bed with a tunneling machine. She didn't trust my strength. What woman would?"

The three bright dots had nearly reached the center of the dome. I saw nothing between them. I hadn't expected to. Angel was still talking to the pilots.

Up from the edge of the dome came something I didn't want anyone to notice. I said, "Is that your excuse for mass murder, Forward? Lack of women?"

"I need give you no excuses at all, Shaeffer. My world will thank me for what I've done. Earth has swallowed the lion's share of the interstellar trade for too long."

"They'll thank you, huh? You're going to tell them?"

"I—"

"Julian!" That was Angel calling. He'd seen it . . . no, he hadn't. One of the tug captains had.

Forward left us abruptly. He consulted with Angel in low tones, then turned back. "Carlos! Did you leave your ship on automatic? Or is there someone else aboard?"

"I'm not required to say," said Carlos.

"I could—no. In a minute it will not matter."

Angel said, "Julian, look what he's doing."

"Yes. Very clever. Only a human pilot would think of that."

Ausfaller had maneuvered the *Hobo Kelly* between us and the tugs. If the tugs fired a conventional weapon, they'd blast the dome and kill us all.

The tugs came on.

"He still does not know what he is fighting," Forward said with some satisfaction.

True, and it would cost him. Three unarmed tugs were coming down Ausfaller's throat, carrying a weapon so slow that the tugs could throw it at him, let it absorb *Hobo Kelly,* and pick it up again long before it was a danger to us.

From my viewpoint *Hobo Kelly* was a bright point with three dimmer, more distant points around it. Forward and Angel were getting a better view, through the phone. And they weren't watching us at all.

I began trying to kick off my shoes. They were soft ship slippers, ankle high, and they resisted.

I kicked the left foot free just as one of the tugs flared with ruby light.

"He did it!" Carlos didn't know whether to be jubilant or horrified. "He fired on unarmed ships!"

Forward gestured peremptorily. Angel slid out of his seat. Forward slid in and fastened the thick seat belt. Neither had spoken a word.

A second ship burned fiercely red, then expanded in a pink cloud.

The third ship was fleeing.

Forward worked the controls. "I have it in the mass indicator," he rasped. "We have but one chance."

So did I. I peeled the other slipper off with my toes. Over our heads the jointed arm of the Grabber began to swing . . . and I suddenly realized what they were talking about.

Now there was little to see beyond the dome. The swinging Grabber, and the light of *Hobo Kelly*'s drive, and the two tumbling wrecks, all against a background of fixed stars. Suddenly one of the tugs winked blue-white and was gone. Not even a dust cloud was left behind.

Ausfaller must have seen it. He was turning, fleeing. Then it was as if an invisible hand had picked up *Hobo Kelly* and thrown her away. The fusion light streaked off to one side and set beyond the dome's edge.

With two tugs destroyed and the third fleeing, the black hole was falling free, aimed straight down our throats.

Now there was nothing to see but the delicate motions of the Grabber. Angel stood behind Forward's chair, his knuckles white with his grip on the chair's back.

My few pounds of weight went away and left me in free fall. Tides again. The invisible thing was more massive than this asteroid beneath me. The Grabber swung a meter more to one side . . . and something struck it a mighty blow.

The floor surged away from beneath me, left me head down above the Grabber. The huge soft-iron puppy dish came at me; the jointed metal arm collapsed like a spring. It slowed, stopped.

"You got it!" Angel crowed like a rooster and slapped at the back of the chair, holding himself down with his other hand. He turned a gloating look on us, turned back just as suddenly. "The ship! It's getting away!"

"No." Forward was bent over the console. "I see him. Good, he is coming back, straight toward us. This time there will be no tugs to warn the pilot."

The Grabber swung ponderously toward the point where I'd seen *Hobo Kelly* disappear. It moved centimeters at a time, pulling a massive invisible weight.

And Ausfaller was coming back to rescue us. He'd be a sitting duck, unless—

I reached up with my toes, groping for the first and fourth buttons on my falling jumper.

The weaponry in my wonderful suit hadn't helped me against Jinxian strength and speed. But flatlanders are less than limber, and so are Jinxians. Forward had tied my hands and left it at that.

I wrapped two sets of toes around the buttons and tugged.

My legs were bent pretzel fashion. I had no leverage. But the first button tore loose, and then the thread. Another invisible weapon to battle Forward's portable bottomless hole.

The thread pulled the fourth button loose. I brought my feet down to where they belonged, keeping the thread taut, and pushed backward. I felt the Sinclair molecule chain sinking into the pillar.

The Grabber was still swinging.

When the thread was through the pillar I could bring it up in back of me and try to cut my bonds. More likely I'd cut my wrists and bleed to death; but I had to try. I wondered if I could do anything before Forward launched the black hole.

A cold breeze caressed my feet.

I looked down. Thick fog boiled out around the pillar.

Some very cold gas must be spraying through the hair-fine crack.

I kept pushing. More fog formed. The cold was numbing. I felt the jerk as the magic thread cut through. Now the wrists—

Liquid helium?

Forward had moored us to the main superconducting power cable.

That was probably a mistake. I pulled my feet forward, carefully, steadily, feeling the thread bite through on the return cut.

The Grabber had stopped swinging. Now it moved on its arm like a blind, questing worm, as Forward made fine adjustments. Angel was beginning to show the strain of holding himself upside down.

My feet jerked slightly. I was through. My feet were terribly cold, almost without sensation. I let the buttons go, left them floating up toward the dome, and kicked back hard with my heels.

Something shifted. I kicked again.

Thunder and lightning flared around my feet.

I jerked my knees up to my chin. The lightning crackled and flashed white light into the billowing fog. Angel and Forward turned in astonishment. I laughed at them, letting them see it. Yes, gentlemen, I did it on purpose.

The lightning stopped. In the sudden silence Forward was screaming, "—know what you've *done?*"

There was a grinding *crunch,* a shuddering against my back. I looked up.

A piece had been bitten out of the Grabber.

I was upside down and getting heavier. Angel suddenly pivoted around his grip on Forward's chair. He hung above the dome, above the sky. He screamed.

My legs gripped the pillar hard. I felt Carlos' feet fumbling for a foothold, and heard Carlos' laughter.

Near the edge of the dome a spear of light was rising. *Hobo Kelly*'s drive, decelerating, growing larger. Otherwise the sky was clear and empty. And a piece of the dome disappeared with a snapping sound.

Angel screamed and dropped. Just above the dome he seemed to flare with blue light.

He was gone.

Air roared out through the dome—and more was disappearing into something that had been invisible. Now it showed as a blue pinpoint drifting toward the floor. Forward had turned to watch it fall.

Loose objects fell across the chamber, looped around the pinpoint at meteor speed or fell into it with bursts of light. Every atom of my body felt the pull of the thing, the urge to die in an infinite fall. Now we hung side by side from a horizontal pillar. I noted with approval that Carlos' mouth was wide open, like mine, to clear his lungs so that they wouldn't burst when the air was gone.

Daggers in my ears and sinuses, pressure in my gut.

Forward turned back to the controls. He moved one knob hard over. Then—he opened the seat belt and stepped out and up, and fell.

Light flared. He was gone.

The lightning-colored pinpoint drifted to the floor, and into it. Above the increasing roar of air I could hear the grumbling of rock being pulverized, dwindling as the black hole settled toward the center of the asteroid.

The air was deadly thin, but not gone. My lungs thought they were gasping vacuum. But my blood was not boiling. I'd have known it.

So I gasped, and kept gasping. It was all I had attention for. Black spots flickered before my eyes, but I was still gasping and alive when Ausfaller reached us carrying a clear plastic package and an enormous handgun.

He came in fast, on a rocket backpack. Even as he decelerated he was looking around for something to shoot. He returned in a loop of fire. He studied us through his faceplate, possibly wondering if we were dead.

He flipped the plastic package open. It was a thin sack with a zipper and a small tank attached. He had to dig for a torch to cut our bonds. He freed Carlos first, helped him into the sack. Carlos bled from the nose and ears. He was barely mobile. So was I, but Ausfaller got me into the sack with Carlos and zipped it up. Air hissed in around us.

I wondered what came next. As an inflated sphere the rescue bag was too big for the tunnels. Ausfaller had thought of that. He fired at the dome, blasted a gaping hole in it, and flew us out on the rocket backpack.

Hobo Kelly was grounded nearby. I saw that the rescue bag wouldn't fit the airlock either . . . and Ausfaller confirmed my worst fear. He signaled us by opening his mouth wide. Then he zipped open the rescue bag and half-carried us into the airlock while the air was still roaring out of our lungs.

When there was air again Carlos whispered, "Please don't do that anymore."

"It should not be necessary anymore." Ausfaller smiled. "Whatever it was you did, well done. I have two well-equipped autodocs to repair you. While you are healing, I will see about recovering the treasures within the asteroid."

Carlos held up a hand, but no sound came. He looked like something risen from the dead: blood running from nose and ears, mouth wide open, one feeble hand raised against gravity.

"One thing," Ausfaller said briskly. "I saw many dead men; I saw no living ones. How many were there? Am I likely to meet opposition while searching?"

"Forget it," Carlos croaked. "Get us out of here. Now."

Ausfaller frowned. "What—"

"No time. Get us out."

Ausfaller tasted something sour. "Very well. First, the autodocs." He turned, but Carlos' strengthless hand stopped him.

"Futz, no. I want to see this," Carlos whispered.

Again Ausfaller gave in. He trotted off to the control room. Carlos tottered after him. I tottered after them both, wiping blood from my nose, feeling half dead myself. But I'd half guessed what Carlos expected, and I didn't want to miss it.

We strapped down. Ausfaller fired the main thruster. The rock surged away.

"Far enough," Carlos whispered presently. "Turn us around."

Ausfaller took care of that. Then "What are we looking for?"

"You'll know."

"Carlos, was I right to fire on the tugs?"

"Oh, yes."

"Good. I was worried. Then Forward was the ship eater?"

"Yah."

"I did not see him when I came for you. Where is he?"

Ausfaller was annoyed when Carlos laughed, and more annoyed when I joined him. It hurt my throat. "Even so, he saved our lives," I said. "He must have turned up the air pressure just before he jumped. I wonder why he did that?"

"Wanted to be remembered," said Carlos. "Nobody else knew what he'd done. *Ahh—*"

I looked, just as part of the asteroid collapsed into itself, leaving a deep crater.

"It moves slower at apogee. Picks up more matter," said Carlos.

"What *are* you talking about?"

"Later, Sigmund. When my throat grows back."

"Forward had a hole in his pocket," I said helpfully. "He—"

The other side of the asteroid collapsed. For a moment lightning seemed to flare in there.

Then the whole dirty snowball was growing smaller.

I thought of something Carlos had probably missed. "Sigmund, has this ship got automatic sunscreens?"

"Of *course* we've got—"

There was a universe-eating flash of light before the screen went black. When the screen cleared there was nothing to see but stars.

Fritz Leiber

Whereas Roger Zelazny is seventeen years younger than I am, and Larry Niven is a year younger than that even, Fritz—like all right-thinking people—is older than I am. Ten years older, in fact. (It's getting harder and harder, each year, I notice, to find right-thinking people. Where will it all end? I wonder.)

It makes it easier to point out that Fritz has already appeared once in Volume Two and twice in Volume Three. He also twice won the Hugo for novels; *The Big Time* in 1958 and *The Wanderer* in 1965, and here is "Catch That Zeppelin!" And that's not all—

The Science Fiction Writers of America, at unpredictable intervals, bestows upon some science fiction personality their Grand Master Award. By 1981, they had done this four times, granting awards to Robert Heinlein, Jack Williamson, Clifford D. Simak, and L. Sprague de Camp, in that order. These were all excellent choices since one and all had been writing more or less continually, and certainly with consistent high quality, for forty years and more. (And one and all were older than I was and had been writing longer—don't think I didn't note that carefully.)

In 1981, the SFWA was preparing to hurl its lightning again. I received a call from Norman Spinrad, then president.

"Isaac," he said, "we're going to make Fritz Leiber a Grand Master and we want you to hand out the award. And don't get excited. He's older than you are and he's been writing just as long as you have."

I haven't the faintest idea what made him think it necessary to say that. I was, in fact, delighted, and considered it a great honor, and said so.

"But it's a dark secret, Isaac. Tell *no* one."

This was a hard cross to bear. I am, by nature, a sunny, talkative individual whose life is an open book. I talk cheerfully about everything I can think of, and my dear wife, Janet, complains, in her sweet way, that she has no private life since she married me.

Nevertheless, I managed to keep my mouth shut. For long, long months, I said nothing, told no one. I merely hugged the secret to myself and kept muttering, just before dropping off to sleep at night, "I'm going to hand out the Grand Master Award. I'm going to hand out the Grand Master Award."

Came Saturday, April 25, 1981, the day on which the award was to be given out. Janet and I were driving to the hotel in a taxi, along with Cliff Simak, and Cliff said to me, "You know, Isaac. Fritz Leiber ought to be getting a Grand Master Award. He is a terribly underestimated writer."

Ordinarily, I would have quietly agreed, but if I had opened my mouth all my teeth would have blown out. I kept silent, at what cost to my psyche I can only guess.

So there I was at the head table. For various reasons, it was all a harrowing experience for everyone, and I clung miserably to my sanity and waited for the award that would make it all worthwhile.

Came the moment! Norman Spinrad arose and, to my utter astonishment, instead of introducing me, calmly handed out the award to Fritz Leiber himself. *Norman* did it.

I've been plotting revenge for three years now, but can't think of anything vicious enough. —What's more, there have been no Grand Master Awards since. What are they waiting for?

3

CATCH THAT ZEPPELIN!

This year on a trip to New York City to visit my son, who is a social historian at a leading municipal university there, I had a very unsettling experience. At black moments, of which at my age I have quite a few, it still makes me distrust profoundly those absolute boundaries in Space and Time which are our sole protection against Chaos, and fear that my mind—no, my entire individual existence—may at any moment at all and without any warning whatsoever be blown by a sudden gust of Cosmic Wind to an entirely different spot in a Universe of Infinite Possibilities. Or, rather, into another Universe altogether. And that my mind and individuality will be changed to fit.

But at other moments, which are still in the majority, I believe that my unsettling experience was only one of those remarkably vivid waking dreams to which old people become increasingly susceptible, generally waking dreams about the past, and especially waking dreams about a past in which at some crucial point one made an entirely different and braver choice than one actually did, or in which the whole world made such a decision, with a completely different future resulting. Golden glowing might-have-beens nag increasingly at the minds of some older people.

In line with this interpretation I must admit that my whole unsettling experience was structured very much like a dream. It began with startling flashes of a changed world. It continued into a longer period when I completely accepted the changed world and delighted in it and, despite fleeting quivers of uneasiness, wished I could bask in its glow forever. And it ended in horrors, or nightmares, which I hate to mention, let alone discuss, until I must.

Opposing this dream notion, there are times when I am completely convinced that what happened to me in Manhattan and in a certain famous building there was no dream at all, but absolutely real, and that I did indeed visit another Time Stream.

Finally, I must point out that what I am about to tell you I am necessarily describing in retrospect, highly aware of several transitions involved and, whether I want to or not, commenting on them and making deductions that never once occurred to me at the time.

No, at the time it happened to me—and now at this moment of writing I am convinced that it did happen and was absolutely real—one instant simply succeeded another in the most natural way possible. I questioned nothing.

As to why it all happened to me, and what particular mechanism was involved, well, I am convinced that every man or woman has rare, brief moments of extreme sensitivity, or rather vulnerability, when his mind and entire being may be blown by the Change Winds to Somewhere Else. And then, by what I call the Law of the Conservation of Reality, blown back again.

I was walking down Broadway somewhere near 34th Street. It was a chilly day, sunny despite the smog—a bracing day—and I suddenly began to stride along more briskly than is my cautious habit, throwing my feet ahead of me with a faint suggestion of the goose step. I also threw back my shoulders and took deep breaths, ignoring the fumes which tickled my nostrils. Beside me, traffic growled and snarled, rising at times to a machine-gun rata-tat-tat, while pedestrians were scuttling about with that desperate ratlike urgency characteristic of all big American cities, but which reaches its ultimate in New York. I cheerfully ignored that too. I even smiled at the sight of a ragged bum and a fur-coated gray-haired society lady both independently dodging across the street through the hurtling traffic with a cool practiced skill one sees only in America's biggest metropolis.

Just then I noticed a dark, wide shadow athwart the street ahead of me. It could not be that of a cloud, for it did not move. I craned my neck sharply and looked straight up like the veriest yokel, a regular *Hans-Kopf-in-die-Luft* (Hans-Head-in-the-Air, a German figure of comedy).

My gaze had to climb up the giddy 102 stories of the tallest building in the world, the Empire State. My gaze was strangely accompanied by the vision of a gigantic, long-fanged ape making the same ascent with a beautiful girl in one paw—oh, yes, I was recollecting the charming American fantasy film *King Kong,* or as they name it in Sweden, *Kong King.*

And then my gaze clambered higher still, up the 222-foot sturdy tower, to the top of which was moored the nose of the vast, breathtakingly beautiful, streamlined, silvery shape which was making the shadow.

Now here is a most important point. I was not at the time in the least startled by what I saw. I knew at once that it was simply the bow section of the German zeppelin *Ostwald,* named for the great German pioneer of physical chemistry and electrochemistry, and queen of the mighty passenger and light-freight fleet of luxury airliners working out of Berlin, Baden-Baden, and Bremerhaven. That matchless Armada of Peace, each titanic airship named for a world-famous German scientist—the *Mach,* the *Nernst,* the *Humboldt,* the *Fritz Haber,* the French-named *Antoine Henri Becquerel,* the American-named *Edison,* the Polish-named *T. Sklodowska Edison,* and even the Jewish-named *Einstein!* The great humanitarian navy in which I held a not unimportant position as international sales consultant and *Fachmann*—I mean expert. My chest swelled with justified pride at this *edel*—noble—achievement of *dem Vaterland.*

I knew also without any mind-searching or surprise that the length of the *Ostwald* was more than one half the 1,472-foot height of the Empire State Building plus its mooring tower, thick enough to hold an elevator. And my heart swelled again with the thought that the Berlin *Zeppelinturm* (dirigible tower) was only a few meters less high. Germany, I told myself, need not strain for mere numerical records—her sweeping scientific and technical achievements speak for themselves to the entire planet.

All this literally took little more than a second, and I never broke my snappy stride. As my gaze descended, I cheerfully hummed under my breath *Deutschland, Deutschland über Alles.*

The Broadway I saw was utterly transformed, though at the time this seemed every bit as natural as the serene presence of the *Ostwald* high overhead, vast ellipsoid held aloft by helium.

Silvery electric trucks and buses and private cars innumerable purred along far more evenly and quietly, and almost as swiftly, as had the noisy, stenchful, jerky gasoline-powered vehicles only moments before, though to me now the latter were completely forgotten. About two blocks ahead, an occasional gleaming electric car smoothly swung into the wide silver arch of a quick-battery-change station, while others emerged from under the arch to rejoin the almost dreamlike stream of traffic.

The air I gratefully inhaled was fresh and clean, without trace of smog.

The somewhat fewer pedestrians around me still moved quite swiftly, but with a dignity and courtesy largely absent before, with the numerous blackamoors among them quite as well dressed and exuding the same quiet confidence as the Caucasians.

The only slightly jarring note was struck by a tall, pale, rather emaciated man in black dress and with unmistakably Hebraic features. His somber clothing was somewhat shabby, though well kept, and his thin shoulders were hunched. I got the impression he had been looking closely at me, and then instantly glancing away as my eyes sought his. For some reason I recalled what my son had told me about the City College of New York—CCNY—being referred to surreptitiously and jokingly as Christian College Now Yiddish. I couldn't help chuckling a bit at that witticism, though I am glad to say it was a genial little guffaw rather than a malicious snicker. Germany in her well-known tolerance and noble-mindedness has completely outgrown her old, disfiguring anti-Semitism—after all, we must admit in all fairness that perhaps a third of our great men are Jews or carry Jewish genes, Haber and Einstein among them—despite what dark and, yes, wicked memories may lurk in the subconscious minds of oldsters like myself and occasionally briefly surface into awareness like submarines bent on ship murder.

My happily self-satisfied mood immediately reasserted itself, and with a smart, almost military gesture I brushed to either side with a thumbnail the short, horizontal black mustache which decorates my upper lip, and I automatically swept back into place the thick comma of black hair (I confess I dye it) which tends to fall down across my forehead.

I stole another glance up at the *Ostwald,* which made me think of the matchless amenities of that wondrous deluxe airliner: the softly purring motors that powered its propellers—electric motors, naturally, energized by banks of lightweight TSE batteries and as safe as its helium; the Grand Corridor running the length of the passenger deck from the Bow Observatory to the stern's like-windowed Games Room, which becomes the Grand Ballroom at night; the other peerless rooms letting off that corridor—the *Gesellschaftsraum des Kapitäns* (Captain's Lounge) with its dark woodwork, manly cigar smoke, and *Damentische* (tables for ladies), the Premier Dining Room with its linen napery and silver-plated aluminum dining service, the Ladies' Retiring Room always set out profusely with fresh flowers, the Schwarzwald bar, the gambling casino with its roulette, baccarat, chemmy, blackjack *(vingt-et-un),* its tables for skat and bridge and dominoes and sixty-six, its chess tables presided over by the delightfully eccentric world's champion Nimzowitch, who would defeat you blindfold, but always brilliantly, simultaneously or one at a time, in charmingly baroque brief games for only two gold pieces per person per game (one gold piece to nutsy Nimzy, one to the DLG), and the supremely luxurious staterooms with costly veneers of mahogany over balsa; the hosts of attentive stewards, either as short and skinny as jockeys or else actual dwarfs, both types chosen to save weight; and the titanium elevator rising through the countless bags of helium to the two-decked Zenith Observatory, the sun deck wind-screened but roofless to let in the ever-changing clouds, the mysterious fog, the rays of the stars and good old Sol, and all the heavens. Ah, where else on land or sea could you buy such high living?

I called to mind in detail the single cabin which was always mine when I sailed on the *Ostwald—meine Stammkabine.* I visualized the Grand Corridor thronged with wealthy passengers in evening dress, the handsome officers, the unobtrusive, ever-attentive stewards, the gleam of white shirtfronts, the glow of bare shoulders, the muted dazzle of jewels, the music of conversations like string quartets, the lilting low laughter that traveled along.

Exactly on time I did a neat *"Links, marschieren!"* ("To the left, march!") and passed through the impressive portals of the Empire State and across its towering lobby to the mutedly silverdoored banks of elevators. On my way I noted the silver-glowing date: 6 May 1937 and the time of day: 1:07 P.M. Good!—since the *Ostwald* did not cast off until the tick of 3 P.M., I would be left plenty of time for a leisurely lunch and good talk with my son, if he had remembered to meet me—and there was actually no doubt of that, since he is the most considerate and orderly minded of sons, a real German mentality, though I say it myself.

I headed for the express bank, enjoying my passage through the clusters of high-class people who thronged the lobby without any unseemly crowding, and placed myself before the doors designated "Dirigible Departure Lounge" and in briefer German *"Zum Zeppelin."*

The elevator hostess was an attractive Japanese girl in skirt of dull silver with the DLG Double Eagle and Dirigible insignia of the German Airship Union emblazoned in small on the left breast of her mutedly silver jacket. I noted with unvoiced approval that she appeared to have an excellent command of both German and English and was uniformly courteous to the passengers in her smiling but unemotional Nipponese fashion, which is so like our German scientific precision of speech, though without the latter's warm underlying passion. How good that our two federations, at opposite sides of the globe, have strong commercial and behavioral ties!

My fellow passengers in the lift, chiefly Americans and Germans, were of the finest type, very well dressed—except that just as the doors were about to close, there pressed in my doleful Jew in black. He seemed ill at ease, perhaps because of his shabby clothing. I was surprised, but made a point of being particularly polite toward him, giving him a slight bow and brief but friendly smile, while flashing my eyes. Jews have as much right to the acme of luxury travel as any other people on the planet, if they have the money—and most of them do.

During our uninterrupted and infinitely smooth passage upward, I touched my outside left breast pocket to reassure myself that my ticket—first class on the *Ostwald!*—and my papers were there. But actually I got far more reassurance and even secret joy from the feel and thought of the documents in my tightly zippered inside left breast pocket: the signed preliminary agreements that would launch America herself into the manufacture of passenger zeppelins. Modern Germany is always generous in sharing her great technical achievements with responsible sister nations, supremely confident that the genius of her scientists and engineers will continue to keep her well ahead of all other lands; and after all, the genius of two Americans, father and son, had made vital though indirect contributions to the development of safe airship travel (and not forgetting the part played by the Polish-born wife of the one and mother of the other).

The obtaining of those documents had been the chief and official reason for my trip to New York City, though I had been able to combine it most pleasurably with a long-overdue visit with my son, the social historian, and with his charming wife.

These happy reflections were cut short by the jarless arrival of our elevator at its lofty terminus on the one hundredth floor. The journey old love-smitten King Kong had made only after exhausting exertion we had accomplished effortlessly. The silvery doors spread wide. My fellow passengers hung back for a moment in awe and perhaps a little trepidation at the thought of the awesome journey ahead of them, and I—seasoned airship traveler that I am—was the first to step out, favoring with a smile and nod of approval my pert yet cool Japanese fellow employee of the lower echelons.

Hardly sparing a glance toward the great, fleckless window confronting the doors and showing a matchless view of Manhattan from an elevation of 1,250 feet minus two stories, I briskly turned, not right to the portals of the Departure Lounge and tower elevator, but left to those of the superb German restaurant *Krähennest* (Crow's Nest).

I passed between the flanking three-foot-high bronze statuettes of Thomas Edison and Marie Sklodowska Edison niched in one wall and those of Count von Zeppelin and Thomas Sklodowska Edison facing them from the other, and entered the select precincts of the finest German dining place outside the Fatherland. I paused while my eyes traveled searchingly around the room with its restful dark wood paneling deeply carved with beautiful representations of the Black Forest and its grotesque supernatural denizens—kobolds, elves, gnomes, dryads (tastefully sexy), and the like. They interested me since I am what

Americans call a Sunday painter, though almost my sole subject matter is zeppelins seen against blue sky and airy, soaring clouds.

The *Oberkellner* came hurrying toward me with menu tucked under his left elbow and saying, *"Mein Herr!* Charmed to see you once more! I have a perfect table for one with porthole looking out across the Hudson."

But just then a youthful figure rose springily from behind a table set against the far wall, and a dear and familiar voice rang out to me with *"Hier, Papa!"*

"Nein, Herr Ober," I smilingly told the headwaiter as I walked past him, *"heute hab' ich Gesellschaft, mein Sohn."*

I confidently made my way between tables occupied by well-dressed folk, both white and black.

My son wrung my hand with fierce family affection, though we had last parted only that morning. He insisted that I take the wide, dark, leather-upholstered seat against the wall, which gave me a fine view of the entire restaurant, while he took the facing chair.

"Because during this meal I wish to look only on you, Papa," he assured me with manly tenderness. "And we have at least an hour and a half together, Papa—I have checked your luggage through, and it is likely already aboard the *Ostwald."* Thoughtful, dependable boy!

"And now, Papa, what shall it be?" he continued after we had settled ourselves. "I see that today's special is *Sauerbraten mit Spätzel* and sweet-sour red cabbage. But there is also *Paprika-huhn* and—"

"Leave the chicken to flaunt her paprika in lonely red splendor today," I interrupted him. *"Sauerbraten* sounds fine."

Ordered by my Herr Ober, the aged wine waiter had already approached our table. I was about to give him direction when my son took upon himself that task with an authority and a hostfulness that warmed my heart. He scanned the wine menu rapidly but thoroughly.

"The Zinfandel 1933," he ordered with decision, though glancing my way to see if I concurred with his judgment. I smiled and nodded.

"And perhaps *ein Tröpfchen Schnapps* to begin with?" he suggested.

"A brandy?—yes!" I replied. "And not just a drop, either. Make it a double. It is not every day I lunch with that distinguished scholar, my son."

"Oh, Papa," he protested, dropping his eyes and almost blushing. Then firmly to the bent-backed, white-haired wine waiter, *"Schnapps* also. *Doppel."* The old waiter nodded his approval and hurried off.

We gazed fondly at each other for a few blissful seconds. Then I said, "Now tell me more fully about your achievements as a social historian on an exchange professorship in the New World. I know we have spoken about this several times, but only rather briefly and generally when various of your friends were present, or at least your lovely wife. Now I would like a more leisurely man-to-man account of your great work. Incidentally, do you find the scholarly apparatus—books, *und so weiter* ("et cetera")—of the Municipal Universities of New York City adequate to your needs after having enjoyed those of Baden-Baden University and the institutions of high learning in the German Federation?"

"In some respects they are lacking," he admitted. "However, for my purposes they have proved completely adequate." Then once more he dropped his eyes and almost blushed. "But, Papa, you praise my small efforts far too highly." He lowered his voice. "They do not compare with the victory for international industrial relations you yourself have won in a fortnight."

"All in a day's work for the DLG," I said self-deprecatingly, though once again lightly touching my left chest to establish contact with those most important documents safely stowed in my inside left breast pocket. "But now, no more polite fencing!" I went on briskly. "Tell me all about those 'small efforts,' as you modestly refer to them."

His eyes met mine. "Well, Papa," he began in suddenly matter-of-fact fashion, "all my work these last two years has been increasingly dominated by a firm awareness of the fragility of the underpinnings of the good world-society we enjoy today. If certain historically minute key events, or cusps, in only the past one hundred years had been decided differently—if another course had been chosen than the one that was—then the whole world might now be plunged in wars and worse horrors than we ever dream of. It is a chilling insight, but it bulks continually larger in my entire work, my every paper."

I felt the thrilling touch of inspiration. At that moment the wine waiter arrived with our double brandies in small goblets of cut glass. I wove the interruption into the fabric of my inspiration. "Let us drink then to what you name your chilling insight," I said. *"Prosit!"*

The bite and spreading warmth of the excellent *Schnapps* quickened my inspiration further. "I believe I understand exactly what you're getting at . . ." I told my son. I set down my half-emptied goblet and pointed at something over my son's shoulder.

He turned his head around, and after one glance back at my pointing finger, which intentionally waggled a tiny bit from side to side, he realized that I was not indicating the entry of the *Krähennest,* but the four sizable bronze statuettes flanking it.

"For instance," I said, "if Thomas Edison and Marie Sklodowska had not married, and especially if they had not had their super-genius son, then Edison's knowledge of electricity and hers of radium and other radioactives might never have been joined. There might never have been developed the fabulous T. S. Edison battery, which is the prime mover of all today's surface and air traffic. Those pioneering electric trucks introduced by *The Saturday Evening Post* in Philadelphia might have remained an expensive freak. And the gas helium might never have been produced industrially to supplement earth's meager subterranean supply."

My son's eyes brightened with the flame of pure scholarship. "Papa," he said eagerly, "you are a genius yourself! You have precisely hit on what is perhaps the most important of those cusp events I referred to. I am at this moment finishing the necessary research for a long paper on it. Do you know, Papa, that I have firmly established by researching Parisian records that there was in 1894 a close personal relationship between Marie Sklodowska and her fellow radium researcher Pierre Curie, and that she might well have become Madame Curie—or perhaps Madame Becquerel, for he too was in that work—if the dashing and brilliant Edison had not most opportunely arrived in Paris in December 1894 to sweep her off her feet and carry her off to the New World to even greater achievements?

"And just think, Papa," he went on, his eyes aflame, "what might have happened if their son's battery had not been invented—the most difficult technical achievement, hedged by all sorts of seeming scientific impossibilities, in the entire millennium-long history of industry. Why, Henry Ford might have manufactured automobiles powered by steam or by exploding natural gas or conceivably even vaporized liquid gasoline, rather than the mass-produced electric cars which have been such a boon to mankind everywhere—not our smokeless cars, but cars spouting all sorts of noxious fumes to pollute the environment."

Cars powered by the danger-fraught combustion of vaporized liquid gasoline!—it almost made me shudder and certainly it was a fantastic thought, yet not altogether beyond the bounds of possibility, I had to admit.

Just then I noticed my gloomy, black-clad Jew sitting only two tables away from us, though how he had got himself into the exclusive *Krähennest* was a wonder. Strange that I had missed his entry—probably immediately after my own, while I had eyes only for my son. His presence somehow threw a dark though only momentary shadow over my bright mood. Let him get some good German food inside him and some fine German wine, I thought generously—it will fill that empty belly of his and even put a bit of a good German smile into those sunken Yiddish cheeks! I combed my little mustache with my thumbnail and swept the errant lock of hair off my forehead.

Meanwhile my son was saying, "Also, Father, if electric transport had not been developed, and if during the last decade relations between Germany and the United States had not been so good, then we might never have gotten from the wells in Texas the supply of natural helium our zeppelins desperately needed during the brief but vital period before we had put the artificial creation of helium onto an industrial footing. My researchers at Washington have revealed that there was a strong movement in the U.S. military to ban the sale of helium to any other nation, Germany in particular. Only the powerful influence of Edison, Ford, and a few other key Americans, instantly brought to bear, prevented that stupid injunction. Yet if it had gone through,

Germany might have been forced to use hydrogen instead of helium to float her passenger dirigibles. That was another crucial cusp."

"A hydrogen-supported zeppelin!—ridiculous! Such an airship would be a floating bomb, ready to be touched off by the slightest spark," I protested.

"Not ridiculous, Father," my son calmly contradicted me, shaking his head. "Pardon me for trespassing in your field, but there is an inescapable imperative about certain industrial developments. If there is not a safe road of advance, then a dangerous one will invariably be taken. You must admit, Father, that the development of commercial airships was in its early stages a most perilous venture. During the 1920s there were the dreadful wrecks of the American dirigibles *Roma,* and *Shenandoah,* which broke in two, *Akron,* and *Macon,* the British *R-38,* which also broke apart in the air, and *R-101,* the French *Dixmude,* which disappeared in the Mediterranean, Mussolini's *Italia,* which crashed trying to reach the North Pole, and the Russian *Maxim Gorky,* struck down by a plane, with a total loss of no fewer than 340 crew members for the nine accidents. If that had been followed by the explosions of two or three hydrogen zeppelins, world industry might well have abandoned forever the attempt to create passenger airships and turned instead to the development of large propeller-driven, heavier-than-air craft."

Monster airplanes, in danger every moment of crashing from engine failure, competing with good old unsinkable zeppelins?—impossible, at least at first thought. I shook my head, but not with as much conviction as I might have wished. My son's suggestion was really a valid one.

Besides, he had all his facts at his fingertips and was complete master of his subject, as I also had to allow. Those nine fearful airship disasters he mentioned had indeed occurred, as I knew well, and might have tipped the scale in favor of long-distance passenger and troop-carrying airplanes, had it not been for helium, the T. S. Edison battery, and German genius.

Fortunately I was able to dump from my mind these uncomfortable speculations and immerse myself in admiration of my son's multi-sided scholarship. That boy was a wonder!—a real chip off the old block, and, yes, a bit more.

"And now, Dolfy," he went on, using my nickname (I did not mind), "may I turn to an entirely different topic? Or rather to a very different example of my hypothesis of historical cusps?"

I nodded mutely. My mouth was busily full with fine *Sauerbraten* and those lovely, tiny German dumplings, while my nostrils enjoyed the unique aroma of sweet-sour red cabbage. I had been so engrossed in my son's revelations that I had not consciously noted our luncheon being served. I swallowed, took a slug of the good red Zinfandel, and said, "Please go on."

"It's about the consequences of the American Civil War, Father," he said surprisingly. "Did you know that in the decade after that bloody conflict, there was a very real danger that the whole cause of Negro freedom and rights—for which the war was fought, whatever they say—might well have been completely smashed? The fine work of Abraham Lincoln, Thaddeus Stevens, Charles Sumner, the Freedmen's Bureau, and the Union League Clubs put to naught? And even the Ku Klux Klan underground allowed free reign rather than being sternly repressed? Yes, Father, my thoroughgoing researchings have convinced me such things might easily have happened, resulting in some sort of re-enslavement of the blacks, with the whole war to be refought at an indefinite future date, or at any rate Reconstruction brought to a dead halt for many decades—with what disastrous effects on the American character, turning its deep simple faith in freedom to hypocrisy, it is impossible to exaggerate. I have published a sizable paper on this subject in the *Journal of Civil War Studies.*"

I nodded somberly. Quite a bit of this new subject matter of his was *terra incognita* to me; yet I knew enough of American history to realize he had made a cogent point. More than ever before, I was impressed by his multifaceted learning—he was indubitably a figure in the great tradition of German scholarship, a profound thinker, broad and deep. How fortunate to be his father. Not for the first time, but perhaps with the greatest sincerity yet, I thanked God and the Laws of Nature that I had early moved my family from Braunau, Austria, where I had been born in 1889, to Baden-Baden, where he had grown up in the ambience of the great new university on the edge of the Black

Forest and only 150 kilometers from Count Zeppelin's dirigible factory in Württemberg, at Friedrichshafen on Lake Constance.

I raised my glass of *Kirschwasser* to him in a solemn, silent toast—we had somehow got to that stage in our meal—and downed a sip of the potent, fiery, white cherry brandy.

He leaned toward me and said, "I might as well tell you, Dolf, that my big book, at once popular and scholarly, my *Meisterwerk*, to be titled *If Things Had Gone Wrong,* or perhaps *If Things Had Turned for the Worse,* will deal solely—though illuminated by dozens of diverse examples—with my theory of historical cusps, a highly speculative concept but firmly footed in fact." He glanced at his wristwatch, muttered, "Yes, there's still time for it. So now"—his face grew grave, his voice clear though small—"I will venture to tell you about one more cusp, the most disputable and yet most crucial of them all." He paused. "I warn you, dear Dolf, that this cusp may cause you pain."

"I doubt that," I told him indulgently. "Anyhow, go ahead."

"Very well. In November of 1918, when the British had broken the Hindenburg Line and the weary German army was defiantly dug in along the Rhine, and just before the Allies, under Marshal Foch, launched the final crushing drive which would cut a bloody swath across the heartland to Berlin—"

I understood his warning at once. Memories flamed in my mind like the sudden blinding flares of the battlefield with their deafening thunder. The company I had commanded had been among the most desperately defiant of those he mentioned, heroically nerved for a last-ditch resistance. And then Foch had delivered that last vast blow, and we had fallen back and back and back before the overwhelming numbers of our enemies with their field guns and tanks and armored cars innumerable and above all their huge aerial armadas of De Haviland and Handley-Page and other big bombers escorted by insect-buzzing fleets of Spads and other fighters shooting to bits our last Fokkers and Pfalzes and visiting on Germany a destruction greater far than our zeps had worked on England. Back, back, back, endlessly reeling and regrouping, across the devastated German countryside, a dozen times decimated yet still defiant until the end came at last amid the ruins of Berlin, and the most bold among us had to admit we were beaten and we surrendered unconditionally—

These vivid, fiery recollections came to me almost instantaneously.

I heard my son continuing, "At that cusp moment in November 1918, Dolf, there existed a very strong possibility—I have established this beyond question—that an immediate armistice would be offered and signed, and the war ended inconclusively. President Wilson was wavering, the French were very tired, and so on.

"And if that had happened in actuality—harken closely to me now, Dolf—then the German temper entering the decade of the 1920s would have been entirely different. She would have felt she had not been really licked, and there would inevitably have been a secret recrudescence of pan-German militarism. German scientific humanism would not have won its total victory over the Germany of the—yes!—Huns.

"As for the Allies, self-tricked out of the complete victory which lay within their grasp, they would in the long run have treated Germany far less generously than they did after their lust for revenge had been sated by that last drive to Berlin. The League of Nations would not have become the strong instrument for world peace that it is today; it might well have been repudiated by America and certainly secretly detested by Germany. Old wounds would not have healed because, paradoxically, they would not have been deep enough.

"There, I've said my say. I hope it hasn't bothered you too badly, Dolf."

I let out a gusty sigh. Then my wincing frown was replaced by a brow serene. I said very deliberately, "Not one bit, my son, though you have certainly touched my own old wounds to the quick. Yet I feel in my bones that your interpretation is completely valid. Rumors of an armistice were indeed running like wildfire through our troops in that black autumn of 1918. And I know only too well that if there had been an armistice at that time, then officers like myself would have believed that the German soldier had never really been defeated, only betrayed by his leaders and by Red incendiaries, and we would have begun to conspire endlessly for a resumption of the war under happier circumstances. My son, let us drink to your amazing cusps."

Our tiny glasses touched with a delicate ting, and the last drops went down of biting, faintly bitter *Kirschwasser.* I buttered a thin slice of pumpernickel and nibbled it—always good to finish off a meal with bread. I was suddenly filled with an immeasurable content. It was a golden moment, which I would have been happy to have go on forever, while I listened to my son's wise words and fed my satisfaction in him. Yes, indeed, it was a golden nugget of pause in the terrible rush of time—the enriching conversation, the peerless food and drink, the darkly pleasant surroundings—

At that moment I chanced to look at my discordant Jew two tables away. For some weird reason he was glaring at me with naked hate, though he instantly dropped his gaze—

But even that strange and disquieting event did not disrupt my mood of golden tranquillity, which I sought to prolong by saying in summation, "My dear son, this has been the most exciting though eerie lunch I have ever enjoyed. Your remarkable cusps have opened to me a fabulous world in which I can nevertheless utterly believe. A horridly fascinating world of sizzling hydrogen zeppelins, of countless evil-smelling gasoline cars built by Ford instead of his electrics, of re-enslaved American blackamoors, of Madame Becquerels or Curies, a world without the T. S. Edison battery and even T.S. himself, a world in which German scientists are sinister pariahs instead of tolerant, humanitarian, great-souled leaders of world thought, a world in which a mateless old Edison tinkers forever at a powerful storage battery he cannot perfect, a world in which Woodrow Wilson doesn't insist on Germany being admitted at once to the League of Nations, a world of festering hatreds reeling toward a second and worse world war. Oh, altogether an incredible world, yet one in which you have momentarily made me believe, to the extent that I do actually have the fear that time will suddenly shift gears and we will be plunged into that bad dream world, and our real world will become a dream—"

I suddenly chanced to see the face of my watch—

At the same time my son looked at his own left wrist—

"Dolf," he said, springing up in agitation, "I do hope that with my stupid chatter I haven't made you miss—"

I had sprung up too—

"No, no, my son," I heard myself say in a fluttering voice, "but it's true I have little time in which to catch the *Ostwald. Auf Wiedersehen, mein Sohn, auf Wiedersehen!"*

And with that I was hastening, indeed almost running, or else sweeping through the air like a ghost—leaving him behind to settle our reckoning—across a room that seemed to waver with my feverish agitation, alternately darkening and brightening like an electric bulb with its fine tungsten filament about to fly to powder and wink out forever—

Inside my head a voice was saying in calm yet death-knell tones, "The lights of Europe are going out. I do not think they will be rekindled in my generation—"

Suddenly the only important thing in the world for me was to catch the *Ostwald,* get aboard her before she unmoored. That and only that would reassure me that I was in my rightful world. I would touch and feel the *Ostwald,* not just talk about her—

As I dashed between the four bronze figures, they seemed to hunch down and become deformed, while their faces became those of grotesque, aged witches—four evil kobolds leering up at me with a horrid knowledge bright in their eyes—

While behind me I glimpsed in pursuit a tall, black, white-faced figure, skeletally lean—

The strangely short corridor ahead of me had a blank end—the Departure Lounge wasn't there—

I instantly jerked open the narrow door to the stairs and darted nimbly up them as if I were a young man again and not forty-eight years old—

On the third sharp turn I risked a glance behind and down—

Hardly a flight behind me, taking great pursuing leaps, was my dreadful Jew—

I tore open the door to the hundred and second floor. There at last, only a few feet away, was the silver door I sought of the final elevator and softly glowing above it the words *"Zum Zeppelin."* At last I would be shot aloft to the *Ostwald* and reality.

But the sign began to blink as the *Krähennest* had, while across the door was pasted askew a white cardboard sign which read "Out of Order."

I threw myself at the door and scrabbled at it, squeezing my eyes several times to make my vision come clear. When I finally fully opened them, the cardboard sign was gone.

But the silver door was gone too, and the words above it forever. I was scrabbling at seamless pale plaster.

There was a touch on my elbow. I spun around.

"Excuse me, sir, but you seem troubled," my Jew said solicitously. "Is there anything I can do?"

I shook my head, but whether in negation or rejection or to clear it, I don't know. "I'm looking for the *Ostwald,*" I gasped, only now realizing I'd winded myself on the stairs. "For the zeppelin," I explained when he looked puzzled.

I may be wrong, but it seemed to me that a look of secret glee flashed deep in his eyes, though his general sympathetic expression remained unchanged.

"Oh, the zeppelin," he said in a voice that seemed to me to have become sugary in its solicitude. "You must mean the *Hindenburg.*"

Hindenburg? I asked myself. There was no zeppelin named *Hindenburg.* Or was there? Could it be that I was mistaken about such a simple and, one would think, immutable matter? My mind had been getting very foggy the last minute or two. Desperately I tried to assure myself that I was indeed myself and in my right world. My lips worked and I muttered to myself, *Bin Adolf Hitler, Zeppelin Fachmann. . . .*

"But the *Hindenburg* doesn't land here, in any case," my Jew was telling me, "though I think some vague intention once was voiced about topping the Empire State with a mooring mast for dirigibles. Perhaps you saw some news story and assumed—"

His face fell, or he made it seem to fall. The sugary solicitude in his voice became unendurable as he told me, "But apparently you can't have heard today's tragic news. Oh, I do hope you weren't seeking the *Hindenburg* so as to meet some beloved family member or close friend. Brace yourself, sir. Only hours ago, coming in for her landing at Lakehurst, New Jersey, the *Hindenburg* caught fire and burned up entire in a matter of seconds. Thirty or forty at least of her passengers and crew were burned alive. Oh, steady yourself, sir."

"But the *Hindenburg*—I mean the *Ostwald!*—couldn't burn like that," I protested. "She's a helium zeppelin."

He shook his head. "Oh, no. I'm no scientist, but I know the *Hindenburg* was filled with hydrogen—a wholly typical bit of reckless German risk-running. At least we've never sold helium to the Nazis, thank God."

I stared at him, wavering my face from side to side in feeble denial.

While he stared back at me with obviously a new thought in mind.

"Excuse me once again," he said, "but I believe I heard you start to say something about Adolf Hitler. I suppose you know that you bear a certain resemblance to that execrable dictator. If I were you, sir, I'd shave my mustache."

I felt a wave of fury at this inexplicable remark with all its baffling references, yet withal a remark delivered in the unmistakable tones of an insult. And then all my surroundings momentarily reddened and flickered, and I felt a tremendous wrench in the inmost core of my being, the sort of wrench one might experience in transiting timelessly from one universe into another parallel to it. Briefly I became a man still named Adolf Hitler, same as the Nazi dictator and almost the same age, a German-American born in Chicago, who had never visited Germany or spoke German, whose friends teased him about his chance resemblance to the other Hitler, and who used stubbornly to say, "No, I won't change my name! Let that *Führer* bastard across the Atlantic change his! Ever hear about the British Winston Churchill writing the American Winston Churchill, who wrote *The Crisis* and other novels, and suggesting he change his name to avoid confusion, since the Englishman had done some writing too? The American wrote back it was a good idea, but since he was three years older, he was senior and so the Britisher should change *his* name. That's exactly how I feel about that son of a bitch Hitler."

The Jew still stared at me sneeringly. I started to tell him off, but then I was lost in a second weird, wrenching transition. The first had been directly from one parallel universe to another. The second was also in time—I aged fourteen or fifteen years in a single infinite instant while transiting from 1937 (where I had been born in 1889 and was forty-eight) to 1973 (where I had been born in 1910 and was sixty-three). My name changed back to my truly own (but what is that?), and I no longer looked one bit like Adolf Hitler the Nazi dictator (or dirigible expert?), and I had a married son who was a sort of social historian in a New York City municipal university, and he had many brilliant theories, but none of historical cusps.

And the Jew—I mean the tall, thin man in black with possibly Semitic features—was gone. I looked around and around but there was no one there.

I touched my outside left breast pocket, then my hand darted tremblingly underneath. There was no zipper on the pocket inside and no precious documents, only a couple of grimy envelopes with notes I'd scribbled on them in pencil.

I don't know how I got out of the Empire State Building. Presumably by elevator. Though all my memory holds for that period is a persistent image of King Kong tumbling down from its top like a ridiculous yet poignantly pitiable giant teddy bear.

I do recollect walking in a sort of trance for what seemed hours through a Manhattan stinking with monoxide and carcinogens innumerable, half waking from time to time (usually while crossing streets that snarled, not purred), and then relapsing into trance. There were big dogs.

When I at last fully came to myself, I was walking down a twilit Hudson Street at the north end of Greenwich Village. My gaze was fixed on a distant and unremarkable pale-gray square of building top. I guessed it must be that of the World Trade Center, 1,350 feet tall.

And then it was blotted out by the grinning face of my son, the professor.

"Justin!" I said.

"Fritz!" he said. "We'd begun to worry a bit. Where did you get off to, anyhow? Not that it's a damn bit of my business. If you had an assignation with a go-go girl, you needn't tell me."

"Thanks," I said, "I do feel tired, I must admit, and somewhat cold. But no, I was just looking at some of my old stamping grounds," I told him, "and taking longer than I realized. Manhattan's changed during my years on the West Coast, but not all that much."

"It's getting chilly," he said. "Let's stop in at that place ahead with the black front. It's the White Horse. Dylan Thomas used to drink there. He's supposed to have scribbled a poem on the wall of the can, only they painted it over. But it has the authentic sawdust."

"Good," I said, "only we'll make mine coffee, not ale. Or if I can't get coffee, then cola."

I am not really a *Prosit!*-type person.

1977
35th CONVENTION
MIAMI BEACH

Spider Robinson

Spider Robinson was born in 1945, and I find this incredible. How can anyone be so young?

Just think! Franklin Roosevelt and Adolf Hitler died the year he was born. They're history to him. World War II ended the year he was born. He probably doesn't even remember the Korean War.

Worse yet is the comparison to *me.* When he was a mere infant, mewling and pewking in the nurse's arms (to coin a phrase), I was a married man. I had already been a professional writer for seven years.

Why am I making a fuss over this? Because Spider Robinson, despite his extreme youth, is a powerhouse writer and to have him be so good so young makes me nervous. I don't know why it should, but it does. For one thing, it's unfair. If I try hard to improve myself, I might get to be that good, too; but what do I do to get that young?

To be sure, this is Spider's first appearance in these volumes but that doesn't mean that he is a stranger to convention triumphs. His first published story appeared in 1973, and at the 1974 convention he shared the John W. Campbell Award with Lisa Tuttle, an award given the most promising new writers. (Fortunately, in 1939, when my first story appeared, there was no John W. Campbell Award, or even its equivalent. If there had been, it would have been shared by Robert Heinlein and A. E. van Vogt for that year, and I would have finished in 491st place—though that high a position would only be conceded, I suspect, by my own prejudiced opinion.)

Spider's first novel, *Telempath,* appeared in 1976, and the novella that won the Hugo the very next year, the one you're about to read, represents a version of the first four chapters of the novel.

This, by the way—the excerpting of novels by the s.f. magazines—is something new in science fiction.

In the old days (before Spider was born), very few science fiction novels were written, and those that *were* written were specifically intended for the magazines, because science fiction did not appear in either hard-cover or soft-cover book form. The novels would appear, usually, as three-part serials (though anything from two to six parts was possible).

Nowadays, however, many novels are written primarily for the book trade, and there is a reluctance to allow them to be serialized because that might delay publication unduly. Besides which, the magazines would like to have some of three or four of them, rather than all of one of them. So they excerpt.

I would object out of my great feeling for the purity of the art. Unfortunately, my own most recent novels were excerpted by magazines. One had three different portions excerpted in three different magazines. That, somehow, puts a different light on things. To be sure, I had nothing to do with it; it was my publisher who made the arrangement. Nevertheless, I found my attitude toward excerpting grow considerably more tolerant as a result. I'm not sure why that should be.

In one respect, by the way, Spider didn't get off scot-free. He didn't win an uncontested Hugo. The novella award at the 1977 convention ended in a tie. (Each tie winner gets a whole Hugo, however, with no indication on either of the other.)

Well, I don't cheat. If two novellas win, my Gentle Readers get two novellas. The second one follows immediately after this one.

4

BY ANY OTHER NAME

There's winds out on the ocean
Blowin' wherever they choose.
The winds ain't got no emotion, babe:
They don't know the blues.
—traditional

CHAPTER ONE

Excerpt from the Journal of Isham Stone

I hadn't meant to shoot the cat.

I hadn't meant to shoot anything, for that matter—the pistol at my hip was strictly defensive armament at the moment. But my adrenals were on overtime and my peripheral vision was straining to meet itself behind my head—when something appeared before me with no warning at all, my subconscious sentries opted for the Best Defense. I was down and rolling before I knew I'd fired, through a doorway I hadn't known was there.

I fetched up with a heart-stopping crash against the foot of a staircase just inside the door. The impact dislodged something on the first-floor landing; it rolled heavily down the steps and sprawled across me: the upper portion of a skeleton, largely intact from the sixth vertebra up. As I lurched in horror to my feet, long-dead muscle and cartilage crumbled at last, and random bones skittered across the dusty floor. Three inches above my left elbow, someone was playing a drumroll with knives.

Cautiously I hooked an eye around the doorframe, at about knee level. The smashed remains of what had recently been a gray-and-white Persian tom lay against a shattered fire hydrant whose faded red surface was spattered with brighter red and less appealing colors. Overworked imagination produced the odor of singed meat.

I'm as much cat people as the One-Sleeved Mandarin, and three shocks in quick succession, in the condition I was in, were enough to override all the iron discipline of Collaci's training. Eyes stinging, I stumbled out onto the sidewalk, uttered an unspellable sound, and pumped three slugs into a wrecked '82 Buick lying on its right side across the street.

I was pretty badly rattled—only the third slug hit the exposed gas tank. But it was magnesium, not lead: the car went up with a very satisfactory roar and the prettiest fireball you ever saw. The left rear wheel was blown high in the air; it soared gracefully over my head, bounced off a fourth-floor fire escape, and came down flat and hard an inch behind me. Concrete buckled.

When my ears had stopped ringing and my eyes uncrossed, I became aware that I was rigid as a statue. *So much for catharsis,* I thought vaguely, and relaxed with an effort that hurt all over.

The cat was still dead.

I saw almost at once why he had startled me so badly. The tobacconist's display window from which he had leaped was completely shattered, so my subconscious sentries had incorrectly tagged it as one of the rare unbroken ones. Therefore, they reasoned, the hurtling object must be in fact emerging from the open door just beyond the window. Anything coming out a doorway that high from the ground just had to be a Musky, and my hand is *much* quicker than my eye.

Now that my eye had caught up, of course, I realized that I couldn't possibly track a Musky by eye. Which was exactly why I'd been keyed up enough to waste irreplaceable ammo and give away my position in the first place. Carlson had certainly made life complicated for me. I hoped I could manage to kill him slowly.

This was no consolation to the cat. I looked down at my Musky gun, and found myself thinking of the day I got it, just three months past. The first gun I had ever owned myself, symbol of man's estate, *mine* for as long as it took me to kill Carlson, and for as long afterwards as I lived. After my father had presented it to me publicly, and formally charged me with the avenging of the human race, the friends and neighbors—and dark-eyed Alia—

had scurried safely inside for the ceremonial banquet. But my father took me aside. We walked in silence through the West Forest to Mama's grave, and through the trees the setting sun over West Mountain looked like a knothole in the wall of Hell. Dad turned to me at last, pride and paternal concern fighting for control of his ebony features, and said, "Isham . . . Isham, I wasn't much older than you when I got my first gun. That was long ago and far away, in a place called Montgomery—things were different then. But some things never change." He tugged an earlobe reflectively, and continued, "Phil Collaci has taught you well, but sometimes he'd rather shoot first and ask directions later. Isham, you just can't go blazing away indiscriminately. Not *ever.* You hear me?"

The crackling of the fire around the ruined Buick brought me back to the present. Damn, you called it again Dad, I thought as I shivered there on the sidewalk. You *can't* go blazing away indiscriminately.

Not even here in New York City.

It was getting late, and my left arm ached abominably where Grey Brother had marked me—I reminded myself sharply that I was here on business. I had no wish to pass a night in any city, let alone this one, so I continued on up the street, examining every building I passed with extreme care. If Carlson had ears, he now knew someone was in New York, and he might figure out why. I was on his home territory—every alleyway and manhole was a potential ambush.

There were stores and shops of every conceivable kind, commerce more fragmented and specialized than I had ever seen before. Some shops dealt only in a *single item.* Some I could make no sense of at all. What the hell is an "rko"?

I kept to the sidewalk where I could. I told myself I was being foolish, that I was no less conspicuous to Carlson or a Musky than if I'd stood on second base at the legendary Shea Stadium, and that the street held no surprise tomcats. But I kept to the sidewalk where I could. I remember Mama—a *long* time ago—telling me not to go in the street or the monsters would get me.

They got her.

Twice I was forced off the curb, once by a subway entrance and once by a supermarket. Dad had seen to it that I had the best plugs Fresh Start had to offer, but they weren't *that* good. Both times I hurried back to the sidewalk and was thoroughly disgusted with my pulse rate. But I never looked over my shoulder. Collaci says there's no sense being scared when it can't help you —and the fiasco with the cat proved him right.

It was early afternoon, and the same sunshine that was warming the forests and fields and work zones of Fresh Start my home seemed to chill the air here, accentuating the barren emptiness of the ruined city. Silence and desolation were all around me as I walked, bleached bones and crumbling brick. Carlson had been efficient, all right, nearly as efficient as the atomic bomb folks used to be so scared of once. It seemed as though I were in some immense Devil's Autoclave that ignored filth and grime but grimly scrubbed out life of any kind.

Wishful thinking, I decided, and shook my head to banish the fantasy. If the city had been truly lifeless, I'd be approaching Carlson from uptown—I would never have had to detour as far south as the Lincoln Tunnel, and my left arm would not have ached so terribly. Grey Brother is extremely touchy about his territorial rights.

I decided to replace the makeshift dressing over the torn biceps. I didn't like the drumming insistence of the pain: it kept me awake but interfered with my concentration. I ducked into the nearest store that looked defensible, and found myself sprawled on the floor behind an overturned table, wishing mightily that it weren't so flimsy.

Something had moved.

Then I rose sheepishly to my feet, holstering my heater and rapping my subconscious sentries sharply across the knuckles for the second time in half an hour. My own face looked back at me from the grimy mirror that ran along one whole wall, curly black hair in tangles, wide lips stretched back in what looked just like a grin. It wasn't a grin. I hadn't realized how bad I looked.

Dad has told me a lot about Civilization, before the Exodus, but I don't suppose I'll ever understand it. A glance around this room raised more questions than it answered. On my left, opposite the long mirror, were a series of smaller mirrors that paralleled it for three-quarters of its length, with odd-looking chairs before them. Something like armchairs made of metal, padded where necessary, with levers to raise and lower them. On my right, below the longer mirror, were a lot of smaller, much plainer wooden chairs, in a tight row broken occasionally by strange frameworks from which lengths of rotting fabric dangled. I could only surmise that this was some sort of arcane narcissist's paradise, where men of large ego would come, remove their clothing, recline in luxuriously upholstered seats, and contemplate their own magnificence. The smaller, shabbier seats, too low to afford a decent view, no doubt represented the cut-rate or second-class accommodations.

But what was the significance of the cabinets between the larger chairs and the wall, laden with bottles and plastic containers and heathen appliances? And why were all the skeletons in the room huddled together in the middle of the floor, as though their last seconds of life had been spent frantically fighting over something?

Something gleamed in the bone heap, and I saw what the poor bastards had died fighting for, and knew what kind of place this had been. The contested prize was a straight razor.

My father had spent eighteen of my twenty years telling me why I ought to hate Wendell Carlson, and in the past few days I'd acquired nearly as many reasons of my own. I intended to put them in Carlson's obituary.

A wave of weariness passed over me. I moved to one of the big chairs, pressed gingerly down on the seat to make sure no cunning mechanism awaited my mass to trigger it (Collaci's training again—if Teach' ever gets to Heaven, he'll check it for booby traps), took off my rucksack, and sat down. As I unrolled the bandage around my arm I glanced at myself in the mirror and froze, struck with wonder. An infinite series of me's stretched out into eternity, endless thousands of Isham Stones caught in that frozen second of time that holds endless thousands of possible futures, on the point of some unimaginable cusp. I knew it was simply the opposed mirrors, the one before me slightly askew, and could have predicted the phenomenon had I thought about it—but I was not expecting it and had never seen anything like it in my life. All at once I was enormously tempted to sit back, light a joint from the first-aid kit in my rucksack, and meditate a while. I wondered what Alia was doing right now, right at this moment.

Hell, I could kill Carlson at twilight, and sleep in his bed—or hole up here and get him tomorrow, or the next day. When I was feeling better.

Then I saw the first image in line. Me. A black man just doesn't bruise spectacularly as a rule, but there was something colorful over my right eye that would do until a bruise came along. I was filthy, I needed a shave, and the long slash running from my left eye to my upper lip looked angry. My black turtleneck was torn in three places that I could see, dirty where it wasn't torn, and bloodstained where it wasn't dirty. It might be a long time before I felt any better than I did right now.

Then I looked down at what was underneath the gauze I'd just peeled off, saw the black streaks on the chocolate brown of my arm, and the temptation to set a spell vanished like an overheated Musky.

I looked closer, and began whistling "Good Morning, Heartache" through my teeth very softly. I had no more neosulfa, damned little bandage for that matter, and it looked like I should save what analgesics I had to smoke on the way home. The best thing I could do for myself was to finish up in the city and get gone, find a Healer before my arm rotted.

And all at once that was fine with me. I remembered the two sacred duties that had brought me to New York; one to my father and my people, and one to myself. I had nearly died proving to my satisfaction that the latter was impossible; the other would keep me no great long time. New York and I were, as Bierce would say, incompossible.

One way or another, it would all be over soon.

I carefully rebandaged the gangrenous arm, hoisted the rucksack, and went back outside, popping a foodtab and a very small dosage of speed as I walked. There's no point in bringing real food to New York—you can't taste it anyway and it masses so damned much.

The sun was perceptibly lower in the sky—the day was in catabolism. I shifted my shoulders to settle the pack and continued on up the street, my eyes straining to decipher faded signs.

Two blocks up I found a shop that had specialized in psychedelia. A '69 Ford shared the display window with several smashed hookahs and a narghile or two. I paused there, sorely tempted again. A load of pipes and papers would be worth a good bit at home; Techno and Agro alike would pay dearly for fine-tooled smoking goods—more evidence that, as Dad is always saying, technology's usefulness has outlasted it.

But that reminded me of my mission again, and I shook my head savagely to drive away the daydreaming that sought to delay me. I was—what was that phrase Dad had used at my arming ceremony?—"The Hand of Man Incarnate," that was it, the product of two years of personal combat training and eighteen years of racial hatred. After I finished the job I could rummage around in crumbling deathtraps for hash pipes and roach clips—my last detour had nearly killed me, miles to the north.

But I'd *had* to try. I was only two at the time of the Exodus, too young to retain much but a confused impression of universal terror, of random horror and awful revulsion everywhere. But I remember one incident very clearly. I remember my brother Israfel, all of eight years old, kneeling down in the middle of 116th Street and methodically smashing his head against the pavement. Long after Izzy's eight-year-old brains had splashed the concrete, his little body continued to slam the shattered skull down again and again in a literally mindless spasm of escape. I saw this over my mother's shoulder as she ran, screaming her fear, through the chaotically twisting nightmare that for as long as she could remember had been only a quietly throbbing nightmare, as she ran through Harlem.

Once when I was twelve I watched an Agro slaughter a chicken, and when the headless carcass got up and ran about I heard my mother's scream again. It was coming from my throat. Dad tells me I was unconscious for four days and woke up screaming.

Even here, even downtown, where the bones sprawled everywhere were those of strangers, I was wound up tight enough to burst, and ancient reflex fought with modern wisdom as I felt the irrational impulse to lift my head and cast about for an enemy's scent. I had failed to recover Izzy's small bones; Grey Brother, who had always lived in Harlem, now ruled it, and sharp indeed were his teeth. I had managed to hold off the chittering pack with incendiaries until I reached the Hudson, and they would not cross the bridge to pursue me. And so I lived—at least until gangrene got me.

And the only thing between me and Fresh Start was Carlson. I saw again in my mind's eye the familiar Carlson Poster, the first thing my father ran off when he got access to a mimeograph machine: a remarkably detailed sketch of thin, academic features surrounded by a mass of graying hair, with the legend: WANTED: FOR THE MURDER OF HUMAN CIVILIZATION—WENDELL MORGAN CARLSON. An unlimited lifetime supply of hot-shot shells will be given to anyone bringing the head to the Council of Fresh Start.

No one ever took Dad up on it—at least, no one who survived to collect. And so it looked like it was up to me to settle the score for a shattered era and a planetful of corpses. The speed was taking hold now; I felt an exalted sense of destiny, and a fever to be about it. I was the duly chosen instrument for mankind's revenge, and that reckoning was long overdue.

I unclipped one of the remaining incendiary grenades from my belt—it comforted me to hold that much raw power in my hand—and kept on walking uptown, feeling infinitely more than twenty years old. And as I stalked my prey through concrete canyons and brownstone foothills, I found myself thinking of his crime, of the twisted motives that had produced this barren jungle and countless hundreds like it. I remembered my father's eyewitness account of Carlson's actions, repeated so many times during my youth that I could almost recite it verbatim, heard again the Genesis of the world I knew from its first historian—my father, Jacob Stone. Yes, *that* Stone, the one man Carlson never expected to survive, to shout across a smashed planet the name of its unknown assassin. Jacob Stone, who first cried the name that became a curse, a blasphemy and a scream of rage in the throats of all humankind. Jacob Stone, who named our betrayer: Wendell Morgan Carlson!

And as I reviewed that grim story, I kept my hand near the rifle with which I hoped to write its happy ending. . . .

CHAPTER TWO

Excerpts from I WORKED WITH CARLSON, *by Jacob Stone, Ph.D., authorized version: Fresh Start Press, 1986 (Mimeo).*

. . . The sense of smell is a curious phenomenon, oddly resistant to measurement or rigorous analysis. Each life form on Earth appears to have as much of it as they need to survive, plus a little. The natural human sense of smell, for instance, was always more efficient than most people realized, so much so that in the 1880s the delightfully eccentric Sir Francis Galton had actually succeeded, by associating numbers with certain scents, in *training himself to add and subtract by smell,* apparently just for the intellectual exercise.

But through a sort of neurological suppressor circuit of which next to nothing is known, most people contrived to ignore all but the most pleasing or disturbing of the messages their noses brought them, perhaps by way of reaction to a changing world in which a finely tuned olfactory apparatus became a nuisance rather than a survival aid. The level of sensitivity which a wolf requires to find food would be a hindrance to a civilized human packed into a city of his fellows.

By 1983, Professor Wendell Morgan Carlson had raised olfactometry to the level of a precise science. In the course of testing the theories of Beck and Miles, Carlson almost absentmindedly perfected the classic "blast-injection" technique of measuring differential sensitivity in olfaction, *without regard for the subjective impressions of the test subject.* This not only refined his data, but also enabled him to work with life forms other than human, a singular advantage when one considers how much of the human brain is terra incognita.

His first subsequent experiments indicated that the average wolf utilized his sense of smell on the order of a thousand times more efficiently than a human. Carlson perceived that wolves lived in a world of scents, as rich and intricate as our human worlds of sight and word. To his surprise, however, he discovered that the *potential* sensitivity of the human olfactory apparatus far outstripped that of any known species.

This intrigued him. . . .

. . . Wendell Morgan Carlson, the greatest biochemist Columbia —and perhaps the world—had ever seen, was living proof of the truism that a genius can be a damned fool outside his own specialty.

Genius he unquestionably was; it was *not* serendipity that brought him the Nobel Prize for isolating a cure for the entire spectrum of virus infections called "the common cold." Rather it was the sort of inspired accident that comes only to those brilliant enough to perceive it, fanatic seekers like Pasteur.

But Pasteur was a boor and a braggart who frittered away valuable time in childish feuds with men unfit to wash out his test tubes. Genius is seldom a good character reference.

Carlson was a left-wing radical.

Worse, he was the type of radical who dreams of romantic exploits in a celluloid underground: grim-eyed rebels planting homemade bombs, assassinating the bloated oppressors in their very strongholds and (although he certainly knew what hydrogen sulfide was) escaping through the city sewers.

It never occurred to him that it takes a very special kind of man to be a guerrilla. He was convinced that the moral indignation he had acquired at Washington in '71 (during his undergraduate days) would see him through hardships and privation, and he would have been horrified if someone had pointed out to him that Che Guevera seldom had access to toilet paper. Never having experienced hunger, he thought it a glamorous state. He lived a compartmentalized life, and his wild talent for biochemistry had the thickest walls: only within them was he capable of logic or true intuition. He had spent a disastrous adolescent year in a seminary, enlisted as a "storm trooper of Mary," and had come out of it apostate but still saddled with a relentless need to Serve a Cause—and it chanced that the cry in 1982 was, once again, "Revolution Now!"

He left the cloistered halls of Columbia in July of that year, and applied to the smaller branch—the so-called Action-Faction—of the New Weathermen for a position as assassin. Fortunately he was taken for crazy and thrown out. The African Liberation Front was somewhat less discerning—they broke his leg in three places. In the Emergency Room of Jacobi Hospital Carlson came to the conclusion that the trouble with Serving a Cause was that it involved associating with unperceptive and dangerously unpredictable people. What he needed was a One-Man Cause.

And then, at the age of thirty-two, his emotions noticed his intellect for the first time.

When the two parts of him came together, they achieved critical mass—and that was a sad day for the world. I myself bear part of the blame for that coming-together—unwittingly I provided one of the final sparks, put forward an idea which sent Carlson on the most dangerous intuitive leap of his life. My own feelings of guilt for this will plague me to my dying day—and yet it might have been anyone. Or no one.

Fresh from a three-year stint doing biowar research for the Defense Department, I was a very minor colleague of Carlson's, but quickly found myself becoming a close friend. Frankly I was flattered that a man of his stature would speak to me, and I suspect Carlson was overjoyed to find a black man who would treat him as an equal.

But for reasons which are very difficult to explain to anyone who did not live through that period—and which need no explanation for those who did—I was reluctant to discuss the ALF with a honky, however "enlightened." And so when I went to visit Carlson in Jacobi Hospital and the conversation turned to the self-defeating nature of uncontrollable rage, I attempted to distract the patient with a hasty change of subject.

"The Movement's turning rancid, Jake," Carlson had just muttered, and an excellent digression occurred to me.

"Wendell," I said heedlessly, "do you realize that you personally are in a position to make this a better world?"

His eyes lit up. "How's that?"

"You are probably the world's greatest authority on olfactometry and the human olfactory apparatus, among other things—right?"

"As for as there is one, I suppose so. What of it?" He shifted uneasily within his traction gear: wearing his radical *persona,* he was made uncomfortable by reference to his scientist mode. He felt it had little to do with the Realities of Life—like nightsticks and grand juries.

"Has it ever occurred to you," I persisted to my everlasting regret, "that nearly all the undesirable by-products of twentieth-century living, Technological Man's most unlovable aspects, quite literally *stink?* The whole *world's* going rancid, Wendell, not just the Movement. Automobiles, factory pollution, crowded cities—Wendell, why couldn't you develop a selective suppressant for the sense of smell—controlled anosmia? Oh, I know a snort of formaldehyde will do the trick, and having your adenoids removed sometimes works. But a man oughtn't to have to give up the smell of frying bacon just to survive in New York. And you know we're reaching that pass—in the past few years it hasn't been necessary to leave the city and then return to be aware of how evil it smells. The natural suppressor mechanism in the brain—whatever it is—has gone about as far as it can go. Why don't you devise a small-spectrum filter to aid it? It would be welcomed by sanitation workers, engineers—why, it would be a godsend to the man on the street!"

Carlson was mildly interested. Such an anosmic filter would be both a mordant political statement and a genuine boon to Mankind. He had been vaguely pleased by the success of his cold cure, and I believe he sincerely wished to make the world a happier place—however perverted his methods tended to be. We discussed the idea at some length, and I left.

Had Carlson not been bored silly in the hospital, he would never have rented a television set. It was extremely unfortunate that *The Late Show* (ed. note: a television show of the period) on that particular evening featured the film version of Alistair MacLean's *The Satan Bug.* Watching this absurd production, Carlson was intellectually repelled by the notion that a virus could be isolated so hellishly virulent that "a teaspoon of it would sweep the earth of life in a few days."

But it gave him a wild idea—a fancy, a fantasy, and a tasty one.

He checked with me by phone the next day, very casually, and I assured him from my experiences with advances in virus-vectoring that MacLean had *not* been whistling in the dark. In fact, I said, modern so-called bacterial warfare made the Satan Bug look like child's play. Carlson thanked me and changed the subject.

On his release from the hospital, he came to my office and asked me to work with him for a full year, to the exclusion of all else, on a project whose nature he was reluctant to discuss. "Why do you need me?" I asked, puzzled.

"Because," he finally told me, "you know how to make a Satan Bug. I intend to make a God Bug. And you could help me."

"Eh?"

"Listen, Jake," he said with that delightful informality of his, "I've licked the common cold—and there are still herds of people with the sniffles. All I could think of to do with the cure was to turn it over to the pharmaceuticals people, and I did all I could to make sure they didn't milk it, but there are still suffering folks who can't afford the damned stuff. Well, there's no need for that. Jake, a cold will kill someone sufficiently weakened by hunger—I can't help the hunger, but I could eliminate colds from the planet in forty-eight hours . . . with your help."

"A benevolent virus-vector . . ." I was flabbergasted, as much by the notion of decommercializing medicine as by the specific nostrum involved.

"It'd be a lot of work," Carlson went on. "In its present form my stuff isn't compatible with such a delivery system—I simply wasn't thinking along those lines. But I'll bet it could be made so, with your help. Jake, I haven't got time to learn your field—throw in with me. Those pharmaceuticals gonifs have made me rich enough to pay you twice what Columbia does, and we're both due for sabbatical anyway. What do you say?"

I thought it over, but not enough. The notion of collaborating with a Nobel Prize winner was simply too tempting. "All right, Wendell."

We set up operations in Carlson's laboratory-home on Long Island, he in the basement and myself on the main floor. There we worked like men possessed for the better part of a year, cherishing private dreams and slaughtering guinea pigs by the tens of thousands. Carlson was a stern if somewhat slapdash taskmaster, and as our work progressed he began "looking over my shoulder," learning my field while discouraging inquiries about his own progress. I assumed that he simply knew his field too well to converse intelligently about it with anyone but himself. And yet he absorbed all my own expertise with fluid rapidity, until eventually it seemed that he knew as much about virology as I did myself. One day he disappeared with no explanation, and returned a week or two later with what seemed to me a more nasal voice.

And near the end of the year there came a day when he called me on the telephone. I was spending the weekend, as always, with my wife and two sons in Harlem. Christmas was approaching, and Barbara and I were discussing the relative merits of plastic and natural trees when the phone rang. I was not at all surprised to hear Carlson's reedy voice, so reminiscent of an oboe lately—the only wonder was that he had called during conventional waking hours.

"Jake," he began without preamble, "I haven't the time or inclination to argue, so shut up and listen, right? Right. I advise and strongly urge you to take your family and leave New York *at once*—steal a car if you have to, or hijack a Greyhound (ed. note: a public transportation conveyance) for all of me, but be at least twenty miles away by midnight."

"But . . ."

". . . Head north if you want my advice, and for God's sake stay away from all cities, towns, and people in any number. If you possibly can, get upwind of all nearby industry, and bring along all the formaldehyde you can—a gun too, if you own one. Goodbye, my friend, and remember I do this for the greater good of mankind. I don't know if you'll understand that, but I hope so."

"Wendell, what in the name of *God* are you . . . ?" I was talking to a dead phone.

Barbara was beside me, a worried look on her face, my son Isham in her arms. "What is it?"

"I'm not sure," I said unsteadily, "but I think Wendell has come unhinged. I must go to him. Stay with the children; I'll be back as quickly as I can. And, Barbara . . ."

"Yes?"

"I know this sounds insane, but pack a bag and be ready to leave town *at once* if I call and tell you to."

"Leave town? Without you?"

"Yes, just that. Leave New York and never return. I'm virtually certain you won't have to, but it's just possible that Wendell knows what he's talking about. If he does, I'll meet you at the cabin by the lake, as soon as I can." I put off her questions then and left, heading for Long Island.

When I reached Carlson's home in Old Westbury I let myself in with my key and made my way toward his laboratory. But I found him upstairs in mine, perched on a stool, gazing intently at a flask in his right hand. Its interior swirled, changing color as I watched.

Carlson looked up. "You're a damned fool, Jake," he said quietly before I could speak. "I gave you a chance."

"Wendell, what on earth is this all about? My wife is scared half to . . ."

"Remember that controlled anosmia you told me about when I was in the hospital?" he went on conversationally. "You said the trouble with the world is that it stinks, right?"

I stared at him, vaguely recalling my words.

"Well," he said, "I've got a solution."

And Carlson told me what he held in his hand. A single word.

I snapped, just completely snapped. I charged him, clawing wildly for his throat, and he struck me with his left hand, his faceted ring giving me the scar I bear to this day, knocking me unconscious. When I came to my senses I was alone, alone with a helpless guilt that careened yammering through the halls of my reason and a terror that clutched at my bowels. A note lay on the floor beside me, in Wendell's sprawling hand, telling me that I had—by my watch—another hour's grace. At once I ran to the phone and wasted ten minutes trying to call Barbara. I could not get through—trunk failure, the operator said. Gibbering, I took all the formaldehyde I could find in both labs and a self-contained breathing rig from Carlson's, stepped out into the streetlit night, and set about stealing a car.

It took me twenty minutes, not bad for a first attempt but still cutting it fine—I barely made it to Manhattan, with superb traffic conditions to help me, before the highway became a butcher shop.

At precisely nine o'clock, Wendell Morgan Carlson stood on the roof of Columbia's enormous Butler Library, held high in the air by fake Greek columns and centuries of human thought, gazing north across a quadrangle within which grass and trees had nearly given up trying to grow, toward the vast domed Low Library and beyond toward the ghetto in which my wife and children were waiting, oblivious. In his hands he held the flask I had failed to wrest from him, and within it were approximately two teaspoons of an infinitely refined and concentrated virus culture. It was the end result of our year's work, and it duplicated what the military had spent years and billions to obtain: a strain of virus that could blanket the globe in about forty-eight hours. There was no antidote for it, no vaccine, no defense of any kind for virtually all of humanity. It was diabolical, immoral, and quite efficient. On the other hand, it was not lethal.

Not, that is, in and of itself. But Carlson had concluded, like so many before him, that a few million lives was an acceptable price for saving the world, and so at 9 P.M. on December 17, 1984, he leaned over the parapet of Butler Library and dropped his flask six long stories to the concrete below. It shattered on impact and sprayed its contents into what dismal breeze still blew through the campus.

Carlson had said one word to me that afternoon, and the word was "Hyperosmia."

Within forty-eight hours every man, woman, and child left alive on earth possessed a sense of smell approximately a hundred times more efficient than that of any wolf that ever howled.

During those forty-eight hours, a little less than a fifth of the planet's population perished, by whatever means they could devise, and every city in the world spilled its remaining life into the surrounding countryside. The ancient smell-suppressing system of the human brain collapsed under unbearable demand, overloaded and burned out in an instant.

The great complex behemoth called Modern Civilization ground to a halt in a little less than two days. In the last hours, those pitiably few city dwellers on the far side of the globe who were rigorous enough of thought to heed and believe the brief bewildered death cries of the great mass media strove valiantly—and hopelessly—to effect emergency measures. The wiser attempted, as I had, to deaden their senses of smell with things like formaldehyde, but there is a limit to the amount of formaldehyde that even desperate men can lay hands on in a day or less, and its effects are generally temporary. Others with less vision opted for airtight environments if they could get them, and there they soon died, either by asphyxiation when their air supply ran out or by suicide when, fervently hoping they had outlived the virus, they cracked their airlocks at last. It was discovered that human technology had produced no commonly available nose plug worth a damn, nor any air-purification system capable of filtering out Carlson's virus. Although the rest of the animal kingdom was not measurably affected by it, mankind failed utterly to check the effects of the ghastly Hyperosmic Plague, and the Exodus began . . .

. . . I don't believe Carlson rejoiced over the carnage that ensued, though a strict Malthusian might have considered it as a long-overdue pruning. But it is easy to understand why he thought it was necessary, to visualize the "better world" for which he spent so many lives: Cities fallen to ruin. Automobiles rotting where they stood. Heavy industry gone to join the dinosaurs. The synthetic-food industry utterly undone. Perfume what it had always been best—a memory—as well as tobacco. A wave of cleanliness sweeping the globe, and public flatulation at last a criminal offense, punishable by death. Secaucus, New Jersey, abandoned to the buzzards. The back-to-nature communalists achieving their apotheosis, helping to feed and instruct bewildered urban survivors (projected catchphrase: "If you don't like hippies, next time you're hungry, call a cop"). The impetus of desperation forcing new developments in production of power by sun, wind, and water rather than inefficient combustion of more precious resources. The long-delayed perfection of plumbing. And a profoundly interesting and far-reaching change in human mating customs as feigned interest or disinterest became unviable pretenses (as any wolf could have told us, the scent of desire can be neither faked nor masked).

All in all, an observer as impartial as Carlson imagined himself to be might have predicted that at an ultimate cost of perhaps thirty to forty percent of its population (no great loss), the world ten or twenty years after Carlson would be a much nicer place to live in.

Instead and in fact, there are four billion fewer people living in it, and in this year, Two A.C., we have achieved only a bare possibility of survival at a cost of eighty to ninety percent of our number.

The first thing Carlson could not have expected claimed over a billion and a half lives within the first month of the Brave New World. His compartmentalized mind had not been monitoring current developments in the field of psychology, a discipline he found frustrating. And so he was not aware of the work of Lynch and others, conclusively demonstrating that autism was the result of sensory overload. Autistic children, Lynch had proved, were victims of a physiochemical imbalance which disabled their suppressor circuitry for sight, hearing, touch, smell, or any combination thereof, flooding their brains with an intolerable avalanche of useless data and shocking them into retreat. Lysergic acid diethylamide is said to produce a similar effect, on a smaller scale.

The Hyperosmic Virus produced a similar effect, on a larger scale. Within weeks, millions of near-catatonic adults and children perished from malnutrition, exposure, or accidental injury. Why some survived the shock and adapted, while some did not, remains a mystery, although there exist scattered data suggesting that those whose sense of smell was already relatively acute suffered most.

The second thing Carlson could not have expected was the War.

The War had been ordained by the plummeting fall of his flask, but he may perhaps be excused for not foreseeing it. It was not such a war as has ever been seen on earth before in all recorded history, humans versus each other or subordinate life forms. There was nothing for the confused, scattered survivors of the Hyperosmic Plague to fight over, few unbusy enough to fight over it; and with lesser life forms we are now *better* equipped to compete. No, war broke out between us bewildered refugees—and the Muskies.

It is difficult for us to imagine today how it was possible for the human race to know of the Muskies for so long without ever believing in them. Countless humans reported contact with Muskies—who at various times were called "ghosts," "poltergeists," "leprechauns," "fairies," "gremlins," and a host of other misleading labels—and not *one* of these thousands of witnesses was believed by humanity at large. Some of us saw our cats stare, transfixed, at nothing at all, and wondered—but did not believe—what they saw. In its arrogance the race assumed that the peculiar perversion of entropy called "life" was the exclusive property of solids and liquids.

Even today we know very little about the Muskies, save that they are gaseous in nature and perceptible only by smell. The interested reader may wish to examine Dr. Michael Gowan's ground-breaking attempt at a psychological analysis of these entirely alien creatures, *Riders of the Wind* (Fresh Start Press, 1986).

One thing we do know is that they are capable of an incredible and disturbing playfulness. While not true telepaths, Muskies can project and often impose mood patterns over short distances, and for centuries they seem to have delighted in scaring the daylights out of random humans. Perhaps they laughed like innocent children as women to whom their pranks were attributed were burned at the stake in Salem. Dr. Gowan suggests that this aspect of their racial psyche is truly infantile—he feels their race is still in its infancy. As, perhaps, is our own.

But in their childishness, Muskies can be dangerous both deliberately and involuntarily. Years ago, before the Exodus, people used to wonder why a race that could plan a space station couldn't design a safe airliner—the silly things used to fall out of the sky with appalling regularity. Often it was simply sheer bad engineering, but I suspect that at least as often a careless, drifting Musky, riding the trades lost in God knows what wildly *alien* thoughts, was sucked into the air intake of a hurtling jetliner and burst the engine asunder as it died. It was this guess which led me to theorize that extreme heat might disrupt and kill Muskies, and this gave us our first and so far only weapon in the bitter war that still rages between us and the windriders.

For, like many children, Muskies are dangerously paranoid. Almost at the instant they realized that men could somehow now perceive them directly, they attacked, with a ferocity that bespoke blind panic. They learned quickly how best to kill us: by clamping itself somehow to a man's face and forcing him to breathe it in, a Musky can lay waste to his respiratory system. The only solution under combat conditions is a weapon which fires a projectile hot enough to explode a Musky—and that is a flawed solution. If you fail to burn a Musky in time, before it reaches you, you may be faced with the unpleasant choice of wrecking your lungs or blowing off your face. All too many Faceless Ones roam the land, objects of horror and pity, supported by fellow men uncomfortably aware that it could happen to them tomorrow.

Further, we Technos here at Fresh Start, dedicated to rebuilding at least a minimum technology, must naturally wear our recently developed nose plugs for long intervals while doing Civilized work. We therefore toil in constant fear that at any moment we may feel alien projections of terror and dread, catch even through our plugs the characteristic odor that gives Muskies their name, and gasp our lungs out in the final spasms of death.

God knows how Muskies communicate—or even if they do. Perhaps they simply have some sort of group mind or hive mentality. What would evolution select for a race of gas clouds spinning across the earth on the howling mistral? Someday we may devise a way to take one prisoner and study it; for the present we are content to know that they can be killed. A good Musky is a dead Musky.

Someday we may climb back up the ladder of technological evolution enough to carry the battle to the Muskies' home ground; for the present we are at least becoming formidable defenders.

Someday we may have the time to seek out Wendell Morgan Carlson and present him with a bill; for the present we are satisfied that he dares not show himself outside New York City, where legend has him hiding from the consequences of his actions.

CHAPTER THREE

From the Journal of Isham Stone

. . . but my gestalt of the eighteen years that had brought me on an intersecting course with my father's betrayer was nowhere near as pedantically phrased as the historical accounts Dad had written. In fact, I had refined it down to four words.

God damn you, Carlson!

Nearly midafternoon now. The speed was wearing off; time was short. Broadway got more depressing as I went. Have you ever seen a bus full of skeletons—with pigeons living in it? My arm ached like hell, and a muscle in my thigh had just announced it was sprained—I acquired a slight but increasing limp. The rucksack gained an ounce with every step, and I fancied that my right plug was leaking the barest trifle around the flange. I couldn't say I felt first-rate.

I kept walking north.

I came to Columbus Circle, turned on a whim into Central Park. It was an enclave of life in this concrete land of death, and I could not pass it by—even though my intellect warned that I might encounter a Doberman who hadn't seen a can of dog food in twenty years.

The Exodus had been good to this place at least—it was lush with vegetation now that swarming humans no longer smothered its natural urge to be alive. Elms and oaks reached for the clouds with the same optimism of the maples and birches around Fresh Start, and the overgrown grasses were the greenest things I had seen in New York. And yet—in places the grass was dead, and there were dead bushes and shrubs scattered here and there. Perhaps first impressions were deceiving—perhaps a small parcel of land surrounded by an enormous concrete crypt was not a viable ecology after all. Then again, perhaps neither was Fresh Start.

I was getting depressed again.

I pocketed the grenade I still held and sat down on a park bench, telling myself that a rest would do wonders for my limp. After a time static bits of scenery moved—the place was alive. There were cats, and gaunt starved dogs of various breeds, apparently none old enough to know what a man was. I found their confidence refreshing—like I say, I'm a peaceful-type assassin. Gregarious as hell.

I glanced about, wondering why so many of the comparatively few human skeletons here had been carrying weapons on the night of the Exodus—why go armed in a park? Then I heard a cough and looked around, and for a crazy second I thought I knew.

A leopard.

I recognized it from pictures in Dad's books, and I knew what it was and what it could do. But my adrenaline system was tired of putting my gun in my fist—I sat perfectly still and concentrated on smelling friendly. My hand weapon was designed for high temperature, not stopping power; grenades are ineffective against a moving target; and I was leaning back against my rifle—but that isn't why I sat still. I had learned that day that lashing out is not an optimum response to fear.

And so I took enough of a second look to realize that this leopard was incredibly ancient, hollow-bellied and claw-scarred, more noble than formidable. If wild game had been permitted to roam Central Park, Dad would have told me—he knew my planned route. Yet this cat seemed old enough to predate the Exodus. I was certain he knew me for a man. I suppose he had escaped from a zoo in the confusion of the time, or perhaps he was some rich person's pet. I understand they had such things in the Old Days. Seems to me a leopard'd be more trouble than an eagle—Dad kept one for four years and I never had so much grief over livestock before or since. Dad used to say it was the symbol of something great that had died, but I thought it was ornery.

This old cat seemed friendly enough, though, now that I noticed. He looked patriarchal and wise, and he looked awful hungry if it came to that. I made a gambler's decision for no reason that I can name. Slipping off my rucksack slowly and deliberately, I got out a few foodtabs, took four steps toward the leopard, and sat on my heels, holding out the tablets.

Instinct, memory or intuition, the big cat recognized my intent and loped my way without haste. Somehow the closer he got, the less scared I got, until he was nuzzling my hand with a maw that could have amputated it. I *know* the foodtabs didn't smell like anything, let alone food, but he understood in some empathic way what I was offering—or perhaps he felt the symbolic irony of two ancient antagonists, black man and leopard, meeting in New York City to share food. He ate them all, without nipping my fingers. His tongue was startlingly rough and rasping, but I didn't flinch, or need to. When he was done he made a noise that was a cross between a cough and a snore and butted my leg with his head.

He was old, but powerful; I rocked backward and fell off my heels. I landed correctly, of course, but I didn't get back up again. My strength left me and I lay there gazing at the underside of the park bench.

For the first time since I entered New York, I had communicated with a living thing and been answered in kind, and somehow that knowledge took my strength from me. I sprawled on the turf and waited for the ground to stop heaving, astonished to discover how weak I was and in how many places I hurt unbearably. I said some words that Collaci had taught me, and they helped some but not enough. The speed had worn off faster than it should have, and there was no more.

It looked like it was time for a smoke. I argued with myself as I reached overhead to get the first-aid kit from the rucksack, but I saw no alternative. Carlson was not a trained fighter, had never had a teacher like Collaci: I could take him buzzed. And I might not get to my feet any other way.

The joint I selected was needle-slender—more than a little cannabis would do me more harm than good. I had no mind to get wrecked in *this* city. I lit up with my coil lighter and took a deep lungful, held it as long as I could. Halfway through the second toke the leaves dancing overhead began to sparkle, and my weariness got harder to locate. By the third I knew of it only by hearsay, and the last hit began melting the pains of my body as warm water melts snow. Nature's own analgesic, gift of the earth.

I started thinking about the leopard, who was lying down himself now, washing his haunches. He was magnificent in decay—something about his eyes said that he intended to live forever or die trying. He was the only one of his kind in his universe, and I could certainly identify with that—I'd always felt different from the other cats myself.

And yet—I was kin to those who had trapped him, caged him, exhibited him to the curious, and then abandoned him to die half a world away from his home. Why wasn't he trying to kill me? In his place I might have acted differently . . .

With the clarity of smoke-logic I followed the thought through. At one time the leopard's ancestors had tried to kill mine, and *eat* them, and yet there was no reason for me to hate *him.* Killing him wouldn't help my ancestors. Killing me would accomplish nothing for the leopard, make his existence no easier . . . except by a day's meal, and I had given him that.

What then, I thought uneasily, *will my killing Carlson accomplish?* It could not put the Hyperosmic Virus back in the flask, or save the life of any now living. Why come all this way to kill?

It was not, of course, a new thought. The question had arisen several times during my training in survival and combat. Collaci insisted on debating philosophy while he was working you over, and expected reply; he maintained that a man who couldn't hold up his end of the conversation while fighting for his life would never make a really effective killer. You could pause for thought, but if he decided you were just hoarding your wind he stopped pulling his punches.

One day we had no special topic, and I voiced my self-doubts about the mission I was training for. What good, I asked Collaci, would killing Carlson do? Teach' disengaged and stood back, breathing a little hard, and grinned his infrequent wolf's grin.

"Survival has strange permutations, Isham. Revenge is a uniquely human attribute—somehow we find it easier to bury our dead when we have avenged them. We have many dead." He selected a toothpick, stuck it into his grin. "And for your father's sake it has to be you who does it—only if his son provides his expiation can Dr. Stone grant himself absolution. Otherwise I'd go kill that silly bastard myself." And without warning, he had tried, unsuccessfully, to break my collarbone.

And so now I sat tired, hungry, wounded, and a little stoned in the middle of an enormous island mausoleum, asking myself the question I had next asked Collaci, while trying—unsuccessfully—to cave in his rib cage: is it moral or ethical to kill a man?

Across the months his answer came back: *Perhaps not, but it is sometimes necessary.*

And with that thought my strength came to me and I got to my feet. My thoughts were as slick as wet soap, within reach but skittering out of my grasp. I grabbed one from the tangle and welded it to me savagely: *I will kill Wendell Morgan Carlson.* It was enough.

And saying goodbye to the luckier leopard, who could never be hagridden by ancient ghosts, I left the park and continued on up Broadway, as alert and deadly as I knew how to be.

When I reached 114th Street, I looked above the rooftops, and there it was: a thin column of smoke north and a little east, toward Amsterdam Avenue. Legend and my father's intuition had been right. Carlson was holed up where he had always felt most secure—the academic womb-bag of Columbia. I felt a grin pry my face open. It would all be over soon now, and I could go back to being me—whoever that was.

I left the rucksack under a station wagon and considered my situation. I had three tracers left in my Musky-killing handgun, three incendiary grenades clipped to my belt, and the scope-sighted sniper-rifle with which I planned to kill Carlson. The latter held a full clip of eight man-killing slugs—seven more than I needed. I checked the action and jacked a slug into the chamber.

There was a detailed map of the Morningside campus in my pack but I didn't bother to get it out—I had its twin brother in my head. Although neither Teach' nor I had entirely shared Dad's certainty that Carlson would be at Columbia, I had spent hours studying the campus maps he gave me as thoroughly as the New York City street maps that Collaci had provided. It seemed the only direct contribution Dad could make to my mission.

It looked as though his effort had paid off.

I wondered whether Carlson was expecting me. I wasn't sure if the sound of the car I'd shot downtown could have traveled this far, nor whether an explosion in a city full of untended gas mains was unusual enough to put Carlson on his guard. Therefore I had to assume that it could have and it was. Other men had come to New York to deal with Carlson, as independents, and none had returned.

My mind was clicking efficiently now, all confusion gone. I was eager. A car-swiped lamppost leaned drunkenly against a building, and I briefly considered taking to the rooftops for maximum surprise factor. But rooftops are prime Musky territory, and besides I didn't have strength for climbing.

I entered the campus at the southwest, through the 115th Street gate. As my father had predicted, it was locked—only the main gates at 116th had been left open at night in those days, and it was late at night when Carlson dropped his flask. But the lock was a simple Series 10 American that might have made Teach' laugh out loud. I didn't laugh out loud. It yielded to the second pick I tried, and I slipped through the barred iron gate without a sound—having thought to oil the hinges first.

A flight of steps led to a short flagstone walkway, gray speckled hexagons in mosaic, a waist-high wall on either side. The walkway ran between Furnald and Ferris Booth halls and, I knew, opened onto the great inner quadrangle of Columbia. Leaves lay scattered all about, and trees of all kinds thrashed in the lusty afternoon breeze, their leaves a million green pinwheels.

I hugged the right wall until it abutted a taller perpendicular wall. Easing around that, I found myself before the great smashed glass and stone façade of Ferris Booth Hall, the student activities center, staring past it toward Butler Library, which I was seeing from the west side. There was a good deal of heavy construction equipment in the way—one of the many student groups that had occupied space in Booth had managed to blow up itself and a sizable portion of the building in 1983, and rebuilding had still been in progress on Exodus Day. A massive crane stood before the ruined structure, surrounded by stacks of brick and pipe, a bulldozer, storage shacks, a few trucks, a two-hundred-gallon gasoline tank, and a pair of construction trailers.

But my eyes looked past all the conventional hardware to a curious device beyond them, directly in front of Butler Library and nearly hidden by overgrown hedges. I couldn't have named it—it looked like an octopus making love to a console stereo—but it obviously didn't come with the landscaping. Dad's second intuition was also correct: Carlson was using Butler for his base of operations. God knew what the device was for, but a man without his adenoids in a city full of Muskies and hungry German shepherds would not have built it further from home than could be helped. This was the place.

I drew in a great chest- and bellyful of air, and my grin hurt my cheeks. I held up my rifle and watched my hands. Rock steady.

Carlson, you murdering bastard, I thought, *this is it. The human race has found you, and its Hand is near. A few more breaths and you die violently, old man, like a harmless cat in a smokeshop window, like an eight-year-old boy on a Harlem sidewalk, like a planetwide civilization you thought you could improve on. Get you ready.*

I moved forward.

Wendell Morgan Carlson stepped out between the big shattered lamps that bracketed Butler Hall's front entrance. I saw him plainly in profile, features memorized from the Carlson Poster and my father's sketches, recognizable in the afternoon light even through white beard and tangled hair. He glanced my way, flinched, and ducked back inside a split second ahead of my first shot.

Determined to nail him before he could reach a weapon and dig in, I put my head down and ran, flat out, for the greatest killer of all time.

And the first Musky struck.

Terror sleeted through my brain, driving out the rage, and something warm and intangible plastered itself across my face. I think I screamed then, but somehow I kept from inhaling as I fell and rolled, dropping the rifle and tearing uselessly at the thing on my face. The last thing I saw before invisible gases seared my vision was the huge crane beside me on the right, its long arm flung at the sky like a signpost to Heaven. Then the world shimmered and faded, and I clawed my pistol from its holster. I aimed without seeing, my finger spasmed, and the gun bucked in my hand.

The massive gasoline drum between me and the crane went up with a *whoom,* and I sobbed in relief as I heaved to my feet and dove headlong through the flames. The Musky's dying projections tore at my mind and I rolled clear, searing my lungs with a convulsive inhalation as the Musky exploded behind me. Even as I smashed into the fender of the crane, my hindbrain screamed *Muskies never travel alone!* and before I knew what I was doing I tore loose my plugs to locate my enemy.

Foul stenches smashed my sanity, noxious odors wrenched at my reason, I was torn, blasted, overwhelmed in abominable ordure. The universe was offal, and the world I saw was remote and unreal. My eyes saw the campus, but told me nothing of the rank flavor of putrefaction that lay upon it. They saw sky, but spoke nothing of the reeking layers of indescribable decay of which it was made. Even allowing for a greenhouse effect it was much worse than it should have been after twenty years, just as legend had said. I tasted excrement, I tasted metal, I tasted the flavor of the world's largest charnel house, population seven millions, and I writhed on the concrete. Forgotten childhood memories of the Exodus burst in my brain and reduced me to a screaming, whimpering child. I couldn't *stand* it, it was unbearable, *how had I walked, arrogant and unknowing, through this stinking hell all day?*

And with that thought I remembered why I had come here, and knew I could not join Izzy in the peaceful, fragrant dark. I could not let go—I had to kill Carlson before I let the blackness claim me. Courage flowed from God knows where, feeding on black hatred and the terrible fear that I would let my people down, let my father down. I stood up and inhaled sharply, through my nose.

The nightmare world sprang into focus and time came to a halt.

There were six Muskies, skittering about before Butler as they sought to bend the breezes to their will.

I had three hot-shot shells and three grenades.

One steadied, banked my way. I fired from the hip and he flared out of existence.

A second caught hold of a prevailing current and came in like an express train. Panic tore through my mind, and I laughed and aimed and the Musky went incandescent.

Two came in at once then, like balloons in slow motion. I extrapolated their courses, pulled two grenades and armed them with opposing thumbs, counted to four and hurled them together as Collaci had taught me, aiming for a spot just short of my target. They kissed at that spot and rebounded, each toward an oncoming Musky. But one grenade went up before the other, killing its Musky but knocking the other one safely clear. It shot past my ear as I threw myself sideways.

Three Muskies. One slug, one grenade.

The one that had been spared sailed around the crane in a wide, graceful arc and came in low and fast, rising for my face as one of its brothers attacked from my left. Cursing, I burned the latter and flipped backwards through a great trail of burning gas from the tank I'd spoiled. The Musky failed to check in time, shot suddenly skyward and burst spectacularly. I slammed against a stack of twelve-inch pipe and heard ribs crack.

One Musky. One grenade.

As I staggered erect, beating at my smoldering turtleneck, Carlson reemerged from Butler, a curious helmet over his flowing white hair.

I no longer cared about the remaining Musky. Almost absentmindedly I tossed my last grenade in its direction to keep it occupied, but I knew I would have all the time I needed. Imminent death was now a side issue. I lunged and rolled, came up with the rifle in my hands and aimed for the O in Carlson's scraggly white beard. Dimly I saw him plugging a wire from his helmet into the strange console device, but it didn't matter, it just didn't matter at all. My finger tightened on the trigger.

And then something smashed me on the side of the neck behind the ear, and my finger clenched, and the blackness that had been waiting patiently for oh! so long swarmed in and washed away the pain and the hate and the weariness and oh God the awful smell. . . .

CHAPTER FOUR

Excerpts from THE BUILDING OF FRESH START, *by Jacob Stone, Ph.D., authorized version: Fresh Start Press, 2001.*

Although Fresh Start grew slowly and apparently randomly as personnel and materials became available, its development followed the basic outline of a master plan conceived within a year of the Exodus. Of course, I had not the training or experience to visualize specifics of my dream at that early stage—but the basic layout was inherent in the shape of the landscape and in the nature of the new world Carlson had made for us all.

Five years prior to the Exodus, a man named Gallipolis had acquired title, by devious means, to a logged-out area some distance northwest of New York City. It was an isolated two-hundred-acre parcel of an extremely odd shape. Seen from the air it must have resembled an enormous pair of green sunglasses: two valleys choking with new growth, separated physically by a great perpendicular extrusion of the eastern mountain range, almost to the western slopes, leaving the north and south valleys joined only by a narrow channel. The perpendicular "nose" between the valley "lenses" was a tall, rocky ridge, sharply sloped on both sides, forming a perfect natural division. The land dropped gently away from the foot of this ridge in either direction, and dirt roads left by the loggers cut great loops through both valleys. The land was utterly unsuited for farming, and too many miles from nowhere for suburban development—it was what real estate brokers called "an investment in the future."

Gallipolis was a mad Greek. Mad Greeks in literature are invariably swarthy, undereducated, poor, and drunk. Gallipolis was florid, superbly educated, moderately well off, and a teetotaler. He looked upon his valleys and he smiled a mad smile and decided to hell with the future. He had a serviceable road cut through the north forest past the lake, to a lonely stretch of state highway which fed into the nearby Interstate. He brought bulldozers down this road and had six widely spaced acres cleared west of the logging road loop in the north valley, and a seventh acre on the lakeshore for himself. On these sites he built large and extremely comfortable homes, masterpieces of design which combined an appearance of "roughing it" with every imaginable modern convenience. He piped in water from spring-fed streams high on the slopes of the Nose (as he had come to call the central ridge). He built beach houses along the lakeshore. It was his plan to lease the homes to wealthy men as weekend or summer homes at an exorbitant fee, and use the proceeds to develop three similar sites in both valleys. He envisioned an ultimate two or three dozen homes and an early retirement, but the only two things he ultimately achieved were to go broke before a single home had been leased and to drop dead.

A nephew inherited the land—and the staggering tax bill. He chanced to be a student of mine, and was aware that I was in the market for a weekend haven from the rigors of the city; he approached me. Although the place was an absurdly long drive from New York, I went up with him one Saturday, looked over the house nearest the lake, made him a firm offer of a quarter of his asking price, and closed the deal on the spot. It was a beautiful place. My wife and I became quite fond of it, and never missed an opportunity to steal a weekend there. Before long we had neighbors, but we seldom saw them, save occasionally at the lake. We had all come there for a bit of solitude, and it was quite a big lake—none of us were socially inclined.

It was for this wooded retreat that my family and I made in the horrible hours of the Exodus, and only by the grace of God did we make it. Certainly none of the other tenants did, then or ever, and it must be assumed that they perished. Sarwar Krishnamurti, a chemist at Columbia who had been an occasional weekend guest at Stone Manor, remembered the place in his time of need and showed up almost at once, with his family. He was followed a few days later by George Dalhousie, a friend of mine from the Engineering Department to whom I had once given directions to the place.

We made them as welcome as we could under the circumstances—my wife was in a virtual state of shock from the loss of our eldest son, and none of us were in much better shape. I know we three men found enormous comfort in each other's presence, in having other men of science with whom to share our horror, our astonishment, our guesses, and our grim extrapolations. It kept us sane, kept our minds on practical matters, on survival; for had we been alone, we might have succumbed, as did so many, to a numb, traumatized disinterest in living.

Instead, we survived the winter that came, the one that killed so many, and by spring we had laid our plans.

We made occasional abortive forays into the outside world, gathering information from wandering survivors. All media save rumor had perished; even my international-band radio was silent. On these expeditions we were always careful to conceal the existence and location of our home base, pretending to be as disorganized and homeless as the aimless drifters we continually encountered. We came to know every surviving farmer in the surrounding area, and established friendly relations with them by working for them in exchange for food. Like all men, we avoided areas of previous urbanization, for nose plugs were inferior in those days, and Muskies were omnipresent and terrifying. In fact, rumor claimed, they tended to cluster in cities and towns.

But that first spring, we conquered our fear and revulsion with great difficulty and began raiding small towns and industrial parks with a borrowed wagon. We found that rumor had been correct: urban areas were crawling with Muskies. But we needed tools and equipment of all kinds and descriptions, badly enough to risk our lives repeatedly for them. It went slowly, but Dalhousie had his priorities right, and soon we were ready.

We opened our first factory that spring, on a hand-cleared site in the south valley (which we christened Southtown). Our first product had been given careful thought, and we chose well—if for the wrong reasons. We anticipated difficulty in convincing people to buy goods from us with barter, when they could just as easily have scavenged from the abandoned urban areas. In fact, one of our central reasons for founding Fresh Start had been the conviction that the lice on a corpse are not a going concern: we did not want our brother survivors to remain dependent on a finite supply of tools, equipment, and processed food. If we could risk Musky attack, so could others.

Consequently we selected as our first product an item unobtainable anywhere else, and utterly necessary in the changed world: effective nose plugs. I suggested them, Krishnamurti designed them and the primitive assembly line on which they were first turned out, and Dalhousie directed us all in their construction. All of us, men and women, worked on the line. It took us several months to achieve success, and by that time we were our own best customers —our factory smelled most abominable. Which we had expected, and planned for: the whole concept of Fresh Start rested on the single crucial fact that prevailing winds were virtually always from the north. On the rare occasions when the wind backed, the Nose formed a satisfactory natural barrier.

Once we were ready to offer our plugs for sale, we began advertising and recruiting on a large scale. Word of our plans was circulated by word of mouth, mimeographed flyer, and shortwave broadcast. The only person who responded by the onset of winter was Helen Phinney, but her arrival was providential, freeing us almost overnight from dependence on stinking gasoline-driven generators for power. She was then and is now Fresh Start's only resident world-class genius, a recognized expert on what were then called "alternative" power sources—the only ones Carlson had left us. She quite naturally became a part of the planning process, as well as a warm friend of us all. Within a short time the malodorous generators had been replaced by waterpower from the streams that cascade like copious tears from the "bridge" of the Nose, and ultimately by methane gas and wind power from a series of eggbeater-type windmills strung along the Nose itself. In recent years the generators have been put back on the line, largely for industrial use—but they no longer burn gasoline, nor does the single truck we have restored to service. Thanks to Phinney, they burn pure grain alcohol which we distill ourselves from field corn and rye, which works *more* efficiently than gasoline and produces only water and carbon dioxide as exhaust. (Pre-Exodus man could have used the same fuel in most of his internal-combustion engines—but once Henry Ford made his choice, the industry he incidentally created tended of course to perpetuate itself.)

This then was the Council of Fresh Start, assembled by fate: Myself, a dreamer, racked with guilt and seeking a truly worthwhile penance, trying to salvage some of the world I'd helped ruin. Krishnamurti, utterly practical wizard at both requirements analysis and design engineering, translator of ideas into plans. Dalhousie, the ultimate foreman, gifted at reducing any project to its component parts and accomplishing them with minimum time and effort. Phinney, the energy provider, devoted to drawing free power from the natural processes of the universe. Our personalities blended as well as our skills, and by that second spring we were a unit: the Council. I would suggest a thing, Krishnamurti would design the black box, Dalhousie would build it, and Phinney would throw power to it. We fit. Together we felt *useful* again, more than scavenging survivors.

No other recruits arrived during the winter, which like the one before was unusually harsh for that part of the world (perhaps owing to the sudden drastic decline in the worldwide production of waste heat), but by spring volunteers began arriving in droves. We got all kinds: scientists, technicians, students, mechanics, handymen, construction workers, factory hands, a random assortment of men seeking Civilized work. A colony of canvas tents grew in Northtown, in cleared areas we hoped would one day hold great dormitories. Our initial efforts that summer were aimed at providing water, power, and sewage systems for our growing community, and enlarging our nose plug factory. A combination smithy-repair-shop-motor-pool grew of its own accord next to the factory in Southtown, and we began bartering repair work for food with local farmers to the east and northwest.

By common consent, all food, tools, and other resources were shared equally by all members of the community, with the single exception of mad Gallipolis's summer homes. We the Council members retained these homes, and have never been begrudged them by our followers (two of the homes were incomplete at the time of the Exodus, and remained so for another few years). That aside, all the inhabitants of Fresh Start stand or fall, eat or starve together. The Council's authority as governing committee has never in all the ensuing years been either confirmed or seriously challenged. The nearly one hundred technicians who have by now assembled to our call continue to follow our advice because it works: because it gives their lives direction and meaning, because it makes their hard-won skills useful again, because it pays them well to do what they do best and thought they might never do again.

During that second summer we were frequently attacked by Muskies, invariably (of course) from the north, and suffered significant losses. For instance, Samuel Pegorski, the young hydraulic engineering major who with Phinney designed and perfected our plumbing and sewage systems, was cut down by the windriders before he lived to hear the first toilet flush in Northtown.

But with the timely arrival of Philip Collaci, an ex-Marine and former police chief from Pennsylvania, our security problems disappeared. A preternaturally effective fighting man, Collaci undertook to recruit, organize, and train the Guard, comprising enough armed men to keep the northern perimeter of Fresh Start patrolled at all times. At first, these Guards did no more than sound an alarm if they smelled Muskies coming across the lake, whereupon all hands made for the nearest shelter and tried to blank their minds to the semitelepathic creatures.

But Collaci was not satisfied. He wanted an offensive weapon—or, failing that, a defense better than flight. He told me as much several times, and finally I put aside administrative worries and went to work on the problem from a biochemical standpoint.

It seemed to me that extreme heat should work, but the problem was to devise a delivery system. Early experiments with a salvaged flame thrower were unsatisfactory—the cone of fire tended to brush Muskies out of its path instead of consuming them. Collaci suggested a line of alcohol-burning jets along the north perimeter, ready to guard Fresh Start with a wall of flame, an idea which has since been implemented—but at the time we could not spare the corn or rye to make the alcohol to power the jets. Finally, weeks of research led to the successful development of "hot-shot"—ammunition which could be fired from any existing heavy-caliber weapon after its barrel had been replaced, that would ignite as it cleared the modified barrel and generate enormous heat as it flew, punching through any Musky it encountered and destroying it instantly. An early mixture of magnesium and perchlorate of potash has since given way to an even slower-burning mix of aluminum powder and potassium permanganate which will probably remain standard until the last Musky has been slain (long-range plans for long-range artillery shot will have to wait until we can find a good cheap source of cerium, zirconium, or thorium—unlikely in the near future). Hot-shot's effective range approximates that of a man's nose on a still day—good enough for personal combat. This turned out to be the single most important advance since the Exodus, not only for mankind, but for the fledgling community of Fresh Start.

Because our only major misjudgment had been the climate of social opinion in which we expected to find ourselves. I said earlier that we feared people would scavenge from cities rather than buy from us, even in the face of terrible danger from the Muskies who prowled the urban skies. This turned out not to be the case.

Mostly, people preferred to do without.

Secure in our retreat, we had misjudged the *Zeitgeist*, the mind of the common man. It was Collaci, fresh from over a year of wandering up and down the desolate eastern seaboard, who showed us our error. He made us realize that Lot was probably more eager to return to Gomorrah than the average human was to return to his cities and suburbs. Cities had been the scenes of the greatest racial trauma since the Flood, the places where friends and loved ones had died horribly and the skies had filled with Muskies. The Exodus and the subsequent weeks of horror were universally seen as the Hammer of God falling on the *idea of city* itself, and hard-core urbanites who might have debated the point were mostly too dead to do so. The back-to-nature movement, already in full swing at the moment when Carlson dropped the flask, took on the stature and fervor of a Dionysian religion.

Fortunately, Collaci made us see in time that we would inevitably share in the superstition and hatred accorded to cities, become associated in the common mind with the evil-smelling steel-and-glass behemoth from which men had been so conclusively vomited. He made us realize something of the extent of the suspicion and intolerance we would incur—not ignored for our redundance, but loathed for our repugnance.

At Collaci's suggestion Krishnamurti enlisted the aid of some of the more substantial farmers in neighboring regions to the east, northeast, and northwest. He negotiated agreements by which farmers who supported us with food received preferential access to Musky-killing ammunition, equipment maintenance, and, one day (he promised), commercial power. I could never have sold the idea myself—while I have always understood public relations well from the theoretical standpoint, I have never been very successful in interpersonal diplomacy—at least, with nontechnicals. The dour Krishnamurti might have seemed an even more unlikely choice—but his utter practicality convinced many a skeptical farmer where charm might have failed.

Krishnamurti's negotiations not only assured us a dependable supply of food (and, incidentally, milled lumber), it had the invaluable secondary effect of gaining us psychological allies, non-Technos who were economically and emotionally committed to us.

Work progressed rapidly once our recruiting efforts began to pay off, and by our fifth year the Fresh Start of today was visible, at least in skeleton form. We had cut interior roads to supplement the northern and southern loops left by gyppo loggers two decades before; three dormitories were up and a fourth a-building; our General Store was a growing commercial concern; a line of windmills was taking shape along the central ridge of the Nose; our sewage plant/methane converter was nearly completed; plans were underway to establish a hospital and to blast a tunnel through the Nose to link Northtown and Southtown; the Tool Shed, the depot which housed irreplaceable equipment and tools, was nearly full; and Southtown was more malodorous than ever, with a large fuel distillery, a chemistry lab, a primitive foundry, and glass-blowing, matchmaking, and weaving operations adjoining the hot-shot and nose plug factories.

Despite these outward signs of prosperity, we led a precarious existence—there was strong public sentiment in favor of burning us to the ground, at least among the surviving humans who remained landless nomads. To combat this we were running and distributing a small mimeographed newspaper, *Got News,* and maintaining radio station WFS (then and now the only one in the world). In addition Krishnamurti and I made endless public relations trips for miles in every direction to explain our existence and purpose to groups and individuals.

But there were many who had no land, no homes, no families, nothing but a vast heritage of bitterness. These were the precursors of today's so-called Agro Party. Surviving where and as they could, socialized for an environment that no longer existed, they hated us for reminding them of the technological womb which had unforgivably thrust them out. They raided us, singly and in loosely organized groups, often with unreasonable, suicidal fury. From humanitarian concerns as much as from public relations considerations, I sharply restrained Guard Chief Collaci, whose own inclination was to shoot any saboteur he apprehended—wherever possible they were captured and turned loose outside city limits. Collaci argued strongly for deterrent violence, but I was determined to show our neighbors that Fresh Start bore ill will to no man, and overruled him.

In that fifth year, however, I was myself overruled.

Collaci and his wife Karen (a tough, quiet, red-headed woman) had been given one of Gallipolis's uncompleted cabins, the one furthest and most isolated from Northtown's residential area. A volunteer house-raising had finished it off handsomely the previous spring. It was either bad judgment or ignorance that brought the seven-man raiding party past the Collaci home on their way to blow up the Tool Shed. But it was unquestionably bad judgment that made them kidnap Karen Collaci when they blundered across her in the forest. She was diabetic, and they had no insulin.

Collaci left his duties without authorization and pursued them, found her body within a few days. He tracked the seven guerrillas over a period of a week. Although they had split up and fled in different directions, those seven days sufficed him. He exacted from them penalties which cannot be repeated here, left each nailed to a tree, and upon his return to Fresh Start slept for three consecutive days.

Collaci's understandably impulsive action seems, in the light of history, to have been more correct than my own policy of tolerance. At any rate, we have never been raided since.

With the advent of Dr. Michael Gowan, a former professor of

psychology from Stony Brook who undertook to create and administer an educational system, all the necessary seeds had, to my mind, been planted. Barring catastrophe, technological man now could and would survive. Someday, perhaps, he might rebuild what had been destroyed.

And then, one day in 1999, I interviewed and "hired" a new arrival named Jordan Washington. Since then . . .

CHAPTER FIVE

". . . and when I came to, Carlson was dead with a slug through the head and the last Musky was nowhere in smell. So I reset my plugs, found the campfire behind the hedges, and ate his supper, and then left the next morning. I found a Healer in Jersey. That's all there is, Dad."

My father chewed the pipe he had not smoked in eighteen years and stared into the fire. Dry poplar and green birch together produced a steady blaze that warmed the spacious living room and peopled it with leaping shadows.

"Then it's over," he said at last, and heaved a great sigh.

"Yes, Dad. It's over."

He was silent, his coal-black features impassive, for a long time. Firelight danced among the valleys and crevices of his patriarch's face, and across the sharp scar on his left cheek (so like the one I now bore). His eyes glittered like rainy midnight. I wondered what he was thinking, after all these years and all that he had seen.

"Isham," he said at last, "you have done well."

"Have I, Dad?"

"Eh?"

"I just can't seem to get it straight in my mind. I guess I expected tangling with Carlson to be a kind of solution, to some things that have been bugging me all my life. Somehow I expected pulling that trigger to bring me peace. Instead I'm more confused than ever. Surely you can smell my unease, Dad? Or are your plugs still in again?" Dad used the best plugs in Fresh Start, entirely internal, and he perpetually forgot to remove them after work. Even those who loved him agreed he was the picture of the absentminded professor.

"No," he said hesitantly. "I can smell that you are uneasy, but I can't smell *why*. You must tell me, Isham."

"It's not easy to explain, Dad. I can't seem to find the words. Look, I wrote out a kind of journal of events in Jersey, while the Healer was working on me, and afterwards while I rested up. It's the same story I just told you, but somehow on paper I think it conveys more of what's bothering me. Will you read it?"

He nodded. "If you wish."

I gave my father all the preceding manuscript, right up to the moment I pulled the trigger and blacked out, and brought him his glasses. He read it slowly and carefully, pausing now and again to gaze distantly into the flames. While he read, I unobtrusively fed the fire and immersed myself in the familiar smells of wood-smoke and ink and chemicals and the pines outside, all the thousand indefinable scents that tried to tell me I was home.

When Dad was done reading, he closed his eyes and nodded slowly for a time. Then he turned to me and regarded me with troubled eyes. "You've left out the ending," he said.

"Because I'm not sure how I feel about it."

He steepled his fingers. "What is it that troubles you, Isham?"

"Dad," I said earnestly, "Carlson is the first man I ever killed. That's . . . not a small thing. As it happens I didn't actually see my bullet blow off the back of his skull, and sometimes it's hard to believe in my gut that I really did it—I know it seemed unreal when I saw him afterward. But in fact I have killed a man. And as you just read, that may be necessary sometimes, but I'm not sure it's right. I *know* all that Carlson did, to us Stones and to the world, I know the guilt he bore. But I must ask you: Dad, was I *right* to kill him? Did he deserve to die?"

He came to me then and gripped my shoulder, and we stood like black iron statues before the raving fire. He locked eyes with me. "Perhaps you should ask your mother, Isham. Or your brother Israfel. Perhaps you should have asked the people whose remains you stepped over to kill Carlson. I do not know what is 'right' and 'wrong'; they are slippery terms to define. I only know what is. And revenge, as Collaci told you, *is* a uniquely human attribute.

"Superstitious Agro guerrillas used to raid us from time to time, and because we were reluctant to fire on them they got away with it. Then one day they captured Collaci's wife, not knowing she was diabetic. By the time he caught up with them she was dead of lack of insulin. Within seven days, every guerrilla in that raiding party had died, and Fresh Start has not been raided in all the years since, for all Jordan's rhetoric. Ask Collaci about vengeance."

"But Jordan's Agros hate us more than ever."

"But they buy our axheads and wheels, our sulfa and our cloth, just like their more sensible neighbors, and they leave us alone. Carlson's death will be an eternal warning to any who would impose their values on the world at large, and an eternal comfort to those who were robbed by him of the best of their lives—of their homes and their loved ones.

"Isham, you . . . did . . . *right.* Don't ever think differently, son. You did right, and I am deeply proud of you. Your mother and Israfel are resting easier now, and millions more too. I know that I will sleep easier tonight than I have in eighteen years."

That's right, Dad, you will. I relaxed. "All right, Dad. I guess you're right. I just wanted to hear someone tell me besides myself. I wanted *you* to tell me." He smiled and nodded and sat down again, and I left him there, an old man lost in his thoughts.

I went to the bathroom and closed the door behind me, glad that restored plumbing had been one of Fresh Start's first priorities to be realized. I spent a few minutes assembling some items I had brought back from New York City and removing the back of the septic tank behind the toilet bowl. Then I flushed the toilet.

Reaching into the tank I grabbed the gravity ball and flexed it horizontal so that the tank would not refill with water. Holding it in place awkwardly, I made a long arm and picked up the large bottle of chlorine bleach I had fetched from the city. As an irreplaceable relic of Civilization it was priceless—and utterly useless to modern man. I slipped my plugs into place and filled the tank with bleach, replacing the porcelain cover silently but leaving it slightly ajar. I bent again and grabbed a large canister —also a valuable but useless antique—of bathroom bowl cleaner. It was labeled "Vanish," and I hoped the label was prophetic. I poured the entire canister into the bowl.

Hang the expense, I thought, and giggled insanely.

Then I put the cover down on the seat, hid the bleach and bowl cleaner, and left, whistling softly through my teeth.

I felt good, better than I had since I left New York.

I walked through inky dark to the lake, and I sat among the pines by the shore, flinging stones at the water, trying to make them skip. I couldn't seem to get it right. I was used to the balancing effect of a left arm. I rubbed my stump ruefully and lay back and just thought for a while. I had lied to my father—it was not over. But it would be soon.

Right or wrong, I thought, removing my plugs and lighting a joint, *it sure can be necessary.*

Moonlight shattered on the branches overhead and lay in shards on the ground. I breathed deep of the cool darkness, tasted pot and woods and distant animals and the good crisp scents of a balanced ecology, heard the faraway hum of wind generators storing power for the work yet to be done. And I thought of a man gone mad with a dream of a better, simpler world; a man who, Heaven help him, meant well. And I thought of the tape recording I planned to leave behind me, explaining what I had done to the Council and the world.

CHAPTER SIX

Transcript of a Tape Recording Made by Isham Stone (Fresh Start Judicial Archives).

I might as well address this tape to you, Collaci—I'll bet my Musky gun that you're the first one to notice and play it. I hope you'll listen to it as well, but that might be too much to ask, the first time around. Just keep playing it.

The story goes back a couple of months, to when I was in the city. By now you've no doubt found my journal, with its account of my day in New York, and you've probably noticed the missing ending. Well, there are two endings to that story. There's the ending I told my father, and then there's the one you're about to hear. The true one.

I drifted in the darkness for a thousand years, helpless as a Musky in a hurricane, caroming off the inside of my skull. Memories swept by like drifting blimps, and I clutched at them as I sailed past, but the ones tangible enough to grasp burned my fingers. Vaguely, I sensed distant daylight on either side, decided those must be my ears and tried to steer for the right one, which seemed a bit closer. I singed my arm banking off an adolescent trauma, but it did the trick—I sailed out into daylight and landed on my face with a hell of a crash. I thought about getting up, but I couldn't remember whether I'd brought my legs with me, and they weren't talking. My arm hurt even more than my face, and something stank.

"Help?" I suggested faintly, and a pair of hands got me by the armpits. I rose in the air and closed my eyes against a sudden wave of vertigo. When it passed, I decided I was on my back in the bed I had just contrived to fall out of. High in my chest, a dull but insistent pain advised me to breathe shallowly.

I'll be damned, I thought weakly. *Collaci must have come along to back me up without telling me. Canny old son of a bitch, I should have thought to pick him up some toothpicks.*

"Hey, Teach'," I croaked, and opened my eyes.

Wendell Morgan Carlson leaned over me, concern in his gaze.

Curiously enough, I didn't try to reach up and crush his larynx. I closed my eyes, relaxed all over, counted to ten very slowly, shook my head to clear it, and opened my eyes again. Carlson was still there.

Then I tried to reach up and crush his larynx. I failed, of course, not so much because I was too weak to *reach* his larynx as because only one arm even acknowledged the command. My brain said that my left arm was straining upwards for Carlson's throat, and complaining like hell about it too, but I didn't see the arm anywhere. I looked down and saw the neatly bandaged stump and lifted it up absently to see if my arm was underneath it and it wasn't. It dawned on me then that the stump was all the left arm I was ever going to find, and whacko: I was back inside my skull, safe in the friendly dark, ricocheting off smoldering recollections again.

The second time I woke up was completely different. One minute I was wrestling with a phantom, and then a switch was thrown and I was lucid. *Play for time* was my first thought, *the tactical situation sucks.* I opened my eyes.

Carlson was nowhere in sight. Or smell—but then my plugs were back in place.

I looked around the room. It was a room. Four walls, ceiling, floor, the bed I was in and assorted ugly furniture. Not a weapon in sight, nor anything I could make one from. A look out the window in the opposite wall confirmed my guess that I was in Butler Hall, apparently on the ground floor, not far from the main entrance. The great curved dome of Low Library was nearly centered in the window frame, its great stone steps partly obscured by overgrown shrubbery in front of Butler. The shadows said it was morning, getting on toward noon. I closed my eyes, firmly.

Next I took stock of myself. My head throbbed a good deal, but it was easily drowned out by the ache in my chest. Unquestionably some ribs had broken, and it felt as though the ends were mismatched. But as near as I could tell the lung was intact—it didn't hurt more when I inhaled. Not much more, anyway. My legs both moved when I asked them to, with a minimum of back talk, and the ankles appeared sound. No need to open my eyes again, was there?

I stopped the inventory for a moment. In the back of my skull a clawed lizard yammered for release, and I devoted a few minutes to reinforcing the walls of its prison. When I could no longer hear the shrieking, I switched on my eyes again and quite dispassionately considered the stump on my left arm.

It looked like a good, clean job. The placement of the cut said it was a surgical procedure rather than the vengeful hostility I'd assumed first—it seemed as though the gangrene had been beaten. *Oh fine,* I thought, *a benevolent madman I have to kill.* Then I was ashamed. My mother had been benevolent, as I remembered her; and Israfel never got much chance to be anything. All men knew Carlson's intentions had been good. I could kill him with one hand.

I wondered where he was.

A fly buzzed mournfully around the room. Hedges rustled outside the window, and somewhere birds sang, breathless trills that hung sparkling on the morning air. It was a beautiful day, just warm enough to be comfortable, no clouds evident, just enough breeze and the best part of the day yet to come. It made me want to go down by the stream and poke frogs with a stick, or go pick strawberries for Mr. Fletcher, red-stained hands and a bellyful of sweet and the trots next morning. It was a great day for an assassination.

I thought about it, considered the possibilities. Carlson was . . . somewhere. I was weaker than a Musky in a pressure cooker and my most basic armament was down by twenty-five percent. I was on unfamiliar territory, and the only objects in the room meaty enough to constitute weaponry were too heavy for me to lift. Break the windowpane and acquire a knife? How would I hold it? My sneakers were in sight across the room, under a chair holding the rest of my clothes, and I wondered if I could hide behind the door until Carlson entered, then strangle him with the laces.

I brought up short. How was I going to strangle Carlson with one hand?

Things swam then for a bit, as I got the first of an endless series of flashes of just how drastically my life was altered now by the loss of my arm. *You'll never use a chain saw again, or a shovel, or a catcher's mitt, or . . .*

I buried the lizard again and forced myself to concentrate. Perhaps I could fashion a noose from my sneaker laces. With one hand? *Could* I? Maybe if I fastened one end of the lace to something, then looped the other end around his neck and pulled? I needn't be strong, it could be arranged so that my weight did the killing. . . .

Just in that one little instant I think I decided not to die, decided to keep on living with one arm, and the question never really arose in my mind again. I was too busy to despair, and by the time I could afford to—much later—the urge was gone.

All of my tentative plans, therapeutic as they were, hinged on one important question: could I stand up? It seemed essential to find out.

Until then I had moved only my eyes—now I tried sitting up. It was no harder than juggling bulldozers, and I managed to cut the scream down to an explosive, "Uh *huh!*" My ribs felt like glass, broken glass ripping through the muscle sheathing and pleural tissue. Sweat broke out on my forehead and I fought down dizziness and nausea, savagely commanding my body to obey me like a desperate rider digging spurs into a dying horse. I locked my right arm behind me and leaned on it, swaying but upright, and waited for the room to stop spinning. I spent the time counting to one thousand by eighths. Finally it stopped, leaving me with the feeling that a stiff breeze could start it spinning again.

All right then. *Let's get this show on the road, Stone.* I swung a leg over the side of the bed, discovered with relief that my foot reached the floor. That would make it easier to balance upright on the edge of the bed before attempting to stand. Before I could lose my nerve I swung the other leg over, pushed off with my arm, and was sitting upright. The floor was an incredible distance below—had I really fallen that far and lived? Perhaps I should just wait for Carlson to return, get him to come close, and sink my teeth into his jugular.

I stood up.

A staggering crescendo in the symphony of pain, ribs still carrying the melody. I locked my knees and tottered, moaning piteously like a kitten trapped on a cornice. It was the closest I could come to stealthy silence, and all things considered it was pretty damn close. My right shoulder was discernibly heavier than the left one, and it played hob with my balance. The floor, which had been steadily receding, was now so far away I stopped worrying about it—surely there would be time for the chute to open.

Well then, why not try a step or two?

My left leg was as light as a helium balloon—once peeled off the floor it tried to head for the ceiling, and it took an enormous effort to force it down again. The right leg fared no better. Then the room started spinning again, just as I'd feared, and it was suddenly impossible to keep either leg beneath my body, which began losing altitude rapidly. The chute didn't open. There was a jarring crash, and a ghastly *bounce.* Many pretty lights appeared, and one of the screams fenced in behind closed teeth managed to break loose. The pretty lights gave way to flaking ceiling, and the ceiling gave way to blackness. I remembered a line from an old song Dr. Mike used to sing, something about ". . . road maps in a well-cracked ceiling . . ." and wished I'd had time to read the map. . . .

I came out of it almost at once, I think. It *felt* as though the room was still spinning, but I was now spinning with it at the same velocity. By great good fortune I had toppled backward, across the bed. I took a tentative breath, and it still felt like my lung was intact. I was drenched with sweat, and I seemed to be lying on someone's rock collection.

Okay, I decided, *if you're too weak to kill Carlson now, pretend you're even weaker. Get back under the sheets and play dead, until your position improves.* Isham Machiavelli, that's me. You'd've been proud of me, Teach'.

The rock collection turned out to be wrinkled sheets. Getting turned around and back to where I'd started was easier than reeling a whale into a rowboat, and I had enough strength to arrange the sheets plausibly before all my muscles turned into peanut butter. Then I just lay there breathing as shallowly as I could manage, wondering why my left . . . why my stump didn't seem to hurt enough. I hated to look a gift horse in the mouth; the psychological burden was quite heavy enough, thanks. But it made me uneasy.

I began composing a square-dance tune in time to the throbbing of my ribs. The room reeled to it, slightly out of synch at first but then so rhythmically that it actually seemed to stumble when the snare drummer out in the hall muffed a paradiddle. The music stopped, but the drummer staggered on off-rhythm, faint at first but getting louder. Footsteps.

It had to be Carlson.

He was making a hell of a racket. Feverishly I envisioned him dragging a bazooka into the room and lining it up on me. Crazy. A flyswatter would have more than sufficed. But what the hell *was* he carrying then?

The answer came through the doorway: a large carton filled with things that clanked and rattled. Close behind it came Wendell Morgan Carlson himself, and it was as well that the square-dance music had stopped—the acceleration of my pulse would have made the tune undanceable. My nostrils tried to flare around the plugs, and the hair on the back of my neck might have bristled in atavistic reflex if there hadn't been a thousand pounds of head lying on it.

The Enemy!

He had no weapons visible. He looked much older than his

picture on the Carlson Poster—but the craggy brow, thin pinched nose, and high cheeks were unmistakable, even if the lantern jaw was obscured by an inordinate amount of gray beard. He was a bit taller than I had pictured him, with more hair and narrower shoulders. I hadn't expected the potbelly. He wore baggy jeans and a plaid flannel shirt, both ineptly patched here and there, and a pair of black sandals.

His face held more intelligence than I like in an antagonist—he would not be easy to fool. *Wendell* who? *Never heard of him. Just got back from Pellucidar myself, and I was wondering if you could tell me where all the people went? Sorry I took a shot at you, and oh yeah, thanks for cutting off my arm; you're a brick.*

He put the carton down on an ancient brown desk, crushing a faded photograph of someone's children, turned at once to meet my gaze, and said an incredible thing.

"I'm sorry I woke you."

I don't know what I'd expected. But in the few fevered moments I'd had to prepare myself for this moment, my first exchange of words with Wendell Morgan Carlson, I had never imagined such an opening gambit. I had no riposte prepared.

"You're welcome," I croaked insanely, and tried to smile. Whatever it was I actually did seemed to upset him; his face took on that look of concern I had glimpsed once before—when? Yesterday? *How long had I been here?*

"I'm glad you are awake," he went on obligingly. "You've been unconscious for nearly a week." No wonder I felt constructed of inferior materials. I decided I must be a pretty tough mothafucka. It was nice to know I wasn't copping out.

"What's in the box?" I asked, with a little less fuzz tone.

"Box?" He looked down. "Oh yes, I thought . . . you see, it's intravenous feeding equipment. I studied the literature, and I . . ." he trailed off. His voice was a reedy but pleasant alto, with rusting brass edges. He appeared unfamiliar with its use.

"You were going to . . ." An ice cube formed in my bowels. Needle into sleeping arm, suck my life from a tube; have a hit of old Isham. *Steady, boy, steady.*

"Perhaps it might still be a good idea," he mused. "All I have to offer you at the moment is bread and milk. Not real milk of course . . . but then you could have honey with the bread. I suppose that's as good as glucose."

"Fine with me, Doctor," I said hastily. "I have a thing about needles." And other sharp instruments. "But where do you get your honey?"

He frowned quizzically. "How did you know I have a Ph.D.?"

Think quick. "I didn't. I assumed you were a Healer. It was you who amputated my arm?" I kept my voice even.

His frown deepened, a striking expression on that craggy face. "Young man," he said reluctantly, "I have no formal medical training of any sort. Perhaps your arm could have stayed on—but it seemed to me . . ." He was, to my astonishment, mortally embarrassed.

"Doctor, it needed extensive cutting the last time I saw it, and I'm sure it got worse while I was under. Don't . . . worry about it. I'm sure you did the best you could." If he was inclined to forget my attempt to blow his head off, who was *I* to hold a grudge? Let bygones be bygones—I didn't need a new reason to kill him.

"I read all I could find on field amputation," he went on, still apologetic, "but of course I'd never done one before." On anything smaller than a race. I assured him that it looked to me like a textbook job. It was inexpressibly weird to have this man seek my pardon for saving my life when I planned to take his at the earliest possible opportunity. It upset me, made me irritable. My wounds provided a convenient distraction, and I moved enough to justify a moan.

Carlson was instantly solicitous. From his cardboard carton he produced a paper package which, torn open, revealed a plastic syringe. Taking a stoppered jar from the carton, he drew off a small amount of clear fluid.

"What's that?" I said, trying to keep the suspicion from my voice.

"Demerol."

I shook my head. "No, thanks, Doc. I told you I don't like needles."

He nodded, put down the spike, and took another object from the carton. "Here's oral Demerol, then. I'll leave it where you can reach it." He put it on a bedside table. I picked up the jar, gave it a quick glance. It said it was Demerol. I could not break the seal around the cap with one hand—Carlson had to open it for me. *Thank you, my enemy.* Weird, weird, weird! I palmed a pill, pretending to swallow it. He looked satisfied.

"Thanks, Doc."

"Please don't call me Doc," he asked. "My name is Wendell Carlson."

If he was expecting a reaction, he was disappointed. "Sure thing, Wendell. I'm Tony Latimer. Pleased to meet you." It was the first name that entered my head.

There was a lull in the conversation. We studied each other with the frank curiosity of men who have not known human company for a while. At last he looked embarrassed again and tore his gaze from mine. "I'd better see about that food. You must be terribly hungry."

I thought about it. It seemed to me that I could put away a quarter horse. Raw. With my fingers. "I could eat."

Carlson left the room, looking at his sandals.

I thought of loading the hypo with an overdose and ambushing him when he returned, but it was just a thought. That hypo was mighty far away. I returned my attention to the jar on the table. It still said it was Demerol—and it *had* been sealed, with white plastic. But Carlson could have soaked off and replaced a skull-and-crossbones label—I decided to live with the pain a while longer.

It seemed like a long time before he returned, but my time sense was not too reliable. He fetched a half loaf of brown bread, a mason jar of soya milk, and some thick, crystallized honey. They say that smell is essential to taste, and I couldn't unplug, but it tasted better than food ever had before.

"You never told me where you get honey, Wendell."

"I have a small hive down in Central Park. Only a few supers, but adequate for my needs. Wintering the bees is quite a trick, but I manage."

"I'll bet it is." Small talk in the slaughterhouse. I ate what he gave me and drank soya milk until I was full. My body still hurt, but not as much.

We talked for about half an hour, mostly inconsequentialities, and it seemed that a tension grew up between us, because of the very inconsequentiality of our words. There were things of which we did not speak, of which innocent men should have spoken. In my dazed condition I could concoct no plausible explanation for my presence in New York, nor for the shot I had fired at him. Somehow he accepted this, but in return I was not to ask him how he came to be living in New York City, I was not supposed to have any idea who Wendell Morgan Carlson was. It was an absurd bargain, a truth level impossible to maintain, but it suited both of us. I couldn't imagine what he thought of my own conversational omissions, but I was convinced that his silence was an admission of guilt, and my resolve was firmed. He left me at last, advising me to sleep if I could and promising to return the next day.

I didn't sleep. Not at first. I lay there looking at the Demerol bottle for a hundred years, explaining to myself how unlikely it was that the bottle wasn't genuine. I could not help it—hatred and distrust of Carlson were ingrained in me.

But enough pain will break through the strongest conditioning. About sundown I ate the pill I'd palmed, and in a very short time I was unconscious.

The next few days passed slowly.

Woops—I'm out of tape. Time to flip over the re—

CHAPTER SEVEN

Stone Tape Transcript, Side Two

The days passed slowly, but not so slowly as the pain. Lucidity returned slowly, but no faster than physical strength.

You've got to understand how it was, Teach'.

The Demerol helped—but not by killing pain. What it did was keep me so stoned that I often forgot the pain was there. In a warm, creative glow I would devise a splendidly subtle and poetic means of Killing Carlson—then half an hour later the same plan would seem hopelessly crackbrained. An imperfection of the glass in the window across the room, warping the clean proud curve of the Low dome, held me fascinated for hours—yet I could not seem to concentrate for five minutes on practical matters.

Carlson came and went, asking few questions and answering fewer, and in my stupor I tried to fire my hate to the killing point, and—Collaci, my instructor and mentor and (I hope) friend—I failed.

You must understand me—I spent hours trying to focus on the hatred my father had passed on to me, to live up to the geas that fate had laid upon me, to do my duty. But it was damned hard work. Carlson was an absurd combination: so absentminded as to remind me of Dad—and as thoughtful, in his way, as you. He would forget his coat when he left at night—but be back on time with a hot breakfast, shivering and failing to notice. He would forget my name, but never my chamber pot. He would search, blinking, in all directions for the coffee cup that sat perched on his lap, but he never failed to put mine where I could reach it without strain on my ribs. I discovered quite by accident that I slept in the only bed Carlson had ever hauled into Butler, that he himself dossed on a makeshift bed out in the hall, so as to be near if I cried out in the night.

He offered no clue to his motivations, no insight into what kept him entombed in New York City. He spoke of his life of exile as a simple fact, requiring no explanation. It seemed more and more obvious that his silence was an admission of guilt: that he could not explain his survival and continued presence in this smelly mausoleum without admitting his crime. I tried, how I tried, to hate him.

But it was damnably difficult. He supplied my needs before I could voice them, wants before I could form them. He sensed when I craved company and when to leave me be, when I needed to talk and when I needed to be talked to. He suffered my irritability and occasional rages in a way that somehow allowed me to keep my self-respect.

He was gone for long periods of time during the day and night, and never spoke of his activities. I never pressed him for information; as a recuperating assassin it behooved me to display no undue curiosity. I could not risk arousing his suspicions.

We never, for instance, chanced to speak of my weapons or their whereabouts.

And so the subconscious tension of our first conversation stayed with us, born of the things of which we did not speak. It was obvious to both of us—and yet it was a curious kind of kinship, too: both of us lived with something we could not share, and recognized the condition in the other. Even as I planned his death I felt a kind of empathy between Wendell Morgan Carlson and myself. It bothered hell out of me. If Carlson was what I *knew* he was, what his guilty silence only proved him to be, then his death was necessary and just—for my father had taught me that debts are always paid. But I could not help but like the absentminded old man.

Yet that tension was there. We spoke only of neutral things: where he got gasoline to feed the generator that powered wall sockets in the ground-floor rooms (we did not discuss what he would store it in now that I'd ruined his two-hundred-gallon tank). How far he had to walk these days to find scavengeable flour, beans, and grains. The trouble he had encountered in maintaining the University's hydroponics cultures by himself. What he did with sewage and compost. The probability of tomatoes growing another year in the miserable sandy soil of Central Park. What a turkey he'd been to not think of using the pure-grain alky in Organic Chem for fuel. Never did we talk of why he undertook all the complex difficulty of living in New York, nor why I had sought him here. He . . . diverted the patient with light conversation, and the patient allowed him to do so.

I had the hate part all ready to go, but I couldn't superimpose my lifetime picture of Carlson over this fuzzy, pleasant old academic and make it fit. And so the hate boiled in my skull and made convalescence an aimless, confused time. It got much worse when Carlson, explaining that few things on earth are more addictive than oral Demerol, cut me off cold turkey in my second week. Less potent analgesics, Talwin, aspirin, all had decayed years ago, and if I sent Carlson rummaging through the rucksack I had left under a station wagon on 114th Street for the remaining weed, he would in all likelihood come across the annotated map of New York given me by Collaci, and the mimeo'd Carlson Poster. Besides, my ribs hurt too much to smoke.

One night I woke in a sweat-soaked agony to find the room at a crazy angle, the candle flame slanting out of the dark like a questing tongue. I had half fallen out of bed, and my right arm kept me from falling the rest of the way, but I could not get back up without another arm. I didn't seem to have one. Ribs began to throb as I considered the dilemma, and I cried out from the pain.

From out in the hallway came a honking snore that broke off in a grunted "Whazzat? Wha?" and then a series of gasps as Carlson dutifully rolled from his bed to assist me. There came a crash, then a greater one attended by a splash, then a really tremendous crash that echoed and reechoed. Carlson lurched into view, a potbellied old man in yellow pajamas, eyes three-quarters closed and unfocused, one foot trapped in a galvanized wastebasket, gallantly coming to my rescue. He hit the doorframe a glancing blow with his shoulder, overbalanced, and went down on his face. I believe he came fully awake a second after he hit the floor; his eyes opened wide and he saw me staring at him in dazed disbelief from a few inches away. And for one timeless moment the absurdity of our respective positions hit us, and we broke up, simultaneous whoops of laughter at ourselves that cut off at once, and a second later he was helping me back into bed with strong, gentle hands, and I was trying not to groan aloud.

Dammit, I liked him.

Then one day while he was away I rose from the bed all by myself, quite gratified to find that I could, and hobbled like an old, old man composed of glass to the window that looked out on the entrance area of Butler and the hedge-hidden quadrangle beyond. It was a chill, slightly off-white day, but to me even the meager colors of shrub and tree seemed unaccountably vivid. From the overfamiliar closeness of the sickroom, the decaying campus had a magnificent depth. Everything was so *far away.* It was a little overwhelming. Moving closer to the window, I looked to the right.

Carlson stood before the front doors, staring up at the sky over the quadrangle with his back to me. On his head was the same curious helmet I had seen once before, days ago, framed in the cross hairs of my rifle. The odd-looking machine was before him, wired to his helmet and his arms. I wondered again what it could be, and then I saw something that made me freeze, made me forget the pain and the dizziness and stare with full attention.

Carlson was staring down the row between two greatly overgrown hedges that ran parallel to each other and perpendicular to Butler, facing toward Low's mighty cascade of steps. But he stared as a man watching something *near* him, and its position followed that of the wind-tossed upper reaches of the hedges.

Intuitively I knew that he was using the strange machine to communicate with a Musky, and all the hatred and rage for which I had found no outlet boiled over, contorting my face with fury.

It seemed an enormous effort not to cry out some primal challenge; I believe I bared my teeth. *You bastard,* I thought savagely, *you set us up for them, made them our enemies, and now you're hand in glove with them.* I was stupefied by such incredible treachery, could not make any sense of it, did not care. As I watched from behind and to the left I saw his lips move silently, but I did not care what they said, what kind of deal Carlson had worked out with the murderous gas clouds. He had one. He dealt with the creatures that had killed my mother, that he had virtually created. He would soon die.

I shuffled with infinite care back to bed, and planned.

I was ready to kill him within a week. My ribs were mostly healed now—I came to realize that my body's repair process had been waiting only for me to decide to heal, to leave the safe haven of convalescence. My strength returned to me and soon I could walk easily, and even dress myself with care, letting the left sleeve dangle. Most of the pain was gone from the stump, leaving only the many annoying tactile phenomena of severed nerves, the classic "phantom arm," and the flood of sweat which seemed to pour from my left armpit but could not be found on my side. Thanks to Carlson's tendency toward sound sleep, I was familiar with the layout of the main floor—and had recovered the weapons he was too absentminded to destroy. He had "hidden" them in the broom closet.

I wanted to take him in a time and place where his Musky pals couldn't help him; it seemed to me certain that the ones I had destroyed were bodyguards. A blustery cold night obliged by occurring almost immediately, breezes too choppy to be effectively used by a windrider.

The kind of night which, in my childhood, we chose for a picnic or a hayride.

We ate together in my room, a bean and lentil dish with tamari and fresh bread, and as he was finishing his last sip of coffee I brought the rifle out from under the blanket and drew a bead on his face.

"End of the line, Wendell."

He sat absolutely still, cup still raised to his lips, gazing gravely over it at me, for a long moment. Then he put the cup down very slowly, and sighed. "I didn't think you'd do it so soon. You're not well enough, you know."

I grinned. "You were expecting this, huh?"

"Ever since you discovered your weapons the night before last, Tony."

My grin faded. "And you let me live? Wendell, have you a death wish?"

"I cannot kill," he said sadly, and I roared with sudden laughter.

"Maybe not anymore, Wendell. Certainly not in another few minutes." *But you have killed before, killed more than anyone in history. Hell, Hitler, Attila, they're all punks beside you!*

He grimaced. "So you know who I am."

"The whole world knows. What's left of it."

Pain filled his eyes, and he nodded. "The last few times I tried to leave the city, to find others to help me in my work, they shot at me. Two years ago I found a man down in the Bowery who had been attacked by a dog pack. He had a tooth missing. He said he had come to kill me, for the price on my head, and he died, cursing me, in my arms as I brought him here. The price he named was high, and I knew there would be others."

"And you nursed me back to health? You must know that you deserve to die." I sneered. "Musky-lover."

"You know even that, then?"

"I saw you talking with them, with that crazy helmet of yours. The ones who attacked me were your bodyguards, weren't they?"

"The windriders came to me almost twenty years ago," he said softly, eyes far away. "They did not harm me. Since then I have slowly learned to speak with them, after a fashion, using the undermind. We might yet have understood one another."

The gun was becoming heavy on my single arm, difficult to aim properly. I rested the barrel on my knee, and shifted my grip slightly. My hands were sweaty.

"Well?" he said gruffly. "Why haven't you killed me already?"

A good question. I swept it aside irritably. "Why did you do it?" I barked.

"Why did I create the Hyperosmic Virus?" His weathered face saddened even more, and he tugged at his beard. "Because I was a damned fool, I suppose. Because it was a pretty problem in biochemistry. Because no one else could have done it, and because I wasn't certain that I could. I never suspected when I began that it would be used as it was."

"Its release was a spur-of-the-moment decision, is that it?" I snarled, tightening my grip on the trigger.

"I suppose so," he said quietly. "Only Jacob could say, of course."

"Who?"

"Jacob Stone," he said, startled by my violence. "My assistant. I thought you said you . . ."

"So you knew who I was all the time," I growled.

He blinked at me, plainly astounded. Then understanding flooded his craggy features. "Of course," he murmured. "Of *course.* You're young Isham—I should have recognized you. I smelled your hate, of course, but I never . . ."

"You *what?*"

"Smelled the scent of hate upon you," he repeated, puzzled. "Not much of a trick—you've been reeking with it lately."

How could he? . . . Impossible, sweep it aside.

"And now I imagine you'll want to discharge that hate and avenge your father's death. That was his own doing, but no matter: it was I who made it possible. Go ahead, pull the trigger." He closed his eyes.

"My father is not dead," I said, drowning now in confusion.

Carlson opened his eyes at once. "No? I assumed he perished when he released the Virus."

My ears roared; the rifle was suddenly impossible to aim. I wanted to cry out, to damn Carlson for a liar, but I knew the fuzzy professor was no actor and all at once I sprang up out of the bed and burst from the room, through wrought-iron lobby doors and out of the great empty hall, out into blackness and howling wind and a great swirling kaleidoscope of stars that reeled drunkenly overhead. Ribs pulsing, I walked for a hundred years, clutching my idiot rifle, heedless of danger from Musky or hungry Doberman, pursued by a thousand howling demons. Dimly I heard Carlson calling out behind me for a time, but I lost him easily and continued, seeking oblivion. The city, finding its natural prey for the first time in two decades, obligingly swallowed me up.

More than a day later I had my next conscious thought. I became aware that I had been staring at my socks for at least an hour, trying to decide what color they were.

My second coherent thought was that my ass hurt.

I looked around: beyond smashed observation windows, the great steel-and-stone corpse of New York City was laid out below me like some incredible three-dimensional jigsaw. I was at the top of the Empire State Building.

I had no memory of the long climb, nor of the flight downtown from Columbia University, and it was only after I had worked out how tired I must be that I realized how tired I was. My ribs felt sand-blasted and the winds that swept the observation tower were very very cold.

I was higher from the earth than I had ever been before in my life, facing south toward the empty World Trade Center, toward that part of the Atlantic into which this city had once dumped five hundred cubic feet of human shit every day; but I saw neither city nor sea. Instead I saw a frustrated, ambitious black man, obsessed with a scheme for quick-and-easy world salvation, conning a fuzzy-headed genius whose eminence he could never hope to attain. I saw that man, terrified by the ghastly results of his folly, fashioning a story to shift blame from himself and repeating it until all men believed it—and perhaps he himself as well. I saw at last the true face of that story's villain: a tormented, guilt-driven old man, exiled for the high crime of gullibility, befriended only by his race's bitterest enemies, nursing his assassin back to health. And I saw as though for the first time that assassin, trained and schooled to complete a cover-up, the embittered black man's last bucket of whitewash.

My father had loaded me with all the hatred and anger he felt for himself, aimed me toward a scapegoat and fired me like a cannon.

But I would ricochet.

I became aware of noise below me, in the interior of the building. I waited incuriously, not even troubling to lift my rifle from my lap. The noise became weary footsteps on the floor below me. They shuffled slowly up the iron stairway nearest me, and paused at the top. I heard hoarse, wheezing breath, struggling to slow itself, succeeding. I did not turn.

"Hell of a view," I said, squinting at it.

"View of a hell," Carlson wheezed behind me.

"How'd you find me, Wendell?"

"I followed your spoor."

I spun, stared at him. "You—"

"Followed your spoor."

I turned around again, and giggled. The giggle became a chuckle, and then I sat on it. "Still got your adenoids, eh, Doc? Sure. Twenty years in this rotten graveyard and I'll bet you've never owned a set of nose plugs. Punishment to fit the crime—and then some."

He did not reply. His breathing was easier now.

"My father, Wendell, now there's an absentminded man for you," I went on conversationally. "Always doing some sort of Civilized work, always forgetting to remove his plugs when he comes home—he surely does take a lot of kidding. Our security chief, Phil Collaci, quietly makes sure Dad has a Guard with him at all times when he goes outdoors—just can't depend on Dad's sense of smell, Teach' says. Dad always was a terrible cook, you know? He always puts too much garlic in the soup. Am I boring you, Wendell? Would you like to hear a lovely death I just dreamed? I am the last assassin on earth, and I have just created a brand-new death, a unique one. It convicts as it kills—if you die, you deserve to." My voice was quite shrill now, and a part of me clinically diagnosed hysteria. Carlson said something I did not hear as I raved of toilet bowls and brains splashing on a sidewalk and impossible thousands of chittering gray rats and my eyes went nova and a carillon shattered in my skull and when the world came back I realized that the exhausted old man had slapped my head near off my shoulders. He crouched beside me, holding his hand and wincing.

"Why have no Muskies attacked me, here in the heights?" My voice was soft now, wind-tossed.

"The windriders project and receive emotions. Those who sorrow as you and I engender respect and fear in them. You are protected now, as I have been these twenty years. An expensive shield."

I blinked at him and burst into tears.

He held me then in his frail old arms, as my father had never done, and rocked me while I wept. I wept until I was exhausted, and when I had not cried for a time he said softly, "You will put away your new death, unused. You are his son, and you love him."

I shivered then, and he held me closer, and did not see me smile.

So there you have it, Teach'. Stop thinking of Jacob Stone as the Father of Fresh Start, and see him as a man—and you will not only realize that his sense of smell was a hoax, but like me will wonder how you were ever taken in by so transparent a fiction. There are a dozen blameless explanations for Dad's anosmia—none of which would have required pretense.

So look at the method of his dying. The lid of the septic tank will be found ajar—the bathroom will surely smell of chlorine. Ask yourself how a chemist could possibly walk into such a trap—*if he had any sense of smell at all?*

Better yet, examine the corpse for adenoids.

When you've put it all together, come look me up. I'll be at Columbia University, with my good friend Wendell Morgan Carlson. We have a lot of work to do, and I suspect we'll need the help of you and the Council before long. We're learning to talk with Muskies, you see.

If you come at night, I've got a little place of my own set up in the lobby of the Waldorf-Astoria. You can't miss me. But be sure to knock: I'm Musky-proof these days, but I've still got those subconscious sentries you gave me.

And I'm scared of the dark.

James Tiptree, Jr.

A few years ago, Theodore Sturgeon, writing a review column in the New York *Times,* listed the new great science fiction writers of the 1970s, and pointed out that, except for James Tiptree, Jr., they were all women.

What Ted didn't know, and what no one knew till 1977 (a year after "Houston, Houston, Do You Read?" was published), was that James Tiptree, Jr., was a woman, too. Her real name is Alice Sheldon.

Tiptree appears also in Volume Three. In the introduction to the earlier tale, written in 1976, I used the male pronoun six times. How was I to know?

So what do I call her? I can't say "Sheldon," and certainly not "Alice." Her literary name is "James Tiptree, Jr.," and as long as I'm dealing with her in her literary persona, I ought to use her literary name. (You say "Lewis Carroll" when speaking of the author of *Alice in Wonderland.* You say "Charles Lutwidge Dodgson" when speaking of the mathematician and dean.)

And yet I can't say "James" or "Jim," either, even though I have exchanged friendly letters with her (not knowing she was a "her"). It seems silly to refer to a known woman that way, especially since I strongly suspect that no one has ever called her "James" or "Jim" to her face in her whole life.

So I'm afraid I am going to have to say "Tiptree."

Tiptree is a psychologist by profession and has a doctorate in the field, which she obtained in 1967.

The doctorate is never mentioned in the literary context, and rightly so. I remember that back in the 1920s, when magazine science fiction was just born, Hugo Gernsback was terribly anxious to give it what respectability he could. When he found that one of his authors had an academic degree, he used it. Thus Miles

J. Breuer appeared always as Miles J. Breuer, M.D., and David H. Keller, as David H. Keller, M.D.

The prize example, however, was Edward Elmer Smith, who had a Ph.D. in chemistry. When his first story, "The Skylark of Space," was published, Gernsback featured him on the cover as "E. E. Smith, Ph.D."

Men like Breuer and Keller, however worthy, faded out in the 1930s, but E. E. Smith was a major force in science fiction for twenty years, and E. E. Smith, Ph.D., he was to the end. No one resented it, or thought it presumptuous or self-aggrandizing, because "Doc" Smith (as he was universally called) was the sweetest, most unassuming character ever invented, and everyone loved him.

I don't think anyone else could get away with it. When, in 1948, I got my own Ph.D., for one wild moment I thought of putting "Isaac Asimov, Ph.D." on my next submission. Just one! It may have even been a half moment. Then sanity swept over me like a great healing wave.

I simply do not use the degree at all in a literary context, not even on my stationery. A friend, I remember, urged me to use it.

"No," I said. "It would seem arrogant."

"It would seem more arrogant," he said, "if you didn't. You would be implying that your name required no artificial additions to make it important."

"True," I said.

I suspect Tiptree feels the same way—and should.

5

HOUSTON, HOUSTON, DO YOU READ?

Lorimer gazes around the crowded cabin, trying to listen to the voices, trying to ignore the twitch in his insides that means he is about to remember something bad. No help; he lives it again, that long-ago moment. Himself running blindly—or was he pushed?—into the strange toilet at Evanston Junior High. His fly open, his dick in his hand, he can still see the gray zipper edge of his jeans around his pale exposed pecker. The hush. The sickening wrongness of shapes, faces turning. The first blaring giggle. *Girls.* He was in the *girls' can.*

He flinches now wryly, so many years later, not looking at the women's faces. The big cabin surrounds him with their alien things, curved around over his head: the beading rack, the twins' loom, Andy's leatherwork, the damned kudzu vine wriggling everywhere, the chickens. So cozy. . . . Trapped, he is. Irretrievably trapped for life in everything he does not enjoy. Structurelessness. Personal trivia, unmeaning intimacies. The claims he can somehow never meet. Ginny: *You never talk to me* . . . Ginny, love, he thinks involuntarily. The hurt doesn't come.

Bud Geirr's loud chuckle breaks in on him. Bud is joking with some of them, out of sight around a bulkhead. Dave is visible, though. Major Norman Davis on the far side of the cabin, his bearded profile bent toward a small dark woman Lorimer can't quite focus on. But Dave's head seems oddly tiny and sharp, in fact the whole cabin looks unreal. A cackle bursts out from the "ceiling"—the bantam hen in her basket.

At this moment Lorimer becomes sure he has been drugged.

Curiously, the idea does not anger him. He leans or rather tips back, perching cross-legged in the zero gee, letting his gaze go to the face of the woman he has been talking with. Connie. Constantia Morelos. A tall moon-faced woman in capacious green pajamas. He has never really cared for talking to women. Ironic.

"I suppose," he says aloud, "it's possible that in some sense we are not here."

That doesn't sound too clear, but she nods interestedly. She's watching my reactions, Lorimer tells himself. Women are natural poisoners. Has he said that aloud, too? Her expression doesn't change. His vision is taking on a pleasing local clarity. Connie's skin strikes him as quite fine, healthy-looking. Olive tan even after two years in space. She was a farmer, he recalls. Big pores, but without the caked look he associates with women her age.

"You probably never wore makeup," he says. She looks puzzled. "Face paint, powder. None of you have."

"Oh!" Her smile shows a chipped front tooth. "Oh yes, I think Andy has."

"Andy?"

"For plays. Historical plays, Andy's good at that."

"Of course. Historical plays."

Lorimer's brain seems to be expanding, letting in light. He is understanding actively now, the myriad bits and pieces linking into patterns. Deadly patterns, he perceives; but the drug is shielding him in some way. Like an amphetamine high without the pressure. Maybe it's something they use socially? No, they're watching, too.

"Space bunnies, I still don't dig it," Bud Geirr laughs infectiously. He has a friendly buoyant voice people like; Lorimer still likes it after two years.

"You chicks have kids back home, what do your folks think about you flying around out here with old Andy, h'mm?" Bud floats into view, his arm draped around a twin's shoulders. The one called Judy Paris, Lorimer decides; the twins are hard to tell. She drifts passively at an angle to Bud's big body: a jut-breasted plain girl in flowing yellow pajamas, her black hair raying out. Andy's red head swims up to them. He is holding a big green spaceball, looking about sixteen.

"Old Andy." Bud shakes his head, his grin flashing under his thick dark mustache. "When I was your age folks didn't let their women fly around with me."

Connie's lips quirk faintly. In Lorimer's head the pieces slide toward pattern. I know, he thinks. Do you know I know? His head is vast and crystalline, very nice really. Easier to think. Women. . . . No compact generalization forms in his mind, only a few speaking faces on a matrix of pervasive irrelevance. Human, of course. Biological necessity. Only so, so . . . diffuse? Pointless? . . . His sister Amy, *soprano con tremulo: Of course women could contribute as much as men if you'd treat us as equals. You'll see!* And then marrying that idiot the second time. Well, now he can see.

"Kudzu vines," he says aloud. Connie smiles. How they all smile.

"How 'boot that?" Bud says happily. "Ever think we'd see chicks in zero gee, hey, Dave? Artits-stico. Woo-ee!" Across the cabin Dave's bearded head turns to him, not smiling.

"And ol' Andy's had it all to hisself. Stunt your growth, lad." He punches Andy genially on the arm, Andy catches himself on the bulkhead. Bud can't be drunk, Lorimer thinks; not on that fruit cider. But he doesn't usually sound so much like a stage Texan either. A drug.

"Hey, no offense," Bud is saying earnestly to the boy, "I mean that. You have to forgive one underprilly, underprivileged brother. These chicks are good people. Know what?" he tells the girl. "You could look stu-pen-dous if you fix yourself up a speck. Hey, I can show you, old Buddy's a expert. I hope you don't mind my saying that. As a matter of fact you look real stupendous to me right now."

He hugs her shoulders, flings out his arm and hugs Andy, too. They float upwards in his grasp, Judy grinning excitedly, almost pretty.

"Let's get some more of that good stuff." Bud propels them both toward the serving rack which is decorated for the occasion with sprays of greens and small real daisies.

"Happy New Year! Hey, Happy New Year, y'all!"

Faces turn, more smiles. Genuine smiles, Lorimer thinks, maybe they really like their New Years. He feels he has infinite time to examine every event, the implications evolving in crystal facets. I'm an echo chamber. Enjoyable, to be the observer. But others are observing, too. They've started something here. Do they realize? So vulnerable, three of us, five of them in this fragile ship. They don't know. A dread unconnected to action lurks behind his mind.

"By God, we made it," Bud laughs. "You space chickies, I have to give it to you. I commend you, by God, I say it. We wouldn't be here, wherever we are. Know what, I jus' might decide to stay in the service after all. Think they have room for old Bud in your space program, sweetie?"

"Knock that off, Bud," Dave says quietly from the far wall. "I don't want to hear us use the name of the Creator like that." The full chestnut beard gives him a patriarchal gravity. Dave is forty-six, a decade older than Bud and Lorimer. Veteran of six successful missions.

"Oh, my apologies, Major Dave, old buddy." Bud chuckles intimately to the girl. "Our commanding ossifer. Stupendous guy. Hey, Doc!" he calls. "How's your attitude? You making out dinko?"

"Cheers," Lorimer hears his voice reply, the complex stratum of his feelings about Bud rising like a kraken in the moonlight of his mind. The submerged silent thing he has about them all, all the Buds and Daves and big, indomitable cheerful, able, disciplined slow-minded mesomorphs he has cast his life with. Meso-ectos, he corrected himself; astronauts aren't muscleheads. They like him, he has been careful about that. Liked him well enough to get him on *Sunbird*, to make him the official scientist on the first circumsolar mission. That little Doc Lorimer, he's cool, he's on the team. No shit from Lorimer, not like those other scientific assholes. He does the bit well with his small neat build and his dead-pan remarks. And the years of turning out for the bowling, the volleyball, the tennis, the skeet, the skiing that broke his ankle, the touch football that broke his collarbone. Watch that Doc, he's a sneaky one. And the big men banging him on the back, accepting him. Their token scientist . . . The trouble is, he isn't any kind of scientist anymore. Living off his postdoctoral plasma work, a lucky hit. He hasn't really been into the math for years, he isn't up to it now. Too many other interests, too much time spent explaining elementary stuff. I'm a half jock, he thinks.

A foot taller and a hundred pounds heavier and I'd be just like them. One of them. An alpha. They probably sense it underneath, the beta bile. Had the jokes worn a shade thin in *Sunbird,* all that year going out? A year of Bud and Dave playing gin. That damn exercycle, gearing it up too tough for me. They didn't mean it, though. We were a team.

The memory of gaping jeans flicks at him, the painful end part —the grinning faces waiting for him when he stumbled out. The howls, the dribble down his leg. Being cool, pretending to laugh, too. You shitheads, I'll show you. I am not a girl.

Bud's voice rings out, chanting. "And a Hap-pee New Year to you-all down there!" Parody of the oily NASA tone. "Hey, why don't we shoot 'em a signal? Greetings to all you Earthlings, I mean, all you little Lunies. Hap-py New Year in the good year whatsis." He snuffles comically. "There is a Santy Claus, Houston, ye-ew nevah saw nothin' like this! Houston, wherever you are," he sings out. "Hey, Houston! Do you read?"

In the silence Lorimer sees Dave's face set into Major Norman Davis, commanding.

And without warning he is suddenly back there, back a year ago in the cramped, shook-up command module of *Sunbird,* coming out from behind the sun. It's the drug doing this, he thinks as memory closes around him, it's so real. Stop. He tries to hang on to reality, to the sense of trouble building underneath.

—But he can't, he is *there,* hovering behind Dave and Bud in the triple couches, as usual avoiding his official station in the middle, seeing beside them their reflections against blackness in the useless port window. The outer layer has been annealed, he can just make out a bright smear that has to be Spica floating through the image of Dave's head, making the bandage look like a kid's crown.

"Houston, Houston, *Sunbird,"* Dave repeats; *"Sunbird* calling Houston. Houston, do you read? Come in, Houston."

The minutes start by. They are giving it seven out, seven back; seventy-eight million miles, ample margin.

"The high gain's shot, that's what it is," Bud says cheerfully. He says it almost every day.

"No way." Dave's voice is patient, also as usual. "It checks out. Still too much crap from the sun, isn't that right, Doc?"

"The residual radiation from the flare is just about in line with us," Lorimer says. "They could have a hard time sorting us out." For the thousandth time he registers his own faint, ridiculous gratification at being consulted.

"Shit, we're outside Mercury." Bud shakes his head. "How we gonna find out who won the Series?"

He often says that, too. A ritual, out here in eternal night. Lorimer watches the sparkle of Spica drift by the reflection of Bud's curly face-bush. His own whiskers are scant and scraggly, like a blond Fu Manchu. In the aft corner of the window is a striped glare that must be the remains of their port energy accumulators, fried off in the solar explosion that hit them a month ago and fused the outer layers of their windows. That was when Dave cut his head open on the sexlogic panel. Lorimer had been banged in among the gravity wave experiment, he still doesn't trust the readings. Luckily the particle stream has missed one piece of the front window; they still have about twenty degrees of clear vision straight ahead. The brilliant web of the Pleiades shows there, running off into a blur of light.

Twelve minutes . . . thirteen. The speaker sighs and clicks emptily. Fourteen. Nothing.

"*Sunbird* to Houston, *Sunbird* to Houston. Come in, Houston. *Sunbird* out." Dave puts the mike back in its holder. "Give it another twenty-four."

They wait ritually. Tomorrow Packard will reply. Maybe.

"Be good to see old Earth again," Bud remarks.

"We're not using any more fuel on attitude," Dave reminds him. "I trust Doc's figures."

It's not my figures, it's the elementary facts of celestial mechanics, Lorimer thinks; in October there's only one place for Earth to be. He never says it. Not to a man who can fly two-body solutions by intuition once he knows where the bodies are. Bud is a good pilot and a better engineer; Dave is the best there is. He takes no pride in it. "The Lord helps us, Doc, if we let Him."

"Going to be a bitch docking if the radar's screwed up," Bud says idly. They all think about that for the hundredth time. It will be a bitch. Dave will do it. That was why he is hoarding fuel.

The minutes tick off.

"That's it," Dave says—and a voice fills the cabin, shockingly.

"Judy?" It is high and clear. A girl's voice.

"Judy, I'm so glad we got you. What are you doing on this band?"

Bud blows out his breath; there is a frozen instant before Dave snatches up the mike.

"*Sunbird,* we read you. This is Mission *Sunbird* calling Houston, ah, *Sunbird One* calling Houston Ground Control. Identify, who are you? Can you relay our signal? Over."

"Some skip," Bud says. "Some incredible ham."

"Are you in trouble, Judy?" the girl's voice asks. "I can't hear, you sound terrible. Wait a minute."

"This is United States Space Mission *Sunbird One,*" Dave repeats. "Mission *Sunbird* calling Houston Space Center. You are dee-exxing our channel. Identify, repeat identify yourself and say if you can relay to Houston. Over."

"Dinko, Judy, try it again," the girl says.

Lorimer abruptly pushes himself up the Lurp, the Long-Range Particle Density Cumulator experiment, and activates its shaft motor. The shaft whines, jars; lucky it was retracted during the flare, lucky it hasn't fused shut. He sets the probe pulse on max and begins a rough manual scan.

"You are intercepting official traffic from the United States space mission to Houston Control," Dave is saying forcefully. "If you cannot relay to Houston get off the air, you are committing a federal offense. Say again, can you relay our signal to Houston Space Center? Over."

"You still sound terrible," the girl says. "What's Houston? Who's talking, anyway? You know we don't have much time." Her voice is sweet but very nasal.

"Jesus, that's close," Bud says. "That is close."

"Hold it." Dave twists around to Lorimer's improvised radarscope.

"There." Lorimer points out a tiny stable peak at the extreme edge of the read-out slot, in the transcoronal scatter. Bud cranes too.

"A bogey!"

"Somebody else out here."

"Hello, hello? We have you now," the girl says. "Why are you so far out? Are you dinko, did you catch the flare?"

"Hold it," warns Dave. "What's the status, Doc?"

"Over three hundred thousand kilometers, guesstimated. Possibly headed away from us, going around the sun. Could be cosmonauts, a Soviet mission?"

"Out to beat us. They missed."

"With a *girl?*" Bud objects.

"They've done that. You taping this, Bud?"

"Roger-r-r." He grins. "That sure didn't sound like a Russky chick. Who the hell's Judy?"

Dave thinks for a second, clicks on the mike. "This is Major Norman Davis commanding United States spacecraft *Sunbird One.* We have you on scope. Request you identify yourself. Repeat, who are you? Over."

"Judy, stop joking," the voice complains. "We'll lose you in a minute, don't you realize we worried about you?"

"*Sunbird* to unidentified craft. This is not Judy. I say again, this is not Judy. Who are you? Over."

"What—" the girl says, and is cut off by someone saying, "Wait a minute, Ann." The speaker squeals. Then a different woman says, "This is Lorna Bethune in *Escondita.* What is going on here?"

"This is Major Davis commanding United States Mission *Sunbird* on course for Earth. We do not recognize any spacecraft *Escondita.* Will you identify yourself? Over."

"I just did." She sounds older with the same nasal drawl. "There is no spaceship *Sunbird* and you're not on course for Earth. If this is an andy joke it isn't any good."

"This is no joke, madam!" Dave explodes. "This is the American circumsolar mission and we are American astronauts. We do not appreciate your interference. Out."

The woman starts to speak and is drowned in a jibber of static. Two voices come through briefly. Lorimer thinks he hears the words "*Sunbird* program" and something else. Bud works the squelcher; the interference subsides to a drone.

"Ah, Major Davis?" The voice is fainter. "Did I hear you say you are on course for Earth?"

Dave frowns at the speaker and then says curtly, "Affirmative."

"Well, we don't understand your orbit. You must have very unusual flight characteristics, our readings show you won't node with anything on your present course. We'll lose the signal in a minute or two. Ah, would you tell us where you see Earth now? Never mind the coordinates, just tell us the constellation."

Dave hesitates and then holds up the mike. "Doc."

"Earth's apparent position is in Pisces," Lorimer says to the voice. "Approximately three degrees from P. Gamma."

"It is not," the woman says. "Can't you see it's in Virgo? Can't you see out at all?"

Lorimer's eyes go to the bright smear in the port window. "We sustained some damage—"

"Hold it," snaps Dave.

"—to one window during a disturbance we ran into at perihelion. Naturally we know the relative direction of Earth on this date, October nineteen."

"October? It's March, March fifteen. You must—" Her voice is lost in a shriek.

"E-M front," Bud says, tuning. They are all leaning at the speaker from different angles, Lorimer is head-down. Space noise wails and crashes like surf, the strange ship is too close to the coronal horizon. "—Behind you," they hear. More howls. "Band, try . . . ship . . . if you can, your signal—" Nothing more comes through.

Lorimer pushes back, staring at the spark in the window. It has to be Spica. But is it elongated, as if a second point-source is beside it? Impossible. An excitement is trying to flare out inside him, the women's voices resonate in his head.

"Playback," Dave says. "Houston will really like to hear this."

They listen again to the girl calling Judy, the woman saying she is Lorna Bethune. Bud holds up a finger. "Man's voice in there." Lorimer listens hard for the words he thought he heard. The tape ends.

"Wait till Packard gets this one." Dave rubs his arms. "Remember what they pulled on Howie? Claiming they rescued him."

"Seems like they want us on their frequency." Bud grins. "They must think we're fa-a-ar gone. Hey, looks like this other capsule's going to show up, getting crowded out here."

"If it shows up," Dave says. "Leave it on voice alert, Bud. The batteries will do that."

Lorimer watches the spark of Spica, or Spica-plus-something, wondering if he will ever understand. The casual acceptance of some trick or ploy out here in this incredible loneliness. Well, if these strangers are from the same mold, maybe that is it. Aloud he says, "*Escondita* is an odd name for a Soviet mission. I believe it means 'hidden' in Spanish."

"Yeah," says Bud. "Hey, I know what that accent is, it's Australian. We had some Aussie bunnies at Hickam. Or-stryle-ya, woo-ee! You s'pose Woomara is sending up some kind of combined do?"

Dave shakes his head. "They have no capability whatsoever."

"We ran into some fairly strange phenomena back there, Dave," Lorimer says thoughtfully. "I'm beginning to wish we could take a visual check."

"Did you goof, Doc?"

"No. Earth is where I said, if it's October. Virgo is where it would appear in March."

"Then that's it." Dave grins, pushing out of the couch. "You been asleep five months, Rip van Winkle? Time for a hand before we do the roadwork."

"What I'd like to know is what that chick looks like," says Bud, closing down the transceiver. "Can I help you into your space suit, miss? Hey, miss, pull that in, psst-psst-psst! You going to listen, Doc?"

"Right." Lorimer is getting out his charts. The others go aft through the tunnel to the small dayroom, making no further comment on the presence of the strange ship or ships out here. Lorimer himself is more shaken than he likes; it was that damn phrase.

The tedious exercise period comes and goes. Lunchtime: They give the containers a minimum warm to conserve the batteries. Chicken à la king again; Bud puts ketchup on his and breaks their usual silence with a funny anecdote about an Australian girl, laboriously censoring himself to conform to *Sunbird*'s unwritten code on talk. After lunch Dave goes forward to the command module. Bud and Lorimer continue their current task of checking out the suits and packs for a damage-assessment EVA to take place as soon as the radiation count drops.

They are just clearing away when Dave calls them. Lorimer

comes through the tunnel to hear a girl's voice blare, "—dinko trip. What did Lorna say? *Gloria* over!"

He starts up the Lurp and begins scanning. No results this time. "They're either in line behind us or in the sunward quadrant," he reports finally. "I can't isolate them."

Presently the speaker holds another thin thread of sound.

"That could be their ground control," says Dave. "How's the horizon, Doc?"

"Five hours; Northwest Siberia, Japan, Australia."

"I told you the high gain is fucked up." Bud gingerly feeds power to his antenna motor. "Easy, eas-ee. The frame is twisted, that's what it is."

"Don't snap it," Dave says, knowing Bud will not.

The squeaking fades, pulses back. "Hey, we can really use this," Bud says. "We can calibrate on them."

A hard soprano says suddenly "—should be outside your orbit. Try around Beta Aries."

"Another chick. We have a fix," Bud says happily. "We have a fix now. I do believe our troubles are over. That monkey was torqued one hundred forty-nine degrees. Woo-ee!"

The first girl comes back. "We see them, Margo! But they're so small, how can they live in there? Maybe they're tiny aliens! Over."

"That's Judy." Bud chuckles. "Dave, this is screwy, it's all in English. It has to be some UN thingie."

Dave massages his elbows, flexes his fists; thinking. They wait. Lorimer considers a hundred and forty-nine degrees from Gamma Piscium.

In thirteen minutes the voice from Earth says, "Judy, call the others, will you? We're going to play you the conversation, we think you should all hear. Two minutes. Oh, while we're waiting, Zebra wants to tell Connie the baby is fine. And we have a new cow."

"Code," says Dave.

The recording comes on. The three men listen once more to Dave calling Houston in a rattle of solar noise. The transmission clears up rapidly and cuts off with the woman saying that another ship, the *Gloria,* is behind them, closer to the sun.

"We looked up history," the Earth voice resumes. "There was a

Major Norman Davis on the first *Sunbird* flight. Major was a military title. Did you hear them say 'Doc'? There was a scientific doctor on board, Dr. Orren Lorimer. The third member was Captain—that's another title—Bernhard Geirr. Just the three of them, all males of course. We think they had an early reaction engine and not too much fuel. The point is, the first *Sunbird* mission was lost in space. They never came out from behind the sun. That was about when the big flares started. Jan thinks they must have been close to one, you heard them say they were damaged."

Dave grunts. Lorimer is fighting excitement like a brush discharge sparking in his gut.

"Either they are who they say they are or they're ghosts; or they're aliens pretending to be people. Jan says maybe the disruption in those super-flares could collapse the local time dimension. Pluggo. What did you observe there, I mean the highlights?"

Time dimension . . . never come back . . . Lorimer's mind narrows onto the reality of the two unmoving bearded heads before him, refuses to admit the words he thought he heard: *Before the year two thousand.* The language, he thinks. The language would have to have changed. He feels better.

A deep baritone voice says, "Margo?" In *Sunbird* eyes come alert.

"—like the big one fifty years ago." The man has the accent, too. "We were really lucky being right there when it popped. The most interesting part is that we confirmed the gravity turbulence. Periodic but not waves. It's violent, we got pushed around some. Space is under monster stress in those things. We think France's theory that our system is passing through a micro-black-hole cluster looks right so long as one doesn't plonk us."

"France?" Bud mutters. Dave looks at him speculatively.

"It's hard to imagine anything being kicked out in time. But they're here, whatever they are, they're over eight hundred kays outside us scooting out toward Aldebaran. As Lorna said, if they're trying to reach Earth they're in trouble unless they have a lot of spare gees. Should we try to talk to them? Over. Oh, great about the cow. Over again."

"Black holes." Bud whistles softly. "That's one for you, Doc. Was we in a black hole?"

"Not in one or we wouldn't be here." If we are here, Lorimer adds to himself. A micro-black-hole cluster . . . what happens when fragments of totally collapsed matter approach each other, or collide, say in the photosphere of a star? Time disruption? Stop it. Aloud he says, "They could be telling us something, Dave."

Dave says nothing. The minutes pass.

Finally the Earth voice comes back, saying that it will try to contact the strangers on their original frequency. Bud glances at Dave, tunes the selector.

"Calling *Sunbird One?*" the girl says slowly through her nose. "This is Luna Central calling Major Norman Davis of *Sunbird One.* We have picked up your conversation with our ship *Escondita.* We are very puzzled as to who you are and how you got here. If you really are *Sunbird One* we think you must have been jumped forward in time when you passed the solar flare." She pronounces it Cockney style, "toime."

"Our ship *Gloria* is near you, they see you on their radar. We think you may have a serious course problem because you told Lorna you were headed for Earth and you think it is now October with Earth in Pisces. It is not October. It is March fifteen. I repeat, the Earth date"—she says "dyte"—"is March fifteen, time twenty hundred hours. You should be able to see Earth very close to Spica in Virgo. You said your window is damaged. Can't you go out and look? We think you have to make a big course correction. Do you have enough fuel? Do you have a computer? Do you have enough air and water and food? Can we help you? We're listening on this frequency. Luna to *Sunbird One,* come in."

On *Sunbird* nobody stirs. Lorimer struggles against internal eruptions. *Never came back. Jumped forward in time.* The cyst of memories he has schooled himself to suppress bulges up in the lengthening silence. "Aren't you going to answer?"

"Don't be stupid," Dave says.

"Dave. A hundred and forty-nine degrees is the difference between Gamma Piscium and Spica. That transmission is coming from where they say Earth is."

"You goofed."

"I did not goof. It has to be March."

Dave blinks as if a fly is bothering him.

In fifteen minutes the Luna voice runs through the whole thing again, ending, "Please, come in."

"Not a tape." Bud unwraps a stick of gum, adding the plastic to the neat wad back of the gyro leads. Lorimer's skin crawls, watching the ambiguous dazzle of Spica. Spica-plus-Earth? Unbelief grips him, rocks him with a complex pang compounded of faces, voices, the sizzle of bacon frying, the creak of his father's wheelchair, chalk on a sunlit blackboard, Ginny's bare legs on the flowered couch, Jenny and Penny running dangerously close to the lawn mower. The girls will be taller now, Jenny is already as tall as her mother. His father is living with Amy in Denver, determined to last till his son gets home. *When I get home.* This has to be insanity, Dave's right; it's a trick, some crazy trick. The language.

Fifteen minutes more; the flat, earnest female voice comes back and repeats it all, putting in more stresses. Dave wears a remote frown, like a man listening to a lousy sports program. Lorimer has the notion he might switch off and propose a hand of gin; wills him to do so. The voice says it will now change frequencies.

Bud tunes back, chewing calmly. This time the voice stumbles on a couple of phrases. It sounds tired.

Another wait; an hour, now. Lorimer's mind holds only the bright point of Spica digging at him. Bud hums a bar of "Yellow Ribbons," falls silent again.

"Dave," Lorimer says finally, "our antenna is pointed straight at Spica. I don't care if you think I goofed, if Earth is over there we have to change course soon. Look, you can see it could be a double light source. We have to check this out."

Dave says nothing. Bud says nothing but his eyes rove to the port window, back to his instrument panel, to the window again. In the corner of the panel is a polaroid snap of his wife. Patty: a tall, giggling, rump-switching redhead; Lorimer has occasional fantasies about her. Little-girl voice, though. And so tall. . . . Some short men chase tall women; it strikes Lorimer as undignified. Ginny is an inch shorter than he. Their girls will be taller. And Ginny insisted on starting a pregnancy before he left, even though he'll be out of commo. Maybe, maybe a boy, a son—*stop it.* Think about anything. Bud. . . . Does Bud love Patty? Who knows? He loves Ginny. At seventy million miles. . . .

"Judy?" Luna Central or whoever it is says. "They don't answer. You want to try? But listen, we've been thinking. If these people really are from the past this must be very traumatic for them. They could be just realizing they'll never see their world again. Myda says these males had children and women they stayed with, they'll miss them terribly. This is exciting for us but it may seem awful to them. They could be too shocked to answer. They could be frightened, maybe they think we're aliens or hallucinations even. See?"

Five seconds later the nearby girl says, "Da, Margo, we were into that, too. Dinko. Ah, *Sunbird?* Major Davis of *Sunbird,* are you there? This is Judy Paris in the ship *Gloria,* we're only about a million kay from you, we see you on our screen." She sounds young and excited. "Luna Central has been trying to reach you, we think you're in trouble and we want to help. Please don't be frightened, we're people just like you. We think you're way off course if you want to reach Earth. Are you in trouble? Can we help? If your radio is out can you make any sort of signal? Do you know Old Morse? You'll be off our screen soon, we're truly worried about you. Please reply somehow if you possibly can, *Sunbird,* come in!"

Dave sits impassive. Bud glances at him, at the port window, gazes stolidly at the speaker, his face blank. Lorimer has exhausted surprise, he wants only to reply to the voices. He can manage a rough signal by heterodyning the probe beam. But what then, with them both against him?

The girl's voice tries again determinedly. Finally she says, "Margo, they won't peep. Maybe they're dead? I think they're aliens."

Are we not? Lorimer thinks. The Luna station comes back with a different, older voice.

"Judy, Myda here, I've had another thought. These people had a very rigid authority code. You remember your history, they peck-ordered everything. You notice Major Davis repeated about being commanding. That's called dominance-submission structure, one of them gave orders and the others did whatever they were told, we don't know quite why. Perhaps they were frightened. The point is that if the dominant one is in shock or panicked, maybe the others can't reply unless this Davis lets them."

Jesus Christ, Lorimer thinks. Jesus H. Christ in colors. It is his father's expression for the inexpressible. Dave and Bud sit unstirring.

"How weird," the Judy voice says. "But don't they know they're on a bad course? I mean, could the dominant one make the others fly right out of the system? Truly?"

It's happened, Lorimer thinks; it has happened. I have to stop this. I have to act now, before they lose us. Desperate visions of himself defying Dave and Bud loom before him. Try persuasion first.

Just as he opens his mouth he sees Bud stir slightly, and with immeasurable gratitude hears him say, "Dave-o, what say we take an eyeball look? One little old burp won't hurt us."

Dave's head turns a degree or two.

"Or should I go out and see, like the chick said?" Bud's voice is mild.

After a long minute Dave says neutrally, "All right. . . . Attitude change." His arm moves up as though heavy; he starts methodically setting in the values for the vector that will bring Spica in line with their functional window.

Now why couldn't I have done that? Lorimer asks himself for the thousandth time, following the familiar check sequence. Don't answer. . . . And for the thousandth time he is obscurely moved by the rightness of them. The authentic ones, the alphas. Their bond. The awe he had felt first for the absurd jocks of his school ball team.

"That's go, Dave, assuming nothing got creamed."

Dave throws the ignition safety, puts the computer on real time. The hull shudders. Everything in the cabin drifts sidewise while the bright point of Spica swims the other way, appears on the front window as the retros cut in. When the star creeps out onto clear glass Lorimer can clearly see its companion. The double light steadies there; a beautiful job. He hands Bud the telescope.

"The one on the left."

Bud looks. "There she is, all right. Hey, Dave, look at that!"

He puts the scope in Dave's hand. Slowly, Dave raises it and looks. Lorimer can hear him breathe. Suddenly Dave pulls up the mike.

"Houston!" he says harshly. "*Sunbird* to Houston, *Sunbird* calling Houston. Houston, come in!"

Into the silence the speaker squeals, "They fired their engines —wait, she's calling!" And shuts up.

In *Sunbird*'s cabin nobody speaks. Lorimer stares at the twin stars ahead, impossible realities shifting around him as the minutes congeal. Bud's reflected face looks downwards, grin gone. Dave's beard moves silently; praying, Lorimer realizes. Alone of the crew Dave is deeply religious; at Sunday meals he gives a short, dignified grace. A shocking pity for Dave rises in Lorimer; Dave is so deeply involved with his family, his four sons, always thinking about their training, taking them hunting, fishing, camping. And Doris his wife so incredibly active and sweet, going on their trips, cooking and doing things for the community. Driving Penny and Jenny to classes while Ginny was sick that time. Good people, the backbone. . . . This can't be, he thinks; Packard's voice is going to come through in a minute, the antenna's beamed right now. Six minutes now. This will all go away. *Before the year two thousand*—stop it, the language would have changed. Think of Doris. . . . She has that glow, feeding her five men; women with sons are different. But Ginny, but his dear woman, his *wife*, his *daughters*—grandmothers now? All dead and dust? *Quit that.* Dave is still praying. . . . Who knows what goes on inside those heads? Dave's cry. . . . Twelve minutes, it has to be right. The second sweep is stuck, no, it's moving. Thirteen. It's all insane, a dream. Thirteen plus . . . fourteen. The speaker hissing and clicking vacantly. Fifteen now. A dream. . . . Or are those women staying off, letting us see? Sixteen. . . .

At twenty Dave's hand moves, stops again. The seconds jitter by, space crackles. Thirty minutes coming up.

"Calling Major Davis in *Sunbird*?" It is the older woman, a gentle voice. "This is Luna Central. We are the service and communication facility for space flight now. We're sorry to have to tell you that there is no space center at Houston anymore. Houston itself was abandoned when the shuttle base moved to White Sands, over two centuries ago."

A cool dust-colored light enfolds Lorimer's brain, isolating it. He will remain so a long time.

The woman is explaining it all again, offering help, asking if they were hurt. A nice dignified speech. Dave still sits immobile, gazing at Earth. Bud puts the mike in his hand.

"Tell them, Dave-o."

Dave looks at it, takes a deep breath, presses the send button.

"*Sunbird* to Luna Control," he says quite normally. (It's "Central" Lorimer thinks.) "We copy. Ah, negative on life support, we have no problems. We copy the course change suggestion and are proceeding to recompute. Your offer of computer assistance is appreciated. We suggest you transmit position data so we can get squared away. Ah, we are economizing on transmission until we see how our accumulators have held up. *Sunbird* out."

And so it had begun.

Lorimer's mind floats back to himself now floating in *Gloria,* nearly a year, or three hundred years, later; watching and being watched by them. He still feels light, contented; the dread underneath has come no nearer. But it is so silent. He seems to have heard no voices for a long time. Or was it a long time? Maybe the drug is working on his time sense, maybe it was only a minute or two.

"I've been remembering," he says to the woman Connie, wanting her to speak.

She nods. "You have so much to remember. Oh, I'm sorry—that wasn't good to say." Her eyes speak sympathy.

"Never mind." It is all dreamlike now, his lost world and this other which he is just now seeing plain. "We must seem like very strange beasts to you."

"We're trying to understand," she says. "It's history, you learn the events but you don't really feel what the people were like, how it was for them. We hope you'll tell us."

The drug, Lorimer thinks, that's what they're trying. Tell them . . . how can he? Could a dinosaur tell how it was? A montage flows through his mind, dominated by random shots of Operations' north parking lot and Ginny's yellow kitchen telephone with the sickly ivy vines. . . . Women and vines. . . .

A burst of laughter distracts him. It's coming from the chamber they call the gym. Bud and the others must be playing ball in there. Bright idea, really, he muses: Using muscle power, sustained mild exercise. That's why they are all so fit. The gym is a glorified squirrel wheel; when you climb or pedal up the walls it revolves and winds a gear train, which among other things rotates the sleeping drum. A real Woolagong. . . . Bud and Dave usually take their shifts together, scrambling the spinning gym like big pale apes. Lorimer prefers the easy rhythm of the women, and the cycle here fits him nicely. He usually puts in his shift with Connie, who doesn't talk much, and one of the Judys, who do.

No one is talking now, though. Remotely uneasy, he looks around the big cylinder of the cabin, sees Dave and Lady Blue by the forward window. Judy Dakar is behind them, silent for once. They must be looking at Earth; it has been a beautiful expanding disk for some weeks now. Dave's beard is moving, he is praying again. He has taken to doing that, not ostentatiously, but so obviously sincere that Lorimer, a life atheist, can only sympathize.

The Judys have asked Dave what he whispers, of course. When Dave understood that they had no concept of prayer and had never seen a Christian Bible, there had been a heavy silence.

"So you have lost all faith," he said finally.

"We have faith," Judy Paris protested.

"May I ask in what?"

"We have faith in ourselves, of course," she told him.

"Young lady, if you were my daughter I'd tan your britches," Dave said, not joking. The subject was not raised again.

But he came back so well after that first dreadful shock, Lorimer thinks. A personal God, a father-model, man needs that. Dave draws strength from it and we lean on him. Maybe leaders have to believe. Dave was so great; cheerful, unflappable, patiently working out alternatives, making his decisions on the inevitable discrepancies in the position readings in a way Lorimer couldn't do. A bitch. . . .

Memory takes him again; he is once again back in *Sunbird*, gritty-eyed, listening to the women's chatter, Dave's terse replies. God, how they chattered. But their computer work checks out. Lorimer is suffering also from a quirk of Dave's, his reluctance to transmit their exact thrust and fuel reserve. He keeps holding out a margin and making Lorimer compute it back in.

But the margins don't help; it is soon clear that they are in big trouble. Earth will pass too far ahead of them on her next orbit, they don't have the acceleration to catch up with her before they cross her path. They can carry out an ullage maneuver, they can kill enough velocity to let Earth catch them on the second go-by; but that would take an extra year and their life support would be long gone. The grim question of whether they have enough to enable a single man to wait it out pushes into Lorimer's mind. He pushes it back; that one is for Dave.

There is a final possibility: Venus will approach their trajectory three months hence and they may be able to gain velocity by swinging by it. They go to work on that.

Meanwhile Earth is steadily drawing away from them and so is *Gloria,* closer toward the sun. They pick her out of the solar interference and then lose her again. They know her crew now: the man is Andy Kay, the senior woman is Lady Blue Parks; they appear to do the navigating. Then there is a Connie Morelos and the two twins, Judy Paris and Judy Dakar, who run the communications. The chief Luna voices are women too, Margo and Azella. The men can hear them talking to the *Escondita,* which is now swinging in toward the far side of the sun. Dave insists on monitoring and taping everything that comes through. It proves to be largely replays of their exchanges with Luna and *Gloria,* mixed with a variety of highly personal messages. As references to cows, chickens, and other livestock multiply Dave reluctantly gives up his idea that they are code. Bud counts a total of five male voices.

"Big deal," he says. "There were more chick drivers on the road when we left. Means space is safe now, the girlies have taken over. Let them sweat their little asses off." He chuckles. "When we get this bird down, the stars ain't gonna study old Buddy no more, no, ma'm. A nice beach and about a zillion steaks and ale and all those sweet things. Hey, we'll be living history, we can charge admission."

Dave's face takes on the expression that means an inappropriate topic has been breached. Much to Lorimer's impatience, Dave discourages all speculation as to what may await them on this future Earth. He confines their transmissions strictly to the problem in hand; when Lorimer tries to get him at least to mention the unchanged-language puzzle Dave only says firmly, "Later." Lorimer fumes; inconceivable that he is three centuries in the future, unable to learn a thing.

They do glean a few facts from the women's talk. There have been nine successful *Sunbird* missions after theirs and one other casualty. And the *Gloria* and her sister ship are on a long-planned fly-by of the two inner planets.

"We always go along in pairs," Judy says. "But those planets are no good. Still, it was worth seeing."

"For Pete's sake, Dave, ask them how many planets have been visited," Lorimer pleads.

"Later."

But about the fifth meal break Luna suddenly volunteers.

"Earth is making up a history for you, *Sunbird,"* the Margo voice says. "We know you don't want to waste power asking, so we thought we'd send you a few main points right now." She laughs. "It's much harder than we thought, nobody here does history."

Lorimer nods to himself; he has been wondering what he could tell a man from 1690 who would want to know what happened to Cromwell—was Cromwell then?—and who had never heard of electricity, atoms, or the U.S.A.

"Let's see, probably the most important is that there aren't as many people as you had, we're just over two million. There was a world epidemic not long after your time. It didn't kill people but it reduced the population. I mean there weren't any babies in most of the world. Ah, sterility. The country called Australia was affected least." Bud holds up a finger.

"And North Canada wasn't too bad. So the survivors all got together in the south part of the American states, where they could grow food and the best communications and factories were. Nobody lives in the rest of the world but we travel there sometimes. Ah, we have five main activities, was 'industries' the word? Food, that's farming and fishing. Communications, transport, and space—that's us. And the factories they need. We live a lot simpler than you did, I think. We see your things all over, we're very grateful to you. Oh, you'll be interested to know we use zeppelins just like you did, we have six big ones. And our fifth thing is the children. Babes. Does that help? I'm using a children's book we have here."

The men have frozen during this recital; Lorimer is holding a cooling bag of hash. Bud starts chewing again and chokes.

"Two million people and a space capability?" He coughs. "That's incredible."

Dave gazes reflectively at the speaker. "There's a lot they're not telling us."

"I gotta ask them," Bud says. "Okay?"

Dave nods. "Watch it."

"Thanks for the history, Luna," Bud says. "We really appreciate it. But we can't figure out how you maintain a space program with only a couple of million people. Can you tell us a little more on that?"

In the pause Lorimer tries to grasp the staggering figures. From eight billion to two million . . . Europe, Asia, Africa, South America, America itself—wiped out. *There weren't any more babies.* World sterility, from what? The Black Death, the famines of Asia—those had been decimations. This is magnitudes worse. No, it is all the same: beyond comprehension. An empty world, littered with junk.

"Sunbird?" says Margo, "Da, I should have thought you'd want to know about space. Well, we have only the four real spaceships and one building. You know the two here. Then there's *Indira* and *Pech,* they're on the Mars run now. Maybe the Mars dome was since your day. You had the satellite stations, though, didn't you? And the old Luna dome, of course—I remember now, it was during the epidemic. They tried to set up colonies to, ah, breed children, but the epidemic got there, too. They struggled terribly hard. We owe a lot to you really, you men I mean. The history has it all, how you worked out a minimal viable program and trained everybody and saved it from the crazies. It was a glorious achievement. Oh, the marker here has one of your names on it. Lorimer. We love to keep it all going and growing, we all love traveling. Man is a rover, that's one of our mottoes."

"Are you hearing what I'm hearing?" Bud asks, blinking comically.

Dave is still staring at the speaker. "Not one word about their government," he says slowly. "Not a word about economic conditions. We're talking to a bunch of monkeys."

"Should I ask them?"

"Wait a minute . . . Roger, ask the name of their chief of state and the head of the space program. And—no, that's all."

"President?" Margo echoes Bud's query. "You mean like queens and kings? Wait, here's Myda. She's been talking about you with Earth."

The older woman they hear occasionally says *"Sunbird?* Da, we realize you had a very complex activity, your governments. With so few people we don't have that type of formal structure at all. People from the different activities meet periodically and our communications are good, everyone is kept informed. The people in each activity are in charge of doing it while they're there. We rotate, you see. Mostly in five-year hitches; for example, Margo here was on the zeppelins and I've been on several factories and farms and of course the, well, the education, we all do that. I believe that's one big difference from you. And of course we all work. And things are basically far more stable now, I gather. We change slowly. Does that answer you? Of course, you can always ask Registry, they keep track of us all. But we can't, ah, take you to our leader, if that's what you mean." She laughs, a genuine, jolly sound. "That's one of our old jokes. I must say," she goes on seriously, "it's been a joy to us that we can understand you so well. We make a big effort not to let the language drift, it would be tragic to lose touch with the past."

Dave takes the mike. "Thank you, Luna. You've given us something to think about. *Sunbird* out."

"How much of that is for real, Doc?" Bud rubs his curly head. "They're giving us one of your science fiction stories."

"The real story will come later," says Dave. "Our job is to get there."

"That's a point that doesn't look too good."

By the end of the session it looks worse. No Venus trajectory is any good. Lorimer reruns all the computations; same result.

"There doesn't seem to be any solution to this one, Dave," he says at last. "The parameters are just too tough. I think we've had it."

Dave massages his knuckles thoughtfully. Then he nods. "Roger. We'll fire the optimum sequence on the Earth heading."

"Tell them to wave if they see us go by," says Bud.

They are silent, contemplating the prospect of a slow death in space eighteen months hence. Lorimer wonders if he can raise the other question, the bad one. He is pretty sure what Dave will say. What will he himself decide, what will he have the guts to do?

"Hello, *Sunbird?*" the voice of *Gloria* breaks in. "Listen, we've been figuring. We think if you use all your fuel you could come back in close enough to our orbit so we could swing out and pick you up. You'd be using solar gravity that way. We have plenty of maneuver but much less acceleration than you do. You have suits and some kind of propellants, don't you? I mean, you could fly across a few kays?"

The three men look at each other; Lorimer guesses he had not been the only one to speculate on that.

"That's a good thought, *Gloria,*" Dave says. "Let's hear what Luna says."

"Why?" asks Judy. "It's our business, we wouldn't endanger the ship. We'd only miss another look at Venus, who cares? We have plenty of water and food and if the air gets a little smelly we can stand it."

"Hey, the chicks are all right," Bud says. They wait.

The voice of Luna comes on. "We've been looking at that, too, Judy. We're not sure you understand the risk. Ah, *Sunbird,* excuse me. Judy, if you manage to pick them up you'll have to spend nearly a year in the ship with these three male persons from a *very different culture.* Myda says you should remember history and it's a risk no matter what Connie says. *Sunbird,* I hate to be so rude. Over."

Bud is grinning broadly, they all are. "Cavemen." He chuckles. "All the chicks land preggers."

"Margo, they're human beings," the Judy voice protests. "This isn't just Connie, we're all agreed. Andy and Lady Blue say it would be very interesting. If it works, that is. We can't let them go without trying."

"We feel that way, too, of course," Luna replies. "But there's another problem. They could be carrying diseases. *Sunbird,* I know you've been isolated for fourteen months, but Murti says people in your day were immune to organisms that aren't around now. Maybe some of ours could harm you, too. You could all get mortally sick and lose the ship."

"We thought of that, Margo," Judy says impatiently. "Look, if you have contact with them at all somebody has to test, true? So we're ideal. By the time we get home you'll know. And how could we get sick so fast we couldn't put *Gloria* in a stable orbit where you could get her later on?"

They wait. "Hey, what about that epidemic?" Bud pats his hair elaborately. "I don't know if I want a career in gay lib."

"You rather stay out here?" Dave asks.

"Crazies," says a different voice from Luna. "*Sunbird,* I'm Murti, the health person here. I think what we have to fear most is the meningitis-influenza complex, they mutate so readily. Does your Dr. Lorimer have any suggestions?"

"Roger, I'll put him on," says Dave. "But as to your first point, madam, I want to inform you that at the time of takeoff the incidence of rape in the United States space cadre was zero point zero. I guarantee the conduct of my crew provided you can control yours. Here is Dr. Lorimer."

But Lorimer cannot, of course, tell them anything useful. They discuss the men's polio shots, which luckily have used killed virus, and various childhood diseases which still seem to be around. He does not mention their epidemic.

"Luna, we're going to try it," Judy declares. "We couldn't live with ourselves. Now, let's get the course figured before they get any farther away."

From there on, there is no rest on *Sunbird* while they set up and refigure and rerun the computations for the envelope of possible intersecting trajectories. The *Gloria*'s drive, they learn, is indeed low-thrust, although capable of sustained operation. *Sunbird* will have to get most of the way to the rendezvous on her own if they can cancel their outward velocity.

The tension breaks once during the long session, when Luna calls *Gloria* to warn Connie to be sure the female crew members wear concealing garments at all times if the men came aboard.

"Not suit liners, Connie, they're much too tight." It is the older woman, Myda. Bud chuckles.

"Your light sleepers, I think. And when the men unsuit, your Andy is the only one who should help them. You others stay away. The same for all body functions and sleeping. This is very important, Connie, you'll have to watch it the whole way home. There are a great many complicated taboos. I'm putting an instruction list on the bleeper. Is your receiver working?"

"Da, we used it for France's black hole paper."

"Good. Tell Judy to stand by. Now listen, Connie, listen carefully. Tell Andy he has to read it all. I repeat, *he* has to read every word. Did you hear that?"

"Ah, dinko," Connie answers. "I understand, Myda. He will."

"I think we just lost the ball game, fellas," Bud laments. "Old mother Myda took it all away."

Even Dave laughs. But later when the modulated squeal that is a whole text comes through the speaker, he frowns again. "There goes the good stuff."

The last factors are cranked in; the revised program spins, and Luna confirms them. "We have a payout, Dave," Lorimer reports. "It's tight but there are at least two viable options. Provided the main jets are fully functional."

"We're going EVA to check."

That is exhausting; they find a warp in the deflector housing of the port engines and spend four sweating hours trying to wrestle it back. It is only Lorimer's third sight of open space but he is soon too tired to care.

"Best we can do," Dave pants finally. "We'll have to compensate in the psychic mode."

"You can do it, Dave-o," says Bud. "Hey, I gotta change those suit radios, don't let me forget."

In the psychic mode . . . Lorimer surfaces back to his real self, cocooned in *Gloria*'s big cluttered cabin, seeing Connie's living face. It must be hours, how long has he been dreaming?

"About two minutes." Connie smiles.

"I was thinking of the first time I saw you."

"Oh yes. We'll never forget that, ever."

Nor will he . . . He lets it unroll again in his head. The interminable hours after the first long burn, which has sent *Sunbird* yawing so they all have to gulp nausea pills. Judy's breathless voice reading down their approach: "Oh, very good, four hundred thousand . . . Oh great, *Sunbird,* you're almost three, you're going to break a hundred for sure—" Dave has done it, the big one.

Lorimer's probe is useless in the yaw, it isn't until they stabilize enough for the final burst that they can see the strange blip bloom and vanish in the slot. Converging, hopefully, on a theoretical near-intersection point.

"Here goes everything."

The final burn changes the yaw into a sickening tumble with the star field looping past the glass. The pills are no more use and the fuel feed to the attitude jets goes sour. They are all vomiting before they manage to hand-pump the last of the fuel and slow the tumble.

"That's it, *Gloria.* Come and get us. Lights on, Bud. Let's get those suits up."

Fighting nausea, they go through the laborious routine in the fouled cabin. Suddenly Judy's voice sings out, "We see you, *Sunbird!* We see your light! Can't you see us?"

"No time," Dave says. But Bud, half suited, points at the window. "Fellas, oh, hey, look at that."

Lorimer stares, thinks he sees a faint spark between the whirling stars before he has to retch.

"Father, we thank you," says Dave quietly. "All right, move it on, Doc. Packs."

The effort of getting themselves plus the propulsion units and a couple of cargo nets out of the rolling ship drives everything else out of mind. It isn't until they are floating linked together and stabilized by Dave's hand jet that Lorimer has time to look.

The sun blanks out their left. A few meters below them *Sunbird* tumbles empty, looking absurdly small. Ahead of them, infinitely far away, is a point too blurred and yellow to be a star. It creeps: *Gloria,* on her approach tangent.

"Can you start, *Sunbird?*" says Judy in their helmets. "We don't want to brake any more on account of our exhaust. We estimate fifty kay in an hour, we're coming out on a line."

"Roger. Give me your jet, Doc."

"Goodbye, *Sunbird,*" says Bud. "Plenty of lead, Dave-o."

Lorimer finds it restful in a childish way, being towed across the abyss tied to the two big men. He has total confidence in

Dave, he never considers the possibility that they will miss, sail by and be lost. Does Dave feel contempt? Lorimer wonders; that banked-up silence, is it partly contempt for those who can manipulate only symbols, who have no mastery of matter? . . . He concentrates on mastering his stomach.

It is a long, dark trip. *Sunbird* shrinks to a twinkling light, slowly accelerating on the spiral course that will end her ultimately in the sun with their precious records that are three hundred years obsolete. With, also, the packet of photos and letters that Lorimer has twice put in his suit pouch and twice taken out. Now and then he catches sight of *Gloria,* growing from a blur to an incomprehensible tangle of lighted crescents.

"Woo-ee, it's big," Bud says. "No wonder they can't accelerate, that thing is a flying trailer park. It'd break up."

"It's a spaceship. Got those nets tight, Doc?"

Judy's voice suddenly fills their helmets. "I see your lights! Can you see me? Will you have enough left to brake at all?"

"Affirmative to both, *Gloria,*" says Dave.

At that moment Lorimer is turned slowly forward again and he sees—will see it forever: the alien ship in the star field and on its dark side the tiny lights that are women in the stars, waiting for them. Three—no, four; one suit light is way out, moving. If that is a tether it must be over a kilometer.

"Hello, I'm Judy Dakar!" The voice is close. "Oh, mother, you're big! Are you all right? How's your air?"

"No problem."

They are in fact stale and steaming wet; too much adrenaline. Dave uses the jets again and suddenly she is growing, is coming right at them, a silvery spider on a trailing thread. Her suit looks trim and flexible; it is mirror-bright, and the pack is quite small. Marvels of the future, Lorimer thinks; Paragraph One.

"You made it, you made it! Here, tie in. Brake!"

"There ought to be some historic words," Bud murmurs. "If she gives us a chance."

"Hello, Judy," says Dave calmly. "Thanks for coming."

"Contact!" She blasts their ears. "Haul us in, Andy! Brake, brake—the exhaust is back there!"

And they are grabbed hard, deflected into a great arc toward the ship. Dave uses up the last jet. The line loops.

"Don't jerk it," Judy cries. "Oh, I'm *sorry.*" She is clinging on them like a gibbon, Lorimer can see her eyes, her excited mouth. Incredible. "Watch out, it's slack."

"Teach me, honey," says Andy's baritone. Lorimer twists and sees him far back at the end of a heavy tether, hauling them smoothly in. Bud offers to help, is refused. "Just hang loose, please," a matronly voice tells them. It is obvious Andy has done this before. They come in spinning slowly, like space fish. Lorimer finds he can no longer pick out the twinkle that is *Sunbird.* When he is swung back, *Gloria* has changed to a disorderly cluster of bulbs and spokes around a big central cylinder. He can see pods and miscellaneous equipment stowed all over her. Not like science fiction.

Andy is paying the line into a floating coil. Another figure floats beside him. They are both quite short, Lorimer realizes as they near.

"Catch the cable," Andy tells them. There is a busy moment of shifting inertial drag.

"Welcome to *Gloria,* Major Davis, Captain Geirr, Dr. Lorimer. I'm Lady Blue Parks. I think you'll like to get inside as soon as possible. If you feel like climbing go right ahead, we'll pull all this in later."

"We appreciate it, ma'am."

They start hand over hand along the catenary of the main tether. It has a good rough grip. Judy coasts up to peer at them, smiling broadly, towing the coil. A taller figure waits by the ship's open airlock.

"Hello, I'm Connie. I think we can cycle in two at a time. Will you come with me, Major Davis?"

It is like an emergency on a plane, Lorimer thinks as Dave follows her in. Being ordered about by supernaturally polite little girls.

"Space-going stews." Bud nudges him. "How 'bout that?" His face is sprouting sweat. Lorimer tells him to go next, his own LSP has less load.

Bud goes in with Andy. The woman named Lady Blue waits beside Lorimer while Judy scrambles on the hull securing their cargo nets. She doesn't seem to have magnetic soles; perhaps ferrous metals aren't used in space now. When she begins hauling in the main tether on a simple hand winch Lady Blue looks at it critically.

"I used to make those," she says to Lorimer. What he can see of her features looks compressed, her dark eyes twinkle. He has the impression she is part black.

"I ought to get over and clean that aft antenna." Judy floats up.

"Later," says Lady Blue. They both smile at Lorimer. Then the hatch opens and he and Lady Blue go in. When the toggles seat there comes a rising scream of air and Lorimer's suit collapses.

"Can I help you?" She has opened her faceplate, the voice is rich and live. Eagerly Lorimer catches the latches in his clumsy gloves and lets her lift the helmet off. His first breath surprises him, it takes an instant to identify the gas as fresh air. Then the inner hatch opens, letting in greenish light. She waves him through. He swims into a short tunnel. Voices are coming from around the corner ahead. His hand finds a grip and he stops, feeling his heart shudder in his chest.

When he turns that corner the world he knows will be dead. Gone, rolled up, blown away forever with *Sunbird.* He will be irrevocably in the future. A man from the past, a time traveler. In the future. . . .

He pulls himself around the bend.

The future is a vast bright cylinder, its whole inner surface festooned with unidentifiable objects, fronds of green. In front of him floats an odd tableau: Bud and Dave, helmets off, looking enormous in their bulky white suits and packs. A few meters away hang two bareheaded figures in shiny suits and a dark-haired girl in flowing pink pajamas.

They are all simply staring at the two men, their eyes and mouths open in identical expressions of pleased wonder. The face that has to be Andy's is grinning openmouthed like a kid at the zoo. He is a surprisingly young boy, Lorimer sees, in spite of his deep voice; blond, downy-cheeked, compactly muscular. Lorimer finds he can scarcely bear to look at the pink woman, can't tell if she really is surpassingly beautiful or plain. The taller suited woman has a shiny, ordinary face.

From overhead bursts an extraordinary sound which he finally recognizes as a chicken cackling. Lady Blue pushes past him.

"All right, Andy, Connie, stop staring and help them get their suits off. Judy, Luna is just as eager to hear about this as we are."

The tableau jumps to life. Afterwards Lorimer can recall mostly eyes, bright curious eyes tugging his boots, smiling eyes upside down over his pack—and always that light, ready laughter. Andy is left alone to help them peel down, blinking at the fittings which Lorimer still finds embarrassing. He seems easy and nimble in his own half-open suit. Lorimer struggles out of the last lacings, thinking: A boy! A boy and four women orbiting the sun, flying their big junky ships to Mars. Should he feel humiliated? He only feels grateful, accepting a short robe and a bulb of tea somebody—Connie?—gives him.

The suited Judy comes in with their nets. The men follow Andy along another passage, Bud and Dave clutching at the small robes. Andy stops by a hatch.

"This greenhouse is for you, it's your toilet. Three's a lot but you have full sun."

Inside is a brilliant jungle, foliage everywhere, glittering water droplets, rustling leaves. Something whirs away—a grasshopper.

"You crank that handle." Andy points to a seat on a large cross-duct. "The piston rams the gravel and waste into a compost process and it ends up in the soil core. That vetch is a heavy nitrogen user and a great oxidator. We pump CO_2 in and oxy out. It's a real Woolagong."

He watches critically while Bud tries out the facility.

"What's a Woolagong?" asks Lorimer dazedly.

"Oh, she's one of our inventors. Some of her stuff is weird. When we have a pluggy-looking thing that works we call it a Woolagong." He grins. "The chickens eat the seeds and the hoppers, see, and the hoppers and iguanas eat the leaves. When a greenhouse is going darkside we turn them in to harvest. With this much light I think we could keep a goat, don't you? You didn't have any life at all on your ship, true?"

"No," Lorimer says, "not a single iguana."

"They promised us a Shetland pony for Christmas," says Bud, rattling gravel. Andy joins perplexedly in the laugh.

Lorimer's head is foggy; it isn't only fatigue, the year in *Sunbird* has atrophied his ability to take in novelty. Numbly he uses the Woolagong and they go back out and forward to *Gloria*'s big control room, where Dave makes a neat short speech to Luna and is answered graciously.

"We have to finish changing course now," Lady Blue says. Lorimer's impression has been right, she is a small light part-Negro in late middle age. Connie is part something exotic, too, he sees; the others are European types.

"I'll get you something to eat." Connie smiles warmly. "Then you probably want to rest. We saved all the cubbies for you." She says "syved"; their accents are all identical.

As they leave the control room Lorimer sees the withdrawn look in Dave's eyes and knows he must be feeling the reality of being a passenger in an alien ship; not in command, not deciding the course, the communications going on unheard.

That is Lorimer's last coherent observation, that and the taste of the strange, good food. And then being led aft through what he now knows is the gym, to the shaft of the sleeping drum. There are six irised ports like dog doors; he pushes through his assigned port and finds himself facing a roomy mattress. Shelves and a desk are in the wall.

"For your excretions." Connie's arm comes through the iris, pointing at bags. "If you have a problem stick your head out and call. There's water."

Lorimer simply drifts toward the mattress, too sweated out to reply. His drifting ends in a curious heavy settling and his final astonishment: the drum is smoothly, silently starting to revolve. He sinks gratefully onto the pad, growing "heavier" as the minutes pass. About a tenth gee, maybe more, he thinks, it's still accelerating. And falls into the most restful sleep he has known in the long weary year.

It isn't till next day that he understands that Connie and two others have been on the rungs of the gym chamber, sending it around hour after hour without pause or effort and chatting as they went.

How they talk, he thinks, again floating back to real present time. The bubbling irritant pours through his memory, the voices of Ginny and Jenny and Penny on the kitchen telephone, before that his mother's voice, his sister Amy's. Interminable. What do they always have to talk, talk, talk of?

"Why, everything," says the real voice of Connie beside him now, "it's natural to share."

"Natural. . . ." Like ants, he thinks. They twiddle their antennae together every time they meet. Where did you go, what did you do? Twiddle-twiddle. How do you *feel?* Oh, I feel this, I feel that, blah blah twiddle-twiddle. Total coordination of the hive. Women have no self-respect. Say anything, no sense of the strategy of words, the dark danger of naming. Can't hold in.

"Ants, beehives." Connie laughs, showing the bad tooth. "You truly see us as insects, don't you? Because they're females?"

"Was I talking aloud? I'm sorry." He blinks away dreams.

"Oh, please don't be. It's so sad to hear about your sister and your children and your, your wife. They must have been wonderful people. We think you're very brave."

But he has only thought of Ginny and them all for an instant—what has he been babbling? What is the drug doing to him?

"What are you doing to us?" he demands, lanced by real alarm now, almost angry.

"It's all right, truly." Her hand touches his, warm and somehow shy. "We all use it when we need to explore something. Usually it's pleasant. It's a laevonoramine compound, a disinhibitor, it doesn't dull you like alcohol. We'll be home so soon, you see. We have the responsibility to understand and you're so locked in." Her eyes melt at him. "You don't feel sick, do you? We have the antidote."

"No . . ." His alarm has already flowed away somewhere. Her explanation strikes him as reasonable enough. "We're not locked in," he says or tries to say. "We talk . . ." He gropes for a word to convey the judiciousness, the adult restraint. Objectivity, maybe? "We talk when we have something to say." Irrelevantly he thinks of a mission coordinator named Forrest, famous for his blue jokes. "Otherwise it would all break down," he tells her. "You'd fly right out of the system." That isn't quite what he means; let it pass.

The voices of Dave and Bud ring out suddenly from opposite ends of the cabin, awakening the foreboding of evil in his mind. They don't know us, he thinks. They should look out, stop this. But he is feeling too serene, he wants to think about his own new understanding, the pattern of them all he is seeing at last.

"I feel lucid," he manages to say, "I want to think."

She looks pleased. "We call that the ataraxia effect. It's so nice when it goes that way."

Ataraxia, philosophical calm. Yes. But there are monsters in the deep, he thinks or says. The night side. The night side of Orren Lorimer, a self hotly dark and complex, waiting in leash. They're so vulnerable. They don't know we can take them. Images rush up: a Judy spread-eagled on the gym rungs, pink pajamas gone, open to him. Flash sequence of the three of them taking over the ship, the women tied up, helpless, shrieking, raped and used. The team—get the satellite station, get a shuttle down to Earth. Hostages. Make them do anything, no defense whatever . . . Has Bud actually said that? But Bud doesn't know, he remembers. Dave knows they're hiding something, but he thinks it's socialism or sin. When they find out . . .

How has he himself found out? Simply listening, really, all these months. He listens to their talk much more than the others; "fraternizing," Dave calls it. . . . They all listened at first, of course. Listened and looked and reacted helplessly to the female bodies, the tender bulges so close under the thin, tantalizing clothes, the magnetic mouths and eyes, the smell of them, their electric touch. Watching them touch each other, touch Andy, laughing, vanishing quietly into shared bunks. *What goes on? Can I? My need, my need—*

The power of them, the fierce resentment. . . . Bud muttered and groaned meaningfully despite Dave's warnings. He kept needling Andy until Dave banned all questions. Dave himself was noticeably tense and read his Bible a great deal. Lorimer found his own body pointing after them like a famished hound, hoping to Christ the cubicles are as they appeared to be, unwired.

All they learn is that Myda's instructions must have been ferocious. The atmosphere has been implacably antiseptic, the discretion impenetrable. Andy politely ignored every probe. No word or act has told them what, if anything, goes on; Lorimer was irresistibly reminded of the weekend he spent at Jenny's Scout camp. The men's training came presently to their rescue, and they resigned themselves to finishing their mission on a super-*Sunbird,* weirdly attended by a troop of Boy and Girl Scouts.

In every other way their reception couldn't be more courteous. They have been given the run of the ship and their own dayroom in a cleaned-out gravel storage pod. They visit the control room as they wish. Lady Blue and Andy give them specs and manuals and show them every circuit and device of *Gloria*, inside and out. Luna has bleeped up a stream of science texts and the data on all their satellites and shuttles and the Mars and Luna dome colonies.

Dave and Bud plunged into an orgy of engineering. *Gloria* is, as they suspected, powered by a fission plant that uses a range of Lunar materials. Her ion drive is only slightly advanced over the experimental models of their own day. The marvels of the future seem so far to consist mainly of ingenious modifications.

"It's primitive," Bud tells him. "What they've done is sacrifice everything to keep it simple and easy to maintain. Believe it, they can hand-feed fuel. And the backups, brother! They have redundant redundancy."

But Lorimer's technical interest soon flags. What he really wants is to be alone a while. He makes a desultory attempt to survey the apparently few developments in his field, and finds he can't concentrate. What the hell, he tells himself, I stopped being a physicist three hundred years ago. Such a relief to be out of the cell of *Sunbird;* he has given himself up to drifting solitary through the warren of the ship, using their excellent 400 mm telescope, noting the odd life of the crew.

When he finds that Lady Blue likes chess they form a routine of biweekly games. Her personality intrigues him; she has reserve and an aura of authority. But she quickly stops Bud when he calls her "Captain."

"No one here commands in your sense. I'm just the oldest." Bud goes back to "ma'am."

She plays a solid positional game, somewhat more erratic than a man but with occasional elegant traps. Lorimer is astonished to find that there is only one new chess opening, an interesting queen-side gambit called the Dagmar. One new opening in three centuries? He mentions it to the others when they come back from helping Andy and Judy Paris overhaul a standby converter.

"They haven't done much anywhere," Dave says. "Most of your new stuff dates from the epidemic, Andy, if you'll pardon me. The program seems to be stagnating. You've been gearing up this Titan project for eighty years."

"We'll get there." Andy grins.

"C'mon, Dave," says Bud. "Judy and me are taking on you two for the next chicken dinner, we'll get a bridge team here yet. Woo-ee, I can taste that chicken! Losers get the iguana."

The food is so good. Lorimer finds himself lingering around the kitchen end, helping whoever is cooking, munching on their various seeds and chewy roots as he listens to them talk. He even likes the iguana. He begins to put on weight, in fact they all do. Dave decrees double exercise shifts.

"You going to make us *climb* home, Dave-o?" Bud groans. But Lorimer enjoys it, pedaling or swinging easily along the rungs while the women chat and listen to tapes. Familiar music: he identifies a strange spectrum from Handel, Brahms, Sibelius, through Strauss to ballad tunes and intricate light jazz rock. No lyrics. But plenty of informative texts doubtless selected for his benefit.

From the promised short history he finds out more about the epidemic. It seems to have been an airborne quasi-virus escaped from Franco-Arab military labs, possibly potentiated by pollutants.

"It apparently damaged only the reproductive cells," he tells Dave and Bud. "There was little actual mortality, but almost universal sterility. Probably a molecular substitution in the gene code in the gametes. And the main effect seems to have been on the men. They mention a shortage of male births afterwards, which suggests that the damage was on the Y-chromosome where it would be selectively lethal to the male fetus."

"Is it still dangerous, Doc?" Dave asks. "What happens to us when we get back home?"

"They can't say. The birthrate is normal now, about two percent and rising. But the present population may be resistant. They never achieved a vaccine."

"Only one way to tell," Bud says gravely. "I volunteer."

Dave merely glances at him. Extraordinary how he still commands, Lorimer thinks. Not submission, for Pete's sake. A team.

The history also mentions the riots and fighting which swept the world when humanity found itself sterile. Cities bombed, and burned, massacres, panics, mass rapes and kidnapping of women, marauding armies of biologically desperate men, bloody cults. The crazies. But it is all so briefly told, so long ago. Lists of honored names. "We must always be grateful to the brave people who held the Denver Medical Laboratories—" And then on to the drama of building up the helium supply for the dirigibles.

In three centuries it's all dust, he thinks. What do I know of the hideous Thirty Years' War that was three centuries back for me? *Fighting devastated Europe for two generations.* Not even names.

The description of their political and economic structure is even briefer. They seem to be, as Myda had said, almost ungoverned.

"It's a form of loose social-credit system run by consensus," he says to Dave. "Somewhat like a permanent frontier period. They're building up slowly. Of course they don't need an army or air force. I'm not sure if they even use cash money or recognize private ownership of land. I did notice one favorable reference to early Chinese communalism," he adds to see Dave's mouth set. "But they aren't tied to a community. They travel about. When I asked Lady Blue about their police and legal system she told me to wait and talk with real historians. This Registry seems to be just that, it's not a policy organ."

"We've run into a situation here, Lorimer," Dave says soberly. "Stay away from it. They're not telling the story."

"You notice they never talk about their husbands?" Bud laughs. "I asked a couple of them what their husband did and I swear they had to think. And they all have kids. Believe me, it's a swinging scene down there, even if old Andy acts like he hasn't found out what it's for."

"I don't want any prying into their personal family lives while we're on this ship, Geirr. None whatsoever. That's an order."

"Maybe they don't have families. You ever hear 'em mention anybody getting married? That has to be the one thing on a chick's mind. Mark my words, there's been some changes made."

"The social mores are bound to have changed to some extent," Lorimer says. "Obviously you have women doing more work outside the home, for one thing. But they have family bonds; for instance, Lady Blue has a sister in an aluminum mill and another in health. Andy's mother is on Mars and his sister works in Registry. Connie has a brother or brothers on the fishing fleet near Biloxi, and her sister is coming out to replace her here next trip, she's making yeast now."

"That's the top of the iceberg."

"I doubt the rest of the iceberg is very sinister, Dave."

But somewhere along the line the blandness begins to bother Lorimer, too. So much is missing. Marriage, love affairs, children's troubles, jealousy squabbles, status, possessions, money problems, sicknesses, funerals even—all the daily minutiae that occupied Ginny and her friend seems to have been edited out of these women's talk. *Edited*. . . . Can Dave be right? Is some big, significant aspect being deliberately kept from them?

"I'm still surprised your language hasn't changed more," he says one day to Connie during their exertions in the gym.

"Oh, we're very careful about that." She climbs at an angle beside him, not using her hands. "It would be a dreadful loss if we couldn't understand the books. All the children are taught from the same original tapes, you see. Oh, there's faddy words we use for a while, but our communicators have to learn the old texts by heart, that keeps us together."

Judy Paris grunts from the pedicycle. "You, my dear children, will never know the oppression we suffered," she declaims mockingly.

"Judys talk too much," says Connie.

"We do, for a fact." They both laugh.

"So you still read our so-called great books, our fiction and poetry?" asks Lorimer. "Who do you read, H. G. Wells? Shakespeare? Dickens, ah, Balzac, Kipling, Brian?" He gropes; Brian had been a bestseller Ginny liked. When had he last looked at Shakespeare or the others?

"Oh, the historicals," Judy says. "It's interesting, I guess. Grim. They're not very realistic. I'm sure it was to you," she adds generously.

And they turn to discussing whether the laying hens are getting too much light, leaving Lorimer to wonder how what he supposes are the eternal verities of human nature can have faded from a world's reality. Love, conflict, heroism, tragedy—all "unrealistic"? Well, flight crews are never great readers; still, women read more. . . . Something *has* changed, he can sense it. Something basic enough to affect human nature. A physical development perhaps; a mutation? What is really under those floating clothes?

It is the Judys who give him part of it.

He is exercising alone with both of them, listening to them gossip about some legendary figure named Dagmar.

"The Dagmar who invented the chess opening?" he asks.

"Yes. She does anything, when she's good she's great."

"Was she bad sometimes?"

A Judy laughs. "The Dagmar problem, you can say. She has this tendency to organize everything. It's fine when it works but every so often it runs wild, she thinks she's queen or what. Then they have to get out the butterfly nets."

All in present tense—but Lady Blue has told him the Dagmar gambit is over a century old.

Longevity, he thinks; by God, that's what they're hiding. Say they've achieved a doubled or tripled life span, that would certainly change human psychology, affect their outlook on everything. Delayed maturity, perhaps? We were working on endocrine cell juvenescence when I left. How old are these girls, for instance?

He is framing a question when Judy Dakar says, "I was in the crèche when she went pluggo. But she's good, I loved her later on."

Lorimer thinks she has said "crash" and then realizes she means a communal nursery. "Is that the same Dagmar?" he asks. "She must be very old."

"Oh no, her sister."

"A sister a hundred years apart?"

"I mean, her daughter. Her, her *grand*daughter." She starts pedaling fast.

"Judys," says her twin, behind them.

Sister again. Everybody he learns of seems to have an extraordinary number of sisters, Lorimer reflects. He hears Judy Paris saying to her twin, "I think I remember Dagmar at the crèche. She started uniforms for everybody. Colors and numbers."

"You couldn't have, you weren't born," Judy Dakar retorts.

There is a silence in the drum.

Lorimer turns on the rungs to look at them. Two flushed cheerful faces stare back warily, make identical head-dipping gestures to swing the black hair out of their eyes. Identical. . . . But isn't the Dakar girl on the cycle a shade more mature, her face more weathered?

"I thought you were supposed to be twins."

"Ah, Judys talk a lot," they say together—and grin guiltily.

"You aren't sisters," he tells them. "You're what we called clones."

Another silence.

"Well, yes," says Judy Dakar. "We call it sisters. Oh, mother! We weren't supposed to tell you, Myda said you would be frightfully upset. It was illegal in your day, true?"

"Yes. We considered it immoral and unethical, experimenting with human life. But it doesn't upset me personally."

"Oh, that's beautiful, that's great," they say together. "We think of you as different," Judy Paris blurts, "you're more hu— more like us. Please, you don't have to tell the others, do you? Oh, *please* don't."

"It was an accident there were two of us here," says Judy Dakar. "Myda *warned* us. Can't you wait a little while?" Two identical pairs of dark eyes beg him.

"Very well," he says slowly. "I won't tell my friends for the time being. But if I keep your secret you have to answer some questions. For instance, how many of your people are created artificially this way?"

He begins to realize he *is* somewhat upset. Dave is right, damn it, they are hiding things. Is this brave new world populated by subhuman slaves, run by master brains? Decorticate zombies, workers without stomachs or sex, human cortexes wired into machines, monstrous experiments rush through his mind. He had been naïve again. These normal-looking women can be fronting for a hideous world.

"How many?"

"There's only about eleven thousand of us," Judy Dakar says. The two Judys look at each other, transparently confirming something. They're unschooled in deception, Lorimer thinks; is that good? And is diverted by Judy Paris exclaiming, "What we can't figure out is why did you think it was wrong?"

Lorimer tries to tell them, to convey the horror of manipulating human identity, creating abnormal life. The threat to individuality, the fearful power it would put in a dictator's hand.

"Dictator?" one of them echoes blankly. He looks at their faces and can only say, "Doing things to people without their consent. I think it's sad."

"But that's just what we think about you," the younger Judy bursts out. "How do you know who you *are*? Or who anybody is? All alone, no sisters to share with! You don't know what you can do, or what would be interesting to try. All you poor singletons, you—why, you just have to blunder along and die, all for nothing!"

Her voice trembles. Amazed, Lorimer sees both of them are misty-eyed.

"We better get this m-moving," the other Judy says.

They swing back into the rhythm and in bits and pieces Lorimer finds out how it is. Not bottled embryos, they tell him indignantly. Human mothers like everybody else, young mothers, the best kind. A somatic cell nucleus is inserted in an enucleated ovum and reimplanted in the womb. They have each borne two "sister" babies in their late teens and nursed them a while before moving on. The crèches always have plenty of mothers.

His longevity notion is laughed at; nothing but some rules of healthy living have as yet been achieved. "We should make ninety in good shape," they assure him. "A hundred and eight, that was Judy Eagle, she's our record. But she was pretty blah at the end."

The clone strains themselves are old, they date from the epidemic. They were part of the first effort to save the race when the babies stopped and they've continued ever since.

"It's so perfect," they tell him. "We each have a book, it's really a library. All the recorded messages. The Book of Judy Shapiro, that's us. Dakar and Paris are our personal names, we're doing cities now." They laugh, trying not to talk at once about how each Judy adds her individual memoir, her adventures and problems and discoveries in the genotype they all share.

"If you make a mistake it's useful for the others. Of course you try not to—or at least make a *new* one."

"Some of the old ones aren't so realistic," her other self puts in.

"Things were so different, I guess. We make excerpts of the parts we like best. And practical things, like Judys should watch out for skin cancer."

"But we have to read the whole thing every ten years," says the Judy called Dakar. "It's inspiring. As you get older you understand some of the ones you didn't before."

Bemused, Lorimer tries to think how it would be, hearing the voices of three hundred years of Orren Lorimers. Lorimers who were mathematicians or plumbers or artists or bums or criminals, maybe. The continuing exploration and completion of self. And a dozen living doubles; aged Lorimers, infant Lorimers. And other Lorimers' women and children . . . would he enjoy it or resent it? He doesn't know.

"Have you made your records yet?"

"Oh, we're too young. Just notes in case of accident."

"Will we be in them?"

"You can say!" They laugh merrily, then sober. "Truly you won't tell?" Judy Paris asks. "Lady Blue, we have to let her know what we did. Oof. But *truly* you won't tell your friends?"

He hadn't told on them, he thinks now, emerging back into his living self. Connie beside him is drinking cider from a bulb. He has a drink in his hand, too, he finds. But he hasn't told.

"Judys will talk." Connie shakes her head, smiling. Lorimer realizes he must have gabbled out the whole thing.

"It doesn't matter," he tells her. "I would have guessed soon anyhow. There were too many clues . . . Woolagongs invent, Mydas worry, Jans are brains, Billy Dees work so hard. I picked up six different stories of hydroelectric stations that were built or improved or are being run by one Lala Singh. Your whole way of life. I'm more interested in this sort of thing than a respectable physicist should be," he says wryly. "You're all clones, aren't you? Every one of you. What do Connies do?"

"You really do know." She gazes at him like a mother whose child has done something troublesome and bright. "Whew! Oh, well, Connies farm like mad, we grow things. Most of our names are plants. I'm Veronica, by the way. And of course the crèches, that's our weakness. The runt mania. We tend to focus on anything smaller or weak."

Her warm eyes focus on Lorimer, who draws back involuntarily.

"We control it." She gives a hearty chuckle. "We aren't all that way. There's been engineering Connies, and we have two young sisters who love metallurgy. It's fascinating what the genotype can do if you try. The original Constantia Morelos was a chemist, she weighed ninety pounds and never saw a farm in her life." Connie looks down at her own muscular arms. "She was killed by the crazies, she fought with weapons. It's so hard to understand . . . And I had a sister Timothy who made dynamite and dug two canals and she wasn't even an andy."

"*An* andy," he says.

"Oh, dear."

"I guessed that, too. Early androgen treatments."

She nods hesitantly. "Yes. We need the muscle power for some jobs. A few. Kays are quite strong anyway. Whew!" She suddenly stretches her back, wriggles as if she'd been cramped. "Oh, I'm glad you know. It's been such a strain. We couldn't even sing."

"Why not?"

"Myda was sure we'd make mistakes, all the words we'd have had to change. We sing a lot." She softly hums a bar or two.

"What kinds of songs do you sing?"

"Oh, every kind. Adventure songs, work songs, mothering songs, roaming songs, mood songs, trouble songs, joke songs—everything."

"What about love songs?" he ventures. "Do you still have, well, love?"

"Of course, how could people not love?" But she looks at him doubtfully. "The love stories I've heard from your time are so, I don't know, so weird. Grim and pluggy. It doesn't seem like love. . . . Oh, yes, we have famous love songs. Some of them are partly sad, too. Like Tamil and Alcmene O., they're fated together. Connies are fated, too, a little." She grins bashfully. "We love to be with Ingrid Anders. It's more one-sided. I hope there'll be an Ingrid on my next hitch. She's so exciting, she's like a little diamond."

Implications are exploding all about him, sparkling with questions. But Lorimer wants to complete the darker pattern beyond.

"Eleven thousand genotypes, two million people: that averages two hundred of each of you alive now." She nods. "I suppose it varies? There's more of some?"

"Yes, some types aren't as viable. But we haven't lost any since early days. They tried to preserve all the genes they could, we have people from all the major races and a lot of small strains. Like me, I'm the Carib Blend. Of course, we'll never know what was lost. But eleven thousand is a lot, really. We all try to know everyone, it's a life hobby."

A chill penetrates his ataraxia. Eleven thousand, period. That is the true population of Earth now. He thinks of two hundred tall olive-skinned women named after plants, excited by two hundred little bright Ingrids; two hundred talkative Judys, two hundred self-possessed Lady Blues, two hundred Margos and Mydas and the rest. He shivers. The heirs, the happy pallbearers of the human race.

"So evolution ends," he says somberly.

"No, why? It's just slowed down. We do everything much slower than you did, I think. We like to experience things *fully.* We have time." She stretches again, smiling. "There's all the time."

"But you have no new genotypes. It is the end."

"Oh but there are, now. Last century they worked out the way to make haploid nuclei combine. We can make a stripped egg cell function like pollen," she says proudly. "I mean sperm. It's tricky, some don't come out too well. But now we're finding both X's viable we have over a hundred new types started. Of course it's hard for them, with no sisters. The donors try to help."

Over a hundred, he thinks. Well. Maybe. . . . But "both X's viable," what does that mean? She must be referring to the epidemic. But he had figured it primarily affected the men. His mind goes happily to work on the new puzzle, ignoring a sound from somewhere that is trying to pierce his calm.

"It was a gene or genes on the X chromosome that was injured," he guesses aloud. "Not the Y. And the lethal trait had to be recessive, right? Thus there would have been no births at all for a time, until some men recovered or were isolated long enough to manufacture undamaged X-bearing gametes. But women carry their lifetime supply of ova, they could never regenerate reproductively. When they mated with the recovered males only female babies would be produced, since the female carries two X's and the mother's defective gene would be compensated by a normal X from the father. But the male is XY, he receives only the mother's defective X. Thus the lethal defect would be expressed, the male fetus would be finished. . . . A planet of girls and dying men. The few odd viables died off."

"You truly do understand," she says admiringly.

The sound is becoming urgent; he refuses to hear it, there is significance here.

"So we'll be perfectly all right on Earth. No problem. In theory we can marry again and have families, daughters anyway."

"Yes," she says. "In theory."

The sound suddenly broaches his defenses, becomes the loud voice of Bud Geirr raised in song. He sounds plain drunk now. It seems to be coming from the main garden pod, the one they use to grow vegetables, not sanitation. Lorimer feels the dread alive again, rising closer. Dave ought to keep an eye on him. But Dave seems to have vanished, too, he recalls seeing him go toward Control with Lady Blue.

"OH, THE SUN SHINES BRIGHT ON PRET-TY RED WI-I-ING," carols Bud.

Something should be done, Lorimer decides painfully. He stirs; it is an effort.

"Don't worry," Connie says. "Andy's with them."

"You don't know, you don't know what you've started." He pushes off toward the garden hatchway.

"—AS SHE LAY SLE-EEPING, A COWBOY CREE-E-EEPING—" General laughter from the hatchway. Lorimer coasts through into the green dazzle. Beyond the radial fence of snap beans he sees Bud sailing in an exaggerated crouch after Judy Paris. Andy hangs by the iguana cages, laughing.

Bud catches one of Judy's ankles and stops them both with a flourish, making her yellow pajamas swirl. She giggles at him upside down, making no effort to free herself.

"I don't like this," Lorimer whispers.

"Please don't interfere." Connie has hold of his arm, anchoring them both to the tool rack. Lorimer's alarm seems to have ebbed; he will watch, let serenity return. The others have not noticed them.

"Oh, there once was an Indian maid," Bud sings more restrainedly, "who never was a-fraid, that some buckaroo would slip it up her, ahem, ahem." He coughs ostentatiously, laughing. "Hey, Andy, I hear them calling you."

"What?" says Judy. "I don't hear anything."

"They're calling you, lad. Out there."

"Who?" asks Andy, listening.

"They are, for Crissake." He lets go of Judy and kicks over to Andy. "Listen, you're a great kid. Can't you see me and Judy have some business to discuss in private?" He turns Andy gently around and pushes him at the bean stakes. "It's New Year's Eve, dummy."

Andy floats passively away through the fence of vines, raising a hand at Lorimer and Connie. Bud is back with Judy.

"Happy New Year, kitten." He smiles.

"Happy New Year. Did you do special things on New Year?" she asks curiously.

"What we did on New Year's." He chuckles, taking her shoulders in his hands. "On New Year's Eve, yes we did. Why don't I show you some of our primitive Earth customs, h'mm?"

She nods, wide-eyed.

"Well, first we wish each other well, like this." He draws her to him and lightly kisses her cheek. "Kee-rist, what a dumb bitch," he says in a totally different voice. "You can tell you've been out too long when the geeks start looking good. Knockers, ahhh—" His hand plays with her blouse. The man is unaware, Lorimer realizes. He doesn't know he's drugged, he's speaking his thoughts. I must have done that. Oh, God. . . . He takes shelter behind his crystal lens, an observer in the protective light of eternity.

"And then we smooch a little." The friendly voice is back, Bud holds the girl closer, caressing her back. "Fat ass." He puts his mouth on hers; she doesn't resist. Lorimer watches Bud's arms tighten, his hands working on her buttocks, going under her clothes. Safe in the lens, his own sex stirs. Judy's arms are waving aimlessly.

Bud breaks for breath, a hand at his zipper.

"Stop staring," he says hoarsely. "One fucking more word, you'll find out what that big mouth is for. Oh, man, a flagpole.

Like steel. . . . Bitch, this is your lucky day." He is baring her breasts now, big breasts. Fondling them. "Two fucking years in the ass end of noplace," he mutters, "shit on me, will you? Can't wait, watch it—titty-titty-titties—"

He kisses her again quickly and smiles down at her. "Good?" he asks in his tender voice, and sinks his mouth on her nipples, his hand seeking in her thighs. She jerks and says something muffled. Lorimer's arteries are pounding with delight, with dread.

"I, I think this should stop," he makes himself say falsely, hoping he isn't saying more. Through the pulsing tension he hears Connie whisper back, it sounds like "Don't worry, Judy's very athletic." Terror stabs him, they don't know. But he can't help.

"Cunt," Bud grunts, "you have to have a cunt in there, is it froze up? You dumb cunt—" Judy's face appears briefly in her floating hair, a remote part of Lorimer's mind notes that she looks amused and uncomfortable. His being is riveted to the sight of Bud expertly controlling her body in midair, peeling down the yellow slacks. Oh, God—her dark pubic mat, the thick white thighs—a perfectly normal woman, no mutation. Ohhh, God. . . . But there is suddenly a drifting shadow in the way: Andy again floating over them with something in his hands.

"You dinko, Jude?" the boy asks.

Bud's face comes up red and glaring. "Bug out, you!"

"Oh, I won't bother."

"Jee-sus Christ." Bud lunges up and grabs Andy's arm, his legs still hooked around Judy. "This is man's business, boy, do I have to spell it out?" He shifts his grip. "Shoo!"

In one swift motion he has jerked Andy close and backhanded his face hard, sending him sailing into the vines.

Bud gives a bark of laughter, bends back to Judy. Lorimer can see his erection poking through his fly. He wants to utter some warning, tell them their peril, but he can only ride the hot pleasure surging through him, melting his crystal shell. Go on, more —avidly he sees Bud mouth her breasts again and then suddenly flip her whole body over, holding her wrists behind her in one fist, his legs pinning hers. Her bare buttocks bulge up helplessly, enormous moons. "Ass-s-s," Bud groans. "Up, you bitch, ahhh-hh —" He pulls her butt onto him.

Judy gives a cry, begins to struggle futilely. Lorimer's shell boils and bursts. Amid the turmoil ghosts outside are trying to rush in. And something *is* moving, a real ghost—to his dismay he sees it is Andy again, floating toward the joined bodies, holding a whirring thing. Oh, no—a camera. The fools.

"Get away!" he tries to call to the boy.

But Bud's head turns, he has seen. "You little pissass." His long arm shoots out and captures Andy's shirt, his legs still locked around Judy.

"I've had it with you." His fist slams into Andy's mouth, the camera goes spinning away. But this time Bud doesn't let him go, he is battering the boy, all of them rolling in a tangle in the air.

"Stop!" Lorimer hears himself shout, plunging at them through the beans. "Bud, stop it! You're hitting a woman."

The angry face comes around, squinting at him.

"Get lost, Doc, you little fart. Get your own ass."

"Andy is a *woman,* Bud. You're hitting a girl. She's not a man."

"Huh?" Bud glances at Andy's bloody face. He shakes the shirt-front. "Where's the boobs?"

"She doesn't have breasts, but she's a woman. Her real name is Kay. They're all women. Let her go, Bud."

Bud stares at the androgyne, his legs still pinioning Judy, his penis poking the air. Andy put up his/her hands in a vaguely combative way.

"A dyke?" says Bud slowly. "A goddam little bull dyke? This I gotta see."

He feints casually, thrusts a hand into Andy's crotch.

"No balls!" he roars. "No balls at all!" Convulsing with laughter, he lets himself tip over in the air, releasing Andy, his legs letting Judy slip free. "Na-ah." He interrupts himself to grab her hair and goes on guffawing. "A dyke! Hey, dykey!" He takes hold of his hard-on, waggles it at Andy. "Eat your heart out, little dyke." Then he pulls up Judy's head. She has been watching unresisting all along.

"Take a good look, girlie. See what old Buddy has for you? Tha-a-at's what you want, say it. How long since you saw a real man, hey, dogface?"

Maniacal laughter bubbles up in Lorimer's gut, farce too strong for fear. "She never saw a man in her life before, none of them has. You imbecile, don't you get it? There aren't any other men, they've all been dead three hundred years."

Bud slowly stops chuckling, twists around to peer at Lorimer. "What'd I hear you say, Doc?"

"The men are all gone. They died off in the epidemic. There's nothing but women left alive on Earth."

"You mean there's, there's two million women down there and no men?" His jaw gapes. "Only little bull dykes like Andy. . . . Wait a minute. Where do they get the kids?"

"They grow them artificially. They're all girls."

"Gawd. . . ." Bud's hand clasps his drooping penis, jiggles it absently. It stiffens. "Two million hot little cunts down there, waiting for old Buddy. Gawd. The last man on Earth. . . . You don't count, Doc. And old Dave, he's full of crap."

He begins to pump himself, still holding Judy by the hair. The motion sends them slowly backward. Lorimer sees that Andy—Kay—has the camera going again. There is a big star-shaped smear of blood on the boyish face; cut lip, probably. He himself feels globed in thick air, all action spent. Not lucid.

"Two million cunts," Bud repeats. "Nobody home, nothing but pussy everywhere. I can do anything I want, anytime. No more shit." He pumps faster. "They'll be spread out for miles begging for it. Clawing each other for it. All for me, King Buddy. . . . I'll have strawberries and cunt for breakfast. Hot buttered boobies, man. 'N' head, there'll be a couple little twats licking whip cream off my cock all day long. . . . Hey, I'll have contests! Only the best for old Buddy now. Not you, cow." He jerks Judy's head. "Li'l teenies, tight li'l holes. I'll make the old broads hot 'em up while I watch." He frowns slightly, working on himself. In a clinical corner of his mind Lorimer guesses the drug is retarding ejaculation. He tells himself that he should be relieved by Bud's self-absorption, is instead obscurely terrified.

"King, I'll be their god," Bud is mumbling. "They'll make statues of me, my cock a mile high, all over. . . . His Majesty's sacred balls. They'll worship it. . . . Buddy Geirr, the last cock on Earth. Oh man, if old George could see that. When the boys hear that they'll really shit themselves, woo-ee!"

He frowns harder. "They can't all be gone." His eyes rove, find

Lorimer. "Hey, Doc, there's some men left someplace, aren't there? Two or three, anyway?"

"No." Effortfully Lorimer shakes his head. "They're all dead, all of them."

"Balls." Bud twists around, peering at them. "There has to be some left. Say it." He pulls Judy's head up. "Say it, cunt."

"No, it's true," she says.

"No men," Andy/Kay echoes.

"You're lying." Bud scowls, frigs himself faster, thrusting his pelvis. "There has to be some men, sure there are. . . . They're hiding out in the hills, that's what it is. Hunting, living wild. . . . Old wild men, I knew it."

"Why do there have to be men?" Judy asks him, being jerked to and fro.

"Why, you stupid bitch." He doesn't look at her, thrusts furiously. "Because, dummy, otherwise nothing counts, that's why. . . . There's some men, some good old buckaroos—Buddy's a good old buckaroo—"

"Is he going to emit sperm now?" Connie whispers.

"Very likely," Lorimer says, or intends to say. The spectacle is of merely clinical interest, he tells himself, nothing to dread. One of Judy's hands clutches something: a small plastic bag. Her other hand is on her hair that Bud is yanking. It must be painful.

"Uhhh, ahh," Bud pants distressfully, "fuck away, fuck—" Suddenly he pushes Judy's head into his groin, Lorimer glimpses her nonplussed expression.

"You have a mouth, bitch, get working! . . . Take it, for shit's sake, *take* it! Uh, uh—" A small oyster jets limply from him. Judy's arm goes after it with the bag as they roll over in the air.

"Geirr!"

Bewildered by the roar, Lorimer turns and sees Dave—Major Norman Davis—looming in the hatchway. His arms are out, holding back Lady Blue and the other Judy.

"Geirr! I said there would be no misconduct on this ship and I mean it. Get away from that woman!"

Bud's legs only move vaguely, he does not seem to have heard. Judy swims through them bagging the last drops.

"You, what the hell are you doing?"

In the silence Lorimer hears his own voice say, "Taking a sperm sample, I should think."

"Lorimer? Are you out of your perverted mind? Get Geirr to his quarters."

Bud slowly rotates upright. "Ah, the reverend Leroy," he says tonelessly.

"You're drunk, Geirr. Go to your quarters."

"I have news for you, Dave-o," Bud tells him in the same flat voice. "I bet you don't know we're the last men on Earth. Two million twats down there."

"I'm aware of that," Dave says furiously. "You're a drunken disgrace. Lorimer, get that man out of here."

But Lorimer feels no nerve of action stir. Dave's angry voice has pushed back the terror, created a strange hopeful stasis encapsulating them all.

"I don't have to take that anymore. . . ." Bud's head moves back and forth, silently saying no, no, as he drifts toward Lorimer. "Nothing counts anymore. All gone. What for, friends?" His forehead puckers. "Old Dave, he's a man. I'll let him have some. The dummies. . . . Poor old Doc, you're a creep but you're better'n nothing, you can have some, too. . . . We'll have places, see, big spreads. Hey, we can run drags, there has to be a million good old cars down there. We can go hunting. And then we find the wild men."

Andy, or Kay, is floating toward him, wiping off blood.

"Ah, no you don't!" Bud snarls and lunges for her. As his arm stretches out Judy claps him on the triceps.

Bud gives a yell that dopplers off, his limbs thrash—and then he is floating limply, his face suddenly serene. He is breathing, Lorimer sees, releasing his own breath, watching them carefully straighten out the big body. Judy plucks her pants out of the vines, and they start towing him out through the fence. She has the camera and the specimen bag.

"I put this in the freezer, dinko?" she says to Connie as they come by. Lorimer has to look away.

Connie nods. "Kay, how's your face?"

"I felt it!" Andy/Kay says excitedly through puffed lips. "I felt physical anger, I wanted to hit him. Woo-ee!"

"Put that man in my wardroom," Dave orders as they pass. He

has moved into the sunlight over the lettuce rows. Lady Blue and Judy Dakar are back by the wall, watching. Lorimer remembers what he wanted to ask.

"Dave, do you really know? Did you find out they're all women?"

Dave eyes him broodingly, floating erect with the sun on his chestnut beard and hair. The authentic features of man. Lorimer thinks of his own father, a small pale figure like himself. He feels better.

"I always knew they were trying to deceive us, Lorimer. Now that this woman has admitted the facts I understand the full extent of the tragedy."

It is his deep, mild Sunday voice. The women look at him interestedly.

"They are lost children. They have forgotten He who made them. For generations they have lived in darkness."

"They seem to be doing all right," Lorimer hears himself say. It sounds rather foolish.

"Women are not capable of running anything. You should know that, Lorimer. Look what they've done here, it's pathetic. Marking time, that's all. Poor souls." Dave sighs gravely. "It is not their fault. I recognize that. Nobody has given them any guidance for three hundred years. Like a chicken with its head off."

Lorimer recognizes his own thought; the structureless, chattering, trivial, two-million-celled protoplasmic lump.

"The head of the woman is the man," Dave says crisply. "Corinthians one eleven three. No discipline whatsoever." He stretches out his arm, holding up his crucifix as he drifts toward the wall of vines. "Mockery. Abominations." He touches the stakes and turns, framed in the green arbor.

"We were sent here, Lorimer. This is God's plan. *I* was sent here. Not you, you're as bad as they are. My middle name is Paul," he adds in a conversational tone. The sun gleams on the cross, on his uplifted face, a strong, pure, apostolic visage. Despite some intellectual reservations Lorimer feels a forgotten nerve respond.

"Oh, Father, send me strength," Dave prays quietly, his eyes closed. "You have spared us from the void to bring Your light to this suffering world. I shall lead Thy erring daughters out of the darkness. I shall be a stern but merciful father to them in Thy name. Help me to teach the children Thy holy law and train them in the fear of Thy righteous wrath. Let the women learn in silence and all subjection; Timothy two eleven. They shall have sons to rule over them and glorify Thy name."

He could do it, Lorimer thinks, a man like that really could get life going again. Maybe there is some mystery, some plan. I was too ready to give up. No guts. . . . He becomes aware of women whispering.

"This tape is about through." It is Judy Dakar. "Isn't that enough? He's just repeating."

"Wait," murmurs Lady Blue.

"And she brought forth a man-child to rule the nations with a rod of iron, Revelations twelve five," Dave says, louder. His eyes are open now, staring intently at the crucifix. *"For God so loved the world that he sent his only begotten son."*

Lady Blue nods; Judy pushes off toward Dave. Lorimer understands, protest rising in his throat. They mustn't do that to Dave, treating him like an animal, for Christ's sake, a man—

"Dave! Look out, don't let her get near you!" he shouts.

"May I look, Major? It's beautiful, what is it?" Judy is coasting close, her hand out toward the crucifix.

"She's got a hypo, watch it!"

But Dave has already wheeled round. "Do not profane, woman!"

He thrusts the cross at her like a weapon, so menacing that she recoils in midair and shows the glinting needle in her hand.

"Serpent!" He kicks her shoulder away, sending himself upward. "Blasphemer. All right," he snaps in his ordinary voice, "there's going to be some order around here starting now. Get over by that wall, all of you."

Astounded, Lorimer sees that Dave actually has a weapon in his other hand, a small gray handgun. He must have had it since Houston. Hope and ataraxia shrivel away, he is shocked into desperate reality.

"Major Davis," Lady Blue is saying. She is floating right at him, they all are, right at the gun. Oh God, do they know what it is?

"Stop!" he shouts at them. "Do what he says, for God's sake.

That's a ballistic weapon, it can kill you. It shoots metal slugs." He begins edging toward Dave along the vines.

"Stand back." Dave gestures with the gun. "I am taking command of this ship in the name of the United States of America under God."

"Dave, put that gun away. You don't want to shoot people."

Dave sees him, swings the gun around. "I warn you, Lorimer, get over there with them. Geirr's a man, when he sobers up." He looks at the women still drifting puzzledly toward him and understands. "All right, lesson one. Watch this."

He takes deliberate aim at the iguana cages and fires. There is a pinging crack. A lizard explodes bloodily, voices cry out. A loud mechanical warble starts up and overrides everything.

"A leak!" Two bodies go streaking toward the far end, everybody is moving. In the confusion Lorimer sees Dave calmly pulling himself back to the hatchway behind them, his gun ready. He pushes frantically across the tool rack to cut him off. A spray canister comes loose in his grip, leaving him kicking in the air. The alarm warble dies.

"You will stay here until I decide to send for you," Dave announces. He has reached the hatch, is pulling the massive lock door around. It will seal off the pod, Lorimer realizes.

"Don't do it, Dave! Listen to me, you're going to kill us all." Lorimer's own internal alarms are shaking him, he knows now what all that damned volleyball has been for and he is scared to death. "Dave, listen to me!"

"Shut up." The gun swings toward him. The door is moving. Lorimer gets a foot on solidity.

"Duck! It's a bomb!" With all his strength he hurls the massive canister at Dave's head and launches himself after it.

"Look out!" And he is sailing helplessly in slow motion, hearing the gun go off again, voices yelling. Dave must have missed him, overhead shots are tough—and then he is doubling downwards, grabbing hair. A hard blow strikes his gut, it is Dave's leg kicking past him but he has his arm under the beard, the big man bucking like a bull, throwing him around.

"Get the gun, get it!" People are bumping him, getting hit. Just as his hold slips, a hand snakes by him onto Dave's shoulder and they are colliding into the hatch door in a tangle. Dave's body is suddenly no longer at war.

Lorimer pushes free, sees Dave's contorted face tip slowly backward looking at him.

"Judas—"

The eyes close. It is over.

Lorimer looks around. Lady Blue is holding the gun, sighting down the barrel.

"Put that down," he gasps, winded. She goes on examining it.

"Hey, thanks!" Andy—Kay—grins lopsidedly at him, rubbing his jaw. They are all smiling, speaking warmly to him, feeling themselves, their torn clothes. Judy Dakar has a black eye starting, Connie holds a shattered iguana by the tail.

Beside him Dave drifts breathing stertorously, his blind face pointing at the sun. *Judas . . .* Lorimer feels the last shield break inside him, desolation flooding in. *On the deck my captain lies.*

Andy-who-is-not-a-man comes over and matter-of-factly zips up Dave's jacket, takes hold of it, and begins to tow him out. Judy Dakar stops them long enough to wrap the crucifix chain around his hand. Somebody laughs, not unkindly, as they go by.

For an instant Lorimer is back in that Evanston toilet. But they are gone, all the little giggling girls. All gone forever, gone with the big boys waiting outside to jeer at him. Bud is right, he thinks. Nothing counts anymore. Grief and anger hammer at him. He knows now what he has been dreading: not their vulnerability, his.

"They were good men," he says bitterly. "They aren't bad men. You don't know what bad means. You did it to them, you broke them down. You made them do crazy things. Was it interesting? Did you learn enough?" His voice is trying to shake. "Everybody has aggressive fantasies. They didn't act on them. Never. Until you poisoned them."

They gaze at him in silence. "But nobody does," Connie says finally. "I mean, the fantasies."

"They were good men," Lorimer repeats elegiacally. He knows he is speaking for it all, for Dave's Father, for Bud's manhood, for himself, for Cro-Magnon, for the dinosaurs, too, maybe. "I'm a man. By God yes, I'm angry. I have a right. We gave you all this, we made it all. We built your precious civilization and your knowledge and comfort and medicines and your dreams. All of it. We protected you, we worked our balls off keeping you and your kids. It was hard. It was a fight, a bloody fight all the way. We're tough. We had to be, can't you understand? Can't you for Christ's sake understand that?"

Another silence.

"We're trying." Lady Blue sighs. "We are trying, Dr. Lorimer. Of course we enjoy your inventions and we do appreciate your evolutionary role. But you must see there's a problem. As I understand it, what you protected people from was largely other males, wasn't it? We've just had an extraordinary demonstration. You have brought history to life for us." Her wrinkled brown eyes smile at him; a small, tea-colored matron holding an obsolete artifact.

"But the fighting is long over. It ended when you did, I believe. We can hardly turn you loose on Earth, and we simply have no facilities for people with your emotional problems."

"Besides, we don't think you'd be very happy," Judy Dakar adds earnestly.

"We could clone them," says Connie. "I know there's people who would volunteer to mother. The young ones might be all right, we could try."

"We've been *over* all that." Judy Paris is drinking from the water tank. She rinses and spits into the soil bed, looking worriedly at Lorimer. "We ought to take care of that leak now, we can talk tomorrow. And tomorrow and tomorrow." She smiles at him, unselfconsciously rubbing her crotch. "I'm sure a lot of people will want to meet you."

"Put us on an island," Lorimer says wearily. "On three islands." That look; he knows that look of preoccupied compassion. His mother and sister had looked just like that the time the diseased kitten came in the yard. They had comforted it and fed it and tenderly taken it to the vet to be gassed.

An acute, complex longing for the women he has known grips him. Ginny . . . dear God. His sister Amy. Poor Amy, she was good to him when they were kids. His mouth twists.

"Your problem is," he says, "if you take the risk of giving us equal rights, what could we possibly contribute?"

"Precisely," says Lady Blue. They all smile at him relievedly, not understanding that he isn't.

"I think I'll have that antidote now," he says.

Connie floats toward him, a big, warmhearted, utterly alien woman. "I thought you'd like yours in a bulb." She smiles kindly.

"Thank you." He takes the small, pink bulb. "Just tell me," he says to Lady Blue, who is looking at the bullet gashes, "what do you call yourselves? Women's World? Liberation? Amazonia?"

"Why, we call ourselves human beings." Her eyes twinkle absently at him, go back to the bullet marks. "Humanity, mankind." She shrugs. "The human race."

The drink tastes cool going down, something like peace and freedom, he thinks. Or death.

Isaac Asimov

At last! At last! At long last!

There were nine stories in Volume One, fourteen stories in Volume Two, fifteen stories in Volume Three, and five stories so far in Volume Four. That's forty-three Hugo Winners in the short categories, before I finally made it in forty-fourth place. (Of course, I had won three Hugos previously in other categories—and a fourth one since—so this is not the tragedy I'm trying to make it sound like.)

The story was originally written for an anthology that was being planned for 1976 and was to be entitled *The Bicentennial Man.* Every story written for the anthology was to be inspired by that title, but in the broadest possible way. I was asked for 7,500 words, but the story got away from me and it became 15,000 words. The anthologist took it anyway.

Unfortunately, the anthology fell apart for a variety of reasons that had nothing to do with my story. I didn't know it fell apart, but Judy-Lynn del Rey, of Ballantine Books, who knows everything, knew. She was annoyed with me, in any case, because I hadn't done a story for one of *her* anthologies, and Judy-Lynn, when annoyed, is a formidable personage.

"I want to see the story," she said. "Show it to me!"

What could I do? I gave her a carbon of the story.

The next day she called me. "I did my best not to like the story," she said, "but I didn't succeed. I want it. Get it back."

I had to write to the original anthologist and return the money paid me. I received a reversion of the rights and Judy-Lynn published the story in her anthology *Stellar Science Fiction #2* in February 1976. Later that year I included it in my collection *The Bicentennial Man and Other Stories.*

The first hint I got that something unusual had taken place was in the reviews that began to appear in the fan magazines. My favorite review line of all time (for one of my s.f. stories) showed up. It went like this: "I read 'Bicentennial Man' and, for a time, I found myself back in the Golden Age."

And then I found I was nominated for a Hugo in the novelette category. That was bittersweet news. Sweet, for obvious reasons, but bitter because the 1977 convention at which the award was to be given out was to be held at Miami Beach and it was out of reach for me.

But was it? Could I not take a train? I had taken a train to Miami Beach in 1976, and back, too, and had survived (not by much). Wasn't a possible Hugo worth a repeat of the effort? I decided it was.

And then, in May 1977, I had a mild coronary, and I decided I had better not subject myself to the stress of long travel. There was nothing to do but wait. (Again this is not quite the tragedy that I'm trying to make it sound like. Shortly before my coronary, "The Bicentennial Man" won the Nebula Award and I was there to collect *that*—but I'm not here to plug the competition. This is a book of *Hugo* Winners.)

At 11 p.m. on Sunday, September 4, 1977, immediately after the award banquet, Barbara Bova (Ben's beautiful and vivacious wife) called with the good news. "The Bicentennial Man" had won the Hugo as well.

6

THE BICENTENNIAL MAN

The Three Laws of Robotics:

1. *A robot may not injure a human being or, through inaction, allow a human being to come to harm.*
2. *A robot must obey the orders given it by human beings except where such orders would conflict with the First Law.*
3. *A robot must protect its own existence as long as such protection does not conflict with the First or Second Law.*

1

Andrew Martin said, "Thank you," and took the seat offered him. He didn't look driven to the last resort, but he had been.

He didn't, actually, look anything, for there was a smooth blankness to his face, except for the sadness one imagined one saw in his eyes. His hair was smooth, light brown, rather fine, and there was no facial hair. He looked freshly and cleanly shaved. His clothes were distinctly old-fashioned, but neat and predominantly a velvety red-purple in color.

Facing him from behind the desk was the surgeon, and the nameplate on the desk included a fully identifying series of letters and numbers, which Andrew didn't bother with. To call him Doctor would be quite enough.

"When can the operation be carried through, Doctor?" he asked.

The surgeon said softly, with that certain inalienable note of respect that a robot always used to a human being, "I am not certain, sir, that I understand how or upon whom such an operation could be performed."

There might have been a look of respectful intransigence on the surgeon's face, if a robot of his sort, in lightly bronzed stainless steel, could have such an expression, or any expression.

Andrew Martin studied the robot's right hand, his cutting hand, as it lay on the desk in utter tranquillity. The fingers were long and shaped into artistically metallic looping curves so graceful and appropriate that one could imagine a scalpel fitting them and becoming, temporarily, one piece with them.

There would be no hesitation in his work, no stumbling, no quivering, no mistakes. That came with specialization, of course, a specialization so fiercely desired by humanity that few robots were, any longer, independently brained. A surgeon, of course, would have to be. And this one, though brained, was so limited in his capacity that he did not recognize Andrew—had probably never heard of him.

Andrew said, "Have you ever thought you would like to be a man?"

The surgeon hesitated a moment as though the question fitted nowhere in his allotted positronic pathways. "But I am a robot, sir."

"Would it be better to be a man?"

"It would be better, sir, to be a better surgeon. I could not be so if I were a man, but only if I were a more advanced robot. I would be pleased to be a more advanced robot."

"It does not offend you that I can order you about? That I can make you stand up, sit down, move right or left, by merely telling you to do so?"

"It is my pleasure to please you, sir. If your orders were to interfere with my functioning with respect to you or to any other human being, I would not obey you. The First Law, concerning my duty to human safety, would take precedence over the Second Law relating to obedience. Otherwise, obedience is my pleasure. . . . But upon whom am I to perform this operation?"

"Upon me," said Andrew.

"But that is impossible. It is patently a damaging operation."

"That does not matter," said Andrew calmly.

"I must not inflict damage," said the surgeon.

"On a human being, you must not," said Andrew, "but I, too, am a robot."

2

Andrew had appeared much more a robot when he had first been—manufactured. He had then been as much a robot in appearance as any that had ever existed, smoothly designed and functional.

He had done well in the home to which he had been brought in those days when robots in households, or on the planet altogether, had been a rarity.

There had been four in the home: Sir and Ma'am and Miss and Little Miss. He knew their names, of course, but he never used them. Sir was Gerald Martin.

His own serial number was NDR— He forgot the numbers. It had been a long time, of course, but if he had wanted to remember, he could not forget. He had not wanted to remember.

Little Miss had been the first to call him Andrew because she could not use the letters, and all the rest followed her in this.

Little Miss— She had lived ninety years and was long since dead. He had tried to call her Ma'am once, but she would not allow it. Little Miss she had been to her last day.

Andrew had been intended to perform the duties of a valet, a butler, a lady's maid. Those were the experimental days for him and, indeed, for all robots anywhere but in the industrial and exploratory factories and stations off Earth.

The Martins enjoyed him, and half the time he was prevented from doing his work because Miss and Little Miss would rather play with him.

It was Miss who understood first how this might be arranged. She said, "We order you to play with us and you must follow orders."

Andrew said, "I am sorry, Miss, but a prior order from Sir must surely take precedence."

But she said, "Daddy just said he hoped you would take care of the cleaning. That's not much of an order. I *order* you."

Sir did not mind. Sir was fond of Miss and of Little Miss, even more than Ma'am was, and Andrew was fond of them, too. At least, the effects they had upon his actions were those which in a human being would have been called the result of fondness. Andrew thought of it as fondness, for he did not know any other word for it.

It was for Little Miss that Andrew had carved a pendant out of wood. She had ordered him to. Miss, it seemed, had received an ivorite pendant with scrollwork for her birthday and Little Miss was unhappy over it. She had only a piece of wood, which she gave Andrew together with a small kitchen knife.

He had done it quickly and Little Miss said, "That's *nice,* Andrew. I'll show it to Daddy."

Sir would not believe it. "Where did you really get this, Mandy?" Mandy was what he called Little Miss. When Little Miss assured him she was really telling the truth, he turned to Andrew. "Did you do this, Andrew?"

"Yes, Sir."

"The design, too?"

"Yes, Sir."

"From what did you copy the design?"

"It is a geometric representation, Sir, that fit the grain of the wood."

The next day, Sir brought him another piece of wood, a larger one, and an electric vibro-knife. He said, "Make something out of this, Andrew. Anything you want to."

Andrew did so and Sir watched, then looked at the product a long time. After that, Andrew no longer waited on tables. He was ordered to read books on furniture design instead, and he learned to make cabinets and desks.

Sir said, "These are amazing productions, Andrew."

Andrew said, "I enjoy doing them, Sir."

"Enjoy?"

"It makes the circuits of my brain somehow flow more easily. I have heard you use the word 'enjoy' and the way you use it fits the way I feel. I enjoy doing them, Sir."

3

Gerald Martin took Andrew to the regional offices of United States Robots and Mechanical Men, Inc. As a member of the

Regional Legislature he had no trouble at all in gaining an interview with the Chief Robopsychologist. In fact, it was only as a member of the Regional Legislature that he qualified as a robot owner in the first place—in those early days when robots were rare.

Andrew did not understand any of this at the time, but in later years, with greater learning, he could re-view that early scene and understand it in its proper light.

The robopsychologist, Merton Mansky, listened with a gathering frown and more than once managed to stop his fingers at the point beyond which they would have irrevocably drummed on the table. He had drawn features and a lined forehead and looked as though he might be younger than he looked.

He said, "Robotics is not an exact art, Mr. Martin. I cannot explain it to you in detail, but the mathematics governing the plotting of the positronic pathways is far too complicated to permit of any but approximate solutions. Naturally, since we build everything about the Three Laws, those are incontrovertible. We will, of course, replace your robot—"

"Not at all," said Sir. "There is no question of failure on his part. He performs his assigned duties perfectly. The point is, he also carves wood in exquisite fashion and never the same twice. He produces works of art."

Mansky looked confused. "Strange. Of course, we're attempting generalized pathways these days. . . . Really creative, you think?"

"See for yourself." Sir handed over a little sphere of wood on which there was a playground scene in which the boys and girls were almost too small to make out, yet they were in perfect proportion and blended so naturally with the grain that that, too, seemed to have been carved.

Mansky said, "*He* did that?" He handed it back with a shake of his head. "The luck of the draw. Something in the pathways."

"Can you do it again?"

"Probably not. Nothing like this has ever been reported."

"Good! I don't in the least mind Andrew's being the only one."

Mansky said, "I suspect that the company would like to have your robot back for study."

Sir said with sudden grimness, "Not a chance. Forget it." He turned to Andrew, "Let's go home now."

"As you wish, Sir," said Andrew.

4

Miss was dating boys and wasn't about the house much. It was Little Miss, not as little as she was, who filled Andrew's horizon now. She never forgot that the very first piece of wood carving he had done had been for her. She kept it on a silver chain about her neck.

It was she who first objected to Sir's habit of giving away the productions. She said, "Come on, Dad, if anyone wants one of them, let him pay for it. It's worth it."

Sir said, "It isn't like you to be greedy, Mandy."

"Not for us, Dad. For the artist."

Andrew had never heard the word before and when he had a moment to himself he looked it up in the dictionary. Then there was another trip, this time to Sir's lawyer.

Sir said to him, "What do you think of this, John?"

The lawyer was John Feingold. He had white hair and a pudgy belly, and the rims of his contact lenses were tinted a bright green. He looked at the small plaque Sir had given him. "This is beautiful. . . . But I've heard the news. This is a carving made by your robot. The one you've brought with you."

"Yes, Andrew does them. Don't you, Andrew?"

"Yes, Sir," said Andrew.

"How much would you pay for that, John?" asked Sir.

"I can't say. I'm not a collector of such things."

"Would you believe I have been offered two hundred and fifty dollars for that small thing? Andrew has made chairs that have sold for five hundred dollars. There's two hundred thousand dollars in the bank out of Andrew's products."

"Good heavens, he's making you rich, Gerald."

"Half rich," said Sir. "Half of it is in an account in the name of Andrew Martin."

"The robot?"

"That's right, and I want to know if it's legal."

"Legal?" Feingold's chair creaked as he leaned back in it.

"There are no precedents, Gerald. How did your robot sign the necessary papers?"

"He can sign his name and I brought in the signature. I didn't bring him in to the bank himself. Is there anything further that ought to be done?"

"Um." Feingold's eyes seemed to turn inward for a moment. Then he said, "Well, we can set up a trust to handle all finances in his name and that will place a layer of insulation between him and the hostile world. Further than that, my advice is you do nothing. No one is stopping you so far. If anyone objects, let *him* bring suit."

"And will you take the case if suit is brought?"

"For a retainer, certainly."

"How much?"

"Something like that," and Feingold pointed to the wooden plaque.

"Fair enough," said Sir.

Feingold chuckled as he turned to the robot. "Andrew, are you pleased that you have money?"

"Yes, sir."

"What do you plan to do with it?"

"Pay for things, sir, which otherwise Sir would have to pay for. It would save him expense, sir."

5

The occasions came. Repairs were expensive, and revisions were even more so. With the years, new models of robots were produced and Sir saw to it that Andrew had the advantage of every new device until he was a paragon of metallic excellence. It was all at Andrew's expense.

Andrew insisted on that.

Only his positronic pathways were untouched. Sir insisted on that.

"The new ones aren't as good as you are, Andrew," he said. "The new robots are worthless. The company has learned to make the pathways more precise, more closely on the nose, more deeply on the track. The new robots don't shift. They do what they're designed for and never stray. I like you better."

"Thank you, Sir."

"And it's your doing, Andrew, don't you forget that. I am certain Mansky put an end to generalized pathways as soon as he had a good look at you. He didn't like the unpredictability. . . . Do you know how many times he asked for you so he could place you under study? Nine times! I never let him have you, though, and now that he's retired, we may have some peace."

So Sir's hair thinned and grayed and his face grew pouchy, while Andrew looked rather better than he had when he first joined the family.

Ma'am had joined an art colony somewhere in Europe and Miss was a poet in New York. They wrote sometimes, but not often. Little Miss was married and lived not far away. She said she did not want to leave Andrew and when her child, Little Sir, was born, she let Andrew hold the bottle and feed him.

With the birth of a grandson, Andrew felt that Sir had someone now to replace those who had gone. It would not be so unfair to come to him with the request.

Andrew said, "Sir, it is kind of you to have allowed me to spend my money as I wished."

"It was your money, Andrew."

"Only by your voluntary act, Sir. I do not believe the law would have stopped you from keeping it all."

"The law won't persuade me to do wrong, Andrew."

"Despite all expenses, and despite taxes, too, Sir, I have nearly six hundred thousand dollars."

"I know that, Andrew."

"I want to give it to you, Sir."

"I won't take it, Andrew."

"In exchange for something you can give me, Sir."

"Oh? What is that, Andrew?"

"My freedom, Sir."

"Your—"

"I wish to buy my freedom, Sir."

6

It wasn't that easy. Sir had flushed, had said "For God's sake!" had turned on his heel, and stalked away.

It was Little Miss who brought him around, defiantly and harshly—and in front of Andrew. For thirty years, no one had hesitated to talk in front of Andrew, whether the matter involved Andrew or not. He was only a robot.

She said, "Dad, why are you taking it as a personal affront? He'll still be here. He'll still be loyal. He can't help that. It's built in. All he wants is a form of words. He wants to be called free. Is that so terrible? Hasn't he earned it? Heavens, he and I have been talking about it for years."

"Talking about it for years, have you?"

"Yes, and over and over again, he postponed it for fear he would hurt you. I *made* him put it up to you."

"He doesn't know what freedom is. He's a robot."

"Dad, you don't know him. He's read everything in the library. I don't know what he feels inside but I don't know what *you* feel inside. When you talk to him you'll find he reacts to the various abstractions as you and I do, and what else counts? If someone else's reactions are like your own, what more can you ask for?"

"The law won't take that attitude," Sir said angrily. "See here, you!" He turned to Andrew with a deliberate grate in his voice. "I can't free you except by doing it legally, and if it gets into the courts, you not only won't get your freedom but the law will take official cognizance of your money. They'll tell you that a robot has no right to earn money. Is this rigmarole worth losing your money?"

"Freedom is without price, Sir," said Andrew. "Even the chance of freedom is worth the money."

7

The court might also take the attitude that freedom was without price, and might decide that for no price, however great, could a robot buy its freedom.

The simple statement of the regional attorney who represented those who had brought a class action to oppose the freedom was this: The word "freedom" had no meaning when applied to a robot. Only a human being could be free.

He said it several times, when it seemed appropriate; slowly, with his hand coming down rhythmically on the desk before him to mark the words.

Little Miss asked permission to speak on behalf of Andrew. She was recognized by her full name, something Andrew had never heard pronounced before:

"Amanda Laura Martin Charney may approach the bench."

She said, "Thank you, your honor. I am not a lawyer and I don't know the proper way of phrasing things, but I hope you will listen to my meaning and ignore the words.

"Let's understand what it means to be free in Andrew's case. In some ways, he *is* free. I think it's at least twenty years since anyone in the Martin family gave him an order to do something that we felt he might not do of his own accord.

"But we can, if we wish, give him an order to do anything, couch it as harshly as we wish, because he is a machine that belongs to us. Why should we be in a position to do so, when he has served us so long, so faithfully, and earned so much money for us? He owes us nothing more. The debt is entirely on the other side.

"Even if we were legally forbidden to place Andrew in involuntary servitude, he would still serve us voluntarily. Making him free would be a trick of words only, but it would mean much to him. It would give him everything and cost us nothing."

For a moment the Judge seemed to be suppressing a smile. "I see your point, Mrs. Charney. The fact is that there is no binding law in this respect and no precedent. There is, however, the unspoken assumption that only a man can enjoy freedom. I can make new law here, subject to reversal in a higher court, but I cannot lightly run counter to that assumption. Let me address the robot. Andrew!"

"Yes, your honor."

It was the first time Andrew had spoken in court and the Judge seemed astonished for a moment at the human timbre of the voice. He said, "Why do you want to be free, Andrew? In what way will this matter to you?"

Andrew said, "Would you wish to be a slave, your honor?"

"But you are not a slave. You are a perfectly good robot, a genius of a robot I am given to understand, capable of an artistic expression that can be matched nowhere. What more can you do if you were free?"

"Perhaps no more than I do now, your honor, but with greater joy. It has been said in this courtroom that only a human being can be free. It seems to me that only someone who wishes for freedom can be free. I wish for freedom."

And it was that that cued the Judge. The crucial sentence in his decision was: "There is no right to deny freedom to any object with a mind advanced enough to grasp the concept and desire the state."

It was eventually upheld by the World Court.

8

Sir remained displeased and his harsh voice made Andrew feel almost as though he were being short-circuited.

Sir said, "I don't want your damned money, Andrew. I'll take it only because you won't feel free otherwise. From now on, you can select your own jobs and do them as you please. I will give you no orders, except this one—that you do as you please. But I am still responsible for you; that's part of the court order. I hope you understand that."

Little Miss interrupted. "Don't be irascible, Dad. The responsibility is no great chore. You know you won't have to do a thing. The Three Laws still hold."

"Then how is he free?"

Andrew said, "Are not human beings bound by their laws, Sir?"

Sir said, "I'm not going to argue." He left, and Andrew saw him only infrequently after that.

Little Miss came to see him frequently in the small house that had been built and made over for him. It had no kitchen, of course, nor bathroom facilities. It had just two rooms; one was a library and one was a combination storeroom and workroom. Andrew accepted many commissions and worked harder as a free robot than he ever had before, till the cost of the house was paid for and the structure legally transferred to him.

One day Little Sir came. . . . No, George! Little Sir had insisted on that after the court decision. "A free robot doesn't call anyone Little Sir," George had said. "I call you Andrew. You must call me George."

It was phrased as an order, so Andrew called him George—but Little Miss remained Little Miss.

The day George came alone, it was to say that Sir was dying. Little Miss was at the bedside but Sir wanted Andrew as well.

Sir's voice was quite strong, though he seemed unable to move much. He struggled to get his hand up. "Andrew," he said, "Andrew— Don't help me, George. I'm only dying; I'm not crippled. . . . Andrew, I'm glad you're free. I just wanted to tell you that."

Andrew did not know what to say. He had never been at the side of someone dying before, but he knew it was the human way of ceasing to function. It was an involuntary and irreversible dismantling, and Andrew did not know what to say that might be appropriate. He could only remain standing, absolutely silent, absolutely motionless.

When it was over, Little Miss said to him, "He may not have seemed friendly to you toward the end, Andrew, but he was old, you know, and it hurt him that you should want to be free."

And then Andrew found the words to say. He said, "I would never have been free without him, Little Miss."

9

It was only after Sir's death that Andrew began to wear clothes. He began with an old pair of trousers at first, a pair that George had given him.

George was married now, and a lawyer. He had joined Feingold's firm. Old Feingold was long since dead but his daughter had carried on and eventually the firm's name became Feingold and Martin. It remained so even when the daughter retired and no Feingold took her place. At the time Andrew put on clothes for the first time, the Martin name had just been added to the firm.

George had tried not to smile, the first time Andrew put on the trousers, but to Andrew's eyes the smile was clearly there.

George showed Andrew how to manipulate the static charge so as to allow the trousers to open, wrap about his lower body, and move shut. George demonstrated on his own trousers, but

Andrew was quite aware that it would take him awhile to duplicate that one flowing motion.

George said, "But why do you want trousers, Andrew? Your body is so beautifully functional it's a shame to cover it—especially when you needn't worry about either temperature control or modesty. And it doesn't cling properly, not on metal."

Andrew said, "Are not human bodies beautifully functional, George? Yet you cover yourselves."

"For warmth, for cleanliness, for protection, for decorativeness. None of that applies to you."

Andrew said, "I feel bare without clothes. I feel different, George."

"Different! Andrew, there are millions of robots on Earth now. In this region, according to the last census, there are almost as many robots as there are men."

"I know, George. There are robots doing every conceivable type of work."

"And none of them wear clothes."

"But none of them are free, George."

Little by little, Andrew added to the wardrobe. He was inhibited by George's smile and by the stares of the people who commissioned work.

He might be free, but there was built into him a carefully detailed program concerning his behavior toward people, and it was only by the tiniest steps that he dared advance. Open disapproval would set him back months.

Not everyone accepted Andrew as free. He was incapable of resenting that and yet there was a difficulty about his thinking process when he thought of it.

Most of all, he tended to avoid putting on clothes—or too many of them—when he thought Little Miss might come to visit him. She was old now and was often away in some warmer climate, but when she returned the first thing she did was visit him.

On one of her returns, George said ruefully, "She's got me, Andrew. I'll be running for the Legislature next year. Like grandfather, she says, like grandson."

"Like grandfather—" Andrew stopped, uncertain.

"I mean that I, George, the grandson, will be like Sir, the grandfather, who was in the Legislature once."

Andrew said, "It would be pleasant, George, if Sir were still—" He paused, for he did not want to say, "in working order." That seemed inappropriate.

"Alive," said George. "Yes, I think of the old monster now and then, too."

It was a conversation Andrew thought about. He had noticed his own incapacity in speech when talking with George. Somehow the language had changed since Andrew had come into being with an innate vocabulary. Then, too, George used a colloquial speech, as Sir and Little Miss had not. Why should he have called Sir a monster when surely that word was not appropriate?

Nor could Andrew turn to his own books for guidance. They were old and most dealt with woodworking, with art, with furniture design. There were none on language, none on the way of human beings.

It was at that moment it seemed to him that he must seek the proper books; and as a free robot, he felt he must not ask George. He would go to town and use the library. It was a triumphant decision and he felt his electropotential grow distinctly higher until he had to throw in an impedance coil.

He put on a full costume, even including a shoulder chain of wood. He would have preferred the glitter plastic but George had said that wood was much more appropriate and that polished cedar was considerably more valuable as well.

He had placed a hundred feet between himself and the house before gathering resistance brought him to a halt. He shifted the impedance coil out of circuit, and when that did not seem to help enough, he returned to his home and on a piece of notepaper wrote neatly, "I have gone to the library," and placed it in clear view on his worktable.

10

Andrew never quite got to the library. He had studied the map. He knew the route, but not the appearance of it. The actual landmarks did not resemble the symbols on the map and he would hesitate. Eventually he thought he must have somehow gone wrong, for everything looked strange.

He passed an occasional field robot, but at the time he decided he should ask his way, there were none in sight. A vehicle passed and did not stop. He stood irresolute, which meant calmly motionless, and then coming across the field toward him were two human beings.

He turned to face them, and they altered their course to meet him. A moment before, they had been talking loudly; he had heard their voices; but now they were silent. They had the look that Andrew associated with human uncertainty, and they were young, but not very young. Twenty perhaps? Andrew could never judge human age.

He said, "Would you describe to me the route to the town library, sirs?"

One of them, the taller of the two, whose tall hat lengthened him still farther, almost grotesquely, said, not to Andrew, but to the other, "It's a robot."

The other had a bulbous nose and heavy eyelids. He said, not to Andrew, but to the first, "It's wearing clothes."

The tall one snapped his fingers. "It's the free robot. They have a robot at the Martins who isn't owned by anybody. Why else would it be wearing clothes?"

"Ask it," said the one with the nose.

"Are you the Martin robot?" asked the tall one.

"I am Andrew Martin, sir," said Andrew.

"Good. Take off your clothes. Robots don't wear clothes." He said to the other, "That's disgusting. Look at him."

Andrew hesitated. He hadn't heard an order in that tone of voice in so long that his Second Law circuits had momentarily jammed.

The tall one said, "Take off your clothes. I order you."

Slowly, Andrew began to remove them.

"Just drop them," said the tall one.

The nose said, "If it doesn't belong to anyone, he could be ours as much as someone else's."

"Anyway," said the tall one, "who's to object to anything we do? We're not damaging property. . . . Stand on your head." That was to Andrew.

"The head is not meant—" began Andrew.

"That's an order. If you don't know how, try anyway."

Andrew hesitated again, then bent to put his head on the ground. He tried to lift his legs and fell, heavily.

The tall one said, "Just lie there." He said to the other, "We can take him apart. Ever take a robot apart?"

"Will he let us?"

"How can he stop us?"

There was no way Andrew could stop them, if they ordered him not to resist in a forceful enough manner. Second Law of obedience took precedence over the Third Law of self-preservation. In any case, he could not defend himself without possibly hurting them and that would mean breaking the First Law. At that thought, every motile unit contracted slightly and he quivered as he lay there.

The tall one walked over and pushed at him with his foot. "He's heavy. I think we'll need tools to do the job."

The nose said, "We could order him to take himself apart. It would be fun to watch him try."

"Yes," said the tall one thoughtfully, "but let's get him off the road. If someone comes along—"

It was too late. Someone had indeed come along and it was George. From where he lay, Andrew had seen him topping a small rise in the middle distance. He would have liked to signal him in some way, but the last order had been "Just lie there!"

George was running now and he arrived somewhat winded. The two young men stepped back a little and then waited thoughtfully.

George said anxiously, "Andrew, has something gone wrong?"

Andrew said, "I am well, George."

"Then stand up. . . . What happened to your clothes?"

The tall young man said, "That your robot, mac?"

George turned sharply. "He's no one's robot. What's been going on here?"

"We politely asked him to take his clothes off. What's that to you if you don't own him?"

George said, "What were they doing, Andrew?"

Andrew said, "It was their intention in some way to dismember me. They were about to move me to a quiet spot and order me to dismember myself."

George looked at the two and his chin trembled. The two

young men retreated no further. They were smiling. The tall one said lightly, "What are you going to do, pudgy? Attack us?"

George said, "No. I don't have to. This robot has been with my family for over seventy years. He knows us and he values us more than he values anyone else. I am going to tell him that you two are threatening my life and that you plan to kill me. I will ask him to defend me. In choosing between me and you two, he will choose me. Do you know what will happen to you when he attacks you?"

The two were backing away slightly, looking uneasy.

George said sharply, "Andrew, I am in danger and about to come to harm from these young men. Move toward them!"

Andrew did so, and the two young men did not wait. They ran fleetly.

"All right, Andrew, relax," said George. He looked unstrung. He was far past the age where he could face the possibility of a dustup with one young man, let alone two.

Andrew said, "I couldn't have hurt them, George. I could see they were not attacking you."

"I didn't order you to attack them; I only told you to move toward them. Their own fears did the rest."

"How can they fear robots?"

"It's a disease of mankind, one of which it is not yet cured. But never mind that. What the devil are you doing here, Andrew? I was on the point of turning back and hiring a helicopter when I found you. How did you get it into your head to go to the library? I would have brought you any books you needed."

"I am a—" began Andrew.

"Free robot. Yes, yes. All right, what did you want in the library?"

"I want to know more about human beings, about the world, about everything. And about robots, George. I want to write a history about robots."

George said, "Well, let's walk home. . . . And pick up your clothes first. Andrew, there are a million books on robotics and all of them include histories of the science. The world is growing saturated not only with robots but with information about robots."

Andrew shook his head, a human gesture he had lately begun

to make. "Not a history of robotics, George. A history of *robots,* by a robot. I want to explain how robots feel about what has happened since the first ones were allowed to work and live on Earth."

George's eyebrows lifted, but he said nothing in direct response.

11

Little Miss was just past her eighty-third birthday, but there was nothing about her that was lacking in either energy or determination. She gestured with her cane oftener than she propped herself up with it.

She listened to the story in a fury of indignation. She said, "George, that's horrible. Who were those young ruffians?"

"I don't know. What difference does it make? In the end they did no damage."

"They might have. You're a lawyer, George, and if you're well off, it's entirely due to the talent of Andrew. It was the money *he* earned that is the foundation of everything we have. He provides the continuity for this family and I will *not* have him treated as a wind-up toy."

"What would you have me do, Mother?" asked George.

"I said you're a lawyer. Don't you listen? You set up a test case somehow, and you force the regional courts to declare for robot rights and get the Legislature to pass the necessary bills, and carry the whole thing to the World Court, if you have to. I'll be watching, George, and I'll tolerate no shirking."

She was serious, and what began as a way of soothing the fearsome old lady became an involved matter with enough legal entanglement to make it interesting. As senior partner of Feingold and Martin, George plotted strategy but left the actual work to his junior partners, with much of it a matter for his son, Paul, who was also a member of the firm and who reported dutifully nearly every day to his grandmother. She, in turn, discussed it every day with Andrew.

Andrew was deeply involved. His work on his book on robots was delayed again, as he pored over the legal arguments and even, at times, made very diffident suggestions.

He said, "George told me that day that human beings have always been afraid of robots. As long as they are, the courts and the legislatures are not likely to work hard on behalf of robots. Should there not be something done about public opinion?"

So while Paul stayed in court, George took to the public platform. It gave him the advantage of being informal and he even went so far sometimes as to wear the new, loose style of clothing which he called drapery. Paul said, "Just don't trip over it on stage, Dad."

George said despondently, "I'll try not to."

He addressed the annual convention of holo-news editors on one occasion and said, in part:

"If, by virtue of the Second Law, we can demand of any robot unlimited obedience in all respects not involving harm to a human being, then any human being, *any* human being, has a fearsome power over any robot, *any* robot. In particular, since Second Law supersedes Third Law, *any* human being can use the law of obedience to overcome the law of self-protection. He can order any robot to damage itself or even destroy itself for any reason, or for no reason.

"Is this just? Would we treat an animal so? Even an inanimate object which has given us good service has a claim on our consideration. And a robot is not insensible; it is not an animal. It can think well enough to enable it to talk to us, reason with us, joke with us. Can we treat them as friends, can we work together with them, and not give them some of the fruit of that friendship, some of the benefit of co-working?

"If a man has the right to give a robot any order that does not involve harm to a human being, he should have the decency never to give a robot any order that involves harm to a robot, unless human safety absolutely requires it. With great power goes great responsibility, and if the robots have Three Laws to protect men, is it too much to ask that men have a law or two to protect robots?"

Andrew was right. It was the battle over public opinion that held the key to courts and Legislature and in the end a law passed which set up conditions under which robot-harming orders were forbidden. It was endlessly qualified and the punishments for violating the law were totally inadequate, but the principle was established. The final passage by the World Legislature came through on the day of Little Miss's death.

That was no coincidence. Little Miss held on to life desperately during the last debate and let go only when word of victory arrived. Her last smile was for Andrew. Her last words were: "You have been good to us, Andrew."

She died with her hand holding his, while her son and his wife and children remained at a respectful distance from both.

12

Andrew waited patiently while the receptionist disappeared into the inner office. It might have used the holographic chatterbox, but unquestionably it was unmanned (or perhaps unroboted) by having to deal with another robot rather than with a human being.

Andrew passed the time revolving the matter in his mind. Could "unroboted" be used as an analogue of "unmanned," or had "unmanned" become a metaphoric term sufficiently divorced from its original literal meaning to be applied to robots—or to women for that matter?

Such problems came frequently as he worked on his book on robots. The trick of thinking out sentences to express all complexities had undoubtedly increased his vocabulary.

Occasionally, someone came into the room to stare at him and he did not try to avoid the glance. He looked at each calmly, and each in turn looked away.

Paul Martin finally came out. He looked surprised, or he would have if Andrew could have made out his expression with certainty. Paul had taken to wearing the heavy makeup that fashion was dictating for both sexes and though it made sharper and firmer the somewhat bland lines of his face, Andrew disapproved. He found that disapproving of human beings, as long as he did not express it verbally, did not make him very uneasy. He could even write the disapproval. He was sure it had not always been so.

Paul said, "Come in, Andrew. I'm sorry I made you wait but there was something I *had* to finish. Come in. You had said you wanted to talk to me, but I didn't know you meant here in town."

"If you are busy, Paul, I am prepared to continue to wait."

Paul glanced at the interplay of shifting shadows on the dial on the wall that served as timepiece and said, "I can make some time. Did you come alone?"

"I hired an automatobile."

"Any trouble?" Paul asked, with more than a trace of anxiety.

"I wasn't expecting any. My rights are protected."

Paul looked the more anxious for that. "Andrew, I've explained that the law is unenforceable, at least under most conditions. . . . And if you insist on wearing clothes, you'll run into trouble eventually—just like that first time."

"And only time, Paul. I'm sorry you are displeased."

"Well, look at it this way; you are virtually a living legend, Andrew, and you are too valuable in many different ways for you to have any right to take chances with yourself. . . . How's the book coming?"

"I am approaching the end, Paul. The publisher is quite pleased."

"Good!"

"I don't know that he's necessarily pleased with the book as a book. I think he expects to sell many copies because it's written by a robot and it's that that pleases him."

"Only human, I'm afraid."

"I am not displeased. Let it sell for whatever reason since it will mean money and I can use some."

"Grandmother left you—"

"Little Miss was generous, and I'm sure I can count on the family to help me out further. But it is the royalties from the book on which I am counting to help me through the next step."

"What next step is that?"

"I wish to see the head of U. S. Robots and Mechanical Men, Inc. I have tried to make an appointment, but so far I have not been able to reach him. The corporation did not cooperate with me in the writing of the book, so I am not surprised, you understand."

Paul was clearly amused. "Cooperation is the last thing you can expect. They didn't cooperate with us in our great fight for robot rights. Quite the reverse and you can see why. Give a robot rights and people may not want to buy them."

"Nevertheless," said Andrew, "if you call them, you may obtain an interview for me."

"I'm no more popular with them than you are, Andrew."

"But perhaps you can hint that by seeing me they may head off a campaign by Feingold and Martin to strengthen the rights of robots further."

"Wouldn't that be a lie, Andrew?"

"Yes, Paul, and I can't tell one. That is why you must call."

"Ah, you can't lie, but you can urge me to tell a lie, is that it? You're getting more human all the time, Andrew."

13

It was not easy to arrange, even with Paul's supposedly weighted name.

But it was finally carried through and, when it was, Harley Smythe-Robertson, who, on his mother's side, was descended from the original founder of the corporation and who had adopted the hyphenation to indicate it, looked remarkably unhappy. He was approaching retirement age and his entire tenure as president had been devoted to the matter of robot rights. His gray hair was plastered thinly over the top of his scalp, his face was not made up, and he eyed Andrew with brief hostility from time to time.

Andrew said, "Sir, nearly a century ago, I was told by a Merton Mansky of this corporation that the mathematics governing the plotting of the positronic pathways was far too complicated to permit of any but approximate solutions and that therefore my own capacities were not fully predictable."

"That was a century ago." Smythe-Robertson hesitated, then said icily, "*Sir.* It is true no longer. Our robots are made with precision now and are trained precisely to their jobs."

"Yes," said Paul, who had come along, as he said, to make sure that the corporation played fair, "with the result that my receptionist must be guided at every point once events depart from the conventional, however slightly."

Smythe-Robertson said, "You would be much more displeased if it were to improvise."

Andrew said, "Then you no longer manufacture robots like myself which are flexible and adaptable."

"No longer."

"The research I have done in connection with my book," said Andrew, "indicates that I am the oldest robot presently in active operation."

"The oldest presently," said Smythe-Robertson, "and the oldest ever. The oldest that will ever be. No robot is useful after the twenty-fifth year. They are called in and replaced with newer models."

"No robot *as presently manufactured* is useful after the twenty-fifth year," said Paul pleasantly. "Andrew is quite exceptional in this respect."

Andrew, adhering to the path he had marked out for himself, said, "As the oldest robot in the world and the most flexible, am I not unusual enough to merit special treatment from the company?"

"Not at all," said Smythe-Robertson freezingly. "Your unusualness is an embarrassment to the company. If you were on lease, instead of having been a sale outright through some mischance, you would long since have been replaced."

"But that is exactly the point," said Andrew. "I am a free robot and I own myself. Therefore I come to you and ask you to replace me. You cannot do this without the owner's consent. Nowadays, that consent is extorted as a condition of the lease, but in my time this did not happen."

Smythe-Robertson was looking both startled and puzzled, and for a moment there was silence. Andrew found himself staring at the holograph on the wall. It was a death mask of Susan Calvin, patron saint of all roboticists. She was dead nearly two centuries now, but as a result of writing his book Andrew knew her so well he could half persuade himself that he had met her in life.

Smythe-Robertson said, "How can I replace you for you? If I replace you as robot, how can I donate the new robot to you as owner since in the very act of replacement you cease to exist?" He smiled grimly.

"Not at all difficult," interposed Paul. "The seat of Andrew's personality is his positronic brain and it is the one part that cannot be replaced without creating a new robot. The positronic brain, therefore, is Andrew the owner. Every other part of the robotic body can be replaced without affecting the robot's personality, and those other parts are the brain's possessions. Andrew, I should say, wants to supply his brain with a new robotic body."

"That's right," said Andrew calmly. He turned to Smythe-Robertson. "You have manufactured androids, haven't you? Robots that have the outward appearance of humans complete to the texture of the skin?"

Smythe-Robertson said, "Yes, we have. They worked perfectly well, with their synthetic fibrous skins and tendons. There was virtually no metal anywhere except for the brain, yet they were nearly as tough as metal robots. They were tougher, weight for weight."

Paul looked interested. "I didn't know that. How many are on the market?"

"None," said Smythe-Robertson. "They were much more expensive than metal models and a market survey showed they would not be accepted. They looked too human."

Andrew said, "But the corporation retains its expertise, I assume. Since it does, I wish to request that I be replaced by an organic robot, an android."

Paul looked surprised. "Good Lord," he said.

Smythe-Robertson stiffened. "Quite impossible!"

"Why is it impossible?" asked Andrew. "I will pay any reasonable fee, of course."

Smythe-Robertson said, "We do not manufacture androids."

"You do not *choose* to manufacture androids," interposed Paul quickly. "That is not the same as being unable to manufacture them."

Smythe-Robertson said, "Nevertheless, the manufacture of androids is against public policy."

"There is no law against it," said Paul.

"Nevertheless, we do not manufacture them, and we will not."

Paul cleared his throat. "Mr. Smythe-Robertson," he said, "Andrew is a free robot who is under the purview of the law guaranteeing robot rights. You are aware of this, I take it?"

"Only too well."

"This robot, as a free robot, chooses to wear clothes. This results in his being frequently humiliated by thoughtless human beings despite the law against the humiliation of robots. It is difficult to prosecute vague offenses that don't meet with the general disapproval of those who must decide on guilt and innocence."

"U. S. Robots understood that from the start. Your father's firm unfortunately did not."

"My father is dead now," said Paul, "but what I see is that we have here a clear offense with a clear target."

"What are you talking about?" said Smythe-Robertson.

"My client, Andrew Martin—he has just become my client—is a free robot who is entitled to ask U. S. Robots and Mechanical Men, Inc., for the right of replacement, which the corporation supplies anyone who owns a robot for more than twenty-five years. In fact, the corporation insists on such replacement."

Paul was smiling and thoroughly at his ease. He went on, "The positronic brain of my client is the owner of the body of my client —which is certainly more than twenty-five years old. The positronic brain demands the replacement of the body and offers to pay any reasonable fee for an android body as that replacement. If you refuse the request, my client undergoes humiliation and we will sue.

"While public opinion would not ordinarily support the claim of a robot in such a case, may I remind you that U. S. Robots is not popular with the public generally. Even those who most use and profit from robots are suspicious of the corporation. This may be a hangover from the days when robots were widely feared. It may be resentment against the power and wealth of U. S. Robots, which has a worldwide monopoly. Whatever the cause may be, the resentment exists and I think you will find that you would prefer not to withstand a lawsuit, particularly since my client is wealthy and will live for many more centuries and will have no reason to refrain from fighting the battle forever."

Smythe-Robertson had slowly reddened. "You are trying to force me to . . ."

"I force you to do nothing," said Paul. "If you wish to refuse to accede to my client's reasonable request, you may by all means do so and we will leave without another word. . . . But we will sue, as is certainly our right, and you will find that you will eventually lose."

Smythe-Robertson said, "Well—" and paused.

"I see that you are going to accede," said Paul. "You may hesitate but you will come to it in the end. Let me assure you, then, of one further point. If, in the process of transferring my client's positronic brain from his present body to an organic one, there is any damage, however slight, then I will never rest till I've nailed the corporation to the ground. I will, if necessary, take every possible step to mobilize public opinion against the corporation if one brain path of my client's platinum-iridium essence is scrambled." He turned to Andrew and said, "Do you agree to all this, Andrew?"

Andrew hesitated a full minute. It amounted to the approval of lying, of blackmail, of the badgering and humiliation of a human being. But not physical harm, he told himself, not physical harm.

He managed at last to come out with a rather faint "Yes."

14

It was like being constructed again. For days, then for weeks, finally for months, Andrew found himself not himself somehow, and the simplest actions kept giving rise to hesitation.

Paul was frantic. "They've damaged you, Andrew. We'll have to institute suit."

Andrew spoke very slowly. "You mustn't. You'll never be able to prove—something—m-m-m-m—"

"Malice?"

"Malice. Besides, I grow stronger, better. It's the tr-tr-tr—"

"Tremble?"

"Trauma. After all, there's never been such an op—op—op— before."

Andrew could feel his brain from the inside. No one else could. He knew he was well and during the months that it took him to learn full coordination and full positronic interplay, he spent hours before the mirror.

Not quite human! The face was stiff—too stiff—and the motions were too deliberate. They lacked the careless free flow of the human being, but perhaps that might come with time. At least he could wear clothes without the ridiculous anomaly of a metal face going along with it.

Eventually he said, "I will be going back to work."

Paul laughed and said, "That means you are well. What will you be doing? Another book?"

"No," said Andrew seriously. "I live too long for any one career to seize me by the throat and never let me go. There was a time when I was primarily an artist and I can still turn to that. And there was a time when I was a historian and I can still turn to that. But now I wish to be a robobiologist."

"A robopsychologist, you mean."

"No. That would imply the study of positronic brains and at the moment I lack the desire to do that. A robobiologist, it seems to me, would be concerned with the working of the body attached to that brain."

"Wouldn't that be a roboticist?"

"A roboticist works with a metal body. I would be studying an organic humanoid body, of which I have the only one, as far as I know."

"You narrow your field," said Paul thoughtfully. "As an artist, all conception is yours; as a historian, you dealt chiefly with robots; as a robobiologist, you will deal with yourself."

Andrew nodded. "It would seem so."

Andrew had to start from the very beginning, for he knew nothing of ordinary biology, almost nothing of science. He became a familiar sight in the libraries, where he sat at the electronic indices for hours at a time, looking perfectly normal in clothes. Those few who knew he was a robot in no way interfered with him.

He built a laboratory in a room which he added to his house, and his library grew, too.

Years passed, and Paul came to him one day and said, "It's a pity you're no longer working on the history of robots. I understand U. S. Robots is adopting a radically new policy."

Paul had aged, and his deteriorating eyes had been replaced with photoptic cells. In that respect, he had drawn closer to Andrew. Andrew said, "What have they done?"

"They are manufacturing central computers, gigantic positronic brains, really, which communicate with anywhere from a dozen to a thousand robots by microwave. The robots themselves have no brains at all. They are the limbs of the gigantic brain, and the two are physically separate."

"Is that more efficient?"

"U. S. Robots claims it is. Smythe-Robertson established the new direction before he died, however, and it's my notion that it's a backlash at you. U. S. Robots is determined that they will make no robots that will give them the type of trouble you have, and for that reason they separate brain and body. The brain will have no body to wish changed; the body will have no brain to wish anything.

"It's amazing, Andrew," Paul went on, "the influence you have had on the history of robots. It was your artistry that encouraged U. S. Robots to make robots more precise and specialized; it was your freedom that resulted in the establishment of the principle of robotic rights; it was your insistence on an android body that made U. S. Robots switch to brain-body separation."

Andrew said, "I suppose in the end the corporation will produce one vast brain controlling several billion robotic bodies. All the eggs will be in one basket. Dangerous. Not proper at all."

"I think you're right," said Paul, "but I don't suspect it will come to pass for a century at least and I won't live to see it. In fact, I may not live to see next year."

"Paul!" said Andrew, in concern.

Paul shrugged. "We're mortal, Andrew. We're not like you. It doesn't matter too much, but it does make it important to assure you on one point. I'm the last of the human Martins. There are collaterals descended from my great-aunt, but they don't count. The money I control personally will be left to the trust in your name and as far as anyone can foresee the future, you will be economically secure."

"Unnecessary," said Andrew, with difficulty. In all this time, he could not get used to the deaths of the Martins.

Paul said, "Let's not argue. That's the way it's going to be. What are you working on?"

"I am designing a system for allowing androids—myself—to gain energy from the combustion of hydrocarbons, rather than from atomic cells."

Paul raised his eyebrows. "So that they will breathe and eat?"

"Yes."

"How long have you been pushing in that direction?"

"For a long time now, but I think I have designed an adequate combustion chamber for catalyzed controlled breakdown."

"But why, Andrew? The atomic cell is surely infinitely better."

"In some ways, perhaps, but the atomic cell is inhuman."

15

It took time, but Andrew had time. In the first place, he did not wish to do anything till Paul had died in peace.

With the death of the great-grandson of Sir, Andrew felt more nearly exposed to a hostile world and for that reason was the more determined to continue the path he had long ago chosen.

Yet he was not really alone. If a man had died, the firm of Feingold and Martin lived, for a corporation does not die any more than a robot does. The firm had its directions and it followed them soullessly. By way of the trust and through the law firm, Andrew continued to be wealthy. And in return for their own large annual retainer, Feingold and Martin involved themselves in the legal aspects of the new combustion chamber.

When the time came for Andrew to visit U. S. Robots and Mechanical Men, Inc., he did it alone. Once he had gone with Sir and once with Paul. This time, the third time, he was alone and manlike.

U. S. Robots had changed. The production plant had been shifted to a large space station, as had grown to be the case with more and more industries. With them had gone many robots. The Earth itself was becoming parklike, with its one-billion-person population stabilized and perhaps not more than thirty percent of its at least equally large robot population independently brained.

The Director of Research was Alvin Magdescu, dark of complexion and hair, with a little pointed beard and wearing nothing above the waist but the breastband that fashion dictated. Andrew himself was well covered in the older fashion of several decades back.

Magdescu said, "I know you, of course, and I'm rather pleased to see you. You're our most notorious product and it's a pity old

Smythe-Robertson was so set against you. We could have done a great deal with you."

"You still can," said Andrew.

"No, I don't think so. We're past the time. We've had robots on Earth for over a century, but that's changing. It will be back to space with them and those that stay here won't be brained."

"But there remains myself, and I stay on Earth."

"True, but there doesn't seem to be much of the robot about you. What new request have you?"

"To be still less a robot. Since I am so far organic, I wish an organic source of energy. I have here the plans—"

Magdescu did not hasten through them. He might have intended to at first, but he stiffened and grew intent. At one point he said, "This is remarkably ingenious. Who thought of all this?"

"I did," said Andrew.

Magdescu looked up at him sharply, then said, "It would amount to a major overhaul of your body, and an experimental one, since it has never been attempted before. I advise against it. Remain as you are."

Andrew's face had limited means of expression, but impatience showed plainly in his voice. "Dr. Magdescu, you miss the entire point. You have no choice but to accede to my request. If such devices can be built into my body, they can be built into human bodies as well. The tendency to lengthen human life by prosthetic devices has already been remarked on. There are no devices better than the ones I have designed and am designing.

"As it happens, I control the patents by way of the firm of Feingold and Martin. We are quite capable of going into business for ourselves and of developing the kind of prosthetic devices that may end by producing human beings with many of the properties of robots. Your own business will then suffer.

"If, however, you operate on me now and agree to do so under similar circumstances in the future, you will receive permission to make use of the patents and control the technology of both robots and the prosthetization of human beings. The initial leasing will not be granted, of course, until after the first operation is completed successfully, and after enough time has passed to demonstrate that it is indeed successful." Andrew felt scarcely any First Law inhibition to the stern conditions he was setting a human being. He was learning to reason that what seemed like cruelty might, in the long run, be kindness.

Magdescu looked stunned. He said, "I'm not the one to decide something like this. That's a corporate decision that would take time."

"I can wait a reasonable time," said Andrew, "but only a reasonable time." And he thought with satisfaction that Paul himself could not have done it better.

16

It took only a reasonable time, and the operation was a success.

Magdescu said, "I was very much against the operation, Andrew, but not for the reasons you might think. I was not in the least against the experiment, if it had been on someone else. I hated risking *your* positronic brain. Now that you have the positronic pathways interacting with simulated nerve pathways, it might be difficult to rescue the brain intact if the body went bad."

"I had every faith in the skill of the staff at U. S. Robots," said Andrew. "And I can eat now."

"Well, you can sip olive oil. It will mean occasional cleanings of the combustion chamber, as we have explained to you. Rather an uncomfortable touch, I should think."

"Perhaps, if I did not expect to go further. Self-cleaning is not impossible. In fact, I am working on a device that will deal with solid food that may be expected to contain incombustible fractions—indigestible matter, so to speak, that will have to be discarded."

"You would then have to develop an anus."

"The equivalent."

"What else, Andrew?"

"Everything else."

"Genitalia, too?"

"Insofar as they will fit my plans. My body is a canvas on which I intend to draw—"

Magdescu waited for the sentence to be completed, and when it seemed that it would not be, he completed it himself. "A man?"

"We shall see," said Andrew.

Magdescu said, "It's a puny ambition, Andrew. You're better than a man. You've gone downhill from the moment you opted for organicism."

"My brain has not suffered."

"No, it hasn't. I'll grant you that. But, Andrew, the whole new breakthrough in prosthetic devices made possible by your patents is being marketed under your name. You're recognized as the inventor and you're honored for it—as you are. Why play further games with your body?"

Andrew did not answer.

The honors came. He accepted membership in several learned societies, including one which was devoted to the new science he had established; the one he had called robobiology but had come to be termed prosthetology.

On the one hundred and fiftieth anniversary of his construction, there was a testimonial dinner given in his honor at U. S. Robots. If Andrew saw irony in this, he kept it to himself.

Alvin Magdescu came out of retirement to chair the dinner. He was himself ninety-four years old and was alive because he had prosthetized devices that, among other things, fulfilled the function of liver and kidneys. The dinner reached its climax when Magdescu, after a short and emotional talk, raised his glass to toast "the Sesquicentennial Robot."

Andrew had had the sinews of his face redesigned to the point where he could show a range of emotions, but he sat through all the ceremonies solemnly passive. He did not like to be a Sesquicentennial Robot.

17

It was prosthetology that finally took Andrew off the Earth. In the decades that followed the celebration of the Sesquicentennial, the Moon had come to be a world more Earth-like than Earth in every respect but its gravitational pull and in its underground cities there was a fairly dense population.

Prosthetized devices there had to take the lesser gravity into account and Andrew spent five years on the Moon working with local prosthetologists to make the necessary adaptations. When not at his work, he wandered among the robot population, every one of which treated him with the robotic obsequiousness due a man.

He came back to an Earth that was humdrum and quiet in comparison and visited the offices of Feingold and Martin to announce his return.

The current head of the firm, Simon DeLong, was surprised. He said, "We had been told you were returning, Andrew" (he had almost said "Mr. Martin"), "but we were not expecting you till next week."

"I grew impatient," said Andrew brusquely. He was anxious to get to the point. "On the Moon, Simon, I was in charge of a research team of twenty human scientists. I gave orders that no one questioned. The Lunar robots deferred to me as they would to a human being. Why, then, am I not a human being?"

A wary look entered DeLong's eyes. He said, "My dear Andrew, as you have just explained, you are treated as a human being by both robots and human beings. You are therefore a human being *de facto.*"

"To be a human being *de facto* is not enough. I want not only to be treated as one, but to be legally identified as one. I want to be a human being *de jure.*"

"Now that is another matter," said DeLong. "There we would run into human prejudice and into the undoubted fact that however much you may be like a human being, you are *not* a human being."

"In what way not?" asked Andrew. "I have the shape of a human being and organs equivalent to those of a human being. My organs, in fact, are identical to some of those in a prosthetized human being. I have contributed artistically, literarily, and scientifically to human culture as much as any human being now alive. What more can one ask?"

"I myself would ask nothing more. The trouble is that it would take an act of the World Legislature to define you as a human being. Frankly, I wouldn't expect that to happen."

"To whom on the Legislature could I speak?"

"To the chairman of the Science and Technology Committee perhaps."

"Can you arrange a meeting?"

"But you scarcely need an intermediary. In your position, you can—"

"No. *You* arrange it." (It didn't even occur to Andrew that he was giving a flat order to a human being. He had grown accustomed to that on the Moon.) "I want him to know that the firm of Feingold and Martin is backing me in this to the hilt."

"Well, now—"

"To the hilt, Simon. In one hundred and seventy-three years I have in one fashion or another contributed greatly to this firm. I have been under obligation to individual members of the firm in times past. I am not now. It is rather the other way around now and I am calling in my debts."

DeLong said, "I will do what I can."

18

The chairman of the Science and Technology Committee was of the East Asian region and she was a woman. Her name was Chee Li-Hsing and her transparent garments (obscuring what she wanted obscured only by their dazzle) made her look plastic-wrapped.

She said, "I sympathize with your wish for full human rights. There have been times in history when segments of the human population fought for full human rights. What rights, however, can you possibly want that you do not have?"

"As simple a thing as my right to life. A robot can be dismantled at any time."

"A human being can be executed at any time."

"Execution can only follow due process of law. There is no trial needed for my dismantling. Only the word of a human being in authority is needed to end me. Besides—besides—" Andrew tried desperately to allow no sign of pleading, but his carefully designed tricks of human expression and tone of voice betrayed him here. "The truth is, I want to be a man. I have wanted it through six generations of human beings."

Li-Hsing looked up at him out of darkly sympathetic eyes. "The Legislature can pass a law declaring you one—they could pass a law declaring a stone statue to be defined as a man. Whether they will actually do so is, however, as likely in the first case as the second. Congresspeople are as human as the rest of the population and there is always that element of suspicion against robots."

"Even now?"

"Even now. We would all allow the fact that you have earned the prize of humanity and yet there would remain the fear of setting an undesirable precedent."

"What precedent? I am the only free robot, the only one of my type, and there will never be another. You may consult U. S. Robots."

" 'Never' is a long time, Andrew—or, if you prefer, Mr. Martin —since I will gladly give you my personal accolade as man. You will find that most Congresspeople will not be willing to set the precedent, no matter how meaningless such a precedent might be. Mr. Martin, you have my sympathy, but I cannot tell you to hope. Indeed—"

She sat back and her forehead wrinkled. "Indeed, if the issue grows too heated, there might well arise a certain sentiment, both inside the Legislature and outside, for that dismantling you mentioned. Doing away with you could turn out to be the easiest way of resolving the dilemma. Consider that before deciding to push matters."

Andrew said, "Will no one remember the technique of prosthetology, something that is almost entirely mine?"

"It may seem cruel, but they won't. Or if they do, it will be remembered against you. It will be said you did it only for yourself. It will be said it was part of a campaign to roboticize human beings, or to humanify robots; and in either case evil and vicious. You have never been part of a political hate campaign, Mr. Martin, and I tell you that you will be the object of vilification of a kind neither you nor I would credit and there would be people who'll believe it all. Mr. Martin, let your life be." She rose and, next to Andrew's seated figure, she seemed small and almost childlike.

Andrew said, "If I decide to fight for my humanity, will you be on my side?"

She thought, then said, "I will be—insofar as I can be. If at any time such a stand would appear to threaten my political future, I may have to abandon you, since it is not an issue I feel to be at the very root of my beliefs. I am trying to be honest with you."

"Thank you, and I will ask no more. I intend to fight this through whatever the consequences, and I will ask you for your help only for as long as you can give it."

19

It was not a direct fight. Feingold and Martin counseled patience and Andrew muttered grimly that he had an endless supply of that. Feingold and Martin then entered on a campaign to narrow and restrict the area of combat.

They instituted a lawsuit denying the obligation to pay debts to an individual with a prosthetic heart on the grounds that the possession of a robotic organ removed humanity, and with it the constitutional rights of human beings.

They fought the matter skillfully and tenaciously, losing at every step but always in such a way that the decision was forced to be as broad as possible, and then carrying it by way of appeals to the World Court.

It took years, and millions of dollars.

When the final decision was handed down, DeLong held what amounted to a victory celebration over the legal loss. Andrew was, of course, present in the company offices on the occasion.

"We've done two things, Andrew," said DeLong, "both of which are good. First of all, we have established the fact that no number of artifacts in the human body causes it to cease being a human body. Secondly, we have engaged public opinion in the question in such a way as to put it fiercely on the side of a broad interpretation of humanity since there is not a human being in existence who does not hope for prosthetics if that will keep him alive."

"And do you think the Legislature will now grant me my humanity?" asked Andrew.

DeLong looked faintly uncomfortable. "As to that, I cannot be optimistic. There remains the one organ which the World Court has used as the criterion of humanity. Human beings have an organic cellular brain and robots have a platinum-iridium positronic brain if they have one at all—and you certainly have a positronic brain. . . . No, Andrew, don't get that look in your eye. We lack the knowledge to duplicate the work of a cellular brain in artificial structures close enough to the organic type to allow it to fall within the Court's decision. Not even you could do it."

"What ought we do, then?"

"Make the attempt, of course. Congresswoman Li-Hsing will be on our side and a growing number of other Congresspeople. The President will undoubtedly go along with a majority of the Legislature in this matter."

"Do we have a majority?"

"No, far from it. But we might get one if the public will allow its desire for a broad interpretation of humanity to extend to you. A small chance, I admit, but if you do not wish to give up, we must gamble for it."

"I do not wish to give up."

20

Congresswoman Li-Hsing was considerably older than she had been when Andrew had first met her. Her transparent garments were long gone. Her hair was now close-cropped and her coverings were tubular. Yet still Andrew clung, as closely as he could within the limits of reasonable taste, to the style of clothing that had prevailed when he had first adopted clothing over a century before.

She said, "We've gone as far as we can, Andrew. We'll try once more after recess, but, to be honest, defeat is certain and the whole thing will have to be given up. All my most recent efforts have only earned me a certain defeat in the coming congressional campaign."

"I know," said Andrew, "and it distresses me. You said once you would abandon me if it came to that. Why have you not done so?"

"One can change one's mind, you know. Somehow, abandoning you became a higher price than I cared to pay for just one more term. As it is, I've been in the Legislature for over a quarter of a century. It's enough."

"Is there no way we can change minds, Chee?"

"We've changed all that are amenable to reason. The rest—the majority—cannot be moved from their emotional antipathies."

"Emotional antipathy is not a valid reason for voting one way or the other."

"I know that, Andrew, but they don't advance emotional antipathy as their reason."

Andrew said cautiously, "It all comes down to the brain, then, but must we leave it at the level of cells versus positrons? Is there no way of forcing a functional definition? Must we say that a brain is made of this or that? May we not say that a brain is something—anything—capable of a certain level of thought?"

"Won't work," said Li-Hsing. "Your brain is man-made, the human brain is not. Your brain is constructed, theirs developed. To any human being who is intent on keeping up the barrier between himself and a robot, those differences are a steel wall a mile high and a mile thick."

"If we could get at the source of their antipathy—the very source of—"

"After all your years," said Li-Hsing sadly, "you are still trying to reason out the human being. Poor Andrew, don't be angry, but it's the robot in you that drives you in that direction."

"I don't know," said Andrew. "If I could bring myself—"

1 (reprise)

If he could bring himself—

He had known for a long time it might come to that, and in the end he was at the surgeon's. He found one, skillful enough for the job at hand, which meant a robot surgeon, for no human surgeon could be trusted in this connection, either in ability or in intention.

The surgeon could not have performed the operation on a human being, so Andrew, after putting off the moment of decision with a sad line of questioning that reflected the turmoil within himself, put the First Law to one side by saying, "I, too, am a robot."

He then said, as firmly as he had learned to form the words even at human beings over these past decades, "I *order* you to carry through the operation on me."

In the absence of the First Law, an order so firmly given from one who looked so much like a man activated the Second Law sufficiently to carry the day.

21

Andrew's feeling of weakness was, he was sure, quite imaginary. He had recovered from the operation. Nevertheless, he leaned, as unobtrusively as he could manage, against the wall. It would be entirely too revealing to sit.

Li-Hsing said, "The final vote will come this week, Andrew. I've been able to delay it no longer, and we must lose. . . . And that will be it, Andrew."

Andrew said, "I am grateful for your skill at delay. It gave me the time I needed, and I took the gamble I had to."

"What gamble is this?" asked Li-Hsing with open concern.

"I couldn't tell you, or the people at Feingold and Martin. I was sure I would be stopped. See here, if it is the brain that is at issue, isn't the greatest difference of all the matter of immortality? Who really cares what a brain looks like or is built of or how it was formed? What matters is that brain cells die; *must* die. Even if every other organ in the body is maintained or replaced, the brain cells, which cannot be replaced without changing and therefore killing the personality, must eventually die.

"My own positronic pathways have lasted nearly two centuries without perceptible change and can last for centuries more. Isn't *that* the fundamental barrier? Human beings can tolerate an immortal robot, for it doesn't matter how long a machine lasts. They cannot tolerate an immortal human being, since their own mortality is endurable only so long as it is universal. And for that reason they won't make me a human being."

Li-Hsing said, "What is it you're leading up to, Andrew?"

"I have removed that problem. Decades ago, my positronic brain was connected to organic nerves. Now, one last operation has arranged that connection in such a way that slowly—quite slowly—the potential is being drained from my pathways."

Li-Hsing's finely wrinkled face showed no expression for a moment. Then her lips tightened. "Do you mean you've arranged to die, Andrew? You can't have. That violates the Third Law."

"No," said Andrew, "I have chosen between the death of my body and the death of my aspirations and desires. To have let my body live at the cost of the greater death is what would have violated the Third Law."

Li-Hsing seized his arm as though she were about to shake him. She stopped herself. "Andrew, it won't work. Change it back."

"It can't be. Too much damage was done. I have a year to live—more or less. I will last through the two hundredth anniversary of my construction. I was weak enough to arrange that."

"How can it be worth it? Andrew, you're a fool."

"If it brings me humanity, that will be worth it. If it doesn't, it will bring an end to striving and that will be worth it, too."

And Li-Hsing did something that astonished herself. Quietly, she began to weep.

22

It was odd how that last deed caught at the imagination of the world. All that Andrew had done before had not swayed them. But he had finally accepted even death to be human and the sacrifice was too great to be rejected.

The final ceremony was timed, quite deliberately, for the two hundredth anniversary. The World President was to sign the act and make it law and the ceremony would be visible on a global network and would be beamed to the Lunar state and even to the Martian colony.

Andrew was in a wheelchair. He could still walk, but only shakily.

With mankind watching, the World President said, "Fifty years ago, you were declared a Sesquicentennial Robot, Andrew." After a pause, and in a more solemn tone, he said, "Today we declare you a Bicentennial Man, Mr. Martin."

And Andrew, smiling, held out his hand to shake that of the President.

23

Andrew's thoughts were slowly fading as he lay in bed.

Desperately he seized at them. Man! He was a man! He wanted that to be his last thought. He wanted to dissolve—die—with that.

He opened his eyes one more time and for one last time recognized Li-Hsing waiting solemnly. There were others, but those were only shadows, unrecognizable shadows. Only Li-Hsing stood out against the deepening gray. Slowly, inchingly, he held out his hand to her and very dimly and faintly felt her take it.

She was fading in his eyes, as the last of his thoughts trickled away.

But before she faded completely, one last fugitive thought came to him and rested for a moment on his mind before everything stopped.

"Little Miss," he whispered, too low to be heard.

Joe Haldeman

Joe Haldeman is a member of the Vietnam generation. He fought in Vietnam and was wounded there, and used his experiences there for his first big success, *The Forever War,* which appeared first in the magazines, beginning in 1972, but then came out in book form in 1974. As a novel, it won the Hugo in 1976, and the very next year he won the short story award, with which he makes his first appearance in these volumes. We can't give you the novel to read, but here is the short story.

I can't say I envy Joe his wartime experiences. A warrior I'm not. I was in the Army, yes, but I think I must have been the most inadequate member of the armed forces ever invented. I am certain the military establishment itself must have had a presentiment of this fact, for I was not drafted until immediately after the Japanese surrendered. (The word flew through the corridors of the Pentagon: "The Japanese have surrendered. The war is over. —It's safe to draft Asimov.")

Then after I had completed Basic Training, I was told in confidence (by a kindly and amused lieutenant) that everyone had been warned away from me by the captain. "With his peculiar background," he said, "no one's ever going to send him to fight anyone, and he doesn't know his left foot from his right, anyway, so ignore him." Of course, no one told me this at the time and I went through Basic Training constantly convinced that I would be court-martialed and shot for various (totally involuntary) examples of misfeasance, malfeasance, and nonfeasance of soldierly duties.

(No, I don't know what that means either.)

I've met Joe at several of the conventions I have attended; also, once, quite unexpectedly, on the *Queen Elizabeth 2,* a meeting which greatly improved the ambience of that trip. The *QE2* is a beautiful ship and we are always happy on it, but I must admit that it never crawls with fellow science fiction writers, and what is as great as a fellow science fiction writer?

Joe is a very quiet and gentle soul, but he has hidden depths.

Let me explain. I am a professional after-dinner speaker and I have the infinite gall to charge high fees and the infinite luck to get them. I think well of myself as a speaker and have no hesitation in telling people that I'm the best off-the-cuff speaker in the world. (I don't know if that's true or not, but saying it is what supplies most of the luck in getting high fees. That, and a ruthless lecture agent.)

So, generally, I don't worry about who I follow on the convention program. Once I followed Joe Haldeman. "Poor guy," I thought. "He's so quiet and gentle. I'll pull my punches afterward. I don't want him to look bad."

Hah! That quiet, gentle guy got up and gave one of the best and funniest talks I ever heard. Pull my punches? When I got up, I had to sweat out my very best just to stay even. You-all watch out for these quiet and gentle guys, you hear?

I must say one more thing about Joe, perhaps because I have a prejudice in favor of the fair sex (as many people have noticed, especially the fair sex). The very nicest thing about Joe is his wife, Gay, who is ever sweet and cheerful. Personally, I think they're both lucky.

7

TRICENTENNIAL

December 1975

Scientists pointed out that the Sun could be part of a double star system. For its companion to have gone undetected, of course, it would have to be small and dim, and thousands of astronomical units distant.

They would find it eventually; "it" would turn out to be "them"; they would come in handy.

January 2075

The office was opulent even by the extravagant standards of 21st-century Washington. Senator Connors had a passion for antiques. One wall was lined with leatherbound books; a large brass telescope symbolized his role as Liaison to the Science Guild. An intricately woven Navajo rug from his home state covered most of the parquet floor. A grandfather clock. Paintings, old maps.

The computer terminal was discreetly hidden in the top drawer of his heavy teak desk. On the desk: a blotter, a precisely centered fountain pen set, and a century-old sound-only black Bell telephone. It chimed.

His secretary said that Dr. Leventhal was waiting to see him. "Keep answering me for thirty seconds," the Senator said. "Then hang it and send him right in."

He cradled the phone and went to a wall mirror. Straightened his tie and cape; then with a fingernail evened out the bottom line of his lip pomade. Ran a hand through long, thinning white hair and returned to stand by the desk, one hand on the phone.

The heavy door whispered open. A short thin man bowed slightly. "Sire."

The Senator crossed to him with both hands out. "Oh, blow that, Charlie. Give ten." The man took both his hands, only for an instant. "When was I ever 'Sire' to you, heyfool?"

"Since last week," Leventhal said, "Guild members have been calling you worse names than 'Sire.' "

The Senator bobbed his head twice. "True, and true. And I sympathize. Will of the people, though."

"Sure." Leventhal pronounced it as one word: "Willathapeeble."

Connors went to the bookcase and opened a chased panel. "Drink?"

"Yeah, Bo." Charlie sighed and lowered himself into a deep sofa. "Hit me. Sherry or something."

The Senator brought the drinks and sat down beside Charlie. "You shoulda listened to me. Shoulda got the Ad Guild to write your proposal."

"We have good writers."

"Begging to differ. Less than two percent of the electorate bothered to vote; most of them for the administration advocate. Now you take the Engineering Guild—"

"*You* take the engineers. And—"

"They used the Ad Guild." Connors shrugged. "They got their budget."

"It's easy to sell bridges and power plants and shuttles. Hard to sell pure science."

"The more reason for you to—"

"Yeah, sure. Ask for double and give half to the Ad boys. Maybe next year. That's not what I came to talk about."

"That radio stuff?"

"Right. Did you read the report?"

Connors looked into his glass. "Charlie, you know I don't have time to—"

"Somebody read it, though."

"Oh, righty-o. Good astronomy boy on my staff; he gave me a boil-down. Mighty interesting, that."

"There's an intelligent civilization eleven light-years away—that's 'mighty interesting'?"

"Sure. Real breakthrough." Uncomfortable silence. "Uh, what are you going to do about it?"

"Two things. First, we're trying to figure out what they're saying. That's hard. Second, we want to send a message back. That's easy. And that's where you come in."

The Senator nodded and looked somewhat wary.

"Let me explain. We've sent messages to this star, 61 Cygni, before. It's a double star, actually, with a dark companion."

"Like us."

"Sort of. Anyhow, they never answered. They aren't listening, evidently; they aren't sending."

"But we got—"

"What we're picking up is about what you'd pick up eleven light-years from Earth. A confused jumble of broadcasts, eleven years old. Very faint. But obviously not generated by any sort of natural source."

"Then we're already sending a message back. The same kind they're sending us."

"That's right, but—"

"So what does all this have to do with me?"

"Bo, we don't want to whisper at them—we want to *shout!* Get their attention." Leventhal sipped his wine and leaned back. "For that, we'll need one hell of a lot of power."

"Uh, righty-o. Charlie, power's money. How much are you talking about?"

"The whole show. I want to shut down Death Valley for twelve hours."

The Senator's mouth made a silent O. "Charlie, you've been working too hard. Another Blackout? On purpose?"

"There won't be any Blackout. Death Valley has emergency storage for fourteen hours."

"At half capacity." He drained his glass and walked back to the bar, shaking his head. "First you say you want power. Then you say you want to turn off the power." He came back with the burlap-covered bottle. "You aren't making sense, boy."

"Not turn it off, really. Turn it around."

"Is that a riddle?"

"No, look. You know the power doesn't really come from the Death Valley grid; it's just a way station and accumulator. Power comes from the orbital—"

"I know all that, Charlie. I've got a Science Certificate."

"Sure. So what we've got is a big microwave laser in orbit that shoots down a tight beam of power. Enough to keep North America running. Enough—"

"That's what I mean. You can't just—"

"So we turn it around and shoot it at a power grid on the Moon. Relay the power around to the big radio dish at Farside. Turn it into radio waves and point it at 61 Cygni. Give 'em a blast that'll fry their fillings."

"Doesn't sound neighborly."

"It wouldn't actually be that powerful—but it would be a hell of a lot more powerful than any natural 21-centimeter source."

"I don't know, boy." He rubbed his eyes and grimaced. "I could maybe do it on the sly, only tell a few people what's on. But that'd only work for a few minutes . . . What do you need twelve hours for, anyway?"

"Well, the thing won't aim itself at the Moon automatically, the way it does at Death Valley. Figure as much as an hour to get the thing turned around and aimed.

"Then, we don't want to just send a blast of radio waves at them. We've got a five-hour program that first builds up a mutual language, then tells them about us, and finally asks them some questions. We want to send it twice."

Connors refilled both glasses. "How old were you in '47, Charlie?"

"I was born in '45."

"You don't remember the Blackout. Ten thousand people died . . . and you want me to suggest—"

"Come on, Bo, it's not the same thing. We know the accumulators work now—besides, the ones who died, most of them had faulty fail-safes on their cars. If we warn them the power's going to drop, they'll check their fail-safes or damn well stay out of the air."

"And the media? They'd have to take turns broadcasting. Are you going to tell the People what they can watch?"

"Fuzz the media. They'll be getting the biggest story since the Crucifixion."

"Maybe." Connors took a cigarette and pushed the box toward Charlie. "You don't remember what happened to the Senators from California in '47, do you?"

"Nothing good, I suppose."

"No, indeed. They were impeached. Lucky they weren't lynched. Even though the real trouble was way up in orbit.

"Like you say: people pay a grid tax to California. They think the power comes from California. If something fuzzes up, they get pissed at California. I'm the Lib Senator from California, Charlie; ask me for the Moon, maybe I can do something. Don't ask me to fuzz around with Death Valley."

"All right, all right. It's not like I was asking you to wire it for me, Bo. Just get it on the ballot. We'll do everything we can to educate—"

"Won't work. You barely got the Scylla probe voted in—and that was no skin off nobody, not with L-5 picking up the tab."

"Just get it on the ballot."

"We'll see. I've got a quota, you know that. And the Tricentennial coming up, hell, everybody wants on the ballot."

"Please, Bo. This is bigger than that. This is bigger than anything. Get it on the ballot."

"Maybe as a rider. No promises."

March 1992

From *Fax & Pix,* 12 March 1992:

ANTIQUE SPACE PROBE ZAPPED BY NEW STARS

1. Pioneer 10 sent first Jupiter pix Earthward in 1973 (see pix upleft, upright).
2. Left solar system 1987. First man-made thing to leave solar system.
3. Yesterday, reports NSA, Pioneer 10 begins a.m. to pick up heavy radiation. Gets more and more to max about 3 p.m. Then goes back down. Radiation has to come from outside solar system.
4. NSA and Hawaii scientists say Pioneer 10 went through disk of synchrotron (sin-kro-tron) radiation that comes from two stars we didn't know about before.

A. The stars are small "black dwarfs."
B. They are going around each other once every forty seconds, and take 350,000 years to go around the Sun.

C. One of the stars is made of *antimatter.* This is stuff that blows up if it touches real matter. What the Hawaii scientists saw was a dim circle of invisible (infrared) light that blinks on and off every twenty seconds. This light comes from where the atmospheres of the two stars touch (see pic downleft).

D. The stars have a big magnetic field. Radiation comes from stuff spinning off the stars and trying to get through the field.

E. The stars are about 5,000 times as far away from the Sun as we are. They sit at the wrong angle, compared to the rest of the solar system (see pic downright).

5. NSA says we aren't in any danger from the stars. They're too far away, and besides, nothing in the solar system ever goes through the radiation.

6. The woman who discovered the stars wants to call them Scylla *(skill*-a) and Charybdis (ku-*rib*-dus).

7. Scientists say they don't know where the hell those two stars came from. Everything else in the solar system makes sense.

February 2075

When the docking phase started, Charlie thought, that was when it was easy to tell the scientists from the baggage. The scientists were the ones who looked nervous.

Superficially, it seemed very tranquil—nothing like the bone-hurting skin-stretching acceleration when the shuttle lifted off. The glittering transparent cylinder of L-5 simply grew larger, slowly, then wheeled around to point at them.

The problem was that a space colony big enough to hold 4,000 people has more inertia than God. If the shuttle hit the mating dimple too fast, it would fold up like an accordion. A spaceship is made to take stress in the *other* direction.

Charlie hadn't paid first-class, but they let him up into the observation dome anyhow; professional courtesy. There were only two other people there, standing on the Velcro rug, strapped to one bar and hanging on to another.

They were a young man and woman, probably new colonists.

The man was talking excitedly. The woman stared straight ahead, not listening. Her knuckles were white on the bar and her teeth were clenched. Charlie wanted to say something in sympathy, but it's hard to talk while you're holding your breath.

The last few meters are the worst. You can't see over the curve of the ship's hull, and the steering jets make a constant stutter of little bumps: left, right, forward, back. If the shuttle folded, would the dome shatter? Or just pop off.

It was all controlled by computers, of course. The pilot just sat up there in a mist of weightless sweat.

Then the low moan, almost subsonic, shuddering as the shuttle's smooth hull complained against the friction pads. Charlie waited for the ringing *spang* that would mean they were a little too fast: friable alloy plates under the friction pads crumbling to absorb the energy of their forward motion; last-ditch stand.

If that didn't stop them, they would hit a two-meter wall of solid steel, which would . . . It had happened once. But not this time.

"Please remain seated until pressure is equalized," a recorded voice said. "It's been a pleasure having you aboard."

Charlie crawled down the pole, back to the passenger area. He walked *rip-rip-rip* back to his seat and obediently waited for his ears to pop. Then the side door opened and he went with the other passengers through the tube that led to the elevator. They stood on the ceiling. Someone had laboriously scratched a graffito on the metal wall:

> *Stuck on this lift for hours, perforce:*
> *This lift that cost a million bucks.*
> *There's no such thing as centrifugal force:*
> *L-5 sucks.*

Thirty more weightless seconds as they slid to the ground. There were a couple of dozen people waiting on the loading platform.

Charlie stepped out into the smell of orange blossoms and newly mown grass. He was home.

"Charlie! Hey, over here." Young man standing by a tandem

bicycle. Charlie squeezed both his hands and then jumped on the back seat. "Drink."

"Did you get—"

"Drink. Then talk." They glided down the smooth macadam road toward town.

The bar was just a rain canopy over some tables and chairs overlooking the lake in the center of town. No bartender: you went to the service table and punched in your credit number, then chose wine or fruit juice, with or without vacuum-distilled raw alcohol. They talked about shuttle nerves a while, then:

"What you get from Connors?"

"Words, not much. I'll give a full report at the meeting tonight. Looks like we won't even get on the ballot, though."

"Now isn't that what we said was going to happen? We shoulda gone with François Pétain's idea."

"Too risky." Pétain's plan had been to tell Death Valley they had to shut down the laser for repairs. Not tell the groundhogs about the signal at all, just answer it. "If they found out they'd sue us down to our teeth."

The man shook his head. "I'll never understand groundhogs."

"Not your job." Charlie was an Earth-born, Earth-trained psychologist. "Nobody born here ever could."

"Maybe so." He stood up. "Thanks for the drink; I've gotta get back to work. You know to call Dr. Bemis before the meeting?"

"Yeah. There was a message at the Cape."

"She has a surprise for you."

"Doesn't she always? You clowns never do anything around here until I leave."

All Abigail Bemis would say over the phone was that Charlie should come to her place for dinner; she'd prep him for the meeting.

"That was good, Ab. Can't afford real food on Earth."

She laughed and stacked the plates in the cleaner, then drew two cups of coffee. She laughed again when she sat down. Stocky, white-haired woman with bright eyes in a sea of wrinkles.

"You're in a jolly mood tonight."

"Yep. It's expectation."

"Johnny said you had a surprise."

"Hoo-boy, he doesn't know half. So you didn't get anywhere with the Senator."

"No. Even less than I expected. What's the secret?"

"Connors is a nice-hearted boy. He's done a lot for us."

"Come on, Ab. What is it?"

"He's right. Shut off the groundhogs' TV for twenty minutes and they'd have another Revolution on their hands."

"Ab . . ."

"We're going to send the message."

"Sure, I figured we would. Using Farside at whatever wattage we've got. If we're lucky—"

"Nope. Not enough power."

Charlie stirred a half spoon of sugar into his coffee. "You plan to . . . defy Connors?"

"Fuzz Connors. We're not going to use radio at all."

"Visible light? Infra?"

"We're going to hand-carry it. In *Daedalus.*"

Charlie's coffee cup was halfway to his mouth. He spilled a great deal.

"Here, have a napkin."

June 2040

From *A Short History of the Old Order* (Freeman Press, 2040):

". . . and if you think *that* was a waste, consider Project Daedalus.

"This was the first big space thing after L-5. Now L-5 worked out all right, because it was practical. But *Daedalus* (named from a Greek god who could fly)—that was a clear-cut case of throwing money down the rathole.

"These scientists in 2016 talked the bourgeoisie into paying for a trip to another *star!* It was going to take over a hundred years—but the scientists were going to have babies along the way, and train *them* to be scientists (whether they wanted to or not!).

"They were going to use all the old H-bombs for fuel—as if we might not need the fuel someday right here on Earth. What if L-5 decided they didn't like us, and shut off the power beam?

"*Daedalus* was supposed to be a spaceship almost a kilometer long! Most of it was manufactured in space, from Moon stuff, but a lot of it—the most expensive part, you bet—had to be boosted from Earth.

"They almost got it built, but then came the Breakup and the People's Revolution. No way in hell the People were going to let them have those H-bombs, not sitting right over our heads like that.

"So we left the H-bombs in Helsinki and the space freaks went back to doing what they're supposed to do. Every year they petition to get those H-bombs, but every year the Will of the People says no.

"That spaceship is still up there, a sky-trillion-dollar boondoggle. As a monument to bourgeoisie folly, it's worse than the Pyramids!!"

February 2075

"So the Scylla probe is just a ruse, to get the fuel—"

"Oh no, not really." She slid a blue-covered folder to him. "We're still going to Scylla. Scoop up a few megatons of degenerate antimatter. And a similar amount of degenerate matter from Charybdis.

"We don't plan a generation ship, Charlie. The hydrogen fuel will get us out there; once there, it'll power the magnetic bottles to hold the real fuel."

"Total annihilation of matter," Charlie said.

"That's right. Em cee squared to the ninth decimal place. We aren't talking about centuries to get to 61 Cygni. Nine years, there and back."

"The groundhogs aren't going to like it. All the bad feeling about the original *Daedalus*—"

"Fuzz the groundhogs. We'll do everything we said we'd do with their precious H-bombs: go out to Scylla, get some antimatter, and bring it back. Just taking a long way back."

"You don't want to just tell them that's what we're going to do? No skin off . . ."

She shook her head and laughed again, this time a little bitterly. "You didn't read the editorial in *Peoplepost* this morning, did you?"

"I was too busy."

"So am I, boy; too busy for that drik. One of my staff brought it in, though."

"It's about *Daedalus?*"

"No . . . it concerns 61 Cygni. How the crazy scientists want to let those boogers know there's life on Earth."

"They'll come make peopleburgers out of us."

"Something like that."

Over three thousand people sat on the hillside, a "natural" amphitheater fashioned of moon dirt and Earth grass. There was an incredible din, everyone talking at once: Dr. Bemis had just told them about the 61 Cygni expedition.

On about the tenth "Quiet, please," Bemis was able to continue. "So you can see why we didn't simply broadcast this meeting. Earth would pick it up. Likewise, there are no groundhog media on L-5 right now. They were rotated back to Earth and the shuttle with their replacements needed repairs at the Cape. The other two shuttles are here.

"So I'm asking all of you—and all of your brethren who had to stay at their jobs—to keep secret the biggest thing since Isabella hocked her jewels. Until we lift.

"Now Dr. Leventhal, who's chief of our social sciences section, wants to talk to you about selecting the crew."

Charlie hated public speaking. In this setting, he felt like a Christian on the way to being cat food. He smoothed out his damp notes on the podium.

"Uh, basic problem." A thousand people asked him to speak up. He adjusted the microphone.

"The basic problem is, we have space for about a thousand people. Probably more than one out of four want to go."

Loud murmur of assent. "And we don't want to be despotic about choosing . . . but I've set up certain guidelines, and Dr. Bemis agrees with them.

"Nobody should plan on going if he or she needs sophisticated medical care, obviously. Same toke, few very old people will be considered."

Almost inaudibly, Abigail said, "Sixty-four isn't very old, Charlie. I'm going." She hadn't said anything earlier.

He continued, looking at Bemis. "Second, we must leave behind those people who are absolutely necessary for the maintenance of L-5. Including the power station." She smiled at him.

"We don't want to split up mating pairs, not for, well, nine years plus . . . but neither will we take children." He waited for the commotion to die down. "On this mission, children are baggage. You'll have to find foster parents for them. Maybe they'll go on the next trip.

"Because we can't afford baggage. We don't know what's waiting for us at 61 Cygni—a thousand people sounds like a lot, but it isn't. Not when you consider that we need a cross section of all human knowledge, all human abilities. It may turn out that a person who can sing madrigals will be more important than a plasma physicist. No way of knowing ahead of time."

The 4,000 people did manage to keep it secret, not so much out of strength of character as from a deep-seated paranoia about Earth and Earthlings.

And Senator Connors' Tricentennial actually came to their aid.

Although there was "One World," ruled by "The Will of the People," some regions had more clout than others, and nationalism was by no means dead. This was one factor.

Another factor was the way the groundhogs felt about the thermonuclear bombs stockpiled in Helsinki. All antiques; mostly a century or more old. The scientists said they were perfectly safe, but you know how that goes.

The bombs still technically belonged to the countries that had surrendered them, nine out of ten split between North America and Russia. The tenth remaining was divided among forty-two other countries. They all got together every few years to argue about what to do with the damned things. Everybody wanted to get rid of them in some useful way, but nobody wanted to put up the capital.

Charlie Leventhal's proposal was simple. L-5 would provide bankroll, materials, and personnel. On a barren rock in the Norwegian Sea they would take apart the old bombs, one at a time, and turn them into uniform fuel capsules for the *Daedalus* craft.

The Scylla/Charybdis probe would be timed to honor both the major spacefaring countries. Renamed the *John F. Kennedy,* it would leave Earth orbit on America's Tricentennial. The craft would accelerate halfway to the double star system at one gee, then flip and slow down at the same rate. It would use a magnetic scoop to gather antimatter from Scylla. On May Day, 2077, it would again be renamed, being the *Leonid I. Brezhnev* for the return trip. For safety's sake, the antimatter would be delivered to a lunar research station near Farside. L-5 scientists claimed that harnessing the energy from total annihilation of matter would make a heaven on Earth.

Most people doubted that, but looked forward to the fireworks.

January 2076

"The *hell* with that!" Charlie was livid. "I—I just won't do it. Won't!"

"You're the only one—"

"That's not true, Ab, you know it." Charlie paced from wall to wall of her office cubicle. "There are dozens of people who can run L-5. Better than I can."

"Not better, Charlie."

He stopped in front of her desk, leaned over. "Come on, Ab. There's only one logical person to stay behind and run things. Not only has she proven herself in the position, but she's too old to—"

"That kind of drik I don't have to listen to."

"Now, Ab . . ."

"No, you listen to me. I was an infant when we started building *Daedalus;* worked on it as a girl and a young woman.

"I could take you out there in a shuttle and show you the rivets that I put in myself. A half century ago."

"That's my—"

"I earned my ticket, Charlie." Her voice softened. "Age is a factor, yes. This is only the first trip of many—and when it comes back, I *will* be too old. You'll just be in your prime . . . and with over twenty years of experience as Coordinator, I don't doubt they'll make you captain of the next—"

"I don't want to be captain. I don't want to be Coordinator. I just want to *go!*"

"You and three thousand other people."

"And of the thousand that don't want to go, or can't, there isn't one person who could serve as Coordinator? I could name you—"

"That's not the point. There's no one on L-5 who has anywhere near the influence, the connections, you have on Earth. No one who understands groundhogs as well."

"That's racism, Ab. Groundhogs are just like you and me."

"Some of them. I don't see you going Earthside every chance you can get . . . what, you like the view up here? You like living in a can?"

He didn't have a ready answer for that. Ab continued: "Whoever's Coordinator is going to have to do some tall explaining, trying to keep things smooth between L-5 and Earth. That's been your life's work, Charlie. And you're also known and respected here. You're the only logical choice."

"I'm not arguing with your logic."

"I know." Neither of them had to mention the document, signed by Charlie, among others, that gave Dr. Bemis final authority in selecting the crew for *Daedalus/Kennedy/Brezhnev.* "Try not to hate me too much, Charlie. I have to do what's best for my people. All of my people."

Charlie glared at her for a long moment and left.

June 2076

From *Fax & Pix,* 4 June 2076:

SPACE FARM LEAVES FOR STARS NEXT MONTH

1. The *John F. Kennedy,* which goes to Scylla/Charybdis next month, is like a little L-5 with bombs up its tail (see pix upleft, upright).

   A. The trip's twenty months. They could either take a few people and fill the thing up with food, air, and water—or take a lot of people inside a closed ecology, like L-5.
   B. They could've gotten by with only a couple hundred people, to run the farms and stuff. But almost all the space freaks wanted to go. They're used to living that way, anyhow (and they never get to go anyplace).

C. When they get back, the farms will be used as a starter for L-4, like L-5 but smaller at first, and on the other side of the Moon (pic downleft).

2. For other Tricentennial fax & pix, see bacover.

July 2076

Charlie was just finishing up a week on Earth the day the *John F. Kennedy* was launched. Tired of being interviewed, he slipped away from the media lounge at the Cape shuttleport. His white clearance card got him out onto the landing strip, alone.

The midnight shuttle was being fueled at the far end of the strip, gleaming pink-white in the last light from the setting sun. Its image twisted and danced in the shimmering heat that radiated from the tarmac. The smell of the soft tar was indelibly associated in his mind with leave-taking, relief.

He walked to the middle of the strip and checked his watch. Five minutes. He lit a cigarette and threw it away. He rechecked his mental calculations: the flight would start low in the southwest. He blocked out the sun with a raised hand. What would 150 bombs per second look like? For the media they were called fuel capsules. The people who had carefully assembled them and gently lifted them to orbit and installed them in the tanks, they called them bombs. Ten times the brightness of a full moon, they had said. On L-5 you weren't supposed to look toward it without a dark filter.

No warm-up: it suddenly appeared, impossibly brilliant rainbow speck just over the horizon. It gleamed for several minutes, then dimmed slightly with the haze, and slipped away.

Most of the United States wouldn't see it until it came around again, some two hours later, turning night into day, competing with local pyrotechnic displays. Then every couple of hours after that, Charlie would see it once more, then get on the shuttle. And finally stop having to call it by the name of a dead politician.

September 2076

There was a quiet celebration on L-5 when *Daedalus* reached the mid-point of its journey, flipped, and started decelerating. The progress report from its crew characterized the journey as "uneventful." At that time they were going nearly two tenths of the speed of light. The laser beam that carried communications was red-shifted from blue light down to orange; the message that turnaround had been successful took two weeks to travel from *Daedalus* to L-5.

They announced a slight course change. They had analyzed the polarization of light from Scylla/Charybdis as their phase angle increased, and were pretty sure the system was surrounded by flat rings of debris, like Saturn. They would "come in low" to avoid collision.

January 2077

Daedalus had been sending back recognizable pictures of the Scylla/Charybdis system for three weeks. They finally had one that was dramatic enough for groundhog consumption.

Charlie set the holo cube on his desk and pushed it around with his finger, marveling.

"This is incredible. How did they do it?"

"It's a montage, of course." Johnny had been one of the youngest adults left behind: heart murmur, trick knees, a surfeit of astrophysicists.

"The two stars are a strobe snapshot in infrared. Sort of. Some ten or twenty thousand exposures taken as the ship orbited around the system, then sorted out and enhanced." He pointed, but it wasn't much help, since Charlie was looking at the cube from a different angle.

"The lamina of fire where the atmospheres touch, that was taken in ultraviolet. Shows more fine structure that way.

"The rings were easy. Fairly long exposures in visible light. Gives the star background, too."

A light tap on the door and an assistant stuck his head in. "Have a second, Doctor?"

"Sure."

"Somebody from a Russian May Day committee is on the phone. She wants to know whether they've changed the name of the ship to *Brezhnev* yet."

"Yeah. Tell her we decided on *Leon Trotsky* instead, though."

He nodded seriously. "Okay." He started to close the door.

"Wait!" Charlie rubbed his eyes. "Tell her, uh . . . the ship doesn't have a commemorative name while it's in orbit there. They'll rechristen it just before the start of the return trip."

"Is that true?" Johnny asked.

"I don't know. Who cares? In another couple of months they won't *want* it named after anybody." He and Ab had worked out a plan—admittedly rather shaky—to protect L-5 from the groundhogs' wrath: nobody on the satellite knew ahead of time that the ship was headed for 61 Cygni. It was a decision the crew arrived at on the way to Scylla/Charybdis; they modified the drive system to accept matter-antimatter destruction while they were orbiting the double star. L-5 would first hear of the mutinous plan via a transmission sent as *Daedalus* left Scylla/Charybdis. They'd be a month on their way by the time the message got to Earth.

It was pretty transparent, but at least they had been careful that no record of *Daedalus'* true mission be left on L-5. Three thousand people did know the truth, though, and any competent engineer or physical scientist would suspect it.

Ab had felt that, although there was a better than even chance they would be exposed, surely the groundhogs couldn't stay angry for twenty-three years—even if they were unimpressed by the antimatter and other wonders . . .

Besides, Charlie thought, it's not their worry anymore.

As it turned out, the crew of *Daedalus* would have bigger things to worry about.

June 2077

The Russians had their May Day celebration—Charlie watched it on TV and winced every time they mentioned the good ship *Leonid I. Brezhnev*—and then things settled back down to normal. Charlie and three thousand others waited nervously for the "surprise" message. It came in early June, as expected, scrambled in a data channel. But it didn't say what it was supposed to:

This is Abigail Bemis, to Charles Leventhal.

Charlie, we have real trouble. The ship has been damaged, hit in the stern by a good chunk of something. It punched right through the main drive reflector. Destroyed a set of control sensors and one attitude jet.

As far as we can tell, the situation is stable. We're maintaining acceleration at just a tiny fraction under one gee. But we can't steer, and we can't shut off the main drive.

We didn't have any trouble with ring debris when we were orbiting, since we were inside Roche's limit. Coming in, as you know, we'd managed to take advantage of natural divisions in the rings. We tried the same going back, but it was a slower, more complicated process, since we mass so goddamn much now. We must have picked up a piece from the fringe of one of the outer rings.

If we could turn off the drive, we might have a chance at fixing it. But the work pods can't keep up with the ship, not at one gee. The radiation down there would fry the operator in seconds, anyway.

We're working on it. If you have any ideas, let us know. It occurs to me that this puts you in the clear—we were *headed back to Earth, but got clobbered. Will send a transmission to that effect on the regular comm channel. This message is strictly burn-before-reading.*

Endit.

It worked perfectly, as far as getting Charlie and L-5 off the hook—and the drama of the situation precipitated a level of interest in space travel unheard-of since the 1960s.

They even had a hero. A volunteer had gone down in a heavily shielded work pod, lowered on a cable, to take a look at the situation. She'd sent back clear pictures of the damage, before the cable snapped.

Daedalus: A.D. 2081
Earth: A.D. 2101

The following news item was killed from *Fax & Pix*, because it was too hard to translate into the "plain English" that made the paper so popular:

SPACESHIP PASSES 61 CYGNI—SORT OF

(L-5 Stringer)

A message received today from the spaceship *Daedalus* said that it had just passed within 400 astronomical units of 61 Cygni. That's about ten times as far as the planet Pluto is from the Sun.

Actually, the spaceship passed the star some eleven years ago. It's taken all that time for the message to get back to us.

We don't know for sure where the spaceship actually is now. If they still haven't repaired the runaway drive, they're about eleven light-years past the 61 Cygni system (their speed when they passed the double star was better than 99% the speed of light).

The situation is more complicated if you look at it from the point of view of a passenger on the spaceship. Because of relativity, time seems to pass more slowly as you approach the speed of light. So only about four years passed for them on the eleven-light-year journey.

L-5 Coordinator Charles Leventhal points out that the spaceship has enough antimatter fuel to keep accelerating to the edge of the Galaxy. The crew then would be only some twenty years older—but it would be twenty *thousand* years before we heard from them. . . .

(Kill this one. There's more stuff about what the ship looked like to the people on 61 Cygni, and howcum we could talk to them all the time even though time was slower there, but it's all as stupid as this.)

Daedalus: A.D. 2083
Earth: A.D. 2144

Charlie Leventhal died at the age of ninety-nine, bitter. Almost a decade earlier it had been revealed that they'd planned all along for *Daedalus* to be a starship. Few people had paid much attention to the news. Among those who did, the consensus was that anything that got rid of a thousand scientists at once was a good thing. Look at the mess they got us in.

Daedalus: Sixty-seven light-years out, and still accelerating.

Daedalus: A.D. 2085
Earth: A.D. 3578

After over seven years of shipboard research and development —and some 1,500 light-years of travel—they managed to shut down the engine. With sophisticated telemetry, the job was done without endangering another life.

Every life was precious now. They were no longer simply explorers; almost half their fuel was gone. They were colonists, with no ticket back.

The message of their success would reach Earth in fifteen centuries. Whether there would be an infrared telescope around to detect it, that was a matter of some conjecture.

Daedalus: A.D. 2093
Earth: ca. A.D. 5000

While decelerating, they had investigated several systems in their line of flight. They found one with an Earth-type planet around a Sun-type sun, and aimed for it.

The season they began landing colonists, the dominant feature in the planet's night sky was a beautiful blooming cloud of gas that astronomers had named the North American Nebula.

Which was an irony that didn't occur to any of these colonists from L-5—give or take a few years, it was America's Trimillennial.

America itself was a little the worse for wear, this three thousandth anniversary. The seas that lapped its shores were heavy with a crimson crust of anaerobic life; the mighty cities had fallen and their remains nearly ground away by the never-ceasing sandstorms.

No fireworks were planned, for lack of an audience, for lack of planners; bacteria just don't care. May Day too would be ignored.

The only humans in the Solar System lived in a glass and metal tube. They tended their automatic machinery, and turned their backs on the dead Earth, and worshipped the constellation Cygnus, and had forgotten why.

1978
36th CONVENTION
PHOENIX

Spider and Jeanne Robinson

Well, well, here's Spider again, as he wins a Hugo for the second year in a row (and to make it worse, with a second novella—though Fritz Leiber did the same in 1970 and 1971).

You will notice that he has a co-author with the same surname and you might guess from that that they are related. I will end the suspense. Jeanne is Spider's wife, they having been married in 1975.

Spider explains the co-authorship. Jeanne read the story as it was typed and argued it out with Spider. The conclusion was, said Spider, that "although she never set finger to typewriter, the resulting novella was at least as much hers as mine."

I'm not sure about the justification of that. I'm thinking of the times when John Campbell helped me a great deal with one story or another, to say nothing of the help I received from other editors, such as Horace Gold and Fred Pohl. Ought I to have given them bylines? Tight-fisted credit-grabbing me? Never. I'm not as generous as Spider.

To be sure, I have collaborated with my wife, Janet, on an anthology, and on two juvenile s.f. novels, but in each case, dear Janet set all ten fingers to typewriter, so to speak. She did the collecting and arranging of the stories in the anthology, and she did the first draft, complete, in the case of the juveniles. That made it difficult for me to keep her name off. (She has also published two novels of her own and has a collection of her short stories in press, so I'm lucky she didn't decide to keep *my* name out of it.)

We can look at the matter from another standpoint, however.

When I was young and naïve (as opposed to being older and naïve) I thought the thing to know, if you wanted to write science fiction, was science. Brush up on your physics and paleontology and plane geometry and you were all set.

All that science stuff is in the background, however. The social milieu of the story is what requires the technological razzle-dazzle. In the foreground is the plot, and that can deal with anything at all. Science fiction is universal.

This means that the widest cultural knowledge can be useful. Joe Haldeman's military experience, James Tiptree's psychological expertise, Roger Zelazny's knowledge of contemporary literature and Hindu mythology, all come in useful, and lead those fine people in directions where, for instance, I can't follow.

But choreography! If I were awakened in the middle of the night and asked to name something a science fiction writer didn't have to know, I would say, "Choreography."

And I would be wrong. Spider has written here a piece of choreographic science fiction and it won the Hugo. You can't remove the choreography and still have the story. Apparently, most of the choreography was supplied by Jeanne. Under those circumstances, even I would have seen the justice of giving her half the byline.

8

STARDANCE

I can't really say that I knew her, certainly not the way Seroff knew Isadora. All I know of her childhood and adolescence are the anecdotes she chanced to relate in my hearing—just enough to make me certain that all three of the contradictory biographies on the current best-seller list are fictional. All I know of her adult life are the hours she spent in my presence and on my monitors—more than enough to tell me that every newspaper account I've seen is fictional. Carrington probably believed he knew her better than I, and in a limited sense he was correct—but he would never have written of it, and now he is dead.

But I was her video man, since the days when you touched the camera with your hands, and I knew her backstage: a type of relationship like no other on Earth or off it. I don't believe it can be described to anyone not of the profession—you might think of it as somewhere between co-workers and combat buddies. I was with her the day she came to Skyfac, terrified and determined, to stake her life upon a dream. I watched her work and worked with her for that whole two months, through endless rehearsals, and I have saved every tape and they are not for sale.

And, of course, I saw the Stardance. I was there; I taped it.

I guess I can tell you some things about her.

To begin with, it was not, as Cahill's *Shara* and Von Derski's *Dance Unbound: The Creation of New Modern* suggest, a lifelong fascination with space and space travel that led her to become the race's first zero-gravity dancer. Space was a means to her, not an end, and its vast empty immensity scared her at first. Nor was it, as Melberg's hardcover tabloid *The Real Shara Drummond* claims, because she lacked the talent to make it as a dancer on

Earth. If you think free-fall dancing is easier than conventional dance, you try it. Don't forget your dropsickness bag.

But there is a grain of truth in Melberg's slander, as there is in all the best slanders. She could *not* make it on Earth—but not through lack of talent.

I first saw her in Toronto in July of 1984. I headed Toronto Dance Theater's video department at that time, and I hated every minute of it. I hated everything in those days. The schedule that day called for spending the entire afternoon taping students, a waste of time and tape which I hated more than anything except the phone company. I hadn't seen the year's new crop yet, and was not eager to. I love to watch dance done well—the efforts of a tyro are usually as pleasing to me as a first-year violin student in the next apartment is to you.

My leg was bothering me even more than usual as I walked into the studio. Norrey saw my face and left a group of young hopefuls to come over. "Charlie . . . ?"

"I know, I know. They're tender fledglings, Charlie, with egos as fragile as an Easter egg in December. Don't bite them, Charlie. Don't even bark at them if you can help it, Charlie."

She smiled. "Something like that. Leg?"

"Leg."

Norrey Drummond is a dancer who gets away with looking like a woman because she's small. There's about a hundred and fifteen pounds of her, and most of it is heart. She stands about five four, and is perfectly capable of seeming to tower over the tallest student. She has more energy than the North American Grid, and uses it as efficiently as a vane pump (have you ever studied the principle of a standard piston-type pump? Go look up the principle of a vane pump. I wonder what the original conception of *that* notion must have been like, as an emotional experience). There's a signaturelike uniqueness to her dance, the only reason I can see why she got so few of the really juicy parts in company productions until Modern gave way to New Modern. I liked her because she didn't pity me.

"It's not only the leg," I admitted. "I hate to see the tender fledglings butcher your choreography."

"Then you needn't worry. The piece you're taping today is by . . . one of the students."

"Oh, fine. I knew I should have called in sick." She made a face. "What's the catch?"

"Eh?"

"Why did the funny thing happen to your voice just as you got to 'one of the students'?"

She blushed. "Dammit, she's my sister."

Norrey and I are the very oldest and closest of friends, but I'd never chanced to meet a sister—not unusual these days, I suppose.

My eyebrows rose. "She must be good, then."

"Why, thank you, Charlie."

"Bullshit. I give compliments right-handed or not at all—I'm not talking about heredity. I mean that you're so hopelessly ethical you'd bend over backward to avoid nepotism. For you to give your own sister a feature like that, she must be *terrific.*"

"Charlie, she is," Norrey said simply.

"We'll see. What's her name?"

"Shara." Norrey pointed her out, and I understood the rest of the catch. Shara Drummond was ten years younger than her sister—and seven inches taller, with thirty or forty more pounds. I noted absently that she was stunningly beautiful, but it didn't deter my dismay—in her best years, Sophia Loren could never have become a modern dancer. Where Norrey was small, Shara was big, and where Norrey was big, Shara was bigger. If I'd seen her on the street I might have whistled appreciatively—but in the studio I frowned.

"My God, Norrey, she's enormous."

"Mother's second husband was a football player," she said mournfully. "She's awfully good."

"If she *is* good, that *is* awful. Poor girl. Well, what do you want me to do?"

"What makes you think I want you to do anything?"

"You're still standing here."

"Oh. I guess I am. Well . . . have lunch with us, Charlie?"

"Why?" I knew perfectly well why, but I expected a polite lie.

Not from Norrey Drummond. "Because you two have something in common, I think."

I paid her honesty the compliment of not wincing. "I suppose we do."

"Then you will?"

"Right after the session."

She twinkled and was gone. In a remarkably short time she had organized the studioful of wandering, chattering young people into something that resembled a dance ensemble if you squinted. They warmed up during the twenty minutes it took me to set up and check out my equipment. I positioned one camera in front of them, one behind, and kept one in my hands for walk-around close-up work. I never triggered it.

There's a game you play in your mind. Every time someone catches or is brought to your attention, you begin making guesses about them. You try to extrapolate their character and habits from their appearance. Him? Surly, disorganized—leaves the cap off the toothpaste and drinks boilermakers. Her? Art-student type, probably uses a diaphragm and writes letters in a stylized calligraphy of her own invention. Them? They look like schoolteachers from Miami, probably here to see what snow looks like, attend a convention. Sometimes I come pretty close. I don't know how I typecast Shara Drummond in those first twenty minutes. The moment she began to dance, all preconceptions left my mind. She became something elemental, something unknowable, a living bridge between our world and the one the Muses live in.

I know, on an intellectual and academic level, all there is to know about dance, and I could not categorize or classify or even really comprehend the dance she danced that afternoon. I saw it, I even appreciated it, but I was not equipped to understand it. My camera dangled from the end of my arm, next to my jaw. Dancers speak of their "center," the place their motion centers around, often quite near the physical center of gravity. You strive to "dance from your center," and the "contraction and release" idea which underlies much of Modern dance depends on the center for its focus of energy. Shara's center seemed to move about the room under its own power, trailing limbs that attached to it by choice rather than necessity. What's the word for the outermost part of the sun, the part that still shows in an eclipse? Corona? That's what her limbs were: four lengthy tongues of flame that followed the center in its eccentric, whirling orbit, writhing fluidly around its surface. That the lower two frequently contacted the floor seemed coincidental—indeed, the other two touched the floor nearly as regularly.

There were other students dancing. I know this because the two automatic video cameras, unlike me, did their job and recorded the piece as a whole. It was called *Birthing,* and depicted the formation of a galaxy that ended up resembling Andromeda. It was only vaguely accurate, literally, but it wasn't intended to be. Symbolically, it felt like the birth of a galaxy.

In retrospect. At the time I was aware only of the galaxy's heart: Shara. Students occluded her from time to time, and I simply never noticed. It hurt to watch her.

If you know anything about dance, this must all sound horrid to you. A dance about a *nebula?* I know, I know. It's a ridiculous notion. And it worked. In the most gut-level, cellular way it worked—save only that Shara was too good for those around her. She did not belong in that eager crew of awkward, half-trained apprentices. It was like listening to the late Stephen Wonder trying to work with a pickup band in a Montreal bar.

But that wasn't what hurt.

Le Maintenant was shabby, but the food was good and the house brand of grass was excellent. Show a Diner's Club card in there and they'd show you a galley full of dirty dishes. It's gone now. Norrey and Shara declined a toke, but in my line of work it helps. Besides, I needed a few hits. How to tell a lovely lady her dearest dream is hopeless?

I didn't need to ask Shara to know that her dearest dream was to dance. More: to dance professionally. I have often speculated on the motives of the professional artist. Some seek the narcissistic assurance that others will actually pay cash to watch or hear them. Some are so incompetent or disorganized that they can support themselves in no other way. Some have a message which they feel needs expressing. I suppose most artists combine elements of all three. This is no complaint—what they do for us is necessary. We should be grateful that there *are* motives.

But Shara was one of the rare ones. She danced because she needed to. She needed to say things which could be said in no other way, and she needed to take her meaning and her living from the saying of them. Anything else would have demeaned and devalued the essential statement of her dance. I know this, from watching that one dance.

Between toking up and keeping my mouth full and then toking again (a mild amount to offset the slight down that eating brings), it was over half an hour before I was required to say anything, beyond an occasional grunted response to the luncheon chatter of the ladies. As the coffee arrived, Shara looked me square in the eye and said, "Do you talk, Charlie?"

She was Norrey's sister, all right.

"Only inanities."

"No such thing. Inane people, maybe."

"Do you enjoy dancing, Miss Drummond?"

She answered seriously. "Define 'enjoy.' "

I opened my mouth and closed it, perhaps three times. You try it.

"And for God's sake tell me why you're so intent on not talking to me. You've got me worried."

"Shara!" Norrey looked dismayed.

"Hush. I want to know."

I took a crack at it. "Shara, before he died I had the privilege of meeting Bertram Ross. I had just seen him dance. A producer who knew and liked me took me backstage, the way you take a kid to see Santa Claus. I had expected him to look even older off stage, at rest. He looked younger, as if that incredible motion of his was barely in check. He talked to me. After a while I stopped opening my mouth, because nothing ever came out."

She waited, expecting more. Only gradually did she comprehend the compliment and its dimension. I had assumed it would be obvious. Most artists *expect* to be complimented. When she did twig, she did not blush or simper. She did not cock her head and say "Oh, come on." She did not say "You flatter me." She did not look away.

She nodded slowly and said, "Thank you, Charlie. That's worth a lot more than idle chatter." There was a suggestion of sadness in her smile, as if we shared a bitter joke.

"You're welcome."

"For heaven's sake, Norrey, what are you looking so upset about?"

The cat now had Norrey's tongue.

"She's disappointed in me," I said. "I said the wrong thing."

"That was the wrong thing?"

"It should have been 'Miss Drummond, I think you ought to give up dancing.'"

"It should have been *'Shara,* I think you ought' . . . *what?"*

"Charlie," Norrey began.

"I was supposed to tell you that we can't all be professional dancers, that they also surf who only sand and wade. Shara, I was supposed to tell you to dump the dance—before it dumps you."

In my need to be honest with her, I had been more brutal than was necessary, I thought. I was to learn that bluntness never dismayed Shara. She demanded it.

"Why you?" was all she said.

"We're inhabiting the same vessel, you and I. We've both got an itch that our bodies just won't let us scratch."

Her eyes softened. "What's your itch?"

"The same as yours."

"Eh?"

"The man was supposed to come and fix the phone on Thursday. My roommate, Karen, and I had an all-day rehearsal. We left a note. Mister telephone man, we had to go out, and we sure couldn't call you, heh heh. Please get the key from the concierge and come on in; the phone's in the bedroom. The phone man never showed up. They never do." My hands seemed to be shaking. "We came home up the back stairs from the alley. The phone was still dead, but I never thought to take down the note on the front door. I got sick the next morning. Cramps. Vomiting. Karen and I were just friends, but she stayed home to take care of me. I suppose on a Friday night the note seemed even more plausible. He slipped the lock with a piece of plastic, and Karen came out of the kitchen as he was unplugging the stereo. He was so indignant he shot her. Twice. The noise scared him; by the time I got there he was halfway out the door. He just had time to put a slug through my hip joint, and then he was gone. They never got him. They never even came to fix the phone." My hands were under control now. "Karen was a damned good dancer, but I was better. In my head, I still am."

Her eyes were round. "You're not Charlie . . . Charles *Armstead."*

I nodded.

"Oh my God. So *that's* where you went."

I was shocked by how she looked. It brought me back from the cold and windy border of self-pity. I began a little to pity her. I should have guessed the depth of her empathy. And in the way that really mattered, we were too damned alike—we *did* share the same bitter joke. I wondered why I had wanted to shock her.

"They couldn't repair the joint?" she asked softly.

"I can walk splendidly. Given a strong enough motivation, I can even run short distances. I can't dance worth a damn."

"So you became a video man."

"Three years ago. People who know both video and dance are about as common as garter belts these days. Oh, they've been taping dance since the seventies—with the imagination of a network news cameraman. If you film a stage play with two cameras in the orchestra pit, is it a movie?"

"You do for dance what the movie camera did for drama?"

"Pretty fair analogy. Where it breaks down is that dance is more analogous to music than to drama. You can't stop and start it, or go back and retake a scene that didn't go in the can right, or reverse the chronology to get a tidy shooting schedule. The event happens and you record it. What I am is what the record industry pays top dollar for—a mix man with savvy enough to know which ax is wailing at the moment and mike it high—and the sense to have given the heaviest dudes the best mikes. There are a few others like me. I'm the best."

She took it the way she had the compliment to herself—at face value. Usually when I say things like that I don't give a damn what reaction I get, or I'm being salty and hoping for outrage. But I was pleased at her acceptance, pleased enough for it to bother me. A faint irritation made me go brutal again, *knowing* it wouldn't work. "So what all this leads to is that Norrey was hoping I'd suggest some similar form of sublimation for you. Because I'll make it in dance before you will."

She stubborned up. "I don't buy that, Charlie. I know what you're talking about, I'm not a fool, but I think I can beat it."

"Sure you will. *You're too damned big, lady.* You've got tits like both halves of a prize honeydew melon and an ass that any actress in Hollywood would sell her parents for, and in Modern dance that makes you d-e-d dead, you haven't got a chance. Beat it? You'll beat your head in first. How'm I doing, Norrey?"

"For Christ's sake, Charlie!"

I softened. I can't work Norrey into a tantrum—I like her too much. "I'm sorry, hon. My leg's giving me the mischief, and I'm stinkin' mad. She *ought* to make it—and she won't. She's your sister, and so it saddens you. Well, I'm a total stranger, and it enrages me."

"How do you think it makes me feel?" Shara blazed, startling us both. I hadn't known she had so much voice. "So you want me to pack it in and rent me a camera, huh, Charlie? Or maybe sell apples outside the studio?" A ripple ran up her jaw. "Well, I will be damned by all the gods in Southern California before I'll pack it in. God gave me the large economy size, but there is not a surplus pound on it and it fits me like a glove and I can by Jesus *dance* it and I will. You may be right—I may beat my head in first. But I will get it done." She took a deep breath. "Now I thank you for your kind intentions, Char—Mr. Armst— Oh shit." The tears came and she left hastily, spilling a quarter cup of cold coffee on Norrey's lap.

"Charlie," Norrey said through clenched teeth, "why do I like you so much?"

"Dancers are dumb." I gave her my handkerchief.

"Oh." She patted at her lap a while. "How come you like me?"

"Video men are smart."

"Oh."

I spent the afternoon in my apartment, reviewing the footage I'd shot that morning, and the more I watched, the madder I got.

Dance requires intense motivation at an extraordinarily early age—a blind devotion, a gamble on the as-yet-unrealized potentials of heredity and nutrition. You can begin, say, classical ballet training at age six—and at fourteen find yourself broad-shouldered, the years of total effort utterly wasted. Shara had set her sights on Modern dance—and found out too late that God had dealt her the body of a woman.

She was not fat—you have seen her. She was tall, big-boned tall, and on that great frame was built a rich, ripely female body. As I ran and reran the tapes of *Birthing,* the pain grew in me until I even forgot the ever-present aching of my own leg. It was like watching a supremely gifted basketball player who stood four feet tall.

To make it in Modern dance, it is essential to get into a company. You cannot be seen unless you are visible. Norrey had told me, on the walk back to the studio, of Shara's efforts to get into a company—and I could have predicted nearly every word.

"Merce *Cunningham* saw her dance, Charlie. Martha Graham saw her dance, just before she died. Both of them praised her warmly, for her choreography as much as for her technique. Neither offered her a position. I'm not even sure I blame them—I can sort of understand."

Norrey could understand all right. It was her own defect magnified a hundredfold: uniqueness. A company member must be capable of excellent solo work—but she must also be able to blend into group effort, in ensemble work. Shara's very uniqueness made her virtually useless as a company member. She could not help but draw the eye.

And, once drawn, the male eye at least would never leave. Modern dancers must sometimes work nude these days, and it is therefore meet that they have the body of a fourteen-year-old boy. We may have ladies dancing with few or no clothes on up here, but by God it is Art. An actress or a musician or a singer or a painter may be lushly endowed, deliciously rounded—but a dancer must be nearly as sexless as a high-fashion model. Perhaps God knows why. Shara could not have purged her dance of her sexuality even if she had been interested in trying, and as I watched her dance on my monitor and in my mind's eye, I knew she was not.

Why did her genius have to lie in the only occupation besides model and nun in which sexiness is a liability? It broke my heart, by empathic analogy.

"It's no good at all, is it?"

I whirled and barked. "Dammit, you made me bite my tongue."

"I'm sorry." She came from the doorway into my living room. "Norrey told me how to find the place. The door was ajar."

"I forgot to shut it when I came home."

"You leave it open?"

"I've learned the lesson of history. No junkie, no matter how strung out he is, will enter an apartment with the door ajar and the radio on. Obviously there's someone home. And you're right, it's no damn good at all. Sit down."

She sat on the couch. Her hair was down now, and I liked it better that way. I shut off the monitor and popped the tape, tossing it on a shelf.

"I came to apologize. I shouldn't have blown up at you at lunch. You were trying to help me."

"You had it coming. I imagine by now you've built up quite a head of steam."

"Five years' worth. I figured I'd start in the States instead of Canada. Go farther faster. Now I'm back in Toronto and I don't think I'm going to make it here either. You're right, Mr. Armstead—I'm too damned big. Amazons don't dance."

"It's still Charlie. Listen, something I want to ask you. That last gesture, at the end of *Birthing*—what was that? I thought it was a beckoning, Norrey says it was a farewell, and now that I've run the tape it looks like a yearning, a reaching out."

"Then it worked."

"Pardon?"

"It seemed to me that the birth of a galaxy called for all three. They're so close together in spirit it seemed silly to give each a separate movement."

"Mmm." Worse and worse. Suppose Einstein had had aphasia. "Why couldn't you have been a rotten dancer? That'd just be irony. This"—I pointed to the tape—"is high tragedy."

"Aren't you going to tell me I can still dance for myself?"

"No. For you that'd be worse than not dancing at all."

"My God, you're perceptive. Or am I that easy to read?"

I shrugged.

"Oh, Charlie," she burst out, "what am I going to do?"

"You'd better not ask me that." My voice sounded funny.

"Why not?"

"Because I'm already two thirds in love with you. And because you're not in love with me and never will be. And so that is the sort of question you shouldn't ask me."

It jolted her a little, but she recovered quickly. Her eyes softened, and she shook her head slowly. "You even know why I'm not, don't you?"

"And why you won't be."

I was terribly afraid she was going to say "Charlie, I'm sorry." But she surprised me again. What she said was "I can count on the fingers of one foot the number of grown-up men I've ever met. I'm grateful for you. I guess ironic tragedies come in pairs?"

"Sometimes."

"Well, now all I have to do is figure out what to do with my life. That should kill the weekend."

"Will you continue your classes?"

"Might as well. It's never a waste of time to study. Norrey's teaching me things."

All of a sudden my mind started to percolate. Man is a rational animal, right? Right? "What if I had a better idea?"

"If you've got another idea, it's better. Speak."

"Do you have to have an audience? I mean, does it have to be *live?*"

"What do you mean?"

"Maybe there's a back way in. Look, they're building tape facilities into all the TVs nowadays, right? And by now everybody has collected all the old movies and Ernie Kovacs programs and such that they always wanted, and now they're looking for new stuff. Exotic stuff, too esoteric for network or local broadcast, stuff that—"

"The independent video companies, you're talking about."

"Right. TDT is thinking of entering the market, and the Graham company already has."

"So?"

"So suppose we go freelance? You and me? You dance it and I'll tape it: a straight business deal. I've got a few connections, and maybe I can get more. I could name you ten acts in the music business right now that never go on tour—just record and record. Why don't you bypass the structure of the dance companies and take a chance on the public? Maybe word of mouth could . . ."

Her face was beginning to light up like a jack-o'-lantern. "Charlie, do you think it could work? Do you really think so?"

"I don't think it has a snowball's chance." I crossed the room, opened up the beer fridge, took out the snowball I keep there in the summer, and tossed it at her. She caught it, but just barely, and when she realized what it was, she burst out laughing. "I've got just enough faith in the idea to quit working for TDT and put my time into it. I'll invest my time, my tape, my equipment, and my savings. Ante up."

She tried to get sober, but the snowball froze her fingers and she broke up again. "A snowball in July. You madman. Count me in. I've got a little money saved. And . . . and I guess I don't have much choice, do I?"

"I guess not."

The next three years were some of the most exciting years of my life, of both our lives. While I watched and taped, Shara transformed herself from a potentially great dancer into something truly awesome. She did something I'm not sure I can explain.

She became dance's analogy of the jazzman.

Dance was, for Shara, self-expression, pure and simple, first, last and always. Once she freed herself of the attempt to fit into the world of company dance, she came to regard choreography per se as an *obstacle* to her self-expression, as a preprogrammed rut, inexorable as a script and as limiting. And so she devalued it.

A jazzman may blow *Night in Tunisia* for a dozen consecutive nights, and each evening will be a different experience, as he interprets and reinterprets the melody according to his mood of the moment. Total unity of artist and his art: spontaneous creation. The melodic starting point distinguishes the result from pure anarchy.

In just this way Shara devalued preperformance choreography to a starting point, a framework on which to build whatever the moment demanded, and then jammed around it. She learned in those three busy years to dismantle the interface between herself and her dance. Dancers have always tended to sneer at improv dancing, even while they practiced it, in the studio, for the looseness it gave. They failed to see that *planned* improv, improv around a theme fully thought out in advance, was the natural next step in dance. Shara took the step. You must be very, very good to get away with that much freedom. She was good enough.

There's no point in detailing the professional fortunes of

Drumstead Enterprises over those three years. We worked hard, we made some magnificent tapes, and we couldn't sell them for paperweights. A home video cassette industry indeed existed—and they knew as much about Modern dance as the record industry knew about the blues when *they* started. The big outfits wanted credentials, and the little outfits wanted cheap talent. Finally we even got desperate enough to try the schlock houses—and learned what we already knew. They didn't have the distribution, the prestige, or the technical specs for the critics to pay any attention to them. Word-of-mouth advertising is like a gene pool—if it isn't a certain minimum size to start with, it doesn't get anywhere. "Spider" John Koerner is an incredibly talented musician and songwriter who has been making and selling his own records since 1972. How many of you have ever heard of him?

In May of 1987 I opened my mailbox in the lobby and found the letter from VisuEnt Inc., terminating our option with deepest sorrow and no severance. I went straight over to Shara's apartment, and my leg felt as if the bone marrow had been replaced with thermite and ignited. It was a very long walk.

She was working on *Weight Is a Verb* when I got there. Converting her big living room into a studio had cost time, energy, skull sweat, and a fat bribe to the landlord, but it was cheaper than renting time in a studio, considering the sets we wanted. It looked like high mountain country that day, and I hung my hat on a fake alder when I entered.

She flashed me a smile and kept moving, building up to greater and greater leaps. She looked like the most beautiful mountain goat I ever saw. I was in a foul mood and I wanted to kill the music (McLaughlin and Miles together, leaping some themselves), but I never could interrupt Shara when she was dancing. She built it gradually, with directional counterpoint, until she seemed to hurl herself into the air, stay there until she was damned good and ready, and then hurl herself down again. Sometimes she rolled when she hit and sometimes she landed on her hands, and always the energy of falling was transmuted into something instead of being absorbed. It was total energy output, and by the time she was done I had calmed down enough to be almost philosophical about our mutual professional ruin.

She ended up collapsed in upon herself, head bowed, exquisitely humbled in her attempt to defy gravity. I couldn't help applauding. It felt corny, but I couldn't help it.

"Thank you, Charlie."

"I'll be damned. Weight *is* a verb. I thought you were crazy when you told me the title."

"It's one of the strongest verbs in dance—and you can make it do *anything.*"

"Almost anything."

"Eh?"

"VisuEnt gave us our contract back."

"Oh." Nothing showed in her eyes, but I knew what was behind them. "Well, who's next on the list?"

"There is no one left on the list."

"Oh." This time it showed. "Oh."

"We should have remembered. Great artists are never honored in their own lifetime. What we ought to do is drop dead—then we'd be all set."

In my way I was trying to be strong for her, and she knew it and tried to be strong for me.

"Maybe what we should do is go into death insurance, for artists," she said. "We pay the client premiums against a controlling interest in his estate, and we insure that he'll die."

"We can't lose. And if he becomes famous in his lifetime he can buy out."

"Terrific. Let's stop this before I laugh myself to death."

"Yeah."

She was silent for a long time. My own mind was racing efficiently, but the transmission seemed to be blown—it wouldn't *go* anywhere. Finally she got up and turned off the music machine, which had been whining softly ever since the tape ended. It made a loud *click.*

"Norrey's got some land in Prince Edward Island," she said, not meeting my eyes. "There's a house."

I tried to head her off with the punch line from the old joke about the kid shoveling out the elephant cage in the circus whose father offers to take him back and set him up with a decent job. "What? And leave show business?"

"Screw show business," she said softly. "If I went out to PEI now, maybe I could get the land cleared and plowed in time to get a garden in." Her expression changed. "How about you?"

"Me? I'll be okay. TDT asked me to come back."

"That was six months ago."

"They asked again. Last week."

"And you said no. Moron."

"Maybe so, maybe so."

"The whole damn thing was a waste of time. All that time. All that energy. All that work. I might as well have been farming in PEI—by now the soil'd be starting to bear well. What a waste, Charlie, what a stinking waste."

"No, I don't think so, Shara. It sounds glib to say that 'nothing is wasted,' but—well, it's like that dance you just did. Maybe you can't beat gravity—but it surely is a beautiful thing to *try.*"

"Yeah, I know. Remember the Light Brigade. Remember the Alamo. They tried." She laughed, a bitter laugh.

"Yes, and so did Jesus of Nazareth. Did you do it for material reward, or because it needed doing? If nothing else, we now have several hundred thousand feet of the most magnificent dance recordings on tape, commercial value zero, real value incalculable, and by me that is no waste. It's over now, and we'll both go do the next thing, but it was *not a waste."* I discovered that I was shouting, and stopped.

She closed her mouth. After a while she tried a smile. "You're right, Charlie. It wasn't waste. I'm a better dancer than I ever was."

"Damn right. You've transcended choreography."

She smiled ruefully. "Yeah. Even Norrey thinks it's a dead end."

"It is *not* a dead end. There's more to poetry than haiku and sonnets. Dancers don't *have* to be robots, delivering memorized lines with their bodies."

"They do if they want to make a living."

"We'll try again in a few years. Maybe they'll be ready then."

"Sure. Let me get us some drinks."

I slept with her that night, for the first and last time. In the morning I broke down the set in the living room while she packed. I promised to write. I promised to come and visit when I could. I carried her bags down to the car, and stowed them inside. I kissed her and waved goodbye. I went looking for a drink, and at four o'clock the next morning a mugger decided I looked drunk enough and I broke his jaw, his nose, and two ribs, and then sat down on him and cried. On Monday morning I showed up at the studio with my hat in my hand and a mouth like a bus-station ashtray and crawled back into my old job. Norrey didn't ask any questions. What with rising food prices, I gave up eating anything but bourbon, and in six months I was fired. It went like that for a long time.

I never did write to her. I kept getting bogged down after "Dear Shara . . ."

When I got to the point of selling my video equipment for booze, a relay clicked somewhere and I took stock of myself. The stuff was all the life I had left, and so I went to the local Al-Anon instead of the pawnshop and got sober. After a while my soul got numb, and I stopped flinching when I woke up. A hundred times I began to wipe the tapes I still had of Shara—she had copies of her own—but in the end I could not. From time to time I wondered how *she* was doing, and I could not bear to find out. If Norrey heard anything, she didn't tell me about it. She even tried to get me my job back a third time, but it was hopeless. Reputation can be a terrible thing once you've blown it. I was lucky to land a job with an educational TV station in New Brunswick.

It was a long couple of years.

Vidphones were coming out by 1990, and I had breadboarded one of my own without the knowledge or consent of the phone company, which I still hated more than anything. When the peanut bulb I had replaced the damned bell with started glowing softly on and off one evening in June, I put the receiver on the audio pickup and energized the tube, in case the caller was also equipped. "Hello?"

She was. When Shara's face appeared, I got a cold cube of fear in the pit of my stomach, because I had quit seeing her face everywhere when I quit drinking, and I had been thinking lately of hitting the sauce again. When I blinked and she was still there, I felt a little better and tried to speak. It didn't work.

"Hello, Charlie. It's been a long time."

The second time it worked. "Seems like yesterday. Somebody else's yesterday."

"Yes, it does. It took me *days* to find you. Norrey's in Paris, and no one else knew where you'd gone."

"Yeah. How's farming?"

"I . . . I've put that away, Charlie. It's even more creative than dancing, but it's not the same."

"Then what *are* you doing?"

"Working."

"Dancing?"

"Yes. Charlie, I need you. I mean, I have a job for you. I need your cameras and your eye."

"Never mind the qualifications. Any kind of need will do. *Where are you?* When's the next plane there? Which cameras do I pack?"

"New York, an hour from now, and none of them. I didn't mean 'your cameras' literally—unless you're using GLX-5000s and a Hamilton Board lately."

I whistled. It hurt my mouth. "Not on my budget. Besides, I'm old-fashioned—I like to hold 'em with my hands."

"For this job you'll use a Hamilton, and it'll be a twenty-input Masterchrome, brand new."

"You grew poppies on that farm? Or just struck diamonds with the rototiller?"

"You'll be getting paid by Bryce Carrington."

I blinked.

"Now will you catch that plane so I can tell you about it? The New Age, ask for the Presidential Suite."

"The hell with the plane, I'll walk. Quicker." I hung up.

According to the *Time* magazine in my dentist's waiting room, Bryce Carrington was the genius who had become a multimillionaire by convincing a number of giants of industry to underwrite Skyfac, the great orbiting complex that kicked the bottom out of the crystals market. As I recalled the story, some rare poliolike disease had wasted both his legs and put him in a wheelchair. But the legs had lost strength, not function—in lessened gravity, they worked well enough. So he created Skyfac, establishing mining crews on Luna to supply it with cheap raw materials, and lived in orbit under reduced gravity. His picture made him look like a reasonably successful author (as opposed to writer). Other than that I knew nothing about him. I paid little attention to news and none at all to space news.

The New Age was *the* hotel in New York in those days, built on the ruins of the Sheraton. Ultra-efficient security, bulletproof windows, carpet thicker than the outside air, and a lobby of an architectural persuasion that John D. MacDonald once called "Early Dental Plate." It stank of money. I was glad I'd made the effort to locate a necktie, and I wished I'd shined my shoes. An incredible man blocked my way as I came in through the air lock. He moved and was built like the toughest, fastest bouncer I ever saw, and he dressed and acted like God's butler. He said his name was Perry. He asked if he could help me as though he didn't think so.

"Yes, Perry. Would you mind lifting up one of your feet?"

"Why?"

"I'll bet twenty dollars you've shined your soles."

Half his mouth smiled, and he didn't move an inch. "Whom did you wish to see?"

"Shara Drummond."

"Not registered."

"The Presidential Suite."

"Oh." Light dawned. "Mr. Carrington's lady. You should have said so. Wait here, please." While he phoned to verify that I was expected, keeping his eye on me and his hand near his pocket, I swallowed my heart and rearranged my face. It took some time. So that was how it was. All right then. That was how it was.

Perry came back and gave me the little button transmitter that would let me walk the corridors of the New Age without being cut down by automatic laser fire, and explained carefully that it would blow a largish hole in me if I attempted to leave the building without returning it. From his manner I gathered that I had just skipped four grades in social standing. I thanked him, though I'm damned if I knew why.

I followed the green fluorescent arrows that appeared on the bulbless ceiling, and came after a long and scenic walk to the Presidential Suite. Shara was waiting at the door, in something like an angel's pajamas. It made all that big body look delicate. "Hello, Charlie."

I was jovial and hearty. "Hi, babe. Swell joint. How've you been keeping yourself?"

"I haven't been."

"Well, how's Carrington been keeping you, then?" Steady, boy.

"Come in, Charlie."

I went in. It looked like where the Queen stayed when she was in town, and I'm sure she enjoyed it. You could have landed an airplane in the living room without waking anyone in the bedroom. It had two pianos. Only one fireplace, barely big enough to barbecue a buffalo—you have to scrimp somewhere, I guess. Roger Kellaway was on the quadio, and for a wild moment I thought he was actually in the suite, playing some unseen third piano. So this was how it was.

"Can I get you something, Charlie?"

"Oh, sure. Hash oil, Tangier Supreme. Dom Pérignon for the pipe."

Without cracking a smile she went to a cabinet, which looked like a midget cathedral, and produced precisely what I had ordered. I kept my own features impassive and lit up. The bubbles tickled my throat, and the rush was exquisite. I felt myself relaxing, and when we had passed the narghile's mouthpiece a few times I felt her relax. We looked at each other then—really looked at each other—then at the room around us and then at each other again. Simultaneously we roared with laughter, a laughter that blew all the wealth out of the room and let in richness. Her laugh was the same whooping, braying belly laugh I remembered so well, an unselfconscious and lusty laugh, and it reassured me tremendously. I was so relieved I couldn't stop laughing myself, and that kept *her* going, and just as we might have stopped she pursed her lips and blew a stuttered arpeggio. There's an old recording called the *Spike Jones Laughing Record,* where the tuba player tries to play "The Flight of the Bumblebee" and falls down laughing, and the whole band breaks up and horse-laughs for a full two minutes, and every time they run out of air the tuba player tries another flutter and roars and they all break up again, and once when Shara was blue I bet her ten dollars that she couldn't listen to that record without at least giggling and I won. When I understood now that she was quoting it, I shuddered and dissolved into great whoops of new laughter, and a minute later we had reached the stage where we literally laughed ourselves out of our chairs and lay on the floor in agonies of mirth, weakly pounding the floor and howling. I take that laugh out of my memory now and then and rerun it—but not often, for such records deteriorate drastically with play.

At last we Dopplered back down to panting grins, and I helped her to her feet.

"What a perfectly dreadful place," I said, still chuckling.

She glanced around and shuddered. "Oh God, it *is,* Charlie. It must be awful to need this much front."

"For a horrid while I thought *you* did."

She sobered, and met my eyes. "Charlie, I wish I could resent that. In a way I do need it."

My eyes narrowed. "Just what do you mean?"

"I need Bryce Carrington."

"This time you can trot out the qualifiers. *How* do you need him?"

"I need his money," she cried.

How can you relax and tense up at the same time? "Oh, *damn* it, Shara! Is *that* how you're going to get to dance? Buy your way in? What does a critic go for these days?"

"Charlie, stop it. I need Carrington to get seen. He's going to rent me a hall, that's all."

"If that's all, let's get out of the dump right now. I can bor . . . get enough cash to rent you any hall in the world, and I'm just as willing to risk my money."

"Can you get me Skyfac?"

"Uh?"

I couldn't for the life of me imagine why she proposed to go to Skyfac to dance. Why not Antarctica?

"Shara, you know even less about space than I do, but you must know that a satellite broadcast doesn't have to be made from a satellite?"

"Idiot. It's the setting I want."

I thought about it. "Moon'd be better, visually. Mountains. Light. Contrast."

"The visual aspect is secondary. I don't want one-sixth g, Charlie. I want zero gravity."

My mouth hung open.

"And I want you to be my video man."

God, she was a rare one. What I needed then was to sit there with my mouth open and think for several minutes. She let me do just that, waiting patiently for me to work it all out.

"Weight isn't a verb anymore, Charlie," she said finally. "That dance ended on the assertion that you can't beat gravity—you said so yourself. Well, that statement is incorrect—obsolete. The dance of the twenty-first century will have to acknowledge that."

"And it's just what you need to make it. A new kind of dance for a new kind of dancer. Unique. It'll catch the public eye, and you should have the field entirely to yourself for years. I like it, Shara. I like it. But can you pull it off?"

"I thought about what you said: that you can't beat gravity but it's beautiful to try. It stayed in my head for months, and then one day I was visiting a neighbor with a TV and I saw newsreels of the crew working on Skyfac Two. I was up all night thinking, and the next morning I came up to the States and got a job in Skyfac One. I've been up there for nearly a year, getting next to Carrington. I can do it, Charlie, I can make it work." There was a ripple in her jaw that I had seen before—when she told me off in Le Maintenant. It was a ripple of determination.

Still I frowned. "With Carrington's backing."

Her eyes left mine. "There's no such thing as a free lunch."

"What does he charge?"

She failed to answer, for long enough to answer me. In that instant, I began believing in God again, for the first time in years, just to be able to hate Him.

But I kept my mouth shut. She was old enough to manage her own finances. The price of a dream gets higher every year. Hell, I'd half expected it from the moment she'd called me.

But only half.

"Charlie, don't just sit there with your face all knotted up. Say something. Cuss me out, call me a whore, *something.*"

"Nuts. You be your own conscience, I have trouble enough being my own. You want to dance, you've got a patron. So now you've got a video man."

I hadn't intended to say that last sentence at all.

Strangely, it almost seemed to disappoint her at first. But then she relaxed and smiled. "Thank you, Charlie. Can you get out of whatever you're doing right away?"

"I'm working for an educational station in Shediac. I even got to shoot some dance footage. A dancing bear from the London Zoo. The amazing thing was how well he danced." She grinned. "I can get free."

"I'm glad. I don't think I could pull this off without you."

"I'm working for you. Not for Carrington."

"All right."

"Where is the great man, anyway? Scuba diving in the bathtub?"

"No," came a quiet voice from the doorway. "I've been sky diving in the lobby."

His wheelchair was a mobile throne. He wore a four-hundred-dollar suit the color of strawberry ice cream, a powder-blue turtleneck, and one gold earring. The shoes were genuine leather. The watch was that newfangled bandless kind that literally tells you the time. He wasn't tall enough for her, and his shoulders were absurdly broad, although the suit tried hard to deny both. His eyes were like twin blueberries. His smile was that of a shark wondering which part will taste best. I wanted to crush his head between two boulders.

Shara was on her feet. "Bryce, this is Charles Armstead. I told you . . ."

"Oh yes. The video chap." He rolled forward and extended an impeccably manicured hand. "I'm Bryce Carrington, Armstead."

I remained seated, hands in my lap. "Oh yes. The rich chap."

One eyebrow rose an urbane quarter inch. "Oh, my. Another rude one. Well, if you're as good as Shara says you are, you're entitled."

"I'm rotten."

The smile faded. "Let's stop fencing, Armstead. I don't expect manners from creative people, but I have far more significant contempt than yours available if I need any. Now I'm tired of this damned gravity and I've had a rotten day testifying for a friend and it looks like they're going to recall me tomorrow. Do you want the job or don't you?"

He had me there. I did. "Yeah."

"All right, then. Your room is 2772. We'll be going up to Skyfac in two days. Be here at eight A.M."

"I'll want to talk with you about what you'll be needing, Charlie," Shara said. "Give me a call tomorrow."

I whirled to face her, and she flinched from my eyes.

Carrington failed to notice. "Yes, make a list of your requirements by tomorrow, so it can go up with us. Don't scrimp—if you don't fetch it, you'll do without. Good night, Armstead."

I faced him. "Good night, Mr. Carrington." Suh.

He turned toward the narghile, and Shara hurried to refill the chamber and bowl. I turned away hastily and made for the door. My leg hurt so much I nearly fell on the way, but I set my jaw and made it. When I reached the door I said to myself, You will now open the door and go through it, and then I spun on my heel. "Carrington!"

He blinked, surprised to discover I still existed. "Yes?"

"Are you *aware* that she doesn't love you in the slightest? Does that matter to you in any way?" My voice was high, and my fists were surely clenched.

"Oh," he said, and then again, "Oh. So that's what it is. I didn't *think* success alone merited that much contempt." He put down the mouthpiece and folded his fingers together. "Let me tell you something, Armstead. No one has ever loved me, to my knowledge. This suite does not love me." His voice took on human feeling for the first time. "But it is *mine.* Now get out."

I opened my mouth to tell him where to put his job, and then I saw Shara's face, and the pain in it suddenly made me deeply ashamed. I left at once, and when the door closed behind me I vomited on a rug that was worth slightly less than a Hamilton Masterchrome board. I was sorry then that I'd worn a necktie.

The trip to Pike's Peak Spaceport, at least, was aesthetically pleasurable. I enjoy air travel, gliding among stately clouds, watching the rolling procession of mountains and plains, vast jigsaws of farmland and intricate mosaics of suburbia unfolding below.

But the jump to Skyfac in Carrington's personal shuttle, *That First Step,* might as well have been an old *Space Commando* rerun. I *know* they can't put portholes in space ships—but dammit, a shipboard video relay conveys no better resolution, color values, or presence than you get on your living-room tube. The only differences are that the stars don't "move" to give the illusion of travel, and there's no director editing the POV to give you dramatically interesting shots.

Aesthetically speaking. The *experiential* difference is that they do not, while you are watching the Space Commando sell hemorrhoid remedies, strap you into a couch, batter you with thunders, make you weigh better than half a ton for an unreasonably long time, and then drop you off the edge of the world into weightlessness. I had been half expecting nausea, but what I got was even more shocking: the sudden, unprecedented, total absence of pain in my leg. At that, Shara was hit worse than I was, barely managing to deploy her dropsickness bag in time. Carrington unstrapped and administered an antinausea injection with sure movements. It seemed to take forever to hit her, but when it did there was an enormous change—color and strength returned rapidly, and she was apparently fully recovered by the time the pilot announced that we were commencing docking and would everyone please strap in and shut up. I half expected Carrington to bark manners into him, but apparently the industrial magnate was not that sort of fool. He shut up and strapped himself down.

My leg didn't hurt in the slightest. Not at all.

The Skyfac complex looked like a disorderly heap of bicycle tires and beach balls of various sizes. The one our pilot made for was more like a tractor tire. We matched course, became its axle, and matched spin, and the damned thing grew a spoke that caught us square in the air lock. The air lock was "overhead" of our couches, but we entered and left it feet first. A few yards into the spoke, the direction we traveled became "down," and handholds became a ladder. Weight increased with every step, but even when we had emerged in a rather large cubical compartment it was far less than Earth normal. Nonetheless, my leg resumed biting me.

The room tried to be a classic reception room, high-level ("Please be seated. His Majesty will see you shortly"), but the low g and the p-suits racked along two walls spoiled the effect. Unlike the Space Commando's armor, a real pressure suit looks like nothing so much as a people-shaped baggie, and they look particularly silly in repose. A young dark-haired man in tweed rose from behind a splendidly gadgeted desk and smiled. "Good to see you, Mr. Carrington, I hope you had a pleasant jump."

"Fine, thanks, Tom. You remember Shara, of course. This is Charles Armstead. Tom McGillicuddy." We both displayed our teeth and said we were delighted to meet each other. I could see that beneath the pleasantries McGillicuddy was upset about something.

"Nils and Mr. Longmire are waiting in your office, sir. There's . . . there's been another sighting."

"God *damn* it," Carrington began, and cut himself off. I stared at him. The full force of my best sarcasm had failed to anger this man. "All right. Take care of my guests while I go hear what Longmire has to say." He started for the door, moving like a beach ball in slow motion but under his own power. "Oh yes—the *Step* is loaded to the gun'ls with bulky equipment, Tom. Have her brought around to the cargo bays. Store the equipment in Six." He left, looking worried. McGillicuddy activated his desk and gave the necessary orders.

"What's going on, Tom?" Shara asked when he was through.

He looked at me before replying. "Pardon my asking, Mr. Armstead, but—are you a newsman?"

"Charlie. No, I'm not. I am a video man, but I work for Shara."

"Mmmm. Well, you'll hear about it sooner or later. About two weeks ago, an object appeared within the orbit of Neptune, just appeared out of nowhere. There were . . . certain other anomalies. It stayed put for half a day and then vanished again. The Space Command slapped a hush on it, but it's common knowledge on board Skyfac."

"And the thing has been sighted again?" Shara asked.

"Just beyond the orbit of Jupiter."

I was only mildly interested. No doubt there was an explanation for the phenomenon, and since Isaac Asimov wasn't around I would doubtless never understand a word of it. Most of us gave up on intelligent nonhuman life when the last intersystem probe came back empty. "Little green men, I suppose. Can you show us the lounge, Tom? I understand it's just like the one we'll be working in."

He seemed to welcome the change of subject. "Sure thing."

McGillicuddy led us through a p-door opposite the one Carrington had used, through long halls whose floors curved up ahead of and behind us. Each was outfitted differently, each was full of busy, purposeful people, and each reminded me somehow of the lobby of the New Age, or perhaps of the old movie *2001*. Futuristic Opulence, so understated as to fairly shriek. Wall Street lifted bodily into orbit—the *clocks* were on Wall Street time. I tried to make myself believe that cold, empty space lay a short distance away in any direction, but it was impossible. I decided it was a good thing spacecraft didn't have portholes—once he got used to the low gravity, a man might forget and open one to throw out a cigar.

I studied McGillicuddy as we walked. He was immaculate in every respect, from necktie down to nail polish, and he wore no jewelry at all. His hair was short and black, his beard inhibited, and his eyes surprisingly warm in a professionally sterile face. I wondered what he had sold his soul for. I hoped he had gotten his price.

We had to descend two levels to get to the lounge. The gravity on the upper level was kept at one-sixth normal, partly for the convenience of the lunar personnel who were Skyfac's only regular commuters, and mostly (of course) for the convenience of Carrington. But descending brought a subtle increase in weight, to perhaps a fifth or a quarter normal. My leg complained bitterly, but I found to my surprise that I preferred the pain to its absence. It's a little scary when an old friend goes away like that.

The lounge was a larger room than I had expected, quite big enough for our purposes. It encompassed all three levels, and one whole wall was an immense video screen, across which stars wheeled dizzily, joined with occasional regularity by a slice of mother Terra. The floor was crowded with chairs and tables in various groupings, but I could see that, stripped, it would provide Shara with entirely adequate room to dance; equally important, my feet told me that it would make a splendid dancing surface. Then I remembered how little use the floor was liable to get.

"Well," Shara said to me with a smile, "this is what home will look like for the next six months. The Ring Two lounge is identical to this one."

"Six?" McGillicuddy said. "Not a chance."

"What do you mean?" Shara and I said together.

He blinked at our combined volume. "Well, *you'll* probably be good for that long, Charlie. But Shara's already had over a year of low g, while she was in the typing pool."

"So what?"

"Look, you expect to be in free fall for long periods of time, if I understand this correctly?"

"Twelve hours a day," Shara agreed.

He grimaced. "Shara, I hate to say this . . . but I'll be surprised if you last a month. A body designed for a one-g environment doesn't work properly in zero g."

"But it will adapt, won't it?"

He laughed mirthlessly. "Sure. That's why we rotate all personnel Earthside every fourteen months. Your body will adapt. One way. No return. Once you've fully adapted, returning to Earth will stop your heart—if some other major systemic failure doesn't occur first. Look, you were just Earthside for three days—did you have any chest pains? Dizziness? Bowel trouble? Dropsickness on the way up?"

"All of the above," she admitted.

"There you go. You were close to the nominal fourteen-month limit when you left. And your body will adapt even faster under no gravity at all. The successful free-fall endurance record of about eight months was set by a Skyfac construction gang with bad deadline problems—and they hadn't spent a year in one-sixth g first, *and* they weren't straining their hearts the way you will be. Hell, there are four men on Luna now, from the original dozen in the first mining team, who will never see Earth again. Eight of their teammates tried. Don't you two know *any*thing about space?"

"But I've got to have at least four months. Four months of solid work, every day. I *must.*" She was dismayed, but fighting hard for control.

McGillicuddy started to shake his head, and then thought better of it. His warm eyes were studying Shara's face. I knew exactly what he was thinking, and I liked him for it.

He was thinking, *How to tell a lovely lady her dearest dream is hopeless?*

He didn't know the half of it. I *knew* how much Shara had

already—irrevocably—invested in this dream, and something in me screamed.

And then I saw her jaw ripple and I dared to hope.

Dr. Panzarella was a wiry old man with eyebrows like two fuzzy caterpillars. He wore a tight-fitting jumpsuit which would not foul a p-suit's seals should he have to get into one in a hurry. His shoulder-length hair, which should have been a mane on that great skull, was clipped securely back against a sudden absence of gravity. A cautious man. To employ an obsolete metaphor, he was a suspenders-*and*-belt type. He looked Shara over, ran tests, and gave her just under a month and a half. Shara said some things. I said some things. McGillicuddy said some things. Panzarella shrugged, made further, very careful tests, and reluctantly cut loose of the suspenders. Two months. Not a day over. Possibly less, depending on subsequent monitoring of her body's reactions to extended weightlessness. Then a year Earthside before risking it again. Shara seemed satisfied.

I didn't see how we could do it.

McGillicuddy had assured us that it would take Shara at least a month simply to learn to handle herself competently in zero g, much less dance. Her familiarity with one-sixth g would, he predicted, be a liability rather than an asset. Then figure three weeks of choreography and rehearsal, a week of taping, and just maybe we could broadcast one dance before Shara had to return to Earth. Not good enough. She and I had calculated that we would need three successive shows, each well received, to make a big enough dent in the dance world for Shara to squeeze into it. A year was far too big a spacing—*and who knew how soon Carrington would tire of her?* So I hollered at Panzarella.

"Mr. Armstead," he said hotly, "I am specifically contractually forbidden to allow this young lady to commit suicide." He grimaced sourly. "I'm told it's terrible public relations."

"Charlie, it's okay," Shara insisted. "I can fit in three dances. We may lose some sleep, but we can do it."

"I once told a man nothing was impossible. He asked me if I could ski through a revolving door. You haven't got . . ."

My brain slammed into hyperdrive, thought about things, kicked itself in the ass a few times, and returned to real time in time to hear my mouth finish without a break: ". . . much choice, though. Okay, Tom, have that damned Ring Two lounge cleaned out, I want it naked and spotless, and have somebody paint over that damned video wall, the same shade as the other three, and I mean *the same.* Shara, get out of those clothes and into your leotard. Doctor, we'll be seeing you in twelve hours. Quit gaping and *go,* Tom—we'll be going over there at once; *where the hell are my cameras?*"

McGillicuddy sputtered.

"Get me a torch crew—I'll want holes cut through the walls, cameras behind them, one-way glass, six locations, a room adjacent to the lounge for a mixer console the size of a jetliner cockpit, and bolt a Norelco coffee machine next to the chair. I'll need another room for editing, complete privacy, and total darkness, size of an efficiency kitchen, another Norelco."

McGillicuddy finally drowned me out. "Mr. *Armstead,* this is the Main Ring of the Skyfac One complex, the administrative offices of one of the wealthiest corporations in existence. If you think this whole Ring is going to stand on its head for you . . ."

So we brought the problem to Carrington. He told McGillicuddy that henceforth Ring Two was *ours,* as well as any assistance whatsoever that we requested. He looked rather distracted. McGillicuddy started to tell him by how many weeks all this would put off the opening of the Skyfac Two complex. Carrington replied very quietly that he could add and subtract quite well, thank you, and McGillicuddy got white and quiet.

I'll give Carrington that much. He gave us a free hand.

Panzarella ferried over to Skyfac Two with us. We were chauffeured by lean-jawed astronaut types, on vehicles looking, for all the world, like pregnant broomsticks. It was as well that we had the doctor with us—Shara fainted on the way over. I nearly did myself, and I'm sure that broomstick has my thigh-prints on it yet —falling through space is a scary experience the first time. Shara responded splendidly once we had her inboard again, and fortunately her dropsickness did not return—nausea can be a nuisance in free fall, a disaster in a p-suit. By the time my cameras and mixer had arrived, she was on her feet and sheepish. And while I browbeat a sweating crew of borrowed techs into installing them faster than was humanly possible, Shara began learning how to move in zero g.

We were ready for the first taping in three weeks.

Living quarters and minimal life support were rigged for us in Ring Two so that we could work around the clock if we chose, but we spent nearly half of our nominal "off-hours" in Skyfac One. Shara was required to spend half of three days a week there with Carrington, and spent a sizable portion of her remaining putative sack time out in space, in a p-suit. At first it was a conscious attempt to overcome her gut-level fear of all that emptiness. Soon it became her meditation, her retreat, her artistic reverie, an attempt to gain from contemplation of the cold black depths enough insight into the meaning of extraterrestrial existence to dance of it.

I spent my own time arguing with engineers and electricians and technicians and a damn fool union legate who insisted that the second lounge, finished or not, belonged to the hypothetical future crew and administrative personnel. Securing his permission to work there wore the lining off my throat and the insulation off my nerves. Far too many nights I spent slugging instead of sleeping. Minor example: Every interior wall in the whole damned second Ring was painted the identical shade of turquoise—and they couldn't duplicate it to cover that godforsaken video wall in the lounge. It was McGillicuddy who saved me from gibbering apoplexy—at his suggestion, I washed off the third latex job, unshipped the outboard camera that fed the wall screen, brought it inboard, and fixed it to scan an interior wall in an adjoining room. That made us friends again.

It was all like that: jury-rig, improvise, file to fit and paint to cover. If a camera broke down, I spent sleep time talking with off-shift engineers, finding out what parts in stock could be adapted. It was simply too expensive to have anything shipped up from Earth's immense gravity well, and Luna didn't have what I needed.

At that, Shara worked harder than I did. A body must totally recoordinate itself to function in the absence of weight—she had to forget literally everything she had ever known or learned about dancing and acquire a whole new set of skills. This turned out to be even harder than we had expected. McGillicuddy had been right: What Shara had learned in her year of one-sixth g was an exaggerated attempt to *retain* terrestrial patterns of coordination—rejecting them altogether was actually easier for *me*.

But I couldn't keep up with her—I had to abandon any thought of handheld camera work and base my plans solely on the six fixed cameras. Fortunately GLX-5000s have a ball-and-socket mount; even behind that damned one-way glass I had about forty degrees of traverse on each one. Learning to coordinate all six simultaneously on the Hamilton Board did a truly extraordinary thing to me—it lifted me that one last step to unity with my art. I found that I could learn to be aware of all six monitors with my mind's eye, to perceive almost spherically, to—not share my attention among the six—to *encompass* them all, seeing like a six-eyed creature from many angles at once. My mind's eye became holographic, my awareness multilayered. I began to really understand, for the first time, three-dimensionality.

It was that fourth dimension that was the kicker. It took Shara two days to decide that she could not possibly become proficient enough in free-fall maneuvering to sustain a half-hour piece in the time required. So she rethought her work plan too, adapting her choreography to the demands of exigency. She put in six hard days under normal Earth weight.

And for her, too, the effort brought her that one last step toward apotheosis.

On Monday of the fourth week we began taping *Liberation.*

Establishing shot:

A great turquoise box, seen from within. Dimensions unknown, but the color somehow lends an impression of immensity, of vast distances. Against the far wall, a swinging pendulum attests that this is a standard-gravity environment; but the pendulum swings so slowly and is so featureless in construction that it is impossible to estimate its size and so extrapolate that of the room.

Because of this *trompe l'oeil* effect, the room seems rather smaller than it really is when the camera pulls back and we are wrenched into proper perspective by the appearance of Shara, prone, inert, face down on the floor, facing us.

She wears beige leotard and tights. Hair the color of fine mahogany is pulled back into a loose ponytail which fans across one shoulder blade. She does not appear to breathe. She does not appear to be alive.

Music begins. The aging Mahavishnu, on obsolete nylon acoustic, establishes a Minor E in no hurry at all. A pair of small candles in simple brass holders appear inset on either side of the room. They are larger than life, though small beside Shara. Both are unlit.

Her body . . . there is no word. It does not move, in the sense of motor activity. One might say that a ripple passes through it, save that the motion is clearly all outward from her center. She *swells,* as if the first breath of life were being taken by her whole body at once. She lives.

The twin wicks begin to glow, oh, softly. The music takes on quiet urgency.

Shara raises her head to us. Her eyes focus somewhere beyond the camera yet short of infinity. Her body writhes, undulates, and the glowing wicks are coals (that this brightening takes place in slow motion is not apparent).

A violent contraction raises her to a crouch, spilling the ponytail across her shoulder. Mahavishnu begins a cyclical cascade of runs, in increasing tempo. Long, questing tongues of yellow-orange flame begin to blossom *downward* from the twin wicks, whose coals are turning to blue.

The contraction's release flings her to her feet. The twin skirts of flame about the wicks curl up over themselves, writhing furiously, to become conventional candle flames, flickering now in normal time. Tabl̥as, tambouras, and a bowed string bass join the guitar, and they segue into an energetic interplay around a minor seventh that keeps trying, fruitlessly, to find resolution in the sixth. The candles stay in perspective, but dwindle in size until they vanish.

Shara begins to explore the possibilities of motion. First she moves only perpendicular to the camera's line of sight, exploring that dimension. Every motion of arms or legs or head is clearly seen to be a defiance of gravity, of a force as inexorable as radioactive decay, as entropy itself. The most violent surges of energy succeed only for a time—the outflung leg falls, the outthrust arm drops. She must struggle or fall. She pauses in thought.

Her hands and arms reach out toward the camera, and at the

instant they do we cut to a view from the left-hand wall. Seen from the right side, she reaches out into this new dimension, and soon begins to move in it. (As she moves backward out of the camera's field, its entire image shifts right on our screen, butted out of the way by the incoming image of a second camera, which picks her up as the first loses her without a visible seam.)

The new dimension too fails to fulfill Shara's desire for freedom from gravity. Combining the two, however, presents so many permutations of movement that for a while, intoxicated, she flings herself into experimentation. In the next fifteen minutes, Shara's entire background and history in dance are recapitulated, in a blinding tour de force that incorporates elements of jazz, Modern, and the more graceful aspects of Olympic-level mat gymnastics. Five cameras come into play, singly and in pairs on split screen, as the "bag of tricks" amassed in a lifetime of study and improvisation are rediscovered and performed by a superbly trained and versatile body, in a pyrotechnic display that would shout of joy if her expression did not remain aloof, almost arrogant. *This is the offering,* she seems to say, *which you would not accept. This, by itself, was not good enough.*

And it is not. Even in its raging energy and total control, her body returns again and again to the final compromise of mere erectness, that last simple refusal to fall.

Clamping her jaw, she works into a series of leaps, ever longer, ever higher. She seems at last to hang suspended for full seconds, straining to fly. When, inevitably, she falls, she falls reluctantly, only at the last possible instant tucking and rolling back onto her feet. The musicians are in a crescendoing frenzy. We see her now only with the single original camera, and the twin candles have returned, small but burning fiercely.

The leaps begin to diminish in intensity and height, and she takes longer to build to each one. She has been dancing flat out for nearly twenty minutes; as the candle flames begin to wane, so does her strength. At last she retreats to a place beneath the indifferent pendulum, gathers herself with a final desperation, and races forward toward us. She reaches incredible speed in a short space, hurls herself into a double roll, and bounds up into the air off one foot, seeming a full second later to push off against empty air for a few more inches of height. Her body goes rigid, her eyes and mouth gape wide, the flames reach maximum brilliance, the music peaks with the tortured wail of an electric guitar, and—she falls, barely snapping into a roll in time, rising only as far as a crouch. She holds there for a long moment, and gradually her head and shoulders slump, defeated, toward the floor. The candle flames draw in upon themselves in a curious way and appear to go out. The string bass saws on, modulating down to D.

Muscle by muscle, Shara's body gives up the struggle. The air seems to tremble around the wicks of the candles, which have now grown nearly as tall as her crouching form.

Shara lifts her face to the camera with evident effort. Her face is anguished, her eyes nearly shut. A long beat.

All at once she opens her eyes wide, squares her shoulders, and contracts. It is the most exquisite and total contraction ever dreamed of, filmed in real time but seeming almost to be in slow motion. She holds it. Mahavishnu comes back in on guitar, building in increasing tempo from a down-tuned bass string to a D with a flatted fourth. Shara holds.

We shift for the first time to an overhead camera, looking down on her from a great height. As Mahavishnu's picking increases to the point where the chord seems a sustained drone, Shara slowly lifts her head, still holding the contraction, until she is staring directly up at us. She poises there for an eternity, like a spring wound to the bursting point . . .

. . . and explodes upward toward us, rising higher and faster than she possibly can in a soaring flight that *is* slow motion now, coming closer and closer until her hands disappear off either side and her face fills the screen, flanked by two candles which have bloomed into gouts of yellow flame in an instant. The guitar and bass are submerged in an orchestra.

Almost at once she whirls away from us, and the POV switches to the original camera, on which we see her fling herself down ten meters to the floor, reversing her attitude in mid-flight and twisting. She comes out of her roll in an absolutely flat trajectory that takes her the length of the room. She hits the far wall with a crash audible even over the music, shattering the still pendulum. Her thighs soak up the kinetic energy and then release it, and once again she is racing toward us, hair streaming straight out behind her, a broad smile of triumph growing larger in the screen.

In the next five minutes all six cameras vainly try to track her as she caroms around the immense room like a hummingbird trying to batter its way out of a cage, using the walls, floor, and ceiling the way a jai alai master does, *existing in three dimensions.* Gravity is defeated. The basic assumption of all dance is transcended.

Shara is transformed.

She comes to rest at last at vertical center in the forefront of the turquoise cube, arms-legs-fingers-toes-face straining *outward,* turning gently end over end. All four cameras that bear on her join in a four-way split screen, the orchestra resolves into its final E Major, and—fade-out.

I had neither the time nor the equipment to create the special effects that Shara wanted. So I found ways to warp reality to my need. The first candle segment was a twinned shot of a candle being blown out from above—in ultra-slow-motion, and in reverse. The second segment was a simple recording of reality. I had lit the candle, started taping—and had the Ring's spin killed. A candle behaves oddly in zero g. The low-density combustion gases do not rise up from the flame, allowing air to reach it from beneath. The flame does not go out: It becomes dormant. Restore gravity within a minute or so, and it blooms back to life again. All I did was monkey with speeds a bit to match in with the music and Shara's dance. I got the idea from Harry Stein, Skyfac's construction foreman, who was helping me design the next dance.

I set up a screen in the Ring One lounge, and everyone in Skyfac who could cut work crowded in for the broadcast. They saw exactly what was being sent out over worldwide satellite hookup (Carrington had sufficient pull to arrange twenty-five minutes without commercial interruption) almost a full half second before the world did.

I spent the broadcast in the Communications Room, chewing my fingernails. But it went without a hitch, and I slapped my board dead and made it to the lounge in time to see the last half of the standing ovation. Shara stood before the screen, Carrington sitting beside her, and I found the difference in their expressions instructive. Her face showed no surprise or modesty.

She had had faith in herself throughout, had approved this tape for broadcast—she was aware, with that incredible detachment of which so few artists are capable, that the wild applause was only what she deserved. But her face showed that she was deeply surprised—and deeply grateful—to be given what she deserved.

Carrington, on the other hand, registered a triumph strangely mingled with relief. He too had had faith in Shara, backing it with a large investment—but his faith was that of a businessman in a gamble he believes will pay off, and as I watched his eyes and the glisten of sweat on his forehead, I realized that no businessman ever takes an expensive gamble without worrying that it may be the fiasco that will begin the loss of his only essential commodity: face.

Seeing his kind of triumph next to hers spoiled the moment for me, and instead of thrilling for Shara I found myself almost hating her. She spotted me, and waved me to join her before the cheering crowd, but I turned and literally flung myself from the room. I borrowed a bottle from Harry Stein and got stinking.

The next morning my head felt like a fifteen-amp fuse on a forty-amp circuit, and I seemed to be held together only by surface tension. Sudden movements frightened me. It's a long fall off that wagon, even at one-sixth g.

The phone chimed—I hadn't had time to rewire it—and a young man I didn't know politely announced that Mr. Carrington wished to see me in his office. At once, I spoke of a barbed-wire suppository and what Mr. Carrington might do with it, at once. Without changing expression, he repeated his message and disconnected.

So I crawled into my clothes, decided to grow a beard, and left. Along the way I wondered what I had traded my independence for, and why.

Carrington's office was oppressively tasteful, but at least the lighting was subdued. Best of all, its filter system would handle smoke—the sweet musk of pot lay on the air. I accepted a macrojoint of "Maoi-Zowie" from Carrington with something approaching gratitude, and began melting my hangover.

Shara sat next to his desk, wearing a leotard and a layer of sweat. She had obviously spent the morning rehearsing for the next dance. I felt ashamed, and consequently snappish, avoiding her eyes and her hello. Panzarella and McGillicuddy came in on my heels, chattering about the latest sighting of the mysterious object from deep space, which had appeared this time in the neighborhood of Mercury. They were arguing over whether it displayed signs of sentience or not, and I wished they'd shut up.

Carrington waited until we had all seated ourselves and lit up, then rested a hip on his desk and smiled. "Well, Tom?"

McGillicuddy beamed. "Better than we expected, sir. All the ratings agree we had about seventy-four percent of the world audience—"

"The hell with the Nielsons," I snapped. *"What did the critics say?"*

McGillicuddy blinked. "Well, the general reaction so far is that Shara was a smash. The *Times*—"

I cut him off again. "What was the less-than-general reaction?"

"Well, nothing is ever unanimous."

"Specifics. The dance press? Liz Zimmer? Migdalski?"

"Uh. Not as good. Praise, yes—only a blind man could've panned that show. But guarded praise. Uh, Zimmer called it a magnificent dance spoiled by a gimmicky ending."

"And Migdalski?" I insisted.

"He headed his review, 'But What Do You Do for an Encore?' " McGillicuddy admitted. "His basic thesis was that it was a charming one-shot. But the *Times*—"

"Thank you, Tom," Carrington said quietly. "About what we expected, isn't it, my dear? A big splash, but no one's willing to call it a tidal wave yet."

She nodded. "But they will, Bryce. The next two dances will sew it up."

Panzarella spoke up. "Ms. Drummond, may I ask why you played it the way you did? Using the null-g interlude only as a brief adjunct to conventional dance—surely you must have expected the critics to call it gimmickry."

Shara smiled and answered, "To be honest, Doctor, I had no choice. I'm learning to use my body in free fall, but it's still a conscious effort, almost a pantomime. I need another few weeks to make it second nature, and it *has* to be if I'm to sustain a whole piece in it. So I dug a conventional dance out of the trunk, tacked on a five-minute ending that used every zero-g move I knew, and found to my extreme relief that they made thematic sense together. I told Charlie my notion, and he made it work visually and dramatically—that whole business of the candles was his, and it underlined what I was trying to say better than any set we could have built."

"So you have not yet completed what you came here to do?" Panzarella asked Shara.

"Oh, no. Not by any means. The next dance will show the world that dance is more than controlled falling. And the third . . . the third will be what this has all been for." Her face lit, became animated. "The third dance will be the one I have wanted to dance all my life. I can't entirely picture it yet—but I know that when I become capable of dancing it, I will create it, and it will be my greatest dance."

Panzarella cleared his throat. "How long will it take you?"

"Not long," she said. "I'll be ready to tape the next dance in two weeks, and I can start on the last one almost at once. With luck, I'll have it in the can before my month is up."

"Ms. Drummond," Panzarella said gravely, "I'm afraid you don't have another month."

Shara went white as snow, and I half rose from my seat. Carrington looked intrigued.

"How much time?" Shara asked.

"Your latest tests have not been encouraging. I had assumed that the sustained exercise of rehearsal and practice would tend to slow your system's adaptation. But most of your work has been in total weightlessness, and I failed to realize the extent to which your body is accustomed to sustained exertion—in a terrestrial environment."

"How much time?"

"Two weeks. Possibly three, if you spend three separate hours a day at hard exercise in two gravities."

"That's ridiculous," I burst out. "Don't you understand about dancers' spines? She could ruin herself in two gees."

"I've got to have four weeks," Shara said.

"Ms. Drummond, I am sorry."

"I've got to have four weeks."

Panzarella had that same look of helpless sorrow that McGillicuddy and I had had in our turn, and I was suddenly sick to death of a universe in which people had to keep looking at Shara that way. "Dammit," I roared, "she needs four weeks."

Panzarella shook his shaggy head. "If she stays in zero g for four working weeks, she may die."

Shara sprang from her chair. "Then I'll die," she cried. "I'll take that chance. I *have* to."

Carrington coughed. "I'm afraid I can't permit you to, darling."

She whirled on him furiously.

"This dance of yours is excellent PR for Skyfac," he said calmly, "but if it were to kill you it might boomerang, don't you think?"

Her mouth worked, and she fought desperately for control. My own head whirled. Die? Shara?

"Besides," he added, "I've grown quite fond of you."

"Then I'll stay up here in space," she burst out.

"Where? The only areas of sustained weightlessness are factories, and you're not qualified to work in one."

"Then for God's sake give me one of the new pods, the small spheres. Bryce, I'll give you a higher return on your investment than a factory pod, and I'll . . ." Her voice changed. "I'll be available to you always."

He smiled lazily. "Yes, but I might not *want* you always, darling. My mother warned me strongly against making irrevocable decisions about women. Especially informal ones. Besides, I find zero-g sex rather too exhausting as a steady diet."

I had almost found my voice, and now I lost it again. I was glad Carrington was turning her down—but the way he did it made me yearn to drink his blood.

Shara too was speechless for a time. When she spoke, her voice was low, intense, almost pleading. "Bryce, it's a matter of timing. If I broadcast two more dances in the next four weeks, I'll have a world to return to. If I have to go Earthside and wait a year or two, that third dance will sink without a trace—no one'll be looking, and they won't have the memory of the first two. This is my only option, Bryce—*let me take the chance.* Panzarella can't guarantee four weeks will kill me."

"I can't guarantee your survival," the doctor said.

"You can't guarantee that any one of us will live out the day," she snapped. She whirled back to Carrington, held him with her eyes. "Bryce, *let me risk it.*" Her face underwent a massive effort, produced a smile that put a knife through my heart. "I'll make it worth your while."

Carrington savored that smile and the utter surrender in her voice like a man enjoying a fine claret. I wanted to slay him with my hands and teeth, and I prayed that he would add the final cruelty of turning her down. But I had underestimated his true capacity for cruelty.

"Go ahead with your rehearsal, my dear," he said at last. "We'll make a final decision when the time comes. I shall have to think about it."

I don't think I've ever felt so hopeless, so . . . impotent in my life. Knowing it was futile, I said, "Shara, I can't let you risk your life—"

"I'm going to do this, Charlie," she cut me off, "with or without you. No one else knows my work well enough to tape it properly, but if you want out I can't stop you." Carrington watched me with detached interest. "Well?"

I said a filthy word. "You know the answer."

"Then let's get to work."

Tyros are transported on the pregnant broomsticks. Old hands hang outside the air lock, dangling from handholds on the outer surface of the spinning Ring. They face in the direction of the spin, and when their destination comes under the horizon, they just drop off. Thruster units built into gloves and boots supply the necessary course corrections. The distances involved are small. Shara and I, having spent more weightless hours than some technicians who'd been in Skyfac for years, were old hands. We made scant and efficient use of our thrusters, chiefly in canceling the energy imparted to us by the spin of the Ring we left. We had throat mikes and hearing-aid-sized receivers, but there was no conversation on the way across the void. I spent the journey appreciating the starry emptiness through which I fell—I had come, perforce, to understand the attraction of sky diving—and wondering whether I would ever get used to the cessation of pain in my leg. It even seemed to hurt less under spin those days.

We grounded, with much less force than a sky diver does, on the surface of the new studio. It was an enormous steel globe, studded with sunpower screens and heat-losers, tethered to three more spheres in various stages of construction, on which p-suited figures were even now working. McGillicuddy had told me that the complex when completed would be used for "controlled density processing," and when I said, "How nice," he added, "Dispersion foaming and variable density casting," as if that explained everything. Perhaps it did. Right at the moment, it was Shara's studio.

The air lock led to a rather small working space around a smaller interior sphere some fifty meters in diameter. It too was pressurized, intended to contain a vacuum, but its locks stood open. We removed our p-suits, and Shara unstrapped her thruster bracelets from a bracing strut and put them on, hanging by her ankles from the strut while she did so. The anklets went on next. As jewelry they were a shade bulky—but they had twenty minutes' continuous use each, and their operation was not visible in normal atmosphere and lighting. Indoor zero-gee dance without them would have been enormously more difficult.

As she was fastening the last strap I drifted over in front of her and grabbed the strut. "Shara . . ."

"Charlie, I can beat it. I'll exercise in *three* gravities, and I'll sleep in two, and I'll make this body last. I know I can."

"You could skip *Mass Is a Verb* and go right to the *Stardance.*"

She shook her head. "I'm not ready yet—and neither is the audience. I've got to lead myself and them through dance in a sphere first—in a contained space—before I'll be ready to dance in empty space, or for them to appreciate it. I have to free my mind, and theirs, from just about every preconception of dance, change the postulates. Even two stages is too few—but it's the irreducible minimum." Her eyes softened. "Charlie—I must."

"I know," I said gruffly, and turned away. Tears are a nuisance in free fall—they don't *go* anywhere. I began hauling myself around the surface of the inner sphere toward the camera emplacement I was working on, and Shara entered the inner sphere to begin rehearsal.

I prayed as I worked on my equipment, snaking cables among the bracing struts and connecting them to drifting terminals. For the first time in years I prayed, prayed that Shara would make it. That we both would.

The next twelve days were the toughest of my life. Shara worked twice as hard as I did. She spent half of every day working in the studio, half of the rest in exercise under two and a quarter gravities (the most Dr. Panzarella would permit), and half of the rest in Carrington's bed, trying to make him contented enough to let her stretch her time limit. Perhaps she slept in the few hours left over. I only know that she never looked tired, never lost her composure or her dogged determination. Stubbornly, reluctantly, her body lost its awkwardness, took on grace even in an environment where grace required enormous concentration. Like a child learning to walk, Shara learned how to fly.

I even began to get used to the absence of pain in my leg.

What can I tell you of *Mass,* if you have not seen it? It cannot be described, even badly, in mechanistic terms, the way a symphony could be written out in words. Conventional dance terminology is, by its built-in assumptions, worse than useless, and if you are at all familiar with the new nomenclature you *must* be familiar with *Mass Is a Verb,* from which it draws *its* built-in assumptions.

Nor is there much I can say about the technical aspects of *Mass.* There were no special effects; not even music. Brindle's superb score was composed *from the dance,* and added to the tape with my permission two years later, but it was for the original, silent version that I was given the Emmy. My entire contribution, aside from editing and installing the two trampolines, was to camouflage batteries of wide-dispersion light sources in clusters around each camera eye, and wire them so that they energized only when they were out-of-frame with respect to whichever camera was on at the time—ensuring that Shara was always lit from the front, presenting two (not always congruent) shadows. I made no attempt to employ flashy camera work; I simply recorded what Shara danced, changing POV only as she did.

No. *Mass Is a Verb* can be described only in symbolic terms, and then poorly. I can say that Shara demonstrated that mass and inertia are as able as gravity to supply the dynamic conflict essential to dance. I can tell you that from them she distilled a kind of dance that could have been imagined only by a group-head consisting of an acrobat, a stunt diver, a skywriter, and an underwater ballerina. I can tell you that she dismantled the last interface between herself and utter freedom of motion, subduing her body to her will and space itself to her need.

And still I will have told you next to nothing. For Shara sought more than freedom—she sought meaning. *Mass* was, above all, a spiritual event—its title pun paralleling its thematic ambiguity between the technological and the theological. Shara made the human confrontation with existence a transitive act, literally meeting God halfway. I do not mean to imply that her dance at any time addressed an exterior God, a discrete entity with or without white beard. Her dance addressed reality, gave successive expression to the Three Eternal Questions asked by every human being who ever lived.

Her dance observed her *self,* and asked, *How have I come to be here?*

Her dance observed the universe in which self existed, and asked, *How did all this come to be here with me?*

And at last, observing her self in relation to its universe, *Why am I so alone?*

And, having asked these questions, having earnestly asked them with every muscle and sinew she possessed, she paused, hung suspended in the center of the sphere, her body and soul open to the universe, and when no answer came, she contracted. Not in a dramatic, ceiling-spring sense as she had in *Liberation,* a compressing of energy and tension. This was physically similar, but an utterly different phenomenon. It was a focusing inward, an act of introspection, a turning of the mind's (soul's?) eye in upon itself, to seek answers that lay nowhere else. Her body too, therefore, seemed to fold in upon itself, compacting her mass, so evenly that her position in space was not disturbed.

And reaching within herself, she closed on emptiness. The camera faded out, leaving her alone, rigid, encapsulated, yearning. The dance ended, leaving her three questions unanswered, the tension of their asking unresolved. Only the expression of patient waiting on her face blunted the shocking edge of the nonending, made it bearable, a small, blessed sign whispering, "To be continued."

By the eighteenth day we had it in the can, in rough form.

Shara put it immediately out of her mind and began choreographing *Stardance,* but I spent two hard days of editing before I was ready to release the tape for broadcast. I had four days until the half hour of prime time Carrington had purchased—but that wasn't the deadline I felt breathing down the back of my neck.

McGillicuddy came into my workroom while I was editing, and although he saw the tears running down my face he said no word. I let the tape run, and he watched in silence, and soon his face was wet too. When the tape had been over for a long time he said, very softly, "One of these days I'm going to have to quit this stinking job."

I said nothing.

"I used to be a karate instructor. I was pretty good. I could teach again, maybe do exhibition work, make ten percent of what I do now."

I said nothing.

"The whole damned Ring's bugged, Charlie. The desk in my office can activate and tap any vidphone in Skyfac. Four at a time, actually."

I said nothing.

"I saw you both in the air lock when you came back the last time. I saw her collapse. I saw you bringing her around. I heard her make you promise not to tell Dr. Panzarella."

I waited. Hope stirred.

He dried his face. "I came in here to tell you I was going to Panzarella, to tell him what I saw. He'd bully Carrington into sending her home right away."

"And now?" I said.

"I've seen that tape."

"And you know the *Stardance* will probably kill her?"

"Yes."

"And you know we have to let her do it?"

"Yes."

Hope died. I nodded. "Then get out of here and let me work."

He left.

On Wall Street and aboard Skyfac it was late afternoon when I finally had the tape edited to my satisfaction. I called Carrington, told him to expect me in half an hour, showered, shaved, dressed, and left.

A major of the Space Command was there with him when I arrived, but he was not introduced and so I ignored him. Shara was there too, wearing a thing made of orange smoke that left her breasts bare. Carrington had obviously made her wear it, as an urchin writes filthy words on an altar, but she wore it with a perverse and curious dignity that I sensed annoyed him. I looked her in the eye and smiled. "Hi, kid. It's a good tape."

"Let's see," Carrington said. He and the major took seats behind the desk, and Shara sat beside it.

I fed the tape into the video rig built into the office wall, dimmed the lights, and sat across from Shara. It ran twenty minutes, uninterrupted, no sound track, stark naked.

It was terrific.

"Aghast" is a funny word. To make you aghast, a thing must hit you in a place you haven't armored over with cynicism yet. I seem to have been born cynical; I have been aghast three times that I can remember. The first was when I learned, at the age of three, that there were people who could deliberately hurt kittens. The second was when I learned, at age seventeen, that there were people who could actually take LSD and then hurt other people for fun. The third was when *Mass Is a Verb* ended and Carrington said in perfectly conversational tones, "Very pleasant; very graceful. I like it," when I learned, at age forty-five, that there were men, not fools or cretins but intelligent men, who could watch Shara Drummond dance and fail to *see.* We all, even the most cynical of us, always have some illusion which we cherish.

Shara simply let it bounce off her somehow, but I could see that the major was as aghast as I, controlling his features with a visible effort.

Suddenly welcoming a distraction from my horror and dismay, I studied him more closely, wondering for the first time what he was doing here. He was my age, lean and more hard-bitten than I am, with silver fuzz on top of his skull and an extremely tidy mustache on the front. I'd taken him for a crony of Carrington's, but three things changed my mind. Something indefinable about his eyes told me that he was a military man of long combat experience. Something equally indefinable about his carriage told me that he was on duty at the moment. And something quite definable about the line his mouth made told me that he was disgusted with the duty he had drawn.

When Carrington went on, "What do you think, Major?" in polite tones, the man paused for a moment, gathering his thoughts and choosing his words. When he did speak, it was not to Carrington.

"Ms. Drummond," he said quietly, "I am Major William Cox, commander of S.C. *Champion,* and I am honored to meet you. That was the most profoundly moving thing I have ever seen."

Shara thanked him most gravely. "This is Charles Armstead, Major Cox. He made the tape."

Cox regarded me with new respect. "A magnificent job, Mr. Armstead." He stuck out his hand, and I shook it.

Carrington was beginning to understand that we three shared a thing which excluded him. "I'm glad you enjoyed it, Major," he said with no visible trace of sincerity. "You can see it again on your television tomorrow night, if you chance to be off duty. And eventually, of course, cassettes will be made available. Now perhaps we can get to the matter at hand."

Cox's face closed as if it had been zippered up, became stiffly formal. "As you wish, sir."

Puzzled, I began what I thought was the matter at hand. "I'd like your own Comm Chief to supervise the actual transmission this time, Mr. Carrington. Shara and I will be too busy to—"

"My Comm Chief will supervise the broadcast, Armstead," Carrington interrupted, "but I don't think you'll be particularly busy."

I was groggy from lack of sleep; my uptake was rather slow.

He touched his desk delicately. "McGillicuddy, report at once," he said, and released it. "You see, Armstead, you and Shara are both returning to Earth. At once."

"What?"

"Bryce, you *can't,"* Shara cried. "You *promised."*

"I promised I would think about it, my dear," he corrected.

"The hell you say. That was weeks ago. Last night you *promised."*

"Did I? My dear, there were no witnesses present last night. Altogether for the best, don't you agree?"

I was speechless with rage.

McGillicuddy entered. "Hello, Tom," Carrington said pleasantly. "You're fired. You'll be returning to Earth at once, with Ms. Drummond and Mr. Armstead, aboard Major Cox's vessel. Departure in one hour, and don't leave anything you're fond of." He glanced from McGillicuddy to me. "From Tom's desk you can tap any vidphone in Skyfac. From my desk you can tap Tom's desk."

Shara's voice was low. "Bryce, two days. God damn you, name your price."

He smiled slightly. "I'm sorry, darling. When informed of your collapse, Dr. Panzarella became most specific. Not even one more day. Alive you are a distinct plus for Skyfac's image—you are my gift to the world. Dead you are an albatross around my neck. I cannot allow you to die on my property. I anticipated that you might resist leaving, and so I spoke to a friend in the"—he glanced at Cox—"*higher* echelons of the Space Command, who was good enough to send the Major here to escort you home. You are not under arrest in the legal sense—but I assure you that you have no choice. Something like protective custody applies. Goodbye, Shara." He reached for a stack of reports on his desk, and I surprised myself considerably.

I cleared the desk entirely, tucked head catching him squarely in the sternum. His chair was belted to the deck and so it snapped clean. I recovered so well that I had time for one glorious right. Do you know how, if you punch a basketball squarely, it will bounce up from the floor? That's what his head did, in low-g slow motion.

Then Cox had hauled me to my feet and shoved me into the far corner of the room. "Don't," he said to me, and his voice must have held a lot of that "habit of command" they talk about, because it stopped me cold. I stood breathing in great gasps while Cox helped Carrington to his feet.

The millionaire felt his smashed nose, examined the blood on his fingers, and looked at me with raw hatred. "You'll never work in video again, Armstead. You're through. Finished. Un-employed, you get that?"

Cox tapped him on the shoulder, and Carrington spun on him. "What the hell do you want?" he barked.

Cox smiled. "Carrington, my late father once said, 'Bill, make your enemies by choice, not by accident.' Over the years I have found that to be excellent advice. You suck."

"And not particularly well," Shara agreed.

Carrington blinked. Then his absurdly broad shoulders swelled and he roared, "Out, all of you! *Off my property at once!*"

By unspoken consent, we waited for McGillicuddy, who knew his cue. "Mr. Carrington, it is a rare privilege and a great honor to have been fired by you. I shall think of it always as a Pyrrhic defeat." And he half bowed and we left, each buoyed by a juvenile feeling of triumph that must have lasted ten seconds.

The sensation of falling that comes with zero g is literal truth, but your body quickly learns to treat it as an illusion. Now, in zero g for the last time, for the half hour before I would be back in Earth's own gravitational field, I felt I was falling. Plummeting into some bottomless gravity well, dragged down by the anvil that was my heart, the scraps of a dream that should have held me aloft fluttering overhead.

The *Champion* was three times the size of Carrington's yacht, which childishly pleased me until I recalled that he had summoned it here without paying for either fuel or crew. A guard at the air lock saluted as we entered. Cox led us to a compartment aft of the air lock where we were to strap in. He noticed along the way that I used only my left hand to pull myself along, and when we stopped he said, "Mr. Armstead, my late father also told me, 'Hit the soft parts with your hand. Hit the hard parts with a utensil.' Otherwise I can find no fault with your technique. I wish I could shake your hand."

I tried to smile, but I didn't have it in me. "I admire your taste in enemies, Major."

"A man can't ask for more. I'm afraid I can't spare time to have your hand looked at until we've grounded. We begin reentry immediately."

"Forget it."

He bowed to Shara, did *not* tell her how deeply sorry he was to et cetera, wished us all a comfortable journey, and left. We strapped into our acceleration couches to await ignition. There ensued a long and heavy silence, compounded of a mutual sadness that bravado could only have underlined. We did not look at each other, as though our combined sorrow might achieve some kind of critical mass. Grief struck us dumb, and I believe that remarkably little of it was self-pity.

But then a whole lot of time seemed to have gone by. Quite a bit of intercom chatter came faintly from the next compartment, but ours was not in circuit. At last we began to talk, desultorily, discussing the probable critical reaction to *Mass Is a Verb,* whether analysis was worthwhile or the theater really dead, anything at all except future plans. Eventually there was nothing else to talk about, so we shut up again. I guess I'd say we were in shock.

For some reason I came out of it first. "What in hell is taking them so long?" I barked irritably.

McGillicuddy started to say something soothing, then glanced at his watch and yelped. "You're right. It's been nearly an hour."

I looked at the wall clock, got hopelessly confused until I realized it was on Greenwich time rather than Wall Street, and realized he was correct. "Chrissakes," I shouted, "the whole bloody *point* of this exercise is to protect Shara from overexposure to free fall! I'm going forward."

"Charlie, hold it." McGillicuddy, with two good hands, unstrapped faster than I. "Dammit, stay right there and cool off. I'll go find out what the holdup is."

He was back in a few minutes, and his face was slack. "We're not going anywhere. Cox has orders to sit tight."

"What? Tom, what the *hell* are you talking about?"

His voice was all funny. "Red fireflies. More like bees, actually. In a balloon."

He simply *could not* be joking with me, which meant he flat out *had* to have gone completely round the bend, which meant that somehow I had blundered into my favorite nightmare where everyone but me goes crazy, and begins gibbering at me. So I lowered my head like an enraged bull, and charged out of the room so fast the door barely had time to get out of my way.

It just got worse. When I reached the door to the bridge I was going much too fast to be stopped by anything short of a body block, and the crewmen present were caught flatfooted. There was a brief flurry at the door, and then I was on the bridge, and then I decided that I had gone crazy too, which somehow made everything all right.

The forward wall of the bridge was one enormous video tank—and just enough off center to faintly irritate me, standing out against the black deep as clearly as cigarettes in a darkroom, there truly did swarm a multitude of red fireflies.

The conviction of unreality made it okay. But then Cox snapped me back to reality with a bellowed *"Off this bridge, mister."* If I'd been in a normal frame of mind it would have blown me out the door and into the farthest corner of the ship; in my current state it managed to jolt me into acceptance of the impossible situation. I shivered like a wet dog and turned to him.

"Major," I said desperately, "What is going on?"

As a king may be amused by an insolent varlet who refuses to kneel, he was bemused by the phenomenon of someone failing to obey him. It bought me an answer. "We are confronting intelligent alien life," he said concisely. "I believe them to be sentient plasmoids."

I had never for a moment believed that the mysterious object which had been leapfrogging around the solar system since I came to Skyfac was *alive.* I tried to take it in, then abandoned the task and went back to my main priority. "I don't care if they're eight tiny reindeer; you've got to get this can back to Earth *now.*"

"Sir, this vessel is on Emergency Red Alert and on Combat Standby. At this moment the suppers of everyone in North America are getting cold. I will consider myself fortunate if I ever see Earth again. Now get off my bridge."

"But you don't *understand.* Sustained free fall might kill Shara. That's what you came up here to prevent, dammit—"

"MR. ARMSTEAD! This is a military vessel. We are facing nearly a dozen intelligent beings who appeared out of hyperspace near here twenty minutes ago, beings who therefore use a drive beyond my conception with no visible parts. If it makes you feel any better, I am aware that I have a passenger aboard of greater intrinsic value to my species than this ship and everyone else on her, and if it is any comfort to you this knowledge already

provides a distraction I need like an auxiliary anus, and I can no more leave this orbit than I can grow horns. Now will you get off this bridge or will you be dragged?"

I didn't get a chance to decide: They dragged me.

On the other hand, by the time I got back to our compartment Cox had put our vidphone screen in circuit with the tank on the bridge. Shara and McGillicuddy were studying it with rapt attention. Having nothing better to do, I did too.

McGillicuddy had been right. They *did* act more like bees, in the swarming rapidity of their movement. It was a while before I could get an accurate count: ten of them. And they *were* in a balloon—a faint, barely tangible thing on the fine line between transparency and translucency. Though they darted like furious red gnats, it was only within the confines of the spheroid balloon—they never left it or seemed to touch its inner surface.

As I watched, the last of the adrenaline rinsed out of my kidneys, but it left a sense of frustrated urgency. I tried to grapple with the fact that these *Space Commando* special effects represented something that was—more important than Shara. It was a primevally disturbing notion, but I could not reject it.

In my mind were two voices, each hollering questions at the top of their lungs, each ignoring the other's questions. One yelled: *Are those things friendly? Or hostile? Or do they even use those concepts? How big are they? How far away? From where?* The other voice was less ambitious but just as loud: all it said, over and over again, was: *How much longer can Shara remain in free fall without dooming herself?*

Shara's voice was full of wonder. "They're . . . they're *dancing.*"

I looked closer. If there was a pattern to the flies-on-garbage swarm they made, I couldn't detect it. "Looks random to me."

"Charlie, look. All that furious activity, and they never bump into each other or the walls of that envelope they're in. They must be in orbits as carefully choreographed as those of electrons."

"Do atoms dance?"

She gave me an odd look. "Don't they, Charlie?"

"Laser beam," McGillicuddy said.

We looked at him.

"Those things have to be plasmoids—the man I talked to said they were first spotted on radar. That means they're ionized gases of some kind—the kind of thing that used to cause UFO reports." He giggled, then caught himself. "If you could slice through that envelope with a laser, I'll bet you could deionize them pretty good—besides, that envelope has to hold their life support, whatever it is they metabolize."

I was dizzy. "Then we're not defenseless?"

"You're both talking like soldiers," Shara burst out. "I tell you they're dancing. Dancers aren't fighters."

"Come on, Shara," I barked. "Even if those things happen to be remotely like us, that's not true. Samurai, karate, kung fu—they're dance." I nodded to the screen. "All we know about these animated embers is that they travel interstellar space. That's enough to scare me."

"Charlie, look at them," she commanded.

I did.

By God, they didn't look threatening. They did, the more I watched, seem to move in a dancelike way, whirling in mad adagios just too fast for the eye to follow. Not like conventional dance—more analogous to what Shara had begun with *Mass Is a Verb.* I found myself wanting to switch to another camera for contrast of perspective, and that made my mind start to wake up at last. Two ideas surfaced, the second one necessary in order to sell Cox the first.

"How far do you suppose we are from Skyfac?" I asked McGillicuddy.

He pursed his lips. "Not far. There hasn't been much more than maneuvering acceleration. The damn things were probably attracted to Skyfac in the first place—it must be the most easily visible sign of intelligent life in this system." He grimaced. "Maybe they don't *use* planets."

I reached forward and punched the audio circuit. "Major Cox."

"Get off this circuit."

"How would you like a closer view of those things?"

"We're staying put. Now stop jiggling my elbow and get off this circuit or I'll—"

"Will you listen to me? I have four mobile cameras in space, remote-control, self-contained power source and light, and better resolution than you've got. They were set up to tape Shara's next dance."

He shifted gears at once. "Can you patch them into my ship?"

"I think so. But I'll have to get back to the master board in Ring One."

"No good, then. I can't tie myself to a top—what if I have to fight or run?"

"Major—how far a walk is it?"

It startled him a bit. "A mile or two, as the crow flies. But you're a groundlubber."

"I've been in free fall for most of two months. Give me a portable radar and I can ground on Phobos."

"Mmmm. You're a civilian—but dammit, I need better video. Permission granted."

Now for the first idea. "Wait—one thing more. Shara and Tom must come with me."

"Nuts. This isn't a field trip."

"Major Cox—Shara *must* return to a gravity field as quickly as possible. Ring One'll do—in fact, it'd be ideal, if we can enter through the 'spoke' in the center. She can descend very slowly and acclimatize gradually, the way a diver decompresses in stages, but in reverse. McGillicuddy will have to come along to stay with her—if she passes out and falls down the tube, she could break a leg even in one-sixth g. Besides, he's better at EVA than either of us."

He thought it over. "Go."

We went.

The trip back to Ring One was far longer than any Shara or I had ever made, but under McGillicuddy's guidance we made it with minimal maneuvering. Ring, *Champion,* and aliens formed an equiangular triangle about a mile and a half on a side. Seen in perspective, the aliens took up about as much volume as Shea Stadium. They did not pause or slacken in their mad gyration, but somehow they seemed to watch us cross the gap to Skyfac. I got an impression of a biologist studying the strange antics of a new species. We kept our suit radios off to avoid distraction, and it made me just a little bit more susceptible to suggestion.

I left McGillicuddy with Shara and dropped down the tube six rings at a time. Carrington was waiting for me in the reception room, with two flunkies. It was plain to see that he was scared silly, and trying to cover it with anger. "Goddammit, Armstead, those are my bloody cameras."

"Shut up, Carrington. If you put those cameras in the hands of the best technician available—me—and if I put their data in the hands of the best strategic mind in space—Cox—we *might* be able to save your damned factory for you. And the human race for the rest of us." I moved forward, and he got out of my way. It figured. Putting all humanity in danger might just be bad PR.

After all the practicing I'd done, it wasn't hard to direct four mobile cameras through space simultaneously by eye. The aliens ignored their approach. The Skyfac comm crew fed my signals to the *Champion* and patched me in to Cox on audio. At his direction I bracketed the balloon with the cameras, shifting POV at his command. Space Command Headquarters must have recorded the video, but I couldn't hear their conversation with Cox, for which I was grateful. I gave him slow-motion replay, close-ups, split screens—everything at my disposal. The movements of individual fireflies did not appear particularly symmetrical, but patterns began to repeat. In slow motion they looked more than ever as though they were dancing, and although I couldn't be sure, it seemed to me that they were increasing their tempo. Somehow the dramatic tension of their dance seemed to build.

And then I shifted POV to the camera which included Skyfac in the background, and my heart turned to hard vacuum and I screamed in pure primal terror—halfway between Ring One and the swarm of aliens, coming up on them slowly but inexorably, was a p-suited figure that had to be Shara.

With theatrical timing, McGillicuddy appeared in the doorway, leaning heavily on the chief engineer, his face drawn with pain. He stood on one foot, the other leg plainly broken.

"Guess I can't . . . go back to exhibition work . . . after all," he gasped. "Said . . . 'I'm sorry, Tom' . . . knew she was going to swing on me . . . wiped me out anyhow. Oh, dammit, Charlie, I'm sorry." He sank into an empty chair.

Cox's voice came urgently. "What the hell is going on? Who is that?"

She *had* to be on our frequency. "Shara!" I screamed. "Get your ass back in here!"

"I can't, Charlie." Her voice was startlingly loud, and very calm. "Halfway down the tube my chest started to hurt like hell."

"Ms. Drummond," Cox rapped, "if you approach any closer to the aliens I will destroy you."

She laughed, a merry sound that froze my blood. "Bullshit, Major. You aren't about to get gay with laser beams near those things. Besides, you need me as much as you do Charlie."

"What do you mean?"

"These creatures communicate by dance. It's their equivalent of speech, it has to be a sophisticated kind of sign language, like hula."

"You can't know that."

"I *feel* it. I know it. Hell, how else do you communicate in airless space? Major Cox, I am the only qualified interpreter the human race has at the moment. Now will you kindly shut up so I can try to learn their 'language'?"

"I have no authority to—"

I said an extraordinary thing. I should have been gibbering, pleading with Shara to come back, even racing for a p-suit to *bring* her back. Instead I said, "She's right. Shut up, Cox."

"What are you trying to do?"

"Damn you, *don't waste her last effort.*"

He shut up.

Panzarella came in, shot McGillicuddy full of painkiller, and set his leg right there in the room, but I was oblivious. For over an hour I watched Shara watch the aliens. I watched them myself, in the silence of utter despair, and for the life of me I could not follow their dance. I strained my mind, trying to suck meaning from their crazy whirling, and failed. The best I could do to aid Shara was to record everything that happened, for a hypothetical posterity. Several times she cried out softly, small muffled exclamations, and I ached to call out to her in reply, but did not. With the last exclamation, she used her thrusters to bring her closer to the alien swarm, and hung there for a long time.

At last her voice came over the speaker, thick and slurred at first, as though she were talking in her sleep. "God, Charlie. Strange. So strange. I'm beginning to read them."

"How?"

"Every time I begin to understand a part of the dance, it . . . it brings us closer. Not telepathy, exactly. I just . . . know them better. Maybe it is telepathy, I don't know. By dancing what they feel, they give it enough intensity to make me understand. I'm getting about one concept in three. It's stronger up close."

Cox's voice was gentle but firm. "What have you learned, Shara?"

"That Tom and Charlie were right. They are warlike. At least there's a flavor of arrogance to them—conviction of superiority. Their dance is a challenging, a dare. Tell Tom they *do* use planets."

"What?"

"I think at one stage of their development they're corporeal, planetbound. Then when they have matured sufficiently, they . . . become these fireflies, like caterpillars becoming butterflies, and head out into space."

"Why?" from Cox.

"To find spawning grounds. They want Earth."

There was a silence lasting perhaps ten seconds. Then Cox spoke up quietly. "Back away, Shara. I'm going to see what lasers will do to them."

"No!" she cried, loud enough to make a really first-rate speaker distort.

"Shara, as Charlie pointed out to me, you are not only expendable, you are for all practical purposes expended."

"No!" This time it was me shouting.

"Major," Shara said urgently, "that's not the way. Believe me, they can dodge or withstand anything you or Earth can throw at them. I *know.*"

"Hell and damnation, woman," Cox said, "what do you want me to do? Let them have the first shot? There are vessels from four countries on their way right now."

"Major, wait. Give me time."

He began to swear, then cut off. "How much time?"

She made no direct reply. "If only this telepathy thing works in reverse . . . it must. I'm no more strange to them than they are to me. Probably less so; I get the idea they've been around. Charlie?"

"Yeah."

"This is a take."

I knew. I had known since I first saw her in open space on my monitor. And I knew what she needed now, from the faint trembling of her voice. It took everything I had, and I was only glad I had it to give. With extremely realistic good cheer, I said, "Break a leg, kid," and killed my mike before she could hear the sob that followed.

And she danced.

It began slowly, the equivalent of one-finger exercises, as she sought to establish a vocabulary of motion that the creatures could comprehend. *Can you see,* she seemed to say, *that* this *movement is a reaching, a yearning? Do you see that* this *is a spurning,* this *an unfolding,* that *a graduated elision of energy? Do you feel the ambiguity in the way I distort this arabesque, or that the tension can be resolved* so?

And it seemed that Shara was right, that they had infinitely more experience with disparate cultures than we, for they were superb linguists of motion. It occurred to me later that perhaps they had selected motion for communication because of its very universality. At any rate, as Shara's dance began to build, their own began to slow down perceptibly in speed and intensity, until at last they hung motionless in space, watching her.

Soon after that Shara must have decided that she had sufficiently defined her terms, at least well enough for pidgin communication—for now she began to dance in earnest. Before, she had used only her own muscles and the shifting masses of her limbs. Now she added thrusters, singly and in combination, moving within as well as in space. Her dance became a true dance: more than a collection of motions, a thing of substance and meaning. It was unquestionably the *Stardance*, just as she had choreographed it, as she had always intended to dance it. That it had something to say to utterly alien creatures, of man and his nature, was not at all a coincidence: It was the essential and ultimate statement of the greatest artist of her age, and it had something to say to God himself.

The camera lights struck silver from her p-suit, gold from the twin air tanks on her shoulders. To and fro against the black backdrop of space, she wove the intricacies of her dance, a leisurely movement that seemed somehow to leave echoes behind it. And the meaning of these great loops and whirls slowly became clear, drying my throat and clamping my teeth.

For her dance spoke of nothing more and nothing less than the tragedy of being alive, and being human. It spoke, most eloquently, of pain. It spoke, most knowingly, of despair. It spoke of the cruel humor of limitless ambition yoked to limited ability, of eternal hope invested in an ephemeral lifetime, of the driving need to try and create an inexorably predetermined future. It spoke of fear, and of hunger, and, most clearly, of the basic loneliness and alienation of the human animal. It described the universe through the eyes of man: a hostile environment, the embodiment of entropy, into which we are all thrown alone, forbidden by our nature to touch another mind save secondhand, by proxy. It spoke of the blind perversity which forces man to strive hugely for a peace which, once attained, becomes boredom. And it spoke of folly, of the terrible paradox by which man is simultaneously capable of reason and unreason, forever unable to cooperate even with himself.

It spoke of Shara and her life.

Again and again, cyclical statements of hope began, only to collapse into confusion and ruin. Again and again, cascades of energy strove for resolution, and found only frustration. All at once she launched into a pattern that seemed familiar, and in moments I recognized it: the closing movement of *Mass Is a Verb* recapitulated—not repeated but reprised, echoed, the Three Questions given a more terrible urgency by this new altar on which they were piled. And as before, it segued into that final relentless contraction, that ultimate drawing-inward of all energies. Her body became derelict, abandoned, drifting in space, the essence of her being withdrawn to her center and invisible.

The quiescent aliens stirred for the first time.

And suddenly she exploded, blossoming from her contraction not as a spring uncoils, but as a flower bursts from a seed. The force of her release flung her through the void as though she were tossed like a gull in a hurricane by galactic winds. Her center appeared to hurl itself through space and time, yanking her body into a new dance.

And the new dance said, *This is what it is to be human: to see the essential existential futility of all action, all striving—and to act, to strive. This is what it is to be human: to reach forever beyond your grasp. This is what it is to be human: to live forever or die trying. This is what it is to be human: to perpetually ask the unanswerable questions, in the hope that the asking of them will somehow hasten the day when they will be answered. This is what it is to be human: to strive in the face of the certainty of failure.*

This is what it is to be human: to persist.

It said all this with a soaring series of cyclical movements that held all the rolling majesty of grand symphony, as uniquely different from each other as snowflakes, and as similar. And the new dance *laughed,* and it laughed as much at tomorrow as it did at yesterday, and it laughed most of all at today.

For this is what it means to be human: to laugh at what another would call tragedy.

The aliens seemed to recoil from the ferocious energy, startled, awed, and faintly terrified by Shara's indomitable spirit. They seemed to wait for her dance to wane, for her to exhaust herself, and her laughter sounded on my speaker as she redoubled her efforts, became a pinwheel, a Catherine wheel. She changed the focus of her dance, began to dance *around* them, in pyrotechnic spatters of motion that came ever closer to the intangible spheroid which contained them. They cringed inward from her, huddling together in the center of the envelope, not so much physically threatened as cowed.

This, said her body, *is what it means to be human: to commit hara-kiri, with a smile, if it becomes needful.*

And before that terrible assurance, the aliens broke. Without warning fireflies and balloon vanished, gone, *elsewhere.*

I know that Cox and McGillicuddy were still alive, because I saw them afterward, and that means they were probably saying and doing things in my hearing and presence, but I neither heard nor saw them then; they were as dead to me as everything except Shara. I called out her name, and she approached the camera that was lit, until I could make out her face behind the plastic hood of her p-suit.

"We may be puny, Charlie," she puffed, gasping for breath. "But by Jesus we're tough."

"Shara—come on in now."

"You know I can't."

"Carrington'll *have* to give you a free-fall place to live now."

"A life of exile? For what? To dance? Charlie, *I haven't got anything more to say.*"

"Then I'll come out there."

"Don't be silly. Why? So you can hug a p-suit? Tenderly bump hoods one last time? Balls. It's a good exit so far—let's not blow it."

"Shara!" I broke completely, just caved in on myself and collapsed in great racking sobs.

"Charlie, listen now," she said softly, but with an urgency that reached me even in my despair. "Listen now, for I haven't much time. I have something to give you. I hoped you'd find it for yourself, but . . . will you listen?"

"Y—yes."

"Charlie, zero-g dance is going to get awful popular all of a sudden. I've opened the door. But you know how fads are, they'll bitch it all up unless you move fast. I'm leaving it in your hands."

"What . . . what are you talking about?"

"About you, Charlie. You're going to dance again."

Oxygen starvation, I thought. But she can't be that low on air already. "Okay. Sure thing."

"For God's sake stop humoring me—I'm straight, I tell you. You'd have seen it yourself if you weren't so damned stupid. Don't you understand? *There's nothing wrong with your leg in free fall!*"

My jaw dropped.

"Do you hear me, Charlie? You can dance again!"

"No," I said, and searched for a reason why not. "I . . . you can't . . . it's . . . dammit, the leg's not strong enough for inside work."

"Forget for the moment that inside work'll be less than half of what you do. Forget it and remember that smack in the nose you gave Carrington. Charlie, when you leaped over the desk, *you pushed off with your right leg.*"

I sputtered for a while and shut up.

"There you go, Charlie. My farewell gift. You know I've never been in love with you . . . but you must know that I've always loved you. Still do."

"I love you, Shara."

"So long, Charlie. Do it right."

And all four thrusters went off at once. I watched her go down. A while after she was too far to see, there was a long golden flame that arced above the face of the globe, waned, and then flared again as the air tanks went up.

There's a tired old hack plot about the threat of alien invasion unifying mankind overnight. It's about as realistic as Love Will Find a Way—if those damned fireflies ever come back, they'll find us just as disorganized as we were the last time. There you go.

Carrington, of course, tried to grab all the tapes and all the money—but neither Shara nor I had ever signed a contract, and her will was most explicit. So he tried to buy the judge, and he picked the wrong judge, and when it hit the papers and he saw how public and private opinion were going, he left Skyfac in a p-suit with no thrusters. I think he wanted to go the same way she had, but he was unused to EVA and let go too late. He was last seen heading in the general direction of Betelgeuse. The Skyfac board of directors picked a new man who was most anxious to wash off the stains, and he offered me continued use of all facilities.

And so I talked it over with Norrey, and she was free, and that's how the Shara Drummond Company of New Modern Dance was formed. We specialize in good dancers who couldn't cut it on Earth for one reason or another, and there are a surprising hell of a lot of them.

I enjoy dancing with Norrey. Together we're not as good as Shara was alone—but we mesh well. In spite of the obvious contraindications, I think our marriage is going to work.

That's the thing about us humans: We persist.

Joan D. Vinge

Maybe it's time to talk about women. (When isn't it time?)

In Hugo Winners, Volume One, the nine stories that were included were written by nine males, and I don't remember, at the time, being surprised at that. Sure, there were competent and well-thought-of women writers—Judith Merril springs to mind—but somehow such was the casual sexist attitude within science fiction that the field was accepted by one and all as primarily of interest to males. Women who wrote science fiction, or even merely read it, were considered somewhat anomalous.

Of the fourteen stories in Volume Two, one was written by a woman, Anne McCaffrey. Of the fifteen stories in Volume Three, two were written by Ursula K. Le Guin and one was written by James Tiptree, Jr., who, it turned out, was a woman.

Le Guin was, in my opinion, the breakthrough. For the first time, people began to speak of a woman as a first-magnitude star without any trace of condescension whatever. She could bear comparison with any male writer whatever. For a while there, I could actually feel the foundations of the Big Three tremble as she moved up to fourth place in some reader polls, and I covered my eyes waiting for the crash.

In Volume Four, we already have three women represented, three different women—James Tiptree, Jr. (again), Jeanne Robinson, and now Joan D. Vinge, making her first appearance. I promise you that before this volume is done there will be a fourth woman.

Mind you, we are not talking merely about the increasing number of women writers of science fiction; we are talking about the increasing number of Hugo-winning women writers of science fiction.

All this is a consummation devoutly to be wished (to put it in my own words).

For one thing, I have a personal sin I can never adequately atone for. One of my most embarrassing memories concerns my anti-feminist stance as a teenager. (Many teenage boys, especially those who feel totally inadequate with respect to teenage girls—as I did—compensate by developing a feeling of lordly superiority to these creatures they both long for and fear.) I remember writing teenage letters to *Astounding Science Fiction* denouncing the mere appearance of women in science fiction stories, and I even think that John Campbell may have carelessly printed one.

I have changed since. My fear of women vanished abruptly with my teens. I now get along with them easily and well, and I am a convinced feminist. I believe that the entrance of more and more women writers into the field will broaden and strengthen science fiction, give it added dimensions and delight, and be, in every way, a good thing.

To be sure, there are still differences. Women writers, I think, tend to avoid hard science fiction more than men do, but that is the same cultural phenomenon that pushes professional women into law and real estate rather than into science; and women who *do* enter science go into biology rather than into physics. It arises out of a supposed feminine distaste for mathematics, which I firmly believe is culturally induced and can be made to vanish with time.

9

EYES OF AMBER

The beggar woman shuffled up the silent evening street to the rear of Lord Chwiul's town house. She hesitated, peering up at the softly glowing towers, then clawed at the watchman's arm. "A word with you, master—"

"Don't touch me, hag!" The guard raised his spear butt in disgust.

A deft foot kicked free of the rags and snagged him off balance. He found himself sprawled on his back in the spring melt, the spear tip dropping toward his belly, guided by a new set of hands. He gaped, speechless. The beggar tossed an amulet onto his chest.

"Look at it, fool! I have business with your lord." The beggar woman stepped back, the spear tip tapped him impatiently.

The guard squirmed in the filth and wet, holding the amulet up close to his face in the poor light. "You . . . you are the one? You may pass—"

"Indeed!" Muffled laughter. "Indeed I may pass—for many things, in many places. The Wheel of Change carries us all." She lifted the spear. "Get up, fool . . . and no need to escort me, I'm expected."

The guard climbed to his feet, dripping and sullen, and stood back while she freed her wing membranes from the folds of cloth. He watched them glisten and spread as she gathered herself to leap effortlessly to the tower's entrance, twice his height above. He waited until she had vanished inside before he even dared to curse her.

"Lord Chwiul?"

"T'uupieh, I presume." Lord Chwiul leaned forward on the couch of fragrant mosses, peering into the shadows of the hall.

"Lady T'uupieh." T'uupieh strode forward into light, letting the ragged hood slide back from her face. She took a fierce pleasure in making no show of obeisance, in coming forward directly as nobility to nobility. The sensuous ripple of a hundred tiny *miih* hides underfoot made her callused feet tingle. *After so long, it comes back too easily . . .*

She chose the couch across the low, waterstone table from him, stretching languidly in her beggar's rags. She extended a finger claw and picked a juicy *kelet* berry from the bowl in the table's scroll-carven surface; let it slide into her mouth and down her throat, as she had done so often, so long ago. And then, at last, she glanced up, to measure his outrage.

"You dare to come to me in this manner—"

Satisfactory. *Yes, very . . . "I* did not come to you. You came to me . . . you sought my services." Her eyes wandered the room with affected casualness, taking in the elaborate frescoes that surfaced the waterstone walls even in this small, private room . . . particularly in this room? she wondered. How many midnight meetings, for what varied intrigues, were held in this room? Chwiul was not the wealthiest of his family or clan: and appearances of wealth and power counted in this city, in this world—for wealth and power were everything.

"I sought the services of T'uupieh the Assassin. I'm surprised to find that the Lady T'uupieh dared to accompany her here." Chwiul had regained his composure; she watched his breath frost, and her own, as he spoke.

"Where one goes, the other follows. We are inseparable. You should know that better than most, my lord." She watched his long, pale arm extend to spear several berries at once. Even though the nights were chill he wore only a body-wrapping tunic, which let him display the intricate scaling of jewels that danced and spiraled over his wing surfaces.

He smiled; she saw the sharp fangs protrude slightly. "Because my brother made the one into the other, when he seized your lands? I'm surprised you would come at all—how did you know you could trust me?" His movements were ungraceful; she remembered how the jewels dragged down fragile, translucent wing membranes and slender arms, until flight was impossible. Like every noble, Chwiul was normally surrounded by servants who answered his every whim. Incompetence, feigned or real, was one more trapping of power, one more indulgence that only the rich could afford. She was pleased that the jewels were not of high quality.

"I don't trust you," she said, "I trust only myself. But I have friends, who told me you were sincere enough—in this case. And of course, I did not come alone."

"Your outlaws?" Disbelief. "That would be no protection."

Calmly she separated the folds of cloth that held her secret companion at her side.

"It is true," Chwiul trilled softly. "They call you Demon's Consort!"

She turned the amber lens of the demon's precious eye so that it could see the room, as she had seen it, and then settled its gaze on Chwiul. He drew back slightly, fingering moss.

" 'A demon has a thousand eyes, and a thousand thousand torments for those who offend it.' " She quoted from the Book of Ngoss, whose rituals she had used to bind the demon to her.

Chwiul stretched nervously, as if he wanted to fly away. But he only said, "Then I think we understand each other. And I think I have made a good choice: I know how well you have served the Overlord, and other court members . . . I want you to kill someone for me."

"Obviously."

"I want you to kill Klovhiri."

T'uupieh started, very slightly. "You surprise me in return, Lord Chwiul. Your own brother?" *And the usurper of my lands. How I have ached to kill him, slowly, so slowly, with my own hands. . . . But always he is too well guarded.*

"And your sister too—my lady." Faint overtones of mockery. "I want his whole family eliminated; his mate, his children . . ."

Klovhiri . . . and Ahtseet. Ahtseet, her own younger sister, who had been her closest companion since childhood, her only family since their parents had died. Ahtseet, whom she had cherished and protected; dear, conniving, traitorous little Ahtseet—who could forsake pride and decency and family honor to mate willingly with the man who had robbed them of everything . . . Anything to keep the family lands, Ahtseet had shrilled; anything to keep her position. But that was not the way! Not by surrendering; but by striking back—T'uupieh became aware that Chwiul was watching her reaction with unpleasant interest. She fingered the dagger at her belt.

"Why?" She laughed, wanting to ask, *"How?"*

"That should be obvious. I'm tired of coming second. I want what he has—your lands, and all the rest. I want him out of my way, and I don't want anyone else left with a better claim to his inheritance than I have."

"Why not do it yourself? Poison them, perhaps . . . it's been done before."

"No. Klovhiri has too many friends, too many loyal clansmen, too much influence with the Overlord. It has to be an 'accidental' murder. And no one would be better suited than you, my lady, to do it for me."

T'uupieh nodded vaguely, assessing. No one could be better chosen for a desire to succeed than she . . . and also, for a position from which to strike. All she had lacked until now was the opportunity. From the time she had been dispossessed, through the fading days of autumn and the endless winter—for nearly a third of her life now—she had haunted the wild swamp and fenland of her estate. She had gathered a few faithful servants, a few malcontents, a few cutthroats, to harry and murder Klovhiri's retainers, ruin his phib nets, steal from his snares and poach her own game. And for survival, she had taken to robbing whatever travelers took the roads that passed through her lands.

Because she was still nobility, the Overlord had at first tolerated, and then secretly encouraged, her banditry: Many wealthy foreigners traveled the routes that crossed her estate, and for a certain commission, he allowed her to attack them with impunity. It was a sop, she knew, thrown to her because he had let his favorite, Klovhiri, have her lands. But she used it to curry what favor she could, and after a time the Overlord had begun to bring her more discreet and profitable business—the elimination of certain enemies. And so she had become an assassin as well—and found that the calling was not so very different from that of noble: both required nerve, and cunning, and an utter lack of compunction. And because she was T'uupieh, she had succeeded admirably. But because of her vendetta, the rewards had been small . . . until now.

"You do not answer," Chwiul was saying. "Does that mean your nerve fails you, in kith-murder, where mine does not?"

She laughed sharply. "That you say it proves twice that your judgment is poorer than mine. . . . No, my nerve does not fail me. Indeed, my blood burns with desire! But I hadn't thought to lay Klovhiri under the ice just to give my lands to his brother. Why should I do that favor for you?"

"Because obviously you cannot do it alone. Klovhiri hasn't managed to have you killed, in all the time you've plagued him; which is a testament to your skill. But you've made him too wary—you can't get near him, when he keeps himself so well protected. You need the cooperation of someone who has his trust—someone like myself. I can make him yours."

"And what will be my reward, if I accept? Revenge is sweet; but revenge is not enough."

"I will pay what you ask."

"My estate." She smiled.

"Even you are not so naïve—"

"No." She stretched a wing toward nothing in the air. "I am not so naïve. I know its value . . ." The memory of a golden-clouded summer's day caught her—of soaring, soaring, on the warm updrafts above the streaming lake . . . seeing the fragile rose-red of the manor towers spearing light far off above the windswept tide of the trees . . . the saffron and crimson and aquamarine of ammonia pools, bright with dissolved metals, that lay in the gleaming melt-surface of her family's land, the land that stretched forever, like the summer . . . "I know its value." Her voice hardened. "And that Klovhiri is still the Overlord's pet. As you say, Klovhiri has many powerful friends, and they will become your friends when he dies. I need more strength, more wealth, before I can buy enough influence to hold what is mine again. The odds are not in my favor—now."

"You are carved from ice, T'uupieh. I like that." Chwiul leaned forward. His amorphous red eyes moved along her outstretched body; trying to guess what lay concealed beneath the rags in the shadowy foxfire-light of the room. His eyes came back to her face.

She showed him neither annoyance nor amusement. "I like no man who likes that in me."

"Not even if it meant regaining your estate?"

"As a mate of yours?" Her voice snapped like a frozen branch. "My lord—I have just about decided to kill my sister for doing as much. I would sooner kill myself."

He shrugged, lying back on the couch. "As you wish . . . ." He waved a hand in dismissal. "Then what will it take to be rid of my brother—and of you as well?"

"Ah." She nodded, understanding more. "You wish to buy my services, and to buy me off, too. That may not be so easy to do. But—" *But I will make the pretense, for now.* She speared berries from the bowl in the tabletop, watched the silky sheet of emerald-tinted ammonia water that curtained one wall. It dropped from heights within the tower into a tiny plunge basin, with a music that would blur conversation for anyone who tried to listen outside. Discretion, and beauty. . . . The musky fragrance of the mossy couch brought back her childhood suddenly, disconcertingly: the memory of lying in a soft bed, on a soft spring night. . . . "But as the seasons change, change moves me in new directions. Back into the city, perhaps. I like your tower, Lord Chwiul. It combines discretion and beauty."

"Thank you."

"Give it to me, and I'll do what you ask."

Chwiul sat up, frowning. "My town house!" Recovering, "Is that all you want?"

She spread her fingers, studied the vestigial webbing between them. "I realize it is rather modest." She closed her hand. "But considering what satisfaction will come from earning it, it will suffice. And you will not need it, once I succeed."

"No . . ." He relaxed somewhat. "I suppose not. I will scarcely miss it after I have your lands."

She let it pass. "Well then, we are agreed. Now, tell me, where is the key to Klovhiri's lock? What is your plan for delivering him —and his family—into my hands?"

"You are aware that your sister and the children are visiting here, in my house, tonight? And that Klovhiri will return before the new day?"

"I am aware." She nodded, with more casualness than she felt; seeing that Chwiul was properly, if silently, impressed at her nerve in coming here. She drew her dagger from its sheath beside the demon's amber eye and stroked the serrated blade of waterstone-impregnated wood. "You wish me to slit their throats, while they sleep under your very roof?" She managed the right blend of incredulity.

"No!" Chwiul frowned again. "What sort of fool do you—" He broke off. "With the new day, they will be returning to the estate by the usual route. I have promised to escort them, to ensure their safety along the way. There will also be a guide, to lead us through the bogs. But the guide will make a mistake . . ."

"And I will be waiting." T'uupieh's eyes brightened. During the winter the wealthy used sledges for travel on long journeys—preferring to be borne over the frozen melt by membranous sails, or dragged by slaves where the surface of the ground was rough and crumpled. But as spring came and the surface of the ground began to dissolve, treacherous sinks and pools opened like blossoms to swallow the unwary. Only an experienced guide could read the surfaces, tell sound waterstone from changeable ammonia-water melt. "Good," she said softly. "Yes, very good. . . . Your guide will see them safely foundered in some slush-hole, and then I will snare them like changeling phibs."

"Exactly. But I want to be there when you do; I want to watch. I'll make some excuse to leave the group, and meet you in the swamp. The guide will mislead them only if he hears my signal."

"As you wish. You've paid well for the privilege. But come alone. My followers need no help, and no interference." She sat up, let her long, webbed feet down to rest again on the sensuous hides of the rug.

"And if you think that I'm a fool, and playing into your hands myself, consider this. You will be the obvious suspect when Klovhiri is murdered. I'll be the only witness who can swear to the Overlord that your outlaws weren't the attackers. Keep that in mind."

She nodded. "I will."

"How will I find you, then?"

"You will not. My thousand eyes will find you." She rewrapped the demon's eye in its pouch of rags.

Chwiul looked vaguely disconcerted. "Will—*it* take part in the attack?"

"It may, or it may not; as it chooses. Demons are not bound to the Wheel of Change like you and me. But you will surely meet it face to face—although it has no face—if you come." She brushed the pouch at her side. "Yes—do keep in mind that I have my safeguards too in this agreement. A demon never forgets."

She stood up at last, gazing once more around the room. "I shall be comfortable here." She glanced back at Chwiul. "I will look for you, come the new day."

"Come the new day." He rose, his jeweled wings catching light.

"No need to escort me. I shall be discreet." She bowed, as an equal, and started toward the shadowed hall. "I shall definitely get rid of your watchman. He doesn't know a lady from a beggar."

"The Wheel turns once more for me, my demon. My life in the swamps will end with Klovhiri's life. I shall move into town . . . and I shall be lady of my manor again, when the fishes sit in the trees!"

T'uupieh's alien face glowed with malevolent joy as she turned away, on the display screen above the computer terminal. Shannon Wyler leaned back in his seat, finished typing his translation, and pulled off the wire headset. He smoothed his long, blond, slicked-back hair, the habitual gesture helping him reorient to his surroundings. When T'uupieh spoke he could never maintain the objectivity he needed to help him remember he was still on Earth, and not really on Titan, orbiting Saturn, some fifteen hundred million kilometers away. *T'uupieh, whenever I think I love you, you decide to cut somebody's throat. . . .*

He nodded vaguely at the congratulatory murmurs of the staff and technicians, who literally hung on his every word waiting for new information. They began to thin out behind him, as the computer reproduced copies of the transcript. Hard to believe he'd been doing this for over a year now. He looked up at his concert posters on the wall, with nostalgia but no regret.

Someone was phoning Marcus Reed: he sighed, resigned.

" 'Ven the fishes sit in the trees'? Are you being sarcastic?"

He looked over his shoulder at Dr. Garda Bach's massive form. "Hi, Garda. Didn't hear you come in."

She glanced up from a copy of the translation, tapped him lightly on the shoulder with her forked walking stick. "I know, dear boy. You never hear anything when T'uupieh speaks. But what do you mean by this?"

"On Titan that's summer—when the triphibians metamorphose for the third time. So she means maybe five years from now, our time."

"Ah! Of course. The old brain is not what it was . . ." She shook her gray-white head; her black cloak swirled out melodramatically.

He grinned, knowing she didn't mean a word of it. "Maybe learning Titanese on top of fifty other languages is the straw that breaks the camel's back."

"Ja . . . ja . . . maybe it is . . ." She sank heavily into the next seat over, already lost in the transcript. He had never, he thought, expected to like the old broad so well. He had become aware of her Presence while he studied linguistics at Berkeley—she was the *grande dame* of linguistic studies, dating back to the days when there had still been unrecorded languages here on Earth. But her skill at getting her name in print and her face on television, as an expert on what everybody "really meant," had convinced him that her true talent lay in merchandising. Meeting her at last, in person, hadn't changed his mind about that; but it had convinced him forever that she knew her stuff about cultural linguistics. And that, in turn, had convinced him her accent was a total fraud. But despite the flamboyance, or maybe even because of it, he found that her now-archaic views on linguistics were much closer to his own feelings about communication than the views of either one of his parents.

Garda sighed. "Remarkable, Shannon! You are simply remarkable—your feel for a wholly alien language amazes me. Whatever vould ve have done if you had not come to us?"

"Done without, I expect." He savored the special pleasure that came of being admired by someone he respected. He looked down again at the computer console, at the two shining green-lit plates of plastic thirty centimeters on a side that together gave him the versatility of a virtuoso violinist and a typist with a hundred thousand keys: His link to T'uupieh, his voice—the new IBM synthesizer, whose touch-sensitive control plates could be manipulated to re-create the impossible complexities of her language. God's gift to the world of linguistics . . . except that it required the sensitivity and inspiration of a musician to fully use its range.

He glanced up again and out the window, at the now familiar fog-shrouded skyline of Coos Bay. Since very few linguists were musicians, their resistance to the synthesizer had been like a brick wall. The old guard of the aging New Wave—which included His Father the Professor and His Mother the Communications Engineer—still clung to a fruitless belief in mathematical computer translation. They still struggled with ungainly programs weighed down by endless morpheme lists that supposedly would someday generate any message in a given language. But even after years of refinement, computer-generated translations were still uselessly crude and sloppy.

At graduate school there had been no new languages to seek out, and no permission for him to use the synthesizer to explore the old ones. And so—after a final, bitter family argument—he had quit graduate school. He had taken his belief in the synthesizer into the world of his second love, music; into a field where, he hoped, real communication still had some value. Now, at twenty-four, he was Shann the Music Man, the musician's musician, a hero to an immense generation of aging fans and a fresh new generation that had inherited their love for the ever-changing music called "rock." And neither of his parents had willingly spoken to him in years.

"No false modesty," Garda was chiding. "What could we have done without you? You yourself have complained enough about your mother's methods. You know we would not have a tenth of the information about Titan we've gained from T'uupieh if she had gone on using that damned computer translation."

Shannon frowned faintly, at the sting of secret guilt. "Look, I know I've made some cracks—and I meant most of them—but I'd never have gotten off the ground if she hadn't done all the preliminary analysis before I even came." His mother had already been on the mission staff, having worked for years at NASA on the esoterics of computer communication with satellites and space probes; and because of her linguistic background, she had been made head of the newly pulled-together staff of communications specialists by Marcus Reed, the Titan project director. She had been in charge of the initial phonic analysis, using the computer to compress the alien voice range into one audible to humans, then breaking up the complex sounds into more, and simpler, human phones . . . she had identified phonemes, separated morphemes, fitted them into a grammatical framework, and assigned English sound equivalents to it all. Shannon had watched her on the early TB interviews, looking unhappy and ill at ease while Reed held court for the spellbound press. But what Dr. Wyler the Communications Engineer had had to say, at last, had held them on the edge of his seat; and unable to resist, he had taken the next plane to Coos Bay.

"Vell, I meant no offense," Garda said. "Your mother is obviously a skilled engineer. But she needs a little more—flexibility."

"You're telling me." He nodded ruefully. "She'd still love to see the synthesizer drop through the floor. She's been out of joint ever since I got here. At least Reed appreciates my 'value.' " Reed had welcomed him like a long-lost son when he first arrived at the institute. . . . Wasn't he a skilled linguist as well as an inspired musician, didn't he have some time between gigs, wouldn't he like to extend his visit, and get an insider's view of his mother's work? He had agreed, modestly, to all three—and then the television cameras and reporters had sprung up as if on cue, and he understood clearly enough that they were not there to record the visit of Dr. Wyler's kid, but Shann the Music Man.

But he had gotten his first session with a voice from another world. And with one hearing, he had become an addict . . . because their speech was music. Every phoneme was formed of two or three superposed sounds, and every morpheme was a blend of phonemes, flowing together like water. They spoke in chords, and the result was a choir, crystal bells ringing, the shattering of glass chandeliers . . .

And so he had stayed on and on, at first only able to watch his mother and her assistants with agonized frustration: His mother's computer-analysis methods had worked well in the initial transphonemicizing of T'uupieh's speech, and they had learned enough very quickly to send back clumsy responses using the probe's echo-locating device, to keep T'uupieh's interest from wandering. But typing input at a keyboard, and expecting even the most sophisticated programming to transform it into another language, still would not work even for known human languages.

And he knew, with an almost religious fervor, that the synthesizer had been designed for just this miracle of communication; and that he alone could use it to capture directly the nuances and subtleties machine translation could never supply. He had tried to approach his mother about letting him use it, but she had turned him down flat: "This is a research center, not a recording studio."

And so he had gone over her head to Reed, who had been delighted. And when at last he felt his hands moving across the warm, faintly tingling plates of light, tentatively re-creating the speech of another world, he had known that he had been right all along. He had let his music commitments go to hell, without a regret, almost with relief, as he slid back into the field that had always come first.

Shannon watched the display, where T'uupieh had settled back with comfortable familiarity against the probe's curving side, half obscuring his view of the camp. Fortunately both she and her followers treated the probe with obsessive care, even when they dragged it from place to place as they constantly moved to camp. He wondered what would have happened if they had inadvertently set off its automatic defense system—which had been designed to protect it from aggressive animals; which delivered an electric shock that varied from merely painful to fatal. And he wondered what would have happened if the probe and its "eyes" hadn't fit so neatly into T'uupieh's beliefs about demons. The idea that he might never have known her, or heard her voice. . . .

More than a year had passed already since he, and the rest of the world, had heard the remarkable news that intelligent life existed on Saturn's major moon. He had no memory at all of the first two flybys to Titan, back in '79 and '81—although he could clearly remember the 1990 orbiter that had caught fleeting glimpses of the surface through Titan's swaddling of opaque, golden clouds. But the handful of miniprobes it had dropped had proved that Titan profited from the same "greenhouse effect" that made Venus a boiling hell. And even though the seasonal temperatures never rose above two hundred degrees Kelvin, the few photographs had shown, unquestionably, that life existed there. The discovery of life, after so many disappointments throughout the rest of the solar system, had been enough to initiate another probe mission, one designed to actually send back data from Titan's surface.

That probe had discovered a life form with human intelligence . . . or rather, the life form had discovered the probe. And T'uupieh's discovery had turned a potentially ruined mission into a success: The probe had been designed with a main, immobile data processing unit, and ten "eyes," or subsidiary units, that were to be scattered over Titan's surface to relay information. The release of the subsidiary probes during landing had failed, however, and all of the "eyes" had come down within a few square kilometers of its own landing in the uninhabited marsh. But T'uupieh's self-interested fascination and willingness to appease her "demon" had made up for everything.

Shannon looked up at the flat wall-screen again, at T'uupieh's incredible, unhuman face—a face that was as familiar now as his own in the mirror. She sat waiting with her incredible patience for a reply from her "demon": She would have been waiting for over an hour by the time her transmission reached him across the gap between their worlds; and she would have to wait as long again, while they discussed a response and he created the new translation. She spent more time now with the probe than she did with her own people. *The loneliness of command* . . . he smiled. The almost flat profile of her moon-white face turned slightly toward him—toward the camera lens; her own fragile mouth smiled gently, not quite revealing her long, sharp teeth. He could see one red pupilless eye, and the crescent nose-slit that half ringed it; her frosty cyanide breath shone blue-white, illuminated by the ghostly haloes of St. Elmo's fire that wreathed the probe all through Titan's interminable eight-day nights. He could see balls of light hanging like Japanese lanterns on the drooping snarl of icebound branches in a distant thicket.

It was unbelievable . . . or perfectly logical; depending on which biological expert was talking . . . that the nitrogen- and ammonia-based life on Titan should have so many analogs with oxygen- and water-based life on Earth. But T'uupieh was not human, and the music of her words time and again brought him messages that made a mockery of any ideals he tried to harbor about her and their relationship. So far in the past year she had assassinated eleven people, and with her outlaws had murdered God knew how many more, in the process of robbing them. The only reason she cooperated with the probe, she had as much as said, was because only a demon had a more bloody reputation; only a demon could command her respect. And yet, from what little she had been able to show them and tell them about the world she lived in, she was no better or no worse than anyone else—only more competent. Was she a prisoner of an age, a culture, where blood was something to be spilled instead of shared? Or was it something biologically innate that let her philosophize brutality, and brutalize philosophy—

Beyond T'uupieh, around the nitrogen campfire, some of her outlaws had begun to sing—the alien folk melodies that in translation were no more than simple, repetitious verse. But heard in their pure, untranslated form, they layered harmonic complexity on complexity: musical speech in a greater pattern of song. Shannon reached out and picked up the headset again, forgetting everything else. He had had a dream, once, where he had been able to sing in chords—

Using the long periods of waiting between their communications, he had managed, some months back, to record a series of the alien songs himself, using the synthesizer. They had been spare and uncomplicated versions compared to the originals, because even now his skill with the language couldn't help wanting to make them his own. Singing was a part of religious ritual, T'uupieh had told him. "But they don't sing because they're religious; they sing because they like to sing." Once, privately, he had played one of his own human compositions for her on the synthesizer, and transmitted it. She had stared at him (or into the probe's golden eye) with stony, if tolerant, silence. She never sang herself, although he had sometimes heard her softly harmonizing. He wondered what she would say if he told her that her outlaws' songs had already earned him his first Platinum Record. Nothing, probably . . . but knowing her, if he could make the concepts clear, she would probably be heartily in favor of the exploitation.

He had agreed to donate the profits of the record to NASA (and although he had intended that all along, it had annoyed him to be asked by Reed), with the understanding that the gesture would be kept quiet. But somehow, at the next press conference, some reporter had known just what question to ask, and Reed had spilled it all. And his mother, when asked about her son's sacrifice, had murmured, "Saturn is becoming a three-ring circus," and left him wondering whether to laugh or swear.

Shannon pulled a crumpled pack of cigarettes out of the pocket of his caftan and lit one. Garda glanced up, sniffing, and shook her head. She didn't smoke, or anything else (although he suspected she ran around with men), and she had given him a long, wasted lecture about it, ending with "Vell, at least they're not tobacco." He shook his head back at her.

"What do you think about T'uupieh's latest victims, then?" Garda flourished the transcript, pulling his thoughts back. "Vill she kill her own sister?"

He exhaled slowly around the words "Tune in tomorrow, for our next exciting episode! I think Reed will love it; that's what I think." He pointed at the newspaper lying on the floor beside his chair. "Did you notice we've slipped to page three?" T'uupieh had fed the probe's hopper some artifacts made of metal—a thing she had said was only known to the "Old Ones"; and the scientific speculation about the existence of a former technological culture had boosted interest in the probe to front-page status again. But even news of that discovery couldn't last forever . . . "Gotta keep those ratings up, folks. Keep those grants and donations rolling in."

Garda clucked. "Are you angry at Reed, or at T'uupieh?"

He shrugged dispiritedly. "Both of 'em. I don't see why she won't kill her own sister—" He broke off, as the subdued noise of the room's numerous project workers suddenly intensified, and concentrated: Marcus Reed was making an entrance, simultaneously solving everyone else's problems, as always. Shannon marveled at Reed's energy, even while he felt something like disgust at the way he spent it. Reed exploited everyone, and everything, with charming cynicism, in the ultimate hype for Science—and watching him at work had gradually drained away whatever respect and goodwill Shannon had brought with him to the project. He knew that his mother's reaction to Reed was close to his own, even though she had never said anything to him about it; it surprised him that there was something they could still agree on.

"Dr. Reed—"

"Excuse me, Dr. Reed, but—"

His mother was with Reed now as they all came down the room; looking tight-lipped and resigned, her lab coat buttoned up as if she was trying to avoid contamination. Reed was straight out of *Manstyle* magazine, as usual. Shannon glanced down at his own loose gray caftan and jeans, which had led Garda to remark, "Are you planning to enter a monastery?"

". . . we'd really like to—"

"Senator Foyle wants you to call him back—"

". . . yes, all right; and tell Dinocci he can go ahead and have the probe run another sample. Yes, Max, I'll get to that . . ." Reed gestured for quiet as Shannon and Garda turned in their seats to face him. "Well, I've just heard the news about our 'Robin Hood's' latest hard contract."

Shannon grimaced quietly. He had been the one who had first, facetiously, called T'uupieh "Robin Hood." Reed had snapped it up and dubbed her ammonia swamps "Sherwood Forest" for the press: After the facts of her bloodthirsty body counts began to come out, and it even began to look like she was collaborating with "the Sheriff of Nottingham," some reporter had pointed out that T'uupieh bore no more resemblance to Robin Hood than she did to Rima the Bird-Girl. Reed had said, laughing, "Well, after all, the only reason Robin Hood stole from the rich was because the poor didn't have any money!" That, Shannon thought, had been the real beginning of the end of his tolerance.

". . . this could be used as an opportunity to show the world graphically the harsh realities of life on Titan—"

"Ein Moment," Garda said. "You're telling us you want to let the public watch this atrocity, Marcus?" Up until now they had never released to the media the graphic tapes of actual murders; even Reed had not been able to argue that that would have served any real scientific purpose.

"No, he's not, Garda." Shannon glanced up as his mother began to speak. "Because we all agreed that we would *not* release any tapes just for purposes of sensationalism."

"Carly, you know that the press has been after me to release those other tapes, and that I haven't, because we all voted against it. But I feel this situation is different—a demonstration of a unique, alien sociocultural condition. What do you think, Shann?"

Shannon shrugged, irritated and not covering it up. "I don't know what's so damn unique about it: a snuff flick is a snuff flick, wherever you film it. I think the idea stinks." Once, at a party while he was still in college, he had watched a film of an unsuspecting victim being hacked to death. The film, and what all films like it said about the human race, had made him sick to his stomach.

"*Ach*—there's more truth than poetry in that!" Garda said.

Reed frowned, and Shannon saw his mother raise her eyebrows.

"I have a better idea." He stubbed out his cigarette in the ashtray under the panel. "Why don't you let me try to talk her out of it?" As he said it, he realized how much he wanted to try; and how much success could mean, to his belief in communication—to his image of T'uupieh's people and maybe his own.

They both showed surprise this time. "How?" Reed said.

"Well . . . I don't know yet. Just let me talk to her, try to really communicate with her, find out how she thinks and what she feels; without all the technical garbage getting in the way for a while."

His mother's mouth thinned, he saw the familiar worry crease form between her brows. "Our job here is to collect that 'garbage.' Not to begin imposing moral values on the universe. We have too much to do as it is."

"What's 'imposing' about trying to stop a murder?" A certain light came into Garda's faded blue eyes. "Now that has real . . . social implications. Think about it, Marcus—"

Reed nodded, glancing at the patiently attentive faces that still ringed him. "Yes—it does. A great deal of human interest . . ." Answering nods and murmurs. "All right, Shann. There are about three days left before morning comes again in Sherwood Forest. You can have them to yourself, to work with T'uupieh. The press will want reports on your progress . . ." He glanced at his watch, and nodded toward the door, already turning away. Shannon looked away from his mother's face as she moved past him.

"Good luck, Shann." Reed threw it back at him absently. "I

wouldn't count on reforming Robin Hood; but you can still give it a good try."

Shannon hunched down in his chair, frowning, and turned back to the panel. "In your next incarnation may you come back as a toilet."

T'uupieh was confused. She sat on the hummock of clammy waterstone beside the captive demon, waiting for it to make a reply. In the time that had passed since she'd found it in the swamp, she had been surprised again and again by how little its behavior resembled all the demon lore she knew. And tonight. . . .

She jerked, startled, as its grotesque, clawed arm came to life suddenly and groped among the icy-silver spring shoots pushing up through the melt at the hummock's foot. The demon did many incomprehensible things (which was fitting) and it demanded offerings of meat and vegetation and even stone—even, sometimes, some part of the loot she had taken from passersby. She had given it those things gladly, hoping to win its favor and its aid . . . she had even, somewhat grudgingly, given it precious metal ornaments of Old Ones which she had stripped from a whining foreign lord. The demon had praised her effusively for that; all demons hoarded metal, and she supposed that it must need metals to sustain its strength: its domed carapace—gleaming now with the witch-fire that always shrouded it at night—was an immense metal jewel the color of blood. And yet she had always heard that demons preferred the flesh of men and women. But when she had tried to stuff the wing of the foreign lord into its maw it had spit him out with a few dripping scratches, and told her to let him go. Astonished, she had obeyed, and let the fool run off screaming to be lost in the swamp.

And then, tonight—"You are going to kill your sister, T'uupieh," it had said to her tonight, "and two innocent children. How do you feel about that?" She had spoken what had come first, and truthfully, into her mind: "That the new day cannot come soon enough for me! I have waited so long—too long—to take my revenge on Klovhiri! My sister and her brats are a part of his foulness, better slain before they multiply." She had drawn her dagger and driven it into the mushy melt, as she would drive it into their rotten hearts.

The demon had been silent again, for a long time; as it always was. (The lore said that demons were immortal, and so she had always supposed that it had no reason to make a quick response, she had wished, sometimes, it would show more consideration for her own mortality.) Then at last it had said, in its deep voice filled with alien shadows, "But the children have harmed no one. And Ahtseet is your only sister, she and the children are your only blood kin. She has shared your life. You say that once you"—the demon paused, searching its limited store of words—"cherished her for that. Doesn't what she once meant to you mean anything now? Isn't there any love left to slow your hand as you raise it against her?"

"Love!" she had said, incredulous. "What speech is that, O Soulless One? You mock me—" Sudden anger had bared her teeth. "Love is a toy, my demon, and I have put my toys behind me. And so has Ahtseet . . . she is no kin of mine. Betrayer, betrayer!" The word hissed like the dying embers of the campfire; she had left the demon in disgust, to rake in the firepit's insulating layer of sulphury ash, and lay on a few more soggy branches. Y'lirr, her second-in-command, had smiled at her from where he lay in his cloak on the ground, telling her that she should sleep. But she had ignored him, and gone back to her vigil on the hill.

Even though this night was chill enough to recrystallize the slowly thawing limbs of the *safilil* trees, the equinox was long past, and now the fine mist of golden polymer rain presaged the golden days of the approaching summer. T'uupieh had wrapped herself more closely in her own cloak and pulled up the hood, to keep the clinging, sticky mist from fouling her wings and ear membranes; and she had remembered last summer, her first summer, which she would always remember . . . Ahtseet had been a clumsy, flapping infant as that first summer began, and T'uupieh the child had thought her new sister was silly and useless. But summer slowly transformed the land, and filled her wondering eyes with miracles; and her sister was transformed too, into a playful, easily led companion who could follow her into adventure. Together they learned to use their wings, and to use the warm updrafts to explore the boundaries and the freedoms of their heritage.

And now, as spring moved into summer once again, T'uupieh clung fiercely to the vision, not wanting to lose it, or to remember that childhood's sweet, unreasoning summer would never come again, even though the seasons returned; for the Wheel of Change swept on, and there was never a turning back. No turning back . . . she had become an adult by the summer's end, and she would never soar with a child's light-winged freedom again. And Ahtseet would never do anything again. Little Ahtseet, always just behind her, like her own fair shadow . . . *No! She would not regret it! She would be glad—*

"Did you ever think, T'uupieh," the demon had said suddenly, "that it is wrong to kill anyone? You don't want to die—no one wants to die too soon. Why should they have to? Have you ever wondered what it would be like if you could change the world into one where you—where you treated everyone else as you wanted them to treat you, and they treated you the same? If everyone could—live and let live . . ." Its voice slipped into blurred overtones that she couldn't hear.

She had waited, but it said no more, as if it were waiting for her to consider what she'd already heard. But there was no need to think about what was obvious: "Only the dead 'live and let live.' I treat everyone as I expect them to treat me; or I would quickly join the peaceful dead! Death is a part of life. We die when fate wills it, and when fate wills it, we kill.

"You are immortal, you have the power to twist the Wheel, to turn destiny as you want. You may toy with idle fantasies, even make them real, and never suffer the consequences. We have no place for such things in our small lives. No matter how much I might try to be like you, in the end I die like all the rest. We can change nothing, our lives are preordained. That is the way among mortals." And she had fallen silent again, filled with unease at this strange wandering of the demon's mind. But she must not let it prey on her nerves. Day would come very soon, she must not be nervous; she must be totally in control when she led this attack on Klovhiri. No emotion must interfere . . . no matter how much she yearned to feel Klovhiri's blood spill bluely over her hands, and her sister's, and the children's . . . Ahtseet's brats would never feel the warm wind lift them into the sky; or plunge, as she had, into the depths of her rainbow-petaled pools; or see her towers spearing light far off among the trees. *Never! Never!*

She had caught her breath sharply then, as a fiery pinwheel burst through the wall of tangled brush behind her, tumbling past her head into the clearing of the camp. She had watched it circle the fire—spitting sparks, hissing furiously in the quiet air—three and a half times before it spun on into the darkness. No sleeper wakened, and only two stirred. She clutched one of the demon's hard, angular legs, shaken; knowing that the circling of the fire had been a portent . . . but not knowing what it meant. The burning silence it left behind oppressed her; she stirred restlessly, stretching her wings.

And utterly unmoved, the demon had begun to drone its strange, dark thoughts once more, "Not all you have heard about demons is true. We can suffer"—it groped for words again—"the—consequences of our acts; among ourselves we fight and die. We *are* vicious, and brutal, and pitiless: But we don't like to be that way. We want to change into something better, more merciful, more forgiving. We fail more than we win . . . but we believe we *can* change. And you are more like us than you realize. You can draw a line between—trust and betrayal, right and wrong, good and evil; you can choose never to cross that line—"

"How, then?" She had twisted to face the amber eye as large as her own head, daring to interrupt the demon's speech. "How can one droplet change the tide of the sea? It's impossible! The world melts and flows, it rises into mist, it returns again to ice, only to melt and flow once more. A wheel has no beginning, and no end; no starting place. There is no 'good,' no 'evil' . . . no line between them. Only acceptance. If you were a mortal, I would think you were mad!"

She had turned away again, her claws digging shallow runnels in the polymer-coated stone as she struggled for self-control. *Madness. . . .* Was it possible? she wondered suddenly. Could her demon have gone mad? How else could she explain the thoughts it had put into her mind? Insane thoughts, bizarre, suicidal . . . but thoughts that would haunt her.

Or, could there be a method in its madness? She knew that

treachery lay at the heart of every demon. It could simply be lying to her when it spoke of trust and forgiveness—knowing she must be ready for tomorrow, hoping to make her doubt herself, make her fail. Yes, that was much more reasonable. But then, why was it so hard to believe that this demon would try to ruin her most cherished goals? After all, she held it prisoner; and though her spells kept it from tearing her apart, perhaps it still sought to tear apart her mind, to drive her mad instead. Why shouldn't it hate her, and delight in her torment, and hope for her destruction?

How could it be so ungrateful! She had almost laughed aloud at her own resentment, even as it formed the thought. As if a demon ever knew gratitude! But ever since the day she had netted it in spells in the swamp, she had given it nothing but the best treatment. She had fetched and carried, and made her fearful followers do the same. She had given it the best of everything —anything it desired. At its command she had sent out searchers to look for its scattered eyes, and it had allowed—even encouraged—her to use the eyes as her own, as watchers and protectors. She had even taught it to understand her speech (for it was as ignorant as a baby about the world of mortals) when she realized that it wanted to communicate with her. She had done all those things to win his favor—because she knew that it had come into her hands for a reason; and if she could gain its cooperation, there would be no one who would dare to cross her.

She had spent every spare hour in keeping it company, feeding its curiosity—and her own—as she fed its jeweled maw . . . until gradually those conversations with the demon had become an end in themselves, a treasure worth the sacrifice of even precious metals. Even the constant waiting for its alien mind to ponder her questions and answers had never tired her, she had come to enjoy sharing even the simple pleasure of its silences, and resting in the warm amber light of its gaze.

T'uupieh looked down at the finely woven fiber belt which passed through the narrow slits between her side and wing and held her tunic to her. She fingered the heavy, richly-amber beads that decorated it—metal-dyed melt trapped in polished waterstone by the jewelsmith's secret arts—that reminded her always of her demon's thousand eyes. *Her* demon—

She looked away again, toward the fire, toward the cloak-wrapped forms of her outlaws. Since the demon had come to her she had felt both the physical and emotional space that she had always kept between herself as leader and her band of followers gradually widening. She was still completely their leader, perhaps more firmly so because she had tamed the demon; and their bond of shared danger and mutual respect had never weakened. But there were other needs which her people might fill for each other, but never for her.

She watched them sleeping like the dead, as she should be sleeping now; preparing themselves for tomorrow. They took their sleep sporadically, when they could, as all commoners did—as she did now, too, instead of hibernating the night through like proper nobility. Many of them slept in pairs, man and woman; even though they mated with a commoner's chaotic lack of discrimination whenever a woman felt the season come upon her. T'uupieh wondered what they must imagine when they saw her sitting here with the demon far into the night. She knew what they believed—what she encouraged all to believe—that she had chosen it for a consort, or that it had chosen her. Y'lirr, she saw, still slept alone. She trusted and liked him as well as she did anyone; he was quick and ruthless, and she knew that he worshipped her. But he was a commoner . . . and more importantly, he did not challenge her. Nowhere, even among the nobility, had she found anyone who offered the sort of companionship she craved . . . until now, until the demon had come to her. No, she would not believe that all its words had been lies—

"T'uupieh," the demon called her name buzzingly in the misty darkness. "Maybe you can't change the pattern of fate . . . but you can change your mind. You've already defied fate, by turning outlaw, and defying Klovhiri. Your sister was the one who accepted . . ." (unintelligible words) ". . . only let the Wheel take her. Can you really kill her for that? You must understand why she did it, how she *could* do it. You don't have to kill her for that . . . you don't have to kill any of them. You have the strength, the courage, to put vengeance aside, and find another way to your goals. You can choose to be merciful—you can choose your own path through life, even if the ultimate destination of all life is the same."

She stood up resentfully, matching the demon's height, and drew her cloak tightly around her. "Even if I wished to change my mind, it is too late. The Wheel is already in motion . . . and I must get my sleep, if I am to be ready for it." She started away toward the fire; stopped, looking back. "There is nothing I can do now, my demon. I cannot change tomorrow. Only you can do that. Only you."

She heard it, later, calling her name softly as she lay sleepless on the cold ground. But she turned her back toward the sound and lay still, and at last sleep came.

Shannon slumped back into the embrace of the padded chair, rubbing his aching head. His eyelids were sandpaper, his body was a weight. He stared at the display screen, at T'uupieh's back turned stubbornly toward him as she slept beside the nitrogen campfire. "Okay, that's it. I give up. She won't even listen. Call Reed and tell him I quit."

"That you've quit trying to convince T'uupieh," Garda said. "Are you sure? She may yet come back. Use a little more emphasis on—spiritual matters. We must be certain we have done all we can to . . . change her mind."

To save her soul, he thought sourly. Garda had gotten her early training at an institute dedicated to translating the Bible; he had discovered in the past few hours that she still had a hidden desire to proselytize. *What soul?* "We're wasting our time. It's been six hours since she walked out on me. She's not coming back. . . . And I mean quit everything. I don't want to be around for the main event, I've had it."

"You don't mean that," Garda said. "You're tired, you need the rest too. When T'uupieh wakes, you can talk to her again."

He shook his head, pushing back his hair. "Forget it. Just call Reed." He looked out the window, at dawn separating the mist-wrapped silhouette of seaside condominiums from the sky.

Garda shrugged, disappointed, and turned to the phone.

He studied the synthesizer's touch boards again, still bright and waiting, still calling his leaden, weary hands to try one more time. At least when he made this final announcement, it wouldn't have to be direct to the eyes and ears of a waiting world: He doubted that any reporter was dedicated enough to still be up in the glass-walled observation room at this hour. Their questions had been endless earlier tonight, probing his feelings and his purpose and his motives and his plans, asking about Robin Hood's morality, or lack of it, and his own; about a hundred and one other things that were nobody's business but his own.

The music world had tried to do the same thing to him once, but then there had been buffers—agents, publicity staffs—to protect him. Now, when he'd had so much at stake, there had been no protection, only Reed at the microphone eloquently turning the room into a sideshow, with Shann the Man as chief freak; until Shannon had begun to feel like a man staked out on an anthill and smeared with honey. The reporters gazed down from on high critiquing T'uppieh's responses and criticizing his own, and filled the time gaps when he needed quiet to think with infuriating interruptions. Reed's success had been total in wringing every drop of pathos and human interest out of his struggle to prevent T'uupieh's vengeance against the innocents . . . and by that, had managed to make him fail.

No. He sat up straighter, trying to ease his back. No, he couldn't lay it on Reed. By the time what he'd had to say had really counted, the reporters had given up on him. The failure belonged to him, only him: his skill hadn't been great enough, his message hadn't been convincing enough—he was the one who hadn't been able to see through T'uppieh's eyes clearly enough to make her see through his own. He had had his chance to really communicate, for once in his life—to communicate something important. And he'd sunk it.

A hand reached past him to set a cup of steaming coffee on the shelf below the terminal. "One thing about this computer," a voice said quietly, "it's programmed for a good cup of coffee."

Startled, he laughed without expecting to; he glanced up. His mother's face looked drawn and tired, she held another cup of coffee in her hand. "Thanks." He picked up the cup and took a sip, felt the hot liquid slide down his throat into his empty stomach. Not looking up again, he said, "Well, you got what you wanted. And so did Reed. He got his pathos, and he gets his murders too."

She shook her head. "This isn't what I wanted. I don't want to see you give up everything you've done here, just because you don't like what Reed is doing with part of it. It isn't worth that. Your work means too much to this project . . . and it means too much to you."

He looked up.

"*Ja,* she is right, Shannon. You can't quit now—we need you too much. And T'uupieh needs you."

He laughed again, not meaning it. "Like a cement yo-yo. What are you trying to do, Garda, use my own moralizing against me?"

"She's telling you what any blind man could see tonight; if he hadn't seen it months ago . . ." His mother's voice was strangely distant. "That this project would never have had this degree of success without you. That you were right about the synthesizer. And that losing you now might—"

She broke off, turning away to watch as Reed came through the doors at the end of the long room. He was alone, this time, for once, and looking rumpled. Shannon guessed that he had been sleeping when the phone call came and was irrationally pleased at waking him up.

Reed was not so pleased. Shannon watched the frown that might be worry, or displeasure, or both, forming on his face as he came down the echoing hall toward them. "What did she mean, you want to quit? Just because you can't change an alien mind?" He entered the cubicle, and glanced down at the terminal—to be sure that the remote microphones were all switched off, Shannon guessed. "You knew it was a long shot, probably hopeless . . . you have to accept that she doesn't want to reform, accept that the values of an alien culture are going to be different from your own—"

Shannon leaned back, feeling a muscle begin to twitch with fatigue along the inside of his elbow. "I can accept that. What I can't accept is that you want to make us into a bunch of damn panderers. Christ, you don't even have a good reason! I didn't come here to play sound track for a snuff flick. If you go ahead and feed the world those murders, I'm laying it down. I don't want to give all this up, but I'm not staying for a kill-porn carnival."

Reed's frown deepened, he glanced away. "Well? What about the rest of you? Are you still privately branding me an accessory to murder, too? Carly?"

"No, Marcus—not really." She shook her head. "But we all feel that we shouldn't cheapen and weaken our research by making a public spectacle of it. After all, the people of Titan have as much right to privacy and respect as any culture on Earth."

"*Ja,* Marcus—I think we all agree about that."

"And just how much privacy does anybody on Earth have today? Good God—remember the Tasaday? And that was thirty years ago. There isn't a single mountaintop or desert island left that the all-seeing eye of the camera hasn't broadcast all over the world. And what do you call the public crime surveillance laws—our own lives are one big peep show."

Shannon shook his head. "That doesn't mean we have to—"

Reed turned cold eyes on him. "And I've had a little too much of your smartass piety, Wyler. Just what do you owe your success as a musician to, if not publicity?" He gestured at the posters on the walls. "There's more hard sell in your kind of music than any other field I can name."

"I have to put up with some publicity push, or I couldn't reach the people, I couldn't do the thing that's really important to me—communicate. That doesn't mean I like it."

"You think I enjoy this?"

"Don't you?"

Reed hesitated. "I happen to be good at it, which is all that really matters. Because you may not believe it, but I'm still a scientist, and what I care about most of all is seeing that research gets its fair slice of the pie. You say I don't have a good reason for pushing our findings: Do you realize that NASA lost all the data from our Neptune probe just because somebody in effect got tired of waiting for it to get to Neptune, and cut off our funds? The real problem on these long outer-planet missions isn't instrumental reliability, it's financial reliability. The public will pay out millions for one of your concerts, but not one cent for something they don't understand—"

"I don't make—"

"People want to forget their troubles, be entertained . . . and who can blame them? So in order to compete with movies, and sports, and people like you—not to mention ten thousand other worthy government and private causes—we have to give the public what it wants. It's my responsibility to deliver that, so that the 'real scientists' can sit in their neat, bright institutes with half a billion dollars' worth of equipment around them, and talk about 'respect for research.' "

He paused; Shannon kept his gaze stubbornly. "Think it over. And when you can tell me how what you did as a musician is morally superior to, or more valuable than, what you're doing now, you can come to my office and tell me who the real hypocrite is. But think it over, first—all of you." Reed turned and left the cubicle.

They watched in silence, until the double doors at the end of the room hung still. "Vell . . ." Garda glanced at her walking stick, and down at her cloak. "He does have a point."

Shannon leaned forward, tracing the complex beauty of the synthesizer terminal, feeling the combination of chagrin and caffeine pushing down his fatigue: "I know he does. But that isn't the point I was trying to get at! I didn't want to change T'uupieh's mind, or quit either, just because I objected to selling this project. It's the *way* it's being sold, like some kind of kill-porn show perversion, that I can't take—" When he was a child, he remembered, rock concerts had had a kind of notoriety; but they were as respectable as a symphony orchestra now, compared to the "thrill shows" that had eclipsed them as he was growing up: where "experts" gambled their lives against a million-dollar pot, in front of a crowd who came to see them lose; where masochists made a living by self-mutilation; where they ran cinema verité films of butchery and death.

"I mean, is that what everybody really wants? Does it really make everybody feel good to watch somebody else bleed? Or are they going to get some kind of moral superiority thing out of watching it happen on Titan instead of here?" He looked up at the display, at T'uupieh, who still lay sleeping, unmoving and unmoved. "If I could have changed T'uupieh's mind, or changed what happens here, then maybe I could have felt good about something. At least about myself. But who am I kidding . . ." T'uupieh had been right all along; and now he had to admit it to himself: that there had never been any way he could change either one. "T'uupieh's just like the rest of them, she'd rather cut off your hand than shake it . . . and doing it vicariously means we're no better. And none of us ever will be." The words to a song older than he was slipped into his mind, with sudden irony. "'One man's hands can't build,'" he began to switch off the terminal, "anything."

"You need to sleep . . . ve all need to sleep." Garda rose stiffly from her chair.

"'. . . but if one and one and fifty make a million,'" his mother matched his quote softly.

Shannon turned back to look at her, saw her shake her head; she felt him looking at her, glanced up. "After all, if T'uupieh could have accepted that everything she did was morally evil, what would have become of her? She knew: It would have destroyed her—we would have destroyed her. She would have been swept away and drowned in the tide of violence." His mother looked away at Garda, back at him. "T'uupieh is a realist, whatever else she is."

He felt his mouth tighten against the resentment that sublimated a deeper, more painful emotion; he heard Garda's grunt of indignation.

"But that doesn't mean that you were wrong—or that you failed."

"That's big of you." He stood up, nodding at Garda, and toward the exit. "Come on."

"Shannon."

He stopped, still facing away.

"I don't think you failed. I think you did reach T'uupieh. The last thing she said was 'only you can change tomorrow' . . . I think she was challenging the demon to go ahead; to do what she didn't have the power to do herself. I think she was asking you to help her."

He turned, slowly. "You really believe that?"

"Yes, I do." She bent her head, freed her hair from the collar of her sweater.

He moved back to his seat, his hands brushed the dark, unresponsive touchplates on the panel. "But it wouldn't do any good to talk to her again. Somehow the demon has to stop the attack itself. If I could use the 'voice' to warn them. . . . Damn the time lag!" By the time his voice reached them, the attack would have been over for hours. How could he change anything tomorrow, if he was always two hours behind?

"I know how to get around the time-lag problem."

"How?" Garda sat down again, mixed emotions showing on her broad, seamed face. "He can't send a varning ahead of time; no one knows when Klovhiri will pass. It would come too soon, or too late."

Shannon straightened up. "Better to ask 'why?' Why are you changing your mind?"

"I never changed my mind," his mother said mildly. "I never liked this either. When I was a girl, we used to believe that our actions *could* change the world; maybe I've never stopped wanting to believe that."

"But Marcus is not going to like us meddling behind his back, anyway." Garda waved her staff. "And what about the point that perhaps we do need this publicity?"

Shannon glanced back irritably. "I thought you were on the side of the angels, not the devil's advocate."

"I am!" Garda's mouth puckered. "But—"

"Then what's such bad news about the probe making a last-minute rescue? It'll be a sensation."

He saw his mother smile, for the first time in months. "Sensational . . . if T'uupieh doesn't leave us stranded in the swamp for our betrayal."

He sobered: "Not if you really think she wants our help. And I know she wants it . . . I *feel* it. But how do we beat the time lag?"

"I'm the engineer, remember? I'll need a recorded message from you, and some time to play with that." His mother pointed at the computer terminal.

He switched on the terminal and moved aside. She sat down, and started a program documentation on the display; he read, REMOTE OPERATIONS MANUAL. "Let's see . . . I'll need feedback on the approach of Klovhiri's party."

He cleared his throat. "Did you really mean what you said, before Reed came in?"

She glanced up, he watched one response form on her face, and then fade into another smile. "Garda—have you met My Son, the Linguist?"

"And when did you ever pick up on that Pete Seeger song?"

"And My Son, the Musician . . ." The smile came back to him.

"I've listened to a few records, in my day." The smile turned inward, toward a memory. "I don't suppose I ever told you that I fell in love with your father because he reminded me of Elton John."

T'uupieh stood silently, gazing into the demon's unwavering eye. A new day was turning the clouds from bronze to gold; the brightness seeped down through the glistening, snarled hair of the treetops, glanced from the green translucent cliff faces and sweating slopes to burnish the demon's carapace with light. She gnawed the last shreds of flesh from a bone, forcing herself to eat, scarcely aware that she did. She had already sent out watchers in the direction of the town, to keep watch for Chwiul . . . and Klovhiri's party. Behind her the rest of her band made ready now, testing weapons and reflexes or feeding their bellies.

And still the demon had not spoken to her. There had been many times when it had chosen not to speak for hours on end; but after its mad ravings of last night, the thought obsessed her that it might never speak again. Her concern grew, lighting the fuse of her anger, which this morning was already short enough; until at last she strode recklessly forward and struck it with her open hand. "Speak to me, *mala 'ingga!*"

But as her blow landed a pain like the touch of fire shot up the muscles of her arm. She leaped back with a curse of surprise, shaking her hand. The demon had never lashed out at her before, never hurt her in any way: But she had never dared to strike it before, she had always treated it with calculated respect. *Fool!* She looked down at her hand, half afraid to see it covered with burns that would make her a cripple in the attack today. But the skin was still smooth and unblistered, only bright with the smarting shock.

"T'uupieh! Are you all right?"

She turned to see Y'lirr, who had come up behind her looking half frightened, half grim. "Yes." She nodded, controlling a sharper reply at the sight of his concern. "It was nothing." He carried her double-arched bow and quiver, she put out her smarting hand and took them from him casually, slung them at her back. "Come, Y'lirr, we must—"

"T'uupieh." This time it was the demon's eerie voice that

called her name. "T'uupieh, if you believe in my power to twist fate as I like, then you must come back and listen to me again."

She turned back, felt Y'lirr hesitate behind her. "I believe truly in all your powers, my demon!" She rubbed her hand.

The amber depths of its eye absorbed her expression, and read her sincerity; or so she hoped. "T'uupieh, I know I did not make you believe what I said. But I want you to"—its words blurred unintelligibly—"in me. I want you to know my name. T'uupieh, my name is—"

She heard a horrified yowl from Y'lirr behind her. She glanced around—seeing him cover his ears—and back, paralyzed by disbelief.

"—Shang'ang."

The word struck her like the demon's fiery lash, but the blow this time struck only in her mind. She cried out, in desperate protest; but the name had already passed into her knowledge, *too late!*

A long moment passed; she drew a breath, and shook her head. Disbelief still held her motionless as she let her eyes sweep the brightening camp, as she listened to the sounds of the wakening forest, and breathed in the spicy acridness of the spring growth. And then she began to laugh. She had heard a demon speak its name, and she still lived—and was not blind, not deaf, not mad. The demon had chosen her, joined with her, surrendered to her at last!

Dazed with exultation, she almost did not realize that the demon had gone on speaking to her. She broke off the song of triumph that rose in her, listening:

". . . then I command you to take me with you when you go today. I must see what happens, and watch Klovhiri pass."

"Yes! Yes, my—Shang'ang. It will be done as you wish. Your whim is my desire." She turned away down the slope, stopped again as she found Y'lirr still prone where he had thrown himself down when the demon spoke its name. "Y'lirr?" She nudged him with her foot. Relieved, she saw him lift his head; watched her own disbelief echoing in his face as he looked up at her.

"My lady . . . it did not—?"

"No, Y'lirr," she said softly; then more roughly, "Of course it did not! I am truly the Demon's Consort now; nothing shall stand in my way." She pushed him again with her foot, harder. "Get up. What do I have, a pack of sniveling cowards to ruin the morning of my success?"

Y'lirr scrambled to his feet, brushing himself off. "Never that, T'uupieh! We're ready for any command . . . ready to deliver your revenge." His hand tightened on his knife hilt.

"And my demon will join us in seeking it out!" The pride she felt rang in her voice. "Get help to fetch a sledge here, and prepare it. And tell them to move it *gently.*"

He nodded, and for a moment as he glanced at the demon she saw both fear and envy in his eyes. "Good news." He moved off then with his usual brusqueness, without glancing back at her.

She heard a small clamor in the camp, and looked past him, thinking that word of the demon had spread already. But then she saw Lord Chwiul, come as he had promised, being led into the clearing by her escorts. She lifted her head slightly, in surprise—he had indeed come alone, but he was riding a *bliell.* They were rare and expensive mounts, being the only beast she knew of large enough to carry so much weight, and being vicious and difficult to train, as well. She watched this one snapping at the air, its fangs protruding past slack, dribbling lips, and grimaced faintly. She saw that the escort kept well clear of its stumplike webbed feet, and kept their spears ready to prod. It was an amphibian, being too heavy ever to make use of wings, but buoyant and agile when it swam. T'uupieh glanced fleetingly at her own webbed fingers and toes, at the wings that could only lift her body now for bare seconds at a time; she wondered, as she had so many times, what strange turns of fate had formed, or transformed, them all.

She saw Y'lirr speak to Chwiul, pointing her out, saw his insolent grin and the trace of apprehension that Chwiul showed looking up at her; she thought that Y'lirr had said, "She knows its name."

Chwiul rode forward to meet her, with his face under control as he endured the demon's scrutiny. T'uupieh put out a hand to casually—gently—stroke its sensuous jewel-faceted side. Her eyes left Chwiul briefly, drawn by some instinct to the sky directly above him—and for half a moment she saw the clouds break open . . .

She blinked, to see more clearly, and when she looked again it was gone. No one else, not even Chwiul, had seen the gibbous disc of greenish gold, cut across by a line of silver and a band of shadow-black: The Wheel of Change. She kept her face expressionless, but her heart raced. The Wheel appeared only when someone's life was about to be changed profoundly—and usually the change meant death.

Chwiul's mount lunged at her suddenly as he stopped before her. She held her place at the demon's side; but some of the *bliell*'s bluish spittle landed on her cloak as Chwiul jerked at its heavy head. "Chwiul!" She let her emotion out as anger. "Keep that slobbering filth under control, or I will have it struck dead!" Her hand fisted on the demon's slick hide.

Chwiul's near-smile faded abruptly, and he pulled his mount back, staring uncomfortably at the demon's glaring eye.

T'uupieh took a deep breath, and produced a smile of her own. "So you did not quite dare to come to my camp alone, my lord."

He bowed slightly, from the saddle. "I was merely hesitant to wander in the swamp on foot, alone, until your people found me."

"I see." She kept the smile. "Well then—I assumed that things went as you planned this morning. Are Klovhiri and his party all on their way into our trap?"

"They are. And their guide is waiting for my sign, to lead them off safe ground into whatever mire you choose."

"Good. I have a spot in mind that is well ringed by heights." She admired Chwiul's self-control in the demon's presence, although she sensed that he was not as easy as he wanted her to believe. She saw some of her people coming toward them, with a sledge to carry the demon on their trek. "My demon will accompany us, by its own desire. A sure sign of our success today, don't you agree?"

Chwiul frowned, as if he wanted to question that, but didn't quite dare. "If it serves you loyally, then yes, my lady. A great honor and a good omen."

"It serves me with true devotion." She smiled again, insinuatingly. She stood back as the sledge came up onto the hummock, watched as the demon was settled onto it, to be sure her people used the proper care. The fresh reverence with which her outlaws treated it—and their leader—was not lost on either Chwiul or herself.

She called her people together then, and they set out for their destination, picking their way over the steaming surface of the marsh and through the slimy slate-blue tentacles of the fragile, thawing underbrush. She was glad that they covered this ground often, because the pungent spring growth and the ground's mushy unpredictability changed the pattern of their passage from day to day. She wished that she could have separated Chwiul from his ugly mount, but she doubted that he would cooperate, and she was afraid that he might not be able to keep up on foot. The demon was lashed securely onto its sledge, and its sweating bearers pulled it with no hint of complaint.

At last they reached the heights overlooking the main road—though it could hardly be called one now—that led past her family's manor. She had the demon positioned where it could look back along the overgrown trail in the direction of Klovhiri's approach, and sent some of her followers to secret its eyes further down the track. She stood then, gazing down at the spot below where the path seemed to fork, but did not. The false fork followed the rippling yellow bands of the cliff face below her—directly into a sink caused by ammonia-water melt seeping down and through the porous sulphide compounds of the rock. There they would all wallow, while she and her band picked them off like swatting *ngips* . . . she thoughtfully swatted a *ngip* that had settled on her hand. Unless her demon—unless her demon chose to create some other outcome . . .

"Any sign?" Chwiul rode up beside her.

She moved back slightly from the cliff's crumbly edge, watching him with more than casual interest. "Not yet. But soon." She had outlaws posted on the lower slope across the track as well; but not even her demon's eyes could pierce too deeply into the foliage along the road. It had not spoken since Chwiul's arrival, and she did not expect it to reveal its secrets now. "What livery does your escort wear, and how many of them do you want killed for effect?" She unslung her bow, and began to test its pull.

Chwiul shrugged. "The dead carry no tales; kill them all. I shall have Klovhiri's men soon. Kill the guide too—a man who can be bought once, can be bought twice."

"Ah—" She nodded, grinning. "A man with your foresight and discretion will go far in the world, my lord." She nocked an arrow in the bowstring before she turned away to search the road again. Still empty. She looked away restlessly, at the spiny silver-blue-green of the distant, fog-clad mountains; at the hollow fingers of upthrust ice, once taller than she was, stubby and diminishing now along the edge of the nearer lake. The lake where last summer she had soared . . .

A flicker of movement, a small unnatural noise, pulled her eyes back to the road. Tension tightened the fluid ease of her movement as she made the trilling call that would send her band to their places along the cliff's edge. *At last*—She leaned forward eagerly for the first glimpse of Klovhiri; spotting the guide, and then the sledge that bore her sister and the children. She counted the numbers of the escort, saw them all emerge into her unbroken view on the track. But Klovhiri . . . where was Klovhiri? She turned back to Chwiul, her whisper struck out at him, "Where is he! Where is Klovhiri?"

Chwiul's expression lay somewhere between guilt and guile. "Delayed. He stayed behind, he said there were still matters at court—"

"Why didn't you tell me that?"

He jerked sharply on the *bliell*'s rein. "It changes nothing! We can still eradicate his family. That will leave me first in line to the inheritance . . . and Klovhiri can always be brought down later."

"But it's Klovhiri I want, for myself." T'uupieh raised her bow, the arrow tracked toward his heart.

"They'll know who to blame if I die!" He spread a wing defensively. "The Overlord will turn against you for good; Klovhiri will see to that. Avenge yourself on your sister, T'uupieh—and I will still reward you well if you keep the bargain!"

"This is not the bargain we agreed to!" The sounds of the approaching party reached her clearly now from down below; she heard a child's high notes of laughter. Her outlaws crouched, waiting for her signal; and she saw Chwiul prepare for his own signal call to his guide. She looked back at the demon, its amber eye fixed on the travelers below. She started toward it. It could still twist fate for her. . . . *Or had it already?*

"Go back, go back!" The demon's voice burst over her, down across the silent forest, like an avalanche. "Ambush . . . trap . . . you have been betrayed!"

"—betrayal!"

She barely heard Chwiul's voice below the roaring; she looked back, in time to see the *bliell* leap forward, to intersect her own course toward the demon. Chwiul drew his sword, she saw the look of white fury on his face, not knowing whether it was for her, or the demon itself. She ran toward the demon's sledge, trying to draw her bow; but the *bliell* covered the space between them in two great bounds. Its head swung toward her, jaws gaping. Her foot skidded on the slippery melt, and she went down; the dripping jaws snapped futilely shut above her face. But one flailing leg struck her heavily and knocked her sliding through the melt to the demon's foot—

The demon. She gasped for the air that would not fill her lungs, trying to call its name, saw with incredible clarity the beauty of its form, and the ululating horror of the *bliell* bearing down on them to destroy them both. She saw it rear above her, above the demon—saw Chwiul, either leaping or thrown, sail out into the air—and at last her voice came back to her and she screamed the name, a warning and a plea, "Shang'ang!"

And as the *bliell* came down, lightning lashed out from the demon's carapace and wrapped the *bliell* in fire. The beast's ululations rose off the scale; T'uupieh covered her ears against the piercing pain of its cry. But not her eyes: the demon's lash ceased with the suddenness of lightning, and the *bliell* toppled back and away, rebounding lightly as it crashed to the ground, stone dead. T'uupieh sank back against the demon's foot, supported gratefully as she filled her aching lungs, and looked away—

To see Chwiul, trapped in the updrafts at the cliff's edge, gliding, gliding . . . and she saw the three arrows that protruded from his back, before the currents let his body go, and it disappeared below the rim. She smiled, and closed her eyes.

"T'uupieh! T'uupieh!"

She blinked them open again, resignedly, as she felt her people cluster around her. Y'lirr's hand drew back from the motion of touching her face as she opened her eyes. She smiled again, at him, at them all; but not with the smile she had had for Chwiul. "Y'lirr—" She gave him her own hand, and let him help her up. Aches and bruises prodded her with every small movement, but she was certain, reassured, that the only real damage was an oozing tear in her wing. She kept her arm close to her side.

"T'uupieh—"

"My lady—"

"What happened? The demon—"

"The demon saved my life." She waved them silent. "And . . . for its own reasons, it foiled Chwiul's plot." The realization, and the implications, were only now becoming real in her mind. She turned, and for a long moment gazed into the demon's unreadable eye. Then she moved away, going stiffly to the edge of the cliff to look down.

"But the contract—" Y'lirr said.

"Chwiul broke the contract! He did not give me Klovhiri." No one made a protest. She peered through the brush, guessing without much difficulty the places where Ahtseet and her party had gone to earth below. She could hear a child's whimpered crying now. Chwiul's body lay sprawled on the flat, in plain view of them all, and she thought she saw more arrows bristling from his corpse. Had Ahtseet's guard riddled him too, taking him for an attacker? The thought pleased her. And a small voice inside her dared to whisper that Ahtseet's escape pleased her much more. . . . She frowned suddenly at the thought.

But Ahtseet had escaped, and so had Klovhiri—and so she might as well make use of that fact, to salvage what she could. She paused, collecting her still-shaken thoughts. "Ahtseet!" Her voice was not the voice of the demon, but it echoed satisfactorily. "It's T'uupieh! See the traitor's corpse that lies before you—your own mate's brother, Chwiul! He hired murderers to kill you in the swamp—seize your guide, make him tell you all. It is only by my demon's warning that you still live."

"Why?" Ahtseet's voice wavered faintly on the wind.

T'uupieh laughed bitterly. "Why, to keep the roads clear of ruffians. To make the Overlord love his loyal servant more, and reward her better, dear sister! And to make Klovhiri hate me. May it eat his guts out that he owes your lives to me! Pass freely through my lands, Ahtseet; I give you leave—this once."

She drew back from the ledge and moved wearily away, not caring whether Ahtseet would believe her. Her people stood waiting, gathered silently around the corpse of the *bliell.*

"What now?" Y'lirr asked, looking at the demon, asking for them all.

And she answered, but made her answer directly to the demon's silent amber eye. "It seems I spoke the truth to Chwiul after all, my demon: I told him he would not be needing his town house after today . . . Perhaps the Overlord will call it a fair trade. Perhaps it can be arranged. The Wheel of Change carries us all; but not with equal ease. Is that not so, my beautiful Shang'ang?"

She stroked its day-warmed carapace tenderly, and settled down on the softening ground to wait for its reply.

Harlan Ellison

Harlan is no stranger to the Hugo volumes. He didn't have one in Volume One, for though he was already writing professionally by then, he had not yet hit his stride in science fiction. In Volume Two, however, he is the author of no fewer than three of the fourteen stories, and in Volume Three he has two more. "Jeffty Is Five," in this volume, is therefore his sixth appearance in these Hugo Winner books.

Harlan is a good friend of mine. I make inordinate fun at his expense (as he does at mine), for we are both thick-skinned where friends are concerned (only friends) and we are both keenly aware that we can give as good as we get. People listening to us at conventions, however, sometimes get the idea we are deadly enemies and might at any moment come to blows. (The Fates forbid! For all that Harlan is several inches—or perhaps feet—shorter than I am, he can break me—or almost anyone—in two with his left hand.) Anyway, I'll never get tired of stressing our friendship, though I know there will always remain many who will cling to the myth of an Asimov-Ellison feud.

Harlan is a Hollywood person. He lives in Los Angeles in what I have heard is a marvelous house, which, of course, I have never seen because I don't fly. He also works with Hollywood people.

Personally, I think this is a fate worse than death. When you write books, you are boss. Your editor may make suggestions, but past a certain point you can override him and get your books published essentially as you've written them. In Hollywood, as I understand it, writing a screenplay is just an act of futility since everyone who lives in Los Angeles has the constitutional right to rewrite it at will—the producer, the director, the actors, the stenographers, the office boys, to say nothing of strangers passing by.

This kills Harlan, but then it would even kill me. Some years ago, he did a screenplay for my book *I, Robot.* It was a terrific screenplay. It was in many ways different from the book, for he added distinctive Harlanesque touches, but there were unmistakable parts of my book included, too, and what he added would have been cinematographically wonderful.

Nothing ever came of it, alas. Partly, it was Harlan's temper. "Harlan," I said to him at the beginning, "whatever they say to you, smile and say 'Yes, sir.' If they want a revision, stir it around a bit and say you've revised. If they want you to do something you don't want to do, say you'll do it, and then don't quite, but say you've done it. Understand?"

"Yes, Isaac," he said docilely.

But then came the time when the head of the studio made one dumb remark too many (which is often just one dumb remark where Harlan is concerned) and Harlan said to him in a fury, "You have the cranial capacity of an artichoke."

As soon as the studio head found out what "cranial capacity" meant, he fired Harlan, and made a great many cursory remarks about him.

Too bad, but I love Harlan as he is, thorns and all.

10

JEFFTY IS FIVE

When I was five years old, there was a little kid I played with: Jeffty. His real name was Jeff Kinzer, and everyone who played with him called him Jeffty. We were five years old together, and we had good times playing together.

When I was five, a Clark Bar was as fat around as the gripping end of a Louisville Slugger, and pretty nearly six inches long, and they used real chocolate to coat it, and it crunched very nicely when you bit into the center, and the paper it came wrapped in smelled fresh and good when you peeled off one end to hold the bar so it wouldn't melt onto your fingers. Today, a Clark Bar is as thin as a credit card, they use something artificial and awful-tasting instead of pure chocolate, the thing is soft and soggy, it costs fifteen or twenty cents instead of a decent, correct nickel, and they wrap it so you think it's the same size it was twenty years ago, only it isn't; it's slim and ugly and nasty-tasting and not worth a penny, much less fifteen or twenty cents.

When I was that age, five years old, I was sent away to my Aunt Patricia's home in Buffalo, New York for two years. My father was going through "bad times" and Aunt Patricia was very beautiful, and had married a stockbroker. They took care of me for two years. When I was seven, I came back home and went to find Jeffty, so we could play together.

I was seven. Jeffty was still five. I didn't notice any difference. I didn't know: I was only seven.

When I was seven years old I used to lie on my stomach in front of our Atwater-Kent radio and listen to swell stuff. I had tied the ground wire to the radiator, and I would lie there with my coloring books and my Crayolas (when there were only sixteen colors in the big box), and listen to the NBC Red network: Jack Benny on the *Jell–O Program, Amos 'n' Andy,* Edgar Bergen and Charlie McCarthy on the *Chase and Sanborn Program, One Man's Family, First Nighter;* the NBC Blue network: *Easy Aces,* the *Jergens Program* with Walter Winchell, *Information Please, Death Valley Days;* and best of all, the Mutual Network with *The Green Hornet, The Lone Ranger, The Shadow,* and *Quiet, Please.* Today, I turn on my car radio and go from one end of the dial to the other and all I get is 100 strings orchestras, banal housewives and insipid truckers discussing their kinky sex lives with arrogant talk show hosts, country and western drivel and rock music so loud it hurts my ears.

When I was ten, my grandfather died of old age and I was "a troublesome kid," and they sent me off to military school, so I could be "taken in hand."

I came back when I was fourteen. Jeffty was still five.

When I was fourteen years old, I used to go to the movies on Saturday afternoons and a matinee was ten cents and they used real butter on the popcorn and I could always be sure of seeing a western like Lash LaRue, or Wild Bill Elliott as Red Ryder with Bobby Blake as Little Beaver, or Roy Rogers, or Johnny Mack Brown; a scary picture like *House of Horrors* with Rondo Hatton as the Strangler, or *The Cat People,* or *The Mummy,* or *I Married a Witch* with Fredric March and Veronica Lake; plus an episode of a great serial like *The Shadow* with Victor Jory, or *Dick Tracy* or *Flash Gordon;* and three cartoons; a James Fitzpatrick TravelTalk; Movietone News; a singalong and, if I stayed on till evening, Bingo or Keeno; and free dishes. Today, I go to movies and see Clint Eastwood blowing people's heads apart like ripe cantaloupes.

At eighteen, I went to college. Jeffty was still five. I came back during the summers, to work at my Uncle Joe's jewelry store. Jeffty hadn't changed. Now I knew there was something different about him, something wrong, something weird. Jeffty was still five years old, not a day older.

At twenty-two I came home for keeps. To open a Sony television franchise in town, the first one. I saw Jeffty from time to time. He was five.

Things are better in a lot of ways. People don't die from some of the old diseases any more. Cars go faster and get you there more quickly on better roads. Shirts are softer and silkier. We have paperback books even though they cost as much as a good hardcover used to. When I'm running short in the bank I can live off credit cards till things even out. But I still think we've lost a lot of good stuff. Did you know you can't buy linoleum any more, only vinyl floor covering? There's no such thing as oilcloth any more; you'll never again smell that special, sweet smell from your grandmother's kitchen. Furniture isn't made to last thirty years or longer because they took a survey and found that young home-makers like to throw their furniture out and bring in all new, color-coded borax every seven years. Records don't feel right; they're not thick and solid like the old ones, they're thin and you can bend them . . . that doesn't seem right to me. Restaurants don't serve cream in pitchers any more, just that artificial glop in little plastic tubs, and one is never enough to get coffee the right color. You can make a dent in a car fender with only a sneaker. Everywhere you go, all the towns look the same with Burger Kings and McDonald's and 7-Elevens and Taco Bells and motels and shopping centers. Things may be better, but why do I keep thinking about the past?

What I mean by five years old is not that Jeffty was retarded. I don't think that's what it was. Smart as a whip for five years old; very bright, quick, cute, a funny kid.

But he was three feet tall, small for his age, and perfectly formed: no big head, no strange jaw, none of that. A nice, normal-looking five-year-old kid. Except that he was the same age as I was: twenty-two.

When he spoke it was with the squeaking, soprano voice of a five-year-old; when he walked it was with the little hops and shuffles of a five-year-old; when he talked to you it was about the concerns of a five-year-old . . . comic books, playing soldier, using a clothespin to attach a stiff piece of cardboard to the front fork of his bike so the sound it made when the spokes hit was like a motorboat, asking questions like *why does that thing do like that,* how high is up, how old is old, why is grass green, what's an elephant look like? At twenty-two, he was five.

•

Jeffty's parents were a sad pair. Because I was still a friend of Jeffty's, still let him hang around with me, sometimes took him to the county fair or miniature golf or the movies, I wound up spending time with *them.* Not that I much cared for them, because they were so awfully depressing. But then, I suppose one couldn't expect much more from the poor devils. They had an alien thing in their home, a child who had grown no older than five in twenty-two years, who provided the treasure of that special childlike state indefinitely, but who also denied them the joys of watching the child grow into a normal adult.

Five is a wonderful time of life for a little kid . . . or it *can* be, if the child is relatively free of the monstrous beastliness other children indulge in. It is a time when the eyes are wide open and the patterns are not yet set; a time when one has not yet been hammered into accepting everything as immutable and hopeless; a time when the hands cannot do enough, the mind cannot learn enough, the world is infinite and colorful and filled with mysteries. Five is a special time before they take the questing, unquenchable, quixotic soul of the young dreamer and thrust it into dreary schoolroom boxes. A time before they take the trembling hands that want to hold everything, touch everything, figure everything out, and make them lie still on desktops. A time before people begin saying "act your age" and "grow up" or "you're behaving like a baby." It is a time when a child who acts adolescent is still cute and responsive and everyone's pet. A time of delight, of wonder, of innocence.

Jeffty had been stuck in that time, just five, just so.

But for his parents it was an ongoing nightmare from which no one—not social workers, not priests, not child psychologists, not teachers, not friends, not medical wizards, not psychiatrists, no one—could slap or shake them awake. For seventeen years their sorrow had grown through stages of parental dotage to concern, from concern to worry, from worry to fear, from fear to confusion, from confusion to anger, from anger to dislike, from dislike to naked hatred, and finally, from deepest loathing and revulsion to a stolid, depressive acceptance.

John Kinzer was a shift foreman at the Balder Tool & Die plant. He was a thirty-year man. To everyone but the man living it, his was a spectacularly uneventful life. In no way was he remarkable

. . . save that he had fathered a twenty-two-year-old five-year-old.

John Kinzer was a small man; soft, with no sharp angles; with pale eyes that never seemed to hold mine for longer than a few seconds. He continually shifted in his chair during conversations, and seemed to see things in the upper corners of the room, things no one else could see . . . or wanted to see. I suppose the word that best suited him was *haunted.* What his life had become . . . well, *haunted* suited him.

Leona Kinzer tried valiantly to compensate. No matter what hour of the day I visited, she always tried to foist food on me. And when Jeffty was in the house she was always at *him* about eating: "Honey, would you like an orange? A nice orange? Or a tangerine? I have tangerines. I could peel a tangerine for you." But there was clearly such fear in her, fear of her own child, that the offers of sustenance always had a faintly ominous tone.

Leona Kinzer had been a tall woman, but the years had bent her. She seemed always to be seeking some area of wallpapered wall or storage niche into which she could fade, adopt some chintz or rose-patterned protective coloration and hide forever in plain sight of the child's big brown eyes, pass her a hundred times a day and never realize she was there, holding her breath, invisible. She always had an apron tied around her waist, and her hands were red from cleaning. As if by maintaining the environment immaculately she could pay off her imagined sin: having given birth to this strange creature.

Neither of them watched television very much. The house was usually dead silent, not even the sibilant whispering of water in the pipes, the creaking of timbers settling, the humming of the refrigerator. Awfully silent, as if time itself had taken a detour around that house.

As for Jeffty, he was inoffensive. He lived in that atmosphere of gentle dread and dulled loathing, and if he understood it, he never remarked in any way. He played, as a child plays, and seemed happy. But he must have sensed, in the way of a five-year-old, just how alien he was in their presence.

Alien. No, that wasn't right. He was *too* human, if anything. But out of phase, out of sync with the world around him, and resonating to a different vibration than his parents, God knows. Nor would other children play with him. As they grew past him, they found him at first childish, then uninteresting, then simply frightening as their perceptions of aging became clear and they could see he was not affected by time as they were. Even the little ones, his own age, who might wander into the neighborhood, quickly came to shy away from him like a dog in the street when a car backfires.

Thus, I remained his only friend. A friend of many years. Five years. Twenty-two years. I liked him; more than I can say. And never knew exactly why. But I did, without reserve.

But because we spent time together, I found I was also—polite society—spending time with John and Leona Kinzer. Dinner, Saturday afternoons sometimes, an hour or so when I'd bring Jeffty back from a movie. They were grateful: slavishly so. It relieved them of the embarrassing chore of going out with him, of having to pretend before the world that they were loving parents with a perfectly normal, happy, attractive child. And their gratitude extended to hosting me. Hideous, every moment of their depression, hideous.

I felt sorry for the poor devils, but I despised them for their inability to love Jeffty, who was eminently lovable.

I never let on, of course, even during the evenings in their company that were awkward beyond belief.

We would sit there in the darkening living room—*always* dark or darkening, as if kept in shadow to hold back what the light might reveal to the world outside through the bright eyes of the house—we would sit and silently stare at one another. They never knew what to say to me.

"So how are things down at the plant?" I'd say to John Kinzer.

He would shrug. Neither conversation nor life suited him with any ease or grace. "Fine, just fine," he would say, finally.

And we would sit in silence again.

"Would you like a nice piece of coffee cake?" Leona would say. "I made it fresh just this morning." Or deep dish green apple pie. Or milk and tollhouse cookies. Or a brown betty pudding.

"No, no, thank you, Mrs. Kinzer; Jeffty and I grabbed a couple of cheeseburgers on the way home." And again, silence.

Then, when the stillness and the awkwardness became too much even for them (and who knew how long that total silence reigned when they were alone, with that thing they never talked about any more hanging between them), Leona Kinzer would say, "I think he's asleep."

John Kinzer would say, "I don't hear the radio playing."

Just so, it would go on like that, until I could politely find excuse to bolt away on some flimsy pretext. Yes, that was the way it would go on, every time, just the same . . . except once.

•

"I don't know what to do any more," Leona said. She began crying. "There's no change, not one day of peace."

Her husband managed to drag himself out of the old easy chair and went to her. He bent and tried to soothe her, but it was clear from the graceless way in which he touched her graying hair that the ability to be compassionate had been stunned in him. "Shhh, Leona, it's all right. Shhh." But she continued crying. Her hands scraped gently at the antimacassars on the arms of the chair.

Then she said, "Sometimes I wish he had been stillborn."

John looked up into the corners of the room. For the nameless shadows that were always watching him? Was it God he was seeking in those spaces? "You don't mean that," he said to her, softly, pathetically, urging her with body tension and trembling in his voice to recant before God took notice of the terrible thought. But she meant it; she meant it very much.

I managed to get away quickly that evening. They didn't want witnesses to their shame. I was glad to go.

•

And for a week I stayed away. From them, from Jeffty, from their street, even from that end of town.

I had my own life. The store, accounts, suppliers' conferences, poker with friends, pretty women I took to well-lit restaurants, my own parents, putting antifreeze in the car, complaining to the laundry about too much starch in the collars and cuffs, working out at the gym, taxes, catching Jan or David (whichever one it was) stealing from the cash register. I had my own life.

But not even *that* evening could keep me from Jeffty. He called me at the store and asked me to take him to the rodeo. We chummed it up as best a twenty-two-year-old with other interests *could* . . . with a five-year-old. I never dwelled on what bound us together; I always thought it was simply the years. That, and affection for a kid who could have been the little brother I never had. (Except I *remembered* when we had played together, when we had both been the same age; I *remembered* that period, and Jeffty was still the same.)

And then, one Saturday afternoon, I came to take him to a double feature, and things I should have noticed so many times before, I first began to notice only that afternoon.

•

I came walking up to the Kinzer house, expecting Jeffty to be sitting on the front porch steps, or in the porch glider, waiting for me. But he was nowhere in sight.

Going inside, into that darkness and silence, in the midst of May sunshine, was unthinkable. I stood on the front walk for a few moments, then cupped my hands around my mouth and yelled, "Jeffty? Hey Jeffty, come on out, let's go. We'll be late."

His voice came faintly, as if from under the ground.

"Here I am, Donny."

I could hear him, but I couldn't see him. It was Jeffty, no question about it: as Donald H. Horton, President and Sole Owner of The Horton TV & Sound Center, no one but Jeffty called me Donny. He had never called me anything else.

(Actually, it isn't a lie. I *am,* as far as the public is concerned, Sole Owner of the Center. The partnership with my Aunt Patricia is only to repay the loan she made me, to supplement the money I came into when I was twenty-one, left to me when I was ten by my grandfather. It wasn't a very big loan, only eighteen thousand, but I asked her to be a silent partner, because of when she had taken care of me as a child.)

"Where are you, Jeffty?"

"Under the porch in my secret place."

I walked around the side of the porch, and stooped down and pulled away the wicker grating. Back in there, on the pressed dirt, Jeffty had built himself a secret place. He had comics in orange crates, he had a little table and some pillows, it was lit by big fat candles, and we used to hide there when we were both . . . five.

"What'cha up to?" I asked, crawling in and pulling the grate closed behind me. It was cool under the porch, and the dirt smelled comfortable, the candles smelled clubby and familiar. Any kid would feel at home in such a secret place: there's never been a kid who didn't spend the happiest, most productive, most deliciously mysterious times of his life in such a secret place.

"Playin'," he said. He was holding something golden and round. It filled the palm of his little hand.

"You forget we were going to the movies?"

"Nope. I was just waitin' for you here."

"Your mom and dad home?"

"Momma."

I understood why he was waiting under the porch. I didn't push it any further. "What've you got there?"

"Captain Midnight Secret Decoder Badge," he said, showing it to me on his flattened palm.

I realized I was looking at it without comprehending what it was for a long time. Then it dawned on me what a miracle Jeffty had in his hand. A miracle that simply could *not* exist.

"Jeffty," I said softly, with wonder in my voice, "where'd you get that?"

"Came in the mail today. I sent away for it."

"It must have cost a lot of money."

"Not so much. Ten cents an' two inner wax seals from two jars of Ovaltine."

"May I see it?" My voice was trembling, and so was the hand I extended. He gave it to me and I held the miracle in the palm of my hand. It was *wonderful.*

You remember. *Captain Midnight* went on the radio nationwide in 1940. It was sponsored by Ovaltine. And every year they issued a Secret Squadron Decoder Badge. And every day at the end of the program, they would give you a clue to the next day's installment in a code that only kids with the official badge could decipher. They stopped making those wonderful Decoder Badges in 1949. I remember the one I had in 1945: it was beautiful. It had a magnifying glass in the center of the code dial. *Captain Midnight* went off the air in 1950, and though I understand it was a short-lived television series in the midFifties, and though they issued Decoder Badges in 1955 and 1956, as far as the *real* badges were concerned, they never made one after 1949.

The Captain Midnight Code–O–Graph I held in my hand, the one Jeffty said he had gotten in the mail for ten cents *(ten cents!!!)* and two Ovaltine labels, was brand new, shiny gold metal, not a dent or a spot of rust on it like the old ones you can find at exorbitant prices in collectible shoppes from time to time . . . it was a *new* Decoder. And the date on it was *this* year.

But *Captain Midnight* no longer existed. Nothing like it existed on the radio. I'd listened to the one or two weak imitations of old-time radio the networks were currently airing, and the stories were dull, the sound effects bland, the whole feel of it wrong, out of date, cornball. Yet I held a *new* Code–O–Graph.

"Jeffty, tell me about this," I said.

"Tell you what, Donny? It's my new Capt'n Midnight Secret Decoder Badge. I use it to figger out what's gonna happen tomorrow."

"Tomorrow how?"

"On the program."

"What program?!"

He stared at me as if I was being purposely stupid. "On Capt'n *Mid*night! Boy!" I was being dumb.

I still couldn't get it straight. It was right there, right out in the open, and I still didn't know what was happening. "You mean one of those records they made of the old-time radio programs? Is that what you mean, Jeffty?"

"What records?" he asked. He didn't know what *I* meant.

We stared at each other, there under the porch. And then I said, very slowly, almost afraid of the answer, "Jeffty, how do you hear *Captain Midnight?"*

"Every day. On the radio. On my radio. Every day at five-thirty."

News. Music, dumb music, and news. That's what was on the radio every day at 5:30. Not *Captain Midnight.* The Secret Squadron hadn't been on the air in twenty years.

"Can we hear it tonight?" I asked.

"Boy!" he said. I was being dumb. I knew it from the way he said it; but I didn't know *why.* Then it dawned on me: this was

Saturday. *Captain Midnight* was on Monday through Friday. Not on Saturday or Sunday.

"We goin' to the movies?"

He had to repeat himself twice. My mind was somewhere else. Nothing definite. No conclusions. No wild assumptions leapt to. Just off somewhere trying to figure it out, and concluding—as *you* would have concluded, as *any*one would have concluded rather than accepting the truth, the impossible and wonderful truth—just finally concluding there was a simple explanation I didn't yet perceive. Something mundane and dull, like the passage of time that steals all good, old things from us, packratting trinkets and plastic in exchange. And all in the name of Progress.

"We goin' to the movies, Donny?"

"You bet your boots we are, kiddo," I said. And I smiled. And I handed him the Code-O-Graph. And he put it in his side pants pocket. And we crawled out from under the porch. And we went to the movies. And neither of us said anything about *Captain Midnight* all the rest of that day. And there wasn't a ten-minute stretch, all the rest of that day, that I didn't think about it.

•

It was inventory all that next week. I didn't see Jeffty till late Thursday. I confess I left the store in the hands of Jan and David, told them I had some errands to run, and left early. At 4:00. I got to the Kinzers' right around 4:45. Leona answered the door, looking exhausted and distant. "Is Jeffty around?" She said he was upstairs in his room . . .

. . . listening to the radio.

I climbed the stairs two at a time.

All right, I had finally made that impossible, illogical leap. Had the stretch of belief involved anyone but Jeffty, adult or child, I would have reasoned out more explicable answers. But it *was* Jeffty, clearly another kind of vessel of life, and what he might experience should not be expected to fit into the ordered scheme.

I admit it: I *wanted* to hear what I heard.

Even with the door closed, I recognized the program:

"There he goes, Tennessee! Get him!"

There was the heavy report of a squirrel-rifle shot and the

keening whine of the slug ricocheting, and then the same voice yelled triumphantly, *"Got him! D-e-a-a-a-d center!"*

He was listening to the American Broadcasting Company, 790 kilohertz, and he was hearing *Tennessee Jed,* one of my most favorite programs from the Forties, a western adventure I had not heard in twenty years, because it had not existed for twenty years.

I sat down on the top step of the stairs, there in the upstairs hall of the Kinzer home, and I listened to the show. It wasn't a rerun of an old program; I knew every one of them by heart, had never missed an episode. Further evidence that this was a new installment: there were occasional references during the integrated commercials to current cultural and technological developments, and phrases that had not existed in common usage in the Forties: aerosol spray cans, laserasing of tattoos, Tanzania, the word "uptight."

I couldn't ignore it: Jeffty was listening to a *new* segment of *Tennessee Jed.*

I ran downstairs and out the front door to my car. Leona must have been in the kitchen. I turned the key and punched on the radio and spun the dial to 790 kilohertz. The ABC station. Rock music.

I sat there for a few moments, then ran the dial slowly from one end to the other. Music, news, talk shows. No *Tennessee Jed.* And it was a Blaupunkt, the best radio I could get. I wasn't missing some perimeter station. It simply was not there!

After a few moments I turned off the radio and the ignition and went back upstairs quietly. I sat down on the top step and listened to the entire program. It was *wonderful.*

Exciting, imaginative, filled with everything I remembered as being most innovative about radio drama. But it was modern. It wasn't an antique, rebroadcast to assuage the need of that dwindling listenership who longed for the old days. It was a new show, with all the old voices, but still young and bright. Even the commercials were for currently available products, but they weren't as loud or as insulting as the screamer ads one heard on radio these days.

And when *Tennessee Jed* went off at 5:00, I heard Jeffty spin the dial on his radio till I heard the familiar voice of the announcer

Glenn Riggs proclaim, *"Presenting Hop Harrigan! America's ace of the airwaves!"* There was the sound of an airplane in flight. It was a prop plane, *not* a jet! Not the sound kids today have grown up with, but the sound *I* grew up with, the *real* sound of an airplane, the growling, revving, throaty sound of the kind of airplanes G-8 and His Battle Aces flew, the kind Captain Midnight flew, the kind Hop Harrigan flew. And then I heard Hop say, *"CX–4 calling control tower. CX–4 calling control tower. Standing by!"* A pause, then, *"Okay, this is Hop Harrigan . . . coming in!"*

And Jeffty, who had the same problem all of us kids had had in the Forties with programming that pitted equal favorites against one another on different stations, having paid his respects to Hop Harrigan and Tank Tinker, spun the dial and went back to ABC, where I heard the stroke of a gong, the wild cacophony of nonsense Chinese chatter, and the announcer yelled, *"T-e-e-e-rry and the Pirates!"*

I sat there on the top step and listened to Terry and Connie and Flip Corkin and, so help me God, Agnes Moorehead as the Dragon Lady, all of them in a new adventure that took place in a Red China that had not existed in the days of Milton Caniff's 1937 version of the Orient, with river pirates and Chiang Kai-shek and warlords and the naive Imperialism of American gunboat diplomacy.

Sat, and listened to the whole show, and sat even longer to hear *Superman* and part of *Jack Armstrong, the All-American Boy* and part of *Captain Midnight,* and John Kinzer came home and neither he nor Leona came upstairs to find out what had happened to me, or where Jeffty was, and sat longer, and found I had started crying, and could not stop, just sat there with tears running down my face, into the corners of my mouth, sitting and crying until Jeffty heard me and opened his door and saw me and came out and looked at me in childish confusion as I heard the station break for the Mutual Network and they began the theme music of *Tom Mix,* "When It's Round-Up Time in Texas and the Bloom Is on the Sage," and Jeffty touched my shoulder and smiled at me, with his mouth and his big brown eyes, and said, "Hi, Donny. Wanna come in an' listen to the radio with me?"

•

Hume denied the existence of an absolute space, in which each thing has its place; Borges denies the existence of one single time, in which all events are linked.

Jeffty received radio programs from a place that could not, in logic, in the natural scheme of the space-time universe as conceived by Einstein, exist. But that wasn't all he received. He got mail-order premiums that no one was manufacturing. He read comic books that had been defunct for three decades. He saw movies with actors who had been dead for twenty years. He was the receiving terminal for endless joys and pleasures of the past that the world had dropped along the way. On its headlong suicidal flight toward New Tomorrows, the world had razed its treasurehouse of simple happinesses, had poured concrete over its playgrounds, had abandoned its elfin stragglers, and all of it was being impossibly, miraculously shunted back into the present through Jeffty. Revivified, updated, the traditions maintained but contemporaneous. Jeffty was the unbidding Aladdin whose very nature formed the magic lampness of his reality.

And he took me into his world with him.

Because he trusted me.

We had breakfast of Quaker Puffed Wheat Sparkies and warm Ovaltine we drank out of *this* year's Little Orphan Annie Shake-Up Mugs. We went to the movies and while everyone else was seeing a comedy starring Goldie Hawn and Ryan O'Neal, Jeffty and I were enjoying Humphrey Bogart as the professional thief Parker in John Huston's brilliant adaptation of the Donald Westlake novel *Slayground.* The second feature was Spencer Tracy, Carole Lombard and Laird Cregar in the Val Lewton-produced film of *Leiningen Versus the Ants.*

Twice a month we went down to the newsstand and bought the current pulp issues of *The Shadow, Doc Savage* and *Startling Stories.* Jeffty and I sat together and I read to him from the magazines. He particularly liked the new short novel by Henry Kuttner, "The Dreams of Achilles," and the new Stanley G. Weinbaum series of short stories set in the subatomic particle universe of Redurna. In September we enjoyed the first installment of the new Robert E. Howard Conan novel, *Isle of the*

Black Ones, in *Weird Tales;* and in August we were only mildly disappointed by Edgar Rice Burroughs's fourth novella in the Jupiter series featuring John Carter of Barsoom—"Corsairs of Jupiter." But the editor of *Argosy All-Story Weekly* promised there would be two more stories in the series, and it was such an unexpected revelation for Jeffty and me that it dimmed our disappointment at the lessened quality of the current story.

We read comics together, and Jeffty and I both decided—separately, before we came together to discuss it—that our favorite characters were Doll Man, Airboy, and The Heap. We also adored the George Carlson strips in *Jingle Jangle Comics,* particularly the Pie-Face Prince of Old Pretzleburg stories, which we read together and laughed over, even though I had to explain some of the esoteric puns to Jeffty, who was too young to have that kind of subtle wit.

How to explain it? I can't. I had enough physics in college to make some offhand guesses, but I'm more likely wrong than right. The laws of the conservation of energy occasionally break. These are laws that physicists call "weakly violated." Perhaps Jeffty was a catalyst for the weak violation of conservation laws we're only now beginning to realize exist. I tried doing some reading in the area—muon decay of the "forbidden" kind: gamma decay that doesn't include the muon neutrino among its products—but nothing I encountered, not even the latest readings from the Swiss Institute for Nuclear Research near Zurich, gave me an insight. I was thrown back on a vague acceptance of the philosophy that the real name for "science" is *magic.*

No explanations, but enormous good times.

The happiest time of my life.

I had the "real" world, the world of my store and my friends and my family, the world of profit&loss, of taxes and evenings with young women who talked about going shopping or the United Nations, of the rising cost of coffee and microwave ovens. And I had Jeffty's world, in which I existed only when I was with him. The things of the past he knew as fresh and new, I could experience only when in his company. And the membrane between the two worlds grew ever thinner, more luminous and transparent. I had the best of both worlds. And knew, somehow, that I could carry nothing from one to the other.

Forgetting for just a moment, betraying Jeffty by forgetting, brought an end to it all.

Enjoying myself so much, I grew careless and failed to consider how fragile the relationship between Jeffty's world and my world really was. There is a reason why the present begrudges the existence of the past. I never really understood. Nowhere in the beast books, where survival is shown in battles between claw and fang, tentacle and poison sac, is there recognition of the ferocity the present always brings to bear on the past. Nowhere is there a detailed statement of how the Present lies in wait for What-Was, waiting for it to become Now-This-Moment so it can shred it with its merciless jaws.

Who could know such a thing . . . at any age . . . and certainly not at my age . . . who could understand such a thing?

I'm trying to exculpate myself. I can't. It was my fault.

•

It was another Saturday afternoon.

"What's playing today?" I asked him, in the car, on the way downtown.

He looked up at me from the other side of the front seat and smiled one of his best smiles. "Ken Maynard in *Bullwhip Justice* an' *The Demolished Man.*" He kept smiling, as if he'd really put one over on me. I looked at him with disbelief.

"You're *kidd*ing!" I said, delighted. "Bester's *The Demolished Man?*" He nodded his head, delighted at my being delighted. He knew it was one of my favorite books. "Oh, that's super!"

"Super *duper,*" he said.

"Who's in it?"

"Franchot Tone, Evelyn Keyes, Lionel Barrymore, and Elisha Cook, Jr." He was much more knowledgeable about movie actors than I'd ever been. He could name the character actors in any movie he'd ever seen. Even the crowd scenes.

"And cartoons?" I asked.

"Three of 'em: a *Little Lulu,* a *Donald Duck* and a *Bugs Bunny.* An' a *Pete Smith Specialty* an' a Lew Lehr *Monkeys is da C-r-r-r-aziest Peoples.*"

"Oh boy!" I said. I was grinning from ear to ear. And then I looked down and saw the pad of purchase order forms on the seat. I'd forgotten to drop it off at the store.

"Gotta stop by the Center," I said. "Gotta drop off something. It'll only take a minute."

"Okay," Jeffty said. "But we won't be late, will we?"

"Not on your tintype, kiddo," I said.

•

When I pulled into the parking lot behind the Center, he decided to come in with me and we'd walk over to the theater. It's not a large town. There are only two movie houses, the Utopia and the Lyric. We were going to the Utopia and it was only three blocks from the Center.

I walked into the store with the pad of forms, and it was bedlam. David and Jan were handling two customers each, and there were people standing around waiting to be helped. Jan turned a look on me and her face was a horror-mask of pleading. David was running from the stockroom to the showroom and all he could murmur as he whipped past was "Help!" and then he was gone.

"Jeffty," I said, crouching down, "listen, give me a few minutes. Jan and David are in trouble with all these people. We won't be late, I promise. Just let me get rid of a couple of these customers." He looked nervous, but nodded okay.

I motioned to a chair and said, "Just sit down for a while and I'll be right with you."

He went to the chair, good as you please, though he knew what was happening, and he sat down.

I started taking care of people who wanted color television sets. This was the first really substantial batch of units we'd gotten in—color television was only now becoming reasonably priced and this was Sony's first promotion—and it was bonanza time for me. I could see paying off the loan and being out in front for the first time with the Center. It was business.

In my world, good business comes first.

Jeffty sat there and stared at the wall. Let me tell you about the wall.

Stanchion and bracket designs had been rigged from floor to within two feet of the ceiling. Television sets had been stacked artfully on the wall. Thirty-three television sets. All playing at the same time. Black and white, color, little ones, big ones, all going at the same time.

Jeffty sat and watched thirty-three television sets, on a Saturday afternoon. We can pick up a total of thirteen channels including the UHF educational stations. Golf was on one channel; baseball was on a second; celebrity bowling was on a third; the fourth channel was a religious seminar; a teenage dance show was on the fifth; the sixth was a rerun of a situation comedy; the seventh was a rerun of a police show; eighth was a nature program showing a man flycasting endlessly; ninth was news and conversation; tenth was a stock car race; eleventh was a man doing logarithms on a blackboard; twelfth was a woman in a leotard doing setting-up exercises; and on the thirteenth channel was a badly animated cartoon show in Spanish. All but six of the shows were repeated on three sets. Jeffty sat and watched that wall of television on a Saturday afternoon while I sold as fast and as hard as I could, to pay back my Aunt Patricia and stay in touch with my world. It was business.

I should have known better. I should have understood about the present and the way it kills the past. But I was selling with both hands. And when I finally glanced over at Jeffty, half an hour later, he looked like another child.

He was sweating. That terrible fever sweat when you have stomach flu. He was pale, as pasty and pale as a worm, and his little hands were gripping the arms of the chair so tightly I could see his knuckles in bold relief. I dashed over to him, excusing myself from the middle-aged couple looking at the new 21″ Mediterranean model.

"Jeffty!"

He looked at me, but his eyes didn't track. He was in absolute terror. I pulled him out of the chair and started toward the front door with him, but the customers I'd deserted yelled at me, "Hey!" The middle-aged man said, "You wanna sell me this thing or don't you?"

I looked from him to Jeffty and back again. Jeffty was like a zombie. He had come where I'd pulled him. His legs were rubbery and his feet dragged. The past, being eaten by the present, the sound of something in pain.

I clawed some money out of my pants pocket and jammed it into Jeffty's hand. "Kiddo . . . listen to me . . . get out of here right now!" He still couldn't focus properly. *"Jeffty,"* I said as tightly as I could, *"listen* to me!" The middle-aged customer and his wife were walking toward us. "Listen, kiddo, get out of here right this minute. Walk over to the Utopia and buy the tickets. I'll be right behind you." The middle-aged man and his wife were almost on us. I shoved Jeffty through the door and watched him stumble away in the wrong direction, then stop as if gathering his wits, turn and go back past the front of the Center and in the direction of the Utopia. "Yes sir," I said, straightening up and facing them, "yes, ma'am, that is one terrific set with some sen*sa*tional features! If you'll just step back here with me . . ."

There was a terrible sound of something hurting, but I couldn't tell from which channel, or from which set, it was coming.

•

Most of it I learned later, from the girl in the ticket booth, and from some people I knew who came to me to tell me what had happened. By the time I got to the Utopia, nearly twenty minutes later, Jeffty was already beaten to a pulp and had been taken to the manager's office.

"Did you see a very little boy, about five years old, with big brown eyes and straight brown hair . . . he was waiting for me?"

"Oh, I think that's the little boy those kids beat up?"

"What!?! *Where is he?"*

"They took him to the manager's office. No one knew who he was or where to find his parents—"

A young girl wearing an usher's uniform was kneeling down beside the couch, placing a wet paper towel on his face.

I took the towel away from her and ordered her out of the office. She looked insulted and snorted something rude, but she left. I sat on the edge of the couch and tried to swab away the blood from the lacerations without opening the wounds where the blood had caked. Both his eyes were swollen shut. His mouth was ripped badly. His hair was matted with dried blood.

He had been standing in line behind two kids in their teens. They started selling tickets at 12:30 and the show started at 1:00.

The doors weren't opened till 12:45. He had been waiting, and the kids in front of him had had a portable radio. They were listening to the ball game. Jeffty had wanted to hear some program, God knows what it might have been, *Grand Central Station, Let's Pretend, Land of the Lost,* God only knows which one it might have been.

He had asked if he could borrow their radio to hear the program for a minute, and it had been a commercial break or something, and the kids had given him the radio, probably out of some malicious kind of courtesy that would permit them to take offense and rag the little boy. He had changed the station . . . and they'd been unable to get it to go back to the ball game. It was locked into the past, on a station that was broadcasting a program that didn't exist for anyone but Jeffty.

They had beaten him badly . . . as everyone watched.

And then they had run away.

I had left him alone, left him to fight off the present without sufficient weaponry. I had betrayed him for the sale of a 21" Mediterranean console television, and now his face was pulped meat. He moaned something inaudible and sobbed softly.

"Shhh, it's okay, kiddo, it's Donny. I'm here. I'll get you home, it'll be okay."

I should have taken him straight to the hospital. I don't know why I didn't. I should have. I should have done that.

•

When I carried him through the door, John and Leona Kinzer just stared at me. They didn't move to take him from my arms. One of his hands was hanging down. He was conscious, but just barely. They stared, there in the semi-darkness of a Saturday afternoon in the present. I looked at them. "A couple of kids beat him up at the theater." I raised him a few inches in my arms and extended him. They stared at me, at both of us, with nothing in their eyes, without movement. "Jesus Christ," I shouted, "he's been beaten! He's your son! Don't you even want to touch him? What the hell kind of people are you?!"

Then Leona moved toward me very slowly. She stood in front of us for a few seconds, and there was a leaden stoicism in her face that was terrible to see. It said, *I have been in this place before, many times, and I cannot bear to be in it again; but I am here now.*

So I gave him to her. God help me, I gave him over to her.

And she took him upstairs to bathe away his blood and his pain.

John Kinzer and I stood in our separate places in the dim living room of their home, and we stared at each other. He had nothing to say to me.

I shoved past him and fell into a chair. I was shaking.

I heard the bath water running upstairs.

After what seemed a very long time Leona came downstairs, wiping her hands on her apron. She sat down on the sofa and after a moment John sat down beside her. I heard the sound of rock music from upstairs.

"Would you like a piece of nice pound cake?" Leona said.

I didn't answer. I was listening to the sound of the music. Rock music. On the radio. There was a table lamp on the end table beside the sofa. It cast a dim and futile light in the shadowed living room. *Rock music from the present, on a radio upstairs?* I started to say something, and then *knew* . . . Oh, God . . . *no!*

I jumped up just as the sound of hideous crackling blotted out the music, and the table lamp dimmed and flickered. I screamed something, I don't know what it was, and ran for the stairs.

Jeffty's parents did not move. They sat there with their hands folded, in that place they had been for so many years.

I fell twice rushing up the stairs.

•

There isn't much on television that can hold my interest. I bought an old cathedral-shaped Philco radio in a second-hand store, and I replaced all the burnt-out parts with the original tubes from old radios I could cannibalize that still worked. I don't use transistors or printed circuits. They wouldn't work. I've sat in front of that set for hours sometimes, running the dial back and forth as slowly as you can imagine, so slowly it doesn't look as if it's moving at all sometimes.

But I can't find *Captain Midnight* or *Land of the Lost* or *The Shadow* or *Quiet, Please.*

So she did love him, still, a little bit, even after all those years. I can't hate them: they only wanted to live in the present world again. That isn't such a terrible thing.

It's a good world, all things considered. It's much better than it used to be, in a lot of ways. People don't die from the old diseases any more. They die from new ones, but that's Progress, isn't it?

Isn't it?

Tell me.

Somebody please tell me.

1979
37th CONVENTION
BRIGHTON, ENGLAND

John Varley

John Varley is two years younger than Spider Robinson, so you can see the situation grows continually worse. To make it still worse, John is of the Heinlein/van Vogt school of writers, who make it big with their very first few stories. (He published his first in 1974.) What makes it worst of all is that I met him at a regional convention in Philadelphia a few years ago and found to my horror that he is six and a half feet tall and as handsome as the day is long.

It doesn't seem right, somehow.

One of the good points of science fiction, it has always seemed to me, was that a writer could work out almost any subtlety without readers turning a hair. If you deal with the future or with a different world or with a radically different society, there is no limit to the oddities you can insert into your social background. You can deliberately violate any taboo, dislodge anything ordinarily taken for granted, and in this way have a lot of fun, to say nothing of doing a little exploring in ordinarily forbidden territory.

Alas, I'm not much good at this myself, but I did once write a story about a society in which mother love was considered obscene. I don't know that I did a very good job of it. Certainly, the story I wrote ended up being one of my most obscure.

Well, to get to the point—John, in "The Persistence of Vision," takes up a society (no, I won't tell you the details; read for yourself) which I found frightening, and in the highest degree unpleasant. In fact, I wondered if, perhaps, for my own peace of mind I ought *not* to read it—but I *had* to read it because I can't shove a story into an anthology without reading it (even though its presence is compelled by the fact of its Hugo award, whether I like it or not).

And as I read on, John won me over. In fact, he ended with a sentence (no, don't look at it now) which is one of those powerful conclusions that will stay with you forever. It will certainly stay with me forever.

This leads on to further thoughts. People ask me sometimes why so much science fiction seems to be so unpleasant these days. I know what they mean. I cut my teeth on stories of science fiction adventure in which the good guys could be told from the bad guys and you could rely on the good guys winning.

As a matter of fact, I still write stories like that. My stories are accessible. I write clearly, with a beginning, middle, and end, and you know where you are at all times.

The newer generation of writers, however, appears to set itself a harder task. They face up to more ambiguous and realistic situations; they deal with worlds in which good and bad are not conveniently compartmentalized, in which there is confusion of emotions and motives, in which understanding comes not only from words but from all kinds of symbols. The result may be more difficult to understand, but, once understood, may be found to mean more.

However, I trust you will all nevertheless continue to read my own non-obscure stories, for old times' sake (and my economic welfare) if nothing else.

11

THE PERSISTENCE OF VISION

It was the year of the fourth non-depression. I had recently joined the ranks of the unemployed. The President had told me that I had nothing to fear but fear itself. I took him at his word, for once, and set out to backpack to California.

I was not the only one. The world's economy had been writhing like a snake on a hot griddle for the last twenty years, since the early seventies. We were in a boom-and-bust cycle that seemed to have no end. It had wiped out the sense of security the nation had so painfully won in the golden years after the thirties. People were accustomed to the fact that they could be rich one year and on the breadlines the next. I was on the breadlines in '81, and again in '88. This time I decided to use my freedom from the time clock to see the world. I had ideas of stowing away to Japan. I was forty-seven years old and might not get another chance to be irresponsible.

This was in late summer of the year. Sticking out my thumb along the interstate, I could easily forget that there were food riots back in Chicago. I slept at night on top of my bedroll and saw stars and listened to crickets.

I must have walked most of the way from Chicago to Des Moines. My feet toughened up after a few days of awful blisters. The rides were scarce, partly competition from other hitchhikers and partly the times we were living in. The locals were none too anxious to give rides to city people, who they had heard were mostly a bunch of hunger-crazed potential mass murderers. I got roughed up once and told never to return to Sheffield, Illinois.

But I gradually learned the knack of living on the road. I had started with a small supply of canned goods from the welfare and by the time they ran out, I had found that it was possible to work for a meal at many of the farmhouses along the way.

Some of it was hard work, some of it was only a token from people with a deeply ingrained sense that nothing should come for free. A few meals were gratis, at the family table, with grandchildren sitting around while grandpa or grandma told oft-repeated tales of what it had been like in the Big One back in '29, when people had not been afraid to help a fellow out when he was down on his luck. I found that the older the person, the more likely I was to get a sympathetic ear. One of the many tricks you learn. And most older people will give you anything if you'll only sit and listen to them. I got very good at it.

The rides began to pick up west of Des Moines, then got bad again as I neared the refugee camps bordering the China Strip. This was only five years after the disaster, remember, when the Omaha nuclear reactor melted down and a hot mass of uranium and plutonium began eating its way into the earth, headed for China, spreading a band of radioactivity six hundred kilometers downwind. Most of Kansas City, Missouri, was still living in plywood and sheet-metal shantytowns till the city was rendered habitable again.

The refugees were a tragic group. The initial solidarity people show after a great disaster had long since faded into the lethargy and disillusionment of the displaced person. Many of them would be in and out of hospitals for the rest of their lives. To make it worse, the local people hated them, feared them, would not associate with them. They were modern pariahs, unclean. Their children were shunned. Each camp had only a number to identify it, but the local populace called them all Geigertowns.

I made a long detour to Little Rock to avoid crossing the Strip, though it was safe now as long as you didn't linger. I was issued a pariah's badge by the National Guard—a dosimeter—and wandered from one Geigertown to the next. The people were pitifully friendly once I made the first move, and I always slept indoors. The food was free at the community messes.

Once at Little Rock, I found that the aversion to picking up strangers—who might be tainted with "radiation disease"—dropped off, and I quickly moved across Arkansas, Oklahoma, and Texas. I worked a little here and there, but many of the rides were long. What I saw of Texas was through a car window.

I was a little tired of that by the time I reached New Mexico. I decided to do some more walking. By then I was less interested in California than in the trip itself.

I left the roads and went cross-country where there were no fences to stop me. I found that it wasn't easy, even in New Mexico, to get far from signs of civilization.

Taos was the center, back in the '60's, of cultural experiments in alternative living. Many communes and cooperatives were set up in the surrounding hills during that time. Most of them fell apart in a few months, or years, but a few survived. In later years, any group with a new theory of living and a yen to try it out seemed to gravitate to that part of New Mexico. As a result, the land was dotted with ramshackle windmills, solar heating panels, geodesic domes, group marriages, nudists, philosophers, theoreticians, messiahs, hermits, and more than a few just plain nuts.

Taos was great. I could drop into most of the communes and stay for a day or a week, eating organic rice and beans and drinking goat's milk. When I got tired of one, a few hours' walk in any direction would bring me to another. There, I might be offered a night of prayer and chanting or a ritualistic orgy. Some of the groups had spotless barns with automatic milkers for the herds of cows. Others didn't even have latrines; they just squatted. In some, the members dressed like nuns, or Quakers in early Pennsylvania. Elsewhere, they went nude and shaved all their body hair and painted themselves purple. There were all-male and all-female groups. I was urged to stay at most of the former; at the latter, the responses ranged from a bed for the night and good conversation to being met at a barbed-wire fence with a shotgun.

I tried not to make judgments. These people were doing something important, all of them. They were testing ways whereby people didn't have to live in Chicago. That was a wonder to me. I had thought Chicago was inevitable, like diarrhea.

This is not to say they were all successful. Some made Chicago look like Shangri-La. There was one group who seemed to feel that getting back to nature consisted of sleeping in pigshit and eating food a buzzard wouldn't touch. Many were obviously doomed. They would leave behind a group of empty hovels and the memory of cholera.

So the place wasn't paradise, not by a long way. But there were successes. One or two had been there since '63 or '64 and were raising their third generation. I was disappointed to see that most of these were the ones that departed last from established norms of behavior, though some of the differences could be startling. I suppose the most radical experiments are the least likely to bear fruit.

I stayed through the winter. No one was surprised to see me a second time. It seems that many people came to Taos and shopped around. I seldom stayed more than three weeks at any one place, and always pulled my weight. I made many friends and picked up skills that would serve me if I stayed off the roads. I toyed with the idea of staying at one of them forever. When I couldn't make up my mind, I was advised that there was no hurry. I could go to California and return. They seemed sure I would.

So when spring came I headed west over the hills. I stayed off the roads and slept in the open. Many nights I would stay at another commune, until they finally began to get farther apart, then tapered off entirely. The country was not as pretty as before.

Then, three days' leisurely walking from the last commune, I came to a wall.

In 1964, in the United States, there was an epidemic of German measles, or rubella. Rubella is one of the mildest of infectious diseases. The only time it's a problem is when a woman contracts it in the first four months of her pregnancy. It is passed to the fetus, which usually develops complications. These complications include deafness, blindness, and damage to the brain.

In 1964, in the old days before abortion became readily available, there was nothing to be done about it. Many pregnant women caught rubella and went to term. Five thousand deaf-blind children were born in one year. The normal yearly incidence of deaf-blind children in the United States is one hundred and forty.

In 1970 these five thousand potential Helen Kellers were all six years old. It was quickly seen that there was a shortage of Anne Sullivans. Previously, deaf-blind children could be sent to a small number of special institutions.

It was a problem. Not just anyone can cope with a blind-deaf child. You can't tell them to shut up when they moan; you can't reason with them, tell them that the moaning is driving you crazy. Some parents were driven to nervous breakdowns when they tried to keep their children at home.

Many of the five thousand were badly retarded and virtually impossible to reach, even if anyone had been trying. These ended up, for the most part, warehoused in the hundreds of anonymous nursing homes and institutes for "special" children. They were put into beds, cleaned up once a day by a few overworked nurses, and generally allowed the full blessings of liberty: they were allowed to rot freely in their own dark, quiet, private universes. Who can say if it was bad for them? None of them were heard to complain.

Many children with undamaged brains were shuffled in among the retarded because they were unable to tell anyone that they were in there behind the sightless eyes. They failed the batteries of tactile tests, unaware that their fates hung in the balance when they were asked to fit round pegs into round holes to the ticking of a clock they could not see or hear. As a result, they spent the rest of their lives in bed, and none of them complained, either. To protest, one must be aware of the possibility of something better. It helps to have a language, too.

Several hundred of the children were found to have IQ's within the normal range. There were news stories about them as they approached puberty and it was revealed that there were not enough good people to properly handle them. Money was spent, teachers were trained. The education expenditures would go on for a specified period of time, until the children were grown, then things would go back to normal and everyone could congratulate themselves on having dealt successfully with a tough problem.

And indeed, it did work fairly well. There are ways to reach and teach such children. They involve patience, love, and dedication, and the teachers brought all that to their jobs. All the graduates of the special schools left knowing how to speak with their hands. Some could talk. A few could write. Most of them left the institutions to live with parents or relatives, or, if neither was possible, received counseling and help in fitting themselves into society. The options were limited, but people can live rewarding lives under the most severe handicaps. Not everyone, but most of the graduates, were as happy with their lot as could reasonably be expected. Some achieved the almost saintly peace of their role model, Helen Keller. Others became bitter and withdrawn. A few had to be put in asylums, where they became indistinguishable from the others of their group who had spent the last twenty years there. But for the most part, they did well.

But among the group, as in any group, were some misfits. They tended to be among the brightest, the top ten percent in the IQ scores. This was not a reliable rule. Some had unremarkable test scores and were still infected with hunger to do something, to change things, to rock the boat. With a group of five thousand, there were certain to be a few geniuses, a few artists, a few dreamers, hell-raisers, individualists, movers and shapers: a few glorious maniacs.

There was one among them who might have been President but for the fact that she was blind, deaf, and a woman. She was smart, but not one of the geniuses. She was a dreamer, a creative force, an innovator. It was she who dreamed of freedom. But she was not a builder of fairy castles. Having dreamed it, she had to make it come true.

The wall was made of carefully fitted stone and was about five feet high. It was completely out of context with anything I had seen in New Mexico, though it was built of native rock. You just don't build that kind of wall out there. You use barbed wire if something needs fencing in, but many people still made use of the free range and brands. Somehow it seemed transplanted from New England.

It was substantial enough that I felt it would be unwise to crawl over it. I had crossed many wire fences in my travels and had not gotten in trouble for it yet, though I had some talks with some ranchers. Mostly they told me to keep moving, but didn't seem upset about it. This was different. I set out to walk around it.

From the lay of the land, I couldn't tell how far it might reach, but I had time.

At the top of the next rise I saw that I didn't have far to go. The wall made a right-angle turn just ahead. I looked over it and could see some buildings. They were mostly domes, the ubiquitous structure thrown up by communes because of the combination of ease of construction and durability. There were sheep behind the wall, and a few cows. They grazed on grass so green I wanted to go over and roll in it. The wall enclosed a rectangle of green. Outside, where I stood, it was all scrub and sage. These people had access to Rio Grande irrigation water.

I rounded the corner and followed the wall west again.

I saw a man on horseback about the same time he spotted me. He was south of me, outside the wall, and he turned and rode in my direction.

He was a dark man with thick features, dressed in denim and boots with a gray battered Stetson. Navaho, maybe. I don't know much about Indians, but I'd heard they were out here.

"Hello," I said when he'd stopped. He was looking me over. "Am I on your land?"

"Tribal land," he said. "Yeah, you're on it."

"I didn't see any signs."

He shrugged.

"It's okay, bud. You don't look like you out to rustle cattle." He grinned at me. His teeth were large and stained with tobacco. "You be camping out tonight?"

"Yes. How much farther does the, uh, tribal land go? Maybe I'll be out of it before tonight?"

He shook his head gravely. "Nah. You won't be off it tomorrow. 'S all right. You make a fire, you be careful, huh?" He grinned again and started to ride off.

"Hey, what is this place?" I gestured to the wall, and he pulled his horse up and turned around again. It raised a lot of dust.

"Why you asking?" He looked a little suspicious.

"I dunno. Just curious. It doesn't look like the other places I've been to. This wall . . ."

He scowled. "Damn wall." Then he shrugged. I thought that was all he was going to say. Then he went on.

"These people, we look out for 'em, you hear? Maybe we don't go for what they're doin'. But they got it rough, you know?" He looked at me, expecting something. I never did get the knack of talking to these laconic Westerners. I always felt that I was making my sentences too long. They use a shorthand of grunts and shrugs and omitted parts of speech, and I always felt like a dude when I talked to them.

"Do they welcome guests?" I asked. "I thought I might see if I could spend the night."

He shrugged again, and it was a whole different gesture.

"Maybe. They all deaf and blind, you know?" And that was all the conversation he could take for the day. He made a clucking sound and galloped away.

I continued down the wall until I came to a dirt road that wound up the arroyo and entered the wall. There was a wooden gate, but it stood open. I wondered why they took all the trouble with the wall only to leave the gate like that. Then I noticed a circle of narrow-gauge train tracks that came out of the gate, looped around outside it, and rejoined itself. There was a small siding that ran along the outer wall for a few yards.

I stood there a few moments. I don't know what entered into my decision. I think I was a little tired of sleeping out, and I was hungry for a home-cooked meal. The sun was getting closer to the horizon. The land to the west looked like more of the same. If the highway had been visible, I might have headed that way and hitched a ride. But I turned the other way and went through the gate.

I walked down the middle of the tracks. There was a wooden fence on each side of the road, built of horizontal planks, like a corral. Sheep grazed on one side of me. There was a Shetland sheepdog with them, and she raised her ears and followed me with her eyes as I passed, but did not come when I whistled.

It was about half a mile to the cluster of buildings ahead. There were four or five domes made of something translucent, like greenhouses, and several conventional square buildings. There were two windmills turning lazily in the breeze. There were several banks of solar water heaters. These are flat constructions of glass and wood, held off the ground so they can tilt to follow the sun. They were almost vertical now, intercepting the oblique rays of sunset. There were a few trees, what might have been an orchard.

About halfway there I passed under a wooden footbridge. It arched over the road, giving access from the east pasture to the west pasture. I wondered, What was wrong with a simple gate?

Then I saw something coming down the road in my direction. It was traveling on the tracks and it was very quiet. I stopped and waited.

It was a sort of converted mining engine, the sort that pulls loads of coal up from the bottom of shafts. It was battery-powered, and it had gotten quite close before I heard it. A small man was driving it. He was pulling a car behind him and singing as loud as he could with absolutely no sense of pitch.

He got closer and closer, moving about five miles per hour, one hand held out as if he was signaling a left turn. Suddenly I realized what was happening, as he was bearing down on me. He wasn't going to stop. He was counting fence posts with his hand. I scrambled up the fence just in time. There wasn't more than six inches of clearance between the train and the fence on either side. His palm touched my leg as I squeezed close to the fence, and he stopped abruptly.

He leaped from the car and grabbed me and I thought I was in trouble. But he looked concerned, not angry, and felt me all over, trying to discover if I was hurt. I was embarrassed. Not from the examination; because I had been foolish. The Indian had said they were all deaf and blind but I guess I hadn't quite believed him.

He was flooded with relief when I managed to convey to him that I was all right. With eloquent gestures he made me understand that I was not to stay on the road. He indicated that I should climb over the fence and continue through the fields. He repeated himself several times to be sure I understood, then held on to me as I climbed over to assure himself that I was out of the way. He reached over the fence and held my shoulders, smiling at me. He pointed to the road and shook his head, then pointed to the buildings and nodded. He touched my head and smiled when I nodded. He climbed back onto the engine and started up, all the time nodding and pointing where he wanted me to go. Then he was off again.

I debated what to do. Most of me said turn around, go back to the wall by way of the pasture, and head back into the hills. These people probably wouldn't want me around. I doubted that I'd be able to talk to them, and they might even resent me. On the other hand, I was fascinated, as who wouldn't be? I wanted to see how they managed it. I still didn't believe that they were *all* deaf and blind. It didn't seem possible.

The Sheltie was sniffing at my pants. I looked down at her and she backed away, then daintily approached me as I held out my open hand. She sniffed, then licked me. I patted her on the head, and she hustled back to her sheep.

I turned toward the buildings.

The first order of business was money.

None of the students knew much about it from experience, but the library was full of Braille books. They started reading.

One of the first things that became apparent was that when money was mentioned, lawyers were not far away. The students wrote letters. From the replies, they selected a lawyer and retained him.

They were in a school in Pennsylvania at the time. The original pupils of the special schools, five hundred in number, had been narrowed down to about seventy as people left to live with relatives or found other solutions to their special problems. Of those seventy, some had places to go but didn't want to go there; others had few alternatives. Their parents were either dead or not interested in living with them. So the seventy had been gathered from the schools around the country into this one, while ways to deal with them were worked out. The authorities had plans, but the students beat them to it.

Each of them had been entitled to a guaranteed annual income since 1980. They had been under the care of the government, so they had not received it. They sent their lawyer to court. He came back with a ruling that they could not collect. They appealed, and won. The money was paid retroactively, with interest, and came to a healthy sum. They thanked their lawyer and retained a real estate agent. Meanwhile, they read.

They read about communes in New Mexico, and instructed their agent to look for something out there. He made a deal for a tract to be leased in perpetuity from the Navaho nation. They read about the land, found that it would need a lot of water to be productive in the way they wanted it to be.

They divided into groups to research what they would need to be self-sufficient.

Water could be obtained by tapping into the canals that carried it from the reservoirs on the Rio Grande into the reclaimed land in the south. Federal money was available for the project through a labyrinthine scheme involving HEW, the Agriculture Department, and the Bureau of Indian Affairs. They ended up paying little for their pipeline.

The land was arid. It would need fertilizer to be of use in raising sheep without resorting to open-range techniques. The cost of fertilizer could be subsidized through the Rural Resettlement Program. After that, planting clover would enrich the soil with all the nitrates they could want.

There were techniques available to farm ecologically, without worrying about fertilizers or pesticides. Everything was recycled. Essentially, you put sunlight and water into one end and harvested wool, fish, vegetables, apples, honey, and eggs at the other end. You used nothing but the land, and replaced even that as you recycled your waste products back into the soil. They were not interested in agribusiness with huge combine harvesters and crop dusters. They didn't even want to turn a profit. They merely wanted sufficiency.

The details multiplied. Their leader, the one who had had the original idea and the drive to put it into action in the face of overwhelming obstacles, was a dynamo named Janet Reilly. Knowing nothing about the techniques generals and executives employ to achieve large objectives, she invented them herself and adapted them to the peculiar needs and limitations of her group. She assigned task forces to look into solutions of each aspect of their project: law, science, social planning, design, buying, logistics, construction. At any one time, she was the only person who knew everything about what was happening. She kept it all in her head, without notes of any kind.

It was in the area of social planning that she showed herself to be a visionary and not just a superb organizer. Her idea was not to make a place where they could lead a life that was a sightless, soundless imitation of their unafflicted peers. She wanted a whole new start, a way of living that was by and for the blind-deaf, a way of living that accepted no convention just because that was the way it had always been done. She examined every human cultural institution from marriage to indecent exposure to see how it related to her needs and the needs of her friends. She was aware of the peril of this approach, but was undeterred. Her Social Task Force read about every variant group that had ever tried to make it on its own anywhere, and brought her reports about how and why they had failed or succeeded. She filtered this information through her own experiences to see how it would work for her unusual group with its own set of needs and goals.

The details were endless. They hired an architect to put their ideas into Braille blueprints. Gradually the plans evolved. They spent more money. The construction began, supervised on the site by their architect, who by now was so fascinated by the scheme that she donated her services. It was an important break, for they needed someone there whom they could trust. There is only so much that can be accomplished at such a distance.

When things were ready for them to move, they ran into bureaucratic trouble. They had anticipated it, but it was a setback. Social agencies charged with overseeing their welfare doubted the wisdom of the project. When it became apparent that no amount of reasoning was going to stop it, wheels were set in motion that resulted in a restraining order, issued for their own protection, preventing them from leaving the school. They were twenty-one years old by then, all of them, but were judged mentally incompetent to manage their own affairs. A hearing was scheduled.

Luckily, they still had access to their lawyer. He also had become infected with the crazy vision, and put on a great battle for them. He succeeded in getting a ruling concerning the rights of institutionalized persons, later upheld by the Supreme Court, which eventually had severe repercussions in state and county hospitals. Realizing the trouble they were already in regarding the thousands of patients in inadequate facilities across the country, the agencies gave in.

By then, it was the spring of 1986, one year after their target date. Some of their fertilizer had washed away already for lack of erosion-preventing clover. It was getting late to start crops, and they were running short of money. Nevertheless, they moved to New Mexico and began the backbreaking job of getting everything started. There were fifty-five of them, with nine children aged three months to six years.

I don't know what I expected. I remember that everything was a surprise, either because it was so normal or because it was so different. None of my idiot surmises about what such a place might be like proved to be true. And of course I didn't know the history of the place; I learned that later, picked up in bits and pieces.

I was surprised to see lights in some of the buildings. The first thing I had assumed was that they would have no need of them. That's an example of something so normal that it surprised me.

As to the differences, the first thing that caught my attention was the fence around the rail line. I had a personal interest in it, having almost been injured by it. I struggled to understand, as I must if I was to stay even for a night.

The wood fences that enclosed the rails on their way to the gate continued up to a barn, where the rails looped back on themselves in the same way they did outside the wall. The entire line was enclosed by the fence. The only access was a loading platform by the barn, and the gate to the outside. It made sense. The only way a deaf-blind person could operate a conveyance like that would be with assurances that there was no one on the track. These people would *never* go on the tracks; there was no way they could be warned of an approaching train.

There were people moving around me in the twilight as I made my way into the group of buildings. They took no notice of me, as I had expected. They moved fast; some of them were actually running. I stood still, eyes searching all around me so no one would come crashing into me. I had to figure out how they kept from crashing into each other before I got bolder.

I bent to the ground and examined it. The light was getting bad, but I saw immediately that there were concrete sidewalks crisscrossing the area. Each of the walks was etched with a different sort of pattern in grooves that had been made before the stuff set—lines, waves, depressions, patches of rough and smooth. I quickly saw that the people who were in a hurry moved only on those walkways, and they were all barefoot. It was no trick to see that it was some sort of traffic pattern read with the feet. I stood up. I didn't need to know how it worked. It was sufficient to know what it was and stay off the paths.

The people were unremarkable. Some of them were not dressed, but I was used to that by now. They came in all shapes and sizes, but all seemed to be about the same age except for the children. Except for the fact that they did not stop and talk or even wave as they approached each other, I would never have guessed they were blind. I watched them come to intersections in the pathways—I didn't know how they knew they were there, but could think of several ways—and slow down as they crossed. It was a marvelous system.

I began to think of approaching someone. I had been there for almost half an hour, an intruder. I guess I had a false sense of these people's vulnerability; I felt like a burglar.

I walked along beside a woman for a minute. She was very purposeful in her eyes-ahead stride, or seemed to be. She sensed something, maybe my footsteps. She slowed a little, and I touched her on the shoulder, not knowing what else to do. She stopped instantly and turned toward me. Her eyes were open but vacant. Her hands were all over me, lightly touching my face, my chest, my hands, fingering my clothing. There was no doubt in my mind that she knew me for a stranger, probably from the first tap on the shoulder. But she smiled warmly at me, and hugged me. Her hands were very delicate and warm. That's funny, because they were callused from hard work. But they felt sensitive.

She made me to understand—by pointing to the building, making eating motions with an imaginary spoon, and touching a number on her watch—that supper was served in an hour, and that I was invited. I nodded and smiled beneath her hands; she kissed me on the cheek and hurried off.

Well. It hadn't been so bad. I had worried about my ability to communicate. Later I found out she learned a great deal more about me than I had told.

I put off going into the mess hall or whatever it was. I strolled around in the gathering darkness looking at their layout. I saw the little Sheltie bringing the sheep back to the fold for the night. She herded them expertly through the open gate without any instructions, and one of the residents closed it and locked them in. The man bent and scratched the dog on the head and got his hand licked. Her chores done for the night, the dog hurried over to me and sniffed my pant leg. She followed me around the rest of the evening.

Everyone seemed so busy that I was surprised to see one woman sitting on a rail fence, doing nothing. I went over to her.

Closer, I saw that she was younger than I had thought. She was thirteen, I learned later. She wasn't wearing any clothes. I touched her on the shoulder, and she jumped down from the fence and went through the same routine as the other woman had, touching me all over with no reserve. She took my hand and I felt her fingers moving rapidly in my palm. I couldn't understand it, but knew what it was. I shrugged, and tried out other gestures to indicate that I didn't speak hand talk. She nodded, still feeling my face with her hands.

She asked me if I was staying to dinner. I assured her that I was. She asked me if I was from a university. And if you think that's easy to ask with only body movements, try it. But she was so graceful and supple in her movements, so deft at getting her meaning across. It was beautiful to watch her. It was speech and ballet at the same time.

I told her I wasn't from a university, and launched into an attempt to tell her a little about what I was doing and how I got there. She listened to me with her hands, scratching her head graphically when I failed to make my meanings clear. All the time the smile on her face got broader and broader, and she would laugh silently at my antics. All this while standing very close to me, touching me. At last she put her hands on her hips.

"I guess you need the practice," she said, "but if it's all the same to you, could we talk mouthtalk for now? You're cracking me up."

I jumped as if stung by a bee. The touching, while something I could ignore for a deaf-blind girl, suddenly seemed out of place. I stepped back a little, but her hands returned to me. She looked puzzled, then read the problem with her hands.

"I'm sorry," she said. "You thought I was deaf and blind. If I'd known I would have told you right off."

"I thought everyone here was."

"Just the parents. I'm one of the children. We all hear and see quite well. Don't be so nervous. If you can't stand touching, you're not going to like it here. Relax, I won't hurt you." And she kept her hands moving over me, mostly my face. I didn't understand it at the time, but it didn't seem sexual. Turned out I was wrong, but it wasn't blatant.

"You'll need me to show you the ropes," she said, and started for the domes. She held my hand and walked close to me. Her other hand kept moving to my face every time I talked.

"Number one, stay off the concrete paths. That's where—"

"I already figured that out."

"You did? How long have you been here?" Her hands searched my face with renewed interest. It was quite dark.

"Less than an hour. I was almost run over by your train."

She laughed, then apologized and said she knew it wasn't funny to me.

I told her it *was* funny to me now, though it hadn't been at the time. She said there was a warning sign on the gate, but I had been unlucky enough to come when the gate was open—they opened it by remote control before a train started up—and I hadn't seen it.

"What's your name?" I asked her, as we neared the soft yellow lights coming from the dining room.

Her hand worked reflexively in mine, then stopped. "Oh, I don't know. I *have* one; several, in fact. But they're in bodytalk. I'm . . . Pink. It translates as Pink, I guess."

There was a story behind it. She had been the first child born to the school students. They knew that babies were described as being pink, so they called her that. She felt pink to them. As we entered the hall, I could see that her name was visually inaccurate. One of her parents had been black. She was dark, with blue eyes and curly hair lighter than her skin. She had a broad nose, but small lips.

She didn't ask my name, so I didn't offer it. No one asked my name, in speech, the entire time I was there. They called me many things in bodytalk, and when the children called me it was "Hey, you!" They weren't big on spoken words.

The dining hall was in a rectangular building made of brick. It connected to one of the large domes. It was dimly lighted. I later learned that the lights were for me alone. The children didn't need them for anything but reading. I held Pink's hand, glad to have a guide. I kept my eyes and ears open.

"We're informal," Pink said. Her voice was embarrassingly loud in the large room. No one else was talking at all; there were just the sounds of movement and breathing. Several of the children looked up. "I won't introduce you around now. Just feel like part of the family. People will feel you later, and you can talk to them. You can take your clothes off here at the door."

I had no trouble with that. Everyone else was nude, and I could easily adjust to household customs by that time. You take your shoes off in Japan, you take your clothes off in Taos. What's the difference?

Well, quite a bit, actually. There was all the touching that went on. Everybody touched everybody else, as routinely as glancing. Everyone touched my face first, then went on with what seemed like total innocence to touch me everywhere else. As usual, it was not quite what it seemed. It was *not* innocent, and it was not the usual treatment they gave others in their group. They touched each other's genitals a lot *more* than they touched mine. They were holding back with me so I wouldn't be frightened. They were very polite with strangers.

There was a long, low table, with everyone sitting on the floor around it. Pink led me to it.

"See the bare strips on the floor? Stay out of them. Don't leave anything in them. That's where people walk. Don't *ever* move anything. Furniture, I mean. That has to be decided at full meetings, so we'll all know where everything is. Small things, too. If you pick up something, put it back exactly where you found it."

"I understand."

People were bringing bowls and platters of food from the adjoining kitchen. They set them on the table, and the diners began feeling them. They ate with their fingers, without plates, and they did it slowly and lovingly. They smelled things for a long time before they took a bite. Eating was very sensual to these people.

They were *terrific* cooks. I have never, before or since, eaten as well as I did at Keller. (That's my name for it, in speech, though their bodytalk name was something very like that. When I called it Keller, everyone knew what I was talking about.) They started off with good, fresh produce, something that's hard enough to find in the cities, and went at the cooking with artistry and imagination. It wasn't like any national style I've eaten. They improvised, and seldom cooked the same thing the same way twice.

I sat between Pink and the fellow who had almost run me down earlier. I stuffed myself disgracefully. It was too far removed from beef jerky and the organic dry cardboard I had been eating for me to be able to resist. I lingered over it, but still finished long before anyone else. I watched them as I sat back carefully and wondered if I'd be sick. (I wasn't, thank God.) They fed themselves and each other, sometimes getting up and going clear around the table to offer a choice morsel to a friend on the other side. I was fed in this way by all too many of them, and nearly popped until I learned a pidgin phrase in handtalk, saying I was full to the brim. I learned from Pink that a friendlier way to refuse was to offer something myself.

Eventually I had nothing to do but feed Pink and look at the others. I began to be more observant. I had thought they were eating in solitude, but soon saw that lively conversation was flowing around the table. Hands were busy, moving almost too fast to see. They were spelling into each other's palms, shoulders, legs, arms, bellies; any part of the body. I watched in amazement as a ripple of laughter spread like falling dominoes from one end of the table to the other as some witticism was passed along the line. It was *fast.* Looking carefully, I could see the thoughts moving, reaching one person, passed on while a reply went in the other direction and was in turn passed on, other replies originating all along the line and bouncing back and forth. They were a wave form, like water.

It was messy. Let's face it; eating with your fingers and talking with your hands is going to get you smeared with food. But no one minded. *I* certainly didn't. I was too busy feeling left out.

Pink talked to me, but I knew I was finding out what it's like to be deaf. These people were friendly and seemed to like me, but could do nothing about it. We couldn't communicate.

Afterwards, we all trooped outside, except the cleanup crew, and took a shower beneath a set of faucets that gave out very cold water. I told Pink I'd like to help with the dishes, but she said I'd just be in the way. I couldn't do anything around Keller until I learned their very specific ways of doing things. She seemed to be assuming already that I'd be around that long.

Back into the building to dry off, which they did with their usual puppy dog friendliness, making a game and a gift of toweling each other, and then we went into the dome.

It was warm inside, warm and dark. Light entered from the passage to the dining room, but it wasn't enough to blot out the stars through the lattice of triangular panes overhead. It was almost like being out in the open.

Pink quickly pointed out the positional etiquette within the dome. It wasn't hard to follow, but I still tended to keep my arms and legs pulled in close so I wouldn't trip someone by sprawling into a walk space.

My misconceptions got me again. There was no sound but the soft whisper of flesh against flesh, so I thought I was in the middle of an orgy. I had been at them before, in other communes, and they looked pretty much like this. I quickly saw that I was wrong, and only later found out I had been right. In a sense.

What threw my evaluations out of whack was the simple fact that group conversation among these people *had* to look like an orgy. The much subtler observation that I made later was that with a hundred naked bodies sliding, rubbing, kissing, caressing, all at the same time, what was the point in making a distinction? There was no distinction.

I have to say that I use the noun "orgy" only to get across a general idea of many people in close contact. I don't like the word, it is too ripe with connotations. But I had these connotations myself at the time, so I was relieved to see that it was not an orgy. The ones I had been to had been tedious and impersonal, and I had hoped for better from these people.

Many wormed their way through the crush to get to me and meet me. Never more than one at a time; they were constantly aware of what was going on and were waiting their turn to talk to me. Naturally, I didn't know it then. Pink sat with me to interpret the hard thoughts. I eventually used her words less and less, getting into the spirit of tactile seeing and understanding. No one felt they really knew me until they had touched every part of my body, so there were hands on me all the time. I timidly did the same.

What with all the touching, I quickly got an erection, which embarrassed me quite a bit. I was berating myself for being unable to keep sexual responses out of it, for not being able to operate on the same intellectual plane I thought they were on, when I realized with some shock that the couple next to me was making love. They had been doing it for the last ten minutes, actually, and it had seemed such a natural part of what was happening that I had known it and not known it at the same time.

No sooner had I realized it than I suddenly wondered if I was right. *Were they?* It was very slow and the light was bad. But her legs were up, and he was on top of her, that much I was sure of. It was foolish of me, but I really had to know. I had to find out *what the hell I was in.* How could I give the proper social responses if I didn't know the situation?

I was very sensitive to polite behavior after my months at the various communes. I had become adept at saying prayers before supper in one place, chanting Hare Krishna at another, and going happily nudist at still another. It's called "when in Rome," and if you can't adapt to it you shouldn't go visiting. I would kneel to Mecca, burp after my meals, toast anything that was proposed, eat organic rice and compliment the cook; but to do it right, you have to know the customs. I had thought I knew them, but had changed my mind three times in as many minutes.

They *were* making love, in the sense that he was penetrating her. They were also deeply involved with each other. Their hands fluttered like butterflies all over each other, filled with meanings I couldn't see or feel. But they were being touched by and were touching many other people around them. They were talking to all these people, even if the message was as simple as a pat on the forehead or arm.

Pink noticed where my attention was. She was sort of wound around me, without really doing anything I would have thought of as provocative. I just couldn't *decide.* It seemed so innocent, and yet it wasn't.

"That's (—) and (—)," she said, the parentheses indicating a series of hand motions against my palm. I never learned a sound word as a name for any of them but Pink, and I can't reproduce the bodytalk names they had. Pink reached over, touched the woman with her foot, and did some complicated business with her toes. The woman smiled and grabbed Pink's foot, her fingers moving.

"(—) would like to talk with you later," Pink told me. "Right after she's through talking to (—). You met her earlier, remember? She says she likes your hands."

Now this is going to sound crazy, I know. It sounded pretty crazy to me when I thought of it. It dawned on me with a sort of revelation that her word for talk and mine were miles apart. Talk, to her, meant a complex interchange involving all parts of the body. She could read words or emotions in every twitch of my muscles, like a lie detector. Sound, to her, was only a minor part of communication. It was something she used to speak to outsiders. Pink talked with her whole being.

I didn't have the half of it, even then, but it was enough to turn my head entirely around in relation to these people. They talked with their bodies. It wasn't all hands, as I'd thought. Any part of the body in contact with any other was communication, sometimes a very simple and basic sort—think of McLuhan's light bulb as the basic medium of information—perhaps saying no more than "I am here." But talk was talk, and if conversation evolved to the point where you needed to talk to another with your genitals, it was still a part of the conversation. What I wanted to know was *what were they saying?* I knew, even at that dim moment or realization, that it was much more than I could grasp. Sure, you're saying. You know about talking to your lover with your body as you make love. That's not such a new idea. Of course it isn't, but think how wonderful that talk is even when you're not primarily tactile-oriented. Can you carry the thought from there, or are you doomed to be an earthworm thinking about sunsets?

While this was happening to me, there was a woman getting acquainted with my body. Her hands were on me, in my lap, when I felt myself ejaculating. It was a big surprise to me, but to no one else. I had been telling everyone around me for many minutes, through signs they could feel with their hands, that it was going to happen. Instantly, hands were all over my body. I could almost understand them as they spelled tender thoughts to me. I got the gist, anyway, if not the words. I was terribly embarrassed for only a moment, then it passed away in the face of the easy acceptance. It was very intense. For a long time I couldn't get my breath.

The woman who had been the cause of it touched my lips with her fingers. She moved them slowly, but meaningfully I was sure. Then she melted back into the group.

"What did she say?" I asked Pink.

She smiled at me. "You know, of course. If you'd only cut loose from your verbalizing. But, generally, she meant 'How nice for you.' It also translates as 'How nice for me.' And 'me,' in this sense, means all of us. The organism."

I knew I had to stay and learn to speak.

The commune had its ups and downs. They had expected them, in general, but had not known what shape they might take.

Winter killed many of their fruit trees. They replaced them with hybrid strains. They lost more fertilizer and soil in windstorms because the clover had not had time to anchor it down. Their schedule had been thrown off by the court actions, and they didn't really get things settled in a groove for more than a year.

Their fish all died. They used the bodies for fertilizer and looked into what might have gone wrong. They were using a three-stage ecology of the type pioneered by the New Alchemists in the '70's. It consisted of three domed ponds: one containing fish, another with crushed shells and bacteria in one section and algae in another, and a third full of daphnids. The water containing fish waste from the first pond was pumped through the shells and bacteria, which detoxified it and converted the ammonia it contained into fertilizer for the algae. The algae water was pumped into the second pond to feed the daphnids. Then daphnids and algae were pumped to the fish pond as food and the enriched water was used to fertilize greenhouse plants in all of the domes.

They tested the water and the soil and found that chemicals were being leached from impurities in the shells and concentrated down the food chain. After a thorough cleanup, they restarted and all went well. But they had lost their first cash crop.

They never went hungry. Nor were they cold; there was plenty of sunlight year-round to power the pumps and the food cycle and to heat their living quarters. They had built their buildings half buried with an eye to the heating and cooling powers of convective currents. But they had to spend some of their capital. The first year they showed a loss.

One of their buildings caught fire during the first winter. Two men and a small girl were killed when a sprinkler system malfunctioned. This was a shock to them. They had thought things would operate as advertised. None of them knew much about the building trades, about estimates as opposed to realities. They found that several of their installations were not up to specifications, and instituted a program of periodic checks on everything. They learned to strip down and repair anything on the farm. If something contained electronics too complex for them to cope with, they tore it out and installed something simpler.

Socially, their progress had been much more encouraging. Janet had wisely decided that there would be only two hard and fast objectives in the realm of their relationships. The first was that she refused to be their president, chairwoman, chief, or supreme commander. She had seen from the start that a driving personality was needed to get the planning done and the land bought and a sense of purpose fostered from their formless desire for an alternative. But once at the promised land, she abdicated. From that point they would operate as a democratic communism. If that failed, they would adopt a new approach. Anything but a dictatorship with her at the head. She wanted no part of that.

The second principle was to accept nothing. There had never been a blind-deaf community operating on its own. They had no expectations to satisfy, they did not need to live as the sighted did. They were alone. There was no one to tell them not to do something simply because it was not done.

They had no clearer idea of what their society would be than anyone else. They had been forced into a mold that was not relevant to their needs, but beyond that they didn't know. They would search out the behavior that made sense, the moral things for blind-deaf people to do. They understood the basic principles of morals: that nothing is moral always, and anything is moral under the right circumstances. It all had to do with social context. They were starting from a blank slate, with no models to follow.

By the end of the second year they had their context. They continually modified it, but the basic pattern was set. They knew themselves and what they were as they had never been able to do at the school. They defined themselves in their own terms.

I spent my first day at Keller in school. It was the obvious and necessary step. I had to learn handtalk.

Pink was kind and very patient. I learned the basic alphabet and practiced hard at it. By the afternoon she was refusing to talk to me, forcing me to speak with my hands. She would speak only when pressed hard, and eventually not at all. I scarcely spoke a single word after the third day.

This is not to say that I was suddenly fluent. Not at all. At the end of the first day I knew the alphabet and could laboriously make myself understood. I was not so good at reading words spelled into my own palm. For a long time I had to look at the hand to see what was spelled. But like any language, eventually you think in it. I speak fluent French, and I can recall my amazement when I finally reached the point where I wasn't translating my thoughts before I spoke. I reached it at Keller in about two weeks.

I remember one of the last things I asked Pink in speech. It was something that was worrying me.

"Pink, am I welcome here?"

"You've been here three days. Do you feel rejected?"

"No, it's not that. I guess I just need to hear your policy about outsiders. How *long* am I welcome?"

She wrinkled her brow. It was evidently a new question.

"Well, practically speaking, until a majority of us decide we want you to go. But that's never happened. No one's stayed here much longer than a few days. We've never had to evolve a policy about what to do, for instance, if someone who sees and hears wants to join us. No one has, so far, but I guess it could happen. My guess is that they wouldn't accept it. They're very independent and jealous of their freedom, though you might not have noticed it. I don't think you could ever be one of them. But as long as you're willing to think of yourself as a guest, you could probably stay for twenty years."

"You said 'they.' Don't you include yourself in the group?"

For the first time she looked a little uneasy. I wish I had been better at reading body language at the time. I think my hands could have told me volumes about what she was thinking.

"Sure," she said. "The children are part of the group. We like it. I sure wouldn't want to be anywhere else, from what I know of the outside."

"I don't blame you." There were things left unsaid here, but I didn't know enough to ask the right questions. "But it's never a problem, being able to see when none of your parents can? They don't . . . resent you in any way?"

This time she laughed. "Oh, no. Never that. They're much too independent for that. You've seen it. They don't *need* us for anything they can't do themselves. We're part of the family. We do exactly the same things they do. And it really doesn't matter. Sight, I mean. Hearing, either. Just look around you. Do I have any special advantages because I can see where I'm going?"

I had to admit that she didn't. But there was still the hint of something she wasn't saying to me.

"I know what's bothering you. About staying here." She had to draw me back to my original question; I had been wandering.

"What's that?"

"You don't feel a part of the daily life. You're not doing your share of the chores. You're very conscientious and you want to do your part. I can tell."

She read me right, as usual, and I admitted it.

"And you won't be able to until you can talk to everybody. So let's get back to your lessons. Your fingers are still very sloppy."

There was a lot of work to be done. The first thing I had to learn was to slow down. They were slow and methodical workers, made few mistakes, and didn't care if a job took all day so long as it was done well. When I was working by myself I didn't have to worry about it: sweeping, picking apples, weeding in the gardens. But when I was on a job that required teamwork I had to learn a whole new pace. Eyesight enables a person to do many aspects of a job at once with a few quick glances. A blind person will take each aspect of the job in turn if the job is spread out. Everything has to be verified by touch. At a bench job, though, they could be much faster than I. They could make me feel as though I was working with my toes instead of fingers.

I never suggested that I could make anything quicker by virtue of my sight or hearing. They quite rightly would have told me to mind my own business. Accepting sighted help was the first step to dependence, and after all, they would still be here with the same jobs to do after I was gone.

And that got me to thinking about the children again. I began to be positive that there was an undercurrent of resentment, maybe unconscious, between the parents and children. It was obvious that there was a great deal of love between them, but how could the children fail to resent the rejection of their talent? So my reasoning went, anyway.

I quickly fit myself into the routine. I was treated no better or worse than anyone else, which gratified me. Though I would never become part of the group, even if I should desire it, there was absolutely no indication that I was anything but a full member. That's just how they treated guests: as they would one of their own number.

Life was fulfilling out there in a way it has never been in the cities. It wasn't unique to Keller, this pastoral peace, but the people there had it in generous helpings. The earth beneath your bare feet is something you can never feel in a city park.

Daily life was busy and satisfying. There were chickens and hogs to feed, bees and sheep to care for, fish to harvest, and cows to milk. Everybody worked: men, women, and children. It all seemed to fit together without any apparent effort. Everybody seemed to know what to do when it needed doing. You could think of it as a well-oiled machine, but I never liked that metaphor, especially for people. I thought of it as an organism. Any social group is, but this one *worked.* Most of the other communes I'd visited had glaring flaws. Things would not get done because everyone was too stoned or couldn't be bothered or didn't see the necessity of doing it in the first place. That sort of ignorance leads to typhus and soil erosion and people freezing to death and invasions of social workers who take your children away. I'd seen it happen.

Not here. They had a good picture of the world as it is, not the rosy misconceptions so many other utopians labor under. They did the jobs that needed doing.

I could never detail all the nuts and bolts (there's that machine metaphor again) of how the place worked. The fish-cycle ponds alone were complicated enough to over-awe me. I killed a spider in one of the greenhouses, then found out it had been put there to eat a specific set of plant predators. Same for the frogs. There were insects in the water to kill other insects; it got to a point where I was afraid to swat a mayfly without prior okay.

As the days went by I was told some of the history of the place. Mistakes had been made, though surprisingly few. One had been in the area of defense. They had made no provision for it at first, not knowing much about the brutality and random violence that reaches even to the out-of-the-way corners. Guns were the logical and preferred choice out here, but were beyond their capabilities.

One night a carload of men who had had too much to drink showed up. They had heard of the place in town. They stayed for two days, cutting the phone lines and raping many of the women.

The people discussed all the options after the invasion was over, and settled on the organic one. They bought five German shepherds. Not the psychotic wretches that are marketed under the description of "attack dogs," but specially trained ones from a firm recommended by the Albuquerque police. They were trained as both Seeing-Eye and police dogs. They were perfectly harmless until an outsider showed overt agression, then they were trained, not to disarm, but to go for the throat.

It worked, like most of their solutions. The second invasion resulted in two dead and three badly injured, all on the other side. As a backup in case of a concerted attack, they hired an ex-marine to teach them the fundamentals of close-in dirty fighting. These were not dewy-eyed flower children.

There were three superb meals a day. And there was leisure

time, too. It was not all work. There was time to take a friend out and sit in the grass under a tree, usually around sunset, just before the big dinner. There was time for someone to stop working for a few minutes, to share some special treasure. I remember being taken by the hand by one woman—whom I must call Tall-one-with-the-green-eyes—to a spot where mushrooms were growing in the cool crawl space beneath the barn. We wriggled under until our faces were buried in the patch, picked a few, and smelled them. She showed me how to smell. I would have thought a few weeks before that we had ruined their beauty, but after all it was only visual. I was already beginning to discount that sense, which is so removed from the essence of an object. She showed me that they were still beautiful to touch and smell after we had apparently destroyed them. Then she was off to the kitchen with the pick of the bunch in her apron. They tasted all the better that night.

And a man—I will call him Baldy—who brought me a plank he and one of the women had been planing in the woodshop. I touched its smoothness and smelled it and agreed with him how good it was.

And after the evening meal, the Together.

During my third week there I had an indication of my status with the group. It was the first real test of whether I meant anything to them. Anything special, I mean. I wanted to see them as my friends, and I suppose I was a little upset to think that just anyone who wandered in here would be treated the way I was. It was childish and unfair to them, and I wasn't even aware of the discontent until later.

I had been hauling water in a bucket into the field where a seedling tree was being planted. There was a hose for that purpose, but it was in use on the other side of the village. This tree was not in reach of the automatic sprinklers and it was drying out. I had been carrying water to it until another solution was found.

It was hot, around noon. I got the water from a standing spigot near the forge. I set the bucket down on the ground behind me and leaned my head into the flow of water. I was wearing a shirt made of cotton, unbuttoned in the front. The water felt good running through my hair and soaking into the shirt. I let it go on for almost a minute.

There was a crash behind me and I bumped my head when I raised it up too quickly under the faucet. I turned and saw a woman sprawled on her face in the dust. She was turning over slowly, holding her knee. I realized with a sinking feeling that she had tripped over the bucket I had carelessly left on the concrete express lane. Think of it: ambling along on ground that you trust to be free of all obstruction, suddenly you're sitting on the ground. Their system would only work with trust, and it had to be total; everybody had to be responsible all the time. I had been accepted into that trust and I had blown it. I felt sick.

She had a nasty scrape on her left knee that was oozing blood. She felt it with her hands, sitting there on the ground, and she began to howl. It was weird, painful. Tears came from her eyes, then she pounded her fists on the ground, going "Hunnnh, hunnnh, *hunnnh!*" with each blow. She was angry, and she had every right to be.

She found the pail as I hesitantly reached out for her. She grabbed my hand and followed it up to my face. She felt my face, crying all the time, then wiped her nose and got up. She started off for one of the buildings. She limped slightly.

I sat down and felt miserable. I didn't know what to do.

One of the men came out to get me. It was Big Man. I called him that because he was the tallest person at Keller. He wasn't any sort of policeman, I found out later; he was just the first one the injured woman had met. He took my hand and felt my face. I saw tears start when he felt the emotions there. He asked me to come inside with him.

An impromptu panel had been convened. Call it a jury. It was made up of anyone who was handy, including a few children. There were ten or twelve of them. Everyone looked very sad. The woman I had hurt was there, being consoled by three or four people. I'll call her Scar, for the prominent mark on her upper arm.

Everybody kept telling me—in handtalk, you understand—how sorry they were for me. They petted and stroked me, trying to draw some of the misery away.

Pink came racing in. She had been sent for to act as a translator if needed. Since this was a formal proceeding it was necessary that they be sure I understood everything that happened. She went to Scar and cried with her for a bit, then came to me and embraced me fiercely, telling me with her hands how sorry she was that this had happened. I was already figuratively packing my bags. Nothing seemed to be left but the formality of expelling me.

Then we all sat together on the floor. We were close, touching on all sides. The hearing began.

Most of it was in handtalk, with Pink throwing in a few words here and there. I seldom knew who said what, but that was appropriate. It was the group speaking as one. No statement reached me without already having become a consensus.

"You are accused of having violated the rules," said the group, "and of having been the cause of an injury to (the one I called Scar). Do you dispute this? Is there any fact that we should know?"

"No," I told them. "I was responsible. It was my carelessness."

"We understand. We sympathize with you in your remorse, which is evident to all of us. But carelessness is a violation. Do you understand this? This is the offense for which you are (—)." It was a set of signals in shorthand.

"What was that?" I asked Pink.

"Uh . . . 'brought before us'? 'Standing trial'?" She shrugged, not happy with either interpretation.

"Yes. I understand."

"The facts not being in question, it is agreed that you are guilty." ("'Responsible,'" Pink whispered in my ear.) "Withdraw from us a moment while we come to a decision."

I got up and stood by the wall, not wanting to look at them as the debate went back and forth through the joined hands. There was a burning lump in my throat that I could not swallow. Then I was asked to rejoin the circle.

"The penalty for your offense is set by custom. If it were not so, we would wish we could rule otherwise. You now have the choice of accepting the punishment designated and having the offense wiped away, or of refusing our jurisdiction and withdrawing your body from our land. What is your choice?"

I had Pink repeat this to me, because it was so important that I know what was being offered. When I was sure I had read it right, I accepted their punishment without hesitation. I was very grateful to have been given an alternative.

"Very well. You have elected to be treated as we would treat one of our own who had done the same act. Come to us."

Everyone drew in closer. I was not told what was going to happen. I was drawn in and nudged gently from all directions.

Scar was sitting with her legs crossed more or less in the center of the group. She was crying again, and so was I, I think. It's hard to remember. I ended up face down across her lap. She spanked me.

I never once thought of it as improbable or strange. It flowed naturally out of the situation. Everyone was holding on to me and caressing me, spelling assurances into my palms and legs and neck and cheeks. We were all crying. It was a difficult thing that had to be faced by the whole group. Others drifted in and joined us. I understood that this punishment came from everyone there, but only the offended person, Scar, did the actual spanking. That was one of the ways I had wronged her, beyond the fact of giving her a scraped knee. I had laid on her the obligation of disciplining me and that was why she had sobbed so loudly, not from the pain of her injury, but from the pain of knowing she would have to hurt me.

Pink later told me that Scar had been the staunchest advocate of giving me the option to stay. Some had wanted to expel me outright, but she paid me the compliment of thinking I was a good enough person to be worth putting herself and me through the ordeal. If you can't understand that, you haven't grasped the feeling of community I felt among these people.

It went on for a long time. It was very painful, but not cruel. Nor was it primarily humiliating. There was some of that, of course. But it was essentially a practical lesson taught in the most direct terms. Each of them had undergone it during the first months, but none recently. You *learned* from it, believe me.

I did a lot of thinking about it afterward. I tried to think of what else they might have done. Spanking grown people is really unheard of, you know, though that didn't occur to me until long after it had happened. It seemed so natural when it was going on that the thought couldn't even enter my mind that this was a weird situation to be in.

They did something like this with the children, but not as long or as hard. Responsibility was lighter for the younger ones. The adults were willing to put up with an occasional bruise or scraped knee while the children learned.

But when you reached what they thought of as adulthood—which was whenever a majority of the adults thought you had or when you assumed the privilege yourself—that's when the spanking really got serious.

They had a harsher punishment, reserved for repeated or malicious offenses. They had not had to invoke it often. It consisted of being sent to Coventry. No one would touch you for a specified period of time. By the time I heard of it, it sounded like a very tough penalty. I didn't need it explained to me.

I don't know how to explain it, but the spanking was administered in such a loving way that I didn't feel violated. *This hurts me as much as it hurts you. I'm doing this for your own good. I love you, that's why I'm spanking you.* They made me understand those old clichés by their actions.

When it was over, we all cried together. But it soon turned to happiness. I embraced Scar and we told each other how sorry we were that it had happened. We talked to each other—made love if you like—and I kissed her knee and helped her dress it.

We spent the rest of the day together, easing the pain.

As I became more fluent in handtalk, "the scales fell from my eyes." Daily, I would discover a new layer of meaning that had eluded me before; it was like peeling the skin of an onion to find a new skin beneath it. Each time I thought I was at the core, only to find that there was another layer I could not yet see.

I had thought that learning handtalk was the key to communication with them. Not so. Handtalk was baby talk. For a long time I was a baby who could not even say goo-goo clearly. Imagine my surprise when, having learned to say it, I found that there were syntax, conjunctions, parts of speech, nouns, verbs, tense, agreement, and the subjunctive mood. I was wading in a tide pool at the edge of the Pacific Ocean.

By handtalk I mean the International Manual Alphabet. Anyone can learn it in a few hours or days. But when you talk to someone in speech, do you spell each word? Do you read each letter as you read this? No, you grasp words as entities, hear groups of sounds and see groups of letters as a gestalt full of meaning.

Everyone at Keller had an absorbing interest in language. They each knew several languages—spoken languages—and could read and spell them fluently.

While still children they had understood the fact that handtalk was a way for blind-deaf people to talk to *outsiders.* Among themselves it was much too cumbersome. It was like Morse Code: useful when you're limited to on-off modes of information transmission, but not the preferred mode. Their ways of speaking to each other were much closer to our type of written or verbal communication, and—dare I say it?—better.

I discovered this slowly, first by seeing that though I could spell rapidly with my hands, it took *much* longer for me to say something than it took anyone else. It could not be explained by differences in dexterity. So I asked to be taught their shorthand speech. I plunged in, this time taught by everyone, not just Pink.

It was hard. They could say any word in any language with no more than two moving hand positions. I knew this was a project for years, not days. You learn the alphabet and you have all the tools you need to spell any word that exists. That's the great advantage in having your written and spoken speech based on the same set of symbols. Shorthand was not like that at all. It partook of none of the linearity or commonality of handtalk; it was not code for English or any other language; it did not share construction or vocabulary with any other language. It was wholly constructed by the Kellerites according to their needs. Each word was something I had to learn and memorize separately from the handtalk spelling.

For months I sat in the Togethers after dinner saying things like "Me love Scar much much well," while waves of conversation ebbed and flowed and circled around me, touching me only at the edges. But I kept at it, and the children were endlessly patient with me. I improved gradually. Understand that the rest of the conversations I will relate took place in either handtalk or shorthand, limited to various degrees by my fluency. I did not speak nor was I spoken to orally from the day of my punishment.

I was having a lesson in bodytalk from Pink. Yes, we were making love. It had taken me a few weeks to see that she was a sexual being, that her caresses, which I had persisted in seeing as innocent—as I had defined it at the time—both were and weren't innocent. She understood it as perfectly natural that the result of her talking to my penis with her hands might be another sort of conversation. Though still in the middle flush of puberty, she was regarded by all as an adult and I accepted her as such. It was cultural conditioning that had blinded me to what she was saying.

So we talked a lot. With her, I understood the words and music of the body better than with anyone else. She sang a very uninhibited song with her hips and hands, free of guilt, open and fresh with discovery in every note she touched.

"You haven't told me much about yourself," she said. "What did you do on the outside?" I don't want to give the impression that this speech was in sentences, as I have presented it. We were bodytalking, sweating and smelling each other. The message came through from hands, feet, mouth.

I got as far as the sign for pronoun, first person singular, and was stopped.

How could I tell her of my life in Chicago? Should I speak of my early ambition to be a writer, and how that didn't work out? And why hadn't it? Lack of talent, or lack of drive? I could tell her about my profession, which was meaningless shuffling of papers when you got down to it, useless to anything but the Gross National Product. I could talk of the economic ups and downs that had brought me to Keller when nothing else could dislodge me from my easy sliding through life. Or the loneliness of being forty-seven years old and never having found someone worth loving, never having been loved in return. Of being a permanently displaced person in a stainless-steel society. One-night stands, drinking binges, nine-to-five, Chicago Transit Authority, dark movie houses, football games on television, sleeping pills, the John Hancock Tower where the windows won't open so you can't breathe the smog or jump out. That was me, wasn't it?

"I see," she said.

"I travel around," I said, and suddenly realized that it was the truth.

"I see," she repeated. It was a different sign for the same thing. Context was everything. She had heard and understood both parts of me, knew one to be what I had been, the other to be what I hoped I was.

She lay on top of me, one hand lightly on my face to catch the quick interplay of emotions as I thought about my life for the first time in years. And she laughed and nipped my ear playfully when my face told her that for the first time I could remember, I was happy about it. Not just telling myself I was happy, but truly happy. You cannot lie in bodytalk any more than your sweat glands can lie to a polygraph.

I noticed that the room was unusually empty. Asking around in my fumbling way, I learned that only the children were there.

"Where is everybody?" I asked.

"They are all out***," she said. It was like that: three sharp slaps on the chest with the fingers spread. Along with the finger configuration for "verb form, gerund," it meant that they were all out ***ing. Needless to say, it didn't tell me much.

What did tell me something was her bodytalk as she said it. I read her better than I ever had. She was upset and sad. Her body said something like "Why can't I join them? Why can't I (smell-taste-touch-hear-see) *sense* with them?" That is exactly what she said. Again, I didn't trust my understanding enough to accept that interpretation. I was still trying to force my conceptions on the things I experienced there. I was determined that she and the other children be resentful of their parents in some way, because I was sure they had to be. They *must* feel superior in some way, they *must* feel held back.

I found the adults, after a short search of the area, out in the north pasture. All the parents, none of the children. They were standing in a group with no apparent pattern. It wasn't a circle, but it was almost round. If there was any organization, it was in the fact that everybody was about the same distance from everybody else.

The German shepherds and the Sheltie were out there, sitting on the cool grass facing the group of people. Their ears were perked up, but they were not moving.

I started to go up to the people. I stopped when I became aware of the concentration. They were touching, but their hands were not moving. The silence of seeing all those permanently moving people standing that still was deafening to me.

I watched them for at least an hour. I sat with the dogs and scratched them behind the ears. They did that choplicking thing that dogs do when they appreciate it, but their full attention was on the group.

It gradually dawned on me that the group was moving. It was very slow, just a step here and another there, over many minutes. It was expanding in such a way that the distance between any of the individuals was the same. Like the expanding universe, where all galaxies move away from all others. Their arms were extended now; they were touching only with fingertips, in a crystal lattice arrangement.

Finally they were not touching at all. I saw their fingers straining to cover distances that were too far to bridge. And still they expanded equilaterally. One of the shepherds began to whimper a little. I felt the hair on the back of my neck stand up. Chilly out here, I thought.

I closed my eyes, suddenly sleepy.

I opened them, shocked. Then I forced them shut. Crickets were chirping in the grass around me.

There was something in the darkness behind my eyeballs. I felt that if I could turn my eyes around I would see it easily, but it eluded me in a way that made peripheral vision seem like reading headlines. If there was ever anything impossible to pin down, much less describe, that was it. It tickled at me for a while as the dogs whimpered louder, but I could make nothing of it. The best analogy I could think of was the sensation a blind person might feel from the sun on a cloudy day.

I opened my eyes again.

Pink was standing there beside me. Her eyes were screwed shut, and she was covering her ears with her hands. Her mouth was open and working silently. Behind her were several of the older children. They were all doing the same thing.

Some quality of the night changed. The people in the group

were about a foot away from each other now, and suddenly the pattern broke. They all swayed for a moment, then laughed in that eerie, unselfconscious noise deaf people use for laughter. They fell in the grass and held their bellies, rolled over and over and roared.

Pink was laughing, too. To my surprise, so was I. I laughed until my face and sides were hurting, like I remembered doing sometimes when I'd smoked grass.

And that was ***ing.

I can see that I've only given a surface view of Keller. And there are some things I should deal with, lest I foster an erroneous view.

Clothing, for instance. Most of them wore something most of the time. Pink was the only one who seemed temperamentally opposed to clothes. She never wore anything.

No one ever wore anything I'd call a pair of pants. Clothes were loose: robes, shirts, dresses, scarves, and such. Lots of men wore things that would be called women's clothes. They were simply more comfortable.

Much of it was ragged. It tended to be made of silk or velvet or something else that felt good. The stereotyped Kellerite would be wearing a Japanese silk robe, hand-embroidered with dragons, with many gaping holes and loose threads and tea and tomato stains all over it while she sloshed through the pigpen with a bucket of slop. Wash it at the end of the day and don't worry about the colors running.

I also don't seem to have mentioned homosexuality. You can mark it down to my early conditioning that my two deepest relationships at Keller were with women: Pink and Scar. I haven't said anything about it simply because I don't know how to present it. I talked to men and women equally, on the same terms. I had surprisingly little trouble being affectionate with the men.

I could not think of the Kellerites as bisexual, though clinically they were. It was much deeper than that. They could not even recognize a concept as poisonous as a homosexuality taboo. It was one of the first things they learned. If you distinguish homosexuality from heterosexuality you are cutting yourself off from communication—*full* communication—with half the human race. They were pansexual; they could not separate sex from the rest of their lives. They didn't even have a word in shorthand that could translate directly into English as *sex.* They had words for male and female in infinite variation, and words for degrees and varieties of physical experience that would be impossible to express in English, but all those words included other parts of the world of experience also; none of them walled off what we call *sex* into its own discrete cubbyhole.

There's another question I haven't answered. It needs answering, because I wondered about it myself when I first arrived. It concerns the necessity for the commune in the first place. Did it really have to be like this? Would they have been better off adjusting themselves to our ways of living?

All was not a peaceful idyll. I've already spoken of the invasion and rape. It could happen again, especially if the roving gangs that operate around the cities start to really rove. A touring group of motorcyclists could wipe them out in a night.

There were also continuing legal hassles. About once a year the social workers descended on Keller and tried to take their children away. They had been accused of everything possible from child abuse to contributing to delinquency. It hadn't worked so far, but it might someday.

And after all, there are sophisticated devices on the market that allow a blind and deaf person to see and hear a little. They might have been helped by some of those.

I met a blind-deaf woman living in Berkeley once. I'll vote for Keller.

As to those machines . . .

In the library at Keller there is a seeing machine. It uses a television camera and a computer to vibrate a closely set series of metal pins. Using it, you can feel a moving picture of whatever the camera is pointed at. It's small and light, made to be carried with the pinpricker touching your back. It cost about thirty-five thousand dollars.

I found it in the corner of the library. I ran my finger over it and left a gleaming streak behind as the thick dust came away.

Other people came and went, and I stayed on.

Keller didn't get as many visitors as the other places I had been. It was out of the way.

One man showed up at noon, looked around, and left without a word.

Two girls, sixteen-year-old runaways from California, showed up one night. They undressed for dinner and were shocked when they found out I could see. Pink scared the hell out of them. Those poor kids had a lot of living to do before they approached Pink's level of sophistication. But then Pink might have been uneasy in California. They left the next day, unsure if they had been to an orgy or not. All that touching and no getting down to business, very strange.

There was a nice couple from Santa Fe who acted as a sort of liaison between Keller and their lawyer. They had a nine-year-old boy who chattered endlessly in handtalk to the other kids. They came up about every other week and stayed a few days, soaking up sunshine and participating in the Together every night. They spoke halting shorthand and did me the courtesy of not speaking to me in speech.

Some of the Indians came around at odd intervals. Their behavior was almost aggressively chauvinistic. They stayed dressed at all times in their Levi's and boots. But it was evident that they had a respect for the people, though they thought them strange. They had business dealings with the commune. It was the Navahos who trucked away the produce that was taken to the gate every day, sold it, and took a percentage. They would sit and powwow in sign language spelled into hands. Pink said they were scrupulously honest in their dealings.

And about once a week all the parents went out in the field and ***ed.

I got better and better at shorthand and bodytalk. I had been breezing along for about five months and winter was in the offing. I had not examined my desires as yet, not really thought about what it was I wanted to do with the rest of my life. I guess the habit of letting myself drift was too ingrained. I was there, and constitutionally unable to decide whether to go or to face up to the problem if I wanted to stay for a long, long time.

Then I got a push.

For a long time I thought it had something to do with the economic situation outside. They were aware of the outside world at Keller. They knew that isolation and ignoring problems that could easily be dismissed as not relevant to them was a dangerous course, so they subscribed to the Braille *New York Times* and most of them read it. They had a television set that got plugged in about once a month. The kids would watch it and translate for their parents.

So I was aware that the non-depression was moving slowly into a more normal inflationary spiral. Jobs were opening up, money was flowing again. When I found myself on the outside again shortly afterward, I thought that was the reason.

The real reason was more complex. It had to do with peeling off the onion layer of shorthand and discovering another layer beneath it.

I had learned handtalk in a few easy lessons. Then I became aware of shorthand and bodytalk, and of how much harder they would be to learn. Through five months of constant immersion, which is the only way to learn a language, I had attained the equivalent level of a five- or six-year-old in shorthand. I knew I could master it, given time. Bodytalk was another matter. You couldn't measure progress as easily in bodytalk. It was a variable and highly interpersonal language that evolved according to the person, the time, the mood. But I was learning.

Then I became aware of Touch. That's the best I can describe it in a single, unforced English noun. What *they* called this fourth-stage language varied from day to day, as I will try to explain.

I first became aware of it when I tried to meet Janet Reilly. I now knew the history of Keller, and she figured very prominently in all the stories. I knew everyone at Keller, and I could find her nowhere. I knew everyone by names like Scar, and She-with-the-missing-front-tooth, and Man-with-wiry-hair. These were shorthand names that I had given them myself, and they all accepted them without question. They had abolished their outside names within the commune. They meant nothing to them; they told nothing and described nothing.

At first I assumed that it was my imperfect command of shorthand that made me unable to clearly ask the right question about

Janet Reilly. Then I saw that they were not telling me on purpose. I saw why, and I approved, and thought no more about it. The name Janet Reilly described what she had been *on the outside,* and one of her conditions for pushing the whole thing through in the first place had been that she be no one special on the inside. She melted into the group and disappeared. She didn't want to be found. All right.

But in the course of pursuing the question I became aware that each of the members of the commune had no specific name at all. That is, Pink, for instance, had no less than one hundred and fifteen names, one from each of the commune members. Each was a contextual name that told the story of Pink's relationship to a particular person. My simple names, based on physical descriptions, were accepted as the names a child would apply to people. The children had not yet learned to go beneath the outer layers and use names that told of themselves, their lives, and their relationships to others.

What is even more confusing, the names evolved from day to day. It was my first glimpse of Touch, and it frightened me. It was a question of permutations. Just the first simple expansion of the problem meant there were no less than thirteen thousand names in use, and they wouldn't stay still so I could memorize them. If Pink spoke to me of Baldy, for instance, she would use her Touch name for him, modified by the fact that she was speaking to me and not Short-chubby-man.

Then the depths of what I had been missing opened beneath me and I was suddenly breathless with fear of heights.

Touch was what they spoke to each other. It was an incredible blend of all three other modes I had learned, and the essence of it was that it never stayed the same. I could listen to them speak to me in shorthand, which was the real basis for Touch, and be aware of the currents of Touch flowing just beneath the surface.

It was a language of inventing languages. Everyone spoke their own dialect because everyone spoke with a different instrument: a different body and set of life experiences. It was modified by everything. *It would not stand still.*

They would sit at the Together and invent an entire body of Touch responses in a night; idiomatic, personal, totally naked in its honesty. And they used it only as a building block for the next night's language.

I didn't know if I wanted to be that naked. I had looked into myself a little recently and had not been satisfied with what I found. The realization that every one of them knew more about it than I, because my honest body had told what my frightened mind had not wanted to reveal, was shattering. I was naked under a spotlight in Carnegie Hall, and all the no-pants nightmares I had ever had came out to haunt me. The fact that they all loved me with all my warts was suddenly not enough. I wanted to curl up in a dark closet with my ingrown ego and let it fester.

I might have come through this fear. Pink was certainly trying to help me. She told me that it would only hurt for a while, that I would quickly adjust to living my life with my darkest emotions written in fire across my forehead. She said Touch was not as hard as it looked at first, either. Once I learned shorthand and bodytalk, Touch would flow naturally from it like sap rising in a tree. It would be unavoidable, something that would happen to me without much effort at all.

I almost believed her. But she betrayed herself. No, no, no. Not that, but the things in her concerning ***ing convinced me that if I went through this I would only bang my head hard against the next step up the ladder.

***

I had a little better definition now. Not one that I can easily translate into English, and even that attempt will only convey my hazy concept of what it was.

"It is the mode of touching without touching," Pink said, her body going like crazy in an attempt to reach me with her own imperfect concept of what it was, handicapped by my illiteracy. Her body denied the truth of her shorthand definition, and at the same time admitted to me that she did not know what it was herself.

"It is the gift whereby one can expand oneself from the eternal quiet and dark into something else." And again her body denied it. She beat on the floor in exasperation.

"It is an attribute of being in the quiet and dark all the time, touching others. All I know for sure is that vision and hearing preclude it or obscure it. I can make it as quiet and dark as I possibly can and be aware of the edges of it, but the visual orientation of the mind persists. That door is closed to me, and to all the children."

Her verb "to touch" in the first part of that was a Touch amalgam, one that reached back into her memories of me and what I had told her of my experiences. It implied and called up the smell and feel of broken mushrooms in soft earth under the barn with Tall-one-with-green-eyes, she who taught me to feel the essence of an object. It also contained references to our bodytalking while I was penetrating into the dark and wet of her, and her running account to me of what it was like to receive me into herself. This was all one word.

I brooded on that for a long time. What was the point of suffering through the nakedness of Touch, only to reach the level of frustrated blindness enjoyed by Pink?

What was it that kept pushing me away from the one place in my life where I had been happiest?

One thing was the realization, quite late in coming, that can be summoned up as "What the hell am I *doing* here?" The question that should have answered that question was "What the hell would I do if I *left?*"

I was the only visitor, the only one in *seven years,* to stay at Keller for longer than a few days. I brooded on that. I was not strong enough or confident enough in my opinion of myself to see it as anything but a flaw in *me,* not in those others. I was obviously too easily satisfied, too complacent to see the flaws that those others had seen.

It didn't have to be flaws in the people of Keller, or in their system. No, I loved and respected them too much to think that. What they had going certainly came as near as anyone ever has in this imperfect world to a sane, rational way for people to exist without warfare and with a minimum of politics. In the end, those two old dinosaurs are the only ways humans have yet discovered to be social animals. Yes, I do see war as a way of living with another; by imposing your will on another in terms so unmistakable that the opponent has to either knuckle under to you, die, or beat your brains out. And if that's a solution to anything, I'd rather live without solutions. Politics is not much better. The only thing going for it is that it occasionally succeeds in substituting talk for fists.

Keller *was* an organism. It was a new way of relating, and it seemed to work. I'm not pushing it as a solution for the world's problems. It's possible that it could only work for a group with a common self-interest as binding and rare as deafness and blindness. I can't think of another group whose needs are so interdependent.

The cells of the organism cooperated beautifully. The organism was strong, flourishing, and possessed of all the attributes I've ever heard used in defining life except the ability to reproduce. That might have been its fatal flaw, if any. I certainly saw the seeds of something developing in the children.

The strength of the organism was communication. There's no way around it. Without the elaborate and impossible-to-falsify mechanisms for communication built into Keller, it would have eaten itself in pettiness, jealousy, possessiveness, and any dozen other "innate" human defects.

The nightly Together was the basis of the organism. Here, from after dinner till it was time to fall asleep, everyone talked in a language that was incapable of falsehood. If there was a problem brewing, it presented itself and was solved almost automatically. Jealousy? Resentment? Some little festering wrong that you're nursing? You couldn't conceal it at the Together, and soon everyone was clustered around you and loving the sickness away. It acted like white corpuscles, clustering around a sick cell, not to destroy it, but to heal it. There seemed to be no problem that couldn't be solved if it was attacked early enough, and with Touch, your neighbors knew about it before you did and were already laboring to correct the wrong, heal the wound, to make you feel better so you could laugh about it. There was a lot of laughter at the Togethers.

I thought for a while that I was feeling possessive about Pink. I know I had done so a little at first. Pink was my special friend, the one who had helped me out from the first, who for several days was the only one I could talk to. It was her hands that had taught me handtalk. I know I felt stirrings of territoriality the first time she lay in my lap while another man made love to her. But if there was any signal the Kellerites were adept at reading, it was that one. It went off like an alarm bell in Pink, the man, and the women and men around me. They soothed me, coddled me, told me in every language that it was all right, not to feel ashamed. Then the man in question began loving *me.* Not Pink, but the man. An observational anthropologist would have had subject matter for a whole thesis. Have you seen the films of baboons' social behavior? Dogs do it, too. Many male mammals do it. When males get into dominance battles, the weaker can defuse the aggression by submitting, by turning tail and surrendering. I have never felt so defused as when that man surrendered the object of our clash of wills—Pink—and turned his attention to me. What could I do? What I did was laugh, and he laughed, and soon we were all laughing, and that was the end of territoriality.

That's the essence of how they solved most "human nature" problems at Keller. Sort of like an oriental martial art; you yield, roll with the blow so that your attacker takes a pratfall with the force of the aggression. You do that until the attacker sees that the initial push wasn't worth the effort, that it was a pretty silly thing to do when no one was resisting you. Pretty soon he's not Tarzan of the Apes, but Charlie Chaplin. And he's laughing.

So it wasn't Pink and her lovely body and my realization that she could never be all mine to lock away in my cave and defend with a gnawed-off thighbone. If I'd persisted in that frame of mind she would have found me about as attractive as an Amazonian leech, and that was a great incentive to confound the behaviorists and overcome it.

So I was back to those people who had visited and left, and what did they see that I didn't see?

Well, there was something pretty glaring. I was not part of the organism, no matter how nice the organism was to me. I had no hopes of ever becoming a part, either. Pink had said it in the first week. She felt it herself, to a lesser degree. She could not ***, though that fact was not going to drive her away from Keller. She had told me that many times in shorthand and confirmed it in bodytalk. If I left, it would be without her.

Trying to stand outside and look at it, I felt pretty miserable. What was I trying to *do,* anyway? Was my goal in life *really* to become a part of a blind-deaf commune? I was feeling so low by that time that I actually thought of that as denigrating, in the face of all the evidence to the contrary. I should be out in the real world where the real people lived, not these freakish cripples.

I backed off from that thought very quickly. I was not totally out of my mind, just on the lunatic edges. These people were the best friends I'd ever had, maybe the only ones. That I was confused enough to think that of them even for a second worried me more than anything else. It's possible that it's what pushed me finally into a decision. I saw a future of growing disillusion and unfulfilled hopes. Unless I was willing to put out my eyes and ears, I would always be on the outside. *I* would be the blind and deaf one. I would be the freak. I didn't want to be a freak.

They knew I had decided to leave before I did. My last few days turned into a long goodbye, with a loving farewell implicit in every word touched to me. I was not really sad, and neither were they. It was nice, like everything they did. They said goodbye with just the right mix of wistfulness and life-must-go-on, and hope-to-touch-you-again.

Awareness of Touch scratched on the edges of my mind. It was not bad, just as Pink had said. In a year or two I could have mastered it.

But I was set now. I was back in the life groove that I had followed for so long. Why is it that once having decided what I must do, I'm afraid to reexamine my decision? Maybe because the original decision cost me so much that I didn't want to go through it again.

I left quietly in the night for the highway and California. They were out in the fields, standing in that circle again. Their fingertips were farther apart than ever before. The dogs and children hung around the edges like beggars at a banquet. It was hard to tell which looked more hungry and puzzled.

The experiences at Keller did not fail to leave their mark on me. I was unable to live as I had before. For a while I thought I could not live at all, but I did. I was too used to living to take the decisive step of ending my life. I would wait. Life had brought one pleasant thing to me; maybe it would bring another.

I became a writer. I found I now had a better gift for communicating than I had before. Or maybe I had it now for the first time.

At any rate, my writing came together and I sold. I wrote what I wanted to write, and was not afraid of going hungry. I took things as they came.

I weathered the non-depression of '97, when unemployment reached twenty percent and the government once more ignored it as a temporary downturn. It eventually upturned, leaving the jobless rate slightly higher than it had been the time before, and the time before that. Another million useless persons had been created with nothing better to do than shamble through the streets looking for beatings in progress, car smash-ups, heart attacks, murders, shootings, arson, bombings, and riots: the endlessly inventive street theater. It never got dull.

I didn't become rich, but I was usually comfortable. That is a social disease, the symptoms of which are the ability to ignore the fact that your society is developing weeping pustules and having its brains eaten out by radioactive maggots. I had a nice apartment in Marin County, out of sight of the machine-gun turrets. I had a car, at a time when they were beginning to be luxuries.

I had concluded that my life was not destined to be all I would like it to be. We all make some sort of compromise, I reasoned, and if you set your expectations too high you are doomed to disappointment. It did occur to me that I was settling for something far from "high," but I didn't know what to do about it. I carried on with a mixture of cynicism and optimism that seemed about the right mix for me. It kept my motor running, anyway.

I even made it to Japan, as I had intended in the first place.

I didn't find someone to share my life. There was only Pink for that, Pink and all her family, and we were separated by a gulf I didn't dare cross. I didn't even dare think about her too much. It would have been very dangerous to my equilibrium. I lived with it, and told myself that it was the way I was. Lonely.

The years rolled on like a Caterpillar tractor at Dachau, up to the penultimate day of the millennium.

San Francisco was having a big bash to celebrate the year 2000. Who gives a shit that the city is slowly falling apart, that civilization is disintegrating into hysteria? Let's have a party!

I stood on the Golden Gate Dam on the last day of 1999. The sun was setting in the Pacific, on Japan, which had turned out to be more of the same but squared and cubed with neo-samurai.

Behind me the first bombshells of a firework celebration of holocaust tricked up to look like festivity competed with the flare of burning buildings as the social and economic basket cases celebrated the occasion in their own way. The city quivered under the weight of misery, anxious to slide off along the fracture lines of some subcortical San Andreas Fault. Orbiting atomic bombs twinkled in my mind, up there somewhere, ready to plant mushrooms when we'd exhausted all the other possibilities.

I thought of Pink.

I found myself speeding through the Nevada desert, sweating, gripping the steering wheel. I was crying aloud but without sound, as I had learned to do at Keller.

Can you go back?

I slammed the citicar over the potholes in the dirt road. The car was falling apart. It was not built for this kind of travel. The sky was getting light in the east. It was the dawn of a new millennium. I stepped harder on the gas pedal and the car bucked savagely. I didn't care. I was not driving back down that road, not ever. One way or another, I was here to stay.

I reached the wall and sobbed my relief. The last hundred miles had been a nightmare of wondering if it had been a dream. I touched the cold reality of the wall and it calmed me. Light snow had drifted over everything, gray in the early dawn.

I saw them in the distance. All of them, out in the field where I had left them. No, I was wrong. It was only the children. Why had it seemed like so many at first?

Pink was there. I knew her immediately, though I had never seen her in winter clothes. She was taller, filled out. She would be nineteen years old. There was a small child playing in the snow at her feet, and she cradled an infant in her arms. I went to her and talked to her hand.

She turned to me, her face radiant with welcome, her eyes staring in a way I had never seen. Her hands flitted over me and her eyes did not move.

"I touch you, I welcome you," her hands said. "I wish you could have been here just a few minutes ago. Why did you go away, darling? Why did you stay away so long?" Her eyes were stones in her head. She was blind. She was deaf.

All the children were. No, Pink's child sitting at my feet looked up at me with a smile.

"Where is everybody?" I asked when I got my breath. "Scar? Baldy? Green-eyes? And what's happened? What's happened to you?" I was tottering on the edge of a heart attack or nervous collapse or something. My reality felt in danger of dissolving.

"They've gone," she said. The word eluded me, but the context put it with the *Mary Celeste* and Roanoke, Virginia. It was complex, the way she used the word *gone.* It was like something she had said before; unattainable, a source of frustration like the one that had sent me running from Keller. But now her word told of something that was not hers yet, but was within her grasp. There was no sadness in it.

"Gone?"

"Yes. I don't know where. They're happy. They ***ed. It was glorious. We could only touch a part of it."

I felt my heart hammering to the sound of the last train pulling away from the station. My feet were pounding along the ties as it faded into the fog. Where are the Brigadoons of yesterday? I've never yet heard of a fairy tale where you can go back to the land of enchantment. You wake up, you find that your chance is gone. You threw it away. *Fool!* You only get one chance; that's the moral, isn't it?

Pink's hands laughed along my face.

"Hold this part-of-me-who-speaks-mouth-to-nipple," she said, and handed me her infant daughter. "I will give you a gift."

She reached up and lightly touched my ears with her cold fingers. The sound of the wind was shut out, and when her hands came away it never came back. She touched my eyes, shut out all the light, and I saw no more.

We live in the lovely quiet and dark.

Poul Anderson

Here's Poul, one top-ranking science fiction writer who comes ahead of me in the alphabetical listing. You didn't think you'd miss him, did you? He is the only writer who has appeared in every one of the four Hugo Winner volumes. He has one in the first, two in the second, two in the third, and now one in the fourth. That gives him six appearances, which ties him with Harlan Ellison. And if you would like to have a little peep into the future, I can assure you that Poul will appear in the forthcoming fifth volume as well.

Poul has been writing steadily and quite prolifically for nearly forty years now, and has clearly won his share of awards, and yet somehow I have always felt that he was underrated. In fact, it's my idea that he is the most highly rated author in the field who manages to be underrated just the same.

Sometimes I speculate idly on why that should be.

It may be a matter of charisma. I remember a top-notch s.f. writer *(not* Poul) once saying to me bitterly that he was of a mind to quit the field because he felt unappreciated.

He said, "Good writing isn't enough. You have to put on a show. If I were willing to make a fool of myself the way you and Harlan do, and jump around like a madman at conventions and chase the girls and yell at people and turn handsprings, then everyone would notice me and decide my books were good. But just because I behave like a quiet, civilized person, they ignore me."

Well, perhaps there's something to that. Certainly Poul is among the most civilized people I know. He is extremely quiet and soft-spoken and, as far as I know, has never offended anyone, but is unfailingly polite, and thoughtful, and considerate. His reward is that people tend to overlook him, which is Not Right.

Of course, I have to defend the charismatics. I don't think for one minute that Harlan, for instance, behaves as he does out of a calculated intention of attracting attention and selling books. I know that *I* don't.

When Harlan loses his temper and lets loose a stream of colorful invective, it's because he can't help it. He sometimes does himself infinite harm in this way, and he would *not* do it if only he knew how not to do it. As for myself, when I kiss the girls that is not because I think to myself that a reputation as a "lovable lecher" (I have a plaque that was awarded to me at a convention with that phrase upon it as my reason for getting it) will lend color to my otherwise colorless stories. I do it because I enjoy kissing girls.

If Harlan or I were forced to attend a convention, or any gathering, and act quiet and civilized, the chances are that we would explode through internal combustion. On the other hand, I don't think that even threats of imminent torture could force Poul Anderson to do some of the crazy things that Harlan and I do as a matter of course.

It's the way it is—but don't worry, Poul, you have more Hugos than I have and we all love you, too.

12

HUNTER'S MOON

We do not perceive reality, we conceive it. To suppose otherwise is to invite catastrophic surprises. The tragic nature of history stems in large part from this endlessly recurrent mistake.

—Oskar Haeml, *Betrachtungen über die menschliche Verlegenheit*

*** Both suns were now down. The western mountains had become a wave of blackness, unstirring, as though the cold of Beyond had touched and frozen it even as it crested, a first sea barrier on the flightway to the Promise; but heaven stood purple above, bearing the earliest stars and two small moons, ocher edged with silvery crescents, like the Promise itself. Eastward, the sky remained blue. There, just over the ocean, Ruii was almost fully lighted, Its bands turned luminous across Its crimson glow. Beneath the glade that It cast, the waters shivered, wind made visible.

A'i'ach felt the wind too, cool and murmurous. Each finest hair on his body responded. He needed but little thrust to hold his course, enough effort to give him a sense of his own strength and of being at one, in travel and destination, with his Swarm. Their globes surrounded him, palely iridescent, well-nigh hiding from him the ground over which they passed; he was among the highest up. Their life-scents overwhelmed all else which the air bore, sweet, heady, and they were singing together, hundreds of voices in chorus, so that their spirits might mingle and become Spirit, a foretaste of what awaited them in the far west. Tonight, when P'a crossed the face of Ruii, there would return the Shining Time. Already they rejoiced in the raptures ahead.

A'i'ach alone did not sing, nor did he lose more than a part of himself in dreams of feast and love. He was too aware of what he carried. The thing that the human had fastened to him weighed very little, but what it was putting into his soul was heavy and harsh. The whole Swarm knew about the dangers of attack, of course, and many clutched weapons—stones to drop or sharp-pointed branches shed by ü trees—in the tendrils that streamed under their globes. A'i'ach had a steel knife, his price for letting the human burden him. Yet it was not in the nature of the People to dread what might sink down upon them out of the future. A'i'ach was strangely changed by that which went on inside him.

The knowledge had come, he knew not how, slowly enough that he was not astonished by it. Instead, a grimness had meanwhile congealed. Somewhere in those hills and forests, a Beast ran that bore the same thing he did, that was also in ghostly Swarm-touch with a human. He could not guess what this might portend, save trouble of some kind for the People. He might well be unwise to ask. Therefore he had come to a resolve he realized was alien to his race: he would end the menace.

Since his eyes were set low on his body, he could not see the object secured on top, nor the radiance beaming upward from it. His companions could, though, and he had gotten a demonstration before he agreed to carry it. The beam was faint, faint, visible only at night and then only against a dark background. He would look for a shimmer among shadows on the land. Sooner or later, he would come upon it. The chance was not bad now at this, the Shining Time, when the Beasts would seek to kill People they knew would be gathered in vast numbers to revel.

A'i'ach had wanted the knife as a curiosity of possible usefulness. He meant to keep it in the boughs of a tree; when the mood struck him, he would experiment with it. A Person did once in a while employ a chance-found object, such as a sharp pebble, for some fleeting purpose, such as scooping open a crestflower pod to release its delicious seedlets upon the air. Perhaps with a knife he could shape wood into tools and have a stock of them always ready.

Given his new insight, A'i'ach saw what the blade was truly for. He could smite from above till a Beast was dead—no, *the* Beast.

A'i'ach was hunting. ***

Several hours before sundown, Hugh Brocket and his wife, Jannika Rezek, had been preparing for their night's work when Chrisoula Gryparis arrived, much overdue. A storm had first grounded aircraft at Enrique and then, perversely moving west, forced her into a long detour on her way to Hansonia. She didn't even see the Ring Ocean until she had traversed a good thousand kilometers of mainland, whereafter she must bend southward an equal distance to reach the big island.

"How lonely Port Kato looks from the air," she remarked. Though accented, her English—the agreed-upon common language at this particular station—was fluent: one reason she had come here to investigate the possibility of taking a post.

"Because it is," Jannika answered in her different accent. "A dozen scientists, twice as many juniors, and a few support personnel. That makes you extra welcome."

"What, do you feel isolated?" Chrisoula wondered. "You can call to anywhere on Nearside that there is a holocom, can you not?"

"Yeah, or flit to a town on business or vacation or whatever," Hugh said. "But no matter how stereo an image is and sounds, it's only an image. You can't go out with it for a drink after your conference is finished, can you? As for an actual visit, well, you're soon back here among the same old faces. Outposts get pretty ingrown socially. You'll find out, if you sign on." In haste: "Not that I'm trying to discourage you. Jan's right, we'd be more than happy to have somebody fresh join us."

His own accent was due to history. English was his mother tongue, but he was third-generation Medean, which meant that his grandparents had left North America so long ago that speech back there had changed like everything else. To be sure, Chrisoula wasn't exactly up-to-date, when a laser beam took almost fifty years to go from Sol to Colchis and the ship in which she had fared, unconscious and unaging, was considerably slower than that . . .

"Yes, from Earth!" Jannika's voice glowed.

Chrisoula winced. "It was not happy on Earth when I left. Maybe things got better afterward. Please, I will talk about that later, but now I would like to look forward."

Hugh patted her shoulder. She was fairly pretty, he thought:

not in a class with Jan, which few women were, but still, he'd enjoy it if acquaintance developed bedward. Variety is the spice of wife.

"You really have had bad luck today, haven't you?" he murmured. "Getting delayed till Roberto—uh, Dr. Venosta went out in the field—and Dr. Feng back to the Center with a batch of samples—" He referred to the chief biologist and the chief chemist. Chrisoula's training was in biochemistry; it was hoped that she, lately off the latest of the rare starcraft, would contribute significantly to an understanding of life on Medea.

She smiled. "Well, then I will know others first, starting with you two nice people."

Jannika shook her head. "I am sorry," she said. "We are busy ourselves, soon to leave, and may not return until sunrise."

"That is—how long? About thirty-six hours? Yes. Is that not long to be away in . . . what do you say? . . . this weird an environment?"

Hugh laughed. "It's the business of a xenologist, which we both are," he said. "Uh, I think I, at least, can spare a little time to show you around and introduce you and make you feel sort of at home." Arriving as she did at a point in the cycle of watches when most folk were still asleep, Chrisoula had been conducted to his and Jannika's quarters. They were early up, to make ready for their expedition.

Jannika gave him a hard glance. She saw a big man who reckoned his age at forty-one Terrestrial years: burly, a trifle awkward in his movements, beginning to show a slight paunch; craggy-featured, sandy-haired, blue-eyed; close-cropped, clean-shaven, but sloppily clad in tunic, trousers, and boots, the style of the miners among whom he had grown up. "*I* have not time," she stated.

Hugh made an expansive gesture. "Sure, you just continue, dear." He took Chrisoula under the elbow. "Come on, let's wander."

Bewildered, she accompanied him out of the cluttered hut. In the compound, she halted and stared about her as if this were her first sight of Medea.

Port Kato was indeed tiny. Not to disturb regional ecology with things like ultraviolet lamps above croplands and effluents off them, it drew its necessities from older and larger settlements on the Nearside mainland. Moreover, while close to the eastern edge of Hansonia, it stood a few kilometers inland, on high ground, as a precaution against Ring Ocean tides, which could get monstrous. Thus nature walled and roofed and weighed on the huddle of structures, wherever she looked—

—or listened, smelled, touched, tasted, moved. In slightly lesser gravity than Earth's, she had a bound to her step. The extra oxygen seemed to lend energy likewise, though her mucous membranes had not yet quite stopped smarting. Despite a tropical location, the air was balmy and not overly humid, for the island lay close enough to Farside to be cooled. It was full of pungencies, only a few of which she could remotely liken to anything familiar, such as musk or iodine. Foreign too were sounds—rustlings, trills, croakings, mumbles—which the dense atmosphere made loud in her ears.

The station itself had an outlandish aspect. Buildings were made of local materials to local design; even a radiant energy converter resembled nothing at home. Multiple shadows carried peculiar tints; in fact, every color was changed in this ruddy light. The trees that reared above the roof were of odd shapes, their foliage in hues of orange, yellow, and brown. Small things flitted among them or scuttled along their branches. Occasional glittery drifts in the breeze did not appear to be dust.

The sky was deep-toned. A few clouds were washed with faint pink and gold. The double sun Colchis—Castor C was suddenly too dry a name—was declining westward, both members so dim that she could safely gaze at them for a short while, Phrixus at close to its maximum angular separation from Helle.

Opposite them, Argo dominated heaven, as always on the inward-facing hemisphere of Medea. Here the primary planet hung low; treetops hid part of the great flattened disc. Daylight paled the redness of its heat, which would be lurid after dark. Nonetheless it was a colossus, as broad to the eye as fifteen or sixteen Lunas above Earth. The subtly chromatic bands and spots upon its face, ever-changing, were clouds more huge than continents and hurricane vortices that could have swallowed whole this moon upon which she stood.

Chrisoula shivered. "It . . . strikes me," she whispered,

"more than anywhere around Enrique or—or approaching from space . . . I have come elsewhere in the universe."

Hugh laid an arm around her waist. Not being a glib man otherwise, he merely said, "Well this *is* different. That's why Port Kato exists, you know. To study in depth an area that's been isolated a while; they tell me the isthmus between Hansonia and the mainland disappeared fifteen thousand years ago. The local dromids, at least, never heard of humans before we arrived. The ouranids did get rumors, which may have influenced them a little, but surely not much."

"Dromids—ouranids—oh." Being Greek, she caught his meanings at once. "Fuxes and balloons, correct?"

Hugh frowned. "Please. Those are pretty cheap jokes, aren't they? I know you hear them a lot in town, but I think both races deserve more dignified names from us. They are intelligent, remember."

"I am sorry."

He squeezed a trifle. "No harm done, Chris. You're new. With a century needed for question and answer, between here and Earth—"

"Yes. I have wondered if it is really worth the cost, planting colonies beyond the Solar System just to send back scientific knowledge that slowly."

"You've got more recent information about that than I do."

"Well . . . the planetology, biology, chemistry, they were still giving new insights when I left, and this was good for everything from medicine to volcano control." The woman straightened. "Perhaps the next step is in your field, xenology? If we can come to understand a nonhuman mind—no, two, on this world—maybe three, if there really are two quite unlike sorts of ouranid as I have heard theorized—" She drew breath. "Well, then we might have a chance of understanding ourselves." He thought she was genuinely interested, not merely trying to please him, when she went on: "What is it you and your wife do? They mentioned to me in Enrique it is quite special."

"Experimental, anyway." Not to overdo things, he released her. "A complicated story. Wouldn't you rather take the grand tour of our metropolis?"

"Later I can by myself, if you must go back to work. But I am fascinated by what I have heard of your project. Reading the minds of aliens!"

"Hardly that." Seeing his opportunity, he indicated a bench outside a machine shed. "If you really would like to hear, sit down."

As they did, Piet Marais, botanist, emerged from his cabin. To Hugh's relief, he simply greeted them before hurrying off. Certain Hansonian plants did odd things at this time of day. Everyone else was still indoors, the cook and bull cook making breakfast, the rest washing and dressing for their next wakeful period.

"I suppose you are surprised," Hugh commenced. "Electronic neuranalysis techniques were in their infancy on Earth when your ship left. They took a spurt soon afterward, and of course the information reached us before you did. The use there had been on lower animals as well as humans, so it wasn't too hard for us—given a couple of geniuses in the Center—to adapt the equipment for both dromids and ouranids. Both those species have nervous systems too, after all, and the signals are electrical. Actually, it's been more difficult to develop the software, the programs, than the hardware. Jannika and I are working on that, collecting empirical data for the psychologists and semanticians and computer people to use.

"Uh, don't misunderstand, please. To *us,* this is nearly incidental. Mindscan—bad word, but we seem to be stuck with it—mindscan should eventually be a valuable tool in our real job, which is to learn how local natives live, what they think and feel, everything about them. However, at present it's very new, very limited, and very unpredictable."

Chrisoula tugged her chin. "Let me tell you what I imagine I know," she suggested, "then you tell me how wrong I am."

"Sure."

She grew downright pedantic: "Synapse patterns can be identified and recorded which correspond to motor impulses, sensory inputs, their processing—and at last, theoretically, to thoughts themselves. But the study is a matter of painfully accumulating data, interpreting them, and correlating the interpretations with verbal responses. Whatever results one gets, they can be stored in a computer program as an *n*-dimensional map off which readings can be made. More readings can be gotten by interpolation."

"Whe-ew!" the man exclaimed. "Go on."

"I am right this far? I did not expect to be."

"Well, naturally, you're trying to sketch in a few words what needs volumes of math and symbolic logic to describe halfway properly. Still, you're doing better than I could myself."

"I continue. Now recently there are systems which can make correspondences between different maps. They can transform the patterns that constitute thought in one mind into the thought-patterns of another. Also, direct transmission between nervous systems is possible. A pattern can be detected, passed through a computer for translation, and electromagnetically induced in a receiving brain. Does this not amount to telepathy?"

Hugh started to shake his head, but settled for: "M-m-m, of an extremely crude sort. Even two humans who think in the same language and know each other inside out, even they get only partial information—simple messages, burdened with distortion, low signal-to-noise ratio, and slow transmission. How much worse when you try with a different life form! The variations in speech alone, not to mention neurological structure, chemistry—"

"Yet you are attempting it, with some success, I hear."

"Well, we made a certain amount of progress on the mainland with both dromids and ouranids. But believe me, 'certain amount' is a gross overstatement."

"Next you are trying it on Hansonia, where the cultures must be entirely strange to you. In fact, the species of ouranid— Why? Do you not add needlessly to your difficulties?"

"Yes—that is, we do add countless problems, but it is not needless. You see, most cooperating natives have spent their whole lives around humans. Many of them are professional subjects of study: dromids for material pay, ouranids for psychological satisfaction, amusement, I suppose you could say. They're deracinated; they themselves often don't have any idea why their 'wild' kinfolk do something. We wanted to find out if mindscan can be developed into a tool for learning about more than neurology. For that, we needed beings who're relatively, uh, uncontaminated. Lord knows Nearside is full of virgin areas. But here Port Kato already was, set up for intensive study of a region that's both isolated and sharply defined. Jan and I decided we might as well include mindscan in our research program."

Hugh's glance drifted to the immensity of Argo and lingered. "As far as we're concerned," he said low, "it's incidental—one more way for us to try and find out why the dromids and ouranids here are at war."

"They kill each other elsewhere too, do they not?"

"Yes, in a variety of ways, for a larger variety of reasons, as nearly as we can determine. Let me remark for the record, I myself don't hold with the theory that information on this planet can be acquired by eating its possessor. For one thing, I can show you more areas than not where dromids and ouranids seem to coexist perfectly peacefully." Hugh shrugged. "Nations on Earth never were identical. Why should we expect Medea to be the same everywhere?"

"On Hansonia, however—you say war?"

"Best word I can think of. Oh, neither group has a government to issue a formal declaration. But the fact is that more and more, for the past couple of decades—as long as humans have been observing, if not longer—dromids on this island have been hell-bent to kill ouranids. Wipe them out! The ouranids are pacifistic, but they do defend themselves, sometimes with active measures like ambushes." Hugh grimaced. "I've glimpsed several fights, and examined the results of a lot more. Not pleasant. If we in Port Kato could mediate—bring peace—well, I'd think that alone might justify man's presence on Medea."

While he sought to impress her with his kindliness, he was not hypocritical. A pragmatist, he had nevertheless wondered occasionally if humans had a right to be here. Long-range scientific study was impossible without a self-supporting colony, which in turn implied a minimum population, most of whose members were not scientists. He, for example, was the son of a miner and had spent his boyhood in the outback. True, settlement was not supposed to increase beyond its present level, and most of this huge moon was hostile enough to his breed that further growth did seem unlikely. But—if nothing else, simply by their presence, Earthlings had already done irreversible things to both native races.

"You cannot ask them why they fight?" Chrisoula wondered.

Hugh smiled wryly. "Oh, sure, we can ask. By now we've

mastered local languages for everyday purposes. Except, how deep does our understanding go?

"Look, I'm the dromid specialist, she's the ouranid specialist, and we've both worked hard trying to win the friendship of specific individuals. It's worse for me, because dromids won't come into Port Kato as long as ouranids might show up anytime. They admit they'd be duty bound to try and kill the ouranids—and eat them, too, by the way; that's a major symbolic act. The dromids agree this would be a violation of our hospitality. Therefore I have to go meet them in their camps and dens. In spite of this handicap, she doesn't feel she's progressed any further than me. We're equally baffled."

"What do the autochthons *say?*"

"Well, either species admits they used to live together amicably . . . little or no direct contact, but with considerable interest in each other. Then, twenty or thirty years back, more and more dromids started failing to reproduce. Oftener and oftener, castoff segments don't come to term, they die. The leaders have decided the ouranids are at fault and must be exterminated."

"Why?"

"An article of faith. No rationale that I can untangle, though I've guessed at motivations, like the wish for a scapegoat. We've got pathologists hunting for the real cause, but imagine how long that might take. Meanwhile, the attacks and killings go on."

Chrisoula regarded the dusty ground. "Have the ouranids changed in any way? The dromids might then jump to a conclusion of *post hoc, propter hoc.*"

"Huh?" When she had explained, Hugh laughed. "I'm not a cultivated type, I'm afraid," he said. "The rock rats and bush rangers I grew up amongst do respect learning—we wouldn't survive on Medea without learning—but they don't claim to have a lot of it themselves. I got interested in xenology because as a kid I acquired a dromid friend and followed her-him through the whole cycle, female to male to postsexual. It grabbed hold of my imagination—a life that exotic."

His attempt to turn the conversation into personal channels did not succeed. "What have the ouranids done?" she persisted.

"Oh . . . they've acquired a new—no, not a new religion. That implies a special compartment of life, doesn't it? And ouranids don't compartmentalize their lives. Call it a new Way, a new *Tao.* It involves eventually riding an east wind off across the ocean, to die in the Farside cold. Somehow, that's transcendental. Please don't ask me how, or why. Nor can I understand—or Jan—why the dromids consider this is such a terrible thing for the ouranids to do. I have some guesses, but they're only guesses. She jokes that they're born fanatics."

Chrisoula nodded. "Cultural abysses. Suppose a modern materialist with little empathy had a time machine, and went back to the Middle Ages on Earth, and tried to find out what drove a Crusade or Jihad. It would appear senseless to him. Doubtless he would conclude everybody concerned was crazy, and the sole possible way to peace was total victory of one side or the other. Which was not true, we know today."

The man realized that this woman thought a good deal like his wife. She continued: "Could it be that human influences have brought about these changes, perhaps indirectly?"

"It could," he admitted. "Ouranids travel widely, of course, so those on Hansonia may well have picked up, at second or third hand, stories about Paradise which originated with humans. I suppose it'd be natural to think Paradise lies in the direction of sunset. Not that anybody has ever tried to convert a native. But natives have occasionally inquired what our ideas are. And ouranids are compulsive mythmakers, who might seize on any concept. They're ecstatics, too. Even about death."

"While dromids are prone to develop militant new religions overnight, I have heard. On this island, then, a new one happens to have turned against the ouranids, no? Tragic—though not unlike persecutions on Earth, I expect."

"Anyhow, we can't help till we have a lot more knowledge. Jan and I are trying for that. Mostly, we follow the usual procedures, field studies, observations, interviews, et cetera. We're experimenting with mindscan as well. Tonight it gets our most thorough test yet."

Chrisoula sat upright, gripped. "What will you do?"

"We'll draw a blank, probably. You're a scientist yourself, you know how rare the real breakthroughs are. We're only slogging along."

When she remained silent, Hugh filled his lungs for talk. "To be exact," he proceeded, "Jan's been cultivating a 'wild' ouranid, I a 'wild' dromid. We've persuaded them to wear miniaturized mindscan transmitters, and have been working with them to develop our own capability. What we can receive and interpret isn't much. Our eyes and ears give us a lot more information. Still, this is special information. Supplementary.

"The actual layout? Oh, our native wears a button-sized unit glued onto the head, if you can talk about the head of an ouranid. A mercury cell gives power. The unit broadcasts a recognition signal on the radio band—microwatts, but ample to lock onto. Data transmission naturally requires plenty of bandwidth, so that's on an ultraviolet beam."

"What?" Chrisoula was startled. "Isn't that dangerous to the dromids? I was taught they, most animals, have to take shelter when a sun flares."

"This is safely weak, also because of energy limitations," Hugh replied. "Obviously, it's limited to line-of-sight and a few kilometers through air. At that, natives of either kind tell us they can spot the fluorescence of gas along the path. Not that they describe it in such terms!

"So Jan and I go out in our separate aircraft. We hover too high to be seen, activate the transmitters by a signal, and 'tune in' on our individual subjects through our amplifiers and computers. As I said, to date we've gotten extremely limited results; it's a mighty poor kind of telepathy. This night we're planning an intensive effort, because an important thing will be happening."

She didn't inquire immediately what that was, but asked instead: "Have you ever tried sending to a native, rather than receiving?"

"What? No, nobody has. For one thing, we don't want them to know they're being scanned. That would likely affect their behavior. For another thing, no Medeans have anything like a scientific culture. I doubt they could comprehend the idea."

"Really? With their high metabolic rate, I should guess they think faster than us."

"They seem to, though we can't measure that till we've improved mindscan to the point of decoding verbal thought. All we've identified thus far is sensory impressions. Come back in a hundred years and maybe someone can tell you."

The talk had gotten so academic that Hugh positively welcomed the diversion when an ouranid appeared. He recognized the individual in spite of her being larger than usual, her globe distended with hydrogen to a full four meters of diameter. This made her fur sparse across the skin, taking away its mother-of-pearl sheen. Just the same, she was a handsome sight as she passed the treetops, crosswind and then downward. Prehensile tendrils streaming below in variable configurations, to help pilot a jet-propelled swim through the air, she hardly deserved the name "flying jellyfish"—though he had seen pictures of Earthside Portuguese men-of-war and thought them beautiful. He could sympathize with Jannika's attraction to this race.

He rose. "Meet a local character," he invited Chrisoula. "She has a little English. However, don't expect to understand her pronunciation at once. Probably she's come to make a quick swap before she rejoins her group for the big affair tonight."

The woman got up. "Swap? Exchange?"

"Yeah. Niallah answers questions, tells legends, sings songs, demonstrates maneuvers, whatever we request. Afterward we have to play human music for her. Schönberg, usually; she dotes on Schönberg."

—Loping along a clifftop, Erakoum spied Sarhouth clearly against Mardudek. The moon was waxing toward solar fullness as it crossed that coal-glow. Its disc was dwarfed by the enormous body behind, was actually smaller to the eye than the spot which also passed in view, and its cold luminance had well-nigh been drowned earlier when it moved over one of the belts which changeably girded Mardudek. They grew bright after dark, those belts; thinkers like Yasari believed they cast back the light of the suns.

For an instant, Erakoum was captured by the image, spheres traveling through unbounded spaces in circles within circles. She hoped to become a thinker herself. But it could not be soon. She still had her second breeding to go through, her second segment to shed and guard, the young that it presently brought forth to help rear; and then she would be male, with begetting of her own to do—before that need faded out likewise and there was time for serenity.

She remembered in a stab of pain how her first birthing had been for naught. The segment staggered about weakly for a short while, until it lay down and died as so many were doing, so many. The Flyers had brought that curse. It had to be them, as the Prophet Illdamen preached. Their new way of faring west when they grew old, never to return, instead of sinking down and rotting back into the soil as Mardudek intended, surely angered the Red Watcher. Upon the People had been laid the task of avenging this sin against the natural order of things. Proof lay in the fact that females who slew and ate a Flyer shortly before mating always shed healthy segments which brought forth live offspring.

Erakoum swore that tonight she was going to be such a female.

She stopped for breath and to search the landscape. These precipices rimmed a fjord whose waters lay more placid than the sea beyond, brilliant under the radiance from the east. A dark patch bespoke a mass of floating weed. Might it be plants of the kind from which the Flyers budded in their abominable infancy? Erakoum could not tell at her distance. Sometimes valiant members of her race had ventured out on logs, trying to reach those beds and destroy them; but they had failed, and often drowned, in treacherous great waves.

Westward rose rugged, wooded hills where darkness laired. Athwart their shadows, sparks danced glittering golden, by the thousands—the millions, across the land. They were firemites. Through more than a hundred days and nights, they had been first eggs, then worms, deep down in forest mold. Now Sarhouth was passing across Mardudek in the exact path that mysteriously summoned them. They crept to the surface, spread wings which they had been growing, and went aloft, agleam, to mate.

Once it had meant no more to the People than a pretty sight. Then the need came into being, to kill Flyers . . . and Flyers gathered in hordes to feed on yonder swarms. Hovering low, careless in their glee, they became more vulnerable to surprise than they commonly were. Erakoum hefted an obsidian-headed javelin. She had five more lashed across her back. A number of the People had spent the day setting out nets and snares, but she considered that impractical; the Flyers were not ordinary winged quarry. Anyhow, she wanted to fling a spear, bring down a victim, sink fangs into its thin flesh, herself!

The night muttered around her. She drank odors of soil, growth, decay, nectar, blood, striving. Warmth from Mardudek streamed through a chill breeze to lave her pelt. Half-glimpsed flitting shapes, half-heard as they rustled the brush, were her fellows. They were not gathered into a single company, they coursed as each saw fit, but they kept more or less within earshot, and whoever first saw or winded a Flyer would signal it with a whistle.

Erakoum was farther separated from her nearest comrade than any of them were. The others feared that the light-beam reaching upward from the little shell on her head would give them away. She deemed it unlikely, as faint as the bluish gleam was. The human called Hugh paid her well in trade goods to wear the talisman whenever he asked and afterward discuss her experiences with him. For her part, she knew a darkling thrill at such times, akin to nothing else in the world, and knowledge came into her, as if through dreams but more real. These gains were worth a slight handicap on an occasional hunt . . . even tonight's hunt.

Moreover—there was something she had not told Hugh, because he had not told her earlier. It was among the things she learned without words from the gleam-shell. A certain Flyer also carried one, which also kept it in eldritch contact with a human.

The big grotesque creatures were frank about being neutral in the strife between People and Flyers. Erakoum did not hold that against them. This was not their home, and they could not be expected to care if it grew desolate. Yet she had shrewdly deduced that they would try to keep in its burrow their equal intimacy with members of both breeds.

If Hugh had been anxious for her to be soul-tied to him this night, doubtless another human wanted the same for a Flyer. It would be a special joy to her to bring that one down. Besides, looking as she fared for a pale ray among firemites and stars might lead her toward a whole pack of enemies. Rested, she began to trot inland.

Erakoum was hunting.—

Jannika Rezek was forever homesick for a land where she had never lived.

Her parents had politically offended the government of the Danubian Federation. It informed them they need not enter a reindoctrination hospice if they would volunteer to represent their country in the next shipful of personnel to Medea. That was scarcely a choice. Nevertheless, her father told her afterward that his last thought, as he sank down into suspended animation, was of the irony that when he awakened, none of his judges would be alive and nobody would remember what his opinions had been, let alone care. As a matter of fact, he learned at his goal that there was no longer a Danubian Federation.

The rule remained in force that, except for crewfolk, no person went in the opposite direction. A trip was too expensive for a passenger to be carried who would land on Earth as a useless castaway out of past history. Husband and wife made the best they could of their exile. Both physicians, they were eagerly received in Armstrong and its agricultural hinterland. By the modest standards of Medea, they prospered, finally winning a rare privilege. The human population had now been legally stabilized. More would overcrowd the limited areas suitable for settlement, as well as wreaking havoc on environments which the colony existed to study. To balance reproductive failures, a few couples per generation were allowed three children. Jannika's folk were among these.

Thus everybody, herself perforce included, reckoned hers a happy childhood. It was a highly civilized one, too. In the molecules of reels kept at the Center was stored most of mankind's total culture. Industry was, at last, sufficiently developed that well-to-do families could have sets which retrieved the data in as full hologrammic and stereophonic detail as desired. Her parents took advantage of this to ease their nostalgia, never thinking what it might do to younger hearts. Jannika grew up among vivid ghosts: old towers in Prague, springtime in the Böhmerwald, Christmas in a village which centuries had touched only lightly, a concert hall where music rolled in glory across a festive-clad audience which outnumbered the dwellers in Armstrong, replications of events which once made Earth tremble, songs, poetry, books, legends, fairy tales. . . . She sometimes wondered if she had gone into xenology because the ouranids were light, bright, magical beings in a fairy tale.

Today, when Hugh led Chrisoula outside, she had stood for a moment staring after them. Abruptly the room pressed in as if to choke her. She had done what she could in the way of brightening it with drapes, pictures, keepsakes. At present, however, it was bestrewn with field gear; and she hated disorder. He cared naught.

The question rose afresh: How much did he care at all, any longer? They were in love when they married, yes, of course, but even then she recognized it was in high degree a marriage of convenience. Both were after appointments to an outpost station where they would maximize their chances of doing really significant, original research. Wedded couples were preferred, on the theory that they would be less distracted from their work than singletons. When they had their first babies, they were customarily transferred to a town.

She and Hugh quarreled about that. Social pressure—remarks, hints, embarrassed avoidance of the subject—was mounting on them to reproduce. Within population limits, it was desirable to keep the gene pool as large as possible. She was getting along in age, a bit, for motherhood. He was more than willing. But he took for granted that *she* would maintain the home, hold down the desk job, while *he* continued in the field. . . .

She must not reprove him when he came back from his flirtatious little stroll. She lost her temper too often these days, grew outright shrewish, till he stormed from the hut or else grabbed the whiskey and started glugging. He was not a bad man—at the core, he was a good man, she amended hastily—thoughtless in many ways but well-meaning. At her time of life, she couldn't likely do any better.

Although— She felt the heat in her cheeks, made a gesture as if to fend off the memory, and failed. It was two days old.

Having learned from A'i'ach about the Shining Time, she wanted to gather specimens of the glitterbug larvae. Hitherto humans had merely known that the adult insectoids swarmed aloft at intervals of approximately a year. If that was important to the inhabitants of Hansonia, she ought to know more. Observe for herself, enlist the aid of biologists, ecologists, chemists— She asked Piet Marais where to go, and he offered to come along. "The idea should have occurred to me before," he said. "Living in humus, the worms must influence plant growth."

Moister soil was required than existed at Port Kato. They went several kilometers to a lake. The walking was easy, for dense foliage overhead inhibited underbrush. Softness muffled footfalls, trees formed high-arched naves, multiple rays of light passed through dusk and fragrances to fleck the ground or glance off small wings, a sound as of lyres rippled from an unseen throat.

"How delightful," Piet said after a while.

He was looking at her, not ahead. She became very conscious of his blond handsomeness. And his youth, she reminded herself; he was her junior by well-nigh a decade, though mature, considerate, educated, wholly a man. "Yes," she blurted. "I wish I could appreciate it as you do."

"It is not Earth," he discerned. She realized that her answer had been less noncommittal than intended.

"I wasn't pitying myself," she said fast. "Please don't think that. I do see beauty here, and fascination, and freedom, oh, yes, we're lucky on Medea." Attempting to laugh: "Why, on Earth, what would I have done for ouranids?"

"You love them, don't you?" he asked gravely. She nodded. He laid a hand on her bare arm. "You have a great deal of love in you, Jannika."

She made a confused effort to see herself through his eyes. Medium-sized, with a figure she knew was stunning; dark hair worn shoulder length, with gray streaks that she wished Hugh would insist were premature; high cheekbones, tilted nose, pointed chin, large brown eyes, ivory complexion. Still, though Piet was a bachelor, someone that attractive needn't be desperate, he could meet girls in town and keep up acquaintance by holocom. He shouldn't be this appreciative of her. She shouldn't respond. True, she'd had other men a few times, before and after she married. But never in Port Kato; too much likelihood of complications, and she'd been furious when Hugh got involved locally. Worse yet, she suspected Piet saw her as more than a possible partner in a frolic. That could break lives apart.

"Oh, look," she said, and disengaged from his touch in order to point at a cluster of seed pyramids. Meanwhile her mind came to the rescue. "I quite forgot, I meant to tell you, I got a call today from Professor al-Ghazi. We think we've found what makes the glitterbugs metamorphose and swarm."

"Eh?" He blinked. "I didn't realize anybody was working on that."

"Well, it was a, a notion that occurred to me after my special ouranid started me speculating about them. He, A'i'ach, I mean, he told me the time is not strictly seasonal—that is not necessary here in the tropics—but set by Jason—the moon," she added, because the name that humans had bestowed on the innermost of the larger satellites happened to resemble a word which humans had adopted, given by dromids in the Enrique area to an analog of the sirocco wind.

"He says the metamorphoses come during particular transits of Jason across Argo," she continued. "Roughly, every four hundredth. To be exact, the figure is every hundred and twenty-seven Medean days, plus or minus a trifle. The natives here are as keenly conscious of heavenly bodies as everywhere else. The ouranids make a festival of the swarming; they find glitterbugs delicious. Well, this gave me an idea, and I called the Center and requested an astronomical computation. It seems I was right."

"Astronomical cues, for a worm underground?" Marais exclaimed.

"Well, you doubtless recall how Jason excites electrical activity in the atmosphere of Argo, like Io with Jupiter"—the solar system, where Earth has her dwelling! "In this case, there's a beaming effect on one of the radio frequencies that are generated, a kind of natural maser. Therefore those waves only reach Medea when the two moons are on their line of nodes. And that is the exact period my friend was describing. The phase is right, too."

"But can the worms detect so weak a signal?"

"I think it is clear that they do. How, I cannot tell without help from specialists. Remember, though, Phrixus and Helle create little interference. Organisms can be fantastically sensitive. Did you know that it takes less than five photons to activate the visual purple in your eye? I suppose the waves from Argo penetrate the soil to a few centimeters' depth and trigger a chain of biochemical reactions. No doubt it is an evolutionary relic from a time when the orbits of Jason and Medea gave an exact match to the seasons. Perturbation does keep changing the movements of the moons, you know."

He was silent a while before he said: "I do know you are a most extraordinary person, Jannika."

She had regained enough equilibrium to control their talk until they reached the lake. There, for a moment, she felt herself shaken again.

A canebrake screened it from them till they had passed through, to halt on a beach carpeted with mosslike amber-hued turf. Untouched by man in its chalice of forest, the water lay scummy, bubbling, and odorous. The sight of soft colors and the smell of living things were not unpleasant; they were normal to Medea—yet how clear and silver-blue the Neusiedler See gleamed in Danubia. Breath hissed between her teeth.

"What's wrong?" Piet followed her gaze. "The dromids?"

A party of them had arrived to drink, some distance off. Jannika stared as if she had never seen their kind before.

Nearest was a young adult, presumably virgin, since she had six legs. From the slender, long-tailed body rose a two-armed centauroid torso, up to the oddly vulpine head, which would reach to Jannika's chest. Her pelt shimmered blue-black under the suns; Argo was hidden by trees.

Four-legged, a trio of mothers kept watch on the eight cubs they had between them. One set of young showed by their size that their parent would soon ovulate again, be impregnated by a mating, shortly thereafter shed her second segment, and attend it until it gave birth. Another member of this group was at that stage of life, walking on two legs, no longer a functional female but with the male gonads still undeveloped.

No male of breeding age was present. Such a creature was too driven, lustful, impatient, violent, for sociability. There were three postsexual beings, grizzled but strong, protective, their biped movements fast by human standards though laggard compared to the lightning fluidity of their companions.

All adults were armed with stone-age spears, hatchets, and daggers, plus the carnivore teeth in their jaws.

They were gone almost as soon as Jannika had seen them, not out of fear but because they were Medean animals whose chemistry and living went swifter than hers.

"The dromids," she got out.

Piet regarded her a while before he said gently: "They pursue your dear ouranids. You tell me that will get worse than ever on the night when the glitterbugs rise. But you must not hate them. They are caught in a tragedy."

"Yes, the sterility problem, yes. Why should they drag the ouranids down with them?" She struck fist into palm. "Let's get to work, let's collect our samples and go home, can we, please?"

He was fully understanding.

—She cast the memory out and flung herself back into preparations for the night.

Hugh Brocket and his wife departed a while after sunset. Their flitters jetted off in a whisper, reached an intermediate altitude, and circled for a minute while the riders got bearings and exchanged radioed farewells. Observed from below, catching the last gleam of sunken Colchis on their flanks, they resembled a pair of teardrops.

"Good hunting, Jan."

"Ugh! Don't say that."

"Sorry," he apologized in a stiff tone, and cut out the sender. Sure, it had been tactless of him, but why must she be so goddamn touchy?

Never mind. He'd plenty to do. Erakoum had promised to be on Shipwreck Cliffs about this time, since her gang meant to proceed north along the coast from its camp before turning inland. Thereafter her location would be unpredictable. He must lock onto her transmitter soon. Jannika's craft dwindled in sight, bound on her own quest. Hugh set his inertial pilot and settled back in his safety harness to double-check his instruments. That was mechanical, since he knew quite well everything was in order. Most of his attention roamed free.

The canopy gave a titanic vista. Below, hills lay in dappled masses of shadow, here and there relieved by an argent thread that was a river or by the upheaving of precipices and scarps. The hemisphere-dividing Ring Ocean turned the eastern horizon to quicksilver. Westward in heaven, the double sun had left a Tyrian wake. Overhead reached a velvety dark, becoming more starry with each of his heartbeats. He saw a pair of moons, close enough to show discs lighted from two sides, rusty and white; he recognized more, which were mere bright points to his eyes, by their positions as they went on sentry-go among the constellations. Low above the sea smoldered Argo—no, shone, because its upper clouds were in full daylight, bands of brilliance splashed over sullen red. Jason was close to transit, with angular diameter exceeding twenty minutes of arc, and nevertheless Hugh had trouble finding it amidst that glare.

The shore came in view. He activated the detector and set his craft to hovering. An indicator light flashed green; he had his contact. He sent the vehicle aloft, a full three kilometers. Partly this was because he would be concentrating on encephalic input and wanted plenty of room for piloting error; partly it was to keep beyond sight or hearing of the natives, lest his presence affect their actions. Having taken station, he connected and secured the receiver helmet to his head—it didn't weigh much—and switched it on. Transmitted, amplified, transformed, relayed, reinduced, the events in Erakoum's nervous system merged with the events in his.

By no means did he acquire the dromid's full awareness. Conveyance and translation were far too primitive. He had spent his professional lifetime gaining sufficient fellow-feeling with the species that, after as much patience as both individuals could maintain over a span of years, he could barely begin to interpret the signals he gathered. The speed of native mental processes was less of a help—through repetition and reinforcement—than an added hindrance. As a rough analogy, imagine trying to follow a rapid and nearly inaudible conversation, missing many a word, in a language you do not know well. Actually, none of what Hugh perceived was verbal; it was sight, sound, a complex of senses, including those interior like balance and hunger, including dream-hints of senses that he did not think he possessed.

He saw the land go by, bush, branch, slope, stars and moons above shaggy ridges; he felt its varying contours and textures as feet went pacing; he heard its multitudinous low noises; he smelled richness; the impressions were endless, most of them vague and fleeting, the best of them strong enough to take him out of himself, draw him groundward toward oneness with the creature below.

Clearest, perhaps because his glands were stimulated thereby, was emotion, determination. Erakoum was out to get herself a Flyer.

It was going to be a long night, quite possibly a harrowing one. Hugh expected he'd need a dose or two of sleep surrogate. Humans had never gotten away from the ancient rhythms of Earth. Dromids catnapped; ouranids went—daydreamy? contemplative?

As often before, he wondered briefly what Jan's rapport with her native felt like. They would never be able to describe their sharings to each other.

***Well into the hills, A'i'ach's Swarm found a grand harvest of starwings. The heights were less densely wooded than the lowlands, which was good, for the bright prey never went far up, and below a forest crown, the People were vulnerable to Beast attack. Here was a fair amount of open ground, turf-begrown and boulder-strewn, scattered through the shadowing timber. A narrow ravine crossed the largest of those glades, a gash abrim with blackness.

Like an endless shower of sparks, the starwings danced, dashed, dodged about, beyond counting, meant for naught save the ecstasy of their mating and of the People who fed upon them. Despite the wariness in him, A'i'ach could resist no more than anyone else. He did refrain from valving out gas in his haste to descend, as many did. That would make ascent slow. Instead, he contracted his globe and sank, letting it reexpand slightly as varying air densities demanded. Nor did he release gas to propel himself. Rhythmically pumping, his siphon worked together with the breezes to zigzag him about at low speed. There was no hurry. The starwings numbered more than the Swarm could eat. Plenty would go free to lay their eggs for the next crop.

Among the motes, A'i'ach inhaled his first swallow of them. The sweet hot flavor sang in his flesh. Thickly gathered around him, bobbing, spinning, rippling, and flailing their corybantic tendrils, filling the sky with music, the People forgot caution. Love began. It was not purposeless, though without water to fall into, the pollinated seeds would not germinate. It united everyone. Life-dust drifted like smoke in the radiance of Ruii; the sight, smell, taste made feverish that joy which the starwing feast awakened. Again and again A'i'ach ejaculated. He went past his skin, he became a cell of a single divine being which was itself a tornado of love. Sometimes when he felt age upon him, he would drift westward across the sea, into the cold Beyond. There, yielding up the last warmth of his body, his spirit would take its reward, the Promise that forever and ever it would be what it was now in this brief night. . . .

A howl smote. Shapes bounded from under trees, out into the open. A'i'ach saw a shaft pierce the globe next to his. Blood spurted, gas hissed forth, the shriveling form fell as a dead leaf falls. Tendrils still writhed when a Beast snatched it the last way down and fangs rent it asunder.

In the crowd and chaos, he could not know how many others died. The greatest number were escaping, rising above missile reach. Those who were armed began to drop their stones and ü boughs. It was not likely that any killed a Beast.

A'i'ach had relaxed the muscles in his globe and shot instantly upward. Safe, he might have joined the rest of the Swarm, to wander off in search of a place to renew festival. But rage and grief seethed too high. A far-off part of him wondered at that; the People did not take hard the death of a Person. This thing he wore, that somehow whispered mysteries—

And he carried a knife!

Recklessly spending gas, he swung about, downward. Most of the Beasts had vanished back into the woods. A few remained, devouring. He cruised at a height near the limits of prudence and peered after his chance. Since he could not drop like a rock, he must feint at one individual, then quickly jet at another, stab, rise, and attack again.

A wan beam of light struck toward him. It came from the head of a Beast which emerged from shadow, halted, and glared upward.

His will blazed forth in A'i'ach. Yonder was the monster which had his kind of bond to humans. If he had already gained a knife thereby, what might that being have gotten, what might it get, to wreak worse harm? If nothing else, killing it ought to shock its companions, make them think twice about their murderousness.

A'i'ach moved to battle. About him, the starwings happily danced and mated.***

Jannika must search for an hour before she made her contact. An ouranid could not undertake to be at an exact spot at a given time. Hers had simply informed her, while she fastened the transmitter on him, that his group was currently in the neighborhood of Mount MacDonald. She flew there and cast about in ever-deepening darkness until her indicator shone green. Having established linkage, she rose to three kilometers and set the autopilot to make slow circles. From time to time, as her subject passed northeast, she moved the center of her path.

Otherwise she was engaged in trying to be her ouranid. It was impossible, of course, but from the effort she was learning what could never have come to her through spoken language. Answers to factual questions she would not have thought to ask. Folkways, beliefs, music, poetry, aerial ballet, which she could not have known for what they were, observing from outside. Lower down in her, dimmer, but more powerful—nothing she could write into a scientific report: a sense of delights, yearnings, wind, shiningness, perfumes, clouds, rain, immense distances, a sense of what it was to be a heaven-dweller. Not complete, no, a few wavery glimpses, hard to remember afterward; yet taking her out of herself into a new world agleam with wonder.

The thrill was redoubled tonight by A'i'ach's excitement. Her impressions of what he was experiencing had never been stronger or sharper. She floated on airstreams, life-scents and song possessed her, she was a drop in an ocean beneath Ruii the mighty, there was no home to hopelessly long for because everywhere was home.

The Swarm came at last upon a cloud of glitterbugs, and Jannika's cosmos went wild.

For a moment, half terrified, she started to switch off her helmet. Reason checked her hand. What was happening was just an extreme of what she had partaken in before. Ouranids seldom took much nourishment at a single time; when they did, it had an intoxicating effect. She had also felt their sexuality; A'i'ach's maleness was too unearthly to disturb her, as his dromid's femaleness had disturbed Hugh when she mated and later shed her hindquarters. Tonight the ouranids held high revel.

She surrendered to it, crescendo after crescendo, oh, if she only had a man here, but no, that would be different, would blur the sacred splendor, the Promise, the Promise!

Then the Beasts arrived. Horror erupted. Somewhere a strange voice screamed for the avenging of her shattered bliss.

—As she trotted along a bare ridge, Erakoum had thought, with a leap of her pulse, that she spied afar a faint blue ray of light in the air. She could not be certain, through the brilliance cast by Mardudek, but she altered her course in hopes. When she had scrambled a long while among stones and thorns, the glimmer disappeared. It must have been a trick of the night, perhaps moonglow on rising mists. That conclusion did nothing to ease her temper. Everything about the Flyers was unlucky!

Because of this, she was behind the rest of the pack. Her first news of quarry came through their yells. *"Hai-ay, hai-ay, hai-ay!"* echoed around, and she snarled in bafflement. Surely she would arrive too late for a kill. Nonetheless she bounded in that direction. If the Flyers did not get a good wind, she could overtake them and follow along from cover to cover, unseen. Maybe they would not go further than she had strength for, before they chanced on a fresh upswelling of firemites and descended anew. Breath rasped in her gullet, the hillside struck at her feet with unseen rocks, but eagerness flung her on till she reached the place.

It was a glade, brightly lit though crisscrossed by shadows, cut in half by a small ravine. The firemites swirled about against the forest murk, like a glinting dustcloud. Several females crouched on the turf and ripped at the remnants of their prey. The rest had departed, to trail the escaped Flyers as Erakoum planned.

She stopped at the edge of trees to pant, looked up, and froze. The mass of Flyers was slowly and chaotically streaming west, but a few lingered to cast down their pitiful weapons. From the top of one, dim light beamed aloft. She had found what she sought.

"Ee-hah!" she screamed, sprang forward, shook her javelin.

"Come, evilworker, come and be slain! By your blood shall you give to my next brood the life you reaved from my first!"

There was no surprise, there was fate, when the eerie shape spiraled about and drew nearer. More would be settled this night than which of them was to survive. She, Erakoum, had been seized by a Power, had become an instrument of the Prophet.

Crouched, she cast her spear. The effort surged through her muscles. She saw it fly straight as the damnation it carried—but her foe swerved, it missed him by a fingerbreadth, and then all at once he was coming directly at her.

They never did that! What sheened in his seaweed grip?

Erakoum grabbed after a new javelin off her back. Each knot in the lashing was supposed to give way at a jerk, but this jammed, she must tug again, and meanwhile the enemy loomed ever more big. She recognized what he held, a human-made knife, sharp as a fresh obsidian blade and more thin and strong. She retreated. Her spear was now loose. No room for a throw. She thrust.

With crazy glee, she saw the head strike. The Flyer rolled aside before it could pierce, but blood and gas together foamed darkly from a slash across his paleness.

He spurted forward, was inside her guard. The knife smote and smote. Erakoum felt the stabs, but not yet the pain. She dropped her shaft, batted her arms, snapped jaws together. Teeth closed in flesh. Through her mouth and down her throat poured a rush of strength.

Abruptly the ground was no more beneath her hind feet. She fell over, clawed with forefeet and hands for a hold, lost it, and toppled. When she hit the side of the ravine, she rolled down across cruel snags. She had an instant's glimpse of sky above, stars and firemites, the Mardudek-lighted Flyer drifting by and bleeding. Then nothingness snatched her to itself.—

Folk at Port Kato asked what brought Jannika Rezek and Hugh Brocket home so early, so shaken. They evaded questions and hastened to their place. The door slammed behind them. A minute later, they blanked their windows.

For a time they stared at each other. The familiar room held no comfort. Illumination meant for human eyes was brass-harsh, air shut away from the forest was lifeless, faint noises from the settlement outside thickened the silence within.

He shook his head finally, blindly, and turned from her. "Erakoum gone," he mumbled. "How'm I ever going to understand that?"

"Are you sure?" she whispered.

"I . . . I felt her mind shut off . . . damn near like a blow to my own skull . . . but you were making such a fuss about your precious ouranid—"

"A'i'ach's *hurt!* His people know nothing of medicine. If you hadn't been raving till I decided I must talk you back with me before you crashed your flitter—"

Jannika broke off, swallowed hard, unclenched her fists, and became able to say: "Well, the harm is done and here we are. Shall we try to reason about it, try to find out what went wrong and how to stop another such horror, or not?"

"Yeah, of course." He went to the pantry. "You want a drink?" he called.

She hesitated. "Wine."

He fetched her a glassful. His right hand clutched a tumbler of straight whiskey, which he began on at once. "I felt Erakoum die," he said.

Jannika took a chair. "Yes, and I felt A'i'ach take wounds that may well prove mortal. Sit down, will you?"

He did, heavily, opposite her. She sipped from her glass, he gulped from his. Newcomers to Medea always said wine and distilled spirits there tasted more peculiar than the food. A poet had made that fact the takeoff point for a chilling verse about isolation. When it was sent to Earth as part of the news, the reply came after a century that nobody could imagine what the colonists saw in it.

Hugh hunched his shoulders. "Okay," he growled. "We should compare notes before we start forgetting, and maybe repeat tomorrow when we've had a chance to think." He reached across to their recorder and flicked it on. As he entered an identification phrase, his tone stayed dull.

"That is best for us too," Jannika reminded him. "Work, logical thought, those hold off the nightmares."

"Which this absolutely was— All right!" He regained a little vigor. "Let's try to reconstruct what did happen.

"The ouranids were out after glitterbugs and the dromids were out after ouranids. You and I witnessed an encounter. Naturally, we'd hoped we wouldn't—I suppose you prayed for that, hm?—but we knew there'd be hostilities in a lot of places. What shocked the wits out of us was when our personal natives got into a fight, with us in rapport."

Jannika bit her lip. "Worse than that," she said. "They were seeking it, those two. It was not a random encounter, it was a duel." She raised her eyes. "You never told Erakoum, any dromid, that we were linking with an ouranid too, did you?"

"No, certainly not. Nor did you tell your ouranid about my liaison. We both know better than to throw that kind of variable into a program like this."

"And the rest of the station personnel have vocabularies too limited, in either language. Very well. But I can tell you that A'i'ach knew. I was not aware he did until the fight began. Then it reached the forefront of his mind, it shouted at me, not in words but not to be mistaken about."

"Yeah, same thing for me with Erakoum, more or less."

"Let's admit what we don't want to, my dear. We have not simply been receiving from our natives. We have been transmitting. Feedback."

He lifted a helpless fist. "What the devil might convey a return message?"

"If nothing else, the radio beam that locks us onto our subjects. Induced modulation. We know from the example of the glitterbug larvae—and no doubt other cases you and I never heard of—how shall we know everything about a whole world? We know Medean organisms can be extremely radio-sensitive."

"M-m, yeah, the terrific speed of Medean animals, key molecules more labile than the corresponding compounds in us. . . . Hey, wait! Neither Erakoum nor A'i'ach had more than a smattering of English. Certainly no Czech, which you've told me you usually think in. Besides, look what an effort we had to make before we could tune them in at all, in spite of everything learned on the mainland. They'd no reason to do the same, no idea of scientific method. They surely assumed it was only a whim or a piece of magic or something that made us want them to carry those objects around."

Jannika shrugged. "Perhaps when we are in rapport, we think more in their languages than we ourselves realize. And both kinds of Medeans think faster than humans, observe, learn. Anyway, I do not say their contact with us was as good as our contact with them. If nothing else, radio has much less bandwidth. I think probably what they picked up from us was subliminal."

"I guess you're right," Hugh sighed. "We'll have to sic the electronicians and neurologists into the problem, but I sure can't think of any better explanation than yours."

He leaned forward. The energy which now vibrated in his voice turned cold: "But let's try to see this thing in context, so we can maybe get a hint of what kind of information the natives have been receiving from us. Let's lay out once more why the Hansonian dromids and ouranids are at war. Basically, the dromids are dying off, and blame the ouranids. Could we, Port Kato, be at fault?"

"Why, hardly," Jannika said in astonishment. "You know what precautions we take."

Hugh smiled without mirth. "I'm thinking of psychological pollution."

"What? Impossible! Nowhere else on Medea—"

"Be quiet, will you?" he shouted. "I'm trying to bring back to my mind what I got from my friend that your friend killed."

She half rose, white-faced, sat down again, and waited. The wineglass trembled in her fingers.

"You've always babbled about how kind and gentle and esthetic the ouranids are," he said, at her rather than to her. "You swoon over this beautiful new local faith they've acquired—the windborne flight to Farside, the death in dignity, the Nirvana, I forget what else. To hell with the grubby dromids. Dromids don't do anything but make tools and fires, hunt, care for their young, live in communities, create art and philosophy, same as humans. What's interesting to you in that?

"Well, let me tell you what I've told you before, dromids are believers too. If we could compare, I'd give long odds their faiths are stronger and more meaningful than the ouranids'. They keep trying to make sense of the world. Can't you sympathize the least bit?

"Okay, they have a tremendous respect for the fitness of things. When something goes seriously wrong—when a great crime or sin or shame happens—the whole world hurts. If the wrong isn't set right, everything will go bad. That's what they believe on Hansonia, and I don't know but what they've got hold of a truth.

"The lordly ouranids never paid much attention to the groundling dromids, but that was not symmetrical. The ouranids are as conspicuous as Argo, Colchis, any part of nature. In dromid eyes, they too have their ordained place and cycle.

"All at once the ouranids change. They don't give themselves back to the soil when they die, the way life is supposed to—no, they head west, over the ocean, toward that unknown place where the suns go down every evening. Can't you see how unnatural that might seem? As if a tree should walk or a corpse rise. And not an isolated incident; no, year after year after year.

"Psychosomatic abortion? How can I tell? What I can tell is that the dromids are shocked to the guts by this thing the ouranids are doing. No matter how ridiculous the thing is, it hurts them!"

She sprang to her feet. Her glass hit the floor. "Ridiculous?" she yelled. "That *Tao,* that vision? No, ridiculous, that's what your . . . your fuxes believe—except that it makes them attack innocent beings and, and eat them—I can't wait till those creatures are extinct!"

He had risen likewise. "You don't care about children dying, no, of course not," he answered. "What sense of motherhood have you got, for hell's sake? About like a balloon's. Drift free, scatter seed, forget it, it'll bud and break loose and the Swarm will adopt it, never mind anything except your pleasure."

"Why, you— Are you wishing you could be a mother?" she jeered.

His empty hand swung at her. She barely evaded the blow. Appalled, they stiffened where they stood.

He tried to speak, failed, and drank. After a full minute she said, quite low: "Hugh, our natives were getting messages from us. Not verbal. Unconscious. Through them"—she choked—"were you and I seeking to kill each other?"

He gaped until, in a single clumsy gesture, he set his own glass down and held out his arms to her. "Oh, no, oh, no," he stammered. She came to him.

Presently they went to bed. And then he could do nothing. The medicine cabinet held a remedy for that, but what followed might have happened between a couple of machines. At last she lay quietly crying and he went out to drink some more.

The wind awakened her. She lay for a time listening to it boom around the walls. Sleep drained out of her. She opened her eyes and looked at the clock. Its luminous dial said three hours had passed. She might as well get up. Maybe she could make Hugh feel better.

The main room was still lighted. He was asleep himself, sprawled in an armchair, a bottle beside it. How deep the lines were in his face.

How loud the wind was. Probably a storm front which the weather service had reported at sea had taken a quick, unexpected swing this way. Medean meteorology was not yet an exact science. Poor ouranids, their festival disrupted, they themselves blown about and scattered, even endangered. Normally they could ride out a gale, but a few might be carried to disaster, hit by lightning or dashed against a cliff or hopelessly entangled in a tree. The sick and injured would suffer most.

A'i'ach.

Jannika squeezed her lids together and struggled to recall how badly wounded he was. But everything had been too confused and terrible; Hugh had diverted her attention; before long she had flitted out of transmission range. Besides, A'i'ach himself could hardly have ascertained his own condition at once. It might not be grave. Or it might. He could be dead by now, or dying, or doomed to die if he didn't get help.

She was responsible—perhaps not guilty, by a moralistic definition, but responsible.

Resolution crystallized. If the weather didn't preclude, she would go search for him.

Alone? Yes. Hugh would protest, delay her, perhaps actually restrain her by force. She recorded a few words to him, wondered if they were overly impersonal, decided against composing something more affectionate. Yes, she wanted a reconciliation, and supposed he did, but she would not truckle. She redonned her field garb, added a jacket into whose pockets she stuffed some food bars, and departed.

The wind rushed bleak around her, *whoo-oo-oo,* a torrent she must breast. Clouds scudded low and thick, tinged red where Argo shone between them. The giant planet seemed to fly among ragged veils. Dust whirled in the compound, gritty on her skin. Nobody else was outdoors.

At the hangar, she punched for the latest forecast. It looked bad but not, she thought, frightening. (And if she did crash, was that such an enormous loss, to herself or anyone else?) "I am going back to my study area," she told the mechanic. When he attempted to dissuade her, she pulled rank. She never liked that, but from the Danubian ghosts she had learned how. "No further discussion. Stand by to open the way and give me assistance if required. That is an order."

The little craft shivered and drummed on the ground. Takeoff took skill—with a foul moment when a gust nearly upset her—but once aloft her vehicle flew sturdily. Risen above the cloud deck, she saw it heave like a sea, Argo a mountain rearing out of it, stars and companion moons flickery overhead. Northward bulked a darkness more deep and high, the front. The weather would really stiffen in the next few hours. If she wasn't back soon, she'd better stay put till it cleared.

The flight was quick to the battleground. When the inertial pilot had brought her there, she circled, put on her helmet, activated the system. Her pulse fluttered and her mouth had dried. "A'i'ach," she breathed, "be alive, please be alive."

The green light went on. At least his transmitter existed on the site. He? She must will herself toward rapport.

Weakness, pain, a racket of soughing leaves, tossing boughs—

"A'i'ach, hang on, I'm coming down!"

A leap of gladness. Yes, he did perceive her.

Landing would be risky indeed. The aircraft had a vertical capability, excellent radar and sonar, a computer and effectors to handle most of the work. However, the clear space below was not large, it was cleft in twain, and while the surrounding forest was a fair windbreak, there would be vile drafts and eddies. "God, into

Your hands I give myself," she said, and wondered as often before how Hugh endured his atheism.

Nevertheless, if she waited she would lose courage. Down!

Her descent was wilder still than she had expected. First the clouds were a maelstrom, then she was through them but into a raving blast, then she saw treetops grab at her. The vehicle rolled, pitched, yawed. Had she been an utter fool? She didn't truly want to leave this life. . . .

She made it, and for minutes sat strengthless. When she stirred, she felt her entire body ache from tension. But A'i'ach's hurt was in her. Called by that need, she unharnessed and went forth.

The noise was immense in the black palisade of trees around her, their branches groaned, their crowns foamed; but down on the ground the air, though restless, was quieter, nearly warm. Unseen Argo reddened the clouds, which cast enough glow that she didn't need her flashlight. She found no trace of the slain ouranids. Well, they had no bones; the dromids must have eaten every scrap. What a ghastly superstition— Where was A'i'ach?

She found him after a search. He lay behind a spiny bush, in which he had woven his tendrils to secure himself. His body was deflated to the minimum, an empty sack; but his eyes gleamed, and he could speak, in the shrill, puffing language of his people, which she had come to know was melodious.

"May joy blow upon you. I never hoped for your advent. Welcome you are. Here it has been lonely." A shudder was in that last word. Ouranids could not long stand being parted from their Swarm. Some xenologists believed that with them consciousness was more collective than individual. Jannika rejected that idea, unless perhaps it applied to the different species found in parts of Nearside. A'i'ach had a soul of his own!

She knelt. "How are you?" She could not render his sounds any better than he could hers, but he had learned to interpret.

"It is not overly ill with me, now that you are nigh. I lost blood and gas, but those wounds have closed. Weak, I settled in a tree until the Beasts left. Meanwhile the wind rose. I thought best not to ride it in my state. Yet I could not stay in the tree, I would have been blown away. So I valved out the rest of my gas and crept to this shelter."

The speech held far more than such a bare statement. The denotation was laconic and stoical, the connotations not. A'i'ach would need at least a day to regenerate sufficient hydrogen for ascent—how long depended on how much food he could reach in his crippled condition—unless a carnivore found him first, which was quite likely. Jannika imagined what a flood of suffering, dread, and bravery would have come over her had she been wearing her helmet.

She gathered the flaccid form into her arms. It weighed little. It felt warm and silky. He cooperated as well as he was able. Just the same, part of him dragged on the ground, which must have been painful.

She must be rougher still, hauling on folds of skin, when she brought him inside the aircraft. It had scant room to spare; he was practically bundled into the rear section. Rather than apologizing when he moaned, or saying anything in particular, she sang to him. He didn't know the ancient Terrestrial words, but he liked the tunes and realized what she meant by them.

She had equipped her vehicle for basic medical help to natives, and had given it on past occasions. A'i'ach's injuries were not deep, because most of him was scarcely more than a bag; however, the bag had been torn in several places and, though it was self-sealing, flight would reopen it unless it got reinforcement. Applying local anesthetics and antibiotics—that much had been learned about Medean biochemistry—she stitched the gashes.

"There, you can rest," she said when, cramped, sweat-soaked, and shaky, she was done. "Later I will give you an injection of gas and you can rise immediately if you choose. I think, though, we would both be wisest to wait out the gale."

A human would have groaned: "It is *tight* in here."

"Yes, I know what you mean, but— A'i'ach, let me put my helmet on." She pointed. "That will join our spirits as they were joined before. It may take your mind off your discomfort. And at this short range, given our new knowledge—" A thrill went through her. "What may we not find out?"

"Good," he agreed. "We may enjoy unique experiences." The concept of discovery for its own sake was foreign to him . . . but his search for pleasures went far beyond hedonism.

Eager despite her weariness, she moved into her seat and

reached for the apparatus. The radio receiver, always open to the standard carrier band, chose that moment to buzz.

Argo in the east glowered at the nearing, lightning-shot wall of storm in the north. Below, the clouds already present roiled in reds and darknesses. Wind wailed. Hugh's aircraft lurched and bucked. Despite a heater, chill seeped through the canopy, as if brought by the light of stars and moons.

"Jan, are you there?" he called. "Are you all right?"

Her voice was a swordstroke of deliverance. "Hugh? Is that you, darling?"

"Yes, sure, who the hell else did you expect? I woke up, played your message, and— Are you all right?"

"Quite safe. But I don't dare take off in this weather. And you mustn't try to land, that would be too dangerous by now. You shouldn't stay, either. Darling, *rostomily,* that you came!"

"Judas priest, sweetheart, how could I not? Tell me what's happened."

She explained. At the end, he nodded a head which still ached a bit from liquor in spite of a nedolor tablet. "Fine," he said. "You wait for calm air, pump up your friend, and come on home." An idea he had been nursing nudged him. "Uh, I wonder. Do you think he could go down into that gulch and recover Erakoum's unit? Those things are scarce, you know." He paused. "I suppose it'd be too much to ask him to throw a little soil over her."

Jannika's tone held pity. "I can do that."

"No, you can't. I got a clear impression from Erakoum as she was falling, before she cracked her skull apart or whatever she did. Nobody can climb down without a rope secured on top. It'd be impossible to return. Even with a rope, it'd be crazy dangerous. Her companions didn't attempt anything, did they?"

Reluctance: "I'll ask him. It may be asking a lot. Is the unit functional?"

"Hm, yes, I'd better check on that first. I'll report in a minute or three. Love you."

He did, he knew, no matter how often she enraged him. The idea that, somewhere in the abysses of his being, he might have wished her death, was not to be borne. He'd have followed her through a heavier tempest than this, merely to deny it.

Well, he could go home with a satisfied conscience and wait for her arrival, after which—what? The uncertainty made a hollowness in him.

His instrument flashed green. Okay, Erakoum's button was transmitting, therefore unharmed and worth salvaging. If only she herself—

He tensed. The breath rattled in his lungs. Did he *know* she was dead?

He lowered the helmet over his temples. His hands shook, giving him trouble in making the connections. He pressed the switch. He willed to perceive—

Pain twisted like white-hot wires, strength ebbed and ebbed, soft waves of nothingness flowed ever more often, but still Erakoum defied. The slit of sky that she could see, from where she lay unable to creep further, was full of wind. . . . She shocked to complete awareness. Again she sensed Hugh's presence.

"Broken bones, feels like. Heavy blood loss. She'll die in a few more hours. Unless you give her first aid, Jan. Then she ought to last till we can fly her to Port Kato for complete attention."

"Oh, I can do sewing and bandaging and splinting, whatever, yes. And nedolor's an analgesic stimulant for dromids too, isn't it? And simply a drink of water could make the whole difference; she must be dehydrated. But how to reach her?"

"Your ouranid can lift her up, after you've inflated him."

"You can't be serious! A'i'ach's hurt, convalescent—and Erakoum tried to kill him!"

"That was mutual, right?"

"Well—"

"Jan, I'm not going to abandon her. She's down in a grave, who used to run free, and the touch of me she's getting is more to her than I could have imagined. I'll stay till she's rescued, or else I'll stay till she dies."

"No, Hugh, you mustn't. The storm."

"I'm not trying to blackmail you, dearest. In fact, I won't blame your ouranid much if he refuses. But I can't leave Erakoum. I just plain can't."

"I . . . I have learned something about you. . . . I will try."

***A'i'ach had not understood his Jannika. It was not believable that helping a Beast could help bring peace. That creature was what it was, a slaughterer. And yet, yet, once there had been no trouble with the Beasts, once they had been the animals which most interested and entertained the People. He himself remembered songs about their fleetness and their fires. In those lost days they had been called the Flame Dancers.

What made him yield to her plea was unclear in his spirit. She had probably saved his life, at hazard to her own, and this was an overpowering new thought to him. He wanted greatly to maintain his union with her, which enriched his world, and therefore hesitated to deny a request that seemed as urgent as hers. Through the union, she helmeted, he believed he felt what she did when she said, with water running from her eyes, "I want to heal what *I* have done—" and that kind of feeling was transcendent, like the Shining Time, and was what finally decided him.

She assisted him from the thing-which-bore-her and payed out a tube. Through the latter he drank gas, a wind-rush of renewed life. His injuries twinged when his globe expanded, but he could ignore that.

He needed her anchoring weight to get across the ground to the ravine. Fingers and tendrils intertwined, they nevertheless came near being carried away. Had he let himself swell to full size, he could have lifted her. Air harried and hooted, snatched at him, wanted to cast him among thorns—how horrible the ground was!

How much worse to descend below it. He throbbed to an emotion he scarcely recognized. Had she been in rapport, she could have told him that the English word for it was "terror." A human or a dromid who felt it in that degree would have recoiled from the drop. A'i'ach made it a force blowing him onward, because this too raised him out of himself.

At the edge, she threw her arms around him as far as they would go, laid her mouth to his pelt, and said, "Good luck, dear A'i'ach, dear brave A'i'ach, good luck, God keep you." Those were the noises she made in her language. He did not recognize the gesture either.

A cylinder she had given him to hold threw a strong beam of light. He saw the jagged slope tumble downward underneath him, and thought that if he was cast against that, he was done for. Then his spirit would have a fearful journey, with no body to shelter it, before it reached Beyond—if it did, if it was not shredded and scattered first. Quickly, before the churning airs could take full hold of him, he jetted across the brink. He contracted. He sank.

The dread as gloom and walls closed in was like no other carouse in his life. At its core, he felt incandescently aware. Yes, the human had brought him into strange skies.

Through the dankness he caught an odor more sharp. He steered that way. His flash picked out the Beast, sprawled on sharp talus, gasping and glaring. He used jets and siphon to position himself out of reach and said in what English he had, "I haff ch'um say-aff ee-you."***

—From the depths of her death-place, Erakoum looked up at the Flyer. She could barely make him out, a big pale moon behind a glare of light. Amazement heaved her out of a drowse. Had her enemy pursued her down here in his ill-wishing?

Good! She would die in battle, not the torment which ripped her. "Come on and fight," she called hoarsely. If she could sink teeth in him, get a last lick of his blood— The memory of that taste was like sweet lightning. During the time afterward which refused to end, she had thought she would be dead already if she had not swallowed those drops.

Their wonder-working had faded out. She stirred, seeking a defensive posture. Agony speared through her, followed by night.

When she roused, the Flyer still waited. Amidst a roaring in her ears, she heard, over and over, "I haff ch'um say-aff ee-you."

Human language? This *was* the being that the humans favored as they did her. It had to be, though the ray from its head was hidden by the ray from its tendrils. *Could Hugh have been bound all the while to both?*

Erakoum strove to form syllables never meant for her mouth and throat. "Ha-watt-tt you ha-wannit? Gho, no bea haiar, gho."

The Flyer made a response. She could no more follow that than he appeared to have followed hers. He must have come down to make sure of her, or simply to mock her while she died. Erakoum scrabbled weakly after a spear. She couldn't throw one, but—

From the unknownness wherein dwelt the soul of Hugh, she suddenly knew: He wants to save you.

Impossible. But . . . but there the Flyer was. Half delirious, Erakoum could yet remember that Flyers were seldom that patient.

What else could befall but death? Nothing. She lay back on the rock shards. Let the Flyer be her doom or be her Mardudek. She had found the courage to surrender.

The shape hovered. Her hair sensed tiny gusts, and she thought dimly that this must be a difficult place for him too. Speech burst and skirled. He was trying to explain something, but she was too hurt and tired to listen. She folded her hands around her muzzle. Would he appreciate that gesture?

Maybe. Hesitant, he neared. She kept motionless. Even when his tendrils brushed her, she kept motionless.

They slipped across her body, got a purchase, tightened. Through the haze of pain, she saw him swelling. He meant to lift her—up to Hugh?

When he did, her knife wounds opened and she shrieked before she swooned.

Her next knowledge was of lying on turf under a hasty, red-lit sky. A human crouched above her, talking to a small box that replied in the voice of Hugh. Behind, the Flyer lay shrunken, clutching a bush. Storm brawled; the first stinging raindrops fell.

In the hidden way of hunters, she knew that she was dying. The human might staunch those cuts and stabs, but could not give back what was lost.

Memory—what she had heard tell, what she had briefly tasted herself—"Blood of the Flyer. It will save me. Blood of the Flyer, if he will give." She was not sure whether she spoke or dreamed it. She sank back into the darkness.

When she surfaced anew, the Flyer was beside her, embracing her against the wind. The human was carefully using a knife on a tendril. The Flyer brought the tendril in between Erakoum's fangs. As the rain's full violence began, she drank.—

A double sunrise was always lovely.

Jannika had delayed telling Hugh her news. She wanted to surprise him, preferably after his anxiety about his dromid was past. Well, it was; Erakoum would be hospitalized several days in Port Kato, which ought to be an interesting experience for all concerned, but she would get well. A'i'ach had already rejoined his Swarm.

When Hugh wakened from the sleep of exhaustion which followed his bedside vigil, Jannika proposed a dawn picnic, and was touched at how fast he agreed. They flitted to a place they knew on the sea cliffs, spread out their food, and sat down to watch.

At first Argo, the stars, and a pair of moons were the only lights. Slowly heaven brightened, the ocean shimmered silver beneath blue, Phrixus and Helle wheeled by the great planet. Wild songs went trilling through air drenched with an odor of roanflower, which is like violets.

"I got the word from the Center," she declared while she held his hand. "It's definite. The chemistry was soon unraveled, given the extra clue we had from the reviving effect of blood."

He turned about. "What?"

"Manganese deficiency," she said. "A trace element in Medean biology, but vital, especially to dromids and their reproduction—and evidently to something else in ouranids, since they concentrate it to a high degree. Hansonia turns out to be poorly supplied with it. Ouranids, going west to die, were removing a significant percentage from the ecology. The answer is simple. We need not try to change the ouranid belief. Temporarily, we can have a manganese supplement made up and offer it to the dromids. In the long run, we can mine the ore where it's plentiful and scatter it as a dust across the island. Your friends will live, Hugh."

He was quiet for a time. Then—he could surprise her, this son of an outback miner—he said: "That's terrific. The engineering solution. But the bitterness won't go away overnight. We won't see any quick happy ending. Maybe not you and me, either." He seized her to him. "Damnation, though, let's try!"

C. J. Cherryh

Here is the fourth woman writer of the book. You may not be able to tell from the initials alone, but they stand for Carolyn Janice.

Actually, I disapprove of the use of initials in identification. For one thing, they mask sex. This may seem to be a matter of indifference. After all, does it matter if a writer is a man or a woman any more than if he/she had yellow hair or brown or black? No, of course not. Still, what if you get a letter from A. B. Smith and have to answer. Do you address him/her as Mr., Mrs., Miss, or Ms. (or Dr. or Prof. or Rev., for that matter.)

I think it is a matter of common courtesy, if your name is ambiguous, either because you use initials or because you have an epicene first name (suitable for either sex), that you indicate how you prefer to be addressed.

In fact, I have just made up my mind. From now on, from this very moment on, if I ever get a letter from A. B. Smith, or from Leslie Smith, with no indication of sex or preferred mode of address, I intend to answer with a Dear Smith.

To be sure, my wife had her first books appear under her maiden name, with initials, so that the author was J. O. Jeppson. There was a reason for that, however. She *was* hiding herself in a way because she did not want to give any indication that she was Mrs. Isaac Asimov, lest anyone accuse her of nepotism or of trying to use me to get ahead. (People, of course, found out, and in her most recent books, she appears as Janet Asimov.)

The use of the name Cherryh is, on the other hand, a masterstroke. Carolyn's real surname is Cherry, but she added an "h" for use in her fiction as a minimal pseudonym.

This is good because it virtually guarantees name recognition. A glance at the author and you say to yourself, " 'H'? How the hell did an 'h' get in there? How do you pronounce the name except Cherry?"

It's possible you may get quite indignant at this, and turn red, and mutter "Damn fool writer" under your breath, but the important thing is that you're not going to forget that name. The next time you see it you will say, "There's that 'h' again." If you happen to read the story and like it, you will decide that this "h" writer is pretty good. You start watching for his/her stories and you never fail to recognize them because there's just no way you can miss an author with that peculiar spelling. In no time at all, Cherryh would become a household word.

I know this because it happened to me. My name, Asimov, is a funny-looking word and a funny-sounding name, until you get used to it. People who saw it on a magazine page would nudge each other and say, "How do you suppose you pronounce that, Joe?" "Good heavens, Bill, never saw anything like it." "You suppose it's a Russian name, Joe?" "Could be anything with that spelling."

So they puzzle it out and by the time they've finished, there's nothing left of the name, but such as it was—they never forget it.

Of course, I didn't know that my name was laughable. I always thought of it as noble and patrician, and born of a heritage of kings.

13

CASSANDRA

Fires.

They grew unbearable here.

Alis felt for the door of the flat and knew that it would be solid. She could feel the cool metal of the knob amid the flames . . . saw the shadow-stairs through the roiling smoke outside, clearly enough to feel her way down them, convincing her senses that they would bear her weight.

Crazy Alis. She made no haste. The fires burned steadily. She passed through them, descended the insubstantial steps to the solid ground—she could not abide the elevator, that closed space with the shadow-floor, that plummeted down and down; she made the ground floor, averted her eyes from the red, heatless flames.

A ghost said good morning to her . . . old man Willis, thin and transparent against the leaping flames. She blinked, bade it good morning in return—did not miss old Willis' shake of the head as she opened the door and left. Noon traffic passed, heedless of the flames, the hulks that blazed in the street, the tumbling brick.

The apartment caved in—black bricks falling into the inferno, Hell amid the green, ghostly trees. Old Willis fled, burning, fell—turned to jerking, blackened flesh—died, daily. Alis no longer cried, hardly flinched. She ignored the horror spilling about her, forced her way through crumbling brick that held no substance, past busy ghosts that could not be troubled in their haste.

Kingsley's Cafe stood, whole, more so than the rest. It was refuge for the afternoon, a feeling of safety. She pushed open the door, heard the tinkle of a lost bell. Shadowy patrons looked, whispered.

Crazy Alis.

The whispers troubled her. She avoided their eyes and their presence, settled in a booth in the corner that bore only traces of the fire.

WAR, the headline in the vender said in heavy type. She shivered, looked up into Sam Kingsley's wraithlike face.

"Coffee," she said. "Ham sandwich." It was constantly the same. She varied not even the order. Mad Alis. Her affliction supported her. A check came each month, since the hospital had turned her out. Weekly she returned to the clinic, to doctors who now faded like the others. The building burned about them. Smoke rolled down the blue, antiseptic halls. Last week a patient ran—burning—

A rattle of china. Sam set the coffee on the table, came back shortly and brought the sandwich. She bent her head and ate, transparent food on half-broken china, a cracked, fire-smudged cup with a transparent handle. She ate, hungry enough to overcome the horror that had become ordinary. A hundred times seen, the most terrible sights lost their power over her: she no longer cried at shadows. She talked to ghosts and touched them, ate the food that somehow stilled the ache in her belly, wore the same too-large black sweater and worn blue shirt and gray slacks because they were all she had that seemed solid. Nightly she washed them and dried them and put them on the next day, letting others hang in the closet. They were the only solid ones.

She did not tell the doctors these things. A lifetime in and out of hospitals had made her wary of confidences. She knew what to say. Her half-vision let her smile at ghost-faces, cannily manipulate their charts and cards, sitting in the ruins that had begun to smolder by late afternoon. A blackened corpse lay in the hall. She did not flinch when she smiled good-naturedly at the doctor.

They gave her medicines. The medicines stopped the dreams, the siren screams, the running steps in the night past her apartment. They let her sleep in the ghostly bed, high above ruin, with the flames crackling and the voices screaming. She did not speak of these things. Years in hospitals had taught her. She complained only of nightmares, and restlessness, and they let her have more of the red pills.

WAR, the headline blazoned.

The cup rattled and trembled against the saucer as she picked it up. She swallowed the last bit of bread and washed it down with coffee, tried not to look beyond the broken front window, where twisted metal hulks smoked on the street. She stayed, as she did each day, and Sam grudgingly refilled her cup, which she would nurse as far as she could and then order another one. She lifted it, savoring the feel of it, stopping the trembling of her hands.

The bell jingled faintly. A man closed the door, settled at the counter.

Whole, clear in her eyes. She stared at him, startled, heart pounding. He ordered coffee, moved to buy a paper from the vender, settled again and let the coffee grow cold while he read the news. She had view only of his back while he read, scuffed brown leather coat, brown hair a little over his collar. At last he drank the cooled coffee all at one draught, shoved money onto the counter, and left the paper lying, headlines turned face down.

A young face, flesh and bone among the ghosts. He ignored them all and went for the door.

Alis thrust herself from her booth.

"Hey!" Sam called at her.

She rummaged in her purse as the bell jingled, flung a bill onto the counter, heedless that it was a five. Fear was coppery in her mouth; he was gone. She fled the cafe, edged round debris without thinking of it, saw his back disappearing among the ghosts.

She ran, shouldering them, braving the flames—cried out as debris showered painlessly on her, and kept running.

Ghosts turned and stared, shocked—*he* did likewise, and she ran to him, stunned to see the same shock on his face, regarding her.

"What is it?" he asked.

She blinked, dazed to realize he saw her no differently than the others. She could not answer. In irritation he started walking again, and she followed. Tears slid down her face, her breath hard in her throat. People stared. He noticed her presence and walked the faster, through debris, through fires. A wall began to fall and she cried out despite herself.

He jerked about. The dust and the soot rose up as a cloud behind him. His face was distraught and angry. He stared at her as the others did. Mothers drew children away from the scene. A band of youths stared, cold-eyed and laughing.

"Wait," she said. He opened his mouth as if he would curse her; she flinched, and the tears were cold in the heatless wind of the fires. His face twisted in an embarrassed pity. He thrust a hand into his pocket and began to pull out money, hastily, tried to give it to her. She shook her head furiously, trying to stop the tears—stared upward, flinching, as another building fell into flames.

"What's wrong?" he asked her. "What's wrong with you?"

"Please," she said. He looked about at the staring ghosts, then began to walk slowly. She walked with him, nerving herself not to cry out at the ruin, the pale moving figures that wandered through burned shells of buildings, the twisted corpses in the street, where traffic moved.

"What's your name?" he asked. She told him. He gazed at her from time to time as they walked, a frown creasing his brow. He had a face well-worn for youth, a tiny scar beside the mouth. He looked older than she. She felt uncomfortable in the way his eyes traveled over her: she decided to accept it—to bear with anything that gave her this one solid presence. Against every inclination she reached her hand into the bend of his arm, tightened her fingers on the worn leather. He accepted it.

And after a time he slid his arm behind her and about her waist, and they walked like lovers.

WAR, the headline at the newsstand cried.

He started to turn into a street by Tenn's Hardware. She balked at what she saw there. He paused when he felt it, faced her with his back to the fires of that burning.

"Don't go," she said.

"Where do you want to go?"

She shrugged helplessly, indicated the main street, the other direction.

He talked to her then, as he might talk to a child, humoring her fear. It was pity. Some treated her that way. She recognized it, and took even that.

His name was Jim. He had come into the city yesterday, hitched rides. He was looking for work. He knew no one in the city. She listened to his rambling awkwardness, reading through it. When he was done, she stared at him still, and saw his face contract in dismay at her.

"I'm not crazy," she told him, which was a lie, that everyone in Sudbury would have known, only *he* would not, knowing no one. His face was true and solid, and the tiny scar by the mouth made it hard when he was thinking; at another time she would have been terrified of him. Now she was terrified of losing him amid the ghosts.

"It's the war," he said.

She nodded, trying to look at him and not at the fires. His fingers touched her arm, gently. "It's the war," he said again. "It's all crazy. Everyone's crazy."

And then he put his hand on her shoulder and turned her back the other way, toward the park, where green leaves waved over black, skeletal limbs. They walked along the lake, and for the first time in a long time she drew breath and felt a whole, sane presence beside her.

They bought corn, and sat on the grass by the lake, and flung it to the spectral swans. Wraiths of passersby were few, only enough to keep a feeling of occupancy about the place—old people, mostly, tottering about the deliberate tranquillity of their routine despite the headlines.

"Do you see them," she ventured to ask him finally, "all thin and gray?"

He did not understand, did not take her literally, only shrugged. Warily, she abandoned that questioning at once. She rose to her feet and stared at the horizon, where the smoke bannered on the wind.

"Buy you supper?" he asked.

She turned, prepared for this, and managed a shy, desperate smile. "Yes," she said, knowing what else he reckoned to buy with that—willing, and hating herself, and desperately afraid that he would walk away, tonight, tomorrow. She did not know men. She had no idea what she could say or do to prevent his leaving, only that he would when someday he realized her madness.

Even her parents had not been able to bear with that—visited her only at first in the hospitals, and then only on holidays, and then not at all. She did not know where they were.

There was a neighbor boy who drowned. She had said he

would. She had cried for it. All the town said it was she who pushed him.

Crazy Alis.

Fantasizes, the doctors said. Not dangerous.

They let her out. There were special schools, state schools.

And from time to time—hospitals.

Tranquilizers.

She had left the red pills at home. The realization brought sweat to her palms. They gave sleep. They stopped the dreams. She clamped her lips against the panic and made up her mind that she would not need them—not while she was not alone. She slipped her hand into his arm and walked with him, secure and strange, up the steps from the park to the streets.

And stopped.

The fires were out.

Ghost-buildings rose above their jagged and windowless shells. Wraiths moved through masses of debris, almost obscured at times. He tugged her on, but her step faltered, made him look at her strangely and put his arm about her.

"You're shivering," he said. "Cold?"

She shook her head, tried to smile. The fires were out. She tried to take it for a good omen. The nightmare was over. She looked up into his solid, concerned face, and her smile almost became a wild laugh.

"I'm hungry," she said.

They lingered long over a dinner in Graben's—he in his battered jacket, she in her sweater that hung at the tails and elbows: the spectral patrons were in far better clothes, and stared at them, and they were set in a corner nearest the door, where they would be less visible. There was cracked crystal and broken china on insubstantial tables, and the stars winked coldly in gaping ruin above the wan glittering of the broken chandeliers.

Ruins, cold, peaceful ruin.

Alis looked about her calmly. One could live in ruins, only so the fires were gone.

And there was Jim, who smiled at her without any touch of pity, only a wild, fey desperation that she understood—who spent more than he could afford in Graben's, the inside of which she had never hoped to see—and told her—predictably—that she was beautiful. Others had said it. Vaguely she resented such triteness from him, from him whom she had decided to trust. She smiled sadly, when he said it, and gave it up for a frown and, fearful of offending him with her melancholies, made it a smile again.

Crazy Alis. He would learn and leave tonight if she were not careful. She tried to put on gaiety, tried to laugh.

And then the music stopped in the restaurant, and the noise of the other diners went dead, and the speaker was giving an inane announcement.

Shelters . . . shelters . . . shelters.

Screams broke out. Chairs overturned.

Alis went limp in her chair, felt Jim's cold, solid hand tugging at hers, saw his frightened face mouthing her name as he took her up into his arms, pulled her with him, started running.

The cold air outside hit her, shocked her into sight of the ruins again, wraith figures pelting toward that chaos where the fires had been worst.

And she knew.

"No!" she cried, pulling at his arm. "No!" she insisted, and bodies half-seen buffeted them in a rush to destruction. He yielded to her sudden certainty, gripped her hand and fled with her against the crowds as the sirens wailed madness through the night—fled with her as she ran her sighted way through the ruin.

And into Kingsley's, where safe tables stood abandoned with food still on them, doors ajar, chairs overturned. Back they went into the kitchens and down and down into the cellar, the dark, the cold safety from the flames.

No others found them there. At last the earth shook, too deep for sound. The sirens ceased and did not come on again.

They lay in the dark and clutched each other and shivered, and above them for hours raged the sound of fire, smoke sometimes drifting in to sting their eyes and noses. There was the distant crash of brick, rumblings that shook the ground, that came near, but never touched their refuge.

And in the morning, with the scent of fire still in the air, they crept up into the murky daylight.

The ruins were still and hushed. The ghost-buildings were solid now, mere shells. The wraiths were gone. It was the fires themselves that were strange, some true, some not, playing above dark, cold brick, and most were fading.

Jim swore softly, over and over again, and wept.

When she looked at him she was dry-eyed, for she had done her crying already.

And she listened as he began to talk about food, about leaving the city, the two of them. "All right," she said.

Then clamped her lips, shut her eyes against what she saw in his face. When she opened them it was still true, the sudden transparency, the wash of blood. She trembled, and he shook at her, his ghost-face distraught.

"What's wrong?" he asked. "What's wrong?"

She could not tell him, would not. She remembered the boy who had drowned, remembered the other ghosts. Of a sudden she tore from his hands and ran, dodging the maze of debris that, this morning, was solid.

"Alis!" he cried and came after her.

"No!" she cried suddenly, turning, seeing the unstable wall, the cascading brick. She started back and stopped, unable to force herself. She held out her hands to warn him back, saw them solid.

The brick rumbled, fell. Dust came up, thick for a moment, obscuring everything.

She stood still, hands at her sides, then wiped her sooty face and turned and started walking, keeping to the center of the dead streets.

Overhead, clouds gathered, heavy with rain.

She wandered at peace now, seeing the rain spot the pavement, not yet feeling it.

In time the rain did fall, and the ruins became chill and cold. She visited the dead lake and the burned trees, the ruin of Graben's, out of which she gathered a string of crystal to wear.

She smiled when, a day later, a looter drove her from her food supply. He had a wraith's look, and she laughed from a place he did not dare to climb and told him so.

And recovered her cache later when it came true, and settled among the ruined shells that held no further threat, no other nightmares, with her crystal necklace and tomorrows that were the same as today.

One could live in ruins, only so the fires were gone.

And the ghosts were all in the past, invisible.